THE CORNISH TRILOGY

Roberston Davies, novelist, playwright, literary cr
born in 1913 in Thamesville, Ontario. He was e
University, Toronto, and Balliol College, Oxford. Whils
became interested in the theatre and from 1938 until 1940 he was a
teacher and actor at the Old Vic in London. He subsequently wrote a
number of plays. In 1940 he returned to Canada, where he was literary
editor of *Saturday Night*, an arts, politics and current affairs journal,
until 1942, when he became editor and later publisher of the *Peter-
borough Examiner*. Several of his books, including *The Diary of Samuel
Marchbanks* and *The Table Talk of Samuel Marchbanks*, had their origins
in an editorial column. In 1962 he was appointed Professor of English
at the University of Toronto, and in 1963 was appointed the first
Master of the University's Massey College. He retired in 1981, but
remained Master Emeritus and Professor Emeritus. He held honorary
doctorates from twenty-six universities in the UK, the USA and
Canada, and he received numerous awards for his work, including the
Governor-General's Award for *The Manticore* in 1973. It is as a writer
of fiction that Robertson Davies achieved international recognition,
with such books as *The Salterton Trilogy* (*Tempest-Tost, Leaven of Malice*,
winner of the Leacock Award for Humour, and *A Mixture of
Frailties*); *The Deptford Trilogy* (*Fifth Business, The Manticore* and *World
of Wonders*); *The Cornish Trilogy* (*The Rebel Angels, What's Bred in the
Bone*, shortlisted for the 1986 Booker Prize, and *The Lyre of Orpheus*);
Murther & Walking Spirits; and *The Cunning Man*. His other work
includes *One Half of Robertson Davies, The Enthusiasms of Robertson
Davies, Robertson Davies: The Well-Tempered Critic, The Papers of Samuel
Marchbanks, High Spirits, A Voice from the Attic* and *The Merry Heart*, a
posthumous collection of autobiography, lectures and essays. Many of
his books are published by Penguin.

Robertson Davies died in December 1995. Malcolm Bradbury described him as 'one of the great modern novelists', and in its obituary
The Times wrote: 'Davies encompassed all the great elements of life …
His novels combined deep seriousness and psychological inquiry with
fantasy and exuberan

ROBERTSON DAVIES

The Cornish Trilogy

THE REBEL ANGELS

WHAT'S BRED IN THE BONE

THE LYRE OF ORPHEUS

PENGUIN BOOKS

PENGUIN BOOKS

Published by the Penguin Group
Penguin Books Ltd, 80 Strand, London WC2R 0RL, England
Penguin Putnam Inc., 375 Hudson Street, New York 10014, USA
Penguin Books Australia Ltd, 250 Camberwell Road, Camberwell, Victoria 3124, Australia
Penguin Books Canada Ltd, 10 Alcorn Avenue, Toronto, Ontario, Canada M4V 3B2
Penguin Books India (P) Ltd, 11 Community Centre, Panchsheel Park, New Delhi – 110 017, India
Penguin Books (NZ) Ltd, Cnr Rosedale and Airborne Roads, Albany, Auckland, New Zealand
Penguin Books (South Africa) (Pty) Ltd, 24 Sturdee Avenue, Rosebank 2196, South Africa

Penguin Books Ltd, Registered Offices: 80 Strand, London WC2R 0RL, England

www.penguin.com

Rebel Angels first published in Canada by Macmillan of Canada 1981
Published in the USA by The Viking Press, 1982
Published in Great Britain by Allen Lane 1982
Published in Penguin Books 1983

Copyright © Robertson Davies, 1981

What's Bred in the Bone first published in Canada by Macmillan of Canada 1985
Published in the USA by Viking Penguin 1985
Published in Great Britain by Viking 1986
Published in Penguin Books 1987

Copyright © Robertson Davies, 1985

The Lyre of Orpheus first published in Canada by Macmillan of Canada 1988
Published in the USA in a limited edition by The Foundation Library 1988
Published in the USA by Viking Penguin 1989
Published in Great Britain by Viking 1988
Published in Penguin Books 1989

Copyright © Robertson Davies, 1988

Published in one volume as *The Cornish Trilogy* in Penguin Books 1991

15

All rights reserved

Printed in England by Clays Ltd, St Ives plc

ISBN-13: 978–0–140–14446–8
ISBN-10: 0–140–14446–3

www.greenpenguin.co.uk

Contents

The Rebel Angels

Second Paradise I

"**P**ARLABANE IS BACK."

"What?"

"Hadn't you heard? Parlabane is back."

"Oh my God!"

I hurried on down the long corridor, through chattering students and gossiping faculty members, and again I overheard it, as another pair of professors met.

"You haven't heard about Parlabane, I suppose?"

"No. What should I have heard?"

"He's back."

"Not here?"

"Yes. In the college."

"Not staying, I hope?"

"Who's to say? With Parlabane, anyhow."

This was what I wanted. It was something to say to Hollier when we met after nearly four months apart. At that last meeting he had become my lover, or so I was vain enough to think. Certainly he had become, agonizingly, the man I loved. All through the summer vacation I had fretted and fussed and hoped for a postcard from wherever he might be in Europe, but he was not a man to write postcards. Not a man to say very much, either, in a personal way. But he could be excited; he could give way to feeling. On that day in early May, when he had told me about the latest development in his work, and I—so eager to serve him, to gain his gratitude and perhaps even his love—did an inexcusable thing and betrayed the secret of the *bomari* to him, he seemed lifted quite outside himself, and it was then he took me in his arms and put me on that horrible old sofa in his office, and had me amid a great deal of confusion of clothing, creaking of springs, and peripheral anxiety lest somebody should come in. That was when we had parted, he embarrassed and I overcome with astonishment and devotion, and now I was to face him again. I needed an opening remark.

So—up the two winding flights of stairs, which the high ceilings in St. John's made rather more like three flights. Why was I hurrying? Was I so eager to see him? No, I wanted that, of course, but I dreaded it as well. How does one greet one's professor, one's thesis director, whom one loves and who has had one on his old sofa, and whom one hopes may love one in return? It was a sign of my mental state that I was thinking of myself as 'one', which meant that my English was become stiff and formal. There I was, out of breath, on the landing where there were no rooms but his, and on the study door was his tattered old hand-written sign saying 'Professor Hollier is in; knock and enter'. So I did, and there he was at his table looking like Dante if Dante had had better upper teeth, or perhaps like Savonarola if Savonarola had been handsomer. Stumbling—a little light-headed—I rattled out my scrap of news.

"Parlabane is back."

The effect was more than I had reckoned for. He straightened in his chair, and although his mouth did not open, his jaw slackened and his face had that look of intentness that I loved even more than his smile, which was not his best expression.

"Did you say that Parlabane was here?"

"That's what they're all saying in the main hall."

"Great God! How awful!"

"Why awful? Who's Parlabane?"

"I dare say you'll find out soon enough.—Have you had a good summer? Done any work?"

Nothing to recall the adventure on the sofa, which was right beside him and seemed to me to be the most important thing in the room. Just professor-questions about work. He didn't give a damn if I'd had a good summer. He simply wanted to know if I had been getting on with my work—which was a niggling little particle of the substructure of *his* work. He hadn't even asked me to sit down, and brought up as I had been I could not sit in the presence of a professor until asked. So I began to explain what work I had been doing, and after a few minutes he noticed that I was standing and waved me to a chair. He was pleased with my report.

"I've arranged that you can work in here this year. Of course you've got your own dog-hole somewhere, but here you can spread out books and papers and leave things overnight. I've been clearing this table for you. I shall want you near."

I trembled. Do girls still tremble when their lovers say they want them near? I did. Then—

"Do you know why I want you near?"

I blushed. I wish I didn't blush but at twenty-three I still blush. I could not say a word.

"No, of course you don't. Couldn't possibly. But I'll tell you, and it will make you jump out of your skin. Cornish died this morning."

Oh, abomination of desolation! It wasn't the sofa and what the sofa meant.

"I don't think I know about Cornish."

"Francis Cornish is—was—undoubtedly the foremost patron of art and appreciator and understander of art this country has ever known. Immensely rich, and spent lavishly on pictures. They'll go to the National Gallery; I know because I'm his executor. Don't say anything about that because it's not to be general knowledge yet. He was also a discriminating collector of books, and they go to the University Library. But he was a not-so-discriminating collector of manuscripts; didn't really know what he had, because he was so taken up with the pictures he hadn't much time for other things. The manuscripts go to the Library, too. And one of those manuscripts will be the making of you, and will be quite useful to me, I hope. As soon as we can get our hands on it you will begin your serious work—the work that will put you several rungs up the scholarly ladder. That manuscript will be the guts of your thesis, and it won't be some mouldy, pawed-over old rag of the kind most students have to put up with. It could be a small bombshell in Renaissance studies."

I didn't know what to say. I wanted to say: am I just a student again, after having been tumbled by you on the sofa? Can you really be so unfeeling, such a professor? But I knew what he wanted me to say, and I said it.

"How exciting! How marvellous! What's it about?"

"I don't really know, except that it's in your line. You'll need all your languages—French, Latin, Greek, and you may have to bone up some Hebrew."

"But what is it? I mean, could you be so interested if you really didn't know?"

"I can only say that it is very special, and it may be a—a bombshell. But I have a great deal to get through before lunch, so we must put off any further talk about it until later. You'd better move your stuff in here this morning and put a sign on the door to say you're inside.— Nice to see you again."

And with that he shuffled off in his old slippers up the steps into the big inner room which was his private study, and where his camp-bed lurked behind a screen. I knew because once, when he was out, I had peeped. He looks at least a million, I thought, but these academic wizards are shape-shifters: if his work goes well he will come out of that door within two hours, looking thirtyish, instead of his proper forty-five. But for the present, he was playing the Academic Old Geezer.

Nice to see me again! Not a kiss, not a smile, not even a handshake! Disappointment worked through me like a poison.

But there was time, and I was to be in his outer room, constantly under his eye. Time works wonders.

I was sufficiently bitten by the scholarly bug to feel another kind of excitement that somewhat eased my disappointment. What was this manuscript about which he was so evasive?

[2]

I WAS ARRANGING my papers and things on the table in the outer room after lunch when there was a soft tap at the door and in came someone who was certainly Parlabane. I knew everyone else in St. John's who might have turned up in such a guise; he was wearing a cassock, or a monkish robe that had just that hint of fancy dress about it that marked it as Anglican rather than Roman. But he wasn't one of the divinity professors of St. John's.

"I am Brother John, or Dr. Parlabane if you prefer it; is Professor Hollier in?"

"I don't know when he'll be in; certainly not in less than an hour. Shall I say you'll come back?"

"My dear, what you are really saying is that you expect me to go away now. But I am not in a hurry. Let us chat. Who might you be?"

"I am one of Professor Hollier's students."

"And you work in this room?"

"After today, yes."

"A very special student, then, who works so close to the great man. Because he is a very great man. Yes, my old classmate Clement Hollier is now a very great man among those who understand what he is doing. I suppose you must be one of those?"

"A student, as I said."

"You must have a name, my dear."

"I am Miss Theotoky."

"Oh, what a jewel of a name! A flower in the mouth! Miss Theotoky. But surely more than that? Miss What Theotoky?"

"If you insist on knowing, my full name is Maria Magdalena Theotoky."

"Better and better. But what a contrast! Theotoky—with the accent firmly on the first 'o'—linked with the name of the sinner out of whom Our Lord cast seven devils. Not Canadian, I assume?"

"Yes, Canadian."

"Of course. I keep forgetting that any name may be Canadian. But quite recently, in your case, I should say."

"I was born here."

"But your parents were not, I should guess. Now where did they come from?"

"From England."

"And before England?"

"Why do you want to know?"

"Because I am insatiably curious. And you provoke curiosity, my dear. Very beautiful girls—and of course you know that you are very beautiful—provoke curiosity, and in my case I assure you a benevolent, fatherly curiosity. Now, you are not a lovely English rose. You are something more mysterious. That name—

Theotoky—means the bringer of God, doesn't it? Not English—oh dear me, no. Therefore, in a spirit of kindly, Christian curiosity, where were your parents before England?"

"Hungary."

"Ah, now we have it! And your dear parents very wisely legged it to hell out of Hungary because of the trouble there. Am I not right?"

"Quite right."

"Confidence begets confidence. And names are of the uttermost importance. So I'll tell you about mine; it is a Huguenot name, and I suppose once, very long ago, some forebear of mine was a persuasive talker, and thus came by it. After several generations in Ireland it became Parlabane, and now, after several more generations in Canada, it is quite as Canadian as your own, my dear. I think we are foolish on this continent to imagine that after five hundred generations somewhere else we become wholly Canadian—hard-headed, no-nonsense North Americans—in the twinkling of a single life. Maria Magdalena Theotoky, I think we are going to be very good friends."

"Yes—well, I must get on with my work. Professor Hollier will not be back for some time."

"How lucky then that I have precisely that amount of time. I shall wait. By your leave, I'll just put myself on this disreputable old sofa, which you are not using. What a wreck! Clem never had any sense of his surroundings. This place looks just like him. Which delights me, of course. I am very happy to be snuggled back into the bosom of dear old Spook."

"I should warn you that the Rector greatly dislikes people calling the college Spook."

"How very right-minded of the Rector. You may be sure that I shall never make that mistake in his presence. But between us, Molly—I think I shall call you Molly as short for Maria—how in the name of the ever-living God does the Rector expect that a place called the College of St. John and the Holy Ghost will not be called Spook? I like Spook. I think it is affectionate, and I like to be affectionate."

He was already stretched out on the sofa, which had such associations for me, and it was plain there would be no getting rid of him; so I was silent and went on with my work.

But how right he was! The room looked very much like Hollier, and like Spook, too. Spook is about a hundred and forty years old and was built in the time when Collegiate Gothic raged in the bosoms of architects like a fire. The architect of Spook knew his business, so it was not hideous, but it was full of odd corners and architecturally indefensible superfluities, and these rooms where Hollier lived were space-wasting and inconvenient. Up two long flights of stairs, they were the only rooms on their landing, except for a passage that led to the organ-loft of the chapel. There was the outer room, where I was working, which was of a good size, and had two big Gothic arched windows, and then, up three steps and somewhat around a corner was Hollier's inner room, where he also slept. The washroom and john were down a long flight, and when Hollier wanted a bath he had to traipse to another wing of the college, in the great Oxbridge tradition. The surroundings were as Gothic as the nineteenth century could make them. But Hollier, who had no sense of congruity, had furnished them with decrepit junk from his mother's house; what had legs was unsteady on them, and what was stuffed leaked stuffing here and there, and had unpleasantly greasy upholstery. The pictures were photographs of college groups from Hollier's younger days here at Spook. Apart from the books there was only one thing in the room that seemed to belong there, and that was a large alchemist's retort, of the kind that looks like an abstract sculpture of a pelican, that sat on top of a bookcase; someone who did not know of Hollier's indifference to objects had given this picturesque object to him many years ago. His rooms were, by ordinary standards, a mess, but they had a coherence, and even a comfort, of their own. Once you stopped being offended by the muddle, neglect, and I suppose one must say dirt, they were oddly beautiful, like Hollier himself.

Parlabane lay on the sofa for almost two hours, during which I do not think he ever ceased to stare at me. I wanted to get away on some business of my own, but I had no intention of leaving him in possession, so I made work for myself, and thought about him. How had he managed to get so much out of me in so short a time? How did he get away with calling me 'my dear' in such a way that I did not check him? And 'Molly'! The man was all of brass, but the brass had such a soft, buttery sheen that one was disarmed. I began to see why people had been so dismayed when they heard that Parlabane was back.

At last Hollier returned.

"Clem! Dear old Clem! My dear man, how good to see you again!"

"John—I heard you were back."

"And isn't Spook delighted to see me! Haven't I had a real Spook welcome! I've been brushing the frost off my habit all morning. But here I am, with my dear old friend, and charming Molly, who is going to be another dear friend."

"You've met Miss Theotoky?"

"Darling Molly! We've been having a great old heart-to-heart."

"Well, John, you'd better come inside and talk to me. Miss T., I'm sure you want to get away."

Miss T. is what he calls me in semi-formality—a way-station between my true name and Maria, which he uses very seldom.

They went up the steps into his inner room, and I trotted down the two long flights of stairs, feeling in my bones that something had gone deeply wrong. This was not going to be the wonderful term I had expected and longed for.

[3]

I LIKE TO BE early at my work; that means being at my desk by half past nine, because academics of my kind begin late and work late. I let myself into Hollier's outer room and breathed in a strong whiff of the stench not very clean men create when they sleep in a room with the windows closed—something like the lion's cage at the zoo. There was Parlabane, stretched out on the sofa, fast asleep. He wore most of his clothes but his heavy monk's robe he had used as a blanket. Like an animal, he was aware of me at once, opened his eyes, and yawned.

"Good morning, dear Molly."

"Have you been here all night?"

"The great man gave me permission to doss down here until Spook finds a room for me. I forgot to give the Bursar proper warning of my arrival. Now I must say my prayers and shave; a monk's shave—in cold water and without soap, unless I can find some in the washroom. These austerities keep me humble."

He pulled on and laced a big pair of black boots, and then from a knapsack he had tucked behind the sofa he brought out a dirty bag which I suppose contained his washing things. He went out, mumbling under his breath—prayers, I assumed—and I opened the windows and gave the room a good airing.

I suppose I had worked for about two hours, getting my papers laid out, and books arranged on the big table, and my portable typewriter plugged in, when Parlabane came back, carrying a big, scabby leather suitcase that looked as if it had been bought in a Lost Luggage shop.

"Don't mind me, my dear. I shall be quiet as a mouse. I'll just tuck my box—don't you think 'box' is the best name for an old case like this?—in this corner, right out of your way." Which he did, and settled himself again on the sofa, and began to read from a thick little black book, moving his lips but making no sound. More prayers, I supposed.

"Excuse me, Dr. Parlabane; are you proposing to stay here for the morning?"

"For the morning, and for the afternoon, and this evening. The Bursar has no place for me, though he is kind enough to say I may eat in Hall. If that is really kind, which my recollection of Spook food makes me doubt."

"But this is my workroom!"

"It is my honour to share it with you."

"But you can't! How can I possibly work with you around?"

"The scholar's wish for complete privacy—how well I understand! But Charity, dear Molly, Charity! Where else can I go?"

"I'll speak to Professor Hollier!"

"I'd think carefully before I did that. He might tell me to go; but then there is a chance—not a bad chance—that he might tell you to go to your carrel, or whatever they call those little cupboards where graduate students work. He and I are very old friends. Friends from a time before you were born, my dear."

I was furious, and speechless. I left, and hung around the Library until after lunch. Then I returned, deciding that I must try again. Parlabane was on the sofa, reading a file of papers from my table.

"Welcome, welcome dear Molly! I knew you would come back. It is not in your heart to be angry for long. With your beautiful name—Maria, the Motherhood of God—you must be filled with understanding and forgiveness. But tell me why you have been making such careful study of that renegade monk François Rabelais? I've been peeping into your papers, you see. Rabelais is not the kind of company I expected to find you keeping."

"Rabelais is one of the great misunderstood figures of the Reformation. He's part of my special area of study."

How I hated myself for explaining! But Parlabane had a terrible trick of putting me on the defensive.

"Ah, the Reformation, so called. What a fuss about very little! Was Rabelais truly one of those nasty, divisive reformers? Did he dig with the same foot as that pestilent fellow Luther?"

"He dug with the same foot as that admirable fellow Erasmus."

"I see. But a dirty-minded man. And a great despiser of women, if I recollect properly, though it's years since I read his blundering, coarse-fibred romance about the giants. But we mustn't quarrel; we must live together in holy charity. I've seen dear Clem since last we talked, and he says it's all right for me to stay. I wouldn't fuss him about it if I were you. He seems to have great things on his mind."

So he'd won! I should never have left the room. He'd got to Hollier first. He was smiling a cat's smile at me.

"You must understand, my dear, that my case is a special one. Indeed, all my life I've been a special case. But I have a solution for all our problems. Look at this room! The room of a medieval scholar if ever I saw one. Look at that object on the bookcase; alchemical—even I can see that. This is like an alchemist's chamber in some quiet medieval university. And fully equipped! Here is the great scholar himself, Clement Hollier. And here are you, that inescapable necessity of the alchemist, his *soror mystica*, his scholarly girlfriend, to put it in modern terms. But what's lacking? Of course, the *famulus*, the scholar's intimate servant, devoted disciple, and unquestioning stooge. I nominate myself *famulus* in this little corner of the Middle Ages. You'll be astonished at how handy I can be. Look, I've already rearranged the books in the bookcase, so that they make sense alphabetically."

Damn! I'd been meaning to do that myself. Hollier could never find what he wanted because he was so untidy. I wanted to cry. But I wouldn't cry in front of Parlabane. He was going on.

"I suppose this room is cleaned once a week? And by a woman Hollier has terrified so she daren't touch or move anything? I'll clean it every day so that it will be as clean—well, not as a new pin, but cleanish, which is the most a scholar will tolerate. Too much cleanliness is an enemy to creation, to speculative thought. And I'll clean for you, dear Molly. I shall respect you as a *famulus* ought to respect his master's *soror mystica*."

"Will you respect me enough not to snoop through my papers?"

"Perhaps not as much as that. I like to know what's going on. But whatever I find, dear girl, I shan't betray you. I didn't get where I am by blabbing all I know."

And where did he think he had got to? Shabby monk, his spectacles mended at the temple with electrician's tape! The answer came at once: he had got into my special world, and had already taken much of it from me. I looked him squarely in the eye, but he was better at that game than I was, so very soon I was trotting down those winding stairs again, angry and hurt and puzzled about what I ought to do.

Damn! Damn! Damn!

The New Aubrey I

AUTUMN, TO ME the most congenial of seasons: the University, to me the most congenial of lives. In all my years as a student and later as a university teacher I have observed that university terms tend to begin on a fine day. As I walked down the avenue of maples that leads toward the University Bookstore I was happy as I suppose it is in my nature to be; my nature tends toward happiness, or toward enthusiastic industry, which for me is the same thing.

Met Ellerman and one of the few men I really dislike, Urquhart McVarish. The cancer look on poor Ellerman's face was far beyond what it was when last I saw him.

"You've retired, yet here you are, on the first day of full term, on the old stamping-ground," said I. "I thought you'd be off to the isles of Greece or somewhere, rejoicing in your freedom."

Ellerman smiled wistfully, and McVarish released one of the wheezes that pass with him as laughter. "Surely you ought to know—you of all people, Father Darcourt—that the dog turns to his own vomit again, and the sow to her wallowing in the mire." And he wheezed again with self-delight.

Typical of McVarish: nasty to poor Ellerman, who was obviously deathly ill, and nasty to me for being a clergyman, which McVarish thinks no man in his right senses has any right to be.

"I thought I'd like to see what the campus looks like when I am no longer a part of it," said Ellerman. "And really, I thought I'd like to look at some young people. I've been used to them all my life."

"Serious weakness," said Urky McVarish; "never allow yourself to become hooked on youth. Green apples give you the belly-ache."

Wanting to see young people—I've observed it often in the dying. Women wanting to look at babies, and that sort of thing. Poor Ellerman. But he was going on.

"Not just young people, Urky. Older people, too. The University is such a splendid community, you know; every kind of creature here, and all exhibiting what they are so much more freely than if they were in business, or the law, or whatever. It ought to be recorded, you know. I've often thought of doing something myself, but I'm out of it now."

"It is being recorded," said McVarish. "Isn't the University paying Doyle to write its history—given her three years off all other work, a budget, secretaries, assistants, whatever her greedy historian's heart can desire. It'll be three heavy volumes of un-illuminated crap, but who cares? It will be a history."

"No, no it won't; not what I mean at all," said Ellerman. "I mean a vagarious history with all the odd ends and scraps in it that nobody ever thinks of recording but which are the real stuff of life. What people said informally, what they did when they were not on parade, all the gossip and rumour without the ne-cessity to prove everything."

"Something like Aubrey's *Brief Lives,*" said I, not thinking much about it but wanting to be agreeable to Ellerman, who looked so poorly. He responded with a vigour I had not expected. He almost leapt where he stood.

"That's it! That's absolutely it! Somebody like John Aubrey, who listens to everything, wonders about everything, scrawls down notes in a hurry without fussing over style. An academic magpie, a snapper-up of unconsidered trifles. This university needs an Aubrey. Oh, if only I were ten years younger!"

Poor wretch, I thought, he is clinging to the life that is ebbing away, and he thinks he could find it in the brandy of gossip.

"What are you waiting for, Darcourt?" said McVarish. "Eller-man has described you to the life. Academic magpie; no con-science about style. You're the very man. You sit like a raven in your tower, looking down on the whole campus. Ellerman has given you a reason for being."

McVarish always reminds me of the fairy-tale about the girl

out of whose mouth a toad leapt whenever she spoke. He could say more nasty things in ordinary conversation than anybody I had ever known, and he could make poor innocents like Ellerman accept them as wit. Ellerman was laughing now.

"There you are, Darcourt! You're a made man! The New Aubrey—that's what you must be."

"You could make a start with the Turd-Skinner," said McVarish. "He must surely be the oddest fish even in this odd sea."

"I don't know who you're talking about."

"Surely you do! Professor Ozias Froats."

"I never heard him called that."

"You will, Darcourt, you will. Because that's what he does, and that's what he gets big grants to do, and now that university money is so closely watched there may be some questions about it. Then—oh, there are dozens to choose from. But you should get on as fast as possible with Francis Cornish. You've heard that he died last night?"

"I'm sorry to hear it," said Ellerman, who was particularly sorry now to hear of any death. "What collections!"

"Accumulations, would perhaps be a better word. Great heaps of stuff and I don't suppose he knew during his last years what he had. But I shall know. I'm his executor."

Ellerman was excited. "Books, pictures, manuscripts," he said, his eyes glowing. "I suppose the University is a great inheritor?"

"I shan't know until I get the will. But it seems likely. And it should be a plum. A plum," said McVarish, making the word sound very ripe and juicy in his mouth.

"You're the executor? Sole executor?" said Ellerman. "I hope I'll be around to see what happens." Poor man, he guessed it was unlikely.

"So far as I know I'm the only one. We were very close. I'm looking forward to it," said McVarish, and they went on their way.

The day seemed less fine than before. Had Cornish made another will? For years I had been under the impression that I was his executor.

[2]

IN THE COURSE of a few days I knew better. I was burying Cornish, as one of the three priests in the slap-up funeral we gave him in the handsome chapel of Spook. He had been a distinguished alumnus of the College of St. John and the Holy Ghost; he was not attached to any parish church; Spook expected that he would leave it a bundle. All good reasons for doing the thing in style.

I had liked Cornish. We shared an enthusiasm for ancient music, and I had advised him about some purchases of manuscripts in that area. But it would be foolish for me to pretend that we were intimates. He was an eccentric, and I think his sexual tastes were out of the common. He had some rum friends, one of whom was Urquhart McVarish. I had not been pleased when I got my copy of the will from the lawyers to find out that McVarish was indeed an executor, with myself, and that Clement Hollier was a third. Hollier was an understandable choice: a great medieval scholar with a world reputation as something out of the ordinary called a paleo-psychologist, which seemed to mean that by a lot of grubbing in old books and manuscripts he got close to the way people in the pre-Renaissance world really thought about themselves and the universe they knew. I had known him slightly when we were undergraduates at Spook, and we nodded when we met, but we had gone different ways. Hollier would be a good man to deal with a lot of Cornish's stuff. But McVarish—why him?

Well, McVarish would not have a free hand, nor would Hollier nor I, because Cornish's will appointed us not quite as executors, but as advisers and experts in carrying out the disposals and bequests of the collections of pictures, books, and manuscripts. The real executor was Cornish's nephew, Arthur Cornish, a young business man, reputed to be able and rich, and we should all have to act under his direction. There he sat in the front pew, upright, apparently unmoved, and every inch a rich man of business and wholly unlike his uncle, the tall, shambling, short-sighted Francis whom we were burying.

As I sat in my stall in the chancel, I could see McVarish in the front pew, doing all the right things, standing, sitting, kneeling, and so forth, but doing them in a way that seemed to indicate that he was a great gentleman among superstitious and uncivilized people, and he must not be suspected of taking it seriously. While the Rector of Spook delivered a brief eulogy on Cornish, taking the best possible view of the departed one, McVarish's face wore a smile that was positively mocking, as though to say that he knew of a thing or two that would spice up the eulogy beyond recognition. Not sexy, necessarily. Cornish had dealt extensively in pictures, including those of some of the best Canadian artists, and in the congregation I could see quite a few people whose throats he might be said to have cut, in a connoisseur-like way. Why had they turned up at these obsequies? The uncharitable thought crossed my mind that they might have come to be perfectly sure that Cornish was dead. Great collectors and great connoisseurs are not always nice people. Great benefactors, however, are invariably and unquestionably nice, and Cornish had left a bundle to Spook, though Spook was not officially aware of it. But I had tipped the wink to the Rector, and the Rector was showing gratitude in the only way college recipients of benefactions can do— by praying loud and long for the dead friend.

Quite medieval, really. However much science and educational theory and advanced thinking you pump into a college or a university, it always retains a strong hint of its medieval origins, and the fact that Spook was a New World college in a New World university made surprisingly little difference.

The faces of the congregation, which I could see so well from my place, had an almost medieval calm upon them, as they listened to the Rector's very respectable prose. Except, of course, for McVarish's knowing smirk. But I could see Hollier, who had not pushed himself into the front row, though he had a right to be there, and his thin, splendid features looked hawkish and solemn. Not far from him was a girl in whom I had found much to interest me, one Maria Magdalena Theotoky, who had come the day before to join my special class in New Testament Greek. Girls who want to work on that subject are usually older and more obviously given to the scholarly life than was Maria. She was beyond doubt a great beauty, though it was beauty of a kind not everybody would notice, or like, and which I suspected did not appeal greatly to her contemporaries. A calm, transfixing face, of the kind one sees in an ikon, or a mosaic portrait—it was oval in shape; the nose was long and aquiline; if she were not careful about her front teeth it would be a hook in middle age; her hair was a true black, the real raven's-wing colour, with blue lights in it, but no hint of the dreadful shade that comes with dye. What was Maria doing at Cornish's funeral? It was her eyes that startled you when you looked at her, because you could see some of the white below the iris, as well as above, and when she blinked—which she did not seem to do as often as most people—the lower lid moved upward as the upper lid moved down, and that is something you rarely see. Her eyes, fixed in what may have been devotion, startled me now. She had covered her head with a loose scarf, which most of the women in the chapel had not done, because they are modern, and set no store by St. Paul's admonition on that subject. But what was she doing there?

The comic turn of the funeral—and many a funeral boasts its clown—was John Parlabane, who was, I had heard, infesting Spook. He was in his monk's robe at the funeral, mopping and mowing in the very Highest of High Anglican style. Not that I mind. At the Name of Jesus, every knee shall bow, but Parlabane didn't stop short at bowing; he positively cringed and crossed himself with that crumb-brushing movement which is supposed to show long custom to which he, born a Protestant of some unritualistic sect, grossly overdid. The scarred skin of his face—I remembered how and when he came by those scars—was composed in a sanctimonious leer that seemed meant to combine regret for the passing of a friend with ecstasy at the thought of the glory that friend was now enjoying.

I am an Anglican, and a priest, but sometimes I wish my coreligionists wouldn't carry on so.

As a priest at this funeral I had my special duty. The Rector had asked me to speak the Committal, and then the choir sang: *I heard a voice from heaven saying unto me, Write: From henceforth blessed are the dead which die in the Lord: even so saith the spirit, for they rest from their labours.*

So Francis Cornish rested from his labours, though whether he had died in the Lord I can't really say. Certainly he had laid labours upon me, for his estate was a big one and was reckoned not simply in money but in costly possessions, and I had to come to grips with it, and with Hollier—and with Urquhart McVarish.

[3]

THREE DAYS LATER the three of us sat in Arthur Cornish's office in one of the big bank towers in the financial district, while he told us who was who and what was what. He was not uncivil, but his style was not what we were used to. We knew all about meetings where anxious deans fluttered and fussed to make sure that every shade of opinion was heard, and strangled decisive action in the slack, dusty ropes of academic scruple. Arthur Cornish knew what had to be done, and he expected us to do our parts quickly and efficiently.

"Of course I am to look after all the business and financial side," he said. "You gentlemen are appointed to attend to the proper disposal of Uncle Frank's possessions—the works of art and that sort of stuff. It could turn out to be quite a big job. The things that have to be shipped and moved to new owners should be put in the hands of a reliable shipper, and I'll give you the name of the firm I've chosen; they'll take orders from you, countersigned by my secretary. She will help you in every way possible. I'd like to get it done as soon as you can manage it, because we want to get on with probate and the dispersal of legacies and gifts. So may I ask you to move as quickly as you can?"

Professors do not like to be asked to move quickly, and particularly not by a man who is not yet thirty. They can move quickly, or so they imagine, but they don't like to be bossed. We had no need to look at one another for Hollier, McVarish, and I to close ranks against this pushy youth. Hollier spoke.

"Our first task must be to find out what has to be disposed of in the way of works of art, and 'that sort of stuff', to use your own phrase, Mr. Cornish."

"I suppose there must be an inventory somewhere."

Now it was McVarish's turn. "Did you know your uncle well?"

"Not really. Saw him now and then."

"You never visited his dwelling?"

"His home? No, never. Wasn't asked."

I thought I had better put in a few words. "I don't think home is quite the word one would use for the place where Francis Cornish lived."

"His apartment, then."

"He had three apartments," I continued. "They occupied a whole floor of the building, which he owned. And they are crammed from floor to ceiling with works of art—and that sort of stuff. And I didn't say over-furnished: I said crammed."

Hollier resumed the job of putting the rich brat in his place. "If you didn't know your uncle, of course you cannot imagine how improbable it was that he possessed an inventory; he was not an inventory sort of man."

"I see. A real old bachelor's rat's-nest. But I know I can depend on you to sort it out. Get help if you need it, to catalogue the contents. We must have a valuation, for probate. I suppose in aggregate it must be worth quite a lot. Any clerical assistance you need, lay it on and my secretary will countersign chits for necessary payments."

After a little more of this we left, passing through the office of the secretary who had countersigning powers (a middle-aged woman of professional charm) and through the office of the other secretaries who were younger and pattered away on muted, expensive machines, and past the uniformed man who guarded the portals—because the big doors really were portals.

"I've never met anybody like that before," I said as we went down sixteen floors in the elevator.

"I have," said McVarish. "Did you notice the mahogany panelling? Veneer, I suppose, like young Cornish."

"Not veneer," said Hollier. "I tapped it to see. Not veneer. We must watch our step with that young man."

McVarish sniggered. "Did you notice the pictures on his walls? Corporation taste. Provided by a decorator. Not his Uncle Frank's sort of stuff."

I had looked at the pictures too, and McVarish was wrong. But we wanted to feel superior to the principal executor because we were a little in awe of him.

[4]

DURING THE WEEK that followed, Hollier, McVarish, and I met every afternoon at Francis Cornish's three apartments. We had been given keys by the countersigning secretary. After five days had passed, our situation seemed worse than we could have imagined and we did not know where to start on our job.

Cornish had lived in one of the apartments, and it had some suggestion of a human dwelling, though it was like an extremely untidy art dealer's shop—which was one of the purposes to which he put it. Francis Cornish had done much in his lifetime to establish and gain recognition for good Canadian painters. He bought largely himself, but he also acted as an agent for painters who had not yet made a name. This meant that he kept some of their pictures in his apartment, and sold them when he could, remitting the price to the painter, and charging no dealer's fee. That, at least, was the theory. In practice he acquired pictures from young painters, stacked them in his flat, forgot them or absent-mindedly lent them to people who liked them, and was surprised and hurt when an aggrieved painter made a fuss, or threatened a lawsuit.

There was no real guile in Francis Cornish, but there was no method in him either, and it was supposed that it was for this reason he had not taken a place in the family business, which had begun in his grandfather's time as lumber and pulpwood, had grown substantially in his father's time, and in the last twenty-five years had left lumber to become a very big bond and investment business. Arthur, the fourth generation, was now the head of the firm. Francis's fortune, partly from a trust established by his father, and partly inherited from his mother, had made him a very rich man, able to indulge his taste for art patronage without thinking much about money.

He had seldom sold a picture for an artist, but when it became known that he had some of them for sale, other and more astute dealers sought out that artist, and in this haphazard way Cornish was a considerable figure in the dealer's world. His taste was as sure as his business method was shaky.

Part of our problem was the accumulation, in apartment number one, of a mass of pictures, drawings, and lithographs, as well as quite a lot of small sculpture, and we did not know if it belonged to Cornish, or to the artists themselves.

As if that were not enough, apartment number two was so full of pictures that it was necessary to edge through the door, and push into rooms where there was hardly space for one person to stand. This was his non-Canadian collection, some of which he had certainly not seen for twenty-five years. By groping amid the dust we could make out that almost every important name of the past fifty years was represented there, but to what extent, or in what period of the artist's work, it was impossible to say, because moving one picture meant moving another, and in a short time no further movement was possible, and the searcher might find himself fenced in, at some distance from the door.

It was Hollier who found four large packages in brown paper stacked in a bathtub, thick in dust. When the dust was brushed away (and Hollier, who was sensitive to dust, suffered in doing it) he found that the packages were labelled, in Cornish's beautiful hand, 'P. Picasso Lithographs—be sure your hands are clean before opening.'

My own Aladdin's cave was apartment number three, where the books and manuscripts were. That is, I tried to make it mine, but Hollier and McVarish insisted on snooping; it was impossible to keep scholars away from such a place. Books were heaped on tables and under tables—big folios, tiny duodecimos, every sort of book ranging from incunabula to what seemed to be a complete collection of first editions of Edgar Wallace. Stacks of books like chimneys rose perilously from the floor and were easily knocked over. There were illuminated books, and a peep was all that was necessary to discover that they were of great beauty; Cornish must have bought them forty years ago, for such things are hardly to be found now, for any money. There were caricatures and manuscripts, including fairly modern things; there was enough stuff by Max Beerbohm alone—marvellous unpublished mock portraits of royalty and of notabilities of the nineties and the early nineteen-hundreds—for a splendid exhibition, and my heart yearned toward these. And there was pornography, upon which McVarish pounced with snorts of glee.

I know little of pornography. It does not stir me. But McVarish seemed to know a great deal. There was a classic of this genre, nothing less than a fine copy of Aretino's *Sonnetti Lussuriosi,* with all the original plates by Guilio Romano. I had heard of this erotic marvel, and we all had a good look. I soon tired of it because the pictures—which McVarish invariably referred to as 'The Postures'—illustrated modes of sexual intercourse, although the naked people were so classical in figure, and so immovably classic in their calm, whatever they might be doing, that they seemed to me to be dull. No emotion illuminated them. But in contrast there were a lot of Japanese prints in which furious men, with astonishingly enlarged privates, were setting upon moon-faced women in a manner almost cannibalistic. Hollier looked at them with gloomy calm, but McVarish whooped and frisked about until I feared he might have an orgasm, right there amid the dust. It had never occurred to me that a grown man could be so powerfully fetched by a dirty picture. During that first week he insisted again and again on returning to that room in the third apartment, to gloat over these things.

"You see, I do a little in this way myself," he explained; "here is my most prized piece." He took from his pocket a snuffbox, which looked to be of eighteenth-century workmanship. Inside the lid was an enamel picture of Leda and the Swan, and when a little knob was pushed to and fro the swan thrust itself between Leda's legs, which jerked in mechanical ecstasy. A nasty toy, I thought, but Urky doted on it. "We single gentlemen like to have these things," he said. "What do you do, Darcourt? Of course we know that Hollier has his beautiful Maria."

To my astonishment Hollier blushed, but said nothing. His beautiful Maria? My Miss Theotoky, of New Testament Greek? I didn't like it at all.

On the fifth day, which was a Friday, we were further from making a beginning on the job of sorting this material than we had been on Monday. As we moved through the three apartments, trying not to show to one another how utterly without a plan we were, a key turned in the lock of apartment number one, and Arthur Cornish came in. We showed him what our problem was.

"Good God," he said. "I had no idea it was anything like this."

"I don't suppose it was ever cleaned," said McVarish. "Your Uncle Francis had strong views about cleaning-women. I remember him saying—'You've seen the ruins of the Acropolis? Of the Pyramids? Of Stonehenge? Of the Colosseum in Rome? Who reduced them to their present state? Fools say it was invading armies, or the erosion of Time. Rubbish! It was cleaning-women.' He said they always used dusters with hard buttons on them for flogging and flailing at anything with a delicate surface."

"I knew he was eccentric," said Arthur.

"When people use that word they always suggest something vague and woolly. Your uncle was rather a wild man, especially about his works of art."

Arthur did not seem to be listening; he nosed around. There is no other expression for what one was compelled to do in that extraordinary, precious mess.

He picked up a little water-colour sketch. "That's a nice thing. I recognize the place. It's on Georgian Bay; I spent a lot of time there when I was a boy. I don't suppose it would do any harm if I took it with me?"

He was greatly surprised by the way we all leapt at him. For the past five days we had been happening on nice little things that we thought there would be no harm in taking away, and we had restrained ourselves.

Hollier explained. The sketch was signed; it was a Varley. Had Francis Cornish bought it, or had he taken it at some low point in Varley's life, hoping to sell it, thereby getting some money for the artist? Who could tell? If Cornish had not bought it, the sketch, which was now of substantial value, belonged to the dead painter's estate. There were scores of such problems, and how were we expected to deal with them?

That was when we found out why Arthur Cornish, not yet thirty, was good at business. "You'd better query any living painter who can be found about anything signed that's here; otherwise it all goes to the National Gallery, according to the will. We can't go into the matter of ownership beyond that. 'Of which I die possessed' is what the will says, and so far as we're concerned he dies possessed of anything that is in these apartments. It will mean a lot of letters; I'll send you a good secretary."

When he went, he looked wistfully at the little Varley. How easy to covet something when the owner is dead, and it has been willed to a faceless, soulless public body.

Second Paradise II

DURING THE FIRST ten days after Parlabane settled himself in Hollier's outer room I went through a variety of feelings about him: indignation because he invaded what I wanted for myself; disgust at having to share a place which he quite soon invested with his strong personal smell; fury at his trick of nosing into my papers and even my briefcase when I was elsewhere; irritation at his way of talking, which mingled a creepy-crawly nineteenth-century clerical manner with occasional very sharp phrases and obscenities; a sense that he was laughing at me and playing with me; feminine fury at being treated mockingly as the weaker vessel. I was getting no work done, and I decided to have it out with Hollier.

It was not easy to catch him, because he was out every afternoon; something to do with the Cornish business, I gathered. I hoped that soon the mysterious manuscript of which he had spoken would be mentioned again. But one day I caught him in the quadrangle and persuaded him to sit on a bench while I told my tale.

"Of course it is tedious for you," he said; "and for me, as well. But Parlabane is an old friend, and you mustn't turn your back on old friends. We were at school together, at Colborne College, and then we went through Spook together and began academic careers together. I know something about his family; that wasn't a happy story. And now he's down on his luck.

"I suppose it's his own fault. But I always admired him, you see, and I don't imagine you know what that means among young men. Hero-worship is important to them, and when it has passed, it is false to yourself to forget what the hero once meant. He was always first in every class, and I was lucky to be fifth. He could write brilliant light verse; I have some of it still. His conversation was a delight to all of our group; he was witty and I'm most decidedly not. The whole College expected brilliant things from him, and his reputation spread far beyond the College, through the whole University. When he graduated with the Governor General's Medal and top honours of all kinds, and whizzed off to Princeton with a princely scholarship to do his doctoral work, the rest of us didn't envy him; we marvelled at him. He was so special, you see."

"But what went wrong?"

"I'm not much good at knowing what goes wrong with people. But when he came back he was immediately grabbed by Spook for its philosophy faculty; he was obviously the most brilliant young philosopher in the University and in the whole of Canada, I expect. But he had become different during those years. Medieval philosophy was his thing—Thomas Aquinas, chiefly—and all that fine-honed scholastic disputation was victuals and drink to him. But he did something not many academic philosophers do; he let his philosophy spill over into his life, and just for fun he would take the most outrageous lines in argument. His specialty was the history of scepticism: the impossibility of real knowledge—no certainty of truth. Making black seem white was easy for him. I suppose it affected his private life, and there were a few messes, and Spook found him too rich for its blood, and by general consent he moved on, leaving rather a stink."

"Sounds like too much intellect and too little character."

"Don't be a Pharisee, Maria; it isn't becoming either to your age or your beauty. You didn't know him as I know him."

"Yes, but this monk business!"

"He does that to spook Spook. And he was a monk. It was his latest attempt to find his place in life."

"You mean he isn't a monk now?"

"Legally, perhaps, but he went over the wall, and it wouldn't be easy for him to climb back again. I had lost touch with him, but a few months ago I had a most pathetic letter saying how unhappy he was in the monastery—it was in the Midlands—and begging for help to get out. So I sent him some money. How could I do otherwise? It never entered my head that he would turn up here, and certainly not in that rig-out he wears. But I suppose it's the only outfit he owns."

"And is he going to stay forever?"

"The Bursar is getting restless. He doesn't mind me having a guest overnight, now and then, but he spoke to me about Parlabane and said he couldn't allow a squatter in the College, and he'd refuse to let Parlabane charge meals in Hall unless he had some assurance that he could pay his bill. Which he can't, you see. So I shall have to do something."

"I hope you won't take him on as a permanent responsibility."

"Ah, you hope that, do you Maria? And what right have you to hope any such thing?"

There was no answer to that one. I hadn't expected Hollier to turn professor on me—not after the encounter on the sofa which had now become Parlabane's bed. I had to climb down.

"I'm sorry. But it's not as if it were none of my business. You did say I was to work in your outer room. How can I do that with Parlabane sitting there all day knitting those interminable socks of his? And staring. He fidgets me till I can't stand it."

"Be patient a little longer. I haven't forgotten you, or the work I want you to do. Try to understand Parlabane."

Then he stood up, and the talk was over. As he walked away I looked upward, and in the window of Hollier's rooms—very high up, because Spook is nothing if not Gothic in effect—I saw Parlabane's face looking down at us. He couldn't possibly have heard, but he was laughing, and made a waggling gesture at me with his finger, as if he were saying, "Naughty girl; naughty puss!"

[2]

TRY TO UNDERSTAND HIM. All right. Up the stairs I went and before he could speak I said: "Dr. Parlabane, could you have dinner with me tonight?"

"It would be an honour, Maria. But may I ask why this sudden invitation? Do I look as if I needed feeding up?"

"You pinched a big block of chocolate out of my briefcase yesterday. I thought you might be hungry."

"And so I am. The Bursar is looking sour these days whenever

I appear in Hall. He suspects I shall not be able to pay my bill, and he is right. We monks learn not to be sensitive about poverty."

"Let's meet downstairs at half past six."

I took him to a spaghetti joint that students frequent, called The Rude Plenty; he began with a hearty vegetable broth, then ate a mountain of spaghetti with meat sauce, and drank the whole of a flask of Chianti except for my single glass. He wolfed a lot of something made with custard, coconut shreds, and plum jam, and then made heavy inroads on a large piece of Gorgonzola that came to the table whole and was removed in a state of wreckage. He had two big cups of frothed coffee, and topped off with a Strega; I even stood him a fearful Italian cigar.

He was a fast, greedy eater and a notable belcher. He talked as he ate, giving a good view of whatever was in his mouth, plying me with questions that called for extended answers.

"What are you doing these days, Maria? That's to say, when you are not glaring at me as I knit my innocent, monkish long socks; we monks wear 'em long, you know, in case the robe should blow aside in the wind, and show a scandalous amount of middle-aged leg."

"I'm getting on with the work that will eventually make me a Doctor of Philosophy."

"Ah, that blessed degree that stamps us for life as creatures of guaranteed intellectual worth. But what's your special study?"

"That's rather complicated. I come under the general umbrella of Comparative Literature, but that's a house of many mansions. Working with Professor Hollier I shall certainly do my thesis on something in his line."

"Which isn't just what I'd call Comparative Literature. Rooting about in the kitchen-middens and trash-heaps of the Middle Ages. What was it he made his name with?"

"A definitive study of the establishment of the Church Calendar, by Dionysius Exiguus. A lot of it had been done before, but it was Hollier who showed why Dionysius reached his conclusions—the popular belief and ancient custom that lay behind the finished work, and all that. It was what established him as a really great paleo-psychologist."

"Have mercy, God! Is that some new kind of shrink?"

"You know it isn't. It's really digging into what people thought, in times when their thinking was a muddle of religion and folk-belief and rags of misunderstood classical learning, instead of being what it is today, which I suppose you'd have to call a muddle of materialism, and folk-belief, and rags of misunderstood scientific learning. Comp. Lit. gets mixed up with it because you have to know a lot of languages, but it spills over into the Centre for the Study of the History of Science and Technology. Hollier is cross-appointed there, you know."

"No, I didn't know."

"There's a lot of talk about establishing an Institute of Advanced Studies; he'd be very important there. It will come as soon as the University can get its hands on some money."

"That may not be soon. Our fatherly government is growing restless about the big sums universities consume. It's the people's money, dear Maria, and don't you ever forget it. And the people, those infallible judges of value, must have what they want, and what they think they want (because the politicians tell them so) is people who can fill useful jobs. Not remote chaps like Clem Hollier, who want to dig in the past. When you've achieved your Ph.D., what the hell good will you be to society?"

"That depends on what you call society. I might just manage to push away a cloud or two from what people are like now, by discovering what they've been at some time past."

"Nobody is going to like you for that, sweetie. Never disturb ignorance. Ignorance is like a rare, exotic fruit; touch it and the bloom is gone. Do you know who said that?"

"Oscar Wilde, wasn't it?"

"Clever girl. It was dear, dead Oscar. By no means a fool when he didn't pretend to be thinking, and just let his imagination run. But I thought you were doing something about Rabelais."

"Yes—well, I've got to have a thesis topic, and Hollier has put me to work to get some notion of what Rabelais's intellectual background was."

"Old stuff, surely?"

"He thinks I might find a few new things, or take a new look at some old things. The Ph.D. thesis isn't expected to be a thunderbolt from heaven, you know."

"Certainly not. The world couldn't stand so many thunderbolts. You haven't written anything yet?"

"I'm making preparations, I've got to bone up on New Testament Greek; Rabelais was very keen on it. It was a big thing in his time."

"Surely, with your name, you know some modern Greek?"

"No, but I know Classical Greek pretty well. And French and Spanish and Italian and German and of course Latin—the Golden, the Silver, and the awful kind they used in the Middle Ages."

"You make me quite dizzy. How so many languages?"

"My father was very great on languages. He was a Pole, and he lived quite a while in Hungary. He made it a game, when I was a child. I don't pretend to be perfect in those languages; I can't write them very well but I can read and speak them well enough. It's not difficult, if you have a knack."

"Yes, if you have a knack."

"When you know two or three, a lot of others just fall into place. People are afraid of languages."

"But your cradle tongues are Polish and Hungarian? Any others?"

"One or two. Not important."

I certainly didn't mean to tell him which unimportant language I spoke at home, when things grew hot. I hoped I had learned a lesson from my indiscretion when I told Hollier about the *bomari*. And I began to fear that if I were not careful, Parlabane might get that out of me. His curiosity was of a special intensity, and he bustled me in conversation so that I was apt to say more than I wanted to. Perhaps if I took the questioning out of his hands I could escape his prying?

Therefore—"You ask a lot of questions, but you never tell anything. Who are you, Dr. Parlabane? You're a Canadian, aren't you?"

"Please call me Brother John; I put aside all my academic pomps long ago, when I fell in the world and discovered that my only salvation lay in humility. Yes, I'm a Canadian. I'm a child of this great city, and also a child of this great university, and a child of Spook. You know why it's called Spook?"

"It's the College of St. John and the Holy Ghost. Spook's the Holy Ghost."

"Sometimes used as a put-down; sometimes, as I told you, affectionately. But you know the reference, surely? Mark one, verse eight: 'I indeed have baptized you with water, but he shall baptize you with the Holy Ghost.' So the college is truly an Alma Mater, a Bounteous Mother, and from one breast she gives her children the milk of knowledge and from the other the milk of salvation and good doctrine. In other words, water without which no man can live, and the Holy Ghost without which no man can live well. But the nasty little brats get Ma's boobs so mixed up they don't know which is which. I only discovered salvation and good doctrine after I had been brought very low in the world."

"How did that happen?"

"Perhaps some day I'll tell you."

"Well, you can't expect to ask all the questions, Brother John. I've been told you had an exceptionally brilliant academic career."

"And so I did. Oh, yes indeed, I was a meteor in the world of the intellect when I still knew nothing about mankind, and nothing whatever about myself."

"That was the knowledge that brought you down?"

"It was my failure to combine those two kinds of knowledge that brought me down."

I decided I would bounce Brother John a bit, and see if I could get something out of him beside all this sparring. "Too much intellect and too little character—was that it?"

That did it. "That is wholly unworthy of you, Maria Magdalena Theotoky. If you were some narrow Canadian girl who had known nothing but the life of Toronto and Georgian Bay, such a remark might seem perceptive. But you have drunk at better springs than that. What do you mean by character?"

"Guts. A good strong will to balance all the book-learning. An understanding of how many beans make five."

"And an understanding of how to get a good academic appointment, and then tenure, and become a full professor without ever guessing what you're really full of, and then soar to a Distinguished Professor who can bully the President into giving you a whopping salary because otherwise you might slip away to Harvard? You don't mean that, Maria. That's some fool talking out of your past. You'd better corner whatever fool it is and tell him this: the kind of character you talk about is all rubbish. What really shapes and conditions and makes us is somebody only a few of us ever have the courage to face: and that is the child you once were, long before formal education ever got its claws into you—that impatient, all-demanding child who wants love and power and can't get enough of either and who goes on raging and weeping in your spirit till at last your eyes are closed and all the fools say, 'Doesn't he look peaceful?' It is those pent-up, craving children who make all the wars and all the horrors and all the art and all the beauty and discovery in life, because they are trying to achieve what lay beyond their grasp before they were five years old."

So—I had bounced him. "And have you found that child, Wee Jackie Parlabane?"

"I think so. And rather a battered baby he has proved to be. But do you believe what I've said?"

"Yes, I do. Hollier says the same thing, in a different way. He says that people don't by any means all live in what we call the present; the psychic structure of modern man lurches and yaws over a span of at least ten thousand years. And everybody knows that children are primitives."

"Have you ever known any primitives?"

Had I! This was a time to hold my tongue. So I nodded.

"What's Hollier really up to? Don't say paleo-psychology again. Tell me in terms a simple philosopher can understand."

"A philosopher? Hollier is rather like Heidegger, if you want a philosopher. He tries to recover the mentality of the earliest thinkers; but not just the great thinkers—the ordinary people, some of whom didn't hold precisely ordinary positions. Kings and priests, some of them, because they have left their mark on the history of the development of the mind, by tradition and custom and folk-belief. He just wants to find out. He wants to comprehend those earlier modes of thought without criticizing them. He's deep in the Middle Ages because they really are middle—between the far past, and the post-Renaissance thinking of today. So he can stand in the middle and look both ways. He hunts for fossil ideas, and tries to discover something about the way the mind has functioned from them."

I had ordered another bottle of Chianti, and Parlabane had drunk most of it, because two glasses is my limit. He had had four Stregas, as well, and another asphyxiating cigar, but drunks and stinks are no strangers to me. He had begun to talk loudly, and sometimes talked through a belch, raising his voice as if to quell the interruption from within.

"You know, when we were at Spook together I wouldn't have given a plugged nickel for Hollier's chances of being anything but a good, tenured professor. He's come on a lot."

"Yes, he's one of the Distinguished Professors you were sneering at. Not long ago, in a press interview, the President called him one of the ornaments of the university."

"Have mercy, God! Old Clem! A late-bloomer. And of course he's got you."

"I am his student. A good student, too."

"Balls! You're his *soror mystica*. A child could see it. Anyhow, that extremely gifted, all-desiring Wee Johnnie Parlabane can see it, long before it reaches the bleared eyes of the grown-ups. He encloses you. He engulfs you. You are completely wrapped up in him."

"Don't shout so. People are looking."

Now he was really shouting. " 'Don't shout, I can hear you perfectly. I have the Morley Phone which fits in the ear and cannot be seen. Ends deafness instantly.'—Do you remember that old advertisement? No, of course you don't; you know too much and you aren't old enough to remember anything." Now Parlabane squeaked in a falsetto: " 'Don't shout so; people are looking!' Who gives a damn, you stupid twat? Let 'em look! You love him. Worse, you're subsumed in him, and he doesn't know it. Oh, shame on stupid Professor Hollier!"

But he does know it! Would I have let him take me on the sofa five months ago if I wasn't sure he knew I loved him? No! Don't ask that question. I can't be sure of the answer now.

The proprietor of The Rude Plenty was hovering. I gave him a beseeching glance, and he helped me get Parlabane to his feet and toward the door. The monk was as strong as a bull, and it was a tussle. Parlabane began to sing in a very loud and surprisingly melodious voice—

> Let the world slide, let the world go,
> A fig for care and a fig for woe!
> If I can't pay, why I can owe,
> And death makes equal the high and the low.

At last I got him into the street, and steered him back to the front door of Spook, where the night porter, an old friend of mine, took him in charge.

As I walked back to the subway station I thought: that's what comes of trying to understand Parlabane; a loud scene in The Rude Plenty. Would I go on? Yes, I thought I would.

The initiative was taken out of my hands. When I arrived at Hollier's outer room the following morning there was a note for me, placed beside a bouquet of flowers—salvia—which had too obviously been culled from the garden outside the Rector's Lodging. The note read:

Dearest and Most Understanding of Created Beings:
Sorry about last night. Some time since I had a really good swig at anything. Shall I say it will not happen again? Not with any degree of sincerity. But I must make reparation. So ask me to dinner again soon, and I shall tell you the Story Of My Life, which is well worth whatever it may cost you.
      Your crawling slave,
                                                  P.

[3]

TO BECOME A PH.D. you must take a few courses relating to your special theme before you get down to work on your thesis. I had done almost all that was necessary, but Hollier suggested that I do two courses this year, one with Professor Urquhart McVarish in Renaissance European Culture and the other in New Testament Greek with Professor the Reverend Simon Darcourt. McVarish lectured dully; his stuff was good but he was too much the scholar to make it interesting, lest somebody should accuse him of 'popularization'. He was a fussy little man who was forever dabbing at his long red nose with a handkerchief he kept tucked in his left sleeve. Somebody told me that this was a sign that he had once been an officer in a first-class British regiment. About twenty people attended the lectures.

Prof. the Rev. was different, a roly-poly parson, as pink as a baby, who did not lecture, but conducted seminars, in which everybody present was expected to speak up and have an opinion, or at least ask questions. There were only five of us: myself and three young men and one middle-aged man, all studying for the ministry. Two of the young men were modern and messy, long-haired and fashionably dirty; they were heading for advanced evangelical church work, and in their spare time assisted in services with rock music, where people like themselves danced away Evil, and embraced one another in tears when the show was over. They were taking the course in hopes, I think, of discovering from the original texts that Jesus was also a great dancer and guitar-player. The other young man was very High Church Anglican, and addressed Darcourt as 'Father' and wore a dark grey suit to which he obviously hoped, very soon, to add a clerical collar. The middle-aged man had given up his job selling insurance to become a parson, and worked like a galley-slave, because he had a wife and two children and had to get himself ordained as fast as he could. Altogether, they were not an inspiring lot. God had presumably called all four to His service, but surely in a fit of absent-mindedness or perhaps as some complicated Jewish joke.

Luckily, Prof. the Rev. was far better than I could have hoped. "What do you expect from this seminar?" he asked, right away. "I'm not going to teach you a language; I suppose you all know classical Greek?" I did, but the four men looked unconfident, and admitted slowly that they had done a bit of it, or crammed some during summer courses. "If you know Greek, it may be assumed that you also know Latin," said Prof. the Rev., and this was received in glum silence. But was he downhearted? No!

"Let's find out how good you are," he said. "I'm going to write a short passage on the blackboard, and in a few minutes I'll ask you for a translation." Widespread discomfort, and one of the long-haired ones murmured that he hadn't brought a Latin dictionary with him. "You won't need it," said Darcourt; "this is easy."

He wrote: *Conloqui et conridere et vicissim benevole obsequi, simul leger libros dulciloquos, simul nugari et simul honestari.* Then he sat down and beamed at us over his half-glasses. "That's the motto, the groundwork for what we shall do in this seminar during the year before us; that's the spirit in which we shall work. Now, let's have a rendering in English. Who'll translate?"

There followed that awful hush that falls on a room when several people are trying to make themselves invisible. "Talk together, laugh together, do good to each other—" murmured the spiky youth, and fell silent. The hairy pair looked as if they hated Darcourt already.

"Ladies first," said Darcourt, smiling at me. So in I plunged.

"Conversations and jokes together, mutual rendering of good services, the reading together of sweetly phrased books, the sharing of nonsense and mutual attentions," said I.

I could see he was pleased. "Admirable. Now somebody else tell me where it comes from. Come on, you've all read the book, even if only in translation. You ought to know it well; the author ought to be a close friend."

But nobody would speak and I suspect nobody knew. Shall I make myself hated, I thought. I might as well; I've been doing it in classes all my life.

"It's Saint Augustine's *Confessions*," I said. The two hairy ones looked at me with loathing, the spiky one with sick envy. The middle-aged one was making a careful note; he was going to conquer this stuff or die; he owed it to the wife and kids.

"Thank you, Miss Theotoky. You gentlemen must learn not to be so shy," he said with what seemed to be a hint of irony. "That's what we're going to attempt here; talk and jokes—I hope—rising out of the reading of the New Testament. Not that it's a great book for jokes, though Christ once made a pun on Peter's new name that he had given him: 'Thou art Peter and upon this rock I will build my church'. Of course Peter is *petras*, a stone, in Greek. If that were translated Thou art Rocky and upon this rock I will build my church, people would get the point, but it would hardly be worth it. Wouldn't have church-goers rolling in the aisles two thousand years later. Of course I suppose Christ went on calling him Cephas, which is Stone in Aramaic, but the pun suggests that Our Lord knew some Greek—perhaps quite a lot of it. And so should you, if you want to serve Him."

It seemed to me that Darcourt was being mischievous; he saw that the hairy ones did not like the line he was taking, and he was getting at them.

"This study can lead in all sorts of directions," he said, "and of course deep into the Middle Ages when the sort of Greek we are going to study was hardly known in Europe, and wasn't in the least encouraged by the Church. But there were some rum people who knew some of it—alchemists and detrimentals of that sort—and the tradition of it persisted in the Near East, where Greek was making its long journey toward the language we know as Modern Greek. Funny how languages break down and turn into something else. Latin was rubbed away until it degenerated into dreadful lingos like French and Spanish and Italian, and lo! people found out that quite new things could be said in these degenerate tongues—things nobody had ever thought of in Latin. English is breaking down now in the same way—becoming a world language that every Tom Dick and Harry must learn, and speak in a way that would give Doctor Johnson the jim-jams. Received Standard English has had it; even American English, that once seemed such an impertinent johnny-come-lately in literature, is fusty stuff compared with what you will hear in Africa, which is where the action is, in our day. But I am indulging myself—a bad professorial habit. You must check me when you see it coming on. To work, then. May I assume that you all know the Greek alphabet, and therefore can count to ten in Greek? Good. Then let's begin with changes there."

I knew I was going to like Prof. the Rev. Darcourt. He seemed to think that learning could be amusing, and that heavy people needed stirring up. Like Rabelais, of whom even educated people like Parlabane had such a stupid opinion. Rabelais was gloriously learned because learning amused him, and so far as I am concerned that is learning's best justification. Not the only one, but the best.

It is not that I wanted to know a great deal, in order to acquire what is now called expertise, and which enables one to become an expert-tease to people who don't know as much as you do about the tiny corner you have made your own. I hoped for a bigger fish; I wanted nothing less than Wisdom. In a modern university if you ask for knowledge they will provide it in almost any form—though if you ask for out-of-fashion things they may say, like the people in shops, 'Sorry, there's no call for it.' But if you ask for Wisdom—God save us all! What a show of modesty, what disclaimers from the men and women from whose eyes intelligence shines forth like a lighthouse. Intelligence, yes, but of Wisdom not so much as the gleam of a single candle.

That was what chained me to Hollier; I thought that in him I saw Wisdom. And as Paracelsus said—that Paracelsus with whom I had to be acquainted because he was part of my study of Rabelais: *The striving for wisdom is the second paradise of the world.*

With Hollier I truly thought that I would have the second paradise, and the first as well.

The New Aubrey II

IS IT EVER a kindness to appoint someone an executor? It is
evidence of trust, certainly, but it may become a tedious servitude. Hollier and I were swept more and more into concern
with Cornish's affairs, at cost of time and energy that we needed
for our own work. There was a note in the will that when everything was dealt with each of the advisers or sub-executors might
choose 'some object that especially pleases him, provided it has
not been designated as a bequest or portion of a bequest elsewhere'. But this made our work more vexatious, because we were
continually coming upon things we would like to have and finding
that they had been earmarked for somebody else. And young
Cornish's lawyers told us that we might not choose or remove
anything until all bequests had been dealt with. We were like
poor relatives at the Christmas Tree of rich children.

Rich, and not as grateful as I thought they should be. The big
recipients were glad enough to take what they liked, but made
it clear that some things that were in their portion didn't especially
please them and weren't welcome.

The National Gallery was one of these. Cornish had left them
dozens of canvases, but he had stipulated that the Canadian
pictures were to be kept together and placed on permanent
exhibition, as the Cornish Bequest. The Gallery people said,
reasonably enough, that they liked to show their pictures in a
historical context, and Cornish's Krieghoffs and other early things
ought to go with their exhibitions of Early Canadian Painting;
they didn't want primitives spotted about all over their galleries.
They said also that they didn't think some of the modern pic-

tures first-rate, whatever Cornish may have thought, and simply couldn't say they would put them on permanent show. If there was to be a Cornish Bequest, Cornish might have discussed it with them beforehand; or might have thought of leaving money to build a special gallery for it; even if he had done so, they had no land on which to build such a gallery. The correspondence was courteous, but only just, and there were frequent hints that donors could be peremptory and inconsiderate, and that anybody without a degree in Fine Arts was rather an amateur.

Hollier didn't like that. He is a man of strong feelings and loyalties, and he thought Cornish's memory was being insulted. I, with my tedious capacity to see both sides of a question, wasn't so sure. McVarish made Hollier even angrier by being frivolous, as if the will and Cornish's wishes didn't matter very much.

"All donors and benefactors are crazy," he said. "What they want is posthumous fame and posthumous gratitude. Every college and faculty on this campus could tell a bloody tale if you asked for it. What about the family that earmarked the income from a million to found a chair of internal medicine, and then craftily snatched it back when they didn't like the politics of the third man appointed to it—years later? What about that old bastard who gave a historical library to the University Library, and frowned everybody down and demanded an honorary degree even when it was shown that the books weren't really his, but the property of a foundation he directed? What about old Mahaffy, who gave a bundle for a Centre for Celtic Studies, on condition that Celtic Studies meant Irish Studies and the Scots and the Welsh and the Bretons could all go and bugger themselves? What about that miserable old hound who founded a lectureship, insisting that it be initiated in his lifetime and that the University foot the bill till he died, and then told the President, years later, with a grin on his face, that he'd changed his mind, and didn't like the lectures anyway? Benefaction means self-satisfaction, nine times out of ten. The guile and cunning that enable benefactors to get their hands on the dough make it almost impossible for them to relinquish it, at the hour of death. Even our dear friend Cornish—a very superior specimen, as we all know—can't entirely relax his grip. But what does it matter, anyhow? If the National Gallery doesn't want a picture, give it to the Provincial Gallery, who are getting lots of pictures anyhow. What does another daub or so matter, in the long run? You know what the will says: anything that's left over after specific pictures have gone to the right places may be disposed of at the discretion of Cornish's executors. And that means us. The nephew won't know and won't care. Our job is to cut up the melon and get these apartments emptied."

But Hollier wouldn't hear of that. I had known him for years in a casual way, but I had never seen very deeply into him. He seemed to me to have more conscience than is good for any man. A powerful conscience and no sense of humour—a dangerous combination.

McVarish, on the other hand, possessed rather too much humour. People tend to talk as if a sense of humour were a wonderful adjunct to a personality—almost a substitute for common sense, not to speak of wisdom. But in the case of McVarish it was a sense of irresponsibility, a sense of the unimportance of anybody else's needs or wishes if they interfered with his convenience; it was a cheerful disguise for the contempt he felt for everybody but himself. In conversation and in the affairs of life he greatly valued what he called 'the light touch'; nothing must ever be taken seriously, and the kind of seriousness Hollier displayed was, so McVarish hinted pretty broadly, ill-bred. I like a light touch myself, but in McVarish's case it was too plainly another name for selfishness. He didn't care about carrying out Cornish's wishes as well as could be managed; he just liked the importance of being an executor to a very rich and special man, and of hob-nobbing with people from the galleries who met his exacting standards. As has so often been my lot, I had to play peacemaker between these irreconcilables.

My special problem was with archivists. The University Library, not content with the promise of a splendid haul of manuscripts and rare books, wanted all Cornish's papers. The National Library in Ottawa, which had been left nothing, put in a courteous but determined request for Cornish's letters, records, papers, everything that could be found relating to his career as a collector and patron. The two libraries squared off and began, politely but intensely, to fight it out. Cornish had never, I suppose, thought that his old letters and junk might be of any interest to anyone;

he kept no records, his method of filing was to throw stuff into cardboard cartons in whatever order came to hand; his note-books—preserved simply because he never threw anything away—were a muddle of scribbled reminders of appointments, notes of unspecified sums of money, addresses, and occasional words and phrases that had meant something to him at some time. I looked through them superficially and found an entry in a book which, as it was not filled, I presumed must have been his last: it said, 'Lend McV. Rab. MS April 16'.

There were treasures, too, and nobody knew about them except myself, because I would not permit the librarians to snoop. There were letters from painters who had subsequently become cele-brated, but who wrote to Cornish when they were young and poor, letters of friendship and often of touching need. They il-lustrated their letters with sketches and scribbles that were funny and delightful, and sometimes of beauty. When I explained all of this to Arthur Cornish, he said: "I leave it up to you; Uncle Frank trusted you and that's quite good enough for me." Which was complimentary but unhelpful, because the librarians were tough.

The National Library's case was that Cornish had been a Great Canadian (how he would have laughed, for he had as little vanity as any man I ever knew) and everything about him that could be preserved should be given the archival treatment, catalogued, cross-indexed, and preserved in acid-free containers so that it would never perish. But the University Library saw Cornish as a great benefactor of the University who had shown his esteem for its Library by leaving it a splendid collection of fine books and manuscripts; his memory should repose, so far as possible, in their hands.

Why? I asked. Were not the treasures themselves sufficient without all the rubbish, much of which seemed to me to be good for nothing but the incinerator? No, said the archivists, in con-trolled voices beneath which I could hear suppressed shrieks of rage and horror at my ignorance and obtuseness. Surely I was not forgetting Research, that giant scholarly industry? Students of art, students of history, students of God knows what else, would want to know everything about Cornish that could be recovered. How did I expect that the official biography of Cornish could be written if all his papers were not in responsible hands, forever?

I was not impressed. I have read two or three official lives of people I have known well, and they never seemed to be about the person I knew. They were, upon the whole, cautiously favourable to their subjects, though they did not neglect what the writers loved to call Flaws. It is part of the received doctrine of modern biography that all characters are Flawed, and as a Christian priest I am quite ready to agree, but the Flaws the biographers exhibited usually meant that the person under discussion had not seen eye to eye with the biographer on matters of politics, or social betterment, or something impersonal. What I thought of as human flaws—Pride, Wrath, Envy, Lust, Gluttony, Avarice, and Sloth, the Deadly Seven, of which Cornish had scored pretty high on the latter four—rarely received an intelligent discussion. As for the Virtues—Faith, Hope, Charity, Prudence, Justice, Fortitude, and Temperance, some of which Cornish had possessed in praiseworthy plenty—biographers never wanted to talk about them under their own names, or even under fashionable modern names. There had been no Love in the biographies of any people I had known personally, and perhaps it was impudent of me to wish that Cornish, if he were to be the subject of a Life, might have a proper measure of Love. Or Hate, or anything but the scholarly incomprehension of a professional biographer.

So I havered and temporized between the two claimants, and lost sleep, and sometimes wished I had the courage to do what I had a right to do, and put the whole mess in a fire. But those wonderful letters from the artists made me stay my hand.

What was all Cornish's hoard of objects worth? Arthur Cornish had the easy job of dealing with the money, which could be reckoned up in terms tax-collectors and probate courts understood. The objects of art were quite another thing; the tax people wanted a sum to put here and there on pieces of paper which were important to them, if to nobody else. We could not appeal to insurance records; Cornish never insured anything. Why insure what is irreplaceable? I persuaded Hollier and McVarish, without difficulty, to let me call in the Toronto branch of Sotheby's to make a valuation. But here again we ran into trouble. The valuers knew their stuff, and could tell us what the hoard might fetch, piece by piece, at auction if it were all catalogued and offered in the right markets. A probate value was something different, because Arthur Cornish was firm in his determination not to have estate duties reckoned on present inflated values for objects of art. The fact that so much of the stuff was left to the public, in one way or another, did not make as much difference as Arthur thought it should.

It was weary work, and kept me from what I was paid by the university to do.

[2]

THE PRINCIPAL EXCUSE for my life, I suppose, is that I am a good teacher. But to teach my best I must have some peace of mind, because I do not simply dole out lectures I prepared long ago; I engage my classes, which are never large, in talk and discussion; every year the shape of the work is different, and the result is different, because as much depends on the quality of the students as depends on me. Cornish's posthumous demands cost me too much in worry for me to teach at my best level.

I was particularly anxious to do so, because for the first time in some years I had an exceptional student, none other than the Maria Magdalena Theotoky whose presence I had taken note of at Cornish's funeral. I asked her if she knew him, and she said no, but that Professor Hollier had said she might find herself greatly obliged to Cornish some day, and suggested that she attend. She seemed to be a special pet of Hollier's, and that surprised me because he was not a man to have much to do with his students outside the classroom. I suppose that, like myself, he was drawn by her real scholarly appetite; she appeared to want knowledge for itself, and not because it could lead to a career. Theologically trained as I was, I wondered if she were one of the Scholarly Elect; I mean it as a joke, but only partly as a joke. As Calvin said that mankind was divided between the Elect, chosen to be saved, and the Reprobate Remainder of mankind, so it seemed to me to be with knowledge; there were those who were born to it, and those who struggled to acquire it. With the Scholarly Elect one seems not so much to be teaching them as reminding them of something they already know; that was how it was with Maria, and she fascinated me.

Of course she was better prepared for New Testament Greek

than students usually are; she knew Classical Greek well, and instead of treating the N. T. stuff as a degenerate language she saw it for what it was, a splendid ruin, like a Greek statue with the nose knocked off, the arms gone, the privy parts lost, but Greek nevertheless, and splendid in decay. A language, furthermore, that had been serviceable to St. Paul and the Four Evangelists, and capable of saying mighty things.

Why was she bothering with it? She said something about her studies in Rabelais, who knew Greek as both a priest and a humanist, at a time when the Church did not encourage Greek studies. Funny about that, I told the seminar; during the Renaissance it was people outside the universities who really dug into the rediscovered classics; even Archimedes, who put forward no disturbing ideas, like Plato, but propounded some scientific discoveries and the theory of the endless screw, was not studied by the academicians. This brought a laugh from my two ultra-modern students who had been nurtured in our permissive age, and who probably thought that the endless screw, in their own interpretation of the words, might be a path to enlightenment. But Maria knew what I was really talking about, which is that universities cannot be more universal than the people who teach, and the people who learn, within their walls. Those who can get beyond the fashionable learning of their day are few, and it looked as if she might be one of them. I believed myself to be a teacher who could guide her.

Dangerous to make pets of students, I reminded myself. But teaching Maria was like throwing a match into oil, and the others were like wet wood I was trying to blow into something like a fire. I was sorry that Cornish was claiming so much of my energy.

Sorry too because I had become enthusiastic about *The New Aubrey*. Poor Ellerman's idea had raised a flame in me, and I wanted to fan it.

Just a few random notes about scholarly contemporaries—that was what he had suggested. But where to begin? It is easy to find eccentrics in universities if your notion of an eccentric is simply a fellow with some odd habits. But the true eccentric, the man who stands apart from the fashionable scholarship of his day and who may be the begetter of notable scholarship in the future, is a rarer bird. These are seldom the most popular figures, because they derive their energy from a source not understood by their contemporaries. Hollier, I had cause to believe, was such a man, and I must take advantage of the special opportunity Cornish had given me to study him. But the more spectacular eccentrics, the *Species Dingbaticus* as I had heard students call them, were attractive to me; I love a mountebank. And in Urquhart McVarish I had been brought close to a very fine mountebank indeed.

Not that he was short on scholarship. As a scholar in Renaissance history he had a good reputation. But he was immodest about it; he is the only man of any respectability in the scholarly world whom I had ever heard refer to himself shamelessly as 'a great scholar'. He had once been Chairman of the Centre for Renaissance Studies and for a time it seemed as if he would gain it an international reputation. He encouraged able students to work with him, but he would not interest himself in their efforts to stand on their own feet; he used them as skilled assistants, and they saw their chances of achieving the Ph.D. degree vanishing. Taxed with this, Urky replied blithely that anybody who had studied with him could go anywhere in the world and get an academic appointment on that qualification alone. No Ph.D. would be required, and anyhow it was a silly degree which manifest fools were granted every year. To be a McVarish man was a far, far better thing. The students didn't believe it for the best of reasons—because it was untrue. So Urky had to be deposed, and the price was that he be raised to the small, highly paid group of Distinguished Professors, too fine for administrative work. Kicked upstairs.

In a university you cannot get rid of a tenured professor without an unholy row, and though academics love bickering they hate rows. It was widely agreed that the only way to get rid of Urky would be to murder him, and though the Dean may have toyed with that idea, he did not want to be caught. Anyhow, Urky was not a bad scholar. It was simply that he was intolerable, and for some reason that is never accepted as an excuse for getting rid of anybody. So Urky became a Distinguished Professor with light duties, a devoted secretary, and few students.

That did not content him. He took his transformation dourly, and developed what he called an 'awfu'scunner' to the University; he ran it down in a jokey style that was all his own to his few favourites, who might also be called toadies, among the students. I heard a few of these scorning Cornish's money bequest to Spook. "A million dollars," they said disdainfully; "what is it when you've invested it, in these days—a couple of mediocre professors, as if we needed any more mediocre professors." It was not hard to tell where that came from. Yes, I really must not fail to capture the essence of Urquhart McVarish.

We were deep in October when Urky asked me to one of his parties. He gave a party every fortnight, usually for students and junior members of faculty, and there had been one famous one at which his hairdresser was the guest of honour; Urky's hair was a quiffed and prinked wonder of silver, and there was a rumour that he wore a hair-net to bed. But I, who had long since had to admit that I possessed not a Shakespearean brow but a substantially bald head, had to be careful that Envy did not trip me up when I thought of that. This party was to include Hollier and myself, and was to have a Cornish flavour.

Indeed it did, for Arthur Cornish was there, the only non-academic present. We assembled pretty promptly at five, for the invitation, in Urky's elegant Italic hand, had said 'Sherry—5 to 7' and our university is great on punctuality. Of course it wasn't sherry only; Scotch and gin were the favourites, but Urky liked the 'sherry' business, as being more elegant than cocktails.

The apartment was a handsome one, and contained fine books on expensive shelves, and a few excellent pictures of a generally Renaissance character—Virgins and Saint Johns and a nude who looked rickety enough to be a Cranach but certainly wasn't, and two or three nice pieces of old statuary. Be careful of Envy, I said to myself, because I like fine things, and have some, though not as good as these. There was an excellent bar on what must once have been an ambry in a small church, and a student friend was dispensing generous drinks from it. It was a splendid setting for Urky.

There he was, in the centre of the room, wearing a smoking-jacket or a dinner-jacket or whatever it was, in a beautiful bottle-green silk. Not for Urky, as for lesser Scots, the obvious tartan jacket. He scoffed at tartans as romantic humbug, virtually unheard of until Sir Walter Scott set the Scotch tourist industry on its feet. Urky liked to play the high-born Scot. His Scots speech was high-born too; just a touch of a Highland lilt and a slight roll on some of the r's; no hint of the Robert Burns folk speech.

I was surprised to see Maria there. Urky had her by the arm, showing her a portrait above his mantel of a man in seventeenth-century lace cravat and a green coat the shade our host himself was wearing, whose nose was as long and whose face was as red as Urky's own.

"There you are, my dear, and surely a man after your own heart. My great forebear Sir Thomas Urquhart, first and still unquestionably the best translator of Rabelais. Hello, Simon, do you know Maria Theotoky? Precious on two counts, because she is a great beauty and a female Rabelaisian. They used to say that no decent woman could read Rabelais. Are you decent, Maria? I hope not."

"I haven't read the Urquhart translation," said Maria. "I stick to the French."

"But what you are missing! A great monument of scholarship and seventeenth-century English! And what rich neologisms! Slabberdegullion druggels, lubbardly louts, blockish grutnols, doddipol jolfheads, lobdotterels, codshead loobies, ninny-hammer flycatchers, and other suchlike defamatory epithets! How on earth do we get along without them? You must read it! You must allow me to give you a copy. And is it true, Maria dear, that the thighs of a gentlewoman are always cool? Rabelais says so, and I am sure you know why he says it is so, but is it true?"

"I doubt if Rabelais knew much about gentlewomen," said Maria.

"Probably not. But my ancestor did. He was a tremendous swell. Did you know that he is supposed to have died of ecstasy on hearing of the Restoration of his Sacred Majesty King Charles the Second?"

"I might give a guess about what kind of ecstasy it was," said Maria.

"Oho, *touché—touché*. And for that you deserve a drink and perhaps you will achieve a measure of ecstasy yourself."

Maria turned away to the bar without waiting for Urky to steer her there. A self-possessed young person, clearly, and not impressed by Urky's noisy, lickerish gallantry. I introduced her to Arthur Cornish, who was the stranger in this academic gathering, and he undertook to get her a drink. She asked for Campari. An unusual and rather expensive drink for a student. I took a more careful look at her clothes, although I don't know much about such things.

Professor Agnes Marley approached me. "You've heard about poor Ellerman? It won't be long now, I'm afraid."

"Really? I must go to see him. I'll go tomorrow."

"They won't let him see any visitors."

"I'm very sorry. There was something he said to me a few weeks ago—a suggestion. I'd like to tell him that I'm acting on it."

"Perhaps if you spoke to his wife—?"

"Of course. That's what I'll do. I think he'd like to know."

Arthur Cornish, and Maria with him, joined us.

"I see that Murray Brown has been taking a swipe at Uncle Frank," he said.

"On what grounds?"

"Having so much money, and leaving so much of it to the University."

"A million to Spook, I hear."

"Oh, yes. But several millions spread around over other colleges and some of the faculties."

"Well, what's wrong with that?"

"The things that are always wrong with Murray Brown. Why should some have so much when others have so little? Why should a man be allowed to choose where his money goes without regard for where money is needed? Why should the University get anything apart from what the government chooses to give it, when it throws its money around on filth and nonsense? You know Murray; the friend of the plain people."

"Murray Brown is what my great ancestor would have called a scurby sneaksby, or perhaps simply a turdy-gut," said Urky, who had joined us.

"Better not say turdy-gut," said Arthur. "That's one of Murray's beefs; he's heard about some scientist in the University who works on human excrement, and he wants to know where the money is coming from to support such nastiness."

"How does he know it's nastiness?" said Hollier.

"He doesn't, but he can make other people think so. He has tied it in with vivisection, which is another of his themes: torture, and now messing about with dirty things. Is this where our money is being spent? You know his line."

"And where has he said all this?"

"At one of his political rallies; he's getting to work early in preparation for the next election."

"He must be talking about Ozy Froats," said Urky, with one of his sniggering laughs; "Ozy has been playing with other people's droppings for several years. A queer way for a once great foot-baller to spend his time. Or is it?"

"I thought science was what the demagogues liked," said Agnes Marley. "They think they can discern some practicality in it. It's usually the humanities they have their knives into."

"Oh, he hasn't neglected the humanities. He says some girl has been boasting that she is a virgin, and has been carrying water in a sieve to prove it. What the hell kind of university game is that, Murray asks, with what he would probably call justifiable heat."

"Oh God," said Maria; "he's talking about me."

"My dear Maria," said Urky, "what have you been up to?"

"Just my job. I'm a teaching assistant, and one of my assign-ments is to lecture first-year engineers on the history of science and technology. Not easy work, because they don't believe sci-ence has any history—it's all here and now. So I have to make it really interesting. I was telling them about the Vestal Virgins, and how they could prove their virginity by carrying water from the Tiber in a sieve. I challenged the handful of girls in my immense class of a hundred and forty to try it, and some of them were good sports and did—and couldn't. Big laughs. Then I car-ried some water about twenty paces in a sieve without spilling a drop, and when they had Oohed and Ahed at that I invited them to examine the sieves. Of course mine was greased, which proved that the Vestal Virgins had a practical understanding of colloid chemistry. It went over very well, and now they are eating out of my hand. But I suppose some of them talked about it, and this man Murray Whatever picked it up."

"Clever girl," said Arthur; "but perhaps too clever."

"Yes," said Agnes Marley, "the first lesson of a teacher or a student should be, don't be too clever unless you want to be in perpetual hot water."

"But does it really work?" said Urky. "I'll get a sieve from my kitchen, and we'll try it."

Which he did, with a great deal of fuss, and smeared it with butter, and managed to get very little water to stick to it, and made a mess on his carpet.

"But of course I'm not a virgin," he said, with more arch giggling than was really called for.

"And you didn't use the right grease," said Maria. "You didn't consider what the Vestal Virgins would have at hand. Try lanolin and perhaps you'll prove yourself a virgin after all."

"No, no, I prefer to believe it is a genuine test," said Urky. "I prefer to believe that you are really a virgin, dear Maria. Are you? You're among friends, here. Are you a virgin?"

This was the kind of conversation Urky loved. The bartending student gave a guffaw; he had a provincial look, and clearly thought he was seeing life. But Maria was not to be put in a corner.

"What do you mean by virginity?" she said. "Virginity has been defined by one Canadian as having the body in the soul's keeping."

"Oh, if you're going to talk about the soul, I can't pretend to be an authority. Father Darcourt must put us straight on that."

"I think the Vestals knew very well what they were doing," I said. "Simple people demand simple proofs of things that aren't at all simple. I think the writer you are talking about, Miss Theotoky, was defining chastity, which is a quality of the spirit; virginity is a physical technicality."

"Oh Simon, what a Jesuit you are," said Urky. "You mean that a girl can have a high old time and then say, 'But of course I am chaste because I had my spiritual fingers crossed'?"

"Chastity isn't a peculiarly female attribute, Urky," said I.

"Anyhow, I made my point with the engineers," said Maria; "they have almost decided that science wasn't invented the day they came to the University, and that maybe the ancients knew a thing or two in their fumbling way. They had a lot of tests, you know; they had a test for a wise man. Do you remember it, Professor McVarish?"

"I take refuge in the scholar's disclaimer, Maria dear; it's not my field."

"If you are a wise man it is certainly your field," said Maria; "they said a wise man could catch the wind in a net."

"And did he grease the net?"

"It was a metaphor for understanding what could be felt but not seen, but of course not many people understood."

Hollier had been looking uncomfortable during this exchange, and now he rather laboriously changed the subject. "It's despicable to attack Froats in that way; he's a very brilliant man."

"But an eccentric," said Urky. "The old Turd-Skinner is unquestionably an eccentric, and you know what capital a politician can make out of attacking an eccentric."

"A man of great brilliance," said Hollier, "and an old friend of mine. Our work is more closely connected than a rabble-rouser like Murray Brown could ever understand. I suppose we are both trying to capture the wind in a net."

[3]

COCKTAIL PARTIES always spoil my appetite for dinner: I eat too many of the dainty bits. So I went directly back to my rooms after Urky's affair, and bought a paper on my way, to see if Murray Brown's attack on the University was still considered to be news.

I am officially on the theological faculty at Spook but I do not live in Spook. I have rooms in Ploughwright College, which is nearby, a comparatively modern building, but not in the economical, spiteful mode of modern university architecture; my rooms are in the tower over the gate, so that I can look inward to the quadrangle of Ploughwright, and also out over a considerable stretch of our large and ragged campus.

I have no kitchen, but I have a hot-plate and a small refrigerator in my bathroom. I made myself toast and coffee and brought out a jar of honey. Not the right thing for a man beginning to be stout, but I have not much zeal for the modern pursuit of trimness. Food helps me to think.

Brown's speech was reported spottily but sufficiently. I had met Murray Brown a few times during my years as a parish clergyman, before I became an academic. He was an angry man, who had turned his anger into a crusade on behalf of the poor. Thinking of the wrongs of the underprivileged, Murray Brown could become deliciously furious, say all kinds of intemperate things, attribute mean motives to anyone who disagreed with him, and dismiss as unimportant anything he did not understand. He was detested by conservatives, and he embarrassed liberals because he was a man without intellectual scope and without fixed aims, but he was popular with enough like-minded people to get himself elected to the Provincial Legislature over and over again. He always had some hot cause or other, some iniquity to expose, and he had turned his attention to the University. In his intellectually primitive way he was an able controversialist. Are we paying good money to keep fellows playing with shit and girls talking horny nonsense in classrooms? Of course we needed doctors and nurses and engineers; maybe we even needed lawyers. We needed some economists and we needed teachers. But did we need a lot of frills? Murray's audience was sure that we did not.

Would Murray think me a frill? Indeed he would. I was a soldier who had deserted his post. Murray's notion of a clergyman was somebody who worked among the poor, not as efficiently, perhaps, as a trained social worker, but doing his best and doing it cheap. I don't suppose that the notion of religion as a mode of thought and feeling that could consume the best intellectual efforts of an able man ever entered Murray's head. But I had done my whack as the kind of parson Murray understood, and had turned to university teaching because I had become convinced, in some words Einstein was fond of, that the serious research scholar in our generally materialistic age is the only deeply religious human being. Having discovered how hard it is to save the souls of others (did I ever, in my nine years of parish work among both poor and not-so-poor, really save anybody's soul?) I wanted to give all the time I could spare to saving my own soul, and I wanted to do work that gave me a little time for that greater work. Murray would call me selfish. But am I? I am hard at the great task with the person who lies nearest and who is most amenable to my best efforts, and perhaps by example I may persuade a few others to do the same.

Oh, endless task! One begins with no knowledge except that what one is doing is probably wrong, and that the right path is heavy with mist. When I was a hopeful youth I set myself to the

Imitation of Christ, and like a fool I supposed that I must try to be like Christ in every possible detail, adjure people to do the right when I didn't really know what the right was, and get myself spurned and scourged as frequently as possible. Crucifixion was not a modern method of social betterment, but at least I could push for psychological crucifixion, and I did, and hung on my cross until it began to dawn on me that I was a social nuisance, and not a bit like Christ—even the tedious *détraqué* Christ of my immature imagination.

Little by little some rough parish work showed me what a fool I was, and I became a Muscular Christian; I was a great worker in men's clubs, and boys' clubs, and I said loudly that Works were what counted and that Faith could be expected to blossom in gymnasiums and craft classes. And perhaps it does, for some people, but it didn't for me.

Gradually it came to me that the Imitation of Christ might not be a road-company performance of Christ's Passion, with me as a pitifully badly cast actor in the principal role. Perhaps what was imitable about Christ was his firm acceptance of his destiny, and his adherence to it even when it led to shameful death. It was the wholeness of Christ that had illuminated so many millions of lives, and it was my job to seek and make manifest the wholeness of Simon Darcourt.

Not Professor the Reverend Simon Darcourt, though that splendidly titled figure had to be given his due, because the University paid him to be both reverend and a professor. The priest and the professor would function suitably if Simon Darcourt, the whole of him, lived in a serious awareness of what he was and spoke to the rest of the world from that awareness as a priest and a professor and always as a man who was humble before God but not necessarily humble before his fellows.

This was the real Imitation of Christ, and if Thomas à Kempis didn't like it, it was because Thomas à Kempis wasn't Simon Darcourt. But old Thomas could be a friend. "If you cannot mould yourself as you would wish, how can you expect other people to be entirely to your liking?" he asked. You can't, of course. But I had decided that the strenuous moulding of my earlier days, the prayers and austerities (there had been a short time when I went in for peas in my shoes and even flirted with a scourge, till my mother found it) and playing the Stupid Ass when I thought I was being the Suffering Servant, was nonsense. I had given up moulding myself externally and was patiently waiting to be moulded from within by my destiny.

Patiently waiting! In my soul, perhaps, but the University does not pay people for patient waiting, and I had my classes to teach, my theologues to push toward ordination, and a muddle of committees and professional university groups to attend to. I was a busy academic, but I found time for what I hoped was spiritual growth.

My greatest handicap, I discovered, was a sense of humour. If Urquhart McVarish's humour was irresponsibility and contempt for the rest of mankind, mine was a leaning toward topsy-tur-veydom, likely to stand things on their heads at inopportune moments. As a professor in a theological faculty I have some priestly duties and at Spook we are ritualists. I am in entire agreement with that. What did Yeats say? 'How else but in custom and ceremony are innocence and beauty born?' But just when custom and ceremony should most incline me toward worship, I may have to contend with a fit of the giggles. Was that what ailed Lewis Carroll, I wonder? Religion and mathematics, two realms in which humour seems to be wholly out of place, drove him to write the *Alice* books. Christianity has no place for topsy-tur-veydom, little tolerance of humour. People have tried to assure me that St. Francis was rich in humour, but I don't believe it. He was merry, perhaps, but that is something else. And there have been moments when I have wondered if St. Francis were not just the tiniest bit off his nut. Didn't eat enough, which is not nec-essarily a path to holiness. How many visions of Eternity have been born of low blood-sugar? (This as I prepare a third piece of toast thickly spread with honey.)

Indeed some measure of what might be called cynicism, but which could also be clarity of vision, tempered with charity, is an element in the Simon Darcourt I am trying to discover and set free. It was that which made it impossible for me not to take note that Urky McVarish's picture of Sir Thomas Urquhart, looking so strikingly like himself, had been touched up to give precisely that impression. The green coat, the hair (a wig), and most of the face were original, but there had been some helpful work on the resemblance. When you looked at the picture sideways, under the light that shone so strongly on it, the over-painting could be plainly seen. I know a little about pictures.

Poor old Urky. I hadn't liked the way he pestered the Theotoky girl about virginity, and gentlewomen's thighs. I looked up the passage in my Rabelais in English: yes, the thighs were cool and moist because women were supposed to pee a bit at odd times (why, I wonder? they don't seem to do it now) and because the sun never shone there, and they were cooled by farts. Nasty old Rabelais and nasty old Urky! But Maria was not to be disconcerted. Good for her!

What a pitiable bag of tricks Urky was! Could it be that his whole life was as false as his outward man?

Was this charitable thinking? Paul tells us that Charity is many things, but nowhere does he tell us that it is blind.

It would certainly be false to the real Simon Darcourt to leave Urky out of *The New Aubrey*. And it would be equally false not to seek out and say something friendly to the much-beset Professor Ozias Froats, whom I once had known fairly well, in his great football days.

Second Paradise III

"NO, I CANNOT GIVE ANY UNDERTAKING that I will not get drunk this time. Why are you so against a pleasing elevation of the spirits, Molly?"

"Because it isn't pleasing. It's noisy and tiresome and makes people stare."

"What a middle-class attitude! I would have expected better from you, a scholar and a Rabelaisian. I expect you to have a scholarly freedom from vulgar prejudice, and a Rabelaisian's breadth of spirit. Get drunk with me, and you won't notice that the common horde is staring."

"I hate drunkenness. I've seen too much of it."

"Have you, indeed? There's a revelation—the first one I have ever had from you, Molly. You're a great girl for secrets."

"Yes, I am."

"It's inhuman, and probably unhealthy. Unbutton a little, Molly. Tell me the story of your life."

"I thought I was to hear the story of your life. A fair exchange. I pay for the dinner: you do the talking."

"But I can't talk into a void."

"I'm not a void; I have a splendid memory for what I hear—better, really, than for what I read."

"That's interesting. Sounds like a peasant background."

"Everybody has a peasant background, if you travel back in the right directions. I hate talking in a place like this. Too noisy."

"Well, you brought me here. The Rude Plenty—a student beanery."

"It's quite a decent Italian restaurant. And it's cheap for what you get."

"Maria, that is gross! You invite a needy and wretched man to dinner—because that's what we call ourselves in the Spook grace, remember, *miseri homines et egentes*—and you tell him to his face that it's a cheap joint, implying that you could do better for somebody else. You are not a scholar and a gentleman, you are a female pedant and a cad."

"Very likely. You can't bounce me with abuse, Parlabane."

"Brother John, if you please. Damn you, you are always so afraid somebody is going to *bounce* you, as you put it. What do you mean? Bounce you up and down on some yielding surface? What Rabelais calls the two-backed beast?"

"Oh shut up, you sound like Urky McVarish. Every man who can spell out the words picks up a few nasty expressions from the English Rabelais and tries them on women, and thinks he's a real devil. It gives me a royal pain in the arse, if you want a Rabelaisian opinion. By bounce I mean men always want to disconcert women and put them at a disadvantage; bouncing is genial, patronizing bullying and I won't put up with it."

"You wound me more deeply than I can say."

"No, I don't. You're a cultivated sponger, Brother John. But I don't care. You're interesting, and I'm happy to pay if you'll talk. I call it a fair exchange. I've told you, I hate talking against noise."

"Oh, this overbred passion for quiet! Totally unnatural. We are usually begotten with a certain amount of noise. For our first nine months we are carried in the womb in a positive hubbub—the loud tom-tom of the heart, the croaking and gurgling of the guts, which must sound like the noise of the rigging on a sailing ship, and a mother's loud laughter—can you imagine what that must be like to Little Nemo, lurching and heaving in his watery bottle while the diaphragm hops up and down? Why are children noisy? Because, literally, they're bred to it. People find fault with their kids when they say they can do their homework better while the radio is playing, but the kids are simply trying to recover the primal racket in which they learned everything from a blob, to a fish, to a human creature. Silence is entirely a sophisticated, acquired taste. Silence is anti-human."

"What do you want to eat?"

"Let's start with a big go of shrimp. Frozen, undoubtedly, but as it's the best you mean to do for me, let's give ourselves up to third-class luxury. And lots of very hot sauce. To follow that, an omelet *frittata* with chicken stuffing. Then spaghetti, again; it was quite passable last time, but double the order, and I'm sure they can manage a more piquant sauce. Tell the chef to throw in a few extra peppers; my friend will pay. Then *zabaglione,* and don't spare the booze in the mixture. We'll top off with lots and lots of cheese; the goatiest and messiest you have, because I like my cheese opinionated. We'll need at least a loaf of that crusty Italian bread, unsalted butter, some green stuff—a really good belch-lifting radish, if you have such a thing—and some garlic butter to rub on this and that, as we need it. Coffee nicely frothed. Now as for drink—God, what a list! Well, no use complaining; let's have a *fiasco* each of Orvieto and Chianti, and don't chill the Orvieto, because God never intended that and I won't be a party to it. And we'll talk about Strega when things are a little further advanced. And make it quick."

The waitress cocked an eye at me, and I nodded.

"I've ordered well, don't you think? A good meal should be a performance; the Edwardians understood that. Their meals were a splendid form of theatre, like a play by Pinero, with skilful preparation, expectation, dénouement, and satisfactory ending. The well-made play: the well-made meal. Drama one can eat. Then of course Shaw and Galsworthy came along and the theatre and the meals became high-minded: the plays were robbed of their delicious adulteries and the meals became messes of pondweed, and a boiled egg if you were really stuffing yourself."

"Is this an introduction to the story of your life?"

"Just about anything leads to the story of my life. Well, here goes: I was born of well-off but honest parents in this city of Toronto, forty-five heavily packed years ago. Your historical sense fills in what is necessary: the war-clouds gathering, Hitler bestrides the narrow world like a Colossus and as usual none of the politicians know a bastard when they see one; war, and fear clutches the heart as Mother Britain fights bravely and alone (though of course the French and several other nations don't quite agree). The U.S. stumbles in, late and loud. At last, victory and a new world rises somewhat shakily on the ruins of the old. Russia, once a wartime chum, resumes its status as a peacetime bum. During all this uproar I went to school, and quite a good school it was, because not only did I learn a few things and acquire an early taste for philosophy, but I met some very glittering and rich boys, like David Staunton, and some brilliantly clever boys, like your present boss Clement Hollier. We were friends, and contemporaries—he's a few months my senior; he thought I was cleverer than I was, because I was a fast talker and could put all my goods in the shop-window, but I knew that he was really the clever one, though he had great trouble putting words together. He stood by me through a very rough time, and I'm grateful. Then I went to the University and swept through the heavens of Spook like a comet, and was such a fool that I had the gall to feel sorry and a little contemptuous of Clem, who had to work hard for a few not very glittering honours.

"I gloried in the freedom of the University. Of course I had no idea what a university is: it's not a river to be fished, it's an ocean in which the young should bathe, and give themselves up to the tides and the currents. But I was a fisherman, and a successful one. Clem was becoming a strong ocean swimmer, though I couldn't see that.—But this is too solemn, and here come the shrimps.

"Shrimps remind me, for some reason, of my early sexual adventures. I was an innocent youth, and for reasons that you can guess by looking at my ruined face I never dared approach girls. But a successful young man is catnip to a certain sort of older woman, and I was taken up by Elsie Whistlecraft.

"You've heard of Ogden Whistlecraft? Now acclaimed as a major Canadian poet? In those days he was what was called a New Voice, and also a junior professor at this University. Elsie, who had a lot of energy and no shame, was building his career at a great rate, but she still had time for amorous adventure, which she thought becoming to a poet's wife. So one night when Oggie was out reading his poetry somewhere, she seduced me.

"It was not a success, from Elsie's point of view, because the orgasm for women was just coming into general popularity then, and she didn't have one. The reason was that she had forgotten to lock up the dog, a big creature called Mat, and Mat found the whole business exciting and interesting, and barked loudly. Trying to shut Mat up took Elsie's mind off her main concern, and at a critical moment Mat nosed me coldly in the rump, and I was too quick for Elsie. I laughed so hard that she became furious and refused to give it another try. We managed things better during the next few weeks, but I never forgot Mat, and took the whole affair in a spirit Elsie didn't like. Adultery, she felt, ought to be excused and sanctified by overwhelming passion, but Mat had learned to associate me with interesting doings, and even when he was tied up outside he barked loudly all the time I was in the house.

"The affair gave me confidence, however, and it was balm to my spirit to have cuckolded a poet. Altogether I didn't fare badly during my university years, but I never did what is called falling in love.

"That came later, when I went to Princeton to do graduate work, and there I fell in love with a young man—fell fathomlessly and totally in love, and it was a thing of great beauty. The only thing of great beauty, I should say, in my story.

"I hadn't had much emotional growth before that. The old university tale, to which you alluded puritanically last time we were here—the over-developed mind and the under-developed heart. I thought I had emotional breadth, because I'd looked for it in art—music, chiefly. Of course art isn't emotion; it's evocation and distillation of emotion one has known. But if you're clever it's awfully easy to fake emotion and deceive yourself, because what art gives is so much like the real thing. This affair was a revolution of the spirit, and like so many revolutions it left in its wake a series of provisional governments which, one after another, proved incapable of ruling. And like many revolutions, what followed was worse than what went before.

"Don't expect details. He grew tired of me, and that was that. Happens in love-affairs of all kinds, and if death is any worse, God is a cruel master.

"Here's the omelet. More Orvieto? I will. I need sustaining during our next big instalment.

"This was a descent into Hell. I'm not being melodramatic; just wait and see. I came back here, and got a job teaching philosophy—which has always been quite a good trade and keeps bread in your mouth—and Spook was happy to reclaim one of its bright boys. Not so happy when they could no longer blind themselves to the fact that I was leading some of their students into what they had to regard as evil courses of life. Kids are awful squealers, you know; you seduce them and they like that, but they also like confessing and bleating about it. And I wasn't a very nice fellow, I suppose; I used to laugh at them when they had qualms of conscience.

"So Spook threw me out, and I got a couple of jobs teaching out West, where the same thing happened, rather quicker. This was before the Dawn of Permissiveness, you must remember.

"I managed to get a job in the States, just as the first rosy gleam of Permissiveness appeared on the horizon. By this time I was in rather a bad way, because rough fun with kids didn't erase the memory of what had happened with Henry, and I was pretty heavily on the booze. A drunk, though I didn't see it quite in those terms. And booze wasn't a complete answer, so, it being the mode of the day, I had a go at drugs, and they were fine. Really fine. I saw myself as a free soul and a great enlightener of the young. . . . Maria, that ring on your finger twinkles most fascinatingly every time you lift your fork to your mouth. Isn't that rather a big diamond for a girl who entertains her friends at The Rude Plenty?"

"Just costume jewellery," I said, and took it off and trucked it into my handbag. I was stupid to wear it, but I had put it on for McVarish's cocktail party the day before and had worn it to dinner with Arthur Cornish, who took me out afterward. I liked it, and absent-mindedly put it on today, breaking my rule never to wear that sort of thing at the University.

"Liar. That's a very good rock."

"Let's go on with your story. I'm spellbound."

"As if by the Ancient Mariner? 'He listens as a three-years child, The Mariner hath his will.' Well, not to drag things out, the Mariner was shipped back to Canada by the F.B.I. because of a little trouble at my American university, and the next thing the Mariner knew he was in a Foundation in British Columbia, where some earnest and skilled people were working to get him off the drugs and the drink. Do you know how that's done? They just take the drugs away from you and for a while you have a thorough foretaste of Hell, and you sweat and rave and roll around and then you feel as I imagine the very old feel, if they're unlucky. Then, for the drink, they fill you full of a special drug and let you have a drink when you feel like one, only you don't feel like one because the drug makes the effect of the booze so awful that you can't face even a glass of sherry. The drug is called, or used to be called when I took it, Antabuse. Get the feather-light pun? Antibooze! God, the humour of the medical world! Then, when you're cleared out physically, and in terrible shape mentally, they set to work to put you on your intellectual feet again. For me that was worst of all—Ah, thank God for spaghetti! And Chianti—no, no, not to worry, Maria, I'm not slipping back into addiction, as they so unpleasantly call it. Just a mild binge with a friend. I can control it, never you fear.

"Let's see, where were we—ah, yes, Group Therapy. Know what that is? Well, you get together with a group of your peers, and you rap together about your problems, and you are free to say anything you like, about yourself or anybody else who feels like talking, and it's all immensely therapeutic. Gets it all out of your system. Real psychological high jinks. Blood all over the walls. Of course I had some private sessions with a shrink, but the Group Therapy was the big magic.

"The only trouble was, I wasn't with a group of my peers. Who are my peers? Brilliant philosophers, stuffed with everything from Plato to the latest whiz-kids of the philosophical world—Logical Positivists, and such intellectual grandees. And there I was with a dismal coven of repentant soaks—a car salesman who had fallen from the creed of Kiwanis, and a Jewish woman whose family misunderstood her attempts to put them straight on everything, and a couple of schoolteachers who can't ever have taught anything except Civics, and some business men whose god was Mammon, and a truck-driver who was included, I gather, to keep our eyes on the road and our discussions hitched to reality. Whose reality? Certainly not mine. So the imp of perversity prompted me to make pretty patterns of our discussions together, and screw the poor boozers up worse than they'd been screwed up before. For the first time in years, I was having a really good time.

"The group protested, and the shrink told me I must show compassion to my fellow-creatures. His idea of compassion was allowing every indefensible statement to pass unchallenged and sugary self-indulgence to pass as insight. He was a boob—a boob with a technique, but still a boob. When I told him so, he was indignant. Let me give you a tip, Maria: never get yourself into the hands of a shrink who is less intelligent than you are, and if that should mean enduring misery without outside help, it will be better for you in the long run. Shrinks aren't all bright, and they are certainly not priests. I was beginning to think that a priest was what I needed, when finally they told me that the Foundation had done all it could for me, and I must re-enter the world. Threw me out, in fact.

"Where does one look for a good priest? I tried a few, because we all have streaks of sentimentality in us and I still believed that there must be holy men somewhere whose goodness would help me. Oh, God! As soon as they found out how highly educated I was, how swift in argument, how ready with authority, they began to lean on me, and tell me their troubles, and expect answers. Some of them wanted to defect and get married. What was I to do? Get out! Get out! But where was I to go?

"I had a little money, now, because my parents had died and although their last, long illnesses had gobbled up a lot of the family substance, I had enough money to go travelling, and where did I go? To Capri! Yes, Capri, that cliché of wickedness, although it is now so overrun with tourists that the wicked can hardly find room to get on with their sin; the great days of Norman Douglas have utterly departed. So, eastward to the Isles of Greece, where burning Sappho loved and sung but has been edged out of the limelight now by the beautiful fisher-boys who will share a seaside place with you for a substantial price, plus gifts, and who may turn ugly and beat you up now and then, just for kicks. One of them put me in the hospital for six weeks, one bad springtime. Am I shocking you, Maria?"

"Certainly not by telling me you're one of the Gays."

"Ah, but I'm not, you see; I'm one of the Sads, and one of the Uglies. The Gays make me laugh; they're so middle class and political about the whole thing. They'll destroy it all with their clamour about Gay Lib. and alternative life-styles, and all love is holy, and 'both partners must be squeaky clean'. That's putting the old game on a level with No-Cal pop or decaffeinated coffee—

appearance without reality. Strip it of its darkness and danger and what is left? An eccentricity, as if I stuck this spaghetti into my ear instead of into my mouth. Now that would be an alternative life-style, and undoubtedly a perversion, but who would care? No: let my sin be Sin or it loses all stature."

"If you prefer men to women, what's it to me?"

"I don't, except for one form of satisfaction. No, I want no truck with 'homo-eroticism' and the awful, treacherous, gold-digging little queens you get stuck with in that caper: I want no truck with Gay Liberation or hokum about alternative life-styles: I want neither the love that dare not speak its name nor the love that blats its name to every grievance committee. *Gnosce teipsum* says the Oracle at Delphi; know thyself, and I do. I'm just a gross old bugger and I like it rough—I like the mess and I like the stink. But don't ask me to like the people. They aren't my kind."

"From what you tell me, Brother John, not many people seem to be your kind."

"I'm not impossibly choosy: I just ask for a high level of intelligence and honesty about things that really matter."

"That's choosy enough to exclude most of us. But something must have happened to get you out of Greece and into that robe."

"You mistrust the robe?"

"Not entirely, but it makes me cautious. You know what Rabelais says—'Never trust those who look through the hole of a hood.'"

"Well, he looked through that hole for much of his life, so he ought to know. You've never told me, Maria, what brings you to devote so much of your time to that dirty-minded, anti-feminist old renegade monk. Could he have been one of my persuasion, do you suppose?"

"No. He didn't like women much, though he seems to have liked one of them enough to have a couple of children by her, and he certainly loved the son. Maybe he didn't meet the right kind of women. Peasant women, and women at court, but did he meet any intelligent, educated women? They must have been rarities in his experience. He couldn't have been like you, Brother John, because he loved greatly, and he rejoiced greatly, and he certainly wasn't a university hanger-on, which is what you are now. He loved learning, and didn't use it as a way of beating other people to their knees, which seems to be your game. No, no; don't put yourself on the same shelf as Master François Rabelais. But the monk—come on, how did you become a monk?"

"Aha, here's the *zabaglione,* which should just see us through. Excuse me for a moment, while I retire to the gentlemen's room. I wish you could come with me; it is always good sport to see the look on the faces of the other gentlemen when a monk strides up to the urinal and hoists his robe. And how they peep! They want to know what a monk wears underneath. Just a cleanish pair of boxer shorts, I assure you."

Off he went, rather unsteadily, and when people at other tables stared at him, he gave them a beaming smile, so unctuous that they turned to their plates as fast as they could.

"That's better! Well now—the robe," said Parlabane, when he returned. "That's quite a tale in itself. You see, I had somewhat dropped in caste, during my stay in Greece; people who had known me were beginning to avoid me, and my adventures on the beaches—because my days of hiring even a humble cottage had passed by—were what I suppose must be called notorious, even in an easy-going society. A bad reputation without money to sweeten it is a heavy burden. Then one day, when I dropped in at the Consulate to ask if they had any mail for me—which they rarely had, but sometimes I could touch somebody for a little money—there actually was a letter for me. And—I can still feel the ecstasy of that recognition—it was from Henry. It was a long letter; first of all, he thought he had treated me badly, and begged my pardon. Next, he had run through whatever there was to run through in very much the kind of life I had been leading (only in his case it was cushioned with a good deal of money) and he had found something else. That something else was religion, and he was determined to yoke himself to a religious life with a brotherhood that worked among wretched people. God, it was a wonderful letter! And to top off the whole thing he offered to send me my fare, if I needed it, to join him and decide whether or not I wanted to accept that yoke as well.

"I suppose I gave rather a display in the Consulate, and wept and wasn't able to speak. But at last things straightened themselves out to the point where I was able to touch the Consul himself for the price of a cablegram to Henry, promising to pay as soon as my money arrived, because Consuls have to be very careful with people like me or they would be continually broke.

"For a few days I really felt I knew what redemption was and when, at last, the reply cable and the assurance of credit at a bank came I did something I had not done in my life before; I went to a church and vowed to God that whatever happened in the future, I would live a life of gratitude for His great mercy.

"That vow was a deeply sacred thing, Maria, and God tested me sternly within a few days. I was returning to North America by way of England, where I had to pick up some things I had left—books of my trade, principally—and in London there was another cable: Henry was dead. No explanation, but when I found out what had happened it was plain enough that he had done for himself.

"This was desolating, but not utterly desolating. Because, you see, I had had that letter, with its assurance of Henry's change of feeling for me, and his concern for me, and that kept me from going right off my head. And I knew what Henry had intended to do, and I knew what I had vowed in that Greek church. I would become a monk, and I would give up my life to the unlucky and unhappy, and I would make it a sacrifice for my own bad mistakes, and for Henry's memory.

"But how do you go about becoming a monk? You shop around, and see who will take you, and that isn't at all easy, because religious orders are pernickety about people who have a sudden yearning for their kind of life; they don't regard themselves as alternatives to the Foreign Legion. But at last I was accepted by the Society of the Sacred Mission; I offered myself to Anglican groups, because I wanted to get right down to the monk business, and didn't want all the fag of becoming a Roman Catholic first. I had some of the right credentials: I had been baptized and was dizzily above the level of education they wanted. I had an interview in London with the Father Provincial, who had positively the biggest eyebrows I have ever seen and who looked from under them with a stare that was humbling, even to me. But I wanted to be humbled. Also, I found his weak spot; he liked jokes and word-play and—very respectfully, mind you—I coaxed a few laughs out of him—or rather shakes of the shoulders, because his laughter made no noise—and after a few days I was on my way to Nottinghamshire, with a tiny suitcase containing what I was permitted to call my own—brush and comb, tooth-brush and so forth, and though Father Prior didn't seem to be any more enchanted with me than Father Provincial, I was put on probation, instructed, confirmed, and in time I was accepted as a novice.

"The life was just what I had been looking for. The Mother House was a huge old Victorian mansion to which a chapel and a few necessary buildings had been added, and there was an un-ending round of domestic work to be done, and done well.

> Who sweeps a room as for Thy laws
> Makes that and th' action fine—

that was the way we were encouraged to think of it. And not just sweeping rooms, but slogging in the garden to raise vegetables— we ate an awful lot of vegetables because there were a great many fast-days—and real labourers' jobs. There was a school attached to the place and I was given a little teaching to do, but nothing that touched doctrine or philosophy or whatever was central to the life of the community; Latin and geography were my jobs. I had to attend instruction in theology—not theology as a branch of philosophy but theology for keeps, you might say. And all this was stretched on a framework of the daily monastic routine.

"Do you know it? You wouldn't believe people could pray so much. *Prime* at 6:15 A.M., and *Matins* at 6:30; *Low Mass* at 7:15, and after breakfast *Terce* at 8:55, followed by twenty minutes of Meditation afterward. Then work like hell till *Sext* at 12:25, then lunch and work again till tea at 3:30, preceding *Nones* at 3:50. Then recreation—chess or tennis and a smoke. After dinner came Evensong at 7:30, and after study the day ended with *Compline* at 9:30.

"You seem to be a great girl for silence. You would have liked it. On ordinary days there was the Lesser Silence from 9:30 until *Sext;* the Greater Silence extended from *Compline* until 9:30 the next morning. In Lent there was silence from *Evensong* until *Compline.* We could speak if absolute necessity demanded it—gored by a bull, or something of that kind—but otherwise we made things known by a sign-language which we were on our honour not to abuse. I soon found a loophole in that; there was nothing in the Rule against writing, and I was often in trouble about passing notes during Chapel.

"Chapel demanded a good deal of mental agility, because you had to learn your way around the *Monastic Diurnal* and know a *Simple* from a *Double* and a *Semidouble First Class* and all the rest of the monkish craft. Like me to give you the lowdown on the *Common of Apostles Out of Paschaltide?* Like me to outline the rules governing the use of bicycles? Like me to describe 'reverent and disciplined posture'—it means not crossing your legs in Chapel and not leaning your head on your hand, when it seems likely to fall off with sleepiness.

"No sex, of course. The boys in the school were to be kept in their place, and monks and novices were strictly enjoined not to permit any familiarity, roughness, or disrespect from them; no boys in men's rooms except those of the priest-tutors, and no going for walks together. They knew the wickedness of the human heart, those chaps. No woman was allowed on the premises without the special permission of the Prior, who was top banana, and in the discharge of his official duty he was to be accorded obedience and respect as if to Christ himself. But of course the Prior had a confessor, who was supposed to keep him from getting a swelled head.

"Sounds like a first-rate system for its purpose, doesn't it? Yet, you know, Maria, within it there was all kinds of difficulty, where what people now call democracy and the old monastic system didn't gibe. So, now and then, somebody was not confirmed as a Brother after his noviciate, and went back to the world. I mean, he became part of the world again; our order did lots of work in the world besides teaching, and there were missions for down-and-outs where particular monks worked themselves almost to death—though I never heard of anybody actually dying. But they were not of the world, you see, though they were certainly in it.

"Now, let me give you a useful tip: always keep your eye on anybody who has been in a monastery and has come out again. He is sure to say that he chose to leave before taking his final vows, but the chances are strong that he was thrown out, and for excellent reasons, even if for nothing more than being a disruptive nuisance. There are more failed monks than you would imagine, and they can all bear watching."

"Including you, Brother John?"

"I wasn't thrown out; I went over the wall. I'd made it, you know; I'd expressed my intention to stay with the Society all my life, and I'd passed the novice stage and was a Lay Brother, vowed to poverty, chastity, and obedience, and I had hopes of going on to priesthood. I knew the Rule inside and out, and I knew where I was weak—Article Nine, which is *Silence,* and Article Fifteen, *Concerning Obedience.* I couldn't hold my tongue and I hated being disciplined by somebody I regarded as an inferior."

"Yes; I thought so."

"Yes, and undoubtedly you thought something totally wrong. I wasn't like some of the sniffy postulants and Brothers who hated being told off by Father Sub-Prior because he had a low-comedy Yorkshire accent. I wasn't a social snob. But I had won my place in a demanding intellectual world before I ever heard of the Missions, and the Rule said plainly: *Everybody is clever enough for what God wants of him, and strong enough for what he is set to do, if not for what he would like to be.* Father Prior and my confessor were always unyielding when I asked, humbly and reverently, for work that would use what was best in me, meaning my knowledge and the intelligence with which I could employ it. They could quote the Rule as well as I: *You cannot seek God's will and your own too, unless your own is perfectly confirmed to it. If it be so, there will be no need to consider it, though if it be not, there will be much need to mortify it.* So they mortified me, but as they too were fallible beings they made one wrong choice and put me on the job of getting things ready for Mass, and that meant that big jugs of Communion wine were right under my hand, and after some sipping, and swigging, and topping the jugs up with water, there was a morning when I forgot myself and they found me pissed to hell in the vestry. Never drink that cheap wine on an empty stomach, Maria. I suppose I took it too lightly, and did my penances in a forward spirit. Anyhow things went from bad to worse, and I knew I was in danger of being thrown out, and the Society made it clear when a postulant was accepted that there would be no argument or explanation if that happened.

"I could have weathered it through, but I began to be hungry for another kind of life. The Society offered a good life, but that was precisely the trouble—it was so unremittingly *good*. I had known another world, and I became positively sick for the existentialist gloom, and malicious joy at the misfortunes of others, and the gallows-humour that gave zest to modern intellectual life outside the monastery. I was like a child who is given nothing but the most wholesome food; my soul yearned for unwholesome trash, to keep me somehow in balance.

"So I sneaked a letter out with a visitor who had come for a retreat, and dear Clem sent me some money, and I went over the wall.

"Just an expression; there was no wall. But one day at recreation time I walked down the drive in a suit and a red wig out of the box of costumes the school used for Christmas theatricals. Monasteries don't send out dogs after escapees. I am sure they were glad to be rid of me.

"Then off with the wig and on with the robe, which I had providentially, if not quite honestly, brought with me. It smooths the path wonderfully. On the plane and back to the embraces of my Bounteous Mother, to dear old Spook.—*Brraaaaaph!* Excuse me if I appear to belch—Molly, may I just have the teeniest peep at that diamond you whipped out of sight so quickly?"

"No. It's just like any other diamond."

"Not in the least, my darling. How could it be like any other diamond when it is *your* diamond? You give it splendour; it is not in the power of any stone to give splendour to you."

"We'd better go, now. I have some things to do before I go home."

"Aha, she has a home! Beautiful Maria Magdalena of God's Motherhood has a home! Where do you suppose it can be?"

"You don't need to know."

"She has a home and she has a diamond ring. And that ring is greatly privileged! You know old Burton—*The Anatomy of Melancholy*—contemporary of Shakespeare? He has something about a diamond ring that I memorized in my pre-monastery days, and which sometimes wickedly crept into my mind in Chapel; the Devil whispered it, one supposes. And it went like this: 'A lover, in Calcagninus' *Apologues,* wished with all his heart he were his mistress's ring, to hear, embrace, see and do I know not what; O thou fool, quoth the ring, if thou wer'st in my room, thou shouldst hear, observe and see *pudenda et poenitenda,* that which would make thee loathe and hate her, yea, peradventure, all women for her sake.' But the ring was a prissy fool, because it saw what the lover would have given his soul to see."

"Come on, Brother John, this is foolish. Let's be on our way."

"No, no, not yet—you understand what I mean? There's even a song about it." He sang loudly, pounding out the time on the table with the handle of a knife:

> *I wish I were a diamond ring*
> *Upon my lady's hand,*
> *Upon my lady's hand;*
> *So every time she wiped her arse*
> *I'd see the Promised Land*
> *I'd see the Promised Land!*

"Come on; time for us to go now."

"Don't be so prim! Do you think I haven't seen through you? You buy my story with a cheap meal and you sit there with a face like a hanging judge. And now you fuss and want to run away as if you'd never heard a dirty song in your whole life. And I bet you haven't! I bet you don't know a single dirty song, you stone-faced bitch—."

I don't know why I did it. No, that's wrong—I do know. My ancestry forbids me to resist a challenge. Ancestry on both sides of my family. I was suddenly furious and disgusted with Parlabane. I threw back my head and in a loud voice—and I have a really loud voice, when I need it—I sang:

There's a nigger in the alley with a hard-on,
'Cause a woman in the window has her pants down—

and so on.

That caused a sensation. When Parlabane sang, the people at the other tables, most of whom were students, took care not to look. Shouting a rowdy song was within their range of what was permissible. But I had been really dirty. I had used an inexcusable racist word. 'Nigger' brought immediate hisses and shushes, and one young man rose to his feet, as though to address a grievance meeting. In no time the proprietor was at my elbow, lifting, urging, bustling me toward the door; he only permitted me time to pay the bill as we passed the cash-desk.

"Not come back—not come back—no you nor priest," he said, in an angry mumble, because he hated trouble.

So there we were, thrown out of The Rude Plenty, and as I was not drunk, though I was aroused, I thought I ought to see Parlabane back to Spook.

"My God, Molly," he said, as we stumbled along the street, "where did you learn a song like that?"

"Where did Ophelia learn *her* dirty song?" I said; "overheard it, probably. Soldiers singing it in the courtyard as she sat at her window, knitting bedsocks for Polonius."

This put Shakespeare into his mind and he began to bellow, 'Sing me a bawdy song! Sing me a bawdy song to make my eyes red,' and kept it up, as I struggled to keep *him* up.

A car passed with two of the University police in it; they hurried by with averted gaze, because trouble of any kind was the last thing they wanted to be involved in. But what had they seen? Parlabane in his robe, and me in a longish cloak, because it was a chilly autumn night, must have looked like a couple of drunken women brawling on the pavement. Suddenly he took a dislike to me, and beat at me with his fists, but I have had a little experience in fighting and gave him a sobering wipe or two. At last I pushed him through the main gate of Spook, and put him in the hands of the porter, who looked as if these goings-on were becoming too much of a good thing.

As indeed they were.

[2]

NEXT MORNING I FELT shaky and repentant. Not hung-over, because I never drink much, but aware of having behaved like a fool. I shouldn't have sung that song about the nigger. Where had I picked it up? At my convent school, where girls sang songs they had learned from their brothers. I have a capacious memory for what I have heard, and dirty songs and limericks never leave me, when sometimes I have to grope for sober facts I have read. But I would not be bounced by Parlabane, and I have never hesitated to take a dare; neither my Mother nor my Father, very different as they were, would have wanted me to back down in the face of a challenge.

I got rid of the diamond ring—miserable object of female vanity and, much worse, of an unstudentlike affluence—and didn't drive my little car to the University. Watch your step, Maria! Parlabane had done something that had a little unhinged me; he had awakened the Maenad in me, that spirit which any woman of any character keeps well suppressed, but shakes men badly when it is revealed. The Maenads, who tore Pentheus to bloody scraps and ate him, are not dead, just sleeping. But I don't want to join the Political Maenads, the Women's Lib sisterhood; I avoid them just as Parlabane said he avoided the Political Gays; they make a public cause of something too deep, too important, for political, group action. My personal Maenad had escaped control, and I had wasted her terrible energy simply to get the better of a bullying, spoiled monk. Repent, Maria, and watch your step!

When I entered Hollier's rooms, Parlabane was not there, but Hollier was.

"I hear that you and Brother John had a gaudy night together," said he.

I could not think of anything to say, so I nodded my head, feeling not more than sixteen, and as if I were being rebuked again by Tadeusz.

"Sit down," said Hollier; "I want to talk to you. I want to warn you against Parlabane. I know that sounds extreme, and that you are perfectly capable of looking after yourself, and the rest of that nonsense. When I told you to try to understand him I had no idea you would go so far. But I mean precisely what I say:

Parlabane is not a man you should become deeply involved with. Why? In the light of the work you and I share I don't have to explain in modern terms; very old terms are quite sufficient and exact—Parlabane is an evil man, and evil is infectious, and you mustn't catch the infection."

"Isn't that rather hard?" I said.

"No. You understand that I'm not talking village morality, but something that truly belongs to paleo-psychology. There are evil people; they're not common, but they exist. It takes just as much energy to be evil as it does to be good and few people have energy enough for either course. But he has. There is a destroying demon in him, and he would drag you down, and then jeer at you because you had yielded to him. Watch your step, Maria."

I was startled to hear him say what I had been saying to myself ever since I woke. That was Hollier—a touch of the wizard. But one can't just bow to the wizard as if one had no mind of one's own. Not yet, at least.

"I think he is rather pathetic."

"So?"

"He was telling me about his life."

"Yes, he must have it nicely polished up by now."

"Well, it's not a happy story."

"But amusingly told, I am sure."

"Are you down on him because he's Gay?"

"He's a sodomite, if there's anything gay about that. But that doesn't make him evil, necessarily. So was Oscar Wilde, and a kinder, more generous man never walked in shoe leather. Evil isn't what one does, it's something one is that infects everything one does. He told you the whole thing, did he?"

"No, he didn't. Most people when they set out on the story of their lives give you quite a passage about childhood; he began much later."

"Then I'll tell you a few things. I've known him since we were boys; at school together, and at summer camp together. Did he tell you what happened to his face?"

"No, and I didn't get a chance to ask."

"Well, it's not much in the telling, but much in the consequence. One summer when I suppose we were fourteen, we were at camp, and Parlabane, who was always very good with his hands, was working at a repair on a canoe. He was under the direction of one of the counsellors, and everything seemed to be in order. But he had set a pot of glue on a flame to heat it, without putting it in a pan of water: what the counsellor was doing at that moment, God knows. It burst and covered his face with the boiling stuff. He was rushed to hospital near by, and some drastic action had to be taken, and on the whole a good job was done, for he was left with a scarred face, but still a face, and his eyes didn't suffer as much as one might have feared. I went with him, and the camp people arranged for me to stay in the hospital because I was his best friend, and they wanted him to have a friend near by. When he wasn't in the operating-room I sat by his bed and held his hand for three days.

"All that time he was raging with anger, because his parents didn't come. They could have made it in a few hours, and the camp people had been in touch, but nobody appeared. On the fourth day they turned up—mousy, ineffectual Father, and his Mother, who was quite another kettle of fish. She was big in city politics—Board of Education, and then an Alderman—and a very busy woman indeed, as she explained. She had come as soon as she could, but she couldn't stay long. She was all affection, all charm, and, as I had cause to know, a really intelligent and capable person, but she was not rich in maternal concern.

"The way Parlabane talked to her was so dreadful that I wanted to creep out of the room, but he wouldn't release my hand. She was his Mother, and when he was suffering what was she doing? Labouring for the public good, and unable to set it aside for the private need.

"She took it very well. Laughed gently and said, 'Oh, come on, Johnny, it's bad but it isn't the end of the world, now, is it?'

"Then he began to cry, and because of the injuries to his eyes, that was excruciatingly painful and soon crying became screaming, coming from the little hole they had left for his mouth in all the bandaging. It was just enough to admit a feeding-tube. When he spoke it was like a child speaking from a well, muffled and indistinct but terrible in meaning.

"The little northern hospital was heavy with summer heat, because there was no air-conditioning in the wards; the bandages must have been insupportably hot, and the wounds sore, and the sedatives sickening to feel at work. The screaming brought a doctor with a syringe and soon John screamed no more, but Mrs. Parlabane never lost her composure.

" 'You'll stay with him, won't you, Clement?' she said to me, 'because I really must get back to the City.' And away she and the biddable husband went. I noticed that he reached out and patted John's insensible hand before he left.

"So that was it, and after a while the bandages came off, and the face you know was seen for the first time. He was no beauty before, but now he was like a man in a red mask, which has faded with time. I am sure Toronto plastic surgeons could have done a good deal for him in the years that followed, but the Parlabane family did nothing about it."

"Didn't make a fuss with the camp?"

"The people who owned the camp were friends; they didn't want to injure them. John thought it a great injustice."

"And that was what made him the way he is?"

"In part, I suppose. Certainly it did nothing to make him otherwise. He and his Mother were cat and dog after that. He called her The Bitch Goddess, after Henry James's Bitch Goddess Success. She was a success, in her terms. He insisted she had deserted him when he most needed her; she said to me more than once that she had seen that everything was done that could be done, and she thought he was making a great deal of a misfortune that could happen to anyone. But that's by the way—though I suppose it throws some light on him, and on her, of course. The fact that he could not bear to tell you—though I am sure he told you in affecting terms about his other great betrayal by that egotistical catamite Henry Loewi III, the Beauty of Princeton—shows how much it affected him.

"I hope things may look up a little for him now. I've managed to get a job for him and he's away at this minute arranging about it. Appleton, who does some lecturing in Extension, has broken his hip, and even when he gets back on the job he will have to lighten his load. So I have persuaded the director of that division to take Parlabane on to finish out the year; once a week on Basic Principles in Philosophy, and twice a week on Six Major Philosophical Texts."

"That's marvellous."

"I'm afraid he doesn't think so. Extension means teaching at night, and most of the people in the classes are middle-aged and opinionated; it won't be the thrill of moulding the young, which is what he likes."

"Rough on the young, I'd imagine."

"His real teaching days are over, I fear. He has a good mind—used to have a fine mind—but he rambles and blathers too much. He wants me to take him on, you know."

"How?"

"Special research assistant."

"But I'm your research assistant!"

"He'd be happy to supplant you. But don't give it a thought; I won't have it."

"The snake!"

"Oh, that's not the worst of him; that's just his normal way of behaving. But there's a limit to what I can, and will, do for him; I've got him a job, and that's as far as it goes."

"I think you've been wonderful to him."

"He's an old friend. And we don't always choose our old friends, you know; sometimes we're just landed with them. You know somebody for a few years, and you're probably stuck with them for life. Sometimes you must do what you can."

"Well, at least he's out of here."

"Don't count on that. I'll urge him to get a room somewhere, but he will have no campus office. He'll be back to mooch books, and he'll be back for you."

"For me?"

"He fancies you, you know. Oh, yes; being a homosexual doesn't matter. Just about all men need a woman in one way or another, unless they're very strange indeed. Tormenting you refreshes him. And you shouldn't underestimate the gratitude all men feel for women's beauty. Men who truly don't like flowers are very uncommon and men who don't respond to a beautiful woman are even more uncommon. It's not primarily sexual; it's a lifting of the spirits beauty gives. He'll be in to torment you, and tease you, and enrage you, but really to have a good, refreshing look at you."

I decided to dare greatly. "Is that why you keep me here?" I asked.

"Partly. But mostly because you're much the best and most intellectually sympathetic student and assistant I've ever had."

"Thank you. I'll bring you some flowers."

"They'd be welcome. I never get around to buying any myself."

What am I to make of that? One of the enchantments Hollier had for me was this quality of possessive indifference. He must know I worship him, but he never gives me a chance to prove it. Only that one time. God, who would want to be me? But perhaps, like Parlabane in the hospital, I should realize that it wasn't the end of the world.

Hollier was obviously trying to put something together in his mind, before speaking. Now it came.

"There are two things I want you to do for me, Maria."

Anything! Anything whatever! The Maenad in me was subdued now, and Patient Griselda was in total possession.

"The first is that I want you to visit my old acquaintance Professor Froats. There's a kinship between his work and mine that I want to test. You know about him—he's rather too much in the news for the University's comfort or his own, I expect. He works with human excrement—what is rejected, what is accounted of no worth to mankind—and in it I suppose he hopes to discover something that is of worth. You know I've been busy for months on the Filth Therapy of the Middle Ages, and of ancient times, and of the East. The Bedouin mother washes her newborn child in camel's urine, or in her own; probably she doesn't really know why but she follows custom. The modern biologist knows why; it's a convenient protection against several sorts of infection. The nomad of the Middle East binds the rickety child's legs in splints and bandages of ass's dung, and in a few weeks the bent legs are straight. Doesn't know why, but knows it works. The porter at Ploughwright, an Irishman, had that done to him by Irish Gypsies when he was three, and today his legs are as straight as mine. Filth Therapy was widespread; sometimes it was superstition and sometimes it worked. Fleming's penicillin began as Filth Therapy, you know. Every woodcutter knew that the muck off bad bread was the best thing for an axe wound. Salvation in dirt. Why? I suspect that Ozias Froats knows why.

"It's astonishingly similar to alchemy in basic principle—the recognition of what is of worth in that which is scorned by the

unseeing. The alchemist's long quest for the Stone, and the biblical stone which the builders refused becoming the headstone of
the corner. Do you know the Scottish paraphrase—

> *That stone shall be chief corner-stone*
> *Which builders did despise—*

and the *lapis angularis* of the Alchemical Cross, and the stone of
the *filus macrocosmi* which was Christ, the Wholly Good?"

"I know what you've written about all that."

"Well, is Froats the scientist looking for the same thing, but
by means which are not ours, and without any idea of what we
are doing, while being on much the same track?"

"But that would be fantastic!"

"I'm very much afraid that is exactly what it would be. If I'm
wrong, it's fantastic speculation. If I'm right, it could just make
things harder for poor old Ozy Froats if it became known. So we
must keep our mouths shut. That's why I want you to take it on.
If I turned up in his labs Ozy would smell a rat; he'd know I was
after something, and if I told him what it was he'd either be over-
impressed or have a scientific fit—you know what terrible puritans
scientists are about their work—no contamination by anything
that can't be submitted to experimental test, and all that—but
you are able to approach him as a student. I've told him you are
curious because of some work you are doing connected with the
Renaissance. I mentioned Paracelsus. That's all he knows, or
should know."

"Of course I'll go to see him."

"After hours; not when his students are around or they would
prevent him from being enthusiastic. They're all green to science
and all Doubting Thomases—wouldn't believe their grandmoth-
ers had wrinkles if they couldn't measure them with a micrometer.
But in his inmost heart, Ozy is an enthusiast. So go some night
after dinner. He's always there till eleven, at least."

"I'll go as soon as possible. You said there were two things you
wanted me to do?"

"Ah, well, yes I did. You don't have to do the second if you'd
rather not."

What a fool I am! I knew it must be something connected with

our work. Perhaps something more about the manuscript he had
spoken of at the beginning of the term. But the crazed notion
would rush into my mind that perhaps he wanted me to live with
him, or go away for a weekend, or get married, or something it
was least likely to be. But it was even unlikelier than any of those.

"I'd be infinitely obliged if you could arrange to introduce me
to your Mother."

The New Aubrey III

ELLERMAN'S FUNERAL WAS a sad affair, which is not as silly as it sounds, because I have known funerals of well-loved or brave people which were buoyant. But this was a funeral without personal quality or grace. Funeral 'homes' are places that exist for convenience; to excuse families from straining small houses with a ceremony they cannot contain, and to excuse churches from burying people who had no inclination toward churches and did nothing whatever to sustain them. People are said to be drifting away from religion, but few of them drift so far that when they die there is not a call for some kind of religious ceremony. Is it because mankind is naturally religious, or simply because mankind is naturally cautious? For whatever reason, we don't like to part with a friend without some sort of show, and too often it is a poor show.

A parson of one of the sects which an advertising man would call a Smooth Blend read scriptural passages and prayers, and suggested that Ellerman had been a good fellow. Amen to that.

He had been a man who liked a touch of style, and he had been hospitable. This affair would have dismayed him; he would have wanted things done better. But how do you do better when nobody believes anything very firmly, and when the Canadian ineptitude for every kind of ceremony reduces the obsequies to mediocrity?

What would I have done if I had been in charge? I would have had Ellerman's war medals, which were numerous and honourable, on display, and I would have draped his doctor's red gown and his hood over the coffin. These, as reminders of what he had been, of where his strengths had lain. But—*Naked came I out of my mother's womb, and naked shall I return thither*—so at the grave I would have stripped away these evidences of a life, and on the bare coffin I would have thrown earth, instead of the rose-leaves modern funeral directors think symbolic of the words *Earth to earth, ashes to ashes, dust to dust;* there is something honest about hearing the clods rattling on the coffin lid. Ellerman had taught English Literature, and he was an expert on Browning; might not somebody have read some passages from *A Grammarian's Funeral?* But such thought are idle; you are asking for theatricalism, Darcourt; grief must be meagre, and mean, and cheap—not in money, of course, but in expression and invention. Death, be not proud; neither the grinning skull nor the panoply of ceremonial, nor the heart-catching splendour of faith is welcome at a modern, middle-class city funeral; grief must be huddled away, as the Lowest Common Denominator of permissible emotion.

I wish I could have seen him near the last, to tell him that his notion of *The New Aubrey* had taken root in me, and thus, whatever his beliefs may have been, something of him should live, however humbly.

He drew a pretty good house; my professional eye put it at seventy-five, give or take a body or so. No sign of McVarish, though he and Ellerman had been cronies. Urky ignores death, so far as possible. Professor Ozias Froats was there, to my surprise. I knew he had been brought up a Mennonite, but I would have supposed that a life given to science had leached all belief out of him in things unseen, of heights and depths immeasurable. I took my chance, as we stood outside the funeral home, to speak to him.

"I hope all this nonsense in the papers isn't bothering you," said I.

"I wish I could say it wasn't; they're so unfair in what they say. Can't be expected to understand, of course."

"It can't do any permanent harm, surely."

"It could, if I had to ease up to satisfy this guy Brown. His political advantage could cost me seven years of work that would have to be repeated if I had to reduce what I'm doing for a while."

I hadn't expected him to be so down in the mouth. Years ago

I had known him when he was a great football star; he had been temperamental then, and seemingly he still was so.

"I'm sure it does as much good as harm," said I; "thousands of people must have been made aware of what you're doing, and are interested. I'm interested myself. I don't suppose you'd let me visit you some day?"

To my astonishment he blossomed, and said: "Any time. But come at night when I'm alone, or nearly alone. Then I'd be glad to show you my stuff and explain. It's good of you to say you're interested."

So it was quite easy. I could have a look at Ozy for *The New Aubrey*.

[2]

IT WOULDN'T BE FAIR to Ozias Froats or to me to suggest that I was bagging him like a butterfly collector. That wasn't the light in which I saw *The New Aubrey*. Of course poor Ellerman, who loved everything that was quaint in English Literature, had relished John Aubrey's delightful style, and the mixture of shrewdness and naivety with which Aubrey recorded his ragbag of information about the great ones of his time. But I wasn't interested in anything like that; undergraduates love to write such stuff for their literary magazines—'The Diary of Our Own Mr. Pepys', and such arch concoctions. What I valued in Aubrey was the energy of his curiosity, his determination to find out whatever he could about people who interested him: that was the quality in him I would try to recapture.

It was not simple nosiness. It was a proper university project. Energy and curiosity are the lifeblood of universities; the desire to find out, to uncover, to dig deeper, to puzzle out obscurities, is the spirit of the university, and it is a channelling of that unresting curiosity that holds mankind together. As for energy, only those who have never tried it for a week or two can suppose that the pursuit of knowledge does not demand a strength and determination, a resolve not to be beaten, that is a special kind of energy, and those who lack it or have it only in small store will never be scholars or teachers, because real teaching demands

energy as well. To instruct calls for energy, and to remain almost
silent, but watchful and helpful, while students instruct themselves, calls for even greater energy. To see someone fall (which
will teach him not to fall again) when a word from you would
keep him on his feet but ignorant of an important danger, is one
of the tasks of the teacher that calls for special energy, because
holding in is more demanding than crying out.

It was curiosity and energy I brought to *The New Aubrey,* as a
tribute to my University, of which it might not become aware
until I was dead. I have done my share of scholarship—two pretty
good books on New Testament Apocrypha, studies of some of
the later gospels and apocalypses that didn't make it into the
accepted canon of Holy Writ—and I was no longer under compulsion to justify myself in that way. So I was ready to give time
and energy—and of course curiosity, of which I have an extraordinary endowment—to *The New Aubrey.* I was making a plan. I
must have order in the work. The Old Aubrey is charming because
it wholly lacks order, but *The New Aubrey* must not copy that.

I didn't go to Ozy's laboratories at once: I wanted to think
about what I was seeking. Not a scientific appraisal, obviously,
for I was incompetent for that and there would be plenty of
appraisal from his colleagues and peers when his work became
known. No, what I was after was the spirit of the man, the source
of the energy that lay behind the work.

I was thinking on those lines one night a few days after Ellerman's funeral when there came a tap on my door, and to my
astonishment it was Hollier.

We have been on good but not close terms since our days
together at Spook, when I had known him fairly well. We were
not intimates then because I was in Classics, heading toward Theology (Spook likes its parsons to have some general education
before they push toward ordination), and we met only in student
societies. Since then we were friendly when we met, but we did
not take pains to meet. This visit, I supposed, must be about the
Cornish business. Hollier was no man to make a social call.

So it proved to be. After accepting a drink and fussing uneasily
for perhaps five minutes on the general theme of our work, he
came out with it.

"There's something that has been worrying me, but because it lies in your part of the executors' work I haven't liked to mention it. Have you found any catalogue of Cornish's books and manuscripts?"

"He made two or three beginnings, and a few notes. He had no idea what cataloguing means."

"Then you wouldn't know if anything were missing?"

"I'd know if it related to his musical manuscripts, because he showed them to me often, and I have a good idea of what he possessed. Otherwise, not."

"There's one I know he had, because he acquired it last April, and I saw it one night at his place. He had bought a group of MSS for their calligraphy; they were contemporary copies of letters to and from the Papal Chancery of Paul III. You know he was interested in calligraphy in a learnedly amateurish way, and it was the writing rather than the content that had attracted him; it was a bundle from somebody's collection, and the prize piece was a letter from Jacob ben Samuel Martino and it made a passing reference to Henry VIII's divorce, on which you know Martino was one of the experts. There were corrections in Martino's own hand. Otherwise the content was of no interest; just a pretty piece of writing. Good for a footnote, no more. McVarish was there, and he and Cornish gloated over that, and as they did I looked at some of the other stuff, and there was a leather portfolio—not a big one, about ten inches by seven, I suppose—with S. G. stamped on it in gold that had faded almost to nothing. Have you come across that?"

"No, but the Martino letter is present and correct. Very fine. And a group that goes with it, which presumably is what you saw."

"Where do you suppose S. G. has got to?"

"I don't know. I have never heard of it till this minute. What was it?"

"I'm not sure that I can tell you."

"Well, my dear man, if you can't tell me, how can I look for it? He may have put it in one of the other divisions—if those old cartons from the liquor store in which he stored his MSS can be called divisions. There is a very rough plan to be discerned in the muddle, but unless I know what this particular MS was about I wouldn't have any idea where to look. Why are you interested?"

"I was trying to find out what it really was when McVarish came along and wanted to see it, and I couldn't very well say no—no in another man's house, about something that wasn't mine—and I never got back to it. But certainly McVarish saw it, and I saw his eyes popping."

"Had your eyes been popping?"

"I suppose so."

"Come on, Clem, cut the scholarly reticence and tell me what it was."

"I suppose there's nothing else for it. It was one of the great, really *great*, manuscripts. I'm sure you know what some of those are."

"They are very common in my field. In the nineteenth century some letters appeared from Pontius Pilate, describing the Crucifixion; they were in French on contemporary notepaper and a credulous rich peasant paid quite a lot for them; it was when the same crook tried to sell him Christ's last letter to his Mother, written in purple ink, that the buyer began to smell a rat."

"I wish you wouldn't be facetious."

"Perfectly true, I assure you. I know the kind of thing you mean: Henry Hudson's lost diary; James Macpherson's Journal about the composition of *Ossian*—that kind of thing. And stuff does turn up. Look at the big haul of Boswell papers, found in a trunk in an attic in Ireland. Was this something of that order?"

"Yes. It was Rabelais's *Stratagems*."

"Don't know them."

"Neither does anybody else. But Rabelais was historiographer to his patron Guillaume du Bellay and as such he wrote *Stratagems, that is to say, prowesses and ruses of war of the pious and most famous Chevalier de Langey at the beginning of the Third Caesarean War;* he wrote it in Latin, and he also translated it into French, and it was supposed to have been published by his friend the printer Sebastian Gryphius, but no copy exists. So was it published or wasn't it?"

"And this was it?"

"This was it. It must have been the original script from which Gryphius published, or expected to publish, because it was marked up for the compositor—in itself an extraordinarily interesting feature."

"But why hadn't anybody spotted it?"

"You'd have to know some specialized facts to recognize it, because there was no title page—just began the text in close writing which wasn't very distinguished, so I suppose the calligraphy people hadn't paid it much heed."

"A splendid find, obviously."

"Of course Cornish didn't know what it was, and I never had a chance to tell him; I wanted to have a really close look at it."

"And you didn't want Urky to get in before you?"

"He is a Renaissance scholar. I suppose he had as good a right as anyone to the Gryphius MS."

"Yes, but you didn't want him to become aware of any such right. I quite understand. You don't have to be defensive."

"I would have preferred to make the discovery, inform Cornish (who after all owned the damned thing), and leave the disposition of it, for scholarly use, to him."

"Don't you think Cornish would have handed it over to Urky? After all, Urky regards himself as a big Rabelais man."

"For God's sake, Darcourt, don't be silly! McVarish's ancestor—if indeed Sir Thomas Urquhart was his ancestor, which I have heard doubted by people who might be expected to know— Sir Thomas Urquhart translated one work—or part of it—by Rabelais into English, and plenty of Rabelais scholars think it is a damned bad translation, full of invention and whimsy and unscholarly blethering just like McVarish himself! There are people in this University who really know Rabelais and who laugh at McVarish."

"Yes, but he is a Renaissance historian, and this was apparently a significant bit of Renaissance history. In Urky's field, and not really in your field. Sorry, but that's the way it looks."

"I wish people wouldn't talk about fields as if we were all a bunch of wretched prospectors and gold-panners, ready to shoot anybody who steps on our claim."

"Well, isn't that what we are?"

"I suppose I've got to tell you the whole thing."

"I wish you would. What have you been holding back?"

"There was the MS of the *Stratagems,* as I've told you. About forty pages, closely written. Not a good hand and no signature, except the signature that was written all over it—the lost Rabelais book. But in another little bundle in the back of the leather portfolio, in a sort of pocket, were the scripts of three letters."

"From Rabelais?"

"Yes, from Rabelais. They were drafts of three letters written to Paracelsus. His rough copies. But not so rough he hadn't signed them. Perhaps he enjoyed writing his name: lots of people do. It jumped at me off the page—that big ornate signature, not really the Chancery Hand, but a Mannerist style of his own—"

"Yes, Urky always insists that Rabelais was a Mannerist author."

"Urky be damned; he picked that up from me. He wouldn't know Mannerism in any art; he has no eye. But Rabelais is a Mannerist poet who happened to write in prose; he achieves in prose what Guiseppe Arcimboldo achieves in painting—fruitiness, nuttiness, leafiness, dunginess, and the wildest kind of grotesque invention. But there were the letters, and there was the unmistakable, great signature. I had to take hold of myself not to fall on my knees. Think of it! Just think of it!"

"Very nice."

"Nice, you call it! Nice! Stupendous! I had a peep—the merest peep—and they contained passages in Greek (quotations, obviously) and here and there a few words in Hebrew, and half a dozen wholly revealing symbols."

"Wholly revealing what?"

"Revealing that Rabelais was in correspondence with the greatest natural scientist of his day, which nobody knew before. Revealing that Rabelais, who was suspected of being a Protestant, was something at least equally reprehensible for a man of the Church—even a nuisance and a renegade—he was, if not a Cabbalist at least a student of Cabbala, and if not an alchemist at least a student of alchemy! And that *is* bloody well in my field, and it could be the making of any scholar who got hold of it, and I'll be damned if I want that bogus sniggering son of a whore McVarish to get his hands on it!"

"Spoken like a true scholar!"

"And I think he has got his hands on it! I think that bugger has pinched it!"

"My dear man, calm down! If it did turn up it would have to go to the University Library, you know. I couldn't simply hand it over to you."

"You know how those things are done; a word to the Chief Librarian would be all that is necessary, and I wouldn't ask you to do it. I could do it myself. First crack at that MS—that's what I want!"

"Yes, yes, I understand. But I've got bad news for you. In one of Cornish's notebooks there's an entry that says 'Lend McV. Rab. MS April 16'. What do you suppose that tells us?"

"Lend. Lend—does that mean he meant to lend it or that he did lend it?"

"How do I know? But I'm afraid you're grasping at a straw. I suspect Urky has it."

"Pinched it! I knew it! The thief!"

"No, wait a minute—we can't jump to conclusions."

"I'm not jumping to anything. I know McVarish. You know McVarish. He winkled it out of Cornish and now he has it! The sodding crook!"

"Please, don't assume anything. It's simple; I have that entry, and I show it to McVarish and ask him for the MS back."

"Do you think you'll get it? He'll deny everything. I've got to have that MS, Darcourt. I might as well tell you, I've promised it to someone."

"Wasn't that premature?"

"Special circumstances."

"Now look here, Clem, I'm not being stuffy, I hope, but the books and manuscripts in Cornish's collection are my charge, and the circumstances have to be very special for you to talk about anything in that collection to anybody else until all the legal business has been completed and the stuff is safely lodged in the Library. What are these special circumstances?"

"Rather not say."

"I'm sure you'd rather not. But I think you should."

Hollier squirmed in his chair. There is no other word for his uneasy twisting, as if he thought that a change of posture would help his inner unease. To my astonishment he was blushing. I didn't like it at all. His embarrassment was embarrassing me. When he spoke his manner was hangdog. The great Hollier, whom the President had described not long ago—to impress the government who were nagging about cutting our grants—as one of the ornaments of the University, was blushing before *me*. I'm not one of the ornaments myself (just a useful table-leg) and I am too loyal to the University to like watching an ornament squirm.

"A particularly able student—it would be the foundation of an academic career—I would supervise, of course—"

I have a measure of the intuition which common belief regards, quite unfairly, as being an attribute of women. I was ahead of him.

"Miss Theotoky, do you mean?"

"How on earth did you know?"

"Your research assistant, a student of mine, working at least in part of Rabelais, a girl of uncommon promise—it's not really second sight, you know."

"Well—you're right."

"What have you said?"

"Spoke of it once, in general terms. Later, when she asked me, I said a little more. But not much, you understand."

"Then it's easy. You explain to her that there will be a delay. It could take a year to get the MS from McVarish, and wind up the Cornish business, and have the MS properly vetted and catalogued by the Library."

"If you can get it away from McVarish."

"I'll get it."

"But then he may want it for himself, or for some pet of his."

"That's not my affair. You want it for a pet of yours."

"Precisely what do you imply by *pet*?"

"Nothing much. A favoured pupil. Why?"

"I don't have pets."

"Then you're a teacher in a thousand. We all have pets. How can we avoid it? Some students are better and more appealing than others."

"Appealing?"

"Clem, you're very hot under the collar. Have another drink."

To my astonishment he seized the whisky bottle and poured himself three fingers and gulped it off in two swallows.

"Clem, what's chewing you? You'd better tell me."

"I suppose it's part of your job to hear confessions?"

"I haven't done much of that since I left parish work. Never did much there, in fact. But I know how it's done. And I know it's not good practice to hear confessions from people you know socially. But if you want to tell me something informally, go ahead. And mum's the word, of course."

"I was afraid of this when I came here."

"I'm not forcing you. Do as you please. But if I'm not your confessor I am your fellow-executor and I have a right to know what's been going on with things I'm responsible for."

"I have something to make up to Miss Theotoky. I've wronged her, gravely."

"How?"

"Took advantage of her."

"Pinched some of her good work? That sounds more like McVarish than you, Clem."

"No, no; something even more personal. I—I've had carnal knowledge of her."

"Oh, for God's sake! You sound like the Old Testament. You mean you've screwed her?"

"That is a distasteful expression."

"I know, but how many tasteful expressions are there? I can't say you've *lain* with her; maybe you didn't. I can't say you've *had* her, because she is still clearly in full possession of herself. 'Had intercourse with her' sounds like the police-court—or do they still say that 'intimacy occurred'? What really happened?"

"It was last April—"

"A month crammed with incident, apparently."

"Shut up and don't be facetious. Simon, can't you see how serious this is for me? I've behaved very wrongly. The relationship between master and pupil is a special one, a responsible one—you could say, a sacred one."

"You could say that, right enough. But we all know what happens in universities. Nice girls turn up, professors are human, and bingo! Sometimes it's rough on the girl; sometimes it may be destructive to the professor, if some scheming little broad throws herself at him. You must make allowance for the Fall of Man, Clem. I doubt if Maria seduced you; she's far too much in awe of you. So you must have seduced her. How?"

"I don't know. I honestly don't know. But what happened was that I was telling her about my work on the Filth Therapy of the Middle Ages, which had been going particularly well, and sud-

denly she told me something—something about her mother—
that added another huge piece to the jigsaw puzzle of what I had
been doing, and I was so excited by it—there was such an upsurge
of splendid feeling, that before I knew what was happening, there
we were, you see—"

"And Abelard and Heloise lived again for approximately ninety
seconds. Or have you persisted?"

"No, certainly not. I've never spoken to her about it since."

"Once. I see."

"You can imagine how I felt at McVarish's party when he was
plaguing her about being a virgin."

"But she handled that brilliantly, I thought. Was she a virgin?"

"Good God, how would I know?"

"There are sometimes indications. You're a medievalist. You
must know what they looked for."

"You don't suppose I looked, do you! Do you take me for a
Peeping Tom?"

"I'm beginning to take you for a fool, Clem. Have you never
had any experience of this sort of thing before?"

"Well, of course. One can hardly avoid it. The commercial
thing, you know, twice when travelling. Years ago. And on a
conference, once, a female colleague, for a couple of days. She
talked incessantly. But this was a sort of daemonic seizure—I
wasn't myself."

"Oh, yes you were; these daemonic seizures are the unadmitted
elements in a lopsided life. So you've promised Maria the Rabelais
manuscript to make it up to her? Is that it?"

"I must make reparation."

"I don't want to talk too much like a priest, Clem, but you
really can't do it like that. You think you've wronged a girl, and
a handsome gift—in terms you both value greatly—will make
everything right. But it won't. The reparation must be on the
same footing as the wrong."

"You mean I ought to marry her?"

"I don't imagine for a minute she'd have you."

"I'm not so sure. She looks at me sometimes, in a certain way.
I'm not a vain man, but you can't mistake certain looks."

"I suppose she's fallen for you. Girls do fall for professors; I've
been telling you about it. But don't marry her; even if she is

enough of a sap to say Yes; it would never work. You'd both be sick to death of it in two years. No, you stop fretting about Maria; she knows how to manage her life, and she'll get over you. It's yourself you need to put back on the rails. If there is any reparation, it must be made there."

"But how? Oh, I suppose you mean a penance?"

"Good medieval thinking."

"But what? I suppose I could give the College chapel a piece of silver."

"Bad medieval thinking. A penance must cost you something that hurts."

"Then what?"

"You really want it?"

"I do."

"I'll give you some tried and true penitential advice. Whom do you hate most in the world? If you had to name an enemy, who would it be?"

"McVarish!"

"I thought so. Then for your penitence go to McVarish and tell him what you have just told me."

"You're out of your mind!"

"No."

"It would kill me!"

"No, it wouldn't."

"He'd blat it all over."

"Very likely."

"I'd have to leave the University!"

"Hardly that. But you could wear a big red 'A' on the back of your raincoat for a year or so."

"You're not being serious!"

"Neither are you. Look here, Clem: you come to me and expect me to play the priest and coax me into prescribing a penance for you, and then you refuse it because it would hurt. You're a real Protestant; your prayer is 'O God, forgive me, but for God's sake keep this under Your hat.' You need a softer priest. Why don't you try Parlabane; you're keeping him, so he's safely in your pocket. Go and confess to him."

Hollier rose. "Good night," he said. "I see I made a great mistake in coming here."

"Don't be a goat, Clem. Sit down and have another drink."

He did—another great belt of Scotch. "Do you know Parla-bane?" he said.

"Not as well as you do. But when we were undergraduates I saw quite a bit of him. An attractive fellow, very funny. Then I lost track of him, but I thought we were still friends. I've been wondering when he would come to see me. I didn't want to invite him; under the circumstances it might embarrass him."

"Under what circumstances?"

"When we knew one another at Spook he made great fun of me for wanting to go into the Church. He was the Great Sceptic, you remember, and he couldn't understand me believing in Christianity in the face of all reason, or what he would call reason. So I nearly fell out of my chair when I had a letter from him a few months ago, telling me that he was a monk in the Society of the Sacred Mission. Such turn-abouts are common enough, especially with people in middle age, but I would never have expected it of Parlabane."

"And he wanted to leave the Brotherhood."

"Yes, that's what he told me. Needed help, which I provided."

"You mean you sent him money?"

"Yes. Five hundred dollars. I thought I'd better send it. If it did him any good it was charity toward him; if it didn't it was a charity to the Sacred Mission. He wanted to get out."

"That cost me five hundred, too."

"I wonder if he sent out a circular letter. Anyhow I don't want to seem to gloat over him, or to be asking about repayment."

"Simon, that fellow is no damned good."

"What's he been up to?"

"Leeching and bumming and sorning. And wearing that monk's outfit. And getting Maria into bad ways."

"Is he pestering Maria? I thought he was a homo?"

"Nothing so simple. A homo is just unusual; I've known some who are unusually good people. Parlabane is a wicked man. That's an old-fashioned term, but it fits."

"But what's he been doing to Maria?"

"They were thrown out of a students' restaurant a few nights ago for shouting filthy songs, and they were seen fighting in the street afterward. I've found him a job—a fill-in in Extension. I've

told him he must find another place to live, but he just yields as
if I were punching a half-filled balloon, and continues to hang
around my rooms and make claims on Maria."

"What kind of claims?"

"Insinuating claims. I think he knows about us. About Maria
and me."

"Do you think she told him?"

"Unthinkable. But he smells things. And I find now that he's
seeing McVarish."

I sighed. "It's as true as it's horrible: one never regrets anything
so profoundly as a kind action. We should have left him in the
Society; they know a few things about penances that might have
sorted him out."

"What I can't understand or forgive is the way he seems to be
turning on me."

"That's his nature, Clem; he can't bear to be under an obligation. He was always proud as Lucifer. When I think back to our
student days, I'd say he was as Luciferian as a not very tall fellow
with a messed-up face could be; we tend to think of Lucifer as
tall, dark, and handsome—fallen angel, you know. But if Parlabane was ever an angel it's a kind unknown to me; just a very
good student of philosophy with a special talent for the sceptical
hypotyposis."

"Mmmm . . .?"

"The brainy over-view or the chilling put-down or whatever
you like. If you said something you thought was fine, and that
meant a lot to you, he would immediately put it in a context that
showed you up as a credulous boob, or a limited fellow who
hadn't read enough or thought enough. But he did it with such
a grand sweep and such a light touch that you felt you had been
illuminated."

"Until you got sick of it."

"Yes, until you gained enough self-confidence to know you
couldn't be completely wrong all of the time and that exposing
things as cheats and shams or follies couldn't do much for you.
Scepticism ran wild in Parlabane."

"Odd about scepticism, you know, Simon. I've known a few
sceptical philosophers and with the exception of Parlabane they
have all been quite ordinary people in the normal dealings of life.

They pay their debts, have mortgages, educate their kids, google over their grandchildren, try to scrape together a competence precisely like the rest of the middle class. They come to terms with life. How do they square it with what they profess?"

"Horse sense, Clem, horse sense. It's the saving of us all who live by the mind. We make a deal between what we can comprehend intellectually and what we are in the world as we encounter it. Only the geniuses and people with a kink try to escape, and even the geniuses often live by a thoroughly bourgeois morality. Why? Because it simplifies all the unessential things. One can't always be improvising and seeing every triviality afresh. But Parlabane is a man with a kink."

"Years ago plenty of people thought he was a genius."

"I remember being one of them."

"Do you think it was that wretched accident to his face that kinked him? Or his family? His mother, do you suppose?"

"Once I would have supposed all those things, but I don't any longer. People triumph over worse families than his could have been, and do astonishing things with ruined bodies, and I'm sick to death of people squealing about their mothers. Everybody has to have a mother, and not everybody is going to draw the Grand Prize—whatever that may be. What's a perfect mother? We hear too much about loving mothers making homosexuals, and neglectful mothers making crooks, and commonplace mothers stifling intelligence. The whole mother business needs radical re-examination."

"You sound as if in a minute you were going to give me a lecture about Original Sin."

"And why not? We've had psychology and we've had sociology and we're still just where we were, for all practical purposes. Some of the harsh old theological notions of things are every bit as good, not because they really explain anything, but because at bottom they admit they can't explain a lot of things, so they foist them off on God, who may be cruel and incalculable but at least He takes the guilt for a lot of human misery."

"So you think there's no explanation for Parlabane? For his failure to live up to expectation? For what he is now?"

"You've lived in a university longer than I have, Clem, and you've seen lots of splendidly promising young people disappear into mediocrity. We put too much value on a certain kind of examination-passing brain and a ready tongue."

"In a minute you'll be saying that character is more important than intelligence. I know several people of splendid character who haven't got the wits of a hen."

"Stop telling me what I'm going to say in a minute, Clem, and take a good look at yourself: certainly one of the most brilliant men in this university and a man of international reputation, and the first time you get into a tiny moral mess with a girl you become a complete simpleton."

"You presume on your cloth to insult me."

"Balls! I'm not wearing my cloth; I only put on the full rig on Sundays. Have another drink."

"You don't suppose, do you, that this discussion is degenerating into mere whisky-talk?"

"Very likely. But before we sink below the surface, let me tell you what twenty years of the cloth, as you so old-fashionedly call it, have taught me. Intellectual endowment is a factor in a man's fate, and so is character, and so is industry, and so is courage, but they can all go right down the drain without another factor that nobody likes to admit, and that's sheer, bald-headed Luck."

"I would have expected you to say God's Saving Grace."

"Certainly you can call it that if you like, and the way He sprinkles it around is beyond human comprehension. God's a rum old joker, Clem, and we must never forget it."

"He's treated us well, wouldn't you say, Simon? Here's to the Rum Old Joker!"

"The Rum Old Joker! And long may he smile on us."

[3]

THE LABORATORIES OF Professor Ozias Froats looked more than anything else like the kitchens of a first-rate hotel. Clean metal tables, sinks, an array of cabinets like big refrigerators, and a few instruments that looked as if they were concerned with very accurate calculations. I cannot say what I expected; by the time I visited him the hullabaloo stirred up by Murray Brown had so coloured the public conception of his work that I would not have been surprised if I had found Ozy in the sort of surroundings one associates with the Mad Scientist in a bad movie.

"Come on in, Simon. You don't mind if I call you Simon, do you? Call me Ozy; you always did."

It was a name he had lifted from the joke-name of a rube undergraduate to the honoured pet-name of a first-rate footballer. In the great days when he and Boom-Boom Glazebrook were the stars of the University team the crowd used to sing a revised version of a song that had been popular years earlier—

> *Ozy·Froats, and dozy doats*
> *And little Lambsie divy—*

and if he was injured in the game the cheer-leaders, led by his own sweetheart, Peppy Peggy, brought him to his feet with the long, yearning cry, 'Come o-o-o-o-n Ozy! Come O-O-O-O-N OZY!' But everybody knew that Ozy was a star in biology, as well as football, and a Very Big Man On Campus. What he had been doing since graduation, and a Rhodes Scholarship, only God and biologists knew, but the President had named him as another Ornament to the University. So I was glad he had not wholly forgotten me.

"Murray Brown is giving you a rough time, Ozy."

"Yes. You saw that there was a parade outside the Legislature yesterday. People wanting education grants cut. Some of the signs read, 'Get the Shit Out of Our Varsity'. That meant me. I'm Murray's great peeve."

"Well, do you actually work with—?"

"Sure I do. And a very good thing, too. Time somebody got to grips with it.—God, people are so stupid."

"They don't understand, and they're overtaxed and scared about inflation. The universities are always an easy mark. *Cut the frills away from education. Teach students a trade so they can make a living.* You can't persuade most of the public that education and making a living aren't the same thing. And when the public sees people happily doing what they like best and getting paid for it, they are envious, and want to put a stop to it. Fire the unprofitable professors. Education and religion are two subjects on which everybody considers himself an expert; everybody does what he calls using his common sense.—I suppose your work costs a lot of money?"

"Not as much as lots of things, but quite a bit. It isn't public money, most of it. I get grants from foundations, and the National Research Council, and so forth, but the University backs me, and pays me, and I suppose I'm a natural scapegoat for people like Brown."

"Your work is offensive because of what you work with. Though I should think it was cheap."

"Oh no, not at all. I'm not a night-soil man, Simon. The stuff has to be special, and it costs three dollars a bucket, and if you multiply that by a hundred to a hundred and twenty-five—and that's the smallest test-group I can use—it's three hundred dollars or more a day, seven days a week, just for starters."

"A hundred buckets a day! Quite a heap."

"If I was in cancer research you wouldn't hear a word said. Cancer's all the rage, you know, and has been for years. You can get any money for it."

"I don't suppose you could say this was related to cancer research?"

"Simon! And you a parson! That'd be a lie! I don't know what it's related to. That's what I'm trying to find out."

"Pure science?"

"Nearly. Of course I have an idea or two, but I'm working from the known toward the unknown. I'm in a neglected field and an unpopular one because nobody really likes messing with the stuff. But sooner or later somebody had to, and it turns out to be me. I suppose you want to hear about it?"

"I'd be delighted. But I didn't come to pry, you know. Just a friendly visit."

"I'm glad to tell you all I can. But will you wait a few minutes; there's somebody else coming—a girl Hollier wants to know about my work, because of something she's doing in his line, whatever that is. Anyway, she should be here soon."

Shortly she appeared, and it was my New Testament Greek student and the thorn in the flesh of Professor Hollier, that unexpected puritan: Miss Theotoky. A queer group we made: I was in my clerical clothes and back-to-front collar, because I had been at a committee dinner where it seemed appropriate, and Maria was looking like the Magdalen in a medieval illumination, though not so gloomy, and Ozias Froats looked like what was left of a great footballer who had been transformed into a controversial research scientist. He was still a giant and still very strong, but his hair was leaving him, and he had what seemed to be a melon concealed in the front of his trousers, when his white lab-coat revealed it. There were pleasantries, and then Ozy got down to his explanation.

"People have always been interested in their faeces; primitive people take a look after they've had a motion, to see if it tells them anything, and there are more civilized people who do that than you'd suppose. Usually they are frightened; they've heard that cancer can give you blood in your stools, and you'd be amazed how many of them rush off to the doctor in a sweat when they've forgotten the Harvard beets they ate the day before. In the old days doctors looked at the stuff, just the way they looked at urine. They couldn't cut into anybody, but they made quite a lot of those examinations."

"Scatomancy, they called it," said Maria. "Could they have learned anything?"

"Not much," said Ozy; "though if you know what you are doing you can find out a few things by smell—the faeces of a drug-addict, for instance, are easy to identify. Of course when real investigative science got going they did some work on faeces— you know, measured the amounts of nitrogen and ether extract and neutral fat and cholalic acid, and all the inspissated mucus and bile and bacteria, and the large amounts of dead bacteria. The quantity of food residue is quite small. That work was useful in a restricted area as a diagnostic process, but nobody carried it very far. What really got me going on it was Osler.

"Osler was always throwing off wonderful ideas and insights that he didn't follow up; I suppose he expected other people would deal with them when they got around to it. As a student I was caught by his brief remarks on what was then called catarrhal enteritis; he mentioned changes in the constitution of the intestinal secretion—said, 'We know too little about the *succus entericus* to be able to speak of influences induced by change in its quantity or quality.' He wrote that in 1896. But he proposed some associations between diarrhoea and cancer, and anaemia, and some kidney ailments, and what he said stuck in my mind.

"It wasn't till about ten years ago that I came on a book that brought back what Osler had said, though the application was radically different. It was a proposal for what the author named Constitutional Psychology—a man called W. H. Sheldon, a respected Harvard scientist. Roughly, what he said was that there was a fundamental connection between physique and temperament. Not a new idea, of course."

"Renaissance writing is full of it," said Maria.

"You wouldn't call it scientific, though. You wouldn't be able to go that far."

"It was pretty good," said Maria. "Paracelsus said that there were more than a hundred, and probably more than a thousand, kinds of stomach, so that if you collected a thousand people it would be as foolish to say they were alike in body, and treat them as if they were alike in body, as it would be to suppose they were identical in spirit. 'There are a hundred forms of health,' he said, 'and the man who can lift fifty pounds may be as able-bodied as a man who can lift three hundred pounds.' "

"He may have said it, but he couldn't prove it."

"He knew it by insight."

"Now, now, Miss Theotoky, that'll never do. You have to prove things like that experimentally."

"Did Sheldon prove what Paracelsus said experimentally?"

"He certainly did!"

"That just proves Paracelsus was the greater man; he didn't have to fag away in a lab to get the right answer."

"We don't know if Sheldon got the completely right answer; we don't have any answers yet—just careful findings. Now—"

"She's teasing you, Ozy," I said. "Maria, you be quiet and let the great man talk. Perhaps we'll give Paracelsus an innings later. You know, of course, that Professor Froats is under great criticism at present, of a kind that could be harmful."

"So was Paracelsus—hounded from one country to another, and laughed at by all the universities. And he didn't have academic tenure, either. But I'm sorry; please don't let me interrupt."

What a contentious girl she was! But refreshing. I had a sneaking feeling for Paracelsus myself. But I wanted to hear about Sheldon, and on Ozy went.

"He wasn't just saying that people are different, you know. He showed *how* they were different. He worked on four thousand college students, altogether. Not the best sample, of course—all young, all intelligent—not enough variety, which is what I'm trying to achieve. But he finally divided his four thousand guinea pigs into three main groups.

"They were the *endomorphs,* who had soft, rounded bodies, and the *mesomorphs,* who were muscular and bony, and then the *ectomorphs,* who were fragile and skinny. He did extensive research into their temperaments and their backgrounds and the way they lived and what they wanted from life, and he found that the fatties were viscerotonics, or gut-people, who loved comfort in all its forms; and the muscular, tough types were somatotonics, whose pleasure was in exercise and exertion; and the skinnies were cerebrotonics, who were intellectual and nervous—head-people, in fact.

"So far this is not big news. I suppose Paracelsus could have done that by simple observation. But Sheldon showed by measurements and a variety of tests that everybody contains some elements of all three types, and it is the mixture that influences— influences, I said, not wholly determines—temperament. He devised a scale running from one to seven to assess the quantity of such elements contained in a single subject. So you see that a 711 would be a maximum endomorph—a fatty with hardly any muscle or nerve—a real slob. And a 117 would be a physical wreck, all brain and nerve and a physical liability. Big brain, by the way, doesn't necessarily mean a capacious or well-managed intellect. The perfectly balanced creature would be a 444 but you don't see many and when you do you've probably found the secretary of an athletic club with a rich membership and first-class catering."

"Do you go around spotting the types?" said Maria.

"Certainly not. You can't type people without careful examination, and that means exact measurement. Want to see?"

Of course we did want to see. Obviously Ozy was loving every minute of this, and in no time he had a screen set up, and a lantern, and was showing us slides of men and women of all ages and appearance, photographed naked against a grid of which the horizontal and lateral lines made it possible to judge with accuracy where they bulged and where they were wanting.

"This isn't what I'd do for the public," said Ozy. "Then the faces would be blacked out and also the genitals. But this is among friends."

Indeed it was. I recognized a paunchy University policeman, and a fellow from Physical Plant who pruned trees. And wasn't that one of the secretaries from the President's office? And a girl from the Alumni House? Several students I had seen flashed by, and—really, this is hardly the place for me—Professor Agnes Marley, heavier in the hams than her tweeds admitted, and with a decidedly poor bosom. All of these unhappy creatures had been photographed in a hard, cruel light. And in big black figures at the bottom right-hand corner of each picture was their ratio of elements, determined by Sheldon's scale. Ozy switched on the lights again.

"You see how it goes?" he said. "By the way, I hope you didn't recognize any of those people. No harm done if you did, but people are sometimes sensitive. Everybody wants to be typed, just as they want to have their fortunes told. Me, now, I'm a 271; not much fat, but enough, as you see, to make some trouble when I'm tied to sedentary work; I'm a seven in frame and muscle— I'd be a Hercules if I had a few more units on either end of my scale. I'm only a one in the cerebrotonic aspect, which doesn't mean I'm dumb, thank God, but I've never been what you'd call nervy or sensitive. That's why this Brown thing doesn't bother me too much.—By the way, I suppose you noticed the varying hirsutism of those people? The women are sensitive about it, but it's extremely revealing to a scientist in my kind of work.

"Typing at a glance—I'd never attempt it seriously. But you can tell a lot about typology by the kind of things people say. Christ, now; tradition and all the pictures represent Him as a cerebrotonic ectomorph, and that raises a theological point that should interest you, Simon. If Christ was really the Son of Man, and assumed human flesh, you'd have thought he'd be a 444, wouldn't you? A man who felt for everybody. But no—a nervy, thin type. Must have been tough, though; great walker, spell-binding orator, which takes strength, put up with a scourging and a lot of rough-house from soldiers; at least a three in the meso-morphic range.

"It's fascinating, isn't it? There you are, Simon, a professional propagandist and interpreter of a prophet who wasn't, literally, your type at all. Just off the top of my head, I'd put you down as a 425—soft, but chunky and possessed of great energy. You write a good deal, don't you?"

I thought of *The New Aubrey,* and nodded.

"Of course. That's your type, when it's combined with superior intelligence. Enough muscle to see you through; sensitive but not ridden with nerves, and a huge gut. Because that's what makes your type come out so far in front, you see? Some of your vis-cerotonics have a gut that is almost double the length of the gut in a real cerebrotonic. They haven't got a lot of gut, but they're beggars for sex. The muscular ones aren't sexy to nearly the same extent and the fatties would just as soon eat. It's the little, skinny ones who can never let it alone. I could tell you astonishing things. But you're a gut-man, Simon. And just right for your kind of parson: fond of ceremony and ritual, and of course a big eater. Fart much?"

How much is much? I did not take up this lead.

"I expect you do, but on the sly, because of that five at your cerebrotonic end. But writers—look at them. Balzac, Dumas, Trollope, Thackeray, Dickens in his later years, Henry James (a lifelong sufferer from constipation, by the way), Hugo, Goethe— at least forty feet of gut in every one of them."

Ozy had quite forgotten about scientific calm and was warming to his great theme.

"You'll want to know, though, what this has to do with faeces. I just got a hunch, remembering Osler, that there might be var-iations in composition, according to type, and that might be in-teresting. Because what people forget, or don't consider, is that the bowel movement is a real creation; everybody produces the stuff in an incidence that ranges within normality from three times a day to about once every ten days, with, say, once every forty-eight hours as a mean. There it is, and it'd be damned funny if there was nothing individual or characteristic about it, and it might just be that it varied according to health. You know the old country saying: 'Every man's dung smells sweet in his own nose'.

But not in anybody else's nose. It's a creation, a highly characteristic product. So let's get to work, I thought.

"Setting up an experiment for something like that is a hell of a job. First of all, Sheldon identified seventy-six types that are within the range of the normal; of course there are some wild combinations in people who are born to severe physical trouble. Getting an experimental group together is a lot of work, because you have to interview so many people, and do a lot of explaining, and rule out the ones who could become nuisances. I guess my team and I saw well over five hundred, and managed to keep things fairly quiet to exclude jokers and nuts like Brown. We ended up with a hundred and twenty-five, who would promise to give us all their faeces, properly contained in the special receptacles we provided (and they cost a pretty penny, let me tell you), as fresh as possible, and over considerable lengths of time, because you want serial inspection if you are going to get anywhere. And we wanted as big a range of temperament as we could achieve, and not just highly intelligent young students. As I told you, Simon, we have to pay our test group, because it's a nuisance to them, and though they understand that it's important they have to have some recompense. We expect them to have tests whenever my medical assistant calls for it, and they have to mark a daily chart that records a few things—how they felt, for instance, on a one-to-seven scale ranging from Radiant to The Pits. I often wish we could do it with rats but human temperament can't be examined in any cheap way."

"Paracelsus would have liked you, Dr. Froats," said Maria; "he rejected the study of formal anatomy for a consideration of the living body as a whole; he'd have liked what you say about faeces being a creation. Have you read his treatises on colic and bowel-worms?"

"I just know him as a name, really. I thought he was some kind of nut."

"That's what Murray Brown says about you."

"Well, Murray Brown is wrong. I can't tell him so for a while— maybe for a few years—but there'll be a time."

"Does that mean you've found what you are looking for?" I said. I felt that I had better get Maria away from Paracelsus.

"I'm not looking for anything. That's not how science works;

I'm just looking to see what's there. If you start with a precon-
ceived idea of what you are going to find, you are liable to find
it, and be dead wrong, and maybe miss something genuine that's
under your nose. Of course we're not just sitting on our hands
here; at least half a dozen good papers from Froats, Redfern, and
Oimatsu have appeared in the journals. Some interesting stuff
has come up. Want to see some more pictures? Oimatsu prepares
these. Wonderful! Nobody like the Japanese for fine work like
this."

These were slides showing what I understood to be extremely
thin slices of faeces, cut transversely, and examined microscopically and under special light. They were of extraordinary beauty,
like splendid cuttings of moss-agate, eye-agate, brecciated agate,
and my mind turned to that chalcedony which John's Revelation
tells us is part of the foundations of the Holy City. But as Maria
had been unsuccessful in persuading Ozy to hear about Paracelsus
I thought I would have no greater success with references to the
Bible. So I fished around for something which I hoped might be
intelligent to say.

"I don't suppose there'd be such a thing as a crystal-lattice in
those examples?"

"No, but that's a good guess—a shrewd guess. Not a crystal-
lattice, of course, for several reasons, but call it a disposition
toward a characteristic form which is pretty constant. And if it
changes markedly, what do you suppose that means? I don't know,
but if I can find out"—Ozy became aware that he was yielding
to unscientific enthusiasm—"I'll know something I don't know
now."

"Which could lead to—?"

"I wouldn't want to guess what it might lead to. But if there is
a pattern of formation which is as identifiable for everybody as a
fingerprint, that would be interesting. But I'm not going to go
off half-cocked. People can do that, after reading Sheldon. There
was a fellow named Huxley, a brother of the scientist—I think
he was a writer—and he read Sheldon and he went to foolish
extremes. Of course being a writer he loved the comic extremes
in the somatotypes, and he lost his head over something Sheldon
keeps harping on in his two big books. And that's humour. Sheldon keeps saying you have to deal with the somatotypes with an

ever-active sense of humour, and damn it, I don't know what he's talking about. If a fact is a fact, surely that's it? You don't have to get cute about it. I've read a good deal, you know, in general literature, and I've never found a definition of humour that made any sense whatever. But this Huxley—the other one, not the scientist—goes on about how funny it would be if certain ill-matched types got married, and he thought it would be a howl to see an ectomorph shrimp and his endomorphic slob of a wife in a museum looking at the mesomorphic ideal of Greek sculpture. What's funny about that? He rushed off in all directions about how soma affects psyche, and how perhaps the body was really the Unconscious that the psychoanalysts talk about—the unknown factor, the depth from which arises the unforeseen and uncontrollable in the human spirit. And how learning intelligently to live with the body would be the path to mental health. All very well to say, but just try and prove it. And that's work for people like me."

It was getting late, and I rose to go, because it was clear that Ozy had shown us all he meant to show. But as I prepared to leave I remembered his wife. Now it is not tactful in these days to ask about the wives of one's friends too particularly, in case they are wives no longer. But I thought I'd plunge.

"How's Peggy?"

"Good of you to ask, Simon. She'll be delighted you remembered her. Poor Peg."

"Not unwell, I hope? Of course I remember her as our top cheer-leader."

"Wasn't she marvellous? Wonderful figure, and every ounce of it rubber, you'd have said. A real fireball. God, you should see her now."

"Very sorry she isn't well."

"She's well enough. But her type, you know—her somatotype. She's a PPJ—what Sheldon calls a Pyknic Practical Joke. Pyknic, you understand? Of course, Greek's your thing. Compact: rubbery. But the balance of her three elements was just that tiny bit off, a 442, and—well, now she weighs well over two hundred, poor kid, and she's barely five foot three. No; no children. She keeps cheerful, though. Takes a lot of night courses at one of the community colleges—Dog Grooming, Awake Alive and Aware

Through Yoga, Writing for Fun and Profit—that crap. I'm here so much at night, you see."

I saw. The Rum Old Joker had been a bit rowdy with Ozy and Peggy, and even if Ozy's sense of humour had been more active than it was, he could hardly have been expected to relish that one.

As we walked up the campus together, Maria said: "I wonder if Professor Froats is a magus."

"I think he'd be surprised if you suggested it."

"Yes, he seemed very dismissive about Paracelsus. But it was Paracelsus who said that the holy men who serve the forces of nature are magi, because they can do what others are incapable of doing, and that is because they have a special gift. Surely Ozias Froats works under the protection of the Thrice-Divine Hermes. Anyway I hope so: he won't get far if he doesn't. I wish he'd read Paracelsus. He said that each man's soul accords with the design of his lineaments and arteries. I'm sure Sheldon would have agreed."

"Sheldon appears to have had a sense of humour. He wouldn't mind a sixteenth-century alchemist getting in ahead of him. But not Ozy."

"It's a pity about science, isn't it?"

"Miss Theotoky, that is very much a humanist remark, and you must be careful with it. We humanists are an endangered species. In Paracelsus's time the energy of universities resided in the conflict between humanism and theology; the energy of the modern university lives in the love-affair between government and science, and sometimes the two are so close it makes you shudder. If you want a magus, look for one in Clement Hollier."

With that we parted, but I thought she gave me a surprised glance.

I walked on toward Ploughwright, thinking about faeces. What a lot we had found out about the prehistoric past from the study of fossilized dung of long-vanished animals. A miraculous thing, really; a recovery of the past from what was carelessly rejected. And in the Middle Ages, how concerned people who lived close to the world of nature were with the faeces of animals. And what a variety of names they had for them: the Crotels of a Hare, the Friants of a Boar, the Spraints of an Otter, the Werderobe of a

Badger, the Waggying of a Fox, the Fumets of a Deer. Surely there might be some words for the material so near to the heart of Ozy Froats better than shit? What about the Problems of a President, the Backward Passes of a Footballer, the Deferrals of a Dean, the Odd Volumes of a Librarian, the Footnotes of a Ph.D., the Low Grades of a Freshman, the Anxieties of an Untenured Professor? As for myself, might it not appropriately be called the Collect for the Day?

Musing in this frivolous strain I went to bed.

[4]

I THOUGHT IT WOULD not be long before Hollier pushed Parlabane in my direction, and sure enough he turned up the night after I had visited Ozias Froats.

I was not in a good mood, because I had been haunted all day by Ozy's humbling estimate of my physical—and by implication my spiritual—condition. A 425, soft, chunky, doubtless headed toward undeniable fat. I make frequent resolves to go to the Athletic Building every day, and get myself into trim, and if I were not so busy I would do it. Now, at a blow, Ozy had suggested that fat was part of my destiny, an inescapable burden, an outward and visible sign of an inward and only partly visible love of comfort. Had I been deceiving myself? Did my students speak of me as Fatso? But then, if the Fairy Carabosse had appeared at my christening with her spiteful gift of adiposity, there had been other and better-natured fairies who had made me intelligent and energetic. But because human nature inclines toward dissatisfaction, it was the fat that rankled.

Worse, he had suggested that I was the sort of man who broke wind a great deal. Everyone recognizes, surely, that with the passing of time this trivial physical mannerism is likely to increase? No priest who has done much visiting among the old must be reminded of it. Need Froats have made a point of it before Maria Magdalena Theotoky?

This was a new reason for disquiet. Why should I care what she thought? But I did care, and I cared about what people thought of her. Hollier's revelation had annoyed me; he ought to keep his great paws off his students (no, no, that's unjust), he should not have taken advantage of his position as a teacher, however elated he was about his work. I thought of Balzac, driven by unconquerable lust, rushing at his kitchen-maid and, when he had taken her against the wall, screaming in her face, 'You have cost me a chapter!' and rushing back to his writing-table. I had not liked the suggestion that Maria was a singer of bawdy songs in public; if she had done so, there must have been some reason for it.

Darcourt, I thought, you are being a fool about that girl. Why? Because of her beauty, I decided; beauty clear through, for it was beauty not only of feature but of movement, and that rarest of beauties, a beautiful low voice. A man may admire beauty, surely, without reproaching himself? A man may wish not to seem fat and ridiculous, a Crypto-Farter, in the presence of such an astonishing work of God? Froats had not, I remembered, made a guess at her type, and it could not have been reticence, for Ozy had none. Was it—good God, could it be?—that he recognized in her a PPJ, another Preppy Peggy who would explode into grossness before she was thirty? No, it could not be: Peggy had been pneumatic and exuberant, and neither word applied to Maria.

My forty feet of Literary Gut was not in the best of moods when Parlabane came; I had denied it a sweet at dinner. This sort of denial may be the path to Heaven for some people, but not for me; it makes me cranky.

"Sim, you old darling? I've been neglecting you, and I'm ashamed. Do you want to beat Johnny? Three on each paddy with a hard, hard ruler?"

I suppose he thought of this as taking up from where we had left off, twenty-five years ago. He had loved to prattle in this campy way, because he knew it made me laugh. But I had never played that game except on the surface; I had never been one of his 'boys', the student gang who called themselves Gentleman's Relish. I was interested in them—fascinated might be a better word—but I never wanted to join them in the intimacies that bound them together, whatever those may have been. That I never really knew, because although they talked a lot about homosexuality, most of them had, after graduation, married and settled into what looked like the uttermost bourgeois respectability, leav-

ened by occasional divorce and remarriage. One was now on the
Bench, and was addressed as My Lord by obsequious or mock-
obsequious lawyers. I suppose that, like Parlabane himself, they
had played the field; one or two, I knew, had been on gusty terms
with omnivorous Elsie Whistlecraft, who had thought of herself
as a great hetaera, inducting the dewy young into the arts of love.
A lot of young men try varied aspects of sex before they settle
on the one that suits them best, which is usually the ordinary one.
But I had been cautious, discreet, and probably craven, and I had
never been one of Parlabane's 'boys'. But it had once tickled me
to hear him talk as if I were.

A foolish state of mind, but who has not been foolish, one way
or another? It would not do now, after a quarter of a century. I
suppose I was austere.

"Well, John, I had heard you were back, and I expected you'd
come to see me some time."

"I've left it inexcusably long. *Mea culpa, mea culpa, mea maxima
culpa,* as we say in the trade. But here I am. I hear great things
of you. Excellent books."

"Not bad, I hope."

"And a priest. Well—better get it over with; you can see from
my habit that I've had a change of mind. I think I have you to
thank for that, at least in part. During the past years, I've thought
of you often, you know. Things you used to say kept recurring.
You were wiser than I. And I turned to the Church at last."

"You had a shot at being a monk. Let's put it that way. But
obviously it hasn't worked."

"Don't be rough on me, Sim. I've had a rotten time. Everything
seemed to go sour. Surely you aren't surprised that I turned at
last to the place where nothing can go sour."

"Can't it? Then what are you doing here?"

"You would understand, if anybody would. I entered the S.S.M.
because I wanted to get away from all the things that had made
my life a hell—the worst of which was my own self-will. Abandon
self-will, I thought, and you may find peace, and with it salvation.
If thou bear the Cross cheerfully, it will bear thee."

"Thomas à Kempis—an unreliable guide for a man like you,
John."

"Really? I'd have thought he was very much your man."

"He isn't. Which is not to say I don't pay him all proper respect. But he's for the honest, you know, and you have never been quite honest. No, don't interrupt, I'm not insulting you; but Thomas à Kempis's kind of honesty is impossible for a man with as much subtlety as you have always possessed. Just as Thomas Aquinas was always too subtle a man to be a safe guide for you, because you blotted up his subtlety but kept your fingers crossed about his principles."

"Is that so? You seem to be a great authority about me."

"Fair play; when we were younger you set up to be a great authority about me.—I gather you were not able to bear the Cross cheerfully, so you skipped out of the monastery."

"You lent me the money for that. I can never be grateful enough."

"Divide any gratitude you have between me and Clem Hollier. Unless there were others on your five-hundred-dollar campaign list."

"You never thought a measly five hundred would do the job, did you?"

"That was certainly what your eloquent letter suggested."

"Well, that's water over the dam. I had to get out, by hook or crook."

"An unfortunate choice of expression."

"God, you've turned nasty! We are brothers in the Faith, surely. Haven't you any charity?"

"I have thought a good deal about what charity is, John, and it isn't being a patsy. Why did you have to get out of the Sacred Mission? Were they getting ready to throw you out?"

"No such luck! But they wouldn't let me move toward becoming a priest."

"Funny thing! And why was that, pray tell?"

"You are slipping back into undergraduate irony. Look, I'll level with you: have you ever been in one of those places?"

"A retreat or two when I was younger."

"Could you face a lifetime of it? Listen, Sim, I won't have you treating me as some nitwit penitent. I'm not knocking the Order, they gave me what I asked for, which was the Bread of Heaven. But I have to have a scrape of the butter and jam of the intellect on that Bread, or it chokes me! And listening to Father Prior's homilies was like first-year philosophy, without any of the doubts given a fair chance. I have to have some play of intellect in my life, or I go mad! And I have to have some humour in life—not the simple-minded jokes the Provincial got off now and then when he was being chummy with the brothers, and not the infant-class dirty jokes some of the postulants whispered at recreation hour, to show that they had once been men of the world. I've got to have the big salutary humour that saves—like that bloody Rabelais I hear so much about these days. I have to have something to put some yeast into the unleavened Bread of Heaven. If they'd let me be a priest I could have brought something useful to their service, but they wouldn't have it, and I think their rejection was nothing but spite and envy!"

"Envy of your learning and intellect?"

"Yes."

"Perhaps that was part of it. Spite and envy are no less frequent behind the monastery wall than outside it, and you have an especially shameless mind that can't disguise itself for the sake of people who are not so gifted. But what's done is done. The question is, what do you do now?"

"I'm doing a little teaching."

"In Continuing Studies."

"They're humbling me."

"Lots of good people teach there."

"But God damn it to hell, Sim, I'm not just 'good people'! I'm the best damned philosopher this University has ever produced and you know it."

"Perhaps. You are also a hard man to get along with, and to fit into anything. Have you any other prospects?"

"Yes, but I need time."

"And money, I'll bet."

"Could you see your way—?"

"What do you want to do?"

"I'm writing a book."

"What about? Scepticism used to be your special thing."

"No no; quite different. A novel."

"I don't suppose you are counting on it to produce much money?"

"Not for a while, of course."

"Better try for a Canada Council grant; they back novelists."

"Will you recommend me?"

"I recommend quite a few people every year; but I'm not known for literary taste. How do you know you can write a novel?"

"Because I have it all clear in my head! And it's really extraordinary! A brilliant account of life as it used to be in this city—the underground life, that's to say—but underlying it an analysis of the malaise of our time."

"Great God!"

"Meaning what, precisely?"

"Meaning that roughly two-thirds of the first novels that people write are on that theme. Very few of them get published."

"Don't be so ugly! You know me; you remember the things I used to write when we were students. With my mind—"

"That's what I'm afraid of. Novels aren't written with the mind."

"With what, then?"

"Ask Ozy Froats; the forty-foot gut, he says. Look at you—a heavy mesomorphic element combined with substantial ectomorphy, but hardly any endomorphy at all. You've lived a terrible life, you've boozed and drugged and toughed around, and you're still built like an athlete. I'll bet you've got a miserable little gut. When did you last go to the w.c.?"

"What the hell is all this?"

"It's the new psychology. Ask Froats.—Now I'll make a deal with you, John—"

"Just a few dollars to tide me over—"

"All right, but I said a deal, and here it is. Stop wearing that outfit. You disgust me, parading around as a man in God's service when you're in no service but your own—or perhaps the Devil's. I'll give you a suit, and you've got to wear it, or no money and not one crumb of help from me."

We looked over my suits. I had in mind one that was becoming a little tight, but Parlabane, by what course of argument I can't recall, walked off with one of my best ones—a smart clerical grey, though not of clerical cut. And a couple of very good shirts, and a couple of dark ties, and some socks, and a few handkerchiefs, and even an almost new pair of shoes.

"You've certainly put on weight," he said, as he preened in

front of the mirror. "But I'm handy with the needle; I can take a reef or two in this."

At last he was going, so—sheer weakness—I gave him one drink.

"How you've changed," he said. "You know, you used to be a soft touch. We seem to have changed roles. You, the pious youth, have become as hard as nails: I, the unbeliever, have tried to become a priest. Has your faith been so eroded by your life?"

"Strengthened, I should say."

"But when you recite the Creed, do you really mean what you say?"

"Every word. But the change is that I also believe a great many other things that aren't in the Creed. It's shorthand, you know. Just what's necessary. But I don't live merely by what is necessary. If you are determined on the religious life, you have to toughen up your mind. You have to let it be a thoroughfare for all thoughts, and among them you must make choices. You remember what Goethe said—that he'd never heard of a crime he could not imagine himself committing? If you cling frantically to the good, how are you to find out what the good really is?"

"I see.—Do you know anything about a girl called Theotoky?"

"She's a student of mine. Yes."

"I see something of her. She's Hollier's *soror mystica,* did you know? And as I'm his *famulus*—though he's doing his damnedest to shake me—I see her quite often. A real scrotum-stirring beauty."

"I know nothing about that."

"But Hollier does, I think."

"Meaning what?"

"I thought you might have heard something."

"Not a word."

"Well, I must go. Sorry you've become such a bad priest, Sim."

"Remember what I said about the habit."

"Oh, come on—just now and then. I like to lecture my mature students in it."

"Be careful. I could make things difficult for you."

"With the bishop? He wouldn't care."

"Not with the bishop. With the R.C.M.P. You've got a record, remember."

"I bloody well have not!"

"Not official. Just a few notes in a file, perhaps. But if I catch you in that fancy-dress again, I'll grass on you, Brother John."

He opened his mouth, then shut it. He had learned something after all; he had learned not to have an answer for everything.

He finished his drink, and after a longing look at the bottle, which I ignored, he went. But there was a pathetic appeal at the door which cost me fifty dollars. And he took his monk's robe, bundled up and tied with its own girdle.

Second Paradise IV

"POSHRAT!"

Mamusia struck me as hard as she could on the cheek with the flat of her hand. It was a rough blow, but perhaps I staggered a little more than was fully justified, and whimpered and appeared to be about to fall to the floor. She rushed toward me and pushed her face as near as possible to mine, hissing fury and garlic.

"*Poshrat!*" she screamed again, and spat in my face. This was a scene we had played many times in our life together, my Mother and I, and I knew better than to try to wipe away the spittle. It was something that had to be endured, and in the end it would probably work out as I wished.

"To tell him that! To chatter to your *gadjo* professor about the *bomari!* You hate me! You want to destroy me! Oh, I know how you despise me, how you are ashamed of me, how you want to ruin me! You grudge me the work by which I earn my poor living! You wish me dead! But do you think I have lived so long that I'm to be trampled and ruined by a *poshrat* slut, and my secrets torn away from me! I'll kill you! I'll come in the night and stab you as you sleep! Don't glare at me with your bold eyes, or I'll blind you with a needle! [I was not glaring, but this was a favourite threat.] Oh, that I should be cursed with you! The fine lady, the *gadjo's* whore—that must be it—you're his whore, are you? And you want to bring him here to spy on me! May the Baby Jesus tear you with a great iron hook!"

On and on she raved, enjoying herself immensely; I knew that in the end she would rave herself into a good temper, and then there would be endearments, and a cold wet poultice of mint for my burning face, and a snort of Yerko's fierce plum brandy, and she would play the *bosh* and sing to me and her affection would be as high-pitched as her wrath. Nothing for me to do but play my part, that of the broken, repentant daughter, supposedly living in the sunshine or shade of a Mother's affection.

Nobody could say my life lacked variety. At the University I was Miss Theotoky, a valued graduate student somewhat above the rest because I was one of the select group of Research Assistants, a girl with friends and a quiet, secure place in the academic hierarchy, with professors who had marked me as one who might some day join their own Druid circle. At home I was Maria, one of the Kalderash, the Lovari, but not quite, because my Father had not been of this ancient and proud strain, but a *gadjo*—and therefore, when my Mother was displeased with me, she used the offensive word *poshrat,* which means half-breed. Everything that was wrong with me, in her eyes, came of being a *poshrat.* Nobody was to blame for this but herself, but it would not have been tactful to say so when she was angry.

I was half Gypsy, and since my Father died the half sometimes seemed in my Mother's estimation to amount to three-quarters, or even seven-eighths. I knew she loved me deeply, but like any deep love there were times when it was a burden, and its demands cruel. To live with my Mother meant living according to her beliefs, which were in almost every way at odds with what I had learned elsewhere. It had been different when my Father was alive, because he could control her, not by shouting or domination—that was her way—but by the extraordinary force of his noble character.

He was a very great man, and since his death when I was sixteen I had been looking for him, or something like him, among all the men I met. I believe that psychiatrists explain such a search as mine to troubled girls as though it were a deep secret the girls could never have uncovered for themselves, but I had always known it; I wanted my Father, I wanted to find a man who was his equal in bravery and wisdom and warmth of love, and once or twice, briefly, I thought I had found him in Clement Hollier. Wisdom I knew he possessed; if it were called for I was sure he would have bravery; warmth of love was what I wanted to arouse in him, but I knew it would never do to thrust myself at him. I must serve; I must let my love be seen in humility and sacrifice; I must let him discover me. As indeed I thought he had, that April day on the sofa. I was not yet disappointed, but I was beginning to be just a little frenzied. When would he show himself the successor to my beloved Tadeusz, to my dear Father?

Can I be a modern girl, if I acknowledge such thoughts? I must be modern: I live now. But like everybody else, as Hollier says, I live in a muddle of eras, and some of my ideas belong to today, and some to an ancient past, and some to periods of time that seem more relevant to my parents than to me. If I could sort them and control them I might know better where I stand, but when I most want to be contemporary the Past keeps pushing in, and when I long for the Past (like when I wish Tadeusz had not died, and were with me now to guide and explain and help me to find where I belong in life) the Present cannot be pushed away. When I hear girls I know longing to be what they call liberated, and when I hear others rejoicing in what they think of as liberation, I feel a fool, because I simply do not know where I stand.

I know where I have been, however, or rather where the people from whom I derive all that I am, had their being and lived out vital portions of their fate. My Father, Tadeusz Bonawentura Niemcewicz, was Polish, and he had the misfortune to be born in Warsaw in 1910. Misfortune, I say, because a great war came soon afterward and his family, which had been well off, lost everything except a strong endowment of pride. He was a man of cultivation, and his profession was that of an engineer, leaning particularly toward the establishment and equipment of factories, and it was this work that took him while he was still young to Hungary, where he soon settled down as one of the Politowski who were numerous in Budapest. In consideration for his Hungarian friends, who thought Niemcewicz hard to pronounce, he added to it the name of his mother, which was Theotoky. She had been of Greek ancestry.

He was a man of romantic temperament—or rather, I should say that is how I like to think of him—and like many such young men he fell in love with a Gypsy girl, but unlike most of the others, he married her. That was my Mother, Oraga Laoutaro.

Not all Gypsies are nomads, and my Mother's family had been musicians in Budapest for generations, because the Gypsy musicians would much rather play in comfortable restaurants, officers' clubs, and the houses of rich people than wander the roads. Indeed, the Gypsy musicians think of themselves as the aristocracy of their people. My Mother was an oddity, because she played her violin in public; usually the Gypsy fiddlers are men, and the women sing and dance. She was beautiful and exciting, and the young Polish engineer pursued her and at last persuaded her to marry him, both in Gypsy form and in the Catholic Church.

When the Second World War was approaching, my Father smelled it on the breeze, or more probably smelled it in the industrial work in which he was occupied. He determined to get out of Europe, and made arrangements which took so much time that he and my Mother barely made it to England before war broke out in the autumn of 1939. There they were joined by my Mother's brother Yerko, who had been travelling in France—for reasons I shall tell in good time—and there they remained until 1946; my Father was in the Army, but not as a fighter; he designed equipment and planned its manufacture, and Yerko worked with him as an artificer, a maker of models. Tadeusz and my Mother had a child, but it died, and it was not until after they had come to Canada and settled in Toronto that I was born, in 1958, when my Mother was already near forty. (She always said she was born in 1920, but I don't think she really knew, and certainly had nothing that would support it.) By that time my Father and Yerko were well set up in a business of their own, manufacturing equipment for hospitals; my Father knew how manufacturing should be managed, and Yerko, who was a brilliant metalsmith, could make and improve the working models of anything my Father could design. Everything seemed to move on a wave of success until my Father died in 1975, not dramatically of overwork but draggingly of a neglected cold which turned into other things and could not be defeated. And with my Father's death our family, which had been pretty much, I suppose, like scores of other European families that had settled in Canada, a little foreign but not markedly at odds with the prevailing North American style of life, took a sharp turn from which it has not recovered.

My Father was a strong character, and though he loved my Mother greatly, and loved to think of her as a Gypsy girl, it was clear that he wanted things in the family to go in the upper-class Polish way. My Mother dressed like a woman of means, and some good shops repressed her taste for gaudy colours and droopy silhouettes. She rarely spoke the Romany that was her cradle language, except to me and to Yerko, and her ordinary language with my Father was Hungarian; she learned a little Polish from him and I learned that language as well as I learned Hungarian; she was sometimes jealous that he and I could speak together in a tongue she did not follow perfectly. English she never learned perfectly, but in Toronto there were quite enough people for her to talk to in Hungarian for that not to be a severe handicap. In the company of English-speaking people she employed a broken English to which she managed to give a certain elegance—English-speaking people being pushovers for that kind of speech. Looking back over the years before my Father's death, I realize now that Mamusia lived a somewhat muted, enclosed life. A beloved man had enveloped her, as now Hollier enveloped me.

Mamusia was what my parents wanted me to call her—the appropriate pet-name of a well-bred Polish child for its Mother. Canadian children who heard me thought I was saying Mamoosha (Canadians are incorrigibly tin-eared) but the proper way to say the word is delicate and caressing. I also, on birthdays and at Christmas, called her Édesanya, which is high-class Hungarian, and I usually called my Father by the Hungarian form, which is Édesapa. When my Mother wanted to vex him, she would encourage me to call her Mamika—which is about equivalent to Mommix in English—and he would frown and click his tongue. He was never angry, but the tongue-clicking was rebuke enough for me.

I think I was rather stiffly brought up, for Édesapa did not like the free-and-easy Canadian ways and could not see that they meant no disrespect. He was startled to discover that at the good convent school to which I was sent we were taught to play softball and lacrosse, and that the nuns bundled up their skirts and played with us. Nuns on skates—which is a very pretty sight—troubled him dreadfully. Of course these were the old nuns, in skirts to their feet; the revolution in convent dress of the sixties almost persuaded him that the sky was falling. I know now that an aging romantic is hardly to be distinguished from an aging Tory, but as a loyal child I tried to share some of his sense of outrage. Not successfully. It was a black day when he learned that, like the other girls at the convent, I referred to the Mother Superior behind her back as The Old Supe.

Poor Édesapa, so sweet, so courteous, so chivalrous but, even I must admit, so stuffy about some things. It was the nobility of spirit and the high ideals that won me and hold me still.

How he made so much money, I do not know. Many people think that business and a fine concept of life cannot be reconciled, but I am not so sure. Make money he undoubtedly did, and when he died we were surprised to learn how much. Yerko could not have carried on alone, but he knew how to sell to advantage to a rival firm, and in the end there was a handsome trust to maintain Mamusia, and a handsome trust for me, and Yerko was quite a rich man. Of course everybody has his own idea about what it is to be rich; truly rich people, I suppose, don't really know what they have. But Yerko was rich beyond anything that a Hungarian Gypsy musician would have thought possible, and he wept copiously and assured me that it would all come to me when he died, and that he felt the hand of death on him very frequently. He was only fifty-eight and as strong as a horse, and lived a life that would have killed any ordinary man years ago, but he spoke of death as something to be expected hourly.

The root of much trouble was that I was to get the whole of the money that was in trust for me when I became twenty-five, and would receive all the capital of Mamusia's trust when she died. It appeared to her—and no amount of explanation or reasoning on my part or that of the puzzled men at the Trust Company's offices could persuade her otherwise—that I had scooped the pile, that her adored Tadeusz had somehow done the dirty on her, and that she was close to destitution. Where was her money? Why was she never able to lay hands on it? She received a substantial monthly cheque, but who was to say when that might not be cut off? In her heart she knew well enough what was what, but she delighted in making a Gypsy row in order to see the Trust men blench and swallow their spittle as she raved.

What had happened was that she was experiencing that intoxicating upsurge of energy some women have when their husbands die. She grieved in true Gypsy style for Tadeusz, declared that she would soon follow him to the grave, and took on tragic airs for several weeks. But working up through this drama, part genuine and part ritual, was the knowledge that she was free, and that the debt of *gadjo* respectability she had owed to her marriage was paid in full. Freedom for Mamusia meant a return to Gypsy ways. She went into mourning, which was old-fashioned but necessary to assuage her grief. But she never really emerged from mourning, the fashionable clothes disappeared from her cupboards, and garments which had a markedly *Ciganyak* look replaced them. She wore several long skirts and, to my dismay, no pants underneath them.

"Dirty things," she said when I protested, "they get very foul in a few days; only a dirty person would want to wear them."

She had returned to Gypsy notions of cleanliness, which are not modern; her one undergarment was a shift which she gave a good tubbing every few months; she did not wash, but rubbed her skin with olive oil, and put a heavier, scented oil on her hair. I would not say that she was dirty, but the North American ideal of freshness had no place in her personal style. Gold chains and a multitude of gold rings, hidden away since her days as a Gypsy restaurant fiddler, reappeared and jingled and clinked musically whenever she moved; she often said you could tell the ring of real gold, which was like no other sound in the world. She was never seen without a black scarf on her head, tied under her chin when she went out into the *gadjo* world, but tied behind when she was indoors. She was a striking and handsome figure, but not everybody's idea of a mother.

Mamusia lived in a world of secrets, and she had in the highest degree the Gypsy conviction that the Gypsies are the real sophisticates, and everybody else is a *gadjo*—which really means a dupe, a gull, a simpleton to be cheated by the knowing ones. This belief ran deep; sometimes sheer necessity required her to accept a *gadjo* as at least an equal, and to admit that they too had their cunning. But the essential sense of crafty superiority was never dormant for long.

It was this conviction that led to the worst quarrels between us. Mamusia was a dedicated and brilliant shop-lifter. Most of what we ate was pinched.

"But they are so stupid," she would reply when I protested; "those supermarkets, they have long corridors stacked with every kind of thing anybody could want, and trash nobody but a *gadjo* would want; if they don't expect it to be taken, why don't they guard it?"

"Because they trust the honesty of the public," I would say, and Mamusia would laugh her terrible, harsh Gypsy laugh. "Well, actually, it costs more to guard it than to put up with a certain amount of thieving," I would go on, rather more honestly.

"Then they expect it. So what's all the bother?"; this was her unanswerable reply.

"But if you get caught, think of the disgrace! You, the widow of Tadeusz Theotoky, what would it be like if you were brought into court?" (I was also thinking of my own shame if it should come out that my Mother was a clouter.)

"But I don't intend to be caught," she would reply.

Nor was she ever caught. She never went to the same supermarket too often, and before she entered she became stooped, tremulous, and confused; as she padded up and down the aisles she made great play with a pair of old-fashioned spectacles—her trick was to adjust them, trying to get them to stick on her nose, and then to make a great business of reading the directions on the label of a tin she held in her right hand; meanwhile her left hand was deftly moving goods from a lower shelf into the inner pockets of a miserable old black coat she always wore on these piratical voyages. When she came at last to the check-out desk she had only one or two small things to pay for, and as she opened her purse she made sure the checker got a good view of her pitiful store of money; sometimes she would scrabble for as many as eighteen single cents to eke out the amount of her bill. Pitiful old soul! The miseries of these lonely old women who have only their Old Age Pensions to depend on! (Fearful old crook, despoiling the stupid *gadje!*)

I ate at home as little as I decently could, not only because I disapproved of Mamusia's method of provisioning, but also because the avails of shop-lifting do not make for a balanced or delicious menu. Gypsies are terrible cooks, by modern standards, anyhow, and the household we maintained when Tadeusz was alive was a thing of the past. The evening meal after our great fight about Hollier's visit was pork and beans, heavily sprinkled with paprika, and Mamusia's special coffee, which she made by adding a little fresh coffee to the old grounds in the bottom of the pot, and boiling until wanted.

As I had foreseen, a calm followed the storm, my bruised face had been poulticed, and we had done some heavy hugging and in my case some weeping. Among Gypsies, a kiss is too important a thing for exchange after a mere family disagreement; it is for serious matters, so we had not kissed.

"Why did you tell him about the *bomari?*" said Mamusia.

"Because it is important to his work."

"It's important to my work, but it won't be if everybody knows about it."

"I'm sure he'll respect your secrecy."

"Then he'll be the first *gadjo* that ever did."

"Oh Mamusia, think of Father."

"Your Father was bound to me by a great oath. Marriage is a great oath. Nothing would have persuaded him to betray any secret of mine—or I to betray him. We were married."

"I'm sure Professor Hollier would swear an oath if you asked him."

"Not to breathe a word about the *bomari?*"

I saw that I had made a fool of myself. "Of course he'd want to write about it," I said, wondering whether the dreadful fight would begin again.

"Write what?"

"Articles in learned journals; perhaps even a book."

"A book about the *bomari?*"

"No, no, not just about the *bomari,* but about all sorts of things like it that wise people like you have preserved for the modern world."

This was Gypsy flattery on my part, because Mamusia is convinced that she is uncommonly wise. She has proof of it; when she was born the ages of her father and mother, added together, amounted to more than a hundred years. This is an indisputable sign.

"He must be a strange teacher if he wants to teach about the *bomari* to all those flat-faced loafers at the University. They wouldn't know how to manage it even if they were told about it."

"Mamusia, he doesn't want to teach about it. He wants to write about it for a few very learned men like himself who are interested in the persistence of old wisdom and old belief in this modern world, which so terribly lacks that sort of wisdom. He wants to do honour to people like you who have suffered and kept silent in order to guard the ancient secrets."

"He's going to write down my name?"

"Never, if you ask him not to; he will say he learned so-and-so from a very wise woman he was so lucky as to meet under circumstances he has vowed not to reveal."

"Ah, like that?"

"Yes, like that. You know better than anyone that even if *gadje* knew about the *bomari* they could never make it work properly, because they haven't had your experience and great inherited wisdom."

"Well, little *poshrat,* you have started this and I suppose I must end it. I do it for you because you are Tadeusz's daughter. Nothing less than that would persuade me. Bring your wise man."

[2]

BRING MY WISE MAN. But that was only the beginning; I must manage the encounter between Mamusia and my wise man so that neither of them was turned forever against me. What a fool I had been to start all this! What a *gadji* fool! Would I get out of it with my skin, not to speak of the admiration and gratitude and perhaps the love I hoped to win from Hollier by what I had done? If only I had not wanted to add something to his research on the Filth Therapy! But I was in the predicament of the Sorcerer's Apprentice; I had started something I could not stop, and perhaps in the end the Sorcerer would punish me.

I had plenty of time to reflect on my trouble, for I had a whole evening with Mamusia, lying on my sofa and changing my poultice every half-hour or so, as she played her fiddle and occasionally sang.

She knew, in her cunning fashion, how irritating this was to me. I am an enthusiast for music, and I like it at its most so-phisticated and intellectual; it is one of the few assurances of order in my confused world. But Mamusia's music was the true

Magyar Gypsy strain, lamenting, mourning, yowling, and suddenly modulating into frenzied high spirits, the fingers sliding up
the fingerboard in *glissandi* that seemed to be primitive screams
of some sort of ecstasy that was never real to me. The Gypsy
scale—minor third, augmented fourth, minor sixth, and major
seventh—fretted my nerves; had not the diatonic scale sufficed
for the noble ecstasy of J. S. Bach? I had to fight this music; its
primitivism and sentimentality grated on everything the University meant to me; yet I knew it for an aspect of my inheritance
that I could never root out, deny it though I might. Oh, I knew
what was wrong with me, right enough; I wanted to be an intellectual, to escape from everything Mamusia and the generations
of Kalderash behind her meant, and I knew I could do it only by
the uttermost violence to myself. Even my agonizing concern with
Hollier, I sometimes suspected, was chiefly a wish to escape from
my world into his. Is that love, or isn't it?

Mamusia now turned to a kind of music that was deeply personal to herself; not the kind of thing she would ever, as a girl,
have played in an officers' mess, or to the diners in a fashionable
restaurant. She called it the Bear Chant; it was the music Gypsy
bear-leaders played or sang to their animals, but I think it was
something older than that; to those gypsies so long ago the bear
was not only a valuable possession and money-spinner, but a
companion and perhaps an object of reverence. Is it unbeliev-
able? Notice how some people talk to their dogs and cats nowadays; the talk is usually the sentimentality they think appropriate
to a not very dangerous animal. But how would one talk to a bear
which could kill? How would one ask it for friendship? How
would one invite its wisdom, which is so unlike the wisdom of a
man, but not impenetrable by a man? This was what the Bear
Chant seemed to be—music that moved slowly, with long inter-
rogative pauses, and unusual demands on that low, guttural voice
of the fiddle, which is so rarely heard in the kind of music I
understand and enjoy. *Croak—croak;* tell me, Brother Martin,
how is it with you? What do you see? What do you hear? And
then: *Grunt—grunt,* Brother Martin (for all Gypsy bears are
called Martin) says his profound say. Would she ever play that
for Hollier? And—I knew nothing of his sensitivity to such
things—would Hollier make anything of it?

Bring my wise man; what would he make of the house in which I lived?

It was a big house and a handsome house, in the heavy banker-like style that prevails in the most secure, most splendidly tree-lined streets of the Rosedale district of Toronto. One Hundred and Twenty Walnut Street was not the handsomest, nor yet the simplest, of the houses to be found there. Solid brick, white-painted woodwork, impressively quoined at the corners; a few fine trees, well attended by professional tree-pruners and patchers; a good lawn, obviously planted by an expert, of fine grass without a weed to be seen. The very house, indeed, for a Polish engineer who had done well in the New World and wished to take the place in that world his money and ability and obvious respectability required. How proud Tadeusz had been of it, and how he had laughed gently when Mamusia said it was too big for a couple with one child, even with a housekeeper who lived in a flat all her own on the third floor. A good house, furnished with good things, and kept in the best of condition by contract cleaners and gardeners. And so it looked still to the passer-by.

Inside, however, there had been catastrophic changes. When Tadeusz died Mamusia had talked distractedly of selling it and looking for some hovel congruous with her widowed and financially fallen state. But her brother Yerko had told her not to be a fool; she was sitting on a fortune. It was Yerko who remembered that when Tadeusz bought the house, it had possessed a rating at City Hall as an apartment and rooming-house; this had been granted because of some temporary necessity, during the war years, and had never been revoked, even though Tadeusz had required the whole thing for his own occupancy. The thing to do, said Yerko, was to restore the place to its former condition as an apartment and rooming-house, and make money from it. The *gadje* always wanted nice places to live.

I do not know what its former condition had been, but after Mamusia and Yerko had finished with it One Hundred and Twenty Walnut Street was surely one of the queerest warrens in a city noted for queer warrens. To save money, Yerko did much of the work himself; he could turn his hand to anything, and with a labourer to help him he turned Tadeusz's beautiful, proud home into ten dwellings: the best apartment, consisting of a living-room, kitchen, and bedroom, and a sun porch, was Mamusia's own. On the ground floor there were, in addition, two bachelor apartments of kennel-like darkness and inconvenience, one of which had no less than seven corners, after the cupboard-like kitchen facility and the doll's bathroom had been created. These were rented to young men, Mr. Kolbenheyer and Mr. Vitrac; Kolbenheyer was skeletonic, and never spoke above a whisper; about Vitrac I had perpetual misgivings, because he looked like a man bent on suicide and his apartment would have been a perfect setting for a miserable departure.

On the middle floor, where once the bedrooms of Tadeusz and Mamusia and I had been, there was a one-bedroom apartment with its own bath, and a tiny kitchen, and a sitting-room which shared its only window with the kitchen, by an architectural twist of Yerko's that split a window down the middle. The queen of our lodgers, Mrs. Faiko, lived here, with her three cats. There were also on this floor three bed-sitters, which shared a kitchen and a bathroom; these were for Miss Gretser, Mrs. Nowaczynski, and Mrs. Schreyvogl, all old, who possessed among them four poodles and two cats. They had agreed among themselves that as they did not use the shower much (danger of being trapped in scalding water) they should keep the lower part of the shower booth filled with torn-up newspaper as a litter-box for the animals. They were supposed to clear it out now and then, but they were feeble and forgetful, so it was usually my job to attend to this. Miss Gretser, after all, was over eighty-seven and so far as anyone knew had not been out of the house in three years; Mrs. Nowaczynski kindly did her small shopping for her.

On the top floor were two single-room apartments, sharing a bathroom. These were occupied by Mr. Kostich, who was said to be associated somehow with a dry-cleaner's business, and Mr. Horne, who was a male nurse. Whenever Mamusia had occasion to mention this in his presence he would shout, "Well, I sure's hell ain't a female´nurse," and this made him the wit of the establishment.

In the basement was a very extensive five-room apartment, where my Uncle Yerko lived, and maintained his still, and Mamusia did some of her most important and secret work.

The decoration of all these flats and rooms had been undertaken by Yerko, who had cleverly picked up a job-lot of paint and wallpaper that nobody wanted to buy. The paper was blue, with large roses in a darker blue, a truly dreadful background for the array of family photographs and wedding pictures with which the old ladies ornamented their rooms. The paint, on the other hand, was pink. Not a faint pink or a shade of pink but *pink*. As Yerko worked on the decoration he had frequent recourse to the plum brandy of his own manufacture with which he supported his energies, and consequently none of the paper was quite straight on the wall, and there were large spatterings of paint on the floor. It was a drunken, debauched, raped house when this Gypsy pair finally began to accept lodgers, with a preference for those not too rich in *gadjo* cunning. The house stank; a stench all its own pervaded every corner. It was a threnody in the key of Cat minor, with a ground-bass of Old Dog, and modulations of old people, waning lives, and relinquished hopes.

Why was this dreadful rookery never condemned by the city's inspectors of such places? Yerko knew what to do. You cannot bribe an inspector; everybody knows that. But inspectors are not well paid, or they think they aren't, and they and their wives all want things like dish-washers, or power-mowers, or air-conditioners which Yerko was able to secure for them at wholesale prices; he had connections with the manufacturing world from his days with Tadeusz. He was obliging to the inspectors, and not only did he see that the goods were delivered direct from the factory, he somehow arranged that no bill, even for the wholesale price, was ever rendered. And as everybody knows, a little friendliness goes a long way in the world of the *gadje*.

Where did I fit into this? Yerko and Mamusia agreed that it would be folly to keep a whole room for a girl who was away all day at the University, and I could easily sleep on Mamusia's sofa. I was a young woman of substantial independent means and there was nothing in the world to prevent me from taking an apartment of my own, answerable to nobody but myself, far from the stink of senile dogs and unwashed old people, and out of earshot of the distressing cries that came through the wall when Mr. Vitrac had a bad dream. Nothing in the world but love and loyalty. Because, agonizing though it often was to live with Mamusia, and tedious as I found the company of Yerko, who was rarely sober,

I loved them both and if I deserted them, I thought, what might not happen to them?

[3]

THE VISIT OF my wise man was soon arranged; he could come on the third day from my asking him. My Mother says will you come to tea, I said, prompted by I cannot say what madness. Did this expression conjure up in his mind some fragrant old soul in a Rosedale house, pouring delicate China tea into thin, rare cups? But in this, as in all social dealings with Hollier, I seemed to lose my head. About academic things I could talk to him sensibly enough but on anything suggesting a personal relationship, however ordinary, I was a fool.

For both of us, the transformation in Parlabane was astonishing. Gone was the monk's robe, and with it had gone the theatrically monkish demeanour. He looked almost smart, in a good grey suit. It seemed to have been made for a somewhat taller and stouter man; there was not quite enough room in the shoulders, and there was more than he needed in the waistcoat; to keep the trousers from dragging at his heels he wore them braced up to the last possible inch. But his sober tie and clean shirt, the white handkerchief tucked in his breast pocket, were all that could be asked of any tidy academic.

Best of all, he had stopped grumbling about the poor pay he got for teaching in Extension. I asked him if he had found some way of increasing his income.

"I'm looking into one or two things," he said, "and I've found avenues around the University that may lead to something that will tide me over until I get an advance on my novel."

Novel? This was unexpected.

"It's rather a big thing," he said, "and needs some touching up. But it's in a condition to be seen. When I've done a little more work on it I'm going to ask Clem to take a look at it, and advise me about publishing."

This was the first I had heard about Hollier as an authority on novels. Surprise must have shown in my face.

"Clem will understand it better than most people. It's not just a best-seller sort of thing, you see. It's the real *roman philosophique*, and I want some informed people to give me their opinion before I hand it over to the publisher."

"Oh, you have a publisher?" I said.

"No, not yet; that's one of the things I want advice about. Which publisher should it be? I don't want it to get into the wrong hands, and have the wrong sort of promotion."

This was a new Parlabane, an innocent, hopeful Parlabane. Women are supposed, from time to time, to see the men they know as little boys. I think that is unjust, but certainly as Parlabane cocked his head at me and talked of his novel, I had a sudden perception of a little boy in that battered, blurred face.

[4]

SINCE I FIRST MET him at McVarish's cocktail party, Arthur Cornish had asked me to have dinner with him three times, and I had gone twice. He was a change from the men I met at the University, who were either married, or of that group called 'not the marrying kind', or young academics who wanted a listener as they talked about themselves and their careers. The first time Arthur talked about food, and politics, and travel, and seemed not to have any personal revelations that couldn't wait. Nor did he seem to think that feeding me put me in his debt in any way at all. He was almost impersonal, but nice, and liked me to talk at least half the time; so I talked about food, and politics, and travel, without really knowing much about any of them. But he had the gift of creating an easy evening, and that was a novelty.

"Let's do this again," he said as he dropped me at One Hundred and Twenty Walnut Street, after that first dinner. "I hate eating alone."

"Surely you know lots of people," I said. He was obviously well off; he drove a modest but expensive car. I supposed young men of means must know lots of girls.

"Not girls as beautiful as you," he said, but not in a way that suggested it was going to lead to further compliments, or any of that grappling which some men think is fair exchange for a meal.

I refuse to pretend that I don't like being told that I am beautiful. It is a fact, and though I would rather be the way I am than ugly, I don't pay much attention to it. Sooner or later almost all the men I know make some comment about it. So I decided that this pleasant, rather cool young man thought I was ornamental, and it was satisfactory to be seen in a restaurant with me, and that was a fair deal. I liked him better for being rich: he liked me better for being beautiful. Reasonable enough.

When I refused his second invitation, because I had to go to a special lecture, I thought that would be the end of it. But he asked me a third time, to dine and go to a symphony concert, and that surprised me a little, because he said nothing about music the first time we were alone together.

We went to a good restaurant, but not to one of the showy ones, and it was clear from the table we were given that Arthur was known there. It was a very good meal, from quite a different world of the imagination than the offerings of The Rude Plenty.

I had made some effort about clothes, and did what I could to look well, and was prepared for another bout of food, politics, and travel, but he surprised me by talking about music. He seemed to have almost a patron's attitude toward it, which reminded me that he was the nephew of Francis Cornish. It was about his uncle he talked now.

"Uncle Frank has left his collection of musical manuscripts to the University; I wish he had left them to me. I'd like to do something in that line myself. Of course it's not difficult to buy manuscripts from modern composers, and I do a little in that way. But I would have liked to have his early things; there's a beauty about them—about the manuscript itself—that the modern works don't have. A lot of the early composers wrote the most exquisite musical hands. Had to, so that the copyist didn't get into trouble. But they also took pride in them."

"You mean you like the manuscript better than the music?"

"No, but there is a quiet beauty about a really fine original manuscript that is like nothing else. People buy manuscripts of authors and get great satisfaction from them, quite apart from any bibliographical interest they may have. Why not music? A Mendelssohn manuscript is wholly Mendelssohnian—precise, beautiful, just the tiniest bit conventional, and sensitive without being weak. It speaks of the man. And Berlioz! Fiery spirit, but splendidly legible, and dotted all over with directions in his handwriting, which is that of a man who was both a Romantic and the possessor of a thoroughgoing classical education. Bach—manuscript of a man who had to be careful with his ruled paper, which cost money he didn't want to spend. Beethoven—scribble, scribble, scribble. It's something of the man. My Uncle had some nice Liszt things, and I wish I had them. We're going to hear Liszt tonight. Egressy is playing the last three Hungarian Rhapsodies."

"I hate that kind of music."

"Really? Too bad."

"I'll turn off my ears while he's playing."

"What do you hate about it?"

"Everything. The spirit of it, the stress of emotion, the unchaste ornamentation."

"The very things I like."

"It's a change for you; I have it all the time."

"Theotoky; a Greek name, isn't it?"

"My Father's; but on my Mother's side I am a Gypsy, and being a Gypsy in the modern world—especially the University world—simply doesn't do."

"You don't like it in yourself?"

"I'd have to believe in heredity more than I do to admit there is much of it in myself. I'm a Canadian woman, setting out on a university career, and I don't want any part of the Gypsy world."

Now what on earth made me say that? I was surprised to hear myself. It sounded so aggressive, so much like the know-it-all girls I liked least at the University. I didn't want to go on with that theme; I had not meant to tell Arthur Cornish that I had Gypsy blood, because it sounded as if I were tyring to make myself interesting in a cheap way. Let's drop that.

"Did you never tell your uncle you were interested in his musical manuscripts?"

"He knew I was."

"Isn't it odd that he didn't leave you even one of them?"

"Not odd at all. It's fatal to let a collector know you're interested in his things; he's quite likely to suspect you of coveting them. He begins to think you are waiting for them. I'll show him, says the collector, and bequeaths them to somebody else."

"What odd people collectors must be."

"Some of the oddest."

"How odd are you? But I suppose working with figures keeps you sane."

"Do I work with figures?"

"What else is working with money?"

"Oh—quite different. Money's something you shove around, like electricity."

"Like electricity?"

"Like large power-grids, and transformers, and that sort of thing. The diffusion of electricity is an extremely important kind of engineering. You decide where to put the energy, and how to get it there, according to the result you expect. Money is a form of power."

"A kind of power most people think they don't have enough of."

"That's quite different. The personal money people are always making such a fuss about depends heavily on where the big power-money is put—what bonds and industries get the heavy support, and when. People who aren't in the money trade talk about *making* money; they are able to do that because of the decisions people like me make about the power-money. The money people want for their personal use is all part of the big scheme, just as the electricity they turn on at a switch in their houses is a tiny part of what happens through the big grid. Brightens things up for them but it isn't much in the large scheme. What anybody can do with money for mere personal satisfaction is extremely limited. It's the power-money that's fascinating."

"It doesn't fascinate me."

"Not the power?"

"It's not my world."

"The University world is a power world, I suppose."

"Oh no, you don't understand universities. They're not just honeycombs of classrooms, where students are labelled this, that, and the other, so they can get better jobs than their parents. It's the world of research; the selfless pursuit of knowledge and sometimes of truth."

"Selfless?"

"Sometimes."

Of course I was thinking of Hollier, and how much I wanted to follow him.

"I can't judge, of course. I never went to a university."

"You didn't!"

"I'm a heavily disguised illiterate. I deceive lots of people. No B.A.—not to speak of an M.A.—yet I usually escape undetected. You won't turn me in, will you?"

"But—how have you—?"

"Where did I achieve my deceptive polish and ease in high-class conversation? In the University of Hard Knocks."

"Tell me about the U. of H.K."

"Not so very long ago there was a positive prejudice against university-trained people in the banking world, especially if they were expected to go to the top. What could a university give me that would be of any practical use? A degree in economics? You can learn economics better and quicker by reading a few books. A training in business administration? I was *born* to business administration. The rich gloss of cultivation? My guardians thought I could get that just as well by travelling and meeting a few Rothschilds and their like. So that's what I did."

"Guardians? Why guardians?"

"Oh, I had a Grandfather, and a fine old crusted money type he was. You'd have loathed him; he thought professors were fellows with holes in their pants who didn't notice the bad food they were eating because they were reading Greek at the same time. He's the one Uncle Frank escaped from. But my Father, who was a very good banker indeed, and not quite such a savage as my Grandfather, married rather late, and having begot me was killed in a motor accident in which my young, beautiful Mother was killed too. So I had Grandfather, and guardians who were members of his banking entourage, and was to all intents and purposes an orphan. What's more, that despair of psychiatrists, a very rich orphan. I had no parents to humble me in the great Canadian upper-bourgeois tradition, to warn me against being myself, to urge me to be like them. So far as a civilized upbringing permits, I was free. And being free I found that I had no special urge toward rebellion, but rather, a pull toward orthodoxy. Now perhaps that's odd, if you are looking for oddity. I had a wonderfully happy childhood, suckled at the twin breasts of Trust and Equity. Then I travelled, and it was while travelling that I developed my great idea."

"What was it?"

"Should I tell you? Why should I tell you?"

"The best of reasons: I'm dying to know. I mean, there has to be more to you than banking."

"Maria, that's patronizing and silly. You know damn-all about banking, and you scorn it because it seems to have nothing to do with university life. How do you think a university keeps its doors open? Money, that's how. The unionized professors and the un-ionized support staff and the meccano the scientists and doctors demand, all cost megatons of money, and how does the Alma Mater get it? Partly from her alumni, I admit; a university must truly be a Bounteous Mother if she can charm so much dough out of the pockets of her children who have long left her. But who manages the money? Who turns it into power? People like me, and don't you forget it."

"All right, all right, all right; I apologize on my knees; I grovel under the table. I just meant, there is something about you that is interesting, and banking doesn't interest me. So perhaps it's your great idea. Please, Arthur, tell me."

"All right, though you don't deserve it."

"I'll be quiet and respectful."

"I've had this notion since my school days, and travel abroad strengthened it because I met some people who had made it work. I am going to be a patron."

"Like your Uncle Frank?"

"No. Wholly unlike my Uncle Frank. He was a patron in a way, but it was part of his being a miser in a much bigger way. He was an accumulator; he acquired works of art and then hated to think of getting rid of them; the result is the mess I'm cleaning up now, with Hollier and McVarish and Darcourt helping me. That's not what I call being a patron. Of course Uncle Frank put some money in the hands of living artists, and spotted some winners and encouraged them and gave them what they want most—which is sympathetic understanding—but he wasn't a pa-tron on the grand scale. Whatever he did was basically for the satisfaction of Francis Cornish."

"What's a patron on the grand scale?"

"A great *animateur;* somebody who breathes life into things. I suppose you might call it a great encourager, but also a begetter, a director who keeps artists on the tracks, and provides the power—which isn't all money, by any means—that makes them go. It's a kind of person—a very rare kind—that has to work in opera, or ballet, or the theatre; he's the central point for a group of artists of various kinds, and he has to be the autocrat. That's what calls for tact and firmness, but most of all for exceptional taste. It has to be the authoritative taste artists recognize and want to please."

I suppose I looked astonished and incredulous.

"You're taken aback because I lay claim to exceptional taste. It's queer what people are allowed to boast about; if I told you I was an unusually good money-man and had a flair for it, you wouldn't be surprised in the least. Why shouldn't I say I have exceptional taste?"

"It's just unusual, I suppose."

"Indeed it is unusual, in the sense that I'm talking about. But there have been such people."

I scurried around in my mind for an example.

"Like Diaghilev?"

"Yes, but not in the way you probably mean. Everybody now thinks of him as an exotic; no, no, he was hard as nails and began life as a lawyer. But Christie at Glyndebourne wasn't exotic at all, and perhaps he achieved more than Diaghilev."

"It all seems a bit—hard to find a word that won't make you angry—but a bit grandiose."

"We'll see. Or I'll see, at any rate. But I don't want to be an art miser, like Uncle Frank; I want to show the world what I've made and what I am."

"Good luck to you, Arthur."

"Thanks. I can be sure of the power, but without luck, it's not worth a damn.—Now it's time we were going. Do you want to meet Egressy afterward? I know him fairly well."

[5]

I DID NOT MUCH LIKE the first part of the concert, which included a Festival Overture by Dohnanyi and something by Kodaly; the conductor was giving us a Hungarian night. When Egressy appeared on the platform to play the Liszt Piano Concerto No. 2

I felt hostile toward him. I turned off my ears, as I had said I
would, but if you really like music you cannot do that completely,
any more than you can turn off the dreadful Muzak in a public
building. You try not to be drawn into it. But when, during the
second part of the program, Egressy played the last three Hungarian Rhapsodies, I could not turn off my ears. Not to hear
demanded an effort, a negation of spirit, that was utterly beyond
me. During the fifteenth, in which the Rakoczy March appears
in so many guises, I became a wreck, emotionally and to some
degree physically, for I wept and wept beyond the power of my
handkerchief to staunch my tears.

Of course Arthur knew that I was weeping; people on all sides
knew it, though I made no noise. The remarkable thing was that
he did nothing about it; no solicitous proffering of large white
handkerchief, no patting of the arm, no murmur of There, there.
Yet I knew he respected my weeping, knew it was private, knew
it was beyond anything he could do to repair, knew it had to be.
When he took me home afterward—he said nothing more about
meeting Egressy—neither of us spoke about it.

Why had I wept? Because I had behaved like a fool at dinner,
for one thing, speaking of my Gypsy blood as if it were a social
embarrassment, instead of a glory and a curse. How bourgeois,
how mean of spirit, how *gadjo!* What ailed me, to speak so to a
stranger about something I never discussed with anybody? As a
child I had thought innocently that it was fun to be part Gypsy,
but my schoolmates soon put me straight on that matter. Gypsies
were dirty, they were thieves, they knew mean tricks. The parents
of several children would not allow me to play with them; I was
the strange child.

True enough, I was a little strange, for I had thoughts that do
not belong to childhood. I wondered what it was like to be one
of those smiling, pale-skinned, and often pale-eyed Canadian
mothers, whose outward pleasantness so often enclosed a hard
and narrow spirit. They lived again in their pale children, who
thought me strange because I was not pale, but had red cheeks
and black eyes and black hair; not even the Canadian winters
could bleach me down to the prevailing skin-colour, which was
like that of an arrowroot biscuit.

Wondering what it was like to be in their skins, it was a short step to doing whatever I could to get into their skins. I used to imitate their walks and postures and their hard, high voices, but most of all their facial expressions. This was not 'taking them off' as some of the girls at the convent school 'took off' the nuns and the Old Supe; it was 'putting them on' like a cloak, to find out what it felt like, as a way of knowing them. When I was fourteen I called it the Theotoky Theory of Exchangeable Personalities, and took huge delight in it. And indeed it taught me a surprising amount; walk like somebody, stand like her, try to discover how she produces her voice, and often astonishing things become clear.

A strange child, perhaps, but I wouldn't give a pinch of dust for a child who was not strange. Is not every child strange, by adult accounting, if we could only learn to know it? If it has no strangeness, what is the use of it? To grow up into another humanoid turnip? But I was stranger than the others. They were proud of being of Scots descent, or French, or Irish, or whatever it was. But Gypsy blood was not a thing to be proud of—unless one happened to have it oneself, and knew what Gypsy pride was like. Not the assertive pride of the boastful Celts and Teutons and Anglo-Saxons, but something akin to the pride of the Jews, a sense of being different and special.

The Jews, so cruelly used by the National Socialists in Germany, so bullied, tortured and tormented, starved and done to death in every way from the most sophisticated to the most brutal, have the small comfort of knowing that the civilized world feels for them; they have themselves declared that the world will never be allowed to forget their sufferings. But the Jews, for all their pride of ancestry, are a modern people in command of all the modern world holds, and so they know how to make their voices heard. The Gypsies have no such arts, and the Gypsies too were victims of the Nazi madness.

What happened to them has that strange tinge of reasonableness that deceived so much of the world when it heard what the Nazis were doing. At first the Fuehrer himself professed an interest in the Gypsies; they were fascinating relics of the Indo-Germanic race, and to preserve their way of life in its purity was a scientifically desirable end. They must be gathered together, and they must be numbered and their names recorded. Scholars must study them, and there is a terrible humour in the fact that they were declared to be, living creatures as they were, under the protection of the Department of Historical Monuments. So they were herded together, and then it was discovered by the same scientists who had acclaimed them that they were an impure ethnic group, and a threat to the purity of the Master Race; the obvious solution to their problem was to sterilize them, bringing an end to their tainted heritage, and the inveterate criminality it fostered. But as Germany gained power over much of Europe it was found simpler to kill them.

Being skilled in escape and evasion, great numbers of Gypsies ran away, and took refuge in the countryside that had always been so kind to them. That was when the greatest horror began; troops hunted them through the woods like animals, and shot on sight. Those who could not escape were in the hands of the *Einsatz-gruppen*, the exterminators, and they were gassed. The Gypsies are not a numerous people, and so the statistics concerning their extermination are unimpressive, if you are impressed chiefly by numbers: there were just a few less than half a million who died thus, but when one human creature dies a whole world of hope and memory and feeling dies with him. To be robbed of the dignity of a natural death is a terrible deprivation.

It was these souls I thought of, Canadian as I am by birth, but half-Gypsy by blood, as I listened to Liszt's three final Hungarian Rhapsodies, all in minor keys, and all speaking the melancholy defiance of a medieval people, living in a modern world, in which their inveterate criminality expresses itself in robbing clothes-lines and face-to-face cheating of *gadje* who want their fortunes told by a people who seem to have the old wisdom they themselves have lost in their complex world of *gadjo* ingenuity, where the cheats and rogueries are institutionalized.

Half a million Gypsies dead, at the command of this *gadjo* world; who weeps for them? I do, sometimes.

I do.

[6]

"SO: MY BAD CHILD has told you about the *bomari?*"

"Very little; nothing that would give me a clue to what it really is. But enough to rouse great curiosity."

"Why do you want to know? What has it to do with you?"

"Well, Madame Laoutaro, I had better explain as briefly as I can. I am an historian, not of wars or governments, not of art or science—at least not science as people think of it now—but of beliefs. I try to recapture not simply the fact that people at one time believed something-or-other, but the reasons and the logic behind their belief. It doesn't matter if the belief was wrong, or seems wrong to us today: it is the fact of the belief that concerns me. You see, I don't think people are foolish and believe wholly stupid things; they may believe what is untrue, but they have a *need* to believe the untruth—it fills a gap in the fabric of what they want to know, or think they ought to know. We often throw such beliefs aside without having truly understood them. If an army is approaching on foot nowadays, the information reaches us by radio, or perhaps by army telephone; but long ago every army had men who could hear the approach of an enemy by putting their heads to the ground. That wouldn't do now, because armies move faster, and we attack them before we can see them, but it worked very well for several thousand years. This is a simple example; I don't want to bore you with complexities. But the kind of sensitivity that made it possible for a man to hear an army marching several miles away without any kind of artificial aid has almost disappeared from the earth. The recognition of oneself as a part of nature and reliance on natural things are disappearing for hundreds of millions of people who do not know that anything is being lost. I am not digging into such things because I think the old ways are necessarily better than the new ways, but I think there may be some of the old ways that we would be wise to look into before all knowledge of them disappears from the earth— the knowledge, and the kind of thinking that lay behind it. And the little I have heard about your *bomari* suggests that it may be very important in my research. Do I make any sense to you?"

To my astonishment, Mamusia nodded. "Good sense indeed," she said.

"Can I persuade you to talk to me about it?"

"I have to be careful; secrets are serious things."

"I understand that perfectly. I assure you that I am not here as a snooper. You and I understand the importance of secrets, Madame Laoutaro."

"Bring tea, Maria," said Mamusia, and I knew that much, perhaps everything, had been gained. This was Hollier at his best. His honesty and seriousness were persuasive, even to my suspicious Mother. And her capacity to understand was far beyond what I had expected. Children often underestimate what their parents can grasp.

As I made the scalding strong tea which Mamusia wanted, and was more appropriate to this meeting than any merely social brew, I could hear her and Hollier talking together confidentially. In transcribing their conversation I shall not attempt to reproduce Mamusia's version of English literally, because it would be wearisome to read and a waste of time. Besides, it would appear to diminish her dignity, which suffered not at all. When I returned, she was apparently putting Hollier on oath.

"Never, never to tell this for money; you understand?"

"Completely. I don't work for money, Madame, though I have to have money to live."

"No, no, you work to understand the world; the whole world, not just the world of little Here and little Now, and that means secrets, eh?"

"Not a doubt of it."

"Secrets are the blood of life. Every big thing is a secret, even when you know it, because you never know all of it. If you can know everything about anything, it is not worth knowing."

"Finely said, Madame."

"Then swear: swear on your Mother's grave."

"She has no grave; she lives about a half a mile from here."

"Then swear on her womb. Swear on the womb that bore you, and the breasts you sucked."

Hollier rose splendidly to this very un-Canadian request. "I swear most solemnly by the womb that bore me, and the breasts that gave me suck, that I shall never reveal what you tell me for gain or for any unworthy reason, whatever it might do for me."

"Maria, I think I heard Miss Gretser fall; there was a thump upstairs a minute ago. See that she is all right."

Damn! But much depended on my obedience, so off I went, and found Miss Gretser in as good a state as might be expected, lying on her bed with Old Azor the poodle, eating stuffed dates, her favourite indulgence. When I returned something had happened to solemnize the oath, but on what Hollier had sworn, apart from the organs of his Mother stipulated, I never knew. Mamusia settled herself on the sofa, prepared to talk.

"My name, you see on the door outside, is Laoutaro; my husband, Niemcewicz-Theotoky, is dead, God rest him, and I have gone back to my family name. Why? Because it tells what I am. It means luthier; you understand luthier?"

"A maker of violins?"

"Maker, mender, lover, mother, bondwoman of violins and all the viol family. The Gypsies I come from held that work as their great craft, and every craft means secrets. It is men's work, but my Father taught me because he sensed a special aptitude in me, and my brother Yerko wanted to be a smith—you know?—work in fine metals and especially copper in the best Gypsy style, and he was so good at it that it would have been a black sin to stop him. Besides, we luthiers needed him, for a reason you shall know in good time. I learned to be a luthier from my Father, who learned from his Father, and so back and back. We were the best. Listen to this—spit in my mouth if I lie—Ysaye never allowed anybody but my Grandfather to touch his violins—the great Eugène Ysaye. I learned everything."

"A very great art, indeed."

"To make violins, you mean? It's more than that. It's keeping violins alive. Who wants a new violin? A child. You make half-size and quarter-size for children, yes, but the big artist doesn't want a new fiddle; he wants an old one. But old fiddles are like old people, they get cranky, and have to be coaxed, and sent to the spa, and have beauty treatments and all that."

"Is repairing your chief work, then?"

"Repairing? Oh yes, I do that in the ordinary way. But it goes beyond repairing. It means resting; it means restoring youth. Do you know what a wolf is?"

"I doubt if I know the sense in which you use the word."

"If you were a fiddler you'd fear the wolf. It's the buzz or the howl that comes in one string when you are using another, and it can be caused by all kinds of little things—even a trifle of loose glue—and it is the devil to repair properly. Of course if you use plastic glues and such stuff, you can do a great deal, but you should repair a fine fiddle with the same sort of glue that was used by the maker, and it is no simple thing to find out what that glue was, because glues were carefully guarded secrets. But there's another way to deal with a wolf, and that's to put him in the *bomari* after you have patched him up. I'm not talking about cheap fiddles, you understand, but the fiddles made by the great masters. A Goffriller now, or a Bergonzi or anything from Marknenkirchen or Mirecourt or a good Banks needs to be approached on the knees, if you want to coax it back to its true life."

"And that is what the *bomari* does?"

"That is what the *bomari* does if you can find a *bomari*."

"And the *bomari* is a kind of heat treatment—a form of cooking? Am I right?"

"How in the Devil's name did you know that?"

"It is my profession to divine such things."

"You must be a great wizard!"

"In the world in which you and I work, Madame Laoutaro, it would be stupid of me to deny what you have said. Magic is producing effects for which there seem to be no causes. But you and I also know that there is always a cause. So I shall explain my wizardry: I suspect—and you behave as if I were right—that *bomari* is a corruption, or a Romany form, of what is ordinarily called a *bain-marie*. You find one in every good kitchen; it is simply a water-bath to keep things warm that will curdle or be spoiled if they grow cool. But why is it called a *bain-marie?* Because tradition has it that it was invented by the second greatest Mary of all—Miriam the sister of Moses and a great sorceress. She died, it is said, of a kiss from God. We may take leave to doubt all that, though traditions should never be thrown aside without careful examination. It seems much more likely that the *bain-marie* was the invention of Maria Prophetissa, to whom books are attributed, and who was believed by Cornelius Agrippa to have been an historical person, even though she lived centuries before his time. She was the greatest of the women-alchemists, a formidable crew, I assure you. She was a Jewess, she discovered hydrochloric acid, and also the *balneus mariae* or *bain-marie,* one of the surviving alchemical instruments; even though it has been humbled and banished to the kitchen it still has a certain glory. So—from *bain-marie* to *bomari*—was I right?"

"Not entirely right, wizard," said Mamusia. "You had better come and take a look."

We went down into the cellar of the house, which was where Yerko lived, and where Mamusia's carefully hidden workroom was. Hers was not a noisy business, nor was Yerko's, though now and then, faintly and musically, the clink of the coppersmith's hammer might have been heard upstairs. Yerko's forge was small; Gypsies do not use the big anvils and huge bellows of the blacksmith, because traditionally they must be able to carry their forges on their backs, and it is not the Gypsy style to carry any more weight than is necessary. In the workroom, wearing his leather apron and tinkering with something small—a pin or a catch that one might have expected a jeweller to produce.

My Uncle Yerko, like Mamusia, had changed his way of life radically when Tadeusz died. While he worked as my Father's junior and principal designer in the factory, he had borne some resemblance to a man of business, though he never looked at home in conventional clothes. But when Tadeusz died he too returned to his Gypsy ways, and gave up his pathetic attempt to be a New World man. How hard he had tried when first they came to Canada! He had even wanted to change his name so that he might become, as he thought, indistinguishable from his new countrymen. His name was Miya Laoutaro, and he wanted to translate it literally into Martin Luther; I do not think he ever understood why my Father forbade it, as being too extreme. Yerko was his pet name, his family name, and I never heard anybody call him Miya. When Tadeusz died he was as stricken as Mamusia; he would sit for hours, brooding and weeping, murmuring from time to time, 'My good Father is dead.'

Indeed Tadeusz had been a father to him, advising him, seeing that his considerable earnings were properly invested, and lifting him as far up in the world of business as it was possible for him to go. That was not beyond the designing and model-making part of the manufacturing work, because Yerko could not direct anyone else, was hopeless at explaining things he could do easily, and was apt to take time off for week-long drunks.

Gypsies are not great drinkers as a rule, but when they do drink they are whole-hoggers, and without becoming a thoroughgoing dissolute boozer, Yerko was unreliable with anyone but Tadeusz. Mamusia tried to make the best of it by assuring my Father that this failing was much to be preferred to an unappeasable appetite for women, but Tadeusz had to keep a tight rein on Yerko who, when drunk, was not unlike Brother Martin the bear—heavy, incalculable, and in need of much humouring. In his workroom Yerko had a still; he objected rigorously to paying government taxes to get feeble liquor, and he made his own plum brandy, which would have stunned a bull, or anybody but Yerko himself.

"Yerko, I am going to show the *bomari*," said Mamusia, and although Yerko was astonished, he made no objection. He never contradicted his sister, though I have known him to hit her, and even to take a swipe at her with his coppersmith's hammer.

Mamusia led Hollier to a heavy wooden door, which was of Yerko's manufacture, and I do not think the cleverest safe-cracker could have opened it, so barred and locked was it. Yerko unfastened the locks—he believed in plenty of complex locks—and we walked into a room where there may once have been electric light, but where we now had to use candles, for all the wiring had been taken out.

It was not unusually big, and I think that in some earlier time in the life of the house it had been a wine-cellar. Now all the bins had been removed. What immediately seized you was the smell, which was not foul, but very strong, heavy, and warm; I can only describe it as a combination of wet wool and stable, but concentrated. All around the walls stood large, heavily elegant shapes; they were rounded, and seemed almost like mute human figures; in racks in the middle of the room were smaller versions of these man-sized cases, plump and gleaming. They gleamed because they were made of copper, and every inch bore the tiny impress of Yerko's hammer, so that they twinkled and took the light in a manner that was almost jewel-like, but subdued. This was not the thin, cheap copper of the commercial jug or ornament, but the finest metal, very costly in the modern market. It seemed to be a cave of treasure.

Mamusia was putting on a show. "These are the great ladies and gentlemen," she said, with a deep curtsy toward them. She waited for Hollier to take it in, to grow eager for more.

"You want to know how it works," she said. "But I cannot disturb these old noblemen in their beauty sleep. However, there is one here that was sealed only a week ago, and if I open her now and re-seal her, no great harm will be done, because she has at least six months to rest."

At her direction, Yerko took a knife and deftly broke the heavy wax seal at the uppermost end of one of the small copper vessels, lifted the lid—which took strength because it was a tight fit— and at once a powerful essence of the prevailing smell escaped. Inside, in a bed of what looked like dark-brown earth, lay a figure swathed in woollen cloth.

"Real wool, carefully spun so that I know that not a thread of rubbish has been sneaked into it. This must be the proper lamb's-wool, or it is not good."

She unwrapped the figure, which was bandaged at least six layers deep, and there we saw a violin.

"The great lady is undressed for her sleep," said Mamusia, and indeed the violin had no bridge, no strings, no pegs, and looked very much like someone in *déshabillé*. "You see that the sleep is coming on her; the varnish is already a little dulled, but she is breathing, she is sinking into her trance. In six months she will be wakened by me, her cunning servant, and I shall dress her again and she will go back to the world with her voice in perfect order."

Hollier put out his hand to touch the brown dust that sur-rounded the woollen cloth. "Damp," he said.

"Of course it is damp. And it is alive, too. Don't you know what that is?"

He sniffed at his fingers, but shook his head.

"Horse dung," said Mamusia. "The best; thoroughly rotted and sieved, and from horses in mighty health. This comes from a racing stable, and you wouldn't believe what they make me pay for it. But the shit of old nags isn't what I want. The very best is demanded for the very best. She's a Bergonzi, this sleeper," she said, tapping the violin lightly. "Ignorant people chatter about Strads, and Guarneris, and they are magnificent. I like a Bergonzi. But the best is a St. Petersburg Leman; that's one over there, in her fourth month—or will be when the moon is new. They must be put to bed according to the moon," she said, cocking an eye at Hollier to see how he would take that.

"And where do they come from, all these great ladies and gentlemen?" he said, looking around the room, in which there were probably forty cases of various sizes.

"From my friends the great artists," said Mamusia. "I must not tell whose fiddles these are. But the great artists know me, and when they come here—and they all do come to this city, sometimes every year—they bring me a fiddle that needs a rest, or has come down with some trouble of the voice. I have the skill and the love to make everything right. Because you see this asks for understanding that goes beyond anything the cleverest craftsman can learn. And you must be a fiddler yourself, to test and judge. I am a very fine fiddler."

"Who could doubt it?" said Hollier. "I hope that some day I may have the great honour of hearing you. It would be like listening to the voice of the ages."

"You may say that," said Mamusia, who was enjoying every instant of the courtly conversation. "I have played on some of the noblest instruments in the world—because these are not just violins, you know, but violas, and those big fellows over there are the violoncellos, and those biggest of all are the big-burly-bumbles, the double basses, which have a way of going very gruff when they have to travel—and I can make them speak secrets like a doctor. The great player, oh yes, he makes them sing, but Oraga Laoutaro makes them whisper what is wrong, and then sing for joy when it is wrong no longer.—This room should not be open; Yerko, cover Madame until I can come back and put her to bed again."

Upstairs then, and after a tremendous exchange of compliments between Hollier and Mamusia, I drove him home in my little car.

What a success it had been! Well worth a few blows and a lot of cursing from Mamusia, for it had brought me near to Hollier again. I could feel his enthusiasm. But it was not directly for me.

"I know you won't be offended, Maria," he said, "but your Mother is an extraordinary discovery, a living fossil. She might have come out of any age, from the nineteenth century in Hungary to anywhere in Europe for six or seven centuries back. That wonderful boasting! It refreshed me to hear her, because it was like Paracelsus himself, that very great man and emperor of boasters. And you remember what he said: Never hope to find wisdom at the high colleges alone—consult old women, Gypsies, magicians, wanderers, and all manner of peasant folk and random folk, and learn from them, for these have more knowledge about such things than all the high colleges."

"What about Professor Froats?" I said, "with his search in the dung-heap for a jewel that he suspects may be there, but of whose nature he can hardly guess?"

"Yes, and if my old friend Ozy finds anything I shall borrow any part of it that can be bent to support my research on the Filth Therapy. What your Mother is doing is Filth Therapy at its highest—though to call that wonderful substance in which she buries the fiddles filth is to be victim to the stupidest modern prejudice. But I am inclined to think of Ozy as a latter-day alchemist; he seeks the all-conquering Stone of the Philosophers exactly where they said it must be sought, in the commonest, most neglected, most despised.—Please take me to see your Mother again. She enchants me. She has in the highest degree the kind of spirit that must not be called unsophisticated, but which is not bound by commonplaces. Call it the Wild Mind."

Another meeting would be easy, as I found the minute I returned to One Hundred and Twenty Walnut Street.

"Your man is very handsome," she said. "Just what I like; fine eyes, big nose, big hands. That goes with a big thing; has he a big thing?"

This was mischief, meant to disconcert me, to make me blush, which it did to my annoyance.

"You watch yourself with him, my daughter; he is a charmer. Such elegant speech! You love him, don't you?"

"I admire him very much. He is a great scholar."

Hoots of laughter from Mamusia. "He is a great scholar," she peeped in a ridiculous falsetto, holding up her skirts and tiptoeing around the room in what I suppose was meant to be an imitation of me, or of whatever my university work suggested to her. "He is a man, in just the way your Father was a man. You had better be careful, or I will take him away from you! I could love that man!"

If you try it, you'll wish you hadn't, I thought. But I am not half-Gypsy for nothing, and I gave her an answer to choke her with butter.

"He thinks you are wonderful," I said. "He raved about you all the way home. He says you are a true *phuri dai*." That is the name of the greatest Gypsy women; not the so-called 'queens' who are often just for show to impress *gadje,* but the great old female counsellors without whose wisdom no Kalderash chief would think of making an important decision. I was right; that fetched her.

"He is truly a great man," she said. "And at my age I would rather be a *phuri dai* than anybody's pillow-piece. I'll tell you what I'll do; I'll make sure you get him. Then we'll both have him."

Oh God, what now?

The New Aubrey IV

I T WAS NEAR the end of November before all Cornish's possessions were sorted and ready for removal to the public bodies
for whom they were intended. The job, which had seemed un-
manageable to begin with, had called for nothing but hard work
to complete it and Hollier and I had worked faithfully, giving up
time we wanted and needed for other tasks. Urquhart McVarish
had not exerted himself to the same extent, and possessed some
magic whereby a lot of his sorting and note-making was undertaken by the secretary from Arthur Cornish's office, who in her
turn was able to provide a couple of strong men who could lift
and lug and shuffle things about.

Hollier and I had nobody to blame but ourselves. McVarish
was in charge of paintings and objects of art, which can be heavy
and clumsy, so he could hardly have been expected to do the
work by himself. But Hollier was in charge of books, and he was
the kind of man who hates to have anyone else touch a book
until he has examined it thoroughly, by which time he might as
well put it in its final place. Except that there rarely is any final
place for books, and people whose job it is to sort them seem
always to be juggling and pushing them hither and yon, making
heaps as tall as chimneys on the floor, when the space on tables
has been filled. My job was to sort and arrange the manuscripts
and portfolios of drawings, and it was not work I could very well
trust out of my own hands. Indeed, I wanted no help.

None of us wanted interference, for a reason we never completely acknowledged. Cornish's will had included a special section naming in detail what was to go to the National Gallery, the

Provincial Gallery, the University Library and the College of St. John and the Holy Ghost. This list had been made two or three years before his death. But between the making of the list and his last days he had continued to buy with his usual avid recklessness. Indeed, large packages continued to arrive after he was buried. Thus there was quite a lot of stuff that was not named in the will, and much of it was of the first quality. But the will had a clause that provided that each of his executors was to be free to choose something for himself, provided it was not already named as a bequest, as a recognition of the work he had undertaken and as a gift from a former friend. All else became part of his estate, under Arthur Cornish's care. Clearly our choice was to be made from these most recent acquisitions. I suppose our behaviour could be described as devious, but we did not want the galleries and the libraries casting a possessive eye over anything that was available, because we did not want to have to argue, or perhaps wrangle with them as to what we might take. Our right was indisputable, but the high-minded covetousness of public bodies is so powerful and sometimes so rancorous that we did not wish to arouse it needlessly.

We kept the librarians and archivists and curators at bay, therefore, until after our final meeting; once that was over they could strip the place to the walls.

I was first on the spot on that great November Friday, and next to come was Urquhart McVarish. This gave me the chance I needed to do the job I dreaded.

"All the stuff in my department is accounted for," I said, "except for one thing that is mentioned in a memo of Cornish's that I can't quite figure out. He speaks of a manuscript I haven't been able to find."

Urky looked inquiring, but non-committal.

"Here it is," I said, producing the pocket-book from one of the boxes that had been packed up for the University archivists. "You see here, he speaks of what he calls a 'Rab. MS' that he lent to 'McV.' last April. What would that have been?"

"Haven't a clue," said Urky.

"But you are obviously McV. Did you borrow something from him?"

"I'm not a borrower, because I hate lending myself."

"How do you explain it?"

"I don't."

"You see it puts me in a spot."

"There's no sense in being too pernickety, Darcourt. Counting all the books and manuscripts and things there must be thousands of items here. Nobody in his senses would expect us to check every scrap of paper and old letter. In my department I've lumped a lot of things together under Miscellaneous, and I presume you and Hollier have done the same. With a man like Cornish, who was fiercely acquisitive but utterly unsystematic, things are bound to be mislaid. Don't worry about it."

"Well, but I do, rather. If there's a manuscript somewhere that ought to be here, I have an obligation to recover it and see that the Library gets it."

"Sorry I can't help you."

"But you *must* be McV."

"Darcourt, you're pressing me in a way I don't much like. Are you by any chance suggesting I've pinched something?"

"No, no; not at all. But you see my position; I really must follow up this note."

"And on the basis of that, taken from a lot of scribbles that seem to be phone numbers and addresses, and reminders of God knows what past events, you are pressing me rather forcibly. Have you traced all the rest of the stuff in all this mess of notebooks?"

"Of course not. But this one is not like the rest; it says he lent something to you. I'm just asking."

"You have my word that I don't know anything about it."

When somebody gives you his word, you are supposed to take it, or else be prepared to make an unpleasant fuss. There is a moment when one should be bold, but I hesitated and the moment passed. In these confrontations the stronger will prevails, and whether it was that I had eaten the wrong things for lunch, or because I am naturally a hater of rows, or because Urky's Sheldonian type has the edge on my Sheldonian type in such matters, I lost my chance. I was resentful, but the code which is supposed to govern the dealings of scholars prevented me from saying any more. Of course I was uncomfortable, and my conviction hardened that Urky had kept the Rabelais manuscript Hollier had described. But if I couldn't make him disgorge it by the sort of inquiry I had made, was I now to denounce him and demand—what? A search of his house? Impossible! An appeal to Arthur Cornish? But would Arthur understand that a misplaced manuscript was a serious matter, and if he did would he be willing to pursue it? Would Hollier stand by me? And if I went through all this uproar, and the manuscript finally reached the Library, would Hollier and his Maria ever get their hands on it? If McVarish produced it, might he not take the important letters from the pocket in the back of the cover, and deny any knowledge of them? All the muddle of arguments that rush into the mind of a man who has been worsted in an encounter streaked through my brain in a few seconds. Better face the fact: I had backed down, and that was all there was to it. Urky had won, and I had probably made an enemy.

More unpleasantness was avoided because the man from the lawyer's office and the man from Sotheby's arrived, and the secretary Cornish had put on the job, and shortly afterward came Hollier and Arthur Cornish. Necessary business was completed: the Sotheby representative swore that the valuation his firm had prepared was in conformity with modern estimates of such things; we three swore that we had carried out our duties to the best of our abilities, and that was that. It was all eyewash, really, because the only way to find the current value of Cornish's art collections was to sell them, and our abilities as executors rested on Cornish's opinion of us, rather than on any professional experience. But documents were necessary for probate, and we did what was necessary. The lawyer and the Sotheby man went away, and the moment came that we had all been waiting for.

"Now gentlemen, what are you going to choose?" said Arthur Cornish. He looked at McVarish, who was the oldest.

"This, for me," said Urky going to a table in a far corner of the room and putting his hand on a bronze figure that stood with a huddle of similar pieces. But though similar, they were not of equal value. Urky had chosen the best, and why not? It was a Venus; the Sotheby man had identified it as a Canova, and a good one.

I was grateful that Urky had in this way set the tone for Hollier and myself; what he had chosen was unquestionably valuable, but among Cornish's treasures it was not conspicuous. There were obviously better things. It was a substantial, but not a grabby, choice.

"Professor Hollier?" said Arthur.

I knew how much Hollier hated having to reveal his choice. There was about it too much the air of the child who is taken into a candy-shop on its birthday and told to choose, under the eye of indulgent adults. For such a private man this was deeply distasteful. But he spoke up.

"These books, if nobody objects."

He had chosen the four volumes of Konrad Gesner's *Historia Animalium*, a splendid piece of sixteenth-century book-making.

"Well done, Hollier," said Urky; "the German Pliny—just your boy."

"Professor Darcourt?" said Arthur.

I suppose I disliked revealing my choice as much as Hollier, but there is no sense in being a fool about such things. When would such an opportunity come again? Never. So after some pretence of not knowing where to look, I laid on the table a brown paper folder containing two caricatures, elegantly drawn and palely coloured, that could have come from one hand only.

"Beerbohms!" said Urky, darting forward. "How sly of you, Simon! If I'd known there were any of those I might have changed my mind."

Not a very serious comment, but why did I feel that I should like to kill him?

Our choices made, we moved the things to a central table, and everybody had a look. The secretary asked us for descriptions that could be included in the information for the lawyers. She was a nice woman; I wished that she too could have something. Arthur Cornish asked Hollier about Gesner, and Hollier was unwontedly communicative.

"He was a Swiss, actually; not a German. An immensely learned man, but greatest as a botanist, I suppose. In these four volumes he brought together everything that was known about every animal that had been identified by scholars up to 1550. It is a treasure-house of fact and supposition, but it aims at being scientific. It's not like those medieval bestiaries that deal simply in legend and old wives' tales."

"I thought old wives' tales were your stock in trade, Hollier," said Urky.

"The growth of scientific knowledge is my stock in trade, if that's what you want to call it," said Hollier, without geniality.

"Let's see the Beerbohms," said Urky. "Oh, marvellous! *College Types;* look at Magdalen, would you! What a swell! And Balliol, all bulging brow and intellectual pride; and Brasenose—huge shoulders and a head like a child's! And Merton—my gosh, it's a lovely little portrait of Max himself!—What's the other one? *The Old Self and the Young Self; Cosmo Gordon Lang.* What are they saying? Young Self: *I really can't decide whether to go on the Stage or into the Church. Both provide such opportunities. . . .* Old Self: *You made the right choice; the Church gave me a rôle in a real Abdication.* Oh Simon, you old slyboots! That's really valuable you know."

Of course it was valuable, but that wasn't the point; it was authentic Max. How Ellerman would have loved it!

"It won't be sold," I said, perhaps more sharply than was wise. "I'll leave it as a treasure in my will."

"Not to Spook, I hope," said Urky.

What a busybody the man was!

Arthur saw that I was being harried. He ran his hand appreciatively over the splendid back of the nude bronze. "Very fine," he said.

"Ah, but do you see what finally decided me?" said Urky. "Look at her. Doesn't she remind you of anyone? Somebody we all four know? . . . Look closely. It's Maria Magdalena Theotoky to the life."

"There's a resemblance, certainly," said Arthur.

"Though we can't—or I'd better say I can't—answer for the whole figure," said Urky. "Still, one can guess at what lies under modern clothes. Who was the model? Being Canova, it was probably a lady from Napoleon's court. He must have known her intimately. Observe the detail of the modelling."

The bronze Venus was about twenty-five inches tall; the figure was seated, one foot resting on the other knee, lovingly tying the laces of a sandal. What was unusual about it was that the vulva, which sculptors usually represent as an imperforate lump of flesh, was here realistically defined. It was not pornographic; it had the grace and the love of the female figure Canova knew so well how to impart to his statuary.

It is hard for me to be just to Urky. Certainly he appreciated the beauty of the figure, but there was a moist gleam in his eye that hinted at an erotic appreciation, as well. . . . And why not, Darcourt, you miserable puritan? Is this some nineteenth-century nonsense about art banishing sensuality, or some twentieth-century nonsense about a human figure being no more than an arrangement of masses and planes? No, I didn't like Urky's attitude toward the Venus because he had linked it with a girl we knew, and whom Hollier knew especially well, and Urky was seeking to embarrass us. What I would have accepted without qualm from another man, I didn't like at all when it came from Urky.

"You agree that it looks like Maria, don't you Hollier?" he said.

"I certainly agree that it looks like Maria," said Arthur, unexpectedly.

"A stunner, isn't she?" said Urky to Arthur, but with his eye on Hollier. "Tell me just as a matter of interest, where would you place her in the Rushton Scale?"

We all looked blank at this.

"Surely you know it? Devised by W. A. H. Rushton, the great Cambridge mathematician? Well, it's this way: Helen of Troy is accepted as the absolute in female beauty, and we have it on a poet's authority that her face launched a thousand ships. But clearly 'face' implies the whole woman. Therefore let us call a face that launches a thousand ships a *Helen*. But what is a face that launches only one ship? Obviously a *millihelen*. There must be a rating for all other faces between those two that have any pretension whatever to beauty. Consider Garbo; probably 750 *millihelens*, because although the face is exquisite, the figure is spare and the feet are big. Now Maria seems to me to be a wonder in every respect that I have had the pleasure of examining, and her clothes are plainly not meant to conceal defects. So what do we say? I'd say 850 *millihelens* for Maria. Anybody bid higher? What do you say, Arthur?"

"I'd say she's a friend of mine, and I don't rate friends by mathematical computation," said Arthur.

"Oh, Arthur, that's very square! Never mention a lady's name in the mess, eh?"

"Call it what you like," said Arthur. "I just think there's a difference between a statue and somebody I know personally."

"And *Vive la différence!*" said Urky.

Hollier was breathing audibly and I wondered what Urky knew—because if Urky knew anything at all, it was a certainty that the whole world would know it very soon, and in a form imposed on it by Urky's disagreeable mind. But I did not see how, under the circumstances, Urky could know anything whatever about Hollier's involvement with Maria. Nor did I see why I should care, but plainly I did care. I thought the time had come to change the subject. The secretary from Arthur's office was looking unhappy; she sniffed a troublesome situation she did not understand.

"I have a suggestion to make," I said. "Our old friend Francis Cornish's will says that his executors are to have something to remember him by, and we have been going on the assumption that he meant the three of us. But isn't Arthur an executor? You mentioned a picture that took your eye the first day we met here, Arthur; it was a little sketch by Varley."

"It was named for the Provincial Gallery," said Urky. "Sorry, it's spoken for."

"Yes, I knew that," I said. There was no reason why Urky should be the only one to know best. "But I've been told you're a music enthusiast, Arthur. A collector of musical manuscripts, indeed. There are one or two things not spoken for that might interest you."

Arthur was flattered, as rich people often are when somebody remembers that they, too, are human and that not everything lies within their grasp. I fished out the envelope I had put handy, and his eyes gleamed when he saw a delicate and elegant four-page holograph of a song by Ravel, and a scrap of six or eight bars in the unmistakable strong hand of Schoenberg.

"I'll take these with the greatest pleasure," he said. "And thanks very much for thinking of me. It had crossed my mind that I might choose something, but after my experience with the Varley I didn't want to push."

Yes, but we knew him and liked him much better than when

he cast longing eyes at the Varley. Arthur improved with knowing.

"If that finishes our business, I'd like to get along," I said. "We're expecting you at Ploughwright at six, and as I'm Vice-Warden I have some things to attend to."

I took up my Beerbohms, Hollier tucked two big volumes of Gesner under each arm, and McVarish, whose prize was heavy, asked the secretary to call him a taxi. To be charged, I had no doubt, to the Cornish estate.

I left Cornish's spreading complex of apartments, where I had often cursed the work he had imposed on me, with regret. Emptying Aladdin's Cave had been an adventure.

[2]

BEING VICE-WARDEN WAS not heavy work, and I accepted it gladly because it ensured me a good set of rooms in the College; Ploughwright was for graduate students, a quiet and pleasant oasis in a busy University. On Guest Nights it was my job to see that things went well, guests properly looked after, and the food and wine as good as the College could manage. They cost us something, these Guest Nights, but they perpetuated a tradition modern universities sometimes appear to have forgotten, the old tradition of scholarly hospitality. This was not food and drink provided so that people might meet to haggle and drive bargains, not the indigestive squalor of the 'working lunch', not the tedium of a 'symposium' with a single topic of conversation, but a dinner held once a fortnight when the Fellows of the College asked some guests to eat and drink and made good cheer for no other reason than that this is one of civilization's triumphs over barbarism, of humane feeling over dusty scholasticism, an assertion that the scholar's life is a good life. Ozy Froats had typed me as a man fond of ceremonies, and he was right; our Guest Nights were ceremonies, and I made it my special care to ensure that they were ceremonies in the best sense; that is to say, that people took part in them because they were irresistible, rather than merely inevitable.

Our guests on this November Friday night were Mrs. Skeldergate, who was a member of the Provincial Legislature at the head of a committee considering the financing of universities, and

I had arranged that the others should be Hollier and Arthur Cornish—which meant the inclusion also of McVarish—as a small celebration of our completion of the work on the Cornish bequests. Arthur might well have asked us to dinner for this purpose, but I thought I would get in ahead of him; I dislike the idea that the richest person in a group must always pay the bill.

Apart from these, fourteen of the Fellows of Ploughwright attended this Guest Night, not including the Warden and myself. We were a coherent group, in spite of the divergence of our academic interests. There was Gyllenborg, who was notable in the Faculty of Medicine, Durdle and Deloney, who were in different branches of English, Elsa Czermak the economist, Hitzig and Boys, from Physiology and Physics, Stromwell, the medievalist, Ludlow from Law, Penelope Raven from Comparative Literature, Aronson the computer man, Roberta Burns the zoologist, Erzenberger and Lamotte from German and French, and Mukadassi, who was a visitor to the Department of East Asian Studies. With McVarish from History, Hollier from his ill-defined but much-discussed area of medievalism, Arthur Cornish from the world of money, the Warden who was a philosopher (his detractors said he would have been happier in a nineteenth-century university where the division of Moral Philosophy still existed), and myself as a classicist, we cast a pretty wide net of interests, and I hoped the conversation would be lively.

I was not alone in this. Urky McVarish took me by the arm as we came downstairs from Hall, to continue our dinner in the Senior Common Room, and murmured in my ear, in his most caressing voice—and Urky had a caressing voice when he wanted to use it.

"Delightful, Simon, totally delightful. Do you know what it reminds me of? Of course you know my Rabelaisian enthusiasm—because of my great forebear. Well, it puts me in mind of that wonderful chapter about the country people at the feast where Gargantua is born, chatting and joking over their drinks. You remember how Sir Thomas translates the chapter-heading?—*How they chirped over their cups;* it's been splendid in Hall, and the junior scholars are so charming, but I look forward to being in the S.C.R. where we shall hear the scholars chirping over their cups even more exuberantly."

He darted off to the men's room. We allow an interval at this juncture in our Guest Nights for everybody to retire, to relieve themselves, rinse their false teeth if need be, and prepare for what is to follow. I know I am absurdly touchy about everything McVarish says, but I wished that he had not compared our pleasant College occasion to a Rabelaisian feast. True, we were going to sit down in a few minutes to nuts and wine and fruit, but chiefly to conversation. No need for Urky to talk as if it were a peasant booze-up as described by his favourite author. Still—Urky was not a fool; as Vice-Warden charged with the duty of ensuring that the decanters were replenished, that Elsa Czermak had her cigar and the gouty Lamotte his mineral water, I should have a freedom given to no one else to move around the table and hear how the scholars chirped over their cups.

"Oh, how lovely this looks!" said Mrs. Skeldergate, entering the Senior Common Room with the Warden. "And how luxurious!"

"Not really," said the Warden, who was sensitive on this point. "And I assure you, not a penny of government money goes to pay for it; you are our guest, not that of the oppressed taxpayers."

"But all this silver," said the government lady; "it's not what you think of in a college."

The Warden could not let the subject alone, and considering who the guest was, I don't blame him. "All gifts," he said; "and you may take it from me that if everything on this table were sold at auction it wouldn't bring enough to support the weekly costs of such a laboratory as that of—" he groped for a name, because he didn't know much about laboratories—"as that of Professor Froats."

Mrs. Skeldergate had a politician's tact. "We're all hoping for great things from Professor Froats; some new light on cancer, perhaps." She turned to her left, where Archy Deloney stood, and said, "Who is that very handsome, rather careworn man near the top of the table?"

"Oh, that's Clement Hollier, who rummages about in the ashheaps of bygone thought. He is handsome, isn't he? When the President called him an ornament of the University we didn't quite know whether he meant his looks or his work. But careworn. 'A noble wreck in ruinous perfection', as Byron says."

"And that man who is helping people find their places? I know I met him, but I have a terrible memory for names."

"Our Vice-Warden, Simon Darcourt. Poor old Simon is struggling with what Byron called his 'oily dropsy'—otherwise fat. A decent old thing. A parson, as you see."

Did Deloney care that I overheard? Did he intend that I should? Oily dropsy, indeed! The malice of these bony ectomorphs! The chances are good that I shall still be hearty when Archy Deloney is writhen with arthritis. Here's to my forty feet of gut and all that goes with it!

Professor Lamotte was looking pale and patting his brow with a handkerchief, and I knew that Professor Burns must have trodden on his gouty foot. She was distressed, but "It doesn't matter in the least," said Lamotte, who is the perfection of courtesy. "Oh, but it does," said Roberta Burns, an argumentative Scot, but a kind heart. "Everything matters. The Universe is approximately fifteen billion years old, and I swear that in all that time, nothing has ever happened that has not mattered, has not contributed in some way to the totality. Would it relieve you to hit me fairly hard, just once? If so, may I suggest a clout over the ear?" But Lamotte was regaining his colour, and tapped her ear playfully.

The Warden had heard this and called out, "I heard you, Roberta, and I agree without reserve; everything matters. This is what gives vitality to the whole realm of ethical speculation."

The Warden has no talent for small talk, and the younger Fellows like to chaff him. Deloney broke in: "Really Warden, you must admit the existence of the trivial, the wholly meaningless. Like the great dispute now raging in Celtic Studies. Have you heard?"

The Warden had not heard, and Deloney continued: "You know how they are always boozing—the real hard stuff, not the blood of the grape like our civilized selves. At one of their pow-wows last week Darragh Twomey was as tight as a drum, and asserted boldly that the *Mabinogion* was really an Irish epic, and the Welsh had stolen it and made a mess of it. Professor John Jenkin Jones took up the gauntlet, and it came to a fist-fight."

"You don't say so," said the Warden, pretending to be aghast.

"That's absolutely not true, Archy," Professor Penelope Raven said; she was circling the table looking for her place-card. "Not a blow was struck; I was there, and I know."

"Penny, you're just defending them," said Deloney. "Blows were exchanged. I have it on unimpeachable authority."

"Not blows!"

"Pushing, then."

"Perhaps some pushing."

"And Twomey fell down."

"He slipped. You're making an epic of it."

"Perhaps. But University violence is so trifling. One longs for something full-blooded. One wants a worthy motive. One must exaggerate or feel oneself a pygmy."

This is not the way a Guest Night is supposed to be conducted. When we are seated we converse politely to left and right, but with people like Deloney and Penny Raven there is a tendency to yell, and interfere in conversations to which they are not party. The Warden was looking woeful—his way of suggesting disapproval—and Penny turned to Aronson, and Deloney to Erzenberger and behaved themselves.

"Isn't it true that when you cut Irishmen open, four out of five have brass stomachs?" Penny whispered. Gyllenborg, a Swede, pondered for a moment, and said, "That has not come within the range of my experience."

HITZIG SAID TO LUDLOW: "What have you been doing today?"

"Reading the papers," said Ludlow, "and I am tired of them. Every day a score of Chicken Lickens announce over their bylines that the sky is falling."

"Don't tell me you are one of those who asks why the big news must always be bad news," said Hitzig. "Mankind delights in mischief; always has, always will."

"Yes, but the mischief is so repetitive," said the lawyer. "Nobody finds a variation on the old themes. As our friends down the way were complaining, crime is trivialized by its dowdiness. That's why detective stories are popular; the crimes are always ingenious. Real crime is not ingenious; the same old story, again and again. If I wanted to commit a murder I should devise a truly novel murder weapon. I think I should go to my wife's freezer, and take out a frozen loaf of bread. Have you looked at those?

They are like large stones. You bash your victim—let's say, your wife—with the frozen loaf, melt it out and eat it. The police seek in vain for the murder weapon. A novelty, you see?"

"They would discover you," said Hitzig, who knew a lot about Nietzsche, and was apt to be dismal; "I think that notion has been tried."

"Very likely," said Ludlow. "But I should have added a novelty to the monotonous tale of Othello. I should go down in the annals of crime as the Loaf Murderer. Admittedly we live in a violent world, but my complaint is that the violence is unimaginative."

"I gather that it is some time since violence has played much part in student life," said Mrs. Skeldergate to the Warden.

"God be praised," said he. "Though I think people exaggerated the violence there was; they spoke and wrote as though it were something wholly without precedent. But European universities are unceasingly violent, and the students are tirelessly political. History rings with the phrase 'The students rioted in the streets'. Of course we treat our students much more humanely than the European universities have ever done. I have colleagues at the Sorbonne who boast that they have never spoken to a student except in the lecture-hall, and do not choose to know them personally. Quite unlike the English and American tradition, as you know."

"Then you don't think the uproars really changed anything, Warden?"

"Oh, they did that, right enough. Our tradition of the relationship between student and professor had always been that of the aspirant toward the adept; part of the disturbances arose from a desire to change it to a consumer-retailer arrangement. That caught the public fancy too, you know, and consequently governments began to talk in the same way, if you will allow me to say so. 'We shall require seven hundred head of engineers in the next five years, Professor; see to it, will you?'—that sort of thing. 'Don't you think philosophy a frill in these stern times, Professor? Can't you cut down your staff in that direction?' Education for immediate effective consumption is more popular than ever, and nobody wants to think of the long term, or the intellectual tone of the nation."

Mrs. Skeldergate, to her dismay, had turned on a tap she could

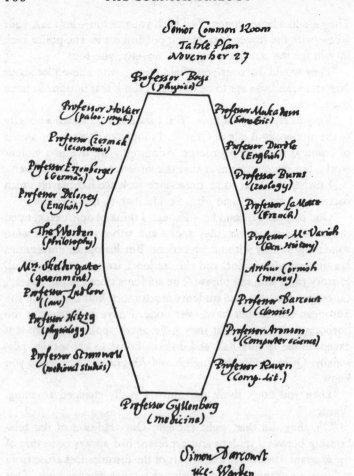

Senior Common Room
Table Plan
November 27

Professor Boys
(physics)

Professor Hollier   Professor Makadam
(paleo-psych.)   (Sanskrit)

Professor Gretmak   Professor Durdle
(economics)   (English)

Professor Erzenberger   Professor Burns
(German)   (zoology)

Professor Deloney   Professor La Motte
(English)   (French)

The Warden   Professor McVarish
(philosophy)   (Ren. History)

Mrs. Skeldergate   Arthur Cornish
(government)   (money)

Professor Ludlow   Professor Darcourt
(law)   (classics)

Professor Hitzig   Professor Aronson
(physiology)   (computer science)

Professor Stromwell   Professor Raven
(medieval studies)   (comp. lit.)

Professor Gyllenberg
(medicine)

Simon Darcourt
vice-Warden

not shut off, and the Warden was in full spate. But she was an experienced listener, and there was no disturbance in her appearance of interest.

PROFESSOR LAMOTTE was still recouping his powers after the assault on his gouty foot, and he was startled when McVarish leaned across him and said to Professor Burns: "Roberta, have I ever shown you my penis-bone?"

Professor Burns, a zoologist, did not turn a hair. "Have you truly got one? I know they used to be common, but it's ages since I saw one."

Urky detached an object with a gold handle from his watch-chain and handed it to her. "Eighteenth century; very fine."

"Oh, what a beauty. Look, Professor Lamotte, it's the penis-bone of a raccoon; very popular as toothpicks in an earlier day. And tailors used them for ripping out basting. Very nice, Urky. But I'll bet you haven't got a kangaroo-scrotum tobacco pouch; my brother sent me one from Australia."

Professor Lamotte regarded the penis-bone with distaste. "Don't you find it rather disagreeable?" he said.

"I don't pick my teeth with it," said Urky; "I just show it to ladies on social occasions."

"You astonish me," said Lamotte.

"Oh come off it, René; you—a Frenchman! Subtle wits like to refresh themselves with a whiff of mild indecency. *La nostalgie de la boue* and all that. Indecency and even filth—letting the hard-run intellect off the chain. Like Rabelais, you know."

"I know Rabelais is very much your man," said Lamotte.

"A family connection," said Urky; "my ancestor, Sir Thomas Urquhart—the first and still the greatest translator of Rabelais into English."

"Yes, he improved on Rabelais a good deal," said Lamotte. But Urky was insensitive to any irony but his own. He proceeded to inform Professor Burns about Sir Thomas Urquhart, with occasional gamy quotations.

AS I PROWLED round the table, about my Vice-Warden's business, Arthur Cornish, I was glad to see, was getting on well with Professor Aronson, the University's big man on computer science. They were talking about Fortran, the language of formula and translation, in which Arthur, as a man deeply concerned with banking and investment, had a professional interest.

"DO YOU THINK we ought to tackle Mrs. Skeldergate later about what is being said in the Legislature about poor Ozias Froats?" said Penelope Raven to Gyllenborg. "Really, they've got him all wrong. Not that I know anything about what he's doing, but nobody could be such a fool as some of those idiots are pretending."

"I wouldn't, if I were you," said Gyllenborg. "Remember our rule: never talk business or ask for favours on Guest Night. And I'll add something: never attempt to explain science to people who want to misunderstand. Froats will be all right; the people who know have no misgivings about him. What's going on in the Legislature is just democracy on the rampage; everybody having his uninformed say. Never explain things; my lifelong rule."

"But I like explaining," said Penny. "People have such nutty ideas about universities and the people who work in them. Did you see the obituary that appeared of poor Ellerman? You wouldn't have known it was the same man we knew. The facts were more or less right, but they gave no sense of what he had been, and he was damned good. If they'd wanted to crucify him, of course, it would have been easy. That crack-brained continuous romance he wrote, which was supposed to be such a secret and which he kept confiding in everybody about; a sort of Dream-Woman he invented for his private delectation, and made love to in quasi-Elizabethan prose. If anybody got hold of that—"

"They won't," said Professor Stromwell, from across the table; "it's gone forever."

"Really?" said Penny. "What happened?"

"I burned it myself," said Stromwell. "Ellerman wanted it out of the way."

"But oughtn't it to have gone to Archives?"

"In my opinion, too much goes to Archives, and anything that is in Archives gains a wholly ridiculous importance because of it. Judge a man by what he publishes, not by what he hides in a bottom drawer."

"Was it as raunchy as he hinted?"

"I don't know. He asked me not to read it, and I didn't."

"And thus another great romance is lost," said Penny. "He may have been a considerable artist in pornography."

"No, not a man who was so devoted to the university ideal as Ellerman," said Professor Hitzig. "If he had been an artist primarily he would not have been so happy here. The characteristic of the artist is discontent. Universities may produce fine critics, but not artists. We are wonderful people, we university people, but we are apt to forget the limitations of learning, which cannot create or beget."

"Oh, come on!" said Penny; "that's going too far. I could name you lots of artists who have lived in universities."

"For every one you name, I'll name you a score who didn't," said Hitzig. "Scientists are what universities produce best and oftenest. Science is discovery and revelation, and that is not art."

"Aha! 'The reverent inquiry into nature'," said Penny.

"Finding a gaping hole in exact knowledge and plugging it, to the world's great benefit," said Gyllenborg.

"Then what do you call the Humanities?" said Penny. "Civilization, I suppose."

"Civilization rests on two things," said Hitzig; "the discovery that fermentation produces alcohol, and voluntary ability to inhibit defecation. And I put it to you, where would this splendidly civilized occasion be without both?"

"Fermentation is undoubtedly science," said Gyllenborg; "but voluntary inhibition must be psychology, and if anybody suggests that psychology is a science I shall scream."

"No, no; you are on my ground now," said Stromwell; "inhibition of defecation is in essence a theological matter, and unquestionably one of the effects of the Fall of Man. And that, as everybody now recognizes, means the dawn of personal consciousness, the separation of the individual from the tribe, or mass. Animals have no such power of inhibition, as every stage-manager who has to get a horse on and off stage without a mishap will assure you. Animals know themselves but dimly—even more dimly than we, the masters of the world. When Man ate the fruit from the Tree of Knowledge he became aware of himself as something other than a portion of his surroundings, and he dropped his last, carefree turd, as he, with wandering steps and slow, from Eden took his solitary way. After that he had, literally, to mind his step, not to speak of his Ps and Qs."

" 'His solitary way'," said Penny Raven. "Just like Milton, the old sour-belly! What about Eve?"

"Every child repeats the experience of recognizing himself as unique," said Hitzig, ignoring the feminist outburst.

"Every child repeats the whole history of life, beginning as a fish, before he begins to experience inhibition," said Gyllenborg.

"Every child repeats the Fall of Man, quits the Paradise of the womb, and is launched into the painful world," said Stromwell. "Sub-Warden, have those people up the way completely forgotten that decanters are supposed to be passed?"

I tore myself away from a disquisition by Arthur Cornish on loan-sharking—of which of course he disapproved, although it fascinated him—and made another tour of the table to see that everyone was all right, and speed the decanters on their way. They had come to rest in front of Professor Mukadassi, who did not drink wine, and seemed absorbed in the talk of Hollier. I was glad Clem was enjoying himself, because he is not really a clubbable man.

"What I call cultural fossils," he was saying, "are parts of human belief or behaviour that have become so imbedded in the surrounding life that nobody questions them. I remember going to church with some English relatives when I was a boy, and noticing that a lot of the country women, as they came in, made a tiny curtsy to a blank wall. When I asked why, nobody knew, but my cousin inquired of the vicar, and he said that before the Reformation a statue of the Virgin had stood there, and although Cromwell's men had destroyed it, they could not destroy the local habit, as evinced in the women's behaviour. Years ago I paid a brief call at Pitcairn Island, and it was like stepping back into the earliest days of the nineteenth century; the last immigrants to that island were soldiers from Wellington's troops, and their descendants still spoke the authentic speech of Sam Weller, and said 'Vell, sir', and 'Werry good'. When my Father was a boy every well-brought-up Canadian child learned that 'herb' was pronounced without the 'h'; you still hear it now and again, and modern Englishmen think it's ignorance, though it's really cultural history. These things are trifles, but among races that keep much to themselves, like some of the nomads of the East, or our surviving real Gypsies, all kinds of ideas persist, that are worth investigating. We tend to think of human knowledge as progressive; because we know more and more, our parents and grandparents are back numbers. But a contrary theory is possible—that we simply recognize different things at different times and in different ways.

Which throws a new light on the whole business of mythology; the myths are not dead, just different in understanding and application. Perhaps superstition is just myth, dimly perceived and unthinkingly revered. If you think superstition is dead, visit one of our examination halls, and count the fetishes and ju-jus that the students bring in with them."

"You don't take that seriously," said Boys.

"Quite seriously," said Hollier.

"You speak of one of the great gaps in understanding between East and West," said Mukadassi. "In India we know that men every bit as good as we believed things that the advanced members of society look on as absurdities. But I agree with you, Professor; our task is not to scorn them but to try to discover what they meant and where they thought they were going. The pride of Science encourages us to this terrible folly and darkness of scorning the past. But we in the East take much more account of Nature in our daily life than you do. Perhaps it is because we are able to be out-of-doors more than you. But if I may say it—and you must not think I would wound your susceptibilities, Professor— no, no, not for the world—but your Christianity is not helpful about Nature. None the less, Nature will have her say, and even that Human Nature that Christianity so often deplores. I hope I do not give offence?"

Hollier was not offended; Mukadassi exaggerated the hold Christianity had on him. "One of my favourite cultural fossils," said he, "is the garden gnome. You have observed them? Very cute objects; very cute indeed. But do people want them simply for cuteness? I don't believe it. The gnomes provide some of that sugar in the drink of belief that Western religion no longer offers, and which the watered-down humanitarianism that passes with so many people for religion offers even less. The gnomes speak of a longing, unrecognized but all the stronger for its invisibility, for the garden-god, the image of the earth-spirit, the kobold, the *kabir,* the guardian of the household. Dreadful as they are, they have a truth you won't find in the bird-bath and the sundial."

PROFESSOR DURDLE WAS airing a grievance to Elsa Czermak, who had been complaining about an economic weekend of seminars she had been attending at a sister university. "But at least you talk about your subject," said he; "you don't have to listen to atmospheric burble."

"Don't we?" said Elsa; "that shows how much you know about it."

"Can one burble about economics? I wouldn't have thought it possible. But surely you don't have to put up with the kind of thing I was listening to this afternoon. A Big Bloomsbury Man is visiting us, you know? And his message to the world about the mighty past of which he was a tiny part was chiefly this sort of thing: 'Of course in Bloomsbury in the great days we were all absolutely *mad*. The servants were *mad*. You might go to sit down and find a plate of *food* on youah chah. Because the maids were simply *mad*. . . . We had a red doah. There were lots of green doahs and blue doahs and brown doahs, but ours was a *red* doah. Completely MAD!' It is quite extraordinary what charity universities extend toward people who have known the great. It's a form of romanticism, I suppose. Any wandering Englishman who remembers Virginia Woolf, or Wyndham Lewis, or E. M. Forster can pick up a fee and eat and drink himself paralytic in any university on this continent. Medieval, really; taking in jugglers and sword-swallowers who are on the tramp. And the American cadgers are just as bad though they are usually poets and min- nesingers who want to show that they are very close to the young. It's this constant arse-creeping to youth that kills me, because it isn't the youth who pay them. God, you should have heard that fatuous jackass this afternoon! 'I shall *nevah* forget the night Vir- ginia stripped *absolutely naked* and wrapped herself in a bath-towel and did Arnold Bennett dictating in the Turkish bath. We simply *screamed! Mad!* MAD!' "

"We have our own lunatic raconteurs," said Elsa. "Haven't you ever heard Deloney telling about the Principal at St. Brendan's who had the mynah bird that could talk Latin? It could say *Liber librum aperit* and a few classical nifties of that sort, but it had had a rough background, and was likely to shout 'Gimme a drink, you old bugger' when the Principal was ticking off a naughty student. I must say Deloney does it very well, but if he ever goes out as a touring lecturer I can see it developing into a star turn. Econ- omists are just the same; long tales about Keynes not being able to make change for taxis, and that sort of thing. Universities are great repositories of trivia. You need a sabbatical, Jim, you're getting sour."

"Perhaps so," said Durdle. "As a matter of fact, I'm working up a turn of my own about the last Canada Council 'site visit' I was mixed up in. You know how they work? It's really like an episcopal visitation in the Middle Ages. You spend months preparing all the material for an application for money to carry on some special piece of work, and then when everything's in order they send a committee of six or seven to meet your committee of six or seven, and you wine them and dine them and laugh at their jokes, and tell them everything you've already told them all over again, and treat them as friends—even equals. Then they go back to Ottawa and write to you that they really think your plan is quite strong enough to merit their assistance. Overpaid, over-pensioned running dogs of bourgeois philistinism!"

"Mit der Dummheit kämpfen Götter selbst vergebens," said Erzenberger.

"Translation, please," said Elsa.

"The gods themselves struggle vainly with stupidity," said Erzenberger and could not keep a note of pity out of his voice as he added, "Schiller."

Elsa ignored the pity and turned again to Durdle. "Well, when you go begging you must sometimes expect to have the door slammed, or the dogs loosed on you. Scholars are mendicants. Always have been, and always will be—or so I hope. God help us all if they ever got control of any real money."

"Oh Christ, Elsa, don't be so po-faced! It's those damned cigars you smoke; they breed resignation. Every academic worth his salt wants to be a Philosopher King, but that takes a lot of money. I wish I had a small independent income; I'd get away from everything and write."

"No you wouldn't, Jim. The University has you in its grip forever. Academicism runs in the blood like syphilis."

NOBODY GETS DRUNK at a Guest Night. The wine performs its ancient magic of making the drinkers more themselves, and what is in the fabric of their natures appears more clearly. Ludlow, the law don, was being legalistic and Mrs. Skeldergate, whose preoccupation was with society, was trying to arouse his indignation, or his pity, or something other than his cool judgematical observation of the degradation she knew about in our city.

"It's the children, of course, that we must think of, because so many of the older people are beyond reclaim. The children, and the young. One of the hardest things I had to learn when I began the sort of work I am doing now is that many women have no concern for their children whatever. And the children are in a world of which they have no comprehension. A little girl told me last week that an old man came to their house and he and her mother fought on the bed. Of course she did not recognize sexual intercourse. What will she be when she does—which must be soon? A child prostitute, one of the saddest things in the world, surely. I have been trying to do something about another child, who cannot speak. Nothing wrong with her speech organs, but neglect has made her dumb. She doesn't know the commonest words. Her buttocks are covered with triangular burns; her mother's lover touches the child up with the iron, to cure her stupidity. Another child dares not speak; he lives in mute terror and his tortured, placatory grimace makes his mother hit him."

"You describe a dreadful, Dostoevskian world," said Ludlow, "and it is grim to know that it exists not more than two miles from where we sit, in circumstances of comfort—indeed, of luxury. But what do you propose to do?"

"I don't know, but something must be done. We can't shut our eyes to it. Have you people no suggestions? It used to be thought that education was the answer."

"University life makes it amply clear that education is not an answer to anything, unless it is united to some basic endowment of common sense, goodness of heart, and recognition of the brotherhood of mankind," said Ludlow.

"And the Fatherhood of God," said the Warden.

"You must allow me to withhold my opinion about that, Warden," said Ludlow. "Wrangling about God is not for lawyers, like me, but for philosophers like you, and priests like Darcourt. Mrs. Skeldergate and I have to come to grips with the actualities of society, she in her social work and I in the courts; we have to deal with what society gives us. And although I do not in the least underestimate the problems you attribute to poverty and ignorance, Mrs. Skeldergate, some rough-and-tumble court work has convinced me that much the same sort of thing comes under the consideration of the law from parts of society that are not poor and not, in the ordinary sense, ignorant. Inhumanity, cruelty, and criminal self-seeking are not the exclusive property of the poor. You can find lots of that sort of thing right here in the University."

"Oh, come, Ludlow, you are simply talking for effect," said the Warden.

"Not at all, Warden. Every senior person in the University world knows how much thieving, for instance, goes on in that world, and everybody conspires to keep quiet about it. Probably the conspiracy is a wise one, because there would be a row if it ever became a matter of public knowledge. But what are you to expect? A university like this is a community of fifty thousand people; if you lived in a town of fifty thousand, wouldn't you expect some of them to be thieves? What is stolen? Everything from trifles to costly equipment, from knives and forks to whole sets of Communion vessels from the chapels, which are whisked off to South America, I happen to know. It is stupid to pretend that students have no part in it, and probably members of faculty, if we knew. There are explanations: all institutions arouse the larceny in the human heart, and pinching something from the Alma Mater is a revenge taken on behalf of some unacknowledged part of the human spirit, for the Bounteous Mother's superiority of pretension. Not for nothing were students known to our ancestors as St. Nicholas's clerks—learned and thievish alike. Good God, Warden, have you forgotten that only three years ago a visiting professor who stayed in this College tried to get away with the curtains off his windows? He was a learned man, but he was also in the grip of the universal desire to steal."

"Come now, Ludlow, you don't expect me to admit any such universal desire."

"Warden, I put it to you: have you never stolen anything in your life? No, I'll retract that; your position is such that you are, by definition, honest; the Warden of a college does not steal, though the man under the Warden's gown might do so. I won't ask the man. But you, Mrs. Skeldergate—have you never stolen?"

"I wish I could say I haven't," said Mrs. Skeldergate with a smile, "but I have. Not very seriously, but a book from a college library. I've tried to make restitution—quite a bit more than restitution. But I can't deny it."

"The soul of mankind is incurably larcenous," said Ludlow, "in the olive-groves of Academe as well as anywhere else; and thefts of books and property by students, servants, and faculty, and betrayal of trust by trusted persons must be expected to continue. A world without corruption would be a strange world indeed— and a damned bad world for lawyers, let me say."

"You talk as if you believed in the Devil," said the Warden.

"The Devil, like God, lies outside the legal sphere, Warden. But I'll tell you this: I've never seen God, but twice I've caught a glimpse of the Devil in court, once in the dock, and once on the Bench."

MCVARISH AND ROBERTA BURNS were at it, hammer and tongs, across the body of Lamotte, who seemed not to relish their conversation.

"It's no good talking to a zoologist about love as if you meant sex," said Professor Burns. "We see sex as it works among the humbler creation—if they are humbler—and you can count on the fingers of two hands the species that seem to show any tenderness for their mates. With the others it's just compulsion."

"And what about mankind?" said Lamotte. "Do you agree with the terrible Strindberg that love is a farce invented by Nature to fool men and women into propagating their species?"

"No, I don't," said Roberta. "Not a farce at all. Mankind did plenty of propagation before the notion of love had any place in his world, or we shouldn't be here. My point is that love and sex needn't be lumped together. You see it among students; some are sick with love and some are roasting with sex; some are both."

"I had a student once who wanted to be a devil with the girls," said Urky, "and he was taking some muck he got from a quack— a sort of soup made of bull's balls. Did him no good, really, but he thought it did, which was probably effective, but don't let Gyllenborg know I said so. At the same time I had another student who was mooning over a ballerina he hadn't a chance of approaching, but he beggared himself sending her an orchid every time she danced. Both silly, of course. But really, Roberta, do you mean to separate love from the old houghmagandy? Isn't that going too far?"

"The old houghmagandy, as you call it, is all very well in its way, but don't take it as a measure of love, or I'll go scientific on you and point out that the greatest lover in Nature is the boar, statistically speaking; he ejects eighty-five billion sperms at every copulation; even a stallion can only rise to thirteen billions or so. So where does man rank, with his measly dribble of a hundred and twenty-five millions? But man knows love, whereas the boar and the stallion hardly look at their mates, once they've done the trick."

"I am glad I have not had a scientific education," said Lamotte; "I have always thought, and shall continue to think, of woman as a miracle of Nature."

"Of course she's a miracle," said Roberta, "but you don't appreciate how much of a miracle. You're too spiritual. Look at a splendid girl—is she a spirit? Of course she is, but she's a lot of other things that are absolutely galvanizing, they are so miraculous. Look at me, even, though I assure you I'm not parading my middle-aged charms; yet here I sit, ears waxing, snots hardening, spit gurgling, tears at the ready, and after a dinner like this one, what miracles within! Gall and pancreas hard at it, faeces efficiently kneaded into nubbins, kidneys at their wondrous work, bladder filling up, and my sphincters—you have no idea what the whole concept of womankind owes to sphincters! Love takes all that for granted, like a greedy child that sees only the icing on the splendid cake!"

"I can manage very happily with the icing," said Lamotte. "To think of a woman as a walking butcher's shop revolts me."

"And the icing is so various that it is a life study in itself," said McVarish. "The tricks women get up to! I know a hairdresser who tells me that women come to the manicurist-and-superfluous-hair lady in his salon, and the things they ask for! The pubic hair plucked and shaped into hearts, or darts, and they will endure any amount of hot-wax treatment to get the desired result. Then they want it hennaed! 'There's fire down below,' as the sailors sing—certainly as they sing when they behold the result!"

"They needn't bother," said Roberta. "People will put up with anything for the old houghmagandy. Or rather, Nature gently assists them to do so. Intercourse brings about a considerable loss of perceptive capacity; sight, hearing, taste, touch, and smell are all dulled, whatever the sex-technique books pretend to the contrary. The plain lover looks handsome for the moment; the broken veins and the red nose are scarcely perceptible, the grunting is not comic, bad breath is hardly noticed. And that's not love, René, but Nature coming to the rescue of love. And man is the only creature to know love as a complex emotion: man is also, in the whole of Nature, the only creature to turn sex into a hobby. Oh, it's a complex study, let me tell you."

" 'Love not as do the flesh-imprisoned men,' " said Lamotte, pretending to stop his ears. "I'll bet neither of you can continue the sonnet."

IT WAS GETTING on for the time when I should suggest to the Warden that we rise for coffee and cognac, if anybody wanted it. I had some trouble getting his attention because he and Mrs. Skeldergate and Ludlow were still hard at it about the nature of a university.

"Ludlow talks about the university as a town," said the Warden, "but I'm not so sure that's the right definition."

"Surely a university is a city of youth," said Mrs. Skeldergate.

"Not a bit of it," said the Warden. "Lots of youth in a university, fortunately, but youth alone could not sustain such an institution. It is a city of wisdom, and the heart of the university is its body of learned men; it can be no better than they, and it is at their fire the young come to warm themselves. Because the young come and go, but we remain. They are the minute-hand, we the hour-hand of the academic clock. Intelligent societies have always preserved their wise men in institutions of one kind or another, where their chief business is to be wise, to conserve the fruits of wisdom and to add to them if they can. Of course the pedants and the opportunists get in somehow, as we are constantly reminded; and as Ludlow points out we have our scoundrels and our thieves—St. Nicholas's clerks, indeed. But we are the preservers and custodians of civilization, and never more so than in the present age, where there is no aristocracy to do the job. A city of wisdom; I would be content to leave it at that."

But he was not permitted to leave it at that, for in universities nobody is ever fully satisfied with somebody else's definition. Deloney spoke: "Not just a city, I think, Warden; more like an Empire, in a large university like this, composed of so many colleges that were once independent, and which still retain a measure of independence under the federation of the University itself. The President is an Emperor, presiding over a multitude of realms, each of which has its ruler, and the Principals, Rectors, Wardens, and so forth are very like the great dukes and rulers of mighty fiefdoms, with here and there a Prince Bishop, like the head of St. Brendan's, or a mitred abbot, like the Rector of Spook; all jealous of their own powers, but all subject to the Emperor. Universities were creations of the Middle Ages, and much of the Middle Ages still clings to them, not only in their gowns and official trappings, but deep in their hearts."

"When you speak of 'learned men', Warden, don't you think you should say 'and women', to avoid any injustice?" said Mrs. Skeldergate.

"As the Warden's legal counsellor I can assure you that whenever he says 'men' the word 'women' is also to be understood," said Ludlow.

"And neuter, to avoid any discrimination or hurt feelings in a university community," said the Warden, who was not wholly without humour.

"Will you take coffee, Warden?" said I, in the approved formula. The Warden rose, and the table broke up, and for the last few minutes of the evening, new groups formed.

Arthur Cornish approached me. "I haven't had a chance to tell you how much I appreciate what you did this afternoon," he said. "Of course everybody assumes that I have inherited enormously from Uncle Frank, but in the complexity of a big family business it becomes impersonal, and I wanted something to remember him by. We were more alike than you might suppose. He got away young and devoted himself to his art collections; I think he pretended to be more impractical than he was to escape the burdens of business. He was extraordinarily sharp, you know, after a bargain. Steal a dead fly from a blind spider, he would, when he was among dealers. But he was kind to lots of painters as well, so I suppose it cancels out, in a sort of way. But tell me, how did you know I was interested in musical manuscripts?"

"A friend of yours, and a friend of mine, told me: Miss Theotoky. We were talking one day after class about methods of musical notation in the early Middle Ages, and she spoke of it."

"I remember mentioning it to her once, but I didn't think she was paying much attention."

"She was. She told me everything you said."

"I'm glad to hear that. Her taste in music and mine aren't very close."

"She's interested in medieval music, and in trying to find out what she can about earlier music. It's very mysterious; we know Nero fiddled, but what precisely did he fiddle? When Jesus and the Apostles had sung an hymn, they went up into the Mount of Olives; but what was the hymn? If we heard it now, would we be appalled to hear the Saviour of Mankind whining and yowling through his nose? It's only in the past few hundred years that music of the past has been recoverable, yet music is the key to feeling, very often. Something Hollier ought to be interested in."

"Perhaps Maria is doing it for Hollier; she seems to be very much under his spell."

"Did I hear the name Maria?" said McVarish, joining us. "That marvellous creature pops up everywhere. By the way, I hope you didn't think I was being too familiar with her presence this afternoon? But ever since I spotted that little Venus among your uncle's bits and pieces I have been obsessed by its resemblance to her, and now I've had it home and studied it in detail I'm even more delighted. I shall have her always near me—tying her sandal, so innocently, as if she were quite alone. If you ever want a reminder, Arthur, do come to my place. She's very fond of you, you know."

"What makes you think so?" said Arthur.

"Because I know a lot about what she thinks. A friend of mine whom you don't know, I believe—a most amusing creature called Parlabane—knows her intimately. He devils for Hollier—calls himself Hollier's *famulus*, which is delightful—and so he sees a lot of Maria, who works in Hollier's rooms. They have great old chats, and Maria tells him everything. Not directly, I gather, but Parlabane is an old hand at reading between lines. And though of course Hollier is her great enthusiasm, she likes you a lot. As who wouldn't, my dear boy."

He touched Arthur lightly on the sleeve, as he had touched me before this evening. Urky is a great toucher.

"You mustn't imagine I'm trying to muscle in," he went on, "although Maria comes to my lectures and sits in the front row. Which gives me immense pleasure, because students are not, on the whole, decorative, and I can't resist decorative women. I adore women, you know. Unlike Rabelais, but very much like Sir Thomas Urquhart, I think." And he moved on to say good night to the Warden.

"Sir Thomas Urquhart?" said Arthur. "Oh, yes, the translator. I'm beginning to hate the sound of his name."

"If you know Urky, you get a good deal of Sir Thomas," I said. Then I added, spitefully I admit but Urky maddened me: "If you look him up in the dictionary of biography, you will find that it is widely agreed that Sir Thomas was crazy with conceit."

Arthur said nothing, but he winked. Then he too moved off to take leave of the Warden, and I remembered that as Sub-Warden I ought to call a taxi for Mrs. Skeldergate. And when that had been done I hurried up to my rooms over the gate, to note down, in *The New Aubrey*, what I had heard during the evening. *How they chirped over their cups.*

[3]

I WAS BEGINNING to dread *The New Aubrey*. What I had begun as a portrait of the University, drawn from life, was becoming altogether too much like a personal diary, and a confessional diary of the embarrassing sort. Not nearly enough about other people; far too much about Simon Darcourt.

I don't drink much, and what I drink doesn't affect me, but I had a feeling after our Guest Night that I wasn't myself in a way that a few glasses of wine, taken between six o'clock and ten, could hardly explain. I had finished a day that ought to have been enjoyable; some good work done in the morning, the completion of the Cornish business in the afternoon, and the acquisition of two first-rate Beerbohms that had never been published, and thus were very much my own and a sop to that desire for solitary possession which collectors know so well; Guest Night, which had gone well, and the Cornish executors entertained at my own expense. But I was melancholy.

A man with a theological training ought to know how to deal with that. A little probing brought the cause to light. It was Maria.

She was a first-rate student, and she was a girl of great personal charm. Nothing unusual there. But she played far too large a part in my thoughts. As I looked at her, and listened to her in class, I was troubled by what I knew about her and Clement Hollier; the fact that he had once had her on his wretched old sofa was not pleasing, but it was the kind of thing that happens and there is no use making a fuss over it—especially as Hollier had seemed to be in the state of lowered perception at the time that Roberta Burns had so briskly described. But Hollier thought she was in love with him, and that troubled me. Whatever for? Of course he was a fine scholar, but surely she wasn't such a pinhead as to fall for an attribute of a man who was in so many other ways wholly unsuitable. He was handsome, if you like craggy, gloomy men who look as if they were haunted, or perhaps prey to acid indigestion. But, apart from his scholarship, Hollier was manifestly an ass.

No, Darcourt, that is unjust. He is a man of deep feeling; look how loyal he is to that miserable no-hoper John Parlabane.

Damn Parlabane! He had been prattling to McVarish about Maria, and when Urky said 'reading between the lines' it was obvious that they had both been speculating in the wholly unjustified way men of unpleasant character speculate about women.

Fond of Arthur Cornish, indeed! No, 'very fond' had been his expression. More exaggeration. But was it? Why had she dragged Arthur Cornish into her conversation with me, when we were talking about medieval musical notation? Something about his uncle's collection, but had that been relevant? I know well enough how people in love drag the name of the loved one into every conversation, simply to utter that magical word, to savour it on the tongue.

The trouble with you, Darcourt, is that you are allowing this girl to obsess you.

More inner tumult, upon which I tried to impose some of the

theological stricture I had learned as a method of examining conscience.

The trouble with you, Darcourt, is that you are falling in love with Maria Magdalena Theotoky. What a name! Mary Magdalene, the woman with seven devils; and Theotoky, the divine motherhood of Mary. Of course people do carry the most extraordinary names, but what a contradiction! It was the contradiction that would not give me any peace.

Oh, fathead! Oh, jackass! Oh, triple-turned goof!

How far can absurdity carry a supposedly sane man? You, a stoutish, middle-aged priest . . . *but not a priest of a church that denies marriage to its priests, remember that* . . . shut up, who said anything about marriage? . . . *it was in your mind and the link between love and marriage marks you forever as a bourgeois and a creature from the past, as well* . . . get back to your point. How far can absurdity carry a supposedly sane man? You have a successful career, and your way of life is comfortable . . . *but lonely* . . . who will smooth the pillow when you lie at the hour of death? . . . *are you seriously expecting that superb creature to slide you into the grave?* How far can absurdity carry a supposedly sane man? What have you to offer her? Devotion. *Pooh, she can expect devotion from scores of men—handsome, young rich men, like Arthur Cornish.* He must love her; remember the way he resented Urky's references to her this afternoon, and again not an hour ago? What chance have you against him? Or Handsome Clem? You are a fool, Darcourt.

Of course I could love her hopelessly. There has been a good deal of that sort of thing throughout the ages. Since the time Roberta Burns speaks of, when our hairy ancestors gave up biting their women and throwing them the bones after they had finished their uncooked feast. A good deal of hopeless love has saddened mankind since the Idealist and the Sex-Hobbyist became different aspects of the same, infatuated human creature.

An Idealist I certainly was. But a Sex-Hobbyist? I am not a wholly inexperienced creature but it has been some little time . . . and I can't really say I've missed it much. But Maria is young and in the flower of her beauty. Adoration and amusing talk wouldn't be enough for her.

Oh, God, how did I ever get into this?

[4]

THAT WAS WHERE I WAS, however. Deep in love with one of my students, a situation in which a professor must appear as either a knave or a fool. For the weeks to come I did the best I could: I never addressed Maria except in class; I was overscrupulous in valuing her work, but as it was admirable that didn't make much difference. I was determined to keep my folly bottled up.

It was a blow to my resolve, but a mighty fire in my heart, therefore, when she lingered after the last lecture before Christmas, and said, shyly: "Professor Darcourt, is there any chance that you could come to my Mother's house for dinner on Boxing Day? We'd be so happy if you could."

Happy! Happy!! Happy!!!

Second Paradise V

PARLABANE HAD BECOME a fixture in my life and I had accepted him, without joy but with philosophy, if I may be allowed to use that word. I cannot be sure, because deeper acquaintance with Parlabane made it clear that philosophy was not a word to be used loosely. It was his academic discipline; he was a professional philosopher, in comparison with whom most people were ill-disciplined muddlers as soon as they turned their minds to large questions. But if I may be allowed to use 'philosophy' merely to mean rueful resignation in the face of the inevitable, I accepted his presence in Hollier's rooms, almost every day for the space of an hour or two, with philosophy.

He had dropped the manner, half-obsequious and half-contemptuous, which went with his monk's robe. He was no longer the beginning friar who secretly scorned those from whom he asked alms. He had his knitting with him, however; he carried it in a brown-paper shopping-bag with a few books, and what looked like a dirty towel. As I remember what he said, I hear the click of the needles as an accompaniment to every word. He was now teaching philosophy in what used to be called Extension Courses, now Continuing Studies, lecturing at night to people who were doing their work for a degree slowly, and in bits. What he was teaching them I fear to think, because what he said to me from time to time almost froze the marrow in my bones.

"I am one of the very few genuine sceptical philosophers in the world, Molly. Oh, there are people who teach scepticism, but their lives prove that they don't believe what they teach. They love their families, give to the Cancer Fund, and listen with tolerance and sometimes with approval to the baloney that makes up most of the talk about politics, society, culture, and whatnot even in a university.

"The real sceptic, however, lives in a constant atmosphere of carefully balanced dubiety about everything; he will not accept that there are any satisfactory grounds for acquiescence in any statement or proposition whatever. Of course if some fool tells him that it is a fine day he will probably nod because he hasn't time to haggle with the fool over what he means by a word like 'fine'. But in all important things he reserves his judgement."

"Doesn't he admit that some things are good and some bad? Some things desirable and some undesirable?"

"Those would be decisions in ethics, and his aim in matters of ethics is to deflate all pretension; the kind of judgement you speak of is pretentious because it rests on some sort of metaphysics. Metaphysics is gibble-gabble, though admittedly often fascinating. Scepticism strives to assist every metaphysic to destroy itself— to hang itself in its own garters, so to speak."

"But that leaves you without anything at all!"

"Not quite. It leaves you with a cautious recognition that the contradictory of any general proposition may be asserted with as much claim to belief as the proposition itself."

"Oh, come on, Parlabane! Only a few weeks ago you were swanning around here dressed up as a monk. Had you no religious belief? Was it just cynical masquerade?"

"By no means. You are making the vulgar assumption that scepticism and cynicism are related. Cynicism is cheap goods, and the cynic is usually a grouchy sentimentalist. Christianity, or perhaps any intellectually respectable faith, is acceptable to the sceptic because he doubts the power of purely human reason to explain or justify anything; but Christianity teaches that it was Man's Fall that brought doubt into the world. Beyond this world of doubt and sorrow lies Truth, and the Faith points the way to it because it is based on the existence of something above human knowledge and experience. Scepticism is of this world, my darling, but God is not of this world."

"Oh God!"

"Precisely. So my faith did not, and does not, debar me from being a sceptic about all the things of this world. Without God the sceptic is in a vacuum and his doubt, which is his crowning achievement, is also his tragedy. The tragedy of man without God is so dreadful that I cannot keep my mind on it for more than a minute or two at a time. The Fall of Man was a much greater calamity than most men are prepared to face."

"Nothing is certain except God?"

"Five words. Allow me five hundred thousand and I would put it for you more convincingly than your *Reader's Digest* summary can achieve."

"Don't trouble yourself. You haven't convinced me."

"Dearest Molly, I am not an old friend, but I hope I am a friend, so allow me to speak frankly: I am not trying to convince you of anything. Because your mind is as it is, and your age and state of health as they are, and your sex a factor which it is now fashionable to discount in intellectual argument, it is most unlikely that I should ever succeed in convincing you of the likelihood of what it has taken me something more than thirty years to decide, with great anguish of mind, for myself. I am not interested in converting you to scepticism. I am not interested in converting anybody. But I am paid rather poorly by this University to say what I believe to be the truth to an odd assortment of students, and that is what I do."

"But if it blasts them? No truth, no certainty anywhere?"

"Then it blasts them. They will be no worse off than millions of others who have been blasted by far less elegant agencies than my philosophical teaching. Of course I tell them what I have just told you: when human reason refuses to admit vassalage to anything other than itself, life becomes tragedy. God is the factor that banishes that tragedy. But very often my students have turned to philosophy to get away from God—some peanut God, usually of their parents' devising. Like so many would-be intellectuals, they have trivial minds and adore tragedy and complexity."

That was one Parlabane. But there was at least one other known to me, quite apart from the Parlabane who stodged pasta and guzzled coarse wine and talked dirtily in The Rude Plenty, and the Parlabane who borrowed money almost every week. This Parlabane was by no means the sceptical philosopher.

"You wouldn't expect me to live always on such dizzy intellectual heights, would you, Molly? I should certainly be the wildest sort of fake if I did, and many philosophers have come to grief that way. For example that high-minded romantic Nietzsche. He never let himself off the chain. Of course he believed implicitly in his nonsense, whereas I, as a sceptic, am committed to non-belief in everything, including my most cherished philosophical ideas. Nietzsche once said that there could be no gods, because he could not endure it if there were gods and he were not one of them himself. Which is as good as saying that nothing can be true if it does not put Friedrich Nietzsche at the top of the tree. I am not like that; I recognize that a tree has a bottom as well as a top, a root as well as a crown. That is to say, I assume it to be so for practical purposes, because I have never seen or heard of a tree that did not fit that description.

"I have thought a good deal about trees; I like them. They speak eloquently of the balanced dubiety which I told you was the sceptical attitude. No splendid crown without the strong root that works in the dark, drawing its nourishment among the rocks, the soil, hidden waters, and all the little, burrowing things. A man is like that; his splendours and his fruits are to be seen, to win him love and admiration. But what about the root?

"Have you ever seen a bulldozer clearing land? It advances upon a great tree and shoves and pushes inexorably until the tree is down and thrust out of the way, and all of that effort is accompanied by a screaming and wrenching sound from the tree as the great roots are torn from the ground. It is a particularly distressing kind of death. And when the tree is upturned, the root proves to be as big as the crown.

"What is the root of man? All sorts of things that nourish his visible part, but the deepest root of all, the tap-root, is that child he once was, of which I spoke to you when I was amusing you with the story of my life. That is the root which goes deepest because it is reaching downward toward the ancestors.

"The ancestors—how grand it sounds! But the root does not go back to those old stuffed shirts with white wigs whose portraits people display so proudly, but to our unseen depths—which means the messy stuff of life from which the real creation and achievement takes its nourishment. The root is far more like a large placenta than it is like those family trees that are all branches."

"You talk like Ozias Froats."

"The Turd-Skinner? Do you know him? I wish you'd introduce me."

"I certainly won't if you talk of him as the Turd-Skinner. I think he's a Paracelsian magus; he has a bigger view of things than any of us—except Professor Hollier, perhaps. Truth lies in the hidden and unacknowledged."

"Yes: shit. But what does he think is hidden in it?"

"He won't say, and I don't expect I'd understand his terms if he did say. But I think it's some sort of individual stamp, and maybe it changes significantly with states of health and mental health; a new measure of—I don't think I know what, but something like personality or individuality. I shouldn't make guesses."

"I know; it's not your field."

"But if he's right, it's everybody's field, because everybody will be the greater for what Ozias Froats has discovered."

"Well, I wish him luck. But as a sceptic I am dubious about science as about everything else, unless the scientist is himself a sceptic, and few of them are. The stench of formaldehyde may be as potent as the whiff of incense in stimulating a naturally idolatrous understanding."

I was beginning to recognize Parlabane as something very much more important than the weighty nuisance I had thought him at first. He carried his own atmosphere about with him, and after he had sat for five minutes on Hollier's old sofa it was the dominating spirit in the room. It would be silly to say it was hypnotic, but it was limiting; it inclined me to agree with him while he was present, only to realize that I had admitted to many things I did not really believe as soon as he was gone. It was that duality of his; when he was the philosopher he had to have his way because he could out-argue me any day in the week, and when he was the other man who talked about the roots of the tree of selfhood he was so outrageous and ingenious that I could not keep up with him.

His outward man was going from bad to worse. As a monk he had looked odd, in the Canadian setting—even in Spook—but now he looked like a sinister bum. The suit somebody had given him was of good grey English cloth, but it had never been a fit and now it was a baggy, food-stained mess. The trousers were too long, and he could no longer endure having them braced up, so now he belted them with what looked like an old necktie, and they dragged at his heels, the bottoms dirty and frayed. His shirt was always dirty, and it occurred to me that perhaps advanced scepticism made ordinary cleanliness seem a folly. He had a bad smell; not just dirty clothes, but a living, heavy stench. As the cold weather came on Hollier gave him an overcoat of his own, already terribly worn; it was what I called his 'animal coat' because it had collar and cuffs of some fur that had become matted and mangy; with it went a fur cap that was too big for Parlabane, and gave the impression of a neglected wig; from under it his un-trimmed hair hung over the back of his collar.

A bum, certainly, but nothing like the bums who haunted the campus, hoping to mooch a dollar from some kindly professor. They were destroyed men, from whose faces no mind shone forth—only confusion and despair. Parlabane looked somehow important; the blurred, scarred face was impressive, and through the thick spectacles his eyes swam with a transfixing stare.

His attitude toward me was much as Hollier had said it would be. He could not leave me alone, and although he apparently thought I was a female nitwit, amusing herself by acquiring a doctorate at the University (don't imagine there is any contra-diction here; nitwits can do it), he plainly wanted to be near me, to talk with me, to bamboozle me intellectually. This was no novelty to me; around universities there is always some 'female-molesting' or 'harassment' or whatever the fashionable word may be, but there is a great deal more of intellectual mauling and pawing by people who don't even know that what they are doing is sexy. Parlabane was different; his intellectual seduction was on a grander scale and vastly more amusing than that of the average run of academics. I certainly didn't like him, but it was fun to play with him, on this level. Sexual thrills are not all physical, and although Parlabane was an unlikely seducer, even on the intel-lectual plane, it was clear that his desire was, by this prolonged tickling, to bring me to an orgasm of the mind.

Late November can be a romantic time of year in Canada; the bare trees, the frosty air and whirling winds, the eerie light which sometimes persists for the whole of the day and then sinks, shortly after four, into steely darkness, dispose me to Gothic thoughts.

In Spook, so Gothic in architecture, it was tempting to indulge northern fantasies, and I found myself wondering if in such a frame of mind I was not working under the eye of Doctor Faustus himself, for Hollier had the intensity of Faust and much of his questing appearance. But then, no Faust without Mephistopheles, and there was Parlabane, as slippery-tongued, as entertaining, and sometimes as frightening as the Devil himself. Of course in Goethe's play the Devil appears handsomely dressed as a travelling scholar; Parlabane was at the other end of the scale, but in his command of any conversation he had with me, and his ability under all circumstances to make the worse seem the better thing, he was acceptable as Mephistopheles.

I have no use for a woman who doesn't want to try conclusions with the Devil at some time in her life. I am no village simpleton, like poor Gretchen whom the Devil delivered over to Faust, for his pleasure; I am my own woman and even if I gained what I desired, and Hollier declared his love for me and suggested marriage or an affair, I would not expect to be subsumed in him. I know this is a bold word, for better women than I have been devoured by love, but I would hope to keep something of myself for myself, even if only to have one more thing in my power to give. In love I do not want to play the old, submissive game, nor have I any use for the ultra-modern maybe-I-will-and-maybe-I-won't-and-anyhow-you-watch-your-step game; Tadeusz's daughter and a girl part Gypsy had no time for such thin, sour finagling. Parlabane was trying to seduce me intellectually, to put me with my back on the floor and leave me gasping and rumpled, and all with words. I decided to see what luck I would have in discombobulating him.

"Brother John," I said one November afternoon when the light in Hollier's outer room was beginning to fade, "I'm going to give you a cup of tea, and a question to answer. You have been telling me about the world of philosophical scepticism, and God as the only escape from a world blighted by tragic ambiguity. But I spend my time working with the writings of men who thought otherwise, and I find them strongly persuasive. I mean Cornelius Agrippa, Paracelsus, and my own dear François Rabelais."

"Spleeny Lutherans, every one of them," said Parlabane.

"Heretics, probably, but not Lutherans," I said. "How could

such soaring spirits agree with the man who declared that society
is a prison filled with sinners, in which order has to be maintained
by force? You see, I know something of Luther, too. But don't
try to sidetrack me with Luther. I want to talk about Rabelais,
who said that a free human creature finds his rule of conduct in
his sense of honour—"

"Just a minute; he didn't say 'a free human creature', he said
men—'men that are free, well born, well-bred, and conversant in
honest companies'."

"You don't have to give it to me in English; I know it in French—
'*gens libères, bien nés, bien instruits, conversantes en compagnies hon-
nêtes*' and if you can prove to me that 'gens' means Men Only I
should like to hear you do it. It means 'people'. You have the
common idea of Rabelais as a woman-hater because you have
only read that gassy translation by Sir Thomas Urquhart—"

"As a matter of fact I have been rereading it because Urquhart
McVarish has lent me a copy—"

"I'll lend you a French copy, and in it you'll discover that where
Rabelais sets out the plan for his ideal community—one might
almost call it a university—he includes lots of women."

"For entertainment, one assumes."

"Don't assume. Read—and in French."

"Molly, what a horrible old academic scissorbill you are getting
to be."

"Abuse cannot shake me. Now answer my question: isn't a
sense of honour a sufficient rule of conduct?"

"No."

"Why not?"

"Because it can be no bigger than the man—or woman, if you
are going to be pernickety—who possesses it. And the honour
of a fool, or a pygmy-in-spirit, or a redneck, or a High Tory, or
a convinced democrat are all wholly different things and any one
of them, under the right circumstances, could send you to the
stake, or stop your wages, or just push you out into the cold.
Honour is a matter of personal limitation. God is not."

"Well, I'd rather be François Rabelais than one of your frozen
sceptics, grabbing at God as a lifebelt in an Arctic sea."

"All right; be anything you please. You are a romantic; Rabelais
was a romantic. His nonsense suits your nonsense. If the lie of

honour as a sole and sufficient guide to conduct suits you, well and good! You'll end up with those English idiots who used to govern their lives by what is or is not cricket."

"Come on, Parlabane, this is just hair-splitting and academic abuse. Don't you make any allowance for quality of life? Isn't the worth of what a man believes shown by what his belief makes of him? Wouldn't you rather live nobly as François Rabelais than be stuck in the deep freeze of scepticism, wondering when, and if, God is going to open the door of the fridge and thaw you out?"

"Rabelais didn't live nobly. Most of his life he was on the run from people who were more accurate reasoners than he was."

"He was a great writer, a broad and copious writer, a man of wide and hospitable mind."

"Romanticism. Sheer romanticism. You are putting forward critical opinions as if they were facts."

"O.K., you have beaten me at the academic game, but you haven't changed my mind, and so I don't admit that you've beaten me at the real game."

"Which is?"

"Well, look at you and look at me. I'm delighted with what I'm doing, and I've never heard you say one pleasant or approving thing about anything you've ever done, except for a single love-affair that turned out badly. So which of us is the winner?"

"You are a fool, Molly. A beautiful fool and you prattle your nonsense in such a lovely voice and with such an enchanting hint of a foreign accent that a young heterosexual like Arthur Cornish might take you for a genuine, solid-gold Aspasia."

"So I am, or at any rate so I may be. You keep telling me that I am a woman, but you haven't any idea what a woman is. Yours is a masculine mind and I suppose it's a pretty good one, though it doesn't originate anything: my mind is feminine, and where yours delights in subtle distinctions it is all one colour, and my mind is in shades that shame the spectrum. I can't beat you at your game, but I don't think you can even guess what my game is."

"Prettily put, but might I suggest that at present your game is romanticism—oh, not in any dismissive sense, but meaning a rich diffusion, and profusion, and—"

"Go on. Confusion. But only if I let you make the rules."

"Please let me finish. I have told you that the crown of my tree is scepticism that leaves nothing untouched but the wonder of God. But I have a root, to nourish my crown, and as usual the root is the contrary of the crown—the crown upside down, in the dark instead of in the light, working toward the depths instead of straining upward to the heights. And my root is romantic, Molly, and in the realm of romance you and I can meet and have the greatest sport together. Why do you think I am writing a novel? Sceptics don't write novels."

"Well, Brother John, from what I have learned about you I cannot imagine why you are writing a novel. You are talkative, but not I think imaginative; you are no romancer, no bard, no unfolder of marvels. I don't know any novelists, but you seem an unlikely candidate for that sort of job."

"My life has been a romance. My novel is my life, slightly disguised but not very much. I don't need imagination: I have rich fact. I am writing about me and all the people I have met who are important to me, and about my ideas, and how they have changed. And I don't mind telling you that when my novel appears there will be some red faces among those I have encountered along the road. I am not writing to justify myself, but to put down the evidence about a remarkable spiritual adventure, so that the readers can judge for themselves. As they certainly will."

"Are you going to let me read it?"

"When it appears I may give you a copy. You are not going to read it in manuscript. I am only permitting that to one or two friends whose literary judgement I trust. And you, with your taste for Rabelais, cannot expect to qualify. This will be a very serious book."

"Thanks for those kind words."

"Meanwhile, you can be of the greatest practical assistance. People don't often think of it, but writing costs the writer a good deal of money, on the way. Can you see your way to letting me have fifty dollars for a few days?"

"My little notebook tells me that you already owe me two hundred and sixty-five dollars. You have a tidy mind, Brother John; you always borrow in multiples of five. Why do you think I can go on lending at this rate?"

"Because you have money, sweet child. Far more money than the run of students."

"What makes you think so?"

"I am an observant man. The possession of money is hard to hide. But you have lots of it.—Maybe you get it from Hollier?"

"Get out!"

But he didn't get out, and I knew too much to get into a shoving-match with anybody as muscular as Parlabane, for even under that awful suit he looked an unusually strong man. He sat on the sofa grinning, and I turned stolidly to my work, and tried to ignore him.

Why had he said that? Surely Hollier had never said anything to him about our solitary and, it now seemed to me, meaningless and gratuitous encounter on that sofa? No; that was quite outside Hollier's character, even allowing for the awful complicity and loyalty among men where women are concerned.

I knew I was blushing, a trick I have never been able to control. Why? Anger, I suppose. As I sat writing and fiddling with papers, increasingly aware of Parlabane's hypnotic stare, I heard his voice, very low and surprisingly sweet, singing the song I hate most in the world—the song with which girls used to torment me at school, after they had wormed out something about my family:

> Slumber on, my little Gypsy sweetheart
> Wild little woodland dove;
> Can you hear the song that tells you
> All my heart's true love?

That was the end. I put my head down on the table and sobbed. What a dirty fighter Parlabane was!

"Why Maria, are you unwell? Does my little song touch some chord in you that you would rather keep silent? There, there, dear little heart, don't weep so. I suppose you are wondering how I found out? Sheer intuition, my darling. I have it, you see, very strongly. It is part of my root, not of my crown. I can sniff out all sorts of things, simply by looking and listening and letting my roots feed my crown. If you'd rather I didn't mention it, you can rely on me. Though, as you probably know, there are people who are curious about you, because you are so beautiful and so desirable to the kind of people who desire women. They torment me for information about you, because they think knowing about you is a step toward possessing you. Sometimes they make it hard for me to resist."

So he got his fifty dollars. He tucked it into an inner pocket and rose to go. Standing at the door he spoke again.

"Don't suppose I think you capable of anything so stupid and low as a desire to conceal your Gypsy blood, my very dear Molly. I am not so coarse in my perceptions as that. I think you are trying to suppress it because it is the opposite of what you are trying to be—the modern woman, the learned woman, the creature wholly of this age and this somewhat thin and sour civilization. You are not trying to conceal it; you are trying to tear it out. But you can't, you know. My advice to you, my dear, is to let your root feed your crown."

[2]

ALL VERY WELL for Parlabane to advise me to come to terms with my root. He could not know, nor would he care, what my root was costing me at home, which I could not accept as some hidden cavern of feeling and inherited wisdom, but a rat's-nest of duplicity and roguery, Gypsy-style. Mamusia was getting Yerko ready for one of his piratical descents on the innocent, credulous city of New York.

Those two had, as the phrase goes, a connection there, with one of the most highly reputed dealers in stringed instruments in that city—a dealer who had also a Paris house, with which the Laoutari had long been associated. Not only some of the finest string players in the world, but an army of lesser though still considerable folk—violinists in first-rate orchestras, and their colleagues who played the viola, the violoncello, and the double-bass, all of whom, from time to time, wanted an instrument for themselves, or for a pupil—came to this celebrated dealer for what they needed, and they accepted his word as truth.

I cannot name the name, for that would betray a secret which is not mine, and I do not suggest that the dealer was a crook. But the supply of fine instruments is not unlimited; there have not been hundreds of great luthiers in the eighteenth and nineteenth centuries, and although there are some thousands of fine fiddles in existence, there are even more that seem just as good, or almost as good, that come from workshops like that of Mamusia and Yerko. So when the dealer said to a buyer: 'If you feel that this Nicolas Lupot is a little more expensive than you want to pay for a stand-by instrument, I have something here which is authentically of the Mirecourt School, but because we do not have a complete dossier on its former owners, we do not feel justified in asking quite so much for it. Probably some rich amateur has had it in his possession for a generation. It's a beauty—and a bargain.' And the player would try it, and probably take it away for a while to get used to it, and at last he would buy it.

I don't pretend he didn't get a good instrument, or that some parts of it had not at some time been fashioned at Mirecourt. But perhaps the scroll—that beautiful, suggestive, not very important part of a fiddle—had been carved by Yerko, eighteen months before, and it might be that the back, or even the belly, had been lovingly shaped by Mamusia from the beautiful silver fir, or the sycamore that she bought from piano-makers. The corner-blocks were almost certainly her work, however authentic the remainder might be. And every fiddle or viola or cello from the basement of One Hundred and Twenty Walnut Street in the city of Toronto had been re-varnished, with layer upon layer of the mixture which was a Laoutaro secret, made in the authentic old way with balsams and fossil amber that cost a lot of money and much ingenuity to secure. Oh, Mamusia and Yerko weren't crooks, supplying cheap goods at high prices; by the time one of their fiddles had been through the *bomari* it was a fine instrument; it was made by piecing together portions of instruments that had come to grief in some way and so could be bought cheap, and rebuilt with new portions wherever they were needed. Wonders of ingenuity, but not precisely what they seemed.

Mamusia and Yerko were sellers of romance—the romance of antiquity. There are makers of violins living today, in unromantic places like Chicago, who make excellent instruments, as good in every physical respect as the work of the great luthiers of the past. All these instruments lack is the romance of age. And although many fiddlers are cynical men, and some are no better than unionized artisans without any more of the artist in them than is necessary to keep a chair in the back row of a modest small-town symphony, they are susceptible to the charm of antiquity. The romance and the antiquity were what Yerko and Mamusia offered, and for which the great dealer charged handsomely, because he too understood the market value of romantic antiquity.

Why did it bother me? Because I had apprenticed myself to the hard trade of scholarship, which shrieks at the thought of a fake, and disgraces a man who, let us say, pretends to the existence of a Shakespeare Quarto that nobody else is able to find. If something is not defensible on every count, it is suspect and probably worthless. A trumpery puritanism, surely? No, but impossible to reconcile with such romantic deceptions as the fine, ambiguous instruments that came from our basement.

For such journeys Yerko assembled what he always called the Kodaly String Quartet; the other three were musicians in some sort of moral or financial disarray who were glad to travel free to New York with him in a station-wagon with perhaps ten instruments which remained with the dealer; Yerko returned to Canada by a different port of entry, without his quartet, but with a good deal of rubbish—broken or dismembered instruments—in the back of the car. Yerko, so large, so dark, long-haired, and melancholy in appearance, was a Customs officer's idea of a musician. Part of the preparation for the journey was getting Yerko sobered up so that he could drive the car and strike bargains without coming to grief, and convincing him that if he went to a gambling-house and risked any of the money Mamusia would certainly search him out and make him sorry for it. The payments were in cash, and Yerko returned from New York with bundles of bills in the lining of his musician's baggy black overcoat. The logic of my Mother and my Uncle was that Yerko was too conspicuous and too farcically musical in appearance to attract the wrong kind of attention.

This was the staple of their business. The perfectly honest work they did for some musicians of the highest rank did not pay so well, but it flattered them as luthiers, and gave them a valuable reputation among the people who provided romance and sound fiddles for the orchestras of North America.

[3]

GYPSIES HAVE A POOR opinion of ill health, and nobody was permitted to ail in our house. Therefore, when I caught quite bad influenza I did what I could to conceal it. Mamusia supposed I had a cold, and there could be no thought of staying in my bed, that couch in the communal living-room; she insisted on her single treatment for all respiratory diseases—cloves of garlic shoved up the nose. It was disgusting, and made me feel worse, so I dragged myself to the University and took refuge in Hollier's outer room, where I sat on the sofa when he was likely to appear, and lay on it when he was not, and was sorry for myself.

Why not? Had I not troubles? My home was a place of discomfort and moral duplicity, where I had not even a proper bed to lie on. (*You are rich, fool; get yourself an apartment and turn your back on them.* Yes, but that would hurt their feelings, and with all their dreadful tricks, I love them and to leave them would be to leave what Tadeusz would have expected me to cherish.) My infatuation with Hollier was wearing me out, because there was never any sign from him that our single physical union might be repeated or that he cared very much for me. (*Then bring him to the point. Have you no feminine resource? You are not of an age, nor is this a time in history for such shilly-shallying.* Yes, but it shames me to think of thrusting myself on him. *All right then, if you won't put out a hand for food you must starve!* But how would I do it?— *'There's a woman in the window with her pants down!'* Shut up! Shut up! Stop singing! *I'm singing from the root, Maria: what did you expect? Fairy bells?* Oh God, this is Gretchen, listening to the Devil in the church! *No, it's your good friend Parlabane, Maria, but you are not worthy of such a friend: you are a simpering fool.*)

My academic work was hanging fire. I was pegging away at Rabelais, whose existing texts I now know well, but I had been promised a splendid manuscript that would bring me just the kind of attention I needed—that would lift me above the world in which Mamusia and Yerko could disgrace me—and apart from that one reference to it in September Hollier had never said a single word about it further. (*Ask him about it.* I wouldn't dare; he would just say that when he had anything further to tell, he would tell me.) I felt dreadful, I had a fever, my head felt as if it were stuffed with oily rags. (*Take two aspirin and lie down*.)

I was lying down, in a deep sleep and almost certainly with my mouth open, when Hollier returned one afternoon. I tried to leap up, and fell down. He helped me back to the sofa, felt my head and looked grave. I wept a few feeble tears and told him why I could not be ill at home.

"I suppose you're worried about your work," he said. "You don't know where you're going, and that is my fault. I had expected to be able to talk to you about that manuscript before this, but the bloody thing has vanished. No, by God, it's been stolen, and I know who has it."

This was exciting, and by the time he had told me about the Cornish bequests, and Professor Darcourt's attempt to nail down Professor McVarish about the manuscript he had certainly borrowed, and McVarish's unsatisfactory attitude toward the whole thing, I felt much better and was able to get up and make us some tea.

I had never seen Hollier in this mood before. "I know that scoundrel has it," he kept saying; "he's hugging it to himself, like the dog in the manger he is. What in God's name does he expect he can do with it?"

I tried being the voice of reason. "He's a Renaissance historian," I said, "so I suppose he wants to make something of it in his own line."

"He's the wrong kind of Renaissance historian! What does he know about the history of thought? He knows politics and he knows something about Renaissance art, but he hasn't the slightest claim to be a cultural or intellectual historian, and I am, and I want that manuscript!"

This was glorious! Hollier was angry and unreasonable; only once before, when I first told him about the *bomari*, had I seen him so excited. I didn't care if he was talking rather foolishly. I liked it.

"I know what you're going to say. You're going to say that eventually the manuscript must come to light because McVarish will write about it, and I'll be able to ask to see it, and undoubtedly expose a lot of his nonsense. You're going to say that I should go to Arthur Cornish and demand a show-down. But what would young Cornish know about such things! No, no; I want that

manuscript before anybody else has monkeyed with it. I told you
I didn't have time to look at those letters for more than a glance.
But a glance is all it needed to show that they are written in Latin,
of course, but Latin with plenty of what I suppose was quotation
in Greek and several words in Hebrew, sticking out in those big,
chunky, uncompromising Hebrew characters—and what do you
suppose that means?"

I had an idea, but I thought I had better let him tell me.

"Cabbala—that's what it could mean! Rabelais writing to Paracelsus about Cabbala. Perhaps he was deep in it; perhaps he
scorned it; perhaps he was making inquiry. Perhaps he was one
of that group who were trying to Christianize it. But whatever it
is, what could be more significant to uncover now? And that's
what I want to do—to discover and make known this group of
letters as they should be made known, and not in some half-baked
interpretation of McVarish's."

"I suppose they could be rather mild stuff. I mean, I hope they
aren't, but it could be."

"Don't be stupid! It wasn't a time, you know, when one great
scholar wrote to another to ask how his garden was coming along.
It was dangerous; the letters could fall into the hands of repressive
Church authorities and once again Rabelais's name would have
been mud. Must I remind you? Protestantism was the Commu-
nism of the time and Rabelais was too near to Protestantism for
safety. But Cabbala could have put him in prison. Pushed far
enough it could have meant death! The stake! Mild stuff! Really,
Maria, you disappoint me! Because I want to count you in on
this, you know; when my commentary on those letters is printed,
your name shall stand with mine, because I want you to do all
the work in verifying the Greek and Hebrew quotations. More
than that; the *Stratagems* shall be all yours, to translate and edit."

In scholarly terms this was fantastic generosity. If he had the
letters I could have the historical commentary. Gorgeous!

Then he did a most uncharacteristic thing. He began to swear
violently, and smashed his teacup on the floor; he snatched mine
and broke it; he smashed the teapot. Then, shouting McVarish's
name over and over again he broke the wooden tray over the
back of a chair and trampled on all the fragments of china, wood,
and tea-leaves. His face was very dark with anger. Without a word

to me he stamped into his inner room and locked the door. I had shrunk myself as small as possible on the sofa, for safety and the better to admire.

Not a word about love, though. I was almost ashamed to notice such a thing when big scholarly matters were in the air. I did notice, however. But Hollier was so furious with McVarish that he had no time for anything else.

None the less, this had been a display of feeling from Hollier; he had shown human concern, even if most of it was for himself. It was when his scholarly zeal was excited that Hollier became something more than the preoccupied, removed scholar which was the man he showed to the world. When I had first told him about the *bomari* he had done something extraordinary: both times he had told me about the Gryphius MS he had been greatly stirred and this time he had flared into anger. On all three occasions he had been a different creature, younger, physically alert, swept by passion into acts that were foreign to his usual self.

This was Hollier's root, not his austere scholarly crown. From time to time I heard him shouting. Sometimes things I could understand like—'And that blockhead wanted me to go to McVarish and tell him everything!' Tell what? Who was the blockhead?

I cleaned up the mess, and was happy to do it. Hollier's rage had cured my influenza.

Or almost cured it. When I went home that evening, Mamusia said: "Your cold is gone, but you look white. I know what is wrong with you, my girl; you are in love. Your professor. How is he?"

"Never better," said I, thinking of the storm I had seen that afternoon.

"A fine man. Very handsome. Has he made love to you?"

"No." I didn't want to go into fine detail with Mamusia.

"Ach, these *gadje*! Slow as snakes in autumn. I suppose there must be social occasions. They think a lot of social occasions. We must show you off to advantage. You must ask him here at Christmas."

We had quite a long argument about that. I was dubious about what Mamusia meant by social occasions; when Tadeusz was alive he and Mamusia never entertained anybody at home; they always took them to restaurants, to concerts or plays. The great change that had come over her since Tadeusz's death had obliterated all that; she had never had friends among the *gadjo* business and professional Hungarians, and she had dropped all the acquaintances. But when Mamusia took an idea into her head it was not in my power to change her. A Christmas party now dominated her imagination, although as a Gypsy, Christmas was not a great festival for her. I tried being outspoken.

"I won't let you ask him here to parade me like a Gypsy pony you want to sell. You don't know how people like that behave."

"So at my age I'm a fool? I will be as high and fine as any *gadji* lady—so slick a louse would slip off me. Parade you? Is that how it's done, *poshrat*? Never! We shall do it like the great ladies of Vienna. We shall make him see he isn't alone in desiring you."

"Mamusia! He doesn't desire me!"

"That's what he thinks. He doesn't know what he desires. You leave that to me. He's the man I want for the father of my grandchildren, and it's high time. We'll make him jealous. You must ask another man."

What other man? Arthur Cornish? Arthur and I had been going out together fairly often, and were becoming real friends, but he had never made a move toward me, except to kiss me good night once or twice, which can't be said to count. Arthur was the last man I wanted to introduce into Mamusia's world.

She had been thinking. "To make Hollier jealous, you must ask somebody who is his equal, or a little better than that. Somebody with prettier manners, better clothes, more jewellery. Another professor! Do you know another professor?"

So that was how I came to ask Professor Darcourt to dine with my family on Boxing Day. He turned rather an odd colour when I wound myself up to the point of speaking about it—a pink that started below his collar and worked up, as if somebody were filling a wineglass. I was terrified. Had he heard that my home was a Gypsy home? Was he afraid he would have to sit on the floor and eat baked hedgehog, which is all the *gadje* ever seem to know about gypsy food? When he said that yes, he would be delighted to come, I was hugely relieved, and as I left his seminar room I was surprised to find that he was still looking at me, and was pinker than ever. But he would do very nicely. He was near to Hollier in age, and he had lovely manners and dressed smartly for a stout man, and though he did not wear what Mamusia would have thought of as jewellery he had a natty little gold cross hanging from his watch chain, which draped over what I assumed was the forty feet of literary gut Professor Froats had mentioned. Yes, Simon Darcourt would be just the thing.

"A priest?" said Mamusia when I told her. "I must warn Yerko to guard his tongue."

"You make sure Yerko is sober," said I.

"Trust me," said Mamusia. Words I interpreted as generously as I could, but with reservation.

[4]

THERE WAS NO NEED to warn Yerko to guard his tongue. He returned from New York heavy with concealed money, but light of heart, for he had found a god to worship, and the name of the god was Bebby Jesus. A friend had taken him to the Metropolitan Museum where, in the medieval section, a Nativity Play was being performed in the celebration of the coming of Christmas. The friend thought that Yerko might be pleased by the medieval music, played on authentic old viols and some instruments of which one resembled the *cimbalom,* the gypsy dulcimer Yerko played like a master. But Yerko's incalculable fancy had settled upon the drama, the Annunciation, the Virgin Birth, the Adoration of the Shepherds, and the Journey of the Magi. In official matters, Gypsies call themselves Catholics, but Yerko's mind, uncluttered by education or conventional religion, was wide open to marvels; at the age of fifty-eight he was transfigured by his newly found belief in the Miraculous Child. Therefore he had purchased an elaborate *crèche* of carved and painted wood, and as soon as he came home he set to work with his great skill as a woodworker and craftsman to make it the most splendid thing of its kind his imagination could conceive. Nor was it anything less than splendid, though a little gaudy and bedizened, in the Gypsy style.

He set it up in our one living-room, already crammed with all the best pieces Mamusia and Tadeusz had spread through the big house when they occupied it all; the *crèche* dominated everything else. Yerko prayed in front of it, and never passed it without a low bow and a murmured greeting to Bebby Jesus who wore, when Yerko had finished his task of improvement, a superb little crown of beautifully worked copper and gold, and a robe of red velvet, made by Mamusia and decorated with tiny pearls.

I was not pleased with Bebby Jesus, who went contrary to what I hoped was my scholarly austerity of mind, my Rabelaisian disdain for superstition, and my yearning for—what? I suppose for some sort of Canadian conventionality, which keeps religion strictly in its place, where it must not be mocked but need not be heeded, either. What would our party guests make of this extraordinary shrine?

They thought it was magnificent. They arrived on our doorstep together, though Hollier had walked and Darcourt travelled by taxi, and they made the somewhat too extravagant protestations of being glad to see each other that people do make around Christmas-time. Before I could take his coat Darcourt had dashed forward and stood in front of the *crèche,* lost in admiration.

I had warned Yerko that one of our guests was a priest, and, being Yerko, he assumed that it must be Hollier, who was the more austere in appearance.

"Good father," he said, bowing deeply, "I wish you all happiness at this Birthday of Bebby Jesus."

"Oh,—ah quite so, Mr. Laoutaro," said Hollier, rather taken aback. I do not think he had heard Yerko speak on his first visit, and Yerko had a voice like someone speaking from a well of thick oil—a basso, profound and oleaginous.

But now Yerko had spied Darcourt's gleaming clerical collar, and I feared for a moment that he was going to kiss his hand, peasant-style. That would have put the party off to a really bad start, from my point of view.

"This is my Uncle Yerko," I said, stepping between them.

Darcourt had lots of social sense, and he knew that 'Mr. Laoutaro' was all wrong. "May I call you Yerko?" he said, "and you must call me Simon. Did you make this superb tableau? My dear Yerko, this brings us very close together. It is by far the loveliest thing I have seen this Christmas." He seemed to mean it. A taste for the Baroque I had not suspected in a medieval scholar, I suppose.

"Dear Father Simon," said Yerko, bowing again, "you make my heart very filled up. Is all for Bebby Jesus." And he cast a swimming eye at the *crèche*. "And this all for Bebby Jesus, too," he said, gesturing at the dining table.

I admit it was a wonder. Mamusia had unpacked treasures not seen since the death of Tadeusz, and the table could have appeared in a pageant of the Seven Deadly Sins as an altar to Gula, or Gluttony. On a tablecloth lumpy with lace was spread a complete service of that china prized by one group of connoisseurs called Royal Crown Derby, gaudy with blue and red and gold and in the extreme Gypsy taste. Tadeusz had given it to Mamusia at a time when they had some notion of entertaining at home, but it had never been used. There it was, plates resting upon larger service plates, and standing amid silver in the most highly wrought pattern Jensen had been able to devise. There was a positive forest-fire of candles burning in stands with many branches, and the flowers I had insisted on providing were already wilting in the heat.

"It isn't only the *gadje* who can do a thing well," Mamusia had said. If Darcourt had feared that he was to be given baked hedgehog, he must now be certain that he would eat it in such style as hedgehog had never known before.

Darcourt had brought a large and splendid Christmas cake, which he offered to Mamusia with ceremony. She took it with approval: such tribute from guests fitted well into her mid-European idea of hospitality. Hollier had no gift, but I was pleased to see him in a good, if unpressed, suit of clothes.

There were no preliminaries. We sat down to eat at once. I had murmured about cocktails, but Mamusia was firm; such things had never appeared in any of the first-class Budapest restaurants in which she had played as a girl; Tadeusz had thought cocktails an American folly and not really high style, in the Polish mode; and so there were no cocktails. Of course Darcourt was asked to say grace, which he did in Greek, as the language most congruous with the Crown Derby, I suppose.

Mamusia sat at the head of the table with Hollier on her left, and Darcourt on her right; Yerko sat at the other end. To my extreme annoyance I had been cast in the role of serving-wench, and though I had a place at table next to Darcourt I was not expected to sit in it often. I was to bring food from the kitchen, where an over-driven Portuguese, who asked double pay for working on a holiday, was in charge, ribbed and confined by Mamusia's orders.

"It becomes a daughter to serve the guests," Mamusia had said. "And take care you smile and beg them to take more. Show yourself open-handed. This is to show your professor that you know how such things should be done. And wear a low dress. *Gadjo* men like to peep."

I know that *gadjo* men like to peep. But Gypsies do not much care if they peep or not. Gypsies are modest about legs, not about breasts, and I suppose Parlabane would have said that it was part of my root asserting itself that I had never been able to bother my head if men peeped down my front. This night I wore skirts to my ankles, as did Mamusia, but we both were pretty well to the fore in the matter of shoulders and bosom.

I did not wear a kerchief, however, as Mamusia did. Nor did I wear any jewellery except for a chain or two and a few rings. But Mamusia was the most ornamented object, save for Bebby Jesus, in the room. She was hung with gold—real gold—and had large hoops in her ears and a necklace made of Maria Theresa thalers that must have weighed thirty ounces.

"You are looking at my gold," she said to Hollier; "this is my dowry-gold. I brought it to my marriage with Maria's father. But it is mine. In case the marriage had not been a success, I would not have been poor. But it was a success. Oh, yes, a great success! We Laoutaro women are wonderful wives. Famous for it." This was said with what I can only call a leer, which embarrassed me horribly and I blushed. Then I was angry and blushed even more because I could see that both Hollier and Darcourt were looking at me, and I was playing the role of the modest maiden before possible husbands. Real Gypsy stuff.

God damn it to hell! Here was I, a modern girl in the New World, rigged up like a Gypsy, serving food at her mother's table, simply because I had not the power to resist Mamusia. Or perhaps because my root was still greater than my crown. My root was assuring me, as I raged inwardly, that I was looking my best, and that it was because I was blushing. How much more complicated life is than the attainment of a Ph.D. would lead one to believe!

The meal was according to the plan Mamusia had observed in the restaurants of her girlhood and I think—indeed I know—it was an astonishment to our guests. Not all of it had been stolen. The wines, in particular, had been purchased, because in our part of the world all wines and spirits are a government monopoly, and stealing from the stores maintained by the Liquor Control Board is difficult even for such a talented booster as Mamusia. The government, which has its hand in everybody's pocket, and its nose thrust deep into everybody's glass, is careful of its own. So the heavy red wine and the Tokaji we drank had been purchased with real money, though in a store that was on the self-serve principle Mamusia had been able to swipe a bottle of a pear liqueur, a Hubertus, and a couple of bottles of apricot Barack. So we were not ill supplied, for five people, not counting an occasional snort for the Portuguese, who needed encouragement.

We began with a lobster soup, stolen in the can by Mamusia and much improved by sherry and the thickest cream that could be bought. We then moved on to a rabbit pie, which was really excellent, and had been bought at a French patisserie. Our guests ate heartily of this unaccustomed dish, and I was glad, for it had cost a fortune. Perhaps they did not realize that a large stuffed carp was to follow, with a garlic sauce in which you could have stood a spoon, and a *mélange* of vegetables, so sophisticated that they hardly seemed to be vegetables at all. Darcourt's brow showed some dampness by the time he had done justice to it.

Hollier, I was concerned to observe, was a noisy eater, and to seem to eat noisily when Yerko was at the table was to be noisy in demanding company. Hollier was a chomper, his jaws working up and down like pistons, and without seeming to be greedy he ate a great deal. Dear man, did he not get enough to eat in his lonely professorial life? Or had his mother, who was not far away from us, loaded him up with the turkey and plum pudding their sort of Canadian thought appropriate to Christmas? But he was of a Sheldonian type that can eat a great deal without putting on any flesh.

The carp was followed by a *sorbet,* a water-ice, served not as a sweet, to bring the meal to a close, but merely, as Mamusia said, to joke a little with our stomachs before getting on with the next serious course. This was a true *gulyás-hus,* again with a lot of garlic, and plentiful, because Mamusia thought it the really serious offering, the crown of the feast.

That was that, except for a fruit flan of apricots, with brandied cream, and a Sachertorte, which Mamusia insisted everyone should try, because it recalled great days in Vienna, and gave therefore a cosmopolitan air to a meal which she insisted was otherwise truly Hungarian. And, of course, we all had to eat a piece of Darcourt's cake.

The guests ate everything, drank the heavy, red wine, and moved on happily to the Tokaji.

Conversation had been animated all through the meal, and became much more animated as it drew toward its close. I was busy taking things to the kitchen, bringing things from the kitchen, and managing the Portuguese, whom I had somewhat over-encouraged with drink. Her sighs and moans could have been overlooked, but as the meal wore on she began to talk animatedly to herself, and now and then opened the door to stare in, with groggy solemnity, to see how things were going.

Mamusia was very much the high-born hostess, as she understood the role, and wanted to talk to our guests about the University and what they did there. Darcourt's work she could understand; he taught priests, like himself. He tried to explain that he was not a priest in quite the meaning of that word known to Mamusia and Yerko.

"I am an Anglican, you see," he said at one point, "and therefore although I am unquestionably a priest, I suppose I might say I am a priest in a Pickwickian sense, if you know what I mean."

They did not know what he meant. "But you love the Bebby Jesus?" said Yerko.

"Oh, yes indeed. Just as much, I assure you, as our brethren at Rome. Or, for that matter, in the Orthodox Church."

Hollier had, at his first visit, explained to Mamusia what his work was; he enlarged on that, without suggesting that he regarded her as a cultural fossil, or a possessor of the Wild Mind. "I look into the past," he said.

"Oho, so do I!" said Mamusia. "All we Romany women can look into the past. Does it give you a pain? When I have looked backward sometimes I have a very bad pain in my women's parts, if I may speak of such things. But we are not children here. Except for my daughter. Maria, go to the kitchen and see what Rosa is doing. Tell her if she chips one of those plates I will cut out her heart. Now, dear Hollier, you teach looking into the past. Do you teach that to my daughter, eh?"

"Maria is busy studying a remarkable man of past times, one François Rabelais. He was a great humorist, I suppose one might say."

"What is that?"

"He was a man of great wisdom, but he expressed his wisdom in wild jokes and fantasies."

"Jokes? Like riddles, you mean?"

"I suppose every joke is a riddle, because it says one thing and means another."

"I know some good riddles," said Yerko. "Mostly not riddles I could ask in front of the Bebby Jesus. But can you guess this one? Now listen good. What big, laughing fellow can go into the queen's bedroom—yes even the Queen of England—without knocking on the door?"

There was the usual embarrassing silence that always follows a riddle, while people pretend to search for the answer, but are really waiting for the asker to tell them.

"You can't guess? A big, laughing, hot fellow, he even maybe lets himself down on the queen's bed and sees through her peignoir? Hey?—You don't know such a fellow?—Oh, yes you do.— The Sun, that's who! Ah, priest Simon, you thought I meant for dirty, eh?" And Yerko laughed loudly and showed the inside of his mouth right back to the pillars of his throat, in enjoyment of his joke.

"I know a better riddle than that," said Mamusia. "Now pay attention to what I say, or you will never guess.—It is a *thing,* you understand? And this thing was made by a man who sold it to a man who didn't want it; the man who used it didn't know he was using it. Now, what is it?—Think very hard."

They thought very hard, or seemed to do so. Mamusia slapped the table emphatically and said, "A coffin!—A good joke for a priest, eh?"

"You must tell me more Gypsy riddles, Madame," said Hollier; "for me such things are like a wonderful long look into the far past. And everything that can be recovered from the past throws light on our time, and guides us toward the future."

"Oh, we could tell secrets," said Yerko. "Gypsies have lots of secrets. That's what makes them so powerful. Look—I'll tell you a Gypsy secret, worth a thousand dollars to anybody. Your dog gets into a fight see; both dogs trying to kill other dog—Rowf-rowf! Grrrrr!—you can't get your dog away. Kick him! Pull his tail! No good! He wants to kill. So what you do? You lick the long finger good—make it good and wet—then you run up and you shove your finger up the arse-hole of one dog—not matter whether your dog or not. Shove up as far as you can. Wiggle it good. Dog surprised. What the hell! he think. He let go, and you kick him good so no more fight.—You got a good dog?"

"My mother has a very old Peke," said Hollier.

"Well, you do that next time he fight. Show who's master.— You got a horse?"

Neither of the professors had a horse.

"Too bad. I could tell you how to make any horse yours forever. I tell you anyway. Just whisper up his nose. What you whisper? Whisper your secret name—the name only you and your mother know. Right up his nose, both nose-holes. Yours forever. Leave anybody he living with when you do it, and follow you. Spit in my face if I lie."

"You see my daughter's hair is uncovered," said Mamusia to Darcourt. "That means, you know, that she is without a husband— not even spoken for, though she has a wonderful dowry. And a good girl. Nobody lay a finger on her. Gypsy girls are very par-ticular about that. No funny business, like these shameless *gadji* girls. What I have heard! You wouldn't believe it! No better than *putani*. But not Maria."

"I am sure she is unmarried by her own choice," said Darcourt. "Such a beauty!"

"Aha, you like the women, though you are a priest. Oh but yes, you priests marry like the Orthodox."

"Not quite like the Orthodox. They may marry, but they must never hope to become bishops if they do. Our bishops are usually married men."

"Much, much better! Keeps them out of scandals. You know what I mean," Mamusia scowled. "Boysss!"

"Well, yes, I suppose so. But bishops have so much of other people's scandals I don't think they would care greatly for that sort of thing, even if they weren't married."

"Will you be a Bishop, Father Simon?"

"Very unlikely, I assure you."

"You don't know. You look just right for a Bishop. A Bishop should be a fine man, with a fine voice. Don't you want to know?"

"Could you tell him?" said Hollier.

"Oh, he doesn't care. And I could not tell him, not on a full stomach."

Cunning Mamusia! Slowly, but not too slowly, Hollier persuaded her to look into the future. The apricot brandy had been going round the table and Hollier was more persuasive, Mamusia more flirtatious, and Darcourt, though he protested, was anxious to see what would happen.

"Bring the cards, Yerko," she said.

The cards were on the top of a cabinet, because nothing in the room was ever to rest higher than they, and Yerko lifted them down with proper reverence.

"Maybe I should cover up Bebby Jesus?"

"Is Bebby Jesus a parrot, to be put under a cloth? Shame on you, brother! Anything I can see in the future, He knows already," said Mamusia.

"Sister, I know what! You read the cards, and we tell Bebby Jesus it is a birthday gift to him, and that way there can be no trouble, you see."

"That is an inspired thought, Yerko," said Darcourt. "Offer up the splendid talent as a gift. I had not thought of that."

"Everybody owes a gift to Bebby Jesus," said Yerko. "Even kings. Look, here are the kings; I made the crowns myself. You know what they bring?"

"The first brings a gift of Gold," said Darcourt, turning toward the *crèche*.

"Yes, Gold; and you must give my sister money—not much, maybe a quarter, or the cards will not fall right. But Gold was not all. The other kings bring Frank Innocence and Mirth."

Darcourt was startled, then delighted. "That is very fine, Yerko; is it your own?"

"No, it is in the story. I saw it in New York. The kings say, We bring you Gold, Frank Innocence, and Mirth."

"*Sancta simplicitas,*" said Darcourt, raising his eyes to mine. "If only there were more Mirth in the message He has left to us. We miss it sadly, in the world we have made. And Frank Innocence. Oh, Yerko, you dear man."

Was it just the apricot brandy, or had the room taken on a golden glow? The candles were burning down, and all the dishes except for plates of chocolates, nougat, and preserved fruits had been removed to the kitchen by me. These trifles were, Mamusia said, to seal up our stomachs, to signal to our digestions and guts, of whatever length, that there would be no more tonight.

Mamusia had opened the delicate box of tortoise-shell, and was preparing the cards. The Tarot pack is a beautiful thing, and her cards were fine ones, more than a century old.

"I cannot do the full pack," she said. "Not after what I have eaten. It must be the Five Cards."

Quickly she divided the pack into five smaller packs, and these were the Coins, the Rods, the Cups, and the Swords, set at four corners; in the centre was the pack containing the twenty-two Higher Arcanes.

"Now we must be very serious," she said, and Darcourt suppressed his social smile. "The money, please." He gave her a twenty-five-cent piece. Mamusia then covered her face for perhaps thirty seconds. "Now, you must shuffle and choose a card from each pack, leaving the middle cards for last, and you must lay them out as I have done here."

So Darcourt did that, and when he had made his choice what we saw on the table was a pentalogy, which Mamusia read as follows: "Your first card, which sets the tone for everything else, is the Queen of Rods, the dark, serious beautiful woman who is much in your thoughts. . . . But next we have the Two of Cups and it comes in the place of the Contrariety; it means that in your love affair with the dark woman, one of you will make a difficulty. But don't worry too much about that until we have looked at the rest. . . . Ah, here is the Ace of Swords, so you will have a worrying time, much to rob you of your sleep. . . . Then last of your enfolding four is the Five of Coins, and that means you will have a loss, but it will be far less than a greater gain that is coming your way. Now, all of these four are under the rule of the fifth card in the middle; it is your Great Trump, and it influences all that you have been told by the other cards. . . . And yours is the Chariot; that is very good, because it means that everything else is under the protection of the Sun and whatever happens will be for your great gain, although you may not see it until after you have had some hard times."

"But you don't see a mitre for me? A Bishop's hat?"

"I have told you; a great gain. What it will be is whatever would look like a great gain to you. If that is a Bishop's hat, perhaps that is what it will be. But unless I did the full pack, which takes at least an hour, I couldn't come any nearer. And it is a very good destiny I have found for you, Father Simon, in return for this quarter, which isn't even silver any more but some kind of government shoddy. You think about what I have said. This beautiful dark woman—if you want her the Chariot is on your side, and it could lead you to her."

"But Madame Laoutaro, be frank with us; you attach meaning to these cards which I suppose are arbitrary. Whoever chooses them has the same fortune as myself. I am sure what you do is much more than a feat of memory."

"Memory has not much to do with it. Of course the cards are of a certain meaning, but you must remember that there are seventy-eight of them, and how many combinations of five does that make? There are twenty-two of the Great Trumps alone, and they influence everything in the other four. Without the Chariot I would have given you a much less happy prospect.

"But all this is under the cloak of time and fate. You are you—if you know who that is—and I am who I am, and what happens between us when I read the cards is not what will happen with anybody else. And this is the night after Christmas, and it is already nearly ten o'clock, and that makes a difference, too. Nothing is without meaning. Why am I reading your cards at this special time, when I have never seen you before? What brings us together? Chance? Don't you believe it! There is no such thing. Nothing is without meaning; if it were, the world would dash to pieces.

"You are not to be left out, dear Hollier. Let me shuffle the cards again, and then you shall make your choice, and we shall see what next year will bring."

Darcourt had been willing, but Hollier was eager and his face glowed. This was what he called the Wild Mind at work, and he was in the presence of a culture-fossil. He chose his cards; as Mamusia looked at them I saw her face darken, and I looked very carefully, because I know something of the cards and I wanted to see if she would tell the truth as it appeared, or sweeten it, or perhaps change it altogether. Because you have to be very careful at the Tarot, even if you are not reading the cards for money, and therefore in danger from the law. You must not be too explicit about the Death card, for instance; that ugly picture of the skeleton with a scythe reaping flowers, and human heads and limbs, should not be associated with the person who sits across the table from you, even though you see death plainly in his face; much better to say, 'A death of Someone known to you may influence the future,' and then perhaps the poor soul will jump at the thought of a legacy; or emancipation, if it is a woman whose marriage is hollow. But with Hollier she was honest, though she softened some of the blows.

"This is very interesting, and you must not think too much of the outcome of what I am going to tell you until I am finished. This Four of Rods, now, means that something that is difficult for you now will be doubly difficult soon. . . . And here, the Four of Cups—you are a great man for fours, Hollier—means that somebody, some third person close to you, is going to make great trouble for you and the person who is even nearer. . . . Now here, where your fortune comes into the place of discussion, is the Three of Swords, and that means hatred, and you must be on your guard against it because whether somebody hates you or you hate somebody, it will make very bad trouble. . . . But your fourth card is the Knave of Coins, and a Knave is a servant, somebody in a position to work for you, and who will send you a very important letter; how it will work with the hatred and the trouble I cannot tell. . . . But here is your Great Trump, and that is the Moon, the changeable woman, and she tells of danger, so as you see the whole thing is very complicated and I dare not try to sort it out for you simply with these cards. So I shall ask you to choose one more card from Major Trumps, and we must all very earnestly desire that it will throw some light on what you have chosen here."

Was Hollier looking rather white? I know I was. I had expected Mamusia to fake his fortune, which I had seen was a dark one, but she must have feared the cards too much to do that. If you cheat the cards, the cards will cheat you, and many a good fortune-teller has become a charlatan and a cheat in that way, and some have been become drunkards or killed themselves when they knew the cards had turned against them.

Hollier chose a card, and rather slowly laid it down. It was the Wheel of Fortune. Mamusia was delighted.

"Aha, now we know! You have put it in front of me upside down, Hollier, so we all see the creatures turning on the wheel, and the Devil King is at the bottom and the top of the wheel is empty! So all your hard fortune will turn to good in the end, and you will triumph, though not without some severe losses. So be brave! Keep your courage and all will be well!"

"Thanks to the Bebby Jesus!" said Yerko. "I was sweating from fear. Professor, have a drink!"

More apricot brandy; by now I seemed to have lost my crown entirely and was living from my root. I suppose I was rather drunk, but so was everybody else, and it was a good drunkenness. To work with the cards, Mamusia had kicked off her shoes, and I had done so too; barefoot Gypsy women. Quite how things developed next I don't properly know, but Mamusia had her violin, and was playing Gypsy music, and I was lost in the heavily emotional contradictions between the *lassu,* so melancholy and indeed lachrymose, and the *friska,* which is the wild merriment of the Gypsies, but in the true, somewhat mad, and undoubtedly archaic style, and not in the sugary mode of such *gadje* confectioneries as *'Die Czardasfürstin'.* As Mamusia played a *friska* it was not the light of the campfire and the flashing teeth and swirling skirts of musical-comedy Gypsies that was evoked, but something old and enduring, something that banished the University and the Ph.D. to a stuffy indoors, something of a time when people lived out of doors more than indoors, and took the calls of birds for auguries, and felt God about and all around them. This was Frank Innocence and Mirth.

Yerko fetched his *cimbalom,* which he had made himself; it hung from his neck by a cord, like a large tray, and he hammered so fast at the resounding strings that his sticks flashed like the whisk of a cook who is beating cream. At four o'clock in the afternoon, when this party was still a dark shadow on my future, I would have cringed from this music; now, when it was after eleven, I thrilled to it, and wished I had the courage to spring up and even in that crowded room to dance, slap a tambourine, and give myself to the moment.

The room could not contain us. "Let's serenade the house!" Mamusia cried above the music, and that is what we did, parading up the stairs, singing, now. What we sang was one of the great Magyar songs, '*Magasan repül a daru*', which is not a Christmas song, but a song of triumph and love. I took my two professors, one on each arm, and sang words for three, because Darcourt sang the tune in a very good voice, but only with la-la-la, whereas Hollier, who seemed to have lots of spirit but no ear, roared in a monotone, and yah-yah-yah was his syllable. When we came to

Akkor leszek kedves rózsám atied,

I kissed them both, because the occasion seemed to call for it. It occurred to me that in spite of what had happened between us, I had never kissed Hollier, nor had he kissed me, till that moment. But it was Darcourt who responded with passion, and his mouth was soft and sweet, whereas Hollier kissed me so hard he almost broke my teeth.

What did the house make of it? The poodles barked furiously. Mrs. Faiko remained invisible, but turned up the volume of her TV. Miss Gretser appeared in her nightdress, supported by Mrs. Schreyvogl, and they nodded and smiled appreciatively, and so did Mrs. Nowaczynski, who had been in the bathroom and made an appearance without teeth or wig that embarrassed her more than it did us. On the third floor Mr. Kostich looked out on the landing in his pyjamas, and smiled and said, "Great! Very fine Madam," but Mr. Horne burst out of his door in a fury, shouting, "Jesus, isn't anybody supposed to get any sleep around here?"

Mamusia stopped playing, and gestured with her bow toward Mr. Horne, who slept in his pyjama jacket only, so that his shrivelled and unpleasing privy parts were offered to our view. "Mr. Horne," she said, grandly; "Mr. Horne is a male nurse."

As if a button had been touched, Mr. Horne screamed, "Well I sure as hell ain't a female nurse! Now stop that fucking row, willya, or I'll beat the bejesus outa you all!"

Yerko approached Mr. Horne very softly. "You not talk like that to my sister. You not talk dirty to my niece, who is a virgin. You not make ugly when we sing for Bebby Jesus. You shut up."

Mr. Horne did not shut up. He shouted, "You're drunk, the whole bunch of you! Maybe it's Christmas for you, but it's a work day for me."

Yerko advanced upon Mr. Horne, and flicked him sharply on the tip of his penis with one of the long, supple hammers of his *cimbalom*. Mr. Horne danced and screamed, and I forgot to maintain my virginal character and laughed loud and long as we retreated down the stairs, where the poodles were still barking. It came to me that Rabelais would have enjoyed this.

Mamusia remembered that she was appearing to my friends as a great lady. In a voice pitched to reach the ear of Mr. Horne she explained, "You must pay no attention. He is a man of low birth and I have him here out of pity."

Mr. Horne's rage could find no words, but he shouted inarticulately until we were back in Mamusia's apartment.

"That song we were singing," said Darcourt; "the tune is familiar. Surely it comes in one of Liszt's Hungarian Rhapsodies?"

"Our music is much admired," said Mamusia. "People steal it, which shows its value. This Liszt, this great musician, he steals from us all the time."

"Mamusia, Liszt is long dead," I said, because the University was not wholly overcome in me and I did not want her to appear ignorant to Hollier.

Mamusia was not one to admit error. "The truly great are never dead," she said, and Hollier shouted, "Magnificently said, Madame!"

"Coffee! You have not yet had coffee," she said. "Yerko, give the gentlemen cigars, while Maria and I prepare coffee."

When we returned to the living-room Hollier was looking on, as Darcourt was handling one of the Kings from the *crèche*; Yerko was explaining some detail of his work of ornamentation.

"Here it is! True Kalderash coffee, black as revenge, strong as death, sweet as love! Maria, give this to Professor Hollier."

I took the cup, and handed it instead to Darcourt, because he was nearer. I thought I heard Mamusia draw her breath rather sharply, but I paid no heed to it. I was having a little trouble not to weave and stagger. Apricot brandy, in quantity, is terrible stuff.

Coffee. More coffee. Long, black cheroots with a tangy smell that could have been camel's dung, so powerfully did it evoke the East. I tried to keep command of myself, but I knew my eyelids were falling, and I wondered if I could stay awake until the guests were gone.

At last they did go, and I went with them to the front door, where we kissed again, to end the party. It seemed to me that Darcourt took longer about it than his professor-uncle status quite justified, but after all he was not really old. He had a pleasant smell. I have always been conscious of how people smell, and that is something civilization does not encourage, and countless advertisements tell us every day that it is not the proper thing to have a recognizable human smell at all. My crown ignores smells, but my root has a keen nose, and after the party my root was wholly in charge. Darcourt had a good smell, like a nice, clean man. Hollier, on the other hand, had a slightly fusty smell, like the smell that comes from a trunk when it is opened after many years. Not a bad smell, but not an attractive smell. Perhaps it was the suit. I thought of this as I stood at the door for a moment, watching them walk away in the light snow, taking deep breaths of the sharp air.

When I went back to the flat, I heard Mamusia say to Yerko, in Romany, "No, don't drink that!"

"Why not? Coffee. Hollier didn't drink his second cup."

"Don't drink it, I tell you."

"Why not?"

"Because I say so."

"Have you put something in it?"

"Sugar."

"Of course. But what else?"

"Just a little of something special, for him."

"What?"

"It doesn't matter."

"You lie! What have you put in the professor's cup? He's my friend. You tell me or I'll beat you."

"Oh, if you must know—a little toasted appleseed."

"Yes, and something else—Woman, you put your secret blood in this coffee!"

"No!"

"You lie! What are you doing? Do you want Hollier to love you? You old fool! Wasn't the dear Tadeusz husband enough for you?"

"Keep quiet. Maria will hear. Not my blood—her blood."

"Jesus!—Oh, forgive me, Bebby Jesus!—Maria's! How did you get it?"

"Those things—you know, those *gadje* things she pushes up herself every month. Squeeze one in the garlic squeezer, and— phtt—there you are. She wants Hollier. But she's a fool. I gave her a cup for Hollier and she gave it to Darcourt! Now what do you think will happen?—And you put that cup down, because I won't have incest in this house!"

I rushed into the room, seized Mamusia by the big gold rings in her ears, and tried to throw her on the floor. But she grabbed my hair, and we clung together, like two stags with locked horns, dragging at each other and screaming at the tops of our voices. It was in Romany that I abused Mamusia—remembering terrible words I had forgotten I ever knew. We fell to the floor, and she thrust her face into mine and bit me very hard and painfully on the nose. I was trying, in all seriousness, to tear off her ears. More screams.

Yerko stood over us, shouting at the top of his voice: "Irreverent cunts! What will Bebby Jesus think?" And he kicked me with all his force in the rump, and Mamusia somewhere else that I could not know, because I was lying on the floor howling with pain and fury from the very depths of my Gypsy root.

Far off, the poodles were barking.

The New Aubrey V

IF I THOUGHT MYSELF in love with Maria before Christmas, I was agonizingly certain of it by the beginning of the New Year. I do not use the word 'agonizingly' without consideration; I was a man pulled apart. My diurnal man could come to terms with his situation; so long as the sun was in the sky I could bring reason to bear on my position, but as soon as night fell—and our nights are long in January—my nocturnal man took over and I was worse off than any schoolboy mooning over his first girl.

Worse, because I knew more, had a broader range of feeling to plague me, had seen more of the world, and knew what happens to a professor who falls in love with a student. Young love is supposed to be absorbing and intense and so I know it to be; as a youth I do not think I was ever out of love for more than a week at a time. But love is expected of the young. The glassy eye, the abstracted manner, the heavy sighs are sympathetically observed and indulgently interpreted by the world. But a man of forty-five has other fish to fry. He is thought to have dealt with that side of his nature, and to be settled in his role as husband and father, or satisfied bachelor, or philanderer, or homosexual, or whatever it may be, and to have his mind on other things. But love as I was experiencing it is a mighty consumer of energy and time; it is the primary emotion in the light of which all else is felt, and at my age it is intensified by a full twenty-five years of varied experience of the world, which gives it strength but does not soften it with philosophy or common sense.

I was like a man with a devouring disease, of which he cannot complain and for which he must expect no sympathy.

That dinner party on Boxing Day had thrown my whole emotional and intellectual life out of kilter. What was Maria's mother telling me when she read my fortune in the Tarot? Was she warning me off, with her talk of the Queen of Rods, and a difficult love affair with a dark woman? Had she guessed something about me and Maria? Had Maria guessed something from my manner, and told her mother? Impossible; I had surely been discreet. Anyhow, what right had I to think that the old woman was faking? She appeared to be a charlatan if I compared her with other Rosedale mothers—Hollier's, for instance, from whom nothing extraordinary was ever to be expected—but Madame Laoutaro was a *phuri dai* and not accountable in those terms. Nothing of that extraordinary evening was in the common run of my experience, and something deep inside me gave assurance that it was not just a night out with some displaced Gypsies, but an encounter of primordial weight and significance.

Not merely my own response to it, but Hollier's, assured me that I had been living in a mode of feeling quite different from anything I had ever known. Hollier's fortune was a dark one, and the intensity with which the *phuri dai* read his cards and he listened, had made me fear that something would be said which might better be left unsaid. If she were faking, she would certainly not have told him so much that was ominous. It is true that a Great Trump came to the rescue of both of us, but in Hollier's case that was not until he had made a second choice. No, her work with the Tarot did not smell of charlatanism; like her necklace of Maria Theresa thalers, it was from a different world, but the ring was that of real gold.

So where did that leave me? With a forecast of a love affair in which somebody was to make a difficulty, and which would end happily, though I was to know both a loss and a gain. A love affair I most certainly had.

What an evening that had been! Every detail of it was clear to my mind, even to the queer garlicky aftertaste of the coffee. Clearest was Maria's kiss. Would I ever kiss her again? Not, I was determined, unless I kissed her as an accepted lover.

To think of her kiss and to make my resolve at night had a fine romantic flourish about it: the same thoughts in the morning filled me with something like terror. It was humiliating to face the fact that my love had a hot head and cold feet. But that was the way of it; I wanted the sweets of love but I shrank from the responsibilities of love, and whatever the rules may be for a youth, that is impossible for a middle-aged man, and, what is more, a clergyman. My love had a Janus head; one face, the youthful face, looked backward toward all the pleasures of my earlier days, the joys of love sought and achieved, the kisses, embraces, and the bedding. But the other face, the elder face, looked toward the farce of the old bachelor who marries a young wife—because for me there could be nothing short of marriage. I would offer nothing dishonourable to Maria, and my priesthood forbade any thought of the easy concubinage of the liberated young. But—marriage? Years ago I had put aside thought of any such thing, and it cost me little effort because at that time I did not want to marry anyone in particular, and had taken the view that a parish clergyman loses much if he lacks a wife, but gains more if he can give all his efforts to his work. Was I not too old to change? To confess oneself too old at forty-five to do something as natural as falling in love and getting married was to be old indeed. The more the youthful face of my Janus love sighed and pined, the sterner the look on its older face became.

Consider the realities, said my diurnal man. You live comfortably, you are answerable to nobody else for any of your ordinary habits, you have time for your profession and your private pursuits, especially that spiritual path on which you toil and which has for so long been your chief joy. You do not have to keep a car; the college servants look after you very well, because you distribute something like five hundred dollars a year in tips to them and others who smooth your path. You do not have to live in the suburbs and sweat under a mortgage and worry about bands on your children's teeth. Your state, if not princely, is better than most men of your kind can command, so watch your step, Darcourt, and do nothing foolish. Slothful, comfort-loving beast, cried the nocturnal man. Do you truly set such pursy vulgarities before the completion of your soul? When you put forward such excuses for thwarting the flesh, how can you hope for advancement of the spirit? Fat slug, you are unworthy of the revelation that has been granted to you.

Because, you see, I had decided that Maria was a revelation, and such a revelation that I hardly dare to set it down even for my own eyes.

I left parish work and became a scholar-priest because I wanted to dig deep in mines of old belief that were related, as I have said, to those texts which the compilers of the Bible had not thought suitable for inclusion in the reputed Word of God. That was what I had done and my work had attracted some favourable attention. But he who troubles his head with apocryphal texts will not do so long before he peeps into heretical texts, and without any intention of becoming a Gnostic I found myself greatly taken up with the Gnostics because of the appeal of so much that they had to say. Their notion of Sophia seized upon my mind because it suited some ideas that I had tentatively and fearfully developed of my own accord.

I like women, and the lack of a feminine presence in Christianity has long troubled me. Oh, I am familiar with all the apologies that are offered on that point: I know that Christ had women among his followers, that he liked to talk to women, and that the faithful who remained with him at the foot of his Cross were chiefly women. But whatever Christ may have thought, the elaborate edifice of doctrine we call his church offers no woman in authority—only a Trinity made up, to put it profanely, of two men and a bird—and even the belated amends offered to Mary by the Church of Rome does not undo the mischief. The Gnostics did better than that; they offered their followers Sophia.

Sophia, the feminine personification of God's Wisdom: 'With you is Wisdom, she who knows your works, she who was present when you made the world; she understands what is pleasing in your eyes, and what agrees with your commandments.' Sophia, through whom God became conscious of himself. Sophia, by whose agency the universe was brought to completion, a partner in Creation. Sophia—in my eyes at least—through whom the chill glory of the patriarchal God becomes the embracing splendour of a completed World Soul.

What has all this to do with Maria Magdalena Theotoky, graduate student, under my eye, of New Testament Greek? Maria who, for what I assume was an astonished and certainly not physically ecstatic three minutes, had been possessed by Clement Hollier on his terrible old wreck of a leather sofa? Oh, God, this is where my scholarly madness shows, I suppose, but anybody who concerns himself with the many legends of Sophia knows about the 'fallen Sophia' who put on mortal flesh and sank at last to being a whore in a brothel in Tyre, from which she was rescued by the Gnostic Simon Magus. I myself think of that as the Passion of Sophia, for did she not assume flesh and suffer a shameful fate for the redemption of mankind? It was this that led the Gnostics to hail her both as Wisdom and also as the *anima mundi,* the World Soul, who demands redemption and, in order to achieve it, arouses desire. Well, was not Maria's name Theotoky—the Motherhood of God? Oh, quite useless to tell me that by the Byzantine era Theotoky was a sufficiently common Greek surname, no more to be given special significance than the fairly common English name of Godbehere. But what might be an interesting fact to most scholars was to me a sign, an assurance that my Maria was, perhaps for me alone, a messenger of special grace and redemption.

I suppose that if a man makes legend and forgotten belief his special and devout study he should not be surprised when legend invades his life and possesses his mind. For me Maria was wholeness, the glory and gift of God and also the dark earth as well, so foreign to the conventional Christian mind. The Persians believed that when a man dies he meets his soul in the form of a beautiful woman who is also infinitely old and wise, and this was what seemed to have happened to me, living though I undoubtedly was.

It is a terrible thing for an intellectual when he encounters an idea as a reality, and that was what I had done.

These were the fantasies of my nocturnal man, and all the worldly counsel of the well-set, nicely fixed, book-keeping diurnal man could not beat them down.

So what was I to do? To go backward was base: to go forward an adventure into splendour and terror. But it was forward I must go.

[2]

THOUGH I SAY, as lovers always do, that thoughts of Maria filled all my waking hours, of course it was not so. Whatever people outside universities may think, professors are busy people, made even more busy by the fact that they are often unbusiness-like by nature and thus complicate small matters, and by the fact that they either do not have secretaries or share an overdriven and not always very competent secretary with several others, so that they are involved in a lot of record-keeping, and filing and hunting for things they have lost. They are daily asked for information they never had or have thrown away, and for reports on students they have not seen for five years and have forgotten. They have a reputation for being absent-minded because they are torn between the work they are paid for—which is teaching what they know and enlarging what they know—and the work they never expected to come their way—which is sitting on committees under the direction of chairmen who do not know how to make their colleagues come to a decision. They are required to be business-like in a profession which is not a business, lacks the apparatus of a business, and deals in intangibles. In my case the usual professorial muddle was further complicated by clerical odd jobs, including the delivery of occasional sermons at short notice, and putting friends and the children of friends through the Christian rites of passage, such as baptism, marriage, and burial. Having no parish of my own I was the man many people thought of immediately whenever a parson, often in a distant suburb, fell ill with flu and somebody had to be jobbed in at short notice to turn the crank of the dogma-mill on Sunday morning. But as I was a professor, I could not claim the usual Monday holiday of the clergyman. I am not complaining: I am merely saying that I was a busy man.

Nevertheless, Maria was never far from my thoughts, even when it seemed that the greater part of my small allowance of spare time was demanded by Parlabane and his dreadful novel.

I was never sure precisely how near the novel was to completion, because he had so many drafts and sketches and alternative versions, and because I was never shown the full text. He had all the jealousy and suspicion of an author about his work, and I really think he believed me capable of pinching his ideas if I saw too much of them. He had this same bugbear about publishers and seemed to be in what I thought a ridiculous process of selling a novel that nobody was allowed to read in full.

"You don't understand," he would say, when I protested. "Publishers are always buying books they haven't seen in a completed form. They can tell from a chapter or so whether the thing is any good or not. You constantly read in the papers about huge advances they have paid to somebody on the promise or mere sketch of a work."

"I don't believe all I read in the papers. But I have published two or three books myself."

"Academic stuff. Quite a different matter. Nobody expects a book of yours to sell widely. But this will be a sensation, and I am confident that if it is brought out in the right way, with the right sort of publicity, it will make a fortune."

"Have you offered it to anybody in the States?"

"No. That will come later. I insist on Canadian publication first, because I want it read by those who are most involved before it reaches a wider public."

"Those who are most involved?"

"Certainly. It's a *roman à clef* as well as a *roman philosophique.* There will be some red faces when it comes out, I can tell you."

"Aren't you worried about libel?"

"People won't be in a hurry to claim that they are the originals of most of the characters. Other people will do that for them. And of course I'm not such a fool as to record and transcribe doings and conversations that are too easily identified. But they'll know, don't you worry. And in time everybody else will know, as well."

"It's a revenge novel, then?"

"Sim, you know me better than that! There's nothing small about it. Not a revenge novel. Perhaps a justice novel."

"Justice for you?"

"Justice for me."

I didn't like the sound of it at all. But little by little, as he trusted me with wads of yellow paper on which were messy carbon copies of parts of the great work, I felt certain that the novel would never see publication. It was terrible.

Not terrible in the sense of being wholly incompetent or illiterate. Parlabane was far too able a man for that sort of amateurishness. It was simply unreadable. Ennui swept over me like the effect of a stupefying drug every time I tried to read some of it.

It was a very intellectual novel, very complex in structure, with what seemed like armies of characters, all of whom were personifications of something Parlabane knew, or had heard about, and they said their say in chapter after chapter of leaden prose. One night I said something of the sort, as tactfully as I knew how.

Parlabane laughed. "Of course you can't appreciate the sweep of it, because you haven't seen it all," he said. "The plan is there, but it reveals itself slowly. This isn't a romance for holiday reading, you know. It's a really great book, and I expect that when it has made its first mark, people will read and reread, and discover new depths every time. As they do with Joyce—though it's my ideas that are complex, not my language. You are deceived by its first impression, which is that of a life-story—the intellectual pilgrimage of an uncommon and very rich mind, linked with a questing spirit. I can say this to you because you're an old friend, and up to a point you comprehend my quality. Other readers will comprehend other things, and some will comprehend more. It's a book in which really devoted and understanding readers will find themselves, and thus will find something of the essence of our times. The world is drawing near to the end of one of the Platonic Aeons—the Aeon of Pisces—and gigantic changes are in the air. This book is probably the first of the great books of the New Aeon, the Aeon of Aquarius, and it foreshadows what lies in the future for mankind."

"Aha. Yes, I see. Or rather, I haven't seen. Frankly, it seemed to me to be about you and everybody you've locked horns with since your childhood."

"Well, Sim, you know I don't mean to be nasty, but I'm afraid that is a criticism of you, rather than of my book. You're a man who uses a mirror to see if his tie is straight, not to look into his own eyes. You're no worse than thousands of others will be, when first they read it. But you're a nice old thing, so I'll give you a few clues. Perhaps another drink, just to start me off. I wish you wouldn't measure drinks with that little dinkus. I'll pour my own."

Helping himself to what was really a tumbler of Scotch, with a little water on top for the sake of appearances, he launched into a description of his book most of which I had heard before and all of which I was to hear several times again.

"It's extremely dense in texture, you see. A multiplicity of themes, interwoven and illuminating each other, and written so that every sentence contains a complex nexus of possible meanings, giving rise to a variety of possible interpretations. Meaning is packed within meaning, so that the whole thing unfolds like the many skins of an onion. The book moves forward in the ordinary literal or historical sense, but its real movement is dialectical and moral, and the conclusion is reached by the pressure of successive renunciations, discoveries of error, and what the careful reader discerns to be partial truths."

"Tough stuff."

"Not really. The simple reader can be quite happy with a *literal* interpretation. It will seem to be the biography of a rather foolish and peculiarly perverse young man, born to live in the Spirit, but determined to escape that fate or postpone it as long as possible because he wants to explore the ways of the world and its creatures. It will be quite realistic, you see, so that it may even appear to be a simple narrative. A fool could find it idle or even tedious, but he'll press on because of the spicy parts.

"That's the literal aspect. But of course there is the *allegorical* aspect. The life of the principal character, a young academic, is the journey of a modern Everyman, on a Pilgrim's Progress. The reader follows the movement of his soul from its infantile fantasies, through its adolescent preoccupation with the mechanical and physical aspects of experience, until he discovers logical principles, metaphysics, and particularly scepticism, until he is landed in the dilemmas of middle age—early middle age—and maturity, and finally to his recovery, through imagination, of a unified view of life, of a synthesis of unconscious fantasy, scientific knowledge, and moral mythology, and wisdom that meets in a religious reconciliation of the soul with reality through the acceptance of revealed truth."

"Whew!"

"Hold on a minute. That isn't all. There's the moral dimension of the book. It's a treatise on folly, error, frustration, and exploration of the blind alleys and false theories about life as currently propagated and ineffectually practised. The hero—a not-too-bright adventurer—is looking for the good life in which intellect is at harmony with emotion, intelligence integrated through recollected experience, sentiment tempered by fact, desire directed toward worldly objects and controlled by a sense of humour and proportion."

"I'm glad to hear there is going to be some humour in it."

"Oh, it's all humour from start to finish. The deep, rumbling humour of the fulfilled spirit is at the heart of the book. Like Joyce, but not so confined by the old Jesuit boundaries."

"That'll be nice."

"But the crown of the book is the *anagogical* level of meaning, suggesting the final revelation of the twofold nature of the world, the revelation of experience as the language of God and of life as the preliminary to a quest that cannot be described but only guessed at, because all things point beyond themselves to a glory which is greater than any of them. And thus the hero of the tale—because it is a tale to the simple, as I said—will be found to have been preoccupied all his life with the quest for the Father Image and the Mother Idol to replace the real parents who in real life were inadequate surrogates of the Creator. The quest is never completed, but the preoccupation with Image and Idol gradually gives way to the conviction of the reality of the Reality which lies behind the shadows which constitute the actual moment as it rushes by."

"You've bitten off quite a substantial chunk."

"Yes indeed. But I can chew it because I've lived it, you see. I gained my philosophy in youth, took it out into the world and tested it."

"But Johnny, I hate to say this, but what you've allowed me to read doesn't make me want to read more."

"You haven't seen the whole thing."

"Has anyone?"

"Hollier has a complete typescript."

"And what does he say?"

"I haven't been able to tie him down to a real talk about it. He says he's very busy, and I suppose he is, though I think reading this ought to come before the trivialities that eat up his time. I'm shameless, I know. But this is a great book, and sooner or later he is going to have to come to terms with it."

"What have you done about publication?"

"I've written a careful description of the book—the plan, the themes, the depths of meaning—and sent it to all the principal publishers. I've sent a sample chapter to each one, because I don't want them to see the whole thing until I know how serious they are and what sort of deal they are prepared to make."

"Any bites?"

"One editor asked me to have lunch with him, but at the last moment his secretary called to say that he couldn't make it. Another one called to ask if there were what he called 'explicit' scenes in it."

"Ah, the old buggery bit. Very fashionable now."

"Of course there's a good deal of that in it, but unless it's taken as an integral part of the book it's likely to be mistaken for pornography. The book is frank—much franker than anything else I've seen—but not pornographic. I mean, it wouldn't excite anybody."

"How can you tell?"

"Well—perhaps it might. But I want the reader to experience as far as possible everything that is experienced by the hero, and that includes the ecstasy of love as well as the disgust and filthiness of sex."

"You won't get far with modern readers by telling them that sex is filthy. Sex is very fashionable at present. Not just necessary, or pleasurable, or natural, but fashionable, which is quite a different thing."

"Middle-class fucking. My jail-buggery isn't like that at all. The one is Colonel Sanders' finger-lickin' chicken, and the other is fighting for a scrap of garbage in Belsen."

"That might sell very well."

"Don't be a crass fool, Sim. This is a great book, and although I expect it to sell widely and become a classic, I'm not writing nastiness for the bourgeois market."

A classic. As I looked at him, so unkempt and messy in the ruin of a once-good suit of my own, I wondered if he could truly have written a classic novel. How would I know? Identifying classics of literature is not my job and I have the usual guilt that is imposed on all of us by the knowledge that in the past people have refused to recognize classics, and have afterward looked like fools because of it. One has a certain reluctance to believe that anybody one knows, and particularly anybody looking such a failure and crook as Parlabane, is the author of something significant. Anyhow, he hadn't permitted me to read the whole thing, so obviously he thought me unworthy, a sadly limited creature not up to comprehending its quality. The burden of declaring his book a great one had not been laid on me. But I was curious. As custodian of *The New Aubrey* it was up to me to find out if I could, and record genius if genius came into my ken.

Identifying classics may be considered outside my capacity, but several fund-granting bodies are prepared to take my word about the abilities of students who want money to continue their studies, and after Parlabane had left I settled to the job of filling in several of the forms such bodies provide for the people they call referees, and the students refer to as 'resource persons'. So I turned off whatever part of me was Parlabane's confidant, and the part which was the compiler of *The New Aubrey,* and the part—the demanding, aching part—that yearned for Maria-Sophia, and set to work on a pile of such forms, all of which had been brought to me at the last moment by anxious but ill-organized students, all of which had to be sent to the grantors immediately, and upon which it was apparently my task to affix the necessary postage; the students had not done so.

Outside my window lay the quadrangle of Ploughwright and although it was still too early to be called Spring, the fountains which never quite froze were making gentle music below their crowns of ice. How peaceful it looked, even at this ruinous time of the year. 'A garden enclosed is my sister; my spouse, a spring shut up, a fountain sealed.' How I loved her! Was it not strange that a man of my age should feel it so painfully? Get to work, Simon. Work, supposed anodyne of all pain.

As I bent over my desk, my mood sank toward misanthropy. What would happen, I wondered, if I filled out these forms honestly? First: *Say how long you have known the applicant.* There were few whom I could claim to know at all, in any serious sense of the word, for I saw them only in seminars. *In what capacity do you know him/her?* As a teacher; why else would I be filling in this form? *Of the students you have known in this way, would you rank the applicant in the first five percent—ten percent—twenty-five percent?* Well, my dear grantor, it depends on your standards; most of them are all right, in a general way. Aha, but here we

get down to cases; *Make any personal comment you consider relevant.*
This is where a referee or resource person is expected to pour
on the oil. But I am sick of lying.

So, after an hour and a half of soul-searching, I found that I
had said of one young fellow, 'He is a good-natured slob, and
there is no particular harm in him, but he simply doesn't know
what work means.' Of another: 'Treacherous; never turn your
back on him.' Of a third: 'Is living on a woman who thinks he is
a genius; perhaps any grant you give him ought to be based on
her earning capacity; she is quite a good stenographer, with a
B.A. of her own, but she is plain and I suspect that once he has
his doctorate he will discover that his affections lie elsewhere.
This is a common pattern, and probably doesn't concern you, but
it grieves me.' Of a young woman: 'Her mind is as flat as Holland—the salt-marshes, not the tulip fields—stretching toward
the horizon in all directions and covered by a leaden sky. But
unquestionably she will make a Ph.D.—of a kind.'

Having completed this Slaughter of the Innocents—innocent
in their belief that I would do anything I could to get them
money—I hastily closed the envelopes, lest some weak remorse
overtake me. What will the Canada Council make of that, I wondered, and was cheered by the hope that I had caused that body
a lot of puzzlement and confusion. Tohubohu and brouhaha, as
Maria loved to say. Ah, Maria!

Next day at lunch in the Hall of Spook I saw Hollier sitting
alone at a table which is used for the overflow from the principal
dons' table, and I joined him.

"About this book of Parlabane's," I said; "is it really something
extraordinary?"

"I've no idea. I haven't time to read it. I've given it to Maria
to read. She'll tell me."

"Given it to Maria! Won't he be furious?"

"I don't know and I don't much care. I think she has a right to
read it, if she wants to; she seems to be putting up the money to
have it professionally typed."

"He's touched me substantially for money to have that done."

"Are you surprised? He touches everybody. I'm sick of his
cadging."

"Has she said anything?"

"She hasn't got far with it. Has to read it on the QT because he's always bouncing in and out of my rooms. But I've seen her puzzling over it, and she sighs a lot."

"That's what it made me do."

But a few days later the situation was reversed, for Hollier joined me at lunch.

"I met Carpenter the other day; the publisher, you know. He has Parlabane's book or part of it, and I asked him what he thought."

"And—?"

"He hasn't read it. Publishers have no time to read books, as I suppose you know. He handed it on to a professional reader and appraiser. The report, based on a description and a sample chapter, isn't encouraging."

"Really?"

"Carpenter says they get two or three such books every year— long, wandering, many-layered things with an elaborate structure, and a heavy freight of philosophy, but really self-justifying autobiographies. He's sending it back."

"Parlabane will be disappointed."

"Perhaps not. Carpenter says he always sends a personal letter to ease the blow, suggesting that the book be sent to somebody else, who does more in that line. You know: the old down-ready-pass."

"Has Maria got on any farther with it?"

"She's beavering away at it. Chiefly because of the title, I think."

"I didn't know it had a title."

"Yes indeed, and just as tricky as the rest of the thing. It's called *Be Not Another*."

"Hm. I'm not sure that I would snatch for a book called *Be Not Another*. Why does Maria like it?"

"It's a quotation from one of her favourite writers. Paracelsus. She persuaded Parlabane to read some of Paracelsus and Johnny stuck in his thumb and pulled out a plum. Paracelsus said, *Alterius non sit, qui suus esse potest;* Be not another's if thou canst be thyself."

"I know Latin too, Clem."

"I suppose you must. Well, that's what it comes from. Rotten, if you ask me, but he thinks it will look well on the title-page, in italic. A hint to the reader that something fine is in store."

"I suppose it is a good title, if you look at it understandingly. Certainly Parlabane is very much himself."

"I wish people weren't so set on being themselves, when that means being a bastard. I'm surer than ever that McVarish has that manuscript you didn't dig out of him. I can't get it out of my mind. It's becoming an obsession. Have you any idea what an obsession is?"

Yes, I had a very good idea what an obsession is. Maria. Sophia.

[3]

"I'VE BEEN SEEING SOMETHING of that girl who was here last time you visited me," said Ozy Froats. "You know the one— Maria."

Indeed I know the one. And what was she doing in Ozy's lab? Not bringing him a daily bucket for analysis, surely?

"She's been introducing me to Paracelsus. He's a lot more interesting than I would have suspected. Some extraordinary insights, but of course without any way of verifying them. Still, it's amazing how far he got by guesswork."

"You won't yield an inch to the intuition of a great man, will you Ozy?"

"Not a millimetre. No, I guess I have to hedge on that. Every scientist has intuitions and they scare the hell out of him till he can test them. Great men are rare, you see."

"But you're one. This award has lifted you right above the clutch of Murray Brown, hasn't it?"

"The Kober Medal, you mean? Not bad. Not bad at all."

"Puts you in the Nobel class, they tell me."

"Oh, these awards—I'm very pleased, of course—but you have to be careful not to mistake them for real achievement. I'm glad to be noticed. I have to give a lecture when I get it, you know. That's when I'll find out what the boys really think, by the way they take it. But I haven't shown all I want to show, by any means."

"Ozy, the modesty of you great men is sickening to those of

us who just plug along, doing the best we can and knowing it isn't very much. The American College of Physicians gives you the best thing they have, and you demur and grovel. It isn't modesty; it's masochism. You like suffering and running yourself down. You make me sick. I suppose it's your Sheldonian type."

"It's a Mennonite upbringing, Simon. Beware of pride. You people are all so nice to me, I have to watch out I don't begin patting myself on the back too much. Maria, now, she insists I'm a magus."

"I suppose you are one, in her terms."

"She wrote me a sweet letter. A quotation from Paracelsus, mostly. I carry it around, which is a sign of weakness. But listen to the quote: 'The natural saints, who are called magi, are given powers over the energies and faculties of nature. For there are holy men in God who serve the beatific life; they are called saints. But there are also holy men who serve the forces of nature, and they are called magi. . . . What others are incapable of doing they can do, because it has been conferred upon them as a special gift.' If a man started thinking of himself in those terms, he'd be finished as a scientist. Doubt, doubt, and still more doubt, until you're dead sure. That's the only way."

"If Maria wrote to me like that, I'd believe her."

"Why?"

"I think she knows. She has extraordinary intuition about people."

"Do you think? She sent me a very queer fish, and he's certainly an oddity in Sheldonian terms, so I've put him on the bucket. An interesting contributor, but only about once a week."

"Anybody I know?"

"Now Simon, you know I couldn't tell you his name. Not ethical at all. Sometimes we talk about doubt. He's a great doubter. Used to be a monk. The interesting thing about him is his Sheldonian type. Very rare; a 376. You follow? Very intellectual and nervy, but a fantastic physique. A dangerous man, I'd say, with a makeup like that. Could get very rough. He's abused his body just about every way that's possible and from the whiff of his buckets I think he's well into drugs right now, but although he's on the small side he's fantastically muscular and strong. He wants the money, but he isn't a big producer. Plugged. That's drugs. I don't like him, but he's a rarity, so I put up with him."

"For Maria's sake?"

"No. For my sake. Listen, you don't think I'm soft about Maria, do you? She's a nice girl enough, but that's all."

"Not an interesting type?"

"Not from my point of view. Too well balanced."

"No chance she might turn out to be a Pyknic Practical Joke?"

"Never. She'll age well. Be a fine old woman. Slumped, probably; that's inherent in the female build. But she'll be sturdy, right up to the end."

"Ozy, about these Sheldonian types; are they irrevocable?"

"How do you mean?"

"Last time I talked to you, you were very frank about me, and my tendency toward fat. Do you remember?"

"Yes; that was the first time Maria came here. What I said about you wasn't the result of an examination, of course. Just a guess. But I'd put you down as a 425—soft, chunky, abundant energy. Big gut."

"The literary gut, I think you said."

"Lots of literary people have it. You can have a big gut without being literary, of course."

"Don't rob me of the one consolation you offered! But what I want to know is this: couldn't somebody of that type moderate his physique, by the right kind of diet and exercise, and general care?"

"To some extent. Not without more trouble than it would probably be worth. That's what's wrong with all these diets and body-building courses and so forth. You can go against your type, and probably achieve a good deal as long as you keep at it. Look at these Hollywood stars—they starve themselves and get surgeons to carve them into better shapes and all that because it's their livelihood. Every now and then one of them can't stand it any more, then it's the overdose. The body is the inescapable factor, you see. You can keep in good shape for what you are, but radical change is impossible. Health isn't making everybody into a Greek ideal; it's living out the destiny of the body. If you're thinking about yourself, I guess you could knock off twenty-five pounds to advantage, but that wouldn't make you a thin man; it'd make you a neater fat man. What the cost would be to your nerves, I couldn't even guess."

"In short, be not another if thou canst be thyself."

"What's that?"

"More Paracelsus."

"He's dead right. But it isn't simple, being yourself. You have to know yourself physiologically and people don't want to believe the truth about themselves. They get some mental picture of themselves and then they devil the poor old body, trying to make it like the picture. When it won't obey—can't obey, of course— they are mad at it, and live in it as if it were an unsatisfactory house they were hoping to move out of. A lot of illness comes from that."

"You make it sound like physiological predestination."

"Don't quote me on that. Not my field at all. I have my problem and it's all I can take care of."

"Discovering the value that lies in what is despised and rejected."

"That's what Maria says. But wouldn't I look stupid if I announced that as the theme of my Kober Lecture?"

" 'This is the stone which was set at naught of your builders, which is become the head of the corner.' "

"You don't talk that way to scientists, Simon."

"Then tell them it is the *lapis exilis,* the Philosopher's Stone of their spiritual ancestors, the alchemists."

"Oh, get away, get away, get away!"

Laughing, I got away.

[4]

I SET TO WORK TO BECOME a neater fat man, as that seemed to be the best I could hope for, and sank rapidly into the ill-nature that overcomes me when I deny myself a reasonable amount of rich food and creamy desserts. I thought sourly of Ozy, and great man though he might be, I reflected that I could give a better Kober Lecture than he, fattening out my scientific information with plums from Paracelsus and giving it a persuasive humanistic gloss that would wake up the audience from the puritan stupor of their scientific attitude. Whereupon I immediately reproached myself for vanity. What did I know about Ozy's work? What was I but a silly fat ass whose pudgy body was the conning-tower from which a thin and acerbic soul peered out at the world? No: that wouldn't do either. I wasn't as fat as that suggested, nor was my spirit really sour when I allowed myself enough to eat. I wasted a lot of time in this sort of foolish inner wrangling, and the measure of my abjection is that once or twice—besotted lover as I was—I wondered if Maria were really worth all this trouble.

One of Parlabane's tedious whims was that he liked to take baths in my bathroom; he said that the arrangements at his boarding-house were primitive. He was a luxurious bather and a great man for parading about naked, which was not unselfconsciousness but calculated display. He was vain of his body, as well he might be, for at the same age as myself he was firm and muscular, had slim ankles and that impressive contour of belly in which the rectus muscles may be seen, like Roman armour. It was surely unjust that a man who had drugged and boozed for twenty years and who was, by Ozy's account, decidedly constipated, should look so well in the buff. His face, of course, was a mess, and he could not see very much without his glasses, but even so he was an impressive and striking contrast to the man who removed my old suit and some lamentable underclothes. Clothed he looked shabby and sinister; naked he looked disturbingly like Satan in a drawing by Blake. Not at all a man with whom one would want to get into a fight.

"I wish I were in as good shape as you are," said I, on one of these occasions.

"Don't wish it if you hope to be remembered as a theologian," said he; "they are all bonies or fatties. Not one like me in the lot. Put on another forty pounds, Simon, and you'll be about the size of Aquinas when he confuted the Manichees. You know he got so fat they had to make him a special altar with a half-moon carved out of it to accommodate his tum? You have a long way to go yet."

"I have it on the assurance of Ozy Froats, now distinguished and justified as the latest recipient of the Kober Medal, that I am of the literary sort of physique," said I. "I have what Ozy calls the literary gut. Perhaps if you had a gently swelling belly like mine, instead of that fine washboard of muscles that I envy, your novel might read more easily."

"I'd gladly take on the burden of your paunch if I could get a decisive answer from a publisher."

"Nothing doing yet?"

"Four rejections."

"That seems decisive, so far as it goes."

He sank into one of my armchairs, naked as he was, and though he was clearly much dejected, his muscles held firm, and he looked rather splendid (except for his thick specs), like a figure of a defeated author by Rodin.

"No. The only decisive answer that I will recognize is an acceptance of the book, on my terms, for publication as soon as possible."

"Oh, come; I didn't mean to be discouraging. But—four rejections! It's nothing at all. You must simply hang on and keep pestering publishers. Lots of authors have gone on doing that for years."

"I know, but I won't. I feel at the end of my tether."

"It's Lent, as I don't have to remind you. The most discouraging season of the year."

"Do you do much about Lent, Simon?"

"I'm eating less, but that's incidental. What I usually do is take on a program of introspection and self-examination—try to tidy myself up a bit. Do you?"

"I'm coming unstuck, Simon. It's the book. I can't get anybody to take it seriously, and it's killing me. It's my life, far more than I had suspected."

"Your autobiography, you mean?"

"Hell no! I've told you it isn't meanly autobiographical. But it's the best of me, and if it's ignored, what of me will survive? You're too fat to have any idea what an obsession is."

"I'm sorry, John. I didn't mean to be flippant."

"It's what I've salvaged from a not very square deal in this miserable hole of a world. It's all of me—root and crown. You don't know what I would do to get it published."

He grew more and more miserable, but did not lose his sense of self-preservation, because before he left he had touched me for two more shirts and some socks and another hundred dollars, which was all I had in my desk. I hate to seem mean-spirited, but I was growing tired of listening to the romantic agonies of his spirit, while forking out to sustain the wants of his flesh.

He earned money. Not much, but enough to keep him. What did he spend my money, and Maria's money, and Hollier's money on?

Could it really be drugs? He looked too well. Drink? He drank a good deal when he could sponge on somebody, but he didn't have any sign of being a drunkard. Where did the money go? I didn't know but I resented being continually asked for contributions.

[5]

LENT, PROPER SEASON for self-examination, perhaps for self-mortification, but never, so far as I know, a season for love. Nevertheless, love was my daily companion, my penance, my hair shirt. Something had to be done about it, but what? Face the facts, Simon; how does a clergyman of forty-five manoeuvre himself into a position where he can tell a young woman of twenty-three that he loves her, and what does she think about that? What might she be expected to think? Face facts, fool.

But can one, in the grip of an obsession, face facts or even judge what facts are relevant?

I worked out several scenarios and planned a number of eminently reasonable but warmly worded speeches; then, as often happens, it all came about suddenly and, considering everything, easily. As Hollier's research assistant, Maria had the privilege of eating with the dons in Spook's Hall at dinner, and one night in late March I met her just after the Rector had said the grace that ended the meal, as we were moving toward coffee in the Senior Common Room. Or rather, I was heading toward coffee and asked her if I could bring some to her. No, she said, Spook coffee wasn't what she wanted at the moment. I saw an opening, and snatched it.

"If you would like to walk over to my rooms in Ploughwright, I'll make you some really good coffee. I could also give you cognac, if you'd like that."

"I'd love it."

Five minutes later she was helping me—watching me, really—as I set my little Viennese coffee-maker on the electric element.

Fifteen minutes later I had told her that I loved her and, rather more coherently than I had ever expected, I told her about the notion of Sophia (with which she was acquainted from her medieval studies) and that she was Sophia to me. She sat silent for what seemed a long time.

"I've never been so flattered in my life," she said at last.

"Then the idea doesn't seem totally ridiculous to you."

"Certainly not ridiculous. How could you think of yourself as ridiculous?"

"A man of my age, in love with a woman of your age, could certainly seem ridiculous."

"But you're not just any man of your age. You are a beautiful man. I've admired you ever since the first class where I met you."

"Maria, don't tease me. I know what I am. I'm middle-aged and not at all good-looking."

"Oh, that! I meant beautiful because of your wonderful spirit, and the marvellous love you bring to your scholarship. Why would anybody care what you look like?—Oh, that sounds terrible; you look just right for what you are. But looks don't really matter, do they?"

"How can you say that? You, who are so beautiful yourself?"

"If your looks attracted as much attention as mine do, and made people think so many stupid things about you, you'd see it all differently."

"Does what I've told you I think about you seem stupid?"

"No, no; I didn't mean that. What you've said, coming from you, is the most wonderful compliment I've ever had."

"So what do we do about it? Dare I ask if you love me?"

"Yes, most certainly I do love you. But I don't think it's the kind of love you mean when you tell me you love me."

"Then—?"

"I must think very carefully about what I say. I love you, but I've never even called you Simon. I love you because of your power to lead me to understand things I didn't understand before, or understand in the same way. I love you because you have made your learning the chief nourisher of your life, and it has made you a special sort of man. You are like a fire; you warm me."

"So what are we to do about it?"

"Must we do something about it? Aren't we doing something about it already? If I am Sophia to you, what do you suppose you are to me?"

"I'm not sure I understand. You say you love me, and I am something great to you. So are we to become lovers?"

"I think we already are lovers."

"I mean differently. Completely."

"You mean a love affair? Going to bed and all that?"

"Is it out of the question?"

"No, but I think it would be a great mistake."

"Oh, Maria, can you be sure? Look, you know what I am; I'm a clergyman. I'm not asking you to be my mistress. I think that would be shabby."

"Well, I certainly couldn't marry you!"

"You mean it's utterly out of the question?"

"Utterly."

"Ah. But I can't make dishonourable proposals to you. Don't think it's just prudery—"

"No, no; I really do understand. 'You could not love me, dear, so much/Loved you not honour more.' "

"Not just honour. You can put it like that, but it's something weightier than honour. I am a priest forever, after the order of Melchisedek; it binds me to live by certain inflexible rules. If I take you without giving you an oath before an altar it wouldn't be long before I was something you would hate; I would be a renegade priest. Not a drunkard, or a lecher, or anything comparatively simple and perhaps forgivable, but an oath-breaker. Can you understand that?"

"Yes, I can understand it perfectly. You would have broken an oath to God."

"Yes. You do understand it. Thank you, Maria."

"I'm sure you will admit I'd cut a strange figure as the wife of a clergyman. And—forgive me for saying this—I don't think it's really a wife you want, Simon. You want someone to love. Can't you love me without bringing in all these side-issues about marriage and going to bed and things that I don't really think have any bearing on what we are talking about?"

"You certainly ask a lot! Don't you know anything about men?"

"Not a great deal. But I think I know quite a lot about you."

As soon as I had said it I wished it unsaid, but the jealous spirit was too quick for me. "You don't know as much about me as you do about Hollier!"

She turned pale, which made her skin an olive shade. "Who told you about that? I don't suppose I need to ask; he must have told you."

"Maria! Maria, you must understand—it wasn't like that! He wasn't boasting or stupid; he was wretched and he told me because I am a priest, and I should never have given you a hint!"

"Is that true?"

"I swear it is true."

"Then listen to me, because this is true. I love Hollier. I love him the way I love you—for the splendid thing you are, in your own world of splendid things. Like a fool I wanted him the way you are talking about, and whether it was because I wanted him or he wanted me I don't know and never shall know, but it was a very great mistake. Because of that stupidity, which didn't amount to a damn as an experience, I think I have put something between us that has almost lost him to me. Do you think I want to do that with you? Are all men such greedy fools that they think love only comes with that special favour?"

"The world thinks of it as the completion of love."

"Then the world still has something important to learn. Simon, you called me Sophia: the Divine Wisdom, God's partner and playmate in Creation. Now perhaps I am going to surprise you: I agree that I am Sophia to you, and I can be that for as long as you wish, but I must be my own human Maria-self as well, and if we go to bed it may be Sophia who lies down but it will certainly be Maria—and not the best of her—who gets up, and Sophia will be gone forever. And you, Simon dear, would come into bed as my Rebel Angel, but very soon you would be a stoutish Anglican parson, and a Rebel Angel no more."

"A Rebel Angel?"

"You don't mean to tell me that I can teach you something, after the very non-academic talk we have had? Oh, Simon, you must remember the Rebel Angels? They were real angels, Samahazai and Azazel, and they betrayed the secrets of Heaven to King Solomon, and God threw them out of Heaven. And did they mope and plot vengeance? Not they! They weren't sore-headed egotists like Lucifer. Instead they gave mankind another push up the ladder, they came to earth and taught tongues, and healing and laws and hygiene—taught everything—and they were often special successes with 'the daughters of men'. It's a mar-vellous piece of apocrypha, and I would have expected you to know it, because surely it is the explanation of the origin of universities! God doesn't come out of some of these stories in a very good light, does He? Job had to tell Him a few home truths about His injustice and caprice; the Rebel Angels showed Him that hiding all knowledge and wisdom and keeping it for Himself was dog-in-the-manger behaviour. I've always taken it as proof that we'll civilize God yet. So don't, Simon dear, don't rob me of my Rebel Angel by wanting to be an ordinary human lover, and I won't rob you of Sophia. You and Hollier are my Rebel Angels, but as you are the first to be told you may choose which one you will be: Samahazai or Azazel?"

"Samahazai, every time! Azazel is too zizzy."

"Dear Simon!"

We talked for another hour, but nothing was said that had not been said already in one way or another, and when we parted I did indeed kiss Maria, not as an ordinary lover or one who had been promised a marriage, but in a spirit I had never known before.

Since the dinner on Boxing Day I had drunk deep of Siren tears, and to my exultant delight that trial seemed to be over. I slept like a child and woke the next day immeasurably refreshed.

[6]

"HELLO? HELLO—ARE YOU the Reverend Darcourt? Listen, it's about this fella John Parlabane: he's dead. Dead in bed with the light on. There's a letter says to call you. So you'll come, eh? Because something's got to be done. I can't be expected to deal with this kinda thing."

Thus Parlabane's landlady, who sounded as if she belonged to the tradition of affronted, put-upon landladies, calling me shortly after six o'clock on the morning of Easter Sunday. Doctors and parish clergymen are old hands at emergencies, and know that

rarely is anything so pressing that there is not time to dress properly, and drink a cup of instant coffee while doing so. Figures of
authority should be composed when they arrive at the scene of
whatever human mess awaits them. Parlabane's boarding-house
was not far from the University, and it was not long before I was
listening to Mrs. Mustard's excited, angry story as we trudged
upstairs. She had risen early to go to seven o'clock church, had
seen a light under his door, was always telling 'em they weren't
to waste current, knocked and couldn't rouse him, so in she went,
expecting to find him drunk as he so often was—him that tried
to pass himself off as some kind of a brother—and there he was
on the bed with what looked like a smile on his face and couldn't
be roused and was icy cold, and no, she hadn't called a doctor,
and she certainly didn't want any trouble.

In the small, humble room, which Parlabane had managed to
invest with a squalor that was not inherent in it, he lay on his
narrow iron bed, dressed in his monk's robe, his Monastic Diurnal
clasped in his hands, looking well pleased with himself, but not
smiling; the dead do not smile except under the embalmer's expert
hand. Propped on his table was a letter addressed to me, with
my telephone number on the envelope.

Suicide, I thought. I cannot say that I reassured Mrs. Mustard,
but I calmed her down as much as I could, and then telephoned
a doctor whom Parlabane and I had both known as a college
friend, and asked him to come. In twenty minutes or so he was
with me, also fully clothed and smelling perceptibly of instant
coffee. Oh, what a boon powdered coffee is to parsons and doctors!

While waiting, I had read the letter, having got rid of Mrs.
Mustard by asking if she would be so good as to make some
coffee—preferably not instant coffee, I said, so as to keep her
out of the way for a while.

It was a characteristic Parlabane letter.

Dear Old Simon:
Sorry to let you in for this, but somebody must cope, and it
is part of your profession, isn't it? I really cannot expect too
much of La Mustard, to whom I owe quite a bit of back rent.
That, and other debts, may be discharged out of the advance

of my novel, which ought to be coming along soon. You think not? Shame on you for a doubter! Meanwhile I do very deeply want a Christian burial service, so will you add that to a long list of favours—see Johnny safely into his beddy-bye as you sometimes did when we were young at Spook—though you would never take the risk of joining him there, you old fraidy-cat. . . . God bless you, Sim—Your brother in Xt.

John Parlabane, S.S.M.

It was a relief when the doctor came, examined the body and said unnecessarily that Parlabane was dead, and surprisingly that he couldn't say why.

"No sign of anything," he said; "he's dead because his heart has stopped beating, and that's all I can put on the certificate. Cardiac arrest, which is what finishes us all really."

"Any suggestion that it was self-induced?" I asked.

"None. That's what I expected, you know, when you called me. But I can't find a puncture or a mark or anything that would account for it. No sign of poison—you know, there's usually something. He looks so pleased with himself, there can't have been any distress at the end. I'd have expected suicide, frankly."

"So would I, but I'm glad it isn't so."

"Yes, I guess it lets you off the hook, doesn't it?"

By which my old friend the doctor paid tribute to the widely held notion that clergymen of my persuasion are not permitted to say the burial service over suicides. In fact, we are allowed great latitude, and charity usually wins the day.

So I did what was necessary, adding extra work to my Easter Sunday, which was already a busy day. There was a little unseemly trouble with Mrs. Mustard, who didn't want the body to be taken out of her house until her debt was paid. So I paid it, wondering how long she would have held out if I had allowed her to keep Parlabane in his present state. Poor woman, I suppose she led a dog's life, and it made her disagreeable, which she mistook for being strong.

The following day, Easter Monday morning, I read the Burial Service for Parlabane at the chapel of St. James the Less, which is handy to the crematorium. As I waited to see if anyone would turn up, I reflected on what I was about to do. There I stood, in cassock, surplice, and scarf, the Professional Dispatcher. How much did I believe of what I was about to say? How much had Parlabane believed? The resurrection of the body, for instance? No use havering about that now; he had asked for it and he should have it. The Burial Service was noble—splendid music not to be examined like an insurance policy.

Besides myself only Hollier and Maria were present. The undertaker, misled by Parlabane's robe into thinking him a priest, had placed the body with its head toward the altar, and I did not trouble to have the position changed. I had already explained to the undertaker that the corpse did not really need underclothes; Parlabane had died naked under his robe, and that was the way I sent him to the flames; I did not want to court a reputation for eccentricity by asking for further revisions in what the undertaker thought was proper.

The atmosphere was understandably intimate, and at the appropriate moment in the service I said: "This is where the priest usually says something about the person whose human shell is being sent on its way. But as we are few, and all friends of his, perhaps we might talk about him for a while. I think he was a man to be pitied, but he would have scorned pity; his spirit was defiant and proud. He asked for a Christian burial service, and that is why we are here. In a manner that was very much his own he professed a great feeling for the Christian faith but seemed to scorn most of the virtues Christians are supposed to hold dear. It was as if faith and pride were at war in him: he knew nothing of humility. I confess I don't know what to make of him; I think he meant to be jokey but was really contemptuous. My belief bids me forgive him, and I do; he asked for this service and it is out of the question for me to refuse it; but I wish I could honestly say that I had liked him."

"He did everything in his power to make it impossible to like him," said Maria. "In spite of all his smiles and caressing jokes and words of endearment, he was deeply contemptuous of everyone."

"I liked him," said Hollier; "but then, I knew him better than either of you. I suppose I looked on him as one of my cultural fossils; the day has gone when people feel that they can be unashamedly arrogant about superior intellect. We are hypocritical about that. He was quite open about it; he thought we were dullards and he certainly thought I was intellectually fraudulent. In this he was a throwback to the great days of Paracelsus and Cornelius Agrippa—yes, and of Rabelais—when people who knew a lot sneered elaborately at anybody they considered an intellectual inferior. There was something refreshing about him. Pity that novel of his was so bad; it was really one huge sneer from start to finish, whatever he may have thought about it."

"He seems to have died believing that it would see publication," I said. "His last letter to me says his debts could be paid out of the advance from his publisher."

"Don't you believe it," said Hollier. "He simply never admitted what he knew to be the truth—that he lived by sponging. And that reminds me, Simon, who's paying the shot for this?"

"I suppose I am," I said.

"No, no," said Hollier; "I must put in for it. Why should you do it all?"

"Of course," said Maria; "that's the way it was while he was alive and it had better be the same to the end. He died owing me just under nine hundred dollars; another hundred won't break me."

"Oh it won't be anything like that," I said; "I arranged this on the cheapest terms. With the burial costs and what he owed his landlady, and odds and ends, I reckon it will run us each about— well, you're closer than I thought, Maria; it will probably be more than two hundred apiece.—Oh, dear, this is very unseemly. I meant that we should think seriously and kindly about him for a few minutes, and here we are haggling about his debts."

"Serve him damned well right," said Hollier. "If he is anywhere about, he's laughing his head off."

"He could have left Rabelais's will," said Maria. " 'I owe much, I have nothing, the rest I leave to the poor,' " and she laughed.

Hollier and I caught the infection and we were laughing loudly when the undertaker's man stuck his head into the chancel from the little room where he was lurking, and coughed. I knew the signal; Parlabane must be whisked off to the crematory before lunch.

"Let us pray," said I.

"Yes," said Hollier; "and afterward—the cleansing flames."

More laughter. The undertaker's man, though he had probably seen some queer funerals, looked scandalized. I have never laughed my way through the Committal before, but I did so now.

We met outside after I had seen the coffin on its way. There was no need for me to return for the burning.

"I can't think when I've enjoyed a funeral so much," said Hollier.

"I feel a sense of relief," said Maria. "I suppose I ought to be ashamed of it—but no, I don't really suppose anything of the kind. I'm just relieved. He was getting to be an awful burden, and now it's gone."

"What about lunch?" said I. "Please let me take you. It was good of you to come."

"Couldn't think of it," said Hollier. "After all, you made the arrangements and actually read the service. You've done enough."

"I won't go unless you let me pay," said Maria. "If you want a reason, let's say it's because I'm happier than either of you that he's gone. Gone forever."

So we agreed, and Maria paid, and lunch stretched out until after three, and we all enjoyed ourselves immensely at what we called Parlabane's Wake. Driving to the University, where none of us had been earlier in the day, we noticed that the flag on the main campus was at half-staff. We did not bother to wonder why; a big university is always regretting the death of one of its worthies.

Second Paradise VI

FEBRUARY: UNQUESTIONABLY CRISIS MONTH in the University, and probably everywhere else in our Canadian winter. Crisis was raging all about me in Mamusia's sitting-room where, for at least an hour, Hollier had been circling his obsession with Urquhart McVarish and the Gryphius MS without ever coming to grips with the realities of the matter. The room seemed darker even than five o'clock in February could explain. I kept my head low and watched, and watched, and feared, and feared.

"Why don't you say what you want, Hollier? Why don't you speak what is in your mind? Do you think you can fool me? You talk and talk, but what you want shouts louder than what you say. Look here—you want to buy a curse from me. That's what you want. No?"

"It is difficult to explain, Madame Laoutaro."

"But not hard to understand. You want these letters, this book, whatever it is. This other fellow has it and he teases you because you can't get it. You hate him. You want him out of your way. You want that book. You want him punished."

"There are considerations of scholarship—"

"You've told me that. You think you can do whatever can be done with this book better than he can. But most of all, you want to be first with whatever that is. No?"

"Very bluntly put, I suppose that's it."

"Why not bluntly? Look: you come and you flatter me and tell me I'm a *phuri dai*, and you tell me this long story about this enemy who is making your life a hell, and you think I don't know what you want? You talk about me becoming your colleague in a fascinating experiment. You mean you want me to be your *cohani*, who casts the evil spell. You talk about the Dark World and the—what's the word—Chthonic Powers and all this professor-talk, but what you mean is Magic, isn't it? Because you're in a situation that can't be dealt with in nice, fancy professor terms and you think maybe the black old stuff might serve you. But you're scared to come right out and ask. Am I right?"

"I'm not a fool, Madame. I have spent twenty years circling round and round the sort of thing we are talking about now. I've examined it in the best and most objective way the scholarly world makes possible. But I haven't swallowed it wholesale. My present problem turns my mind to it, of course, and you are right—I do want to invoke some special means of getting what I want, and if that brings harm to my professional rival, I suppose that is inevitable. But don't talk to me of magic in simple terms. I know what it is: that's to say, I know what I think it is. Magic—I hate the word because of what it has come to mean, but anyway— magic in the big sense can only happen where there is very strong feeling. You can't set it going with a sceptical mind—with your fingers crossed, so to speak. You must desire, and you must believe. Have you any idea how hard that is for a man of my time and a man of my training and temperament? At the deepest level of your being you are living in the Middle Ages, and magic comes easily—I won't say logically—to you. But for me it is a subject of study, a psychological fact but not necessarily an objective fact. A thing some people have always believed but nobody has quite been able to prove. I have never had a chance to experiment with it personally because I have never had what is necessary—the desire and the belief.

"But now, for the first time in my life—for the very first time— I want something desperately. I want that manuscript. I want it enough to go to great lengths to get it. I've wanted things before, things like distinctions in my professional work, but never like this."

"Never wanted a woman?"

"Not as I want that manuscript. Not very much, I suppose, at all. That kind of thing has meant very little to me."

"So the first great passion in your life has its roots in hatred and envy? Think, Hollier."

"You simplify the whole thing in order to belittle me."

"No. To make you face yourself. All right; you have the desire. But you can't quite force yourself to admit you have the belief."

"You don't understand. My whole training is to suspend belief, to examine, to experiment, to try things out, to test them."

"So, just for an experiment, you want a curse on your enemy."

"I never spoke of a curse."

"Not in words. But to my old-style ears, that inform my old-style mind, you don't have to use the old-style word. You can't say it because you want to leave yourself a way out; if it works, so—and if it doesn't work, it was all Gypsy bunk anyway, and the great professor, the modern-style man, is still on top. Look; you want this book. Well, get somebody to steal it. I can put you on to a good, clever thief."

"Yes; I've thought of that. But—"

"Yes—but if you stole it and then wrote about it, your enemy would know you stole it. No?"

"That had occurred to me."

"Ho! Occurred to you! So let's face the facts as you have already faced them inside your heart, and as you won't admit to me, or even admit straight out to yourself: if you are to have this book or whatever it is, and be safe to use it, the fellow who has it now must be dead. Are you prepared to wish somebody dead, professor?"

"Thousands of people wish somebody dead every day."

"Yes, but do they really mean it? Would they do it if they could? So: why not get him murdered? I won't find you a murderer, but Yerko might be able to tell you where to look."

"Madame, I didn't come here to hire thieves and murderers."

"No, you are too clever; too modern. Suppose your murderer gets caught; they are often very clumsy, those fellows. He says, 'The professor hired me,' and you are in trouble. But if you are found out and say, 'I hired an old Gypsy woman to curse him,' the judge laughs and wags his finger at you for a big joker. You are a clever man, Hollier."

"You are treating me like a fool."

"Because I like you. You are too good a man to be acting like this. You're lucky you have come to me. But why did you come?"

"At Christmas you read my fortune in the Tarot, and it has

proved true. The obsession and the hatred of which you spoke have become terrible realities."

"Making trouble for you and somebody near to you. Who is that?"

"I had forgotten that. I don't know who it could be."

"I do. My daughter Maria."

"Oh yes; of course. Maria has to work with me on the manuscript, if I can get it."

"That's all about Maria?"

"Well, yes, it is. What else could there be?"

"God, Hollier, you are a fool. I remember your fortune well. Who is the Knave of Coins, the servant with a letter?"

"I don't know. He hasn't appeared yet. But the figure in your prediction that has brought me back to you is the Moon, the changeable woman, who speaks of danger. Who can that be but yourself? So naturally I turn to you for advice."

"Did you look good at that card? The Moon, high in the sky, and she is both the Old Woman, the full moon, and the Virgin, the crescent moon, and neither of them is paying any attention to the wolf and the dog who are down on the earth barking at the Moon: and at the bottom of the card, under the earth, do you remember, there is the Cancer, and that is the earth spirit that governs the dark side of all the Moon sees, and the Cancer is many bad things—revenge and hate and self-destruction. Because it devours, you see; that is why the devouring disease bears its name. When I see the Moon card coming up, I always know that something bad could happen because of revenge and devouring hate and that it could ruin the person I am talking to. Now listen to me, Hollier, because I am going to tell you some things you won't like, but I hope I can help you by telling you the truth.

"You have been hinting for more than an hour that as an experiment—just as a joke, just to see what happens—I might try one of those old Gypsy spells on your enemy. What old Gypsy spells? Do you know of any? You talk as if you knew much more about Gypsies than I do. I only know maybe a hundred Gypsies, and most of them are dead—killed by people like you who must always be modern and right. All that spell business is just to concentrate feeling.

"But a curse? That needs the strongest feeling. Suppose I sell you a curse? I don't hate your enemy; he is nothing to me. So to curse him I have to be very well in with—*What?*—if I am to escape without harm to myself. Because *What?* is very terrible. *What?* does not deal in the Sweet Justice of civilized man, but in Balance, which is not nearly so much concerned with man, and may seem terrible and evil to him. You understand me? When Balance decides the time has come to settle the scales awful things happen. Much of what we do not understand is Balance at work. We attract what we are, you know, Hollier; we always get the dog or the fiddle that is right for us, even though we may not like it, and if we are proud Balance may be rough in showing us how weak we are. And the Lord of Balance is *What?*, and if I call down a curse just for your benefit, believe me, Balance must be satisfied, or I shall be in deep trouble. I do not think I want to stretch my credit with *What?* to oblige you, Hollier. I do not want to call on *What?*, who lives down there in the darkness where Cancer dwells, and whose army is all the creatures of the dark, and the spirits of the suicides and all the terrible forces, to get an old book for you. And do you know what frightens me about this talk we are having? It is your frivolity in asking such a thing of me. You don't know what you are doing. You have the shocking frivolity of the modern, educated mind."

Hollier was not taking this well. As Mamusia talked his face grew darker and darker until it was the colour people mean when they say a face is black; it was bloody from within. Now he faced her, and all the reasonable, professorial manner with which he had been talking for the past hour was gone. He looked terrible as I had never seen him before, and his voice was choked with passion.

"I am not frivolous. You cannot understand what I am, because you cannot know anything of intellectual passion—"

"Pride, Hollier, give it its real name."

"Be silent! You have said all you have to say, which is No. Very well then, say no more. You may have it your own way. When I came here I probably did hope that somehow you might consent to use your powers for my sake. I took you for a *phuri dai* and a friend. Now I know how far your friendship goes, and

I have revised my ideas about the extent of your wisdom. I am no worse off than when I came. Good afternoon."

"Wait, Hollier wait! You do not understand what danger you are in! You have not understood what I have been saying! It is the feeling that is the power of the curse. If I say to *What?* 'My friend here feels very deeply about so-and-so; what will you do for him?' I am only your messenger. To be the messenger I must have belief. You don't need me for a curse; you have already cursed your enemy in your heart, and you have reached *What?* without me. Man, I fear for you! I have seen terrible hate before, but never in a man so stupid about himself as you are."

"Now you tell me I can do it without you?"

"Yes, because you have pushed me to it."

"So, listen to me, Madame Laoutaro: you have done one great thing for me this afternoon. I know now that I have both feeling and belief! I believe! Yes—I *believe!*"

"Oh God, Hollier my friend, I am in great distress for you! Maria, drive the professor home—and be very careful how you drive!"

I did not speak a word as I drove Hollier back to the gate of Spook. I had not spoken a word during his angry hour with Mamusia, though I was terrified by the awful feeling that mounted in that room, like a poison. What was there for me to say? As he got out of my car he slammed the door so hard I feared it might fall off.

[2]

THE NEXT DAY HOLLIER seemed calm, and said nothing to me about his row with Mamusia. Indeed, to judge from appearances, it affected him much less than it did me. I was being forced to come to new terms with myself. I had struggled hard for freedom from my Mother's world, which I saw as a world of superstition, but I was being forced to a recognition that it was out of my power to be wholly free. Indeed, I was beginning to think more kindly about superstition than I had done since the time, when I was about twelve, when I first became aware of the ambiguous place it had in the world in which I lived.

Everybody I knew at school was terribly hard on superstition, but I had only to watch them to see that all of them had some irrational prejudice. And where was I to draw the line between the special veneration some of the nuns had for particular saints, and the tricks the girls played to find out if their boy-friends loved them? Why was it all right to bribe St. Anthony of Padua with a candle to find you the spectacles you had mislaid but not all right to bribe The Little Flower to keep Sister St. Dominic from finding out you hadn't done your homework? I despised superstition as loudly as anyone, and practised it in private, as did all my friends. The mind of man is naturally religious, we were taught; it is also naturally superstitious, I discovered.

It was this duality of mind, I suppose, that drew me to Hollier's work of uncovering evidence of past belief and submerged wisdom. Like so many students I was looking for something that gave substance to the life I already possessed, or which it would be more honest to say, possessed me; I was happy and honoured to be his apprentice in this learned grubbing in the middens of supposedly outworn faith. Especially happy because it was recognized by the university as a scientific approach to cultural history.

But what was going on around me was getting uncomfortably near the bone of real superstition, or recognition that what I thought of as superstition might truly have some foundation in the processes of life. Long before Hollier told me he wanted me to take him to Mamusia again, I knew that what she had seen in the Tarot was manifesting itself in his life—and because in his, in mine as well. Growing difficulties and dissatisfaction with the way his work was going; the trouble-maker?—it was plain enough to me that Urquhart McVarish was the source of the disquiet and that Hollier's response was hatred—real hatred and not just the antagonism that is common enough in academic life. In the old expression, he was Cain Raised to get his hands on the Gryphius portfolio; the fact that he knew very little about what was in the letters merely served to persuade him that they were of the uttermost importance. What new light he expected on Rabelais and Paracelsus I could not guess; he dropped hints about Gnosticism, or some sort of crypto-protestantism, or mystical alchemy, about herbal cures, or new insights into the link between soul and body that were counterparts of the knowledge Ozy Froats was so patiently seeking. It seemed that he expected anything and everything if he could only get his hands on the letters that were tucked into the back flap of that leather portfolio. McVarish was thwarting him, and Cain was raised.

This at least had nothing to do with imagination. Urky was behaving in an intentionally irritating way, and betrayed that he knew what was in Hollier's mind. When they met, as they sometimes did at faculty meetings or more rarely on social occasions, he was likely to be affectionate, saying, 'How's the work going, Clem? Well, I hope? Run across anything in your special line lately? I suppose it's impossible to put your hand on anything really new?'

It was the sort of talk which, when it was said with one of Urky's teasing smiles, was enough to make Hollier uncivil, and afterward, when he was talking to me, furious and abusive.

He was angry because Darcourt would not accuse Urky to his face, and threaten to put the police on him, which I could see plainly was not something Darcourt could do on wobbly evidence. All Darcourt knew was that Urky seemed to have borrowed a manuscript from Cornish, which could not now be traced, and it takes more than that to spur one academic to set the cops on another. Hollier, by the time he demanded that I take him to Mamusia, had grown thinner and more saturnine; feeding on his obsession. Chawing his own maw, like that Dragon in the *Faerie Queene*.

When Hollier told Mamusia he did not recognize the Knave of Coins, the unjust servant, I could not believe my ears. Parlabane was worse than ever, and his demands for money, which had been occasional before Christmas, were now weekly and sometimes more than weekly. He said he needed money to pay for the typing of his novel, but I couldn't believe it, for he would take anything from two dollars to fifty, and when he sponged from Hollier he would come to me and demand further tribute.

When I say 'demand' I mean it, because he was not an ordinary borrower; his words were civil enough but behind them I felt a threat, though what the threat might be I never found out—took care not to find out. He begged me with intensity, a suggestion that to refuse him would provoke more than just abuse; he seemed not far from violence. Would he have struck me? Yes, I know he would, and it would have been a terrible blow, for he was a very strong little man, and very angry, and I feared the anger even more than the pain.

So I kept up a modern woman's pretence that I was acting from my own choice, however unwillingly; but not far below that I was simply a woman frightened by masculine strength and ferocity. He bullied money out of me, and I never reached the point of anger where I would rather run the risk of a blow than submit to further bullying.

He didn't bully Hollier. Nobody could have done that. Instead he worked on the loyalty men feel for old friends who are down on their luck, which I suppose has at least one of its roots in guilt. *There but for the Grace of God . . .* ; that nonsense. He could whine ten dollars out of Hollier and within thirty seconds be in the outer room twisting another ten out of me. It was an astonishing performance.

His novel was to him what the Gryphius MSS were to Hollier. He lugged masses of typescript around in one of those strong plastic bags you get at supermarkets. There must have been at least a thousand pages of that typescript, for the bag was full even when Parlabane at last handed Hollier a wad which was, he said, almost a complete and perfect copy of the book. He hinted, but did not actually say, that a typist somewhere had the final version, and was making copies for publishers, and that what he still had in the bag was a collection of notes, drafts, and unsatisfactory passages.

Parlabane made rather a ceremony of handing over his typescript, but after he had gone, Hollier glanced at it, retreated in dismay, and asked me to read it for him and make a report, and perhaps to offer some criticism that he could pass on as his own. Whether Parlabane ever suspected this deceit I do not know, but I took care that he never found me grappling with his rat's-nest of fiction.

Some typescripts are as hard to read as bad handwriting, and Parlabane's was one of these. It was on that cheap yellow paper that does not stand up to correction in ink and pencil, to frequent crossings-out, and especially to that pawing a book undergoes when it is in the writing process. Parlabane's novel, *Be Not Another,* was a limp, dog-eared mess, unpleasing to the touch, ringed by glasses and cups, and smelly from too much handling by a man whose whole way of life was smelly.

I read it, though I had to flog myself to the work. It was about a young man who was studying philosophy at a university that was obviously ours, in a college that was obviously Spook. His parents were duds, unfit to have such a son. He had long philosophical pow-wows with his professors and friends, and these gurgled with such words as 'teleological' and 'epistemological', and there was much extremely fine-honed stuff about scepticism and the whole of life being a can of worms. There was a best friend called Featherstone, who seemed to be Hollier; he was just bright enough to play straight man to the Hero, who of course was Parlabane himself. (He had no name and was referred to throughout as *He* and *Him* in italics.) There was a clown friend called Billy Duff, or Plum Duff, who never got any good lines; this was undoubtedly Darcourt. There were sexual scenes with girls who were too stupid to recognize what an intellectual bonanza *He* was, and they either refused to go to bed with *Him,* or did and failed to come up to expectation. Light dawned when *He* went to another university for advanced study and met a young man who was like a Greek God—no, he did not deny himself that cliché—and with the G.G. *He* was fulfilled spiritually and physically.

He denied himself nothing. Everybody wrangled far too much and didn't do nearly enough—even in the sexy parts. They weren't much fun except with the G.G. and those encounters were described so rhapsodically that it was hard to figure out what was happening except in a general way, because they talked so learnedly about it.

I cannot pretend to be a critic of modern fiction; for the moment, Rabelais was in the front of my mind; but anyhow I question whether this thing of Parlabane's was really a modern novel or perhaps a novel at all. It just seemed to be a discouragingly dull muddle, and so I told Hollier.

"It's his life, though not nearly so interesting as what he told me in The Rude Plenty; everything is seen from the inside, so microscopically that there's no sense of narrative; it just belly-flops along, like a beached whale."

"Doesn't it come to anything at all?"

"Oh yes; after much struggle *He* finds God, who is the sole reality, and instead of scorning the world *He* learns to pity it."

"Very decent of him. Plenty of caricatures of his contemporaries, I suppose?"

"I wouldn't recognize them."

"Of course; before your time. But I dare say there are some recognizable people who wouldn't be too happy to have their youthful exploits recalled."

"There's scandalous stuff, but it isn't described with much selection or point."

"I thought we would all be in it; he made enemies easily."

"You don't come off too badly, but he's rather hard on Professor Darcourt; he's the butt, who thinks he has found God, but of course it isn't the real eighteen-karat philosopher's God that *He* finds after his spiritual pilgrimage. Just a peanut God for tiny minds. But the queerest thing is that he hasn't a scrap of humour in it. Parlabane's a lively talker, but he seems to have no comic perception of himself."

"Would you expect it? You, a scholar of Rabelais? What he has is wit, not humour, and wit alone never turns inward. Wit is something you possess, but humour is something that possesses you. I'm not surprised that Darcourt and I appear in a poorish light. No such bitter judge of old friends as a brilliant failure."

"He certainly seems to be a failure as a novelist—though I don't set up to know."

"You can't make a novelist out of a philosopher. Ever read any of Bertrand Russell's fiction?"

There was never any question of Hollier's reading the book himself. He was too much taken up with his rage against McVarish. It was in February he made me take him to visit Mamusia, and during that miserable hour I kept in the background, terrified by what she was able to corkscrew out of him. It had never entered my mind that he would ask her for a curse. I suppose it is a measure of how stupid I am that I was able to read and write of such things in his company and under his direction, as part of the tissue of past life we were studying, but it never occurred to me that he might seize upon a portion of that bygone life—at least it seemed to me that it belonged to the past—as a way of revenging himself on his adversary. I had never admired Mamusia so much;

her severity of calm, good sense made me proud of her. But Hollier was transformed. Whose was the Wild Mind now?

From that day onward he never mentioned the matter to me.

Not so Mamusia. "You were angry about my little plan at Christmas," she said, "but you see how well everything is turning out. Poor Hollier is a madman. He will be in deep trouble. No husband for you, my girl. It was the hand of Fate that directed the cup of coffee to the priest Darcourt. Have you heard anything from him yet?"

[3]

HAD I HEARD ANYTHING from the priest Darcourt? It was easy for Mamusia to talk about Fate as if she were Fate's accomplice and instrument; beyond a doubt she believed in the power of her nasty philtre, made of ground appleseed and my menstrual blood, because its action was as much taken for granted by her as were the principles of scientific method by Ozy Froats. But for me to admit that there could be any direct relationship between what she had done and the attitude toward me that I now detected in Simon Darcourt would mean a rejection of the modern world and either the acceptance of coincidence as a factor in daily life— a notion for which I harboured a thoroughly modern scorn—or else an admission that some things happened that ran on separate but parallel tracks, and occasionally flashed by one another with blazes of confusing light, like trains passing one another in the night. There was a stylish word for this: synchronicity. But I did not want to think about that: I was a pupil of Hollier's and I wanted to examine the things that belonged to Mamusia's world as matter to be studied, but not beliefs to be accepted and lived. So I tried not to pay too much attention to Simon Darcourt, so far as being his pupil and the necessities of common civility allowed.

This would have been easier if I had not been troubled by disloyal thoughts about Hollier. I still loved him, or cherished feeling for him which I called love because there seemed to be no other appropriate name. Now and then, in the talks I had with him about my work, he said something that was so illuminating that I was confirmed in my conviction that he was a great teacher, an inspirer, an opener of new paths. But his obsession with the Gryphius MSS and the things he said about them and about Urquhart McVarish seemed to come from another man; an obsessed, silly, vain man. I had put out of my head all hope that he would spare any loving thoughts for me, and though I pretended I was ready to play the role of Patient Griselda and put up with anything for the greater glory of Hollier, another girl inside me was coming to the conclusion that my love for him was a great mistake, that nothing would come of it, and that I had better get over it and move on to something else, and of this practical femininity I was foolishly ashamed. But could I love Cain Raised?

All you want is a lover, said the scholar in me, with scorn. *And what's wrong with that,* said the woman in me, with a Gypsy jut of the hip. *If you are looking for a lover,* said a third element (which I could not identify, but which I suppose must be called common awareness), *Simon Darcourt has lover written all over him.*

Yes, but—. *But what? You seem to be yearning after one of these Rebel Angels, who people the universities and have established what Paracelsus calls The Second Paradise of Learning, and who are ready and willing to teach all manner of wisdom to the daughters of men.* Yes, but Simon Darcourt is forty-five, and stoutish, and a priest in the Anglican church. *He is learned, kind, and he obviously loves you.* I know; that satisfies the scholar, but the Gypsy girl just laughs and says it won't do at all. What sort of a figure would I cut as a parson's wife? *A scholar—and you have hopes of a reputation in that work—would be just the wife for a scholar-parson.* And again the Gypsy girl laughs. I tell the Gypsy girl to go to hell; I am not prepared to admit (not yet, anyway) that a Gypsy trick with a love philtre has plumped poor Simon and me into this pickle, but certainly I am not going to put up with Gypsy mockery in my present position. What a mess!

This inner confusion plagued me night and day. I felt that it was destroying my health, but every morning, when I looked in the mirror expecting to see the ravages of a tortured spirit etched into my face in crow's-feet and harsh lines, I was forced to admit that I was looking as well as I ever had in my life, and I will not pretend that I wasn't glad of it. Scholar I may be, but I refuse to play the game some of the scholarly women in the University play, and make the worst of myself, dress as if I stole clothes out of the St. Vincent de Paul box, and had my hair cut in a dark cellar by a madman with a knife and fork. The Gypsy strain, I suppose. On with the earrings and the gaudy scarves; glory in your long black hair, and walk proudly, holding your head high. That is at least a part of what God made you for.

This, I concluded, was what life involved at my age: confusion, but at least an intensely interesting confusion. Since I was old enough to conceive of such a thing, I have longed for enlightenment. In private prayer, at school, I lifted my eyes to the altar and begged *O God, don't let me die stupid.* What I was going through now must be part of the price that had to be paid if that prayer were to be answered. *Feed on this in thy heart and be thankful, Maria.*

An unexpected sort of enlightenment broke upon me in mid-March, when Simon manoeuvred me into his rooms at Plough-wright (he thought he was being clever, but there was clearly a good deal of planning to it) and gave me coffee and cognac and told me he loved me. He did it wonderfully well. What he said didn't sound in the least contrived, or rehearsed; it was simple and eloquent and free from any extravagances about eternal devotion, or not knowing what he would do if I could not return his love, or any of that tedious stuff. But what really shook me out of my self-possession was his confession that in his life I had taken on the character of Sophia.

I suppose that most men, when they fall in love, hang some sort of label on the woman they want, and attribute to her all sorts of characteristics that are not really hers. Or should I say, not completely hers, because it is hard to see things in somebody else that have no shred of reality, if you are not a complete fool. Women do it, too. Had I not convinced myself that Hollier was, in the very best sense, a Wizard? And could anyone deny that Hollier was in a considerable measure (though probably less than I imagined) a Wizard? I suppose the disillusion that comes after marriage, about which so much is said now, is the recognition that the label was not precise, or else the lover had neglected to read the small print on the label. But surely only the very young, or the people who never know much about themselves, hang labels on those they love that have no correspondence whatever with reality? The disillusion of stupid people is surely just as foolish as their initial illusion? I don't pretend to know; only the wiseacres who write books about love, and marriage, and sex, seem to possess complete certainty. But I do think that without some measure of illusion life becomes intolerable.

Still—Sophia! What a label to hang on Maria Magdalena Theotoky! Sophia: the feminine personification of Wisdom; that companion figure to God who urged Him on to create the Universe; God's female counterpart whom the Christians and the Jews have agreed to hush up, to the great disadvantage of women for so many hundreds of years! It was overwhelming. But was it utterly ridiculous?

No, I don't think so. Granting freely that I am not Sophia, which no living woman could be except in tiny measure, what am I in the world of Simon Darcourt? I am a woman from far away, because of my Gypsy heritage; a woman, I suppose, of the Middle Ages. A woman who can in some measure talk Simon's language of learning and the kind of speculation learning begets. A woman not afraid of the possibilities that lurk in the background of modern life, but which so much of modern life denies utterly—a woman whom one can call Sophia with the certainty that she will know what is being said. A woman, in fact, whom a beglamoured man might think of as Sophia without being a fool.

Ah, but there is the word that pulls me up sharp—beglamoured. The word glamour has been so battered and smeared that almost everybody has forgotten that it means magic and enchantment. Could it really be that poor Simon was a victim of my Gypsy mother's cup of hocussed coffee, and saw wonders in me because he had been given a love philtre, a sexy Mickey Finn? I hate the idea, but I cannot say with absolute certainty that there is no truth in it. And if I cannot say that, what sort of Divine Wisdom am I, what possible embodiment of Sophia? Or is it not Sophia's part to split hairs in such matters?

Whatever the answers to these hard questions, I had the gumption to tell Simon that I did indeed love him, which was true, and that I could not possibly think of marrying him, which was also true. And as he could not consider doing anything about a physical love without marriage (for reasons that I understood and thought greatly to his credit, though I did not share his reluctance) that was that. The love was a reality, but it was a reality within limits.

What astonished me was his relief when the limits had been defined. I knew, as I don't suppose he did for a long time afterward, that he had never in the truest sense wanted to marry me—didn't even want unbearably to make sexual love to me. He wanted a love that excluded those things, and he knew that such a love was possible, and he had achieved it. And so had I. When we parted each was richer by a loving and enduring and delightful friend, and I was perhaps the happier of the two because in the hour I had wholly changed my feeling about Hollier.

The knowledge of Simon's love made it easier for me to endure the painful tensions in Hollier's rooms from this time until Easter, and to respond whole-heartedly when Simon telephoned me shortly after seven o'clock on the morning of Easter Sunday.

"Maria, I thought you should know as soon as possible that Parlabane is dead. Very sudden, and the doctor says it was heart—no, no suspicion of anything else, though I feared that, too. I'll attend to everything, and there seems to be no reason to wait, so I'm arranging the funeral for tomorrow morning. Will you bring Clem? We're his only friends, it appears. Poor devil? Yes, that's what I said: poor devil."

[4]

HOLLIER, DARCOURT, AND I drove back from the funeral happy because we seemed to have regained something that Parlabane had taken from us. We were refreshed and drawn together by this shared feeling, and did not want to part. That was why Hollier asked Darcourt if he would come up to his rooms for a cup of tea. We had just finished a long, vinous lunch but it was a day for hospitality.

I stopped in the porter's lodge to see if there was any mail for Hollier; there is no postal delivery on Easter Monday, but the inter-college service in the University might have something from the weekend that had begun the previous Thursday.

"Package for the Professor, Miss," said Fred the porter, and handed me an untidy bundle done up in brown paper, to which a letter was fastened with sticky tape. I recognized Parlabane's ill-formed writing and saw that there was a scrawl of direction: *Confidential: Letter before Package, Please.*

"More of the dreadful novel," said Hollier when I showed it to him. He threw it down on the table, I made tea, and we went on with our chat, which was all of Parlabane. At last Hollier said, "Better see what that is, Maria. I suppose it's an epilogue, or something of the kind. Poor man, he died full of hope about his book. We'll have to decide what to do about it."

"We've all done what we could," said Darcourt. "The only thing we can do now is recover the typescript and get rid of it."

I had opened the letter. "It seems awfully long, and it's to both of us," I said to Hollier; "do you want me to read it?"

He nodded, and I began.

"*Dear Friends and Colleagues, Clem and Molly:*

—As you will have guessed, it was I who gave his quietus to Urky McVarish."

"Christ!" said Hollier.

"So that's who the flag was at half-staff for," said Darcourt.

"Does he mean it? He can't mean murder?"

"Get on, Maria, get on!"

"—Not, I assure you, for the mere frivolous pleasure of disposing of a nuisance, but for purely practical reasons, as you shall see. It lay in Urky's power to help me forward in my career, by his death, and—a secondary but I assure you not a small consideration with me—to do some practical good to both of you and to bring you closer together. I cannot tell you how distressed I have been during the recent months to see Molly pining for you, Clem—"

"Pining? What's he talking about," said Hollier.

I hurried on.

"—while your mind was elsewhere, pondering deep considerations of scholarship, and hating Urky. But I hope my little plan will unite you forever. At this culminating hour of my life that gives me immense satisfaction. Fame for me, fame and wedded bliss for you; lucky Urky to have been able to make it all possible."

"This is getting to be embarrassing," I said. "Perhaps you'll take over the reading, Simon? I wish you would."

Darcourt took the letter from me.

"—You knew that I was seeing a good deal of Urky during the

months since Christmas, didn't you? Maria once let something drop about me getting *thick* with him; she appeared to resent it. But really, Molly, you were so tight with your money I had to turn somewhere for the means of subsistence. I still owe you— whatever the trifling sum is—but you may strike it off your books, and think yourself well repaid by Parlabane, whom you used less generously than a beautiful girl should. Beautiful girls ought to be open-handed; parsimony ruins the complexion after a while. And you, Clem—you kept trying to get me rotten little jobs, but you would not move a finger to get my novel published. No faith in my genius—for now that I no longer have to keep up the pretence of modesty I must point out unequivocally that I *am* a genius, admitting at the same time that, like most geniuses, I am not an entirely nice fellow.

"—I tried to get a living by honest means, and after that by means that seemed to present themselves most readily. Fatty Darcourt can tell you about that, if you are interested. Poor old Fatty didn't think much of my novel either, and it may have been because he recognized himself in it: people are ungenerous about such things. So, as a creature of Renaissance spirit, I took a Renaissance path, and became a parasite.

"—Parasite to Urquhart McVarish. I supplied him with flattery, an intelligent listener who was in no sense a rival, and certain services that he would have had trouble finding elsewhere.

"—Why was I driven to assume this role, which seems distasteful to people like you whose cares are simple? Money, my dears; I had to have money. I am sure you were not entirely deceived by my explanation about the cost of having my novel fair-copied. No: I was being blackmailed. It was my ill luck to run into a fellow I had once known on the West Coast, who knew something I thought I had left behind. He was not a blackmailer on the grand scale, but he was ugly and exigent. Earlier this evening I sent the police a note about him, which will cook his goose. I couldn't have done that if I had intended to hang around and see the fun, gratifying though that would have been. But the thought warms me now.

"—The police will not be surprised to hear from me. I have been doing a little work for them since before Christmas. A hint here, a hint there. But they pay badly. God, how mean everybody is about money!

"—The paradox of money is that when you have lots of it you can manage life quite cheaply. Nothing so economical as being rich. But when you are on the rocks, it's all hand to mouth and no peace of mind. So I had to work hard to keep afloat, begging, cadging, squealing to the cops, and slaving at the ill-requited profession of parasite to a parsimonious Scot.

"—Urky, you see, had specialized needs that only someone like myself could be trusted to understand and supply. In our modern world, where there is so much bibble-babble about sexual preferences, people in general still seem to think that these must lie either in heterosexual capers or in one of the varieties of homosexuality. But Urky was, I suppose one must say, a narcissist; his fun was deeply personal and his fun-shop was his own mind and his own body, exclusively. I rumbled him at once. All that guff about 'my great ancestor, Sir Thomas Urquhart' was not primarily to impress other people, but to provide the music to which his soul danced its solitary galliard. You have often heard it said of somebody that he loves himself? That was the simple truth about Urky. He was a pretty good scholar, Clem; that side of him was real enough, though it would not have suited you to admit it. But he was such a self-delighted ass that he got on the nerves of sterner egotists, like you.

"—He needed somebody who would be wholly subservient, do his will without question, bring to the doing a dash of style and invention, and provide access to things he didn't like to approach himself. I was just his man.

"—There are more things in heaven and earth, my dears, than are dreamed of in your philosophy, or in mine when I was safe in the arms of the academic life. It was the jails and the addiction-cure hospitals that rounded out my experience, taught me how to find my way in the shadowy streets and to know at sight the people who hold the keys to inadmissible kinds of happiness. Really, I know when I look back on our association that Urky got a bargain in me, because he was very mean with money. Rather like you two. But he needed a parasite and I knew the role as a mere unilluminated groveller never could. I was well up in the literature of parasitism, and I could give to my servitude the panache Urky wanted.

"—He was mad on what he called his 'ceremonies'. A sociologist would probably call them 'role-playing', but Urky had no use for sociologists or their lingo, which turns the spiciest adventure into an ill-written entry in a case-book. Urky liked to be able to explain a ceremony to his parasite, and then forget that he had ever done so; it was the parasite's job to make the ceremony seem fresh, truthful, and inevitable.

"—Shall I describe a Saturday night at Urky's? I was up in the morning early because I had to be at the St. Lawrence Market betimes to buy the pick of the vegetables, find a nice piece of fish and something for an entrée—brains, or sweetbreads or kidneys to be done up in a special way, because Urky was fond of offals. Then up to Urky's apartment (I had no key but he let me in with head averted—didn't even say good morning) where I made preparations for the evening's dinner (those offals take a lot of getting ready) and called a French patisserie to order a sweet. I picked up the sweet in the afternoon, bought flowers, opened wine, and did all the jobs that go toward making a first-rate little dinner, which somebody is going to demolish as if it were not a work of art. I was on me feet all day, as we domestics say.

"—You didn't know I was a cook? Learned it in jail during one of my periods as a trusty; there was a pretty good course for inmates who wanted a trade that would lead them toward an honest life. I had a little gift in that direction—the cooking, I mean, not the life.

"—One of my jobs was to bake some of the special little confectioneries needed for the evening's entertainment. Grass-brownies we called them in jail, but Urky didn't like low expressions. That meant cutting up some marijuana so that it was fine enough but not too fine, and mixing a delicate batter so that the cookies could be baked quickly, without killing the goodness of the grass. Also, I had to be sure there was enough of the old Canadian Black to make a pot of Texas Tea, and this might involve a visit to a Dutch Mill, where I was known, but not too well known.

"—Why was I known there? I don't want to embarrass you, my

dears, but you were so unrelentingly stingy toward me that I had to pick up a little money by telling curious friends—policemen, I believe they were—who was selling Aunt Mary, and Aunt Hazel, and even jollybeans. I suppose in my own small way I was a double agent in the drug world, which is not pretty but can be modestly rewarding. Every time I dropped into a Dutch Mill I had a tiny *frisson* lest the boys should have rumbled me, which could have been embarrassing and indeed dangerous, because those boys are very irritable. But they never found me out, and now they never will.

"—Where was Urky, while I was so busy in his kitchen? Lunching sparely but elegantly at his club, going to a foreign film, and finally having a jolly good sweat at a sauna. L'après-midi d'un gentleman-scholar.

"—I saw nothing of him until he returned in time to dress for dinner. I had laid out his clothes, including his silk socks turned halfway inside out, so that he could put them on with the greatest ease, and his evening shoes which had to be gleaming, and the insteps polished as highly as the toes. (Urky said you knew a gentleman that way; no decent valet would allow his master to have soiled insteps.) By this time I had changed into my own first costume, which was a houseman's outfit, with a snowy shirt and a mess-jacket starched till it was almost like the icing on a wedding-cake. (I did the washing on Wednesdays, when he was busy teaching the impressionable young, like you, Maria.)

"—Sherry before dinner set things going. Sherry is a good drink, but the way Urky sucked it was more like *fellatio* than drinking; he smacked and relished it with his beautifully shined shoes stuck out toward the fire, which I had laid, and which it was my job to keep burning brightly during the evening.

"—'The McVarish is served,' I said, and Urky strolled to the table and set about the fish. He would never hear of soup; low, for some reason. I said 'The McVarish is served' with a Highland accent. I don't know quite what character in Urky's imagination I was bodying forth, but I think it may have been some faithful clansman who had followed Urky to the wars as his personal servant, and was now back with the laird in private life.

"—He never spoke to me. Nodded when he wanted a plate removed, nodded when I offered the decanter of claret for his inspection, nodded when he had gobbled up as much as he wanted of the *gâteau* and it was time for the walnuts and port. Nodded when I brought the coffee and fine old whisky in a quaich. I played the self-effacing servant pretty well; stood behind his chair as he ate, so that he couldn't see me munching mouthfuls I had snatched of the food he had not eaten—though that was little enough. Urky was close about food; not much in the way of crumbs from the rich man's table.

"—This was the first part of the evening, after which Urky retired to his bedroom and I cleared away and washed up and set the stage for the second act.

"—By half past nine or thereabout I had washed up, changed into my second costume, and made things ready. I tiptoed into Urky's bedroom, drew back the covers and exposed Urky, stark naked and a pretty pink from his sauna, lying on his tum. Very carefully I parted his buttocks and—aha! you are expecting something spicy to happen? A bit of the old Brown Eye? You think I may be about to give Urky the keister-stab? No such low jailbird tricks for the fastidious Urky, I assure you. No; I gently and carefully inserted into his rectum what I thought of as 'the deck', because it looked rather like a small pack of cards; it was a piece of pink velvet ribbon, two inches wide and ten feet long, folded back and forth on itself so that it formed a package about two inches square, and four inches thick; a length of two or three inches was left hanging out. Urky did not move or seem to notice, as I tiptoed out again.

"—I had rearranged the living-room so that two chairs were before the fire; for Urky, one of those old-fashioned deck-chairs made of teak that used to be seen on CPR liners, which I had filled with cushions and a steamer-rug in the McVarish tartan; for me a low chair of the sort that used to be called a 'lady's chair', without arms; between the chairs I placed a low tea-table with cups and saucers, and the marijuana tea in a pot covered with a knitted cosy, made in the shape of a comical old woman. I set the record-player going and put on Urky's entrance music; it was a precious old seventy-eight of Sir Harry Lauder singing 'Roamin' in the Gloamin' '. I wore a baggy old woman's dress (bad style that, but I really did look like an old bag, so let it stand) and a straggly grey wig. I must have looked like one of the witches in

Macbeth. When Urky came in, wearing a long silk dressing-gown and slippers, I was ready to make my curtsy.

"—This was the build-up for the ceremony that Urky called The Two Old Edinburgh Ladies.

"—Innocent fun, in comparison with some parties at which I have assisted, but kinky in the naughty-nursery style that appealed to Urky. We assumed Edinburgh accents for this game; I hadn't much notion what an Edinburgh accent was, but I copied Urky, and screwed up my mouth and spoke as if I were sucking at a peppermint, and he seemed satisfied with my efforts.

"—We assumed names, too, and here it becomes rather complicated, for the names were Mistress Masham (that was me) and Mistress Morley. You get it? Probably not. Know then that Masham was the name of Queen Anne's *confidante,* and Morley was the name the Queen assumed when she chatted informally with her toady, and drank brandy out of a china cup, calling it her 'cold tea'. What this pair had to do with Edinburgh or with Urky you must not ask, because I don't know, but in the world of fantasy the greatest freedom is allowed."

Darcourt's eye had run ahead of his reading, and he was embarrassed. "Do you really want me to go on?" he said. Of course we did.

"—It was his fantasy, not mine, and it wasn't easy to improvise conversation to puff it out, and the burden was on me. What Urky liked was scandalous University gossip, offered on my part as if unwillingly and prudishly, as we sipped the marijuana tea and nibbled the marijuana cookies (I tried once or twice to get Urky to advance toward something a little more adventurous— a little acid on a sugar cube, or the teeniest jab with the monkey-pump—but he is what we call a chipper, flirting with drugs but scared to go very far. A Laodicean of vice.) So what kind of thing did I provide for him? Here is a sample that may interest you.

MRS. MORLEY: And what do you hear of that sweet girl Miss Theotoky, Mistress Masham, my dear?

MRS. MASHAM: Och, she keeps up with her studies, the poor lamb.

MRS. MORLEY: The poor lamb—and why the poor lamb, Mistress Masham?

MRS. MASHAM: Heaven defend us, Mistress Morley, my dear,

how you take a poor body up! I meant nothing—nothing at all. Only that I hope she may not be falling into dissolute ways.

MRS. MORLEY: But how could that be, when she has good Brother John to give her advice? Brother John, that best of holy men. Put aside your knitting, dear friend, and speak plainly.

MRS. MASHAM: I fear good Brother John has lost all influence with her, Mistress Morley. If she has an adviser I doubt but it's that fat priest Father Darcourt, may Heaven stand between her and his great belly.

MRS. MORLEY: Preserve us, Mistress Masham, what do you mean by such hints?

MRS. MASHAM: God send I suspect nobody wrongfully, Mistress Morley, but I have seen him looking after her with a verra moist eye, almost like a man enchanted.

MRS. MORLEY: You make me tremble, ma'am! Does not her good mentor, Professor Hollier, do anything to keep her from harm?

MRS. MASHAM: Och, Mistress Morley, ma'am, how should any-one of your known goodness understand the wickedness of men! I fear that same Hollier—!

MRS. MORLEY: You are not going to speak any evil of him?

MRS. MASHAM: Not unless the truth be evil, ma'am. But I fear he has—

MRS. MORLEY: Another cup of tea!—Go on, I can bear the worst.

MRS. MASHAM: I never said whoremaster! Mind, I never said it! Who's to say he was not tempted? The girl—the Theotoky girl—I blush to say it—she's no better than a wee besom! She can entice the finest of them! Have ye looked at her likeness lately? That bronze figure now, that you had from poor Mr. Cornish—

"—Then Urky looked at the bronze and—nothing personal, you understand, Molly, but simply in aid of Urky's little game and in the line of duty as a parasite—I had previously put a dab of salad oil on the cleft of the *mons,* which is such a charming feature of that work, so that it seemed moist and inviting. An imaginative stroke, don't you think? It threw Urky into a regular spasm, so that it was touch and go whether or not he might anticipate his Little Xmas, which was supposed to be held back for the topper of the evening.

"—That was the object of this elaborate masquerade; to bring Urky very slowly to the boil. Dirty gossip and plenty of tea and cookies did the trick—the gossip to excite, the Mary Jane to hold back—with the pink ribbon as the fuse to his rocket.

"—You two were not the only ones to cut a figure in these fantasies, but you were regular favourites. Urky had a weak hankering after you, Molly, and as for Clem, I liked to toy with him to please Urky, because though I fully understand and forgive, I was well aware that Clem felt he couldn't drag me after his splendid career more than so much; one does what one can for old friends, but of course some must drop by the way. Clem did what he felt he could for me, but he was damn certain I wasn't going to be allowed to be too much of a nuisance. So I had some fun with you two, but as you will discover, I have recompensed your real kindness in fullest measure, pressed down and running over.

"—Another favourite figure in the ceremonies was Ozy Froats— always good for a giggle. There were lots of others; Urky's vast spite could embrace them all. But it was only play, you know. The popular sex-manuals urge their readers to give spice to the old familiar act by building fantasies around it. Who would grudge Urky his pleasure, or blame me for ministering to it, when the role of parasite was the only one left to me? Not you, dear friends; certainly not you.

"—Urky liked a good hour and a half of this sort of thing, during which his pleasure mounted, his laughter became harder to conceal under the role of Mrs. Morley. The lewd gossip pricked him on, while Old Mary Jane held him back. As he talked and listened he worked his legs up in the deck-chair and his dressing-gown fell apart so that his bare bottom was to be seen. That was the cue for my culminating sequence, thus:

MRS. MASHAM: Mistress Morley, ma'am, forgive the freedom in an old, though humble, friend, but your gown is disordered, ma'am.

MRS. MORLEY: No, no, I'm sure.

MRS. MASHAM: Yes, yes, *I'm* sure.

MRS. MORLEY: It's nothing. Don't distress yourself, ma'am.

MRS. MASHAM: But for your own good, ma'am, as a friend, ma'am, I shall be compelled to bind you, ma'am. Indeed I shall.

MRS. MORLEY: Nay, nay, my good creature, you don't know what
    you're doing.

MRS. MASHAM: That I do. It's the Urquhart blood declaring itself.
    See—there's old Sir Thomas himself looking down at you and
    laughing, the sly old Rabelaisian. He knows your nature may
    declare itself, and it's for me to act to preserve you from shame
    before him. Bound you must be.

"—Then I would produce some nice white sash-cord and bind
Urky into the chair, just tight enough to give him the thrill of
being under constraint, but not enough to hurt him. By this time
he was well and truly sexually aroused. Not a pretty sight, but I
was not supposed to notice. Instead—

MRS. MASHAM: You must forgive me, ma'am. It's a deeply per-
    sonal thing, but I cannot help observing, ma'am—because of
    the disorder of your dress—that you have a wee thing—

MRS. MORLEY: A wee thing? You are bold, ma'am.

MRS. MASHAM: Aye, a wee thing. I'll go further—a wee pink
    tail. Yes, a wee pink tailie—I can see it, I can see it, I can
    see it—

MRS. MORLEY: You must not peep!

MRS. MASHAM: Aye, but I will peep! And I'll—how my fingers
    itch—I'll pull it—

MRS. MORLEY: Creature, you dare not!

MRS. MASHAM: I dare all! I'll pull it, I'll pull it, I'll pull it—

"—And when the tease was almost at its climax, I did pull it.
Pulled Urky's little tag of ribbon, and ran with it across the room
so that it unfolded rapidly and softly and ticklishly inside him,
and he reached what he called his Little Xmas.
"—Then I ran to the kitchen and kept out of the way until Urky
had freed himself from the easy bonds and retired to his bedroom.
I cleaned up, put everything in order, and left, having picked up
the envelope which he had left for me on the table by the door.
"—It contained twenty-five dollars. Twenty-five measly bucks for
a day that had started at six in the morning and never ended
before one! Twenty-five lousy bucks for a man of my attainments
to serve as cook, butler, drug-supplier, coosie-packer, character

actor, sex-tease, and scholarly parasite for nineteen hours! Once, when I hinted to Urky that it was sweated labour, he looked hurt, and said he had supposed I got as much fun out of it as he did! All that delicious exciting pretence! His egotism was phenomenal in my experience, which has been great. If he hadn't nosed out a few things I preferred not to have known, I would have squealed on him long ago. Now I no longer have to dread blackmail, for I speak from the threshold of eternity, my dears. Pray for Brother John. Necessity, not my will, consented. Until tonight, when I decided I had had enough. Even a buzzard sometimes gags.

"—Not that my decision was a sudden one; I do not make up my mind about important things in an instant. It is at least three weeks since I decided that the time had come for me to disappear as Brother John, the joke-monk, and to re-emerge as John Parlabane, author of one of the few unquestionably great novels of our time. For that is what *Be Not Another* is: the greatest and in time the most influential *roman philosophique* written by anyone since Goethe. And when I am not around to be punished and patronized and belittled by my inferiors that is how it will be seen. It is jealousy—yours, Clem, God forgive you, and that of many others—that stands in the way of the book; you know me and you know me in my inferior guise as a needy friend who has taken some wrong turnings in his life, and so has not made his way to the scholar's safe harbour. You refuse to see me as what I truly am—a man of strongly individual nature, richly perceptive and an original moralist of the first order. I should not have been this if I had refused to get my shoes muddy, as you have done.

"—As an original moralist I value a truly fine work of art above human life, including my own. To ensure the publication of my book and its recognition for what it is, I am ready to give my own life, but I recognize that such an act would attract little attention. In the eyes of the world I am nobody; if I am to get the attention that is my due, I must become somebody. What easier way than by taking another into the shadows with me? All the world loves a murderer.

"—Few murders have been undertaken to ensure the publication of a book; offhand, I can't think of one, but as there may be some other instances I must speak with caution. People murder for other sorts of gain, or in passion. I do not even admit that I have polished off Urky for gain, because I shall reap no direct advantage—the advantage will all be the world's, which will be persuaded by this rough means to give fair consideration to my book, and in the course of time the world will see how enormously it is the gainer. Which would you rather have, Maria—the great romance of François Rabelais, or a living, breathing, sniggering Urquhart McVarish? Indeed, I am providing Urky with a kind of immortality he could not aspire to if he died by what are called natural causes. (Not, of course, that I write in Rabelais's vein, which I have always considered needlessly gross, but as a work of humanist learning my book is measurably finer than his.)

"—Why Urky? Well, why not Urky? I need someone and he fills the bill because his taking-off will cause a stir, especially in the way I have managed it, without in any serious way depriving the world of a useful human creature. Besides, I have become impatient with his hoity-toity ways with me, as well as his stinginess. It is an oddity of people with unusual sexual tastes that they must enjoy them in the company of somebody whom they can patronize and look down on; I think Oscar Wilde really liked his grooms and messenger boys better than he ever liked aristocratic Bosie. There are men who like vulgar women, as well as women who prefer vulgar men; snobbery in sex has never been carefully investigated. But I, to whom Urky was what a dog is to a man, have grown tired of playing the gossiping old Edinburgh wifie, to be snubbed and put down by The McVarish. The worm turns: the parasite punishes.

"So, a few hours ago when the tedious charade of the Two Old Edinburgh Ladies had sniggered toward its close, I made a change in the script, which Urky at first saw as an ingenious variation designed for his pleasure. Oh, invaluable parasite!

"—Imagine him, tied up and giggling like a schoolgirl as I lean closer and closer.

MRS. MASHAM: Mistress Morley, my dear, you do giggle so! It can't be good for you. I shall have to punish you, you naughty girlie. Look how you've disturbed your frock! I shall have to tie you up tight, my wee lassie, verra tight indeed.—But och! what a foolish giggler! Can ye not laugh a guid hearty laugh! Here, let me show you how. See, I am going to put this record

on the machine; it's Sir Harry Lauder singing 'Stop Your Tickling, Jock'.—Now, listen how Sir Harry laughs; that's a laugh,
eh? A guid, hearty laugh? Come on, Mistress Morley, sing with
me and Sir Harry:

> *I'm courtin' a fairmer's dochter,*
> *She's one o' the fairest ever seen;*
> *Her cheeks they are a rosy red,*
> *And her age is just sweet seventeen—*

I'll just turn up the volume a bit to encourage you. And I'll tickle
you! Yes, I will! See, I'm coming at you to tickle you!—Och,
do ye call that a laugh? I know what! Ordinary tickling will
never do the job. Now watch: ye see I have here my knitting
needles. If I just insert this one up your great red nose, Mistress
Morley, and wiggle it a wee bit to tickle the hairs, eh? Ticklish,
eh? But still not enough; let's put the other needle up the other
hole in yer neb. See, when I wiggle them both how easy it is
to laugh? Laugh right along with Sir Harry? Och, that's not
laughin'. That's more like shriekin'. I'll just push them in a wee
bit further. No, no, it's no good rollin' yer een and greeting,
Mistress Morley, my dear.—D'ye know, a great idea occurs to
me! Juist suppose now—I'll need some sort of a hammer—so
juist suppose I take off my shoe, so. Then wi' the heel o't I gie
the ends o' the needles a sharp tap—one, two: But Mistress
Morley, ye're no longer laughin'. Only Sir Harry is laughin'.

"—And indeed only Sir Harry was laughing, for Urky with two
aluminum knitting-needles well up into his brain was quite quiet.
Whether it was the needles, or fright, or heart failure, or all three,
Urky was dead, or too close to it to make a sound.
"—So—out of Mistress Masham's old gown in a flash, set the
repeating-device and turn up the volume on the record-player to
the full, so that Sir Harry will go on singing his song and laughing
heartily until a neighbour phones the caretaker, and out of the
flat, not forgetting my envelope. But no need to worry about
fingerprints; I wanted to leave plenty of those, so that there would
be no danger of anybody else stealing my murder.
"—No fingerprints, however, on one little thing I removed from
Urky's apartment; he had it locked up in his desk, and like so

many vain people he had a simple faith in simple locks. You may open your gifts now, children.—Package Number One: yes, it's the Gryphius Portfolio and it's yours, my dears, to gloat over and keep for your own dear little selves. Especially those letters concealed in the back flap. Urky knew all about them, and he hinted about what he knew, underestimating my power to comprehend, as he always did, the poor sap.

"—The other package, the big one, is the complete typescript of my novel *Be Not Another.* I am writing to the papers, Clem, to tell them what I have told you here, and to say that you have my book, that it is rare and fine, and that applications from publishers who hope to get it must be made to you. And there will be applications! Oh, indeed there will be applications! Publishers will fight to publish a murderer, when they had no time to spare for a philosopher. It's a hot property, so make the toughest deal you can, dear Clem. Revenge me, dear old boy; roast 'em, squeeze 'em, gouge 'em for every possible dollar. And keep a sharp eye on the kind of publicity they give it; I have provided the material for a first-rate campaign—'The book a man murdered to place in your hands!—A great, misunderstood genius speaks to his times!—The philosopher-criminal bares his soul!'—that's the first line of fire, after which you'll easily get some eminent critic to plump it all out with praise as the distilled essence of a mighty, ruined spirit.

"—As for the monies accruing, I leave it to you to set up a handsome research fund at Spook, so that people like yourself can get some of the dibs to further their work. And I want it named the Parlabane Bounty, so that every pedant who wants a hand-out has to burn a tiny pinch of incense to my memory. You know how these things are managed. Don't worry that Spook won't take the money. The dear old coll. will sanctify my gift to its use, never fear.

"—That's all, I think. I hope you and Molly won't come to quarrelling over the Gryphius. Because I mean it for both of you, and if either one tries to bag it all, or cheat the other out of her due— you, Clem, appear to me as the most likely to try a dirty trick— there will certainly be hell to pay, if I have any influence in hell.

"—All that now remains is for me to put myself beyond the reach of the law. Not, let me assure you, because I fear it, but because

I despise it. I could get a lot of interest in my book by hanging around, going to trial, and having my say from the dock. But you know what would happen in a modern court. Could I expect justice? Could I, who have planned a murder and killed a man in cold blood, expect to have my own life exacted as poetic justice (the only really satisfactory kind) demands? Not a chance! What a parade there would be of psychiatrists, eager to 'explain' me! They would assure the court that I was 'insane' because of course no man in his right mind ever wants revenge or personal advancement. People drunk with the cheap wine of compassion would assure one another that I was 'sick'. But I'm not insane and I am in robust health, and I will not expose myself to the pity of my inferiors.

"—So, one last tiny joke. Everybody will assume that I have committed suicide. Well, if I have, let them prove it. But you, dear friends, shall know. I am going to dress myself now in my habit; then I shall lie down on my bed with my prayerbook at hand, and I shall inject into a vein in my foot—there are lots of them—a few c.c.s of potassium; in thirty seconds I shall be dead, and that will just give me time, I trust, to drop the needle through a hole in the floor under Ma Mustard's bedside carpet. Neat, don't you think? I shall be encharnelled (good, romantic word) before anybody thinks to look under the carpet. Keep this under your hat. I should like to puzzle my old friends, the police. Their doctors are very unimaginative.

"—However, should any snooper decide to dig me up, I make a final bequest under the provision of the Human Tissue Gift Act of 1971. I leave my arse-hole, and all necessary integument thereto appertaining, to the Faculty of Philosophy; let it be stretched upon a steel frame so that each New Year's Day, the senior professor may blow through it, uttering a rich, fruity note, as my salute to the world of which I now take leave, in search of the Great Perhaps.

My blessings on you both, my dears,

John Parlabane

(sometime of the Society of the Sacred Mission)

When Darcourt had finished reading, Hollier was already deep in the letters from the back flap of the Gryphius; his face glowed, and when Darcourt spoke to him he seemed at first not to hear.

"Clem?"

"Hmm."

"We ought to talk about that manuscript."

"Yes, yes; but I'll have to go through it carefully before I can say anything definite."

"No, Clem."

"What?"

"You mustn't go through it. I know it's exciting, and all that, but you must realize it isn't yours."

"I don't follow you."

"It's stolen goods, you know."

"McVarish stole it. Now we've got it back."

"No. Not 'we'. You have no right to it whatever. It belongs to the Cornish Estate, and it's my job to see that it is returned to its owners."

Darcourt rose, and took the Gryphius Portfolio and the precious letters out of Hollier's hands, folded it up in its original wrappings, and left the room.

[5]

THE FOLLOWING TEN DAYS were sheer hell for me. First, there was all the worry about Hollier, who collapsed within a few minutes of Darcourt's masterful recovery of the Gryphius Portfolio, and was in such a dreadful way that I feared he might die. I have often heard about people 'collapsing' but what does it mean? In Hollier's case it meant that I could not get him to speak, or apparently to hear, and his eyes fixed on nothingness. He was cold to the touch. He sat crumpled up in an armchair, and kept turning his head slowly toward the left and back again, for all the world like a sturdied sheep; I could not shake him into attention, or get him to his feet. In my alarm I could not think of anything except to call Darcourt back, and in half an hour he reappeared, accompanied by a doctor friend who was, I afterward learned, the same one who had been called to certify the death of Parlabane.

Dr. Greene pushed Hollier about, and tapped him under the knees, and listened to his heart, and waved his hand in front of his eyes, and eventually came up with a diagnosis of shock. Had

Hollier had some severe shock? Yes, said Darcourt, a severe setback related to his research, quite unavoidable; I was impressed by Simon's firmness, his refusal to budge an inch. Aha, said the doctor, he understood completely; such metaphysical ills sometimes came his way in his treatment of academics, who were a delicately balanced lot. But he had known old Clem since their days at Spook, and he was sure he would come round. Would need nursing and tender, loving care, however. So the two men heaved Hollier to his feet, and manhandled him into my small car, which was not really big enough for four people, one of whom was too ill to squeeze himself into a small space, and I drove to Hollier's mother's house in Rosedale—not very far from my own home.

It was not a place I would have chosen to provide tender, loving care. It was one of those houses stiff with Good Taste, and Mrs. Hollier, whom I had never met, was stiff with Good Taste too. I was left in the drawing-room—positively the palest, most devitalized room I have ever been in—while the men and Mrs. Hollier lugged the invalid upstairs; after a while an elderly housekeeper toiled upward with what looked like a cup of bouillon; after an even longer while Darcourt, and Dr. Greene, and Mrs. Hollier returned and I was introduced as a student of the professor's, and Mrs. Hollier gave me a look that could have etched glass, and nodded but did not speak. The doctor was talking reassuringly about a drop in blood pressure that was dramatic but not really alarming, and the necessity for rest, light diet, and detective stories when the patient seemed ready for them. He would keep in touch.

I felt very much out of things. Darcourt and Dr. Greene were the kind of Canadians who understood and could cope with such refrigerated souls as Mrs. Hollier. A Northern land and its Northern people can be brisk and bracing when faced with a metaphysical ill, but I was not of their kind. I had a disquieting feeling that, when Hollier was ill, this was the place where he belonged. However much an intellectual adventurer he might be, this cold home was his home.

That night, therefore, I told Mamusia everything, or as much as she would comprehend, because she insisted on seeing the situation from a point of view entirely her own.

"Of course he is cold and cannot speak," she said; "the curse has been thrown back on him and he is looking inward at his own evil. I told him. But would he listen? Oh, no! Not the great professor, not Mr. Modern! He thought he would be happy if he killed his enemy—because that is what he has done and don't you try to tell me otherwise—but now he knows what it is to kill with hate. The knife, the gun—perhaps you can get away with it if you are made of coarse stuff. But a man like Hollier to kill with hate—he's lucky he didn't die at once."

"But Mamusia, it was the other man—the monk—who killed Professor McVarish."

"The monk was a sly one. A real bad man. I wish I had known him. Such people are rare. But the monk was just a tool, like a knife or a gun—"

"No, no, Mamusia, the monk had terrible hatred for McVarish! For Hollier, too—"

"Sure! All that hate slinking around, looking for a place to explode itself. To think Hollier wanted to pull me in such a mess! He is a fool, Maria. No husband for you. Lucky the Priest Simon drank the spiked coffee."

"You won't look at it as it really is."

"Won't I? Let me tell you, you fool, that my way is the way it really is: all this other stuff is just silly talk by people who don't know anything about hate, or jealousy, or any of the things that rule their lives because they don't accept them as realities, real force. Now you listen to me: I want your car keys."

"What for? You can't drive."

"I don't want to drive. And you shall not drive. Not for forty days. You are mixed up in this, you know. How much I can't say, because I don't believe you have told me the whole truth. But you are not going to drive any car for the next forty days. Not while those men can still reach you."

"What men are you talking about?"

"McVarish and the monk. Don't argue. Give me the keys."

So I did, pretending a reluctance I did not altogether feel. I did not want to figure in one of those accidents in which, the newspapers ambiguously report, a car 'goes out of control'. Perhaps; but into whose control?

I was in great anxiety about what the newspapers would say.

Had Parlabane written to them in the same unbuttoned spirit that he had written to me and Hollier? No: a joker in this as in everything, Parlabane had written his letter to us and delivered it by hand on the Saturday night after he had killed McVarish. The much abbreviated accounts that he had written for the three Toronto papers and which were, I later learned, terrible muddles of crossing out and misused carbon copying, he had posted—but in a mailbox that was intended for overseas post only; upon each he had put a few details in his own hand, so that no paper received quite the same story. This confusion, and the fact that there was no postal delivery on Easter Monday, meant that the papers did not have their story until Thursday; the police, who had been sent a carbon and some further details, did not get their letter until Friday, such is the caprice of modern postal service. Therefore, the story of Urky's taking-off appeared on the Monday as a report of an inexplicable murder, and at the weekend figured again with all the rich embroidery of Parlabane's confession. God be praised, he had not named either me or Hollier in his accounts of the 'ceremonies'—only as custodians of his great book. The police let it be known that they had information not granted to anyone else, and that they were not going to tell all they knew; great destruction among the drug-pushers was predicted by the press.

Between the news of the murder on Monday, and the revelation of its nature and its cause on Thursday, University authorities had lavished much praise on the character of Urky; a devoted teacher, a great scholar, a man of fine character and irreproachable conduct, a loss to the academic community never to be replaced— he was given the works, in a variety of distinguished styles. There was great speculation about The Demon Knitter who had slain the blameless scholar and grossly 'interfered' with his body by stuffing him with velvet ribbon. This was a relief from the bread-and-butter murders with guns and hammers upon obscure and uninteresting victims, with which the press has to do the best it can. This came to an abrupt stop when the real story broke; the plans that had been going forward for a splendid memorial service in Convocation Hall were abandoned. Murray Brown spoke in the Legislature, pointing out that the education of the young was in dubious hands and something like a purge of the whole University community would not be amiss. And of course the news about Parlabane's book galvanized the publishers. The telephone began to ring.

Who was there to answer it but myself? I had been mentioned in Parlabane's letter as one of the two people who had access to the complete typescript, and Hollier could not be reached. He was still cosy, lucky man, in his bed at his mother's house and could not speak on the telephone, his mother said. So I temporized, and evaded direct questions and commitments, and refused to see people, and then was forced to see them when they pushed through the door of Hollier's rooms. Unwillingly I was photographed by newspapermen who lay in wait outside Spook, and hounded by literary agents who wanted to free me from tedious cares; I experienced all the delights of unsought notoriety. I was offered a lot of money for my story, *John Parlabane as I Knew Him*, and the services of a ghost to write it up from my verbal confession. (It was assumed that, as a student, I would not be capable of coherent expression.) I was invited to appear on TV. Hollier's mother was outraged by the newspaper publicity and suspected, by the sixth sense given to mothers, that I had designs on her innocent son, and seemed convinced that the whole thing was my fault. After someone had attempted a clumsy robbery of Hollier's rooms I put the typescript of *Be Not Another* in the vault at Spook and attempted to have the telephone disconnected, but that took several days to accomplish. O tohubohu and brouhaha!

Another thing for which I had cause to thank the spirit of Parlabane was that in none of his letters to police or newspapers had he mentioned the Gryphius Portfolio. Where it was now I had no idea. But late on the Friday of the second week of this siege by newspapers and publishers I was sitting in Hollier's outer room, trying to get on with some of my own work, and not managing to do so, when there came a knock at the door.

"Go away," I shouted.

The knock was repeated, more powerfully.

"Bugger off!" I called, in something like a roar.

But I had not locked the door, and now it opened and Arthur Cornish poked his head around it, grinning.

"That's no way to speak to an old friend, Maria."

"Oh, it's you! If you're an old friend, why didn't you come sooner?"

"I assumed you would be busy. I've been reading about you in the papers, and they all said you were closeted with publishers for twelve hours a day, making juicy terms about your friend's book, over magnums of champagne."

"It's all very well for you to be facetious; I've been living like a hunted animal."

"Do you dare to come out with me for dinner? If you wear a heavy veil, nobody will recognize you. A veil and perhaps a pillow under the back of your coat. I'll say you are an unpresentable aunt; a Veiled Hunchback. Anyhow, I'd thought of going to a nice dark place."

I was not in the mood to be teased, but I was very much in a mood to be fed. I had not dared to eat in a restaurant since the trouble began, and I was sick of Mamusia's grim meals. He took me to a very good place, sat in a dark corner, and ordered a very good meal. It was deeply soothing to the spirit—a far cry from The Rude Plenty in the company of Parlabane. Of course we talked about the murder, the excitement, and the trouble I had been having. There was no pretence of rising above the most interesting thing either of us knew about at the moment, but it was possible, in these circumstances, to see it in a different light.

"So Hollier has taken to his bed and left you holding the bag?"

"The loss of the Gryphius Portfolio was the last straw. He simply couldn't believe Darcourt would take it. Where is it now?"

"I have it. Darcourt was evasive about how he came by it, but I gathered it had something to do with McVarish."

"What are you going to do with it?"

"I'd rather thought of giving it as a wedding present."

"Who to?"

"Why, to you and Hollier, of course. You *are* marrying him, aren't you?"

"No, I'm not."

"Then I am mistaken."

"You never thought any such thing."

"But you and he were so absorbed in your work. You were so very much his disciple. What did the murderer-monk call you— his *soror mystica*."

"You're being very objectionable."

"Not intentionally; I only want to get things straight."

"I wouldn't marry him even if he asked me. Which he won't. His mother wouldn't let him."

"Really? Is he under her thumb, then?"

"That's not fair. He lives for his work. People do, you know, in the University. But when I saw him in his mother's house, I knew that was where his emotions live still. His mother is on to me."

"Meaning?"

"When she looks at me I see a balloon coming out of her head with Gypsy Bitch written in it, like somebody in the comics."

"Not Bitch, surely."

"To people like her all Gypsy girls are bitches."

"That's a shame. I looked forward to giving you that Portfolio as a wedding present. Well, when you decide to marry somebody else, it's yours."

"Oh, please don't say that. Please give it to the University library, because Hollier wants it more than you can guess."

"You forget that it is mine. It was not included in the gifts to the University, and in fact I paid the bill for it less than a month ago; those dealers in rare manuscripts are slow with their bills, you know. Perhaps because they are ashamed of the prices they ask. I feel no yearning to oblige Professor Hollier; I once told you I'm a man of remarkable taste; I don't like a man who doesn't know a good thing when he sees it."

"Meaning—?"

"Meaning you. I think he's treated you shabbily."

"But you wouldn't expect him to marry me just to get the Gryphius, would you? Do you think I'd say yes to such a proposal?"

"Don't tempt me to give you an answer to either of those questions."

"You think very poorly of me, I see."

"I think the world of you, Maria. So let's stop this foolishness and talk to the point. Will you marry me?"

"Why should I marry you?"

"That would take a long time to answer, but I'll give you the best reason: because I think we have become very good friends, and could go on to be splendid friends, and would be very likely to be wonderful friends forever."

"Friends?"

"What's wrong with being friends?"

"When people talk about marriage, they generally use stronger words than that."

"Do they? I don't know. I've never asked anyone to marry me before."

"You mean you've never been in love?"

"Certainly I've been in love. More times than I can count. I've had two or three affairs with girls I loved. But I knew very well that they weren't friends."

"You put friendship above love?"

"Doesn't everybody? No, that's a foolish question; of course they don't. They talk about love to people with whom they are infatuated, and sometimes involved to the point of devotion. I've nothing against love. Most enjoyable. But I'm talking to you about marriage."

"Marriage. But you don't love me?"

"Of course I love you, fathead, but I'm serious about marriage, and marriage with anyone whom I do not think the most splendid friend I've ever had doesn't interest me. Love and sex are very fine but they won't last. Friendship—the kind of friendship I am talking about—is charity and loving-kindness more than it's sex and it lasts as long as life. What's more, it grows, and sex dwindles: has to. So—will you marry me and be friends? We'll have love and we'll have sex, but we won't build on those alone. You don't have to answer now. But I wish you'd think very seriously about it, because if you say no—"

"You'll go to Africa and shoot lions."

"No; I'll think you've made a terrible mistake."

"You think well of yourself, don't you?"

"Yes, and I think well of you—better of you than of anybody. These are liberated days, Maria; I don't have to crawl and whine and pretend I can't live without you. I can, and if I must, I'll do it. But I can live so much better with you, and you can live so much better with me, that it's stupid to play games about it."

"You're a very cool customer, Arthur."

"Yes."

"You don't know much about me."

"Yes, I do."

"You don't know my mother, or my Uncle Yerko."

"Give me a chance to meet them."

"My mother is a shop-lifter."

"Why? She's got lots of money."

"How do you know?"

"In a business like mine there are ways of finding out. You aren't badly off yourself. But your mother is something more than a shop-lifter; you see, I know that, too. She's by way of being famous among my musical friends. In such a person the shop-lifting is an eccentricity, like the collections of pornography some famous conductors are known to possess. Call it a hobby. But must I point out that I'm not proposing to marry your mother?"

"Arthur, you're very cool, but there are things you don't know. Comes of having no family, I suppose."

"Where did you get the idea I have no family?"

"You told me yourself."

"I told you I had no parents I could remember clearly. But family—I have platoons of family, and though most of them are dead, yet in me they are alive."

"Do you really think that?"

"Indeed I do, and I find it very satisfying. You told me you hadn't much use for heredity, though how you reconcile that with rummaging around in the past, as you do with Clement Hollier, I can't imagine. If the past doesn't count, why bother with it?"

"Well—I think I said more than I meant."

"That's what I suspected. You wanted to brush aside your Gypsy past."

"I've thought more carefully about that."

"So you should. You can't get rid of it, and if you deny it, you must expect it to revenge itself on you."

"My God, Arthur, you talk exactly like my mother!"

"Glad to hear it."

"Then don't be, because what sounds all right from her sounds ridiculous from you. Arthur, did anybody ever tell you that you have a pronounced didactic streak?"

"Bossy, would you call it?"

"Yes."

"A touch of the know-it-all?"

"Yes."

"No. Nobody's ever hinted at any such thing. Decisive and strongly intuitive, are the expressions they use, when they are choosing their words carefully."

"I wonder what my mother would say about you?"

"Generous recognition of a fellow-spirit, I should guess."

"I wouldn't count on it. But about this heredity business—have you thought about it seriously? Girls grow to be very like their mothers, you know."

"What better could a man ask than to be married to a *phuri dai*; now, how long do you suppose it might take you to make up your mind?"

"I've made it up. I'll marry you."

Some confusion and kissing. After a while—

"I like a woman who can make quick decisions."

"It was when you called me fathead. I've never been called that before. Flattering things like Sophia, and unflattering things like irreverent cunt, but never fathead."

"That was friendly talk."

"Then what you said about being friends settled it. I've never had a real friend. Rebel Angels, and such like, but nobody ever offered me friendship. That's irresistible."

The New Aubrey VI

I WILL NOT MARRY couples with whom I have had no previous discussion; I insist on finding out what they think marriage is, and what they suppose they are doing. In part this is self-preservative caution; I will not become involved with people who want to write their own wedding service, devising fancy vows for their own use, and substituting hogwash from Kahlil Gibran or some trendy shaman for the words of the Prayer Book. On the other hand, I am ready to make excisions for people who find the wording of the marriage service a little too rugged for their modern concepts. I am fussy about music and will permit no 'O Promise Me' or 'Because God Made Thee Mine'; I discourage the wedding march by Mendelssohn, which is theatre music, and the other one from *Lohengrin,* which was a prelude to a notably unsuccessful marriage. I do not regard myself as a picturesque adjunct to a folk ceremony performed by people who have no scrap of religious belief, though I do not require orthodoxy, because I have unorthodox reservations of my own.

I was startled, therefore, by the orthodoxy insisted on by Arthur Cornish and Maria. Startled, and somewhat alarmed, for in my experience too much orthodoxy can lead to trouble; a decent measure of come-and-go is more enduring.

My interview with Arthur and Maria took place in my rooms in Ploughwright before dinner on the Monday preceding their wedding. Maria arrived early, which pleased me, because I wanted some private talk with her.

"Does Arthur know about you and Hollier?"

"Oh yes, I told him all about that, and we've agreed it doesn't count."

"What do you mean by count?"

"It means that as far as we are concerned I'm still a virgin."

"But Maria, it isn't usual nowadays for the virginity of the bride to be an important issue. Love, trust, and seriousness of intention are what really count."

"Don't forget that I am part Gypsy, Simon, and it counts for Gypsies. The value of virginity depends on whose it is; for trivial people, it is no doubt trivial."

"Then what have you told him? That you had your fingers crossed?"

"I hadn't expected you to be frivolous, Simon."

"I'm not frivolous. I just want to be sure you aren't kidding yourselves. It doesn't matter to me, but if it matters to you, I'd like to be sure you know what you are doing. What really matters is whether you have got Hollier completely out of your system."

"Not completely. Of course I love him still, and as Arthur is giving me the Gryphius Portfolio for a wedding present I'll certainly be working on it with Hollier. But he's a Rebel Angel, like you, and I love him as I love you, Simon dear, though of course you're a priest and he's a sort of wizard, which makes all the difference."

"How?"

"Wizards don't count. Merlin and Klingsor and all those were incapable of human love and usually impotent as well."

"What a pity Abelard and Heloise didn't know that."

"Yes. They got themselves into a terrible muddle. If Heloise had been more clear-headed she'd have seen that Abelard was a frightful nerd in human relationships. Of course, she was only seventeen. Those letters! But let's not forget about them: Hollier has led me to some recognition of what wisdom and scholarship are, and that's what matters, not a tiny stumble on the path. You've shown me as much as I am able to understand at present about the generosity and pleasure of scholarship. So I love you both. But Arthur is different, and what I bring to Arthur is untouched by any other man."

"Good."

"Arthur says the physical act of love is a metaphor for a spiritual encounter. That certainly was so with Hollier. Whatever I felt about it, he was ashamed of himself right away."

"I hadn't realized Arthur was such a philosopher about these things."

"Arthur has some amazing ideas."

"So have you. I thought you were in flight from all the Gypsy part of your heritage."

"So I was till I met Parlabane, but his talk about the need to recognize your root and your crown as of equal importance has made me understand that my Gypsy part is inescapable. It has to be recognized, because if it isn't it will plague me all my life as a canker at the root. We're doing a lot of Gypsy things—"

"Maria, be careful; I want to be the priest at your wedding, but I'll have nothing to do with cutting wrists and mingling blood, or waving bloody napkins to show that you have been deflowered, or anything of that sort. I thought you wanted a Christian marriage."

"Don't worry, there'll be none of that. But Yerko is taking himself very seriously as a substitute for my Father; as my Mother's brother he's far more important, really, in Gypsy life. Yerko has demanded, and received, a purchase-price from Arthur in gold. And Yerko has ceremonially accepted Arthur as a 'phral'— you know, a *gadjo* who has married a Gypsy, and who is regarded as a brother, though of course not as a Gypsy. And Mamusia has given us the bread and salt; she breaks a nice crusty roll and salts it and gives us each half and we eat it while she says that we shall be faithful until we tire of bread and salt."

"Well, you seem to be going the whole Romany hog. Are you certain you need a marriage ceremony after all that?"

"Simon, how can you ask such a thing! Yes, we want our marriage to be blessed. We're serious people. I am much more serious, much more real, for having accepted my Gypsy root."

"I see. What about Arthur's root?"

"Very extensive, apparently. He says he has a cellar full of dried roots."

When Arthur came he didn't want to talk about his root; he seemed more inclined to lecture me about orthodoxy, of which he had an unexpectedly high opinion. The reason so many modern marriages break down, he informed me, was because people did not dare to set themselves a high enough standard; they went into marriage with one eye on all the escape-hatches, instead of accepting it as an advance from which there was no retreat.

I think he expected me to agree enthusiastically, but I didn't. Nor did I contradict him; I have had too much experience of life to attempt to tell a really rich person anything. They are as bad as the young; they know it all. Arthur and Maria had agreed that they wanted no revised service as it appears in modern Prayer Books, and he brought along a handsome old volume dated 1706 with a portrait of Queen Anne, of all people, as a frontispiece, which was obviously from the possessions of the late Francis Cornish. I knew the form, of course, but felt I should take them through it, to make sure they knew what they were letting themselves in for, and sure enough they insisted on the inclusion of the passage in the Preamble which debars those who marry 'to satisfie mens carnal lusts and appetites, like brute beasts, that have no understanding'. They wanted to be enjoined publicly 'to avoid fornication' and Maria wanted to vow to 'obey, serve, love, honour and keep' her husband; indeed in the order of service they wanted she would use the word 'obey'—so hateful to the liberal young—twice, and when I questioned it she said that it seemed to her to be like the oath of loyalty to the monarch— which is another vow that most people are too modern to take seriously.

I would have resisted all this antiquarianism if they had not both been so touching in their delight that marriage 'was ordained for the mutual society, help and comfort that the one ought to have of the other'. This was plainly what they were looking for, and Arthur was eloquent about it. "People don't talk to one another nearly enough," he said. "The sex-hobbyists go on tediously about their preoccupation without ever admitting that it is bound to diminish as time passes. There are people who say that the altar of marriage is not the bed, but the kitchen stove, thereby turning it into a celebration of gluttony. But who ever talks about a lifelong, intimate friendship expressing itself in the broadest possible range of conversation? If people are really alive and alert it ought to go on and on, prolonging life because there is always something more to be said."

"I used to think it was horrible to see couples in restaurants, simply eating and never saying a word to one another," said Maria, "but I am beginning to know better. Maybe they don't have to talk all the time to be in communication. Conversation in its true meaning isn't all wagging the tongue; sometimes it is a deeply shared silence. But Arthur and I have never stopped talking since we decided to marry."

"I'm beginning to wonder if we haven't got the legend of Eden all wrong," said Arthur. "God threw Adam and Eve out of the Garden because they gained knowledge at the price of their innocence, and I think God was jealous. 'The Kingdom of the Father is spread upon the earth and men do not see it'—you recognize that, Simon?"

"One of the Gnostic Gospels," said I, a little nettled at being instructed in my own business by this young man.

"*The Gospel of Thomas,* and very juicy stuff," said Arthur, who was in a condition to lecture the Archbishop of Canterbury and the Pope, if they needed any help. "Adam and Eve had learned how to comprehend the Kingdom of the Father, and their descendants have been hard at it ever since. That's what universities are about, when they aren't farting around with trivialities. Of course God was jealous; He was being asked to share some of His domain. I'll bet Adam and Eve left the Garden laughing and happy with their bargain; they had exchanged a know-nothing innocence for infinite choice."

This was all very well, and a great improvement on what I usually meet with when I talk to young couples who are approaching marriage. How dumb a lot of them are, poor dears; quite incapable of putting their expectations into words. They don't even seem to comprehend what my function in the service is—not as somebody who publicly licenses them to sleep together and use the same towels, but as an intermediary between them, the suppliants, and Whatever It Is that hears their supplication. But I had my reservations. These two were a little too articulate for my complete satisfaction. And I wanted to be satisfied, for I still loved Maria deeply.

She knew that I was not easy in my mind, and before they went she said: "What you told us in the first class I took with you is the motto for our marriage. You remember that passage from Augustine?"

"*Conloqui et conridere . . .*"

"Yes. 'Conversations and jokes together, mutual rendering of good services, the reading together of sweetly phrased books, the sharing of nonsense and mutual attentions'. And the mutual attentions of course include sex. So you mustn't look worried, Simon dear."

I would have had to be more than human not to worry. I was losing a great gifted pupil. I was losing a woman whom I had regarded, for a time, as the earthly embodiment of Sophia. Though I knew I could never possess her, I loved her still, and I was going to bind her to a man against whom I knew nothing that was not good, but who somehow bothered me.

I decided this was jealousy. I suppose the Rebel Angels were not above jealousy. It is an unpopular passion; people will confess with some degree of self-satisfaction that they are greedy, or have terrible tempers, or are close about money, but who admits to being jealous? It cannot easily be presented as a good quality with a dark complexion. But my job as a priest is to look human frailty in the face and call it by its right name. I was jealous of Arthur Cornish because he was going to be first in the heart of a woman I still loved. But as Maria had said, a Rebel Angel takes something of a woman's innocence as he leads her toward a larger world and an ampler life, and it is not surprising if the man who has done that is jealous of the man who reaps the benefit. I could understand and value Maria as he never could, I was sure of that; but I was equally sure that Maria could never be mine except on the mythological plane she had herself explained. *What ails you, Father Darcourt, is that you want to eat your cake and have it too; you want to be first with Maria, without paying the price of that position.* All right, I understand. But it still hurts.

Why was I so withholding in my feelings about Arthur? It was because, although I had seen quite a lot of his crown, I knew nothing about his root except what might be inferred from his deep feeling for music. Maria seemed to have yielded to him completely; whatever she had said in the interview just closed had a—no, not a falsity, but a somewhat un-Marialike quality that spoke of Arthur. I had observed that in plenty of brides, but Maria was not to be judged as one of them.

All this orthodoxy—what could it lead to? In my experience the essentials of Christianity, rightly understood, may form the best possible foundation for a life and a marriage, but in the case of people of strongly intellectual bent these essentials need extensive farcing out—I use the word as cooks do, to mean the extending and amplifying of a dish with other, complementary elements—if they are to prove enough. One cannot live on essences.

Young couples whom I interview before marriage are sincere in their faith, or pretend to a sincerity they think I expect, but I know that in the household they set up there will be other gods than the one God. The Romans talked of household gods, and they knew what they were talking about; in every home and every marriage there are the lesser gods, who sometimes swell to extraordinary size, and even when they are not consciously acknowledged they have great power. Every one of the household gods has a dark side, a mischievous side, as when Pride disguises itself as self-respect, Anger as the possession of high standards of behaviour, or Lust as freedom of choice. Who would be the household gods under the Cornish roof?

I knew of the special bee in Maria's bonnet; it was Honour, a concept she had seized from the work of François Rabelais, and made her own. Honour which was said to prompt people to virtuous action and hold them back from vice; was there a dark side to that god? Fruitless to speculate, but I could imagine Honour raising quite a lot of hell if it were to swell to a size where it darkened the face of the one God.

[2]

MARIA'S MARRIAGE WAS, all things considered, a great success, though there were a few oddities. Standing at the altar, waiting for the bride, I could see her, at the back of Spook Chapel, slipping off her shoes, so that she was barefoot when she confronted me, though her long white wedding-gown concealed her feet most of the time. It made her a little shorter than I had ever seen her before, and although Arthur Cornish was not especially tall, he seemed to tower above her. He was handsomely and conventionally dressed; it was plain that his morning clothes were made for him and not hired. I have seen many a wedding given a decided list toward comedy when the groom wore badly fitting hired clothes, and was all too plainly ill at ease in his first stiff collar. (I think it a bad omen when the groom is the clown of the circus; it is usually the top hat that is the betrayer.) Arthur and his best man were impeccable. The best man was Geraint Powell, a rising young actor from the Stratford Festival, handsome, self-assured, and somewhat larger than life as actors tend to be on ceremonial occasions. Where, I wondered, had Arthur picked up such a friend, who was as near as our modern age allows to what used to be called a matinee idol.

The music, too, was impeccable and I suppose it was Arthur's choice. It was strange to see Maria walking with the splendid poise of a barefoot Gypsy down that long aisle on the arm of Yerko, who padded like a huge bear, and made a great business of smiling through tears, which he clearly thought was the proper emotional tone for his role. Somewhere—God knows where— Yerko had found a purple Ascot stock, and it was pinned with a garnet like an egg.

Mamusia, in the first seat of the first pew on the bride's side of the chapel, was a *phuri dai* in state attire, a complexity of skirts, gaudy petticoats, not less than three shawls, and her hair greased until she was like the God of Sion; her paths dropped fatness. No tears for Mamusia; matriarchal dignity was her role.

I had no eyes for anyone but Maria, when once she appeared, and as she drew near me the ache I felt changed to astonishment, for she was wearing the longest necklace I have ever seen. The Lord Mayor of a great city might have envied it. It was made of gold roundels at least two inches in diameter, stamped with the image of some horned beast; without rude peering I could not read the inscription on each piece, but I could make out a word that looked like 'Fyngoud'. What was this? Some Scottish treasure? Mamusia's Maria Theresa thalers, which she wore for the occasion, were nothing to this. To increase the resemblance to a mayoral chain it was pinned far out on her shoulders and quite a lot of it hung down her back, beneath her veil; if it had simply depended from her neck, like an ordinary necklace, it would have reached almost to her thighs.

There she was, my darling and my joy, standing beside the man to whom I was to marry her. Time to begin.

" 'Dearly beloved, we are gathered together here in the sight of God, and in the face of this congregation' (and what a crew they are—nobody but Mamusia on the bride's side of the chapel, except Clement Hollier, who looked about as well pleased as I felt, and on the groom's side a considerable group of people who could have been relatives, though some were probably board members and business associates) 'to joyn together this man and this woman in Holy Matrimony.' " Which I did, marvelling, not for the first time, how short the marriage service is, and how easy and inevitable the answers are, compared with the tedious rigmarole involved in a divorce. And at the end, in duty bound, I implored God to fill Maria and Arthur with spiritual benediction and grace, so that they might so live together in this life that in the world to come they might have life everlasting. I don't think I have ever spoken those words with a stronger sense of ambiguity.

It was a morning wedding—the orthodox Arthur again—and afterward there was a reception, or party, or whatever you like to call it, in one of the rooms Spook sometimes makes available for such affairs, a room of oaken academic solemnity. It was here that Mamusia held court, and was gracious in what she appeared to think an Old World Viennese style toward Arthur's business friends, who all seemed to be called Mr. Mumble and Ms. Clackety-Clack. Maria had set aside her veil for a kerchief tied in the married woman's style. Yerko was rather drunk and extremely communicative.

"You saw the necklace, Priest Simon?" he said. "What you think it worth, eh? You'll never guess, so I'll tell you." Warmly and boozily he whispered an astounding sum into my ear. "I make it myself; took me a week working hours and hours every day. Now, this is the big thing; all that gold except the chains, which I made out of some personal gold left by her father, Tadeusz, was Maria's purchase price! You know—what Arthur paid me, as her uncle, to marry her. Sounds funny, you say, but it is the

Gypsy way and because Arthur is rich and a *gadjo,* he has to pay plenty. My sister and me, we are people of wealth, too, but an old custom is an old custom. That's why we give it back, in the necklace. You saw those big pieces? A full ounce of gold, every one. Guess what they were; come on, guess—Krugerrands, that's what they are. Pure gold and Maria has them for her own if anything goes wrong. Because these *gadji,* their money is all paper anyways and could go *phtttt* any day. What do you think of that for generosity, eh? What do you say to a family that gives back all of the purchase price?"

I could only say that it seemed extremely open-handed. Hollier was listening; he said nothing and looked sour. But Yerko was not finished with me.

"Tell me, Priest Simon, what kind church is this? I know you are a good priest—real priest, very strong in power—but I look everywhere and what do I see? Bebby Jesus? Nowhere! Not a picture, not a figure. Lots of old saints behind the altar, but not Bebby Jesus or his Mother. Doesn't this church know who Bebby Jesus is?"

"Bebby Jesus is everywhere in our chapel, Yerko, don't doubt it for a moment."

"I didn't see him. I like to see, then I believe." And Yerko padded off to get himself some more champagne, which he drank in gulps.

"There you are," said I to Hollier. "I think I agree with Yerko; we ought to make the evidences of faith more obvious in our churches. We've refined faith almost out of existence."

"Nonsense," said Hollier. "You don't think anything of the sort. That sort of thing leads directly to plaster statuary of the most degraded kind. I'm hating all this, Sim. I loathe this self-conscious ethnicity—purchase price, and bare feet. In a few minutes we'll all be dancing around shouting and spilling wine."

"I thought that was just your thing," I said; "the Wild Mind at work. Whoop-de-doo and unbuttoned carousing."

"Not when it's done simply for show. It's like those rain-dances Indians are coaxed to do for visiting politicians."

He still looked unwell from his collapse, so I didn't contradict him. But he felt what I was thinking.

"Sorry," he said. "I have to toast the bride, and making speeches always puts me in a bad state."

He needn't have worried; the Mumbles and the Clackety-Clacks were real Canadian Wasps and unlikely to take off their shoes, or sing. Powell, the actor, was master of ceremonies, and in a few minutes he called for silence, so that Hollier might speak—which he did, with what I thought a degree of solemnity too severe for a wedding, though I was grateful for what he said.

"Dear friends, this is a happy occasion, and I am particularly honoured at having been asked to propose the health of the bride. I do so with the deepest feeling of tenderness, for I love her as a teacher to whom she has been the most enriching and rewarding of pupils. We teachers, you know, can only rise to our best when we have great students, and Maria has made me surpass myself and surprise myself, and what I have given to her—which I will not pretend with foolish modesty has been little—she has equalled with the encompassing warmth of her response. She is surrounded at this moment by her two families. Her mother and her uncle, who so clearly represent the splendid tradition of the East and of the past, and by Father Darcourt and myself, who are here as devoted servants of that other tradition which she has claimed as her own and to which she has brought great gifts. One mother, the *phuri dai,* the Mother of the Earth, is splendidly present among us: but the other, the Alma Mater, the bounteous mother of the University and the whole great world of learning and speculative thought of which the University is a part, is all about us. With such a heritage it is almost superfluous to wish her happiness, but I do so from my heart, and wish her and her husband long life and every joy that the union of root and crown can bring. Those of you who know of Maria's enthusiasm for Rabelais will understand why I wish her happiness in words of his: *Vogue la galère—tout va bien!*"

Polite applause rose from the Mumbles and the Clackety-Clacks, who seemed a little subdued by what Hollier had said; probably they had expected the usual avuncular facetiousness that goes with such toasts. Then Arthur made a speech that did nothing to lighten the atmosphere. To marry, he said, was to take a hand in a dangerous game where the stakes are the highest—

a fuller life or a life diminished and confined. It was a game for adult players.

The speeches of bridegrooms are usually awful, but I found this one particularly embarrassing.

When toasts were over, and it was time to go—for as priest I know that I should leave before anybody gets obviously drunk, and family quarrels or fist-fights occur—I went to take my leave of Maria.

"Shall we see you again next term?" I said, because I could think of nothing that was not banal.

"I can't be sure, just yet. I may take a year out to get used to being married. But I'll be back. As Clem said, this is my home and you and he are my family. Thank you, thank you, dear Simon, for marrying me to Arthur, and thank you for the year past. I learned so much from you and Clem."

"Very sweet of you to say so."

But then there came over the face of my Maria a look I had never seen on it before, a look of teasing and mischief. "But I think I learned most from Parlabane," she said.

"What could you have learned from that ruffian?"

" 'Be not another if thou canst be thyself'."

"But you learned that from Paracelsus."

"I *read* it in Paracelsus. But I *learned* it from Parlabane. He was a Rebel Angel too, Simon."

Hollier came away with me, and he seemed so desolate that I hesitated to leave him. "Better go home and get some rest," I said.

"I don't want to go home."

I could understand that. The society of Hollier's mother was not precisely what a man needs who has relinquished his love to another man. Time I spoke out.

"Look Clem, there's no use whatever in either of us feeling sorry for ourselves. We've had all of Maria that was coming to us, and we gave her all that our nature and circumstances allowed. Let's not delight ourselves with the bitter-sweet pleasures of Renunciation. No 'It is a far, far better thing I do—' for us. We must be ourselves and know ourselves for what we are: Rebel Angels, we hope, and not a couple of silly middle-aged professors boo-hooing about what could never have been."

"But I was such a fool; I found out too late."

"Clem, don't spit on your luck. You think you have lost Maria; I think you are free of her. Remember your destiny that the *phuri dai* read for you at Christmas? The last card was Fortune, with her ever-turning wheel? It has turned in your favour, hasn't it? You have the Gryphius Portfolio as soon as you and Maria can get together again. That's your destiny, at your age and with your character. You're not a Lover; you're too much a Wizard. Now look here; go to your rooms and have a good afternoon's rest, and come to dinner at Ploughwright at six o'clock sharp. It's a Guest Night."

"No, no, I'll crowd your table."

"Not a bit of it; a guest has dropped out at the last moment, so there's a place which Fate has obviously cleared for you. Six o'clock for drinks. Sharp, mind. Don't keep the Warden waiting."

[3]

IT WAS AN ESPECIALLY GENIAL Guest Night, because it was our last before the long summer break, and also because the calendar and a public holiday had intervened in such a way that it was our first following Easter. Downstairs, when the first part of dinner was over and the students had gone about their own affairs, all our regulars were present, and as well as Hollier, there were two other guests, George Northmore, who was a Judge of the Supreme Court of the province, and Benjamin Jubilei, from the University Library.

I wondered how long it would be before somebody brought up the murder of Urquhart McVarish, and who would do so; I had made a mental bet with myself that it would be Roberta Burns, and I won. Once again, for *The New Aubrey*, I give some notion of how they chirped over their cups.

"Poor old Urky. Don't you remember him dining with us last autumn, and how proud he was of his penis-bone, poor devil? He tried to get a squeak out of me with that, but I was one too many for him; Urky simply had no idea what a tough nut an intelligent middle-aged woman can be."

"He was an Oxonian of the old dispensation," said Penny Raven; "thought women were lovely creatures whose sexual coals could be blown into warmth by raunchy academic chit-chat. Well, well; one down and a few score around this campus still to go."

"Penny, that isn't like you," said Lamotte.

"No, no, Penny," said Deloney; "the poor fellow is dead. Let's not beat the bones of the vanquished."

"Yes," said Hitzig, "we're not hyenas or biographers, to pee on the dead."

"Okay. *De mortuis nil nisi hokum,*" said the unrepentant Penny.

"I was myself at Oxford at least as long ago as McVarish," said the Warden, "and I have never thought meanly of women."

"Oh, but you were Balliol, Warden. Always in the van. Urky was Magdalen—quite another bed of cryptorchids."

The warden smirked; Oxford rivalries died hard in him.

"I wonder what is to become of all his erotica," said Roberta Burns. "He had a pornographic bootjack at his door that always interested me."

"A pornographic b—!" Lamotte was playing the innocent, as he loved to do with women.

"Indeed. A naked woman rendered in brass, lying on her back with her legs astraddle. You put one foot on her face, forced the other into her crotch, and hoiked off your galosh. Practical enough, but offensive to my lingering female sensibilities."

"I never know what people want with such nasty toys," said Lamotte. "It has been my observation, over a long life, that a man's possessions are a surer clue to his character than anything he does or says. If you know how to interpret the language of possessions." Lamotte looked as if he considered himself such a man.

"All we'll ever find in your cupboards are pieces of rare old china," said Deloney; "and from what I hear, René, they don't provide guarantees of a blameless taste."

"What? What? We must hear about this," said Roberta. Lamotte was blushing.

"René is reputed to have a fine collection of bourdaloues," said Deloney.

"Being—?"

"Eighteenth-century china piss-pots for elegant ladies to slip under their skirts on long, cold coach journeys."

"No, no," said Lamotte. "Named for the Abbé Bourdalue who

preached inordinately long sermons—extreme tests of human endurance. But who says this—?"

"Aha, wouldn't you like to know? Are they really painted with naughty pictures?"

"As long as I keep on drinking mineral water while you are sipping port, it will be quite a while before you find out."

"Minds that are too refined slip into grossness. Watch your step, René; we have our eyes on you."

Here it was Lamotte who smirked.

"Do I hear you discussing the deep damnation of Urky McVarish's taking-off?" It was Durdle, shouting down the table, which the etiquette of the occasion forbade him to do.

"Ah, the Pink Ribbon Murder," said Ludlow, the law don. "What did you make of that, Judge?"

"I didn't make much of it," said Mr. Justice Northmore. "I read everything that appeared in all three papers, and the accounts were so muddled and contradictory that I couldn't be sure of anything except that a professor had been murdered under somewhat imaginative circumstances. I wish it had come to trial, so we could have got to the bottom of it—"

Roberta Burns snorted. The Warden raised his eyebrows.

"So that we could have found out the truth about the ten feet of pink ribbon that were concealed in the rectum of the body. Now why would anybody want to do that?"

"There was talk in one of the confessions of 'ceremonies'."

"Yes, yes, Mr. Ludlow, but *what* ceremonies?"

"The full explanation of that was given only in the letter that reached the police, which I had an opportunity of examining," said Ludlow. "Something very complicated about Queen Anne."

"Can we not talk of anything else?" said the Warden.

"Tell me later, Ludlow," hissed the Judge.

But the Warden's mild plea could not stop the flow.

Deloney was querying Ludlow: "Whatever became of the body?"

"McVarish's body, do you mean? I suppose the police released it to the family, when they had found out whatever they could."

"I never knew there was any family."

Here I was able to intervene with special knowledge. "There isn't. So the University took over and there was a very private funeral. Just a couple of people from the President's office at the crematorium."

"That can't have been much of a 'ceremony'. But a parson, one presumes? Who was it? Not you, Simon?"

"No, not me. I read the service for the murderer, however, if you collect such information. I'd known him all my life."

"I think that fellow—the murderer—deserves public thanks," said Elsa Czermak.

"Elsa, we never knew you had it in for Urky!"

"I mean for finishing himself off and not putting the public to heavy expense in the matter of a trial. He must have been a man of considerable quality."

"He was, I can assure you," said Hollier.

"Suicide, wasn't it?" The curious Deloney again. "I heard he drank a whole can of Dog-Off."

Strange to hear Hollier defending Parlabane. "Nothing of the sort I assure you. He was an exceptional man, a man of formidable abilities, with a sense of style that would utterly reject death by Dog-Off."

"Of course, the book! The great book. Is it really magnificent?" said Durdle.

"When will it be published?" said Aronson. "You are supposed to be attending to that, aren't you, Hollier?"

"Somebody else has been dealing with it while I have been ill," said Hollier. "I understand the bidding among the publishers is not yet concluded. The film rights have been in demand from people who haven't even seen the book."

"The really important point is that the original manuscript should be lodged in the University Library," said Jubilei, who was an expert in archival work. "It sprang from this University, it led to an incident in University history that is inescapable, however reprehensible, and we must have it where it properly belongs."

"It's been left to his old college library," said Hollier. "St. John and the Holy Ghost. Spook, to you."

"I am not convinced such a small library will know how to deal with it," said Jubilei. "Can you guarantee that it will be preserved, page by page, between sheets of acid-free paper?"

I thought of Parlabane's squalid mess of typescript, and smiled a private smile.

"I don't see how you can possibly speak of it as 'an incident'," said Durdle. "It's our Crime, don't you see, and a real beauty! How many other universities can boast a crime—an acknowledged, indisputable *crime*, that's to say? It gives us a quality all our own, lifts us high above every other university on this continent. It was international news! Worth at least three Nobel Laureates! Raises us all immeasurably in our professional stature!"

"Oh rubbish! How can you possibly say such a thing?" said Stromwell.

"You can ask that? You, a medievalist! What were the great scholars of the past? Venal, cadging, saucy, spiteful, contumelious, and quarrelsome—Urky and his murderer are right in the pattern—and they were also great humanists. What is the modern scholar? A frowsy scarecrow of bourgeois conventionality."

"Speak for yourself," said Stromwell.

"I do! I do! I was saying precisely that to my wife this morning at breakfast."

"And what did she say?"

"I think she said Yes dear, and went on making a list for her shopping. But that's beside the point, which is that some grotesquerie, some wrenching originality, is a necessary part of real scholarship, and brings a special glory with it. We all share in the dark splendour of Urky's murder; we are the greater for his passing, and his murderer's book is in a special sense our book."

"You don't even know whether or not it is a good book."

As they wrangled, some of the others were trying to change the subject, to please the Warden.

"I have it on very good authority that we shall shortly have another Nobel Laureate in this University," said Boys.

"You mean he's got it?" said Gyllenborg.

"Can't be absolutely certain until the announcement is made, but there are only three possible contenders this year, and I hear our man is top of the list."

"I thought it might be so when I read his Kober Lecture. Ozy spoke like a man who knew he had come to disturb the sleep of the world. We shall have to revise our thinking. Excrement: daily barometer of whether the body—perhaps even the mind—is tending toward health or sickness. Of course he stands on Sheldon's shoulders, but don't we all stand on somebody's past work?"

"That is what lends splendour to a university," said the Warden. "Not these dreadful interruptions of the natural order."

"You lean always toward the light, Warden; perhaps both are necessary, for completeness."

"Quite so," said the Warden. "I confess I never really liked McVarish, but it is good modern theology to acknowledge every man's right to go to hell in his own way."

As I listened, I felt a sadness creeping over me that was unquestionably tinged by the self-pity I had condemned in Hollier earlier in the day. Ah, well; a little self-pity is perhaps not amiss in circumstances where we cannot reasonably expect pity from anyone else. So I gave way to a measure of the harlot-emotion, and to my immense satisfaction it turned in a few minutes to a deep tenderness.

Vogue la galère, Maria. Let your ship sail free.

What's Bred in the Bone

"What's bred in the bone will not
out of the flesh."

ENGLISH PROVERB
FROM THE LATIN, 1290

PART
One

Who Asked the Question?

"THE BOOK MUST BE DROPPED."

"No, Arthur!"

"Perhaps only for a time. But for the present, it must be dropped. I need time to think."

The three trustees in the big penthouse drawing-room were beginning to shout, which destroyed all atmosphere of a business meeting—not that such an atmosphere had ever been strong. Yet this was a business meeting, and these three were the sole members of the newly founded Cornish Foundation for Promotion of the Arts and Humane Scholarship. Arthur Cornish, who was pacing up and down the room, was unquestionably a business man; a Chairman of the Board to his business associates, but a man with interests that might have surprised them if he had not kept his life in tidy compartments. The Reverend Simon Darcourt, pink, plump, and a little drunk, looked precisely what he was: a priest-academic pushed into a tight corner. But the figure least like a trustee of anything was Arthur's wife Maria, barefoot in gypsy style, and dressed in a housecoat that would have been gaudy if it had not been made by the best couturier of the best materials.

There is an ill-justified notion that women are peacemakers. Maria tried that role now.

"What about all the work Simon's done?"

"We acted too quickly. Commissioning the book, I mean. We should have waited to see what would turn up."

"What's turned up may not be as bad as you think. Need it, Simon?"

"I haven't any idea. It would take experts to decide, and they could be years doing it. All I have is suspicions. I'm sorry I ever mentioned them."

"But you suspect Uncle Frank faked some Old Master drawings he left to the National Gallery. Isn't that bad enough?"

"It could be embarrassing."

"Embarrassing! I admire your coolness. A member of a leading Canadian financial family may be a picture-faker!"

"You're neurotic about the business, Arthur."

"Yes, Maria, I am, and for the best of reasons. There is no business so neurotic, fanciful, scared of its own shadow, and downright loony as the money business. If one member of the Cornish family is shown to be a crook, the financial world will be sure that the whole Cornish family is shady. There'll be cartoons of me in the papers: 'Would You Buy an Old Master from This Man?' That kind of thing."

"But Uncle Frank was never associated with the business."

"Doesn't matter. He was a Cornish."

"The best of the lot."

"Perhaps. But if he's a crook, all his banking relations will suffer for it. Sorry: no book."

"Arthur, you're being tyrannous."

"All right; I'm being tyrannous."

"Because you're scared."

"I have good reason to be scared. Haven't you been listening? Haven't you heard what Simon has been telling us?"

"I'm afraid I've been clumsy about this whole thing," said Simon Darcourt. He looked miserable; his face was almost as white as his clerical collar. "I shouldn't have told you my suspicions—because that's all they are, you know—the very first thing. Will you listen while I tell you what is really bothering me? It isn't just your Uncle Frank's cleverness with his pencil. It's the whole book.

"I'm a disciplined worker. I don't mess about, waiting for inspiration, and all that nonsense. I sit down at my desk and wire in and make prose out of my copious notes. But this book has twisted and turned under my hands like a dowser's hazel twig. Does the spirit of Francis Cornish not want his life to be written? He was the most private man I've ever known. Nobody ever got much out of him that was personal—except two or three, of whom Aylwin Ross was the last. You know, of course, that Francis and Ross were thought to be homosexual lovers?"

"Oh my God!" said Arthur Cornish. "First you suspect he was a picture-faker and now you tell me he was a poofter. Any other little surprises, Simon?"

"Arthur, don't be silly and coarse," said Maria; "you know that homosexuality is an O.K. kink nowadays."

"Not in the money-market."

"Oh, to hell with the money-market."

"Please, my dears," said Darcourt. "Don't quarrel, and if I may say so, don't quarrel foolishly about trivialities. I've been busy on this biography for eighteen months and I'm not getting anywhere. You don't frighten me by threatening to quash it, Arthur. I've got a mind to quash it myself. I tell you I can't go on. I simply can't get enough facts."

Arthur Cornish had his full share of the human instinct to urge people to do what they do not want to do. Now he said, "That's not like you, Simon; you're not a man to throw in the towel."

"No, please don't think of it, Simon," said Maria. "Waste eighteen months of research? You're just depressed. Have a drink and let us cheer you up."

"I'll gladly have a drink, but I want to tell you what my position is. It's more than just author's cold feet. Please listen to my problem. It's serious."

Arthur was already getting drinks for the three of them. He set a glass that was chiefly Scotch with a mere breathing of soda in front of Darcourt, and sat down on the sofa beside his wife.

"Shoot," he said.

Darcourt took a long and encouraging swig.

"You two married about six months after Francis Cornish died," said he. "When at last his estate was settled, it became apparent that he had a lot more money than anybody had supposed—"

"Well, of course," said Arthur. "We didn't think he had anything but his chunk of his grandfather's estate, and what his father left, which could have been considerable. He was never interested in the family business; most of us thought of him as an eccentric— a man who would rather mess around with his collections of art than be a banker. I was the only member of the family who had an inkling of what made him feel that way. Banking isn't much of a life if you have no enthusiasm for it—which fortunately I have, which is why I'm now Chairman of the Board. He had a comfortable amount of money; a few millions. But ever since he died, money has been turning up in substantial chunks from unexpected places. Three really big wads in numbered accounts in Switzerland, for instance. Where did he get it? We know he got big fees for authenticating Old Masters for dealers and private collectors, but even big fees don't add up to additional millions. What was he up to?"

"Arthur, shut up," said Maria. "You promised to let Simon tell us his problem."

"Oh, sorry. Go ahead, Simon. Do you know where the extra money came from?"

"No, but that's not the most important thing I don't know. I simply don't know who he was."

"But you must. I mean, there are verifiable facts."

"Indeed, there are, but they don't add up to the man we knew."

"I never knew him at all. Never saw him," said Maria.

"I didn't really know him," said Arthur. "I saw him a few times when I was a boy, at family affairs. He didn't usually come to those, and didn't seem at ease with the family. He always gave me money. Not like an uncle tipping a nephew, with a ten-dollar bill; he would slip me an envelope on the sly, often with as much as a hundred dollars in it. A fortune to a schoolboy, who was being brought up to respect money and look at both sides of a dollar bill. And I remember another thing; he never shook hands."

"I knew him much better than either of you, and he never shook hands with me," said Darcourt. "We became friends because we shared some artistic enthusiasms—music, and manuscripts, and calligraphy, and that sort of thing—and of course he made me one of his executors. But as for shaking hands—not Frank. He did once tell me that he hated shaking hands. Said he could smell mortality on his hand when it had touched somebody else's. When he absolutely had to shake hands with some fellow who didn't get his clear signals, he would shoot off to the washroom as soon as he could and wash his hands. Compulsive behaviour."

"That's odd," said Arthur. "He always looked rather dirty to me."

"He didn't bathe much. When we cleared out his stuff he had three apartments, with six bathrooms among them, and every bathtub was piled high with bundles of pictures and sketches and books and manuscripts and whatnot. After so many years of disuse I wonder if the taps worked. But he had preserved one tiny washroom—just a cupboard off an entry—and there he did his endless hand-washing. His hands were always snowy white, though otherwise he smelled a bit."

"Are you going to put that in?"

"Of course. He hadn't a bad smell. He smelled like an old, leather-bound book."

"He sounds rather a dear," said Maria; "a crook who smells like an old book. A Renaissance man, without all the boozing and sword-fighting."

"Certainly no boozing," said Darcourt. "He didn't drink—at least not in his own place. He would take a drink, and even several drinks, if somebody else was paying. He was a miser, you know."

"This is getting better and better," said Maria. "A bookysmelling, tight-fisted crook. You can surely make a wonderful biography, Simon."

"Shut up, Maria; control your romantic passion for crooks. It's her gypsy background coming out," said Arthur to Darcourt.

"Would you two *both* shut up and let me get on with what I have to say?" said Darcourt. "I am not trying to write a sensational book; I am trying to do what you asked me to do nearly two years ago, which is to prepare a solid, scholarly, preferably not deadly-dull biography of the late Francis Cornish, as the first act of the newly founded Cornish Foundation for Promotion of the Arts and Humane Scholarship, of which you two and I are at present the sole directors. And don't say you 'commissioned' it, Arthur. Not a penny changed hands and not a word was written in agreement. It was a friendly thing, not a money thing. You thought a nice book about Uncle Frank would be a nice thing with which to lead off a laudable Foundation devoted to the nice things that you thought Uncle Frank stood for. This was a typically Canadian act of smiling niceness. But I can't get the facts I want for my book, and some of the things I have not quite uncovered would make a book which—as Arthur so justifiably fears—would cause a scandal."

"And make the Foundation and the Cornish name stink," said Arthur.

"I don't know about the Cornish name, but if the Foundation had money to give away I don't think you'd find artists or scholars fussing about where it came from," said Darcourt. "Scholars and artists have no morals whatever about grants of money. They'd take it from a house of child prostitution, as you two innocents will discover."

"Simon, that must have been an awfully strong drink," said Maria. "You're beginning to bully us. That's good."

"It was a strong drink, and I'd like another just like it, and I'd like to have the talk to myself to tell you what I know and what I don't know."

"One strong Scotch for the Reverend Professor," said Arthur, moving to prepare it. "Go on, Simon. What have you actually got?"

"We might as well begin with the obituary that appeared in the London *Times,* on the Monday after Francis died. It's a pretty good summing up of what the world thinks, up to now, about your deceased relative, and the source is above suspicion."

"Is it?" said Maria.

"For a Canadian to be guaranteed dead by *The Times* shows that he was really somebody who could cut the mustard. Important on a world level."

"You talk as if the obituary columns of the London *Times* were the Court Circular of the Kingdom of Heaven, prepared by the Recording Angel."

"Well, that's not a bad way of putting it. *The New York Times* had a much longer piece, but it isn't really the same thing. The British have some odd talents, and writing obituaries is one of them. Brief, stylish, no punches pulled—so far as they possessed punches. But either they didn't know or didn't choose to say a few things that are public knowledge. Now listen: I'll assume a *Times* voice:

MR. FRANCIS CHEGWIDDEN CORNISH

On Sunday, September 12, his seventy-second birthday, Francis Chegwidden Cornish, internationally known art expert and collector, died at his home in Toronto, Canada. He was alone at the time of his death.

Francis Cornish, whose career as an art expert, especially in the realms of sixteenth-century and Mannerist painting, extended over forty years and was marked by a series of discoveries, reversals of previously held opinions, and quarrels, was known as a dissenter and frequently a scoffer in matters of taste. His authority was rooted in an uncommon knowledge of painting techniques and a mastery of the comparatively recent critical approach called iconology. He seemed also to owe much to a remarkable intuition, which he displayed without modesty, to the chagrin of a number of celebrated experts, with whom he disputed tirelessly.

Born in 1909 in Blairlogie, a remote Ontario settlement, he enjoyed all his life the freedom which comes with ample means. His father came of an old and distinguished family in Cornwall; his mother (née McRory) came of a Canadian family that acquired substantial wealth first in timber, and later in finance. Cornish never engaged in the family business, but derived a fortune from it, and he was able to back his intuitions with a long purse. The disposition of his remarkable collections is as yet unknown.

He received his schooling in Canada and was educated at Corpus Christi College, Oxford, after which he travelled extensively, and was for many years a colleague and pupil of Tancred Saraceni of Rome, some of whose eccentricities he was thought to have incorporated in his own rebarbative personality. But in spite of his eccentricities it might always have been said of Francis Cornish that for him art possessed all the wisdom of poetry.

During and after the 1939–45 war he was a valuable member of the group of Allied experts who traced and recovered works of art which had been displaced during the hostilities.

In his later years he made generous gifts of pictures to the National Gallery of Canada.

He never married and leaves no direct heirs. It is authoritatively stated that there was no foul play in the manner of his death.

"I'm not mad about that," said Maria. "It has a snotty undertone."

"You don't know how snotty a *Times* obit can be. I suspect most of that piece was written by Aylwin Ross, who thought he would outlive Francis, and have a chuckle over the last sentence. In fact, that obit is Ross's patronizing estimate of a man who was greatly his superior. There's a question in it that is almost Ross's trade mark. It's quite decent, really, all things considered."

"What things considered?" said Arthur. "What do they mean, 'no foul play'? Did anybody suggest there was?"

"Not here," said Darcourt, "but some of the people on the Continent who knew him might have wondered. Don't find fault with it; obviously Ross chose to suppress a few things the *Times* certainly has in its files."

"Like—?"

"Well, not a word about the stinking scandal that killed Jean-Paul Letztpfennig, and made Francis notorious in the art world. Reputations fell all over the place. Even Berenson was just the teeniest bit diminished."

"Obviously you know all about it, though," said Arthur, "and if Uncle Frank came out on top, that's all to the good. Who was Tancred Saraceni?"

"Queer fish. A collector, but known chiefly as a magnificent restorer of Old Masters; all the big galleries used him, or consulted him, at one time or another. But some very rum things went through his hands to other collectors. Like your Uncle Frank, he was rumoured to be altogether too clever with his paintbox; Ross hated him."

"And that *Times* piece is the best that was said about Francis?" said Maria.

"Do you notice they say he went to school in Canada but was *educated* at Oxford?" said Arthur. "God, the English!"

"*The Times* was generous in its own terms," said Darcourt. "They printed the piece I sent to them as soon as I saw their obit. Listen to this: published in their issue of September 26:

FRANCIS CORNISH

Professor the Rev. Simon Darcourt writes:

Your obituary of my friend Francis Cornish (Sept. 13) is correct in all its facts, but gives a dour impression of a man who was sometimes crusty and difficult, but also generous and kind in countless personal relationships. I have met no one who knew him who thought for an instant that his death might have been from other than natural causes.

Many leading figures in the art world regarded him as a knowledgeable and co-operative colleague. His work with Saraceni may have gained him the mistrust of some who had felt the scorn of that ambiguous figure, but his authority, based on unquestioned scholarship, was all his own, and it is known that on several occasions his opinion was sought by the late Lord Clark. In a quarrel it was rarely Cornish who struck the first blow, although he was not quick to resolve a dispute or forget an injury.

His fame as an authority on painting overshadowed his substantial achievements in the study and scientific examination of illumination and calligraphy, an area not much favoured by critics of painting and sculpture, but which seemed to him to be significant, as providing clues to work on a larger scale. He was also a discriminating collector of music MSS.

During his years in Canada after 1957 he did much to encourage Canadian painters, though his scorn for what he regarded as psychological fakery in certain modern movements generated a good deal of heat. His own aesthetic approach was carefully considered and philosophically founded.

An eccentric, undoubtedly, but a man of remarkable gifts who shunned publicity. When his collections have been examined it may emerge that he was a more significant figure in the art world of his time than is at present understood.

"That's a lot better, Simon," said Maria, "but it's still a long way from being a rave."

"It's not my business to write raves, but to speak the truth, as a friend who is also a scholar and a man with his eyes open."

"Well, can't you do that in the biography?"

"Not if it means exposing Uncle Frank as a picture-faker," said Arthur.

"Listen, Arthur, you're going too far. The most you can say is that my book won't have any Cornish money behind it unless it presents a whitewashed portrait of Francis. You forget that I could find a commercial publisher. I don't write bad books, and a book you would think scandalous might appeal to them as a good commercial proposition."

"Simon—you wouldn't!"

"If you bully me, I might."

"I don't mean to bully you."

"But that's what you're doing. You rich people think you have unlimited power. If I decided to write this book entirely on my own responsibility you couldn't do a thing to stop me."

"We could withhold information."

"You could if you had any, but you haven't and you know it."

"We could sue you for defamation."

"I'd take care not to defame the living Cornishes, and surely you know the law doesn't care about defamation of the dead."

"Please, will you men stop being silly and threatening one another," said Maria. "If I understand Simon rightly, it's this very lack of information and creeping suspicion that's holding him up. But you must have some stuff, Simon. Anybody's life can be dug up to some extent."

"Yes, and used by cheap writers with lots of spicy innuendo to make a trumpery book. But I'm not that kind of writer. I have my pride; I even have my tiny reputation. If I can't do a first-rate job on old Frank I won't do anything."

"But all this stuff about Saraceni, and what *The Times* doesn't say about this other fellow—the one who died or was killed or whatever happened—surely can be tracked down, and fleshed out. Though if it means a book that suggests Francis Cornish was a crook, I hope you'll do what you can about that." Arthur seemed to be climbing down.

"Oh, that—I can get that right enough. But what I want is what lies behind it. How did Francis get into such company? What was it in his character that disposed him to that part of the art world, instead of keeping his skirts clear like Berenson, or Clark? How did a rich amateur—which is what he was, to begin with—get mixed up with such shabby types?"

"Just luck, probably," said Arthur. "What happens to people is so often nothing but the luck of the game."

"I don't believe that," said Darcourt. "What we call luck is the inner man externalized. We make things happen to us. I know that sounds horrible and cruel, considering what happens to a lot of people, and it can't be the whole explanation. But it's a considerable part of it."

"How can you say that?" said Arthur. "We are all dealt a hand of cards at birth; if somebody gets a rotten hand, full of twos and threes and nothing above a five, what chance has he against the fellow with a full flush? And don't tell me it's how he plays the game. You're not a poker-player or a bridge-player, Simon, and you just don't know."

"Not a card-player, I admit, but I am a theologian, and rather a good one. Consequently I have a different idea of the stakes that are being played for than you have, you banker. Of course everybody is dealt a hand, but now and then he has a chance to draw another card, and it's the card he draws when the chance comes that can make all the difference. And what decides the card he draws? Francis was given a good, safe hand at birth, but two or three times he had a chance to draw, and every time he seems to have drawn the joker. Do you know why?"

"No, and neither do you."

"I think I do. Among your uncle's papers I found a little sheaf of horoscopes he had prepared for him at various points in his life. He was superstitious, you know, if you call astrology superstition."

"Don't you?"

"I reserve judgment. What is important is that he obviously believed in it to some extent. Now—your uncle's birthday fell at a moment when Mercury was the ruling sign of his chart, and Mercury at the uttermost of his power."

"So?"

"Well? Maria understands. Isn't her mother a gifted card-reader? Mercury: patron of crooks, the joker, the highest of whatever is trumps, the mischief-maker, who upsets all calculations."

"Not just that, Simon," said Maria; "he is also Hermes, the reconciler of opposites—something out of the scope of conventional morality."

"Just so. And if ever there was a true son of Hermes, it was Francis Cornish."

"When you begin to talk like that, I must leave you," said Arthur. "Not in disgust, but in bafflement. Life with Maria has given me a hint of what you are talking about, but just at this moment I can't continue with you. I have to catch a plane at seven tomorrow, and that means getting up at five and being at the airport not much after six—such is the amenity and charm of modern travel. So I'll give you another drink, Simon, and bid you good-night."

Which Arthur did, kissing his wife affectionately and telling her not to dare to wake early to see him off.

"Arthur pours a very heavy drink," said Darcourt.

"Only because he thinks you need it," said Maria. "He's wonderfully kind and observant, even if he does make noises like a banker about this book. You know why, don't you? Anything that challenges the perfect respectability of the Cornishes stirs him up, because he has secret doubts of his own. Oh, they're unimpeachable so far as money-dealers go, but banking is like religion: you have to accept certain rather dicey things simply on faith, and then everything else follows in marvellous logic. If Francis was a bit of a crook, he was the shadow of a great banking family, and they aren't supposed to cast shadows. But was Francis a crook? Come on, Simon, what's really troubling you?"

"The early years. Blairlogie."

"Where exactly is Blairlogie?"

"Now you're beginning to sound like The Times. I can tell you a little about the place as it is now. Like a good biographer I've made my pilgrimage there. It's in the Ottawa Valley, about sixty miles or so north-west of Ottawa. Rough country. Perfectly accessible by car now, but when Francis was born it was thought by a lot of people to be the Jumping-Off Place, because you couldn't get there except by a rather primitive train. It was a town of about five thousand people, predominantly Scots.

"But as I stood on the main street, looking for evidence and hoping for intuitions, I knew I wasn't seeing anything at all like what little Francis saw at the beginning of the century. His grand-father's house, St. Kilda, is cut up into apartments. His parents' house, Chegwidden Lodge, is now the Devine Funeral Parlours—yes, Devine, and nobody thinks it funny. All the timber business that was the foundation of the Cornish money is totally changed. The McRory Opera House is gone, and nothing remains of the McRorys except some unilluminating stuff in local histories written by untalented amateurs. Nobody in modern Blairlogie has any recollection of Francis, and they weren't impressed when I said he had become quite famous. There were some pictures that had come from his grandfather's house that had passed into the possession of the public library, but they had stored them in the cellar, and they were perished almost beyond recognition. Just tenth-rate Victorian junk. I drew almost a total blank."

"But are the childhood years so important?"

"Maria, you astonish me! Weren't your childhood years important? They are the matrix from which a life grows."

"And that's all gone?"

"Gone beyond recovery."

"Unless you can wangle a chat with the Recording Angel."

"I don't think I believe in a Recording Angel. We are all our own Recording Angels."

"Then I am more orthodox than you. I believe in a Recording Angel. I even know his name."

"Pooh, you medievalists have a name for everything. Just somebody's invention."

"Why not somebody's revelation? Don't be so hidebound, Simon. The name of the Recording Angel was Radueriel, and he wasn't just a book-keeper; he was the Angel of Poetry, and Master of the Muses. He also had a staff."

"Wound with serpents, like the caduceus of Hermes, I suppose."

"Not that kind of staff; a civil service staff. One of its important members was the Angel of Biography, and his name was the Lesser Zadkiel. He was the angel who interfered when Abraham was about to sacrifice Isaac, so he is an angel of mercy, though a lot of biographers aren't. The Lesser Zadkiel could give you the lowdown on Francis Cornish."

Darcourt by now was unquestionably drunk. He became lyrical.

"Maria—dear Maria—forgive me for being stupid about the Recording Angel. Of course he exists—exists as a metaphor for all that illimitable history of humanity and inhumanity and inanimate life and everything that has ever been, which must exist some place or else the whole of life is reduced to a stupid file with no beginning and no possible ending. It's wonderful to talk to you, my dearest, because you think medievally. You have a personification or a symbol for everything. You don't talk about ethics: you talk about saints and their protective spheres and their influences. You don't use lettuce-juice words like 'extraterrestrial'; you talk frankly about Heaven and Hell. You don't blather about neuroses; you just say demons."

"Certainly I haven't a scientific vocabulary," said Maria.

"Well, science is the theology of our time, and like the old theology it's a muddle of conflicting assertions. What gripes my gut is that it has such a miserable vocabulary and such a pallid pack of images to offer to us—to the humble laity—for our edification and our faith. The old priest in his black robe gave us things that seemed to have concrete existence; you prayed to the Mother of God and somebody had given you an image that looked just right for the Mother of God. The new priest in his whitish lab-coat gives you nothing at all except a constantly changing vocabulary which he—because he usually doesn't know any Greek—can't pronounce, and you are expected to trust him implicitly because he knows what you are too dumb to comprehend. It's the most overweening, pompous priesthood mankind has ever endured in all its recorded history, and its lack of symbol and metaphor and its zeal for abstraction drive mankind to a barren land of starved imagination. But you, Maria, speak the old language that strikes upon the heart. You talk about the Recording Angel and you talk about his lesser angels, and we both know exactly what you mean. You give comprehensible and attractive names to psychological facts, and God—another effectively named psychological fact—bless you for it."

"You're raving ever so slightly, darling, and it's time you went home."

"Yes, yes, yes. Of course. This instant. Can I stand up? Ooooh!"

"No, wait a minute, I'll see you out. But before you go, tell me what it is about Francis you want and can't discover?"

"Childhood! That's the key. Not the only key, but the first key to the mystery of a human creature. Who brought him up, and what were they and what did they believe that stamped the child so that those beliefs stuck in his mind long after he thought he had rejected them? Schools—schools, Maria! Look what Colborne has done to Arthur! Not bad—or not all of it—but it clings to him still, in the way he ties his tie, and polishes his shoes, and writes amusing little thankees to people who have had him to dinner. And a thousand things that lurk below the surface, like the conventionality he showed when he heard Francis might be rather a crook. Well—what were the schools of Blairlogie? Francis was never out of the place until he was fifteen. Those were the schools that marked him. Of course, I could fake it. Oh, I wish I had the indecency of so many biographers and dared to fake it! Not crude faking, of course, but a kind of fiction, the sort of fiction that rises to the level of art! And it would be true, you know, in its way. You remember what Browning says:

> . . . Art remains the one way possible
> Of speaking truth, to mouths like mine, at least.

I could serve Francis so much better if I had the freedom of fiction."

"Oh, Simon, you don't have to tell me that you are an artist at heart."

"But an artist chained to biography, which ought to bear some resemblance to fact."

"A matter of moral conscience."

"And a matter of social conscience, as well. But what about artistic conscience, which people don't usually pay much attention to? I want to write a really good book. Not just a trustworthy book, but a book people will like to read. Everybody has a dominant kind of conscience, and in me the artistic conscience seems to be pushing the other two aside. Do you know what I really think?"

"No, but you obviously want to tell me."

"I think that probably Francis had a daimon. As a man so much under the influence of Mercury, or Hermes, it would be quite likely. You know what a daimon is?"

"Yes, but go on."

"Oh, of course you'd know. I keep forgetting what a knowing girl you are. Since you became the wife of a very rich man, it somehow seems unlikely that you should know anything really interesting. But of course you're your mother's child, splendid old crook and sibyl that she is! Of course you know what Hesiod calls daimons: spirits of the Golden Age, who act as guardians to mortals. Not tedious manifestations of the moral conscience, like Guardian Angels, always pulling for Sunday-school rightness and goodiness. No, manifestations of the artistic conscience, who supply you with extra energy when it is needed, and tip you off when things aren't going as they should. Not wedded to what Christians think of as what is right, but to what is your destiny. Your joker in the pack. Your Top Trump that subdues all others!"

"You could call that intuition."

"Bugger intuition! That's a psychological word, grey and dowdy. I prefer the notion of a daimon. Know the names of any good daimons, Maria?"

"I've only come across the name of one, engraved on an old gem. It was Maimas. D'you know, Simon, I think I'm getting a little drunk too. Now, if you could just get the ear of the Lesser Zadkiel and—well, call him Maimas—you'd have all you want about Francis Cornish."

"Wouldn't I, by God! I'd have what I want. I'd know what was bred in the bone of old Francis. Because what's bred in the bone will come out in the flesh, and we should never forget it.—Oh, I really must go."

Darcourt gulped the remainder of his drink, kissed Maria impressionistically—in the region of the nose—and stumbled toward the door.

Not too steadily, Maria rose and took him by the arm. Should she offer to drive him home? No, that might make things worse than if he made it himself, refreshed by the cool night air. But she went with him to the hallway of the penthouse on top of the condominium where she and Arthur lived, and steered him toward the elevator.

The doors closed, but as he descended, she could hear him shouting, "What's bred in the bone! Oh, what was bred in bone?"

THE LESSER ZADKIEL and the Daimon Maimas, who had been drawn by the sound of their own names to listen to what was going on, found it diverting.

—Poor Darcourt, said the Angel of Biography. Of course he'll never know the whole truth about Francis Cornish.

—Even we do not know the entire truth, brother, said the Daimon Maimas. Indeed, I've already forgotten much of what I did know when Francis was my entire concern.

—Would it amuse you to be reminded of the story, so far as you and I can know it? said the Angel.

—Indeed it would. Very generous of you, brother. You have the record, or the film, or the tape or whatever it must be called. Could you be bothered to set it going?

—Nothing simpler, said the Angel.

What Was Bred in
the Bone?

To BEGIN, when Francis was born there, Blairlogie was not the Jumping-Off Place, and would have strongly resented any such suggestion. It thought of itself as a thriving town, and for its inhabitants the navel of the universe. It knew itself to be moving forward confidently into the twentieth century, which Canada's great Prime Minister, Sir Wilfrid Laurier, had declared to be peculiarly Canada's. What might have appeared to an outsider to be flaws or restrictions were seen by Blairlogie as advantages. The roads around it were certainly bad, but they had always been bad so long as they had been roads, and the people who used them accepted them as facts of their existence. If the greater world wished to approach Blairlogie, it could very well do so by the train which made the sixty-mile journey from Ottawa over a rough line, much of it cut through the hardest granite of the Laurentian Shield, a land mass of mythic antiquity. Blairlogie saw no reason to be easily accessible.

The best of the town's money and business was firmly in the hands of the Scots, as was right and proper. Below the Scots, in a ranking that was decreed by money, came a larger population of Canadians of French descent, some of whom were substantial merchants. At the bottom of the financial and social heap were the Poles, a body of labourers and small farmers from which the upper ranks drew their domestic servants. Altogether the town numbered about five thousand carefully differentiated souls.

The Scots were Presbyterian, and as this was Canada at the turn of the century their religious belief and their political loyalty were the important conditioning factors in their lives. These Presbyterians might have had some trouble in formulating the doctrine of predestination or foreordination which lay deep in their belief, but they had no practical difficulty in knowing who was of the elect, and who belonged to a creation with a less certain future in Eternity.

The French and the Poles were Roman Catholics, and they too knew precisely where they stood in relation to God, and were by no means displeased with their situation. There were a few Irish, also Catholics, and some odds and ends of other racial strains—mongrels of one sort and another—who had mean churches suited to their eccentricities, dwindling toward a vacant-store temple that changed hands from one rampaging evangelist to another, in whose windows hung gaudy banners displaying the Beasts of the Apocalypse, in horrendous detail. There were no Jews, blacks, or other incalculable elements.

The town could have been represented as a wedding-cake, with the Poles as the large foundation layer, bearing the heaviest weight; the French, the middle layer, were smaller but central; the Scots were the topmost, smallest, most richly ornamented layer of all.

No town is simple in every respect. People who liked perfection and tidiness of structure were puzzled by the quirk of fate which decreed that the Senator, by far the richest and most influential man in Blairlogie, cut right across accepted ideas: though a Scot, he was an R.C., and though rich he was a Liberal, and his wife was French.

The Senator was the person to begin with, for he was Francis Chegwidden Cornish's grandfather, and the origin of the wealth that supported Francis's life until he gained a mysterious fortune of his own.

The Senator was the Honourable James Ignatius McRory, born on the Isle of Barra in the Hebrides in 1855, who had been brought to Canada in 1857 by parents who were, like so many of their kind, starving in their beautiful homeland. They never succeeded in getting the ache of starvation and bitter poverty out of their bones, though they did better in the New World than they could have done at home. But their son James—called Hamish by them, because that was his name in the Gaelic they customarily spoke between themselves—hated starvation and resolved as a child to put poverty well behind him, and did so. Necessity sent him early to work in the forests which were a part of the wealth of Canada, and ambition and daring, combined with an inborn long-headedness (to say nothing of his skill with his fists, and his feet when fists were not enough), made him a forest boss very young, and a contractor for lumber companies shortly after, and the owner of a lumber company of his own before he was thirty, by which time he was already a rich man.

A common enough story, but, like everything else connected with Hamish, not without its individual touches. He did not marry into a lumbering family, to advance himself, but made a love-match with Marie-Louise Thibodeau when he was twenty-seven and she was twenty, and he never desired any other woman afterward. Nor did the life in the camps make him hard and remorseless; he treated his men fairly when he was an employer, and when he came to have money he gave generously to charity and to the Liberal Party.

Indeed, the Liberal Party was, after Marie-Louise and one other, the great love of his life. He never stood for Parliament, but he supported and financed men who did so; in so far as there was a party machine in Blairlogie, where he settled as soon as he no longer had to live near the forests, Hamish McRory was the brains behind the machine; thus nobody was surprised when Sir Wilfrid Laurier appointed him to the Senate when he was not yet forty-five, making him the youngest man, and demonstrably one of the ablest, in the Upper House.

A Canadian senator was, in those days, appointed for life, and some senators were known to give up all political effort once they felt their feet on the red carpet of the Upper Chamber. But Hamish had no intention of relaxing his party zeal because of his new honour, and as a senator he was more Sir Wilfrid's man in an important area of the Ottawa Valley than ever before.

WHEN ARE WE GOING to get to my man? said the Daimon Maimas, who was eager to make his contribution to the story.

—In due season, said the Lesser Zadkiel. Francis must be seen against his background, and if we are not to start at the very beginning *of all things, we must not neglect the Senator. That's the biographical way.*

—I see, you want to do it on the nature and nurture principle, said Maimas, and the Senator is both.

—Nature and nurture are inextricable; only scientists and psychologists could think otherwise, and we know all about them, don't we?

—We should. We've watched them since they were tribal wizards, yelping around the campfire. Go on. But I'm waiting for my chance.

—Be patient, Maimas. Time is for those who exist within its yoke. We are not time-bound, you and I.

—I know, but I like to talk.

APART FROM MARIE-LOUISE, and of a different order, the Senator's deep love was his elder daughter, Mary-Jacobine. Why so named? Because Marie-Louise had hoped for a son, and Jacobine was a fancy derivation from Jacobus, which is James, which is also Hamish. It suggested also a devotion to the Stuart cause, and called up that sad prince James II and his even sadder son, Bonnie Prince Charlie. The name was suggested with implacable modesty by the Senator's sister, Miss Mary-Benedetta McRory, who lived with him and his wife. Miss McRory, known always as Mary-Ben, was a formidable spirit concealed in a little, wincing spinster. It was her romantic notion that her forebears, as Highland Scots, must necessarily have been supporters of the Stuarts, and none of the books she read on that subject suggested that James II and his son, as well as being handsome and romantic, were a couple of pig-headed losers. So Mary-Jacobine it was, affectionately shortened to Mary-Jim.

There was a second daughter, Mary-Teresa—Mary-Tess inevitably—but Mary-Jim was first by birth and first in her father's heart, and she lived the life of a small-town princess, without too much harm to her character. She was taught at home by a governess of unimpeachable Catholicism and gentility, and by Miss McRory; when she was old enough she went to a first-rate convent school in Montreal, the Superior of which was yet another McRory, Mother Mary-Basil. The McRorys were strong for education; Aunt Mary-Ben had gone to the same convent school as the one over which Mother Mary-Basil now ruled. Education and gentility must go hand in hand with money, and even the Senator, whose schooling had been brief, read consistently and well all his life.

The McRorys had offered their full due to the church, for as well as Mother Mary-Basil there was an uncle, Michael McRory, a certainty for a bishopric, probably in the West, as soon as some veteran vacated a likely see. The other men of the family had not done so well; the whereabouts of Alphonsus were unknown since last he had been heard of in San Francisco, Lewis was a drunk, somewhere in the Northern Territories, and Paul had died, in no distinguished way, in the Boer War. It was in the Senator's daughters that the future of the family resided, and Mary-Jim could not help knowing it.

If she thought about the matter at all, it caused her no misgiving, for she was clever at school, possessed some measure of charm, and, because she was prettier than most girls, was thought of— by herself as well as by the rest of the family—as a beauty. Oh, it is a fine thing to be a beauty!

The Senator had great plans for Mary-Jim. Not for her the life of Blairlogie. She must marry well, and marry a Catholic, so she must know a wider circle of suitable young men than Blairlogie could ever afford.

Money makes the mill turn. With his money behind her, Mary-Jim could certainly marry not merely well, but brilliantly.

On January 22, 1901, when Mary-Jim was sixteeen, Queen Victoria died, and King Edward VII ascended the throne. This pleasure-loving prince made no secret of his intention to change the social structure of the Court, decreeing that in future young ladies of good family should be presented to their Sovereign not at subdued afternoon receptions, as in his mother's day, but at evening Courts, which were in effect balls, and that the doors of the Court should be open to people who were not of the old, assured aristocracy, but who had some "go" in them, as His Majesty phrased it. Even the daughters of magnates from the Dominions, if possessed of sufficient "go", might aspire to this honour.

The Senator had made his fortune by seizing opportunities

while lesser people failed to see what was before their eyes. Mary-Jim should be presented at Court. Gently, methodically, and implacably, the Senator set to work.

In the beginning, luck was with him. The King-Emperor's Coronation had to wait until a year of mourning for the Old Queen had been observed; a royal illness intervened, so there were no Courts until the royal household moved into Buckingham Palace in the spring of 1903, and initiated a splendid season of Court Balls. Mary-Jim was presented then, but it was a close thing, and it took the Senator all the time at his disposal to manage it.

He began, logically, by writing to the secretary of the Governor-General of Canada, Lord Minto, asking for advice and, if possible, help. The answer, when it came, said that the matter was a delicate one, and the secretary would put it before His Excellency when a propitious moment turned up. The moment must have been elusive, and several weeks later the Senator wrote again. It had not been possible to put the matter before His Excellency, who was understandably much involved in the ceremonies preceding and following the Coronation. By this time it was August. The secretary suggested that the matter was not one of great urgency, as the young lady was still of an age to wait. The Senator began to wonder if Government House was still shy of the McRorys, remembering that awkward affair of more than twenty years ago. He also came to understand the nature of courtiers in some degree. He decided to go elsewhere. He asked for a few minutes of the Prime Minister's time, on a personal matter.

Sir Wilfrid Laurier was always ready to make time to see Hamish McRory, and when he heard that the personal matter was a request that he should politely speed up affairs at Government House, he was all smiles. The two men spoke together in French, for the Senator had always spoken in Canada's other tongue with his wife. The two men were staunch Catholics, and, without putting too much stress on it, felt themselves other than the very English group at Government House, and were determined not to be slighted. Sir Wilfrid, like many men who have no children, dearly loved a family, and was warmed by a father's desire to launch his daughter into the world with every advantage.

"Be sure that I shall do my very best, my dear old friend," said he, and his leave-taking of Hamish was in his most gracious style.

It was less than a week later that Hamish received a message that he should call again on Sir Wilfrid. The great man's advice was brief.

"I don't think we shall get far with His Excellency," said he. "You should write to our representative in London, and tell him what you want. I shall write also; I shall write today. If the presentation can be managed, it will certainly be done."

It was done, but not quickly or easily.

The representative in London was the resoundingly titled Baron Strathcona and Mount Royal, but the Senator's letter began "Dear Donald", because they knew each other well through the Bank of Montreal, of which the Baron, as plain Donald Smith, was president. He was well aware of Hamish McRory through the freemasonry of the rich, which overrides even politics. A letter from the Baron came as soon as a mailboat could carry it; the thing would be done, and his wife would be pleased to present Mary-Jim at Court. But he warned that it would take time and diplomacy, and possibly even a little arm-twisting, for the desire to appear at Court was by no means confined to the McRorys.

Reports followed over several months. Things were going well; the Baron had dropped a word to a Secretary. Things were hanging fire: the Baron hoped to meet the Secretary at his club, and would jog his memory. Things were rather clouded, for the Secretary said there were people with prior claims, and the list of debutantes must not be too long. A stroke of luck: a New Zealand magnate had choked to death on a fishbone and his daughter had reluctantly been forced into mourning. The thing was virtually assured, but it would be premature to make any moves until official invitations had been received; meanwhile Lady Strathcona was doing some backstairs haggling, for which, as the daughter of a former Hudson's Bay official, she had an inherited aptitude.

At last, in December of 1902, the impressive cards arrived, and the Senator, who had bottled the matter up inside himself for more than a year, was able to reveal his triumph to Marie-Louise and Mary-Jim. Their response was not entirely what he had foreseen. Marie-Louise was in an immediate fuss about clothes, and Mary-Jim thought it nice, but did not seem greatly impressed. Neither understood the immensity of his triumph.

As letters began to arrive from Lady Strathcona, they learned better. The matter of clothes was carefully explained, and as these included garments not only for the Court Ball, but for the London Season it initiated, mother and daughter should lose no time in getting to London and into the dressmakers' salons. A suitable place to live would have to be found, and already the rentable houses in appropriate parts of London were being snapped up. What jewels had Marie-Louise? Mary-Jacobine must undergo a rigorous training in Court etiquette, and Lady Strathcona had booked her into a class being conducted by a decayed Countess who would, for a substantial fee, explain these rites. The curtsy was all-important. There must be no toppling.

Lord Strathcona was even more direct. Bring a large cheque-book and get here in time to have some knee-breeches made, were his principal pieces of advice to the Senator.

The McRorys did as they were bid, and set out for London early in January with a mass of luggage, including two of those huge trunks with rounded lids that used to be called Noah's Arks.

It had been impossible to get them a London house of the right kind, and a house outside the West End was unthinkable, so Lord Strathcona had booked them into the best suite at the Cecil Hotel, in the Strand. If the Court were grander than the Cecil, the McRorys wondered if they would be worthy of it. At the time the hotel outfitted its male staff with three liveries: sleeve-waistcoats and white stocks for morning, blue liveries with brass buttons and white ties for afternoon, and in the evening the full grandeur of plush breeches, plum-coloured coats with cut-steel buttons, and powdered wigs. It was sumptuous in a manner un-dreamed of in Blairlogie, where a housemaid marked the pinnacle of domestic service; but the McRorys, being naturally thrivers and intelligent, determined not to play the farcical role of colonial cousins any more than they could help, and behaved themselves unassumingly, until they got the hang of things.

The sessions with the decayed Countess presented some dif-ficulty at the beginning, for she showed a tendency to behave as if Mary-Jim's inelegant Canadian speech gave her pain. Snotty old bitch, thought Mary-Jim, who was a convent girl and knew how to deal with tedious instructresses. "Would you prefer that I speak in French, Your Grace?" she asked, and continued for some time, very rapidly, in that language, which the decayed

Countess spoke slowly and indifferently. The decayed Countess understood that she had a Tartar in the McRory child, and mended her ways. When she had recovered herself she dropped a remark about the difficulty of understanding a patois, but nobody was deceived.

At last, in May of 1903, the great night came. Marie-Louise, still a pretty woman, was resplendent in pale-blue chiffon and cloth of silver, embroidered with stripes of brilliants, the swathed bodice (over a repressive new corset) fastened with diamonds, which had been hired from a discreet jeweller, who did a large trade in such rentals. Mary-Jim was modestly done up in tulle and mousseline-de-soie. The Senator wore his accustomed tailcoat and white waistcoat above, and his unaccustomed corded-silk knee-breeches and double black-silk stockings below. They were photographed in the drawing-room of their suite at four o'clock in the afternoon, in their grandeur; the ladies had been put to rights by the hairdresser between one and half past two, and had then been forced to bathe with the uttermost care, so as not to wet or tumble their careful head-arrangements. An expert maid from the hotel had encased them in their splendid gowns. After the photographer had gone they ate a light meal in their suite, and then had nothing to do but sit and fret inwardly until half past nine, when the carriage arrived to take them to the Palace. They could have walked there in fifteen minutes, but with the crush of people going to Court, it took a full three-quarters of an hour to make the journey, during which they were inspected, at every stop, by crowds who had gathered to have a look at the toffs.

They had been fretting because they were sure they would know no one at Court—how could they? They would hang dejectedly around the walls, pretending that they were solitary from choice. In their panicky moments they were sure they would bump into things, break ornaments, spill food. The Lord Chamberlain would strike the floor with his wand, crying, "Throw those colonial rubes out!" But that was not the way the King-Emperor entertained.

As soon as they had arrived, and given up their cloaks, a smiling aide swooped upon them, saying, "Ah, there you are, Senator! Madame! Mademoiselle! The High Commissioner and Lady

Strathcona are upstairs; I'll take you to them at once. Awful crush, isn't it"—and much more genial, meaningless, but reassuring chatter until they were safe under the wing of the Strathconas, and Mary-Jim had been hived off into a group, not too obviously defined, of the girls who were to be presented.

There were thrones on a dais at the end of the room but—what, no trumpets? No, just a quiet entry—or as quiet as a royal entry can ever be—of a very stout, shortish man in uniform and a blaze of orders, and a lady of great beauty, wearing enough jewels, thought the Senator, to finance a railway. Ladies curtsied; gentlemen bowed. The King and Queen were seated.

Without preamble the ladies in the special group began to lead forward their protégées. An aide with a list in his hand murmured to the blue-eyed man and the smiling, beautiful, deaf woman. The moment came: taking Mary-Jim's hand, Lady Strathcona led her forward to the steps of the dais, and together they curtsied; the aide murmured, "Miss Mary-Jacobine McRory." It was over. The campaign which had taken twenty-two months was complete.

The Senator, from the crowd, had watched intently. Had the royal eyes lightened at Mary-Jim's beauty? This was a king who admired beauty—had he been impressed? Impossible to tell, but at least the prominent blue eyes had not been veiled. The child looked so lovely it gripped his heart. Dark, high-coloured from her Highland ancestry, Mary-Jim was unquestionably a beauty.

The presentations were quickly over, and the royal couple left their thrones. The aide swooped upon the McRorys again.

"Must introduce you to some people. May I present Major Francis Cornish? He's going to help me in seeing that you get everything you want."

Major Francis Cornish was not very young, not very old. Not very handsome, but not precisely plain. If he were called distinguished, it would be because of the eyeglass he wore in his right eye, and his fine moustache, which defied all laws of facial hair by growing sidewise instead of straight down, and turning up at the ends. He wore the dress uniform of an excellent regiment, but not a Guards regiment. He bowed to the ladies, extended the forefinger of his right hand to the Senator, and said, almost inaudibly, "Howjahdo?" But he stayed with the McRorys, whereas the other aide, murmuring that he had some people to see to, vanished.

The music began: a Guards band, but with string players turning it into a splendid orchestra. Dancing, and Major Cornish saw that Mary-Jacobine had as many suitable partners as she needed. He himself waltzed with her, and with Marie-Louise. Time passed without the McRorys ever feeling out of things or overlooked. And, astonishingly soon to Mary-Jacobine, it was time for supper.

Royalty was supping in an inner room with a few personal friends, but something of their magic lingered in the large supper-room, where Marie-Louise exclaimed over *Blanchailles à la Diable, Poulardes à la Norvégienne, Jambon d'Espagne à la Basque, Ortolans rôtis sur Canapés,* and ate them all, following with a great many patisseries and two ices. The splendour of the meal quite overcame any lingering coldness she, as a French Canadian, might feel about British royalty. They knew what food was, these people! As she ate, and under the influence of an 1837 sherry, an 1892 champagne, an 1874 Château Langoa, and—"Oh, I shouldn't, Major, but this is my weakness, you know?"—some 1800 brandy, she confided to the Major more than once that his Sovereign really knew how to do things properly. She ate until the new corset began to take its vengeance, for Marie-Louise had not the fashionable lady's art of picking at the splendid supper.

Mary-Jacobine ate very little; she had suddenly become aware of what being presented at Court meant; until then she had only known that it was another step in her life, with lessons to be learned, that meant a great deal to her father. But here she was, suddenly awakened in a real palace, among such people as she had never seen, dancing to such a band as she had never heard. That lady with the splendid diamonds, making her way to the inner room, was the Marchioness of Lansdowne. The lady in black satin? The Countess of Dundonald. That was the Countess of Powis in blue satin, diamond-embroidered; one of the great Fox beauties; known to be a daring gambler. Major Cornish was ready with all information, and when she became accustomed to his murmuring manner of speech she engaged him in what might almost pass as conversation, though on her side it was almost entirely questions, and on his almost telegraphic answers. But he was unquestionably attentive, securing more and more food for the mother, and showing the most respectful, but never slavish, admiration for the daughter.

A stir in the room. The King and Queen were withdrawing. More bowing and curtsying. "Shall I see you to your carriage?" That must be the way courtiers got rid of guests. Marie-Louise, a little overcome with food and wine, pats the front of her bodice indulgently, and her daughter wishes she might sink through the floor. Could any of the countesses have noticed? At last, after some waiting that the aides make as agreeable as possible, the carriage comes and the Senator's name is shouted very loudly by a footman. The Major hands them into the carriage. He leans toward Marie-Louise when she is safely seated and murmurs something that sounds like "Permission to call?" Sure, Major, whatever you please. Then back to the Cecil Hotel.

Marie-Louise kicks off her tight shoes. The maid comes back and delivers her from the cruel constriction of her corset. The Senator is melancholy, but exalted. His darling is launched into the world where she truly belongs. In future he will cut his beard in the fashion of the King-Emperor, though the Senator's beard is black, and his physique, developed in his youth in the forests where he had plied the axe and the saw, would make two of the King-Emperor, fat though that monarch undoubtedly is. He kissed his daughter an affectionate good-night.

She retired to her room. Like her father she was melancholy, but exalted, but she was also very young. A Court Ball, her presentation, countesses, splendidly uniformed young men—and now it was over, forever! The maid appeared. "Shall I help you to undress, miss?"

"Yes. Then tell somebody to bring me a bottle of champagne."

OF COURSE, IT WAS *the mother stuffing herself that did the mischief, said the Daimon Maimas.*

—*I fear so, said the Lesser Zadkiel. The McRorys held up very well, otherwise. They were not less accustomed to court than many other people who were there. They had a certain native gumption that kept them in good order, except for the eating and drinking. Do you think it is time now for us to take a look at Major Francis Cornish?*

FRANCIS CORNISH WAS A MAN OF FASHION, in terms of his era, and within the rules governing an officer of a good regiment. In consequence he was something outside the experience of the McRorys, who found his quiet, drawling voice, his reticence, his eyeglass, and his air of not being wholly alive quite unlike anything they had met with. He was a man with his way to make, for he was a younger son of a good family, without much money except his Army pay, and that would shortly cease. The Major had served well, but not conspicuously, in the Boer War, and had been wounded seriously enough to cause him to be invalided back to England, and he knew that the Army had not much in store for him in the future. He had decided to retire from his regiment, therefore, and he must do something, must find his place in the world, for the next portion of his life. It took him no time at all to decide that marriage was his aim and his hope.

Marriage could be a career for a man like the Major. Englishmen without money had for some time been establishing themselves in the world by marrying rich American girls, and everybody knew about the most significant marriages that had taken place. It was not unknown for fortunes of two million pounds, and even more, to cross the Atlantic through such matches, where the daughter of an American railway king or steel monarch was united with an English nobleman. It was a fair enough exchange, in the eyes of the great world: aristocracy on the one hand, and great wealth on the other, seemed to have been ordained for each other in Heaven. There are Heavens for all kinds of people, including those who think chiefly in terms of aristocracy and wealth. Major Cornish thought there might be a modest place in the world of wealth for himself.

The Major was no fool. He knew what he had to offer: unimpeachable family descent, but without title; a good Army career and the knowledge of how to behave in the world of fashion as well as when confronting Boers who had no notion of how to fight like gentlemen; a reasonable person, though not much in the way of wit or learning, beyond what it took to be a decent chap and an efficient soldier. Therefore, it would be foolish for him to aspire to one of the great American fortunes. But a lesser fortune, though still a substantial one, might be discovered among the young ladies from the Colonies. He had friends at Court, brother officers who would let him know what was coming up, so to speak. The McRory girl, with a large, though not clearly estimated, timber fortune behind her, and herself a beauty— though not yet in the duchess category—would do him nicely. It was as simple as that.

The Court had, of course, its aides, its gentlemen-in-waiting, its special group who might be called upon to look after guests when the Court entertained; it was known as "doing the agreeable". But there was always room for another presentable man who knew the ropes and would do his duty by some of the waifs and strays who always had to be looked after on great occasions. The Major spoke to a friend who was an aide; the aide spoke to a chamberlain; the Major was given the nod for the right Court occasion and gained his introduction to the McRorys. The Senator was not the only man who knew how to plan and contrive.

The London Season that followed the McRorys' appearance at Court was brilliant as no season had been for decades, and although they certainly were not in the thick of it, they managed to appear, somehow, at the principal events. Lady Strathcona was helpful; guided by her husband, who knew which English magnates might like to meet a Canadian magnate who was knowledgeable about investments in that rich colony, they were invited here and there, spent weekends at country houses, and managed to get themselves to Henley and Ascot under good auspices. Marie-Louise's talent for bridge gained her a place in a world that was mad for bridge, and the French-Canadian intonation of her speech, so embarrassing to her daughter, seemed to her hostesses provincial but not disagreeable. The Senator could talk to anybody about money in any of its multifarious aspects without sounding too much like a banker, and his fine looks and Highland gallantry made him acceptable to the ladies. They did not move in the very highest society, but they did pretty well.

As for Mary-Jacobine, her prettiness became something very

like beauty in the sunshine of this unfamiliar world. She gained a new bloom. Impressionable as the young are, she moderated her own speech considerably to meet English expectations, and learned to call pleasing things "deevie" and unpleasing things "diskie" like the girls she met. Doubtless it was the unaccustomed rich food and unaccustomed wine that disturbed her convent-bred digestion, for sometimes she was unwell in the mornings, but she learned how to be a delightful companion (it is not a natural accomplishment) and she was a very good dancer. She acquired admirers.

Of these Major Francis Cornish was the most persistent, though he was far from being her favourite. She made fun of him to some of her more lively dancing partners, and they, with the disloyalty of flirtatious young men, took up her name for him, which was the Wooden Soldier. He did not manage to appear everywhere the McRorys went, and that did not trouble him, for to be too pervasive would not have suited his plan of campaign. But he had what was needed to be a man modestly in the fashion: he had a small flat near Jermyn Street, and he was a member of three good clubs, to which he was able to introduce the Senator. It was in one of these, after luncheon, that he asked the Senator for permission to put the decisive question to Mary-Jacobine.

The Senator was surprised, and demurred, and said he would like to think about it. That meant talking with Marie-Louise, who thought her daughter might do much, much better. He mentioned the matter to Mary-Jacobine, who laughed, and said she would marry for love, and did Papa really suppose anybody could love the Wooden Soldier? Papa thought it unlikely, and told Major Cornish that the time was not yet ripe for his daughter to marry, and perhaps they should defer the question for a while. His daughter, in spite of her blooming appearance, was not as well as he wished her to be. Could they talk of it later?

August came, and of course it was out of the question for the fashionable world to remain in London. It dispersed toward Scotland, and the McRorys went with it to two or three northern estates. But they were back in London, at the Cecil, by the end of September, and Major Cornish happened to be in town as well, and as attentive as good manners permitted.

So frequent had Mary-Jim's digestive difficulties become that Marie-Louise thought they had gone beyond what Blairlogie called "bilious attacks" and the simple remedies Blairlogie used in such cases, so she summoned a doctor. A fashionable one, of course. His examination was swift and decisive, and his diagnosis was the worst possible.

Marie-Louise broke the news to her husband in bed, which was their accustomed place for conferences on the highest level. She spoke in French, which was another indication of high seriousness.

"Hamish, I have something awful to tell you. Now don't shout, or do anything stupid. Just listen."

Some hired jewels lost, thought the Senator. Insurance would take care of it. Marie-Louise had never understood insurance.

"Mary-Jim is pregnant."

The Senator turned cold, then heaved himself up on his elbow and looked at his wife in horror.

"She can't be."

"She is. The doctor says so."

"Who was it?"

"She vows she doesn't know."

"That's ridiculous! She must know."

"Well then, you talk to her. I can't get any sense out of her."

"I'll talk to her right now!"

"Hamish, don't you dare. She's miserable. She is an innocent, sweet girl. She knows nothing about such things. You would put shame on her."

"What has she put on us?"

"Calm down. Leave things to me. Now go to sleep."

The Senator could as well have slept on hot ploughshares, but though he tossed and turned and gave his wife a night like nothing she had experienced except at sea, he said no more.

After breakfast the next morning his wife left him with Mary-Jacobine. The Senator made the worst possible beginning.

"What's this your mother tells me?" he said.

Tears. The more he demanded that she dry her eyes and

speak up, the harder they flowed. So there had to be a great deal of paternal petting and plying of the handkerchief (for Mary-Jim had not so far left the convent that she could be depended on to have one with her) and at last something like a story emerged.

After the Presentation at Court she had felt both elevated and depressed. The Senator understood that, for he had felt precisely the same. Never before in her life had she drunk champagne, and she had fallen in love with it. Understandable, thought the Senator, if dangerous. She felt very flat, going to bed after all the gaiety, the splendour of Court, the attention of the aides, the presence of high-born beauties, and so—she had told the maid to get her some champagne. But when it arrived, it was not the maid but one of the splendidly liveried footmen of the Cecil Hotel. He seemed a nice fellow, and she was so lonely that she asked him to take a glass himself. One thing led to another, and—more tears.

The Senator was reassured, if not comforted. His daughter was not a woman, but a child who had got herself into a situation that was beyond her. He had been sure that Mary-Jacobine was the wronged party, and now he was in a position to do something about it. He went to the manager of the hotel, told him that on the night of the Ball his daughter had suffered grave affront from one of the hotel's employees, and demanded to see the man. What sort of place was it that sent a footman, late at night, to a young lady's room? And much more, in a high strain. The manager promised to look into the matter at once.

It was not until late in the afternoon that the manager had anything to report. It was a most unfortunate business, said he, but the man could not be found. It was the custom of the hotel on particularly busy evenings—and the occasion of a Court Ball meant a very busy evening with people who were attending and the much greater number who were not but who wished somehow to have a special celebration—to engage extra men, usually soldiers who were supplied by a Regimental Sergeant-Major who had a sideline in such things, to wear livery and adorn the corridors and public rooms, but not to perform any duty as servants. Through some inexplicable muddle—the Senator could not believe how difficult it was to keep perfect discipline everywhere on a great night—one of these had been charged to take the champagne to Mary-Jacobine, and as the men had been paid off when they left the hotel at three o'clock, it was now impossible to trace the culprit. Precisely what was it he had said or done which had given such offence? If the manager had known earlier he might have traced the man, but now, three months later, he greatly feared it was out of the question. He did not know what to suggest in the way of amends, but he would certainly apologize to the young lady on behalf of his hotel. He had indeed already ventured to send some flowers to her room.

The Senator did not wish to be explicit about the insult. He had been defeated, and as men who are defeated often do, he made a great tale about it to his wife.

Marie-Louise was not a weeper, but a woman of sterling common sense, so far as her beliefs and experience allowed.

"We mustn't lose our heads," said she. "Perhaps nothing will come of it after all."

She set to work to see what could be done to secure a satisfactory outcome. The notion of abortion never entered her head, for it was utterly repugnant to her faith, but in rural Quebec it was not unknown for a pregnancy to fail to reach its term. In any case, a pregnant girl should be in robust health. She adjusted her mind accordingly. Her daughter had been suffering from digestive troubles, and obviously it was too rich a diet that had disturbed her. A good dose of castor oil would put that right. She gave the protesting Mary-Jacobine, who was not now in a position to make too much trouble about anything, a dose that would have astonished a lumberjack. It took the girl a week to recover, but the only effect was to leave her with a look resembling that favourite picture of the period called *The Soul's Awakening,* in which a pale maiden gazes to Heaven with glowing eyes.

Very well. A stubborn case. Next, for her own good, Marie-Louise demanded that her daughter jump to the floor from a table, several times. The only result was exhaustion and despair in the victim. But Marie-Louise had not finished her schemes to give nature a necessary nudge. This time it was not champagne,

but a substantial glass of gin—as much as the mother considered
to be safe—and a very hot bath.

Mary-Jacobine was even more unwell than after the castor oil,
but the tedious little intruder did not budge. All the natural aids
Marie-Louise knew were now exhausted, and she confessed to
her husband that she was beaten, and something would have to
be done.

For a miserable week, the parents argued about the possibilities.
They could take their daughter to the Continent, wait out the
pregnancy, and put the infant in a foundling hospital. They did
not like the idea, and after talking with Mary-Jacobine they liked
it even less. Everything that lay deep in their composition—the
convent, the brother and sister in religious orders, a simple sense
of decency—spoke powerfully against it.

There was, of course, marriage.

They thought highly of marriage and it was the only means
possible of salvaging morality as they understood it. Could a
marriage be achieved?

The Senator was a man for direct action and he knew something
of how the world wagged. This time it was he who asked Major
Cornish to luncheon, at the Savoy.

Luncheon in a fashionable dining-room, even outside the
Season, when really there is not a soul in London, is not the
best place for such delicate negotiations, but the Senator said
what he had to say, and asked Major Cornish if, under the
circumstances, he was still of the same mind? The Major,
coolly eating an ice, said that he would like to think about it, and
arranged another luncheon with the Senator for a week from that
day.

When the meeting came, the Major looked as if he had
grown a few inches. He said that yes, he was prepared to maintain
his offer of marriage, but the Senator would understand that
things were not altogether as they had been. It was distasteful
to talk of one's people, said he, but the Senator should be
aware that the Cornishes were an old county family of, understandably, Cornwall. The family seat, Chegwidden (he pronounced it Cheggin, and explained that it meant, in the old
Cornish tongue, the White House), was close to Tintagel, the

birthplace of King Arthur, and Cornishes had lived there (the memory of man going not to the contrary) so long that they had probably counted King Arthur as a neighbour. When Cornwall had become a royal duchy, several Cornishes at various times served the Dukes of Cornwall as Vice-Warden of the Stannaries. It was a proud record, and an association with such a family might be accounted an honour.

The Major was, however, a younger son, and the family was not a rich one, so it was unlikely that he would ever live at Chegwidden himself, as its master. But he was a Cornish of Chegwidden, all the same. He had served his country honourably as a soldier, but now that he was about to leave the Army, he was undeniably hard up.

The Senator was not utterly unprepared for this, and hastened to say that an alliance with his daughter would certainly include a settlement that would put her husband's mind at ease about the future.

Very generously put, said the Major, but he wanted it to be clear that his suit to Mary-Jacobine was not prompted by any mercenary motive. The Senator would understand that the personal detail he had confided when last they talked could not be a matter of total indifference. Nevertheless he loved her dearly, and over the week past he had come to love her even more, because she had suffered the gravest misfortune that could befall an innocent girl. The Major touched lightly and tactfully upon Our Lord's behaviour toward the woman taken in adultery, and the Senator could not repress a tear or two at this show of fine religious feeling, though he had never thought of Christ as an Englishman with a monocle and an improbable moustache. Here was chivalry, and from the Wooden Soldier! Oh, God be praised!

It would be as well, said the Major, for them to understand one another thoroughly. This surprised the Senator, who thought an understanding had been reached. But at this point the Major drew from an inner pocket two pieces of paper which he handed across the table, saying: "These few matters should be understood between us, and if you will be good enough to sign both copies of this agreement I shall ask Mary-Jacobine to marry me tomorrow morning at eleven o'clock. Take your time in reading it over. It is not complicated, but I assure you I have thought carefully about what would best work toward our married happiness, and I should not like to abridge that memorandum in any way."

He's as cool as a cucumber, thought the Senator, but he did not find himself particularly cool after he had read what was written, in a very fine hand, on the document—for it could not be otherwise described.

(1) It will be clear that I do not wish to enter upon marriage burdened with debt, and I have some outstanding obligations of the sort that accrue to my position in the Army and in Society. Therefore immediately upon my acceptance by Mary-Jacobine, I should be obliged to receive a draft for ten thousand pounds (£10,000).

(2) I estimate that the expenses of marriage, wedding-tour, and subsequent travel to Canada will not be less than twenty-five thousand pounds (£25,000) for which I should be pleased to accept a draft before the wedding ceremony.

(3) My experience with men, and also with finance, as Adjutant of my regiment, appears to me to fit me for a position in industry in the New World, to which I propose that my wife and myself should emigrate after our wedding tour and the birth of the first child. As we must live in a manner congruous with your position and my own, and not below that to which Mary-Jacobine has been accustomed, I propose a settlement upon her of one hundred and twenty-five thousand pounds (£125,000) to be invested or otherwise disposed on my sole authority. In addition, we shall require a dwelling suitable for your daughter and son-in-law and any family we may have, and I think it best that this be a newly-built house, the construction and planning of which I shall be glad to oversee, submitting all bills for building and furnishing to you for settlement. I shall be ready to discuss the position I shall take in your business enterprises and the salary attaching thereto at your convenience.

(4) I undertake to bring up and show every proper care for any children attaching to the union, with the proviso that

they be reared in the Protestant faith as evinced in the
Church of England.

(signed)

FRANCIS CHEGWIDDEN CORNISH

(agreed)

. . . .

For a time the Senator breathed deeply and audibly through
his nose. Should he tear the agreement up and hit the Wooden
Soldier on the head with a bottle? He had expected to be generous, but to have his generosity prescribed for him, and in such
figures, hit him very hard in his Highland pride. To be tied down
to a deal! The Wooden Soldier was sipping a glass of claret with
total self-composure; the light falling on his eyeglass gave him
the air of a miniature Cyclops, about to eat a sheep.

"There are two copies, of course," he murmured; "one for you
and one for me."

Still the Senator glared. He could afford the money, though it
had never occurred to him that he might pay his son-in-law's
debts acquired before marriage. It was Number Four that struck
in his craw. Protestants! His grandchildren Protestants! He had
no quarrel with Protestants so long as religion did not become
an issue; let them be wrong, let them even be damned, if that
was their perverse desire. But his grandchildren—and then he
bethought himself of that small, obstinate grandchild who had
precipitated this whole hateful affair. If Mary-Jacobine did not
marry the Wooden Soldier, then who? Where in the time could
he find a Catholic who would take her—a Catholic as outwardly
suitable, if not really desirable, as Major Cornish?

"Anything troubling you?" said the Major. "I worked out the
financial terms as exactly as I could, and I don't think I could
bring any of the figures down."

The figures! How crass these English could be! To hell with
the figures! But Number Four—

"This fourth item," said the Senator in a voice that trembled a little; "it will not be easy to persuade my wife or my daughter that it is desirable or necessary."

"Not negotiable, I'm afraid," said the Major. "All the Cornishes have been C. of E. since Reformation times."

Like his daughter, the Senator was subject to sudden changes of mood. His fury left him naked and weak. What use to struggle? He was beaten.

He took out his fountain pen and signed the prettily written paper—both copies—in his bold, poorly formed hand.

"Thank you," said the Major; "I'm glad we understand each other. If you would ask Mary-Jacobine to be at home tomorrow at eleven o'clock, I shall have the honour of calling upon the ladies."

SURELY THE SENATOR *might have argued a little more, said the Daimon Maimas. He buckled under very quickly, wouldn't you say?*

—*No, I wouldn't say that, said the Lesser Zadkiel. It was the temperament of the man, you see, as it was of his daughter. They were so good when they were cool but quite out of their element when they were overcome with feeling. Not that they didn't feel, or couldn't feel; not a bit. The trouble was that they felt so powerfully it utterly overset them and brought them sometimes near to panic. A Celtic temperament; a difficult heritage. Often they made terrible mistakes when an intelligent approach to feeling was called for. You know what happened? In later life the Senator became something of a philosopher, which is a great escape from feeling, and Mary-Jim acquired the trick of banishing or trivializing anything that was troublesome.*

—*What about the scene in the Cecil Hotel? said the Daimon.*

—*Oh, that was a real Celtic hullabaloo. Mary-Jacobine wept and vowed that she'd rather die than marry the Wooden Soldier, and after half an hour of that she caved in and said yes, she'd do it. Her parents didn't browbeat her; it was the situation itself that overwhelmed her. It was panic and despair.*

—*Yes, indeed, said the Daimon. I had to deal with the same temperament in Francis, and sometimes it was hard work. He never became either a philosopher or a trivializer; he faced his troubles head-on. It*

*was a lucky thing for him that he had me at his elbow, more than
once.*

*—Yes, that's what they call it; luck. It's interesting, isn't it, to
observe the parents. It would be quite wrong to say that they sold their
daughter to preserve their respectability; they wouldn't have done that.
But you have to understand what respectability meant to those people.
It was much more than just What will the neighbours think? It was
How will the poor child face the world with such a clouded beginning
in life? It was What can I do to save my darling from hurt? It was
emotion, disguising itself as reason, that governed the Senator. Marie-
Louise had a good hard Norman head on her shoulders, but the Church
had relieved her of any necessity to use it for thinking. She had done
the best she knew, and failed. They faced real wretchedness in their
terms. It wasn't worry about London, which wouldn't have cared even
if it knew. It was Blairlogie. How Blairlogie would have gloried in
the fall of a virgin McRory! How she would have felt the whip, all
her life!*

IN BLAIRLOGIE, Aunt Mary-Ben McRory was, in her own phrase,
"holding the fort" while her brother and his wife and dear Mary-
Jim disported themselves in the fashionable world. She did not
mind. She knew she had been born to serve, and she was willing
to serve, and if any hint of longing or jealousy entered her mind
she prayed it away at once. She was a mighty prayer. In her
bedroom she had a little prie-dieu—padded but not overpadded
on the kneeling portion—before a fine oleograph of a Murillo
Virgin, and the worn upholstery on the kneeler showed how much
it was used.

When she was not much older than Mary-Jim was now, God
had made it plain to her that her portion was to serve. Dr. J.A.
and many other people had referred to it as a freak accident, but
she knew it was God's way of defining her role in life.

It had happened at a Garden Party in Government House—
or Rideau Hall as it was familiarly called—in Ottawa. That was
during Lord Dufferin's last months as Governor-General and
Hamish had been asked, as a rising young man and already a
political figure, to a Garden Party in late July. Being still unmar-

ried he had taken his sister Mary-Ben, and for the occasion she had bought a splendid hat covered with black and white plumes. How romantic it had been! Delighting in the romanticism, she had wandered into the shrubbery, her mind on the romantic figure of Vergile Tisserant, who had been increasingly attentive, when suddenly—

It is now part of ornithological history, and even has its footnote in medical history, that at that time the Great Horned Owl—a species referred to by the Canadian naturalist Ernest Thompson Seton as "winged tigers among the most pronounced and savage birds of prey"—had been making occasional forays into the more inhabited parts of the country, and now and then had swooped upon humans, and especially upon ladies who were wearing those fashionable black and white hats; for to the owls they looked like skunks. As Mary-Ben strolled musing in the vice-regal shrubbery, an owl swooped, seized the hat, and soared away with it—and with a considerable portion of the wearer's scalp in its terrible talons.

For weeks she had lain in hospital, her head swathed in bandages and her spirit in ruins. How had those girls in mythology survived the fearful, birdlike descents of Jove? But of course they had been singled out for a special destiny, hadn't they? Had she been so chosen by the God of her own faith, and if so, for what? She found out when, little by little, the bandages were removed and her ravaged skull, with only a few locks of hair still remaining, was revealed. A wig was out of the question, for her scalp was now too tender to endure it. She had to make do with little caps, like turbans, of the softest materials. She never made any attempt to ornament the little caps, for she knew what they were. They were the head-dress of servitude, and she had been marked to serve. So—serve she did, in her brother's household, with the little caps protecting her little skull. Not even Dr. J.A. had been so harsh as to mention that the swooping god had mistaken her for a skunk.

She had been keeper of her brother's household for three years before his marriage to Marie-Louise Thibodeau and there was never any question that she should make way for the wife; no, indeed, she served her, and kept tedious duties from her, and when the first child was born she was invaluable, even suggesting the romantic name by which she was known. Marie-Louise, who found the social obligations of a rising man's wife wholly agreeable, was glad enough to let Mary-Ben—who was known even more often as Aunt, as soon as Mary-Jim began to speak—see to the household.

Besides, Aunt had Taste, which can be a form of power in those who possess it.

Aunt's taste and Aunt's judgment came into full sway when Hamish decided to build a fine house, and move up to the hill which dominated the southern horizon of Blairlogie. Marie-Louise had no ideas about houses, but Aunt had enough for three, and it was she who told the builder what was wanted, and drew little pictures, and gently domineered over the workmen. It was a brick house, of course, and not just your common brick but a finely surfaced rosy brick, as impenetrable as tile. Because Hamish was in lumber, the interior finish had all the latest things in turned wood, matched wood, wooden lace worked on the band-saw, and, in the room called the library, wooden panelling, not as it is generally known, but in octagons of what looked like hardwood flooring, set on the bias. Hideous, but of course very hard for the workmen to do, said Dr. J.A., who always had an opinion, and usually a disagreeable one.

Aunt furnished. Aunt chose wallpapers, showing a fondness for flock papers in which a pattern stood out from the background in a substance rather like velvet. Aunt chose pictures, spending money in a way that astonished her brother, in the shops of art dealers in Montreal. Aunt selected the subject for the stained-glass window that did not really light the landing on the staircase; it was Landseer's *The Monarch of the Glen,* a very choice thing. All of this choosing Aunt called "helping wherever she could, without interfering".

Aunt's desire not to interfere influenced the shape of the house, which had a substantial sun parlour attached to the north side that was rarely warmed by any sun. Above the sun parlour was a suite of rooms that was Aunt's alone. She could go in there and shut the door, she said, and be totally out of the way in her little sitting-room—it was quite big, really—and her bedroom with the little prayer-alcove off it, and her bathroom where she could do things she had to do—by which she implied difficult attentions to her destroyed scalp. Hamish and Marie-Louise need never know she was in the house when they were entertaining, or wanted to be by themselves, as married folk very properly should do.

Busy as a bee, nodding and smiling sweetly, deferring to everybody, Aunt built the house and even chose its name; 26 Scott Street simply would not do, and Aunt proposed St. Kilda, as a lovely name, and a link with Barra. As neither Marie-Louise nor Hamish had any alternative, that was what appeared in the stained-glass fanlight over the front door.

Aunt's mind, busy as it was, never strayed toward introspection or the making of significant connections. If it had done so she might have wondered why one of her evening prayers was so particularly dear to her—that which ran:

> God, who ordainest the services of angels and men in a wonderful order, be pleased to grant our life on earth may be guarded by those who stand always ready to serve thee in heaven. . . . God, who in thy transcendent providence delightest to send thy holy angels to watch over us, grant our humble petition that we may be safe under their protection, and may rejoice in their companionship through all eternity.

Did Aunt think of herself as one of those divinely appointed guardians and servers? God forbid that she should be guilty of such pride! But beneath what the mind chooses to admit to itself lie convictions that shape our lives.

There had never been any suggestion that Aunt might go with the family on the great expedition to launch Mary-Jacobine upon the world. Aunt did not repine. She knew she was unsightly. Yes, yes, she insisted upon it, and when Marie-Louise or Mary-Jacobine or the Senator protested that it was not so, she would smile sweetly and say, Now dear, you don't have to be kind. I know what I look like, and I have offered it up.

This business of "offering up" figured largely in Aunt's religious life. After that terrible affair at Rideau Hall, she had offered up her attachment to Vergile Tisserant, as a sacrifice she hoped would be acceptable at the Heavenly Throne. Before Vergile there had been Joseph Crone, who had decided that he would rather be a Jesuit than Aunt's husband, and she had offered him up, too. She offered up her ugliness, as an act of acceptance and humility. Oh, Aunt had plenty of gifts for God, and perhaps God was grateful, for He had given her quite a lot of power in her small sphere.

Letters from Marie-Louise and less often from Mary-Jacobine kept her aware of how things were going in England. Neither of the ladies had much gift for writing but—the mother in French, the daughters in English—they tried for as long as they could to keep Aunt informed. But a new kind of life, and new people, so far removed from anything Aunt had known, were not in their power to describe, and the letters grew fewer and briefer.

Aunt accepted this without complaint. She had much to do, maintaining St. Kilda in good order, and keeping the servants up to the mark. These were a Polish housemaid, Anna Lemenchick, who was so short as to be almost a dwarf, but broad beyond the ordinary, and a cook, Victoria Cameron, who was always on the verge of being dismissed because she had a fiery Highland temper and was apt, in the phrase Aunt used, to "kick right over the traces" if she were crossed. Everything was against Victoria; to begin, she was a Protestant, and there were plenty of Catholic cooks to be had; as well as a temper she had a rough tongue in her head, and gave saucy answers; she was also astonishingly bow-legged, and could be heard all over the house, tramping around the kitchen like a great horse. With these disadvantages it was not surprising that nobody noticed that she had a beautiful dark face, like one of the Spanish Madonnas Aunt admired so whole-heartedly. But who ever heard of a beautiful cook? Victoria's trump card was that she was by many lengths the best cook in Blairlogie, a natural genius, and the Senator would not hear of letting her go. These, with visits twice a week from Mrs. August, a Pole who did the rough cleaning, made up the indoor staff.

The outdoor staff was all embodied in a drunken detrimental called Old Billy, who cared for and drove the horses, shovelled snow, cut grass, exterminated the flowers, and was supposed to do heavy lifting and any odd jobs that turned up. But Old Billy was a devout Catholic and a noisy repenter of his misdeeds and frequent toots, so it was impossible to get rid of him, grave trial that he was.

It was Aunt who looked after young Mary-Tess when she was home on holiday from the convent. That was easy, for Mary-Tess

was a cheerful girl, and skating and tobogganing were her great
pleasures. Aunt had little pleasures of her own. There was her
music; she played and sang. And there was a weekly visit from
the Senator's mother-in-law, old Madame Thibodeau, a stately
lady far gone in fat, who spoke no English but enjoyed a gossip
in French, in which Aunt was as fluent as her brother. Old Billy
was sent with the barouche, or in winter with the elegant scarlet
cutter, to haul her up the hill every Thursday at four, and haul
her back again, substantially heavier because of the great tea she
had eaten, at half past five. Each month there was a visit from
Father Devlin and Father Beaudry, of St. Bonaventura's; as a
guarantee of total chastity, they visited the old maid together,
and devoured huge meals in gloomy silence, occasionally punctuated by the more edifying bits of parish news. Irregular and
unforeseeable were visits from Dr. J.A.—Dr. Joseph Ambrosius
Jerome, the leading Catholic physician of Blairlogie, who kept
an eye on Aunt because she was supposed to be frail.

He was by far her liveliest visitor. A little, spare, very dark,
grinning man, saturnine in his appearance and alarming in his
opinions, he was locally believed to have powers of healing verg-
ing on the miraculous. He "brought back" lumbermen who had
chopped themselves in the foot with one of their terrible axes
and were in danger of blood-poisoning. He sewed up Poles who
had decided some obscure point of honour with knives. He saw
people through double pneumonia with poultices and inhalations
and sheer exercise of his healing power. He told women to have
no more babies, and threatened their husbands with dreadful
reprisals if this were not so. He blasted out the constipated and
salved their angry hemorrhoids with ointments of opium. He
could diagnose worms at a glance, and drag a tapeworm from its
lair with horrible potions.

If not actually an atheist, the Doctor was known to have dark
beliefs nobody wanted to explore. He was rumoured to know
more theology than Father Devlin and Father Beaudry clapped
together. He read books that were on the Index, some of them
in German. But he was trusted, and nobody trusted him more
than Aunt.

He understood her case, you see. He knew her nerves as nobody else knew them. He hinted darkly that to be a maiden lady

at her age was not altogether a safe thing, and to her terrible embarrassment he sometimes demanded to squeeze her pallid little breasts, and peep up her most secret passage, assisted by a flashlight and a cold tube called a speculum. A man who had done that has a very special place in a virgin's life. And he teased her. Teased her and taunted her and refused to take her at all seriously; if she had known anything intimate about herself, she would have realized that she loved him. As it was, she knew him as a close, terrifying friend, upon whom she placed the uttermost reliance. He was almost more than a priest—a priest with a strong whiff of the Devil about him.

It was to the Doctor that she first confided the news, contained in a letter that had come from Marie-Louise, that Mary-Jim was to be married! Yes, married to an Englishman, a Major Francis Cornish, very much a swell, it appeared. Well, wouldn't you know that Mary-Jim wouldn't be long without a husband. Such a lovely girl! And it looked as if they would be coming to Blairlogie to live. We shall have to polish up our manners for the English swell, won't we? Whatever would he think of such an old auntie as herself—such a figure of fun!

"I dare say it won't be long before he'll want to know what's under that cap," said the Doctor. "What'll you tell him, then, Mary-Ben? If he's a soldier as you say, I suppose he's seen worse things." And the Doctor departed, laughing and scooping the remains of the cake-tray into his pocket. It was for some children in the Polish section, but he took care to make it look like greed.

At a later visit, Aunt was bursting with news. They'd been married! Somewhere in Switzerland, apparently. A place called Montreux. And they were going to stay there for a while, on a honeymoon, before coming home. Madame Thibodeau had been delighted; a honeymoon in a French-speaking land seemed somehow to mitigate the Major's terrible Englishness.

The Senator and Marie-Louise returned to Blairlogie late in the autumn, and were less communicative than Aunt had expected. Very soon, of course, it had to come out—some of it, anyhow. Mary-Jacobine and the Major had been married by the English chaplain in Montreux, in the English Church. Now it's no good taking it like that, Mary-Ben; the thing's done, and we can't change it. We can pray, of course, that he may see the light at last, though I don't think he's much of a man for changes. Now, put a good face on it, and stop weeping, because I'll have to tell Father Devlin, and he'll tell Father Beaudry, and only God knows what the town will make of it. Yes, I did all I could, and I might as well have saved my breath. I'll have to tell Mary-Tess, too, what her sister's done, and believe me I'll make her understand that there's to be no more of that sort of thing in this family. Oh, Mother of God, there'll be Mother Mary-Basil to tell, and that won't be an easy letter to write; you'll have to help me. Hamish just takes it like a mule; there's no getting anything out of him.

The regrettable baby was not brought into the conversation at this point, or later, till at last a telegram came: "My wife delivered of a boy last night. Regards, Cornish." The telegram came sufficiently late in the year following to still the counting fingers, Aunt's among them, with which Blairlogie greeted all first children.

Of course the town knew all about it, and supposed much that nobody had told. The local paper, *The Clarion,* had announced the wedding in a brief piece, without saying anything about the Protestant aspect of the marriage, but as the name of the officiating clergyman was the Rev. Canon White, it was not necessary. There was the spite of that Tory rag for you! They knew that everybody would understand at once. Thank God the proviso number four was still a secret, but how long would that last! Later *The Clarion* announced the good news of the birth of Francis Chegwidden Cornish, son of Major and Mrs. Francis Chegwidden Cornish; grandson of our popular Senator, the Hon. James Ignatius McRory and Mrs. McRory; and great-grandson of Madame Jean Telesphore Thibodeau. But these were bare bones; rumour supplied ample flesh. The Tory-Scots talked.

You'd have thought the girl could have found a Canadian now, wouldn't you?—Oh, but nobody'd be good enough. The Senator has made a proper fool of that girl.—What foot d'you suppose he digs with?—Oh, sure to be an R.C. with all that raft of priests and nuns in the family and old Mary-Ben with her holy pictures all over the house (some of them right in the sitting-room, wouldn't it give you the creeps!)—he couldn't be anything but an R.C. Not that I ever heard of an Englishman that was.—Anglicans, so far as they're anything. But somebody told me she met this fella at the Court.—Yes, and more than that, the King himself had a hand in the match—sort of hinted, you know, but that's just like an order—Well, no doubt we'll find out soon enough. Not that they'll be telling *me,* a Tory through and through. Would you believe it, I've lived in Blairlogie for sixty-seven years, and generations before me, and a McRory has never so much as given me a good-day?—They smell the Protestant blood in you, that's what it is.—Yes, the black drop, they call it.

But at last, more than a year later, Major and Mrs. Cornish and their infant son arrived in Blairlogie on the afternoon train from Ottawa. If ever the town looked well, it did so in autumn, when the maples were blazing, and close watchers said Mary-Jim wept a little as she stepped into the barouche in which Old Billy drove them to St. Kilda. The child was in her arms, in a long shawl. The Major, without hesitation, took the two seats facing forward for himself and his wife, leaving the seats with their backs to Old Billy for the Senator and Marie-Louise. Watchers did not fail to notice that. There was a mass of luggage on the station platform for Old Billy to pick up later—military trunks, metal boxes, and queer-shaped leather cases that might be guns.

When they retired that night, the Major had some questions to ask.

"Precisely who is the old party in the little cap?"

"I've told you times without number. She's my aunt, my father's sister, and she lives here. It's her home."

"Rum old soul, isn't she? Wants to call me Frank. Well, no harm in that, I suppose. What did you say her name was?"

"Mary-Benedetta, but you'd better call her Mary-Ben. Everybody does."

"You're all Mary-Something, aren't you? Jolly rum!"

"Family Catholic custom. And listen—you're not the one to talk about caps."

The Major was applying the special mixture, which smelled like walnuts, to his hair, before he put on the woollen cap that supposedly hugged the dressing to his head and delayed baldness, of which he had a dread.

"Eats a lot for a little 'un, doesn't she?"

"I've never noticed. She has terrible indigestion. A martyr to gas."

"I'm not surprised. Let's hope she doesn't go the way of Jesse Welch."

"Who was he?"

"I only know his epitaph:

> Here lies the body of Jesse Welch
> Who died of holding back a belch:
> The belch did in his pipes expand
> And blew him to the Promised Land."

"Ah, but Mary-Ben couldn't belch to save her life. Too much a lady."

"Well, it had better go somewhere, or—BANG!"

"Don't be diskie, Frank. Come to bed."

The Major now did what he always did last thing before going to bed. He removed his monocle, for the first time in the day, polished it carefully, and laid it in a little velvet box. Then he tied on a strap of pink netting which held his moustache in place overnight and enabled it to defy its natural instinct. He climbed into the high bed and took his wife in his arms.

"The sooner we build our own house, the better, wouldn't you say, old girl?"

"My very thought," said Mary-Jim, and kissed him. She regarded the moustache-strap as no detriment. It was a conjugal rather than a romantic kiss.

Contrary to probability, during the year past they had become fond of one another. But neither was fond of the child that lay silent in the crib at the foot of the bed.

There was no use delaying the matter, and the next day Dr. J. A. Jerome was asked to take a look at the baby. Dr. Jerome investigating a case was not the jokey, chattering man he was in social meetings, and he did a number of things without speaking. Clapped his hands near the baby's ear, passed a lighted match before its eyes, poked it here and there and even pinched it, then pinched it again, to make sure he had heard its curious cry. He measured its scalp and probed the fontanelle with a long finger.

"The Swiss man was right," he said at last. "Now we must see what we can do."

To the Senator, upon whom he dropped in that night for a dram, he was more communicative.

"They'll never raise that one," said he. "No point in sparing you, Hamish; the child's an idjit, and the mercy is it won't live long."

THE CORNISHES LOST NO TIME in building their house on a piece of land that was visible from St. Kilda, being beyond the big house's garden and across a road. It was not as large as the Senator's mansion, but it was a large house all the same, and Blairlogie people joked that perhaps the Major intended to take boarders. What did two young people, with one child, want with a house the like of that? It was modern, too, in the manner that passed as modern at the time, and word got around that several of the rooms weren't meant to have wallpaper, and were plastered in a gritty way that must be intended to take paint. There were a great many windows, too, as if it wasn't hard enough to heat a house in that climate without having so much glass. It had steam-heating, expensive though it was, and so many bathrooms that the thing was a perfect scandal—bathrooms right off the bedrooms, and a washroom with a toilet in it on the ground floor, so that you couldn't decently conceal where you were going when you went. Snoopers were not encouraged, though it was the local custom to visit any house during its building, just to see what was going on.

The scandal of the house, however, was minor compared to the scandal of seeing the Major and his wife walking to the Anglican church, most Sunday mornings. That was a slap in the eye for the McRorys, now wasn't it? A mixed marriage! Just wait till the boy grows up a little. He'll be an R.C. right enough. The Papists would never let him go.

But the boy was not seen. He was never taken out in his baby-carriage, and when Mary-Jim was asked about him directly, she said he was delicate and needed special care. Probably born with one glass eye, like his father, said the ribald. Maybe he was a cripple, said the people who failed to add that in Blairlogie there were more cripples than he. They would find out, in time.

They did not find out when the house was completed, and

furnished. (Did you see the carloads of furniture coming into the station, from Ottawa and as far away as Montreal?) Mary-Jim knew what had to be done, and in due time a small notice appeared in *The Clarion* announcing that on a certain day in June Mrs. Francis Cornish would be At Home at Chegwidden Lodge.

This meant, according to local custom, that anyone not positively Polish was free to come, drink a cup of tea, and look around. They came in hundreds, trudged all over the house, rubbed fabrics between their fingers, covertly looked in drawers and cupboards, sucked in their lips, and murmured jealously among themselves. Didn't it beat the band! The money that must have been poured out! Well, it was nice for them that had it. And Chegwidden Lodge—what were you to make of that? The postmaster's wife said that her husband had half a mind to insist that letters be addressed to 17 Walter Street, which is what the vacant lot had been before this mansion was set up. Everybody agreed, out of her earshot, that the postmaster had only half a mind at the best of times, and nothing of the sort happened. The postmaster's wife reported that letters were posted with Chegwidden Lodge plainly printed on the envelopes. Their own stationery! And Mary-Jim correcting everybody about the way to say it, and wanting them to say Cheggin, as if they couldn't read plain English—if that word was English, mind you.

The day Mary-Jim received Blairlogie was also the last day she did anything of the sort; she had only agreed to a single occasion because of her father's political position. There was no sign of the baby. It was usual for babies to hold court, and be exclaimed over, as the wonders they were.

The baby had a nurse, a starched, grim-faced woman from Ottawa, who made no friends. A rumour went around that when the baby cried, its cry was queer—the queerest thing you ever heard. Victoria Cameron made it her business to track down the source of this rumour, and, as she suspected, it was Dominique Tremblay, the maid at Chegwidden Lodge. Victoria descended upon Dominique and told her that if she ever dared to open her mouth about family matters again, she, Victoria Cameron, would rip the soul-case out of her. Dominique, terrified, said no more. But when she was questioned, she rolled her eyes dramatically, and laid her fingers to her lips; this made rumour worse.

Rumour whispered that the ailing child was the victim of some fault in the father (you know what those old English families are) or—hush!—one of those diseases soldiers pick up from foreign harlots. That would be why Mary-Jim had no more children. Was it choice or inability? Rumour knew of women whose insides were simply a mass of corruption from diseases communicated to them by their husbands. Such speculation kept Rumour pleasantly engaged in dispute for some time.

Rumour was checked after February 1909 when Dr. Jerome told Mary-Jim that she was pregnant again. This was both good and bad news to the Cornishes. The Major was delighted that there was to be a child of his loins—a son, he was certain—and so was Mary-Jim. Although they would not have passed as a loving couple, they were congenial, and invariably as polite to one another as if they weren't married at all, Blairlogie said. But with the caprice of domestics, the starched, grim woman from Ottawa chose this moment to leave. People who discharge employees have to give reasons; employees are under no obligation to explain why they leave. Still, the starched, grim woman volunteered the opinion that another year in Blairlogie would be the death of her, and added insultingly that she had always heard it was the Jumping-Off Place, and now she knew it. So Mary-Jim was pregnant, and had the care of the sick child, except for such help as Victoria Cameron could give her. Victoria showed every sign of becoming a family retainer and champion, although she was still not much more than thirty. Dominique Tremblay was not to be trusted, and was kept out of the nursery.

This was inconvenient, for the Senator wanted his cook in his own kitchen. The Major fussed over his wife like a bridegroom, and was angry with fate when she was tired and in low spirits. Dr. Jerome said something had to be done, and, having said it to the Cornishes and to Marie-Louise and Aunt Mary-Ben, he said it with special emphasis to the Senator, once again as they sat in the uniquely panelled library, over a dram.

"I won't make strange on you, Hamish, it would be far better for everybody if that child had not lived. It's a burden, and it will always be a burden, and it'll be a burden to the new child, because a dooley elder brother is a weight to carry."

"You said it wouldn't live when first they brought it home."

"I know I did, and I was right. It's the child that's wrong. It has no business to be going on living, the way it is. Five years! It's utterly unscientific."

"And of course there's nothing in the world to be done about it."

The Doctor paused: "I'm not so sure of that."

"Joe—you don't suggest—?"

"No, I don't. I'm a Catholic like yourself, Hamish, and a pillar of the Church, even if I'm an external pillar. A life is sacred, whatever its quality may be. But if that Swiss man had had any sense he wouldn't have been such a busybody when it was born. The first five minutes, you know—you don't invite death, but you let nature make its choice. I've done it myself scores of times, and never a twinge of conscience. Some of these fellows, you know, are too anxious to show their skill to have any discretion or humanity. But I tell you plump and plain, I wish that boy were out of the way. He's bad for Mary-Jim, and he's bad for all of you!"

"Well, but what did you mean, Joe, when you said you weren't sure? What weren't you sure of?"

"The child isn't what it was a few months ago. We may be quit of it yet—and the sooner the better."

Apparently Dr. Jerome's suspicions were well founded, for a few days later, after a blazing row with the Major, Marie-Louise summoned Father Devlin in a hurry, and the sick child was baptized for the second time, as a Catholic. And it was only a day or two later that one of the top workmen at the Senator's planing-mill made a small coffin—made it beautifully. And at night a little procession of two carriages took its way to the Catholic ceme-tery—a bleak, wind-swept, treeless place and in March dreadfully cold. It was as private as such an affair can be. Old Billy had dug the little grave with pick and shovel breaking the frost-bound soil, and he it was who stood in the background as the Senator and Marie-Louise, Aunt Mary-Ben, and Major Cornish heard Father Devlin read the burial service. The Senator and the Major carried coal-oil lamps to light the scene. There were no tears as the Senator's first grandchild was buried in the otherwise empty McRory plot.

When the spring came, it was Aunt Mary-Ben who saw to the

placing of a little white marble marker—it was only a foot wide, and lifted itself above the earth no more than three inches—on which raised letters said FRANCIS.

Mary-Jim's pregnancy went splendidly after that, and on September 12 the subject of Simon Darcourt's biography was born, and christened, in the Anglican Church, Francis Chegwidden Cornish.

SO YOUR MAN *makes his appearance on the scene at last, said the Lesser Zadkiel. You were at the birth, of course?*

—*Where else would I be? said the Daimon Maimas. I'd been on the job, so to speak, since the boy was conceived on December the tenth, 1908, at* 11:37 *p.m.*

—*What precisely was it you needed to do? said the Biographical Angel.*

—*Obey orders, of course. When Francis was conceived—at the very moment of the Major's fortunate orgasm, They summoned me and said This is yours; do well by him but don't show off.*

—*Had you been showing off?*

—*I never think that a few flourishes do any harm to a life and perhaps I have overdone it, once or twice. But They take a very different view. When They gave me Francis They said, don't show off, and I tried my best not to show off. That family needed an influence like me.*

—*You found them dull?*

—*My dear Zadkiel, we haven't even touched on Blairlogie. There was dullness for you! But it's been my experience, over several aeons, that a good dull beginning does no harm to an interesting life. Your man runs so hard to get away from the dullness he was born to that you can do very interesting things with him. Put them into his head to do himself, that's to say. Without me, Francis would just have been a good, solid citizen like the rest of them. Of course, I knew all there was to know about the burial of the first Francis. There was a rum thing, as the Major said at the time.*

—*You haven't any pity, Maimas.*

—*Neither have you, Zadkiel, and don't pretend you have. Long, long ago—if we must talk as though time had any meaning for us— I learned that when a tutelary spirit like myself is given a life to watch over, pity merely makes a mess of things. Far better to put your man* over the hurdles and scrape him through the hedges, and toughen him up. It is not my work to protect softies.

—Well, shall we get on with the story, now that we have reached Francis? It was necessary to tell about his immediate forebears in some detail, because they were what was bred in his bone, which poor Darcourt wants to find out.

—Yes, but now I am on the job—I, Maimas the Daimon, the Tutelary Spirit, the Indwelling Essence. Though he was a McRory, and a Cornish, and all that goes with such a mixture, I also was what was bred in his bone, right from the instant of his conception. And that made all the difference.

PART
Two

IT WAS IN A GARDEN that Francis Cornish first became truly aware of himself as a creature observing a world apart from himself. He was almost three years old, and he was looking deep into a splendid red peony. He was greatly alive to himself (though he had not yet learned to think of himself as Francis) and the peony, in its fashion, was also greatly alive to itself, and the two looked at each other from their very different egotisms with solemn self-confidence. The little boy nodded at the peony and the peony seemed to nod back. The little boy was neat, clean, and pretty. The peony was unchaste, dishevelled as peonies must be, and at the height of its beauty. It was a significant moment, for it was Francis's first conscious encounter with beauty—beauty that was to be the delight, the torment, and the bitterness of his life—but except for Francis himself, and perhaps the peony, nobody knew of it, or would have heeded if they had known. Every hour is filled with such moments, big with significance for someone.

It was his mother's garden, but it would be foolish to pretend that it was Mary-Jim's creation. She cared little for gardens, and had one only because it was the sort of thing a young matron in her position was expected to possess. Her husband would have protested if she had not had a garden, for he had determined ideas about what women liked. Women liked flowers; on certain occasions one gave them flowers; on certain occasions one told them they were like flowers—though it would not have done to tell a woman she looked like a peony, a beautiful but whorish flower. The garden was the work of Mr. Maidment, and it reflected the dull, geometrical character of Mr. Maidment's mind.

It was uncommon for Francis to be in the garden unattended. Mr. Maidment did not like boys, whom he knew to be plant-tramplers and bloom-snatchers, but at this magical moment Bella-Mae had left him to himself because she had to go indoors for a moment. Francis knew she had gone to pee, which she did frequently, having inherited the weak bladder of her family, the Elphinstones. Bella-Mae did not know that Francis knew, because one of her jobs was to protect Francis from bruising contacts with reality, and in her confused and grubby mind, little boys ought not to know that adults had such creatural needs. But Francis did know, even though he was not fully aware who Francis was, and he felt a minute guilt at his knowledge. He was not yet such a close reasoner as to suspect that if Bella-Mae were thus burdened with the common needs of life, his parents might also share them. The life of his parents was god-like and remote. Their clothes did not come off, obviously, though they changed several times a day; but he had seen Bella-Mae take off her clothes, or at least shrug and struggle them off under her nightdress, because she slept in the nursery with him. She also brushed her coarse rusty hair a hundred times every night, for he had heard her counting, and was usually fast asleep before she had reached the century stroke.

Bella-Mae was called Nanny, because that was what the Major insisted she be called. But Bella-Mae, who was Blairlogie to the core of her being, thought it a silly thing to call her by a name that was not hers. She thought Major and Mrs. Cornish stuck-up and she took no pride in being a child's nurse. It was a job, and she did it as well as she could, but she had her own ideas, and sometimes smacked Francis when he had not been very bad, as a personal protest against the whole Cornish manner of life, so out of tune with Blairlogie ideas.

Within the time between his meeting and recognition of the peony and his fourth year, Francis came to know that Bella-Mae was Awful. She was plain, if not downright ugly, and grown women ought to be beautiful, like his mother, and smell of expensive scent, not starch. Bella-Mae frequently made him clean his teeth with brown soap, as she did herself, and declared it to be wholesome; she took no stock in the tooth-powder with which the nursery was supplied. This was Awful. More Awful still was her lack of respect for the holy ikons which hung on the nursery wall. These were two vividly coloured pictures of King Edward VII and Queen Alexandra, and once a month she scrubbed their glass with Bon Ami, saying under her breath: "Come on, you two, and get your faces washed." If the Major had known that, he would have given Bella-Mae whatfor. But of course he did not know, because Francis was not a squealer, a kind of person Bella-Mae held in abhorrence. But if he was not a squealer, Francis was a noticer, and he kept a mental dossier on Bella-Mae which would certainly have led to her dismissal if his parents had known what it contained.

There was, for instance, her contumelious attitude, expressed physically but not verbally, toward the other picture in the nursery, which was of A Certain Person. Bella-Mae did not hold with images or idols; she belonged to the small assembly of the Salvation Army in Blairlogie, and she knew what was right, and a picture of A Certain Person, in a room like the nursery, was not right.

To remove the picture, or alter its position, was out of the question. It had been hung beside Francis's bed by Aunt, Miss Mary-Benedetta McRory, who ought by rights to be called Great-Aunt. Bella-Mae was not the only one to have reservations about pictures of A Certain Person; the Major was not happy about it, but rather than have a row with Aunt he tolerated it, on the ground that women and children had soft heads about religion, and when the boy grew older he would put an end to all that nonsense. So there it hung, a brightly coloured picture of Jesus, smiling sadly as though a little pained by what his large brown eyes beheld, and with his lovely long white hands extended from his blue robe in the familiar Come-unto-me gesture. Behind him were a good many stars, and he seemed to be floating.

From time to time Aunt Mary-Ben had a secret little whisper with Francis. "When you say your prayers, dear, look first at the picture of Jesus, then close your eyes but keep the picture in your mind. Because that's Who you're praying to, isn't it? And He knows all about little boys and loves them dearly."

Bella-Mae was sure that Jesus didn't like to see little boys naked, and she hustled Francis out of his clothes and into them with great speed and certain modest precautions. "You don't think he wants to look at your bare B.T.M. with his big eyes, do you?" she said, managing to include both Francis and the picture in her displeasure. For her displeasure was immense. The faith of the Salvation Army expressed itself in her through a repertoire of disapprovals; she lived strongly in the faith of the Army, and from time to time she murmured the Army warcry, "Blood and Fire", with the vigour usually reserved for an oath.

She saw that the Army figured in Francis's life as much as possible, though she would not have dared to take him to the Temple; the Major would not have stood for that. But at least twice a week he beheld her in the splendour of her uniform, and he was the first to see her in the glory of the Chapeau.

The Army uniform cost a good deal of money, and Bella-Mae bought hers garment by garment, as she could afford it. The sensible shoes, the black stockings, the skirt, and the tunic with its wonderful buttons, were achieved one by one, and then the great decision had to be made. Should she buy the bonnet, which was the familiar headgear of the Salvation Lassies, or should she opt for the Chapeau, a flat-crowned, broad-brimmed hat of blue fur felt, glorious with its red-and-gold ribbon, and strongly resembling (though Bella-Mae did not know this) the hats worn by Catholic priests in nearby Quebec. After deep inward searching, and prayer for guidance, she chose the Chapeau.

In full Salvation rig at last, she marched around the nursery, for Francis, singing in a style of her own, which included noises indicative of the band's contribution:

> At the Cross, at the Cross
> Where I first saw the light
>   And my heart's great burden roll'd away (pom, pom)
> It was there through Blessed Jesus
> That I turned to the Right
>   And now I am happy all the day! (Pish! scolded the cymbal)

>   At the Cro—s—s—s!
>   At the Cro—o—o—s!
> At the Cross where I first saw the light (boomty-boom)
>   It was there through His mercy

That I turned toward the Right
And now I am happy all the day! (Boom, boom!)

It was irresistible. Francis hopped off his bed and paraded behind Bella-Mae, and under her guidance was able to shout, "Thine the glory!" and "Blest Redeemer!" ecstatically at the right intervals. He was elevated. He was free of the repressive influence of A Certain Person, whose sad eyes he ignored. He did not know what he was singing about, but he sang from a happy heart.

The nursery door opened. It was Aunt Mary-Ben, tiny and smiling, her little soft cap nodding pleasantly, for she was not a bit disapproving. Oh, not she! She motioned Francis back to his bed, and drew Bella-Mae toward the window, where she spoke very softly for a few minutes, after which Bella-Mae ran out of the room, crying.

Then Aunt said, "Shall we say our prayers, Frankie? Or I'll tell you what—you shall hear me say mine." And Aunt knelt by the bed with the little boy, and brought out of her pocket a sort of necklace he had never seen before, made of black beads of different sizes, strung together with silver chain, and as Aunt passed the beads through her fingers she murmured what sounded like poetry. When she had finished she reverently kissed the cross that hung on the necklace and, with a sweet smile, held it out to Francis, who kissed it, too. Liked kissing it, liked the reverential quietness, liked the effect of poetry. This was every bit as good as Bella-Mae's march, in an entirely different way. He held the cross in his hand, reluctant to let it go.

"Would you like it for your very own, Frankie?" said Aunt. "I'm afraid you can't have it right now, dear, but perhaps after a little while I shall be able to give you one of these. It's called a rosary, dear, because it's a rose-garden of prayer. It's the garden of Jesus' dear Mother, and when we say our prayers with it, we are very near Her, and we may even see Her sweet face. But this is our secret, dear. Don't say anything to Daddy."

No fear of that. Conversation between Francis and the Major was in a very different mode. "Come here and I'll show you my gun, Frank. Look down the barrel. See! Clean as a whistle. Always keep your gun clean and oiled. It deserves it. A fine gun deserves decent care. When you're older I'll get you one, and show you how to use it. Must learn to shoot like a sportsman, not like a killer." Or it might be, "Come with me, Frank, and I'll show you how to tie a trout-fly." Or, "Look at my boots, Frank. Bright, what? I never let the girls do my boots. You'd never think these were eleven years old, would you? That's what proper care does. You can always judge a man by his boots. Always get 'em from the best maker. Only cads wear dirty boots." Or, in passing, "Stand straight, Frank. Never slump, however tired you are. Arch your back a bit, too—looks smart on parade. Come tomorrow after breakfast and I'll show you my sword."

A good father, determined that his son should be a good man. Not entirely what might have been expected of the Wooden Soldier. There were depths of affection in the Major. Affection, and pride. No poetry.

Mother was entirely different. Affectionate, but perhaps she turned it on at will. She did not see a great deal of Francis except by accident, for she had so much to do. Amusing Father, and taking care that there were no unfortunate encounters when the Cornishes set out for St. Alban's church on Sunday morning, and the McRorys' carriage might be making toward St. Bonaventura; reading a succession of novels with pretty pictures on the covers; and playing the phonograph, which gave out with *Gems from The Wizard of the Nile,* and a piece Francis loved, the words of which were:

> *Everybody's doing it*
> *Doing it, doing it*
> *Everybody's doing it*
> *Doing what? The turkey-trot;*
> *See that rag-time couple over there,*
> *See them throw their feet in the air—*
> *It's a bear, it's a bear, it's a BEAR!*

It was wonderful—better than anything. Just as good as Father's sword, or Aunt's mysterious beads, and far better than Bella-Mae in her uniform, which he never saw now, anyway. Mother took his hands and they danced the turkey-trot round and round her pretty drawing-room. All wonderful!

As wonderful, in their own way, as the ecstatic first moment with the peony, but perhaps not quite, because that was all his own, and he could repeat it in summer and remember it in winter without anybody else being involved.

All wonderful, until the shattering September morning in 1914 when he was led away by Bella-Mae to school.

This would have figured more prominently in the life of Chegwidden Lodge if the household had not been in disorder because of the many absences, which extend from days to weeks and then to months, of the Major and his wife in Ottawa, where they were increasingly favourites at Government House. In addition there were mysterious colloquies with military authorities; the Major acted as a go-between for the Governor-General, the Duke of Connaught, who was a field marshal and knew rather more about military affairs than most of the Canadian regulars. As the representative of the Crown, the Duke could not make himself too prominent, or cause the Canadians to lose face, and it was somebody's job to carry information to and advice from Rideau Hall without being tactless. That somebody was Major Cornish, who was tact personified. And when, at last, war was officially declared against Germany and what were called the Central Powers, the Major became something which was slow to be named, but was, in fact, Chief of Military Intelligence, in so far as Canada had such an organization, and he moved himself and Mary-Jim to Ottawa. They would not be in Blairlogie, he told the Senator, for the duration, which was not expected to be long.

The business of arranging for Francis's education had not been much considered. Ottawa and the pleasures and intrigues of the Vice-regal world were foremost in Mary-Jacobine's mind, and she was the sort of mother who is certain that if she is happy, all must certainly be well with her child. Francis was too small to be sent to boarding-school, and, besides, he tended to have heavy colds and bronchial troubles. "Local schools for a while," said the Major, but not to Francis. Indeed, nobody said anything to Francis until the evening before school opened, when Bella-Mae said, "Up in good time tomorrow; you're starting school." Francis, who knew every tone of her voice, caught the ring of malice in what she said.

The next morning Francis threw up his breakfast, and was assured by Bella-Mae that there was to be none of that, because

they had no time to spare. With her hand holding his firmly—
more firmly than usual—he was marched off to Blairlogie's Central School, to be entered in the kindergarten.

It was by no means a bad school, but it was not a school to
which children were escorted by nursemaids, or where boys were
dressed in white sailor suits and crowned with a sailor cap with
H.M.S. *Renown* on the ribbon. The kindergarten was housed in
an old-fashioned schoolhouse, to which a large, much newer
school had been joined. It stank, in a perfectly reasonable way,
of floor oil, chalk powder, and many generations of imperfectly
continent Blairlogie children. The teacher, Miss Wade, was a
smiling, friendly woman, but a stranger, and there was not a child
in the thirty or more present whom Francis had ever seen before.

"His name's Francis Cornish," said Bella-Mae, and went home.

Some of the children were crying, and Francis was of a mind
to join this group, but he knew his father would disapprove, so
he bit his lip and held in. Obedient to Miss Wade, and a student
teacher who acted as her assistant, the children sat in small chairs,
arranged in a circle marked out on the floor in red paint.

To put things on a friendly footing at once, Miss Wade said
that everybody would stand up, as his turn came, and say his name
and tell where he lived, so that she could prepare something
mysteriously called the Nominal Roll. The children complied,
some shouting out their names boldly, some sure of their names
but in the dark as to their addresses; the third child in order, a
little girl, lost her composure and wet the floor. Most of the other
children laughed, held their noses, and enjoyed the fun, as the
student teacher rushed forward with a damp rag for the floor and
a hanky for the eyes. When Francis's turn came, he announced,
in a low voice: Francis Chegwidden Cornish, Chegwidden Lodge.

"What's your second name, Francis?" said Miss Wade.

"Chegwidden," said Francis, using the pronunciation he had
been taught.

Miss Wade, kindly but puzzled, said, "Did you say Chicken,
Francis?"

"Cheggin," said Francis, much too low to be heard above
the roar of the thirty others, who began to shout, "Chicken,
Chicken!" in delight. This was something they could understand
and get their teeth into. The kid in the funny suit was called

Chicken! Oh, this was rich! Far better than the kid who had peed.

Miss Wade restored order, but at recess it was Chicken, Chicken! for the full fifteen minutes, and a very happy playtime it made. Kindergarten assembled only during the morning, and as soon as school was dismissed, Francis ran home as fast as he could, followed by derisive shouts.

Francis announced next morning that he was not going to school. Oh yes you are, said Bella-Mae. I won't, said Francis. Do you want me to march you right over to Miss McRory? said Bella-Mae, for in the absence of his parents, Aunt Mary-Ben had been given full authority to bind and loose if anything went beyond the nursemaid's power. So off to school he went, in Bella-Mae's jailer grip, and the second day was worse than the first.

Children from the upper school had got wind of something extraordinary and at recess Francis was surrounded by older boys, anxious to look into the matter.

"It's not Chicken, it's Cheggin," said Francis, trying hard not to cry.

"See—he says his name's Chicken," shouted one boy, already a leader of men, and later to do well in politics.

"Aw, come on," said a philosophical boy, anxious to probe deeper. "Nobody's called Chicken. Say it again, kid."

"Cheggin," said Francis.

"Sounds like Chicken, all right," said the philosophical boy. "Kind of mumbled, but Chicken. Gosh!"

If the boys were derisive, the girls were worse. The girls had a playground of their own, on which no boy was allowed to set foot, but there were places where the boundary, like the equator, was an imaginary line. The boys decided that it was great fun to harry Francis across this line, because anybody called Chicken was probably a girl anyway. When this happened, girls surrounded him and talked not to but at him.

"His name's Chicken," some would say, whooping with joy. These girls belong to what psychologists would later define as the Hetaera, or Harlot, classification of womanhood.

"Aw, let him alone. His parents must be crazy. Look, he's nearly bawling. It's mean to holler on him if his parents are crazy. Is your name really Chicken, kid?" These were what the psychologists would classify as the Maternal, fostering order of womankind. Their pity was almost more hateful than outright jeering.

Teachers patrolled both playgrounds, carrying a bell by its clapper, and usually intent on studying the sky. Ostensibly guardians of order, they were like policemen in their avoidance of anything short of arson or murder. Questioned, they would probably have said that the Cornish child seemed to be popular; he was always . in the centre of some game or another.

Life must be lived, and sometimes living means enduring. Francis endured, and the torment let up a little, though it broke out anew every two or three weeks. He no longer had to go to school in the care of Bella-Mae. Kindergarten was hateful. There was stupid, babyish paper-cutting, which was far beneath his notice, and which he did easily. There was sewing crudely punched cards, so that they formed a picture, usually of an animal. There was learning to tell the time, which he knew anyway. There was getting the Twenty-third Psalm by heart, and singing a tedious hymn that began

> *Can a little child like me*
> *Thank the Father fittingly?*

and dragged on to a droning refrain (for Miss Wade had no skill as a choral director) of

> *Father, we thank Thee:* (twice repeated)
> *Father in Heaven, we thank Thee!*

Francis, who had a precocious theological bent, wondered why he was thanking the Father, whoever He might be, for this misery and this tedium.

It was in kindergarten that the foundations for Francis Cornish's lifelong misanthropy were firmly established. The sampling of mankind into which he had been cast badgered and mocked him, excluded him from secrets and all but the most inclusive games, sneered at his clothes, and in one instance wrote PRICK in indelible pencil on the collar of his sailor middy (for which Bella-Mae gave him a furious scolding).

He could say nothing of this at home. When, infrequently, his parents came back to Blairlogie for a weekend, he was told by his mother that he must be a particularly good boy, because Daddy was busy with some very important things in Ottawa, and was not to be worried. Now: how was school going?

"All right, I guess."

"Don't say 'I guess' unless you really do guess, Frankie. It's stupid."

> Love the Lord and do your part:
> Learn to say with all your heart,
> Father, we thank Thee!

AND SO FRANCIS LEFT *the garden of childhood for the kindergarten, said the Lesser Zadkiel.*

—*It was his second experience of the Fall of Man, said the Daimon Maimas. The first, of course, is birth, when he is thrust out of the paradise of his mother's body; the second is when he leaves his happy home—if he is lucky enough to have such a thing—and finds himself in the world of his contemporaries.*

—*Surely it was stupid to send him to school in white, with a nursemaid?*

—*Nobody thought about it. The Major and his wife thought of nothing but the Major's work in Ottawa, which of course was never defined for the child. But the Major was no fool, and had smelled a war in the air, long before more important people did.*

—*You sound rather pleased with what happened to Francis.*

—*I had a rough idea of the direction in which I was going to push him, and I always like to begin tempering my steel early. A happy childhood has spoiled many a promising life. And it wasn't all unhappy. Go on with the story, and you'll see.*

AS CHRISTMAS DREW NEAR it seemed that the War was going to last longer than had been expected, so the Major thought he had better close Chegwidden Lodge and move to Ottawa. It would be foolish to take Francis, for both parents were busy. Mary-Jim was deep in women's committee work, and looked adorable in the severe clothes she thought appropriate to her role. It was arranged that Francis should move the short distance from the

Lodge to St. Kilda, and live under the guidance of his grandparents and Aunt Mary-Ben.

This meant a great improvement in his lot, for Aunt immediately bought him clothes that were more what other children in Blairlogie wore, and he was happy in his corduroy knickerbockers and a mackinaw coat, and the tuque that replaced his little velvet hat with earflaps. He was happy, too, in his room, not a nursery but full of grown-up furniture. Best of all, Bella-Mae was left at the Lodge as a caretaker, and Aunt made it gently clear that there was no need for her to bother her head about Francis. That suited Bella-Mae, as she said to herself, down to the ground, because it gave her more time to devote to advancement in her own particular Army.

There were some great changes. Francis now ate at the table with the adults, and the manners he had learned while eating with Bella-Mae needed amendment. No grunting, to begin with; Bella-Mae had been a hearty eater and a great grunter as she ate, and as Francis never sat at his parents' table his grunting had passed unnoticed. He had to learn to murmur grace and cross himself before and after meals. He learned to be neat with his knife and fork, and was forbidden to hound morsels of food around his plate. Most significant change of all, he had to learn to speak French.

This had been a matter of some debate. Grand-père and Grand'mère thought it would be useful if they could speak together at table without being understood by the boy. But, said Aunt, he would certainly learn anyhow, and had best learn properly. So he sat beside her at meals, and learned to ask for things in polite form, and finally to make a few remarks of his own, in the pleasing, clear French that Aunt had learned in her convent days; but he also learned the patois (called by Aunt woods-French) into which his grandparents retreated when they had secrets to discuss.

The whole business of French opened a new world to Francis. Of course, he had noticed that a lot of people in Blairlogie spoke this language, with varying degrees of elegance, but he now discovered that the hardware store kept by somebody called Dejordo was, in reality, the property of Emile Desjardins, and that the Legarry family were, to those who spoke French, Legaré. Some tact had to be exercised here, because it was a point of honour among the English-speaking populace to mispronounce any French name, as a rebuke to those who were so foolish, and probably sneaky and disloyal as well, as to speak a private lingo. But Francis was a quick boy—"gleg in the uptake" as his Scots grandfather put it—and he learned not only two kinds of French, but two kinds of English as well. In the schoolyard a substantial quantity of anything whatever was always described as "a big bunch", and any distance beyond what could be covered on foot was "a fur piece of a ways". When adults greeted one another with "Fine day, eh?", the proper reply was "Fine day altogether". He mastered all these niceties with the same ease with which he digested his food and grew, and by the time he was nine he was not merely bilingual, but multilingual, and could talk to anybody he met in their own language, be it French, patois, Canadian-Scots English, or the speech of the Upper Ottawa Valley. He learned manners, too, and would never be so gross as to *tutoyer* Madame Thibodeau, whose social magnificence grew with her fat.

As he had hitherto been chiefly the creation of Bella-Mae, he was now moulded and spiritually surrounded by Aunt. This caused the good lady many anxious hours, for the Major, when it was arranged that Francis should stay for a while at St. Kilda, had said, hastily and with obvious discomfort, that Frank was, of course, a Protestant, and furthermore C. of E., and he had asked Canon Tremaine to look in now and then to see that the boy was alright. But Canon Tremaine, who was a lazy man and not anxious to antagonize anyone so important as the Senator, had called at St. Kilda only once, to the astonishment of Marie-Louise, who had said that of course the little boy was very well, and of course he was going to the Protestant school, and of course he had his prayers, and would the Canon like another piece of cake? Which the Canon ate with pleasure, and forgot that he had meant to ask why Frank never appeared at St. Alban's. But upon Aunt fell the burden of caring for the child's soul.

Aunt knew all about souls. A neglected soul was an invitation for the Evil One to take it over, and, once in, he was almost impossible to banish. Francis knew a prayer—*Now I lay me down to sleep*—and of course he knew who Jesus was, because that picture of A Certain Person had been in the nursery for as long as he could remember. But just why Jesus was important, and that He was always present, watching you, and that although He had died long ago, He was still lurking, unseen, he did not know. As for the Holy Mother, friend and guardian of children, Francis had never heard of her. Such neglect of a child filled Aunt with pity; she could not understand how dear Mary-Jim had been so utterly consumed by her Protestant husband as to permit such a thing. What was she to do?

Little use to seek advice from Marie-Louise, whose comfortable, practical mind, when it could be said to be active at all, was now devoted to bridge. Bridge parties and vast Progressive Euchre parties at the church, devoted to raising money for war charities, possessed her. Not easy work, for so many of the Blairlogie Catholics were also French Canadians, and their zeal for a war against the enemies of England was wavering at best. But Marie-Louise had eaten the splendid cuisine of the English King, and was an ardent royalist. Madame Thibodeau was even less useful in the campaign to rescue Francis; the child had been baptized a Protestant, and was damned, and what was all the fuss about? The Senator was more helpful, but he was a man of honour and he had signed the Wooden Soldier's hateful paper guaranteeing that Francis should be a Protestant, and he would not go back on his word; but neither would he interfere if Mary-Ben moved on her own authority. She had better talk to Dr. J.A., who had a long head on him. Don't go to the priests till you've had a word with Dr. J.A.

Excellent advice! Dr. J. A. Jerome knew just what to do. "Frank's a clever lad," he said; "reads a great deal for a boy of his years. Lead him gently, Mary-Ben. Have you ever talked to him about his patron saint, for instance?"

Because he was born on September 12, Francis's only possible patron was the grubby Guy of Anderlecht, a Belgian who had lost all his money in a bad speculation and turned to God in his bankruptcy. Nothing there to light the flame of devotion in a boy of nine. But it was also the day devoted to the Holy Name of Mary, a feast not much heeded, having lost out to the Feast of the Holy Name of Jesus, but it would do for a beginning. So one day Francis found a large oleograph of Mary hanging in his room; it was a reproduction of a Murillo, and, contrary to what might have been expected, he liked it very much. Its soft beauty reminded him of his own mother, whom he saw so rarely, and he listened with interest as Aunt explained how tender and kind the Mother of God was, and how watchful of the fate of little boys. Dr. J.A. was right, as always.

"Not that I approve of what you're doing, Mary-Ben," said he. "But I have to give a lot of advice that I wouldn't think of taking myself. Far better the Blessed Mother than that Son of hers. I never knew a boy yet that I'd trust who really took to that searching, seeking fella."

"Oh, Joe, you just say that to make me shudder."

"Maybe I do; maybe I don't. Half the time I don't know what I mean. But you seem to be on the right track."

Francis had never heard of anybody's mother at St. Alban's, when he went there with his parents. But he was open to stories about someone who pitied those who were in distress, and increasingly he was in distress.

This was because he had been summarily moved from the Central School, which was not far from St. Kilda, to Carlyle Rural School, which was almost two miles distant, but which included St. Kilda in the outermost reaches of its domain. His transfer was an act of covert spite directed at the Senator by the local school board; the secretary of that board, checking the lists, had discovered that Francis Cornish, by moving a hundred yards from his father's house to his grandfather's, had moved into the Carlyle school district, and one September morning when he was in the third grade he and two other children were told at ten o'clock to bundle up their books and report to Miss Helen McGladdery at their new school. Within an hour Francis, for all purposes sufficient to his age and stage of life, descended into Hell, and stayed there for what seemed to him an eternity.

Carlyle Rural School was not, at that time, particularly rural, for it was on the outskirts of Blairlogie in an area inhabited by workers in the Senator's various mills and factories; it was with their children, and the children of farmers who worked the stony, wretched soil just outside the town, that Francis pursued his academic education and his vastly more significant social, ethical, and economic education.

Having now gained some measure of craftiness, he told Miss

McGladdery that his name was Francis Cornish, but she had fore-knowledge of his coming, and demanded to know what the C. on the secretary's message stood for, and the misery of Chicken began all over again with new and ingenious tormentors.

At the first recess a large boy approached him, hit him hard in the face, and said, "Come on, Chicken, let's see if you can fight." They fought, and Francis was beaten disastrously.

After that he had to fight twice a day for three weeks, and he was beaten every time. Small boys are not skilled fighters, and though he was hurt and shaken, he suffered no serious damage. But after recess he sat at his desk, wretched and aching, and Miss McGladdery was angry with him because he was inattentive. Miss McGladdery was fifty-nine, and she was soldiering through her teaching career until, at sixty-five, she would be able to retire and, with God's help, never see any of her former pupils again.

A strong Scots background, and thirty years at Carlyle Rural, had made her an expert disciplinarian. A short, fat, implacable woman, she ruled her three groups—for Carlyle Rural had only two rooms and she took the most advanced classes—not with a rod of iron, but with the leather strap that was issued by the school board as the ultimate instrument of justice. She did not use it often; she had only to take it from a drawer and lay it across her desk to quell any ordinary disobedience. When she did use it, she displayed a strength that even the biggest, most loutish boy dreaded, for not only did she flail his hands until they swelled to red, aching paws, but she tongue-lashed him with a virtuosity that threw her classes into an ecstasy of silent delight.

"Gordon McNab, you're a true chip off the McNab block. (*Slash!*) I've given the strap to your father (*Slash!*), and both your uncles (*Slash!*), and I once gave it to your mother (*Slash!*), and I'm here to tell the world that you are the stupidest, most ignorant, no-account ruffian of the whole caboodle. (*Slash!*) And that's saying something. (*Slash!*) Now go to your seat, and if I hear a peep out of you except in answer to a question, you'll get it again and get it worse, because I've got it right here in my desk, all ready for you. Do you hear me?"

"Bluh."

"What? Speak up. What do you say?"

"Yes, Miss McGladdery."

McNab would slink to his seat, as boys held hands in front of their mouths, and girls, greatly daring, sharpened their fingers at him in disdain. It was useless for McNab to snarl in the schoolyard that Miss McGladdery was a dirty old bitch and her pants stank. He had lost face. Miss McGladdery had the total authority of the captain of a pirate ship.

She knew what happened in the schoolyard, but she did not interfere. Young Cornish's grandfather was the leading Grit—the hated Liberal Party—and Miss McGladdery was an unwavering Conservative, or Tory. If the boy had so much grit in him, let him show it; she would do nothing until he complained, in which case she would take steps, but she would despise him as a complainer.

He did not complain, but one day a boy hit him in the eye hard enough to blacken it, and he went home knowing that there would be trouble.

It was not the kind of trouble he expected.

Aunt Mary-Ben, horrified, took him at once to Dr. J.A. Jerome. A black eye was nothing, said the doctor; no great harm at all. But then—

"They're giving you a rough time, Frank? You don't have to tell me. I know. I know everything that goes on in this town. Did you know that? They're a rough lot at Carlyle Rural. Do you know the Queensberry Rules?"

Francis had heard something of this code from his father. You didn't hit below the belt.

"Do you not? Well, Frank, the Queensberry Rules are all very fine in the ring but they've never heard of them at Carlyle Rural, or anywhere in Blairlogie, so far as I know. Did you never see the lumbermen fighting on a Saturday night? No, I don't suppose you have. Those French boys know something about rough fighting. Now look here: you have two fists, and they wouldn't dent a pound of butter. But you've two feet and good strong boots. So the trick is to let your man get close, then you rear back and let him have your right boot slap in his wind. Don't kick him in the groin; that's for later. But get his wind. He'll probably fall down, if you do it right. Then jump on him and beat the stuffing out of him. Give it all you've got. He'll be too busy trying to get his breath to do much. Don't kill him, but get as near it as you dare. Get him by the ears and bang his head on the ground; you can't hurt their heads."

"Oh, Joe, you'll make a tough of the boy," said Mary-Ben, in distress.

"Just so, my dear. That's the whole idea. If you've got any brains at Carlyle Rural you have to be a tough in order to keep them for yourself. In fact, Frank, it's a good principle of life to let people understand that you're really a terrible tough; then they'll let you alone and you can be as delicate as you please, so long as they don't find you out. Now, here's some arnica to paint on the eye. Twice a day is enough. And keep him at home for the rest of the week, Mary-Ben, just to give Miss McGladdery a fright. Let her think she's gone too far."

And it all came to pass very much as Dr. J.A. expected. When Frank did not appear at school, Miss McGladdery was worried, and when she was worried her hemorrhoids tormented her. Of course she would not dream of consulting a Catholic doctor, but when Dr. J.A. buttonholed her on the steps of the Post Office on Saturday she could not escape.

"I hear Carlyle Rural is just as rough as it's always been. Did you ever think you might have an ugly situation there one of these days, Miss McGladdery? It'd be a sad thing if anybody was seriously injured."

A nod was as good as a wink to Miss McGladdery, and on Monday morning she announced that there had been too much fighting in the schoolyard, and if there were any more of it, she would strap the fighters.

Of course Frank was blamed; he had squealed. But obviously he wielded some power, and he had no more trouble with fighting. He was no better liked, and when the great spring game began, he watched from the sidelines.

Most of the boys were watchers, but unlike Frank they enjoyed what they saw. It fed something deep in them.

There was a pond in a field across the road from Carlyle Rural, and in spring it was full of frogs. The game was to catch a frog, stick a straw up its cloaca, and blow it up to enormous size. As the frog swelled, there was a delightful apprehension that it might burst. There was an even more splendid hope that the boy who was blowing might, if enough funny things were said to him, stop blowing for a moment and suck and then—why, he might even die, which would richly crown the fun.

Frank's eyes were upon the frog, whose contortions and wildly waving legs pierced his heart with a vivid sense of the sufferings of Jesus, which Aunt had begun to describe to him. When His Name was used as an oath, Jesus suffered, and when boys were naughty Jesus' wounds were opened and bled afresh. How Jesus must have been agonized by the tortures of the frogs! And—horror!—what must Jesus have felt the day some boys caught a tomcat and cut off its testicles, and let it loose to rush away, howling and bleeding! Francis was dimly becoming aware of his own testicles, which were somehow associated with something Awful about which he could not get any exact information.

Animals did it, as you hurried past with blushes and shame. But surely the boys could not be right who said that people did it, too? That your own parents—but that did not bear thinking of; it was horrible and wholly incredible. Frank's mind was becoming a horror of sick speculation. And, young as he was, his body seemed to be in the conspiracy against him.

Aunt was not his only source of information about the mysteries of life. He found great solace in the company of Victoria Cameron, his grandfather's cook. Aunt did not like him to talk too much to Victoria, who was not simply a Protestant but a Presbyterian of the darkest hue. She knew what was going on in the Senator's house, and she knew it was wrong. Miss McRory was trying to suck that poor boy into the abyss of Catholicism and, although Victoria, as a great artist of the kitchen, was glad enough of the high wages—a resounding thirty-seven dollars a month, and board!—that the Senator paid her, she called her soul her own, and resisted Rome as stoutly as she could without provoking a row. She knew enough about the McRorys to hang them, she told herself, but she held her tongue. Judge not that ye be not judged. Of course, you can't be a Calvinist without judging, but as a Calvinist you know what God's ordinances are, so it isn't really judging. It is just knowing right from wrong.

As is so often the case with people who hold their tongues, Victoria had a vast accretion of bottled-up disapproval, and it could be sensed from the darkness of her gaze, and spells of breathing deeply through her nose that could be heard at a considerable distance.

All she could properly do, as a loyal servant, eating the Senator's bread, was to befriend that boy, and befriend him she did, in her own stern fashion.

He asked her outright about the great mystery: did people do what animals did? Her reply was that there was an awful lot of Bad in the world, and the less you know about it the luckier you were, and he was not to ask that question again.

Aunt Mary-Ben, dimly aware but not well informed about the opposition in the kitchen, told Frank many a wondrous story about the mercy of God's Mother, as she had seen it evinced in the visible world. Oh, you could always go to Her, Frankie, when you were troubled. Aunt kept her promise, and during the trouble of the black eye she gave him a pretty little rosary, which she told him had been blessed by the Bishop in Ottawa; he was to keep it under his pillow, and soon she would teach him the poetry that went with it.

Frank was deeply troubled, but it would never do to ask her the question he had put to Victoria. She wouldn't know about such things, or if she did she would be sorrowful because he knew about them. And there was always the risk of opening the wounds of Jesus afresh.

The question plagued and puzzled. There was the time that a travelling company came to the theatre his grandfather owned— the McRory Opera House and Blairlogie's principal centre of culture—offering a play tantalizingly called *The Unwanted Child*. There were special matinees for Women Only, at which a Well-Known Authority would lecture on the theme of the play, which was of concern to everyone. Francis knew that Victoria had attended one of these matinees, and he pestered her without mercy to know what the play had been about.

At last she yielded. "Frankie," she said with great solemnity, "it was about a girl who Went The Limit." No more would she say.

The Limit? Oh, what was the Limit?

POOR WRETCH, *said the Lesser Zadkiel, breaking off in his narrative; don't you pity him?*

—*No, no, no, said the Daimon Maimas. Pity is a human feeling, and I have nothing whatever to do with it. Your work is so much taken up with human creatures, brother, that you are infected by their weaknesses. Those children at Carlyle Rural, for instance; they were simply what they were. But you tell the tale of Francis as if to condemn them. I never condemn. My job was to make something of Francis with the materials I had at hand. If those materials were rough, they were good enough to grind his spirit down to a surface that showed up several veins of gold. Fine polishing will come later.*

—*But it made the boy thin and pale and sad.*

—*Now, now—that's another of your pitying judgements. Put aside pity, Zadkiel. But I forget—you can't; it's not in your welkin. But I can, and indeed I must, if I am to be the grinder, the shaper, the refiner. We work like the classical Greek sculptors, you and I. I must hew the creature out of my own intractable piece of rock and put a fine surface on it. Then you apply the rich colours, of which Pity and Charity are very popular pigments. They seem to give my creation a life that human beings understand and love, but when the colours are washed away by time, the reality is revealed, and I know that the reality has been there since the beginning.*

—*But this struggle for the boy's soul, as they call it. Pull Devil, pull Baker.*

—*I hope you use the phrase metaphorically. It would be unjust to call Aunt Mary-Ben a devil; she was about as honest and well-intentioned as human beings generally are, and she wanted her own way because she thought it was the best way. You may call Victoria Cameron a baker, if you choose. There is some justice in that.*

JUSTICE, INDEED, FOR VICTORIA sprang from a long line of bakers, and her father and her brothers Hugh and Dougal ran the best bakery in Blairlogie. One Friday night Victoria got permission from Aunt to rouse Francis at two o'clock in the morning and take him to the bakery to see the Cameron men knead their dough.

The dough was an immense mass in a large round wooden trough that was built with a huge pole at its centre to which were attached three long bands of linen. The three Camerons were sitting with their trouser legs rolled up to the knee, scrubbing their feet in a low sink. Scrub, scrub, scrub till you might think the skin would come off. Then they dried their feet on fresh towels, powdered their feet with flour, leapt from the sink into the dough-trough, seized a linen band each, and began what looked like a wild dance in the dough. Round and round, until the linen bands were as close to the pole as they could be; then they turned and danced the other way, as the bands unfolded, shouting Heigh, heigh, heigh, as they danced.

"D'ye want to scrub up, young master, and dance with us?" shouted Old Cameron. And, quick as a wink, Victoria had his shoes and stockings off, washed his feet and floured them, and popped him into the trough with the men, where he danced as well as he could, for the dough was resistant, like treading on some sort of flesh; but that added to the fun. Francis never forgot that night, or the heat of the ovens, into which had been thrown many bundles of fern, which burned down to a fine white ash. After the dancing, the dough was cut with paddles into what would be pound loaves, and set out to rise again, before they went into the fiercely hot, sweet-smelling brick ovens.

At breakfast the next day, Victoria assured him that he was eating bread he had helped to bake himself.

The boy's life was not at all dark; he was not clever at school, but he attracted Miss McGladdery's attention by the seriousness with which he applied himself in the weekly half-hour that was given to Art. Miss McGladdery taught Art, as she taught everything, and she instructed all three classes at once in the mysteries of drawing a pyramid and shading one side of it so that it appeared to have a third dimension—or as she put it the shaded side "went back" and the unshaded part "stuck out". A pyramid and a circle which shading made into a ball, and, as the culmination of Art, an apple. Shading was done by scuffling down one side of the object with the flat of the pencil's point. But Frank did not think that good enough; he had learned a craft at home in which shading was done with tiny parallel lines, achieved with great patience, and even by cross-hatching.

"If you take the time to do all that tick-tack-toe on your apple you won't be finished by four, and you'll have to stay in till it's done," said Miss McGladdery. So he did "stay in" with half a dozen other culprits who had work to finish before they were released for the weekend, and when he showed Miss McGladdery his apple at half past four she admitted reluctantly that it was "all right", for she did not want to encourage the boy to be "fancy" and try to go beyond what the class demanded and what she herself knew. Frank could draw, which was something not required in Art, and Miss McGladdery had come upon a caricature of herself done in the back of his arithmetic workbook. Miss McGladdery, who was a fairminded woman, except about religion and politics, and had no vanity, admitted to herself that it was good, so she said nothing about it. Frank was an oddity, and, like a true Scot, Miss McGladdery had a place in her approval for "a chiel o' pairts", so long as he did not go too far.

Almost every Saturday Frank could escape into a world of imagination by going to the matinee at the McRory Opera House, where movies were shown. He got in for nothing, because the girl at the ticket office recognized him, and as he pushed his ten-cent piece across the little counter she winked and quietly pushed it back again.

Then inside, and into his favourite seat, which was on the aisle at the back; he did not crowd into the front rows, as did the other children. Riches unfolded. An episode—locally pronounced "esi-pode"—of a serial, in which, every week, a noble cowboy was brought to the point of a horrible death by remorseless villains who sought to rob him of the equally noble girl he loved. Of course, it all came out right at the end of Episode Twelve, and then another great adventure was announced for the weeks to follow. After the serial, a hilarious comedy, sometimes about the Keystone Komedy Kops, who were as incapable of dealing with disaster as the girl in the serial. Occasionally Charlie Chaplin appeared, but Francis did not like him. He was a loser, and Francis knew too much about being a loser to make a pet of one. Then the feature, in several reels; the ones Francis most enjoyed were not usually those that appealed to the other children. *Lorna Doone,* which came from England, was certain proof that the nasty mystery about what animals did and really good people surely didn't was a lie; the image of the beautiful Lorna, who looked exactly like the Holy Mother, but was attainable by a truly good man, who might then kiss her chastely and adore her forever, did more to shape his ideas about womanhood than Aunt's pious confidences. Certainly Lorna was a girl who would never venture within miles of the Limit, whatever the Limit might be. A companion picture in this special group was *The Passing of the Third Floor Back*, in which the great English tragedian Forbes-Robertson (much was made of his eminence in the advertisements and prices were slightly raised) played the role of a man who showed a group of shabby people that they didn't have to be shabby, and who looked so noble, so distinguished, so totally incapable of laughter or any other lively emotion, that he was plainly intended to be A Certain Person, but wearing a fine cloak and a broad-brimmed hat, instead of those sappy robes in which A Certain Person usually appeared. Frank had not yet been taken to Mass, and he had forgotten St. Alban's, but at the movies he fed upon these things in his heart, and was thankful.

Francis had an eye for the movies that took in more than the action; he saw backgrounds, landscapes (many of them painted, if you looked carefully), and angles; he even saw light. It was to his grandfather, the Senator, that he owed this extension of his understanding, for the Senator was an amateur photographer. His techniques were not sophisticated in terms of the Great War period when Francis was so often his companion; he worked with a large box-camera and a tripod. With this load he trudged happily around Blairlogie, taking pictures of the town, and such of its more picturesque citizens as he could persuade to stand or sit still for the necessary number of seconds, and he drove out to the lumber camps from which his growing fortune flowed, and took pictures of the men at work, or standing by giant trees lying on their sides. He took pictures in his mills. He took pictures of young Blairlogie men who were going off to war, with their rifles and kit, and gave copies to their families. The Senator never thought of himself as an artist, but he had an eye for a picture and he was an enthusiastic pursuer of all the many sorts of light the Canadian seasons afford. He talked to Francis about it as if the boy were of his own age. His senatorial and grandpaternal aloofness quite disappeared on these expeditions in search of what he called "sun-pictures".

"It's all a question of the light, Frank," he said repeatedly; "the light does it all." And he explained that all that painstaking shading in Art was related to light—something which certainly had never occurred to Miss McGladdery.

His detestation was pictures that had been taken by artificial light, and he particularly liked to take portraits in a shelter he caused to be made in the garden, to which furniture and draperies and other decorations could be laboriously lugged, and in which—apparently indoors but in fact in some version of the sun's light—he took countless pictures of Madame Thibodeau, of Marie-Louise, of the children of his second daughter, Mary-Teresa, and of his son-in-law, Gerald Vincent O'Gorman, the rising man in the McRory industrial empire. Aunt resolutely refused to be photographed. "Oh, Hamish, I'd break the camera," she laughed. But at her insistence he photographed Father Devlin and Father Beaudry, each leaning over a table in scholarly abstraction, apparently reading a leather-bound book, one forefinger supporting a brow plainly crammed with edifying knowledge. He even persuaded Dr. Jerome to pose for him, his hand resting on a skull which was a prized possession.

Taking pictures was great fun, but it was not so entrancing as what followed, when Francis and Grand-père were locked in a bathroom with no light save that from a dim red lamp, swishing and sloshing the film in smelly liquids in the wash-basin and the bathtub, watching for each sun-picture to declare itself, with just the right quality to satisfy the Senator's careful eye. And then—

What followed was best of all, for then Grand-père set to work with an exquisitely pointed pencil to improve on his work by retouching the negative, emphasizing shadows, or giving richness to special aspects of the picture with an intricate shading done sometimes in tiny dots, sometimes in little spiral squiggles, sometimes in cross-hatching, so that the appearance of the sitter was enhanced in a flattering way.

Or, it might be, in a way that was not wholly flattering. Gerald Vincent O'Gorman had a dark beard, and when the Senator was finished with him, his close-shaven jaw had a faintly criminal shadow on it. And Father Beaudry's fleshy wen—not large but emphatic—on the left side of his nose was given a prominence which startled the priest when he received the print that was to be sent to his mother in Trois Rivières. Not even the dignity of soutane and biretta could diminish the prominence of that wen. But Mary-Teresa, who already had a perceptible double chin, lost it in the retouching process. The Senator never commented on these alterations to Francis, but he could be seen to smile as he brought them into being with his delicate pencil, and Francis learned, without knowing that he was learning, that a portrait is, among other things, a statement of opinion by the artist, as well as a "likeness", which was what everybody wanted it to be.

Francis was allowed to do some retouching himself, and he longed to transform the sitters with squints and lumps and deforming wrinkles. This was not permitted, but when Grandfather was momentarily absent he did, on one occasion, manage to sharpen one of Father Devlin's front teeth in a way that seemed to him more expressive of Father Devlin's personality than the unaided truth. Whether Grandfather saw what had been done was never known to Francis. But Grandfather did indeed notice, and a spirit of mischief to which he could not often give rein, and a pride in the psychological perception shown by his grandson, made him hold his peace, and he printed the improved portrait. Father Devlin never understood it, and although repeated examination in the mirror, and exploratory licking, told him that his dog-tooth was not really that of a vampire, he was of that simple group of mankind that believes the camera cannot lie, and besides, he did not like to criticize the Senator.

So, in one way and another, Francis managed to get some joy in life despite the shadow of school and the harassment of virtually all other children. Without being aware of it, he took into his mind and spirit forever a world that was passing away, a world of isolated communities like Blairlogie, which knew little of the world outside that they did not learn from *The Clarion* or, in one or two hundred uncharacteristic households, from the Ottawa papers. There was no entertainment from outside save the films and occasional road-shows at the McRory Opera House; entertainment was provided by church groups, by fraternal orders, by innumerable card parties, and of course by gossip, often cruel and bizarre in its nature.

At the top of the class structure were a few families who kept "maids", an order of being who paradoxically conferred distinction, but were themselves held in disdain as underlings. When a maid bought a coat at Thomson and Howat, for instance, Archie Thomson always telephoned her employer (there were about two hundred telephones in the town) to ask if the girl was "good" for it, and to find out if he could what she was paid monthly. If a maid was so audacious as to attract a suitor, her mistress never failed to pop into the kitchen suddenly, to find out if they were up to anything. To employ a maid was splendid: to be a maid was to be sneered at, especially by those ladies who did not have a servant themselves. Protestant ministers were insistent that employers should release their maids on Sunday evenings, so that they could attend late services, but they gave the maids warmed-over sermons.

It was a world in which the horse played a crucial part. Few of these horses were of the noble breed with arching neck and flashing eye; most were miserable screws, rackers, the broken-winded, the spavined, often far gone with the botts, or with nostrils dribbling from the glanders. Even the splendid Percherons that drew the Senator's great sleighs laden with tree-trunks were not objects of pride to their drivers, for they were seldom washed or combed, and the accusation that somebody smelled like a horse had a pungency now forgotten. But all of these creatures were hearty producers of manure, and in spring, when the unploughed roads gradually lost their layers of snow, the droppings of November perfumed the air of April, appearing with the lost overshoes and the copious spittings of the tobacco-chewers that had accumulated during the last months of frost.

Where there are horses there must be smiths. Francis spent many a happy hour, of which Aunt would have disapproved, hanging around Donoghue's, where the big horses that pulled the lumber-sleighs were shod with pointed shoes that would strike into the icy roads. There, warmed by the horses and the fire of the forge, he learned rich blasphemy and objurgation from Vincent Donoghue, learned the stench that rises when the hot shoe is placed on the horse's hoof, and the sharper stench when a spark landed on the blacksmith's apron. But he learned no obscenity. Donoghue was puritanical and his horse-vocabulary was for talking to horses as he understood them; he would permit no smutty stories in his forge.

The taxicab was yet to come, and people who needed a carriage for a funeral, or a visit to the hospital, rode in lurching vehicles like droshkys; for winter their wheels were removed and they were mounted on runners; inside they stank of old leather, and of the mangy buffalo-robes that were drawn over the knees of the passengers; the drivers sat on a box in front, wrapped in fur coats of incalculable age.

There were a few horses of the better, proud sort, and of these the Senator's were the best: a team of good bays, and a dancing pony or two to pull the governess-cart in which Marie-Louise and frequently Madame Thibodeau went shopping. Undertakers also had good horses, for that was part of the panoply of death, and of these Devinney's black team were the most admired.

Good horses need good keeping, and when Old Billy finally drank himself into the grave, the Senator made one of the loose arrangements that were common in Blairlogie to have Devinney's driver and groom take care of his horses as well, and it was not long before this man, whose name was Zadok Hoyle, spent more time at St. Kilda than he did at Devinney's Furniture and Undertaking Parlours.

Zadok Hoyle presented a fine figure on the box of carriage or hearse, for he was a large, muscular man of upright bearing, black-haired and dark-skinned, possessed of a moustache that swept from under his nose in two fine ebony curls. On closer inspection it could be seen that he was cock-eyed, that his nose was of a rich red, and that his snowy collar and stock were washed less often than they were touched up with chalk. The seams of the frock coat he wore when driving the hearse would have been white if he had not painted them with ink. His top hat was glossy, but its nap was kept smooth with vaseline. His voice was deep and caressing. The story was that he was an old soldier, a veteran of the Boer War, and that he had learned about horses in the army.

He became Francis's hero, second only to Grandfather. Zadok Hoyle was a Cornishman by birth, and had never lost his Cornish turn of speech; he usually called Francis "me little dear", which did not sound odd from him, and sometimes he called him "poor worm", which was meant in an affectionate and not a derogatory way. He spoke to the horses in the same terms, and they loved him, in so far as a horse can love anybody. Best of all, he had lived near to Chegwidden Hall in Cornwall when he was a boy, and did not have to be told how to pronounce the name in the proper style. When Francis confided to him the shame of being called Chicken, Zadok said: "Pity their ignorance, me liddle dear; pity their ignorance and despise 'em."

ON NOVEMBER 11, not long after Francis's ninth birthday, the First World War, which for so long was called the Great War, ended, but that did not mean that Major Cornish and Mary-Jacobine returned to Blairlogie. Everyone understands that when a war is over, the cleaning-up and the arranging, and the vengeance toward the vanquished, take just as much time and clashing of brains as the conflict itself. The Major had a very good war; he remained a major, because it gave him a certain protective colouring. There were plenty of majors, and the fact that this one was apparently an unusually clever major, attached to the Canadian forces but a familiar figure in the War Office in London, was better concealed from curious people. "High up in Intelligence" was the phrase people used about him, and that was much better than being a lieutenant-colonel, for instance. Such a man could not be spared when there was so much to do, and he and his wife, that popular beauty, had to go to London almost at once, and for an indefinite time.

The fighting had finished, but disease was busily at work. Spreading, unquestionably, from the putrefying dead lying on the battlefields—Blairlogie knew this to be a fact—the Influenza walked the earth, and killed an additional twenty millions before it subsided. But in Blairlogie, as well as the influenza there was whooping-cough, and that had hardly subsided before there was a rush of what was then called infantile paralysis, the terrible inflammation of the spinal marrow that left so many children on crutches with legs cased in cruel cages, or confined to wheelchairs, if it did not kill them. But Francis, who was not an unusually robust or sickly child, somehow managed to avoid all of these epidemics. Indeed, his first encounter with a severe illness was with whooping-cough four years later. At thirteen this encounter left him whooping, as Dr. J.A. put it, like an Indian on the war-path.

"No school for this young man at least until after Christmas, Mary-Ben," he said to Aunt, who was of course the family nurse. "Perhaps not then. We'll see. He's badly run down and he'll be marked for we-both-know-what if he goes among other children too soon. Keep him in bed as much as you can, and load him up with egg-nogs. Doesn't matter if they come up when he whoops; quite a bit of it will stay."

So Francis settled to a long, reflective holiday, as soon as Miss McGladdery had been convinced that there was no point in send-ing him sheets of arithmetic problems to be solved; she was de-termined that the sick body should not beget the idle mind, and arithmetic was just the thing for a boy who was too weak to sit up in bed. Francis was very ill, and the injections Dr. J.A. gave him every three days, just above the kidneys, did nothing to make him placid. Indeed, on one very bad day, Aunt got into a panic and sent for Father Devlin, who murmured and sprinkled some drops of water on him. Francis was in delirium, and did not understand what had happened, but Aunt was greatly comforted. When at last he seemed a little better, the Doctor said that he was greatly "run down", and gentle steps must be taken to "build him up."

I SUPPOSE *that was your doing, said the Lesser Zadkiel.*

—*Certainly, said the Daimon Maimas, though of course I take no responsibility for the epidemics. It gave me a chance to put our young friend out of the world of action for a while and introduce him to the world of thought and feeling. He had been bullied too much for any good it might do, and the insults to his mother and nasty talk about his family were beginning to wear on him. So I took the means that came to hand to put him out of action for a while. We do that often, you know, with our special people; they need leisure of the sort a bustling, active holiday can never provide. A good long illness can be a blessing. Go on with your chronicle, and you'll see.*

—You are a fierce spirit, brother.
—So it may seem, if you take a purely human point of view.

BETWEEN BOUTS OF WHOOPING Francis had plenty of time to reflect. He was glad to be secure from the torments of Alexander Dagg, who was a psychological rather than a physical bully.

"D'you know what I'm goin' to tell yuh?" he would demand. "There's bad blood in your family. Your old aunt has a bielding head. Did yuh know that? My Maw says so. D'you know what that comes from? Rotting brains. You'll likely end up with a bielding head yourself."

A bielding head? It was a Blairlogie word, used not in the kindly Scots sense of sheltering, but meaning scabby, overgrown with suppurating outbreaks. Children often had bielding fingers, and displayed them with pride; they were neglected whitlows. But a bielding head? Aunt's head was never discussed, and Francis had never seen her without one of her little caps. He loved Aunt, and hated such talk, but he could not escape it.

"D'you know what I'm goin' to tell yuh? Yer Maw's riding for a fall. My Maw says so. Pride riding for a fall. When she come here last time she was lallygagging around and piling on the agony as if she were better than anybody else. That's what my Maw says: she piles on the agony!"

Piling on the agony? To Francis it seemed that his beautiful, distant mother had an air of distinction unequalled by anyone else he knew. Of course she was better than anybody else. It was unendurable that Alexander Dagg and his sluttish mother should take her name into their mouths. But—riding for a fall? Francis could not cast out the barbs planted by Alexander Dagg. All his life he would be naked to criticism, however foolish or unjust.

"D'you know what I'm going to tell yuh? There's something funny about your house. People see the lights where a light's got no right to be. My Maw says there's a looner in there somewheres. Somebody chained up. Does yer old aunt have to be chained up when her head gets too bad? People wonder a lot about your house. Do you know that?"

Yes, Francis knew that. Whoever lives in the finest house in a small Canadian town dwells in a House of Atreus, about which a part of the community harbours the darkest mythical suspicions. Sycophancy is present, but in small store; it is jealousy, envy, detraction, and derision that proliferate. In lesser houses there may be fighting, covert abortions, children "touched up" with a hot flat-iron to make them obedient, every imaginable aspect of parsimony, incest, and simple, persistent cruelty, but these are nothing to whatever seems amiss at the Big House. It is the great stage of its town, on which are played out the dramas that grip the imagination for years after the actors are dead, or have assumed new roles. With St. Kilda was linked its neighbour, Cheg-widden Lodge, which provided in the Major and his beautiful wife a splendid addition to the cast of older actors. But only Francis had to listen, day after day, to what Blairlogie, as represented by Alexander Dagg's Maw, thought about it.

Most of all, Francis reflected about Dr. Upper. The local board of education, persuaded by who can tell what impulse toward modernity, had secured the services of Dr. G. Courtney Upper, who was making a tour of that part of Ontario, going to any school that asked for him, giving instruction in the mysteries of sex to boys and girls. The process took two days. For the first day Dr. Upper talked mysteriously and in general terms about the necessity to love and respect one's body, which was part of that British Empire that had shown its moral splendour in the war just ended. Any falling-off from the highest standards of clean speech, clean thought, deep breathing, daily washing of the armpits, was letting the Empire down. If you told dirty jokes you would quickly grow to look like a dirty joke. Girls were the future mothers of the Empire, and it behooved them to be models of daintiness and refinement in every possible way; boys would be the fathers of the Empire, and a slouching gait, sloppy grammar, smoking cig-arettes, and spitting in the street would bring the Empire down as the Hun had never been able to do.

The Doctor himself was a pursy little man in a shabby black suit; his face was round and pudgy; his eyes ran and needed frequent mopping. But in the street he was a remarkable figure in an Inverness cape made for a bigger man, crowned by a bowler hat. His name was all over Blairlogie an hour after his arrival, for he had gone to Jim Murphy's barber-shop for a shave, and, hearing an oath from some patron who obviously sought to undermine the Empire, he had leapt from the chair, denounced the astonished blasphemer, and rushed into the street with half his face covered with lather. Before an audience of children his manner was hypnotic and powerfully emotional.

It was on the second day of his evangel that the Doctor really got down to serious business. The girls had been taken off to another room, where a lunar nurse initiated them in lunar mysteries of their own, and the boys were at the mercy of Dr. Upper.

He began with motherhood. His style was lyrical; he seemed almost to sing to the harp. No figure in a boy's life was so influential, so totally embracing, so holy and so good, as his mother. To her he owed the gift of life, for at the time of his birth she had gone down, down to the very gates of Hell itself, her body torn with pain, in order that her son might live. Just how this was done was not explained, which made the mystery doubly horrible. But that was what she had done, in the greatness of her love for the child she had not yet seen. Could any boy hope, however long he lived, to recompense her for that sacrifice, in which she had purchased his life at the danger of her own?

Plainly no boy could do so; but by complete obedience, and unfailing love, he might make a poor stab at it. Dr. Upper, assuming a whining voice and a cringing demeanour, spoke to a mother—whom he called Mommy—in a monologue in which worship and obedience were mingled. It would have brought blushes to the cheek of anyone not wholly under his spell, but the Doctor was a brilliant, if sickening, rhetorician. He had worked up his great Apostrophe to Mommy over many years, and of its kind it was a masterpiece.

In the afternoon the pressure was doubled—trebled. Boys had it in their power to be the fathers of a great race, but they would never do so if they relaxed for an instant their determination to be pure in every respect. Purity of mind; he had spoken of that. Purity of speech; he had shown them how unmanly were swearing and dirty talk. But purity of body—on that all else depended, and without that the race would sink into the degeneracy so plainly to be seen among foreigners.

Purity of body meant a sentimental regard for one's testicles that was only slightly less whimpering than one's love for Mommy. Save for occasional washing they must never be touched, though they might be addressed, if they seemed to demand attention, in the Mommy-style of love but, in this case, also of rebuke. They must be told to be patient until the day when some lovely girl, who had kept herself pure, would become your wife on her way to the final apotheosis of motherhood. Were you going to throw away what was rightfully hers on base self-gratification—or worse? (What was worse was not defined.) Dr. Upper had known a boy so curious about his testicles that he had opened them up with his pocket-knife, to see what they were like, and had died of blood-poisoning in Dr. Upper's arms, imploring the Doctor with his last breath to warn other youths against his fatal lack of respect for his body.

If the testicles needed some stern talking-to from time to time, even more so did the penis. Yes, the Doctor urged boys always to use the medical terms, and not to sin by applying filthy names to these precious jewels. The penis might, from time to time, show a mind of its own, and when that happened, it had to be talked to kindly, but firmly (here the Doctor gave a little monologue that would bring any right-thinking penis to its senses), and wrapped in a cold wet towel until it was in a better frame of mind. On no account was it to be encouraged by thought or deed that would lead it to betray that noble mother or that almost equally wonderful girl who trusted you to bring her a love that was wholly pure and manly. Such thoughts, such deeds, were called masturbation, and it led rapidly to total degeneration of body and spirit. The Doctor had seen terrible ravages brought about by this sin of sins, and he could tell at a glance any boy who had succumbed to the loathsome practice.

Loathsome, yes, and dangerous, for the mighty gift of sex was not everlasting. Abuse it, and it would leave you, and then—what followed was too dreadful for the Doctor to say.

His peroration, the top of the show, came when the Doctor produced, after some rummaging, his own penis as an example of the adult member in its full splendour. He held it in his hand, as he thanked God for assisting him in bringing the great message of purity of life to the boys of Blairlogie.

During the two days he listened to Dr. Upper, Francis was sickening for whooping-cough, and shortly afterward he was in bed, warm under the blankets and loaded regularly with egg-nog by dutiful Aunt. The miseries of his illness were compounded by the urgings of his body, of those very organs upon which Dr. Upper had placed such spooky emphasis. They were unruly; they demanded attention and try as he might he could not banish their assertiveness by thoughts of his mother, or the Empire, or anything at all. He was sick not only in body but in mind.

The Doctor had told something, but not all, about the great mystery. That boys possessed some power that could make a girl a mother was clear enough, but how was it done? Not—oh, surely not by what he had seen, furtively and without comprehension, done by animals? What was the Limit, which was visited by such terrible consequences that a whole play was made about it, with Matinees for Ladies Only? There was nobody whom he could ask, of course. The atmosphere of St. Kilda was sternly Catholic, and Dr. Upper had not been asked to speak to Catholic children. Francis had made no mention of the Doctor at home, and he was sure that his knowledge was guilty knowledge, that might even reopen the wounds of Jesus. As for the Holy Mother, she must know of his plight, and would it not strain even her great pity? He was in misery, and his misery made the whooping-cough worse. When at last it abated, after six long weeks, he was left with his old enemy, tonsillitis, and looked, Victoria Cameron assured him, like a ghost.

There were compensations, the best of which was that a return to school lay unimaginably far in the future. Even Miss McGladdery had given up her notion that pages of arithmetic problems would do anything for him. The next best thing was that during the daytime he was moved, partly dressed and bundled up in rugs and shawls, into Aunt's own sitting-room.

It was by far the most personal room in St. Kilda, for Marie-Louise's notions of decoration were strictly French-Canadian, and the downstairs rooms were stiff and grand with furniture almost too delicately upholstered in blue brocade to be sat upon by mortal man. But Aunt's room was a splendid muddle of all the things Aunt liked best, and there was a sofa for Francis in front of the fireplace, where Zadok Hoyle made him a fine fire every day. Zadok was a cheerful visitor, although his daily news for Francis consisted of a notice of what funerals he was driving for in the morning (Catholic) and afternoon (Protestant).

"I'm driving Madame V. de P. Delongpré at eleven," he would say. "A huge woman; not easy to embalm, let me tell you. Then back to the shop and get the Cross off the top of the hearse and put on the draped Urn to get old Aaron Wrong to the Presbyterian church by two sharp. He made it to ninety-four, you know. A tiny man at the last—very easy to embalm because there was so little left of him. I'll just have time for a sandwich in between, but Miss Cameron has promised me a great feed tonight. I'll look in before me dinner and bring you some more wood. Keep your pecker up, dear man."

An unfortunate expression to use to Francis, for though Zadok meant it in its English sense of keeping cheerful, it had quite another message for Francis, who was aware that his pecker was too often indefensibly up and assertive during the day. Did Zadok know? Was Zadok mocking him? Adults were incomprehensible.

Zadok never broke his promise to return in the evening, with more wood and news of the day's diversions.

"Madame Delongpré would have been mortified," he would say. "Church not much more than a third full. But she was a bitter old gossip. Aaron Wrong, now, pulled a full church at St. Andrew's. I suppose it shows you what money and great old age can do. Long funeral. I was hard set to get back here to drive Madame Thibodeau home after the card-party. Between you and me, Francis, she's getting too old and too fat for the pony-trap. But she's still a great hand with the cards. She cleared over three dollars at the table this afternoon. D'you think she cheats?"

By such cheerful irreverences he relieved the warm, happy, but remorselessly devotional atmosphere created by Aunt, who would appear at eight o'clock to say the rosary, at its full length, with Francis, who now knew it by heart. It was not something to be mentioned to the Major, even if he should appear, which was unlikely. But now that Francis had been baptized by Father Devlin he was certainly a Catholic, and was not the poetry of the rosary his by right?

HOW MUCH OF Aunt's total dominance of their household was understood by the Senator and his wife? She was so humble, so deferential to Marie-Louise as the mistress, the wife, the mother;

Aunt was so soft-voiced, so smiling, that her control of everything was hardly noticed. Marie-Louise often said that dear Mary-Ben was her Right Bower—an expression from Aunt's favourite game of euchre. She did not aspire to bridge, which was still new in Blairlogie, and fashionable, and beyond the understanding of a poor, addled old maid like herself; that was for such powerful intellects as Marie-Louise, and Madame Thibodeau, and the card-crazed group with whom they played five times a week, displaying astonishing avarice over the modest stakes. Of course, it could not be called gambling; the money was merely to give a little additional interest to the contest of wits, the severe post-mortems, and the occasional sharping which was not quite cheating. Ample meals and the green baize table were all Marie-Louise asked of life, now. As for the Senator, he had his business, his attendance in the Chamber in Ottawa, his politics, and his sun-pictures. Let his sister manage the household; he made her an ample allowance, most of which seemed to go to the Church.

Not all, however. Mary-Benedetta had her own craze. It was oil-paintings. She bought expensive reproductions from shops in Montreal, where she visited Reverend Mother Mary-Basil twice a year. Not all of these could be hung on the walls of her sitting-room, which were full from the ceiling to within three feet of the floor with Murillos, Ary Scheffers, Guido Renis, and all the masters of sweet piety that appealed to her; scores of others, un-framed, were kept in portfolios, over which she brooded happily when the rosary had been said, and Francis was seated at her side, wrapped in shawls, in a reverential atmosphere. Masters of the Renaissance and masters of the nineteenth century were here, and not all the pictures were on sacred themes. Ladies languished on balconies, listening to cavaliers who played the guitar and sang in the garden below. Here was that lovely thing *Sir Galahad*, by G. F. Watts, O.M., R.A.—"the Order of Merit, dear, and a Royal Academician, truly a great man"—in which the purity of the young man—"not a saint, dear, but a great lover of our Lord"—and the purity of his horse were finely linked. And see, Francis, here is the Infant Samuel, wakened from his sleep by God's summons; can't you almost see the words on his lips, "Speak, for Thy servant heareth"? Remember that, Francis, if you should ever hear the Voice in the darkness. Oh, and look, dear, here is the

Virgin of Consolation; see the poor soul who has lost her baby, comforted by the Holy Mother; painted by a Frenchman, dear, William Adolphe Bouguereau; oh, he must be a troubled soul, Francis, for he has painted some dreadful pagan pictures, but here he is, you see, painting this truly sacred picture that assures us of the Virgin's mercy. And here is *The Doctor* by Luke Fildes; doctors are very wonderful men, Francis, right next to priests in their pity and concern for human suffering; see him as he looks at the sick little boy, just as Uncle Doctor sat and looked at you when you were so bad with the whooping-cough. Well now, this one has got in here by mistake; it's called *Flaming June,* and you can see the girl is asleep, but why Lord Leighton wanted to shove her B.T.M. right into the front of the picture I'll never know; you may well ask why I bought it, but now I have it I can't quite bring myself to throw it away. Isn't the colour fine?

Francis could look at pictures for hours, absorbed in the world of fantasy they created, and their assurance of a life far beyond the reach of Carlyle Rural, and the moral squalor of Alexander Dagg's Maw. His convalescence began only a week or so before Christmas and when that day came Aunt had two gifts for him, in the choice of which she acknowledged him as a kindred spirit.

One was a head of Christ, for the picture of A Certain Person had been left in the nursery at Chegwidden Lodge. But that had been for a little child; this was unquestionably a work of the highest art. It was called *St. Veronica's Napkin,* because you know, dear, that when Our Lord stumbled and fell on the terrible walk to Calvary St. Veronica wiped His dear Face with her napkin (no, not a dinner napkin, dear, more a hanky) and lo! His Image was imprinted on it forever. Just like the Shroud of Turin. As one looked at the calm face, its closed eyes seemed to open and gaze directly into your own. The work of a great Belgian master, dear; we'll hang it where you can see it from your bed, and you'll know He's looking at you all night long.

The other was secular, but though it was "nude" it was not sensational; a boy, about Francis's own age, stood weeping at a door that the painter's art had made to look very firmly closed, but also as though it gave entry to something wholly delightful; it was called *Love Locked Out.* Painted by a lady, Francis—an American lady—but what a truly masculine grasp of art she must have to be able to think of and paint such a wonderful picture!

Love locked out. Francis knew all about that. Oh, Mother, darling Mother, why are you so far away? Why are you never here? Mother's visits were so few and so brief. Of course, it was her work in England, in the hospitals for Canadian soldiers, that kept her away, and Francis must be a brave soldier too, and not mind. Parcels at Christmas, and occasional brief letters that seemed to be written to a much younger boy, did not really make up for Mother's absence. Love Locked Out—even a brave little soldier could not keep back tears. The picture gave an outward, visible form to a longing that lived deep inside him, and surged to the surface whenever he was sad, or lonely, or when dusk was gathering outside the windows, and the fire made changing shadows on the wall.

That Christmas night, when Aunt thought he was fast asleep, Francis stood naked against the wall of his bedroom, and with a hand mirror he looked over his shoulder at his image in the big looking-glass on the other side of the room. Carefully composing his body, he assumed the attitude of the picture, and looked long and with sadness mixed with approval at what he saw. He could do it. He could enter and become the picture. He could do it well. He crept back into his pyjamas and returned to bed, his sadness mingled with a pleasure he did not understand but which was comforting. He would repeat that experience many times in the days to come.

YOU ARE LETTING *your boy become rather odd, aren't you? said the Lesser Zadkiel.*

—*My dear colleague, you are allowing yourself to talk like Alexander Dagg, said the Daimon Maimas. I am pushing him gently in the direction dictated by his destiny, and I have not infinite means of doing that. I must work with whatever is at hand. He is to be a connoisseur, a patron of art, a man who understands art—though there will be dozens of Alexander Daggs of a more sophisticated sort to assert rancorously that he knew nothing whatever about it. Don't expect me to make an omelette without breaking eggs.*

—*I was thinking about breaking hearts.*

—*Oh, hearts! Nobody gets through life without a broken heart. The important thing is to break the heart so that when it mends it will be stronger than before. If you will allow me to say so, my dear Zadkiel, you angels are very easily pulled toward sentimentality. If you had my work to do, you would know how ruinous that can be.*

—*I am disposed sometimes toward pity, if that is what you are talking about.*

—*If Francis was an ordinary boy he might have been lucky enough to have a guardian angel assigned to him, to keep him out of trouble and put pretty things in his way. But I am no guardian angel, as you well know: I am a daimon, and my work must sometimes seem rough. We haven't seen the last of Francis before the mirror, and next time he won't have his back to it.*

—*Ah, well. Let us go on with our story.*

AS AUNT MANAGED everything in St. Kilda her taste was apparent not only in her own room, but everywhere, and especially in the pictures. In the dining-room, for instance, hung two large paintings by François Brunery, which had cost the Senator a pretty penny but which were, as Aunt explained to him, emblematic of his position in the world.

One was called, on the medallion at the bottom of the frame, *The Point of the Story*. At a dining-table in what was plainly a palace in Rome sat five cardinals in scarlet, and a bishop in purple. Oh, how shrewd, how intelligent were the faces (three plump, two thin) that were inclined forward, intent upon the sixth, a cardinal whose upraised forefinger and twinkling eyes showed that the point of the good story was about to break upon his hearers. What could it be? Some tale of Vatican intrigue, some subtle reverse of fortune in the Curia, or, perhaps, some scandal about a lady? The look of discreet enjoyment on the face of the major-domo in the background suggested the last. And look at the table! What gold and silver objects, what crystal glasses, what ruby wine. (Oh, that's clever, contrasting the colour of the wine with the scarlet of the robes, without letting them swear at one another!) And what promise of further wine in the gorgeous silver wine cistern that stands in the foreground, on the finely painted hardwood floor, (Look, Hamish, there's wood for you!) A great picture, a real work of art, and just the thing for a dining-room.

On the opposite wall was an even jollier picture; jolly, but perhaps a little sly. It was called *The Tired Model*. A young monk, a Dominican by his robe, stands before the easel in his studio, upon which is a picture of a saintly old cardinal, his hands pressed against his breast. Just look at that delicate old flesh against the scarlet moiré, and his gaze raised to Heaven, from which is coming the light that enfolds him! But on the model-throne sits the old man, slumped in his chair, fast asleep; the artist—a handsome young fellow with curly hair around his tonsure—is scratching his head in dismay.

Are not these pictures reverential, showing a devotion to the things of the Church and especially to its hierarchy, yet asserting that their owner shares a common humanity with the red-robed cardinals? These are such pictures as you might expect to find in the dining-room of a B.C.L. (as a Big Catholic Layman was jokingly called in Church circles), a man who knew his place, but who also knew his worth—a man who could re-gild a spire or contribute a splendid bell without having to think twice about the bill. Aunt had taken care that Hamish had what was right for him. When Father Devlin and Father Beaudry dined in that room they understood the subtle message; no domineering priests' ways in this house, if you please, gentlemen. Drink your wine and mind your manners.

Canada had officially embraced Prohibition in 1916, in order that when the brave boys returned after the War they would find a country purged of one of the major causes of evil-doing. In such houses as the Senator's the cellars contained stocks of wine bought long before, and there was no stint. But even substantial stocks dwindled, and this was reason for some unease. A good cellar needs regular replenishing. Marie-Louise's friends could nip their way through a surprising amount of white wine in an afternoon of bridge, before it was time for a substantial tea.

By the standards of Blairlogie, quite a lot of entertaining was done at St. Kilda, and in this, as in everything else, Aunt was the unobtrusive manager. Unobtrusive, that is, until it came to music, and then she shone. In every realm, without any hint of undesirable bohemianism or deviation from the strictest morality, Aunt was "artistic".

"Shall we have a little music?" she would say when, after dinner, the guests had had an hour in which to chat and digest. Nobody would think of replying that it might be more fun to go on talking; that would be an affront to the high aesthetic atmosphere of St. Kilda, which Aunt had created, to the greater glory of her brother and his wife.

When it had been enthusiastically agreed that nothing could be pleasanter than a little music, Aunt would go to the piano and, if there were someone present who had not been to dinner before, she would plunge immediately into a difficult and noisy piece, such as a Liszt Hungarian Rhapsody. The guest, if not of a positively turnip-like insensitivity, would be astonished at the noise, the pell-mell speed, the sheer cultivated racket that Aunt was producing. Even more astonished when, at the conclusion, when he was about to say, "Miss McRory, I never dreamed—" the other guests would break into mocking applause, and Aunt herself would turn on the piano stool, shaking with laughter.

For the piano was a Phonoliszt (World Renowned Pianists At Your Beck and Call . . . no pedals to push, no levers to learn . . .) and this was Aunt's little joke. The pianist had been the great Teresa Carreño, a famous matador of the instrument, imprisoned forever on a perforated roll of paper.

"But if you would like me to sing—" she would say, and all the guests agreed eagerly that they would like her to sing.

Aunt sang in English and French and it was generally agreed that her repertoire was very chaste. What was not chaste was the sound she made. She had a good voice, a true contralto, and produced a big, fruity tone surprising in such a small woman. She had always sung, and had been "finished" in Montreal in twelve lessons with Maestro Carboni. The maestro's method was simple, and effective: "All moving utterance is based upon the cry of the child," said he; "make a sound like a child crying—not in anger, but for love—and refine on it, Mademoiselle, and everything else will fall into place." Aunt had done so, and her singing was both good and astonishing, for it moved and troubled even musical ignoramuses.

The songs she sang were, in one way or another, cries for love. Songs in French, from the pen of Guy d'Hardelot, or in English, by Carrie Jacobs-Bond. Strongly emotional songs. Had Aunt known it, songs orgasmic in their slow, swelling climaxes.

But beyond any doubt Aunt's finest effort, her unfailing warhorse, was "Vale", by Kennedy Russell. Although Francis could see plainly on the music that its name was "Vale", Aunt and all cultivated persons pronounced it "Wally", because it was Latin and meant "Farewell". In two brief verses by de Burgh d'Arcy (obviously an aristocrat of some kind) it caught the very soul of Aunt, and most of her hearers.

It was about a man who was dying. He begged somebody (wife? lover?—oh, surely not a lover, not when one was dying) to stay at his side during the creeping, silent hours.

> *Mourn not my loss, you lov'd me faithfully*

(Obviously a wife, who had done her wifely duty.) The conclusion was dramatically splendid:

> *Then, when the cold grey dawn breaks silently,*
> *Hold up THE CROSS . . . and pray for me!*

For a dying person, Aunt made a remarkable amount of noise at *Hold up* THE CROSS and then faded almost into silence at *and pray for me!* as if the singer were actually pegging out. This was done by what Maestro Carboni called "spinning the tone", a very good Italian trick, and not easy to acquire.

Aunt sang this song often. It was always in demand when St. Bonaventura's had one of its concerts to raise money, and Father Devlin had said, in language that might have been more happily phrased, that when Miss McRory sang "Wally" we all got as near to dying as we'd get before our time actually came.

Aunt's music had a lighter side, not for parties, but for those quiet evenings when it was just herself and the Senator and Marie-Louise, and Dr. J.A., who often dropped in after his evening rounds, tired out and wanting relaxation.

"Sing 'Damn Stupid', Mary-Ben," he would say, as he stretched his legs toward the fire.

"Oh, Joe, you do love to make fun of me," Aunt would say, and then sing the ballad from *Merrie England*:

> *Dan Cupid hath a garden*
> *Where women are the flowers—*

Which went on to declare that the sweetest flower loved by Cupid was the Lovely English Rose. She, the wholly Highland Scots old maid, and he, the wholly Irish old bachelor, found a distilment of their own stifled, unacknowledged romance in this very English song by Edward German Jones, born on the Welsh Border. Music, as Aunt often told Francis, knows no frontiers.

Francis heard it all. Sometimes he sat in the drawing-room, already in his pyjamas, but wrapped in rugs, because he had begged to hear Aunt sing, and what singer can refuse such a tribute, so obviously sincere? Sometimes, when there were guests and he was supposed to be in bed, he sat on the stairs, in his pyjamas and without any rugs. To the pictures he responded with mind and heart, eager not only to understand what they had to say, but to know how they were made; to the music he listened with his heart alone.

He was finding out one or two things about pictures. He had the run of Aunt's collection of prints, and a number of books she possessed, with names like *Gems From the World's Great Galleries*. He was probably the only boy within a five-hundred-mile radius who knew what the Pitti was, or what *putti* were. But better than that, he was getting some notion of how pictures were put together.

His teacher was an unlikely one. Among Aunt's books was one which she had bought long ago, glanced at, and decided that it had nothing to say to her. It was called *How to Draw in Pen and Ink*, and the author was Harry Furniss. Indeed, he was still alive, and would be alive for a further five years after Francis met with his book. Furniss was a remarkable caricaturist, but, as he explained in his genial prose, to draw caricatures it is first necessary to be able to draw people, and if you want to draw people you had better try your hand at drawing anything and everything. You cannot make Mr. Gladstone look like an old eagle if you cannot draw a serious Mr. Gladstone and a serious old eagle. You must develop an eye; you must see everything in terms of line and form. Andrea del Sarto was no Raphael, but he could correct Raphael's drawing; you could aim at drawing like del Sarto even if you hadn't a hope of being anything better than a Harry Furniss—which wasn't the easiest thing in the world to be, either.

Francis had access to unlimited paper and pencils; he had but to ask Aunt and plentiful supplies appeared. He did not tell Aunt about Harry Furniss, whom she had rejected as unworthy, and doubtless coarse in his methods. But a man who had been able, as a youth, to attend a London fire, make pages of rapid sketches, and then work them up into a full-page engraving for the *London Illustrated News* was just the man to catch Francis's imagination. A man who could make such vivid caricatures of people whom Francis had never heard of, but whose essence he felt in Furniss's drawings, was just the man to dispel the impression given by Aunt that it all had to be done by geniuses, usually foreigners, in studios, under the spooky guidance of the Holy Mother and perhaps even of A Certain Person. This was a gust of fresh air in art. This made art a possibility—remote, but still a possibility— for somebody like himself.

Always have paper in your pocket, said Harry Furniss. Never be without a notebook. Never miss a significant figure in the streets or at the theatre or in Parliament. Catch every turn of the head, every gleam in the eye. You can't draw pretty girls if you can't draw gutter crones. If you can't keep files of your notes, don't; but once having disciplined your hand and eye to capture every detail and nuance, perhaps you don't need files, for these things are filed in your brain and your hand.

Just the sort of sea-breeze to blow away the odour of sanctity. Francis was conscious of his notebook, which marked him as an artist. But where many a boy would have made a parade of what he was doing, and attracted attention from adults who wanted to see what he was up to, he mastered the trick of sitting quietly, making his rapid sketches without signalling.

A few weeks after Christmas he was able to go outside for limited airings, but he was not anxious to attract attention from Nosy Parkers who would want to know why he was in the streets when all decent boys were either in school, or at home with infantile paralysis, or simply with swollen glands. Not to be easily noticed is an acquirement, as is always being noticed; Francis studied the art of invisibility, and made sketches wherever he was.

He was perched on a bale of straw in the stable one February day, making sketches of the horses as they ate, when Zadok Hoyle said to him: "Frank, it's a fine day and I have to go over to The Portage this afternoon; why don't you ask your Aunt if you can come with me?" Aunt demurred a little, but finally said yes, he might go, but he must be well bundled up.

Bundled up he was, almost to the point of immobility, as he sat beside Zadok on the driver's seat. The wagon was not one of his grandfather's, but an odd cart with a low, boxed-in back; its purpose could not be immediately guessed. They drove perhaps four miles in the sharp air to a hamlet on a river-bank, which had a name of its own but from long custom was always called The Portage. Zadok pointed far beyond the river with his whip. "See that, Frankie? That's Quebec. And some funny things happen on this river."

They stopped on the river-bank at a shed, from which a fat, dark-jowled man appeared, nodded to Zadok, returned to the shed, and shortly returned carrying a box; between them he and Zadok loaded six such boxes into the back of the cart. Not a word was said, as they drove off.

"That was the happy call," said Zadok. "Now we make the sad call." Happy? What was happy about it? Not a word said and the fat man had what Francis thought was a bad eye, and he wished he could have made a rapid sketch of it. And now—the sad call?

They drove somewhat less than a mile to a farmhouse, where Zadok spoke briefly with a woman in black; another, older woman, also in black, was to be seen in the background. A man appeared from the barn, and helped Zadok to carry a large package out of the house; a long package, wrapped in rough brown holland; it was clearly a man. They shoved it into the back of the cart, with the boxes, Zadok said something kindly, the man nodded and spat, and the horse was turned in the direction of Blairlogie.

"Is that a dead person, Zadok? Why are we carrying a dead person?"

"Why do you suppose, Frankie? It's Mr. Devinney's business;

I pick 'em up, and I get 'em ready. I drive the hearse. Mr. Devinney does the business end. He sees to putting the death notice in *The Clarion,* and ordering and sending out the deathcards. He marches in the procession in his plug hat. He does all the condoling, which isn't easy work, but he has quite a poetic turn, sometimes. And of course he does all the billing, reckons up the number of plumes on the hearse, and all that. This one in the back is Old McAllister—a mean old sodbuster, but a customer now—and I'll have to get him ready for the funeral, lug him out to the farm again, and lug him back again on Friday, for the burial. Lot o' hauling in this business. We're riding on the death-cart, Frankie. Didn't you know? Aw, but then a lot o' things are kept from a boy like you."

When they reached Blairlogie they drove up Dalhousie Street, which was the main and only business street, and stopped at a side door of Devinney's Furniture and Undertaking Parlours. Briskly, Zadok leaped down, opened the door of the shop, pulled out a light table on rubber wheels, shifted Old McAllister on to it, threw a sheet over him and had him into the shop in approximately fifteen seconds.

"Have to be quick. People don't like to see how things are done. A funeral's a work of art, y'see, dear boy, and all the rough part is no business of the public's."

This was as he was wheeling Old McAllister on his cart through the furniture part of the store, toward the back, which was closed off by a partition with a curtained double door. Beyond the curtains, Zadok switched on the light—it was a dim light, afforded by two bulbs of modest power—and opened another double door, very heavy and with broad hinges. From inside came a cold breath, damp and stuffy, the smell of slowly melting ice. Quickly Old McAllister was wheeled inside, and doors were closed.

"Don't want too much melting," said Zadok. "Mr. Devinney is always complaining about the ice bill."

"But Zadok, what are you going to do with him?" said Francis. "Do you just leave him in there till the funeral?"

"I should say not," said Zadok. "I make him look better than he ever looked in his life. It's an art, Frankie, and though anybody can learn the elements of it, the real art's inborn.—You didn't know I was an artist, did you?"

It was then that Francis made his great confession. "Zadok, I think I'm an artist too." He rummaged in his outer clothes, and produced his sketch-book.

"By the Powers of Old Melchizedek," said Zadok (this was his mighty oath), "you are, dear boy, and no mistake. Here's Miss McRory to the life. Ah, Frankie, you've been a bit severe with the little cap, dear man. Ah, never be cruel, me dear. But b'God it's true enough, even if it is sharp. And here's Miss Cameron. You've made her look almost like one of your Aunt's spooky pictures. But it's true, too. And here's me! To think I was once accounted a handsome man! Ah, ye devil! That's the red nose to the life! Ah, Frankie, y'rascal! You make me laugh at myself. Oh, you're an artist. And what are you going to do about it?"

"Zadok—Zadok, promise me you won't tell. They'd be after me, and Aunt would want me to have lessons, and I don't want that yet. I have to find my own way first, you see. Harry Furniss says so; find your own way, and then let anybody teach you that can, but hang on to your own way."

"Here's Madame Thibodeau—ah, ye little scallawag—look at the way you've made her great bum hang off both sides of the chair. She'd have you killed if she ever saw that!"

"But that's it, Zadok! I've got to learn to see what's in front of my nose. That's what Harry Furniss says; most people don't see what's in front of their nose. They just see what they think they ought to see."

"True enough, Frankie, and don't I know that in my own art; you just have to encourage people to see what they think they ought to see. But come along, now. I've got to get you home, and the horse'll be gettin' cold."

On the way back to St. Kilda, Francis pleaded to know what Zadok was going to do with Old McAllister. If it was art of any kind, hadn't he the right of a fellow-artist to know? So at last it was clapped up between them that right after he had his supper Francis was to join Zadok again, because Aunt had to go out to a meeting at St. Bonaventura's—something about the poor and needy—and he would see Zadok at his art, and Zadok would get him home in time to slip into his bed so that nobody, not even Miss Victoria Cameron, would suspect that he had been out.

In the barn Zadok's first care was to unload the six boxes which remained in the death-cart, and lock them in an unused stall in the stables.

"What is that, Zadok?"

"Oh, it's just some stuff your grandfather gets from a trusted man in Quebec. Mr. Devinney gets a little slice for the use of the cart. It's a sideline of his business that we never discuss. Everybody has his secret, Frankie. You have yours; Mr. Devinney has his." And as he heaved the last case into the stall, Francis thought he heard Zadok say, "And I have mine."

I QUESTION WHETHER *it was a good thing to steer a boy of thirteen into an undertaking parlour that is run by a bootlegger, said the Lesser Zadkiel.*

—*I don't, said the Daimon Maimas. He had been old-womaned far too much by Aunt. He needed a man in his life, and where was the Wooden Soldier? Saving the Empire across the ocean. And his mother was being wonderful to wounded soldiers, but had no time for her son. His grandfather was far too broken to be more than another gentle presence in the boy's life, though he was very kind, when he thought about it.*

—*Grandfather broken?*

—*The Senator never got over the destruction of his idol. When Mary-Jacobine got into trouble and had to be married off to the likeliest comer—and a Protestant at that—he never quite believed in anything again. He was a strong man in business and in politics, but those are external things: only a fool gives his soul to them. The pith had been scooped out of him. Look at Marie-Louise: an aging, fat gambler. Look at Mary-Ben: she idolized her brother but she never understood more than half of him. Zadok was the strongest man around the place, as you well know.*

—*A rogue, my dear colleague. A rogue.*

—*Very well, but a kindly, decent rogue, in the thick of life and death. I had to work with what was at hand, you know.*

—*As you say. I have not had to do your work, so I certainly must not find fault with the way you did it.*

—*Quite so. And Zadok was something of an artist, as we'll see, if you will be so good as to go on with your narrative. By the way, do you know how it comes out?*

—I cannot remember all of these lives in detail. Like yourself, I am simply being reminded of the life of Francis Cornish.

THE LIGHT in Mr. Devinney's workroom was like the light in Rembrandt, thought Francis; two mean bulbs, hanging above the narrow, slanted table on which Zadok had now placed the bundle which was all that was left of Old McAllister, a mean old sod-buster. Zadok was scrubbing his hands fiercely with yellow soap at a sink.

"Cleanliness is essential," he said. "Respect for the dead, and precaution for the living. You never really know what these people died of. So I'll just throw around some carbolic, and you keep well in your corner, me dear."

Well in his corner, perched on two coffin crates so that he had a good view of the scene, Francis had his notebook and pencil ready.

Respect for the dead; Zadok was gentle in unwrapping Old McAllister, who had apparently died in his long underwear, a baggy, liver-coloured extra skin. Quickly Zadok ripped the underwear with a curved knife which Francis recognized as a pruning-knife, and soon old McAllister was naked, an unimpressive sight, but a Golconda for Francis.

This was something he had never reckoned on. He would be able to draw the nude figure, which even Harry Furniss insisted was the foremost necessity—after seeing what was in front of your eyes—in becoming an artist.

Old McAllister was balding and scrawny. His face and hands were tanned a deep brown by sixty-seven years of Ottawa Valley weather, but the rest of him was a bluey-white. His legs were like sticks, and his feet fell outward and sideways. Zadok had cut off his underwear because Old McAllister, according to local custom, had been sewed into it for the winter. Francis knew all about that; most of the children in Carlyle Rural were so encased and they stank amazingly.

"A bath, for a starter," said Zadok. "First, though, a thorough swilling-out." With a large squirt he neatly washed out the rectum of the corpse into a bucket. Then, with a dribble from a short hose, and frequent dabblings of carbolic, Zadok washed Old

McAllister; the water fell to the cement floor and vanished down a drain. He washed Old McAllister's hands, with plentiful lathering of yellow soap, and cleaned the nails with his jack-knife.

"Always a problem, this," he said to the busily scribbling Francis. "These fellas never clean their nails from Easter to Easter, but they have to have hands like a barber for the viewing. It's part of the art, you see. At the end they must look as they'd have looked on their wedding-day, or better. Probably better."

He shaved Old McAllister with ample lather and hot water. "Lucky I have some experience as a valet," he said, "but of course no valet could get away with this." He deftly poked a finger into the corpse's mouth to push out the hollow cheeks. The scrape of the razor told the toughness of Old McAllister's beard. "Never been shaved more than once a week in his life, I don't suppose," said Zadok.

"Now didn't I have a roll of cotton-wool? For what we call the orifices."

The orifices were the ears, the nostrils, and, to Francis's surprise, the anus; into each a sufficient plug of wool was stuffed. Then a big chunk into the mouth, and before it was closed a large gob of beeswax was popped in and Zadok held the jaws until they were firmly clamped.

"This is easy enough in a winter funeral," he said, "but in summer it's another thing altogether. I've seen funerals where the wax went soft and the mouth opened unexpectedly and you wouldn't believe the screaming and fainting. But we'll have none of that with you, old boy, will we?" he said, and gave Old McAllister a friendly pat on the shoulder. "There, now we've done the clean-up jobs. Now comes the science. If you feel queer, dear soul, there's the bucket just by you."

Francis did not feel queer. He had got Old McAllister's right hand—what a hand for knots and lumps! He had got both feet, corns and bunions complete. He was now busy on a full-length, with difficult perspective. That picture that Aunt didn't like him to linger over in *Gems*—the *Anatomy Lesson,* was it called?—lived in his memory and came to his aid. This was great! This was life!

Zadok had drawn up a machine that sat on a wheeled cart, and looked like a tank with a hose coming out of it, beside his worktable. With a little fleam he lifted a vein in Old McAllister's arm, inserted a thickish needle that was attached to the hose, and began slowly and watchfully to work a pump-handle on his machine. As he pumped, he sang, in a fine bass, but *sotto voce:*

> *Yes! let me like a soldier fall*
> *Upon some open plain,*
> *This breast, expanding for the ball*
> *To blot out every stain.*

This went on for quite a long time—time enough for Francis to do another drawing, with Zadok's dark figure standing beside the body. He was proud of his professionalism in roughing in Old McAllister's privy parts; just six quick lines and a shadow, like Rembrandt. Nothing of the grossness of the boys who drew such things on fences. But of course they were not artists.

"Here we go for the big one," said Zadok. Quickly he nicked Old McAllister's navel, thrust in a larger needle—he called it a trocar—and pumped again. Then, something very delicate, involving the corner of the eye.

"There, old lad," he said. "That'll hold you for a week or two. Now for the real art, Frankie."

As he worked, Zadok, always a genial man, became positively merry. "No time to waste; don't want him to harden on me," he said, as he seemed to wrestle with Old McAllister, quickly getting him into socks, trousers, and a shirt that had come in a bundle from the farm. "On with your dancing-pumps, gaffer," he said, as he fitted the huge, misshapen feet into soft kid slippers. "Now, before the collar and tie, the real fancy-work."

"Where were you a valet, Zadok?" asked Francis.

"Oh, before the war—the Boer War, that's to say—I was a lot o' things. Footman for a while; very good experience that, for any future job. Then a valet, because in the war I was batman to my young lord; I'd been a footman in his father's house, and we went into the Army together, you might say, but him as an officer and me as a private, of course. But we were never apart, not really. Keeping a young officer smart in the field, with them rotten Boers popping up everywhere you didn't expect them, was a job, I can tell you. Do you know them Boers didn't wear uniforms? Just fought in their farm clothes? You can't call that war. But I learned to dress a gentleman to look like a gentleman, dead or alive, so I don't have any trouble with a chap like this."

"But where did you learn all that—about the cotton-wool, and the needles and everything?"

"Always had a turn that way. I remember when I was just a little lad, at my grandfather's funeral. 'I want to see Granda, I want to see Granda' I kept on at my mother. She thought it was love, and very creditable to me, but it was just nosiness. He went by the palsy route, you see, and I was amazed that he'd stopped shaking. I thought it was the undertaker, old Smout, that had stopped him. Of course, Smout was just a Cornish village undertaker; coffin-maker, really; and he didn't have the scientific advantages of today. By my standards, Granda was just a mess, rigged up in a cheap shroud, his hair all combed the wrong way. But it was my start.

"Then in the war we had to bury the dead, and in my lot that work was done under a farrier-sergeant who had no training and no ideas, but he wanted it done proper. That was where my talent came to light. There wasn't much we could do; no embalming, of course, but we could make 'em look like soldiers of the Queen, poor lads. With a face wound you could put on a decent piece of plaster. I would have got a medal for my work if it hadn't been for a misunderstanding, for which I bear no grudge, not now. Other outfits copied our methods, but they went too far. There was one bugger did a nasty business in hearts. He was an officer, so his mail wasn't censored—gentlemen don't read other gents' letters, you see—and he would write home, 'Dear Madam please accept my condolences on the death of your brave son, who fell like a man with the respect of all his regiment. His dying wish was that his heart should return to England and lay in the church where he learned to be a man when a boy. Can deliver said heart to you on my return to England, suitably preserved, at a very moderate fee. Yours, etc.' Rotten trick, but what mother could resist? God damn him, wherever he is now.

"Then I got a bit of real pro training in England, and that's where I picked up all this. Not that I learned the art of make-up in the embalmers' parlours. Not the real art. I had that off a pal of mine who played minor clowns in the panto at Christmas. Powder. That's the great secret."

Zadok raised a cloud of violet-scented *poudre de riz* around the head. "That's the foundation," he said.

Old McAllister's face, which had turned a dark putty shade, was swiftly painted with a wash that left him a light salmon, and over the cheekbones Zadok brushed some dry rouge of a startling crimson. Next he worked on Old McAllister's mouth, gently massaging the grim, grey lips into an unaccustomed smile; this he touched up with a red salve that a harlot might have thought excessive. Then he rapidly massaged some vaseline into the thin hair, and combed it forward.

"How do you suppose he did his hair—when he did it? No indications, so we'll give him Old Faithful." He combed the hair with a left-hand parting, then quiffed the right-hand portion over his finger, giving Old McAllister a nifty, almost a dandified air. Quick work with the collar, the necktie; into the waistcoat; draping a huge silver watch-chain, from which the watch had been removed, over the sunken belly. On with the coat. A piece of card on the tip of which some white cambric was sewn was tucked into the breast pocket of the coat (Old McAllister had not used, or possessed, handkerchiefs of his own). The hands were folded on the breast, as if in Christian acceptance, and Old McAllister was a finished work of art.

Then, further astonishing Francis after an astonishing, rapturous evening, Zadok took Old McAllister's right hand in his own and shook it cordially. "Godspeed, old man," said he. Noticing Francis's astonishment, he said, "I always do that. I'm the last, most personal attendant, you see; the priest is quite another matter. So I always shake the hand, and wish 'em well. You'd better shake, too, Frankie, as you've been here, and drawing pictures, and all."

Tentative, but game, Francis shook Old McAllister's chilly paw.

"There, old cully, back into the cooler with you, and I'll deliver you first thing in the morning, in plenty of time for the viewing. And as for you, Frankie my lad, I must get you home and to bed before anybody notices."

To Francis's surprise, Zadok not only took him back to St. Kilda, but came upstairs with him, and after the door had closed on his bedroom went—where? The sound was not of feet going downstairs, but of feet going upstairs, to the third floor, which was Victoria Cameron's private domain, and to which Francis was forbidden to mount under threat of the severest reprisals. Never, never up there, Francis. So why was Zadok going up there? Another astonishment at the end of an astonishing, enlarging, enlightening day. A memorable day on his journey toward being an artist, a man of the great world of events, like Harry Furniss.

IN THE WEEKS that passed, Francis spent many an enraptured hour in Mr. Devinney's back room, watching Zadok at work, and sketching for dear life. A variety of subjects came under his view and his pencil. The old predominated, of course, but now and then there was somebody who had, in the prime of life, suffered an accident or an unaccountably severe illness. Once there was a girl of sixteen, whom Francis did not positively know, but whom he had seen in the streets and at the McRory Opera House.

With female subjects, Zadok's behaviour was exemplary. As he stripped them on the table, he draped a towel over the pubic region, so that Francis never saw a woman fully naked, much as he wished to do so.

"Professional discretion," said Zadok. "No Nosy-Parkering with the ladies. So we always lay a towel over The Particular, you see, dear soul, because no man, professional though he may be, has any call to behold The Particular of any female he deals with in a purely professional capacity."

But, oh, how Francis longed to see The Particular, about which he speculated so painfully. What could it be? The very few nudes in Aunt's collection seemed to have no Particular, or had averted it from the gaze, or put a hand over it. What was The Particular? He put the matter tactfully to Zadok; he was an artist, and ought to know everything about the human body.

"You must find out your own way, Francis," said Zadok solemnly; "the buzzem—well, it's very widely seen and indeed it's one of the first things any of us do see, but The Particular is quite another matter."

One night in March, as he took Francis to Devinney's, Zadok seemed depressed. "I don't care for this, dear lad; don't care for it at all."

What he did not care for, when it was taken out of the cooler, was the body of François Xavier Bouchard, a dwarf tailor, known to Blairlogie's English-speakers as Bushy.

His one-storey tailor-shop was a mean building at the top end of Dalhousie Street, and winter and summer Bushy could be seen leaning in the door, waiting for a custom. It cannot have been much; sewing on a button or perhaps turning a suit for some thrifty soul, but he seemed to keep bread in his mouth, although, like many tailors, he was shabby in his own dress. He grinned without cease, a dog-like grin that seemed to implore tolerance, respect being beyond his hopes.

There he lay, on Mr. Devinney's table, his head huge and his trunk barrel-like, his arms and legs so short that there seemed to be little between shoulder and elbow, elbow and hand, his private parts huge above his tiny legs, although they would not have been excessive on a full-grown man. His head lay at an unusual angle.

"Hanged himself," said Zadok. "They found him this morning. Did it two or three days ago, I should guess. Poor, poor little soul. We've got to do our best for old F.X., Francis, not that anything can make up for a life like his."

The scene which preceded the final scene of Bushy's life, as Zadok recounted it, was something wholly outside any experience known to Francis, except those terrible quarter-hours in the playground of Carlyle Rural, when boys blew up frogs and tortured cats. This would certainly have reopened the wounds of Jesus.

"The men in one of the lodges, Francis. I'm not going to tell you which one. Do you know what a lodge is? It's a lot of chaps who get together for a kind of religion that isn't quite the same as the real religion; they have altars and whim-whams, and they dress up in trick clothes and talk a lot of rubbish to one another. All very secret but somehow anybody who cares can find out.

"Every so often they let in some new members, and it's all very solemn; then they have to have some fun. You know how it is: after a solemn time you have to have a change. Like at funerals, where they joke and quarrel at the party after the burial. Well, these boys got the idea a while ago that it would be great fun to shanghai Bushy and take him up to the lodge-rooms over De Marche's hardware, and give him a bath. They did it quite a few times. Everybody had a grab at him, or pushed the soap in his face, or tried to take the hide off him with the towel. Then they'd make him run up and down the room; they'd flick him with wet towels and sool him on so they could see his little legs go, and his big what's-its-name whack and thrash around. They had one of those affairs three days ago, and I guess the poor little mortal couldn't stand it any more, and went home and hanged himself. In a pair of braces, I understand. Christ, Frankie, I hardly know whether to weep or puke. I've had a taste of humiliation myself, but poor old F.X.—" Zadok could not go on, but he bent to his work with special gentleness. Yes, let me like a soldier fall, upon some open plain.

Francis had seen pictures in Aunt's books called *The Entombment*. What dignity, what compassion was shown in the faces of those who handled the body of the dead Saviour. He had seen those pictures but he did not know them, encompass them, feel them, until he saw Zadok working over the body of the dead tailor. He sketched away like a man and an artist, but now and then he could not repress a sniff. That hour was to stay with him all his life.

When all was done, Zadok and Francis both shook hands with Bushy and wished him Godspeed. And then, as always, for Zadok would not have it otherwise, he washed his hands carefully.

AT NIGHT, when he was supposed to be in bed and asleep, Francis was sometimes very much awake, and engaged in—what were they? It would not be quite exact to call them games, and he himself could not have described them if he had been called on by some indignant or sorrowing adult to do so.

Thoughts and physical urges about sex rose to torment him several times a day, and even Dr. Upper's remedy of the cold towel was ineffective; Francis tried it once or twice, and then decided that it was silly; he did not really want to rebuke his penis for its insistence on being noticed. And noticed not only when his thoughts strayed to the mystery of The Particular, but often when he was thinking of something innocuous like food, or where he had put his tube of Chinese white. Was he wicked? But the wickedness was also thrilling. Was he in some special way afflicted or diseased, that he should be so teased by a part of his body he could not control? There was nobody to ask.

But the demand was frequent, and in an alarming way delicious. Sometimes he provoked it, knowing that he should not, by looking at his small store of movie magazines. These he had bought, from time to time, at a local store called The Beehive, which sold not only movie magazines but false-faces, rings made in the shape of serpents with glittering red-glass eyes, and books which told you how to be a magician or a ventriloquist. The movie magazines showed the screen favourites of the time—Mae Murray, Margarita Fisher, Gladys Walton—in bathing suits that exposed their legs to the knee, or in short skirts with rolled stockings; a picture of Gloria Swanson in some historical epic of a period when people were obviously dead to shame (or enjoyed it) showed one of her thighs almost to the hip. Long gazing at this picture was a hot excitement. So much more exciting than the few nudes to be found in Aunt's books, so often monumental people by Thorwaldsen, or some nineteenth-century artist with a strong hint of Dr. Upper in his attitude toward sex. They were no fun; the movie stars were alive, and exciting. But most exciting of all were the pictures of Julian Eltinge.

Francis had seen this popular female impersonator in *The Countess Charming* at Grand-père's theatre. Eltinge was a plump man of unremarkable appearance who could disguise himself as a woman of elegance and charm; the film showed the lacy undergarments, the corset, the wig that made the transformation. With some odds and ends of curtains and bits of silk he concealed in his chest of drawers Francis attempted to do what Eltinge did, and although the result would not have impressed anyone else it satisfied him deeply. He had to know about the human figure: he stuffed enough rags into his top to produce a buzzem something like that of Eltinge. The legs were a great feature of the pictures of movie stars: he disposed his legs in the manner of Gloria Swanson. He had no wig but he wrapped his head in a scarf. The effect in the mirror was gratifying to the point of urgency. What had Eltinge done about The Particular? Francis's own particular made it plain that disguise must have been extremely difficult.

Bedtime fantasies were partnered by night horrors. In dreams he was set upon succubi who were nothing like Gloria Swanson or the tantalizing Clarine Seymour; no, in his dreams hags and women horribly like those he had seen in the embalming room tormented and whispered, until he awoke with the hot gush on his thighs that made him leap from his bed, dab at the sheets with a dampened cloth, and do what he could to wash the pants of his pyjamas. Suppose somebody found out? Suppose that Anna Lemenchick, who made the beds, told Victoria Cameron? What would happen? He could not guess, but it would be shame even beyond the rich vocabulary of Dr. Upper to describe. But he could not stop; posturing in the manner of Julian Eltinge was seductive beyond his power of resistance.

WHAT DO YOU MAKE OF THAT, *my friend? said the Daimon Maimas.*

—You had better tell me what you make of it, said the Lesser Zadkiel. I suppose you were at the root of it all?

—Indeed I was, said the Daimon Maimas, and I took care that nobody found Francis at his games, for he was right in supposing that there would have been a pious uproar. But surely you see what the boy was doing?

—Looking for something that his life denied him, obviously. Trying to cope with a problem for which his life in Blairlogie terms offered no solution and no solace. He seems not to have known any girls except in the most distant fashion, and the screen images were unlike anything he would have met with even if he had known some girls at school.

—Just as well, for it wasn't any palpable girl he was trying to evoke in front of his mirror, and it certainly wasn't Julian Eltinge. Of course, he didn't know it—they never do—but he was looking for The Girl, the girl deep in himself, the feminine ideal that has some sort of existence in every man of any substance, and my Francis was a man of substance. It wasn't effeminacy, which is what anybody who discovered him would have supposed. It certainly wasn't homosexuality, for Francis never had more than the usual dash of that. He was groping for the Mystical Marriage, the unity of the masculine and the feminine in himself, without which he would have been useless in his future life as an artist and as a man who understood art. Useless as any sort of man— rich man, poor man, beggar man, thief; not to speak of tinker, tailor, soldier, sailor—who is destined to see more than a few inches beyond the end of his nose. This was the beginning of the search for the Mystical

Marriage, which is one of the great quests, and as usual the quest was longer and more important than the eventual discovery.

—*Aha! And I suppose the quest is what poor Simon Darcourt, labouring over his biography of Francis, apprehends dimly, but without really knowing what it is.*

—*We mustn't be extreme. And we certainly mustn't underestimate Darcourt. But he wouldn't think of describing Francis's quest as a search and a yearning to know the feminine side of his own nature, in order that he might be a complete and spiritually whole man. An idea like that, encountered head-on, is usually rather too much for human beings. They begin to see things they don't understand, and of course if they don't understand them, they are sure they must be monsters.*

—*Like yourself, my dear Maimas?*

—*Yes, like me. Look at me, Zadkiel; what do you see?*

—*A handsome figure. Splendid breasts that any Venus might envy; a fine complexion and a glowing eye, and hyacinthine tresses of the deepest black. So far, a woman. But those elegantly narrow hips and sinewy legs; those handsome masculine organs of generation, which move and stir constantly with every change of your attitude and alteration of your thoughts. Hermes and Aphrodite wonderfully united in a single form. A simulacrum of a complete human creature, though of course you could not be what you are—a daimon—if you were not far above humanity as it now exists. Perhaps you are the creature of the future?*

—*Only as a symbol, brother. If humanity ever took on this form, they would have great trouble in reproducing themselves.*

—*Let us get on with the quest. As the Angel of Biography, that is what I have to record—indeed have recorded, for what we are watching is a record of the past. But as I have said, I can't remember everything about all these people. Did he follow the quest through to the discovery, I wonder? Not many of them do.*

—*No, but every quester has hints and intimations that are very precious and bring sudden light into his life. And of course you've noticed that forecast, that strong hint, that we see as we watch Francis, ludicrously garbed as a woman.*

—*I am being very dense, I fear, said the Angel.*

—*Look behind the boy in his pathetic rags at the picture on the wall—the picture Aunt hung there in the goodness of her modestly wincing, power-greedy heart. Did she know it was a prophecy? Not consciously, but it was a prophecy and also the essence of life as everybody lived it at St. Kilda. The picture of* Love Locked Out.

—Is Francis never to find love?

You are unfolding the story, my dear friend. Please go on.

BUT IT IS IMPOSSIBLE to go on without taking notice at this point of something with which Francis had nothing whatever to do, but which influenced his future decisively. This was the downfall—temporary only, as we shall see—of Gerald Vincent O'Gorman, who was, as the husband of Mary-Tess, his uncle.

G.V. O'Gorman was an unusually able man of business, and the Senator, with his fine eye for talent, had advanced him rapidly until Gerry, as everybody called him, was his second-in-command and managed everything in the ordinary way, giving advice when he was asked—and sometimes when he wasn't—but leaving the major decisions to the Senator himself.

He was a big, fleshy, fine-looking Canadian-Irishman, jolly and kind of heart, a loving husband to Mary-Tess and a careful father of their sons, Gerald Lawrence and Gerald Michael. He was a staunch Catholic, and after the Senator the most prominent B.C.L. in Blairlogie and its district.

The O'Gormans came to dinner at St. Kilda every Sunday, and it did Aunt's heart good to see how loving they were. Their amorous speciality, in public, was a sort of graveyard chivalry, a declaration that each had a proven right to "go first" into the afterlife.

"Aw, Mary-Tess, if you go first, I'll never forgive you as long as I live, for my life would be a mockery without you, darlin'."

"Gerry, don't talk that way! You know it would kill me if you went before me; for the love of God, sweetness, let me go first! It will be the last of the thousand-and-one happinesses you've given me!"

"Aw, well; let's hope under God it'll be many a long day off, whichever it is. But I'll give no promise." Then a kiss—right at the table, after Gerry had gallantly wiped his lips with his napkin, as Aunt beamed, and Marie-Louise nodded approvingly, and the Senator looked down at his plate.

What could have been better? But then came the awful day when Mary-Tess, finding herself not far from the head office of the Senator's business affairs, dropped in after five o'clock, to walk home with her Gerald, and found him in his office, strenuously "at it" on his desk with his secretary, Blondie Utronki.

Oh, the tears! Oh, the protestations! Oh, the dreadful comedown! For Mary-Tess's howls attracted one of the cleaning women, who spread the tale through the whole of the Polish layer of the great fruit-cake, from which it mounted rapidly to the French layer, and in no time at all had reached the top, the Scots layer, where it was a cause of righteous jubilation.

Wouldn't you know it? Of course Blondie Utronki would be just the one for that sort of game! As if Gerry O'Gorman hadn't been shoving her forward whenever he could: getting her those chances to sing—at a hefty five dollars a warble—in the McRory Opera House, just before the feature film, when it was a specially good one! "I'm Forever Blowing Bubbles", and "Smile Awhile, I'll Kiss You Sad Adieu" and all that! Well, she'd blown her last bubble in Blairlogie, and she'll be kissing Gerry sad adieu now, you can bet!

And from Alexander Dagg's Maw: bad blood in that family! I've always said so. Piling on the agony, and now shamelessness on a glass-topped desk! We'll see the McRorys topple! Rot of the brain! Look at the old aunt!

Nor was this the worst. Aunt, that tireless backstairs arranger of destinies, had laboured for two years to bring about her latest coup in St. Bonaventura. Father Devlin was now Monsignor Devlin, and it was Aunt who had pushed and shoved at the Bishop to get him nominated for that honour. Indeed, it had been she who presented him with his first two pairs of violet socks, one of the distinguishing marks of his new splendour. But this was not Aunt's finest achievement.

St. Bonaventura had been very much to the fore in wartime charities, and Gerald Vincent O'Gorman, who was a little too old to be called up, and who felt that his brother-in-law, Major Francis Chegwidden Cornish, was brilliantly upholding the family honour in the Forces, had worked like a slave, and a dog, and a Trojan, for war charities. The whist-drives, the concerts, the fowl suppers!

So successful was he that St. Bonaventura left all the Protestant churches nowhere in the extent of its contributions. Look at the Cigarette Fund—a triumph of organization and achievement! And everyone knew, because Aunt let it be heard, that Gerry did innumerable good works and paid for many a beautification of the church out of his own pocket, and never breathed a word about it. Surely something was owing for devotion like that?

Devotion was rewarded, for Aunt kept on at the Bishop, who kept on at the Cardinal of Apostolic Briefs, until Gerry was honoured by the Papacy itself, and Monsignor Devlin announced one Sunday morning at High Mass that henceforth Gerry was a Knight of St. Sylvester, as a recognition of his work for the Church, the Holy See and society at large.

Mary-Tess was the soul of modesty. Of course, it wasn't a Commander, or a Knight Grand Cross; just a simple Knight of St. Sylvester. No, no; nothing of the honour appertained to the spouse; it was wholly a man's thing—but of course she was very proud. External badges of honour? Well, in future on great occasions, like a visit from the Bishop or at High Mass on St. Bonaventura's festal day, July 15, Gerry would be obliged to wear his coat with the gold buttons, and the gold embroidery on the velvet collar and cuffs, and the gold stripe down the side of the pants, and the bicorne hat with the Papal cockade. And the medal of the Order, with the Golden Spur hanging from it. And of course the sword. He'd have to put it on, whether he wanted to or not, and she'd have the job of making sure he got it all right, because you know what men are. Well, yes, Mary-Tess would admit under pressure, it was very nice.

Then—Blondie Utronki!

Monsignor Devlin, whose life was not a bed of roses, found that the hardest thing he had ever had to do was to inform Gerry that this sort of thing did not become a Papal Knight, and the Bishop had sent a peremptory inquiry. He would have to make a formal report to the Bishop, who would speed it to Rome, and the Knight would be un-knighted. Miserable in his violet socks, Monsignor Devlin made it as easy as he could. But Gerry was not inclined to take it easily.

"All I want to know—all I demand to know, Father Mick—is, who was the squealer?"

"Aw now, Gerry, no squealer was needed. The thing was all over town."

"A little bit of local gossip. Who squealed to the Bishop? That's what I want to know."

"Now Gerry, you know I have to write the report myself, even if my hand withers as I do it."

"All right; you have your duty. But who squealed to you?"

"The whole town, I tell you. The Presbyterians are laughing at us. When I met Mr. McComas in the Post Office he said to me: 'I'm very sorry to hear of your trouble,' he said. Me, to be pitied by a Presbyterian minister! They're jeering at us behind our backs."

"Yes, and to our faces, let me tell you! Yesterday in the office some joker stuck a memo up on the board saying, 'All swords that are to be returned to Rome must be left in the umbrella stand before Friday.'"

"Aw, that's very small! You must frown 'em down."

"D'you know who I bet it was? Now, don't take offence, but you know I've never liked him. Father Beaudry! I'll bet it was his letter put the Bishop on to you!"

"Now Gerry, I can't listen to that kind of thing."

"Oh, can't you? Well, priest though he is, he's a squealer and a whistle-tricker, and you can bet he'll never wear violet socks if I can stop it!"

"Now Gerry, you know the Order prescribes 'Unblemished character' and that's all there is to it. No more to be said.— Where's Blondie?"

"Gone to Montreal."

"Not the worst girl I've known. I hope you gave her something handsome? You've ruined her, you know."

"Aw Mick, don't talk so soft! She was wise enough when she came to me. I'm the one that's ruined."

Besides much of this, Monsignor Devlin had to listen to the wails and beseechings of his benefactress, Mary-Ben.

This was the Dark Night of the Soul for the McRorys, except perhaps for the Senator, who had government business that kept him in Ottawa for several weeks.

FRANCIS KNEW NOTHING of the domestic and public miseries of the O'Gormans, as he was not going to school, and the morose atmosphere in St. Kilda did not greatly affect him. He had a scandal of his own.

He now knew for a certainty that several nights in every week Zadok Hoyle mounted the staircase that was forbidden to himself, because it led to Victoria Cameron's private domain. What went on up there? What was the relationship between these two important figures in his own life? If there was nothing fishy about it, why did Zadok take off his boots and go upstairs in his socks?

There were noises, too. Laughter, which he could distinguish as belonging to Zadok and Victoria. Singing, in what was plainly Zadok's voice. Sometimes thumps and bumps and scuffling. Seldom, but often enough to puzzle him, there was a sound that might have been a cat, but louder than a cat. He didn't like to ask Aunt; it might be squealing. Certainly he couldn't ask Zadok and Victoria, because if they were up to something they shouldn't be up to—something to do with the great mystery, perhaps, and related to the dark world half-unveiled by Dr. Upper—they would be angry with him, and his long, philosophical talks with Victoria, and his visits to Devinney's embalming parlour which were so necessary to his study of drawing, would be at an end. But he must know.

So, one night as Lent began, he crept slowly up the stairs in his pyjamas, feeling his way in the darkness until he became aware that the walls were covered with something soft, which felt like blanketing. On the landing he could see, by moonlight from a window high in the wall, that it was indeed blanketing, and that a heavy curtain of blankets hung directly in front of him. This was odd, for he knew that Victoria's room was in the other direction, and what lay toward the front of the house, beyond this curtain, was above his grandparents' large bedroom. An unlucky stumble, though a boy in his bare feet does not make much noise. But suddenly light, as a door opened, and there stood Zadok.

"You see, Miss Cameron, I told you he'd find his way up here one of these days. Come in, me little dear."

"Are you prepared to take responsibility for this?" said Victoria's voice. "You know what my orders are."

"Circumstances alter cases: Shorter pants need longer braces," said Zadok. "He's here, and if you turn him away now, you'll regret it." And he beckoned Francis into the room, the door of which had been thickened and padded amateurishly but effectively.

The room was large and bare, and suggested a sick-room, for there was a table covered with white oilcloth, on which were a basin and pitcher. The floor was covered with what used to be called battleship linoleum. The light was harsh, from a single large bulb hanging from the ceiling, with a white glass shade that threw the light downward. But what Francis saw first, and what held his eyes for a long time, was the bed.

It was a hospital bed with sides that could be slid up and down, so that at need it became a sort of topless cage. In the cage was an odd being, smaller than Francis himself, dressed in crumpled flannelette pyjamas; its head was very small for its body, and the skull ran, not to a point, but to a knob, not very big, on which grew black hair. Because the top of the head was so small, the lower part seemed larger than it was, the nose longer, the jaw broader, and the very small eyes peeped out at the world without much comprehension. They were now fixed on Francis. The child, or the creature, or whatever it was, opened its lips and made the mewing sound that Francis had sometimes heard downstairs.

"Come along, Francis, and shake hands with your older brother," said Zadok. Then to the figure in the bed, "This is your brother, Franko, come to see you."

Francis had been taught to obey. He walked toward the cage, his hand out, and the figure sank back on its blankets, whimpering.

"This is Francis the First," said Zadok. "Be gentle with him; he's not very well."

Francis the Second had been ill for some months, and he was still weak. He fainted.

When he came to himself again, he was in his bed, and Victoria was sitting by him, dabbing at his brow with a cold towel.

"Now Frankie, you must promise me on your Bible oath that you will never tell where you've been or what you've seen. But

I expect you want to know what's going on, and I'll answer a few questions. But not too many."

"Victoria, is that really my brother?"

"That is Francis Chegwidden Cornish the first."

"But he's in the graveyard. Aunt showed me the stone."

"Well, as you've seen, he's not in the graveyard. That was just something I can't explain. Maybe you'll find out when you're older."

"But he's not like a human person."

"Don't say that, Frankie. He's not well and he'll never be any better, but he's human right enough."

"But why is he up there?"

"Because it would be very hard on everybody if he was down here. There are problems. It wouldn't be nice for your grandparents. Or your parents. He may not live a long time, Frankie. Nobody expected he'd live as long as this."

"But you and Zadok spend a lot of time with him."

"Somebody must, and I was asked to do it by your grandfather, and I'm doing it. I'm not much good at cheering him up. Zadok does that. He's wonderful at it. Your grandfather trusts Zadok. Now you'd better go to sleep."

"Victoria—"

"Well?"

"Can I go to see him again?"

"I don't think it would be for the best."

"Victoria, I get so lonesome. I could be up there with you and Zadok sometimes. Maybe I could cheer him up."

"Well—I don't know."

"Oh, please!"

"Well, we'll see. Now you go to sleep."

Grown-ups always think children can go to sleep at will. An hour later, when Victoria looked in again, Francis was still awake, and she had to take the extraordinary step of giving him a glass of hot milk with some of his grandfather's rum in it to induce sleep.

During that hour his mind had raced over and over the same ground. He had a brother. His brother was very strange. This must be the Looner that Alexander Dagg's hateful Maw declared

that McRorys kept in their attic. A Looner! He could not encompass the idea.

But one thing was uppermost and demandingly powerful in his
mind. He wanted to draw the Looner.

The very next night he was there, with his pad and pencil, and
Victoria Cameron was angry: did he mean to mock the poor boy,
and make a display of his trouble? No, certainly not; nothing
more than he had been doing at Devinney's—just carrying out
the advice of Harry Furniss to draw anything and everything. But
in his heart Francis knew that his urge to draw the Looner was
more than art-student zeal; drawing was his way of making something his own, and he could not hope to comprehend the Looner,
to accept him as something related to himself, if he could not
draw him, and draw him again, and capture his likeness in every
possible aspect.

How much Victoria understood of that Francis could not tell,
but the revelation about Devinney's made her open her eyes very
wide, and breathe heavily through her nostrils, and look fiercely
at Zadok. But Zadok showed no discomposure.

"We have to recognize, Miss C., that Francis isn't just your
run-of-the-mill young scallawag, and circumstances alter cases, as
I'm always saying. I wouldn't take just any boy to Devinney's,
but for Francis, it's part of his education. It's not that he's nosy;
he's a watcher, and a noter, and they're not the commonest people. Francis is deep, and with a deep 'un you have to give 'em
something deeper than a teacup to swim in. This here's a deep
situation. Francis the Second downstairs, sharp as a razor; Francis
the First up here, and Dr. J.A. giving orders right and left about
how to keep him as he ought to be. Aren't they ever to meet?
Haven't they anything for one another? I put it to you fairly, Miss
C., haven't they?"

Was Victoria convinced? Francis could not tell. But it was plain
that she put great trust in the coachman-embalmer.

"I don't know, Zadok. I know what my orders are, and it wasn't
easy for me to convince His Nibs that you should come up here
sometimes—which you've extended to nearly every night."

"Ah, but the Senator trusts me. Would he let me make the
journeys to The Portage if he didn't?"

"Well—I don't know. But you're a soldier, and you've travelled, and I just hope you know what you're doing."

"I do. Francis the First needs a new face to cheer him up. Shall we sing?"

Zadok struck up "Frère Jacques", which he sang in French, pretty well. But Victoria sang

> *Are you sleeping, are you sleeping*
> *Brother John? Brother John?*

because she spoke no French—could not "parley-voo the ding-dong" as the English speakers in Blairlogie put it—and would not try. But Francis piped up with the third voice, and they made a reasonable bilingual job of it.

The Looner was enchanted. It would be false to say that his face brightened, but he stood clinging to the raised side of his bed, and turned his little eyes from face to face of the singers.

Then Zadok sang "Yes, let me like a soldier fall", which was obviously a favourite. Most of it was in an extremely manly vein, but, as he explained to Francis, he always "came the pathetic" on

> *I only ask of that proud race*
> *Which ends its blaze in me,*
> *To die the last, and not disgrace*
> *Its ancient chivalry!*

"That's the way the Captain went in South Africa," he said solemnly, but who the Captain was he did not reveal.

This fine operatic piece was the gem of his repertoire, but as several evenings passed, Francis came to know it all. Zadok was a very personal performer. When he sang

> *There ain't a lady*
> *Livin' in the land*
> *As I'd swan for my dear old Dutch . . .*

he looked languishingly at Victoria, who pretended not to notice, but blushed becomingly. There were rowdy music-hall songs of

the Boer War period, and "Good-bye, Dolly Gray". And there
were songs that must have been the fag-ends of folksongs of great
antiquity, but the words Zadok sang were those he had heard as
a child, among the real folk, and not the cleansed and scholarly
versions known to the English Folk Song Society.

> *The cock sat up in the yew-tree,*
> *King Herod come riding by,*
> *If you can't gimme a penny*
> *Please to gimme a mince-pie.*
> *God send you happy* (three times)
> *A Happy New Year.*

And there was a rough version of "The Raggle-Taggle Gypsies-
O" that made the Looner hop up and down in his bed. When he
did this he was likely to fart loudly, and Victoria would say, almost
automatically, "Now then, none o' that, or I'll go downstairs."
But Zadok said, "Aw now, Miss Cameron, the boy's a natural,
and you know it." And, genially, to the Looner, "Better an empty
house than a bad tenant, eh, Franko me dear?" Which seemed to
comfort the dismayed Looner, who did not know what he had
done that was wrong. Did he comprehend anything of the story
of the gentle lady who left her noble husband and her goose-
feather bed to go with the bright-eyed vagabonds? Nobody could
tell how much the Looner understood of anything, but he responded to rhythm, and his favourite, which ended every concert,
was a rollicking song to the beat of which Zadok, and Francis,
clapped their hands:

> *Rule Britannia!*
> *God Save The Queen!*
> *Hard times in England*
> *Are very seldom seen!*
> *Hokey-pokey, penny a lump,*
> *A taste before you buy,*
> *Singing O what a happy land is England!*

After which Victoria demanded quieter entertainment, or Some
Of Us would never get off to sleep.

Sometimes there were impromptu picnics, when Victoria brought up good things from the kitchen, and they all ate, the Looner noisily and merrily, but with an enjoyment that Francis saw as parody of the refined greed of Aunt and Grand'mère. In one caricature in his Harry Furniss manner he drew them all three at table. Yes, Grand'mère, and Aunt, and the Looner, all tucking into a huge pie. Zadok thought it wonderful, but Victoria seized and destroyed it, and gave Francis a scolding for his "badness".

As the Looner could not talk, Zadok and Victoria talked, with now and then a nod to include the quiet, attentive figure in the bed. Zadok would wave his pipe-stem at him, and interject "Isn't that right, old son?" as if the Looner were silent by choice, and reflecting deeply. Francis rarely spoke, but drew and drew and drew, until he had books full of pictures of the scene—the two adults, not fashionable or stylish figures but people who might have belonged to any of five preceding centuries, Victoria knitting or mending, and Zadok leaning forward with his hands on his knees. Zadok sat in the old countryman's fashion: his back never touched the back of the chair. And, of course, there were countless quick studies of Francis the First, which were grotesque to begin, but with time became perceptive, and touched with an understanding and pity not to be expected in so young an artist.

"Is he really so bad, Victoria? Couldn't he come downstairs now and again?"

"No, Frank, he couldn't. Not ever. You haven't seen all of him. He's shameful."

"He's strange, right enough, but why shameful?"

Victoria shook her head. "You'd know if you had to watch over him every day. He has a festering mind."

A festering mind? Was it rotten brains, as charged by Alexander Dagg's Maw?

It was a few weeks before the explanation came. One night, at the beginning of Easter Week, the Looner was more than ordinarily stirred by Zadok's rendering of a seasonable hymn, "Who is this in gory garments?". The Looner began to puff and blow, and claw at the crotch of his pyjamas.

"Easy, Franko. Easy, old man," said Zadok.

But Victoria was harsh. "Frank, you cut that right out, do you hear? Do you want me to get your belt? Eh? Do you?"

But the Looner paid no heed. He was now masturbating, gobbling and snorting. A sight to strike shame into .Francis the Second.

Quickly Zadok rose and restrained him. Victoria brought from the chest of drawers a strange affair of wire and tapes, and as Zadok pulled down the Looner's pyjama pants she fastened it around his waist, slipped a wire cage over his bobbing genitals, pulled a tape between his legs, and fastened the whole at the back with a little padlock.

The Looner fell to his mattress, whimpering in his catlike voice, and continued to whine.

"You shouldn't have seen that, me dear," said Zadok. "That's the trouble, you see. He can't leave himself alone, and in the daytime, when Miss Cameron is needed downstairs, we have to keep that on him, or nobody knows what might come of it. Sad, and that cage is a hateful thing, but Dr. J.A. says that's how it has to be. Now you and me had better go downstairs, and leave Miss Cameron to settle him for the night."

So that was it! This was plain evidence of the truth of what Dr. Upper had said. Self-abuse and the festering mind, and the shameful secret of the Looner, were all part of a notion of life which began to haunt Francis again, just as he had thought he was breaking free from that torment.

He dreamed terrible dreams, and thought fearful thoughts, as he lay looking without seeing it at the picture of *Love Locked Out*. Sometimes he wept, though tears were a shameful thing in a boy of his age. But what was he to make of this terrible house where the pious refinement of Aunt was under the same roof as the animal lust of the Looner, and the sweet music that Aunt played in the drawing-room was set against Zadok's singing in the attic, singing which was so vigorous, so full of gusto, that there seemed to be a hint of danger—something Dr. Upper would not have approved—about it. This house where there was so much deep concern for his welfare, but nothing of the love he needed except for the two servants, who did not precisely love him so much as accept him as a fellow-being. This house where he, the cherished Francis, was aware that in a sort of hospital-prison there was another Francis whom nobody ever mentioned, and, so far as he could find out, nobody ever visited, except the Presbyterian cook-nurse, whose opinions on the matter he sometimes heard, when she reluctantly spoke of the matter.

"We're not to judge, Frank, but something like what's upstairs doesn't happen just by chance. Nothing comes by chance. Everything's written down somewhere, you know, and we have to live the lives that are foreseen for us long before the world began. So you mustn't look on your brother as a judgement on anyone. But I won't say he isn't a warning—a rebuke to pride, maybe.

> *In Adam's Fall*
> *We sinned all.*

My grandmother worked that into a sampler when she was a girl, and we've still got it on the wall."

"All sinners, Victoria?"

"All sinners, Frank, however your aunt throws scent over it with her religious pictures and fancy prayers. That's just the R.C. way of deceiving yourself, as if life was a fancy-dress party, with purple socks, and all. Life isn't just for fun, you know."

"But aren't we ever to be happy?"

"Show me the place in the Bible where it says we are to be happy in this world. Happiness for sinners means sin. You can't get away from it."

"Are you a sinner, Victoria?"

"Maybe the worst of sinners. How can I tell?"

"Then why are you so good to the fellow upstairs?"

"We sinners have to stick together, Frank, and do the best we can in our fallen state. That's what religion is. I don't make the judgements. For all the silver and thick carpets and hand-painted pictures—your pictures too, clever though they are—this is a House of Sin."

"But Victoria, that's awful. And it isn't an answer. If you're a sinner, why don't you sin?"

"Too proud, Frank. God made me a sinner, and I can't change that. But I don't have to give in, even to Him, and I won't. I won't give it to Him to say. Though He slay me, yet will I worship Him. But I won't throw in the towel, even if He's damned me."

Thus, in addition to a little lukewarm Anglicanism, and much hot, sweet Catholicism, Frank imbibed a stern and unyielding Calvinism. It was no help with his personal difficulties. But he loved Victoria and he believed her, just as he believed Aunt. The only person who didn't seem to have a God who was out for his scalp was Zadok.

Zadok's religion, if it may be so called, was summed up briefly. "Life's a rum start, me little dear. I've good cause to know!"

THE HOUSE OF SIN was, in its way, splendid, and Frank took satisfaction in its richness without having a clear idea of its ugliness. The drawing-room, so silvery blue, so crammed with uncomfortable "Louis" furniture, relieved only by the fierce mahogany gloss of the Phonoliszt, and the portly Victrola, repository of great music, including several records by the mangod Caruso. The dining-room, battleground of two great indigestions—Aunt's manifesting itself in sternly repressed gas, and Grand'mère's in a recurrent biliousness. Neither lady ever thought of moderating her diet. "I can take cream," Aunt would say, as if many other luxuries were denied her; she took cream at every meal. "Oh, I shouldn't, but I'll venture," was what Grand'mère would say, as she helped herself to another slice of Victoria's superb pastry, usually manifesting itself as the casing of a sweet fruit pie. The dining-room, with its red velvety paper and its pictures of cardinals, seemed an outward enlargement of two outraged, overloaded stomachs. And then, Grand-père's study, so complex and tormented in its panelling, where much the most interesting books were his many albums of sun-pictures. A House of Sin? Certainly a house of vexations and disappointments, quite apart from those that plagued Francis.

Late on the night of Good Friday, when in deference to Mary-Ben and Marie-Louise the Senator had taken no wine at the salmon dinner (a day of abstention and fasting, you see), the Senator sat in the hideous study, refreshing himself with a little of his excellent bootleg whiskey. A tap at the door, which opened just wide enough for Dr. Joseph Ambrosius Jerome to slip in, smiling widely but not mirthfully, as was usual with him.

"Come in, Joe; I was hoping you'd look in. Will you take any spirits?"

"In spite of the day, Hamish, I will. And I'd like a word with you about the fellow upstairs."

"No change?"

"Just growing older, like the rest of us. You well know, Hamish, that I didn't give him long, years ago, when we moved him up there. He's proved me wrong."

"That was a bad decision, Joe."

"Don't I know it! But you remember we went into all that, and decided for Mary-Jim's sake, and the sake of the baby that was coming, it was the best we could do."

"Yes, but to pretend he had died! To pretend even to Mary-Jim! That awful pretended funeral—if Mick Devlin had known there was nothing in the coffin but some gravel he'd have had the hide off us both!"

"We had the support of Marie-Louise and Mary-Ben; they were sure we were doing the best thing. Do they ever speak of it now?"

"Not a word from either of them in years. Nobody goes up there but Victoria Cameron, and I believe Zadok, sometimes. I never go up. Can't stand the sight of him. My grandson! Now why, Joe, why?"

"Reasons better not gone into, Hamish."

"That's not an answer. Have you any notion, yourself? What's science got to say about it?"

"Did you read the book I lent you?"

"By that fellow Krafft-Ebing? I read some of it. When I read about the fellow who liked to eat his mistress's earwax, b'God I thought I'd spew. You can take it away with you when you go. What's all that got to do with Mary-Jacobine McRory, a beautiful, sweet-souled girl who got into a mess that might have happened to any girl, under the circumstances."

"Ah, but what were the circumstances? I told you at the time: go whoring after the English and a life of fashion, I said, and you'll be a sorry man. And what are you today, and what have you been ever since? A sorry man."

"Oh, of course, Joe, we know you're always right. And what has your rightness got you? You're a cranky, half-crazy old bachelor, and my sister is a cranky, religious-crazy old maid, and however much you boked at her torn-off scalp you'd have been better together than the way you are now—which is together but tortured apart. So don't preach to me."

"There, there, Hamish. Don't let's have any of your Hielan'-man's hysterics. It hasn't been all bad. When last I saw Mary-Jim she looked happy enough."

"Happy enough isn't as happy as can be. Perhaps I was wrong. But I was trying to do the best for my child."

"God, Hamish, nobody can do the *best* for anyone. People can only rarely do the best for themselves. Mary-Jim's not over-bright, but God knows she's beautiful, and that entirely robbed you of good sense. Good intentions can make terrible mischief, but so long as love lasts, they'll last, and there you are. You didn't do too badly. You landed your Englishman."

"I wasn't fishing for any Englishman! But she had to marry, and where in this place, or in Ottawa even, would there have been anybody good enough for her?"

"The old problem of the rich Catholic girl: where is she to find a husband on her own level?"

"I met some very fine Catholics in England."

"Very fine? Well-born, I suppose you mean, and rich and educated? And I'm not saying that doesn't count for a lot. But you ended up with Cornish."

"And what's so bad about Cornish?"

"Oh, get away, Hamish! You know fine what's wrong with Cornish. What about that paper he made you sign?"

"He overreached me; I don't say he didn't. But he's not turned out so badly. Listen, Joe, keep this under your hat, but there's to be some interesting news soon of Cornish."

"What's he up to now?"

"It's what he was up to all through the War. Working very much on the Q.T. and sometimes in serious danger, I understand. Well, when the next Honours List appears, he'll be a K.B.E.— Sir Francis—and my girl will be Lady Cornish. What d'you think of that?"

"I think I'm happy for you, Hamish, and for Mary-Jim. Maybe not so happy for Gerry O'Gorman and Mary-Tess. To lose one knighthood only to have another pop up in the same family won't sit well with them."

"Oh, that was only a Papal knighthood; this is a far more solid thing."

"Hamish, you astonish me! 'Only a Papal knighthood'! You're beginning to sound almost like a Prot."

"In this country if you're in the money business you have to learn to sit at the table with the Prots. They have most of it their own way. R.C.s and Jews needn't apply. And I'm thinking very hard about the money business."

"Surely you have all you need?"

"What a man needs and what he wants may be very different things. Don't forget, I came from very poor people, and the hatred of poverty is in my blood. Now listen: the lumbering business isn't what it was; it's changing, and I don't want to change with it; I want something new."

"At your age?"

"What about my age? I'm only sixty-seven. I've other people to think of. Now, you know that for years people—widows and old people and the like—have been coming to me and asking me to look after their money for them."

"And you've done it, and made money for them. For me, too."

"Yes, but I don't like it. You trust me, and I'm pleased you do, but this thing of private trust is no way to do business; in business nobody should have total responsibility for anybody else's money. So I'm thinking of unloading the lumber trade, and setting up one of these trust companies."

"In Blairlogie? Wouldn't it be very small potatoes?"

"No, not in Blairlogie. In Toronto."

"Toronto? Man, are you crazy? Why not Montreal, where the big money is?"

"Because there's other big money, and it's in the West, and Toronto will be the centre for that. Not yet, but you have to be ahead of the procession."

"You're away ahead of me."

"And properly so. Why wouldn't I be? You're a doctor and you look after my health; I'm a financier, and I look after your money."

"Well—when do you take the big step?"

"I've taken it. Not many people know, but recent events are pushing me ahead fast. Gerry O'Gorman and Mary-Tess want to get out of Blairlogie; after that come-down over the Knight of St. Sylvester business they're very much out of love with this little place. They'll move to Toronto, and Gerry'll set the thing on its feet."

"God! Is Gerry up to a big thing like that?"

"Yes. Gerry has powers that have never been roused. And he's honest."

"Honest! What about Blondie Utronki?"

"Honest about money. Women are quite a different thing. And I've told Gerry there's to be no more of that monkey-business, and Mary-Tess has him under her thumb forever. He can do it. Gerry has great ability as an organizer, and people like him."

"He's no Prot."

"Not yet. But Gerry isn't nearly as good a Catholic as he was before that little sanctified rat Beaudry did the dirty on him. Give him time, and give him Toronto, and we shall see what we shall see. Anyhow, that needn't show too clearly. Didn't I tell you Cornish is to be a knight?"

"I don't follow you at all."

"Well—look here. The Cornish Trust—Gerry is Managing Director, I'm Chairman of the Board (and I'll keep the real power in my own hands, you may be sure), and Sir Francis Cornish is President, and the grand show-piece of the business. And Cornish is a bigoted Prot, as I have good cause to know."

"Will he do it?"

"Indeed he will. He's always been pestering me for a place in the business, and now there's a place just right for him."

"Can he manage it?"

"He's very far from being a fool. He's got a splendid war record, and that counts for a lot. And he doesn't want to come back to Blairlogie. As president he'll have no power I don't choose to give him, and Gerry'll watch him like a hawk. It's tailor-made, Joe."

"Hamish, I've always said you were a downy one, but this beats everything."

"It's not bad. Not bad at all. Everything has suddenly clicked into place."

"All things work together for good for those that love the Lord."

"Don't be cynical, Joe. But if you mean that, you're right. Even the third generation is taken care of. Gerry's boys are good lads, and they'll grow up to banking and trust business."

"And what about young Francis? Will Cornish let you cut his son out of this big game?"

"Francis is a fine boy. I like him best of the lot, and I won't see him pushed aside. But he's not just what I look for in a boy who's to grow up to be a banker. However, that's not too great a problem; Mary-Jim writes to her mother that there's another young Cornish on the way. If it's a boy—and as you always tell your patients, it's fifty-fifty that it will be—he can grow up to the family trade, which will be money, and a very good trade it is."

"I just hope he's all right."

"What do you mean, Joe?"

"Are you forgetting the lad upstairs?"

"He wasn't Cornish's son. Cornish is sound. The father of the poor creature must have been a degenerate."

"But he is Mary-Jim's son as well."

"I don't follow you."

"Now Hamish, you know I hate to say unpleasant things—"

"I know only too well that you love to say unpleasant things, Joe."

"That's a nasty dig at an old friend, Hamish. But you must remember I'm a man of science, and science has to come to terms with facts, however unpleasant they may be. It takes two to make a child, and if there's something wrong with the child, which of the two is responsible? You told me the father of that poor idjit upstairs was an unknown man, a soldier—"

"God knows what he may have been. Rotten with disease, probably."

"No, not probably at all, for Mary-Jim has never shown any hint of what you'd expect from any such association, so you can't blame it all on the man."

"Are you blaming it on my daughter?"

"Easy, now, Hamish! Easy, man. Just give me another dram of that fine whisky, and I'll explain. Because I've thought a lot about this matter, I can tell you, and I've read every book I can get hold of that might throw light on it. I lent you that book by Krafft-Ebing hoping you'd get a clue, but it seems you haven't."

"That book was full of dirty rubbish."

"Life's full of dirty rubbish. I'm a doctor and I know. If you'd read that book in a scientific spirit you'd have understood what it says. Krafft-Ebing's the great name in this field still, you know, though he died a while back. But I've been reading Kraepelin, his successor, who's the foremost man in this sort of medicine now, and there are certain points on which he and Krafft-Ebing are in full agreement. Now, if you'd read that book instead of skipping over to the earwax stories, you'd have taken in a very pertinent fact to what we're discussing: a healthy, well-brought-up young woman has no sexual desire whatever. Oh, some romantic notions out of books, maybe, but not the real thing. She's no notion of it, even if she has a rough idea how babies come. Now, look here: A very closely guarded, well-educated Catholic girl finds herself in a hotel room with a strange man. A servant, trained to keep his mind on his job, never to betray anything you might call humanity. Does he rape her? Not so far as we've been told. She said to you that one thing led to another. What thing was that one thing, Hamish?"

"That's enough, Joe. You'd better be on your way."

"No, it's not enough, Hamish. You've got your head in the sand, man. And don't order me to go, because I'm speaking to you as your family's medical adviser—have been since I don't know when—and this is nasty medicine I'm giving you, to make you well. I'm not saying Mary-Jim is a light woman. May this whiskey be my poison if I ever thought any such thing! But even the purest woman may be victim of a disease of the mind—"

"Joe—you don't mean Mary-Jim's touched?"

"It's not a permanent thing, Hamish, so far as I know. But it exists, and it attacks the young. In the profession we call it the *furor uterinus*."

"You know I have no Latin. What's that mean?"

"Well—I'd translate it as the rage o' the womb. Uncontrollable

desire. I've seen it in some cases of women—low women down
at the end o' the town—and God forbid you should ever meet
with such a thing. I mean, desire—well, sometimes a married
woman, accustomed to that way of life—might feel something.
On a hot night, for instance, in July. But many fine women never
know any such trouble. So—what are we to make of it in poor
Mary-Jim?"

"God! You tell me a terrible thing!"

"There are a lot of terrible things known to science, Hamish.
And I don't say that some terrible people don't make capital of
them. For instance this fellow Freud that we're beginning to hear
about now that we're getting hold of medical books in German
again. But nobody heeds him, and he'll soon peter out—or be
run out of the profession. But well-authenticated medical science,
based on great experience—you can't go against it."

"Joe, you hint at a world ridden and rotted with sex."

"I don't hint. I know. Why do you suppose I'm a single man?
Even though I know that Mary-Ben would have taken me years
ago, and perhaps even now. It's because I've seen too much, and
I decided against it. Science has its celibates, as well as religion.
And now the craze is for blathering about sex all over the place.
Like that scoundrel Upper who was speaking in the public schools
here, and telling innocent children God knows what! Did Francis
say anything about him?"

"I never heard him mention the name."

"Perhaps he escaped, then. He's a frail lad. I don't imagine
anything like that has come into his head yet. When the time
comes, I'd better have a talk with him. Put him on his guard."

"Perhaps so. But—Joe, do you suggest that this—this trouble
you say Mary-Jim had—might affect the child that's coming?"

"I can say truthfully that I don't know. But she has been leading
the life of a married woman for many years now, and perhaps it's
burned itself out. That's what we'll hope."

"Another like that one upstairs would kill Marie-Louise. It
might finish me. Joe—can nothing be done?"

"Hamish, I told you once I wouldn't kill, and that's my answer
now. Indeed, I'm sworn to keep that idjit alive; it's my sacred
profession. That's why I had that wire affair made, to restrain his
lust. Without it, he might rage and rip himself into the grave, but

that's not for me to encourage or condone. We must all of us just wait it out. But listen, Hamish: if family interests are moving to Toronto, why don't you send Francis to school there? Mary-Tess and Gerry would keep an eye on him. I hear the Christian Brothers have a fine school in Toronto. Get him out of here. Get him away from these women. Just suppose by bad luck he happens on that thing upstairs. What a brother for him!"

Dr. Jerome finished his third drink, shook hands warmly with his old friend, and left, with the warm consciousness that he was a man who had done a duty certainly painful, but in the best interests of everyone concerned.

STILL NO PITY for Francis, brother? said the Lesser Zadkiel, pausing in the unfolding of his story.

—I have told you repeatedly, said the Daimon Maimas, that pity is not one of the insruments with which such agencies as I do our work. Pity at this stage of his life would not make Francis better; it would dull his perceptions and rob him of the advantages I have managed for him.

—Rough on the bystanders, would you not say?

—The bystanders are no concern of mine. I am Francis's daimon, not theirs. He has already met his Dark Brother. Everybody has one, but most people go through their lives without ever recognizing him or feeling any love or compassion for him. They see the Dark Brother in the distance, and they hate him. But Francis has his Dark Brother securely in his drawing-books, and more than that. He has him in his hand, and his artist's sensibility.

—Nevertheless, my dear colleague, reluctant as I am to criticize or appear to teach you your business, is it good to conceal from everyone who the Dark Brother is, or how he came about?

—Well, in the obvious, physical sense, the Dark Brother in Francis's life is the outcome of Marie-Louise's well-intentioned meddling in London, when she made her daughter do everything she knew that might bring about a miscarriage. Those people thought a child had no real life until it was pushed into the outer world; they know nothing of the life in the womb, which is the sweetest and most secure time of all. If you jolt and shake and parboil the child, and batter it with cathartics and stun it with gin, you may kill it, or if it is very strong—and

Francis the First was very strong or he wouldn't have survived the dance they led him—you may have an oddity to deal with. But Francis's Dark Brother is much more than an obvious, physical thing. He's a precious gift from me, and I think I did rather well to seize my opportunity of bringing him to Francis's notice so early.

—I suppose you know best, brother.

—I do. So let us go on and see how my gift to Francis shows itself. It's begun by getting him out of Blairlogie.

PART
Three

WHEN THE SENATOR CONFIDED to Dr. J.A. that the Cornish Trust was in prospect, he was not entirely candid with his old friend; the Trust had been in his mind for at least five years, and had been in the process of assemblage for the last three. The business of the Papal knighthood had somewhat hurried matters, so far as the O'Gormans were concerned, and Gerry and Mary-Tess had already bought a house in Toronto on fashionable St. George Street. Major Cornish and Mary-Jim were talking with an architect about building a house in the rising suburb of Rosedale, appropriately near the residence of the Lieutenant-Governor. The Senator spoke to Dr. J.A. at Easter, and it was less than a month before the O'Gormans moved to Toronto, and at once made themselves known at St. James' Anglican Cathedral.

"It's no use trying to get a trust company on its feet unless you're seen and known where money is," said Gerald Vincent to his wife. She agreed, because he knew Toronto better than she; had he not been making visits to it for the last eighteen months? But she wondered aloud if in a city sometimes called "the Rome of Methodism" it might not be better to ally themselves with one of the Methodist churchs where affluence and the godliness of John Wesley were mingled in a peculiarly Torontonian brew. When she discovered that the Methodist ladies appeared in the evening in a characteristic sort of gown in which the bosom was hidden as high as to the chin, and no jewellery was worn except a few discreet, chunky diamonds (good investments), she plumped for the more easygoing Anglicans. In their first three months of Toronto residence, before the Trust opened its doors to the public, the O'Gormans had caused themselves to be noticed in Toronto society. Noticed—and favourably noticed.

The question that was asked, of course, was whether they were Old Money, or New Money? The difference, though subtle to the vast population which was No Money, was important. Old Money usually reached back to colonial days, and some of it was Empire Loyalist; Old Money was Tory of an indigo that put to shame the weaknesses and follies of such wobblers as the first Duke of Wellington; Old Money sought to conserve and strengthen whatever was best in the body politic and knew precisely where this refined essence was to be found; it was in themselves and all that pertained to them. Even in the early twenties of this century, Old Money clung to its carriages, at least for ladies making calls, and had other tribal customs that spoke of assured distinction. The high priests of Old Money frequently wore top hats on weekdays, if they were going to do something priestly with money. They fought furiously against short coats for dinner dress, and white waistcoats with tailcoats. They kept mistresses, if at all, of such dowdiness they might almost have been mistaken for wives. For them the nineteenth century had not quite ended.

New Money, on the other hand, had taken its cue from Edward VII, who had a high regard for wealth however it was come by, and liked people with some "go" in them. New Money aspired to be Big Money, and did not greatly care if the drawing-rooms of Old Money were not easily opened. New Money wore dinner suits, which it called tuxedos, and smoked big cigars from which it removed the band before lighting up—an unthinkable solecism, for what if you should get a tobacco stain on your white glove? The O'Gormans knew they were New Money, but were aware that a trust company which was not on good terms with Old Money could run into quite unnecessary obstructions. The Senator, too, presented a problem. His gallant manners and handsome person recommended him anywhere, but it could not be concealed from the never-sleeping vigilance of Old Money that he was a Roman Catholic and a Liberal in politics. A difficult situation was avoided by the Cornish family, just as the Senator had foreseen.

Everything fell into place on June 3, when the Birthday Honours were announced, and Major Francis Cornish, President of the soon-to-be-opened Cornish Trust, became Sir Francis Cornish, K.B.E. How did he get it? The whisper was that he had done extraordinary work in Intelligence during the War, and not simply Canadian Intelligence, which was rather small potatoes. Non-military people, and even a lot of military people, have a notion that Military Intelligence implies uncommon brilliance of intellect, extraordinary resource and daring, ability to solve codes over which the enemy has toiled for years, and iron control over beautiful and alluring female spies. Of course, this may be quite true, but nobody knows, and everybody speculates. The passing of time had given the Wooden Soldier an air of distinction, of the grizzle-headed, frozen-faced, uncommunicative variety. His monocle gleamed with suppressed secrets; his moustache spoke of Nature subdued, tamed, domineered over. Just the man to trust your money to: just the man to ask to dinner. And his wife! What a stunner! Could she have been a spy, do you think?

Thus the Cornish name shed lustre over the sturdy understructure of McRorys and O'Gormans. Long before the announcement of the honour, and before its doors were officially opened for business, the Cornish Trust was a financial certainty. No trust company opens for business until a great deal of solid and profitable business has already been done, and promises and assurances have been given. Sir Francis's knighthood gave strong assurance to what was already a reality.

This should by no means be taken as evidence that Toronto's social and business communities were snobbish. They would assure you, almost before you asked, that they were pioneers and democrats to a man, or a woman. But they were well-connected pioneers and democrats, and if they kept a sharp eye on Roman Catholics and Jews it was not to be interpreted as prejudice, but because Roman Catholics and Jews—fine people among them, mind you!—had not been particularly visible when the colony began its long pull toward nationhood. Their time would come, no doubt. But just for the present it was as well for Old Money, and such New Money as showed itself worthy, to keep things on an even keel. And what better guarantee of evenness of keel than a president of the trust company who had served his country well in war, whose intelligence was of a guaranteed respectable sort, and who *looked* so trustworthy?

What Sir Francis thought about it, nobody ever knew. Probably he believed some of what was said about him. Undoubtedly he understood the language of finance, and had the good sense to leave the deployment of finance to his father-in-law and his brother-in-law, and to take his generous reward while keeping his mouth shut.

In these circumstances, Dr. J.A.'s ludicrously provincial notion that the third generation of the family should attend the big school kept by the Christian Brothers played no part. The young O'Gormans, Gerald Lawrence and Gerald Michael, were entered at Colborne College, a great stronghold of Old Money. At the same time the "Gerald" was discreetly dropped from their names; Mary-Tess sensed that the family habit of tacking the same dynastic label on several children might be very well for Blairlogie, but did not suit their changed situation.

Sir Francis also decided on Colborne for his son. The cousins did not see much of one another in their new school; the O'Gormans were in the Lower School because of their age, and were day-boys because their parents lived in Toronto. Sir Francis knew, and his wife (who had ceased to be Mary-Jim to anyone but her McRory family, and was known to everyone else as Jacko, which was what her husband called her) knew also, that they did not intend to be in Toronto for many months of the year. Sir Francis let it be known that his continuing relationship (never specified) with Very Important People in England would take him abroad often, and Jacko did not choose to be left behind. So Francis was to be a boarder at Colborne. Thus it was that Francis entered what looked like a new world, but which was not, in several respects that mattered to him, as new as it might appear.

Since Francis's days at Colborne, the reading world has been subjected to a flood of books written by men who hated their boarding-schools, and whose sensitive natures were thwarted and warped by early experience. It was not so with Francis. His life hitherto had made him philosophical and ingenious—not to say devious—in his dealings with his superiors and his contemporaries, and at Colborne he was philosophical and ingenious. He was not brilliant, in the prize-winning, examination-passing mode that makes for a splendid school career, but he was not stupid.

He took life as it came, and some of what came was uncommonly like what had come at Carlyle Rural.

Much may be learned about any society by studying the behaviour and accepted ideas of its children, for children—and sometimes adults—are shadows of their parents, and what they believe and what they do are often what their parents believe in their hearts and would do if society would put up with it. The dominant group, though by no means the majority of the boys at Colborne College, were the sons of Old Money, and in their behaviour the spirit of Old Money was clear. They were the conservers of tradition, and they imposed tradition without discrimination and without mercy. The tradition best calculated to reduce a New Boy to his lowest common denominator was fagging.

On the first day of the autumn term, each senior boy was assigned, by decision of the prefects, a New Boy who was to be his fag for the year that followed, and it was clearly understood that the fag was the slave and creature of his fag-master, to do his bidding without question at any hour. There was an understanding that if a fag were seriously ill-used he could complain to the prefects, but to do so was squealing, and incurred contempt. Like all such systems it was conditioned by the people who practised it, and some fags had an easy time; it was even known for a fag-master to help a junior boy with his work. A few fag-masters were brutes, and a few fags lived in hell; the majority, like all slave classes, were genially derisive of their masters when they could get away with it, respectful when they had to be, and cleaned boots and put away laundry as badly as they could without incurring punishment. If the system taught them anything at all it was that all authority is capricious, but may be appeased by a show of zeal, unaccompanied by any real work.

Francis was assigned to a large boy named Eastwood, who came from Montreal, and who was on the whole good-natured and untroubled by intelligence. He was an officer in the Cadet Corps, and it was one of his fag's duties to polish the buttons on his uniform, and to bring his sword up to a high finish every Sunday night, ready for Monday's parade. Francis was never guilty of cheek; he allowed Eastwood to think that he admired him and took pride in his appearance on parade, and that did the trick. In his heart he thought Eastwood was a mutt.

Fagging had been good enough for your father, and it was therefore good enough for you. A certain amount of servitude and humiliation made a man of you. There may even have been some truth in this belief. Everybody ought to have some experience of being a servant; it is useful to know what virtually unlimited authority is like for those on the receiving end.

Francis was good enough at his work to escape any particular notice; he was always in the upper half of his form, undistinguished but respectable. He was able to hold his place, while having plenty of time to study the masters, whose personal character was often more educational than anything they taught.

It was on Prize Day that they presented the most interesting spectacle, when they appeared on the platform of the Prayer Hall in their gowns, beneath which they wore, in some cases, old-fashioned morning coats, preserved from far-off weddings. About half of them were Englishmen, and rather more than half were veterans of the recent war. They wore their medals of honour, some of substantial distinction. One or two limped; Mr. Ramsay had a wooden leg and walked with a clumping gait; Mr. Riviere had an artificial hand under a black glove; Mr. Carver had a silver plate in his head, and was known to have had spells when he climbed the water-pipes in his classroom and taught from that elevation. Their hoods were old and crumpled, but some of them were from ancient universities and spoke of a brilliance that had not brought any reward except a position as a schoolmaster. In the eyes of the boys as a whole, they were glorious; but to Francis there was an air of melancholy about them, for he was perhaps the only person in the Hall who saw what was in front of his nose, who really observed how they stood, and what their faces were really saying. Of course, he never spoke to anyone about what he saw.

His life held many secrets—things he could not talk about to anyone, although he had friends, and was passably well-liked. The religion of the School, for instance; it was a kind of middle-brow Anglicanism, not too heavily stressed because the School contained boys of all denominations, including several Jews, and some richly coloured boys from South America who were probably

Papists. The hymns were loud, chiefly unexceptionable admonitions to live decently and honourably, and the music to which they were sung was superior stuff from the Public School Hymnal—Holst, Vaughan Williams, and unsentimental tunes that would not have been strange to Luther. The Headmaster preached a short extempore sermon every Sunday night, and because he was a man whose enthusiasms sometimes outran his judgement, he was likely to say things which a more discreet man would have left unsaid. Musing on the theme of sin and perhaps forgetting where he was, he once quoted Nietzsche, declaring: "Sins are necessary to every society organized on an ecclesiastical basis; they are the only reliable weapons of power; the priest lives upon sins; it is necessary to him that there be sinning." Fortunately few boys were listening, and of those who were, few understood what he was saying. Francis may have been the only one of those who hugged this wisdom to his heart. But upon the whole the School's religion puzzled him. It seemed to lack heart. There was nothing in it of the mystery, the embracing warmth, the rich gravy of the religion of Mary-Ben. It was a religion well suited to Old Money and to the toadies of Old Money. It was a religion that Never Went Too Far.

Never too far. That was the constant admonition of Old Money and the toadies of Old Money. Those who had any pretension to classical education likened it to the Greek doctrine: Nothing in excess. Some, who had dabbled a little in Shakespeare, might say "Look that you o'erstep not the modesty of Nature". Of the blatant immodesty of Nature they had no conception. But Francis had; he had sensed it in the abyss that lay at his feet in Carlyle Rural, and in what he had seen of the exactions and vengeance of life among the corpses in Devinney's embalming room. Francis knew in his heart that life was broader, deeper, higher, more terrifying, and more wonderful than anything dreamed of by Old Money. A schoolboy is not supposed to know such things, and he scarcely admitted them even to himself. But they emerged, sometimes, in his drawings.

In the circumstances of life in a large boarding-school it is impossible to draw without being observed. As a fag he was required to do an extensive business in decorating raincoats; these were slickers made of yellow oilskin, on the back of which, between the shoulders, it was demanded that he draw a funny face, which was then shellacked, so that it was permanent. These raincoats were greatly prized. Two or three came dangerously near to being identifiable caricatures of masters; one in particular, a severe Scottish face with beetling brows and an extraordinary amount of hair growing from its nose, was certainly Mr. Dunstan Ramsay, the history master. Mr. Ramsay called Francis into his study one night after prayers.

"Caricature is a rare and fine gift, Cornish, but you ought to consider it carefully before it gets you completely in its grip. It's the exaggeration of what is most characteristic, isn't it? But if you see nothing as characteristic except what is ugly, you'll become a man who values nothing but ugliness, because it's his trade. And that will make you a sniggering, jeering little creature, which is what most caricaturists have been—even the best. There are some quite good art books in the library. Look at them, and learn something larger than caricature. Don't forget it, but don't make it the whole of what you can do."

Francis was glad not to be caned for *lèse-majesté* and super-cheek, and promised that he would look at the art books in the library. And there, in a not very extensive or distinguished collection, he found what he missed in the religion of the school.

As is likely to happen (to people who have a daimon) the discovery coincided with something else, not obviously related to it. The fags often sang, when they were mustered to haul the big roller over the cricket pitch, or sweep snow from the open-air hockey rink, and what they sang was what they liked, not what the music master made them sing in class; his taste was for "Searching for Lambs" and other folksongs he valued because they were in five-quarter time and demanded some musical skill. But the fags sang a sentimental song in waltz time that a few of them knew and the others quickly learned:

> To the knights in the days of old,
> Keeping watch on the mountain height,
> Came a vision of Holy Grail
> And a voice in the silent night,
> Saying—
> Follow, follow the gleam

Banners unfurled, o'er all the world;
Follow, follow the gleam
Of the chalice that is the Grail.

How many knew what the Grail was, or why it should gleam, does not matter. Francis knew, for he had read it in a book that came, of course, from Aunt Mary-Ben. The Grail was the Cup from which Christ had drunk at the Last Supper, and anybody lucky enough to catch sight of it was ensured a very special life forever after.

Among the art books recommended by Buggerlugs—which was what the boys called Mr. Ramsay—was one that dealt with the work of the Pre-Raphaelite Brotherhood, and in the illustrations—Francis did not bother much with the text—was something of the Grail in the light that shone from the eyes of the men, and the rich, swooning beauty of the women. It was a light that fed the hunger he felt because of the starved, wholly external religion of the school, and a lush depiction of Nature that balanced the world of wretched desks, spattered ink, chalk dust, constipating food, and the unceasing, unimaginative, perfunctory obscenity of schoolboys' talk. It was an enlargement that made even compulsory games and the Rifle Corps open up to a light that came from somewhere outside the school. And then the Headmaster, who kept his ears open, seized upon the slave-song of the fags and preached one of his Sunday-night sermons about the Grail, as a vision, an unresting aspiration, and with his usual fine disregard of probability urged the boys to read Malory at once, and to make the Grail quest a part of their own lives.

Francis hunted down *Le Morte d'Arthur* in the school library, and was soon compelled to recognize that it was a dense, intractable, difficult book and he could not get through enough of it to find the Grail or anything else he wanted. Nor was the encyclopedia more helpful, with its tedious explanation of where parts of the legend came from, and its dowdy, scholarly rejection of all the good stuff about Joseph of Arimathea and King Arthur—the stuff that fed his imagination and made the Grail a glowing reality. So he hugged the book about the Pre-Raphaelites, and kept it out of the library far longer than was permitted, even though nobody else wanted it. He considered stealing it, but a strong feeling from the Blairlogie past told him that A Certain Person would not like it—His wounds might even be reopened— and that a life of noble feeling could not be founded on a crime, especially a crime that would be so easily detected.

All boys were expected to be "keen". The most admired form of keenness was not obvious success, but pitting yourself against some form of school contest where you were not likely to succeed, but where your quality as "a good loser" might be seen and admired. Francis found it in the Oratory Contest.

Of course, nobody expected anything that could be seriously called oratory. To excel at verbal expression was a suspect gift. But a sufficient number of boys came forward every year who could force themselves to stand before an audience of the staff and their peers, and control their terror as they talked for ten minutes on a topic that was handed to them on a folded slip of paper by the Headmaster, who arranged that each contestant should have ten minutes in a secluded room—most certainly not the library—to collect whatever thoughts he might have. The slip handed to Francis read "The Gift of Sight".

That was why Francis mounted the platform and embarked with considerable confidence on a criticism of the portraits that hung on all four sides of the Prayer Hall. These were, he said, pictures that everybody in the school saw every day, but that nobody really was aware of except as interruptions of the walls. The pictures were not good as works of art, and if they were not good works of art, had they a place in an institution of education? Were they worthy of the finest school in Canada? (He thought this a fine touch, certain to please his audience.) He pointed out the low level of artistic competence they represented, and asked rhetorically if any of them were by painters who could be named by anybody in the audience? Two or three of them, he mentioned, were already flaking badly, although they could not be more than fifty years old, and it was clear that they had been done in inferior pigments. He was lightly jocose about the fact that the ample beard of one Headmaster of the nineteenth century was rapidly going green. He said that the painters had obviously been hacks or amateurs. He spent his last three minutes explaining how a painter of acknowledged genius, such as Michelangelo or Bou- guereau, would have presented these grave figures, making them not only records of Heads past, but vivid evocations of strong intelligence and character, and a daily refreshment to the eyes of the school. He sat down amid a heavy silence.

The Headmaster, in his judgement of the speeches, praised Cornish's obvious sincerity. But it was a boy who laboured mightily with "Sabbath Observance: For or Against", and who came down heavily for the closed Toronto Sunday, who was awarded the cup.

Afterward the Head said: "That was good, Cornish. Unexpected and I suppose true. But tactless, Cornish, tactless. There were two or three of our governors in the audience, and they didn't like it. You must be careful with words like 'hack': the world's full of hacks, unfortunately. You must learn to keep your claws in. But there was one Governor who thought you ought to have some recognition. So go to the school bookseller with a note I'll give you, and get yourself a book about art. But don't tell anybody how you came by it. That's an order."

That was the beginning of the substantial library about art in its various forms that was one of the valuable things Francis left behind him when he died. The bookseller, a kindly man, found him Burckhardt's *History of the Renaissance* for four dollars—it was illustrated, and thus expensive—and threw in a second-hand set of Vasari's *Lives of the Painters*, which was marked at a dollar-fifty, but which he reduced for a promising boy.

Francis obediently kept quiet about his special prize, but he could not avoid the reputation he now had for knowing about pictures, and being what some of the hostile masters hissingly condemned as an "ESS-thete". Francis had not heard the word before, though he knew what "aesthetic" meant; but it was plain from the way it was said that an "ESS-thete" was a pretty feeble chap, wasting his time on art when he ought to be building up his character and facing the realities of life—as the hostile masters, failures to a man, understood life. But not all the masters shared this view, and in particular Mr. Mills, the senior classics master, began to look on Francis with favour.

It was the same among the boys. Most of them thought that being interested in pictures was girls' stuff, and not even for the kind of girls they knew—girls who were simply themselves in a different biological package. Old Money girls, in fact. But there were others, including most of the Jews, who wanted to talk about art to Francis. Art as they understood it, that is to say.

For some years a few Canadian painters, who came to be called the Group of Seven, had been trying to reveal the Canadian landscape in a new way, seeing it freshly, and not as it would have appeared to an eye darkened by a nineteenth-century English landscape painter's notion of what Nature ought to be. Their work was of course much derided and they were thought to be outrageously modern, although they would not have seemed so to a European or an American critic. What the parents said was parroted by the children, and Francis was beset with "Whaddya think of the Group of Seven? My mother says it looks like what our Swedish cook used to paint on her day off. My father says he could do as well, if he had the time. I mean—look at it? Can you see Georgian Bay in it? My father says he's hunted through all that country every autumn since he was a boy, and he says he knows it better than any of those birds, and he never sees anything like that. Blue snow! I ask you!"

Francis gave non-committal answers, not because he had any interest in new painting, but because the world he wanted to paint was not the world of Nature but the world of his imagination, dominated by the Grail Legend. This was now the food upon which he fed his spirit, and so far as he retained any of the Catholicism Aunt Mary-Ben had bootlegged into his supposedly Anglican world, it was attached to what he knew about the Grail. That was almost entirely what he derived from Tennyson; if by chance he hit on anything that associated the great legend with the pre-Christian world he left it unread; what he wanted was the world of Rossetti, of Burne-Jones, of William Morris. It was not easy to be a Pre-Raphaelite in Canada in the third decade of the twentieth century, in a school that was cheerfully Philistine about art (though certainly not about scholarship), but in so far as it could be done, Francis did it.

This involved a certain amount of mental contortion, and even something approaching a double consciousness. To his school companions he was just Cornish, not a bad fellow, but with a bee in his bonnet about pictures. To his schoolmasters he was Cornish, a boy somewhat above the middle except in Classics, where he showed ability. To both companions and masters Francis paid his dues; he was mediocre at games, but he played, and he took part in enough other school activities to avoid being despised as a slacker; he worked conscientiously at his studies, was always top of his class in French (but this was discounted by the School, because he had been raised to speak French, which the School regarded less as a key to another culture than as an obstacle course and a brain-teaser), and was good in Latin and Greek, which were also brain-teasers. Nobody knew how his mind was seized by the heroes of Virgil and Homer, and how easy Classics became if you cared about what they said. It was a period when educators believed that the brain could be strengthened, like a muscle, by attacking and conquering anything it might at first find difficult. Algebra, geometry, and calculus were the best developers of mental muscle; to master them was really pumping iron; but Classics wasn't bad—indeed sufficiently repellent to the average boy's mind to rank as a first-rate subject of study. But the inner chamber of Francis's mind was dominated by the Grail, as it appeared to him to be—something fine, something better than his life at present could provide, something to be sought elsewhere, something that made sudden, fleeting appearances at home.

Whether Francis's parents neglected him is a matter about which there could be many opinions. They had left him for long periods in the care of his grandparents and Aunt Mary-Ben, but surely that was not neglect? They had not noticed that his schooling in Blairlogie had been at odds with his life at St. Kilda. They had sent him to Colborne College because it was the kind of school Sir Francis understood, without any consideration of what kind of school Francis might need. They had done everything for him that money could provide, and that they could imagine, but they had not seen much of him or given much thought to him. Their reason was, of course, the War, and the part Sir Francis had played in it as what would be called in a later, different war "a back-room boy", and the necessity for Mary-Jacobine to do what complemented her husband's career and augmented his position. Long after the War was officially over, these necessities seemed to prevail over any serious attention to Francis.

Did this make him feel neglected, rejected, bitter? Far from it. It made it possible for him to idealize his parents and love them as distant, glorious figures, quite apart from the everyday

world. At school, and at the expensive camps where he spent his
summers, he had always with him a folder in which were pictures
of his father, looking distinguished, and his mother, looking beautiful, and these were holy ikons that comforted and reassured
him when he doubted himself. And as the Grail took command
of his inner life, they were associated with it, not directly and
foolishly, but as the kind of people who made such splendour
possible and perpetuated it in the modern world.

When the business of the Cornish Trust required Sir Francis
to be in Canada for much of each year, his son saw him at weekends, talked with him, was sometimes taken for splendid meals
at his club, and was often shown his medals. But, as the Major
explained, medals were not the measure of a man's service; it was
what the chaps at the War Office and the Foreign Office thought
of you that established your true measure. It was the degree of
access you had to the People Who Really Knew. These people
were not named, but that was not because they had no reality,
for there was nothing of the phoney about the Major when it
came to his profession; these significant people were not named
because they were not in the limelight, although in a very real
sense they controlled the limelight and chose the people on whom
it should shine. These people were by no means all soldiers; some
of them were scientists, some were officially explorers, some were
dons. It was never said, but it was clear enough that the Major
was associated in some way with what was still called the Secret
Service. Secrecy was bred in Francis's bones.

As for his mother, she was a beauty, in a time before beauties
had become entirely professional beauties. It would have been
vulgar and un-Grail-like to say it, but she was a Society Beauty.

Being a beauty always means constellating some ideal related
to the historical period where it appears, and Mary-Jacobine, now
known as Jacko Cornish, was a Beauty of the Twenties. She did
not languish; she danced vigorously and joyously. She was not
swathed in embroideries; she wore tight sheaths that came barely
to her beautiful knees. Her figure was boyish but not flat or
muscular. She smoked a great deal, and had a variety of long
holders for her Turkish cigarettes. She drank cocktails to the
extent that made her laugh delightfully, but never until she hic-
cuped. Her hair was cut short in styles that had various names

from year to year, but were basically the Eton Crop. She used make-up, but her own high complexion made make-up an ornament rather than a disguise. Her underclothes were few, and although they were splendidly embroidered they were never so much so as to spoil the set of her wonderful frocks. Her scent was bought in Paris, and only somebody like the President of the Cornish Trust could have afforded it. She flirted with everybody, even her elder son.

For there was now a second son, old enough to be sent to the Lower School at Colborne, and he was Francis's brother Arthur. There was more than ten years between them, and Arthur did not figure largely in Francis's life, but he was a nice kid, and Francis was civil to him. Arthur was everything Francis was not, a noisy, exuberant, strong little boy, and a great success at school. If Francis had not sat on Arthur from time to time, for his soul's good, Arthur would have patronized Francis, whom he recognized with the instinct of his kind as the sort of fellow who would never be Captain of Games in the Upper School, which was the goal Arthur had set for himself, and which after the required number of years he attained. Francis never knew it—it was not proper that he should know it—but the Major thought more highly of Francis than he did of Arthur. The younger boy was the type who would some day be a good soldier, if he were so unlucky as to be involved in a war, but he was not a Secret Service type, and the Major rather suspected that Francis was precisely that.

It was in May 1929, when Francis was nineteen, going on twenty, that several matters which had been hanging fire resolved themselves.

The first came when he was training for Track, on the oval path that surrounded the school's main cricket pitch. Francis was a fair runner, but not a star. On this day he ran a few yards, felt short of breath, pressed on in the best School tradition, lost consciousness, and fell to the ground. Sensation! Boys collected; the drill-sergeant rushed up shouting, "Back, back all of you; give him air!", and when Francis came round, which he did in a few seconds, detailed four boys to take him up to the Infirmary, where Miss Grieve, the school nurse, packed him into bed at once. It was a Thursday, which was one of the days when the doctor visited the School; he listened to Francis's heart, looked grave to hide his want of opinion, and said that he would arrange a visit to a specialist, immediately.

The following morning Francis felt perfectly well, went to Prayers as usual, and was astonished when the Headmaster announced a list of awards, in which his name appeared as winner of the School Prize in Classics. He was also named as one of those who should report to the Head's secretary immediately Prayers were over.

"Oh, Cornish," said Miss Semple; "you're to be excused classes this morning. You're to go to the General Hospital to see Dr. McOdrum at ten. So you'd better hurry."

Dr. McOdrum was very important, but he worked in a mercilessly overheated, windowless little kennel in the basement of the big hospital, and was himself so pale and stooped and overburdened in appearance that he was a poor advertisement for his profession. He made Francis strip, hop up and down, pretend to run, step on the seat of a chair and then step down again, and finally lie on a cold, medical-smelling trolley while he went over him very carefully with a stethoscope.

"Aha," said Dr. McOdrum, and having delivered himself of this opinion, allowed Francis to go back to school, greatly puzzled.

As it was a Friday, and Francis was a prize-winner, he was given special leave to go home for the weekend. Ordinarily he would have had to wait until Saturday morning. So it was about five o'clock when he went into the new house in Rosedale, and made for the drawing-room, hoping there might still be some tea left. There he found his mother, kissing Fred Markham.

They did not start like guilty creatures. The smiling Markham offered Francis a cigarette, which he took, and his mother said, "Hello darling, what brings you home tonight?"

"Special leave. I won the Classics Prize."

"Oh, you clever creature! Kiss me, darling! This calls for a celebration!"

"Sure does," said Fred Markham. "White Lady, Francis?"

"Oh, Fred, are you sure? He doesn't have cocktails."

"Then it's time he started. Here you are, old man."

The White Lady was delicious, specially the white of egg part. Francis drank, chatted, and felt worldly. Then he went up to his room, dropped on his bed, and burst into tears. Mum! Imagine it, Mum! With Fred Markham, who had a gold inlay in one of his front teeth, and must be forty if he was a day! Mum—she wasn't a bit better than Queen Guenevere. But that would set Fred Markham up as Sir Launcelot, which was ridiculous. If Fred was anything, he was a base cullion, or perhaps a stinkard churl. Anyway, he was an insurance broker, and who did he think he was, getting fresh with Lady Cornish? But it had looked as if Mum were in on the kiss; she wasn't resisting, and maybe it wasn't the first. Mum! God, she must be almost as old as Markham! He had never before thought of his mother as anything but young. Older than he, but not in any exact chronological way.

The door opened and his mother came in. She saw his tears.

"Poor Francis," she said, "were you very surprised, darling? No need to be. Doesn't mean a thing, you know. It's just the way people go on nowadays. You wouldn't believe how things have changed, since I was your age. For the better, really. All that tiresome formality, and having to be old so soon. Nobody has to be old now, unless they want to. I met a man last year when we were in London who had had the Voronoff operation— monkey glands, you know—and he was simply amazing."

"Was he like a monkey?"

"Of course not, silly! Now give me a kiss, darling, and don't worry about anything. You're almost done with school, and it's time you grew up in some very important ways. Did you like the White Lady?"

"I guess so."

"Well, they're always rather strange at first. You'll get to like them soon enough. Just don't like them too much. Now you'd better wash your face and come down and talk to Daddy."

But Francis did not hurry to talk to Daddy. Poor Father, deceived like King Arthur! What did Shakespeare call it? A cuckold. A wittoly cuckold. Francis was not pleased with the part he had played in the talk with his mother; he should have carried on like Hamlet in his mother's bedroom. What had Hamlet accused Gertrude of doing? "Mewling and puking over the nasty sty" was it? No, that was somewhere else. She had let her lover pinch wanton on her cheek, and had given him a pair of reechy kisses, and let him paddle in her neck with his damned fingers. God, Shakespeare had a nasty mind! He must look *Hamlet* up again. It was a year since Mr. Blunt had coursed his special Lit. class through it, and Mr. Blunt had gloated a good deal over Gertrude's sin. For sin it was. Had she not made marriage vows as false as dicers' oaths? Well—must wash up and talk to Father.

Sir Francis was greatly pleased about the Classics Prize, and opened a bottle of champagne. Poor innocent, he did not know that his house was falling about his ears, and that the lovely woman who sat at the table with him was an adulteress. Francis had two glasses of champagne, and the White Lady was not altogether dead in his untried stomach. So it was that when Bubbler Graham phoned after dinner he was more ready to fall in with her suggestion that they should go to the movies than he would otherwise have been.

He still had to say where he was going at night, and what he was going to do.

"Bubbler Graham wants to go to the movies," he mumbled.

"And you don't want to? Oh, Francis, come off it! You don't have to pretend to Daddy and me. She's charming."

"Mum—is it all right for Bubbler to call me? I thought the boy was supposed to do the calling."

"Darling, where do you get these archaic ideas? Bubbler is probably lonely. Frank, give the prize-winner five dollars. He's going to have a night out."

"Ah? What? Oh, of course. Do you want the car?"

"She said she'd bring her car."

"There, you see? A thoroughly nice girl. She doesn't want you to carry all the expense. Have a marvellous time, darling."

Bubbler wanted to see a film with Clara Bow in it, called *Dangerous Curves,* and that was where they went. Bubbler had taken Clara Bow as her ideal, and in restless energy and lively curls she was a good deal like her idol. During the show she let her hand stray near enough to Francis's for him to take it. Not that he greatly wanted to, but he was rather in the position of the man upon whom a conjuror forces a card. Afterward they went to an ice-cream parlour, and sat on stools at the counter and consumed very rich, unwholesome messes of ice cream, syrup, and whipped cream, topped with fudge and nuts. Then, as they drove home through one of Toronto's beautiful ravines—which was certainly not on their direct route—Bubbler stopped the car.

"Anything wrong?" said Francis.

"Out of gas."

"Oh, come on! The tank registers more than half full."

Bubbler bubbled merrily. "Don't you know what that means?"

"Out of gas? Of course I do. No gas."

"Oh, you mutt!" said Bubbler, and rapidly and expertly threw her arms around Francis's neck and kissed him, giving a very respectable version of the way Clara Bow did it. But Francis was startled and did not know how to respond.

"Let me show you," said the practical Bubbler. "Now ease up, Frank; it isn't going to hurt. Easy, now." And under her instruction Francis showed himself a quick study.

Half an hour later he was decidedly wiser than he had been. At one point Bubbler unbuttoned his shirt and put her hand over his heart. Tit for tat. Francis opened her blouse, and after some troublesome rucking up of her brassiere, and accidentally breaking a strap on her slip, he put his hand on her heart, and his scrotum (if schoolboy biology were true) sent a message to his brain that was the most thrilling thing that he had ever known, because her heart lay beneath her breast, and although she was a girl of the twenties, Bubbler had a substantial breast, crushed and bamboozled though it was by a tight binder. His kisses were now, he felt, as good as anything in the movies.

"Don't snort so much," said the practical Bubbler.

When she dropped him at his house Francis said slowly and intently, "I suppose this means we're in love?"

Bubbler bubbled more than she had done at any time during a bubbling evening. "Of course not, you poor boob," she said. "It's just nice. Isn't it? Wasn't it nice, Frank?"—and she gave him another of her Clara Bow kisses.

Just nice? Frank prepared for bed, very much aware that he was "all stewed up" as Victoria Cameron would have put it. Bubbler had stewed him up, and to Bubbler it was just nice. Did girls really do all that—fumbling under the blouse and hot kissing— just because it was nice?

He was, after all, a Classics prize-winner. A line of Virgil rose in his mind—a line that Mr. Mills read with sad insistence:

Varium et mutabile semper
Femina

Even in his mind he was careful to get the arrangement of lines correct. *Fickle and changeable always is woman.*

Stewing, regretting, yearning for more but angry to have been used for somebody else's pleasure, Francis went to bed, but for a long time he could not sleep.

"FRANK, I'D LIKE YOU to have lunch with me at my club," said Sir Francis, when he met his son at breakfast.

His club was large, gloomy, untouched by any sort of modern taste, and extraordinarily comfortable. Ladies were not allowed, except on special occasions and under heavy restraints. His father ordered two glasses of sherry—not too dry—and Francis reflected that in his experience this was a weekend of heavy boozing.

"Now, about luncheon—what do you say to a bowl of oxtail, with grilled chops to follow and—Oh, I say, they've got tapioca pudding down for today. I always say, it's the best tapioca pudding I get anywhere. So we'll have that, and—waiter—a couple of glasses of club claret.

"This is a celebration, Frank. A celebration of your Classics prize."

"Oh—thanks, Father."

"A good sort of prize to get—what?"

"Well, lots of the fellows don't think much of Classics. Even some of the masters wonder what use it is."

"Pay no attention. Classics is good stuff. Anything that gives you a foot in the past is good stuff. Can't understand the present if you don't know the past, what? I suppose you'll do Classics at Spook? Or will you leave that till Oxford?"

"Oxford?"

"Well, I've always assumed you'd go to Oxford after you'd been to Varsity here. Of course, you must go here, and I suppose Spook's the best college for you. I mean, as I'm head of a big Canadian business, it wouldn't do to send you out of the country for your 'varsity work altogether. Spook, then Oxford. Give you lots of time."

"Yes, but oughtn't I to be getting on?"

"With what?"

"I don't know, yet. But everybody at school thinks he ought to get on with whatever he's going to do as fast as possible."

"I don't think what you're going to do needs to be hurried."

"Oh? What am I going to do?"

"What do you want to do?"

"I'd really like to be a painter."

"Excellent. Nothing wrong with that. That fellow who painted your mother—de Laszlo, was it?—he seems to do extremely well at it. Mind you, he has talent. Have you got talent?"

"I don't really know. I'd have to find out."

"Excellent."

"I thought perhaps you might want me to go into the business."

"Your grandfather doesn't think you're cut out for it. Neither do I, really. Perhaps Arthur will lean that way. He's more the type than you are. I'd thought that you might skip the business and have a look at the profession."

"I don't follow—"

"My profession. Let's not be coy about this. You know, or you probably guess, that I've been pretty close to Intelligence for the past while. Fascinating world. You don't know what I've done, and you shan't. I don't have to tell you that it's a matter of honour never to hint that I've even been near such work. The real work, I mean. People get wrong ideas. But I think you might have what's wanted, and this Classics prize is nearer to what's wanted than it would be in the financial game. But some of the best Intelligence men must be seen by the world to be doing something else— something that looks as if it took all their time. Being a painter would be very good cover. Able to mix widely, and people wouldn't be surprised if you travelled and were a bit odd."

"I've never thought about it."

"Just as well. People who dream about it and hanker for it are just bloody hell at it. Too much zeal. At best they're just gumshoe men—and women. You know you've got a heart?"

A heart? Did Father mean Bubbler Graham?

"I see McOdrum didn't tell you. Yes, you've got a dicky heart, it appears. Not bad, but you mustn't push yourself too hard. Now, that's just the thing for the profession. Anybody wants to know why you're loafing around, you must tell 'em you've got a heart, and most of 'em will assume you're a bit of an invalid. Loaf and paint. Couldn't be better. They thought I was just a soldier. Still do. Nobody expects a soldier to have any brains. Rather like being an artist."

"You mean—I'd be a spy?"

"Oh, for God's sake, Frank, don't use that word! That's Phillips Oppenheim stuff. No, no; just a noticing sort of chap who goes anywhere and does what he pleases, and meets all sorts of people. Not false whiskers and covering your face with walnut juice and letting on to be Abdul the Water-Carrier. Just be yourself, and keep your eye peeled. Meanwhile, go to Spook and then Oxford and pack your head with everything that looks interesting, and don't listen to fools who want you to do something that looks important to them. You've got a heart, you see."

"But what would I have to do?"

"I can't say. Perhaps just write letters. You know—friendly letters to chaps you know, about this and that. Mind you, I'm talking rather freely. There'd be nothing doing for a while. But you ought to meet some people, as soon as possible. I can arrange for you to meet them when you're in England this summer."

"Am I going to England?"

"Don't you want to?"

"Oh yes; it's just that I hadn't thought about it."

"It's time you met some of my people. I haven't said anything about it, Frank, because after all they're your mother's people, but there's more to you than just that lot at St. Kilda. I mean old Mary-Ben with her priests and her fusspot ways, and your grandmother—nice woman, of course, but she's going to end up like old Madame Thibodeau. There are other people in your life. You ought to meet my lot. We're half of you, you know. Maybe the half that will appeal to you more than the Blairlogie crowd."

"Did you hate Blairlogie, Father?"

"Not hate, exactly; I don't let myself hate any place where I have to be. But a little of Blairlogie was enough. Why do you ask?"

"I remember at the farewell party you gave at the hotel at Blairlogie, and you and Grandfather were the only men who wore evening dress, and Alphonse Legaré came up to you half-slewed and laughed in your face and struck a match on the front of your dress shirt."

"I remember."

"You didn't move an inch or bat an eye. But it was worse than if you had hit him, because you didn't think he was in the same world as you were. He couldn't touch you. I admired that. That was real class."

"Awful word."

"It's the word we use for the real goods. You had the real goods."

"Well—thanks, my boy. That's the profession, you understand. No losing your temper. No doing stupid things."

"Not even if your honour is affected? Not if somebody you trusted with everything turned out to be not worthy of it?"

"You don't trust people till you've learned a lot about them. Obviously you are thinking of someone. Who is it?"

"Father, what do you really think of Fred Markham?"

The Wooden Soldier rarely laughed, but he laughed now.

"He's good enough for what he is, but that isn't much. I think I know what's on your mind, Frank; don't let Fred Markham worry you. He's a trivial person, a kind of recreation for a lot of women. But he hasn't got what you call the real goods."

"But Father, I saw him—"

"I know you did. Your mother told me. She thought you were taking it quite the wrong way. People must have recreations, you know. Change. But a day on the golf-course isn't running off across the world. So don't worry. Your mother can take care of herself. And take care of me, too."

"But I thought—vows—"

"Loyalties, you mean? You find out that loyalties vary and change outwardly, but that doesn't mean they are growing weaker inwardly. Don't worry about your mother and me."

"Does that mean that Mother is just another form of what you call cover?"

"True, and not true. Frank—I don't suppose you know much about women?"

Who likes to admit he doesn't know much about women? Every man likes to think he knows more about women than his father. Frank would have bet that he had seen more naked women than his father had ever dreamed of, though he was not boastful about the quality of what he had seen. Those pallid figures at Devinney's. No beauty chorus. But Francis had long outgrown the ignorance of Blairlogie days; he knew what people *did*. Like animals, but love made it splendid. He thought patronizingly of poor Woodford at school, who had revealed during a bull-session that he thought children were begotten through a woman's navel! At seventeen! How they had kidded Woodford and pictured what it would be like on his wedding night! Francis knew all about the Particular that the encyclopedia and a lot of Colborne school-biology could tell him. And he knew anatomy, and could draw a woman without her skin on—out of a book. Father obviously meant intimacy with women, and Francis was aware that though he could draw quite a decent flayed woman he had never touched a warm one until Bubbler Graham had made it easy for him. The Wooden Soldier was going on.

"I've had quite a bit to do with women. Professionally, as well as personally. They can be useful in Intelligence work. D'you know, I even met the famous Mata Hari a few times. A stunner. Fine eyes, but chunkier built than they like 'em today. When they shot her at last she was forty-one—just about the age your mother is now and every bit as beautiful as your mother. In the profession, you know, their usefulness is limited, because it's all business with them, and they're always looking for a better deal. Now the men—lots of them are mercenary, of course, but some of the best will work for a cause, or love of country. I sometimes think a woman has no country; only a family. And of course there are the men who can't resist adventure. Not women, though they're often called adventuresses. They work with their bodies, you see, and of course their outlook is different. Mind you, I've met some astonishing women in the profession. Marvellous at code and cypher, but they're an entirely different sort—the puzzle-solving mentality. Those are the bluestockings; not usually very inter-esting as women. The adventuresses are bitches. Always on the take.

"Still—I didn't ask you here to talk about that. Just about women in general. My advice is: never have anything to do with a woman, high or low, who expects to be paid. They're all crooks, and unless you pay very high you're likely to end up with something you never wanted to buy. No pay: that's a good rule. I'd say—stick to widows. There are lots of them, especially since the War, and you don't have to go outside your own class, which is important if you have any real respect for women. Be generous, of course, and play decent and straight, and you'll be all right. That's that, I think. Now, what do you intend to do?"

"I don't think I know any widows."

"Oh, you will. But that's not what I meant. Will you go to England this summer? Spook in the autumn?"

"Yes, Father. It sounds great."

"Good. And when you're in England you'd better meet one or two of the chaps. I'll arrange it."

FRANK MISSED HIS CHANCE to ask his father about the Looner, said the Lesser Zadkiel.

—Did you think he had a chance? The Major was a very accomplished talker—which took the form of not seeming to be accomplished at all, but never losing his grip on the way things were going. He overwhelmed Francis with new ideas—the profession, going to England to meet the Cornishes, how to cope with women. With a glass of sherry and a glass of club wine in his unhabituated gizzard, Francis never had a chance to initiate any new subject, or challenge a long-held secret. You know about secrets: they grow more and more mysterious, then suddenly they crumple away and everybody wonders why they were ever secret. The secret of the Looner was some years behind him in Blairlogie, and Francis couldn't keep up with the extraordinary things his father was telling him—that he didn't much mind his mother kissing Fred Markham, that he had really been in the Secret Service, that widows were the thing. The Major was an old hand at important conversations.

FRANCIS SAT IN THE RUINS of the Castle of Tintagel, trying to think about King Arthur. This was holy ground, the very place in which Arthur was begotten by Uther Pendragon upon the beautiful Igraine, wife of the Duke of Cornwall. The enchanter Merlin had made that possible. But try as he would to think about the great story, all Francis could do was to look north-west over the heaving, gleaming sea from which came, so it seemed, all the

light of Cornwall. This sea-light, reflected back toward the sky as
if the sea itself had some source of light beneath it, had puzzled
and dominated him during the whole month he had spent with
the Cornishes of Chegwidden. The light gave new meaning to
the legends he had brought, as appropriate luggage for a Cornish
holiday. This was not the light of the pre-Raphaelite pictures, the
moony glow that bathed those impossibly noble men and per-
versely beautiful women; this was a world-light, a seemingly illimitable light that the sea, like a dull mirror, yielded in a form
so diffused that the whole peninsula of Cornwall was pervaded
by it, and although manifestly there were shadows to be seen,
nevertheless the light seemed to defy shadows, and cast itself on
every side of every object.

In this extraordinary, unfamiliar light—unfamiliar to Francis,
who had never lived near the sea—it was surely possible to plunge
oneself into the world of legend? Looking from this storied head-
land might one not imagine one saw the painted sails of the ship
that bore Tristan and Iseult toward their meeting with King Mark?
But try as he would to bully his thoughts into this legendary and
poetic mode, all Francis could think of was the Cornishes of
Chegwidden, and how odd they were.

Odd because they lived in this enchanted land, and appeared
to be utterly impervious to enchantment. Odd because they lived
where the saints of the ancient Celtic Church had proclaimed
Christ's gospel in a truly Celtic voice, long before the dark-
skinned missionaries of Augustine had come from Rome with
their Mediterranean Catholicism, to preach and impose belief
with all the fanaticism of their kind. Apparently the Cornishes of
Chegwidden had never heard of Celtic Christianity, or, if they
had, could not understand that it might be something more interesting than the Low Church faith of St. Ysfael, in whose parish
they lived and were the great folk. Surely the name of St. Ysfael
was Celtic enough and old enough to nudge the most sluggish
historical sense? The church had been there, in one form or
another, since the sixth century; they knew that. But what really
interested them was that in the nineteenth century a devout Cornish had contributed the thumping sum of five hundred pounds
to have St. Ysfael done up in the height of Victorian Gothic style,
and they were determined that not a brass ornament or an en-

caustic tile should be changed. There was a family story that this pious Cornish had caused a lot of old panelling—fifteenth-century or something of the sort—to be ripped out and burned, as rubbish, when the great work of restoration was done.

Odd because they seemed unaware that King Arthur might have ridden over what were now their own parklands, and that some of their oldest trees might have grown from grandacorns of trees under which the great King—the *dux bellorum* of the earliest records—had reined in his horse to rest and look about him in the mysterious light of the peninsula that was Cornwall. When Francis had mentioned this as a possibility, his uncle—who was named Arthur Cornish, of all things—had looked at him queerly and said that unquestionably there was a tree in the park that had been planted to celebrate the coronation of Queen Victoria, and it was coming into promising maturity, for an oak, at this very moment, having survived two serious periods of blight.

What really interested Uncle Arthur was something called the Local Bench, upon which he sat as a magistrate as every Cornish had done for as long as there had been a Bench, and which he was now disagreeably expected to share with tradesmen and even a local socialist, who could not understand that the essence of local justice lay in knowing the local people—which ones were decent folk and which were known poachers and riff-raff—and treating them accordingly. Uncle Arthur owned a good deal of property in lands and cottages, and it was on the rents of these that Chegwidden and all its ancient glory depended. If Uncle Arthur had ever heard of Oscar Wilde as anything but a damned bad type who would have received no mercy from the Local Bench, he had certainly never heard Wilde's comment that land gives one position and prevents one from keeping it up. He would have agreed that there, at least, the bugger knew what he was talking about. The merciless exactions of modern government on landowners was his favourite topic, and if any of his kin had ever heard the word paranoia, they might have recognized that on this theme Uncle Arthur was distinctly paranoid. Modern government, he was sure, was a gigantic plot to ruin him, and in him all that was best in rural England.

His wife, Aunt May, would have described herself with appropriate modesty as a religious woman, for the doings of the parish and the services at St. Ysfael's were her chief concern. Helping the poor, so far as the waning fortunes of the Cornishes would allow, and a repressive hand on any clergyman who showed a tendency to be High, were her great cares. What she believed, nobody knew, for she was firm in her reticence on all matters relating to the inner life. In church she was seen to pray, but to What, and what she said to It, and how It worked in her daily life, nobody knew. The chances were strong that she prayed for her son Reginald, who was with his regiment in India, and her son Hubert, who was in the Navy and hoped for a command soon, and her daughter Prudence, who had married Roderick Glasson, another oppressed neighbouring squire. Unquestionably she prayed for her tribe of grandchildren, but how efficacious such prayers were was a matter of speculation, for they were a wild lot and gave Francis a good deal of trouble.

He never, during his month at Chegwidden, got them properly sorted into families, for they came and went inexplicably, roaring in and out of the house with cricket bats and bicycles, and small guns, if they were boys. As for the girls, they were doing their uttermost, it seemed to the quiet Canadian, to get themselves killed, riding ponies in a horrible parody of polo, which they played in a meadow full of rabbit holes, so that the ponies were always stumbling, and the girls were always pitching over their heads into the path of other charging ponies. They all regarded him as a huge joke, even when he tried to impress them with his skill (learned at an expensive boys' camp) in making a fire without matches. Because of this they called him the Last of the Mohicans, and treated his enthusiasm for King Arthur as a form of American madness. He never could be sure whose were Reginald's, and whose Hubert's, though he knew that two of the girls must be Prudence's, because they assured him daily that if their older sister, Ismay Glasson, could only meet him, she would soon put him to rights. They were very proud of Ismay because she was a Terror, even among the Chegwidden lunatics. But Ismay was abroad, staying with a French family to improve her accent, and doubtless terrorizing the French.

At the family table, over bad food in restricted quantities, Francis had tried to introduce some topic that would reveal whether or not the Chegwidden Cornishes knew what a great man his father was, and how intimate he was with the Chaps Who Knew, up in London. But he discovered that Sir Francis was merely a younger brother, so far as Uncle Arthur was concerned, and that in Aunt May's mind it was a pity that if there had to be a Lady Cornish at all, that Lady Cornish should be an American—for the Cornishes were pig-headedly determined that the pretence of Canadians not to be Americans was sheer affectation, to be rebuked whenever possible. As for the fortune that the Wooden Soldier had acquired by his marriage and his value as a trust company figurehead, it was plainly a sore touch at Chegwidden; to be a younger son, and to have money, when the elder son was struggling to keep his head above water, was intolerable cheek. So Francis was made to feel that he was not only the Last of the Mohicans, but a Rich American. He was sure the Chegwidden Cornishes did not mean it unkindly; it was simply that their excellent manners were not strong enough to keep their jealousy in complete abeyance.

From the family table Francis sometimes lifted his eyes above his plate of congealing mutton stew to look at the family portraits that hung above the wainscot. They were, he had to admit, ghastly. They were worse, because older and more blackened and scabby, than the portraits in the Prayer Hall at school. But out of them all, though the form varied, stared the family face, a long, horsy face with gooseberry eyes in which, in some portraits, a distinction, an air of intelligence and command, showed itself. As he looked around the table, at Uncle Arthur and at the grandchildren (for of course Aunt May did not count, being a mere breeding machine in the great complex of Cornishes), that face, disappointed and severe in Uncle Arthur, and peering through puppy-fat, or schoolboy awkwardness, or under ill-braided pigtails, was repeated in a variety of styles, but always, in form and mannerism, the same. And, when he went to bed in his chilly room, he could see, in the whorled mirror, that even under the black hair he had from the McRorys, it was his own face, and that his black hair and his gooseberry eyes gave him a look which would some day be startling.

Chegwidden: a disappointment, really. After all he had suffered because of that difficult name, which was not only queer in itself but a nuisance in pronunciation, he had at least expected an impressive dwelling and, as the name suggested, a white building. But no: Chegwidden was a large, low grubby-looking mansion of brownish-grey stone, with a lowering, unfriendly front door, pinched little windows, and a slate roof on which moss grew in patches. Old it unquestionably was; such inconvenience could not have been achieved in anything less than four centuries. Smelly it was, too, for a much-tinkered Victorian system of plumbing had never really come to terms with what was demanded of it. As it seemed to be a family habit never to throw anything away, it was cluttered with furniture and ornaments, pride of place being given to things that various Cornishes had brought home from military or naval service abroad. But the total effect was faded, down-at-heel, uncomfortable, and valetudinarian. School had habituated Francis to shabbiness and discomfort and stinks, but his notion of a family dwelling was the rich, velvety ugliness of St. Kilda, or his mother's uncompromisingly fashionable house in Toronto. How did the Cornishes put up with a house where every chair, in the midst of summer, embraced the sitter like a cold sitzbath, and every bed was dank from the sea mists?

Yet Father had assured him that at least half his root was here.

Try as he might, he could not evoke King Arthur, even in the ruins of Tintagel. He bicycled back through Camelford to Chegwidden, glad that tomorrow he could return to London, and after a few days take ship for Canada.

"DID YOU ENJOY your visit to Cornwall?"

"Thank you, sir. It was very interesting."

"But not enjoyable?"

"Oh, very enjoyable. But I thought people living there would have been more aware of the history of the place."

"The Cornishes *are* the history of the place. I suppose they think of history as something that happens elsewhere. A bit provincial, was it?"

"I wouldn't like to say that."

"You're a cautious fellow, aren't you, Francis?"

"I don't like to make hasty judgements. This is my first time in England, you see."

"But it certainly won't be your last, your father tells me. Going up to Oxford eventually?"

"That's the plan."

"By that time you might be quite a useful chap. Your father tells me you might end up in the profession."

So that was what it was! That was why Colonel Copplestone had asked him to lunch in the Athenaeum, an impressive club in the West End, though certainly not much ahead of Chegwidden in the matter of food. Francis had been expecting something like this, Colonel Copplestone must be one of the Chaps Who Knew.

"Father spoke about it."

"And you liked the idea?"

"I was flattered."

"Well—no promises, of course. Just follow your nose. But we're always on the lookout for promising young men, and if they're promising enough, we might make a few promises later on."

"Thank you, sir."

"Are you a letter-writer?"

"Sir?"

"Write interesting letters, do you? If you're really interested, I want you to write letters to me."

"What about?"

"About what you're doing—and seeing—and thinking. I'd like a letter from you not less than once a fortnight. Write to me at this address; it's my country place. And in the letters you address me as Uncle Jack, because I'm an old friend of your father's, and that's appropriate. I'm your godfather."

"Are you, sir? I hadn't known."

"Neither had I, till I met you today. But that's what I am now. So you write to me as a godfather, which is a very good relationship, because it can mean nothing very much, or quite a lot. Just one thing, though; don't mention that your father, or your godfather, has anything whatever to do with the profession."

"I'm not really very sure what the profession is."

"No, of course not. For the present, it's just the profession of men who follow their noses and see whatever's to be seen. I don't think we want any blancmange, do you? Let's take our mud coffee upstairs."

Dear Uncle Jack:

Cornwall was really great, but I liked London better. I have never seen such pictures before. Our gallery in Toronto is small, and not very good, because we have no money to buy the really first-rate pictures. Not yet. Maybe it will come. I am trying now to find out about the new pictures, by the new men, and I went to as many private galleries in London as I could, and saw a lot of stuff that puzzled me. I might as well tell you, though, that the people who ran the galleries, or perhaps I should say the young men who showed off the pictures to possible buyers, were as interesting as the pictures themselves. They are so *silky,* and they talk so easily about tactile values and *nouveau vague,* and a lot of things that were away over my head. I hadn't really understood what an ignoramus I am.

I've read a bit about the new stuff. Quite a lot, really. And I understand (or think I do) that a picture shouldn't really be *about* anything. Not like those awful pictures that tell a story, or show upper-class kids feeding robins in the snow, or show you Hope, or the Soul's Awakening or something that is intended to make you feel religious, or wistful. No, a picture is just patterns of line and colour arranged on a flat surface, because it's no good kidding yourself that it isn't flat, is it? I mean, perspective is all very fine if it's mathematics, but if it tries to kid you that you are looking into depth it's a cheat. Pictures are pure form and colour. Anyway, that's what the new books say, and certainly that is what the silky chaps in the galleries say. Nix on emotion. Perhaps even nix on meaning anything except what is in front of one's nose.

The trouble is that in some of the best of the new stuff emotion and meaning keep breaking in. Like this chap Picasso. I saw some of his stuff at one of the galleries, and if it's just form and colour on a flat surface, I'm dreaming. It's a statement of some sort. Not that I could tell you what the statement is, but I'm sure it's there, and I'm sure that if I can stick with it long enough, I'll find the meaning.

And Old Masters! Of course I've done my best with the new painting, but I admit I liked the Old Masters best. I think I know why. As you know, I was raised a Catholic—or perhaps not exactly *raised* one but a lot of Catholicism was bootlegged into my early days by a great-aunt, and unless I can drain every drop of it out of me—and I don't seem to have much luck doing that—those Nativities and Adorations and Crucifixions and Transfigurations can never be simply clever arrangements of line, volume, and colour for me. They are statements, some strong, some not so strong, some fancy, some terribly plain. Were the old boys wrong? I try to think so, but it won't work.

You are partly to blame, godfather. You say follow your nose, and if I do it takes me in some very unmodern and unfashionable directions. If I'm to see pictures the modern way, and no other way, I guess I'll have to cut off my nose. And that would spite my face, wouldn't it?

I don't intend to spite my face, ever, or turn my back on old friends. Do you know of a caricaturist and illustrator called Harry Furniss? I owe a lot to him, or I should say to a book of his that was my Bible for a while. The other day, in a shop that sells drawings and pictures, I found an original sketch of an actor called Lewis Waller (never heard of him) by H.F. and I bought it, just for old sake's sake, for ten pounds. Which is pretty steep for my pocket. But I couldn't resist it. Just to have something H.F. had touched. How the silky boys would despise it, but it's a wonder of artistic economy.

I have sore feet from trudging through the National Gallery, the Tate, the Wallace, the Victoria and Albert. All full of marvels. And what do you think? I have a favourite picture! I know I shouldn't, and crushes on works of art are the worst kind of amateurism, but it absolutely stuns me. In the Nat. Gal. a big picture called *An Allegory of Time* by Bronzino; 1502-72 it says and otherwise I know nothing about him. But what a statement! And what is the statement and what is the allegory? I stare and stare and can't figure it out.

Do you know it? What hits you first is the nude figure of a beautiful woman, superbly fleshly and naked as a jaybird except for a coronet of jewels. I mean she isn't just nude, which can be like a corpse on the embalmer's table, but astonishingly naked. A youth who looks about fourteen stoops toward her from the left, kissing her, and it's plain that her tongue is pushing between his lips—French kissing they call that, godfather—and if they are really mother and son it's a pretty queer situation; furthermore his right hand is on her left breast, the nipple peeping between his index and second fingers, which it wouldn't do unless the kiss meant more than just good-morning or something like that. His left hand is drawing her head toward him. On the right a stout baby, with a knowing smile, is winding up to throw some roses over them. So far, so good. But a vigorous, muscular old man, looking as though he wasn't very pleased by the goings-on, is either drawing a blue curtain over this scene, or else he is revealing it. Can't be sure. A woman is helping him, only her head visible, but beneath her and just behind Cupid's out-thrust rump is another woman whose face is torn with pain—is it? or could it be jealousy? Behind the fat baby is a creature with a childlike but not an innocent face, and the body attaching to it ends in a serpent's tail and the terrible feet of a lion. Two masks, one young and one old, lie on the ground.

What do you make of that fine thing? God only knows, at present, but I mean to make it my business to know, because it's saying something, just as my great-aunt's awful, skilful pictures of Cardinals joking and boozing say something. Those are saying that the Church is powerful and classy, but Bronzino says—something about a very different world, and a world I want to learn about. Nobody is going to tell me it's just an arrangement of form and colour. It's what my great-aunt calls A Good Lesson.

I am learning fast. I have already caught on that Bouguereau wasn't really a great painter, though he was an astonishing technician. Bought another drawing yesterday, just some scratches of the Virgin and Child, with a scribble that might be one of the Magi. Cost me twenty-five pounds and I shall not be eating at the Café Royal tonight I assure you. But I'm sure it's a Tiepolo. Maybe School Of.

Off on the boat-train in the morning. It was wonderful to
see you. Shall write again soon.

Yr. affct. godson

Frank

Not bad for a lad of nineteen, thought Colonel John Copplestone, as he tucked the letter into a newly opened file.

BY THE TIME FRANCIS had completed four years at the College
of Saint John and the Holy Ghost (irreverently called Spook by
all students and by faculty members when they were not obliged
to be on their best behaviour) in the University of Toronto, the
file in Colonel John Copplestone's study was a fat one, and there
was an additional file, not so fat, in which the Colonel's old friend
and an honoured member of the profession who simply signed
himself J.B. reported now and then on things which Francis might
not have told his godfather. J.B. was officially the Warden of the
Students' Union at the University of Toronto, but he was a great
letter-writer, and although most of his letters were simply dutiful
communications with his aged mother in Canterbury, quite a few
of them went to Colonel Copplestone, and some of these went
farther still, to the Chaps Who Knew. Even in a trusted, if not
beloved, Dominion, things may happen about which inside information is welcome to the Secret Service of the mother country,
and J.B. supplied a good deal of it.

His comments on Francis, boiled down, would not have seemed
particularly significant unless one happened to be recruiting for
the profession. Francis was fairly well liked, but was not one of
the most popular undergraduates; nothing of the Big Man on
Campus about him. He seemed not to have much to do with
girls, although he was not indifferent to them. On the other hand,
his friendships with young men were not intense. Francis had
made one or two attempts to appear in productions at the University Theatre, and was a wooden, disastrous actor, his black
hair and green eyes making him look odd under theatre circumstances. Outside his studies he did not cut much of a figure, but
he was a surprisingly useful member of the Union Pictures Com-

mittee; he could spot a good thing, and urge that it be bought, when the other undergraduates who worked with J.B. simply didn't know their Picassos from a hole in the ground. Francis was already buying Canadian pictures for himself in the twenty-five-to hundred-dollar range. Though he came of a rich family he didn't have a lot of money to throw around, and once J.B. had asked him why he was wearing no overcoat on a sub-zero day, to be told that Francis had hocked his coat to buy a Lawren Harris that he couldn't resist. He hoarded what money he had in order to buy pictures. Spent none of it on himself, and had the reputation of being "close" with money, which probably accounted for his lack of contact with girls, who are great eaters and drinkers. He drew a good deal, and had decided talent as a caricaturist, but for some reason didn't choose to exploit it; nevertheless the caricaturist's gleam was often seen in his green eye, when he thought nobody was looking. Did pretty well in his studies, and astonished everybody when at the end of his fourth year he took the Chancellor's Prize in Classics, even though Classics wasn't in vogue. This would give him a good push forward at Oxford, and J.B., who had drag at Oxford, would see that it did not go unheeded.

A candidate for the profession? Possibly. The Oxford days would tell, thought Colonel Copplestone. After all, the boy was still only twenty-three.

DURING THE SUMMER before his departure for Oxford, Francis paid a visit to Blairlogie. He might not have thought of doing so if his mother had not urged him to make the effort. The people there are getting old, she said; you see Grand-père now and then, but Grand'mère and Aunt have not seen you for—oh, more than ten years. It's the least you can do, darling. So, in hot August weather, off he went.

The journey, once he had left the main line and taken the train which struck northward toward Blairlogie, seemed to be almost violent in its reversal of time. From the excellent modern train in which, because his parents had paid for his ticket, he travelled in the chair-car, which had radio earphones at every seat, he changed to a primitive affair in which an ancient, puffing engine pulled a baggage coach and one passenger coach at a stately twenty miles an hour through the hinterland. The passenger coach was old without being venerable; it had a great deal of fretwork ornamentation in wood that had once been glossy, but the green plush seats were mangy and slick, the floor was poorly swept, and it stank of coal-dust and long use. Because of the heat the windows that would still open were opened, and grit and smoke from the engine occasionally swept through the car. There were stops at tiny stations in the middle of nowhere, usually in order that some small piece of freight might be unloaded. There were other stops in order that the journal-boxes might cool; the train was prone to that plague of old running-stock, the hot-box.

At noon the train halted in the midst of rocky scrubland where there was not a roof in sight. "If any of yez haven't brought yer lunch, yez can get dinner up on the hill at th' old lady's. Costs a quarter," said the conductor, and himself led a small procession up the hill where, in the old lady's kitchen, chunks of fat bacon and fried potatoes were ready on the back of the wood-stove; on top of each plate of meat was laid a slab of rhubarb pie. The etiquette, Francis saw, was to remove the pie delicately (so as not to break it) and lay it on the pine table beside the plate, until the latter had been cleared and wiped with a chunk of bread; then the pie was lifted back to the plate to be devoured with the well-sucked fork, and washed down with the old lady's coffee, which was boiling hot, but not strong. Fifteen minutes were allowed for this repast, and when the conductor rose everybody rose, and put a quarter into the hand of the unsmiling, unspeaking old lady. The conductor, it seemed, did not pay; he led his pilgrims in single file down the hill to the waiting train. The engine-driver and the fireman (who doubled as a brakeman) had eaten thriftily from lunch-boxes by the side of the line. They clambered back into the cab, belching enjoyably, and the train resumed its sleepy, stately course.

Late in the afternoon the conductor tramped importantly through the car, shouting, "Blairlogie! End of the line! Blairlogie!", as if some passengers could possibly have been in doubt about the matter. Then the conductor hastened to be first off the train and was well away up the street toward his home before Francis could get his suitcase down from the overhead rack, and set foot once again in the place of his birth.

Blairlogie had changed, if the old train had not. Few horses were to be seen on the streets, and some of the streets themselves had been paved. Shops bore different names, and the Ladies' Emporium, where Grand'mère had always bought her hats (because the Misses Sim, though Protestants, had undoubtedly the best taste, and the deftest hands with artificial cherries and roses, in town), had vanished altogether, and weeds grew where it had stood. There was a movie-house, too, which seemed to mean that a gaudy front had been stuck on a failed grocery-store. The McRory Opera House, farther up the street, was closed, and had an offended, snubbed look. Trees were taller but buildings were smaller. Donoghue's blacksmith-shop was not to be seen and, most significant change of all, a motor truck laden with cut timber was making its way up the street, and the name on its side was not his grandfather's name.

But when he got away from the business street and up the hill, St. Kilda looked as it always had looked, and when he rang the bell it was undoubtedly Anna Lemenchick, though broader and seemingly shorter, who answered. She said nothing—she never did say anything when she answered the door—but there was a scampering upstairs, and Aunt Mary-Ben came rattling down, rather dangerously on the polished hardwood, and threw herself at him. She was so tiny; had he really grown so much?

"Francis! Dear, *dear* boy! How big you are! Oh, and so handsome! Oh, Mother of God, isn't this a happy day! Did you take the taxi? We'd have sent, only there's nobody to send just now— Zadok in hospital and all. Oh, what will Grand'mère say when she sees you! Come, come right away and see her, Frankie, my own dear. It'll do her more good than anything!"

Grand'mère was in bed, a mountain of flesh, but yellow and sour-smelling. Conversation with her was in French, because she found English an effort now. She was considerably younger than the Senator—who was, as usual, away in Ottawa, or in Montreal, or in Toronto, on some business or other—but chronology had nothing to do with what ailed her, and she might have been ten years older than her real age, which was sixty-eight.

"Dr. J.A. is reserved about dear Marie-Louise," said Aunt Mary-Ben, as she and Francis ate the bad dinner that evening. "We fear what's wrong, of course, but he won't be plain about it. You remember how he always was. You can't undo nearly seventy years of overeating, he says. But could hearty eating really bring on *that?* I pray for her, of course, but Dr. J.A. says the age of miracles is past. Oh, Frankie, Frankie, it's a dreadful thing, but we must all go in the end, mustn't we, and your dear Grand'mère has led such a *good* life—not a thing to reproach herself with—so though it's hard for us, we must bow to His will."

The ruling passion, it appeared, was still strong. That night Francis played for three hours with Aunt and Grand'mère, who could summon up spirit for the game. It was euchre. The deck of thirty-two cards was ready when they went upstairs, and on and on, remorselessly and almost without speaking, they played hand after hand. Francis, as the least experienced, was euchred again and again, and he could not but notice that frequently his grandmother's hand would disappear beneath the covers, presumably to press some aching part or to ease her bedgown, and when it reappeared—could that have been the flash of a card that had not been there before? An unworthy thought, and he pushed it down, but not quite out of sight. Mary-Ben was willing enough to lose, but Francis had not come to the time of life when he understood that winning is not always a matter of taking the trick.

As they parted at bedtime, he whispered to Aunt, "What's the news of Madame Thibodeau?"

"She doesn't get out much now, Francis; she's become so stout you see. But she's wonderful. Stone deaf, but she plays cards three times a week. And wins! Oh dear me, yes; she wins! Eighty-seven, now."

WHERE WAS VICTORIA CAMERON? Who was caring for the Looner?

It appeared that Aunt had been forced to get rid of Victoria Cameron. She had kicked over the traces just once too often, and Aunt had turned her out lock, stock, and barrel. She had not been replaced as cook, but Anna Lemenchick did her best, helped out by old Mrs. August's youngest girl, who was willing, though not very bright. Anna's best was not good, but with poor Marie-Louise reduced to a diet of liquids, Aunt had no heart to look for another first-rate cook, in spite of her brother's urging. It seemed heartless, didn't it, to hire somebody to cook dishes poor Grand'mère could not hope to taste?

Francis was still incapable of telling Aunt that he knew about the Looner, but on his first night at St. Kilda he crept upstairs while he knew Aunt would be busy on her prie-dieu. All the curtains that had deadened sound were gone. Nobody slept up there because Anna Lemenchick came by the day. He tried the door of the room which had once been hospital and madhouse and prison, but it was locked.

In his childhood room, which seemed to have lost substance, like everything else at St. Kilda, Francis caught sight of himself as he undressed, in the long mirror before which he had once postured in a mockery of women's attire. A young man, with hair on his chest and legs, black curls clustering about his privates; moved by an impulse he could have denied, but to which he yielded, he once again drew the bed cover about him and looked at what he saw—looked hungrily for the girl who should have been behind the mirror, but was not. Where was she? He had not found her in any of the girls with whom, at Spook, he had sought her. She must be somewhere, that girl from the world of myth, from the real Cornwall of his imagination. He would not believe it could be otherwise. But the consequence of his gazing brought on such arousal that he had to "choke the ghost", which was school slang for masturbation. As always, the act brought relief and disgust, and he fell asleep in a bad temper. He didn't want crushes and affairs and the student amusements he heard so much about at Spook. He wanted love. He was twenty-three, which he thought very old to be without love, and he wondered what could possibly be the matter with him, or with his fate, or whatever decreed such things. Hell!

He had no trouble, the next morning, in finding Victoria Cameron. She was smack in the middle of the main street, in a small shop which said, over the door, CAMERON FANCY BAKED GOODS, and inside she stood behind the counter amid a profusion of her best work.

"Well, you never thought leaving your grandfather's house would be the ruin of me, did you, Frankie? It's been the making of me. Dad and the boys baking the bread as always, and me making the fancy stuff here, we're doing a land-office business, let me tell you. No, I'm not married, nor will I ever be, though it's not for want of offers, let me tell you. I've better things to do than slaving for some man, and you can bet on that."

"Zadok? That's a sad story. He wanted to marry me, but can you imagine that? I told him straight: Not as long as you do what you do at Devinney's, I told him, and don't give it up, because I wouldn't marry you even if you gave it up. I'm too fond of my own way, I said. But it hurt him. You could see that. I don't pretend that was all of it, but it may have been part of it.

"I think it was that poor boy's death that hit him hardest. You hadn't heard about that? No, I don't suppose there'd be anybody tell you. Zadok felt he'd done it, in a way."

A pause, during which a group of customers, who looked curiously at Francis, were accommodated with a half-dozen of lemon-curd tarts, another half-dozen of the raspberry tarts, two lemon pies promised for a wedding anniversary, and a big bag of cream puffs. Not to speak of two crusty white and two brown and two raisin loaves. When this press of business was completed, Victoria continued. "Zadok was always one for his beer, you remember. And after I told him flat there was nothing doing so far as I was concerned he took to bringing it up to that room on the top floor, to drink while he sang to Frankie—the other Frankie. You know, Francis, he loved that boy. You might almost have thought he was his own. Zadok had a heart in him, you've got to give him that. I didn't like him bringing in the beer, but I couldn't have stopped it without more trouble than it seemed to me to be worth. And I think there was some spite in it. Men are funny, you know, Francis. I think Zadok wanted to show me that if I wouldn't have him, he'd go to the Devil, hoping maybe I'd change my mind to save him. But I wasn't raised to think you can save people. If they can't save themselves—that's to say, as far as anybody *can*—nobody else can do it for them. We all have our fate to live out, and I knew it wasn't my fate to save Zadok. So he'd drink a lot, and get silly, and drink healths to Frankie, and Frankie knew something cheerful and jolly was meant, and he'd laugh in that sort of lingo that was all he could manage. But I was firm on the one thing: I wouldn't let Zadok give Frankie any of the beer.

"Probably that's what did it. Instead of beer, Frankie drank a lot of water. Harmless, wouldn't you say? He'd just piss it into his diaper, and no harm done. But one night Zadok and I had a real knock-down row, because he was drinking more than usual and making too much noise, and at last I walked out on the two of them and told Zadok he could get Frankie ready for sleep by himself.

"Of course I knew he couldn't. The boy relied on me to get him ready for the night, and I wouldn't fail him. So after an hour or so, when I knew Zadok had gone, I went in to settle Frankie down, and I did, but I thought he looked a little queer, and he was heavy to lift. In the morning he was dead.

"Do you know what it was? *Drownded!* I had to get the old Aunt, and she sent for Dr. J.A., and after he looked at Frankie he said that was what it was. Drownded! You see, that poor boy wasn't like other people. There was some gland right in the top of his head that wasn't right, and when he went on that water toot with Zadok he must have drunk about—I don't know—gallons maybe, and it was more than he could stand. The doctor said some of it must have got into his blood, and then into his lungs, and he drownded. The doctor called it pulmonary oedema. I've remembered it, because—well, you wouldn't expect me to forget it, would you? So there had to be another funeral at night, though there was no priest this time, and now there really is a Frankie under that stone that was a fake for so long.

"No, they didn't tell your parents. In fact, your mother never knew what was up there in the attic all those years. But your grandfather knew, of course, and he and Dr. J.A.—well, it'd be hard to say exactly what happened. They were both relieved, but it wouldn't have done to let that show. I knew some money changed hands, to make sure Zadok kept his mouth shut. And in an awful way I suppose it was gratitude.

"The money was the end of him. Drank worse and worse, and his work at Devinney's suffered; he did some jobs that scared the bereaved when they looked into the coffins—all swollen around the face, and a kind of boiled colour. So Devinney had to get rid of him. And the upshot of that was that he fell down drunk one winter night in the lane behind Devinney's—because he had a sort of unnatural pull toward the place—and nearly froze, and they had to take both his legs off, and even at that they don't seem to have been able to stop the gangrene. He's up in the hospital now. It would be kind of you to go and see him. Yes, I go, once a week, and take a few tarts and things. That hospital food is worse than Anna Lemenchick's.

"After poor Frankie was buried for the second time I didn't last a week at St. Kilda. One morning the old Aunt and I went right to the mat, there in the kitchen, and she told me to go. Go, I said! It's you that'll go if I leave this kitchen! You and the Missus cramming yourselves at every meal worse than Zadok and his beer! Don't think you're firing me! I'm the one that's doing the firing! Just see how you get along without me! *You pair of old stuff-puddings!* That was common of me, Francis, but I was worked up. Not even your grandfather could persuade me to stay after that. How could I stay in a place where I'd showed myself common?"

Francis knew that something had to be said, and though it is not easy for young people to say such things, he said it.

"Victoria, I don't suppose anybody will ever know what you did for that fellow—Francis the First, I call him—but you were wonderful, and I thank you for him, and for everybody. You were an angel."

"Well, I don't see any need to get soft about it, Francis. I did what had to be done. As for thanks, your grandfather was very generous when the parting came. Your grandfather sees farther than most people. Who do you suppose is paying for Zadok in the hospital? And the money that allowed me to set up this place was a gift from him."

"I'm glad. And you can play the tough Presbyterian all you please, Victoria, but I'll go right on thinking of you as an angel." And Francis kissed her soundly.

"Frank—for Heaven's sake! Not in the shop! Suppose somebody saw!"

"They'd think there were more tarts in here than the ones in the showcase," said Francis, and dodged through the door as the outraged Victoria called after him.

"That's quite enough of that sort of talk. You're worse than Zadok."

WAS IT POSSIBLE to be worse than Zadok? When Francis visited
him in the hospital later that day it seemed that Zadok's decline
could not be equalled. The ward was hot and stuffy; there were
no patients in the other two beds, so Francis could talk freely to
the wasted trunk that lay in the bed nearest the window, with a
kind of cage under the sheet to lift it from where the legs had
once been. The stench of disinfectant was oppressive, and from
Zadok's bed there came, from time to time, a whiff of something
disgusting, a scent of evil omen.

"It's this gang-green, they call it, Frankie. I can feel it all through
me. B'God I can taste it. Can't seem to stop it, though they've
taken my legs. It's an eating sore, y'know. Dr. J.A. says he's never
seen it so bad, though he's seen some bad cases in the lumber
camps. Says he doesn't know why I'm not dead, because I'm a
mass of corruption. He can talk like that to me because I'm an
old soldier, me dear, and I can bear the worst. He's not unkind;
it's just that he sees the world as a huge disease, and we're all
part of it."

"It's very, very bad luck, Zadok."

"I've known very bad luck in my time, me dear. I've looked it
right in its ugly mug, and it's a terror. Yes, it's a rum start what
can happen to a man. I've never told you about South Africa,
have I?"

"I knew you'd fought there."

"I fought well there. I did some good work. I was up for
promotion and a decoration. Then it all fell to pieces because of
love. You wouldn't think of that, would you? But love it was,
and I'm not ashamed of it now.

"I was in a regiment raised in Cornwall, you see, and I went
under the lead of a young man who was the son of the great
family in my part. His father was an Earl, so he was a Lord. The
Captain, he was. God, he was a handsome man, Frankie! We'd
grown up together, almost, because I'd followed him all my life,
hunting, fishing, roving, everything boys do. So of course I joined
the regiment under him, and I was his batman—his personal
servant, like. Before I joined I'd been two or three years in his

father's house as an under-servant, a footman that was, so it seemed a very natural thing that I should go on looking after his clothes, and even trimming his hair, like. We were friends, great friends, the way a master and a servant can be. And I swear to God he never laid a finger on me nor I on him in a way that would bring shame on either of us. It wasn't like that; I've seen some o' that, in the Army and out of it, and I swear it wasn't like that. But I loved the Captain, the way you'd love a hero. And he was a hero. A very brave, fine man.

"Like many a hero, he was killed. Stopped a Boer sniper's bullet. So we buried him, and I did my best for him right to the end. Dressed him, and saw his hair was washed, and he looked very fine in the cheap coffin that was all there was, of course. 'Yes, let me like a soldier fall.' Remember that song?

"I thought I'd die, too. At night I used to sneak out after Lights Out, and sit by his grave. One night a picket noticed me, lying on the grave and crying my heart out, and he reported me, and there was an awful fuss. I was charged, and the Colonel had a lot to say about how such behaviour was unworthy of a soldier and could be harmful to morale, and how such immoral relationships must be sharply discouraged, and I was discharged without honour and sent back home, and bang went my medal, and a big part of my life. The Colonel wasn't one of our lot. Not a Cornishman, and he didn't understand me. I wonder if he ever loved anything or anybody in his life. So that was very bad luck."

"Terrible bad luck, Zadok. But I understand. It was like the love that held the Grail knights together, and the people who served them in innocent love."

"Ah, well, I don't know anything about that. But of course you're part Cornish, aren't you, Frankie? Not that I'd say they were a very loving lot, on the whole. But they're a loyal lot."

"What did you do in England?"

"Whatever I could. Servant, mostly, and some jobs for undertakers. But there was one thing that seemed almost as if it was meant to make up for the other, and it was love too, in a funny way.

"It was like a dream, really. That's the way it seems to me now.

"There was one regimental sergeant-major—good bloke—that I'd known, and he was kind to me now and then. He had a funny sideline. Used to supply men—soldiers mostly—to places that wanted servants for big dos, just to dress the place up, you know; not really do much except wear the livery and look tall and trustworthy. Well, I'd been a footman, hadn't I? Get a few bob for an easy night's work.

"One night was a big night in one of the big hotels, and I was on the job, all gussied up in breeches and a velvet clawhammer and white wig. No moustache then, of course. A servant must shave clean. We'd done our job and I was just about to take off the fancy clobber when some fellow—one of the upper waiters—rushed up to me and said, 'Here, we're short-handed; just take this up to number two-four-two will you, and give it in before you leave.' And he handed me a tray with a bottle of champagne and some glasses on it, and dashed away. So up I went, knocked on the door, very soft as I'd been taught in the castle, and went in.

"Girl in there. Alone, so far as I could see. Beautiful girl, I remember, though I couldn't say now what her face was like, because she was so beautifully dressed, and a servant isn't supposed to stare, or even look anybody in the eye, unless asked. 'Open it, please,' she said. Soft voice; might have been French, I thought. So I opened and poured, and said, 'Will that be all, madam?' Because orders were that any lady had to be 'madam', not 'miss'. 'Wait a minute,' said she. 'I want to have a good look at you.' And I still didn't raise my eyes, you see, Frankie. I don't know how long she looked. Might have been a minute. Might have been two. Then she says, very soft, 'Do you ever go to the theatre?' 'Not much in my line, madam,' said I. 'Oh, you should,' says she. 'I've been and it's perfectly wonderful. You haven't seen *Monsieur Beaucaire?*' 'Don't know the gentleman, madam,' I said. 'Of course you don't,' she said; 'he's imaginary. He's in a play. He's a valet who's really a prince. And the actor who plays Monsieur Beaucaire is the most beautiful man in the world. His name is Mr. Lewis Waller,' she said.

"Well, then I knew a little more. I'd heard of Lewis Waller. Matinee idol, they used to call him. A real swell. Then what she said really surprised me, and I had to look in her face.

" 'You're the very image of him in *Monsieur Beaucaire*,' she said. 'The costume, the white wig. It's astonishing! You must have a glass of champagne.'

" 'Strictly against orders, miss,' I said, forgetting myself when I called her that.

" 'But strictly according to my orders,' said she, very much the little princess. 'I'm lonely, and I don't like to drink alone. So you must have a glass with me.'

"I knew that was just swank. She wasn't used to drinking much any time, not to speak of alone. But I did what she said. And I made my glass last, but she had three. We talked. She did, that's to say. I kept mum.

"There was something amiss with her. Don't know what it was. All excited, and yet not happy, as if she'd lost a shilling and found a sixpence, if you follow me.

"Well, I soon saw what it was. I had seen something of life, and I'd seen a good deal of women, of all kinds. She wanted it. You know what I mean? Not like some old woman who's crazy with vanity and foolishness and fear of her own age. She wanted it, and I swear, Frankie, I didn't take advantage of her. I just lived in the present, so to speak, and after some more talk I did what she wanted—not that she asked bolt outright or even seemed to know much about how it was managed. And I swear to you I was perfectly respectful, because she was a sweet kiddie and I wouldn't have harmed her for the world. It was lovely. Lovely! And when it was over she wasn't crying or anything, but looked as if she was ready for bed, so I carried her into the bedroom and laid her down, and gave her one good kiss, and left.

"Frank, it was the sweetest thing that ever happened in my whole life! A dream! It'd be hard to tell it to most people. They'd grin and know best, and think badly of her, and that would be dead wrong, for it wasn't that way at all.

"When I was out in the corridor I passed a big mirror, and saw myself, in the livery and the white wig. I looked hard. Maybe I was Monsieur Beaucaire, whoever he was. Anyhow, it did something wonderful for me. I was able to put the Army disgrace and the dishonourable discharge behind me, and try to get on in the world.

"Not that I did, not in any big way. But after a while I decided to try my luck in Canada, and fetched up here. And now I've ended like this.

"No, I never saw her again. Never knew her name. A rum start, me dear. That's all you can say about it. A rum start."

Zadok was weary, and Francis rose to go. "Is there anything I can do for you, Zadok?"

"Nobody can do anything for me, me dear. Nothing at all."

"That's not like you. You'll get well. You'll see."

"Kindly meant, Frankie, but I know better. Suppose I did get well? No legs—what'd that add up to? Old soldier with no legs, playing the mouth-organ in the street? Not me! Not for Joe! So it's good-bye, me dear."

Zadok smiled a gap-toothed, red-nosed smile, but his moustache, once proudly dyed and now a yellowish grey, had still a dandified twist.

Francis, moved by an impulse he had no time to consider, leaned over the bed and kissed the ruined man on the cheek. Then he hurried from the room, for fear Zadok should see that he was weeping.

The little hospital was at some distance from the town. As Francis emerged, one of Blairlogie's two taxis had just set down a passenger and was about to drive away. But the driver pulled up suddenly, and shouted: "Hey, Chicken! D'yuh want a taxi?" It was Alexander Dagg.

"No, thanks. I'll walk."

"Where yuh been?"

"I haven't lived here for a good many years."

"I know that. I ast yuh where yuh been."

Francis did not answer.

"Visiting somebody in the hospital? That old bum Hoyle, I'll bet. He's dying, isn't he?"

"Maybe."

"No maybe about it. Say—d'yuh know what I'm going to tell

yuh? Nobody was surprised what happened. My Maw says what happened to him is a warning to all boozers."

During his time at Colborne College and Spook, Francis had learned a few things in the gymnasium he had not known when he was at Carlyle Rural. He was now more than six feet tall, and strong. He walked to the taxi, reached through the window by the driver's seat, seized Alexander Dagg by the front of his shirt, and yanked him sharply toward the door.

"Hey! Go easy, Chicken. That hurts!"

"It'll hurt worse if you don't shut your big, loud mouth, Dagg. Now you listen to me: I don't give a good god-damn what you think or what your evil-minded old bitch of a Maw thinks. Now you be on your way, or I'll beat the shit out of you!" Francis thrust Alexander very hard against the steering wheel, then wiped his hands on his handkerchief.

"Oh, so that's how it is! Oh, I'm very sorry, Mr. Cornish, very sorry indeed, your royal highness. Say—d'yuh know what I'm going to tell yuh? My Maw says the McRorys are all a bunch of bloodsuckers, just using this town for whatever they can get out of it. Bloodsuckers, the lot of yez!"

This was hurled bitterly from the window as Alexander Dagg drove away, his head dangerously twisted so that he could not see where he was going; he narrowly missed hitting a tree. Francis should have kept his dignity and his undoubted victory, but he was not quite old enough for that. He picked up a stone and hurled it at the flying car, and had the satisfaction of hearing it strike with a force that undoubtedly damaged the taxi's paint.

"OH DEAR, I HAD PROMISED a duck for your last dinner, Francis, but this doesn't seem to be a duck, does it? So what I said must have been *un canard*."

"Certainly *un canard*, and this is *un malard imaginaire*, Mary-Ben. Look at this! The blood follows the knife as you cut it."

"I'm afraid you're right, J.A. Don't eat it, Francis. You don't have to be polite here."

"I was brought up to be polite at this table by you, Aunt. I can't stop now."

"Yes, but not to the point of eating raw—what do you suppose it is, J.A.?"

"At a rough guess I should say that whatever is on our plates approached the oven believing itself to be a capon," said the Doctor. "Mary-Ben, you can't go on like this; Anna Lemenchick can't cook and that's all there is to it."

"But J.A., she believes herself to be the cook."

"Then you must shatter her illusion, before she kills you and Marie-Louise. I insist, on behalf of my patients. Ah, it was a sorry day when you let Victoria Cameron leave this house."

"J.A., there was no help for it. She had become a tyrant—an utter tyrant. Kicked right over the traces if I made the slightest criticism—"

"Mary-Ben, learn to know yourself before it's too late to learn anything! You nagged her without mercy because she was a Black Protestant, and you hadn't the bigness of spirit to see that her quality as an artist raised her above mere matters of sect—"

"Joe, you are unkind! As if I could nag."

"You're a sweet nagger, Mary-Ben—the very worst kind. But we mustn't wrangle on Francis's last evening here. Now, what's to follow this horrible duck or whatever it is? A pie, is it? God send the pastry isn't raw."

But the pastry was raw. Anna Lemenchick, stolid and indifferent to the amount of uneaten food she removed on the plates, now brought in a tray on which was a bowl of hot bread-and-milk for the patient upstairs. Aunt excused herself, and hurried off with the tray to feed Marie-Louise, who liked company with her meals of slops. Dr. J.A. rose and fetched a bottle of the Senator's port from the sideboard, and sat down with Francis.

"Thank God, Anna can't get her murderer's hands on this," he said, pouring out two large glasses. "This house is sinking into the earth, Francis, as you well can see."

"I'm worried, Uncle Doctor. Nothing seems to be right here. Not just the food, but the whole feel of the place."

"Francis, it's stinginess. Senile parsimony is what ails Mary-Ben. She's rolling in money, but she thinks she's poor and won't hire a decent cook. Your grandmother can't eat the stuff, and Mary-Ben just eats this garbage to prove she's right."

"Uncle Doctor, tell me honestly—is Grand'mère going to die?"

"Oh yes, eventually. We all are. But when I couldn't say. She hasn't got cancer, if that's what you're worried about. Just a totally ruined digestion and gallstones like baseballs. But she and Mary-Ben carry on as if the retribution of a lifetime of over-eating the richest possible foods was something unique in the annals of medicine. B'God they make it almost religious. 'Behold and see, if there be any acidity like unto my acidity.' The oddity is that Mary-Ben's eaten the same stuff, chew for chew, as her sister-in-law, and she's still at it—a mighty little knife-and-fork is Mary-Ben. D'you know she visits old Madame Thibodeau every day for tea? Christian charity? Get away! It's because Madame Thibodeau gets all her cakes and tartlets from the infidel Victoria Cameron, that's why! That's female logic for you, Francis."

"Then Grand'mère is not as bad as she looks?"

"No, she's just as bad as she looks, but if she keeps on bread-and-milk and my peppermint mixture she could last a good long time. But Mary-Ben's the one to last. The McRory strain is a very strong strain, Francis. So look after it in yourself. It's a golden inheritance."

"Is it all good?"

"How do you mean?"

"No madness? No oddity? I know about the fellow that was upstairs; what explains him?"

"That's not for me to tell you, Francis. That may have been a matter of chance—what they call a sport. Or it may be something that is bred in the bone."

"Well—it's very important to me. If I married, and had children, how great is the danger—?"

"On chance, perhaps not very great. Look at you, and look at your brother Arthur; both perfectly sound. Or it could happen again. But let me give you some advice—"

"Yes?"

"Go ahead. Keep on with your life. If you want to have children, take the risk. Don't stay single or childless on some sort of principle. Obey instinct; it's always right. Look at me and Mary-Ben. There's a lesson for you! Yes, Francis, I've come to the time of life when I'm less of a teacher or adviser than I'm an object lesson:

> *The sin I impute to each frustrate ghost*
> *Is—the unlit lamp and the ungirt loin—*

D'you know any Browning?"

"Not really."

"Mary-Ben and I used to read him together, long ago. Very clever fellow. Away ahead of all these so-called psychologists you hear about nowadays."

WHEN THE LONG, TEDIOUS BOUT of euchre was completed in Grand'mère's room, Aunt Mary-Ben insisted that Francis should come into her sitting-room for a last chat. He was leaving early in the morning. The room was almost unchanged, only somewhat shabby from use and the passing of time.

"Aunt, why is Grand-père so seldom here now?"

"Who's to say, Francis? He has so much business to attend to. And I dare say he finds it dull here."

"It wouldn't have anything to do with the food, would it?"

"Oh, Francis! What a thing to say!"

"Well, you heard what Uncle Doctor said. It'll kill you."

"No, no it won't; Dr. J.A. must have his joke. But the truth is, Frank, I can't hurt Anna Lemenchick. She's the last of the old servants, and the only one who has never cost me a moment's uneasiness. Old Billy, you remember, drank so terribly, and Bella-Mae has given herself up totally to that Salvation Army, and do you know sometimes they have the neck to play right outside the church, just before High Mass! and Zadok—well you know I never really trusted him; there was a look in his eye, as if he were thinking impermissible thoughts when he was driving the carriage. D'you know I once caught him imitating Father Devlin? Yes, right in the kitchen! He had a tablecloth over his shoulders, and was bowing up and down with his hands clasped, and moaning, 'We can beat the Jews at do-min-oes!', pretending he was singing Mass, you see. And Victoria Cameron was laughing, with her hand over her mouth! I don't care what your grandfather and Uncle Doctor say, Francis, that woman was evil at heart!"

On the subject of Victoria Cameron, Aunt was implacable, and declared furthermore that with the wages servants wanted now-adays—forty dollars a month had been heard of!—you had to look out that you weren't simply made use of. So Francis led the conversation to his future, in which Aunt was passionately—the word is not too strong—passionately interested.

"To be a painter! Oh, Frankie, my dear boy, if ever there was a dream come true, that's it, for me! When you were so ill as a child, and used to sit in this room and look at the pictures, and draw pictures of your own, I used to pray that it might flower into something wonderful like this!"

"Don't say wonderful, Aunt. I don't know even if I have any talent, yet. Facility—probably. But talent's something very much beyond that."

"Don't doubt yourself, dear. Pray that God will help you, and He will. What God has begun, He will not desert. Painting is the most wonderful thing—of course, after a life in the Church—that any man can aspire to."

"You've always said that, Aunt. But I've wondered why you say it. I mean—why painting, rather than music, for instance, or writing books?"

"Oh, music's all very well. You know I love it. And anybody can write; it just takes industry. But painting—it makes people *see*. It makes them see God's work truly.

> . . . *we're made so that we love*
> *First, when we see them painted, things we have passed*
> *Perhaps a hundred times, nor cared to see:*
> *And so they are better painted.*

That's Browning—*Fra Filippo Lippi*. I used to read a lot of Brown-ing once, with a great friend, and that always made me cry Yes, yes, it's true! The painter is a great moral force, Frankie. It's truly a gift of God."

"Well—I hope so."

"Don't hope. Trust. And pray. You still pray, don't you, Fran-cis?"

"Sometimes. When things are bad."

"Oh my dear, pray when they are good, too. And don't just ask. Give! Give God thanks and praise! So many people treat Him like a banker, you know. It's give, give, give, and they can't see that it's really lend, lend, lend. Frankie—you've never forgotten what happened when you were so sick that time?"

"Well—wasn't that just a bit of panic?"

"Oh, Frank! Shame on you! That was when Father Devlin baptized you. You're a Catholic forever, my dear. It's not something you can shrug off at a fashionable school, or among unthinking people, like your father, though I'm sure he's a good man so far as he understands goodness. Frank—you still have your rosary?"

"It's somewhere, I suppose."

"Dear boy, don't talk like that! Now look, Frankie; you always liked my rosary, and it's a fine one. I want you to have it—no, no, I have others—and I want you to take it with you everywhere, and use it. Promise, Frank!"

"Aunt, how can I promise?"

"By doing so now. A solemn promise, made in love. A promise made to me. Because you know, I'm sure, that at least in part you are my child, and the only one I'll ever have."

So, after some further weak demurrers, Frank took the rosary, and gave the promise, and the next morning he left Blairlogie, as he then thought, forever.

SO THAT POOR WRETCH the Looner was the outcome of a chance meeting between the romantic Mary-Jacobine and the destroyed soldier Zadok? said the Lesser Zadkiel.

—If you wish to talk of Chance, said the Daimon Maimas. But you and I know how deceptive the concept of Chance—the wholly random, inexplicable happening—is as a final explanation of anything.

—Of course. But I am keeping in mind how dear the notion of Chance is to the people on Earth. Theirs is the short view. Rob them of Chance and you strike at their cherished idea of Free Will. They are not granted the time to see that Chance may have its limitations, just as Free Will has its limitations. Odd, isn't it, that they are glad enough to have their scientists show them evidence of pattern in the *rest of Nature, but they don't want to recognize themselves as part of Nature. They seem persuaded that they, alone of all Creation, so far as they know it, are uninfluenced by the Anima Mundi.*

—Well, we see that they have some choice within the pattern, but the pattern is strong, and now and then it shows itself nakedly. Then something like this happens: Mary-Jacobine chooses Zadok—against probability, but because she has a crush on an actor; Zadok begets a child in a single coupling with a virgin—again against probability, but because he is a compassionate, unhappy man. Do we call that chance? But then, she does not recognize her chance lover when he appears and he does not recognize her because they are in a world they think of as the New World. Then—Marie-Louise destroys a child in the womb, which is very probable considering who and what she was. Zadok does not know his own son—how would he? Just Chance and Likelihood in their old familiar muddle, said the Daimon.

—I suppose they would call it coincidence.

—A useful, dismissive word for people who cannot bear the idea of pattern shaping their own lives.

—Coincidence is what they call pattern in which they cannot discern something they are prepared to accept as meaning, said the Lesser Zadkiel.

—But we see the meaning, do we not, brother? Of course we do. The Looner brought love back into the life of Zadok, for only love can explain his behaviour toward him. The Looner brought motherhood into the life of Victoria Cameron, who did not choose—probably feared—to seek it in the usual way.

—And for your man Francis, my dear colleague?

—Ah—for Francis the Looner was a lifelong reminder of the inadmissible primitive in the most cultivated life, a lifelong adjuration to pity, a sign that disorder and abjection stand less than a hair's breadth away from every human creature. A continual counsel to make the best of whatever fortune had given him.

—But surely, also, a constant pointer to humility? said the Angel.

—Very much so. And I think that although I had nothing to do with the begetting of the Looner, I made good use of him in the shaping of Francis. So the Looner did not live in vain.

—Yes, you did well there, brother. And where is the helm set for now?

—For Oxford.

—*Oxford certainly won't strengthen the Blairlogie strain*, said the Angel.

—*Oxford will strengthen whatever is bred in the bone. And I have already made sure that the Looner, in every aspect, is bred in the bone of Francis. Francis will need all his wits and all his pity at Oxford, said the Daimon.*

PART
Four

What Would Not
Out of the Flesh?

"EVERYBODY AGREES that your first year at Oxford was a triumph," said Basil Buys-Bozzaris.

"That's very kind of everybody," said Francis. He was being patronized by the fat slob Buys-Bozzaris and he was beginning to wonder how much longer he would put up with it.

"Now, now; let's have no false modesty. You have made a nice little name as a speaker in the Union; you have gained a place on the committee of the O.U.D.S.; your sketches of Oxford Notables in the *Isis* are admitted to be the best things of their kind since Max Beerbohm. You are known as one of the aesthetes, but you are not a posturing fool. You must admit that's very good."

"Those are pastimes; I came to Oxford to work."

"Why?"

"Well, there's a widely accepted notion that one comes here to learn."

"To learn what?"

"The foundation for whatever one means to do with one's life."

"Which is—?"

"I haven't really decided."

"Oh, God be praised! For a few moments I feared you might be one of those earnest Americans with a career before you. *Too* middle-class! But Roskalns says you told him you meant to be a painter."

Roskalns? Who was he? Oh yes; that grubby chap who hung about the edges of the O.U.D.S. and was a private coach in modern languages. Had Francis confided in him? Possibly he had

said something to somebody else when Roskalns was listening—
as Roskalns always seemed to be doing. Francis decided he had
had quite enough of Buys-Bozzaris.

"I think I'd better be going," he said. "Thanks for the tea."

"Don't hurry. I'd like to talk a little more. I know some people
you might like to meet. You're fond of cards, I hear."

"I play a little."

"For pretty high stakes?"

"Enough to make it interesting."

"And you win pretty consistently?"

"About enough to come out even."

"Oh, better than that. Your modesty is charming."

"I really must go."

"Of course. But just one moment; I know some people who
play regularly—really good players—and I thought you might
care to join us. We don't play for pennies."

"Are you asking me to join some sort of club?"

"Nothing so formal. And we don't just play; we talk, as well.
I hear you like to talk."

"What do you talk about?"

"Oh, politics. World affairs. These are lively times."

"Several people have gone to Spain, to see what they can do
there. Even more say they would be in Spain in a moment, if
they could see their way clear. Is that the sort of talk?"

"No, that is youthful romanticism. We are much more serious."

"Perhaps I could look in once or twice?"

"Of course."

"Tonight?"

"Admirable. Any time after nine."

A FEW DAYS LATER Francis wrote one of his letters to Colonel
Copplestone:

Dear Uncle Jack:

Second year at Oxford is a great improvement. One knows
where the things are that one is likely to want and where the
people are one is certain not to want. The nice thing about
being at Corpus is that it is so small. But that means that

only first-year men and a few specials can live in college, so I am in digs, and have secured a very nice set of rooms virtually on the college doorstep. Canterbury House the place is called, because it's by the Canterbury Gate of Christ Church. I have the top floor; big living room and small bedroom; superb view down Merton Street, which must be the prettiest street in Oxford, and the only drawback is that when Great Tom gets off his 101 peal at 9 P.M. it is almost as if he were in my bedroom. I am thinking of writing to the Dean and suggesting that this ancient custom be discontinued. Do you suppose he would listen?

Have met a few new people. The ground-floor set of rooms here—most expensive, worst view—is occupied by a man called Basil Buys-Bozzaris, which is a name to conjure with, don't you think? He conjures a bit; a few days ago as I was running up the stairs beside his door he popped his head out and said, "A Virgo; I know him by his tread!" which was arresting enough to make me stop and chat, and he waffled a bit about astrology; rather interestingly, as a matter of fact. I don't go for astrology by any means, but I have found that sometimes it provides useful broad clues about people. Anyhow, he wanted me to come to tea with him, and yesterday I did.

In the interim I made a few inquiries about BBB. Our landlord was very forthcoming: rich, he said, and a count, and a Bulgarian. He entertains a lot, and whenever he is having people to lunch, he has the same lunch served to himself the day before, wines and all, and then edits it for errors of cooking or choice! This impresses the landlord no end, as well it might.

Somebody else who knew a bit about him said he was an oddity. Probably thirty-five, and is here ostensibly studying international law; I am sure you know what a vague area that can be, if somebody wants to hang around a university. BBB seems to be interested in Conflict of Laws, which is of course an even more tangled briar-patch. My informant says he is one of those hangers-on all universities attract. As for being a count, I don't know whether Bulgaria has them or has ever had them, but it is a vague title roughly indicative of some distance from the peasant class. So I knew a bit about him before going to tea.

Usual polite questions, to establish the ground. What was I studying? Flattery about some sketches I did last spring for the *Isis* of Oxford people who are in the eye of the University. Velvety request for my birth date and hour, as he would be delighted to cast my horoscope. I yielded; no reason not to, and I cannot resist horoscopes. And what are you interested in, I said. I am a connoisseur, said he, and this surprised me, because the room was not that of a connoisseur; just the landlord's perfectly good, dull furniture, and a few photographs framed in silver of Middle-European-looking people—choker collars and fancy whiskers on the men, and the women with an awful lot of hair and that kind of fat that is kindly referred to as "opulence". Not a good object anywhere, and across one corner an ikon of the Virgin in the most offensively sweet nineteenth-century taste, with a *riza* in decidedly *not* sterling silver covering all but the face and hands. BBB smiled, for he must have seen my surprise. Not a connoisseur of art, he said, but of ideas, of attitudes, of politics in the broad sense. Then he talked a bit about the present European situation, about this man Hitler in Germany, about the misery in Spain, all in a distant, removed fashion, as if only ideas and not people were involved. Asked me to come back, to play cards, and I said I would, not because I liked him but because I didn't.

The card-playing, when I went back, was interesting enough to repay me for an evening I would not ordinarily have chosen to spend in such uncomfortable circumstances. Lots to drink and expensive cigars for the grabbing, but the concentration was on two tables of bridge—all the room would comfortably hold. The atmosphere was very serious for a friendly game. BBB was the leader at one and a rather scruffy fellow called Roskalns, who coaches first-year men in Latin and does a variety of languages for others who want them (not employed by the University, an independent coach), took care of the other. The rest of us changed tables from time to time but these two remained where they were. Brisk play, and the stakes were substantially above what is usual here, where anybody who loses a pound in an evening feels he has been living dangerously. I was particularly interested in another man—in his second year at Christ Church—named Fremantle, because he is a Canadian though he has lived a good deal in England.

Fremantle had the real wild gambler's eye. Life with my mother and grandmother and great-grandmother has taught me quite a bit about cards, and the first rule is—keep calm, don't *want* to win, because the cards, or the gods, or whatever rules the table will laugh at you and take your last penny. Only what my mother calls "intelligent, watchful indifference" will carry you through. If you see that look in somebody's eye—that hot, craving gleam—you see somebody who has lost himself first, and will probably lose his money so long as he sits at the table. When the time came to settle up at the end of the evening Fremantle was in hock to BBB about twelve quid, and he didn't look happy about it. I came out exactly seven shillings to the good, which was part luck and part my fourth-generation skill with the pasteboards. Anybody who has played skat with my gran and great-gran knows at least how to shuffle without dropping the cards.

Knows a few other things, too, and I kept my eye open for those. Nothing to be seen except that Roskalns has just the teeniest inclination to deal from the bottom of the deck now and then, though not very injuriously, so far as I could tell. I enjoy a mild flutter, and shall go to BBB's evening game from time to time, though I can play cards more comfortably in several other places.

Why go, then? You know how inquisitive I am, godfather. Why has BBB one Dutch name as well as his genuine Bulgarian one? Does he float his heavy hospitality on what he makes at the table? Is Charles Fremantle really as hell-bent on ruin as he seems to be? And why, as I was leaving, did BBB give me an envelope that contained a pretty good horoscope which said, among other things, "You are very shrewd at piercing through what is hidden from others"? Sounds like a come-on. I have never found anything in my horoscope that suggested unusual perception—beyond what a caricaturist might have, of course.

Obedient to your advice, I am not writing this on College stationery, as you see. I swiped this paper the other day when I visited the Old Palace to pay my yearly respects to the R.C. chaplain, Monsignor Knollys, as my Aunt Mary-Benedetta strictly charged me to do. The chaplain is a queer bird and rather dismissive to Canadians, whom he merrily terms "colonials". I'll colonial him if I get the chance.

> Yr. affct. godson,
> Frank

TWO DAYS AFTER HIS EVENING with Buys-Bozzaris, Frank was working in his sitting-room when the door burst open after a short, loud knock, and a girl burst in.

"You're Francis Cornish, aren't you?" said she, and dumped an armful of books on his sofa. "I thought I'd better have a look at you. I'm Ismay Glasson, and we're sort of cousins."

Since his visit to Cornwall and Chegwidden House five years ago, Frank had forgotten that he had a cousin named Ismay, but he recalled her now as the terrible older sister of the obnoxious Glasson children, who had assured him that if Ismay had been at home, she would have given him a rough time. He had been rather afraid of girls then, but in the interval had gained greatly in self-possession. He would give her a rough time first.

"Marry come up, m'dirty cousin," said he; "don't you usually wait to be asked before you barge into a room?"

"Not usually. 'Marry come up, m'dirty cousin'—that's a quotation, isn't it? You're not reading Eng.Lit., I hope?"

"Why do you hope that?"

"Because the men who do are usually such dreadful fruits, and I'd hoped you'd be nice."

"I am nice, but apt to be formal with strangers, as you observe."

"Oh balls! How about giving me a glass of sherry."

During his first year, Francis had become thoroughly habituated to the Oxford habit of swimming in sherry. He had also discovered that sherry is not the inoffensive drink innocent people suppose.

"What'll you have? The pale, or the old walnut brown?"

"Old walnut. If not Eng.Lit., what are you reading?"

"Modern Greats."

"That's not so bad. The kids said something about Classics."

"I considered Classics, but I wanted to expand a bit."

"Probably you needed it. The kids said you mooned about and talked about King Arthur and said Cornwall was enchanted ground, like a complete ass."

"If you judge me by the standards of your loathsome and barbarous young relatives, I suppose I was a complete ass."

"Golly! We're not precisely hitting it off, are we?"

"If you burst into my room when I am working and insult me, and tuck up your muddy feet on my sofa, what do you expect? You've been given a glass of sherry; isn't that courtesy above and beyond anything you've deserved?"

"Come off it! I'm your cousin, aren't I?"

"I don't know. Have you any papers of identification? Not that they would say any more than your face. You have the Cornish face."

"So have you. I'd have known you anywhere. Face like a horse, you mean."

"I have not said you have a face like a horse. I am too well-bred, and also too mature, for this kind of verbal rough stuff. And if that means to you that I am a complete ass, or even a fruit, so be it. Go and play with your own coarse kind."

Francis was enjoying himself. At Spook he had learned the technique of bullying girls: bully them first and they may not get to the point of bullying you, which, given a chance, they will certainly do. This girl talked tough, but was not truly self-assured. She was untidily and unbecomingly dressed. Her hair needed more combing than she had given it recently and the soft woman's academic cap she wore was dusty and messy, as was her gown. Good legs, though the stockings had been worn for too many days without washing. But in her the Cornish face was distinguished and spirited. Like several other girls he had seen in Oxford, she might have been a beauty if she had possessed any firm conception of beauty, and related it to herself, but in her the English notion of neglected womanhood was firmly in command.

"Let's not fight. This is good sherry. May I have another shot? Tell me about yourself."

"No, ladies first. You tell me about yourself."

"I'm in my first year at Lady Margaret Hall. Scholarship in modern languages, so that's what I'm doing here. You know Charlie Fremantle, don't you?"

"I think I've met him."

"He says you met at a card game. He lost a lot. You won a lot."

"I won seven shillings. Does Charlie fancy himself as a card player?"

"He adores the risk. Says it makes his blood run around. He adores danger."

"That's expensive danger. I hope he has a long purse."

"Longish. Longer than mine, anyhow. I'm poor but deserving. My scholarship is seventy pounds a year. My people, with many a deep-fetched groan, bring it up two hundred."

"Not bad. Rhodes Scholars only get three hundred, at present."

"Oh, but they get lots of additional money for travel and this and that. What have you got?"

"I look after my own money, to some extent."

"I see. Not going to tell. That's your Scotch side. I know about you from Charlie, so you can't hide anything. He says your family is stinking rich, though a bit common. The kids said you were bone mean. Wouldn't even stand them an ice cream."

"If they wanted ice cream, they shouldn't have put an adder in my bed."

"It was a dead adder."

"I didn't know that when I put my foot on it. Why are you at Oxford? Are you a bluestocking?"

"Maybe I am. I'm very bright in the head. I want to get into broadcasting. Or film. If not Oxford, what? The days are gone when girls just came out and went to dances and waited for Prince Charming."

"So I hear. Well—is there anything I can do for you?"

"Doesn't look like it, does it?"

"If you have no suggestions, I suppose I could take you to lunch."

"Oh splendid! I'm hungry."

"Not today. Tomorrow. That will give you time to smarten up a little. I'll take you to the O.U.D.S. Ever been there?"

"No. I'd love that. I've never been. But why do you say O.U.D.S.? Why don't you call it OUDS? Everybody does, you know."

"Yes; I know, but I wasn't sure you would know. Well—my club, and ladies are admitted at lunch."

"Isn't it full of dreadful fruits? People with sickening upper-class names like Reptilian Cork-Nethersole? Isn't it crammed with fruits?"

"No. About one in four, at the outside. But dreadful fruits, as you so unpleasantly call them, have good food and drink and usually have lovely manners, so no throwing buns or any of that rough stuff you go in for at women's colleges. Meet me here— downstairs, outside the door marked Buys-Bozzaris—at half past twelve. I like to be punctual. Don't trouble to wear a hat."

Francis thought that he had sat on his young cousin enough for the moment.

THE ADVICE ABOUT THE HAT was not simply gratuitous insult. When Ismay found herself lunching in the O.U.D.S. dining-room the following day there were two elegant ladies wearing hats at the President's table. They were actresses, they were beauties, and the hats they wore were in the Welsh Witch fashion of the moment—great towering, steeple-crowned things with scarves of veiling hanging from the brim to the shoulders. The hats, as much as their professional ease and assurance, separated them irrevo-cably from the five hatless Oxford girls, of whom Ismay was one, who were dining with male friends. The O.U.D.S. did not admit women as members.

Ismay was not the aggressive brat of the day before. She was reasonably compliant, but Francis saw in her eye the rolling wickedness of a pony, which is pretending to be good when it means to throw you into a ditch.

"The ladies in the hats are Miss Johnson and Miss Gunn. They're playing in *The Wind and the Rain* at the New Theatre over the way; next week they go to London. Smart, aren't they?"

"I suppose so. It's their job, after all."

But this indifference was assumed. Ismay was positively school-girlish when, after lunch, a handsome young man stopped by their table and said: "Francis, I'd like to introduce you and your sister to our guests."

When the introductions and polite compliments to the actresses were over, Francis said, "I should explain that Ismay is not my sister. A cousin."

"My goodness, you two certainly have the family face," said Miss Johnson, who seemed to mean it as a compliment.

"Is that chap really the president of the club?" said Ismay, when the grandees had gone.

"Yes, and consequently a tremendous Oxford swell. Jervase Featherstone; everybody agrees he's headed for a great career. Did you see him last winter in the club production of *Peer Gynt?* No, of course you didn't; you weren't here. The London critics praised him to the skies."

"He's wonderfully good-looking."

"I suppose so. It'll be part of his job, after all."

"Sour grapes!"

FRANCIS HAD ACHIEVED IN A HIGH DEGREE the Oxford pretence of doing nothing while in fact getting through a great deal of work. He had learned how to study at Colborne, where success was expected, and he had improved on his technique at Spook. At Oxford he more than satisfied his tutor, hung about the O.U.D.S. meddling a little with the decorative side of its productions, contributed occasional caricatures to the *Isis,* and still had time to spend many hours at the Ashmolean, acquainting himself with its splendid collection of drawings by Old Masters, almost Old Masters, and eighteenth- and nineteenth-century artists whom nobody though of as masters, but whose work was, to his eye, masterly.

The Ashmolean was not at that time a particularly attractive or well-organized museum. In the university tradition, it existed to serve serious students, and wanted no truck with whorish American ideas of drawing in and interesting the general public. Was it not, after all, one of the oldest museums in the Old World? It took Francis some time during his first year to persuade the museum authorities that he was a serious student of art; having done so, he was able to investigate the museum's substantial riches without much interference. He wanted to be able to draw well. He was not so vain as to think that he might draw like a master, but it was the masters he wished to follow. So he spent countless hours copying master drawings, analysing master techniques, and to his astonishment surprising within himself ideas and insights and even flashes of emotion that belonged more to the drawings than to himself. He did not trust these whispers from the past until he met Tancred Saraceni.

That came about because Francis was a member, though not a very active one, of the Oxford Union. He would not have joined if he had not been assured in his first year that it was the thing to do. He sometimes attended debates, and on two or three occasions he had even spoken briefly on motions related to art or aesthetics about which he had something to say. Because he knew what he was talking about, when most of the other debaters did not, and because he spoke what he believed to be the truth in plain and uncompromising language, he gained a modest reputation as a wit, which amazed him greatly. He was not interested in politics, which was the great preoccupation of the Union, and his interest in the place was chiefly in its dining-room.

In his second year, however, a House Committee that was looking for something significant to do decided that the lamentable state of the frescoes around the walls of the Union's library must be remedied. What was to be done? The budding politicians of the membership knew nothing much about painting, though they were sufficiently aware of the necessity to have some sort of taste to decorate their rooms with reproductions of Van Gogh's *Sunflowers* or—greatly daring—the red horses of Franz Marc. The library frescoes were, they knew, of significance; had they not been done by leaders of the Pre-Raphaelite Brotherhood? This was just the kind of thing the Union liked and understood, for they could make a debate of it: should relics of a dead past be brought back to life, or should the Union advance fearlessly into the future, getting the frescoes replaced by artists of undoubted reputation, but equally undoubted fearless modernity?

The first thing, of course, was to find out if the frescoes could be restored at all, and to this end, guided by a couple of dons who knew something about art, the Union House Committee invited the celebrated Tancred Saraceni to examine them.

The great man appeared, and demanded a ladder, from which he examined the frescoes with a flashlight and picked at them with a penknife; descending, he declared himself ready for lunch.

Francis was not a member of the House Committee but he was invited to lunch because he was supposed, from his three or four brief speeches, to know something about art. Did he not do those drawings, almost but not quite caricatures, for *Isis?* Was he not known to have drawings—"originals", not reproductions—in his rooms? Just the man to talk to Saraceni. And, when asked, he was eager to meet the man who had the reputation of being the greatest restorer of pictures in the world. Even French museums, so reluctant to look outside their own country for art experts, had called upon Saraceni more than once.

Saraceni was small, very dark, and very neat. He did not look particularly like an artist; the only unusual aspect of his appearance was a pair of discreet side-whiskers that crept down beside his ears and stopped modestly just at the point where they could be described as side-whiskers at all. His customary expression was a smile, which was not mirthful, but ironic. Behind spectacles his brown eyes wandered, not perfectly synchronized, so that he sometimes seemed to be looking in two directions at once. He spoke softly and his English was perfect. Too perfect, for it betrayed him as a foreigner.

"The points to be considered are, first, whether the frescoes can be restored at all, and second, are they worth the cost of restoration?" said the President of the Union, who saw himself as a cabinet minister in embryo, and liked clarifying the obvious. "What is your frank opinion, sir?"

"As works of art, their value is very much a matter of debate," said Saraceni, the ironical smile working at full force. "If I restore them, or supervise their restoration, they will appear as they were originally seen when the artists took down their scaffolds seventy-five years ago, and in their restored form they will last for two or three hundred years, if they are properly cared for. But of course then they will be paintings by me, or my pupils, painted precisely as Rossetti and Burne-Jones and Morris originally meant them to be, but in greatly superior paint, on properly prepared surfaces, and sealed with substances that will preserve them from damp, and smoke, and influences that have turned them into

almost incomprehensible smudges. In short, I shall do professionally what the original painters did as virtual amateurs. They
knew nothing about painting on walls. They were enthusiasts."
He spoke the last word over a tiny giggle.

"But isn't that what restoration always is?" asked another committee member.

"Oh no; a picture that has suffered damage through war, or
accident, may be repaired, re-backed, re-painted where nothing
of the original remains, but it is still the work of the master,
sympathetically and knowledgeably revived. These pictures are
ruins, because they were painted in the wrong way with the wrong
kind of paint. Faint ghosts of the original paintings remain, but
to bring them to life again would mean re-painting, not restoration."

"But you could do that?"

"Certainly. You must understand: I make little claim to being
an artist in the romantic sense of that mauled and blurred word.
I am a fine craftsman—the best at my trade, it is said, in the world.
I should rely on what craft could do; I should not call upon the
Muse, but on a great deal of chemistry and skill. Not that the
Muse might not assert herself, now and then. One never knows."

"I don't follow you, sir."

"Well—it is an aspect of my work I do not talk about very
much. But if you work on a painting with all your skill, and
sympathy, and love, even if you have to re-invent much of it—
as would be the case here—something of what directed the first
painter may come to your aid."

It was at this point that Francis, who had been listening attentively, felt as though he had been given a sharp, quickening tap
on the brow with a tiny hammer.

"Do I understand, Signor Saraceni, that the spirit of the Pre-
Raphaelites might infuse you, from time to time, as you worked?"

"Ah—ah—ah! This is why I do not usually speak of such things.
People like you, Mr. Cornish, may interpret them poetically—
may speak of something almost like possession. I have had too
much experience to speak so boldly. But consider: these men
who painted the pictures we are talking about were poets; better
poets than painters, except for Burne-Jones, and as you probably
know he wrote very well. What was their theme? The pictures

illustrate The Quest for the Grail, and that is much more a theme for a poet than a painter. Surely one can evoke the Grail spirit better in words than in images? Am I a heretic to say that each art has its sphere of supremacy, and invades another's at its deep peril? Painting that is illustrative of a legend is only that legend at second-best. Pictures that tell a story are useless because they are immobile—they have no movement, no nuance or possibility of change, which is the soul of narrative. I suppose it is not unduly fanciful to think that the poets who made asses of themselves with these old, dirty, obliterated pictures might have something to say to somebody who was a masterly painter, even though he might be no poet?"

"You have known that to happen?"

"Oh yes, Mr. Cornish, and there is nothing spooky about it when it happens, I assure you."

"So we might get these pictures back on our walls as Morris and Rossetti and Burne-Jones would have painted them if they had understood fresco-work?"

"Nobody can say that. Certainly they would be much better pieces of craftsmanship. And such inspiration as the original painters possessed would still be there."

"Surely that answers all our questions," said Francis.

"Oh no. Pardon me, there is one question of the uttermost importance that we have not touched on," said the cabinet-minister-in-embryo. "What would you judge the cost to be?"

"I couldn't tell you, for I have not thoroughly examined the walls under the pictures, or even measured the extent of wall that is covered," said Saraceni. "But I am sure you know the story about the American millionaire who asked another American millionaire what it cost him to maintain his yacht? The second American millionaire said, If you have to ask that question, you can't afford it."

"You mean it might run up to—say, a thousand?"

"Many thousands. There would be no point in doing it any way but the best way, and the best way always runs into money. When I had done my work you would have some enthusiastic illustrations of the Grail Legend, if that is what you want."

That effectively concluded the conversation, though there were further courtesies and assurances of mutual esteem. The House Committee was by no means displeased. It had done something, something no previous committee had done in many years. It could make a report on what it had done. So far as the pictures were concerned it really did not care if they were restored or not. The Union was, after all, a great school for budding politicians and civil servants, and this was how politicians and civil servants worked: they consulted experts and ate lunches and worked up a happy sense of behaving with great practicality. But practicality was against spending much money on art.

Francis, however, was in a high state of excitement, and with the full concurrence of the President—who was glad to have Saraceni taken off his hands, once the issue of the pictures had been settled—he invited the little man to dine with him that evening at the Randolph Hotel.

"QUITE CLEARLY, MR. CORNISH, you were the only member of the committee who knew anything about pictures. You also showed keen interest when I spoke of the influence of the original painter on the restorer. Now I must tell you once again that I meant nothing at all mystical by that. I am no spiritualist; the dead do not guide my brush. But consider: in the world of music many composers, when they have completed an opera, rough out the plan of the overture and give it to some trusted, gifted assistant, who writes it so much in the style of the master that experts cannot tell one from t'other. How many passages in Wagner's later work were written by Peter Cornelius? We know, pretty well, but not because the music reveals it.

"It is the same in painting. Just as so many of the great masters entrusted large portions of their pictures to assistants, or apprentices, who painted draperies, or backgrounds, or even hands so well that we cannot tell where their work begins and leaves off, it is possible today for me—I don't say for every restorer—to play the assistant to the dead master and paint convincingly in his style. Some of those assistants, you know, painted copies of masterworks for people who wanted them, but the master did not emphasize that when he presented his bill. And today it is very hard to tell some of those copies from originals. Who painted them? The master or an assistant? The experts quarrel about it all the time.

"I am the heir, not to the masters—I am properly modest, you observe—but to those gifted assistants, some of whom went on to become masters themselves. You see, in the great days of what are now so reverently called the Old Masters, art was a trade as well. The great men kept ateliers which were in effect shops, where you could go and buy anything that pleased you. It was the Romanticism of the nineteenth century that raised the painter quite above trade and made him scorn the shop—he became a child of the Muses. A neglected child, very often, for the Muses are not maternal in the commonplace sense. And as the painter was raised above trade, he often felt himself raised above crafts-manship, like those poor wretches who painted the frescoes we were looking at earlier today. They were full up and slopping over with Art, but they hadn't troubled to master Craft. Result: they couldn't carry out their ideas to their own satisfaction, and their work has dwindled into some dirty walls. Sad, in a way."

"You don't think much of the Pre-Raphaelites."

"The ones with the best ideas, like Rossetti, could hardly draw, let alone paint. Like D.H. Lawrence, in our own time. He had more ideas than any half-dozen admired modern painters, but he couldn't draw and he couldn't paint. Of course, there are fools who say it didn't matter; the conception was everything. Rubbish! A painting isn't a botched conception."

"Is that what's wrong with modern art, then?"

"What's wrong with modern art? The best of it is very fine."

"But so much of it is so puzzling. And some of it's plain messy."

"It is the logical outcome of the art of the Renaissance. During those three centuries, to measure roughly, that we call the Ren-aissance, the mind of civilized man underwent a radical change. A psychologist would say that it changed from extraversion to introversion. The exploration of the outer world was partnered by a new exploration of the inner world, the subjective world. And it was an exploration that could not depend on the old map of religion. It was the exploration that brought forth *Hamlet,* instead of *Gorboduc*. Man began to look inside himself for all that

was great and also—if he was honest, which most people aren't—
for all that was ignoble, base, evil. If the artist was a man of scope
and genius, he found God and all His works within himself, and
painted them for the world to recognize and admire."

"But the moderns don't paint God and all His works. Sometimes I can't make out what they are painting."

"They are painting the inner vision, and working very hard at
it when they are honest, which by no means all of them are. But
they depend only on themselves, unaided by religion or myth,
and of course what most of them find within themselves is revelation only to themselves. And these lonely searches can quickly
slide into fakery. Nothing is so easy to fake as the inner vision,
Mr. Cornish. Look at those ruined frescoes we were examining
this morning; the people who painted those—Rossetti, Morris,
Burne-Jones—all had the inner vision linked with legend, and
they chose to wrap it up in Grail pictures and sloe-eyed, sexy
beauties who were half the Mother of God and half Rossetti's
overblown mistresses. But the moderns, having been hit on the
head by a horrible world war, and having understood whatever
they can of Sigmund Freud, are hell-bent for honesty. They are
sick of what they suppose to be God, and they find something
in the inner vision that is so personal that to most people it looks
like chaos. But it isn't simply chaos. It's raw gobbets of the psyche
displayed on canvas. Not very pretty and not very communicative,
but they have to find their way through that to something that is
communicative—though I wonder if it will be pretty."

"It's hell for anybody who thinks of being an artist."

"As you do? Well—you must find your inner vision."

"That's what I'm trying to do. But it doesn't come out in the
modern manner."

"Yes, I understand that. I don't get on very well with the
modern manner, either. But I must warn you: don't try to fake
the modern manner if it isn't right for you. Find your legend.
Find your personal myth. What sort of thing do you do?"

"Might I show you some of my stuff?"

"Certainly, but not now. I must leave first thing in the morning.
But I shall be back in Oxford before long. Exeter College wants
to consult me about its chapel. I'll let you know in plenty of time,

and I shall keep some time for you. Where shall I send a note?"

"My college is Corpus Christi. I pick up letters there. But before you go, won't you have another cognac?"

"Certainly not, Mr. Cornish. Some of the masters drank a great deal, but we assistants and apprentices, even three centuries afterward, must keep our hands steady. I won't have another cognac, and unless you are certain that you are a master, you won't have one either. We must be the austere ones, we second-class men."

It was said with the ironic grin, but for Francis, suckled at least in part on the harsh creed of Victoria Cameron, it was like an order.

LATE IN THE AUTUMN, and not long after his meeting with Saraceni, Francis was surprised and not immediately pleased to receive the following letter:

My dear grandson Francis:

I have never written to you at Oxford before this, because I did not feel that I had anything to say to a young man who was deep in advanced studies. As you know, my own education was scant, for I had to make my way in the world very young. Education makes a greater gulf in families even than making a lot of money. What has the uneducated grandfather to say to the educated grandson? But there are one or two languages I hope we still speak in common.

One is the language, which I cannot put a name to, that you and I shared when you were a lad, and used to come on afternoon jaunts with me, making the sun-pictures with my camera. It was a language of the eye, and also I think chiefly a language of light, and it gives me the greatest satisfaction to think that perhaps your turn for painting and your interest in pictures had a beginning, or at least some encouragement, there. You now speak that language as I never did. I am proud of your inclination toward art, and hope it will carry you through a happy life.

Another language is something I won't call religion, because all through my life I have been a firm Catholic, without truly accepting everything a Catholic ought to believe. So I cannot urge you sincerely to cling to the Faith. But don't forget it, either. Don't forget that language, and don't be one of those handless fellows who believes nothing. There is a fine world unknown to us, and religion is an attempt to explain it. But, unhappily, to reach everybody religion has to be an organization, and a trade for a lot of its priests, and worst of all it has to be reduced to what the largest mass of people will accept and can be expected to understand. That's heresy, of course. I remember how angry I was when your father demanded that you be raised a Protestant. But that was a while since, and in the meantime I have wondered if the Prots are really any bigger turnip-heads than the R.C.s. As you grow old, religion becomes a lonely business.

The third language we speak in common is money, and it is because of that I am writing to you now. Money is a language I speak better than you do, but you must learn something of the grammar of money, or you cannot manage what your luck has brought you as my grandson. This is much on my mind now, because the doctors tell me that I have not a great way farther to go. Something to do with the heart.

When my will is executed, you will find that I have left you a substantial sum, for your exclusive use, apart from what you will share with my other descendants. The reason I give in my will is that you do not seem to me to be suited by nature to the family business, which is the banking and trust business, and that therefore you must not look for employment or advancement there. This looks almost like cutting you out, but that is not so at all. And this is between us: the money will set you free, I hope, from many anxieties and from a kind of employment that I do not think you would like, but only if you master the grammar of money. Money illiteracy is as restrictive as any other illiteracy. Your brother Arthur promises well as a banker, and in that work he will have opportunities to make money that will not come your way. But you will have another kind of chance. I hope this will suit your purpose.

Do not reply to this letter, for I may not be able to deal

with my own letters for very long, and I do not want anyone
else to read what you might say. Though if you chose to
write a farewell, I should be glad of that.

> With affct. good wishes . . .
> James Ignatius McRory

Francis wrote a farewell at once, and did his utmost with it,
though he was no more a master of the pen than his grandfather;
lacked, indeed, the old man's self-taught simplicity. But a telegram
told him that it came too late.

Was there anything to be done? He wrote to Grand'mère and
Aunt Mary-Ben, and he wrote to his mother. He considered going
to Father Knollys at the Old Palace and asking for—and paying
for—a requiem mass for his grandfather, but in the light of what
the letter had said he thought that would be hypocritical and
would make the old colonial laugh, if he knew.

Was his feeling of grief hypocritical? It struggled in his heart
with a sense of release, and new freedom, a feeling of joy that
he could now do with his life what he liked. His grief for the old
Scots woodsman quickly turned to elation and gratitude. Hamish
was the only one of his family who had ever really looked at him,
and considered what he was. The only one of the whole lot,
perhaps, who had ever loved the artist in him.

CHRISTMAS WAS DRAWING NEAR, and Francis decided that duty
called him back to Canada. After one of those penitential mid-
winter sea voyages across the Atlantic he was once again in the
up-to-the-minute decor of his mother's house, and little by little
became aware of what his grandfather had meant to the Cornishes
and the McRorys, and the O'Gormans. To the bankers a real
regard for the old man was greatly tempered by the delightful
business of administering his affairs. He seemed more splendid
in death than he had ever been in life. Gerald Vincent O'Gorman
in particular was loud in his praise for the way the old man had
disposed of his estate. There was something for everybody. This
was a Christmas indeed!

Gerry O'Gorman was understandably better pleased than was
Sir Francis Cornish, for Gerry now succeeded his father-in-law

as Chairman of the Board, while Sir Francis remained in his honourable but less powerful place as President. But then Lady Cornish inherited substantially, which was very agreeable to Sir Francis, and took much of the salt out of the tears of his wife. Even Francis's younger brother, Arthur, who was just twelve, seemed enlarged by Grand-père's death, for his future in the Cornish Trust, always sure, was now clearer than it had been before, and Arthur, at school, was taking on the air of a young financier, stylish, handsome, well-dressed, and adroit in his dealing with contemporaries and elders.

The stricken ones, of course, were Grand'mère and Mary-Ben, but even they had their benefit from the Senator's death; had not Reverend Mother Mary-Basil from Montreal, and His Grace the Rev. Michael McRory from his archdiocese in the West, come to Blairlogie for the funeral, and stayed on to visit the two old women, dispensing comfort and good counsel that was none the less sweet for the handsome remembrances the Senator had made of his brother and sister in the great will?

The will! It seemed that they talked of nothing but the will, and the part that Francis played in it, singularized as he was by the largest of all the personal bequests (his mother and Mary-Tess were beneficiaries of a special trust), surprised and puzzled his family. It was Gerry O'Gorman who summed it up briefly and bluntly: you would think Frank could study art on less than the income from a cool million.

Not that he was just to have the income; the old man had left it to him outright. Now, what would Frank know about handling money in that quantity? But Francis remembered what his grandfather had said about learning the grammar of money, and before he took the dismal voyage back to Oxford he had given directions as to what was to be done with his money when it became available, and even Gerry had to admit that he had handled it well.

So Francis returned to Corpus Christi and Canterbury House, and the inner rooms of the Ashmolean, a rich man, in terms of what he was and what responsibilities he had. Rich, and with the prospect of being richer, for his grandfather had made him a participant in that family trust which at the moment carried Grand'mère, and Aunt, and his mother and Mary-Tess, and as these died off his portion would increase. You're sitting pretty, boy, said Gerry, and Sir Francis, putting it with the dignity of a President, said that his future was assured.

How quick people are to say that someone's future is assured when they mean only that he has enough money to live on! What young man of twenty-four thinks of his future as assured? In one respect, Francis knew that his future was painfully uncertain.

He had known something of girls at Spook—a little hugging and tugging at parties, though the girls of that time were cautious about what he still thought of as The Limit. He had experienced The Limit in a Toronto brothel with a thick-legged woman who came from a country district—a township—not inappropriately named Dummer, and for a month afterward he had fretted and fussed and examined himself for the marks of syphilis, until a doctor assured him that he was as clean as a whistle. On these slender experiences he was sure he knew a good deal about sex, but of love he had no conception. Now he was in love with his cousin Ismay Glasson, and she was plainly not in love with him.

Perhaps she was in love with Charlie Fremantle. He met them together often, and when he was with her she talked a good deal about Charlie. Charlie found Oxford painfully confining; he wanted to get out into the world and change it for the better, whether the world wanted it or not. He had advanced political ideas. He had read Marx—though not a great deal of him, for Charlie found thick, dense books a clog upon his soaring spirit. He had made a few Marxist speeches at the Union, and was admired by other untrammelled spirits like himself. His Marxism could be summed up as a conviction that whatever was, was wrong, and that the destruction of the existing order was the inevitable preamble to any beginning of the just society; the hope of the future lay with the workers, and all the workers needed was sympathetic leadership by people like himself, who had seen through the hypocrisy, stupidity, and bloody-mindedness of the upper class into which they themselves had been born. In all of this Ismay was his submissive disciple. If anything, she was even more vehement than he against the old (people over thirty) who had made such a mess of affairs. Of course, they dressed their ideas up in language more politically resonant than this, and they had plenty of books—or Ismay had—that supported their emotions, which they called their principles.

Charlie was just twenty-one and Ismay was nineteen. Francis, who was twenty-four, felt middle-aged and dull when he listened to them. His was not a political mind, nor was he quick in argument, but he was convinced that something was wrong with Charlie's philosophy. Charlie had not spent three years at Carlyle Rural, or he might have thought differently about the aspirations and potentialities of the workers. Charlie's grandfather had not hacked his way out of the forest and into the seat of a Chairman of the Board with a woodsman's broadaxe. Educate the workers, said Charlie, and you will see the world changed within three generations. Thinking of Miss McGladdery, Francis was not so sure the workers took readily to education or to any change that went beyond their immediate and obvious betterment. Charlie was a Canadian like himself, but Charlie's family were Old Money. Francis had seen enough of Old Money at Colborne College to know that hypocrisy, stupidity, and bloody-mindedness were just as natural to that class as Charlie said they were. Francis was cursed with an ability, not great but real, to see both sides of the question. It never occurred to him that three years in age might make a difference in Charlie's outlook, and certainly it never entered his head that he himself had the temperament of the artist, detesting both high and low, and anxious only to be let alone to get on with his own work. Charlie was the upper class flinging itself into the struggle for justice on behalf of the oppressed; Charlie was Byron, determined to free the Greeks without having any clear notion of what or who the Greeks were; Charlie was a Grail knight of social justice.

Francis cared little what might happen to Charlie, but he grieved and brooded over Ismay. He had a strong intuition that Charlie was a bad influence, and the more he saw of Charlie at Buys-Bozzaris's gambling sessions the stronger that intuition became. There were now too many regulars at the evening sessions for bridge, and the game had become poker; for poker Charlie had no aptitude at all. Not only was he a rash gambler; he delighted in the role of the rash gambler. He seemed almost to claw his chips toward him; he flung down his cards with an air of defiance; he took stupid risks—and lost. He did not pay, he gave IOUs which Buys-Bozzaris tucked in his waistcoat pocket almost as if he did not notice them. Francis knew quite enough of the grammar of money to know that an IOU is a very dangerous scrap of paper. Worst of all, on the rare occasions when Charlie won, he exulted in an unseemly way, as if by pillaging the Oxonians around him he was vindicating the have-not class. Francis fretted about Charlie, without quite seeing that Charlie was a fool and a gull. For Charlie had something that looked like romantic sweep and dash, and these were qualities that Francis knew he lacked utterly.

He saw a lot of Ismay, for Ismay was drawn by the easy glasses of excellent sherry, the meals at the George, the visits to the cinema and the theatre that Francis could provide, and was eager to provide. Ismay was even willing to let Francis kiss her and paw her (paw was her expression when she was impatient and wanted him to stop) as a reasonable return for the luxuries he commanded. This gave Francis even deeper anxiety; if she allowed him such liberties, what did she permit to Charlie?

He was miserable, as only a worried lover can be, but his love had another and happier aspect. Ismay was willing to pose for drawings, and he did many sketches of her.

When he had completed a particularly good one she said: "Oh, may I have that?"

"It's not much more than a study. Let me try for a really good one."

"No, this is terrific. Charlie would love it."

Charlie did not love it. He was furious and tore it up, and made Ismay cry—she did not often cry—because he said he would not have that oaf Cornish looking at her in the way the sketch made it very clear that he did look at her—as a lover, an adorer.

Ismay, however, rather enjoyed Charlie's pique, so much more fiery than Francis's sluggish jealousy, disguised as concern, so stuffy and possessive. So things went further, and when one day Francis worked himself up to the pitch of asking Ismay if he might draw her in the nude, she consented. He was overjoyed, until she said, "But none of the old Artists-and-Models-in-Paris stuff, you understand?" which he thought reflected on his phlegmatic, objective artist's attitude toward the unclothed figure. He admitted to himself that Ismay had a coarse streak—but that was part of her irresistible allurement. Coarse, like some splendid woman of the Renaissance aristocracy.

So he sketched Ismay in the nude, as she lay on the sofa in his sitting-room on the top floor of Canterbury House, where the light was so good and the coal fire kept the room so warm, and on many subsequent occasions he sketched her in the nude, and though his excellent experience in Mr. Devinney's embalming parlour enabled him to do it very well, the thought of all those work-worn corpses never entered his head.

One day, when he had finished a good effort, he threw down his pad and pencil and knelt beside her on the sofa, kissing her hands and trying to keep back the tears that rushed to his eyes.

"What is it?"

"You are so beautiful, and I love you so much."

"Oh Christ," said Ismay. "I thought it might come to this."

"To what?"

"To talk about love, you prize ass."

"But I do love you. Have you no feeling for me at all?"

Ismay leaned toward him, and his face was buried between her breasts. "Yes," she said. "I love you, Frank—but I'm not in love with you, if you understand."

This is a nice distinction, dear to some female hearts, which people like Francis can never encompass. But he was happy, for had she not said she loved him? Being in love might follow.

So, when he had agreed to her condition that he must not talk about love, it was decided by Ismay that the afternoons of posing in the nude might continue from time to time. She liked it. It gave her a sense of living fully and richly, and Francis's adoring eyes warmed her in places where the glow of his generous coal fire could not reach—places that Charlie did not seem to know existed.

"WHO TAUGHT YOU TO DRAW?"

In one of the guest-rooms at Exeter, where he was staying for a few days in the Spring Term, Saraceni was looking over the sketches and finished pictures that Francis had brought him.

"Harry Furniss, I suppose."

"Extraordinary! Just possible, but—he died—let me see—surely more than ten years ago!"

"But only from a book. *How to Draw in Pen and Ink*—it was my Bible when I was a boy."

"Well, you have his vigour, but not his coarse style—his jokey, jolly-good-fellow superficial style."

"Of course, I've done a great deal of copying since those days, as you can see. I copy Old Master drawings, at the Ashmolean every week. I try to capture their manner as well as their matter. As you said you did when you restored pictures."

"Yes, and you didn't learn anatomy from Harry Furniss, or from copying."

"I picked it up in an embalming parlour, as a matter of fact."

"Mother of God! There is a good deal more in you than meets the eye, Mr. Cornish."

"I hope so. What meets the eye doesn't make much impression, I'm afraid."

"There speaks a man in love. Unhappily in love. In love with this model for these nude studies that you have been trying to palm off on me as some of your Old Master copies."

Saraceni laid his hand on a group of drawings of Ismay that had cost Francis great pains. He had coated an expensive hand-made paper with Chinese white mixed with enough brown bole to give it an ivory tint, and on the sheets thus prepared he had worked up some of his sketches of the nude Ismay, drawing with a silver-point that had cost him a substantial sum, touching up the drawing at last with red chalk.

"I didn't mean to deceive you."

"Oh, you didn't deceive me, Mr. Cornish, though you might deceive a good many people."

"I mean I wasn't trying to deceive anybody. Only to work in the genuine Renaissance style."

"And you have done so. You have imitated the manner admirably. But you haven't been so careful about the matter. This girl, now: she is a girl of today. Everything about her figure declares it. Slim, tall for a woman, long legs—this is not a woman of the Renaissance. Her feet alone give the show away; neither the big feet of the peasant model nor the deformed feet of a woman of fortune. The Old Masters, you know, when they weren't copying from the antique, were drawing women of a kind we do not see today. This girl, now—look at her breasts. She will probably never suckle a child, or not for long. But the women of the Renaissance did so, and their painters fancied the great motherly udders; as soon as those women had given up their virginity they seemed to be always giving suck, and by thirty-five they had flat, exhausted bladders hanging to their waists. Their private parts were torn with child-bearing, and I supposed a lot of them had piles for the same reason. Age came early in those days. The flesh that showed such rosy opulence at eighteen had lost its glow, and fat hung on bones far too small to support it well. This girl of yours will be a beauty all her life. This is the beauty you have captured with a tenderness that suggests a lover.

"I am not pretending to be clairvoyant. Looking deep into pictures is my profession. It is simple enough to see that this model is a woman of today, and the attitude of the artist to his sitter is always apparent in the picture. Every picture is several things: what the artist sees, but also what he thinks about what he sees, and because of that, in a certain sense it is a portrait of himself. All those elements are here.

"None of this is to say that this is not good work. But why go to such pains to work in the Renaissance style?"

"It seems to me to be capable of saying so much that can't be said—or I should say that can't be said by me—in a contemporary manner."

"Yes, yes, and to compliment the sitter—I hope she is grateful—and to show that you see her as beyond time and place. You draw pretty well. Drawing is not so lovingly fostered now as it used to be. A modern artist may be a fine draughtsman without depending much on his skill. You love drawing simply for itself."

"Yes. It sounds extreme, but it's an obsession with me."

"More than colour?"

"I don't know, I haven't really done much about colour."

"I could introduce you to that, you know. But I wonder how good a draughtsman you really are. Would you submit to a test?"

"I'd be flattered that you thought it worth your trouble."

"Taking trouble is much of my profession, also. You have your pad? Draw a straight line from the top of the page to the bottom, will you? And I mean a *straight* line, done freehand."

Francis obeyed.

"Now: draw the same line from the bottom to the top, so exactly that the two lines are one."

This was not so easily done. At one point Francis's line varied a fraction from the first one.

"Ah, that was not simple, was it? Now draw a line across the page to bisect that line—or I should say those two indistinguishable lines. Yes. Now draw a line through the centre point where those two lines bisect; draw it so that I cannot see a hint of a triangle at the middle point. Yes, that is not bad."

The next part of the test was the drawing of circles, freehand, clockwise and anti-clockwise, concentric and in various ways eccentric. Francis managed all of this with credit, but without perfection.

"You should work on this sort of thing," said Saraceni. "You have ability, but you have not refined it to the full extent of your capabilities. This is the foundation of drawing, you must understand. Now, will you try a final test? This is rather more than command of the pencil; it is to test your understanding of mass and space. I shall sit here in this chair, as I have been doing, and you shall draw me as well as you can in five minutes. But you shall draw me as I would look if you were sitting behind me. Ready?"

Francis was wholly unprepared for this, and felt that he made a mess of it. But when Saraceni looked at the result, he laughed.

"If you think you might be interested in my profession, Mr. Cornish—and I assure you it is full of interest—write to me, or come and see me. Here is my card; my permanent address, as you see, is in Rome, though I am not often there; but it would reach me. Come and see me anyhow. I have some things that would interest you."

"You mean I might become a restorer of old paintings?" said Francis.

"You certainly could do so, after you had worked with me. But I see you do not take that as a compliment; it suggests that your talent is not first-rate. Well, you asked me for an opinion, and you shall have it. Your talent is substantial, but not first-rate."

"What's wrong?"

"A lack of a certain important kind of energy. Not enough is coming up from below. There are dozens of respected artists in this country and elsewhere who cannot begin to draw as well as you, and who have certainly not as fine an eye as you, but they have something individual about their work, even when it looks crude and stupid to the uninstructed eye. What they have is what comes from below. Are you a Catholic?"

"Well—partly, I suppose."

"I might have known. You must either be a Catholic, or not be one. The half-Catholics are not meant to be artists, any more than the half-anything-elses. Good night, Mr. Cornish. Let us meet again."

"WHAT WOULD YOU LIKE FOR YOUR BIRTHDAY?"

"Money, please."

"But Ismay, money isn't a present. I want to give you something real."

"What's unreal about money?"

"Will you promise to buy something you really want?"

"Frank, what do you expect me to do with it?"

So Francis gave her a cheque for ten pounds. When Charlie came to Buys-Bozzaris's poker-night two days later with ten pounds to risk, Francis was immediately suspicious.

"Did you give Charlie that ten quid?"

"Yes. He was in a hole."

"But I meant it for you!"

"Charlie and I believe in property in common."

"Oh? And what does Charlie share with you?"

"What right have you to ask that?"

"Damn it, Ismay, I love you. I've told you so more times than I can count."

"I think the porter at the Examination Schools loves me; he always looks sheepish when I speak to him. But that doesn't give him the right to ask me about my private life."

"Don't talk like a fool."

"All right, I won't. You think I'm sleeping with Charlie, don't you? If I were—and I don't say I am—what would it be to you? Aren't you pushing the cousin thing a bit far?"

"It isn't the cousin thing."

"Do you remember what you said, the first time you spoke to me? 'Marry come up, m'dirty cousin.' I said I'd trace that, and I have. A chap in Eng.Lit. ran it down for me. It's from an old play:

'Marry come up, m'dirty Cousin; he may have such as you by the Dozen.' Is that what you mean, Frank? Do you think I'm a whore?"

"I never heard that; I just thought it was something you said to pushy people. And you were very pushy and you still are. But not a whore. Certainly not a whore."

"No; not a whore. But Charlie and I have ideas far beyond yours. You've some frightfully backwoods notions, Frank. You must understand: I won't be questioned and I won't be uncled by you. If that's the way you want it, we're through."

Apologies. Protestations of lover-like concern for her welfare—which made her laugh. An expensive lunch at the George. An afternoon during which she posed for him again; before they settled to work, Ismay struck a number of whorish poses which tormented him, and made her laugh at his torment. And before she went, he gave her another cheque for ten pounds, because she must have a present for herself, and no, no, no, don't stake Charlie at poker if you really care for him at all, because it will be his ruin.

What Ismay bought with the cheque Francis never knew, for he dared not ask her, and he knew from his bank statement that the cheque was not cashed. Doubtless she was keeping it until something appeared that she really wanted.

WHAT BASIL BUYS-BOZZARIS WANTED was becoming clear. After the poker sessions he always asked Francis to stay and talk for a while, and as they lived in the same house there was no need for Francis to leave before midnight; they were free of the rule governing all junior members of the University, who must be in their lodgings or their colleges by midnight, or risk expulsion. Roskalns stayed, as well, because he was not a member of the University, and could come and go as he pleased. And what was the drift of the talk?

Francis understood it long before Buys-Bozzaris knew that he did. The count (if he were a count) from Bulgaria (if that were his place of origin) had what he called advanced political ideas, and although these were not so naive as Charlie's, they tended in Charlie's direction. It was not difficult to broach such subjects at Oxford at that time, where it was common talk among shoals of undergraduates that the political world was, in the popular expression, "polarized". Democracy had failed, and its forms of government might be expected to collapse at any time. Everybody with a head on his shoulders was aware, whether he formulated the thought clearly or not, that he was either a fascist or a communist, and if his head was a good head, there was only one choice. Not to take a side was to be an "indifferentist", and when the show-down came the indifferentists would surely suffer for their foolishness. Buys-Bozzaris knew which way the cat would jump.

Certainly this political cat would not jump toward fascism, which was essentially a bourgeois concept, under the guidance of people like Hitler and Mussolini who wanted to found strong nations—even empires—on the impossible foundations of some version of capitalism. Only a Marxist world, which was to say a world in which the primary doctrines of Marx had been refined and hammered out through trial and error, had any chance of survival. Was it not time for anybody who had his eye on that jumping cat to throw in his lot with the side that would dominate the civilized world, probably in less than ten years? Wasn't it every intelligent man's duty to push things along?

Francis could be of help, perhaps of very great help, but until he had made a firm decision, it was not possible for Buys-Bozzaris to say precisely how it was to be done. Francis was, as Buys-Bozzaris knew—oh, yes, he was not so much the simple student of international law as a casual observer might think—a young man with a certain background. He had money; that was easily to be seen, if you knew what money was, and Buys-Bozzaris knew. He had an invaluable possession in his Canadian citizenship and his Canadian passport, because with those credentials he could go almost anywhere without arousing suspicion. Surely Francis knew that Canadian passports were greatly valued in the world of international espionage? The genuine article, capable of surviving any amount of probing, was a gift of the gods. If Francis chose, he could be immensely useful, and in the course of time his usefulness would not go unrewarded. Had Francis any idea what he was talking about?

Francis admitted that he could dimly guess what lay behind

such conversation. But it was such a novel idea. He needed time to think. Gee, it had never been put to him quite that way before. (Francis thought "Gee" a good stroke; it was just what somebody like Buys-Bozzaris would expect a Canadian to say, when the heavens of political opportunity were opened to him.) Could they talk further? He had to get it sorted out, and in such matters as this, he was a slow thinker.

Take plenty of time, said Buys-Bozzaris.

FRANCIS DID TAKE plenty of time. He did not want to attract the attention of the Bulgarian count, who seemed to watch all his comings and goings, by doing anything uncommon. So he waited until the Easter vacation to meet Colonel Copplestone and tell him all he knew. Once again they lunched at the Athenaeum. Francis understood that the Colonel thought a crowded room, with lots of noise, the best place for confidences. Two people leaning across a table, talking as quietly as possible, attracted no attention. The Colonel listened to all he had to say.

"Your man is quite well known to the profession," he said, when Francis had finished. "Not a very serious person. Rather an ass, in fact. Quite a common type; he has no important contact with the people he talks about, and no real influence. But he likes to suggest that he has a lot of power. Of course, he scorns the out-in-the-open student Communist group: he likes subtlety and secrecy and all the allurement of the classy spy. He isn't one, believe me. Your fellow-Canadian is much more interesting, really. Hot-heads like that can reveal quite a lot by what they do, or try to do, rather than what they know. Keep me posted."

"I'm sorry not to have been more useful," said Francis. This was his first attempt to show that he was worthy of the profession, and it was disappointing to find that he had not really uncovered anything.

"Oh, but you have been useful," said the Colonel. "You've corroborated some information, and that's useful. My job needs an enormous amount of work that isn't at all dramatic, you know. Don't be influenced by novels that suggest that extraordinary things are done by some wonderful chap working entirely on his own."

"Aren't there any wonderful chaps?"

"There may be. But there are far more who just get on quietly, noticing something here, something there, corroborating something for the fifteenth time."

"Wasn't Father wonderful?"

"You should ask him. I can guess what he'd tell you. His best work was understanding and collating things he heard from dozens of chaps who were doing what you're doing. He was awfully good at putting two and two together."

"And I'm likely to go on doing this for quite a while?"

"Quite a while, I should say. Yes."

"I'm not likely to be a permanency, then?"

"Paid, you mean. Oh, my dear fellow, don't be silly. Chaps with incomes like yours don't get paid for the kind of thing you're doing."

"I see. That seems to be the English way. A while ago I was talking to the chief of the curators of the Ashmolean, asking if there were any chance of my getting an appointment there when I've taken my degree. 'What private income have you?' he asked, very first thing. Listen, Uncle Jack, suppose BBB were to offer me a job—a job with money—wouldn't it be a temptation?"

"Not if you've got any brains at all. He won't, you know, but if he did, you should tell me at once. Because you'd never get away with it. You aren't as much alone, or as unknown, as you might suppose. But why are you fussing about money? You've got plenty, haven't you?"

"Yes, but everybody seems to think I'm to be had cheap. Everybody thinks I'm a money-bags. Haven't I any value, apart from my money?"

"Of course you have. Would I be talking to you now if you hadn't? But nobody gets rich in the profession. And nobody who is once in it—even as far in as you are, which isn't far—ever quite gets out of it. Do you think for a moment that your man has lashings of money from his side, to pass out to people like you? He's probably being squeezed, and that can be very uncomfortable. Now, you just get on with what you're doing, and if the time ever comes when we should talk about money, I'll bring the subject up myself."

"Very sorry, Uncle Jack."

"Don't mention it, Francis. And I mean that in every sense of the words."

There had been a look in Colonel Copplestone's eye that surprised and humbled Francis. The benevolent uncle had suddenly turned tough.

IT WAS THE FOURTH WEEK of the Oxford summer term; Trinity Term, as the ancient custom of the University called it. It was Eights Week, when the colleges raced their boats to determine which college should be Head of the River. Francis was taking a leaf out of Colonel Copplestone's book, and he was having a very important conversation with Ismay in the open air, sitting comfortably on the upper deck of the Corpus barge, amid a din of cheering, as they ate strawberries and cream and watched the sweating oarsmen.

"I had a queer message from my bank a couple of days ago."

"I never get anything but queer messages from my bank."

"I'm not surprised if you go on the way you're going."

"Meaning what?"

"I think you know very well what. A cheque made out to you and signed by me, for a hundred and fifty pounds."

Ismay seemed to be chewing a difficult strawberry. "What did they say?"

"Called me in to have a look at it and inquire a little."

"What did you say?"

"Oh, we just chatted. Banker and client, you know."

"Frank, you've got to understand about this. My bank cashed the cheque and I haven't got the money."

"I didn't suppose you had. Charlie's got it, hasn't he?"

"Do we have to talk here?"

"Why not? Just keep your voice down, and if you have anything particularly important to say, whisper it when I'm shouting 'Well rowed, Corpus!' I'll hear you. I have excellent hearing."

"Oh for God's sake don't be so facetious! Do you suppose I'm a forger?"

"Yes. And if you want to know, I've suspected it for some time. Do you think I was taken in when you admired my elegant Italic hand suddenly, and wanted me to show you how it was done?

You're one of Nature's scrawlers, Ismay; if you wanted to learn Italic, it was so you could write like me. Enough to change a cheque, for instance. And why would you want to do that, you little twister?"

"Why did the bank ask you, anyway?"

"The banks all have an agreement with the Proctors that if a junior member of the University cashes a particularly big cheque they will tip the Proctors off. It's a way of keeping an eye on gambling. I suppose the money went to pay off Charlie's debts to Buys-Bozzaris?"

"It will. But you've got to understand; Charlie was being threatened."

"By the fat count? Don't be funny."

"No, by some other chaps—real thugs. Frank, Buys-Bozzaris is a crook."

"You amaze me! Crooks on all sides! You make me tremble!"

"Oh, for God's sake be serious!"

"I am serious. These races stir the blood. Listen to those people shouting. 'Well rowed, Balliol!' Doesn't that excite you?"

"Some terrible toughs came to see Charlie and threatened him. They had all his IOUs that he gave to Buys-Bozzaris. That fat bugger had sold them!"

"Mind your language. This is the barge of the College of Corpus Christi, and we must not disgrace our sacred name. Are you surpised that BBB sold the IOUs? I suppose he needed ready cash and sold them at a discount."

"I've never heard of anything like it!"

"Oh, but you will, Ismay, you will. When you've gone a little farther in the forging game, you'll hear some things that will astonish you. The conversation in prison is most illuminating, I'm told."

"Be serious, Frank. Please!"

"I can be awfully serious about a hundred and fifty nicker. That's an underworld expression, by the way; you'll pick up the lingo soon."

"What did you tell the bank about the cheque?"

"As they'd cashed it, I didn't think I needed to say much. They were looking very coy, you know the way bankers do when they think you're a perfect devil of a fellow."

"You mean you didn't tell?"

"And shame my bank? When you had done such a lovely job, neatly transforming that birthday cheque for ten quid? How could they have faced me, if I'd told them it was a forgery?"

"Oh, Frank, you are a darling!"

"A darling or a complete mug, do you mean?"

"Well—it was one of those tight squeezes. I'll make it up to you, honestly I will."

"Honestly you will? What could you do honestly, Ismay? Sleep with me, do you suppose?"

"If that's what you want."

"You know it's what I want. But not with a price on it, the price being Charlie's skin. I don't think that would have quite the right romantic savour, do you? Though, let's see: woman sacrifices herself to the lust of her wealthy pursuer, to save the honour of her lover. Rather good, isn't it? Only I don't like the casting; either I'm the lover and Charlie is the villain, or it's no deal. May I get you some more strawberries?"

FRANCIS WAS LOOKING FORWARD to his visit to Buys-Bozzaris. His confusion and ineptitude which had made it impossible to cope with a blow in the face or a kick in the rump at Carlyle Rural was long behind him; he was prepared to be moderately rough with the fat count if that should be necessary. His banker's blood, which he had not known he possessed, was running hot, and he wanted his money. After dinner at Corpus he made his way the short distance back to Canterbury House, and knocked on the familiar door.

"Cornish? Happy to see you. Let me give you a drink. Am I to suppose that you have made up your mind about joining us in our political work? You can talk freely. Roskalns here is one of us, and this isn't a poker-night, so nobody else is likely to drop in."

"I've come about those IOUs that Charlie Fremantle gave you."

"Oh—no need to worry. That's all over. Charlie has paid, like an honest chap."

"Come on, Basil. You flogged those notes."

"Well—same thing, isn't it? Charlie is clear."

"No, Charlie bloody well isn't clear. The money to pay came from a cheque that was forged in my name. I want a hundred and fifty pounds from you."

"A hundred and fifty—Oh, come, Cornish, Charlie owed me exactly ninety-seven pounds, fourteen and elevenpence, and I haven't had it yet. I am expecting a visit from the collectors, this evening, as a matter of fact. Did that naughty boy sophisticate a cheque for a hundred and fifty? That wasn't very honest of him, was it?"

"No, and it wasn't very honest of you to give those notes to collectors, as you call them, who are shaking Charlie down for a hundred and fifty, out of which you will presumably get your ninety-seven, fourteen and eleven. I want the names of those fellows. I'm going to turn them over to the Proctors."

"Now, now, Cornish, you're heated. You wouldn't do that. There are rules, unwritten rules, among gentlemen about debts of this sort. Not bringing in the Proggins is almost Rule Number One. Of course Rule Number One is, always pay up."

"But not with my money."

"What about *my* money? Why are you talking to me? Talk to Charlie. He's the naughty boy."

"I'll certainly talk to Charlie. But I'm out a hundred and fifty, and I thought you might have been paid already."

"Not a bean. I'm waiting, as I told you. And I shall have something to say to those collectors. A hundred and fifty pounds for a debt of ninety-seven, fourteen and eleven. It's outrageous!"

"Yes, and so is selling IOUs. Why didn't you collect yourself?"

"Oh, Cornish, you're impossible. One has a certain position. One doesn't go about with a little greasy book, rapping on doors. Or do they, where you come from?"

"Never mind where I come from."

This might have become rancorous, if there had not been a tap on the door. If Francis had not been so busy with Buys-Bozzaris, he could have heard shuffling and whispering outside. Roskalns answered, tried to shut the door after he had peeped through a crack, and was flung backward, as two determined men thrust their way in. In Oxford there are several gradations of society: members of the University, in all their diversity, attendants and servants of members of the University, in all *their* diversity, and people who are not associated with the University, who are also various, but look entirely different from the other two classes. These men were very plainly of class number three.

"Look here, Mr. Booze-Bozzaris, this will never do. Young Fremantle has scarpered."

"You mean he has gone?"

"What I said. Scarpered."

"I don't understand."

"Well then, let me put you straight. We visited him, as per arrangement, and he said, gimme a little time to get the money together, and we said rightyho, but no funny stuff, see? Let's have it, and in cash. Because we are well aware that there can be dishonesty in these matters of collection, and we didn't want none of that. So we kept an eye on the place, and he came and went, and came and went, quite normal. It's one of the colleges he's in; New College. Whenever we inquires, the porter says he's in. But those fellows would say anything. When we didn't see him yesterday we went quiet up to his rooms, and the long and short of it is, he scarpered."

"You're telling me you can't pay me?"

"What do you mean, pay you, Mr. Booze-Bozzaris? We paid you fifty quid on account for those notes, agreeing to make up the rest of the ninety-seven, fourteen and eleven after we'd collected from Fremantle—"

"After you collected a hundred and fifty quid from him, you mean," said Buys-Bozzaris.

"That's by the way. We have to have something for our trouble and risk, haven't we? But now we shall have to ask for that fifty quid back, because we been diddled."

"But not by me."

"Never mind who by. Let's have it."

"Don't be absurd."

"Now look, Mr. Booze-Bozzaris, we don't want trouble in any shape nor form, but it's pay up now or my colleague here may have to do a little persuading."

The colleague, who said nothing, cleared his throat softly, and flexed his hands, rather like a pianist. For the first time the collector who did the talking spoke to Francis. "You'll want to leave, sir," he said; "this is just some private business."

"Not private from me," said Francis. "I have some money to recover from Charlie myself."

"This is getting too complicated altogether," said the collector. "We got no time to waste. Now just stand perfectly still, Mr. Booze-Bozzaris, and you two other gents keep out of the way, while my colleague makes a search that will be perfectly polite and easy, so long as there is no resistance."

The colleague moved toward Basil gently but firmly, his hands extended as if he might be going to tickle him. Buys-Bozzaris backed toward a corner, and as he did so his hand went to the pocket of his jacket.

"Oh no you don't!" said the talking collector. The colleague seized the arm that Buys-Bozzaris jerked upward. The pistol caught in the top of his pocket, went off with a roar that was like a cannon in the room, and Buys-Bozzaris fell to the floor with a scream that was louder still.

"Christ! Shot himself!" said the collector.

"Shot off his goolies!" said the colleague, speaking for the first time. The two rushed to the door, through the small hall and into the street, and were gone.

Gunfire in Oxford is uncommon. The University Statutes strictly forbid it. In a few seconds Mr. Tasnim Khan from the first floor, Mr. Westerby from the second, Mr. Colney-Overend from across the hall, and the landlord were all in the room, shouting contradictory advice. It was Francis who lugged Buys-Bozzaris into a chair, and it became apparent that he had shot himself, not very seriously, in the foot.

Half an hour later the injured man, moaning like a cow in labour, had been taken by Roskalns to the Radcliffe Infirmary in a taxi. Francis had been with the landlord to hunt up the Proctors, and give an account of the affair which said only that two men had visited the Bulgarian, demanded money related apparently to a debt, that nobody had fired a gun at anyone, and the wound was pure accident. The Junior Proctor, who heard it all, raised his eyebrows at the word "pure", took names, warned Francis not to leave Oxford until the matter had been fully investigated, and called the hospital to say that Buys-Bozzaris was not to be released until he had been questioned.

Francis went to Lady Margaret Hall, where, as it still lacked a quarter of an hour before the closing of the gate, he was able to have a short talk with Ismay.

"Oh yes, Charlie's scarpered. I knew he would."

"Where's he gone?"

"I don't suppose it matters if you know, because he won't be back and he won't be found. He's gone to Spain to join the Cause."

"Which of the many possible Causes would that be?"

"The Loyalists, obviously. Thinking as he does."

"Well—at least your name hasn't been mentioned. And won't be, if you have enough sense to keep your mouth shut."

"Thanks, Frank. You're sweet."

"That's what I'm beginning to be afraid of."

BEING SWEET MIGHT MEAN being a gull, but there were compensations. Francis was invited by his Aunt Prudence Glasson to spend a fortnight at St. Columb Hall, the Glasson family seat, when the Oxford term ended. He seemed, said Aunt Prudence, to have become a great chum of Ismay's, and they would be delighted to welcome him, as it was such a long time since he had stayed at nearby Chegwidden. At that time, Francis remembered, the Glassons had not troubled to ask him to visit them, though Aunt Prudence was his father's sister, and her pestilent younger children had seen a great deal of him and found him mockable. But he had no mind for resentment; the thought of having Ismay under his eye for two weeks, without Charlie and the pleasures of Oxford to distract her, was irresistible.

The horrible children had become more tolerable since last he saw them. The two girls, Isabel and Amabel, were lumpy, fattish schoolgirls, who blushed painfully if he spoke to them and giggled and squirmed when he reminded them of the dead adder in his bed. Their older brother, Roderick, who was seventeen, was at this stage very much a product of Winchester, and seemed to have become a Civil Servant without ever having been a youth; but he was not seen much, as he spent a lot of time winding himself up for a scholarship examination that lay some time in the future. Ismay alone retained any of the wildness he had associated with his Glasson cousins.

She was offhand and dismissive with her mother, and contradicted her father on principle. The older Roderick Glasson, it is true, provoked contradiction; he was of the same political stripe as Uncle Arthur Cornish—that is to say, his Toryism was a cautious echo of an earlier day—and though he never quite sank to saying that he didn't know what things were coming to, he used the word "nowadays" frequently in a way that showed he expected nothing from a world gone mad, a world that had forgotten the great days before 1914. This extended even to female beauty.

"You should have seen your mother when your father married her," he said to Francis. "An absolute stunner. There aren't any women like that now. They've broken the mould."

"If he had seen his mother when his father married her," said Ismay, "it would have been rather a scandal, wouldn't it?"

"Ismay, darling, don't catch Daddy up on everything he says," said Aunt Prudence, and a familiar wrangle was renewed.

"Well, why can't people say what they mean, and not simply waffle?"

"You know perfectly well what I meant, but you can't resist any opportunity to show how clever you've become at Oxford."

"If you didn't want me to become clever at Oxford, you shouldn't have nagged me to go for that miserable, inadequate scholarship. I could have stayed at home and studied stupidity. That would have had the advantage of being cheap."

"As I suppose you are too old to be sent from the table, Ismay, I have no recourse but to leave it myself. Francis, would you like a cigar?"

"We've finished anyway, and I wish you wouldn't take refuge in Christian-martyring, Daddy. It isn't argument."

"I do so well remember your mother's wedding," said Aunt Prudence, the peacemaker. "But Francis, didn't you have an older brother? I seem to remember a letter from Switzerland, from your father."

"There was an older brother, also Francis, but he died."

It was the memory of that older Francis that softened the opinions of the living Francis about Ismay and her parents. In a world that contained such secrets as the Looner, these disputes seemed trivial. What did Wordsworth call it? The still, sad music of humanity—to chasten and subdue? Something like that. The underlying, deep grief of things. One must try to understand, to overlook sharp edges. Of course he was on Ismay's side, but certainly not as a combatant. Her parents were dull and tedious, and she was too young, too radiant and full of life, to have learned to be patient. Probably she had never had to be patient about anything. Without knowing it, Francis's view of family life was much like that of Shakespeare; parents, unless they happened to be stars like King Lear, were minor roles, obstructive, comic, and not to be too much heeded. Only Coriolanus paid attention to his mother, and look what happened to him!

If Shakespeare was not present in his mind, the Grail legend had returned to it in full force. Once again he was on the holy ground of Cornwall, and the pedal-point of his passion for Ismay was the story of Tristan and Iseult, and another more primitive and magical tale.

A passion it certainly was. He was twenty-four years old, so he did not moon and brood like a boy, but he ached for Ismay, and longed to see her happy and pleased with life. He had the lover's unjustified belief that love begets love. It was impossible that he should love Ismay so much without her loving him by infection. He did not think ill of himself; he did not consider himself deficient, compared with other young men. But faced with the splendour of Ismay he could only hope that she might let him serve her, devote his life to her and whatever she wanted.

Ismay knew all of this, and therefore it was perhaps surprising that she let him persuade her to spend a day with him at Tintagel. She tormented him, of course. Shouldn't they take Isabel and Amabel, who did not get many outings; they mustn't be selfish, must they? But it was Francis's intention, on this occasion, to be wholly selfish.

They had a fine day for their picnic, though as it was Cornwall it was certainly not a dry day. Ismay had never been to Tintagel, and Francis held forth about its history: the castle of the Black Prince, and before that the monastic community that had gathered around the hermitage of St. Juliot, and, far back in the mists, Arthur, that mysterious fifth-century figure who might have been the last preserver of Roman order and Roman culture in a Britain overrun by savage northerners, or—even better—have been the mighty figure of Welsh legend.

"Did he live here?" said Ismay, who seemed to be yielding a little to the nature of the story and the spirit of the place.

"Born here, and strangely begotten here."

"Why strangely?"

"His mother was a wonderfully beautiful princess, who was wife to the Duke of Cornwall. Her name was Ygraine. A very great Celtic chieftain, Uther Pendragon, saw her and desired her and could not rest until he had possessed her. So he took counsel of the magician, Merlin, and Merlin surrounded this castle with a magical spell, so that when her husband was absent Uther Pendragon was able to come to her in her husband's guise, and it was here that he begot the marvellous child who grew to be Arthur."

"Didn't the Duke ever find out?"

"The Duke had no luck; he was killed and cuckolded the same night, though not by the same man. Arthur was brought up by another knight, Sir Ector, and educated by Merlin."

"Lucky lad."

"Yes. Didn't you ever learn any of this at school? You, a Cornish girl—a Cornish princess."

"My school thought mythology meant Greeks."

"Not a patch on the great Northern and Celtic stuff."

Thus Francis began the casting of a spell that had been long working in his mind, and with such success that Ismay yielded to it, becoming tenderer and more compliant than he had ever known her, until at last on a motor rug in the embrace of what might have been part of the Black Prince's castle, or one of the hermitages of the companions of St. Juliot, or just possibly a remnant of that castle of Duke Gorlois (who figures ignominiously in legend as cuckolds must) in which Arthur was begotten, he possessed Ismay, and it seemed to him that the world could never have been so splendid, or blessing so perfect, since the days of the great legend.

Ismay was subdued as they made their way back to the Glasson family car (itself almost a vehicle of legend) and walked somewhat uneasily.

"Anything wrong?"

"Not seriously. But there were a few stones under that rug. Frank, do you know the one—

> *There was a young fellow named Dockery*
> *Who was screwing his girl in a rockery;*
>   *Oh what did she wail*
>   *As they thumped on the shale?*
> *'This isn't a fuck—it's a mockery!'*

Francis was so lost in the splendour of the afternoon that he was ready to accept this as the plain-spoken jesting of the age of legend, befitting a Celtic princess.

FRANCIS HAD TAKEN SERIOUSLY Saraceni's advice that he should stop flirting with colour and find out what it truly was. That meant working in oils, and except for some tentative messing he had never done much with oils, and knew he must make a serious beginning. When he left Cornwall, reluctantly but aware that his fortnight could not be extended, he went to Paris, and during the summer months worked almost every day at La Grande Chaumière, an art school directed at the time by Othon Friesz. He bought the tickets that were sold by the concierge, arrived early and left late, spoiled a substantial amount of canvas, and achieved some dreadful messes of dirty colour until, in time, he was able to put into practice the few precepts Friesz threw to him, almost inaudibly and apparently with contempt.

Always paint fat on lean. Always lay in your warms over your colds. The groundwork should be done in paint well thinned with turpentine: afterward your fat colour, mixed with mastic or Venice turps. Don't mess your paint about on the palette: fresh paint gives the best quality. Never put more of a colour over the same colour. Always paint warm on cold and after your body coat every successive coat must be thinner until you get to the top. Always fat on lean.

Simplicity itself, like the few notes Mozart wrote on the back of a letter and gave to his pupil Sussmayer to explain how to compose music. But not easy to do. It was Francis's skill in drawing that saved him from abject failure. There were plenty of students in the atelier who knew nothing of drawing, and from their easels Friesz sometimes turned with a murmured "Quelle horreur!" But Friesz did not turn up often. Having given advice, he allowed the student to struggle until he had mastered it or abandoned the contest. Friesz provided a place to work, an ambience, a name, and infrequent, good advice; it was enough.

After ten weeks of hard work Francis thought he had earned a holiday, and would go to Rome. He would see the sights of Rome, and he would find out if Tancred Saraceni had meant anything more than pleasantry when he said to hunt him up.

Saraceni meant much more than that. He insisted that Francis stay with him, and allow him to display the wonders of the great city. There was more than enough room in his apartment.

The apartment was a marvel of splendid clutter. For thirty years Tancred Saraceni had never been able to deny himself a bargain, or a good piece of painting or furniture, or tapestry, or embroidery, or sculpture, whenever one turned up that he could afford, and in his life such things turned up all the time. It was not a pack-rat's nest and there was not a thing in it that was not fine of its own kind; everything was disposed with taste and effect, so far as space allowed. But even in the generous space of that apartment there were limitations, and though Saraceni would not have admitted it, the limitations had long ago been exceeded. The effect was overwhelming.

Why overwhelming? Because it was vastly more than the sum of its parts. It was a collection various in kind, but coherent in representing the taste of one avid, brilliant, greatly gifted connoisseur. It was Saraceni swollen to immense proportions. It was a man's mind, the size of a house.

The apartment itself was part of an old palace that faced what had once been a charming little square with a fountain playing gently in its middle. But that had been in the days before the motor car degraded and despoiled Rome as it has degraded and despoiled so many cities. Now the little square was every day parked full of cars that came and went, leaving their stink on the heavy September air. The little fountain still played, but its basin was full of food wrappers and trash, rarely cleared out. Because the air outside was fouled by cars, Saraceni logically refused to open his windows, and this did nothing to lighten the oppressive feeling of his dwelling. Literally it had an air of an earlier day.

He was alone. A woman came every morning and did such cleaning as he would permit; he dusted all the objects of art, and himself polished whatever needed to be polished. He had been married, yes, to a wonderful English lady who had at last decided that she could no longer bear to live under such circumstances, and they had parted amicably. Tancredo, she had said, you must make a decision—shall it be the collection or me? He had not needed long to decide. My dearest one, he had said, the collection is timeless and you, alas that it should be so, are trapped in time. She had laughed so marvellously that he had almost been tempted to change his mind, but had not done so, in the end. A wonderful woman! They met and had delightful encounters every time he visited England. He had a daughter, also, but she was happily married and lived in Florence, where he saw her from time to time. She could not be tempted back to the apartment, even for a brief visit.

Saraceni was philosophical about the lonely state. He had made his choice. If it was art or human relationships, art unquestionably had the prior call.

He was an admirable host. He took Francis everywhere, and showed him things that even a privileged tourist could not have seen. It may not be said that at the Vatican doors flew open, because they moved gently on oiled hinges, but there were few doors that did not move for Saraceni; there were cardinalical palaces to which the public was not admitted, but where the chamberlain knew Saraceni as a privileged friend of the household. And in many great churches, chapels, and palaces he let it be known, with modesty, that such-and-such a splendid piece had regained its beauty because he had worked on it.

"You keep the Renaissance in repair," said Francis, meaning it as a joke.

But Saraceni did not take it as a joke. "I do," said he; "it is a trust that must be taken very seriously. But it is not repair. Call it re-creation. That demands special knowledge and special techniques. But if you want to know what there are, you must come and work with me." And he looked intently at Francis.

"I must get my degree first. No sense spending two years on it and then chucking it away. I have a third year to go. Then, if you will have me."

"By then I shall be busy on a long and trickly problem. A

private collection that has been allowed to decline fearfully. But I think much of it may be reclaimed. I shall want an assistant. I promise that you could learn a great deal."

"I have everything to learn. Working in Paris I have found out what a totally incompetent painter I am."

"No, no, no; you have learned some basic things, and it takes time to make them work for you. All that you tell me about laying fat over lean, and so forth, is excellent, and you were doing it with modern paint. If you come to me you will have to learn to do it with old paint, which is harder in some ways, easier in others."

"Old paint? Where does it come from?"

"I make it. Make it as the masters made it. They did not buy their paint in tubes, you know. They mixed their own, and much of the work is to discover what they used, and how they mixed it. Did you know that Nicholas Hillyard used ear-wax in those splendid Elizabethan miniatures? What is ear-wax, when you have painstakingly gathered the yield of many ears? I know. Chemistry is the secret. You cannot satisfactorily repair an old picture with a paint that is too much unlike what the painter used. And when you have done that—Ah, well, you shall see what follows, what *must* follow if restoration is to be that, and not simply cobbler's work."

At night they sat in the awesome apartment sipping Scotch whiskey, which was Saraceni's preferred tipple, and as they mellowed, Francis talked about his own taste in art. He was inclined to deplore the fact that, strive as he would, he liked the painting of an earlier day better than that of contemporary artists. What was he to make of himself? How could he hope to be an artist, even of the humblest rank, if he did not live and feel in tune with his own time? When the paintings that haunted him were not modern either in technique or in taste? The Bronzino, for instance . . .

"Ah, the Bronzino, The so-called *Allegory of Love*. Who gave it that inexpressive name, I wonder? It is not about love at its highest, but about Luxury—the indulgence of the senses. For all its erotic splendour and evocation of sensual pleasure it is a profoundly moral picture. Those old painters were great moralists, you know, even such a man as Angelo Bronzino, who so many imperceptive critics have called a cold and heartless artist. Surely you have seen the morality behind it?"

"I've looked at it literally for hours, and the more I look the less I know what is behind it."

"Then you must look again. You, who once won a prize for Classics!"

"It isn't really a classical theme. Venus and Cupid are the principal figures, but not doing anything I can associate with any classical reference I know."

"You must understand the classics as the Renaissance understood them, which is not the way a boys' school understands them. You must penetrate the classical world, which is by no means dead, I assure you; classical morality, classical feeling. Venus is tempting her son Cupid to a display of love that is certainly not simply filial. Is not that what many mothers do? Since Freud there has been a great deal of cocktail-hour chatter about the Oedipus complex and the love of a son for his mother, but who ventures on the dangerous theme of the mother's part in that affair? Come now, Francis, has your mother, whose beauty I have heard you praise, never flirted with you? Never caressed you in a way that was not strictly maternal?"

"She never put her tongue in my mouth or coaxed me to play with her breast, if that is what you are talking about."

"Well—but the possibility—was there never the possibility? If you had been of the pagan world and hot for pleasure, and not frightened out of your wits by Christianity, might you have recognized the possibility?"

"Maestro, I don't really follow you."

"I puzzle over it sometimes. So much talk since Dr. Freud about fathers who rouse erotic feeling in their daughters: never any talk about mothers who do the same with their sons. Does such one-sidedness seem really likely?"

"Where I grew up we had lots of incest. I knew one fellow, the son of a logger who was killed in the forest, and from twelve years of age onward he had to stand and deliver for his mother at least five times a week. When last I heard of him he had two brothers who were probably his sons. He never married; no necessity, I suppose. But that was in what the Renaissance would call very primitive conditions."

"Don't be too sure what the Renaissance would call it. But I speak of possibilities, not of completed acts. Possibilities—things that merely float in the air and are never brought to earth—can be extremely influential. It is the artist's privilege to seize such possibilities and to make pictures of them, and such pictures are among the most powerful we have. What is a picture of the Madonna—and we have seen many of them this week—but a picture of a Mother and her Son."

"A Holy Mother and the Son of God."

"In the worlds of myth and art all mothers are holy because that is what we feel in the depths of our hearts. No, not the heart: that is where modern people think they feel. During the Renaissance they would have said, the liver. In the gut, in fact. Worship of the Mother, real or mythical, comes from the gut. Have you never wondered why in so many of those pictures Joseph, the earthly father, looks such a nincompoop? In the very best of them Joseph is not even permitted to enter. That is one of the unspoken foundation stones of our mighty Faith, Francis; the love affair between Mother and Son, and according to the Scriptures no other woman ever challenged her place of supremacy. But in these Madonnas there is nothing overtly erotic. There is in Bronzino; in that picture he cast off the Christian chains and showed truth as he saw it, of love despised and rejected.

"Have you really looked at the picture? You have looked at the artist's achievement, but have you understood what he is saying? Venus holds an apple in one hand, and an arrow in the other. What does that say? I tempt you, and I have a wound for you. And look at all the secondary figures—the raving figure of Jealousy behind Cupid, speaking so clearly of despair, of love despised and rejected; the little figure of Pleasure who is about to pelt the toying lovers with rose leaves—see at his feet the thorns and those masks of the concealments and cheats of the world, marked with the bitterness of age; and who is that creature behind the laughing Pleasure—a wistful, appealing face, a rich gown that might almost blind us to her lion's feet, her serpent's sting, and her hands that offer both a honeycomb and something beastly—that must be the Cheat—Fraude, in Latin—who can so prettily turn love to madness. Who are the old man and the young woman at the top of the picture? They are plainly Time and Truth, who are drawing aside the mantle that shows the world what is involved in such love as this. Time—and his daughter Truth. A very moral picture, is it not?"

"Certainly as you interpret it, and as I have never heard anyone else explain it I cannot quarrel with you. But I'm horrified that Bronzino thought of love in that way."

"So you might well be. But he didn't, you know. The picture that has enthralled you in the National Gallery in London was half of a design that was meant to be two tapestries. One tapestry is completed and you can see it in Florence, in the Arazzi Gallery. It is called L'Innocentia del Bronzino and it shows Innocence threatened by a dog (for Envy), a lion (for Fury), a wolf (for Greed), and a snake (for Treachery); Innocence is being powerfully protected by Justice, a female figure with a mighty sword, and there again you will see Time with his hourglass and his wings (because he flies, as every parrot knows) and he is taking the cloak from a naked girl, who of course is Truth, his daughter. So really the pictures ought to be called the Allegories of Truth and Luxury, and they are splendid Renaissance sermons. Together they tell us much about life and about love, as it appeared to a Christian mind refreshed by the newly found classicism."

"Maestro, you remind me very much of my dear old Aunt Mary-Ben. She insisted that pictures were moral lessons, and told stories. But you should have seen the pictures she showed me to prove it."

"I am quite sure I have seen many of them. Their morality is of their own time, and the stories they tell are sweet and pretty, suited to people who wanted a sweetly pretty, stunted art. But they are in a long tradition quite different from those innumerable landscapes and figure pictures, and abstracts painted by men who did not want to tell anybody anything except what their personal vision discovered in easily accessible things. The tradition that your aunt and I admire, in our different ways, is not to be brushed aside, nor should its works be discussed as though they belonged to the other, purely objective tradition. There is nothing in the least wrong with having something to say, and saying it as best you can, even if you are a painter. The best moderns often do it, you know. One thinks of Picasso. Think about him."

IT WAS IMPOSSIBLE TO THINK of Picasso, or of anything but immediate concerns, after Frank had read the letter which was sent on from Corpus and reached him two days before he was to return to England.

Dear Frank:

The news is that I am well and truly up the spout. Two months gone. I had meant to keep this jolly secret from the parents until you were back in England, but that hasn't been possible. Not that I am all bagged out, and stumbling about in my bare feet like Tess of the D'Urbervilles, but some determined chucking up in the a.m. gave the show away. So there have been great family conferences, and after Daddy had had his prolonged and mournful say, and Mum had wept, the question was: what to do? My suggestion that I go to London and have the little intruder given a what-for by a really competent doctor was shouted down. Daddy is a churchwarden and takes it greatly to heart. What they want is a wedding. Keep your hair on. They do not in the least regard you as an old black ram who has tupped their white ewe. (Shakes.) Indeed there were one or two nasty hints that they thought their white ewe might have been a not-unwilling collaborator. No, they think you a highly desirable *parti*, as they used to say in Mum's day. When I said that I didn't know if you would want to marry me they said that blood was thicker than water (messier, too) and we were cousins (which in other circs they might well have thought an objection), and there was a lot more to be said for it than just saving face. The Glassons, as you will have divined, have an awful lot of face and precious little else. So—what about it? Don't waste time. Think hard and let me know. If my plan is to be taken, it must be done pretty soon.

Love, and all that that implies,

Ismay

After a morning's reflection Francis sent a telegram:

PROCEED WEDDING PLANS INSTANTER STOP WITH
YOU IN A WEEK   LOVE TO ALL

                                                        FRANK

The eagerness in the telegram was not from the heart. Francis
did not want to marry Ismay, or anybody; he discovered that what
he really wanted was to be in love, but not tied down to marriage,
of which his experience had not been particularly appetizing.
Against abortion he had an insuperable Catholic objection, partnered by an equally insuperable Calvinist objection that sprang
from his association with Victoria Cameron. How had it happened? Why had he not taken precautions? The answer to that
was that he thought precautions unromantic, and with Ismay at
Tintagel, everything must be romantic. A standing prick has no
conscience; that was a piece of bleak wisdom he had acquired at
Colborne College, and that would certainly be the way the Glassons would look at it. The fact that he had not meant it in that
spirit at all simply could not be explained and was irrelevant to
the situation. What was to be done? He couldn't for a moment
think of leaving Ismay in the lurch, quite apart from the fact that
the Glassons and his own parents would probably hunt him down
and kill him if he did such a dirty trick. His career, about which
he had no firm plans but vast, unmoulded expectations, would
be a ruin, for Ismay only fitted into that scene as The Ideal
Beloved, not by any means as a wife and mother. He was to be
the Grail Knight who ventured forth, returning to his lady only
between adventures. But after all thoughts of this sort had been
rehearsed again and again, the nagging feeling crept into his consciousness that he was really a very dim young man, considering
that he was twenty-six and thought to be clever.

Greeting the Glassons in his new character caused him greater
dread than reunion with a pregnant Ismay. He had not then got,
nor would he ever get, Dr. Upper fully out of his system, and
deep within himself he thought that he had done a dirty thing,
and would doubtless be appropriately punished. But when he
arrived at the nearest railway station to St. Columb's Hall the

Glasson parents greeted him with more warmth than they had ever shown before, and his most difficult task was to kiss Ismay on the station platform with the proper sort of affection—as accepted wooer rather than as too successful seducer. Nobody said anything about what was in all their minds until after tea, when Roderick Glasson suggested with terrible casualness that he and Francis might take a walk.

All that was said on that walk was said a score of times afterward, the intention becoming clearer every time. It was too bad that things had been a little premature, but Francis must realize that we were living in 1935, and not in the dark ages of Queen Victoria, and with clever management all would be well. The marriage would take place in a little over a fortnight's time; the banns had already been called once in the parish church. It would be a quiet affair—not more than sixty or seventy people. Then Ismay and Francis would go somewhere on an extended wedding trip, and when they returned in a year or so with a child, who was to be the wiser? Whose business was it, after all, but the family's?

Francis was aware that this was a path that had already been travelled in the family history, but Roderick Glasson could not have known why it struck so coldly into his heart. It was from Victoria Cameron that he had heard of his parents' return from such a wedding trip with the Looner. God! Would this child be another such goblin as that? Did he carry that dark inheritance? Reason was against it, but a strain of the mythical in Francis's thinking put reason firmly in its place. Was the Looner a punishment for something? He dared not contemplate what it might be, for he was sure his parents had never put themselves in such a pickle as he and Ismay had done. Everything about them made it unthinkable. In any case he was unquestionably his father's truly begotten son; the family face was the clearest evidence. The Looner must have been bad luck of some sort. But what sort?

It was incoherent; it was superstitious; it was irrational, this mass of torturing speculation, but it was unquestionably real. And what did the telegram mean that reached him from Canada?

NEWS TODAY FROM RODERICK WE SEND LOVE AND CONGRATULATIONS CANNOT ATTEND WEDDING

WORD TO WISE BE VERY CAREFUL ABOUT ALL
MONEY ARRANGEMENTS

                                        FATHER

Money arrangements? He had already had some hint of that.
The Glassons, Roderick explained during another walk, were
feeling the pinch, as did all landowners. Rents had not kept up
with expenditures; taxes were punitive; without heavy investment
in equipment agriculture could not survive. New money spent
on the estate was imperative if large sales of portions of land that
had been part of the Glasson patrimony for generations were to
be avoided. Not that sales would bridge the gap for long. Roderick
had looked into the future fearlessly, and he saw only one hope
for St. Columb Hall and its estates, and that hope was—new
money. It was a case of substantial refinancing now or—well,
eventual ruin.

Had Francis ever given any thought to agriculture? No, Francis had not. He didn't think he wanted to be a landowner and
farmer.

Roderick laughed, almost musically. No question of that. The
estate must go to Roderick, his only son. Not that it was tied
down by law, but that was how it had always been. However,
young Roderick had set his heart on a career in Whitehall, and
certainly he seemed to have a talent that way. Now if—just suppose—Francis and Ismay lived at a very decent dower house on
the property, and Roderick and Prudence lived at the Hall until
at last they were forced by the inevitable to leave it (manly acceptance of age and death here, almost like the "business" of a
none too accomplished actor), it would be possible to totally re-
finance the estate, and a family property—Francis was already a
cousin and would soon be doubly family—would be revitalized
in the best possible way. Francis wouldn't have to worry about
the farm; Roderick knew farming like the palm of his hand, and
they had an excellent agent who, with real money strength behind
him, would put things in apple-pie order before you knew it. In
time, young Roderick would return, and anyway he would always
have St. Columb's behind him. Francis could do whatever he
pleased. Paint, if he liked. Mess about with Cornish history and
legend, if it suited him. He would be, Roderick thought the phrase

was, a sleeping partner. It was not said how the sleeping partner was to benefit, except in terms of moral satisfaction.

Slowly, it sank in. This was why the Glassons were so philosophical about Ismay's false step, over which they might otherwise be raising the roof. The price of Ismay was—one million Canadian dollars, with accrued interest, because Francis had not been drawing heavily on his income. Of course, they knew all about it; the Cornishes of Chegwidden would have gossiped and probably exaggerated. One million Canadian dollars was rather more than two hundred thousand pounds, which to people like the Glassons was wealth illimitable.

That was where the price began. The largest part would be his thraldom to life in a dower house, under the shadow of St. Columb's and the shadow of Chegwidden, free to paint and dream about myth if he were fool enough to want to do that. He was to be the money-bags, that was plain. More kids, undoubtedly. But such a fate could be avoided; the Glassons could not trap him there. No; after thinking about it painfully and honestly, Francis recognized that it was the money that really meant most, and he was brought to the shameful conclusion that he wanted Ismay, but he didn't like her price.

Still, as Grandfather McRory always said, nobody has your money so long as it's still in your own pocket. Roderick Glasson seemed to think that money would be made over to him in lumps. Francis made it clear that the uttermost he could manage, so far ahead as he could see, was four thousand pounds paid quarterly for the first year. This was not true, for not only had he his grandfather's handsome bequest, but he also received enough from the trust that included his aunts and his mother to make up a good income in itself. But as Francis sat in his bedroom and did reckonings, he was astonished to find how fond of money he was, and how reluctant to let any of it out of his grasp. When he stated his terms to his uncle, Roderick's face fell, but as he had no way of knowing what Francis really possessed, he had to make the best of it. After all, Francis pointed out, he would have to support Ismay and probably Aunt Prudence somewhere on the Continent for the greater part of a year, and that would be another call on his income. Capital, he explained, was not a thing one ever diminished. Roderick nodded sagely at this, knowing very well that he had himself diminished his capital almost to invisibility, and that this was what had brought him to his present position. But he was optimistic; after the first year things might look very different.

Ismay and Aunt Prudence on the Continent, said Roderick, as it sank in. But where would Francis be? At Oxford, said Francis. He was determined not to sacrifice his degree and he had another year to go. But what did he need with a degree? It would be useless if he were living the life of a country gentleman. Roderick had no degree; he had come out of the Navy to assume the splendours and miseries of St. Columb's when he inherited it, and had never felt the want of a university training. It was at this point that Ismay joined in the genteel wrangling; she too wanted to complete her studies and receive some sort of university stamp. Francis had thought about that, too. She certainly could not return to Oxford; the colleges did not encourage married undergraduates—indeed objected to them, and understandably so. But she could go to the continent, and pursue her modern-language studies very effectively at Lausanne, and live near by at Montreux; continental universities did not give as much individual concern to their students as did Oxford. Such a stay abroad would dissemble the early arrival of the child, which was also a consideration. He would pay—within reason.

"You've got it all planned, haven't you?" said Ismay to him when her parents were not near. "You've got them completely outgeneralled." She spoke with admiration.

"It's a short plan," said he; "but it gives us a year to think about what we intend to do. I don't want to settle here and become 'Francis Cornish, whose sensitive landscapes follow in the path of B. W. Leader'." He was really thinking about the profession, of which he had said nothing to Ismay, and which he was determined not to mention unless it became inescapable. Ismay as the Desired One was being replaced in his heart and mind by Ismay the Promised One, not to say the Inescapable One, and there were some things she must not know. She was worse than a blabber; she was a hinter. It gave her pleasure to rouse curiosity and speculation about dangerous things.

These family deliberations took place in the evenings, after Aunt Prudence and in a lesser degree Uncle Roderick had spent a toilsome day planning the wedding. So much to do! And all to be done on a shoestring—for the Glassons insisted that it would be indefensible, and even perhaps unchancy, to let Francis pay for any part of that. They greatly enjoyed the excitement, protesting that they did not know how they could get through another day like the one just completed.

Two nights before the wedding day Francis and Ismay escaped from the general hubbub, and were walking in a lane at dusk. Overhead the sky was deepening from a colour which reminded Francis of the cloak that Time and Truth deploy so effectively in the Bronzino *Allegory*.

"You feel trapped, don't you?" said Ismay.

"Do you?"

"Yes, but my trap is a physical one. The kid. That has to be dealt with before I can do anything else. But you're not trapped in that way."

"No, but I have an obligation. Surely you see that? Apart from loving you, and wanting to marry you, of course."

"Oh Frank, don't be so stuffy! I hate to think what your upbringing must have been. You've still got a chance."

"How?"

"Scarper, of course."

"Desert you? Now?"

"It's been done."

"Not by me. I'd feel the most terrible shit."

"I wouldn't think so."

"Maybe not. But I'd think so."

"All right, my dear-O-dear. It's your neck."

"I'm really surprised you think I might."

"Don't you ever say I didn't give you a chance."

"You're a tough little nut, Ismay."

"Not the Celtic princess of your dreams? Maybe I'm more like a Celtic princess of reality than you suppose. From all I've heard they could be very tough nuts, too."

When the wedding day came neighbours arrived from far and wide: county families, the professional bourgeoisie, tenants of St. Columb's (who had been badgered by the agent into presenting the couple with a mantel clock, engraved in suitably modified feudal terms), such old women as attended all weddings and funerals without distinction of class, and the Bishop of Truro, who did not read the Marriage Service, but gave the blessing afterward. Ismay, tidy for once, and robed in virgin white, looked so lovely that Francis's heart ached toward her. The Service was read by the local parson, who was from the very lowest shelf of the Low Church cupboard. He stressed the admonition that marriage was not to be taken in hand wantonly, to satisfy men's carnal lusts and appetites, like brute beasts that have no understanding, but for the propagation of children. All of this he spat out with such distaste that he alarmed Ismay's two sisters, Isabel and Amabel, present in white dresses to signify virginity in its rawest and meatiest guise, and caused the Glassons and Francis to wonder if the good man smelt a rat. But it was soon over, "The Voice That Breathed o'er Eden" was sung, the Bishop said his say, and Francis and Ismay had been licensed to go to bed in future without shame.

The wedding had not bothered Francis unduly, but the wedding breakfast was a different matter. At this affair, which was held on the lawn at St. Columb's because it was a fineish day, Roderick Glasson the Younger took charge, and conducted the affair in the manner of a Best Man who was aimed at Whitehall, and wanted everything to be done with precision, and with only such enthusiasm as was compatible with his ideal of elegance—which kept enthusiasm well in check.

Roderick gave a good impression of what he would be like at forty-five. He read, like one communicating a knotty minute to a Civil Service superior, some telegrams of congratulation, most of which were from Canada and one or two from Oxford friends which had to be read with restraint. The Bride was toasted by Uncle Arthur Cornish, who described her in terms that made Ismay giggle unsuitably and chilled Francis, who detected in it allusions to his money, and satisfaction that it was not going out of the family. Francis replied, briefly, and made insincere protestations of humility and gratitude toward the Bride's parents, who liked that part of his speech very much, but thought it could have been even more forcibly put. As he spoke, Francis had to overcome whispering among the guests who had not met him, and hissed, "An American? Nobody told me he was an American." "Not American—Canadian." "Well, what's the difference?" "They're touchier, that's what." "They say he's very wealthy."

"Oh, so that's it." Then the Best Man toasted the bridesmaids, and was arch about the fact that, as they were his little sisters, he could not say too much in their favour, but he had hopes that they would improve. The bridesmaids took this with scarlet faces and occasional murmurs of Oh, I say, Roddy, pack it in, can't you? Roderick told about the time he and his sisters had put a dead adder in the groom's bed, and an indecency had to be frowned down when Old George Trethewey, a cousin but not a favourite, shouted drunkenly that they'd put something a damned sight better in his bed now. And finally the tenant who farmed the biggest of St. Columb's farms toasted The Happy Couple, and was somewhat indiscreet in hinting that the coming of new blood (he did not say new money) into the family promised well for the future of agriculture at St. Columb's. But at last it was over, the wedding cake had been deflowered and distributed, every hand had been shaken; the Bride had flung her bouquet from the front door with such force that it took her sister Amabel full in the face, and the couple sped away in a hired car toward Truro, where they were to catch a train.

In Lausanne there was no difficulty about having Ismay entered as a student, with credit for the year she had already completed at Oxford. In Montreux it was not hard to find a pension with a living room and a bedroom, the latter containing a couch on which she or Aunt Prudence could sleep when they occupied the place together. But it all meant laying out money in sums small and large, and Francis, who had never had experience of this sort of slow bleeding, undertaken in a cause which was not nearest his heart, suffered an early bout of the outraged parsimony which was to visit him so often in later life. Stinginess does nothing to improve the looks, and Ismay commented that he was becoming hatchet-faced.

His life with Ismay was agreeable, but it had none of the old lustre. She was more beautiful than ever, and the carelessness with which she had always dressed now seemed a fine disdain for trivialities. Only a very sharp eye would have discerned that she was pregnant, but when she was naked she had a new opulence, and Francis drew her as often as was possible. A really beautiful woman should have a figure like a 'cello, he said, running his hand appreciatively over her swelling belly. But though he loved her, he had ceased to worship her, and sometimes they snapped at one another, because Ismay's broad speech, which he had once thought so delightful, grated on his nerves now.

"Well, if you didn't like the way I talk, you shouldn't have knocked me up."

"I wish you wouldn't use vulgar expressions like that, as if we were that sort of person. If you want to talk dirty, talk dirty, but for God's sake don't talk common."

Irritatingly, Ismay would respond to this sort of thing by singing Ophelia's song, quietly and reflectively, in a Cockney accent:

> *B'Jeez and by Saint Charity,*
> *Alack and fie for shame!*
> *Young men will do't, if they come to't;*
> *By cock, they are to blame.*
> *Quoth she, before you tumbled me,*
> *You promised me to wed,*
> *So would I ha' done, by yonder sun,*
> *An thou hadst not come to my bed.*

"That should be all right," she murmured, apparently to the walls. "Shakespeare. Good old Shakers, the darling of the OUDS. Nothing common about him. You can't get classier than Shakers."

Francis could not linger in Montreux. He had to return to Oxford, and he did so with no time to spare before the beginning of the Michaelmas Term. He had made a mess of things with Ismay, he told himself. Not that he was sorry to have married her, but that should have come later. Now he had to leave her when surely she needed him with her—though she had been calm enough when he went. After all, Aunt Prudence was going to her in a few weeks. He knew nothing about the matter, but he had a vague impression that a pregnant woman needed her husband close by, to run out and get her pickles and ice cream if she should have a sick fancy for them in the middle of the night, and to gloat romantically over the new life that was gathering within her. The doctor in Montreux had taken it philosophically when he explained that he must return to England, and assured him that everything would be quite all right. Well—it had to be all right.

He was determined to get his degree, and get the best class he could manage. This sudden bump in the road should not rob him of that. So he settled to work, and worked very hard, almost entirely giving up drawing and painting, and refusing a tempting offer to assist a distinguished designer in preparing a garden performance of *The Tempest* for the OUDS.

He was able to spend Christmas with Ismay, and found her, now obviously pregnant, and even more obviously a European student, accustomed to speak French more often than English, and deep in Spanish studies. She had enjoyed herself, once she had persuaded her mother to return to England and stop fussing over her. This sort of student life suited her as the formality of Oxford had never done. They spent, on the whole, a very amicable Christmas holiday, much of it in Ismay's living-room, smoking countless stinking French cigarettes and pursuing their university work. They conversed entirely in French and Ismay liked his lingering French-Canadian accent. It was "of the people" she said and she approved of anything that was of the people.

He was with her in February, when the child was born. Pensions are not accommodated to childbirth, and Ismay was in a small private hospital, which cost a lot of money. Aunt Prudence was there, too, and she and Francis had an uneasy time of it in the pension rooms. Francis hauled the couch out of the bedroom into the sitting-room for himself, and Aunt Prudence, though well aware that the bed was due to her sex and seniority, nevertheless accused herself daily of being a nuisance.

The child was born without incident, but surrounded by the usual grandmotherly and fatherly anxiety. Indeed, Francis was nervously wretched until he had seen the little girl and been assured by the doctor that she was perfect in every way. Had he expected anything else? Francis did not say what he had feared.

"She's the absolute image of her father," said Aunt Prudence, smiling at Francis.

"Yes, she's the image of her father," Ismay agreed, smiling at no one.

To Francis the child looked like every baby he had ever seen, but he did not say so.

The question of a name for the child arose almost at once.

Francis had no ideas, but Ismay was perhaps more maternal than she liked to admit. The child was sucking at her breast when she made a suggestion.

"Let's call her Charlotte."

"All right. But why?"

"After her father."

Francis looked blank.

"Frank, I've been trying to get around to this for quite a while, but the time never seemed just right. But this is it. You know, of course, that this is Charlie's child?"

Francis still looked blank.

"Well, it is. I know for a certainty. We were very close before he scarpered."

"And you sucked me in to give cover for Charlie's child?"

"I suppose I did. But don't think I liked doing it. You're a dear, and you've behaved beautifully. But there's a basic difference between you and Charlie: He's the kind that makes things happen, and you're the kind things happen to, and for me there's no question of choice. Don't forget that before the wedding I gave you a chance to get away, and you decided not to take it. This is Charlie's child."

"Does Charlie know?"

"I don't suppose he knows or cares. I've had some indirect news of him, and you know how things are hotting up in Spain, so I suppose that if he did know he couldn't do anything about it. He's got bigger fish to fry."

"Ismay, this puts the lid on it."

"I didn't expect you to be pleased, and I honestly meant to say something earlier, but you see how it is. I wanted to be square with you, and now I have."

"Oh, so that's what you've been, is it? Square? Ismay, I'd hate to be near when you were being crooked."

BACK TO OXFORD, miserable and beaten so far as his marriage was concerned, but with a compensating fierce ambition to distinguish himself in his Final Schools, which he faced in June. It is impossible to prepare for Final Schools by extreme exertions during the last ten weeks; preparation should have been well begun two years before. That was when Francis had started to work, and thus his last ten weeks was free for finishing touches, rather than the acquirement of basic knowledge. His tutor was pleased with him—or as pleased as a tutor ever admits to being—and polished him up to a fine gloss. The consequence was that when he had written his papers and waited out the obligatory period during which they were read and marked, he had the satisfaction of seeing his name posted in the First Class. He telegraphed to Canada, and the next day received an answer: "Congratulations. Love to Ismay and Charlotte." Did his parents, then, see them as a happy trio, a Holy Family, with Baby Bunting prettily innocent of Daddy's distinction?

Ismay and the child were at St. Columb's; Aunt Prudence had insisted that a summer in the country, with country food and air, was just what Ismay and Baby needed. It was to St. Columb's, therefore, that Francis sent his second telegram about his academic success. He was surprised to receive a telephone call on the following day. The telephone was not a favourite agent of the Glassons, nor was Oxford, with its great population of students and its paucity of telephones, an easy place with which to communicate. But Uncle Roderick called, and Francis was found by the Porter of Corpus, and there, in the Porter's lodge, while one undergraduate bought a stamp and another inquired about the whereabouts of his bicycle, he heard his uncle, distant and mouse-like of voice, saying that Ismay was not at St. Columb's but had said she was going up to Oxford for a couple of days to see Francis. That had been a week ago. Was she not with him?

It was on the following day that he received a letter from Lausanne:

Dear Frank:

It's no good pretending something will work when it obviously won't. By the time this reaches you I shall be in Spain. I know where Charlie is, and I'm joining him. Don't try to find me, because you won't. But don't worry. I shall be all right, or if I'm not I shall be all wrong in a cause I think is more important than any personal considerations. You are the best of chaps, I know, and won't let Little Charlie down, and of course when I get back (and if I do) I'll take on again. Sorry about the money. But really you love that stuff too much for your own good. Love,

                                                                    Ismay

The money, he discovered, was what he had deposited in an account for her use. She had cleared it out.

Scarpered!

"I WANT TO BEAT UP a woman with my fists. Are you interested, and if so what would your price be?"

Francis had put his question to at least eight prostitutes on Piccadilly, and had had eight refusals, ranging from amusement to affront. Obviously he was in the wrong district. These girls, most of them fragile and pretty, were high-priced tarts, not hungry enough to consider his proposal. He found his way into Soho, and on the fourth try had better luck.

She was fortyish, with badly dyed hair and a gown trimmed with imitation fur. On the stout side, and underneath a heavy paint job her face was stupid but kindly.

"Well—I don't know what to say. I've had gentlemen who had special tastes, of course. But usually it's them that wants to be beaten up. A few slaps, you know, and some rough talk. But I don't know. With your fists, was it you said?"

"Yes. Fists."

"I'd have to think it over. Talk it over with my friend, really. Have you got a moment?"

From the depths of her bosom she pulled out a crucifix which, when she put it in her lips, proved to be a little whistle, on a chain. She gave a discreet double tweet. Very soon a small, dark man, quietly dressed and wearing a statesman's black Homburg, appeared, and the woman whispered to him.

"How rough would this be?" asked the man.

"Hard to say, till I got into it."

"Well—it could come very dear. Broken teeth, now. Bruising. That could put her out of business for a fortnight. No; I don't think we could look at it, not at any price that would make sense."

"Would one good punch be any help?" said the woman, who seemed to have a pitying heart. "One good punch at, say, ten quid?"

"Twenty," said the man, hastily.

They went to the woman's flat, which was near by.

"You understand I've got to stick around," said the man. "This isn't your ordinary call. You might get carried away, and not in control of yourself. I've got to stick around, for both your sakes."

The woman was undressing, with rapid professional skill.

"No need for that," said Francis.

"Oh, I think she'd better," said the man. "In fact, I'd say she'd rather, seeing as you're paying. Professional, you understand. Her birthday suit is her working clothes, isn't it?"

"Okay. Ready when you are," said the woman, now naked and bracing herself on stout legs. She had, Francis saw with an embalmer's eye, an appendicitis scar of the old-fashioned kind that looks rather like a beetle with outspread legs.

Francis raised his fist, and to summon anger he thought hard of Ismay at her most defiant, her most derisive, her most sluttish. But it would not come. It was the Looner who dominated his feeling, not as an image, but as an influence, and he could not strike. He sat down suddenly on the bed, and to his deep shame burst into sobs.

"Oh, the poor love," said the woman. "Can't you, darling?" She pushed a box of tissue handkerchiefs toward him. "Don't feel it so. There's lots that can't, the other way, you know. They've very good reasons, too."

"He needs a drink," said the man.

"No, I think he needs a cup of tea," said the woman. "Just put on the electric, will you, Jimsie? There, there, now. You tell me about it." She sat beside Francis and drew his head down on her large scented breast. "What did she do to you, eh? She must have done something. What was it? Come on, tell me."

So Francis found himself sitting on the bed with the woman, who had pulled a silk peignoir trimmed with rather worn marabou about her, and her ponce, or her bully, or whatever the term might be for Jimsie, sipping hot, strong tea, giving a shortened, edited version of what Ismay had done. The woman made comforting noises, but it was Jimsie who spoke.

"Don't take me up wrong," he said, "but it certainly looks as if she done the dirty on you. But why? That's the way we have to look at it. There's always a reason, and it may not be one you'd ever think of. Why, would you say?"

"Because she loves another man," said Francis.

"O Gawd; sod love!" said Jimsie. "You never know where you are with it. A great cause of trouble." And as he went on to anatomize love, as it appeared to him both as a man and as a professional dealer in sexual satisfaction, it seemed to Francis that he heard the voice of Tancred Saraceni, explaining the Bronzino *Allegory*. The face that was clearest in the picture, as he thought of it, was the woman-headed beast with a lion's claws and a dragon's tail, who proffered the sweet and the bitter in her outstretched hands. The figure called the Cheat, or in Saraceni's Latin explication, Fraude. He must have whispered the name.

"Fraudy? I should think it was fraudy, and rotten, too, walking out on you and the baby," said the woman.

When at last Francis was fit to go, he offered the woman two ten-pound notes.

"Oh, no dear," said she; "I couldn't think of it. You never had your punch, you see. Not that I'd have blamed you if you'd really socked me."

"No, that wasn't the agreement," said the man, taking the notes himself, swiftly but delicately. "You've got to consider time spent, and an agreement entered into even if not carried out. But I'll say this, sir. This night does you credit. You've behaved like a gentleman."

"Oh, sod being a gentleman," said Francis, then regretted it, and shook hands with them both before running down the stairs into the Soho street.

THE PREMISES OF SIR GEOFFREY DUVEEN and Company were elegant and awesome; Francis would never have presumed to enter on his own volition, but it was here that Colonel Copplestone had said he was to meet him, and the wording of the message had suggested without actually saying so that it was a matter of importance. Something of importance was just what Francis needed. He had never felt so insignificant, so diminished, so exploited in his life since the days at Carlyle Rural. He was smartly dressed and punctual as he presented himself in the great London centre of art dealing and art exportation. The Colonel was in a small panelled room in which hung three pictures that made Francis's eyes pop. This was the sort of thing that very rich collectors could afford, and that they looked to the Duveen Company to supply.

"But you have your degree. First Class honours; I saw it in *The Times*. Just remind me of what that degree implies."

The Colonel seemed inclined to brush aside Francis's story of his marriage and its outcome as something of secondary importance. How callous these old fellows were!

"Well, it's called Modern Greats, but the formal name is Philosophy, Politics, and Economics. I concentrated on philosophy, and having a Classics degree already I had a certain advantage over the men who worked with translations; you begin at Descartes, but it's very useful to know what came before. And modern languages: mine were French and German. The politics is pretty much British constitutional stuff. I did as little economics as I could. Not my thing: I prefer my astrology without water."

"Aha. Well, you didn't waste your time at Oxford," said the Colonel. "Don't let the other thing bother you too much. Painful, of course, but I can offer you something that will make you forget it—or almost forget it."

"In the profession?"

"Yes. Not bang in the middle of the profession, of course. That's for quite a different sort of chap. But something you can do very well, I should think. Better than anyone else available at the moment, certainly. I want you to work with Tancred Saraceni."

"Is he—?"

"Most certainly not. And you must never let him think you are, or you'll be in the soup. No; Saraceni is in a queer game of his own, which interests us at the moment, and could be important. By the way, quite a few people who believe in that sort of thing say he has the Evil Eye. I don't completely dismiss that, so watch your step. You told me he had suggested that you might like to work with him? Learn his special trade, or craft, or whatever he calls it?"

"Yes, but I'm not really sure that's what I want. I want to be a painter, not a craftsman who tarts up paintings that have been allowed to decay."

"Yes, but what the profession wants is that somebody should be with Saraceni on the job he's undertaking now. Do you know anything about the Düsterstein collection?"

"Never heard of it."

"It's not well known, though these people here at Duveen's know about it, of course. It's their business to know such things. It's a lot of Renaissance and post-Renaissance and Counter-Reformation pictures—not all of them the best, I believe, but still remarkable—that are housed in Schloss Düsterstein in Lower Bavaria, about seventy miles from Munich. The owner is the Gräfin von Ingelheim, and she is interested in having her pictures put in A-1 condition, with a view to sale. Not a vulgar sell-out, you understand; not an 'Everything Must Be Sold To The Walls By The End Of The Month' thing. No, a gradual, very high-class unloading that should bring in a great deal of money. We want to know where the pictures are going. She's persuaded Saraceni to do the work of getting the stuff ready, rather on the quiet, without actually being secret. Saraceni needs an assistant, and we would like the assistant to be a member of the profession. And that's you, my boy."

"I'm to report to you? But what? And how?"

"No written reports to me, unless something totally unlikely happens. But you'll come back to England now and then, won't you? Don't you want to see little Charlotte and find out how she is getting on? What kind of a father would you be if you didn't? But there will also be another form of written report, and this afternoon you had better go to Harley Street, where Sir Owen Williams-Owen will see you, and take a look at your heart, and tell you how to report back to him on how it's getting on."

It was plain to Francis that Uncle Jack was enjoying being

mysterious, and that his best course was to play straight man, and let his instructions come in due course.

"Williams-Owen knows all about hearts. He will give you a regimen of health that you must follow, which will include regular reports to him on how your heart is functioning. How many heartbeats after strenuous exercise—that sort of thing. But in actual fact it will be a key to observations we want you to make about trains.

"Schloss Düsterstein sits in a considerable estate, with some parkland and a lot of farms. Less than a mile from the house, or the castle or whatever it is, there is a branch of a railway, and that branch leads to a large compound—a concentration camp, as Lord Kitchener called them, to which freight and cattle cars are taken from time to time, not on any regular schedule but always late at night. You can tell how many cars there are because the train travels quite slowly—what they call a Bummelzug—and at one place it crosses an intersection point, and makes a characteristic sound with its wheels. If you keep your ears open, and count the times you hear that sound, and then divide by two, you can reckon the number of freight or goods vans that have passed over the point, and are thus bound for the camp. And that's what you report to Williams-Owen, every fortnight, according to a scheme he will give you, in a letter in which you can whimper and play the hypochondriac as much as you please. He'll see that the information gets to the right place."

"It's better than staying here and feeling sorry for myself, I suppose."

"Much better. It's your first professional job, and if you haven't thought so already, you're damned lucky to get it."

"Well, but what about—oh, sod being a gentleman! Sorry to be sordid, Uncle Jack, but—am I paid anything?"

"As I told you, this is something of a sideline, and we haven't any appropriation for it. But I think you may count on something eventually. Anyhow, you needn't pretend to me that you need money. I've heard about your grandfather's will. Your father mentioned it in a letter."

"I see. I'm in training, as it were?"

"No; it's a real job. But take my advice, Frank, don't fuss about money. The profession is run on a shoestring, and there are lots of people fighting for a quarter-inch of the string already. When there's anything for you, you can rely on me to let you know. But if there's no money, I can at least offer you some information. We know where Charlie Fremantle is."

"Is she with him?"

"I suppose so. He's in a very hot place to be at the moment. If those two are counting on a peaceful old age, they're out of their minds. Oh, and your friend Buys-Bozzaris is dead."

"What? How?"

"Carelessness. Actually he was a futile agent, and his recruiting was a joke; Charlie Fremantle was the only fish he caught, and even Charlie—who is an idiot—managed to cheat him about some gambling money. So Basil found himself in what we might call an untenable position, and it looks as if he shot himself."

"I don't believe it. I doubt if he could hit himself—on purpose, anyhow."

"Perhaps not. Perhaps he had expert assistance—Well, anything more?"

"Just a matter of curiosity, Uncle Jack. These goods vans—these freight cars—what's in them?"

"People."

YOUR MAN WAS LUCKY to be quit of Ismay, said the Lesser Zadkiel.

—My man was lucky to have known her, said the Daimon Maimas. She doesn't show up well in Francis's story: an unscrupulous little sexual teaser and a crook about money; if she had stayed with him, what sort of cat-and-dog life would they have had? They would have torn one another apart and quite soon she would have betrayed him with somebody. But she thought herself a free agent, and that always leads to trouble.

—Oh, quite. She was really an adjunct of Charlie Fremantle; one aspect of his fate. Odd, isn't it, that these adventurous, feather-brained fools like Charlie always have some woman who is ready to put up with anything to serve him and his folly? My records show it again and again.

—What lies before her in Spain? Scampering around from one squalid, endangered hovel to another, always under threat, often under *gunfire, imagining she is serving the people's cause—which neither she nor Charlie could have defined—but really just Charlie's woman and slave. If pity lay in my sphere, said the Daimon, I think I should pity her.*

—But pity is not in your sphere, brother. You don't even pity poor Francis, who broke his heart over her.

—Certainly not. A heart is never really stout until it has broken and mended at least once. Francis might be grateful to me for finding him such an interesting heart-breaker. Lots of men break their hearts over women who are no more interesting than turnips.

—Yet he knew she was no good. Not to him, anyway. What was she to him?

—Surely you remember how, in his bedroom at Blairlogie, he used to posture in front of his mirror, rigged up as a sort of woman? Searching for the Mystical Marriage, though he didn't know it; looking for the woman in himself, for the completion of himself, and he thought he had found it in Ismay. And he most certainly did find part of it in Ismay, for she was what he was not, she had qualities he would never possess, and she had the beauty and the sluttish irresistible charm to make him love her whatever she did, and whatever he knew about her. I think I did rather well in enlarging his life with Ismay.

—As when she told him he was the kind of man things happened to, and not the kind that made them happen?

—Oh, come, brother, you were not taken in by that old chestnut, were you? You know as well as I that people often make the most astonishing reversals of what seems to be their basic nature, when they are compelled to do it. Really, my dear colleague, you astonish me! I don't wish to be offensive, but here we are, a couple of Minor Immortals, watching Francis's life unfold before us, as you have it filed away in your archive, and yet sometimes you talk as if we were no wiser than a pair of human beings watching television, where the unexpected, the unpredictable is rigorously forbidden to happen. The laws of such melodrama are not binding on us, brother. You have typed Francis, and you talk of Ismay as if she were vanished forever. As for me, you seem to degrade me to the level of that detestable theological fraud, a Guardian Angel! Come, come!

—Don't scold, brother. I am sorry if I have appeared to underestimate your daimonic role in this affair. But I have so much to do with

mortals that sometimes I think a little of their sentimentality is rubbing off on me.

—Don't be distracted by trivialities, said the Daimon Maimas. What do the theologians say? Circumcise yourself as to the heart and not as to the foreskin. And never neglect what is bred in the bone. Do you think it was bred in Francis to be a victim all his life? How would that reflect on me? As a rather superior mortal once said to a sentimental friend, Clear your mind of cant! Shall we continue?

PART
Five

CLICK-CLACK ... CLICK-CLACK ... twenty-four repititions of the sound, and a melancholy toot as if from an entirely innocent Bummelzug passing over a switch-point. But why would an innocent Bummelzug be rumbling through the Bavarian countryside at half past eleven at night, when all decent freight-trains were at rest on their sidings? Twenty-four click-clacks meant twelve vans. Twelve vans, loaded, perhaps, with people, were being hauled to the internment camp that lay obscurely in a nearby valley.

Francis made a note in the book he carried always in his breast pocket. Tomorrow he would write to Sir Owen Williams-Owen in Harley Street, to report on the condition of his heartbeat under particular conditions of stress.

This was the first such observation he had made during his first week at Schloss Düsterstein. It was providential that his bedroom lay on the side of the great house that was nearest to the railway line.

The great house had been a surprise—was still a surprise, after a week's exploration. To begin, in spite of its name it was not particularly suggestive of melancholy. Old it unquestionably was, and large even as country houses go, but its chief quality was that of the centre of a large farming district, and on its own lands and tenant-farms adjacent the Gräfin von Ingelheim conducted a big agricultural industry with exemplary efficiency. Motor trucks took vegetables, fowls, and veal or pork every week to the railway that carried them on to Munich, where wholesale dealers awaited them, and distributed them to a number of hotels, restaurants,

and butchers. In a wing of the castle was an office from which
the farms were managed and the dispatching of the foodstuffs
was arranged, probably in some of the goods vans that now and
then visited the camp in the hills. Schloss Düsterstein was, as
agricultural matters go, big business.

Castle it was called, but there was nothing of the medieval
fortress about it. There were reminders of the seventeenth century and a large square tower that was considerably earlier, but
its appearance and plan were of the latter part of the eighteenth
century; if shabby in some of its details and furnishings—the sort
of shabbiness that suggests an aristocratic indifference to new-
fangledness rather than poverty—it was comfortable and as pleasant as a decidedly grand house could be. It was not domestic in
the English sense, but it was not a comfortless imitation of a
French château, either. Francis's bedroom, for instance: a heavily
furnished room so large that the big bed seemed accidental rather
than central, with armchairs and a desk and plenty of room for
all his artist's equipment, and in one corner a large and fine porcelain stove. True, he washed in a little closet concealed in one
of the walls, to which hot water was brought through an inner
passage, so that he never saw the servant who carried it; but the
ewer and basin, the two large chamber-pots, and the slop-pail
were of an expensive eighteenth-century china, marked with the
crest of Ingelheim. Slops were spirited away every day by means
of the same inner passage. Baths were to be taken in a large
chamber set out with Empire furniture and a marble tub of almost
Roman aspect, into which rather rusty water gushed through huge
brass taps; it was a long walk from the bedroom, but as an Oxford
man Francis was accustomed to distant baths.

Francis's room was in the rear of the castle; the family were in
another wing into which he never penetrated, but he met them
in the living quarters, a series of large drawing-rooms and a dining-
room behind the rooms of state, which were now never used
except for the display of the collection of pictures that had made
Düsterstein and the Ingelheim family famous among connoisseurs
for two centuries. Not that the pictures in these private rooms
were inconsiderable; they were family portraits by a variety of
masters, not always of the foremost rank, but by no means unknown or lightly esteemed.

Ever since his arrival Francis had looked with astonishment from the pictures on the walls to the two representatives of the family who sat below them, the Countess Ottilie and her granddaughter, Amalie, whose features the portraits reflected in a bewildering but always recognizable variety. Here was the Family Face indeed, the Countess's square and determined as became a great landowner and a farmer of formidable talents, and that of Amalie, which was oval, still unmarked by experience but filled with beautiful expectancy. The Countess was not yet sixty; Amalie was probably fourteen. He conversed with them in English, as the Countess was anxious that Amalie should be perfect in that language.

These evenings were not long. Dinner was at eight, and was never over before nine, for though not a heavy meal it was served with what seemed to Francis extraordinary deliberation. Saraceni talked with the Countess. Francis was expected to talk to Miss Ruth Nibsmith, the governess. Amalie spoke only when spoken to by her grandmother. After dinner they sat for an hour, during which the Countess made one cup of coffee and one glass of cognac last the full time; sharp at ten Amalie kissed her grandmother, curtsied to Saraceni and Francis, and retired under the care of Miss Nibsmith. Then the Countess went to her private room, where, Saraceni told him, she worked over the farm accounts until eleven, at which hour she went to bed, in order to rise at six and spend two hours out of doors, directing her workers, before breakfast at eight.

"A very regular existence," said Saraceni.

"Does nothing else ever happen?" said Francis.

"Never. Except that on Sundays the priest comes for Mass at seven; you aren't expected to attend, but it will give satisfaction if you do, and you shouldn't miss the chapel; it is a Baroque marvel that you won't see otherwise. But what do you mean— 'Does nothing else ever happen?' What do you suppose is happening? Money is being made, to begin with. This family was almost beggared during the War and the Countess's father and now Countess Ottilie have made them almost as rich as they ever were—out of veal, which, as you know, is the staple diet of people in this part of the world. Amalie is being prepared for a brilliant marriage to somebody who hasn't been chosen yet, but who will have to measure up to exacting standards. Great fortunes don't go to fools—not at Düsterstein, anyhow. And there is the collection to be put into first-class order, and you and I will work on that like galley-slaves, for the Countess expects it. Isn't that enough activity to satisfy your North American soul?"

"Sorry to bring it up, but—do I get paid?"

"Most certainly you do. First of all, you are privileged to work with me, and there are hundreds of young artists who would give anything for that high distinction. Next, you have an opportunity to study one of the very few notable collections still to remain in private hands. That means that you will be able to make an intimate day-by-day and mood-by-mood study of pictures that even the directors of world-famous galleries see only by carefully controlled appointment. The greatest are on loan to the Munich gallery, but there are splendid things here—things any of those galleries would be glad to possess. You are privileged to live on familiar terms with artistocrats—the Ingelheims of blood, myself of talent—in beautiful country surroundings. Every day you are given real cream and the best of veal. You have the cultivated conversation of La Nibsmith, and the transporting silences of Amalie. You can keep your little car in the stables. But as for money—no, no money; that would be adding sugar to honey. The Countess receives you here as my assistant. I am paid, of course, but not you. What do you want money for? You're rich."

"I'm beginning to be afraid that stands between me and being an artist."

"There are worse disabilities. Want of talent, for instance. You have talent, and I shall show you how to use it."

To begin with, learning to use his talent seemed to mean a lot of dirty work, about the performance of which Saraceni was tyrannical and sarcastic. The silky expert Francis had met at Oxford and the patrician connoisseur he visited in Rome was an unappeasable slave-driver in the studio. During his first few days Francis did no work at all, but wandered freely through the castle to get the feel of things, as Saraceni put it.

But on the first Sunday there was a violent change. Francis was up in time for chapel, and, as Saraceni had said, it was a Baroque marvel. At first sight it seemed to have a splendid dome in which the Last Judgement was set forth in swirling movement, but on examination this proved to be a *trompe-l'oeil* work of extraordinary skill, painted on a flat ceiling, and effective only if the observer did not go too far forward toward the altar; viewed from that point the supposed dome was distorted, and the *sotto in su* figures of the Trinity looked toadlike. The worshipper who went forward to receive the Host was not wise if he looked upward when he returned to his seat, for he would see a fiercely distorted God the Father and God the Son spying on him from the contrived dome. The chapel itself was small, but seemed big; the fat priest had to squeeze himself into the tiny elevated pulpit as if he were putting on tight trousers. The whole room was a wonder of gilding and plaster painted in those pinks and blues that look like confectioner's work to the critic who refuses to surrender himself to their seductions. Francis was surprised to find himself alone in the chapel with Saraceni; the Countess and her granddaughter sat at the back, in an elevated box, as if at the opera, invisible to the less distinguished worshippers below. Theirs was the best view of the magical ceiling.

After chapel, breakfast, at which Saraceni and Francis were served by themselves.

"Now, to work," said Saraceni. "Have you brought any overalls?"

Francis had no overalls, but Saraceni fitted him out with a garment that might once have been a laboratory technician's white coat, filthy with paint and oil.

"Now to the studio," said Saraceni, "and when we are in the studio, you had better call me Meister. Maestro is not quite right for these surroundings. And I shall call you Cornish, not Francis, when we are at work. Corniche. Yes, you shall be Corniche."

What was happening to the Meister? In the studio he was shorter, more darting and nervous in movement, and his nose seemed hookier than elsewhere. At work, Saraceni was not the urbane creature of his social life. Francis recalled what Uncle Jack had said about the Evil Eye, though of course he did not believe in any such thing.

The studio was like a studio only in its fine north light, which came from a wall of windows that opened on the park. It had been, explained Saraceni as Francis gaped in wonderment, one of those amusements that pleased the aristocracy of the eighteenth century. It was a very long room the walls of which were encrusted with shells in many varieties, so set in the plaster that the inner sides of some and the convexities of others were outward toward the light, and they had been used to form an intricate decoration of panels, pillars, and baroque festoons. Not only shells, but minerals of several varieties had been used to decorate the walls, forming pilasters of white and pink and golden marble and—could it be?—lapis lazuli, between which depended clustered ropes of shells, each of which culminated at its fattest richness in a huge piece of brain coral. When it was new, and when it was loved and admired, it must have been a splendid folly, a rococo pavilion to lift the heart and sharpen the senses. But now the shells were dusty and dingy, the dry fountain in the wall showed rust and dirt in its basin, and the occasional mirrors were like eyes over which cataracts had grown. The shell benches had been shoved into a jumble at one end, and the room was dominated by several easels, a laboratory bench whose water supply came from visible, ugly piping that made a toe-catcher in the floor, and a large metal affair, suggesting a furnace, that had been hitched up to the castle's meagre dynamo with equal disregard for the propriety of the room.

"What love and skill must have gone into the making of this," said Francis.

"No doubt, but the less must give way to the greater, and now it is my workroom," said Saraceni. "This was a costly, ingenious toy, and those who played in it are dust. Ours is the greater task."

What was the task? Francis was never told directly; he made his discoveries by deduction, with growing incredulity. From after breakfast until four o'clock in the afternoon, when the light changed too much for Saraceni's needs, with a short interval for sandwiches and a glass of good Munich beer, he toiled at a variety of jobs from early September until mid-December. He learned to grind minerals to powder in a mortar, and mix them with various oils; the mixing was a tedious process. He learned to use and prepare mineral colours and gums—cinnabar, manganese dioxide, calcined umber, and sticky, messy gamboge. He learned to chip bits from the least visible parts of the splendid lapis pilasters, and grind his chippings fine with mortar and pestle before uniting the powder with lilac oil, to make a splendid ultramarine. It gave him particular pleasure to make the acquaintance of woad, the *isatis tinctoria,* from the juice of which a dark blue could be extracted. At the laboratory bench he learned to make up a compound of carbolic acid and formaldehyde (the whiff of which reminded him poignantly of nights with Zadok in Devinney's embalming parlour) and bottle it firmly against evaporation.

"I don't suppose you ever thought painting involved so much chemistry and cooking," said Saraceni. "You are making the true colours used by the Old Masters, Corniche. These are the splendid shades that do not fade with age. Nowadays you can buy colours somewhat like them in shops, but they are not the same at all. They are labour-saving and they save time. But you and I have precisely the same amount of time as the Old Masters— twenty-four hours in every day. There is no more, and never any less. For the true work of restoration on an old panel or canvas you must use the colours the original master employed. The honesty of your craft demands it. It is also undetectable.

"Oh, I suppose some very clever investigator with rays and chemicals might be able to say what parts of a picture had been restored—though I prefer to say revived—but our task is to do a job of revival that will not provoke foolishly inquisitive persons to resort to rays and chemicals. It is not the purpose of a picture to arouse unworthy suspicions, but to give pleasure—delight, or awe, or religious intimations, or simply a fine sense of the past, and of the boundless depth and variety of life."

This had a fine ring of morality and aesthetic probity about it. Saraceni making the past live again. But there were elements in what was really happening that Francis did not understand.

If the past was to be recovered, why not the best of the past? There were pictures hanging in Schloss Düsterstein that plainly needed the attention of a restorer, pictures by distinguished masters—a Mengs, a van Bylert, even a Van Dyck that wanted cleaning—but these did not come to the shell-pavilion. Instead there were several pictures, usually painted on panels, some of which were in bad repair and all of which were dirty. One of Francis's jobs was to wipe these as clean as possible with soft, damp cloths and then—but why?—wash these cloths in as little water as possible and dry out the pan until the dust from the picture was dust again, and could be sucked up with a syringe and put in a numbered small bottle.

Most of the little pictures were portraits of Nobody in Particular, in all his and her dull variety; just noblemen and merchants, burgomasters and scholars, and their pie-faced wives. But Saraceni would place one of these competent, uninteresting daubs on his easel, and study it with care for hours before removing certain portions with a solvent so that the painting beneath was blurred, or else the undercoating of the panel was revealed. Then he would repaint the face, so that it was the same as before but with a greater distinction—a keenness of aristocratic eye, a new look of *bürgerlich* astuteness, a fuller beard; women, if they had hands, were given rings, modest but costly, and better complexions. Sometimes he placed, in the upper left-hand corner of the panel, some little heraldic device, which might indicate the status of the sitter, and on one picture, rather larger than the rest, he introduced an ornamental chain, the collar and emblem of the Saint-Esprit. He is tarting up these four-hundred-year-old dullards, thought Francis, but why, and for whom?

Saraceni's method of painting was wholly new to Francis. On the palette he laid out his colours—the colours that Francis had so laboriously prepared—in small, almost parsimonious dibbets; but elsewhere on the palette was some of the phenol and formaldehyde mixture mingled with a little oil, and before he took paint on his brush he dipped it first in this resinous gum, which served him as a medium. A strange way to paint, surely? Late in November Francis decided that the time had come to ask a question.

"You shall see why I do that," said the Meister. "Indeed, you cannot help but see. Overpainting on a restored—or revived—picture is easily detected with the naked eye. As a picture ages, and the paint dries out—it takes about fifty years—it cracks in a certain pattern. What we call the *craquelure*. The cracks are mere hair-lines; only a poor picture develops a hide like a crocodile. But those hair-lines penetrate right through all the coatings of paint, as deep as to the ground you have used to prepare your canvas—or panel—like these I have been working on. So—how do I produce a *craquelure* in the new work I have done that blends undetectably with the old work? Well, as you see I am using a fast-drying paint—or rather, that phenol mixture that I use as my medium. Tomorrow I shall show you how I produce the *craquelure*."

So this was what the electric furnace was for! Francis had assumed it might be to heat the cold, damp grotto-room, but such heat as there was came from a brazier—not much more than a pan of burning charcoal set on a tripod, which gave out about as much heat as a dying baby's last breath, in Francis's opinion. On the day following their talk about *craquelure* Saraceni turned on the electricity in the furnace, and in time, with much rumbling and moaning, it achieved a heat by no means great, but which taxed the primitive electrical system of the castle, where electric light was scant and dim, and did not proceed above the ground floor.

When Saraceni declared the heat to be sufficient he and Francis carefully inserted the painted panels and after about fifty minutes of slow baking they emerged with, sure enough, tiny hairlines that satisfied the Meister. While they were still warm he surprised Francis yet again.

"Before these cool, you must take a sable brush and put back as much as you can of the dust that was originally on these pictures, taking special pains to get it into the tiny cracks over the new work. Don't be too eager; but be sure to cover the whole picture and especially whatever is new. Of course, you will use the dust from the bottle that bears the number of the picture. We must not insult Bürgermeister A with dirt that the hand of time has sown on the portrait of the wife of Bürgermeister B. And hurry up. The dust must adhere. Now—on with your work, you understudy of Father Time."

THE NEXT DAY Saraceni was in high excitement. "Everything now will have to wait until I return from Rome. I must visit my apartment before Christmas; I cannot be separated forever from my darlings, my pictures, my furniture—not even from my bed-curtains, which once belonged to the Empress Josephine. Antaeus had to touch his foot to the earth to gain strength, and I must touch and see my beauties if I am to have the resolution I need for this work.—You are looking at me oddly, Corniche? Does my passion for my collection really surprise you so much?"

"No, Meister, not that. But—precisely what is it you are doing here?"

"What do you suppose?"

"I don't want to be presumptuous, but this restoration, or re-vitalizing, or whatever you call it, seems to go a bit farther than is necessary."

"Oh, Corniche, speak what is in your mind. The word you want to use is faking, isn't it?"

"I wouldn't use that word to you, Meister."

"Certainly not."

"But it does look rather fishy."

"Fishy is just the right word! Now, Corniche, you shall know everything that is proper for you to know in good time. Indeed, you shall know a great deal when Prince Max visits us. He is coming for Christmas, and I shall be back in plenty of time to show him all these greatly improved panels. Prince Max talks a great deal more freely than I do. Of course, it is his right.

"Meanwhile, during the fortnight that I am absent, you shall have a little treat. A treat and a rest. You have seen how I work, and I promised to teach you as much of what I know as you can take in. While I am away, I want you to paint a picture for me. See, here is this little panel. Almost a ruin as a picture, but the panel is sound enough, and so is the leather that covers it. Paint me a picture that is all your own, but would not look out of place among the other panels. Do the best you can."

"What is the subject to be? One of these *bürgerlich* turnip-heads?"

"What you think best. Use your invention, my dear fellow. But make it congruous with the others. I want to see what you can do. And when I return we shall have a splendid Christmas, show-ing these pretty baked cakes to Prince Max."

USE HIS INVENTION? Well, if that was what Saraceni wanted, that is what Francis would do, and he would surprise the Meister, who seemed to think his invention would be limited. Saraceni set off for Rome the day after he told Francis how to use his time, and

Francis sat down to his table in the chilly shell-grotto to plan his surprise.

Saraceni was not the only one to leave the castle. The Countess and Amalie left on the same day, to go to Munich to enjoy some of its pleasures before Christmas, and Francis and Miss Ruth Nibsmith were left in possession.

Miss Nibsmith was by no means bad company; in the absence of the Countess she expanded considerably, and although Francis never saw her during the day, they met at dinner, which was served at the same stately pace as always. To fill up the time between courses they drank a good deal of the Countess's excellent wine, and resorted after dinner to the brandy bottle.

"I can never really settle myself in these German rooms," said Miss Nibsmith, kicking off her substantial shoes and putting her feet on the side of the splendid porcelain stove in the family drawing-room. "They have no focus. You know what I mean? *Focus,* in the true Latin meaning of the word. No hearth. I long for an open fire. It is as good as a dog in a room to give it life. These German stoves are beautiful, and they are certainly practical. This room is warmer than it would be if it had a fireplace, but where does one look for the centre of the room? Where does one stand when making a pronouncement? Where does one warm one's bottom?"

"I suppose the focus is wherever the most important person is," said Francis. "When the Countess is here, she is obviously the focus. Now—you ought to know these things, as an intimate of Düsterstein: I understand that for Christmas we are to entertain a Prince Max—will he be the focus? Or does the Countess always top the heap in her own castle?"

"Prince Max will be the focus," said Miss Nibsmith, "but not just because of his rank. He is quite the bounciest man I have ever met, and his laugh and his chatter make him the centre wherever he is. The Countess adores him."

"A relative?" said Francis.

"A cousin—not the nearest sort. A Hohenzollern, but poor. Poor, that is, for a prince. But Maxi is not one to repine and blame Fortune. No, no; he stirs his stumps and deals extensively in wine, and he gets rid of a lot of it in England and especially in the States. Maxi is what our Victorian ancestors would have called a smooth file. He will be the focus, you will see. The hot air from Prince Max will keep us all warm, and perhaps uncomfortably hot."

What did Miss Nibsmith do with herself all day? Francis made a polite inquiry.

"I write letters for the Countess in French, English, and German. At the moment I keep an eye on the business. I type quite well. I give lessons to Amalie, chiefly in history; she reads a lot and we talk. History is my thing. My Cambridge degree is in history. I'm a Girton girl. If I have any spare time I work on my own notes, which might be a book some day."

"A book? About what?"

"You'll laugh. Or no, I think you have too much intelligence to laugh. Anybody who works with Tancred Saraceni must be used to odd ventures. I'm making a study of astrology in Bavaria, particularly during the sixteenth and seventeenth centuries. What do you make of that?"

"I don't make anything of it. Tell me about it."

"Astrology is part of the science of the past, and of course the science of the present has no place for it, because it is rooted in a discredited notion of the universe, and puts forward a lot of Neo-Platonic ideas that don't make much sense—until you live with them for a while."

"Does that remark mean that you believe in astrology yourself?"

"Not as hard-boiled science, certainly. But as psychology— that's quite another thing. Astrology is based on a notion nobody wants to accept in our wonderfully reasonable Western World, which is that the position of the stars at the moment of your birth governs your life. 'As above, so below' is the principle in a nutshell. Utterly dotty, obviously. Lots of people must be born under the same arrangement of stars, and they don't have similar fates. Of course, it's necessary to take careful heed of precisely *where* you were born, and that varies greatly, so far as the stars are concerned. But anyhow, if the astrologer has your date, and time, and place of birth he can cast a horoscope, which can sometimes be quite useful—sometimes no good at all."

"You sound as if you half believe it, Ruth."

"Half yes: half not. But it's rather like the *I Ching*. Your intuition has to work as well as your reason, and in astrology it's the intuition of the astrologer that does the trick."

"Are you strongly intuitive?"

"Well, Girton girl though I am, I have to say yes, against what my reason tells me. Anyhow, what I'm studying is how widespread and how influential astrology was in this part of the world at the time of the Reformation and Counter-Reformation, when most people here were fierce Catholics and were supposed to leave all spiritual things—and that meant all psychological things as well—to the Church, which of course knew best, and would see you through if you were a good child. But lots of people didn't want to be good children. They couldn't fight down the pull of whatever was in the depths of their being; couldn't fight it down and couldn't channel it into being a contemplative, or whatever the Church approved. So they sought out astrologers, and the astrologers were usually in hot water with the Church. Very much like our modern world, where we are supposed to leave everything to science, even when science is something as spook-ridden as psychoanalysis. But people don't. Astrology is very big business in the extraverted, science-ridden U.S.A., for instance. The Yanks are always whooping it up for Free Will, and every man's fate being his own creation, and all that, but they're just as superstitious as the Romans ever were."

"Well! You're a funny historian, Ruth."

"Yes I am, aren't I?"

"But as a wise man I know—or knew, for the poor fellow is dead now—used to say, Life's a rum start."

"The very rummest. Like this room, in a way. Here we are, cosy as can be, even if we have no focus. What makes us so snug?"

"The stove, obviously."

"Yes, but have you never thought what makes the stove so warm?"

"I've wondered—yes. How is it fed?"

"That's one of the interesting things about these old castles. Dividing all the main rooms are terribly narrow passages—not more than eighteen inches wide, some of them, and as dark as night—and through those corridors creep servants in soft slippers who poke firewood into these stoves from the back. Unseen by us, and usually unheard. We don't give them a thought, but they are there, and they keep life in winter from being intolerable. Do they listen to us? I'll bet they do. They keep us warm, they are necessary to us, and they probably know a lot more about us than we would consider comfortable. They are the hidden life of the house."

"A spooky idea."

"The whole Universe is a spooky idea. And in every life there are these unseen people and—not people exactly—who keep us warm.—Have you ever had your horoscope cast?"

"Oh, as a boy I sent away money for a horoscope from some company in the States that advertised them in a boys' magazine. Awful rubbish, illiterate and printed on the worst kind of paper. And at Oxford a Bulgarian chap I met insisted on casting a horoscope for me, and it was blatantly obvious that what he found in the stars was pretty much what he wanted me to do, which was join some half-assed Communist spy outfit he thought he commanded. Not a very deep look into astrology, I am sure you would say."

"No, though the Bulgarian one has a familiar ring. Lots of horoscopes used to be cast that way, and still are, obviously. But I'll do one for you, if you like. The genuine article, no punches pulled. Interested?"

"Of course. Who can resist anything so flattering to the ego?"

"Dead right. That's another element. A horoscope means somebody is really paying attention to you, and that is rarer than you might think. Where, and when, were you born?"

"September 12, apparently at seven o'clock in the morning, in 1909."

"And where?"

"A place called Blairlogie, in Canada."

"Sounds like the Jumping-Off Place. I shall have to consult the gazetteer to get the exact position. Because the stars over Blairlogie weren't precisely like the stars over anywhere else."

"Yes, but suppose somebody else had been born at just that moment, in Blairlogie, wouldn't he be my twin, in all matters of Fate?"

"No. And now I shall let the cat out of the bag. This is what separates me from your boys'-paper fraud, and your Bulgarian Commie fraud. This is my great historical discovery that the real astrologers guarded with their lives, and if you breathe it to any-body before my book comes out, I shall hunt you down and kill you very imaginatively. When were you conceived?"

"God, how would I know? In Blairlogie; I'm sure of that."

"The usual answer. Parents are terribly niminy-piminy about telling their children these things. Ah, well; I shall just have to count backward and make an approximation. But anyhow—when were you baptized and christened?"

"Oh, I can tell you that, right enough. It was about three weeks later, September 30, actually, at roughly four o'clock in the after-noon. Church of England rite. Oh, and now I come to think of it, I was baptized again, years later, Catholic, that time. I'm sure I can remember the date if I try. But how does that come in?"

"When you were begotten is obviously important. As you seem to be a healthy chap I presume you were a full-term baby, so I can get the date fairly near. Date of entry upon the stage in the Great Theatre of the World is important, and that is the only one the commoner sort of astrologers bother with. But the date when you were formally received into what your community looked upon as the world of the spirit, and were given your own name, is important because it supplies a few shades to your central chart. And to be baptized twice!—spiritual dandyism, I'd call it. You let me have all that on a piece of paper at breakfast, and I'll get to work. Meanwhile, just one more teensy cognac before we retire to our blameless couches."

DAYS ALONE IN THE SHELL-GROTTO and nights with Ruth Nib-smith were doing much to restore Francis's battered self-esteem. Getting away from England had been a bruising experience. There was all the trouble of explaining to Ismay's parents what had happened, and putting up with their obvious, though unex-pressed, opinion that it must have been his fault. Then there was the trouble of making arrangements about the child Charlotte—Little Charlie as everybody but Francis insisted on calling her, slurring the "Ch" so it sounded like "Sharlie"—because the Glas-sons wanted to have control over her, but did not particularly want to be bothered with her. Their days of bringing up children were, they said reasonably, in the past. Were they now to take on a baby, who needed care every hour of the day? They worried, understandably, about Ismay, who was God knows where with God knows who in a country on the brink of civil war. The girl, they admitted, was a fool, but that did not seem to lessen their conviction that Francis was to blame for everything that had happened. When he was pushed at last to the point of telling them that Little Charlie was not his child, Aunt Prudence wept and Uncle Roderick swore, but they were no more sympathetic toward Francis. Cuckolds are fated to play ignominious and usually comic roles.

Never had Francis felt so low as when at last he came to an arrangement with the Glassons; in addition to the money already promised to keep the estate afloat, he agreed to pay all the costs of maintaining Little Charlie, which were substantial, because the child must have a first-rate nanny, and money for whatever a child needs—and the Glassons were not prepared to stint their granddaughter—and also a sum indefinitely allocated but definitely estimated for unforeseen costs. It was all reasonable enough, but Francis had the feeling that he was being exploited, and when his honour and his affections were under ruinous attack, he was astonished to find how greatly the assault on his bank-account affected him also. It was ignoble, under the circumstances, to think so much about money, but think about it he did. What did he care about Little Charlie, at present a dribbling, squalling, slumbrous lump?

In the circumstances, it was not surprising that he had jumped at Uncle Jack's offer of something to do, some place to go, a necessary task to undertake. But that had resolved itself into three months of grubby devilling for Tancred Saraceni, who had kept him grinding away with mortar and pestle, boiling up the smelly muck that went into the "black oil" the painter needed for his work, and generally acting as chore-boy and sorcerer's apprentice.

What was the sorcerer up to? Faking pictures, or at least improving existing worthless pictures. Could the great Saraceni really be sunk in this worst sort of artistic sin? Certainly that was what it looked like.

Well, if this was the game, if this was what he had been dragged into, he might as well play it to the hilt. He would show Saraceni that he could daub in the sixteenth-century German manner as well as anyone. He was to paint a picture that would agree in quality and style with the panels that had been completed and that now sat all around the shell-grotto, staring at him with the speculative eyes of the unknown dead. As Francis sat down to plan his picture he laughed for the first time in several months.

He did many preliminary drawings, and just to show what a conscientious faker he was, he did them on some of the expensive old paper culled from old books and artists' leavings he had from his Oxford days, coating it with an umber base, and making his careful preliminaries (for they were not sketches in the modern sense) with a silver-point. Yes, it was coming quite well. Yes, that was what he wanted and what would surprise the Meister. Rapidly and surely, he began to paint on his miserable old panel, in the Meister's own careful mode, with unexceptionable, authentic colours, and every stroke mixed with the magical formula of phenol and formaldehyde.

He realized with surprise that he was happy. And in his happiness, he sang.

Many painters have sung at their work, as a form of incantation, an evocative spell. What they sing may not impress an outsider as having much to do with their painting. What Francis sang was an Oxford student song to the tune of the Austrian national anthem of an earlier and happier time, *"Gott erhalte Franz den Kaiser"*:

> *Life presents a dismal picture,*
> *Home is gloomy as the tomb:*
> *Poor old Dad has got a stricture,*
> *Mother has a fallen womb;*
> *Brother Bill has been deported*
> *For a homosexual crime,*
> *And the housemaid's been aborted*
> *For the forty-second time.*

On and on he moaned, happy at his work. The Happy Faker, he thought. As I do this, no one can touch me.

"ARE YOU HAPPY? I am." Ruth Nibsmith turned her head on the pillow to look at Francis. She was not a beautiful woman, or a pretty woman, but she was well-formed and she was incontestably a jolly woman. Jolly was the only possible word. A fresh, high-spirited, merry, and, it proved, an amorous woman, who had in no way set out to lure Francis into her bed, but had cheerfully agreed to his suggestion that they advance their friendship in this direction.

"Yes, I am happy. And it's nice of you to say that you are. I haven't had much luck making anyone happy in this way."

"Oh, but it's good sport, isn't it? How would you rank our performance, in university terms?"

"I'd give us a B+."

"An excellent second class. Well, I dunno—I'd call it an A−. That's modest, and keeps us well below the Romeo and Juliet level. Anyhow, I've enjoyed it immensely these last few days."

"You speak as if it were over."

"It is over. The Countess brings Amalie back from Munich tomorrow, and I must take to my role as the model of behaviour and discretion. Which I do without regret, or not too much regret. One has to play fair with one's employers, you know; the Countess trusts me, and so I can't be having it off with another of the upper servants in the Castle when I am watching over Amalie. Oh, if Amalie could see us now she'd be green with envy!"

"What? That kid?"

"Kid my foot! Amalie's fourteen, and warm as one of those porcelain stoves. She adores you, you know."

"I've hardly spoken to her."

"Of course. You are distant, unattainable, darkly melancholy. Do you know what she calls you? Le Beau Ténébreux. She's eating her heart out for you. It would plunge her into despair to think you were content with her governess."

"Oh, shut up about the governess! And about upper servants; I'm nobody's servant."

"Balls, my boy! One's lucky if that's all one is. The Countess isn't a servant; she's a slave to this place, and to her determination to restore the family fortunes. You and I are just paid hands, able to leave whenever we please. I like being an upper servant. Lots of my betters have been upper servants. If it wasn't too much for Haydn to wear the livery of the Esterhazys, who am I to complain? There's a lot to be said for knowing one's place."

"That's what Victoria Cameron used to say."

"One of the women in your gaudy past?"

"No. Something like my nurse, I suppose. I have no gaudy past, as I'm sure you've read in the stars. My wife was always rubbing it in."

"A wife? So that's the woman in the horoscope?"

"You've found her, then?"

"A woman who gave you the most frightful dunt."

"That's Ismay, right enough. She always said I was too innocent for my own good."

"You're not innocent, Frank. Not in any stupid way. Your horoscope makes that extremely clear."

"When are you going to unveil the great horoscope? It'd better be soon, if the Countesss comes back tomorrow."

"Tonight's the night. And we must get out of this nest of guilty passion right away, because I've got to dress and so have you, and we both want a wash."

"I'd been thinking about a bath. We both reek, in an entirely creditable way."

"No, no bath. The servants would be on to us at once if we bathed during the late afternoon. In the Bavarian lexicon of baths, an afternoon bath means sex. No, you must be content with a searching wash, in your pre-dinner allowance of hot water."

"Okay. 'Ae fond kiss, and then we sever'."

" 'Ae farewell, alas, forever'."

"Oh Ruth, don't say forever."

"Of course not. But until dinner, anyhow. And now—up and out!"

"I hope there's something good for dinner."

"What would you guess?"

"Something utterly unheard of in Düsterstein. What would you say to veal?"

"Bang on! I saw the menu this morning. *Poitrine de veau farci*."

"Ah, well; in the land of veal, all is veal.

> *I'm wearin' awa', Jean*
> *Like snow-wreaths in thaw, Jean*
> *I'm wearin' awa'*
> *In the land o' the veal."*

"Lucky to get it. I could eat a horse."

"Hunger is the best sauce."

"Frank, that's magnificent. What an encapsulation of universal experience! Is it your own?"

Francis gave her a playful punch, and went back to his own room, for a searching wash before dinner.

AFTER DINNER, THE HOROSCOPE. Ruth had an impressive clutch of papers, some of which were zodiacal charts, upon which she had added copious notations in a handsome Italic hand.

"The writing oughtn't to swear at the material, you see, so I learned to write like this."

"Yes. Very nice. The only trouble is that it's so easily forged."

"Think so? I'm sure you could spot a forgery of your own fist."

"Yes, I've done so."

"There you go, being Le Beau Ténébreux. Could it have been the Dream Girl who appears so strongly in your chart?"

"It was. Clever of you to guess."

"A lot of this work is clever guessing. Making hints from the chart fit in with hints from the subject. The girl is an important figure for you."

"Thank God she's gone."

"Not gone. She'll be back."

"What then?"

"Depends if she's still the Dream Girl. You ought to get wise to yourself, Francis. If she treated you badly, some of it was your own fault. When men go about making Dream Girls out of flesh-and-blood girls, it has the most awful effect on the girl. Some fall for it, and try to embody the dream, and that is horribly phoney and invites trouble; others become perfect bitches because they can't stand it. Is your wife a bitch?"

"Of the most absolute and triple-distilled canine order."

"Probably only a food. Fools make more trouble than all the

bitches ever whelped. But let's look at your full chart. Let's get down on the floor, where I can spread it out. Put some books on the corners to hold it down. That's it. Now—"

It was a handsome chart, handsome as the zodiac can be, and as neatly annotated as a governess could make it.

"I won't overwhelm you with astrological jargon, but take a look at these principal facts. The important thing is that your Sun is in midheaven, and that's terrific. And your eastern horizon—the point of ascent—is in conjunction with Saturn, who is a greatly misunderstood influence, because people immediately think, Oh yes, Saturn, he must be saturnine, or sour-bellied, but that's not what it really means at all. Your Moon is in the north, or subterranean midheaven. And—now this is very significant—your Sun is in conjunction with Mercury. Because of your very powerful Sun, you have lots of vitality, and believe me you need it, because life has given you some dunts, and has some others in waiting. But that powerful Sun also assures you of being right in the mainstream of psychic energy. You've got spiritual guts, and lots of intuition. Then that wonderful, resilient, swift Mercury. Psychologically, Francis, you are very fast on your feet.

"Now—here's that very powerful and influential Saturn. That's destiny. You remember about Saturn? He had it tough, because he was castrated, but he did some castrating himself. What's bred in the bone, you know. Patterns necessarily repeat themselves. All kind of obstacles, burdens to be borne, anxieties, depressions and exhaustion—there's your Beau Ténébreux personality for you—but also some compensations because you have the strong sense of responsibility that carries you through, and at last, after a struggle, a sense of reality—which is a fine thing to have, though not always very comfortable. Your Mars supports your Sun, you see, and that gives you enormous endurance. And—this is important—your Saturn has the same relationship to your Moon that Mars has to your Sun, but it's a giver of spiritual power, and takes you deep into the underworld, the dream world, what Goethe called the realm of the Mothers. There's a fad now for calling them the Archetypes, because it sounds so learned and scientific. But the Mothers is truer to what they really are. The Mothers are the creators, the matrixes of all human experience."

"That's the world of art, surely?"

"More than that. Art may be a symptom, a perceptible form, of what the Mothers are. It's quite possible to be a pretty good artist, mind you, without having a clue about the Mothers.

"Saturn on the ascendant and the Sun in midheaven is very rare and suggests a most uncommon life. Perhaps even some special celestial guardianship. Have you ever been aware of anything like that?"

"No."

"You really are a somebody, Francis."

"You're very flattering."

"Like hell I am! I don't fool around with this stuff. I don't make a chancy living by casting horoscopes for paying customers. I'm trying to find out what it's all about, and I've been very lucky in discovering that old astrologers' secret I told you about. I'm not kidding you, Francis."

"I must say my remarkableness has taken its time about showing itself."

"It should start soon, if it hasn't started already. Not worldly fame, but perhaps posthumous fame. There are things in your chart that I would tell you if I were in the fortune-telling and predicting business. Being at Düsterstein is very important; your chart shows that. And working with Saraceni is important, though he simply shows up as a Mercurial influence. And there are all kinds of things in your background that aren't showing up at present. What's happened to all that music?"

"Music? I haven't been much involved with music. No talent."

"Somebody else's music. In your childhood."

"I had an aunt who sang and played a lot. Awful stuff, I suppose it was."

"Is she the false mother who turns up? There are two. Was one the nurse?"

"My grandfather's cook, really."

"A very tough influence. Like granite. But the other one seems to be a bit witchy. Was she queer to look at? Was she the one who sang? It doesn't matter that what she sang wasn't in the most fashionable taste. People are so stupid, you know, in the way they discount the influence of music that isn't right out of the top drawer; if it isn't Salzburg or Bayreuth quality it can't be influential. But a sentimental song can sometimes open doors where

Hugo Wolf knocks in vain. I suppose it's the same with pictures. Good taste and strong effect aren't always closely linked. If your singing aunt put all she had into what she sang, it could have marked you for life."

"Perhaps. I often think of her. She's failing, I hear."

"And who's this—this messy bit here? Somebody that doesn't seem fully human. Could it have been a much-loved pet?"

"I had a brother who was badly afflicted."

"Odd. Doesn't look quite like a brother. But influential, whatever it was. It's given you a great compassion for the miserable and dispossessed, Francis, and that's very fine, so long as you don't let it swamp your common sense. I don't think it can; not with that powerful Mercury. But immoderate compassion will ruin you quicker than brandy. And the kingdom of the dead— what were you doing there?"

"I really believe I was learning about the fragility and pitiful quality of life. I had a remarkable teacher."

"Yes, he shows up; a sort of Charon, ferrying the dead to their other world. What I would call, if I were writing an academic paper, which God be thanked I'm not, a Psycho-pomp."

"Handsome word. He'd have loved to be called a Psycho-pomp."

"Was he your father, by any chance?"

"Oh, no; a servant."

"Funny, he looks like a father, or a relative of some kind. Anyhow—what about your father? There's a Polyphemus figure in here, but I can't make out if he's your father."

Francis laughed. "Oh yes, a Polyphemus figure sure enough. Always wears a monocle. Nice man."

"Just shows how careful you have to be about interpreting. Polyphemus wasn't at all a nice man. But he was certainly one-eyed. But was he your real father? What about the old man?"

"Old man? My grandfather?"

"Yes, probably. The man who truly loved your mother."

"Ruth, what are you talking about?"

"Don't get up on your ear. Incest. Not the squalid physical thing, but the spiritual, psychological thing. It has a sort of nobility. It would dignify the physical thing, if that had occurred. But I'm not suggesting that you are your grandfather's child in the flesh, rather his child in the spirit, the child he loved because you were born of his adored daughter. What about your mother? She doesn't show up very clearly. Do you love her very much?"

"Yes, I think so. I've always told myself so. But she has never been as real as the aunt and the cook. I've never really felt that I knew her."

"It's a wise child that knows his father, but it's one child in a million who knows his mother. They're a mysterious mob, mothers."

"Yes. So I've been told. They go down, down, down into the very depths of hell, in order that we men may live."

"That's very Saturnine, Francis. You sound as if you hated her for it."

"Who wouldn't? Who needs such a crushing weight of gratitude toward another human being? I don't suppose she thought about the depths of hell when I was begotten."

"No. That seems to have been quite a jolly occasion, if your first chart isn't lying. Have you told her about your wife? Running off with the adventurous one?"

"No I haven't. Not yet."

"Or about the child?"

"Oh yes, she knows about the child. 'Darling, you horrible boy, you've made me a grandmother!' was what she wrote."

"Have you relieved her mind by telling her that she isn't really a grandmother?"

"Damn it, Ruth, this is too bloody inquisitorial! Did you really see that in this rigmarole?"

"I see the cuckold's horns, painfully clear. But don't fuss. It's happened to better men. Look at King Arthur."

"Bugger King Arthur—and Tristan and Iseult and the Holy sodding Grail and all that Celtic pack. I made a proper jackass of myself about that stuff!"

"Well, you could make a jackass of yourself about much more unworthy things."

"Ruth, I don't want to be nasty, but really this stuff of yours is far too vague, too mythological. You don't honestly take it seriously, do you?"

"I've told you already; it's a way of channelling intuitions and things that can't be reached by the broad, floodlit paths of science.

You can't nail it down, but I don't think that's a good enough reason for brushing it aside. You can't talk to the Mothers by getting them on the phone, you know. They have an unlisted number. Yes, I take it seriously."

"But this stuff you've been telling me is all favourable, all things I might like to hear. Would you tell me if you saw in this chart that I would die tonight?"

"Probably not."

"Well, when will I die? Come on, let's have some hard information, hot from the planets."

"No astrologer in his right mind ever tells somebody when they are going to die. Though there was once a wise astrologer who told a rather short-tempered king that he would die the day after the astrologer died himself. It assured him of a fine old age. But I will tell you this: you'll have a good innings. The war won't get you."

"The war?"

"Yes, the coming war. Really, Francis, you don't have to be an astrologer to know that there's a war coming, and you and I had better get out of this charming, picturesque castle before it does, or we may find ourselves making the journey on the Bummelzug that passes behind here every few days."

"You know about that?"

"It's not much of a secret. I'd give a lot to have a peep at that place, but the first rule for aliens is not to be too snoopy. I hope you don't go too near there when you are out for spins in your little car. Francis, surely you know that we are living in the grasp of the greatest tyranny in at least a thousand years, and certainly the most efficient tyranny in history. And where there's tyranny, there's sure to be treachery, and some of it is of a rarefied sort. You don't know what Saraceni's doing?"

"I'm beginning to wonder."

"You'll have to know soon. Really, Francis, for a man with your strong Mercury influence you are very slow to catch on. I said you weren't stupid, but you *are* thick. You'd better find out what you've got yourself into, my boy. Maybe Max will tell you. Listen—Mercury is the spirit of intelligence, isn't he? And also of craft, and guile, and trickery, and all that sort of thing. Something of the greatest importance is very near you. A decision. Francis,

I beg you, be a crook if you must, but for the love of God, don't be a dumb crook. You, with Saturn and Mercury so strong in your chart! You want me to tell you the dark things in your chart—there they are! And one thing more: money. You're much too fond of money."

"Because everybody is trying to gouge it out of me. I seem to be everybody's banker and unpaid bottle-washer and snoop and lackey—"

"Snoop? So that's why you're here! Well, it relieves me that you're not just a lost American wandering around in a fog—"

"I'm not an American, damn it! I'm a Canadian. You English never know the difference!"

"Sorry, sorry, sorry! Of course you're a Canadian. Do you know what that is? A psychological mess. For a lot of good reasons, including some strong planetary influences, Canada is an introverted country straining like hell to behave like an extravert. Wake up! Be yourself, not a bad copy of something else!"

"Ruth, you can talk more unmitigated rubbish than anybody I have ever known!"

"Okay, my pig-headed friend. Wait and see. The astrological consultation is now over and it's midnight and we must be fresh and pretty tomorrow to greet our betters when they come from Munich, and Rome, and wherever the ineffable Prince Maximilian is arriving from. So, give me one more cognac, and then it's goodnight!"

"HEIL HITLER!" Prince Maximilian's greeting rang like a pistol shot.

Saraceni started, and his right arm half rose in response to the Nazi salute. But the Countess, who had sunk half-way down in a curtsy, ascended slowly, like a figure on the pantomime stage, rising through a trapdoor.

"Max, do you have to say that?"

"My dear cousin, forgive my little joke. May I?" And he kissed her affectionately on the cheek. "Saraceni, dear old chap! Dear little cousin, you're prettier than ever. Miss Nibsmith, how d'you do? And we haven't met, but you must be Cornish, Tancred's right hand. How d'you do?"

It was not easy to get a word in with Prince Max. Francis shook his outstretched hand. Max did not stop talking.

"So kind of you to ask me to spend Christmas with you, cousin. It's not celebrated as cheerfully in Bavaria as we remember, though I saw a few signs of jollification on the road. I came by way of Oberammergau, because I thought that there, if anywhere, the birth of Our Lord would be gratefully acknowledged. After all, they must sell and export several hundred thousand board-feet of crêches and crucifixes and holy images every year, and even they can't utterly forget why. In Switzerland, now, Christmas is in full, raving eruption. Paris is *en fête,* almost as if Christ had been a Frenchman. And in London people otherwise quite sane are wallowing in the Dickensian slush, and looting Fortnum's of pies and puddings and crackers and all the other artifacts of their national saturnalia. And here—I see you've put up some ever-greens—"

"Of course. And tomorrow there will be Mass, as usual."

"And I shall be there! I shall be there, not having eaten a crumb or drunk a swallow since midnight. I shall not even clean my teeth, lest a Lutheran drop might escape down my gullet. What a lark, eh? Or should I say, 'Wot larks', Cornish? Should I say 'Wot larks'?"

"I beg your pardon, sir?"

"Oh, not sir, please! Call me Max. 'Wot larks' because of Dickens. You must be a real Dickensian Protestant, no?"

"I was brought up a Catholic, Max."

"You don't look in the least like one."

"And exactly how does a Catholic look?" said the Countess, not pleased.

"Oh, it's a most becoming look, cousin, an other-worldly light in the eyes, never seen among Lutherans. Isn't that so, Miss Nib-smith?"

"Oh, but our eyes shine with the light of truth, sir."

"Good, very good! No trapping the governess, is there? Are you taking on any of that light, Amalie?"

Amalie blushed, as she always did when she was singled out for special notice, but had nothing to say. There was no need. The Prince rattled on.

"Ah, a real Bavarian Christmas, just like childhood! How long will it last, eh? I suppose so long as none of us are Jews we shall be allowed to celebrate Christmas in our traditional way, at least in privacy. You're not a Jew, by any chance, Tancred? I've always wondered."

"God forbid," said Saraceni, crossing himself. "I have worries enough as it is."

Amalie found her tongue. "I didn't know Jews celebrated Christmas," she said.

"Poor devils! I don't think they get much chance to celebrate anything. We'll drink to better times at dinner, won't we?"

The Prince had arrived in a small, sporting, snorting, coughing, roaring, farting car, loaded with packages and big leather cases, and when the company assembled for dinner, these proved to contain presents for everybody, all speaking loudly of Bond Street. For the Countess a case of claret and a case of champagne. For Amalie, a photograph of Prince Max in dress uniform, in a costly frame from Asprey's. For Miss Nibsmith a beautiful if somewhat impractical diary bound in blue leather, with a gold lock and key—for astrological notations, said Prince Max, slyly. For Saraceni and Francis leather pocket diaries for the year to come, obviously from Smythson's. And for the servants, all sorts of edible luxuries in a hamper from Fortnum's.

Of course there were other gifts. The Countess gave Francis a book that had been written about the Düsterstein pictures by some toilsome scholar many years before. Amalie, with much blushing, gave him six handkerchiefs which she had embroidered with his initials. Saraceni gave everybody books of poetry, bound in Florence. Francis won high distinction by giving the Countess and Amalie sketches of themselves, done in his Old Master style, in which he had taken special care to emphasize the family resemblance. He had nothing for the men, or for Miss Nibsmith, but it did not seem to matter. And when the gift-giving was finished, they sat down to a dinner of greater length than usual, with venison, and roast goose, and a stuffed carp, which was nicer to look at than to eat. And when cheese had been consumed the Countess announced that in special compliment to Francis they would conclude with a traditional English dish, which the chef identified, he being an Italian-Swiss, as *Suppe Inglese*. It was a dashing attempt at a sherry trifle, rather too wet but kindly meant.

The meal was accompanied by what was less a conversation than a solo performance by Prince Max, filled with casual references—fairly casual but by no means inevitable—to "my cousin Carol, the King of Rumania" and one or two stories about "my ancestor, Friedrich der Grosse (though of course we are of the Swabian branch of the family)" and quite a long account of how he had studied canon law as a boy "so that the priests couldn't cheat us—we had more than fifty parishes, you know." And at last when toasts were to be proposed and the Countess, and Amalie, and Miss Nibsmith, and the splendours of Italian art "as represented by our dear Maestro, Tancred Saraceni", and the King of England, had all been drunk, the Prince insisted with much merriment that they drink also to "the Pretender to the British Throne, my cousin Prince Rupert of Bavaria, whose claim is through his Stuart ancestry, as of course you know." After this toast Francis insisted on smashing his glass (having made sure it was not too precious) in order that no lesser toast should ever be drunk from it.

Francis emerged somewhat too abruptly from his character as Le Beau Ténébreux, for he was feeling the wines stirring within him. When Amalie, daring greatly, asked him if it were true that there were many bears in Canada, he replied that when he was a boy a child had been eaten by a bear within three miles of Blairlogie. That was true, but not content, he went on to say that the bear had later been seen, walking on its hind legs, wearing the child's tuque and carrying its satchel of books, making its way toward Carlyle Rural. Even Amalie refused to believe him.

"My dear Amalie, the English wit tends always toward some *fantaisie*," said the Countess with grandmotherly solemnity. And then Prince Max took over again, to tell about a boar-hunt he had once enjoyed in the company of several highly placed relatives.

"What does Prince Max do now?" Francis asked Ruth Nibsmith, after dinner.

"Travels for a wine company that has headquarters in London," she whispered. "Lives on what he makes, which is pretty good, but not of course a fortune. He's a real aristocrat, a shameless, joyful survivor. Hitler will never down Max. Did you notice the little Wittelsbach thingummy on the door of his car? Max is the real goods, but not tongue-tied, like our English hogen-mogens."

CHRISTMAS MORNING. Mass had been heard, breakfast had been eaten, and without any words having been spoken about it—though Prince Max talked without a stop about other things—Saraceni led the way to the shell-grotto workroom, and the Countess, the Prince, and Francis followed. The panels on which Saraceni had been working all through the autumn were propped up on tables and walls and against the pillars of lapis lazuli.

Slowly the Prince made a tour of inspection.

"Marvellous," he said; "really, Tancred, you are greater than your reputation. How you have transformed these dismal daubs! I would never have believed it if I did not have the evidence before me. And you say it is truly undetectable?"

"A determined critic, armed with various testing acids, and special rays to pick up inevitable discrepancies in the brushwork, could probably see what was done—but I doubt if even then he would be sure. But as I have been telling our friend Corniche every day, our task is to do our work so well that suspicion will not be aroused, and prying investigators will not come with their rays and begin to arouse suspicions. As you see, the pictures are rather dirty. And the dirt on them is their very own. No Augsburg dirt where one might expect Nürnberg dirt. Doubtless they will be given a good cleaning before they are hung in the great gallery."

"Perhaps you will be called in to supervise the cleaning. That would be rather good, wouldn't it?"

"I should certainly enjoy it."

"You know, some of these are so good I almost covet them for myself. You have really made it seem as if some uncommonly clever, and quite unknown and unrecognized, portraitists of authentic German style had been at work among the rich merchants of the fifteenth and sixteenth centuries in these parts. The one thing you have not been able to disguise is your talent, Meister."

"You are very kind."

"Look at this one. The Fuggers' jester. Unquestionably this is one of the Fools whom we know the Fuggers always kept in their entourage after they became Counts, but which one? Do you think it could be Drollig Hansel, the favourite of Count Hans? Look at him. What a face!"

"Poor wretch," said the Countess; "to be born a dwarf and kept as a Fool. Still, I suppose it was better than being a dwarf whom nobody kept."

"This one will certainly delight our friends when they see it," said Prince Max.

"I am sorry, but that one is not included with the others," said Saraceni.

"Not included! But it's the pick of the lot! Why is it not included!"

"Because it is not a touched-up genuine picture. It is wholly and simply a fabrication, made by our young friend Corniche. I have been teaching him the technique of this sort of painting, and as an exercise I left him to produce something solely on his own responsibility, to show how well he had mastered the art."

"But it is superb!"

"Yes. A superb fake."

"Well—but could anybody spot it?"

"Not without a scientific examination. The panel is old and quite genuine, and it is covered in leather as old as itself. The colours are correct, made in the true manner. The technique is impeccable, except that it is rather too good for a wholly unknown painter. And this ingenious scoundrel Corniche has even seen that the *craquelure* incorporates some authentic dust. I don't suppose one observer in a thousand would have any doubt about it."

"Oh, but Meister—that observer would surely spot the old Fugger *Firmenzeichen,* the pitchfork and circle, that can just barely be perceived in the upper left-hand corner. He would pride himself on having spotted it and guessed what it is, although it is almost obscured."

"Yes. But it is a fake, my dear Max."

"Perhaps in the substance. Certainly not in the spirit. Consider, Meister: this is not imitating any known painter's work—that would be a fake, of course. No, this is simply a little picture in a sixteenth-century manner. Now what makes it different from these others?"

"Only the fact that it has been done in the past month."

"Oh, that is almost Lutheran pernickety morality! That is an unworthy servitude to chronology. Cousin, what do you say? Isn't it a little gem?"

"I say it speaks of the dull, inescapable misery of being a dwarf, of having to make oneself ridiculous in order to be tolerated, of feeling that God has not used you well. If it makes me feel these things so strongly, it is certainly a picture of unusual quality. I should like to see it make the journey with the others."

"Of course, cousin. Just the sort of good sense I should expect from you. Come on, Tancred, relent."

"If you say so. The greatest risk is yours."

"Let me worry about the risk. Is everything ready for the journey, cousin?"

"The six big hogsheads are in the old granary."

"Then let us get to work at once."

Francis, Max, the Countess, and Saraceni spent the next three hours wrapping the panels—eighteen of them, including the picture of the jester—in oiled paper, after which they were sewn into packages of oiled silk and the seams caulked with tar Saraceni heated on the brazier. To the silken packages a number of small lead weights were attached. Then they carried them to the old granary, where there were no workmen because of the holiday, and there they removed the tops from the six hogsheads, and carefully sank the packages in the white wine they contained—fifty-two gallons to a barrel. When Prince Max tapped the last top back into place, eighteen pictures had been drowned, snug and dry in their casings, and were ready to travel to England, to the warehouses of a highly respected London wine-merchant. It was a good morning's work, and even the Countess relaxed some of her usual reserve, and invited the conspirators to take Madeira with her in her private room, where Francis had never been before.

"I feel a splendid glow of achievement," said Prince Max, sniffing at his glass. "I am rejoicing in the breadth and ingenuity of our cleverness. I am wondering if I shall be able to resist pinching the little Fugger Jester for myself. But no—that would be unprofessional. He must go with the others. You know, it seems to me to be damn funny that our friend Francis has not said a word—not a single word—about what we have done with his picture."

"I had a good reason for keeping quiet," said Francis. "But I would certainly like to know what is going on, if that is permissible. The Meister has quelled me so completely during the past four months that I don't feel that I have any right to ask questions. I suppose that is what apprenticeship means. Keep your eyes open and your mouth shut. But I'd like to know a little, if I may."

"Tancred, what an old tyrant you must be," said Prince Max. "Cousin, do you think we should explain, just a little?"

"Yes, I do. Though I doubt your ability to explain, or do anything else, just a little, Max. But Mr. Cornish is now in—you shall say in what—farther than he knows, and it would be illusage not to tell him what he is letting himself in for."

"Here it is, my dear Cornish. You know that our Führer is a great connoisseur of art? Understandable, as he was himself a painter in his young days, before his mighty destiny declared itself. Because of his determination that the full glory of the German Volk should be made plain to the whole world, as well as to the Volk itself, he wishes to acquire and bring back to Germany whatever German works of art are owned abroad. Repatriation of our heritage, he calls it. That will take some doing, of course. There was a great dispersal of German religious art during the Reformation. Who wanted that ridiculous stuff? Certainly not the Lutherans. But much of it found its way to other countries, and travelled even further toward America, from which it probably will not return. But what is in Europe may be persuaded to return. There was another great dispersal of German art during the eighteenth and early nineteenth centuries, when every young sprig who made the Grand Tour felt obliged to take a few pretty things home with him, and not all of those pretty things were acquired in Italy. Some fine Gothic things went from here. The Führer wants to get it all together, the first-rate and the second-rate—not that the Führer would regard anything authentically German as second-rate—and he is planning a great Führermuseum in Linz to house it."

"But surely Linz is in Austria?"

"Yes, and not a great distance from the Führer's birthplace. By

the time the pictures have been assembled, Austria will be glad
to have the Führermuseum. Austria is ripe for the picking. Are
you beginning to catch on?"

"Yes, but does the Führer really want the kind of thing the
Meister and I have been working on? That's very small potatoes,
surely? And why send it to England? Why not offer it here?"

"Well—that is a complicated story. First, the Führer wants
everything that is German; when it has been acquired, somebody
will sort the good from the mediocre. And I may say that you
and dear Tancred have lifted these pictures above mediocrity.
They are bürger-portraits of considerable interest. How intelligent, how German they look now! Second, the Führer, or I should
say his agents, are ready to make deals with foreign dealers. They
like to do swaps. For a German picture, a picture of roughly
corresponding worth that is not German but now hangs in a
German gallery may be exchanged. The Kaiser Friedrich Museum
in Berlin and the Alte Pinakothek in Munich have already—under
the gentle persuasion of the Führer's artistic advisers—swapped
a Ducio di Buoninsegna, a Raphael, some Fra Filippo Lippis, and
God knows what else for German paintings that could be made
available. There are scores of them in England, you know."

"I suppose there must be."

"And we are just about to ship some more to England for
swapping purposes. Things that might have been found in English
country houses. Small things, but the Führer's principal agent
likes quantity, as well as quality."

"He has an eye for quality, as well," said the Countess, with
something like a snort.

"Oh yes, he has, and he has had his eyes on the pictures here
at Düsterstein," said Prince Max. "The Führer's principal artistic
agent, as you may know, is that very busy man, Reichsmarschall
Göring, and he has already visited my cousin to discover whether
she would like to present her family collection to the Führermuseum as a token of her fidelity to German ideals. The Reichsmarschall is extremely fond of pictures, and he has an enviable
collection of his own. I understand," said Max, turning to the
Countess, "that he has asked the Führer to revive in his favour
the title that Landgrave Wilhelm III of Hesse gave to his adviser
on art—Director-General of the Delights of My Eye."

"What effrontery," said the Countess. "His taste is very vulgar, as one might expect."

"Well, my dear Cornish, there you have it," said Prince Max.

"And you are doing this as a sort of quixotic anti-Hitler thing?" said Francis. "Just to do him in the eye? Surely the risk is immense?"

"We are quixotic, but not so quixotic as all that," said the Prince. "There is a certain recognition for this work, which is, as you say, dangerous. Friendly English firms are most generous. Certain art dealers are involved. They arrange the swaps, and they sell the Italian treasures that go to England in return for the sort of thing we have been dealing with this morning. Such a group of lesser pictures as this may be exchanged for a single canvas—a Tiepolo, even a Raphael. The work is quixotic, certainly, but—not totally selfless. Some money *does* change hands, depending on how well we do."

Francis looked at the Countess, and although he was pretty good at controlling his features, astonishment must have showed. The Countess did not flinch.

"One does not restore a great fortune by shrinking from risks, Mr. Cornish," she said.

THAT GIRL DID WELL with Francis's horoscope, said the Lesser Zadkiel. She even hinted at your involvement in his fate, brother. That must have surprised you.

—I am not so easily surprised, said the Daimon Maimas. In the days when people understood about the existence and influence of daimons like myself we were often recognized and called upon. But she did well enough, certainly. She warned Francis of an impending crisis, and against his increasing preoccupation with money.

—He has good reason for it, said the Angel. As he says, everybody exploits him and he is open to exploitation. Look at that gang at Düsterstein! Prince Max assumes that Francis will be delighted to be included in the picture hoax—to give it the least objectionable name— because he regards it as an aristocratic lark, and it honours Francis to be one of the jokers. The Countess thinks, in her heart, that a bourgeois like Francis is lucky to be allowed into an aristocratic secret, and to work for his keep to sustain it. And Saraceni has the genial

contempt of the master for the neophyte. But if that scheme were ever uncovered, Francis would suffer most, because he is the only one who has actually forged a picture.

—No, brother, he has forged nothing. He has painted an original picture in a highly individual style, and if any connoisseur misdates it, the more fool he. It is Prince Max and the Countess who are passing it off as what it is not. They are aristocrats, and, as you well know, aristocrats did not always achieve their position by a niggling scrupulosity. As for money, the whole story has not yet been told.

—I bow to your superior knowledge of the case, my dear Maimas. What pleases me is that François Xavier Bouchard, the dwarf tailor of Blairlogie, is at last about to burst upon the world, and be admired, as the Fuggers' Jester, Drollig Hansel. And all because Francis learned to observe, and remember, under the influence of Harry Furniss.

—These are the little jokes that relieve the tedious work of being a Minor Immortal, said the Daimon Maimas.

"DO YOU SUPPOSE THAT La Nibsmith will take Prince Max's broad hint?" said Saraceni. "You heard what he said when he gave her that book: for astrological notations. He is mad to have her cast his horoscope."

"And won't she?" said Francis.

"Apparently not. He has been begging—in so far as so aristocratic a person can beg—for several months. She is capricious, which is her right. She does not do it professionally, but she is very good. A genuine psychic. Of course, casting horoscopes depends a good deal on the psychic gifts of the astrologer. Germans are just as keen for that sort of thing as Americans. The Führer has an astrologer of his own."

"She doesn't look like my idea of a psychic."

"Psychics often don't—the real ones. They are frequently rather earthy people. Has she cast your horoscope yet?"

"Well—yes, as a matter of fact, she has."

"Have you a good destiny?"

"Odd, apparently. Odder than I would have thought."

"Not odder than *I* would have thought. I chose you for my apprentice because you were odd, and you have revealed new depths of oddity ever since. That picture you painted while I was in Rome, for instance. It was a portrait, wasn't it?"

"Yes."

"I won't pry. It had the unmistakable quality of a portrait, a feeling between subject and painter, which cannot be faked—not to my eye, that's to say. Where are your preliminary drawings?"

Francis produced them from a portfolio.

"You are a thorough creature, aren't you? Even your preliminaries on the right paper, in the right style. Not your Harry Furniss style. Nevertheless, I'll wager that when you first drew that dwarf, it was in your Harry Furniss manner."

"It was. He was dead, and I did a few sketches while he was being prepared for burial."

"You see? Odd, as I said. How you profited from Harry Furniss's book! Forget nothing; learn the trick of remembering through the hand. I shall be interested to hear what they think of it in London."

"Meister, who are 'they'? Haven't I a right to know what I'm mixed up in, working here with you? There must surely be some risk. Why am I kept in the dark?"

" 'They' are a few very distinguished dealers in art, who make all the business arrangements in this little game which, as you say, involves some risk."

"They're swapping these worthless, or at least trivial, pictures for pictures of greatly superior quality?"

"They are exchanging certain pictures for others, for complicated reasons."

"All right. But is it no more than what Prince Max said? An elaborate hoax on the German Reich?"

"It would be a very bold man who would try to hoax the German Reich."

"Well, somebody seems to be doing it. Is this a government thing? Some sort of Secret Service lark?"

"The British government knows about it, and very likely the American government knows—but only a very few people, who would deny all knowledge if there should be a discovery and a row."

"It's for private gain, then?"

"There is money involved. This work we are doing is not un-requited."

" 'Unrequited'! What a word for such a thing! You mean that you and the Countess and Prince Max are getting damn well paid!"

"For services rendered. The Countess supplies the pictures on which we work. Where else but in such a place as this, where there are two pictures stacked in those innumerable service corridors for every one on the walls, would you find things of the right age, right character, and indeed authentic? I supply a quality of craftsmanship that makes those pictures look rather more desirable to the agents of the great Reichsmarschall than they did in their earlier, neglected state. Prince Max sees that the pictures arrive in England and reach the dealers, which involves substantial risk. Such services do not come cheap, but what we receive is not comparable to what the London dealers receive, because they get fine Italian art for mediocre German art, and they sell it at splendid prices."

"A huge international fraud, in fact."

"If there is fraud, it is not the kind you suggest. If the German experts consider our pictures so desirable that they will exchange Italian pictures of great value for them, are we to say that they do not know what they are doing? No money changes hands—not at that point. The Reich is not anxious that large sums of German money should leave the country even for works of German art; that is the reason for the exchange arrangement. The German experts have a task; it is to form the finest and most complete and most impressive collection of German art in the world. They need both quantity and quality. The work we do here does not aim at quality in the highest reaches—no Dürers, no Grünewalds, no Cranachs. To provide those we should have to resort to faking—from which, of course, I shrink in holy horror. We simply make old, undistinguished pictures into old pictures of some distinction."

"Except for *Drollig Hansel*. He's a fake and he's gone to England."

"My dear man, don't allow yourself to become heated, or you may say things you will wish you had not said. *Drollig Hansel* is a student exercise, undertaken in the style of an earlier day, as a test of skill. The test has been splendidly passed. I am the judge, and I know what I am talking about. If an expert, seeing it among the others, cannot tell that it is modern, what greater proof can you have of my achievement? But you are blameless. You did not paint to deceive, you signed nobody else's name to it, and you did not yourself send it to England."

"That's casuistry."

"Much talk in the art world is casuistry."

CASUISTRY: the study of Ethics as it relates to questions of conscience. That was how the Church used the word. But in Francis's mind it had a Protestant ring, and it meant quibbling—teetering on the tightrope above a dangerous abyss. His conscience twinged sorely after the Countess received a letter from Prince Max, relating how a newly uncovered picture was causing a small sensation among a score or so of art experts in London.

Pictures of dwarfs are not uncommon, and some of the subjects can be identified. Van Dyck painted Queen Henrietta Maria with her dwarf, Sir Jeffrey Hudson; Bronzino painted the dwarf Morgante in the nude—a front view and a back one so that no detail should be missed; the Prado has the female dwarf Eugenia Martinez Vallego, clothed and nude. The dwarfs of Rizi and Velasquez, who seem to observe royal splendour from a remote, half-comprehending world of their own, are not known by name, but by the pain in their intent regard. Less squeamish ages were delighted by dwarfs, and some of them were used in much the manner that had driven F. X. Bouchard of Blairlogie to put his head in a noose.

The Countess read her cousin's letter to Saraceni and Francis with as much excitement as that reserved lady ever chose to show. The experts had given the painting a little cleaning, and what had they found? That what had looked like the Fuggers' *Firmenzeichen*, their family mark, was perhaps something more; true, it looked like a pitchfork, or a three-branched candlestick with an O beside it, but it could also be a gallows with a noose hanging from it! The experts were delighted by their find, and the puzzle it suggested. Had the dwarf been a hangman, then? That it was indeed Drollig Hansel, known as an obscure figure in history but never before seen, they did not choose to doubt. This was really a find for the Führermuseum, a real whiff from an earlier, spiritually fearless Germany, which did not shrink from realities, even when they were also grotesqueries.

Prince Max's letter was carefully phrased. No inquiring secret police, peeping into the letters that a German aristocrat wrote to his high-born cousin, could have understood anything more than the facts that were stated. But there was rejoicing at Düsterstein.

Francis did not rejoice. His intention to make some record, to offer some comment, on the fate of the dwarf he had known had been unveiled, and he had not expected that to happen. His picture had been a very private affair, an *ex voto* almost, a memorial to a man he had never spoken to, and had come to know only after his death. He could not contain his dismay and torment, and he had to say so to Saraceni.

"Are you really surprised, my dear man? There are very few secrets in this world, as you are quite old enough to have found out. And art is a way of telling the truth."

"That's what Browning said. My aunt was always quoting him."

"Well? Your aunt must have been a wise woman. And Browning a deep psychologist. But don't you see? It is the quality of truth, of depth of feeling, in your picture that has made all these learned gentlemen take notice."

"But it's a cheat!"

"I have carefully explained to you that it is no cheat. It is a revelation of several things about its subject and about you, but it is not a cheat."

If Francis did not rejoice to have his private comment on the incalculability and frequent malignancy of fate acclaimed as a reminder of a long-dead dwarf, he could not help being warmed by the praise he was receiving as a painter, though unidentified. He thought he was being subtle in the way he afforded chances for Saraceni to comment on *Drollig Hansel,* its quality of workmanship, its evocation of a past time, its colour and the sense it gave of being a big picture when it was, by actual measurement, a small one. His subtlety did not deceive the Italian, who laughed at him as fishing for compliments.

"But I am happy to provide the compliments," he said; "why are you not happy to ask for them like a real artist, instead of demurring and hemming like some little old maid who does a few water-colours of her garden?"

"I don't want to over-value the little thing."

"Oh, I see; you don't want to fall into the sin of pride? Well, don't shrink from pride only to fall into hypocrisy. You've had a dog's life, Corniche, brought up half Catholic and half Protestant, in a wretched hole where you got the worst of both those systems of double-dealing."

"Easy, Meister! I have detected a good Catholic in you."

"Perhaps, but when I am working as an artist I banish all that. Catholicism has begotten much great art; Protestantism none at all—not a single painting. But Catholicism has fostered art in the very teeth of Christianity. The Kingdom of Christ, if it ever comes, will contain no art; Christ never showed the least concern with it. His church has inspired much but not because of anything the Master said. Who then was the inspirer? The much-maligned Devil, one supposes. It is he who understands and ministers to man's carnal and intellectual self, and art is carnal and intellectual."

"You work under the wing of the Devil, do you?"

"I must, if I am to work at all. Christ would have had no time for a man like me. Have you noticed how, in the Gospels, He keeps so resolutely clear of anybody who might be suspected of having any brains? Good-hearted simpletons and women who were little better than slaves, those were His followers. No wonder Catholicism had to take a resolute stand in order to include people of intellect and artists; Protestantism has tried to reverse the process. Do you know what I should like, Corniche?"

"A new revelation?"

"Yes, that might come of it. I should like a conference to which Christ would bring all His saints, and the Devil would bring all his scholars and artists, and let them have it out."

"Who would judge the result?"

"That's the sticker. Not God, certainly, as the father of both leaders."

Saraceni did praise *Drollig Hansel*, as both he and Francis now called the picture. He did more. Without declaring it to be so, he included Francis in a closer fellowship with himself, and as they worked he talked untiringly about what he believed to be the philosophy of art. It was a philosophy deformed by that disease so fatal to philosophers—personal experience.

The Countess also became more genial toward Francis. Not that she had ever treated him with anything but courtesy, but now she talked freely about what he and Saraceni were doing, and there were more of those conferences in her private room when Amalie and Miss Nibsmith had retired. The Countess wanted to improve the product she was exporting. If an original like *Drollig Hansel* was so well received, could not Saraceni bring about a greater change in some of the old pictures on which he was working?

"Surely you are not urging me toward fakery, Countess?"

"Certainly not. Just a little more boldness, Meister."

In the course of these talks things leaked out that gave Francis a better idea of what was actually involved in what he could not help considering an elaborate fraud. The Countess and Saraceni were receiving, for the pictures they sent, a full quarter of whatever the dealers could get for the Italian pictures the German museums offered in exchange, and the prices made his eyes start in his head. Where was the money going? Not to Düsterstein; nothing so direct or so dangerous. To Swiss banks, and by no means all to one bank.

"A quarter is not too much," said the Countess. "After all, that is what Bernard Berenson gets for a mere letter of authentication when he writes it for Duveen. We provide the actual works of art and all the authentication they need is the approval of the great German experts who buy them—who must be assumed to know what they are doing."

"Sometimes I wonder if they don't know more than they are telling," said Saraceni.

"They are working under the gleaming eye of the Reichsmarschall," said the Countess, "and he expects them to deliver the goods. And some of the goods—the choicest pieces—are said to find their way into the Reichsmarschall's personal collection, which is large and fine."

"The whole thing sounds crooked as a dog's hind leg," said Francis, falling into the idiom of Blairlogie.

"If that is so, which I do not admit, we are not the leaders in the deception," said the Countess.

"You do not see it as dishonest?"

"If it were a simple matter of business, I would think so," said the Countess, "but it is far from simple. I see it as a matter of natural justice. My family lost everything—well, not quite everything, but a very great deal—in the War, and lost it willingly for Germany. Since 1932 my Germany has been whittled away until I no longer know it, and my task in rebuilding my family's fortunes has been made unbelievably hard. And why? Because I am the wrong kind of aristocrat, which is something much nearer to a democrat than National Socialism can endure. Do you know what an aristocrat is, Mr. Cornish?"

"I know the concept, certainly."

"I know the reality. An aristocrat, when my family rose to prominence, was someone who gained power and wealth through ability, and that meant daring and taking chances, not steering a careful course through a labyrinth of rules that had been made for their own benefit by people without either daring or ability. You know my family's motto? You have seen it often enough."

"Du sollst sterben ehe ich sterbe," said Francis.

"Yes, and what does it mean? It is not one of your nineteenth-century, bourgeois mottoes—a mealy-mouthed assertion of a tradesman's idea of splendour. It means: 'Thou shalt perish ere I perish.' And I do not mean to perish. That is why I am doing what I am doing."

"THE COUNTESS SEEMS to have decided to march under the banner of the Devil," said Francis to the Meister.

"We all meet the Devil in different forms, and the Countess is sure that she has found him in the Führer."

"A dangerous conclusion for a German citizen."

"The Countess would be surprised if you defined her as a citizen. She told you what she was: an aristocrat, a daring survivor. Certainly not a drivelling eccentric, as P. G. Wodehouse would have it."

"But suppose Hitler is right? Suppose the Reich lasts for a thousand years?"

"As an Italian I am sceptical of claims to last for a thousand years according to any plan; Italy has lasted far longer chiefly by muddle and indirection, and how gloriously she has done it. Of course, we have our own buffoon at present, but Italy has seen many buffoons come and go."

"I gather I am being invited to march under the Countess's banner? The Devil's banner."

"You can do that, Corniche, or you can go back to your frozen country, with its frozen art, and paint winter lakes and wind-blown pine trees, to which the Devil is understandably indifferent."

"You suggest that I shall have missed my chance?"

"You will certainly have missed your chance to learn what I can teach you."

"Really? You forget that now I can mix paint, and prepare grounds on the best principles, and I have painted one picture which seems to have met with a good deal of approval."

Saraceni laid down his brush and applauded gently. "Now that is what I have been hoping to hear for quite a while. Some show of spirit. Some real artist's self-esteem. Have you read and reread Vasari's *Lives of the Painters* as I told you?"

"You know I have."

"Yes, but attentively? If so, you must have been struck by the spirit of those men. Lions, all the best of them, even the gentle Raphael. They may have doubted their own work at bad moments, but they did not allow anyone else to do so. If a patron doubted, they changed patrons, because they knew they had something wholly beyond anybody's power to command—a strong individual talent. You have been hinting and manoeuvring to get me to say that *Drollig Hansel* is a fine painting. And I have. After all, you have been drawing and painting for—what—nineteen years? You have had good masters. *Drollig Hansel* will do, for the present. It's a pretty good painting. It shows that you, nipped by the frosty weather of your homeland, and stifled by the ingenious logic-chopping of Oxford, have at last begun to know yourself and respect what you know. Well—there have been late bloomers before you. But if you think you have learned all I can teach you, think again. Technique—yes, you have a measure of that. The inner conviction—not yet. But now you are in a frame of mind where we can begin on that paramount necessity."

THIS SOUNDED PROMISING, but Francis had learned to mistrust Saraceni's promises; the Italian not only reproduced faithfully the painting technique of an earlier day, but also the harsh, unappeasable spirit of a Renaissance master toward his apprentice. What new trial could he possibly devise?

"What do you see here?" The Meister stood ten feet away from Francis and unrolled a piece of paper, obviously old.

"It seems to be a careful pen drawing of the head of Christ on the Cross."

"Yes. Now come nearer. You see how it is done? It is calligraphy. A picture rendered in exquisite, tiny Gothic script in such a way that it depicts Christ's agony, while writing out every word—and not one word more—of Christ's Passion as it is recorded in the Gospel of St. John, chapters seventeen to nineteen. What do you think of it?"

"An interesting curiosity."

"A work of art, of craft, of devotion. Done, I suppose, by some seventeenth-century chaplain, or tutor to the Ingelheim family. Take it, and study it closely. Then I want you to do something in the same manner, but your text shall be the Nativity of Our Lord, as recorded in Luke's Gospel, chapter one, and chapter two up to verse thirty-two. I want a Nativity in calligraphy, and I make only one concession to your weakness: you may do it in Italic, rather than Gothic. So sharpen your quills, boil yourself some ink of soot and oak-galls, and go to work."

It was a job of measuring, scheming, and pernickety reckoning that might have brought despair to the heart of Sir Isaac Newton, but at last Francis had his plan, and set himself carefully to work. But what was there here to inspire inner conviction? This was drudgery, pedantry, and gimmickry. His concentration was not helped by an endless flow of reflection and comment from Saraceni, who was touching up a series of conventional seventeenth-century still-life paintings of impossibly opulent flowers, fish and vegetables on kitchen tables, bottles of wine, and dead hares with the glaucous bloom of death on their staring eyes.

"I sense your hatred of me, Corniche. Hate on. Hate greatly.

It will help your work. It gives you a good charge of adrenaline. But reflect on this: I ask you to do nothing that I have not done in my day. That is how I have achieved mastery that has not its equal in the world. Mastery of what? Of the techniques of the great painters before 1700. I do not seek to be a painter myself. Nobody would want a painting done today in the manner of, let us say, Goveart Flink, the best pupil of Rembrandt. Yet that is how I truly feel. That is my only honest manner. I do not want to paint like the moderns."

"Your hatred is reserved for the moderns, as mine is for you?"

"Not at all. I do not hate them. The best of them are doing what honest painters have always done, which is to paint the inner vision, or to bring the inner vision to some outer subject. But in an earlier day the inner vision presented itself in a coherent language of mythological or religious terms, and now both mythology and religion are powerless to move the modern mind. So—the search for the inner vision must be direct. The artist solicits and implores something from the realm of what the psychoanalysts, who are the great magicians of our day, call the Unconscious, though it is actually the Most Conscious. And what they fish up— what the Unconscious hangs on the end of the hook the artists drop into the great well in which art has its being—may be very fine, but they express it in a language more or less private. It is not the language of mythology or religion. And the great danger is that such private language is perilously easy to fake. Much easier to fake than the well-understood language of the past. I do not want to make you dizzy with flattery, but your picture of Drollig Hansel whispered something of that very deep, dark well."

"Jesus Christ!"

"No, not at all. As I have told you, Our Blessed Lord wanted something quite different from that dark well, and drew from it like the Master He was."

"But the Moderns—surely one must paint in the manner of one's day?"

"I don't admit any such necessity. If life is a dream, as some philosophers insist, surely the great picture is that which most potently symbolizes the unseizable reality that lies behind the dream. If I—or you—can best express that in terms of mythology or religion, why should we not do so?"

"Because it's a kind of fakery, or a deliberate throw-back, like those Pre-Raphaelites. Even if you are a believer, you cannot believe as the great men of the past believed."

"Very well. Live in the spirit of your time, and that spirit alone, if you must. But for some artists such abandonment to the contemporary leads to despair. Men today, men without religion or mythology, solicit the Unconscious, and usually they ask in vain. So they invent something and I don't need to tell you the difference between invention and inspiration. Supply such inventions and you may come to despise those who admire you, and play games with them. Was that the spirit of Giotto, Titian, Rembrandt? Of course, you may become something rather like a photographer. But remember what Matisse said: 'L'exactitude ce n'est pas la vérité.' "

"Isn't exactitude what you are devilling and driving me to achieve with this bloody piece of handwriting?"

"Only as a means of training you so that you will be able to set down, as well as lies in your power, what the Unconscious may choose to put on your hook, and offer it to those who have eyes to see."

"You are teaching me to paint reality so well that it might deceive—like that Roman painter who painted flowers, or a jar of honey, or something so truly that bees settled on his pictures. How do you equate that with the kind of reality you are talking about—the reality that rises from the dark well?"

"Don't despise *things*. Every *thing* has a soul that speaks to our soul, and may move it toward love. To understand that is the real materialism. People speak of our age as materialistic, but they are wrong. Men do not believe in matter today any more than they believe in God; scientists have taught them not to believe in anything. Men of the Middle Ages, and most of them in the Renaissance, believed in God and the *things* God had made, and they were happier and more complete than we. Listen, Corniche: modern man wants desperately to believe in something, to have some value that cannot be shaken. This country in which we live is giving fearful proof of what mankind will do in order to have something on which to fasten his yearning for belief, for certainty, for reality."

"I don't like it, and neither do you. Nor does the Countess."

"But we cannot deny it, or change it. These Nazi fanatics are picturesque, so one can take some comfort from that."

Francis thought of the trains, whose journey to the concentration camp in the hills he was recording, and did not find it picturesque. But he said nothing.

Saraceni went on, serenely. "The modern passion for the art of the past is part of this terrible yearning for certainty. The past is at least done with, and anything that we can recover from it is solid goods. Why do rich Americans pay monstrous prices for paintings by Old Masters which they may, or may not, understand and love, if it is not to import into their country the certainty I am talking about? Their public life is a circus, but in the National Gallery at Washington something of God, and something of the comfort of God's splendour, may be entombed. It is a great cathedral, that gallery. And these Nazis are ready to swap splendid Italian masters for acres of German pictures, because they want to make manifest on the walls of their Führermuseum the past of their race, and so give substance to the present of their race, and provide some assurance of the future of their race. It is crazy, but in a crazy world what can you expect?"

"What I can expect, it appears, is that some day I shall finish this idiotic job, or I shall go mad and kill you."

"No, no, Corniche. What you can expect is that when you have finished that idiotic job you will be able to write a splendid hand like the great Cardinal Bembo. And by so doing you will achieve at least something of the outlook upon the world of that great connoisseur, for the hand speaks to the brain as surely as the brain speaks to the hand. You will not kill me. You love me. I am your Meister. You dote upon me."

Francis threw an ink-bottle at Saraceni. It was an empty bottle, and he took care to miss his mark. Then they both laughed.

SO THE WEEKS AND THE MONTHS passed and Francis had been at Düsterstein for almost three years, during which he had worked without a holiday as Saraceni's slave, then colleague, then trusted friend. True, he had been back to England twice, for a week each time, meeting the Colonel and—for colour—visiting Williams-Owen. But these jaunts could not be called holidays. He was on easier terms with the Countess, though no one was ever fully at ease with the Countess. Amalie had found her tongue and lost her love for Francis, and he taught her some trigonometry (of which Ruth Nibsmith knew nothing) and the elements of drawing, and a great deal about gin rummy and bridge. Amalie was on the way to becoming a great beauty, and although nothing much was said, it was apparent that Miss Nibsmith's reign must soon give way to a broader education, probably in France.

"You don't care, I suppose," said Francis to Ruth, on one of their afternoon walks. "You're not really a governess—not in the nineteenth-century Brontë sense—and surely you want to do something else."

"So I shall," said Ruth, "but I shall stay here as long as there is work for me to do. Like you."

"Ah, well: I'm learning my craft, you see."

"And practicing your other craft. Like me."

"Meaning?"

"Come on, Frank. You're in the profession, aren't you?"

"I'm a professional painter, if that's what you mean."

"Go on with you! You're a snoop, and so am I. The *profession*."

"You've left me behind."

"Frank, nobody at Düsterstein is thick. The Countess has rumbled you, and so has Saraceni, and I rumbled you the first night I noticed you looking out of your open window, counting the cars on the Bummelzug. I was on the ground below, doing the same thing, just for the fun of it. A fine snoop you are! Standing in a window with a light behind you!"

"All right, officer. It's a fair cop. I'll come quietly. So you're in the profession, too?"

"Born to it. My father was in it until he died on the job. Killed, very likely, though nobody really knows."

"And what are you doing here?"

"That's not a question one pro asks another pro. I'm just looking about. Keeping an eye on what you and the Meister are doing, and what the Countess and Prince Max do with that."

"But you've never been in the shell-grotto."

"Don't need to go. I write the Countess's letters, and I know what happens, however much she pretends it's something else."

"Doesn't the Countess rumble *you*?"

"I hope not. It would be awful to think there were two snoops in one's house, wouldn't it? And I'm not very high-powered, you know. Just write the occasional letter home to my mum, who is a pro's widow, and knows how to read them and what to pass on to the big chaps."

"I know it's nosy to ask, but do you get paid?"

"Ha ha; the profession relies to what might be considered a dangerous degree on unpaid help. The old English notion that nobody who is anybody really works for money. No, I work for nothing, on the understanding that if I shape up well I will be in line for a paid job some day. Women don't get on very fast in the profession, unless they are elegant love-goddesses, and then they don't last long. But I don't grumble. I'm acquiring a useful command of Bavarian rural dialect and a peerless knowledge of the borderland between the Reich and Austria."

"Not casting any horoscopes?"

"Plenty, but chiefly of people long dead. Why?"

"It was hinted to me that Prince Max would like to know what you think of his."

"Oh, I know that. But I won't bite. Anyhow, it would be bad for his character. Max is going to be rather famous."

"How?"

"Even if I were sure I wouldn't tell you."

"Aha, I see in you the iconological figure of Prudence."

"Meaning what?"

"The Meister has me hard at it studying all that sort of thing. So that I can read old pictures. All those symbolic women—Truth with her mirror, Charity suckling her child, Justice with her sword and balances, Temperance with her cup and ewer—scores of them; they are the sign language of a particular kind of art."

"Well, why not? Have you anything better to do?"

"I have a block about that sort of thing. This Renaissance and pre-Renaissance stuff, where you make out the figures of Time, and his daughter Truth, and Luxury, and Fraud, and all those creatures, seems to me to pull a fine painting down to the level of moral teaching, if not actual anecdote. Could a great painter like Bronzino really have been so much of a moralist?"

"I don't see why not. It's just romantic nonsense to suppose that painters have always been rowdies and wenchers. Most of them were daubing away like billy-o in order to get the means to live the bourgeois life."

"Oh well—it's very dull learning iconology and I am beginning to wish something interesting would happen."

"It will, and soon. Just hang on a bit. Some day you will be really famous, Francis."

"Are you being psychic?"

"Me? What put that into your head?"

"Saraceni did. He says you are very much a psychic."

"Saraceni is a mischief-making old nuisance."

"Rather more than that. Sometimes when I listen to him going on about the picture exporting and importing business that he and the Countess are up to, I feel like Faust listening to Mephistopheles."

"Lucky you. Would anybody ever have heard of Faust if it hadn't been for Mephistopheles?"

"All right. But he has in a high degree the trick of making the worse seem the better cause. And he says it's because conventional morality takes no heed of art."

"I thought he said art was the higher morality."

"Now you are beginning to sound like him. Listen, Ruth, aren't we ever going to get together in bed again?"

"Not a hope, unless the Countess goes away on one of her jaunts and takes Amalie with her. In the Countess's house and under her eye I play by the Countess's rules, and I can't be having it off with you when I am supposed to be gently watching over the precious virginity of her granddaughter. Fair's fair, and that's a little too much in the line of eighteenth-century castle intrigue for my taste."

"Okay—I just thought I'd ask. 'Hereafter, in a better world than this—' "

" 'I shall desire more love and knowledge of you.' I'll hold you to that."

"And I'll hold *you* to that."

"CORNICHE! I WANT YOU to go to the Netherlands and kill a man."

"At your service, Meister. Shall I take my dagger or rely on the poisoned chalice?"

"You will rely on the poisoned word. Only that will do the job."

"Then I suppose I'd better know his name."

"His name, unfortunately for him, is Jean-Paul Letztpfennig. I am a great believer in the influence of names on destiny, and Letztpfennig is not a lucky name. Nor is he a lucky man. He wanted a career as a painter, but his stuff was dull and derivative. A failure, indeed, but just at the moment he is attracting a lot of attention."

"Not from me. Never heard of him."

"His notoriety is not mentioned in the German papers, but he is of great interest to Germany. The glassy eye of Reichsmarschall Göring is on him. He wants to sell the Reichsmarschall a ridiculous fake painting."

"If it's ridiculous how did the Reichsmarschall ever cast his glassy eye on it?"

"Because Letztpfennig, who is probably the most left-handed schlemiel in the art world at present, is hawking his fake around, and if it were real it would be the great find of the century. Nothing less than a major work by Hubertus van Eyck."

"Not Jan van Eyck?"

"No; Hubertus, Jan's brother who died in 1426, quite young. But Hubertus was a very great painter. It was he who designed and painted quite a bit of the magnificent *Adoration of the Lamb,* which is at Ghent. Jan finished it. There aren't many pictures by Hubertus, and the appearance of one now is bound to create a sensation. But it is a fake."

"How do you know?"

"I know because I feel it in my bones. It is my ability to feel things in my bones that lifts me above the general run of art experts. We all have sensitive bones, of course. But I am a painter myself, and I know more about how the great painters of the past worked than even Berenson, because Berenson is not a painter, and his bones keep changing their mind; he has attributed some very remarkable pictures to as many as three painters over a period of twenty years, to the dismay of their owners. When I know a thing I know it forever. And Letztpfennig's van Eyck is a fake."

"You've seen it?"

"I don't have to see it. If Letztpfennig vouches for it, it's a fake. He has made a tiny reputation among gullible people, but I know him through and through. He is the worst kind of scoundrel—an unlucky, muddling scoundrel. And he must be destroyed."

"Meister—"

"Yes?"

"I have never mentioned this, because it seems tactless, but I have been told that you possess the Evil Eye. Why don't you simply destroy Letztpfennig yourself?"

"Oh, what a dreadful world we live in! How spitefully people talk! The Evil Eye! Of course, I know that stupid people say that, merely because one or two people to whom I have taken a dislike have had unfortunate accidents. Only a broken bone, or losing their sight, or something of that sort. Never anything fatal. I am still a Catholic, you know; I would recoil from killing a rival."

"But don't you want me to kill Letztpfennig?"

"I spoke in terms of melodramatic exaggeration, to get your full attention. I only want you to kill him professionally."

"Oh, I see. Nothing serious."

"If he dies of chagrin, that is because he is over-sensitive. Nobody's fault but his own. Psychological suicide. Not uncommon."

"This is just a matter of professional rivalry, is it?"

"Do you suppose I would elevate such an idiot as Letztpfennig to the status of a rival? A rival to me! You must think I hold my abilities in low esteem. No, he must go because he is dangerous."

"Dangerous to the trade of selling dubious pictures to the Reich?"

"How coarsely you judge these things! It is the Lutheran streak in you—a perverse, self-destroying concept of morality. You refuse to see things as they are. I, and several people of whom you know one or two, am carefully securing some Italian art from the German Reich in exchange for pictures they like better. And not one of those pictures has been a fake—only a picture that has been assisted to put its best face foremost. The chain of action is carefully calculated. Everything goes through people with unex-

ceptionable credentials, and we never pitch the note too high—
no Dürers, no Cranachs. And now this Flemish buffoon appears
with a fake Hubertus van Eyck, and wants gigantic sums either
in cash or in paintings the Reich thinks it can spare, and he has
the effrontery to haggle, and bring in an American bidder for his
picture, with the result that the Dutch government is intervening
in the matter, and God alone knows what beans may be spilled."

"Could you give me some facts? I now know the range of your
passion; I'd just like to know what Letztpfennig has done, and
what you want me to do."

"There is a very nice strain of common sense in you, Corniche.
Your family background is in banking, is it not? Not that my
experience of bankers puts them above art dealers in matters of
probity. But they manage to look and sound so trustworthy, even
when they are not. Well—this all began about two years ago when
Jean-Paul Letztpfennig let it be known that during a jaunt to
Belgium he had come upon a picture in an old country house
that he bought because he wanted an old canvas. Idiot! Who wants
an old canvas unless he means to fake something with it? Anyhow—he says he cleaned the picture and found it to be a painting
of *The Harrowing of Hell*. You know the subject?"

"I know what it is. I've never seen a painting of it."

"They are extremely rare. It was a favourite theme in manuscript illuminations and sometimes in stained glass, but it did not
appeal to painters. It is Christ redeeming the souls of the better
class of pagans from Hell, where they had presumably languished
until His death on the Cross. Well—if it were real and not something Letztpfennig had fudged up himself, it would be interesting,
and if it were in the Gothic style it might reasonably go to the
Führermuseum, if the German experts passed it. Though those
highly intelligent men have so far shown themselves willing to
deal only with reputable people like the group with whom I—
and you, now that *Drollig Hansel* has given such satisfaction—are
associated. But Letztpfennig, like the blockhead he is, asserts that
a signature—by which he means a monogram—is on the picture
that establishes it as the work of Hubertus van Eyck.

"When that leaked out, there was a sensation, and an immediate
request for information and a chance to bid from an American
collector. One of the biggest, and when I tell you that his agent

and expert is Addison Thresher you will know whom I am talking about. And there were complications, because, as you know, the Reichsmarschall is a keen collector himself, and if there were a Hubertus van Eyck to be had, he wanted it. To be paid for, I need hardly tell you, by paintings from German museums. Great men are above trivialities in such negotiations. He offered, or his agents offered on his behalf, some splendid Italian things, and Letztpfennig was out of his meagre wits trying to decide whether he should grab the American dollars at once, or grab the Italian pictures, for resale in the States.

"That was when the Dutch government stepped in. You know how dearly they love the Reich. Their Ministry of Fine Art said that a great masterpiece by Hubertus van Eyck was a national treasure and could not leave the country. You would have thought that Belgium would have intervened and said that the picture had, after all, been found in Belgium, but nothing was heard from Belgium and that made Addison Thresher suspicious that the picture had never been in Belgium and was probably a fake.

"Not to toil through all the details, the picture is now in the protection of the Dutch Ministry of Fine Art, and all sorts of people have been visiting it, trying to decide whether it is genuine or not. Medland and Horsburgh from the British Museum and National Gallery laboratories in London have seen it, and can't give an opinion unless they are permitted to use X-rays and chemical tests—which the Dutch so far won't allow. Lemaire and Bastogne and Baudoin from Paris and Brussels have hemmed and hawed. Two Dutch experts, Dr. Schlichte-Martin and Dr. Hausche-Kuypers, are at each other's throats. Addison Thresher is now almost ready to break off all negotiations on grounds that the thing is a fake, and the German experts Frisch and Belmann are outraged because he suggests that they are afraid to speak their minds for fear of being proved wrong.

"They are running out of experts. Of course, they can't have Berenson, ostensibly because his area is confined to Italian art, but really because he is a Jew and the Reichsmarschall would be outraged. Duveen can't get near it or bring anybody to look at it for the same reason. It's the old wrangle between scientific testing and aesthetic sensibility, and Huygens, the judge who is in charge of the matter, is tired of it and wants to have somebody say that the thing is genuine, or that it is dubious and the scientific tests should proceed. So he has sent for me. And I'm not going."

"Why not?"

"Because of the delicacy of the situation in which our group finds itself. It must never for one moment be thought that we want to destroy Letztpfennig, but Letztpfennig must be destroyed or the Germans may become more suspicious than they naturally and quite rightly are, as professionals in art appreciation. We don't want every fool with an old picture horning in on the work we are doing. So I have written to Judge Huygens saying that my health is precarious, but that I shall send my trusted assistant to his aid, and if it proves absolutely necessary, I shall make the journey to the Hague myself. You are going."

"To do what?"

"To decide whether *The Harrowing of Hell* is by Hubertus van Eyck, or not. To show, if you can, that Letztpfennig either painted it himself on an old canvas, or at least over-painted an existing picture, and put in the van Eyck monogram. This is your chance to establish yourself as an art expert. Don't you understand, Corniche? This is one of your great tests, and I am putting it in your way."

"But what is being tested? You are sending me with instructions to declare the picture a fake and to discredit a rival. It doesn't sound like art criticism to me."

"It is a part of art criticism, Corniche. Your North American innocence—to use an absurdly kind word for it—must come to terms with the world in which you have chosen to put your life. It is a cruel world and its morality is not simple. If I had the least feeling that this thing in The Hague was a genuine Hubertus van Eyck I would be on my knees before it, but the chances are ten thousand to one that it's a fake, and the fake must be exposed. Art is very big money, these days, owing to the extraordinary exertions of certain geniuses, of whom Duveen is certainly the greatest. Fakes cannot be endured. Good art must drive out bad."

"But the morality of that—which I understand—won't square with what we have been doing here."

"The morality of the art world is not square, my dear pupil and colleague; it is a polyhedron. But it is a morality, none the less. So—go and win your spurs!"

"And what if I don't?"

"Then I shall come and do what you have failed to do, by one means or another, including even the Evil Eye—if anyone is so foolish as to believe in it, which I don't, as I have made clear—and if you and I have any further association, it will be simply as master and perpetual apprentice. You will have failed and I shall have to find another successor to myself. In this affair you are being tested as well as Letztpfennig."

THE DUTCH MINISTRY OF FINE ART treated its guests well—indeed, in princely style—and when Francis arrived in The Hague he was put up at the Hotel Des Indes, and ate a splendid meal into which he admitted no scrap of veal. The next morning he presented himself to Judge Huygens, who looked precisely as a judge should, and who took him after an exchange of civilities to a handsome room, where the disputed painting was displayed on an easel. Francis settled to his work, and it was soon clear that the Judge meant to stay in the room all the time he was there. A large, watchful, uniformed attendant was also on guard at the door.

The Harrowing of Hell was a most impressive picture, larger than Francis had expected, and obviously meant for a church. The colours glowed with the extraordinary light and appearance of transparency that the brothers van Eyck were reputed to have perfected and brought to the world of painting in oils; colour had been used at its greatest strength above a light ground, which created the magical glow of even the darkest pigment. In the middle of the picture was the figure of Christ, triumphantly bearing the banner-cross of the Resurrection in His left hand and gesturing toward Adam and Eve, the prophets Enoch and Elijah, and figures of Isaiah, Simeon, and Dismas, the Repentant Thief, with His right hand; He was beckoning them to follow Him through the gates of Hell, which stood open behind Him. On His left, averting their faces from His glory, cringing, gnashing their teeth, and seeking to escape, were Satan and his attendant fiends. The background was a true Dutch sky, flecked with delicate clouds, beneath which was to be seen some parts of a truly Dutch landscape, lying behind the gates of

Hell—and Hell obviously employed a brilliant and imaginative metalsmith.

Francis studied the picture for perhaps half an hour. If it were a fake it was a magnificent fake, done by a painter of enviable talent. But there have been magnificent fakes in the history of art. Well, that's enough aesthetic judgement, thought Francis; now we get down to the really inquisitorial inspection. He had brought, in a brief-case, what he thought of as his Little Jiffy Bernard Berenson Art Expert's Set, consisting of a pair of binoculars, a large magnifying glass, and a brush of medium size. He looked at the picture through the binoculars, from the greatest distance the room allowed; then looked at it through the wrong end of the binoculars. Neither magnification nor diminution suggested anything peculiar about the composition. He looked at the picture through his magnifying glass, inch by inch, and then at his request the large attendant stood the picture on its head, and he examined it again from that aspect. With a reassuring nod to the Judge he dabbed at it here and there with his soft brush. He examined the back, tapped the canvas, inspected the workmanship of the stretchers. To the astonishment of Huygens and the guard he crumpled his handkerchief, warmed it with a cigarette-lighter, and held it to the canvas for perhaps ninety seconds. He sniffed the heated area loudly. No: not a whiff of formaldehyde. Then he sat down again and looked at the picture for another hour, occasionally turning away and suddenly rounding on it, as though it might have relaxed some of its pervasive van Eyckishness while his back was turned. He spent a good deal of time peering at the monogram, small but easily enough seen when you knew where to look, hidden in the folds of Isaiah's robe. It might have been many things: Hubert of Ghent? Signatures didn't matter, anyhow; the real signature was the quality of the painting, and try as he might he couldn't find anything wrong with it.

Fakes, as he well knew, tend to declare themselves a generation or two after they have appeared and been accepted as originals. Truth, the daughter of Time, reveals indications of another age, another temper and taste, in a picture which is painted long after the period to which it has been attributed. Paint ages in the wrong way. Fashions in faces change, and the change may be seen when the fashion for a certain comformation of features has passed. But he did not have fifty years to wait. His job was to declare the picture a fake, and to do so as soon as possible.

When at last he said to the Judge that he had seen enough he received a shock. "Several of your fellow-experts are in the city at present," said Huygens. "They are anxious to hear what you have to say, as I am myself. You speak, we know, with the authority and probity of Tancred Saraceni and we have agreed that your opinion shall carry great weight, and indeed will doubtless prove decisive. Will you meet us here tomorrow at eleven o'clock? The painter will be here also. Understandably he expects a triumphant vindication."

"And you, Edelachtbare Heer?"

"I? Oh, my opinion is of no importance. I am simply the director of the investigation. Indeed, it would be improper if anyone holding strong opinions about this sort of painting had been appointed to preside. I do, of course, represent the Netherlands government."

AT LUNCHEON, as Francis was treating himself to another veal-free blow-out at the expense of his hosts, he was joined by a smiling American.

"Mind if I sit down? I am Addison Thresher, and I'm here from the Metropolitan Museum in New York. Also representing one or two other interested parties. There's no harm in our talking; Huygens said it was perfectly all right. What did you think?"

Addison Thresher was an expensively dressed, conservatively dressed, more than ordinarily tastefully dressed man, with silver-rimmed glasses and those American teeth, so disconcerting to the European eye, that always seem to have been furiously brushed not more than an hour ago. His manners were wonderful and he smelled of a costly toilet water. But in his eyes there was a steely glint.

Warily, Francis told him what he thought, which in effect was nothing at all.

"I know," said Thresher; "that's the trouble, isn't it? Not a thing you can quite lay your hand on. The signature is a fake, of course, but that's not important. But there is something about the whole affair I don't like. You've seen the composition before, of course?"

Francis shook his head, his mouth being full.

"Have you ever looked at that late-medieval manuscript of the Cooks and Innkeepers Play, in the Chester group? There's a miniature of the *Harrowing*. Very suggestive. Could van Eyck have seen it? Barely possible. But a faker could know it. There's nothing that hints at the Fra Angelico or the Bronzino of the *Harrowing;* that would have been a dead give-away, for Hubertus van Eyck couldn't have seen either. But there is also a strong feeling of that big wall painting at Mount Athos, and that would be funny, wouldn't it—two minds with but a single thought, and God knows how many centuries between them? The influences, if they are influences, are so damned scholarly. Nothing in any of the work of either of the van Eycks suggests that they were learned in that way. Painters in those days simply weren't."

"Yes, I see what you mean," said Francis, trying to conceal the fact that he was learning fast. "But still—nothing that proves fakery."

"That's what the Germans say. And also what the Dutch say. They want it to be genuine, of course, because it would be a marvellous acquisition for a Dutch gallery. The man from the Mauritshuis is particularly keen. If it proves to be a national treasure they'll never let it out of the country, and they'd love to thwart Göring. They fight about details but they're wholly agreed on that. They'll pay Letztpfennig a goodish price, but not the really big money he would get from the States, or the splendid swaps he could get from the Germans."

"What do you know about Letztpfennig?"

"Nothing to his discredit. Indeed, he is rather an impressive figure. Lectures learnedly on Dutch art, and is probably the best restorer in Europe—except for Saraceni, of course. Knows perhaps a little too much about Old Master painting techniques to be entirely trustworthy in a situation like this. But I mustn't let my suspicions run away with me. It's just that in my bones I sense something wrong, and as long as the scientific boys from London are kept at bay, I have to rely on my bones. Aesthetic sensibility, we call it in the trade, but it comes down to a feeling in the bones."

"Like Berenson."

"Yes, Berenson has wonderfully shrewd bones. But when Joe Duveen is paying you a full twenty-five per cent of the sale price of a picture for an authentication, I wonder if your bones can always be heard above the sweet music of the cash register. It costs a lot of dough to live like Berenson. Of course, it's all academic to me; whatever happens I won't get the picture. But I hate a faker. Bad for business."

Addison Thresher's manners left nothing to be desired. He did not hover over Francis but took himself off, saying that they would meet again in the morning. And what was Francis to do? Go to the Mauritshuis and look at the pictures? He had been there before and he was sick of looking at pictures. Encouraged by his good lunch he went to the Wassenaar, and spent the afternoon at the zoo.

JEAN-PAUL LETZTPFENNIG'S HAND, when he gave it to Francis to shake, was unpleasantly damp, and Francis immediately drew out his handkerchief and wiped his own hand somewhat too obviously. Some of the other men in the room were quick to notice. Professor Baudoin, whom Francis had already decided was the nasty one, sucked in his breath audibly. This was much better than when he blew it out, generously, as he did in conversation, for his breath suggested that he was dying from within, and had completed about two-thirds of the job. It was a striking contrast to Addison Thresher, whose breath smelled of the very best caries-defying toothpaste. He was dressed this morning in a completely different outfit, somewhat formal and suggestive of great affairs.

Indeed, great affairs were in hand. Expectancy was in the air, and all the sensitive bones of all the experts must have felt it. Dr. Schlichte-Martin, ample and red-faced, Dr. Hausche-Kuypers, young and merry, were like men playing a game of Snakes and Ladders; if the van Eyck were real, the fat old man advanced and the young jolly one was thrown back, but if it were the other way round, youth rejoiced and age grieved. Frisch and Belmann, the Germans, wore iron-grey suits and iron-grey expressions, for they were losers whatever happened. They rather hoped Letzt-pfennig would be exploded and regretted their earlier excitement about his find. Lemaire and Bastogne and Baudoin were philo-sophical, but inclined to negative opinions; the two Frenchmen would have liked the picture to be genuine, but doubted if it could be; the Belgian wanted it to be a fake, for he was a friend of whatever was negative. They were all hedging their bets in the guarded manner of critics the world over.

"Everyone knows everyone else, I believe? Shall we proceed to our business, which may be brief? Mr. Cornish, will you tell us what your conclusions are?" The Judge was by far the calmest man present. The Judge, and the big guard at the door.

Francis approached his task with inward shrinking, but outward calm. He was inclined to like Letztpfennig, though he wished he could wash the corpse-sweat from his right hand. Letztpfennig was by no means the comic figure of Saraceni's derision. A grey man, with the appearance of a deeply intellectual man, thickly spectacled and possessing a mop of grey hair which might have suggested an artist if the man were not so obviously cast in the mould of a professor. A carefully dressed man, with a white handkerchief peeping from his breast pocket in just the right proportion. A man whose shoes gleamed with loving care. His appearance of calm impressed nobody.

Well, here goes, thought Francis. Thank God I can be both decisive and honest.

"I fear the picture cannot be accepted as genuine," said he.

"That is your opinion?" said Huygens.

"More than simply an opinion, Edelachtbare," said Francis; the occasion he thought deserved the fullest formality. "The picture may indeed be an old picture. The quality of the painting is superb, and it strongly suggests van Eyck. Any painter at any time might be proud to have painted it. But you cannot even attribute it to *alunno di* van Eyck or *amico di* van Eyck; it is probably a century after van Eyck."

"You speak with great certainty," said Professor Baudoin, with unconcealed gloating. "But you are—if you will allow me to speak of it—a very young man, and the certainty of youth is not always appropriate to such matters as this. You will give us reasons, of course."

Indeed I shall, thought Francis. You think Letztpfennig is virtually destroyed and now you want to destroy me because I am young. Well—bugger you, you bad-breathed old nuisance.

"I am sure your colleague will be glad to give his reasons," said Huygens, the peacemaker. "If they are truly convincing, we shall call back the experts from Britain, who will make scientific appraisals."

"I don't think you will need to do that," said Francis. "The picture has been put forward as a van Eyck, and it certainly is not by van Eyck, either Hubertus or Jan. Have any of you gentlemen visited the zoo lately?"

What was this about the zoo? Was the young man trifling with them?

"A detail of the painting tells us all we need to know," Francis continued. "Observe the monkey who hangs by his tail from the bars of Hell, in the upper left-hand corner of the picture. What is he doing there?"

"It is an iconographical detail that one might expect in such a picture," said Letztpfennig somewhat patronizingly toward the young man, glad to defend the monkey. "The chained monkey is an old symbol of the fallen mankind that preceded the coming of Christ. Of souls in Hell, in fact. He belongs with the defeated devils."

"But he is hanging by his tail."

"Since when do monkeys not hang by their tails?"

"They did not do so in Ghent in van Eyck's day. That monkey is a *Cebus capucinus*, a New World monkey. The chained monkey of iconography is the *Macacus rhesus*, the Old World monkey. Such a monkey as that, a monkey with a prehensile tail, was unknown in Europe until the sixteenth century, and I need not remind you that Hubertus van Eyck died in 1426. The painter, whoever he is—or was—wanted to complete his composition with a figure, not too commanding, in that particular spot, so the chained monkey had to be hanging by his tail from the bars of Hell. There are several examples of both *Cebus capucinus* and *Macacus rhesus* informatively labelled in your very good local zoo. That is why I mentioned it."

In the melodrama of the nineteenth century there may frequently be found such stage directions as *Sensation! Astonishment! Tableau!* This was the gratifying effect produced by Francis's judgement. None of the experts tried to suggest that they were well up in the lore of monkeys, but when they were shown the obvious they made haste to declare that it was indeed obvious. This is one of the things experts are frequently called on to do.

As they chattered learnedly, assuring each other that they had had some uneasiness about the monkey, Letztpfennig was understandably undergoing great stress. The big guard brought him a chair, and he sat on it and drew his breath painfully. But he regained his self-possession, rose to his feet, clapped his hands authoritatively, like a professor calling a class to order.

"Gentlemen," said he, "you shall know that I painted this picture. Why did I do so? In part as a protest against the fanatical adoration that is accorded to our Dutch masters of an earlier day, that is so frequently linked with a depreciation of modern painters. It is a bad principle that nothing may be praised without dispraising something else. Nobody nowadays can paint like the Old Masters! That is untrue. *I* have done so, and I know there are many others who could do it as well as I. It is not done, of course, because it is a kind of artistic fancy-dress, an insincerity, an imitation of another man's style. I fully agree that a painter should work in the mode—speaking very generally—of his own time. But that is not because it is a degenerate mode, adopted because he cannot paint as well as his great artistic predecessors.

"Now listen to me patiently, if you please. You have all praised this painting for its skill in colour and design, and its power to lift the heart as only a great picture can do. At one time or another you have all spoken highly of it, and several of you have professed yourselves delighted with it. What delighted you? The magic of a great name? The magic of the past? Or was it the picture before your eyes? Even you, Mr. Thresher, before you found that under no circumstances could you buy this picture for your great client, spoke of it to me in terms that made my heart sing in my breast. The work of a very great master, you said, if not indubitably a van Eyck. Well—? I am the very great master. Do you take back everything you said?"

Thresher said nothing, and none of the other experts were

inclined to speak, except Baudoin, who was hissing in Belmann's ear that he had never trusted the *craquelure*.

It was the Judge who spoke, and he spoke like a judge. "We must bear in mind, Mynheer Letztpfennig, that you offered the picture for sale as a genuine van Eyck, and with it you offered a tale about its origins which we now know to be untrue. That cannot be explained away as part of a protest on behalf of the skill of modern painters."

"But how else was I to get attention for my picture? How else was I to make my point? If I had made it known that Jean-Paul Letztpfennig, professor of art, restorer of Old Masters, known as a painter condemned to mediocrity by those who profess to rank artists as if they were schoolboys, had painted a great painting in an old style, how many of you would have crossed your doorstep to see it? Not one! Not one! But as things are you have used words like masterpiece, and transporting beauty. At what were they directed? Toward what you saw, or merely toward what you thought you saw?"

"The Judge is right," said Addison Thresher. "You wanted the top dollar for your picture, not only for its beauty—which I don't deny—but for the glamour of age and a great name. And we fell for it! It's a fine painting, but where can you sell it? I guess it's a draw. Certainly so far as I am concerned, it's a draw."

OF COURSE, IT WASN'T A DRAW, and the international press turned it into a sensation. How did they find out what had happened? When eleven men are in a room and something of unusual interest takes place, at least one of them is likely to let something drop which the press seizes on, and the hunt is up. The one who was supposed to have leaked the story was Sluyters, the guard, who was not nearly so impassive as he looked, and who would have been glad to tell what he knew for a consideration. But did nobody else say a word? Certainly Francis didn't until he was back at Düsterstein, but who can answer for Addison Thresher? Did the Judge drop a word to his wife, who may have told an intimate friend in the uttermost confidence? The Germans certainly were not silent when they reported to their superiors, and through them to the Reichsmarschall, who was not known for being close-mouthed. The two Frenchmen and the Belgian would not be inclined toward silence; they had risked little and gained much, for they had been in on a great unmasking which gave the international art world something to talk about for many months.

"Monkey Blows Hoax" was the headline in one form or another, and one paper carried a caricature of Francis instructing the experts, based on a famous painting of the Boy Christ Teaching in the Temple.

"I see that the Letztpfennig file is now closed," said Saraceni, raising his eyes from the *Völkischer Beobachter* he had been reading in the shell-grotto.

"Are they dropping all charges?" said Francis.

"No charges are effective now. He has killed himself."

"Oh God! The poor devil!"

"Do not reproach yourself, Corniche. I told you to kill him, and you killed him. You destroyed him professionally on my instruction and now he has yielded up his life of his own volition. In a very interesting way, too. He lived in Amsterdam in one of those lovely old houses on a canal. You know how they have projecting mounts for cranes hanging over the canal bank, so that in the old days those merchant houses could have goods hauled up to the top floor for storage? Picturesque old things. It seems Letztpfennig hanged himself on his crane, right out over the canal. When he was retrieved by the police they found a note pinned to his coat. Oddly enough, he had worn his overcoat and hat to die in. The note said: 'Let them say what they will now; in the beginning they said it was a great picture.'—My dear man, are you unwell? Perhaps you had better take the day off. You have done quite enough for art, for the present."

THAT WAS THE MAKING of Francis, said the Daimon Maimas.

—You are not gentle in your methods, brother, said the Lesser Zadkiel.

—Not always, but I am often subtle. It was I, of course, who nudged Francis to visit the zoo, and I made sure he had a good look at the monkeys.

—A bad moment for Letztpfennig.

—Letztpfennig was not my care. And he was not too badly used.

He wanted fame and he wanted to be recognized as a great painter. He had both his wishes—posthumously. His death gave a note of pathos to what was, considering all things, a remarkable career. It was the rest of mankind that felt the pathos, as it usually is in pathetic fates. When everything is added up, Letztpfennig did not do too badly. He is a footnote in the history of art. And Francis gained at a stroke a very nice little reputation.

—And that was the fame that Ruth predicted? said the Lesser Zadkiel.

—Oh, by no means. I can do better than that, said the Daimon Maimas.

THE DOWNFALL OF LETZTPFENNIG was of interest to the world, as somebody's downfall always is, but by the autumn of 1938, not long after Francis's twenty-ninth birthday, the Munich Crisis took precedence over all other news, and the apparent triumph of Neville Chamberlain in concluding an agreement with the German Führer gladdened the hearts of millions of innocents who wanted peace and were ready to believe anything that seemed to promise peace. But not everyone trusted that pact; the Countess and Saraceni were two of these. There was uneasiness and change at Düsterstein. Amalie was sent off to a distinguished school in Switzerland, and though Ruth Nibsmith stayed on to help the Countess in secretarial work, she knew that her time in that capacity was short, and before Christmas she had taken affectionate farewells of everyone and returned to England. Saraceni likewise found that he had imperative business in Rome, and could not say how long it would be before he returned—though he assured the Countess that he would certainly return. And the Countess announced that pressing work in Munich, relating to her sales of farm produce, would keep her in that city for several weeks and perhaps for months.

Saraceni and Francis had, between them, in the year past, completed a substantial amount of work, some of which was ambitious. Bigger and bigger pictures were making their way to the wine merchants' cellars—pictures so large the canvases had to be dismounted from their stretchers, and packed around the insides of the big barrels, carefully wrapped to protect them from the wine.

The stretchers and the old nails that belonged to the pictures travelled in two large bags of golf clubs, which Prince Max had added to his luggage. These were ambitious pictures of battle scenes, and a number of portraits of minor historical figures, all greatly improved by Saraceni and also by Francis, who was trusted with increasingly significant work. What was to become of Francis during the Meister's long absence? The day before he left, Saraceni told him.

"You have done well, Corniche, and you have done it much quicker than I thought you would. The explosion of Letztpfennig has given you a name—a modest name, but nevertheless a name. Still, before you are ready to appear before the world as *amico di Saraceni* instead of the lesser *alunno di Saraceni* there is an important test I want you to accept now. Quite simply it is this: can you paint as well as Letztpfennig? He was a master, you know, in this lesser realm of art. I can say it, now that you have disposed of him. I am not talking of course of faking, for this is contemptible, but I mean the ability to work truly in the technique and also in the spirit of the past. Unless you can satisfy me of that I shall not feel absolutely certain about you. *Drollig Hansel* was good. What you have done during the past year is good. But when you are not under my eye and subject to my advice and relentless criticism—I know I'm a bastard, but all great teachers must be so—can you really bring it off? So: while I am away I want you to paint an original picture on a large scale—not just big, but big in conception—and I want you to do it not in imitation of anyone, but as you would paint yourself if you were living in the fifteenth or sixteenth century. Find your subject. Grind your colours. I have found a groundwork for you.

"Look here; it is, as you see, a triptych, an altar-piece of fair size in three panels that hung in the chapel here before it was done over in the great Baroque style. It is a wreck, of course. It has been standing for at least two hundred years in one of the innumerable service corridors of this castle from which we have recovered so many discarded paintings, but it was never very good and now it is rubbish. Clean it, right down to the wood, and go to work. I am expecting something that will tell me just how good you are, when you work independently. You will have plenty of time. I shall return in the spring, or perhaps a little later. But I shall certainly return."

SO, SHORTLY BEFORE CHRISTMAS of 1938, Francis found himself the virtual master of Düsterstein. The family rooms, as well as the great rooms of state, were transformed by dust-sheets and muslin wraps for the chandeliers into the habitations of ghosts. One small room was left for his use, and there he sat and ate his meals when he was not busy in the shell-grotto. He took walks in the grounds, squelching over mossy paths under weeping trees. Another man might have found it melancholy, but Francis welcomed the solitude and the dimness, for he was turned in upon himself and wanted no distraction, no invitation to play. He was seeking his picture.

The philosophy of Saraceni, as distinguished from the avarice and opportunism of Saraceni, was not something he had learned as Amalie learned her lessons. He had absorbed it, and ingested it, and had made it part of his own wholeness. What was so plainly unworthy in the Meister he regarded with amusement; he was not such a fool as to suppose that great men do not have their foibles, and that such flaws might not be great ones. He had consumed the wheat and discarded the chaff, and the wheat was now bone of his bone. It was his belief, not his lesson.

What did he now believe, at the end of a toilsome and sometimes humiliating apprenticeship? That a great picture must have its foundation in a sustaining myth, which could only be expressed through painting by an artist with an intense vocation. He had learned to accept and cherish his vocation, which was none the less real because it had been reached by such a crooked path. He had worked in the shell-grotto as a man under orders, but now he was to work under no orders but his own, even though he must express himself in a bygone mode of painting. But what was his picture, the masterpiece which would conclude his apprenticeship, to be?

Rooted in a myth, but what myth? In the tangle of mythology, the cosmic bedroom farce and vulgar family wrangles of the gods of Olympus or their diminished effigies as conceived by the Romans? Never! In the finer myth of the Christian world, as seen in a thousand forms in the Age of Faith? Catholicism he certainly possessed, but it was still the sweet Catholicism of Mary-Ben rather than that of the rigorous Church Fathers. In the myth of the greatness of Man, as the Renaissance had asserted, or the myth of Man Diminished and Enchained as it appeared to the Age of Reason? What about Romanticism, the myth of the Inner Man sharply declining to the myth of Egotism? There was even the nineteenth-century myth of Materialism, the exaltation of the World of Things, which had evoked so many great pictures from the Impressionists. But these must be rejected at once, even if they had strongly attracted him (which they did not), because his orders—and he was still under orders—were to paint a picture in the manner of the Old Masters, a picture that would contain some technical instruction even for the ingenious Letztpfennig.

Alone, and only vaguely aware of the Europe that was boiling up toward a war of hitherto unexampled horror almost on his doorstep, Francis found his answer, and it was the only possible, the inescapable answer. He would paint the myth of Francis Cornish.

But how? He was not free to work as a painter might who was not seeking to advance from *alunno* to *amico* in the fierce school of Saraceni. He could not descend, so far as his talent allowed, into the Realm of the Mothers and return with a picture that might evade the understanding of even the most intuitive and sympathetic of observers, but that would perhaps explain itself after twenty years as a prophecy, or a cry of despair. He must have a subject that could be identified as the subjects of the Old Masters are identified, however much these say that is not contained in the obvious subject.

He made and destroyed unnumerable sketches, but even as he rejected them he felt that he was moving nearer to his goal. At last a subject began to assert itself, and then to show that it was inescapable, a subject that might be invited to body forth the myth of Francis Cornish. It was at this point that he began to make the preparatory studies and drawings in the old manner, on prepared paper with a silver-point; studies which might, at some distant time, puzzle the experts. His theme, his subject, his myth, was to be contained in a triptych of *The Marriage at Cana*.

It had not been one of the most popular themes of the masters who painted before the High Renaissance, the masters who painted in the mode that preceded the lush depictions of that wedding feast—so improbable in terms of the biblical story—which were, in fact, glorifications of the splendours and luxuries of this world. Francis must work in terms of the austere but not starveling manner of the sunset of the Gothic world. And as he made his drawings he found that this was a manner that would serve him very well; the myth of Francis Cornish was not a Renaissance myth, or a myth of Reason or of self-delighted egotism, or the myth of the World of Things. If he could not speak in the voice of his century he would speak in the final accents of the Gothic voice. And so he worked, not furiously but with concentration and devotion, and when at last his preliminary cartoons were done, and the ruinous old picture on the triptych was scoured and scraped off, and his colours were chosen and prepared down to the last grinding of the lapis lazuli that lay so readily at hand, he began to paint.

IT WAS MIDSUMMER 1939 before Saraceni returned, and Francis was growing anxious. He had received a letter in late June from Sir Owen Williams-Owen, saying:

> Your record of your heart's action for the past several months is causing me some concern, and I think it advisable that I examine you again. I suggest that you return to England as soon as you conveniently can, so that I may have another look at you. Your godfather, whom I saw the other day, sends his regards.

That was not hard to interpret, even by a preoccupied painter who had not been paying much attention to the world's news. But he must see the Meister before he left Düsterstein. In late July, Saraceni was with him in the shell-grotto, and Francis, not without a sense of drama, unveiled *The Marriage at Cana*, baked and with Augsburg dust in its *craquelure*.

The Meister followed the familiar routine. He looked at the picture for a quarter of an hour without speaking. Then he went through the inspections with the field-glasses, the large magnifying glass, the poking at the back of the canvas, the sniffing, the rubbing of a corner with a wetted finger—all the ceremonies of expertise. But then he did something which was not usual; he sat down and looked at the picture for a considerable time, grunting now and then with what Francis hoped was satisfaction.

"Well, Corniche," he said at last, "I expected something good from you, but I confess you have astonished me. You know what you have done, of course?"

"I think I do, but I'd be glad if you would reassure me."

"I can understand your bewilderment. Your picture is by no means an exercise in a past manner; those things always betray a certain want of real energy, and this has plenty of energy, the unmistakable impression of here and now. Something unquestionably from the Mothers. Reality of artistic creation, in fact. You have found a reality that is not part of the chronological present. Your here and now are not of our time. You seem not to be trapped, as most of us are, in the psychological world of today. I hate such philosophical pomposities, but your immanence is not tainted by the calendar. One cannot predict with certainty, but this should wear well—which Letztpfennig fakery and fancy-dress painting never does."

"So—am I out of my apprenticeship?"

"So far as this picture goes, you are indeed. Whether you can keep this up, or whether you want to do that, remains to be seen. Offhand, I should say that if you continue to paint in this manner, and let it be known, your goose is cooked. The whole world of criticism would be down on you like hawks attacking a—what? A phoenix? Some very rare bird, certainly."

"So what do I do?"

"Ah, well, that is a question I can answer without hesitation. You get back to England as soon as you can. And I am off to Italy in the morning. Things are growing very uncomfortable, if you haven't noticed."

"What about the picture?"

"If I can arrange it, I shall see that it is sent to you. But it is big, and too stiff to go in a cask, and that may not be easy. But for a while I think it must go into one of the dark service corridors here."

"That isn't quite what I meant. You know how I regard you, Meister. Have I satisfied you? That is what has been gnawing me."

"Satisfied me? I find it very hard to say, because satisfaction is not part of my metier, and I rarely step outside my metier. But here I have no choice, and little time to delay. So, for the present, *a rivederci*—Meister."

PART
Six

WARS ARE NATIONAL and international disasters, but everyone in a warring nation fights a war of his own and sometimes it cannot be decided whether he has won or lost. Francis Cornish's war was long and painful, even though he was a noncombatant.

Indeed, being a non-combatant was one of his lesser, if more obvious, troubles. To be an able-bodied man in his thirties, not apparently doing any important work, required frequent explanation, and aroused dislike and suspicion. He had, of course, his letter from Sir Owen Williams-Owen, guaranteeing his troublesome heart and exemption from service, but he could not wear it pinned to his coat; from Uncle Jack, for whom he was working long hours, he had nothing at all, because it was unthinkable, if he should be injured, or challenged, that he should be identified with what he now called, not "the profession", but frankly MI5.

As soon as he returned to England in late July of 1939, Francis became officially—in the sense that he was paid a rather small salary—a counter-intelligence man, which meant that his job was to find out whatever he could about people representing themselves as refugees from Europe, who were in fact German agents. It was not Secret Service in the romantic style; what it meant was that by day he worked with an agency that interviewed refugees and helped them, and at night he hung about in doorways watching who entered and left certain buildings that were under observation. Careful reports of what he learned, which were chiefly timetables, he took as unobtrusively as he could to Uncle Jack, who worked from a small office at the back of a house in Queen Anne's Gate.

It was drudgery, but he managed to give it an individual touch, for which he blessed the name of Harry Furniss and those long hours in Blairlogie, where he had sketched everybody and everything, alive and dead. Once he had seen a man or woman, he could produce a useful likeness, and he was not deceived by disguises. Few people have any aptitude for disguise; they put too much faith in dyed hair, changes of clothes, and peculiar walks; they disguise their fronts, but they neglect to disguise their backs, and Francis, who had learned the lesson from Saraceni, could identify a back when he might be puzzled by a face. So he amused himself by decorating his reports with sketches that were doubtless more useful than he knew, because Uncle Jack was not communicative, and never praised. He was not permitted to use a typewriter, because the sound, late at night, might rouse the suspicion of a landlady; his reports, written in an exquisite, tiny Italic hand, and ornamented with sketches, were little works of art. But Uncle Jack seemed impervious to art, and filed them without comment on their appearance.

What was drudgery for the first months of the war became dangerous misery after the coming of the air raids on London, by day and night in the autumn of 1940, and by night until May of 1941. It was in the great fire-raid of December 29 that Francis lost what had become his chief treasure.

He had rediscovered Ruth Nibsmith, meeting her by chance one October night in a Lyons restaurant where he had gone for a meal before taking up one of his long vigils across the street from a suspected house.

"Le Beau Ténébreaux! What a piece of luck! What are you up to? Not that I need to ask; you look the complete snoop. Who are you snooping on?"

"What do you mean, I look a snoop?"

"Oh, my dear—the stained felt hat, the seedy raincoat, the bulge in the pocket where the notebook is kept—of course you're a snoop."

"You only say that because you're a psychic. My disguise is impenetrable. I am The Unknown Civilian, who is catching it so hard these bad days."

"Not half so hard as he'll be catching it before the end of the year—speaking as a psychic."

"You're right, of course. I am doing confidential work. What are you doing?"

"Also confidential." But after some chat it came out that Ruth was in Government Code and Cipher. "Of course, I have the puzzle-solving sort of mind," she said; "I think it was my ability to do the *Times* crossword in half an hour that got me the job. But being a psychic does no harm, either. And that's enough of that." She glanced up at the poster on the wall, which was a picture by Fougasse of Hitler with an enormous ear cocked, and the legend "Careless Talk Costs Lives".

They renewed their friendship, so far as Francis's peculiar assignments and Ruth's occasional night duties allowed, and this meant renewal of their happy hours in bed. Ruth lived in a very small flat in Mecklenburgh Street where the landlady was either indulgent or indifferent and perhaps once a week they contrived a happy hour or so. In wartime London, which had become so grey and stuffy, where laundry was a difficulty and baths were uncertain because of broken water-pipes, it was bliss to strip off their clothes and tumble into the not very clean sheets and lose themselves in a communion where no rules of security had to be remembered and tenderness and kindness were all that mattered. Perhaps it was odd that they never talked of love, or exchanged promises of fidelity; but they felt no need of such words. Without ever saying so, they knew that time was short and the present everything, and a union achieved when chance permitted was a treasure snatched from destruction.

"If a bomb were to blow us up now," said Francis, one night when they had disobeyed the sirens and stayed in the warm bed when they ought to have gone to the nearest chilly shelter, "I would feel I had died at the peak of my life."

"Don't worry, Frank. No bomb is going to get you. Don't you remember your horoscope at Düsterstein? Old age and fame for you, my darling."

"And you?"

She kissed him. "That's Classified Information," she said. "I'm the decoder, not you."

On the night of December 29, when the great fire-raid struck,

Francis was on the job, watching a door through which nobody came or went, until it became impossible to keep at his post any longer, and he went to a Tube station, where he lay on the hard pavement with some hundreds of others, unsleeping and in terror. When at last the all-clear sounded he went as far toward Ruth's flat as was possible, for fires were raging and whole streets of houses had disappeared.

She had been rescued, and in a shorter time than he had dared to hope he found her in a hospital. Rather, he found a body swathed in packs of saline solution, a body so heavily sedated that only one hand could be seen, and he sat for several hours, holding it, and praying as he had not prayed since childhood that by holding it he was being of some comfort. But the time came when the ward sister beckoned him away.

"No use now. She's gone. Was she your wife? A friend?"

"A friend."

"Do you want a cup of tea?" It was not much, but it was everything the hospital had to offer. Francis did not want a cup of tea.

So ended the greatest comfort he had ever known, which had lasted, he reckoned, a little less than ten weeks. Nothing during the forty-one years of life and a kind of distinction that remained to him brought anything to equal it.

A hero of romance might have undergone what is called, not very descriptively, a nervous breakdown, or might have thrown away his letter of exemption and pushed his way into the armed services, seeking death or revenge. Francis's heroism was of another sort; he pulled about him a harsh cloak of stoicism, shut the door on love, and drudged on at his tedious work until Uncle Jack, perhaps sensing a great change in him, or finding new worth in him, promoted him to something a little more interesting. He next sat for several months in a small office in a building that did not in the least suggest MI5, and coordinated reports that had been brought in by watchers like himself, and tried to make sense of information that was usually uninformative. Only once, in all this time, did he have any certainty that he had been instrumental in uncovering an enemy agent.

It was not wholly loneliness and drudgery. Early in 1943 his father turned up, now revealed as MI5's Security Liaison Officer for Canada, and rather a bigwig, for he stayed at Claridge's and could have commanded a car for his use, if he had not preferred to walk. The Wooden Soldier was more wooden than ever, and his monocle was, if possible, more a part of his face than it had been before. He brought news of home.

"Grand'mère and Aunt Mary-Ben won't be long with us, I'm afraid. They're old, of course; the old lady is well over eighty, and Aunt is eighty-five if she's a day. But it isn't age that ails them; it's parsimony and bad food. That miserable Doctor is even older, but he is remarkably bobbish and keeps the old girls ticking. I never liked him. The worst sort of Irishman. Your mother is well, and as beautiful as the first day I saw her, but she's developing some odd tricks; faulty memory—that kind of thing. The surprise of the park is your young brother Arthur. No university for him; he says you went to two and that's enough for the family. He's been deep in the business already, and very sharp. But he's in the Air Force now; I expect he'll do well.

"And you're doing well, Jack Copplestone tells me."

"I wish he'd tell *me* once in a while. I sometimes think he's forgotten me."

"Not Jack. But you're not the easiest man to place, Frank. Not a swashbuckler, thank God. He'll use you when the right thing turns up. Still, I'll say a word to him. Not as though you had said anything to me, of course. But just to keep the wheels turning.

"You know that both the O'Gorman boys are in the Army? Very junior, mind you, but keen. Unfortunately not very bright— not in a Service way—but full of beans. And of course O'Gorman is up to his neck in what he calls his War Work—selling Victory Bonds and that sort of thing. I suppose somebody has to do it. You know, I think that fat ass is pushing for some kind of official recognition. He's never recovered from that Knight of St. Sylvester fiasco. He wants something nonretractable."

It occurred to Francis that his father could not be very young. He must be at least ten years older than his mother. But Sir Francis Cornish, never having looked young, had not grown to look old, and as he was still part of the profession he must have been good at whatever it was he did. Certainly he looked like a revenant from an Edwardian past, but his step was light, and he was slim without being scrawny.

"You know, Frank, looking back over the years, and the Canadian part of the family, I think I liked the old Senator best of all. If he had had a chance, he might have been a remarkable man."

"I always thought he was remarkable. He certainly became very rich."

"And founded the Trust. You're right, of course; I was thinking of—well, of social advantages. The Cornish Trust—that always surprised me. He thought I was a figure-head, and I suppose I was, really. We lived in different worlds, and it's rum that our worlds should ever have intersected. But they did, to everybody's advantage."

"Grand-père was a man of deep feeling."

"Ah? I suppose so. I never understood much about that, myself. Y'know, Frank, you really must get some decent clothes. You look dreadful. It's still possible to get good clothes, y'know. You've got lots of cash, haven't you?"

"I suppose so. I never think about clothes. They don't seem relevant to what's going on."

"Trust me, my boy, they're always relevant. Even in the profession, you know, protective colouring is of different kinds. If you look like an underling you'll be taken for an underling, because people haven't always time to find out what you really are. So do smarten up. Go to my man, and get him to make you the best suit he can for your coupons. You should wear a school tie, or a college tie. Suppose you get knocked over in one of these raids? When they found you, how would they know who you were?"

"Would it matter?"

"Of course it would. Looking like a lout when you aren't one is just as much affectation as being a dandy. Affectation in death is as ridiculous as affectation in life."

The next day Francis was marched to Savile Row, measured, and promised a suit of dark grey, to be followed by a blue one, in God's and the ration's good time. Sir Francis, having cowed his son, pressed his advantage and gave Francis some decent socks and shirts from his own wardrobe. They were not too bad a fit. To be dressed by one's father when one is thirty-three perhaps suggests unusual compliance of character, but Francis took it humorously; he had been aware for some time that his profession as a lurker had made him look like a lurker, and that something would have to be done about it. The Major provided the necessary shove.

He was well dressed, if still somewhat doubtful in the matter of shoes, when he called on Signora Saraceni at her house in South London. A note from the Meister, smuggled from Paris, had asked him to do so.

The Signora was very English, but perhaps some life in Italy had given her the swooning, fruity manner which she probably thought proper in the wife of an artist. She was confiding.

"Sometimes I wonder if, when this dreadful war is over, Tancred and I will live together again. It will have to be here. I keep my English passport still, you know. I never really liked Rome. And that apartment—well, it really was a bit much, wasn't it? I mean, what domesticity can survive in the middle of so much history? There wasn't a chair that didn't have a lineage, and one really cannot relax perched on a lineage, can one? Not, you must understand, that there was any unkindness between Tancred and me. The war has kept us apart, but before that he visited me every year, and we were lovers. Oh, indeed we were! But I don't suppose Tancred could ever settle happily in this house, and I love it. These chintzes, and this marvellous pickled-wood furniture—isn't it divine? Really, Mr. Cornish, artist though you are, and friend of Tancred's, isn't it divine? From Heal's, every stick of it, and nothing more than a few years old. One ought to live in one's age, don't you think? But I do hope we may live together again."

Her wish was not to be granted. A few weeks later a stray bomb, which was probably meant for the City, wiped out the Signora's street, and the Signora as well, and it was Francis's miserable job to write to the Meister about it, and find a way of reaching him.

"She was the blood of my heart," wrote the Meister in the reply which at last found its way to Francis, "and I truly believe that she would say the same of me. But Art, my dear Cornish, is a cruel obsession, as you may yet learn."

This letter came shortly before Uncle Jack called Francis to him, and at last gave notice that he had never really forgotten about him. Forgetting was not Colonel Copplestone's way.

"You know that we are going to win this war, don't you? Oh yes we are, appearances to the contrary. It will take a while, but it's perfectly clear that we shall win, in so far as anybody wins. The Americans and the Russians will probably be the big winners. And victory will bring some tricky problems, and we shall have to get to work on them now, or be caught unprepared. One of them will be the Art thing.

"It's important, you know. Psychologically. A kind of barometer of psychological and spiritual strength. The losers mustn't seem to be getting away with a lot of spiritual swag, or they'll look too much like winners. So we must be ready to recover a lot of stuff that has gone astray—looted, quite frankly—during the fighting. That's why I'm sending you to South Wales to work with some people who have been keeping an eye on all that. You have a name, you see. That Letztpfennig business gave you a name, but not too big a name, and you must be ready to move as soon as the time is right. Glad to see you've done something about your clothes. You had better do a little more in that direction. Mustn't go to conference tables and sit on commissions looking like a loser, must you?"

Two weeks later Francis was in a quiet place near Cardiff, where what had been a manor-house was now, without attracting too much notice, a part of MI5's curious domain. There, during some of the harshest days of the war, he studied for the coming victory.

It was here, so far from London, that he gained a better idea than ever before of what he was working for, and who he was working with. In London he had been a lowly kind of agent, a snoop, hoofing around dark streets making notes of the journeys and walks and appointments of suspects. He had studied to acquire the knack of invisibility. He learned the psychological hazard of the snoop's trade; anybody one follows for a few days begins to look furtive. He had begun to feel foolish, but it was not for him to ask questions; his job was to lurk in doorways and around corners, to peep into shop windows at the image of the suspect as he passed, to take care that he did not himself attract suspicion, for a few of Uncle Jack's snoops had made themselves ridiculous by reporting on unknown colleagues. In his long hours of waiting he had begun to hate his work, to hate all "systems" and all nationalism. He had begun, indeed, to fall into the state of mind that makes a snoop a possible recruit for the enemy; the lure of becoming a double agent. For what high principle can a man cling to when he has been brought to the lowly employment and personal bankruptcy of a snoop?

In Cardiff he had the job of interviewing many snoops, and weighing them in the balance of his information and judgement. Some of them had been working in MI6, the overseas branch. Again and again Ruth's voice sounded in his head, in a wisdom pieced together from many of their conversations.

"Some of our best agents are very bad boys, Frank, and some of the worst are members of the Homintern—you know, the great international brotherhood of homosexuals. Imagine squealing on somebody you had gone to bed with! But a lot of it's done, and more by the men than the women, I believe. Really, they need more women in the secret-service game: men are such frightful goofs. You can trust a woman—except in love, maybe—because women are proud of what they know, but men are proud of what they can tell. It's a nasty world, and you and I are too innocent ever to get any of the top jobs in the profession."

Yet there he was, in Cardiff, in a job which, if not anywhere near the top, seemed pretty important. Had he sunk so low? Or had Ruth simply spoken from the goodness of her decent heart, without really knowing what she was talking about?

As well as the job, he had to find time for some of the obligations, and the nuisances, of common life. Roderick Glasson wrote to him about once a month, bemoaning the lot of the agriculturist in wartime, and hinting strongly that if more money were not forthcoming which would make possible really big reforms on his estate, all would be lost, and Francis would have his own close-fistedness to blame for bringing the family to ruin. Aunt Prudence wrote less often, but perhaps more pointedly, to report on the growth and progress of Little Charlie, for whom more money was needed if the child were to be brought up in a manner befitting a Cornish. It was in one of these that Aunt Prudence said frankly that it was time Little Charlie had a proper home with parents in it, and should not Francis and Ismay reconsider their position?

This letter was followed in a few days by one from Ismay herself, written from Manchester, saying nothing about Little

Charlie, or a proper home, or that she had his address from her
mother. But stating plainly that she was very hard up, and did
Francis feel like doing anything about it?

So Francis absented himself from his work for a few days,
making the roundabout journey, doubly difficult in wartime, from
Cardiff to Manchester, and met Ismay again, after almost ten
years, over a bad dinner in a good hotel.

"I should judge that this substance had once been whale," he
said, turning over the stuff on his plate. But Ismay was not fastidious; she was eating with avidity. She was very thin and, though
still a beauty in her own particular way, she was now bony, almost
gaunt, and her hair looked as if she might have cut it herself. Her
clothes were grubby and of several dark colours, and everything
about her spoke of a woman devoted to a cause.

So it was: Ismay was now a full-time zealot, but for what it was
hard to tell. Hints that she dropped suggested that she was doing
everything in her power to bring about a Revolt of the Workers.
Such a revolt, in all the warring countries, would force the conflict
to a halt in a matter of weeks, and substitute a Workers' International that would create order and justice in a much-wronged
world.

"You don't have go to into detail," said Francis. "As I came
through London I was allowed, as a great favour, to look at the
file on you at our offices. How you have kept out of jail I don't
really know, but my guess is that you are too small fry to worry
about."

"Balls!" said Ismay, whose vocabulary had not greatly changed
from her student years. "Your lot simply hope that if they leave
me at large I'll lead them to people they really want. Catch me!"
she said rancorously through a mouthful of whale.

"Well, that's not what we need to talk about," said Francis. "I
gather that you have been having some sort of correspondence
with your mother, who naturally has no idea what you're up to;
she thinks we ought to get together again."

"Fat chance," said Ismay.

"I fully agree. So what have we to talk about?"

"Money. Will you let me have some?"

"But why?"

"Because you've got a lot of it, that's why."

"Charlie used to have some. What's happened to Charlie?"

"Charlie's dead. Spain. Charlie was a fool."

"Did he die for the Loyalists?"

"No, he died because he didn't settle some gambling debts."

"I can't say you surprise me. Charlie never understood the grammar of money."

"The what?"

"I am pretty good at the grammar of money. Money is one of the two or three primary loyalties. You might forgive a man for trifling with a political cause, but not with your money, especially money that Chance has sent your way. That's why I'm not rushing to give you money now. Chance sent it to me, and I hold it in trust far more than if I had earned it by hard work."

"Come on, Frank. Your family is rich."

"My family are bankers; they understand the high rhetoric of money. I am simply a grammarian, as I said."

"You want me to beg."

"Listen, Ismay, if I am to help you, you must answer a few straight questions in a straight way and shut up about the people's war. What's chewing you? What's all this underdoggery about? Are you simply revenging yourself on your parents? Why do you hate me? I'm just as much against tyranny as you are, but I see lots of tyranny on your side. Why is a tyranny of workers any better than a tyranny of plutocrats?"

"That's so simple-minded I won't even discuss it. I don't hate you; I merely despise you. Your mind works in clichés. You can't imagine any great cause that doesn't boil down to a personal grievance. You can't think and you have no objectivity. The fact is, Frank, you're simply an artist and you don't give a sweet God-damn who rules as long as you can paint and mess about and stick spangles on an unjust society. My God, you must know what Plato had to say about artists in society?"

"The best thing about Plato was his good style. He liked inventing systems, but he was too fine an artist to trust his systems fully. Now I've come to hate systems. I hate your pet system, and I hate Fascism, and I hate the system that exists. But I suppose there must be some system and I'll take any system that leaves me alone to get on with my work, and that probably means the least efficient, ramshackle, contradictory system."

"Okay. No use talking. But what about money? I'm still your wife and the cops know it. Do you want me to have to go on the streets?"

"Ismay, you astound me! Don't try that sentimental stuff on me. Why should I care whether you go on the streets or not?"

"You used to say you loved me."

"A bourgeois delusion, surely?"

"What if it was? It was real to you. You haven't forgotten how you used to work up artistic reasons for getting me to strip so that you could stare at me for hours without ever getting down to anything practical?"

"No, I haven't forgotten that. A fine, high-minded ass I was, and a slippery little cockteaser you were, and I dare say the gods laughed fit to bust as they watched us. But time has passed since then."

"I suppose that means you've found another woman."

"For a time. An immeasurably better woman. Unforgettable."

"I'm not going to beg, so don't think it."

"Then what are we doing here?"

"You want me to beg, don't you? You shit, Frank! Like all artists and idealists, a shit at the core! Well, I won't beg."

"It would do no good if you did. I won't give you a penny, Ismay. And it's no good murmuring about cops, because you deserted me—scarpered. I'll go on supporting Little Charlie, because the poor brat isn't to blame for any of this, but I won't support her like a princess, which seems to be your mother's idea. I'll even go on for a few more years pouring money into that ill-managed mess your father calls an estate. But I won't give you anything."

"Just for the interest of the thing, would you have given me money if I'd grovelled?"

"No. You tried the sentimental trick and I choked you off. Grovelling would have served you no better."

"Will you order some more food? And drink? Not that I'm grovelling, mind you, but I am a guest."

"And we both grew up under a system where a guest is sacred. For the moment I acknowledge that system."

"*Noblesse oblige.* A motto dear to the heart of bourgeois with pretensions to high breeding."

"I know a bit more about high breeding than I did when last we met. *Thou shalt perish ere I perish.* Ever hear that one? And if I fell for your beauty again—and you are still beautiful, my dear wife—I should certainly perish, and deservedly, of stupidity. I have made myself a promise: I shan't die stupid."

IN DUE COURSE the war did end. That is to say, the fighting with fire and explosives ended, and the fighting with diplomacy burst into action. The special task of what was called victory in which Francis was to play a part began to take shape. Something like peace had to be restored in the world of art, that barometer of national good and bad weather, that indefinable afflatus that a modern country must possess for its soul's good. But that would not begin until many other things had been settled, and Francis put in for leave to make a visit to Canada on compassionate grounds. Grand'mére had indeed died in the early days of 1945, and Aunt Mary-Ben, being no longer anybody's Right Bower, had not been long in following her. Indeed, Mary-Tess said, somewhat unfeelingly, that Grand'mére, arriving in Heaven, had needed somebody to manage eternity for her, and had rung the bell for Mary-Ben.

Francis was not surprised, or reluctant, when the family laid on him the task of going to Blairlogie and settling affairs there, and, in effect, ending the McRory family's long connection with the place. His brother Arthur and his cousins Larry and Mick were still abroad in the services, and anyhow they were young for such work; G. V. O'Gorman (a very big man now in the world of finance) certainly could not be spared, and Sir Francis was too grand for an extended errand of that kind. Besides, Sir Francis had had a stroke, and although his condition was not grave, he tended, as his wife phrased it, to look wonky by the end of the day. After all, he was well over seventy, though nobody said quite how much "over" implied.

As for Mary-Jim (all the family had called her Jacko for years) she was now sixty-one, and although she had the ability to look the best possible for her age, her speech and behaviour were disturbing and Francis felt tenderness and affection for her, which was something other than the obligatory, forced worship he had offered her since childhood. If ever he was to speak to her about the Looner, now was the time.

"Mother: I've always wondered about my elder brother—Francis the First, you know. Nobody has ever said anything to me about him. Can't you tell me anything?"

"There's nothing to tell, darling. He was never a thriving child, and he died very young and very sadly."

"What did he die of?"

"Oh—of whatever very tiny babies do die of. Of not living, really."

"He had something wrong with him?"

"Mm? He just died. It was a long time ago, you know."

"But he must have lived for at least a year. What was he like?"

"Oh, a sweet child. Why do you ask?"

"I just wondered. Odd to have a brother one's never known."

"A sweet child. I'm sure if he'd lived you would have loved him very much. But he died as a baby, you see."

Francis got nothing more from his father.

"I don't really remember anything about him, Frank. He died very young. You saw his marker up there in the graveyard."

"Yes, but that suggested he died a Catholic. You've always insisted that I'm a Protestant."

"Of course. All the Cornishes have been Protestants since the Reformation. I forget how he came to be buried there. Does it matter? He was too young to be anything, really."

Is that so, thought Francis. You don't know anything about it. You don't even know that I'm a Catholic by strict theological reckoning. Neither you nor Mother know one damn thing about me, and all the talk about love was a sham. So far as my soul is concerned neither of you ever gave a sweet damn. Only Mary-Ben, and for all her gentle ways she was a fierce old bigot. None of you ever had a thought that wasn't a disgrace to anything it would be decent to call religion. Yet somehow I've drifted into a world where religion, but not orthodoxy, is the fountain of everything that makes sense.

At Blairlogie, to which he made a last journey, taking sandwiches so that he would not have to eat at the dreadful table of "th'old lady", Francis went at once to Dr. Joseph Ambrosius Jerome, now ninety, a tiny figure whose blazing eyes still spoke of an alert intelligence.

"Well, if you must know, Francis—and you once told me you knew about that fellow in the attic—he was an idjit. I was the one who arranged for him to live up there. Your grandfather would have thanked me if I'd killed him, but none o' that for me. My profession is not that of murderer."

"But it was such a wretched existence. Couldn't he have been put some place to be cared for that wasn't so much like a prison?"

"Had you had no education at Oxford? Don't you remember what Plato says? 'If anyone is insane let him not be openly seen in the city, but let the family of such a person watch over him at home in the best manner they know of, and if they are negligent let them pay a fine.' Well—they did their best, but they paid a fine, right enough. That thing in the attic rotted St. Kilda. It cost them all dear in the coin of the spirit, in spite of your grandmother's card mania, and your grandfather keeping himself busy in Ottawa."

"Were they afraid that whatever ailed him might come out again in me?"

"They never said boo to me about it if they did."

"But why not: I had the same parents."

"Had you so?" Dr. J.A. burst into loud laughter. Not the cackle of a nonagenarian, but a robust laugh, though not a particularly merry one.

"Didn't I?"

"You'll not get that out of me. Ask your mother."

"Do you suggest—?"

"I don't suggest anything, and I'm not answering any more questions. But I'll tell you something that few people ever get told. They say it's a wise child that knows its own father, but it's a damn sight wiser child that knows its own mother. There are corners of a mother no son ever penetrates, and damn few daughters. There was a taint in your mother, and so far it hasn't turned up in you or Arthur—not that Arthur isn't such a blockhead that a taint could pass unnoticed—but you've plenty of time yet. You may live to be as old as me, and God grant you manage it with a safe hide. What's bred in the bone will come out in the flesh:

never was a truer word spoken. Have a dram, Frank, and don't look so dawny. Whatever became of all that first-rate whisky your grandfather had tucked away in his cellar?"

"There's some there still, and it must be dealt with. I'll send it over to you, shall I?"

"God bless you, dear lad! That stuff'll be proper old man's milk by this time. And at my age I need regular draughts of that very milk."

CLEARING OUT ST. KILDA was a weary job, and it took Frank, with two men to fetch and carry and drag loads of stuff to the auctioneer, and to the dump, three weeks to achieve it. He could not live in the house, though Anna Lemenchick was still on the strength as caretaker; he could not face Anna's dreadful food. He stayed at the Hotel Blairlogie, which was miserable, but had no clinging memories. He insisted on dealing with the contents of every room himself: to the auctioneer, all the Louis furniture; to the presbytery, all Aunt's holy pictures and such of her furniture as the priests might use. Francis left the nudes in the portfolio, thinking the priests might appreciate them. To the Public Library went the books and some further prints, and (this was in despair, and rather against the wishes of the librarian) the lesser oil paintings. The Cardinal pictures went to an art dealer in Montreal and fetched a goodish price. Victoria Cameron, now a woman of property, was invited to take anything she wanted, and, characteristically, wanted nothing but a drawing Francis had made, many years ago, of Zadok in top hat and white choker, driving Devinney's hearse. In his own old room he had some things to dispose of, which would not have attracted the attention of anyone else, but which were full of meaning for him.

There was a small collection of old movie magazines, now crumbling and yellow, over which he had once gloated with the ignorant lust of an adolescent boy. The beauty queens of an earlier day showed their knees daringly, and peeped from beneath grotesquely marcelled hair. There were some pictures cut from Christmas Editions of *The Tatler*, the *Bystander*, and *Holly Leaves* that his grandfather had brought home as part of the seasonal celebration, and in these were drawings of coy girls of the twenties in "teddies", or transparent nightgowns, or (very daringly) playing with a dear doggie whose body concealed the breasts and The Particular—but not quite. He saw these now as part of the pathology of Art, the last gasps of the school of erotic painting that had flowered under Boucher and Fragonard. Kitsch, as Saraceni called it.

What he was most anxious to find and destroy was a small bundle of rags—odds and ends of silk and chiffon—in which, in his adolescent days, he had absurdly rigged himself up as a girl, in what he believed was the manner of Julian Eltinge. He now knew, or thought he knew, what that had meant; it was the yearning for a girl companion, and for the mystery and tenderness he thought he might find in such a creature. He had even some intimation that he sought this companion in himself. Browning's lines, written when he was still very young, came to mind:

> *And then I was a young witch, whose blue eyes,*
> *As she stood naked by the river springs,*
> *Drew down a god . . .*

But even Ruth had not been that young witch, and Ismay, who so completely looked the part, was a sardonic parody of its spirit. Where was the young witch? Would she ever come? It was not as a lover he wished for her, but as something even nearer; as a completion of himself, as a desired, elusive dimension of his spirit.

Thus Francis came to terms, as he thought, with his strange boyhood, in which there had been so much talk of love, and so little to warm the heart. He did not feel lonely in Blairlogie, even as he sat for long evenings in the hotel, rereading—how many times had he read those pages—his favourite parts of Vasari's *Lives of the Most Excellent Painters, Sculptors, and Architects.* He did not feel lonely when he visited the Catholic cemetery, and found the marker for Francis the First, the Looner, the shadow of his boyhood and, if Uncle Doctor was to be believed, still an unexploded bomb in his manhood—the secret, the inadmissible element which, as he now understood, had played so great a part in making him an artist, if indeed he might call himself an artist.

But had not Saraceni, that stern judge, called him Meister, without irony and without offering an explanation?

He could not visit the grave of Zadok. Not even Victoria knew where it was, except that it was in that part of the Protestant cemetery which was called, with Blairlogie harshness, the Potter's Field. But Francis was not by nature a hunter of tombs, and he did not care. He remembered Zadok tenderly, and that was what mattered.

So St. Kilda was put up for sale at auction, as was also Cheg-widden Lodge, which had been on rental for several years. A local speculator bought them both, cheap, and there was the end of an old song, as Francis told the family in Toronto, wondering if any of them would understand the reference. From his childhood home he took nothing, except the picture that had hung in his bedroom. No, not the remarkable picture of Christ that opened its eyes when you looked at it, but *Love Locked Out*.

IN THE MANOR NEAR CARDIFF in 1946, there was much to be done, many files to be digested and put in order, and hundreds of photographs to be catalogued. Francis needed an assistant who knew what was in the wind, and Aylwin Ross, not long out of the Canadian Navy, was sent to him.

Aylwin Ross was not at all the sort of young man Francis had come to associate with the work of MI5 and MI6. There was no hint of the snoop about him, and he had some trouble concealing his amusement at the cautious, official way in which Francis ex-plained what had to be done.

"I get you, chief," he said. "We've got to know all these pictures well enough to recognize them, even if they reappear somewhat hocussed to deceive the eye, and so far as we can we've got to get them back to the people with the best claim to them. I'm pretty good at recognizing pictures, even from rotten black-and-white photographs like these. And if any ownership is in doubt, as will certainly be the case, we've got to nab as many as we can for the people we're working for."

Francis was shocked. Of course, what Ross said was true, but that wasn't at all the way to phrase it. He protested.

"Oh come on, Frank," said Ross. "We're both Canadian. We don't have to kid each other. Let's make it as simple as we can."

. . .

SO, WHEN AT LAST the Allied Commission on Art moved into action, and the sector of it in which Francis and Ross were to work assembled in Munich, that was indeed the way they worked, and Ross had so far loosened Francis from his official persona that he greatly enjoyed himself.

Their part in the Commission's work was a large one, and there were many familiar figures in the splendid room—a section of a palace—before which pictures recovered from the enemy were deployed for identification and reclamation. Francis and Ross were by no means the whole deputation from the United Kingdom. The formidable Alfred Nightingale was there, from the Fitzwilliam Museum in Cambridge, and Oxford was represented by the no less knowledgeable John Frewen. From the National Gallery and the Tate there were, predictably, Catchpoole and Seddon. But Francis and Ross were the experts on what paintings had gone astray in the war years, and what paintings might have vanished beyond recovery in the New World.

Saraceni was there, wearing conspicuously on his left arm a black band which Francis interpreted as mourning for the Signora, although it was fully three years since she had been obliterated in her South London refuge of pickled oak and cheery chintz.

"I shall never forget her," the Meister said, "a woman of the greatest, most tender spirit, even though we did not see eye to eye on matters of taste. While I live I shall not cease to mourn." But grief had in no way clouded his fearful vision—could it really be the Evil Eye?—or diminished the ironic mirth with which he treated the opinions of colleagues who disagreed with his judgements. The chief of these was Professor Baudoin, from Brussels, more evil-smelling than ever and not mellowed by wartime sufferings. From Holland Dr. Schlichte-Martin was present, and with him Hausche-Kuypers, who had been in a resistance group and lost an arm, but was merry as ever, and greeted Francis with a shout.

"Aha, the Giant-Killer! Poor Letztpfennig! How you polished him off!"

"Ah yes, the young man who knows so much about (sniff)

monkeys," said Professor Baudoin. "We shall have to keep our eyes open for any zoological problems that evade our mere connoisseur's estimations."

"Who's the old bugger with the charnel-house breath?" whispered Ross. "He's got it in for you, chief; I can see it in his eye."

The German members of the commission were not Frisch and Belmann; their eagerness in the matter of the Führermuseum had discredited them. Germany was represented instead by Professors Knüpfer and Brodersen. From France came Dupanloup and Rudel, and there were men from Norway, Luxembourg, and a number of other interested states. From the U.S. Francis was glad to see Addison Thresher, who would certainly be a voice of reason, as his country had lost no art in the conflict, though what it might have gained it would not be tactful to inquire.

"One of the problems I have had to face is to find some way of preventing high-ranking Air Force officers from sending home planes packed with art loot. They don't know much about art but they certainly know what they like, and they've heard that hand-painted oils fetch big money. I needn't tell you I haven't solved the problem. Still—it's the nature of fighting men to loot." Thresher was a cheerful cynic.

In all, fourteen states were represented, usually by two experts and a secretary, who was aspiring to be an expert. Ross was one of these. An Englishman, Lieutenant-Colonel Osmotherley, who was not an art expert but a redoubtable administrator, acted as chairman.

"What an array of boffins," said Ross. "I feel totally out of my league."

"You *are* out of your league," said Francis. "So keep your trap shut, at the sessions and everywhere else. Leave everything to me."

"Am I not even to have an opinion?" said Ross.

"Not out loud. Just keep your eyes and ears open."

ROSS'S CHEERFUL ESTIMATE of the Commission's work showed total lack of acquaintance with the way in which such things are done. After a war in which art had not been a first consideration, the experts were determined to assert its importance. After years of serving as air-raid wardens, standing in queues for coffee made of tulip bulbs, watching powerless as the invaders snatched their dearest treasures, being snubbed by Occupation forces, and being in most cases made to feel the weight of their years, they were once again men of importance, to whom their governments turned for expert advice. After wretched food, shortages of tobacco and drink, cold rooms, and no hot water, they were lodged in a hotel which, if not functioning at pre-war standard, was the best place they had known in years. Best of all, they were once again in that world of scholarship, of connoisseurship, of hair-splitting, haggling, wrangling, and quarrelling which was their very own, and in which they moved like wizard-kings. Were they going to hurry, to cut corners, to compromise, to take any steps whatever to hasten the evil day when their work would be done and they would have to go home? As Francis explained to Ross, only a dumb-bell Canadian, fresh out of the Navy, could suppose any such absurd thing.

Of course, he knew long before they went to Munich that Ross was no dumb-bell. He was brilliant; he had, in terms of his years and experience, extraordinary knowledge of art. Best of all, he had flair. His perception was swift and sure. But what especially endeared him to Francis was that Ross was lighthearted, and thought that art was for the delight and enlargement of man, rather than a carefully guarded mystery, a battleground for experts, and a treasure-house to be plundered by the manipulators of taste, the merchants of vogue, the art dealers.

Ross was self-educated in art, but a graduate of a Canadian Western university and later of Oxford (he had been some sort of Commonwealth scholar), where he had studied modern languages. Like many young men from the prairies, he had been drawn toward the Navy, where he was fairly useful, and very ornamental. Ross was that unusual creature, a male beauty, fair but not a Scandinavian blond, fine-skinned, fine-featured, and with a good, though not markedly athletic, figure. There was nothing epicene about him: he was, quite simply, beautiful and knew it. Among the commissioners, and their serious secretaries (most of whom were already gripped by the premature age of the

intellectual), he glowed like a rosebush in a forest of evergreens—
a rosebush that had not already succumbed to the acid, evergreen
soil.

"You preserve my sanity, Aylwin," Francis said one night in
the Munich hotel, when he had drunk rather too much. "If I have
to listen once again to Schlichte-Martin and Dupanloup hashing
it out about whether a canvas is a Rembrandt or simply a Goveart
Flink, or if what looks like a Gerard Dou is really a Donner, I
may scream and froth and have to be led from the room and
plunged in a cold shower. What does it matter? Get the things
back to wherever they came from."

"You take it all too seriously," said Ross. "You've simply got
to hang on and not care too much. Do you realize that there were
over five thousand of these pictures, most of them nothing more
than classy crap, in that salt mine at Alt Aussee where so much
of the Führermuseum stuff was stashed? And what about all the
stuff that has turned up near Marburg? Not to speak of Göring's
immense personal loot. We shall have to consider them all, and
if we did fifty a day, how many days does that make? Why don't
you relax and stop listening? Just look at the pictures, the pictures
we do look at. Wonderful! How many *Temptations of St Anthony*
have we seen already? And in every one of them an old geezer
nearly dead of starvation is being tempted by a few pesky demons
but chiefly by meaty girls over whom he is in no condition to
throw a saintly leg. If I were a painter I would show him being
offered a lobster *à la* Newburg. That would have tempted him!
Temptation works in the place where the weakness is greatest."

"You speak with a banal wisdom beyond your years."

"Always have. Born wise. You weren't born wise, Francis. Not
wise and not banal; you were born with a skin too few."

Saraceni was not so greatly taken with Aylwin Ross as was
Francis. "He has talent," said he to Francis one day when they
met over lunch, "but he is at heart a careerist. And why not?
He is not an artist. He creates nothing, preserves nothing. What
has he?"

"Insight," said Francis, and told him what Ross had said about
St. Anthony's temptations.

"Shrewd," said Saraceni. "Commonplace, but it takes shrewdness to see the wisdom in the commonplace. The temptation gets

us at the point of weakness. What is your weak point, Corniche? You'd better take care it isn't Aylwin Ross."

Francis was offended. Of course, he was usually seen in the company of the beauty of the Commission, and he had not quite understood that some of the other commissioners, for reasons best not examined, interpreted this in their own way. In 1947 homosexuality was not so easily accepted as it became later, but for that reason it was much on people's minds.

Because Saraceni was still the Meister in his world, Francis faced what he had said. Of course he liked Ross. Was he not a fellow-Canadian, and one for whom it was not necessary to make apologies to people who saw Canadians as a pseudo-nation of beaver-skinners? Was Ross not witty and merry in a group where wit never arose except as a weapon with which to strike down a rival? Was he not comely among the swag-bellied and the wrinkled? And—Francis did not face this quite honestly—was he not the nearest thing he had ever met to the elusive figure, apparently a girl, who was needed for the completion of himself? To make a friend, and a close and dear friend, of Aylwin Ross was the most natural thing in the world. In this association Francis did not feel himself a pupil, as he was aware that he had always been with Ruth, nor was he a gull, as he had been with the desirable, treacherous Ismay. This was, he told himself, a relationship in which emotion played as little part as it can play in anything, and kinship of mind and friendship were everything.

Nevertheless, he thought he ought to tell Ross what was apparently being said. Ross laughed.

" 'Helter-skelter, hang sorrow, care kill'd a cat, up-tails all, and a louse for the hangman'."

"What's that?"

"Ben Jonson. I did a lot of work on him at one time. Full of excellent good sense, expressed with a trumpeting masculinity. It simply means, Screw 'em all! What does it matter what they think? We know it isn't so, don't we?"

Did they? Did they know that? Francis thought he knew it, but Francis's conception of what was being hinted at was to be seen in the bold-eyed, painted youths who hung about in the shadows of the Munich nights. Of the subtler sodomy of the soul he knew nothing. As for Aylwin Ross, he knew only that he often got what he wanted by enchanting those whose lives had been poor in enchantment, and he saw no harm in it. And indeed, could there be any harm in it?

IT WOULD HAVE BEEN absurd for the Commission to examine every picture that had changed its ground during the war. Its job was to concentrate on treasures. Francis recognized in the lists that were distributed pictures by Nobody-in-Particular of Nobody Special which were certainly from the Düsterstein studio where he had worked with Saraceni; they were in the Führer-museum group, and nobody wanted them, so they were allowed to stay where they were. Because it was known to a few experts and had caused some sensation in London just before the war, *Drollig Hansel* appeared before the Commission in person—that is to say, exhibited on an easel—and was admired as a pleasing minor work, but as it had no known provenance, and was clearly marked with what looked like the Fugger family *Firmenzeichen*, it was decided that it had better go to Augsburg. This decision sat well with Knüpfer and Brodersen, and was firm evidence of the Commission's desire to be fair.

Francis felt no emotion he could not dissemble when *Drollig Hansel* was on the easel, and he was pleased that Ross thought highly of it.

"There's a kind of controlled *grotesquerie* about it I've never seen before," said he. "Not the rowdy horrors of all those *Temptations* of poor old St. Anthony, but something deeper and colder. Must have been an odd chap that painted it."

"Very likely," said Francis.

It was a different matter, however, when unexpectedly, on a November afternoon, *The Marriage at Cana* was carried in by the porters and put on the easel.

"This picture is something out of series," said Lieutenant-Colonel Osmotherley. "No provenance at all, except that it comes from Göring's personal collection, if you call that robber's cave a collection. But it's thought to be important, and you must make a decision about it."

"The Reichsmarschall knew a good thing when he saw it," said Brodersen, who ought to have known, for the Reichsmarschall had taken all the best things from his own gallery, leaving behind cynical receipts, saying that the pictures had been removed for their own protection. Brodersen had not been a Nazi, and only his reputation, and his unstained Aryanism, had kept him in his appointment.

It *was* a good thing. Seeing it after almost ten years, Francis knew it was a good thing. He said nothing and left the superior experts to say their say, which they did at such length that the light faded and the chairman adjourned the sitting until the following morning.

What the experts said was flattering and alarming to the Calvinist side of Francis's conscience. Could this possibly be a hitherto unknown Mathis Neithart? The vigour and brilliance of the colour, and the calligraphic line, the distortion of some of the figures and the *grotesquerie* (that word again!) supported such an attribution, but there were Italianate, Mannerist features that made it unlikely—indeed impossible. The experts plunged into an orgy of happy haggling, of high-powered knowing-best, that filled a whole day.

Ross simply could not keep his mouth shut.

"I know that I shouldn't speak in such company," he said, smiling at the great men about him. "But if you will be good enough to indulge my amateurish hunch, may I ask if anyone sees a quality in this picture that suggests the *Drollig Hansel* we examined a few weeks ago? Merely a hunch." And he sat down, smiling with a boyish charm that might perhaps have been a little overdone.

This started a dispute in a new direction. There were those who said they had felt something of the kind and had meant to bring it up until Mr. Cornish's secretary anticipated them: there were others who brushed the suggestion aside as absurd. But was there not some whiff of Augsburg about both pictures, said others who fancied such intuitions. Knüpfer and Brodersen did not want to hear anything about Mathis der Maler, who had not been a favourite in Germany for some time because Hindemith's opera about him had made his name unacceptable. Anyhow, elements in the picture put such an attribution out of the question. Strive as he might, Colonel Osmotherley could not push them toward a decision.

"What were they looking at?

The picture was a triptych, of which the central panel was five feet square, and the two flanking panels were of the same height, but only three feet wide. What impressed at first sight was the complexity of the composition and its jewel-like richness of colour, so arranged as to throw primary emphasis on the three figures that dominated the central panel, and indeed the whole picture. Two of these were plainly the couple who had been married; they wore fine clothing in the style of the early years of the sixteenth century, and their expressions were serious, indeed elevated; the man was pressing a ring on the fourth finger of his bride's left hand. Their faces seemed to be male and female versions of the same features: a long head, prominent nose, and light eyes that might have been thought at variance with their black hair. The smiling woman who was third of this dominant group must surely be the Mother of Jesus, for she wore a halo—the only halo to be seen in the whole composition; she was offering the bridal pair a splendid cup from which a radiance mounted above the brim.

There were no figures on the right side of this group, but on their left stood a stout old man of a merry, bourgeois appearance, who seemed to be making a sketch of the scene on an ivory tablet, and somewhat behind him, but clearly to be seen, was a woman, smiling like the Virgin, who was holding an astronomical, or perhaps an astrological, chart. Completing this group was a man who might have been a superior groom or huissier, with a smiling, sonsy face, richly liveried; he held a coachman's whip in one hand, but in the other what might have been a scalpel, or small knife; almost concealed behind his back hung a leather bottle; obviously this guest was feeling no thirst. This lesser group—wedding guests? specially favoured friends?—was completed by the figures of a dwarf, in full ceremonial armour, but with no weapon unless the onlooker chose so to define the rope that was coiled around his left arm; with his right hand he was holding out toward the stout artist a bundle of what looked like very sharp pencils, or silver-points.

The startling figure in this otherwise spirited but not inexplicable composition was a creature floating high on the left above the heads of the bridal pair. Was he an angel? But he had no wings, and although his face was at once sanctified and inhuman, the effect was idiotic; the small head rose almost to a point. From the lips of this creature, or angel, or whatever it was, issued an ornate ribbon, or scroll, on which was wriitten, in Old German script. *Tu autem servasti bonum vinum usque adhuc.* Over the heads of the wedded pair it held, in its left hand, a golden crown, while with its right it seemed to point at the couple who dominated the right wing of the triptych.

The background of this central panel, which also appeared in varied form in the other two panels, was a landscape merging in the farthest distance to a range of sun-tipped mountains.

Compared with this arresting central portion, the flanking wings were subdued, almost in some areas to a treatment in *grisaille,* though here and there were some relieving accents of colour. The wing on the left might seem at first to be readily understood; in it Christ was kneeling amid the six water-pots of stone, his hands extended in blessing. In the foreground, in shadow, were three figures easily identified as disciples: Simon Zelotes, a vigorous man of middle age in whose girdle hung a broad-headed woodsman's axe; St. John, identifiable by his pen and inkhorn hanging at his waist, and by the youthful beauty of his features; and—surely not?—yes, it must be Judas, red-haired and with the purse of the holy community safe under his left hand while with his right he calls the attention of his brethren to figures in the central panel.

But before the eye followed that gesture, what was it to make of the two women with Christ, the one standing in what might almost have been an attitude of anger over the kneeling figure, one hand raised as if in rhetorical condemnation, while the other, reaching bare from a servant's smock, pointed downward at the wine-pots. The other woman, kneeling and seeming almost to protect her Lord, was small, and beneath a curious enveloping cap upon her head her expression was sweet with adoration. Around the head of Christ was a radiance, not strongly emphasized, and otherwise the figure was unremarkable, almost humble.

Following Judas's gesture the eye moves toward the righthand panel. The figures here might be taken for wedding guests; a knightly figure, one eye obliterated by a bandage, wears a sword but has a warning finger at its lips, as if cautioning to silence; his companion is a lady of great but cold beauty. If any connoisseur were so pernickety as to extend a string from the pointing finger of Judas to its termination in this picture, it would strike a wealthy merchant and his wife, apparently concerned only with themselves; the male figure carries a heavy purse at his girdle. The physician, somewhat apart, stands with his lancet ready in his hand, ready to let blood from any of the marriage group, all of whom are included in the scope of his penetrating, rodent eyes. But if these are wedding guests, surely those others in the background must be beggars at the feast—that rabble of children with twisted, ugly, hungry faces. They are not looking toward the marriage scene, but are concentrated on one of their number who is gouging the eye from a cat with a sharp stone. In this panel the background is markedly desolate, as compared with the landscape elsewhere.

A strange picture, and the experts were happy to sink their learned teeth into it and worry it to some sort of satisfactory interpretation or attribution.

It was in vain that Colonel Osmotherley reminded them that their task was to say what should be done with the picture, and not to decide beyond question who had painted it, or what its curious assemblage of elements might mean. Schlichte-Martin said that he did not think it could ever have been intended for a Christian church; the relegation of the Saviour to a place on a side wing made it wholly unacceptable. Knüpfer wanted to know why the dwarf was in armour; of course, everyone had seen ceremonial armour that had been made for dwarfs, but why was this dwarf wearing it to hold pencils, and had anybody noticed how much the dwarf looked like Drollig Hansel? (Ross nodded vigorously at this.) Everybody was puzzled by the fact that the Virgin had a halo, but her Son did not. And the floating figure? What was anyone to make of that?

Predictably, it was Professor Baudoin who said the disagreeable thing. As the others disputed he glared at the picture from very close range, plied the flashlight and the magnifying glass, rubbed an inch of paint with his spittle, and at last said loudly, "I don't like the *craquelure;* I don't like it at all; much too even; seems to have happened all at once. I recommend that we get the scientific men to work on it. I will lay any money it proves to be a fake."

This brought an opinion—protest, demur, some inclination to agree—from all the experts. But even in his deep discomfort Francis could not miss the glance that Saraceni threw toward Baudoin, from his ill-coordinated blazing eyes. It had an impact like a blow, and Baudoin retreated to his chair as if a fierce gust of hot air had passed him.

When Colonel Osmotherley had quieted the uproar he explained that the Commission had no instructions to act as Baudoin suggested, and it would take a long time to get them, if that were possible. Could the experts not reach some conclusion based simply on what they saw? Giving every consideration to their widely acknowledged ability to see beyond what was given to lesser people, added the Colonel, who had a turn for diplomacy.

It was at this point that Francis, who had been suffering for two days and a half the torments of an inflamed conscience, disputing with a mischievous inclination to let the experts go on and commit themselves to positions from which they could not retreat, felt that he should rise to his feet and make a speech in the manner of the late Letztpfennig: "Gentlemen, I cannot tell a lie. I did it with my little paintbox." And then, what? Not hang himself, certainly, with his hat and overshoes on, as poor Letztpfennig had ridiculously done. But what a sea of explanations, of excuses or denials would follow any such declaration! The only person who could corroborate anything he said was Saraceni, and steadfast as the Meister could be in some things, he might prove altogether too supple in such a matter as this.

He had underestimated Saraceni, who now rose to his feet. This was in itself significant, for the experts usually spoke seated.

"Mr. Chairman; Esteemed Colleagues," he began with heavy formality; "please permit me to point out that our attempts to explain the curious nature of this picture in terms of Christian iconography are bound to fail, because it is not solely—perhaps not even primarily—a Christian picture. Of course, it demands to be called *The Marriage at Cana* because of the words issuing from the mouth of that curious floating figure—*Thou hast kept the good wine until now*. In the Scripture story it is the so-called 'governor of the feast' who says that; here it is this mysterious figure who seems to be addressing the parents—the Knight and his Lady in the right-hand panel. This strange figure holds a unifying crown over the heads of Bride and Groom. Who are they? You will not have missed that they look more like brother and sister than a wedded pair. These facial resemblances are surely crucial to an interpretation of the picture? Look at the face of Christ. Is he not kin to the Bride and Groom? Look at the Knight and his Lady in the right-hand wing; are they not plainly the parents of both the married ones? Look at the old artist; a fat, elderly version of the same face. We cannot pretend that these resemblances come about because the artist can only draw one face; the man with the whip, the astrologer, the dwarf, the old woman in the curious cap, the Judas, all show how adept he was at portraiture and revelation of character. No, no, gentlemen; there is only one way to explain this picture, and I suggest, humbly, that I know what it is.

"Consider where it comes from. You don't know? Of course not, because it has been hidden. But I know. It comes from Schloss Düsterstein, where, as you do know, there is an extraordinary collection of masterworks (or was, until General Göring took the best of them under his protection) upon which I was engaged for some years in repair and restoration work, before the war. But this picture was not among those that were hung. These panels were under wraps in a storage room very near the Chapel, where they had served as the altar-piece until the Chapel was wholly transformed in the Baroque taste by Johann Lys at some time during the first quarter of the seventeenth century. The old altar-piece was replaced by one painted by Lys, or one of his pupils, an inoffensive Madonna and Child with saints, which may still be seen. The old altar-piece had by that time become disagreeable to the taste of the Ingelheim family.

"Why? The picture we see here had grown out of fashion, and it was also, to a strict Christian taste, heretical. Look at it: this is a picture with strong alchemical suggestions. Of course, alchemy and Christianity were never incompatible, but to seventeenth-century theological orthodoxy, which was that of the Counter-Reformation, it was too near a rival to the true Faith.

"I don't know what you may know of alchemy, and you must forgive me if I seem to tell you what is already clear in your minds. But this is plainly a depiction, given a Christian gloss, of what was called The Chymical Wedding. The alchemical uniting of the elements of the soul, that is to say. Look at it: the Bride and Groom look like brother and sister because they are the male and female elements of a single soul, which it was one of the higher aims of alchemy to unite. I won't harass you with alchemical theory, but that unity—that wedding—was not achieved in youth or with ease, and so the Groom, at least, is not a man in his first youth. That such a unity is brought about by the intervention of the highest and purest element in the soul—which is, of course, what Christ has long been, and was to the Middle Ages, and is still in a somewhat altered but not destructively altered sense— is plain enough. Here we see Christ as a beneficent power at the Wedding. But in this picture it is the Holy Mother—what unorthodox but not heretical thinkers sometimes call Mother Nature—who blesses the Marriage of the Soul, the achievement of spiritual union. Am I making myself clear?"

"Clear so far as you go, Maestro," said Professor Nightingale. "But who are these other figures? That creature in the sky, for instance; a very nasty-looking piece of work, like a pinhead in a circus. Who may he be?"

"I cannot tell you, though of course we all know that in Gothic and late-Gothic art—there are lingering elements of Gothicism in this picture—such an angelic figure often represented a relative—big brother, it might be—who had died before The Chymical Wedding was achieved, but whose memory or spiritual influence might have been helpful in bringing it about."

"All very fine, but I don't trust the *craquelure*," said Professor Baudoin.

"Oh for God's sake forget the *craquelure*," said John Frewen.

"With your permission," said Baudoin, "I shall not forget the *craquelure,* and I would thank you, sir, not to snarl at me."

"I do well to snarl," said Frewen, who was a Yorkshireman and hot-tempered. "Do you suppose anybody would trouble to fake such a farrago of forgotten rubbish as this? Alchemy! What's alchemy?"

> " 'That alchemy is a pretty kind of game
> Somewhat like tricks o' the cards,
>   to cheat a man
> With charming.' "

It was the irrepressible Aylwin Ross who spoke.

"No, Mr. Ross, not that!" said Saraceni. "Some alchemists were cheats, of course, as some priests of all faiths are cheats. But others were truly sincere seekers after enlightenment, and are we who have suffered so much during the past five years under the evil alchemy of science to jeer at any sincere belief of the past, whose style of thought and use of words has grown rusty?"

"Mr. Ross, I should remind you that your position here does not extend to expressing opinions," said Colonel Osmotherley.

"I am very sorry," said Ross. "Just a few words from Ben Jonson, that slipped out."

"Ben Jonson was a great cynic, and a great cynic is a great fool," said Saraceni, with unwonted severity. "But, gentlemen, I do not pretend to explain all the elements in this picture. That would give an iconographer work for many days. I merely suggest that we could be looking here at a picture prepared to the taste of Graf Meinhard, who, four and a half centuries ago, was reputed to be an alchemist himself—a friend and patron of Paracelsus— and to do things at Düsterstein in what was the most advanced science of his time. His chapel was not, after all, a public place of worship. May he not have pleased himself in this way?"

The experts, credulous perhaps in a matter not within the range of their own knowledge, were inclined to agree that this could have been so. Their discussion was long and cloudy. When he thought it had gone on long enough, Saraceni summed it up.

"Might I suggest, Mr. Chairman and Esteemed Colleagues, that we agree that these panels, which certainly came from Düster- stein, be returned to the great collection there, and that we at- tribute this picture, which we are all agreed is a splendid previously unknown work of art, and a great curiosity as well, to The Alchemical Master, whose name, alas, we cannot determine more exactly?"

And so it was agreed, Professor Baudoin abstaining.

"YOU SAVED MY BACON," said Francis, catching Saraceni on the great staircase, as they left the session.

"I will confess to being a little pleased with myself," said the Meister. "I hope you listened attentively, Corniche; I did not utter one word of untruth in anything I said, though of course I was not officious in stripping Truth naked, as so many painters have done. You never knew I studied theology for a few years in my youth? I recommend it to every ambitious young man."

"I'm grateful forever," said Francis. "I really didn't want to confess. Not because of fear. It was something else that I can't just put a name to."

"Justifiable pride, I should say," said Saraceni. "It is a very fine picture, wholly unique in its approach to a biblical subject. Yet a masterpiece of religious art, if one means religion in the true sense. I forgive you, by the way, for giving Judas my features, if not my hair. The Masters must find their models somewhere. I did not call you Meister idly or mockingly, you know. You have made up your soul in that picture, Francis, and I do not joke when I call you The Alchemical Master."

"I don't know anything about alchemy, and there are things in that picture I don't pretend to explain. I just painted what demanded to be painted."

"You may not have a scholar's understanding of alchemy, but plainly you have lived alchemy; transformation of base elements and some sort of union of important elements has worked alchemically in your life. But you do know painting as a great technical skill, and such skills arouse splendid things in their possessors. What you do not understand in the picture will probably explain itself to you, now that you have dredged it up from the depths of your soul. You still believe in the soul, don't you?"

"I've tried not to, but I can't escape it. A Catholic soul in Protestant chains, but I suppose it's better than emptiness."

"I assure you that it is."

"Meister—I shall always call you Meister, though you say I've graduated from *alunno* to *amico di Saraceni*—you have been very good to me, and you have not spared the rod."

"He that spareth his rod, hateth his son. I am proud to be your father in art. So do something for me: I ask it as a father. Watch Ross."

Nothing more could be said, because of a commotion that broke out on the great staircase behind them. Professor Baudoin had misjudged his step, fallen on the marble, and broken his hip.

• • •

—THAT WAS SARACENI'S *Evil Eye*, I suppose, said the Lesser Zadkiel.

—Nobody becomes as great a man as Saraceni without extraordinary spiritual energy, and it isn't all benevolent, said the Daimon Maimas. The Masters and Sibyls turn up in lucky people's lives, and I am glad I could put such good ones in Francis's path.

—Lucky people? I suppose so. Not everybody finds Masters and Sibyls.

—No, and at the present time—I mean Francis's time, of course, because you and I have no truck with Time ourselves, brother—many people who are lucky enough to come into the path of a Master or a Sibyl want to argue and have their trivial say, and prattle as if all knowledge were relative and open to argument. Those who find a Master should yield to the Master until they have outgrown him.

—If Francis has really made up his soul, as Saraceni said, what lies ahead of him? Hasn't he achieved the great end of life?

—You are testing me, brother, but you won't catch me that way. Having got his soul under his eye, so to speak, Francis must now begin to understand it and be worthy of it, and that task will keep him busy for a while yet. Making up the soul isn't an end; it's the new beginning in the middle of life.

—Yes, it will take some time.

—You are fond of that foolish word time. Time in his outward life will run much faster for him now, but in the inward life it will slow down. So we can get on much faster with this record, or film, or tape, or whatever fashionable word Francis's contemporaries would apply to it, because his external life occupies less of his attention. Onward, brother!

WHAT WAS FRANCIS NOW in the world of MI5? Not one of the great ones, who inspire novelists to write about danger and violence and unexplained deaths. His work with the Allied Commission on Art continued when the conferences in Europe were completed, because the decisions of the conferees created all sorts of problems that had to be settled diplomatically, with much bargaining, much soothing of ruffled national pride, and a few arbitrary judgements in which he played a significant if not a leading role. He had a liaison association with the British Council. But only Uncle Jack knew that he was expected to keep a watchful eye on some people who were important in the world of art but who had other loyalties that did not jibe with those of the Allied cause.

It was this secret aspect of his work that gave him the air of Civil Servant, a conventional man, a clubman who might turn up anywhere in the art world, the country-house world, the fashionable world, and sometimes even close to the Court. Anywhere, in fact, where there were clever people who did not think him clever, or quite one of themselves—not a Cambridge man—and who therefore sometimes talked less discreetly when he was present than they would otherwise have done. He was thought to be rather a dull dog who somehow managed to have a finger in the art pie. But he was also a useful man who could arrange things.

For instance, he arranged that Aylwin Ross should receive favours that might not otherwise come his way and Ross, being what he was, showed gratitude but not for long, because he thought the favours the natural outcome of his own brilliant abilities. It was through Francis that Ross gained a good appointment in the Courtauld Institute, and began his rapid climb toward influence as a critic and creator of taste.

Saraceni had warned Francis to watch Ross, so watch him he did, and saw nothing but a brilliant, attractive young man whose career it was a pleasure to advance. He would have watched Ross at closer range if Ross had not been so busy with his concerns and a little inclined to patronize Francis.

"I really think you misjudge Ross," he said to Saraceni on one of his yearly visits to the crammed, cluttered flat in Rome. "He is coming on like a house on fire; soon he will be a very big figure in the critical world. But you hint as though he were somehow dishonest."

"No, no; not dishonest," said the Meister. "Probably he is all you say. But my dear Corniche, I mean that he is not an artist, not a creator; he is a politician of art. He turns with the wind, and you stand like a rock against the wind—except when it is Ross's wind. You are a little too fond of Ross, and you don't understand how."

"If you suggest that I am in love with him, you are totally mistaken."

"You don't want to snuggle up with Ross and whisper secrets on the pillow—or I don't suppose you do. That might not be so dangerous, because lovers are egotists and may quarrel. No: I think you see in Ross the golden youth you never were, the free spirit you never were, the lucky man you think you never were. There is some grey in your hair. Youth has flown for you. Do not try to be young again through Ross. Do not fall for the charm of that sort of youth. People who are young in the way Ross is young never grow old, and never to grow old is a very, very evil fate, though the twaddle of our time says otherwise. Remember what that angel, or whatever it was, says in the great painting you have made: *Thou has kept the good wine until now*. Do not pour out the good wine on the altar of Aylwin Ross."

ROSS MET FRANCIS on an autumn day, walking along Pall Mall.

" 'Thou look'st like Antichrist in that lewd hat,' " said he, in greeting.

"Jonson, I suppose. What's wrong with my hat?"

"It is the epitome of what you have become, my dear Frank. It is an Anthony Eden hat. Sedate, gloomy, and out of fashion. Come with me to Locke's and we'll get you a decent hat. A hat that speaks to the world of the Inner Cornish, the picture-restorer—but of the highest repute."

"I haven't restored a picture for years."

"But I have! I most certainly and indubitably have! I'm restoring it to its proper place in the world of Art. And it's a picture you know, so why don't you take me to Scott's for lunch, and I'll tell you all about it."

Over the Sole Mornay at Scott's Ross told his news with exuberance extraordinary even for him.

"You remember that picture we saw at Munich? *The Marriage at Cana?* You remember what happened to it?"

"It went back to Schloss Düsterstein, didn't it?"

"Yes, but not to oblivion. No indeed. I was tremendously taken with that picture—that triptych, I should say. And don't you remember that I spoke about a link between it and the *Drollig*

Hansel we had seen earlier? The picture that was clearly marked as having belonged to the Fuggers of Augsburg? I've proved the link."

"Proved it?"

"The way we prove things in our game, Frank. By the most careful examination of brushwork, quality of paint, colours, and of course a great deal of flair backed up with expertise. The full Berenson bit. Short of all that really rather inconclusive scientific stuff, I've proved it."

"Aha. A nice footnote."

"If I weren't eating your lunch, I'd kill you. Footnote! It makes clearer the whole affair of that unknown painter Saraceni called The Alchemical Master. Now look: this is obviously a man who loves to deal in puzzles and hints to the observant. That device in the corner of *Drollig Hansel* could have been the Fuggers' family trademark, or it could have been a gallows. A hangman, you see? A dwarf hangman. And who turns up in *The Marriage at Cana* but the same dwarf hangman, and this time he is holding his rope! And he is glorious in his dress armour!"

"That bothered me for years, until at last I was able to get a grant—never do anything without a grant, Frank—to go to Düsterstein and persuade the old Countess to let me see *The Marriage*. She's tremendously chuffed with it now, you know. It hangs in the best gallery. I stayed for three days—she was very hospitable (lonely I suppose, poor old duck)—and I've cracked the code."

"Cracked what code?"

"What *The Marriage* is really about, of course. The alchemical Master cloaked it all in alchemical mystery, and for a very good reason, but it's not really an alchemical picture. It's political."

"You astonish me. Go on."

"What do you know about The Interim of Augsburg?"

"Not a thing."

"It's not on everybody's tongue, but it was important when that picture was painted. It was a scheme to reconcile the Catholics and the Protestants in 1548. It was a compromise that led up to the Council of Trent. The Catholics made certain concessions to the Protestants, the biggest one being communion in both kinds, if you know what that means."

"Don't insult me, you prairie Protestant. It means the laity receive both the bread and the wine at Communion."

"Good boy. So—the Marriage at Cana, where Christ certainly gave everybody the wine, the best they'd ever had. But look who's the principal figure in the picture: Mother Church, personified as the Virgin Mary, offering the Cup. So that's one-up for the Catholics because they are graciously yielding something very precious to the Protestants. The married couple are the Catholic and Protestant factions united in amity."

"There's a hole in your explanation. Mary may be yielding the Cup to the Protestants, but she certainly isn't giving it to the Catholics, and they haven't got it yet."

"I thought of that, but I don't think it really matters. The ostensible point of the picture is not to shout its message to every chance visitor to the Düsterstein Chapel, but to offer an altarpiece representing the Marriage at Cana."

"Well—what about the other figures?"

"Some can be identified. The old man with the writing-tablet is obviously Johann Agricola, one of the framers of the Interim of Augsburg. Who is holding his spare writing materials? Who but Drollig Hansel, the hangman with his rope, but he is in parade armour and thus dressed for a celebration, which he assists by holding the pens. Symbolic of the cessation of persecution, do you see? The Knight and the Lady in the righthand wing of the triptych are surely Graf Meinhard and his wife—the donors of the picture, just where you would expect to find them. Even Paracelsus is there—that shrewd little chap with the scalpel."

"And what about all the others?"

"I don't see that they really matter. The significant thing is that the picture celebrates the Interim of Augsburg, by linking it with the Marriage at Cana. The message of the angel, about the good wine, obviously refers to the Protestant-Catholic reconciliation. Those women quarrelling over Christ—Protestant preaching versus Catholic faith, obviously. And The Alchemical Master has laid out the whole squabble so that the picture, if necessary, could be explained in a number of different ways."

"What did the Gräfin say to all this?"

"Just smiled, and said I astonished her."

"Yes, I see. But Aylwin, I really do think you ought to be

careful. It's ingenious, but a historian could probably blow it full of holes. For instance, why would the Ingelheims want such a thing? They were never Protestants, surely?"

"Perhaps not avowedly so. But they were—or Graf Meinhard was—alchemists, and they chose a painter with this obvious alchemical squint. Graf Meinhard probably had something up his sleeve, but that's not my affair. I shall simply write about the picture."

"Write about it?"

"I'm doing a large-scale article for *Apollo*. Don't miss it."

FRANCIS CERTAINLY DID NOT MISS IT. He worried for many weeks before the article appeared. Obviously he should tell Aylwin the history of *The Marriage at Cana*. But why "obviously"? Because conscience required it? Yes, but if conscience were given a foremost place in the matter, it would be Ross's duty, as a matter of conscience, to denounce Francis as a faker, who had sat in silence while *The Marriage* was praised by the Munich experts. Conscience would involve the Gräfin, who, if she were really as innocent as she seemed about *The Marriage,* was certainly not innocent in the matter of *Drollig Hansel.* And if the Gräfin were involved, what about all those other pictures that had been so stealthily prepared by Saraceni and palmed off on the collectors for the Führermuseum? This was not a time to expose impostures practised on the Third Reich by Anglo-Franco-American entrepreneurs, which had involved the loss to Germany of genuine and splendid pictures; Germany, as the loser, was in the wrong, and must be firmly kept in the wrong for a time, to satisfy public indignation. Francis's dilemma had a bewildering array of horns.

And there was the matter of Ross himself. He counted on his article about *The Marriage* to provide a fine step upward in his career. Was Francis to hold him back by a confession which, if it were to be made at all, should have been made years earlier?

Finally, Francis had to admit, there was sheer pride in having brought off a splendid hoax. Had not Ruth Nibsmith warned him about the strong Mercurial element in his nature? Mercury, who added so much that was uplifting and delightful in the world, was also the god of thieves and crooks and hoaxers. The division between art and deviousness and—yes, it had to be admitted—crime was sometimes as thin as a cigarette paper. Beset by conscience on the one hand, he enjoyed a deep, chuckling satisfaction on the other. He was no Letztpfennig, to be brought down to ruin by a monkey: his picture, though anonymously, was to be given wide exposure and an interesting ambience by a rising young expert in the Mercurial world of connoisseurship. Francis decided to keep mum.

The article, when it did appear, was everything he could have wished. It was soberly, indeed elegantly written, without any of the gee-whiz enthusiasm Ross had shown when he told Francis what he was about to do. It was modest in tone: this very fine picture, hitherto unknown, had at last come to light, and except for *Drollig Hansel* it was the only example from the brush of The Alchemical Master, whoever he might be. He must have been known to the Fuggers, and to Graf Meinhard, and these facts and the quality of the painting put it with the best of the Augsburg group, of whom Holbein had been the finest master. Was The Alchemical Master a pupil or associate of Holbein? It was more than likely, for Holbein had delighted in pictures that offered concealed messages to those who had the historical knowledge and the flair to read them. Fuller explication of the iconographic intricacies of the masterpiece Ross was happy to leave to scholars of greater insight than himself.

It was a fine article, and it caused a sensation among those who cared about such things, which meant several hundred thousand professional critics, connoisseurs, and that large body of people who could never hope to own a great picture, but who cared deeply for great pictures. Perhaps best of all, it offered a fine colour reproduction of the triptych as a whole, and a detailed picture of each of its three parts. *The Marriage at Cana*, now dated and explicated, became art history, and Francis (the Mercurial Francis, not the possessor of the tormented Catholic-Protestant conscience) was overjoyed.

The Countess refused all subsequent requests to examine the picture. She was, she said, too old and too busy with her great farm to oblige the curious. Did she smell a rat? Nobody ever knew. *Thou shalt perish ere I perish.*

THE ARTICLE DESTROYED Francis forever as a painter. Clearly he could not go on in the style which he had, with so much pain and under the whip of Saraceni, made his own. The danger was too great. But with the perversity of his Mercurial aspect, he now found himself eager to paint again. He had done nothing since the end of the war except amuse himself with a few drawings in the Old Master manner and executed with his Old Master technique. After Ross's article appeared he enlarged his portfolio of sketches in this style that had been preliminary studies for *The Marriage at Cana;* created them, so to speak, after the fact. They had to be kept locked up. Now he wanted to paint. The obvious thing—he had grown fond of Ross's word "obvious"—was to learn to paint in a contemporary style. He bought new, ready-made paints and canvases prepared by an artist's supplier, and remembering his early enthusiasm for Picasso he set to work to find a style related to that of the greatest of modern painters, but which would be the true style of Francis Cornish.

That could never have been easy but it became wholly impossible after Picasso made a statement to Giovanni Papini, which was included in an interview that appeared in *Libro Nero* in 1952. The Master said:

> In art the mass of people no longer seeks consolation and exaltation, but those who are refined, rich, unoccupied, who are distillers of quintessences, seek what is new, strange, original, extravagant, scandalous. I myself, since Cubism and before, have satisfied these masters and critics with all the changing oddities which passed through my head, and the less they understood me, the more they admired me. By amusing myself with all these games, with all these absurdities, puzzles, rebuses, arabesques, I became famous and that very quickly. And fame for a painter means sales, gains, fortune, riches. And today, as you know, I am celebrated, I am rich. But when I am alone with myself, I have not the courage to think of myself as an artist in the great and ancient sense of the term. Giotto, Titian, Rembrandt were great

painters. I am only a public entertainer who has understood
his times and exploited as best he could the imbecility, the
vanity, the cupidity of his contemporaries. Mine is a bitter
confession, more painful than it may appear, but it has the
merit of being sincere.

He lost no time in bringing this interview to the attention of
Ross. He had to translate it, because Ross had only a smattering
of tourist-Italian; he was always meaning to learn the language
properly, so that he could read things like *Libro Nero*, but he
never did so.

"What do you make of that?" said Francis.

"I make nothing whatever of it," said Ross. "You know how
artists are; they have bad days and fits of self-doubt and self-
accusation when they think their work is rubbish, and abase themselves before the artists of the past. Often they are trying to coax
whoever they are talking to into contradicting them—giving them
new assurance. I suppose Papini, whoever he may be, caught
Pablo on a bad day, and took all that rubbish for his real opinion."

"Papini is a rather well-regarded philosopher and critic. He
doesn't write to create sensations and I am certain he would have
asked Picasso to reread and consider such a statement as this
before he published it. You can't brush it aside as a passing comment, made in a fit of depression."

"Yes I can. And I do. Listen, Frank: when you want opinions
about an artist's work you don't ask the artists for them. You ask
somebody who knows about art. A critic, in fact."

"Oh, come on! Do you really think artists are inspired simpletons who don't know what they're doing?"

"Artists have tunnel vision. They see what they are doing themselves, and they are plagued by all sorts of self-doubt and misgivings. Only the critic can stand aloof and see what's really going
on. Only the critic is in a position to make a considered and
sometimes a final judgement."

"So Picasso doesn't know what he's talking about when he talks
about Picasso?"

"You've put your finger on it. He is talking about Picasso the
man—troubled, influenced by ups and down in his health, his
love-life, his bank account, his feelings about Spain—everything

that makes the man. When I talk about Picasso I talk about the genius who painted *Les Demoiselles d'Avignon,* the master of every genre, the Surrealist, the visionary who painted the prophetic *Guernica*—one of the greatest things to come out of this rotten era—*The Charnel House,* the whole bloody lot. And about that Picasso, the mere man Picasso knows buggerall, because he is sitting inside himself and has too close a view of himself. About the artist Picasso I know more than Pablo Picasso does."

"I envy your assurance."

"You're not a critic. You're not even a painter. You're a craftsman, a creation of that old scamp Saraceni. And you ought to understand this, Frank, because it's part of the truth. A very big part of it. Too much rides on the reputation of Picasso to allow any rubbish like that interview to rock the boat."

"Money, you mean? Fashion in taste?"

"Don't be cynical about fashion in taste. Among other things, art is very big business."

"But what about what he says about seeking consolation and exaltation in art?"

"That was the fashion of an earlier day. That was probably true about the Age of Faith, which has been bleeding badly ever since the Renaissance, and which got its death blow with the revolutions in America and France. The Age of Faith took a deadly disease from the Reformation. Ever see a really great picture inspired by Protestantism? But the passing of the Age of Faith didn't mean the death of art, which is the only immortal, everlasting thing."

"But he says in so many words that he was serving fashion, pleasing the crowd, devising absurdities and puzzles."

"Don't you hear what I'm telling you? What he *says* is rubbish. It's what he *does* that counts."

FRANCIS COULD NOT WIN the argument, but he was not convinced, and it was his determination that consolation and exaltation must somewhere and somehow be the chief care of the artists that pushed him to his decision to return to Canada, where art was still not big business, where art was indeed little considered, and where therefore art might be persuaded to remain true to the path he was convinced was the right one.

He could not embark on this great missionary journey, this return to his roots, quickly or easily. First of all he had to detach himself from MI5, and to his surprise Uncle Jack was not willing to release him without argument.

"My dear boy, perhaps you feel that you've been neglected—not pushed ahead in the profession as you might have been. But you don't understand how we work—how we are compelled to work. We get a trustworthy, first-rate man in a key job, and we leave him there. You are just what we need in this art connection. Knowledgeable, respected, but not too visible; able to go anywhere without making too much of a stir; a Canadian and therefore supposed to be a bit dumb by people who value a glittering cleverness above everything else. You've got enough money not to be always nagging me for extras. I'd describe you as ideal for what you are doing. You've provided quite enough useful tips about dangererous people to have fully earned your passage in this work. And now you want to throw it up."

"Nice of you to say all that. But where does it lead?"

"I can't possibly promise that it leads anywhere other than where you are at present. Doesn't that satisfy you? Your father never worried about where things led."

"For him it led to a knighthood."

"Do you want a knighthood? What would you get it for? Most of the chaps you are keeping an eye on are pestering for knighthoods for themselves. A thing like that would tip off every clever rogue that you were something more than you seemed."

"Well, I'm grateful for everything, but in fact I am certain that I am something more than I seem, and I want to go home, and be what I am in my own country."

That would have been that, if another upheaval—not a blow or a misfortune, but a disturbing change of circumstances—had not shaken Francis profoundly.

Saraceni died, and as his wife had died in the Blitz, and his daughter had died from a less dramatic cause, Francis discovered that he was the Meister's sole heir.

That meant going to Rome and spending long hours with Italian lawyers and civil servants who explained to him the complexities of inheriting a large private collection of art—not all of it art of the highest quality but every bit of it of museum quality—in a country that had been virtually beggared by a war it had never really wanted.

The Italian lawyers were rueful, and very courteous, but firm that the law must be served in every respect. Serving the law in Italy, as in every civilized country, was an extremely expensive business, but Saraceni had left plenty of money to take care of that and leave some over. What the Italian lawyers could not control, though they tried, was whatever Saraceni had deposited in numbered accounts in Switzerland.

This was what shocked Francis, for he had never thought of the Meister as a very rich man. But the Meister must have made some remarkably good deals with the people who paid him and Prince Max and the Gräfin for the pictures that had made their way to England from Düsterstein. When he made himself known to the quiet men at the banks, and established his undoubted right to Saraceni's wealth, Francis could not believe the record of millions in good hard currency that were his. He came of a banking family and money in substantial sums was not strange to him. But until now his income had reached him from Canada without any necessity for him to think about the capital sums that generated it. Money, to him, meant a lump that appeared in his account every quarter, a lump from which he allotted sums for the miserable estate in Cornwall that never fulfilled the promises that were made for it by Uncle Roderick, and an increasing sum for the maintenance of Little Charlie, who was now almost grown up and appeared to eat money, so great were the demands made on her behalf by Aunt Prudence. Francis, who thought of himself as "careful", sighed and sometimes cursed whenever he signed these cheques, and although he never spent anything like the remainder of his income, he considered himself as a man financially somewhat straitened.

It was a two-year job to shake himself loose from MI5 and make the best he could of Saraceni's estate, but at last it was done, and he returned to the land of his birth.

THE LAND OF HIS BIRTH had not stood still in the years since Francis had left it to go to Oxford. The war had taught it something about its place in the world, and about the exploitative attitude taken by great countries toward small countries—small in population and influence, however gigantic they might be in physical dimension. Canada the wide-eyed farm boy was becoming streetwise, though not truly wise. Large numbers of immigrants from every part of Europe saw a future for themselves in Canada, and their attitude was understandably exploitative and somewhat patronizing. Nevertheless, they could not wholly abandon the sort of intelligence they had gained as a birthright in Europe, and in some respects the Canadian surface became observably smoother. Perhaps the most significant change, in the long term, was that of which Ruth Nibsmith—intuitive as always—had spoken at Düsterstein; the little country with the big body, which had always been introverted in its psychology—an introversion that had shown itself in a Loyalist bias, a refusal to be liberated by the military force of its mighty neighbour from what the mighty neighbour assumed was an intolerable colonial yoke—was striving now to assume the extraversion of that mighty neighbour. Because Canada could not really understand the American extraversion, it imitated the obvious elements in it, and the effect was often tawdry. Canada had lost its way, had suffered what anthropologists call Loss of Soul. But when the Soul was such a doubting, flickering, shy entity, who would regret its loss when there were big, obvious, and immediate gains to be had?

Thus Francis returned to a homeland he did not know. His real homeland, compounded of the best of Victoria Cameron and Zadok Hoyle, of the broad adventurous spirit of Grand-père, of the sentimental goodness of Aunt Mary-Ben, was nowhere to be found in the city of Toronto. Like many another, Francis thought his homeland was the world of childhood, and it had fled.

What he did find in Toronto was a new version of the Cornish and McRory family, with Gerald Vincent O'Gorman a very big man in the financial community and a power of great but undefined influence in the Conservative Party. If the Tories ever came to power, Gerry was a sure bet for a seat in the Senate, an appointment safer and richer than a knighthood of St. Sylvester, and something which would, in his opinion and his wife's, make him the true successor to Grand-père. Gerry was Chairman of the Board of the Cornish Trust, which was now very big business; the President, succeeding Sir Francis (who had died while Francis was deep in financial affairs in Rome, and could not return to Canada), was a Tory senator of unimpeachable dullness and respectability, and he gave Gerry no trouble. Gerry's sons Larry and Michael were high in the Trust and they were as friendly to Francis as he would allow them to be. But he missed his younger brother Arthur, who, with his wife, had been killed in a car crash, leaving their son Arthur to the care of the O'Gormans, who did their best, but confided Arthur chiefly to men and women Trust officers. Francis didn't want any help with his money; his fortune from Saraceni was the first money he had ever possessed—apart from the miserable stipend paid him by MI5—that was not controlled and managed by the family, and he was determined not to reveal its extent or let any part of it be ruled by another hand.

"Frank, you must do as you think best, but for God's sake don't get skinned," said Larry.

"Don't worry," said Francis. "I've been skinned enough in my time to know my way around."

As soon as it could be managed he settled a modest—in the light of his wealth, a mingy—sum on Little Charlie, and informed Uncle Roderick and Aunt Prudence that the girl was to be maintained out of the interest on it until she was twenty-five, when she could take over the management of it herself. He also informed them that under his new circumstances—which he did not explain—he could no longer provide anything more than a very small annual sum for the maintenance of the estate, and he left unanswered the wailing, beseeching letters that followed. He thought it was good of him to give them anything at all.

He then settled himself to the task of devoting his very large income (for he never thought of touching his correspondingly larger capital) to the encouragement of art in Canada, and the experience was like that of a man who bites into a peach and breaks a tooth on the stone.

It was not that the Canadian painters whom he very quickly sought out were disagreeable, but they were strongly independent. More accurately, the good ones were independent and the ones who responded with glee to the appearance of a possible patron were not good. Francis could not get rid of his money because he would not divorce it from his advice, and the painters did not want advice. He tried to band some of them together to do work that consoled and exalted, and his words fell on politely deaf ears.

"You seem to want to create a new Pre-Raphaelite Brotherhood," said one of the best, a large man of Ukrainian antecedents named George Bogdanovich. "You can't get away with it, y'know. Buy some pictures. Sure, we're glad to sell pictures. But don't try to be a big influence. Just leave us alone. We know what we're doing."

What they were doing was respectable enough, but it did not appeal to Francis. They were utterly in love with the Canadian landscape, and tried to come to terms with it in a variety of ways, some of which, Francis knew, were admirable, and a handful splendid.

"But no people ever appear in your pictures," he said, again and again.

"Don't want 'em," said Bogdanovich, answering for all. "The people stink. Most of 'em, anyway. We paint the country, and maybe after a while the people will learn about the country from the pictures, and stink a little less. Got to begin with the country. That's consolation and exaltation. We have to do it our own way."

There could be no quarrelling with that. There were painters, of course, who followed the newest, fashionable trends. Without being pressed, they would explain that they dipped deep into their own Unconscious—a word that was new to Francis in this context—and drew up conceptions that were expressed in pictures that might be gaudy and rather messy rearrangements of what they saw, or felt; some were carefully wrought arrangements of colours, usually dingy. These messages from the Unconscious were deemed to be infinitely precious, evoking in sensitive viewers some hint of an Unconscious deeper than any they could explore unaided. But Francis was not impressed. What had Ruth said? "You can't talk to the Mothers by getting them on the phone. They have an unlisted number." These delvers clearly did not have the number. It was such fakers of a chthonic inner vision whom Francis grew to detest above all others.

So Francis had to content himself with buying pictures that he thought good, but did not much like. Without being quite sure how it happened he found that he was taking pictures from painters who lived in inaccessible places, and keeping them in his

Toronto dwelling, where from time to time he was able to sell them and remit the money to the painter. He took no fee, but in a way he was a dealer. The world of collectors, not large in Canada, understood that he knew a good picture when he saw one, and his recommendation was a guarantee of quality. But this did not satisfy him, though in a desultory way it occupied him.

His satisfaction came from the pictures that had been in Saraceni's collection, which he was able to sneak into Canada by not altogether blameless means, and store in his Toronto headquarters.

These headquarters were on the top floor of an apartment house he owned in a decent, though not a fashionable, part of Toronto. He had bought it, years before, on the advice of his cousin Larry, who had told him that he ought to diversify his holdings, and get some good real estate. There were three apartments on the top floor of the dull building, product of an unadventurous period of architecture, and Francis spread his possessions among all three. To begin, this top floor looked like a richly if oddly furnished large single apartment, but as time went on the rooms became more and more cluttered, and the space in which Francis lived grew smaller and smaller.

"God, what a magpie's nest," said Aylwin Ross, the first time he visited it. " 'Blind Fortune still bestows her gifts on such as cannot use them.' Jonson, not me, but apt, I'm sure you will admit. Where in God's name did all this stuff come from?"

"Inherited," said Francis.

"From Saraceni. You don't have to tell me."

"In part. Much of it I have bought."

"With the ghost of Saraceni looking over your shoulder," said Ross. "Frank, how do you endure it?"

Frank endured it because he never thought of it as a permanent state. He was always meaning to go through his possessions carefully, banishing some to storage, perhaps selling some others, and arriving at last at a dwelling space over-furnished and over-decorated, perhaps, but recognizable as a human habitation. Meanwhile he lived in something like an antique dealer's warehouse, to which he was continually adding the contents of new crates, cartons, and parcels. It was fortunate that his apartment house possessed a freight elevator, as well as the shuddering,

murmurous bronze cage in which visitors ascended to what Ross
named The Old Curiosity Shop.

Ross was a frequent visitor, for he had taken to returning to
Canada several times a year, to give a lecture here, offer advice
to an aspiring municipal or provincial gallery there, and contribute
articles to Canadian periodicals on the state of art and the dizzy
ascent of art prices in the international sale-rooms. He brought
Francis the gossip of the art world—the sort of thing that could
not be printed—and stories about its personalities, some of whom
were people Francis had watched on behalf of Uncle Jack. Not
that Francis ever mentioned his real London work to Ross; he
was as close-mouthed as ever about that, and he was expert in
deflecting delicate inquiries that might give a hint as to the extent
of his fortune. But it could not be concealed that he was rich,
and very rich, for such eccentricity as he was developing could
not be sustained by less than a large fortune. He bought pictures
at Christie's and Sotheby's at high prices, and although he did so
through an agent, Ross was the kind of man who could ferret out
who the real buyer was. What Ross did not know was that such
heavy purchasing was Francis's way of assuaging the great yearning
he felt to paint himself. More than once he tried to find a new
style, and every time he gave it up in disgust. The Mothers would
not speak to him in a contemporary voice.

Ross's preoccupation with the art world of Canada, which might
have puzzled a less astute person, was no mystery to Francis. Ross
wanted to be the Director of the National Gallery in Ottawa, and
to secure such an appointment it was well to lay his plans some
years ahead of the event.

"I really am a Canadian, you know," he said; "a Canadian in
my bones, and I want to do something important here. I want to
raise the Gallery to a level of world importance, which it isn't
now. Of course, it has some fine things. The collection of eighteenth-century drawings is enviable, and there are other good
individual holdings. But not enough. Not nearly enough. The
buying has usually been unexceptionable in terms of a budget
that is simply derisory; but there is far too much that has merely
been donated, and we know what that can mean, in a country
without many real connoisseurs. It's hard to turn down donations,
or to stick 'em in the cellar when you've got 'em. Too many

feelings to be hurt. But the time must come. There must be some ruthless weeding and some major buying.—Look here, Frank, what are you going to do with the best of what you have?"

"I haven't really thought about it," said Francis, which was a lie.

"My dear man, the time to think about it is now."

And so, after much haggling about choices, Francis gave his six finest Canadian pictures to the Gallery, and Ross let it leak out in the proper places that it was he who had secured this benefaction, and from whom it came, although Francis tried his best to keep the gift anonymous.

"If it gets out every gallery in the country will be after me," he said.

"Do you blame them? Come on, Frank, get wise to yourself. If you're not a benefactor, what in God's name are you? When are you going to give the gallery some of that fine Italian stuff?"

"Give away? But why? Why is it assumed that someone who has fine things is under an obligation to give them away?"

In the course of time, and quite a short time as such things go, the Director of the National Gallery had to be replaced, and who was a more obvious candidate for the post than Aylwin Ross?

True to Canadian style in such matters, the committee that was empowered to recommend a successor to the relevant Minister of the Crown fretted and agonized before they did so. Would Ross, now a man with a wide and brilliant reputation, think of accepting such a post? Should not some worthy but relatively unknown scholar from a Canadian university, who for rather vague reasons was thought to deserve something from his country, be appointed instead? Were there not rumours about Ross's private life? Would Ross want more money than the job at present paid? It was possible for Francis to exercise some influence with certain members of the committee, and he did so, but with caution lest the other members of the committee, who hated him for his knowledge and his wealth, should discover that he was interfering. But at last, when the committee had enjoyed as much of this obligatory Gethsemane as could be endured, the recommendation was made to the Minister, the Minister wrote to Ross, Ross asked for a month in which to consider whether he could see his way clear to making the inevitable sacrifice of an international career as a critic, and in the end he agreed to make the sacrifice—at a substantially increased stipend.

The Minister announced the appointment, and as things happened it was the last appointment he did announce, for the Government of which he was a member fell, and after the hubbub and pow-wow incidental to a General Election had been completed, a new Ministry was formed, and the Minister to whom Ross was to be responsible proved to be a woman. What could be more suitable? Among a large number of Canadians it was assumed that women were good at art and culture. After all, in pioneer days, such things, embodied chiefly in quilts and hooked rugs, had lain entirely in their hands, and there was a great deal of pioneer opinion still operative in a fossilized state in the political world.

Ross had not paid much attention to the election. He said himself that he was in no way a political man. He had not heeded, if indeed he heard, the vehement promises made by the political party that now formed the Government to cut expenditures, to lance the boil of a swollen Civil Service, and above all to get rid of what the politicians assured the voters were "frills". But expenditures, especially when so many of them are baby bonuses, mothers' allowances, medical subventions, or pensions to the old and the disabled, are not easy to reduce; indeed, the clamour of the deserving and the needy is always mounting and always for more. Nor is it really possible to reduce the Civil Service without offending multitudes of voters, for all Civil Servants, and especially those on the humbler levels, come not from families but from tribes, engorged with tribal loyalty. This leaves only frills to provide showy economies. And when a country has a National Gallery already full of pictures, as any fool who visits it on a wet day may plainly see, are not more pictures frills, and frills of a peculiarly dispensable, elitist, and effete nature?

Nothing of this struck in upon the consciousness of Aylwin Ross, who was jaunting from one side of Canada to the other, and back again by a different path, explaining to interested groups that it was time Canada had a National Gallery worthy of it, that its present Gallery was not even in the second rank of excellence, and that something decisive must be done, and done at once. His eloquence was much admired. We cannot take our place in the world as a nation of millions of hockey-watchers and a few score hockey-players, he said. He quoted from Ben Jonson: "Whosoever loves not picture is injurious to truth, and all the wisdom of poetry. Picture is the invention of Heaven, the most ancient, and most akin to Nature." (He did not continue the passage, in which Jonson says flatly that painting is inferior to poetry; the art of the quoter is to know when to stop.) His splendid voice, in which the Canadian accent was softened but not obliterated, was in itself a guarantee of his sincerity. His great good looks enchanted the women and not a few of the men. This was a Canadian presence of a kind to which they were not accustomed. And how he could joke, and drink, and tell good stories of the art world at the receptions that followed his public addresses. Ross's popularity grew like a pumpkin, and was as bright and shiny. When he had completed his great tour, by which time the new Ministry was comfortably in the saddle, Ross exploded his firework.

A firework that misfires can be like a bomb. Ross let it be known, in an unwise press conference, that it lay in his power, at a stroke, to lift the National Gallery to a new level, and set it well on the way to recognition as a collection of world importance. He had, by long negotiation and a lightning trip to Europe, succeeded in pledging all the Gallery's allocation for acquisitions for the forthcoming year, and in addition a sum that would gobble it up for six years to come. He had agreed to purchase six pictures, six pictures of world importance, from a great private collection in Europe. He had got them at bargain rates, by dint of keen negotiation and, it was hinted in the gentlest terms, by personal charm.

Who was the owner? Ross let it be teased out of him that the owner was Amalie von Ingelheim, who had recently inherited the collection from her grandmother, and as the Gräfin—for so Ross incorrectly but impressively called her—had need of money (her husband, Prince Max, was taking over a large cosmetic empire with its headquarters in New York), she was letting some of her private treasures out into the world, where they had never been seen before. For a few paltry millions Canada could put itself on the map as a country possessing a notable national collection.

Comparatively few people know what a million dollars actually is. To the majority it is a gaseous concept, swelling or decreasing as the occasion suggests. In the minds of politicians, perhaps more than anywhere, the notion of a million dollars has this accordion-like ability to expand or contract; if they are disposing of it, the million is a pleasing sum, reflecting warmly upon themselves; if somebody else wants it, it becomes a figure of inordinate size, not to be compassed by the rational mind. When the politicians learned that one of their functionaries, an understrapper holding a minor post in a *cul de sac,* had promised several millions abroad, for the acquirement of pictures—*pictures,* for God's sake—they burst into flames of indignation, and none were more indignant than those of the party, now Her Majesty's Loyal Opposition, who had appointed Ross just before they fell from power.

The Minister was under the gun. She did not like Ross, whom she had met two or three times, and her Assistant Deputy Minister, who dealt directly with Ross, was another woman who liked him even less. He had quoted Jonson to her, and she had assumed that he was talking about Samuel Johnson, and had made a goat of herself. (Or so it seemed to her, for Ross, who was used to this misunderstanding, paid little attention.) The Assistant Deputy Minister was a feminist, and certain that Ross's deferential manner toward women was mockery. She had her suspicions that Ross was a homosexual—so handsome a man, and unmarried—and she detailed a trusted henchman (one of the Palace Eunuchs of her Department) to get the goods on Ross if he could, by any means short of making him a proposition in a Parliamentary lavatory. Ross, in his dealings with this lady, was unquestionably tactless; in the words of his favourite author, he was "plagued with an itching leprosy of wit", and he could not dissemble it in his dealings with politicians and Civil Servants.

The Minister relied on the advice of her Deputy, who relied on the advice of her assistant (who was not quite her lover but would have been if they were not both so busy and so tired), and her path was clear. A Civil Servant under her Ministry had behaved with unwarrantable freedom, making deals involving money not yet allocated, and without a word to her. She made a statement in the House repudiating the purchases, and assuring the Commons that no one was more zealous in cutting down unwarrantable expenditures than she. Piously, she said that she yielded to no one in her love of art in all its forms, but there were times when even she had to regard art as a frill. When grave financial problems confronted the country, she knew where her priorities lay. She went no further, but it was assumed that these priorities lay in the Maritimes, or on the Prairies, where money problems are endemic.

Without an election, the press was in need of a political punching-bag, and Ross provided one for at least two weeks. The most conservative insisted that he be humbled, made to understand the facts of Canadian life, taught a sharp lesson: the more extreme papers demanded that his appointment be revoked, and hinted that he ought to go back to Europe, where he obviously belonged, having learned that decent people didn't blaspheme against hockey.

THE RIGHTEOUS UPROAR was almost over when Ross appeared one night in the Old Curiosity Shop. Looking at him, in his painfully reduced state, Francis knew that he loved him. But what was there to say?

"The Ark of the Lord seems to have fallen into the hands of the Philistines" was what he did say.

"I have never met this kind of thing before. They hate me. I think they wish me dead," said Ross.

"Oh, not at all. Politicians get far worse abuse all the time. It will blow over."

"Yes, and I will be left discredited in the eyes of my staff and perpetually school-marmed by the Minister, who will grudge me every penny that goes to the Gallery. I'll be nothing more than a caretaker, looking after a cat-and-dog collection and without any hope of improving it."

"Well, Aylwin, I don't want to be stuffy, but you really shouldn't have spent money you didn't have in your grip. And the Minister—you know that as a woman she has to show herself tougher than any of the men; she can't afford a single feminine weakness. The Prime Minister reserves all those for himself."

"She's out to get me, you know. Wants to prove me a fairy."

"Well—are you? I've never known."

"Not more than most men, I suppose. I've had affairs with women."

"Well, why don't you make a pass at the Minister? That would answer her question."

"Grotesque suggestion! She smells of drug-store perfume and cough-drops! No, there's only one thing that will put me right."

"And that is—?"

"If only I could get one of those pictures for the Gallery. Just one would raise enough interest in the international art world to show the Minister I wasn't completely a fool."

"Yes, but how could you do that?" But even as he spoke, Francis knew.

"If I could get a private benefactor to give one to the Gallery, it would do an immense amount to put me right, and eventually it would put me totally right. If I could get the one I want, that's to say."

"Benefactors are very elusive creatures."

"Yes, but not unknown. Frank—will you?"

"Will I what?"

"You know damn well what. Will you stump up for one of those pictures?"

"With art prices what they are at present? You flatter me!"

"No I don't. I know what you have been paying in London in the past two or three years. You could do it."

"Even if I could, which I don't for a moment admit, why would I?"

"Haven't you any patriotism?"

"It is variable. I take off my hat when our flag goes by—heraldic eyesore though it is."

"For friendship?"

"From what I've seen of the world the worst thing that can happen to friendship is to put a price on it."

"Frank, you're making me beg. All right, damn it, I'll beg.— Will you?"

Never in his life, which had not been sparing of discomfort, had Francis been so cornered. Ross looked so wretched, so beaten, and so beautiful in his wretchedness. In the biblical phrase, his bowels yearned toward Ross. But his compassion was not the whole of Francis's complex of emotions. The more money he had, the more he loved money. And—he couldn't explain it but he felt it—having relinquished his work as an artist, so much of what was deepest in him was now caught up with possessions, and therefore with money. To give a picture to the nation—very fine in the saying, and so dangerous in the doing. Be known as a benefactor and everybody wants something, often to sustain mediocrity. Yet—there was Ross, the last of his loves, and miserable. He had loved Ismay with his whole heart—and like a fool. He had loved Ruth like a man, and Ruth had died with hundreds of thousands of others, a victim of the world's cruel stupidity. He loved Ross, not because he wanted Ross physically, but for his daring youth, which the years had not touched, for his defiance of conventions that Francis knew had kept himself in chains, had made him the sustainer of a failing estate and the supporter of a child who was not his own, had held him back from claiming a great painting as his work. Yes, he must yield, whatever the hurt to his purse, which was now almost his soul. Almost; not wholly.

And so Francis was about to say yes, and would have done if Ross had been able to hold his tongue. But his fatal urge toward speech stepped between Ross and his success.

"The gift could be anonymous, you know."

"Of course. I would insist on that."

"Then you agree.—Frank, I love you!"

The words startled Francis more than any blow. Oh God, this was putting a price on friendship, and no doubt about it!

"I haven't agreed yet."

"Oh yes you have! Frank, this will put everything right! Now, about price—let me get in touch with Prince Max tomorrow!"

"Prince Max?"

"Yes. Even you, drinker of cheap schlock though you are, must know about Prince Max, head of the great Maximilian wine-importers in New York? He's acting on behalf of his wife. She was Amalie von Ingelheim and she inherited the whole collection from the old Gräfin."

"Amalie von Ingelheim. I didn't know she'd married Max! I know her—knew her."

"Yes, she remembers you. Calls you Le Beau Ténébreux. Said you taught her to play skat when she was a kid."

"Why is she selling?"

"Because she's a girl with a head on her shoulders. She and Max are a thriving pair of aristocratic survivors. They even look alike, though he must be a good deal older than she is. She's had a good career already as a model, but you know those careers don't run much more than eighteen months. She's been on the covers of the two biggest fashion magazines, and there's no place else to go. She and Prince Max are buying a cosmetic business— a really good one—and she'll make herself a hugely rich, international beauty."

"And the pictures?"

"She says she never gave a damn about the pictures."

"So? Little Amalie has certainly grown up—in a way."

"Yes, but she's not without heart. She'll listen to reason. And if I tell her you are the buyer, everything will work out well. That's to say, as cheaply as we have any right to expect—from aristocratic survivors. The picture could be here and in the Gallery before Christmas. What a gift to the nation!"

"There are six pictures, I believe. I've never seen any report that said which pictures. I can guess which ones might make a big price in the market. Is it the little Raphael?"

"No, not that one."

"The Bronzino portrait?"

"No. Nor the Grunewald. Since the row here other buyers have appeared and five are gone. But she's holding the one I want."

Ruth had told Francis he had plenty of intuition. It had been slow in acting, but it worked now with full force.

"Which picture?"

"Not the greatest name, but the very picture we need, because it has mystery, you see, and historical importance, and it's virtually unique because only one other picture from the same hand is known to exist. It's a picture that I dearly love, because it did more than anything else to establish me in my present place as an expert. You've seen it! A prize! *The Marriage at Cana*, by the so-called Alchemical Master!"

Intuition was now working furiously. "Why has she kept it? Aylwin, did you tell her you might still be able to arrange to buy it?"

"I may have dropped a hint to Max. You know how one talks in these deals."

"Did you hint that I might put up the money?"

"Certainly your name came into it. And as you're an old friend they have agreed to hold it for a month or so."

"In other words, you have once again spent some money that you didn't have assured. My money."

"Come on, Frank, you know what these situations are like. Don't talk like a banker."

"I won't buy it."

"Frank—listen—I simply did what had to be done. Buying art on this level is extremely sensitive business. When I had Max and Amalie in the right mood I had to move quickly. You'll see it all quite differently tomorrow."

"No, I won't. I will never buy that picture."

"But why? Is it the money? Oh, Frank, don't say it's the money!"

"No, I give you my word it isn't the money."

"Then why?"

"I have personal reasons that I can't explain. The Raphael, the Bronzino, two or three others—yes, I would have done it for you. But not *The Marriage at Cana.*"

"Why, why, why! You've got to tell me. You owe it to me to tell me!"

"Anything I owed you, Aylwin, has been paid in full with six excellent modern paintings. I won't buy that picture, and that's flat."

"You shit, Frank!"

"Oh come, I should have thought that under these circumstances you could have found a quotation from Ben Jonson."

"All right 'Turd in your teeth'."

"Pretty good. Nothing else?"

" 'May dogs defile thy walls,

And wasps and hornets breed beneath thy roof,

This seat of falsehood and this cave of cozenage!' "

And Ross flung out of the room. To Francis it seemed that he was laughing at his own apt quotation, but in truth he was weeping. The two grimaces are not so far apart.

Francis washed his hands and retired to the narrow space he had kept for his bed. Before he went to sleep he looked long at a picture that puzzled those of his friends who had seen it, and that still hung over his bed's head. It was not a great picture. It was a cheapish print of *Love Locked Out* and to him at present it was more poignant than any of his heaped-up masterworks.

OF COURSE FRANCIS *did the only possible thing. He couldn't under any circumstances have allowed the friend he loved to be taken in by a picture he knew to be a fake, and his own fake at that, to place it in the principal gallery of the country to which they were both supposed to owe their first allegiance, said the Lesser Zadkiel.*

—*I disagree totally, said the Daimon Maimas. He could certainly have done it, and what he called his Mercurius influence—myself, really—urged him to do it. I reminded him of what Letztpfenning had said: What is being sold, a great picture or the magic of the past? Is it a work of grave beauty that is being purchased; or such a work given its real worth by the seal of four centuries? I was disgusted with Francis. Indeed, I nearly deserted him at that instant.*

—*Can you do that?*

—*You know I can. And when a man's daimon leaves him, he is finished. You remember that when Mark Antony was playing the fool with that Egyptian woman his daimon left him in disgust. That was because of a stupid love, as well.*

—*Francis's love for Ross was not stupid, brother. I thought it had a flavour of nobility, because it asked nothing.*

—*It made him betray what was best of himself.*

—*Questionable, brother. Love, or worldly gratification? Love, or vanity? Love, or a wry joke on the world of art that seemed to have no place for him? If poor Darcourt, who longs to know the truth about Francis, knew what we know, he would rank Francis very high.*

—*Darcourt is a Christian priest, and Christianity cost Francis dear. It gave him that double conscience we have seen plaguing him throughout his life. Darcourt would have said he did the right thing. I do not.*

—*Yet you did not reject him.*

—*I was disgusted with him. I hate to leave a job uncompleted. I was told to make Francis a great man, and he went directly contrary to my urging.*

—*Perhaps he was indeed a great man.*

—*Not the great man I would have made.*

—*You are not the final judge, brother.*

—*Nor was I wholly defeated, brother. Greatness is achieved in more than one way. Watch what follows.*

THE SUICIDE OF AYLWIN ROSS caused the usual curiosity, the flow of easy pity, the satisfaction at having been witness at second hand to something that newspapers describe as a tragedy, in the public at large. The world of connoisseurship mourned him as a fine talent brought untimely to an end. In Canada it was assumed that he had been unable to bear public disgrace, and there were expressions of regret, mingling guilt with covert contempt that a man had broken under stress, when he should have taken his medicine like a little soldier. There was some speculation of the easy psychological kind that he had killed himself in order to make his enemies and detractors feel cheap, and although some of them did feel cheap they were angry with themselves for having been manipulated in such a way. In Parliament the Minister spoke briefly of Ross as a man who had meant well, but who was not a realist in public affairs; nevertheless, the Honourable Members were charged to think of him as a great Canadian. And the Honourable Members, who are accustomed to such work, obediently did so for a full minute. A memorial service was mounted at the National Gallery and the dead savant was accorded the usual public honours: poetry was spoken, some Bach was played, and the Deputy Minister read a carefully worded tribute, written by a minor poet from the pool of governmental speech-writers; it said many splendid things, but admitted nothing. It enjoined the National Gallery staff, and the nation, never to forget Aylwin Ross in its upward journey toward prudent, economical greatness.

As for Francis, who had suffered no nervous breakdown when Ruth was killed, he allowed himself such a collapse of the spirit now, and he toughed it out by himself in his cave of cozenage, living on beer and baked beans, cold from the can. Perhaps because he sought no professional help in dealing with his misery, he was as much himself in a few weeks as he would ever be again.

HIS FINAL YEARS were productive, in their way, and he had his satisfactions. These were years when it was fashionable to speak of the Century of the Common Man, but Francis saw little real evidence that it was so, and as he remembered his years at Carlyle Rural, spent with the Common Child, he was neither surprised nor regretful. People who met him casually thought him a misanthrope, but he had friends, drawn chiefly from the academic community. Extensive and curious knowledge of European life during the few centuries that most appealed to him established a kinship between Francis and Professor Clement Hollier, who sought historical truths in what many historians chose to overlook. Professor the Reverend Simon Darcourt (the splendour of his title amused Francis) became a great friend because he and Francis were fellow enthusiasts for rare books, manuscripts, old calligraphy, caricatures, and a ragbag of half a dozen other things about which he was not always deeply informed, but that came within the net of his swelling collections. It was Darcourt who revived Francis's sleeping love of music—better music than had ever been known to Mary-Ben—and they were often seen at concerts together.

There were evenings when these cronies gathered in the Old Curiosity Shop and while Hollier sat almost silent, Francis listened as Darcourt poured out a stream of lively, amusing, endearing talk, like wine bubbling out of the bottles that Darcourt always remembered to bring, for Francis was tight about hospitality. It amused him that Darcourt, something of a connoisseur, favoured vintages that bore the distinguished label of Prince Max on which the motto "Thou shalt perish ere I perish" was of course assumed to refer to the wine.

Another friend, not so close but valued, was Professor Urquhart McVarish, whose appeal to Francis (though McVarish never guessed it) was that in him there was something of the Mercurial spirit he felt so strongly in himself, though he kept it hidden, whereas McVarish let it rip, and boasted, and lied and cheated, with a vigour Francis found amusing and refreshing. It was Darcourt who persuaded Francis to read the works of Ben Jonson in a fine First Folio, and because of that Francis often addressed McVarish as Sir Epicure Mammon—a reference McVarish never troubled to check, and assumed to be complimentary. Indeed, in Jonson Francis discovered a spirit he would never have divined from the carefully chosen quotations of Aylwin Ross—a spirit apparently harsh, but inwardly tender, much like Francis himself.

McVarish had the Mercurial trait of thievery, as well; his method was the tried-and-true one of borrowing something which somehow he never remembered to return, and after the disappearance of a valued old gramophone record—Sir Harry Lauder singing "Stop Your Tickling, Jock"—Francis had to take care that only lesser objects got out of his hands to this merry, amoral Scot. But McVarish never felt the need to do anything in return for what arose from his friendship with Francis. It was Hollier and Darcourt who contrived to have Francis elected an honorary member of the Senior Common Room at the College of St. John and the Holy Ghost in the University of Toronto—Francis's old college, affectionately known as Spook. This was the reason why Francis put Spook down for a handsome inheritance in his will—the will that he now delighted to revise, daub with codicils, and play with.

The will cost him much thought, and some anxiety. He had the document acknowledging that what he had done about Little Charlie was all that the child could expect; but he prudently, though not very agreeably, had his London lawyers secure a document from Ismay, who was still pursuing The Workers' Cause in the Midlands, guaranteeing that Little Charlie was not the child of his loins, and that neither Ismay nor Little Charlie could make any claim on his estate. This was not easy, because Ismay was still in law his wife, but Francis provided his lawyers with the names of one or two members of the profession who knew a good deal about Ismay, and could make things uncomfortable for her if she did not toe the line.

He was still enough of a McRory to feel that he must remember relatives in his will, and he arranged bequests—mean, in the light of his great wealth—to Larry and Michael. Something better, but by no means lavish, was left to his nephew Arthur, son of his brother Arthur. Now and then Francis felt some guilt about this young Arthur, some stirring of a parental instinct that was never really strong. But what has a man in his sixties to say to a boy? Francis had an un-evolved Canadian idea that an uncle ought to teach a boy to shoot, or fish, or make a wigwam out of birch bark, and such ideas filled him with dismay. The notion that the boy could be interested in art never entered his head. So to Arthur he remained a taciturn, rather smelly, un-Cornish old party who turned up now and then at family affairs, and who was always good at Christmas and birthdays for a handsome money gift. But although Francis was convinced that a boy must necessarily be interested only in what he himself thought of as boyish things, he saw a glint in Arthur's eye which persuaded him, as the years passed and the boy became a man and an innovative, imaginative figure in the Cornish Trust, to name Arthur as his executor. With his three cronies, of course, to guide the supposedly Philistine young man in the disposal of his now unwieldy accumulation of art. For a collection it could no longer be called.

Once a week, if he remembered, he visited his mother, now in her mid-eighties, beautiful and frail, and with all her wits, if she chose to use them. They were both old people and it was possible for Francis to admit that he had never been on close terms with her, but that now he was past the obligatory, unquestioning love that had been required of him earlier, he quite liked her. She had once taken refuge in her useful vagueness when he asked about the first Francis, whom he still thought of as the Looner, but he thought he might sound her out about those flirtations, which had so embarrassed him as a boy, and which his father had brushed aside as insignificant.

"Mother, you have never told me anything about your youth. Were you and Father very much in love?"

"Franko, what an odd question! No: I wouldn't say we were much in love, but he understood me wonderfully, and we were the greatest friends."

"But were you never in love?"

"Oh—dozens of times. But I never took it very seriously, you know. How can one? It's such a troublesome feeling if you let it go too far. I knew lots of men, but I never gave your father cause for anxiety. He was always Number One, and he knew it. He was rather a strange man, you know. He rode his life on a very easy rein."

"I'm awfully glad to hear that."

"Once, before your father came along, I was desperately in love, the way young girls are. He was the most beautiful man I have ever seen. Beauty is such a disturbing thing, isn't it? I was so young, and he was an actor, and I never met him—only saw him on the stage, but that was the love that really hurt."

"There were a lot of very handsome actors then. It was the fashion. Do you remember which one he was?"

"Oh, indeed I do. I think I've got a picture postcard of him somewhere still, in a play called *Monsieur Beaucaire*. His name was Lewis Waller. What a perfect man!"

So much, then, for Dr. J.A. and his scientific malice about an unspecified taint. This cool, ancient, beautiful flirt had loved once, and with abandonment, and the fruit of that passion was the Looner!

What a punishment! What a slap in the face for a Catholic girl from the God she had been taught to worship! No wonder she had put all passion from her, and had become, like Venus in the Bronzino *Allegory*, someone to whom love was a toy. Francis thought a great deal about it, and formed some highly philosophical conclusions. They were utterly mistaken, of course, because he knew nothing of the well-intentioned, maternally solicitous meddlings of Marie-Louise. Nobody ever knows the whole of anything. But if he had known, his compassion would doubtless have extended to his grandmother, as it now embraced more fully than ever before his mother, Zadok Hoyle, and that poor wretch, the Looner.

THUS IT WAS that when Francis came to die, he had pretty well made up his accounts with all the principal figures in his life, and although he seemed to the world, and even to his few close friends, an eccentric and crabbed spirit, there was a quality of completeness about him that bound those friends tighter than would have been the case if he had been filled with one-sided, know-nothing sweetness and easy acceptance.

The end of his life, though not of his fame, came on a September night, following a Sunday that had been close and humid as Toronto often is in September. As it was his birthday he had made himself go out to dinner, although he was not hungry, and afterward he lay on a sofa in the Old Curiosity Shop, hoping that a breeze from the window would help him to breathe more easily. The sofa had been Saraceni's, and it was beautiful, but it was not well suited to lying; it was for some reclining beauty of the early nineteenth century, who saw herself in the image of Madame Récamier. But Francis could not make himself go to bed, and so when he felt the first shock of his quietus he was fully clothed, and in a position that was neither sitting nor lying. And after that shock, he knew he could not move.

Indeed, he knew he would never move again.

So this was it? Death, whom he had seen so often represented in art, usually as a figure of cruel menace, was there in the Old Curiosity Shop, and Francis was surprised to understand that he had no fear, though his breathing was now laborious and increasingly so. Well, one had always understood that there must be some struggle.

His vision was clouding, but his mind was clear; uncommonly clear. The reflection drifted through his consciousness that this was very different from what Ross must have felt, dying of a surfeit of sleeping-pills washed down with gin. How different was it from the last hours of Ruth? Who could say what that burned body enveloped of an active, certainly courageous and wise mind? But death, though people prate about its universality, is doubtless individual in the way it comes to everyone.

His feeling was going, but another sort of feeling was taking its place. Was this the famous cliché of all one's life passing before one's eyes that drowning men are supposed to experience? It was not all of his life. Rather it was a sense of the completeness of his life, and an understanding—oh, this was luck, this was mercy!—of the fact that his life had not been such a formless muddle, not quite such a rum start, as he had come to believe. He was humble in the recognition that he had not done too badly, and that even things that he had often wished otherwise—the crushing of the wretched Letztpfennig, for instance—were part of a pattern not of his making, and the fulfilling of a destiny that was surely as much Letztpfennig's as it was his own. Even his denial of Ross, which he had so often looked back on as a denial of love itself—death to the soul!—had been brought about as much by Ross as by any fault in himself. Ross was dear, as dear as Ruth, in another way, but something else was dearer and had to be protected. That was his one masterwork, *The Marriage at Cana*, now in a position of honour in a great gallery in the States, gloated over by lovers of art and by countless students who had university degrees in Fine Art, guaranteeing the infallibility of their knowledge and taste. If that bomb ever exploded, it would not explode in Canada, and ruin a friend.

No: that was hypocrisy, and he had no time now for hypocrisy. Surely Death had given a hint of His coming a week ago when he had carefully bundled up the preliminary studies, and those he had done after the fact, for *The Marriage at Cana*, and labelled them in careful Italic "My Drawings in Old Master style, for the National Gallery". Some day, somebody would tumble to it.

Discover who The Alchemical Master had been—that was a certainty and it would give the wiseacres a great deal to chatter about, anatomize, and discuss in articles and even books. Lives would be written of The Alchemical Master, but would they ever come close to the truth, or even the facts? In the picture in which, Saraceni had said, he had made up his soul, both as it had been and as it was yet to be, the figure of Love was indeed the two figures at the very centre, but it was love of the ideal wholeness that was shown there, and not the real loves of his life. Would they read his allegory, as he had once read the great allegory of Bronzino? In that picture, so dear to him, Time and his daughter Truth were unveiling the spectacle of what love was, as some day Time and Truth would unveil *The Marriage at Cana*. And when that day came there would be, to begin with, a great deal of harsh talk about deceit and fakery. But had not Bronzino said much that was relevant about deceit and fakery in the wonderfully painted figure of Fraude, the sweet-faced girl offering the honeycomb and the scorpion, whose lower parts were depicted as the chthonic dragon's claws and swingeing serpent tail? This was Fraude not simply as a cheat, but as a figure from the deep world of the Mothers, whence came all beauty, and also all that was fearful to timid souls seeking only the light, and determined that Love must be solely a thing of light. How lucky he was to have known Fraude, and to have tasted her enlarging, poisoned kiss! Had he, at the end, found the allegory of his own life? Oh, blessing on the angel in *The Marriage at Cana* who declared, so mysteriously, "Thou hast kept the best wine till the last."

Francis was laughing now, but laughter was such an effort that there came another shock, and he dropped deeper into the gulf that was enclosing him.

Where was this? unknown, yet familiar, more the true abode of his spirit than he had ever known before; a place never visited, but from which intimations had come that were the most precious gifts of his life.

It must be—it was—the Realm of the Mothers. How lucky he was, at the last, to taste this transporting wine!

After that, nothing, for to any outward observer it would have seemed that Francis had stood on the threshold of death some time before, and now he had taken the last step.

SO YOU STOOD BY HIM to the end, brother, said the Lesser Zadkiel.

—The end is not yet. Though he had sometimes defied me, I obey my orders still, said the Daimon Maimas.

—Your orders were to make him a great, or at least a remarkable man?

—Yes, and posthumously he will be seen as both great and remarkable. Oh, he was a great man, my Francis. He didn't die stupid.

—You had your work cut out for you.

—It is always so. People are such muddlers and meddlers. Father Devlin and Aunt Mary-Ben with their drippings of holy water, and their single-barrelled compassion. Victoria Cameron with her terrible stoicism masked as religion. That Doctor with his shallow science. All ignorant people determined that their notions were absolutes.

—Yet I suppose you would say they were bred in the bone.

—They! How can you talk so, brother? Of course, we know that it is all metaphor,.you and I. Indeed, we are metaphors ourselves. But the metaphors that shaped the life of Francis Cornish were Saturn, the resolute, and Mercury, the maker, the humorist, the trickster. It

*was my task to see that these, the Great Ones, were bred in the bone,
and came out in the flesh. And my task is not yet finished.*

"I'VE BEEN THINKING."

Arthur had returned from his two-day absence, and, having
eaten grapefruit, porridge with cream, and bacon and eggs, had
now moved into the coda of his usual breakfast and was busy with
toast and marmalade.

"I'm not at all surprised. You think quite often. What now?"
said Maria.

"That life of Uncle Frank. I was wrong. We'd better tell Simon
to go ahead."

"No more worry about possible scandal?"

"No. Suppose a few drawings turn up at the National Gallery
that look like Old Masters but are really by Uncle Frank? That
doesn't make him a faker. He was an art student once, in the
days when a lot of them copied Old Master drawings and even
drew that way themselves, just to find out how it was done. Not
faking at all. The Gallery people will spot them at once, though
of course Darcourt mightn't. Nothing will come of it, you mark
my words. Simon's a literary type, not an art critic. So let's give
him the go-ahead, and get on with the real work of the Foundation. We ought to get some applications soon from needy geniuses."

"I have a few on my desk already."

"You call Simon, darling, and tell him I'm sorry I was arbitrary.
Could he come in tonight? We could look at your letters and get
on with the real job. Being patrons."

"The modern Medici?"

"No immodesty, please. But it should be sport."

"Blow your whistle, Arthur, and let the sport begin."

The Lyre of Orpheus

"The lyre of Orpheus opens the door
of the underworld."

E. T. A. HOFFMAN

ONE

A RTHUR, WHO HAD A MASTERLY WAY with meetings, was
gathering this one together for a conclusion.

"Are we agreed that the proposal is crack-brained, absurd,
could prove incalculably expensive, and violates every dictate of
financial prudence? We have all said in our different ways that
nobody in his right mind would want anything to do with it.
Considering the principles to which the Cornish Foundation is
committed, are these not all excellent reasons why we should
accept the proposal, and the extension of it we have been discussing, and go ahead?"

He really has musical flair, thought Darcourt. He treats every
meeting symphonically. The theme is announced, developed in
major and minor, pulled about, teased, chased up and down dark
alleys, and then, when we are getting tired of it, he whips us up
into a lively finale and with a few crashing chords brings us to a
vote.

There are people who cannot bear to come to an end. Hollier
wanted more discussion.

"Even if, by a wild chance, it succeeded, what would be the
good of it?" he said.

"You have missed my point," said Arthur.

"I am simply speaking as a responsible member of the Cornish
Foundation."

"But my dear Clem, I am urging you to speak as a member of
a special sort of foundation with unusual aims. I am asking you
to use your imagination, which is not what foundations like to
do. I am asking you to take a flyer at an extreme outside chance,

with the possibility of unusual gains. You don't have to pretend to be a business man. Be what you are—a daring professor of history."

"I suppose if you put it like that—"

"I do put it like that."

"But I still think my question is a good one. Why should we present the world with another opera? There are lots of operas already, and people busily writing them in every square mile of the civilized world."

"Because this would be a very special opera."

"Why? Because the composer died before he had gone very far with it? Because this girl Schnak-whatever-it-is wants to get a doctorate in music by completing it? I don't see what's special about that."

"That's reducing the whole plan to the obvious."

"That's leaving out the heart of it. That's forgetting our proposal to mount the finished opera and offer it to the public," said Geraint Powell, a theatre man with a career to make, who already looked on himself as the person to get the opera on the stage.

"I think we should bear in mind the very high opinion of Miss Schnakenburg that is expressed by all her supporters. They hint at genius and we are looking for genius, aren't we?" said Darcourt.

"Yes, but do we want to get into show business?" said Hollier.

"Why not?" said Arthur. "Let me say it again: we have set up the Cornish Foundation with money left by a man who was a great connoisseur, who took all kinds of chances, and we have to decide what sort of foundation it is to be. And we've done that. It's a foundation for the promotion of the arts and humane scholarship, and this plan is both art and scholarship. But haven't we agreed that we don't want another foundation that gives money to good, safe projects, and then stands aside, hoping for good, safe results? Caution and non-intervention are the arthritis of patronage. Let's back our choices and stir the pot and raise some hell. We've already made our obeisance to safety; we've established our good, dull credentials by getting Simon here to write a biography of our founder and benefactor—"

"Thank you, Arthur. Oh, many, many thanks. This estimate of my work is more encouragement than I can accept without blushes." Simon Darcourt knew too well that the biographical job was not as easy as Arthur seemed to think, and was strongly aware also that he had not so far asked for or received a penny for the work he had done. Simon, like many literary men, was no stranger to feelings of grievance.

"Sorry, Simon, but you know what I mean."

"I know what you think you mean," said Darcourt, "but the book may not be quite such a dud as you imagne."

"I hope not. But what I am getting at is that the book may cost a few thousands, and, without being by any means the richest foundation in the country, we have quite a lot of money to dispose of. I want to do something with a bit of flash."

"It's your money," said Hollier, still determined to be the voice of caution, "and I suppose you can do as you please."

"No, no, no, and again no. It isn't my money; it's Foundation money and we are all directors of the Foundation—you Clem, and you Simon, and you Geraint, and, of course, Maria. I am simply the chairman, first among equals, because we have to have a chairman. Can't I persuade you? Do you really want to be safe and dull? Who votes for safety and dullness? Let's have a show of hands."

There were no votes for safety and dullness. But Hollier had a sense of having been pushed aside by totally unfair rhetoric. Geraint Powell didn't like meetings and wished this one to be over. Darcourt felt he had been snubbed. Maria knew well how right Hollier was and that the money was really Arthur's money, in spite of all legal fictions. She knew that it most certainly wasn't her money, even though, as Arthur's wife, she might be supposed to have some extra pull. She had not been married very long, and she loved Arthur dearly, but she knew that Arthur could be a great bully when he wanted something, and he wanted passionately to be a vaunting, imaginative, daring patron. He is a bully just as I suppose King Arthur was a bully when he insisted to the Knights of the Round Table that he was no more than the first among equals, she thought.

"Are we agreed, then?" said Arthur. "Simon, would you draw up a resolution? It doesn't have to be a final form; we can tidy it up later. Have you all got drinks? Isn't anybody going to eat anything? Help yourselves from the Platter of Plenty."

The Platter of Plenty was a joke, and, as jokes will, it had become a little too familiar. It was a large silver epergne that stood in the middle of the round table at which they sat. From a central, richly ornamented pedestal it extended curving arms at the end of which were little plates of dried fruits and nuts and sweets. A hideous object, thought Maria, unjustly, for it was a fine thing of its kind. It had been a wedding gift to Arthur and herself from Darcourt and Hollier and she hated it because she knew it must have cost them a great deal more than she supposed they could afford. She hated it because it seemed to her to embody much of what she disliked about her marriage—needless luxury, an assumption of a superiority based on wealth, a sort of grandiose uselessness. Her passionate desire, after making Arthur happy, was to gain a reputation for herself as a scholar, and big money and big scholarship still seemed to her to be irreconcilable. But she was Arthur's wife, and as nobody else took anything from the epergne she took a couple of nuts, for the look of the thing.

As Darcourt worked over the resolution, the directors chatted, not altogether amicably. Arthur was flushed, and Maria was aware that he was speaking rather thickly. It couldn't be that he had drunk too much. He never did that. He had taken a chocolate from the Platter of Plenty, but it seemed to have a bad taste, and he spat it into his handkerchief.

"Will this do?" said Darcourt. " 'It was resolved that the meeting should comply with the request made jointly by the Graduate Department of the Faculty of Music and Miss Hulda Schnakenburg for support to enable Miss Schnakenburg to flesh out and complete the manuscript notes now reposing in the Graduate Library (among the musical MSS left in the bequest of the late Francis Cornish) of an opera left incomplete at his death in 1822 by Ernst Theodor Amadeus Hoffmann, the work to be done in a manner congruous with the operatic conventions of Hoffmann's day and for such an orchestra as he would have known; this to be done as a musicological exercise in partial fulfilment of the requirements of Miss Schnakenburg's attainment of the degree of Doctor of Music. It was further resolved that if the work proved satisfactory the opera should be mounted and presented in public performance under Hoffmann's title of *Arthur of Britain*. This part of the proposal has not yet been communicated to the Faculty of Music or Miss Schnakenburg.' "

"It'll be a nice surprise for them," said Arthur, who took a sip of his drink, and then set it down, as if it were disagreeable.

"A surprise, no doubt," said Darcourt. "Whether a nice surprise is open to doubt. By the way, don't you think we ought to give the work its full title in the minutes?"

"Is there more than *Arthur of Britain?*" said Geraint.

"Yes. In the fashion of his day Hoffmann suggested a double title."

"I know the kind of thing," said Geraint; "*Arthur of Britain, or—something. What?*"

"*Arthur of Britain, or The Magnanimous Cuckold,*" said Darcourt.

"Indeed?" said Arthur. The bitterness in his mouth seemed to be troubling him. "Well, I don't suppose we need to use the full title if we don't need it."

Again he spat into his handkerchief, as unobtrusively as he could. but he need not have troubled, because at the announcement of the full title of the opera nobody was looking at him.

The three other directors of the Foundation were looking at Maria.

[2]

THE DAY AFTER THE MEETING, Simon Darcourt was interrupted, just as he sat down to his day's work, by a telephone call from Maria; Arthur was in hospital with mumps, which the doctors called parotitis. They had not told Maria what Darcourt knew; mumps in the adult male is not trivial, because it causes painful swelling of the testicles, and can do permanent damage. Arthur would be out of commission for some weeks, but he had mumbled to Maria through his swollen jaws that he wanted the work of the Foundation to go on as fast as possible, and she and Darcourt were to take care of it.

How like Arthur! He had in the highest degree the superior business man's ability to delegate responsibility without relinquishing significant power. Darcourt had known him since the death of his friend Francis Cornish; Francis's will had made Darcourt one of his executors, to act beneath the overriding authority of Francis's nephew Arthur, and it had been apparent at once that

Arthur was a born leader. Like many leaders he was rough at times, because he never thought about anyone's feelings, but there was nothing personal in it. He was Chairman of the Board of the huge Cornish Trust, and was admired and trusted by people who dealt in big money. But, apart from his business life, he was cultivated in a way not common among bankers; genuinely cultivated, that is to say, and not simply benevolent toward the arts as a corporation duty.

His rapid establishment of the Cornish Foundation, using his Uncle Frank's large fortune to do it, was proof of his intention. Arthur wanted to be a patron on a grand scale, for the fun and adventure. There could be no doubt that the Foundation was his. For the look of the thing he had set up a board to administer it, but whom had he invited to join it? Clement Hollier, because Maria had been his student and had a special affection for him. And what had Hollier proved to be? A great objector, a determined looker-on-the-other-hand whose reputation as a scholar in the realm of medieval history did little to mitigate his gloomy insufficiency as a human being. Geraint Powell was Arthur's own choice, reputedly a rising man in the theatre, with all the exuberance and charm of the breed, who backed up Arthur's most extravagant ideas with his Welsh superficiality. And Maria, Arthur's wife; dear Maria, whom Darcourt had loved, and loved still, perhaps the more poignantly because there was no longer the least danger that he would ever have to play the full role of a lover, but could slave for his lady in a condition of mild romantic dejection.

These were Darcourt's estimates of his colleagues on the Foundation. What did he think about himself?

To the world he knew he was the Reverend Simon Darcourt, a professor of Greek, much respected as a scholar and teacher; he was the Vice-Warden of Ploughwright College, an institution for advanced studies within the university; there were people who thought him a wise and genial companion. But Arthur called him the Abbé Darcourt.

What is an abbé? Was it not a title used for several centuries to describe a clergyman who was really an educated upper servant? Your abbé ate at your table, but had a small room off your palace library where he slaved away as a confidential secretary, intermediary, and fixer. Abbés on the stage or in novels were great fellows for intrigue and amusing the ladies. It is a category of society that has disappeared from the modern world under that name, but the world is still in need of abbés, and Darcourt felt himself to be one of them, but was not pleased that Arthur had put his finger on the matter so plainly.

It is to be presumed that abbés in an earlier day had salaries. Darcourt's canker was that he received no salary from the Foundation, although he was its secretary and, as he put it to himself, worked like a dog on its behalf. Nevertheless, as he received no salary, he felt that his independence was secure. Independent as a hog on ice, he thought, in one of the Old Loyalist Ontario expressions which popped up, unbidden, in his mind when least expected. But if his university work were not to suffer, he had to slave away day and night, and he was a man to whom a certain amount of ease and creative lassitude is a necessity.

Creative lassitude, not to doze and dream but to get matters arranged in his head in the best order. This life of Francis Cornish, for instance; it was enough to drive a man mad. He had accumulated a mass of detail; he had passed an expensive summer in Europe, finding out what he could about Francis Cornish's life in England, where it appeared he had been something-or-other in the Secret Service, about which the Secret Service maintained a blandly closed mouth. Francis had, of course, played an important part in the work of restoring looted works of art to their original owners, in so far as that could be done. But there had been something else, and Darcourt could not find out what it was. Before the Second World War Francis had been up to something in Bavaria which sounded fishier and fishier the more Darcourt dug into it, but the fish could not be hooked. There was a huge hole, amounting to about ten years, in the life of Francis Cornish, and somehow Darcourt had to fill that hole. There was a lead, possibly a valuable one, in New York, but when was he to find time to go there, and who would foot the bill? He was tired of spending what were to him large sums of money to get material for a book that Arthur treated as a matter of small consequence. Darcourt was determined that the book should be as good and as full as it was in his power to make it, but after a year of investigation he felt thoroughly ill-used.

Why did he not simply state his case and say that he had to be paid for his services, and that the writing of the book was costing him more money than he could ever expect to recover from it? Because that was not the light in which he wished to appear to Maria.

He was a fool, he knew, and rather a feeble fool, at that. It is no comfort to a man to think of himself as a feeble fool, secretary to a dummy board of directors, and burdened with an exhausting task.

And now Arthur had mumps, had he? Christian charity required that Darcourt should be properly regretful, but the Old Harry, never totally subdued in him, made him smile as he thought that Arthur's balls were going to swell to the size of grapefruit, and hurt like the devil.

The day's work called imperiously. After he had done some college administration, interviewed a student who had "personal problems" (about a girl, of course), taken a seminar in New Testament Greek, and eaten a sufficient but uninteresting college lunch, Darcourt made his way to the building where the Graduate Faculty of Music existed in what looked, to the rest of the university, like unseemly luxury.

The Dean's office was handsome, in the modern manner. It was on a corner of the building and two walls were entirely of glass, which the architect had meant to give the Dean a refreshing prospect of the park outside, but, as it also gave passing students a splendid view of the Dean at work, or perhaps in creative lassitude, he had found it necessary to curtain the windows with heavy net so that the office was rather dim. It was a large room, and the decanal desk was diminished by the piano and the harpsichord—the Dean was an expert on baroque music—and the engravings of eighteenth-century musicians that hung on the walls.

Dean Wintersen was pleased that money would be forthcoming to support the research work and reasonable living expenses of Miss Hulda Schnakenburg. He became confidential.

"I hope this solves more than one problem," said he. "This girl—I'd better call her Schnak because everybody does and it's what she seems to like—is greatly gifted. The most gifted student, I would say, that we've ever had in my time or in the memory of anybody in the faculty. We get lots of people here who will do very well as performers, and a few of them may go to the top. Schnak is something rarer; she may be a composer of real gift. But the way she is going now could land her in a mess, and perhaps finish her!"

"Eccentricity of genius?" said Darcourt.

"Not if you're thinking of picturesque behaviour and great spillings of soul. There is nothing picturesque about Schnak. She is the squalidest, rudest, most offensive little brat I have ever met as Dean, and I've dealt with some lulus, let me tell you. As for soul, I think she would strike you if you used the word."

"What ails her?"

"I don't know. Whoever does know? Background the essence of mediocrity. Parents utterly commonplace. Father a watch-repairer for one of the big jewellery stores. A dull, grey fellow who seems to have been born with a magnifying-glass in his eye. Mother a sad zero. The only thing that singles them out at all is that they are members of some ultra-conservative Lutheran group, and they never stop saying that they have given the girl a good, Christian upbringing. And what have they brought up? A failed anorexic who never washes her hair or anything else, snarls at her teachers, and habitually bites the hand that feeds her. But she has talent, and we think it is the real, big, enduring thing. Just now she's on the uttermost extreme thrust of all the new movements. The computer stuff and the aleatory stuff is old hat to Schnak."

"Then why does she want to do this work on the Hoffmann notes? That sounds like antiquarian stuff."

"That's what we all want to know. What makes Schnak want to fling herself back more than a hundred and fifty years to complete an unfinished work by a man we generally write off as a gifted amateur? Oh, Hoffmann had a few operas performed in his lifetime, but I'm told they are run-of-the-mill. In music he has a reputation as a critic; he praised Beethoven intelligently when nobody else did. Schumann thought a lot of him, and Berlioz despised him, which was a kind of inverted praise. He inspired a lot of far better talents. A literary man, I suppose one would say."

"Is that a bad thing to be? Mind you, I only know him through that opera—you know, Offenbach's *Les Contes d'Hoffmann*. It's a Frenchified version of three of his stories."

"Odd that it's another unfinished work; Guiraud pulled Offenbach's score together after his death. Not a favourite of mine."

"You're the expert, of course. As a mere happy opera-goer I like it very much, though it's not often intelligently done; there's more in it than meets the eye of most opera directors."

"Well, the puzzle of why Schnak wants to take on this job can only be solved by her. But we on the faculty are pleased, because it fits nicely into musicological research and we'll be able to give her a doctorate for it. She'll need that. With her personality she needs every solid qualification she can get."

"Are you trying to coax her away from her ultra-modernity?"

"No, no; that's fine. But for a doctoral exercise something more readily measurable is better. This may steady her, and make her more human."

Darcourt thought this was the moment to tell the Dean about the Cornish Foundation's plan to present the revived and refreshed opera as a stage piece.

"Oh, my God! Do they really mean that?"

"They do."

"Have they any idea what it might mean? It could be such a flop as operatic history has never known—and that's saying a lot, as you probably know. I know she'll do a good job, but only so far as the material permits. I mean—cosmetic work on the orchestration, and reorganization and pulling-together and general surgery can only go so far. The Foundation, the Hoffmann basis, may not support anything the public could possibly want to see."

"The Foundation has voted to do it. I don't have to tell you that eccentricity isn't confined to artists; patrons can suffer from it too."

"You mean it's a bee in the bonnet."

"I've said nothing. As secretary of the Foundation I am just telling you what they intend. They know the risks, and they are still prepared to put a good deal of money into the project."

"They'll have to. Have they any idea what mounting a full-scale new opera, that nobody knows or has studied, could run to?"

"They're game for it. They leave it to you, of course, to see that Schnak delivers the goods—in so far as there are any goods to deliver."

"They're mad! But don't think I'm quarrelling with anybody's generosity. If this is what's in the cards, Schnak will need supervision on the highest level we can manage. A musicologist of great reputation. A composer of some distinction. A conductor who has wide experience of opera."

"Three supervisors?"

"Just one, if I can get the one I want. But with a lot of money I think I can coax her."

The Dean did not say who he meant.

[3]

THE WEEK AFTER ARTHUR FELL ILL, Maria could do no work at all.

Ordinarily she had much to keep her busy. Her marriage had temporarily interrupted her academic career, but she had once again taken up her thesis on Rabelais, though marriage made it seem less pressing—she would not say less important—than before. And she had a great deal to do on behalf of the Cornish Foundation. Darcourt thought he was overworked but Maria had her own burden. It was she who first read all the applications for assistance, and it was tedious work. The applicants seemed to want to do the same few things—write a book, publish a book, edit a manuscript, show their paintings, give a concert of music, or simply to have money to, as they always put it, "buy time" to do any of these things. Probably many of these requests were worthy, but they did not fit into Arthur's notion of the Cornish Foundation, and it was Maria who wrote polite personal notes advising the applicants to look elsewhere. Of course there were the visionaries, who wanted to dam and dredge the Thames to discover the foundations of Shakespeare's Globe Theatre; or who wanted to establish a full-scale *carillon de Flandres* in every provincial capital in Canada and endow the post of *carillonneur;* or who wanted to be supported while they painted a vast series of historical pictures showing that all the great military commanders had been men of less than average stature; or who yearned to release some dubiously identified wreck from the Arctic ice. These had to be discouraged firmly. Borderline cases, and they were many, she discussed with Darcourt. The few proposals that might appeal to Arthur were sifted from the mass, and circulated to all the members of the Round Table.

The Round Table was a joke Maria did not like. Of course the Foundation met at a circular table which was a handsome antique and had perhaps, two or three centuries ago, served as a rent-table in the workroom of some aristocrat's agent; it was the most convenient table for their purpose in the Cornishes' apartment. Geraint Powell insisted that, as Arthur presided over this table, it had some jokey association with the great British hero. Geraint knew a lot about the Arthurian legend, though Maria suspected that it was coloured by Geraint's lively fancy. It was he who insisted that Arthur's determination that the Foundation should take an unusual and intuitive path was truly Arthurian. He urged his fellow directors to "press into the forest wherever we saw it to be thickest" and would emphasize it by repeating, in what he said was Old French, *là où ils la voient plus expresse*. Maria did not like Geraint's theatrical exuberance. She was in flight from exuberance of another sort, and, like a real academic, she was wary of people outside the academic world—"laymen" they called them—who seemed to know a lot. Knowledge was for professionals of knowledge.

Sometimes Maria wondered if this administrative work was what she had married Arthur to do, but she dismissed the question as foolish. This was what came immediately to hand, and she would do it as what marriage seemed to require of her. Marriage is a game for adult players, and the rules in every marriage are different.

As the wife of a very rich man, she could have become "a society woman"—but what does that mean in a country like Canada? Social life in the old sense of calls, teas, dinners, weekends, or fancy-dress parties was utterly gone. The woman who has no gainful job devotes herself to good causes. There are plenty of dogsbody jobs associated with art and music which wealthy volunteers are graciously permitted to do by the professionals. There is the great Ladder of Compassion, on which the community arranges a variety of diseases in order of the social prestige they carry. The society woman slaves on behalf of the lame, the halt, and the blind, the cancerous, the paraplegic, those variously handicapped, and, of course, the great new enthusiasm, AIDS. There are also the sociologically pitiable: the battered wives, battered children, and the raped girls, who seem to be more numerous than ever before, or else their plight is more often revealed. The "society woman" shows herself concerned with society's problems, and patiently fights her way up the Ladder of Compassion through a net of committees, convenorships, vice-presidencies, presidencies, past presidencies, and government investigatory bodies. For some there waits, after years of work, a decoration in the Order of Canada. Now and again she and her husband eat an absurdly expensive dinner in the company of their peers, but not for pleasure; no, no, it is to raise money for some worthy cause, or for "research", which has the prestige that belonged, a century ago, to "foreign missions". The possession of wealth brings responsibilities; woe to the wealthy who seek to avoid them. It is all immensely worthy, but it is not much fun.

Maria had an honourable escape from this charitable treadmill. She was a scholar, engaged in research of her own, and thus she justified her seat in the social lifeboat. But with Arthur seriously ill she knew precisely what she had to do: she had to sustain Arthur in every way she could.

She visited Arthur as often and as long as the hospital would permit, chatting to a silent husband. He was very miserable, for the swelling was not only of his jaws; the doctors called it orchitis, and every day Maria lifted his sheets when the nurse was elsewhere, and grieved over the miserable swelling of his testicles, which gave him wretched pain in all the abdominal area. She had never seen him ill before, and his suffering made him dear to her in a new way. When she was not with him she thought about him too much to be able to do any other work.

The world is no respecter of such feelings, and one day she had a visit that troubled her greatly. As she sat in her handsome study—it was the first workroom she had ever had that was entirely her own, and she had made it perhaps a little too fine—her Portuguese housekeeper came to tell her that a man was anxious to speak with her.

"What about?"

"He won't say. He says you know him."

"Who is he, Nina?"

"The night porter. The one who sits in the lobby from five till midnight."

"If it's anything to do with the building, he should talk to Mr. Calder at the Cornish Trust offices."

"He says it's private."

"Damn. Well, show him in."

Maria did not know him when he appeared. Out of his porter's uniform he might have been anybody. He was a small, not very engaging person, with a shrinking air, and Maria disliked him on sight.

"Good of you to see me, Mrs. Cornish."

"I don't think I know your name."

"Wally. I'm Wally the night man."

"Wally what?"

"Crottel. Wally Crottel. The name won't mean anything to you."

"What did you want to see me about?"

"Well, I'll come right to it. You see, it's about m'dad's book."

"Has your father made an application to the Foundation about his book?"

"No. M'dad's dead. You knew him. You know the book. M'dad was John Parlabane."

John Parlabane, who had committed suicide more than a year ago, and had thereby hastened the courtship and marriage of Arthur Cornish. But when Maria looked at Crottel she could see nothing whatever of the stocky frame, the big head, the compelling look of malicious intelligence that had distinguished the late John Parlabane. Maria had known Parlabane far too well for her own comfort. Parlabane the runaway Anglican monk, the police spy, the drug-pusher, and parasite to the most disagreeable man she had ever known. Parlabane, who had intruded himself into her relations with her academic adviser and, as she had once hoped, lover, Clement Hollier. When Parlabane committed suicide, after having murdered his nasty master, Maria had thought she was rid of him forever, forgetting Hollier's repeated warning that nothing is finished until all is finished. Parlabane's book! This called for deep cunning, and Maria was not sure she had cunning of the right kind.

"I never heard that John Parlabane had any children."

"It's not widely known. Because of my ma, you see. For my ma's sake it was kept dark."

"Your mother was a Mrs. Crottel?"

"No, she was a Mrs. Whistlecraft. Wife of Ogden Whistlecraft, the great poet. You'll know the name. He's been dead for quite a while. I must say he was nice to me, considering he was not my real dad. But he didn't want me to have his name, you see. He didn't want any Whistlecrafts hanging around that weren't the genuine article. Not of the true seed, he used to say. So I was raised under my ma's maiden name, which was Crottel. I was supposed to be their nephew. An orphan nephew."

"And you think your father was Parlabane."

"Oh, I know that. My ma leaked it out. Before she passed away she told me Parlabane was the only man she'd ever had a first-class organism with. I hope you'll excuse me mentioning it but that's what she said. She became very liberated, you see, and talked a lot about the organism. Whistlecraft didn't seem to have the knack of the organism. Too much the poet, I guess."

"Yes, I see. But what was it you wanted to talk to me about?"

"The book. M'dad's book. The big important book he wrote that he left in your care when he passed away."

"John Parlabane left a mass of material to me and Professor Hollier. He left it with a letter when he killed himself."

"Yeah, but when he passed away he probably didn't know he had a natural heir. Me, you see."

"I'd better tell you at once, Mr. Crottel, that the typescript John Parlabane left was a very long, somewhat incoherent philosophical work which he had tried to give special interest by including some disguised biographical material. But he had no skill with fiction. Several people who would know about such things read it, or as much of it as they could, and said it was unpublishable."

"Because it was too raw, wasn't that it?"

"I don't think so. It was just incoherent and dull."

"Aw, now, lookit, Mrs. Cornish, m'dad was a very intelligent man. You're not going to tell me anything he wrote was dull."

"That's exactly what I am telling you."

"I heard there was some stuff in it about people high up— government people, some of them—in their youths, that they wouldn't want the public to know about."

"I don't remember anything like that."

"That's what you say. I don't want to be nasty, but maybe this is a cover-up. I heard a lot of publishers wanted it."

"Several publishers saw it, and decided they didn't want it."

"Too hot for them to handle, eh?"

"No. They simply didn't see any way of making a book of it."

"You got letters saying that?"

"Mr. Crottel, you are becoming very pressing. Now listen: the typescript of the book by the man you tell me, without showing me any evidence, was your father was left outright to Professor Hollier and me. And I have the letter that says so. We were to deal with it as we saw fit, and that is what we have done. That's all there is to it."

"I'd like to see that book."

"Impossible."

"Well then, I guess I'll have to take steps."

"What steps?"

"Legal. I've been mixed up with the law, you know, and I know my rights. I'm an heir. Your right may not be as strong as you think."

"Take it to law, then, if you feel you must. But if you hope to get anything out of that book, I can tell you you're in for a disappointment. I don't think we have anything more to say."

"Okay. Be like that if you want. But you'll be hearing from my legal man, Mrs. Cornish."

It looked as if Maria had won. Arthur always said that if someone threatened legal action the thing to do was to tell them to see what it would get them. Such talk, he said, was probably bluff.

But Maria was unhappy. When Simon Darcourt came to see her that evening she greeted him in a familiar phrase:

"Parlabane is back."

It was an echo of what a lot of people had said, with varying degrees of dismay, two years earlier, when John Parlabane, garbed in the robes of a monk, had returned to the university. Many people remembered him and many more were aware of his legend, as a brilliant student of philosophy who had, years ago, left the university under a cloud—the usual cloud, that old, familiar cloud—and had banged about the world making trouble of several ingenious kinds. He turned up at the College of St. John and the Holy Ghost (familiarly "Spook") as a runaway and renegade from the Society of the Sacred Mission, in England, and the Society showed no sign of wanting to get him back. Maria, Darcourt, and Hollier, and many others, hoped that his suicide about a year later—and the suicide note in which he confessed with glee to the murder of Professor Urquhart McVarish (monster of vanity and sexual weirdo)—had closed the chapter of Parlabane. Maria could not help reopening it with this theatrical flourish.

Darcourt was satisfactorily astonished and dismayed. When Maria explained, he looked a good deal better.

"The solution is simple," he said. "Give him the typescript of the book. You don't want it. Let him see what he can do with it."

"Can't be done."

"Why not?"

"I haven't got it."

"What did you do with it?"

"Threw it away."

Now Darcourt was really horrified.

"You *what?*" he roared.

"I thought it was done with. I put it down the garbage chute."

"Maria! And you call yourself a scholar! Haven't you learned rule number one of scholarship: *never, under any circumstances, throw anything away?*"

"What was the use of it?"

"You know the use of it now! You've delivered yourself, bound and gagged, into this man's hands. How can you prove the book was worthless?"

"If he goes to court, you mean? We can call some of those publishers who turned it down. They'll say what it was."

"Oh, yes; I can hear it now. 'Tell me, Mr. Ballantyne, when did you read the book?' 'Mmm? Oh, I don't read books myself. I turned it over to one of my editors.' 'Yes, and did your editor present you with a written report?' 'That wasn't necessary. She took a look and said it was hopeless. Just what I suspected. I took a quick peep into it myself, of course.' 'Very well, Mr. Ballantyne, you may stand down. You see, ladies and gentlemen of the jury, there is no evidence that the book was given serious professional attention. Are masterpieces of what is called *le roman philosophe* to be assessed in this casual way?'—That's the kind of thing, Maria, that you'll hear until every one of your publisher witnesses has trotted in and out of the witness-box. Crottel's lawyer can assert anything he likes about this book—a philosophical masterwork, a sulphurous exposure of sexual corruption in high places—anything at all. He will say that you and Clem Hollier were professionally jealous of Parlabane, and depreciated his talent for the trivial reason that he was a self-confessed murderer. The lawyer will positively sing to the harp about Genêt, the criminal genius, and tie him up in pink string with Parlabane. Maria, you have put your foot in it right up to the hip."

"You're not being very helpful, Simon. What do we do next?—Can't we get rid of Crottel? Fire him, perhaps?"

"Maria, you numbskull! Haven't you understood that under our splendidly comprehensive Charter of Rights it is practically impossible to fire anybody—particularly not if they are making your life a misery? Crottel's lawyers would crucify you.—Look, child, you need the best legal advice, and at once."

"Well, where do we get it?"

"Please don't talk about 'we' as if I were somehow involved in this mess."

"Aren't you my friend?"

"Being your friend is a very taxing experience."

"I see. A fair-weather friend."

"Stop being feminine. Of course I'm with you. But you must let me have my grievance. Do you think I haven't enough trouble with this bloody opera scheme of Arthur's? It's enough to drive me mad! Do you know what?"

"No. What?"

"We've gone ahead much too fast. We've undertaken to back Schnak—I haven't met Schnak but I hear ominous things about her—in putting this sketch for an opera together, and naturally I wanted to see what these Hoffmann papers consist of. It should have been done earlier, but Arthur has rushed ahead. So I had a look. And do you know what?"

"I wish you'd stop asking me if I know what. It's illiterate and unworthy of you, Simon. Oh, don't sulk, sweetie.—Well, what?"

"Only this. There's no libretto. Only a few words to suggest what ought to go with the music. That's what."

"So—?"

"So a libretto has to be found, or else provided. A libretto in the early nineteenth-century manner. And where is that to come from?"

It seemed to Maria that the time had come to get out the whisky. She and Darcourt rolled and wallowed in their problems till after midnight, and although Maria had only one drink, Simon had several, and she had to push him into a taxi. Fortunately it was after midnight, and the night porter had gone off duty.

[4]

SIMON DARCOURT HAD A BAD NIGHT, and in the morning he had a hangover. He endured something more than the layman's self-reproach. He was drinking too much, no doubt about it. He refused to think of it in the modern sociological term as "a drinking problem"; he told himself that he was becoming a boozer, and of all boozers the clerical boozer was the most contemptible.

Excuses? Yes, plenty of them. Wouldn't the Cornish Foundation drive a saint to the bottle? What a pack of irresponsible blockheads! And headed by Arthur Cornish, who was thought in the financial world to be such a paragon of good judgement. But, provocation or no provocation, he must not become a boozer.

This business of Parlabane's alleged son could be a nuisance. After a queasy breakfast, which he made himself eat because not eating was one of the marks of the boozer, he put through a call to a man who was a private detective, and owed him a favour, for Simon had pushed and pulled his promising son toward a B.A.; the man had connections that were very useful. Then he talked on the telephone to Dean Wintersen, not stressing his worry about the missing libretto, but probing to see what the Dean knew. The Dean was reassuring. Probably the relevant papers had been mislaid or temporarily catalogued under another name, possibly that of the librettist himself, who was thought to be James Robinson Planché. Neither the Dean nor Darcourt knew who Planché was, but they sparred in the accustomed academic manner to find out what the other knew, and worked up a cloud of unknowing which, again in the academic manner, seemed to give them comfort. They arranged a time when Darcourt could meet Miss Hulda Schnakenburg.

When that time came, Darcourt and the Dean cooled their heels in the many-windowed office for twenty minutes.

"You see what I mean," said Wintersen. "Don't think I would put up with this from anyone else. But as I told you, Schnak is special."

Special, it seemed to Darcourt, in a disagreeable way. At last the door opened, and in she came and sat down without waiting to be asked or greeted, saying, "She said you wanna see me."

"Not I, Schnak, but Professor Darcourt. He represents the Cornish Foundation."

Schnak said nothing, but gave Darcourt a look of what might have been malignance. She was not as unusual as he had expected, but certainly she was unusual in a Dean's office. It was not simply that she was sloppy and dirty; lots of girls thought such an appearance obligatory because of their principles, but they were sloppy and dirty in the undergraduate fashion of their time. Schnak's dirt was not a sign of feminine protest, but the real thing. She looked filthy, ill, and slightly crazed. Her dirty hair hung in hanks about a face that was sharp and rodent-like. Her eyes were almost closed in squinting suspicion, and on her face were lines in improbable places, such wrinkles as one does not often see today, even on ancient crones. Her dirty sweater had once been the property of a man, and was ravelled out at the elbows; below she wore dirty jeans, again not the fashionable dirt of rebellious youth, which has a certain coquetry about it; these were really dirty and even disgusting, for there was quite a large yellow stain around the crotch. Her dirty bare feet were thrust into worn-out running shoes without laces. But this very dirty girl was not aggressively dirty, as if she were a *bourgeoise* making some sort of statement; there was nothing striking about her. If it is possible to say so, Schnak was distinguished only by her insignificance; if Darcourt had met her on the street he would probably not have noticed her. But as someone on whom large sums of money were to be risked she struck chill into his heart.

"I suppose the Dean has told you that the Cornish Foundation is giving serious thought to presenting your enlargement of the Hoffmann score as a stage piece, Miss Schnakenburg?" he said.

"Call me Schnak. Yeah. Sounds crazy, but it's their dough." The voice was dry, rebarbative.

"True. But you realize that without your full co-operation it could not be done?"

"Yeah."

"The Foundation could count on that?"

"I guess so."

"They'll want better assurance than a guess. You are still a minor, aren't you?"

"Naw. Nineteen."

"Young for a doctoral candidate. I think I should talk with your parents."

"Fat lot of good that'll be."

"Why?"

"They don't know shit about this stuff."

"Music, you mean? I'm talking about responsibility. We must have some guarantee that you will do what you say. I'd want their agreement."

"Their idea of a musician is a church organist."

"But you think they would agree?"

"How the hell should I know what they'll do? I just know what I'll do. But if it's money they'll probably go for it."

"The Foundation is considering a grant that would pay all your expenses—living, tuition, whatever is necessary. Have you any idea what the amount might be?"

"I can live on nothing. Or I could develop some expensive habits."

"No, Miss Schnakenburg, you couldn't. The money would be carefully supervised. I would probably supervise it myself and anything that looked like the kind of expensive habit you hint at would conclude the agreement at once."

"You told me you had stopped all that nonsense, Schnak," said Wintersen.

"Pretty much. Yeah. I haven't really got the temperament for it."

"I'm glad to hear that," said Darcourt. "Tell me, as a matter of interest, would you pursue this plan—this opera plan—if you did not get the grant?"

"Yeah."

"But I understand that you have been exploring very modern paths in composition. Why this enthusiasm for the early nineteenth century?"

"It kinda grabs me, I guess. All those crazy guys."

"Well then, tell me how you would support yourself if this grant were not forthcoming?"

"Job of some kind. Anything."

Darcourt had had enough of Schnak's indifference. "Would you consider, for instance, playing the piano in a bawdy-house?"

For the first time Schnak showed some sign of animation. She laughed, dustily. "That dates you, prof," she said. "They don't have pianos in bawdy-houses any more. It's all hi-fi and digital, like the girls. You oughta go back and take another look."

Important rule of professorcraft: never show resentment at a student insult—wait and get them later. Darcourt continued, silkily.

"We want you to have freedom to get on with your work, so you needn't worry about jobs. But have you considered all the problems? There doesn't seem to be much of a libretto to go with these scraps of music, for one thing."

"Not my problem. Somebody would have to fix it up. I'm music. Just music."

"Is that enough? I'm no expert on these things, but I would have imagined that the completion of an opera that exists only as sketches and rough plans would call for some dramatic enthusiasm."

"That's what you'd imagine, is it?"

"Yes, that's what I'd imagine. You force me to remind you that nothing has been concluded about this matter. If your parents don't stand behind you, and if you are so indifferent to the money and the encouragement it implies, we're certainly not anxious to force it on you."

Wintersen intervened. "Look, Schnak, don't play the fool. This is a very big chance for you. You want to be a composer, don't you? You told me so."

"Yeah."

"Then get this through your skull: the Cornish Foundation and the Faculty are offering you such a chance, such a springboard toward a career, such a shortcut to important attention, as very great people in the past would have given ten years of life to have. I'm telling you again: don't play the fool."

"Shit."

Darcourt decided the time had come for a strategic loss of temper, a calculated outburst.

"Look here, Schnak," he said, "I won't be talked to in that way. Remember, even Mozart got his arse kicked when he couldn't be civil. Make up your mind. Do you want our help or don't you?"

"Yeah."

"Don't yeah me, young woman. Yeah what?"

"Yeah, I do."

"No. I want the magic word. Come on, Schnak—you must have heard it somewhere in the distant past."

"Please—I guess."

"That's more like it. And keep it that way from now on. You'll be hearing from me."

When Schnak had gone, the Dean was genial. "I enjoyed that," he said. "I've wanted to talk to Schnak like that for months, but you know how cautious we have to be with students nowadays; they're very quick to complain to the Governors that they're being harassed. But money still gives power. Where did you learn your lion-taming technique?"

"As a young parson I was a curate in some very tough parishes. That girl isn't nearly as tough as she wants us to think. She doesn't eat enough, and what she eats is junk. I suppose she has been on drugs, and I wouldn't be surprised if now she was on the booze. But there's something about her I like. If she's a genius, she's a genius in the great romantic tradition."

"That's what I hope."

"I think Hoffmann would have liked her."

"I'm not very well up on Hoffmann. Not my period."

"Very much in the great romantic tradition. As a writer, he

was one of its German inspirers. But there are aspects of the great romantic tradition we can do without, nowadays. Schnak will have to learn that."

"Will she learn it from Hoffmann? Doesn't sound like the teacher I would choose."

"Who would you choose? Have you got the supervisor you want?"

"I'll be talking with her by long-distance tomorrow. I'll be as persuasive as I can and it may take time. I suppose I send the phone bill to you?"

That remark assured Darcourt that the Dean was an old hand at dealing with foundations.

[5]

DARCOURT KNEW THAT, although he had compelled Schnak to say "please", it was no more than a nursery victory. He had made the bad child behave herself for a moment, but that was nothing. He was deeply worried about the whole matter of *Arthur of Britain*.

He grumbled a lot, but he was a faithful friend, and he did not want the Cornish Foundation to fall flat on its face in its first important venture in patronage. News of Arthur's grandiose ambitions were sure to leak out, not from Foundation directors, but from Arthur himself; he would not leak to the press intentionally, but the worst leaks are unintentional. Arthur was riding very high; he was making no secret of his wish to do what other Canadian foundations did not do; he was turning a deaf ear to proven good causes and worthy projects and if he fell, there would be a grand, eight-part chorus of "We told you so" from the right-minded. Arhur was prepared to risk large sums on what were no more than hunches, and that was un-Canadian, and the country that longed for certainties would not forgive him. It made no difference that the money was not public money; in an age when all spending is subjected to ruthless investigation and criticism, any suggestion that large sums were being employed capriciously by a private citizen would inflame the critics who, though not themselves benefactors, knew exactly how benefaction ought to be managed.

Why did Darcourt worry so about Arthur? Because he did not want Maria to be drawn into public rebuke and criticism. He still loved Maria, and remembered with gratitude that she had refused him as a suitor, and offered friendship instead. He still suffered from the lover's idea that the loved one should be, and could be, protected from the vicissitudes of fortune. In a world where everybody gets their lumps, he did not want Maria to get any lumps. If Arthur made a goat of himself, Maria would loyally suppose herself to be a nanny-goat. But what could he do?

A man who is disposed toward the romantic aspect of religion cannot wholly divorce himself from superstition, though he may pretend to hate it. Darcourt wanted reassurance that all was well, or some unmistakable warning that it was not. And where was such a thing to be found? He knew. He wanted to consult Maria's mother, and he knew that Maria would be strongly against any such course, because she was trying to escape from everything her mother represented.

She was not having much success.

Maria thought of herself as a determined scholar, not as a rich man's wife, or a woman of a remarkable beauty which drew all sorts of unscholarly things into her path. She wanted a new mother, the Bounteous Mother, the Alma Mater, the university. Learning and scholarship would surely help her to rise above the fact that she was half Gypsy, and all the Romany inheritance that was abhorrent to her. Her mother was a great stone in her path.

Her mother, a Madame Laoutaro (she had returned to her family name after the death of her husband), practised the respectable profession of a luthier, a doctor of sick violins, violas, cellos, and double basses; her family had a tradition of such work, as her name implied. But she was also in partnership with her brother Yerko, a man of dark skills who saw no reason why he should not palm off instruments that were made of scraps and bits of ruined fiddles, pieced out with portions of his own and his sister's manufacture, on people who accepted them as genuine ancient instruments. Madame Laoutaro and Yerko were not crooks in the ordinary way; it was simply that they had no moral sense at all in such matters. Gypsies through and through, aristocrats of that enduring and despised people, they thought that taking every possible advantage of the *gadjo* world was the normal course of life. The *gadje* wanted to hunt and crush their people; very well, let the *gadje* find out who was cleverest. Madame Laoutaro was a shop-lifter and a fiddle-faker who gloried in her witty impostures, and she supposed that her daughter had taken to education as a means of carrying on the Gypsy battle. Clement Hollier, who was Maria's supervisor in her studies, understood and appreciated Maria's mother pretty well; he thought of her as a wonderful cultural fossil, a hold-over from a medieval world where the dispossessed were cunningly at war with the possessors. But Maria had married a possessor, a priest of the money-morality of Canada, not to despoil him but because she loved him, and Madame Laoutaro could not fully believe it. Small wonder that Maria wanted to get as far as possible from her mother.

Fate—incorrigible joker—saw things differently.

Maria and Arthur had not been married three months before Madame Laoutaro's house burned down, and she and Yerko were homeless. The house, so respectably situated in the Rosedale area of Toronto, looked every bit as blamelessly respectable as it had done in the days of Madame Laoutaro's blamelessly respectable and well-doing Polish *gadjo* husband, the late Tadeusz Theotoky. But no sooner had Tadeusz died, rich and well-regarded, than Madame (having noisily mourned a man she had loved as deeply as Maria loved Arthur) reverted to her maiden name, and her Gypsy ways, which were the only ways she really knew, and she and Yerko despoiled the house. They cut it up into a squalor of mean apartments in which a variety of hopeless people, chiefly old women, were able to dwell, paying much more than the apartments were worth, but trusting to the protective power of their landlady. One such old woman, Miss Gretser, a virgin of ninety-two (though she gave out that she was a mere eighty-eight), fell asleep with a cigarette in her fingers and it was not much more than an hour before Miss Gretser was a cinder, and Madame Laoutaro, luthier, and her ingenious brother Yerko were homeless. Madame declared, with much outcry, that they were also penniless.

They were certainly not penniless. As soon as the fire broke out Madame and Yerko hurried to their cellar workshops, pulled two cement blocks out of a wall, and rushed to the back garden, where they threw a leather bag of money into an ornamental pool.

Then they returned to the front of the house for much enjoyable despair, hair-tearing, and noisy grief. When the last ember was quenched, and the excitement was over, they rescued the bag, hurried to Maria's splendid penthouse, and set to work to pin sodden currency in bills of large denomination to all the uphol-stery and curtains, to dry it out. They insisted on sleeping on the floor of the handsome drawing-room till every bill was dried, ironed, and counted; they were suspicious of Nina, the Portu-guese housekeeper, who made no secret of the fact that she looked on the Laoutaros as riff-raff. Which, of course, from a Portuguese Catholic point of view, they were.

Oh no, not in the least penniless. In addition to the funds in the bag, the late Tadeusz had left a lot of money behind him, tied up in a trust fund, which provided them with an ample in-come. There was also the matter of insurance. To Yerko and Madame Laoutaro, insurance was a form of wager; you bet with the insurance company that your house would not burn down, and if it did you were deemed the winner, and cleaned up hand-somely. Unfortunately, however, when the Laoutaros converted the handsome mansion into a crowded lodging-house, they did not reinsure it as a commercial venture; they continued to pay the lower rate applicable to a dwelling. The insurance company, pernickety about such matters, threatened suit for fraud. Arthur was displeased, but Yerko managed to persuade him to allow the Gypsies to deal with the matter in their own way. Would a great financial company harass and oppress two poor Gypsies, ignorant of the complexities of business? Surely not! The Laoutaros were happily confident that they would get big money out of the in-surance. But to the Gypsy mind all invisible money is fairy money and a fire is an immediate disaster. Where were these two home-less victims to go?

Madame's proposal that they might stay for an indefinite time in the penthouse, which was, she pointed out, big enough for a whole tribe of Gypsies, was immediately ruled out of the question by Maria. Yerko had a plan, which was that they should rent an ancient stable behind a shop a Gypsy friend of his kept on Queen Street East. A little work would make it habitable, and the luthier business and his coppersmith's forge would be handsomely ac-commodated.

This might have been acceptable if Madame had not had a bright idea which would, she said, repair their ruined fortunes. A lot of women, not nearly so gifted as herself, were advertising themselves as palm-readers, clairvoyants, and purveyors of personal counsel. A few of them openly promised restoration of lost sexual power, and reports were that business was brisk. As Madame said with scorn, these women were crooks, but if people appeared with money in their hands and positively demanded to be cheated, who was she to spit in the face of Providence?

Darcourt asked her if she would really prostitute her considerable gift as a psychic for money. Her reponse was positive.

"Never!" she said. "Never would I use my real gift in such trashy work! I would just give them the sort of thing they would get from some low sideshow mitt-camp. It would just be a hobby. I have my pride and my ethics, like anyone else."

This notion put a sharp spur into Arthur. As the chairman of the board of an important trust company, he could not have it known that his mother-in-law was running a mitt-joint in a depressed part of the city. Arthur had not liked the coroner's remarks in the inquest on Miss Gretser. The coroner had been rough about the lack of proper safety precautions in a house which he described, all outer appearances to the contrary, as a slum. Had Madame Laoutaro no advisers to keep her straight in such matters? Arthur had not been at the inquest, but he felt the gimlet eye of the coroner in his luxurious office in the Cornish Tower. Therefore Arthur declared that he would find a place for the refugees to repose themselves. To Maria's horror he offered them accommodation in the basement of the very apartment house in which she and Arthur lived, where he could keep his eye on them.

Hollier tactlessly pointed out to her the almost mythical beauty of the scheme. She, at the very top of the splendid building, exposed to sun and air: her roots, the matrix of her being, ever present in the lowest depths of the same building. The root and the flower, beautifully exemplified. Maria could snarl, and she snarled at Hollier when he said that.

She became accustomed to it. The Laoutaros never came up to the penthouse, not because they were forbidden, but because they did not like it; the air was thin, the food was unwholesome, they would be expected to sit on chairs at all times, the conversation was boring, and Yerko's pungent farting was reprehended. It was no place for people with any real zest for life.

When Darcourt next visited Maria he talked of Schnak but his mind was on Madame Laoutaro. He was a favourite with that lady, who respected him as a priest, though of a somewhat eccentric kind. She sensed the superstition in the heart of the holy man, and it established a kinship. The matter of a visit to the sibyl had to be approached with tact.

"I've been boning up on Hoffmann," said Maria. "It's time somebody on the Foundation knew what kind of world we are getting ourselves into."

"Have you been reading the famous *Tales*?"

"A few. I didn't read his music criticism because I don't know anything about the technical side of music. I've found out a little about his life, and obviously this opera, *Arthur of Britain*, was what he was working on when he was dying. He had lucid fits when he would call for pen and a paper and do something, though his wife, who seems to have been rather a simple woman, didn't say what it was. He was only forty-six. Rotten life, knocking about from pillar to post because Napoleon was making things so difficult for people like him; not as a musician or an author, of course, but as a lawyer, which is what he was when he had the chance. He drank, not habitually but on toots. He had two miserable love affairs, of which the marriage was not one. And he never made it as a composer, which was what he wanted more than anything."

"Sounds like the complete Romantic."

"Not quite. Don't forget his being a lawyer. He was much respected as a judge, when Napoleon allowed it. I think that's what gives his writing its wonderful quality; it's so matter-of-fact and then—bang! You're right out of this world. I'm trying to get a wild autobiographical novel he wrote in which half is the work of a nasty Philistine tom-cat, who jeers at everything Hoffmann held dear."

"A real tom-cat, or a human tom-cat?"

"A real one. Name of Kater Murr."

"Ah well—you read German. I don't. But what about the music?"

"It doesn't get very good marks, because musicians don't like dabblers, and literary men don't like people who cross boundaries—especially musical boundaries. If you're a writer, you're a writer, and if you're a composer, you're a composer—and no scabbing."

"But lots of composers have been splendid writers."

"Yes—but in their letters."

"Let's hope the music was better than its reputation, or Schnak is in the soup, and so are we."

"My hunch is that the poor man was just hitting his stride when he died. Maybe it'll be wonderful."

"Maria, you're taking sides. Already you're an advocate for Hoffmann."

"Why not? I don't think of him as Hoffmann any more. His name was Ernst Theodor Amadeus (he took the name of Amadeus because he worshipped Mozart) Hoffmann. E. T. A. H. I think of him as ETAH. Makes a good pet-name."

"ETAH. Yes, not bad."

"So. Have you found out anything about Crottel?"

"Not yet. But my spies are everywhere.

"Hurry them up. He gives me funny looks when I come in at night."

"A security man has to give funny looks. What kind of look does he give Yerko?"

"Yerko has his own entrance, through the professional part of the building. He and Mamusia have a special key."

This seemed the moment to propose a visit to the Laoutaros. Maria hummed and hawed.

"I know I sound like a miserable daughter, but I don't want to encourage too much coming and going."

"Has there been any coming? No? Then just for this once, Maria, might we do a little going? I terribly want to get your mother's slant on this business."

So, after a little more demur, they sank down as far into the building as the elevator would carry them, into the basement where the owners of the condominiums had their garage space.

" 'The lyre of Orpheus opens the door of the underworld'," said Maria, softly.

"What's that?" said Darcourt.

"A quotation from ETAH," said Maria.

"So? I wonder if it does. We're none of us musicians, on the Foundation. Are we headed toward the underworld? Maybe your mother can say."

"You can depend on her to say something, relevant or not, " said Maria.

"That's unkind. You know your mother is a very deft hand with the cards."

They walked to the farthest end of the basement, in the rather sinister light that seems appropriate to parking areas, went round an unobtrusive corner, and tapped at a faceless metal door. This gave access to an unused space where the architect had meant to put a sauna and exercise room, but in the end that idea had been abandoned.

Tapping was useless. After some banging, the door was opened a very little way on a chain, and Yerko's voice, in its deepest bass register, was heard to say: "If it's a professional visit please use the entrance on the floor above. I will meet you."

"It's not professional, it's friendly," said Darcourt. "It's me, Yerko—Simon Darcourt."

The door opened wide. Yerko, in a purple shirt and corduroy trousers that had once been a rich crimson, clasped Darcourt in a bear's embrace. He was a huge and impressive man with a face as big as one of his own fiddles, and a Gypsy's mane of inky hair.

"Priest Simon! My very dear friend! Come in, come in, come in! Sister, it's Priest Simon. And your daughter," he added in a markedly less welcoming tone.

Only the Laoutaros could have turned a derelict space, enclosed in concrete and in the highest degree impersonal and comfortless, into a version of Aladdin's cave, part workshop and part chaotic dwelling, stinking of glue, fumes from the forge, the reek of two raccoon skins that were drying on the wall, the wonderful scent of precious old wood, and food kept too long without refrigeration. Some of the concrete walls were bare, covered with calculations done in chalk and corrected by erasures of spit, and here and there hung rugs of Oriental designs. Hovering over a pan of burning charcoal, the fumes from which escaped through a stovepipe that ran to one of the windows just below the ceiling, was Maria's mother, the *phuri dai* herself, stirring something smelly in a pan.

"You are in time for supper," she said. "Maria, get two more bowls. They are in the *abort*. I've been making *rindza* and *pixtia*. Wonderful against this flu that everybody has. Well, my daughter, you have been a long time coming, but you are welcome."

It was wonderful to Darcourt to see how the beautiful Maria was diminished in the presence of her mother. Filial respect works in many ways, and Maria was suddenly a gypsy daughter, disguised in some fine contemporary clothes, though she immediately kicked off her shoes.

The Gypsies are not great kissers, but Maria kissed her mother, and Darcourt kissed her sooty hand, which he knew she liked, because it recalled her youthful days as an admired gypsy musician in Vienna.

They all ate bowls of *rindza* and *pixtia*, which was tripe seethed in pig's-foot jelly, and not as bad as it sounds. Darcourt showed great appetite, as was expected; those who consult oracles must not be choosy. The dish was followed by something heavy and cheesy called *saviako*. Darcourt thanked God for a strong shot of Yerko's home-made plum brandy, which was stupefying to the palate, but burned a hole through the heavy mixture in the stomach.

The god of hospitality having been adequately appeased, there followed at least half an hour of general conversation. When consulting an oracle, there should be no haste. At last it was possible to get to Darcourt's questions.

He told Mamusia—for that was what Maria called her—about the Cornish Foundation, of which she had some slight and inaccurate knowledge.

"Yes, yes; it is the Platter of Plenty," she said.

"The Platter of Plenty is just a joke," said Maria.

"It doesn't sound like a joke," said Mamusia.

"Yes, it is a joke," said Darcourt. "It is that big silver epergne that Maria puts on the table when we meet. It is filled with snacks—olives and anchovies, and pickled oysters, and sweets and little biscuits, and things like that. Calling it the Platter of Plenty is a joke by one of our directors. He's a Welshman, and he says it reminds him of a Welsh legend about a chieftain who had a magic platter on his table from which his guests could ask for and receive anything they desired."

"I know that story from other lands. But it's a good name. Isn't that what your Foundation is? A heaping platter from which anybody can get anything he wants?"

"We hadn't really thought of that."

"This Welshman must have a good head on him. You are guardians of plenty, aren't you? It's simple."

Darcourt thought it might be a little too simple, when he thought of what the Platter of Plenty was offering to Schnak. He explained as well as he could, in terms he thought Mamusia would understand, about the uncompleted opera, and Schnak, and his misgivings. He made the easy mistake of being too simple with someone who, although not educated in the ordinary sense, was highly intelligent and intuitive. Maria did not speak; in her mother's presence she was silent unless spoken to. Mamusia's glance moved constantly between her daughter's face and Darcourt's and in her own terms she understood them better than they knew.

"So—you want to know what is going to happen and you think I can tell you. Don't you feel shame, Father Darcourt? You are not a real Catholic, but you are some kind of priest. Isn't there something in the Bible that tells you to keep away from people like me?"

"In several places we are warned against them that have familiar spirits, and wizards that peep and mutter. But we live in a fallen world, Madame. Last time I visited my bishop he was very busy over Church investments, and he could not see me because he was deep in discussion with an investment counsel, who was peeping and muttering about the bond market. If there is any risk to my soul in consulting you, I take it upon me gladly."

So the Tarot cards were brought out, in their fine tortoise-shell box, and Mamusia shuffled them deftly. Carefully, too, for they were a fine old pack and somewhat limp with age.

"The nine-card deal, I think," said she.

At her bidding Darcourt cut the deck, which had been reduced to the picture cards; he began by setting aside four cards, face down; then he put the top card in the middle of the table. It was

the Empress, ruler of worldly fortune and a strong card to stand
at the heart of the prediction. The next card he drew went to the
left of the Empress, and it was Force, the handsome lady who is
subduing a lion by tearing open its jaws, apparently without any
special effort on her part. Above the Empress went the Lover,
and Mamusia's quick eye saw a change in Maria's face. Next card,
placed on the right of the Empress, was the Female Pope, the
Great Mother. Last card, to go below the Empress, made Darcourt
wince, for it was the Death card, the dreadful skeleton which is
scything up human bodies. He hated the Death card, and hesitated.

"Down it goes," said Mamusia. "Don't worry about it until you
see what it means. Turn up your oracle cards."

These were the four that had been set aside, and they were the
Tower of Destruction, at the top, the card of Judgement, next in
order, the Hermit, and last of all, the Fool.

"How do you like it?" said Mamusia.

"I don't like it."

"Don't be afraid because there are some dark cards. Look at
the Empress, who can get you men out of any mess you can
make. This is a very womanly hand of cards you have found,
and lucky for you, because men are awful bunglers. Look at
Strength, or Force, or whatever you want to call her; is she just
brute force, like a man's? Never! She is irresistible force and she
does not get it from being a man, let me tell you. And this High
Priestess—this Female Pope. Who do you suppose she is? It's a
fine spread."

"I can never see that Death card without shuddering."

"Pooh! Everybody shudders at the Death card, because they
don't think what it means. But you—a priest! Doesn't Death mean
transfiguration, change, turning the whole spread into something
else—and you tell us into something better? And look at your
oracle cards. The Tower—well probably somebody will take a
tumble; it would be queer if they didn't considering what you tell
me about your Foundation. And Judgement. Who escapes it? But
look at the Hermit—the man who lives alone—that sounds like
you, Priest Simon. And most powerful of all—the Fool! What's
the Fool's number in the pack?"

"The Fool has no number."

"Of course not! The Fool is zero! And what is zero? Power, no? Put zero to any number and in a wink you increase its power by ten. He is the wise joker who makes everything else in the hand conditional, and he is in the place of greatest power. The Empress and the Fool govern the spread, and with the Tower of Destruction in the first place among the oracles that probably means that there will be a lot of—what's the word—is it higgledy-piggledy? Lots of upsets and turn-arounds—"

"Topsy-turveydom," said Maria.

"Is that the word?"

"Topsy-turveydom seems all too likely," said Darcourt.

"Don't fear it! Love it! Give it the big kiss! That's the way to deal with destiny. You *gadje* are always afraid of something."

"I didn't ask you about my own fate, Madame, but about this venture of the Foundation's. They are my friends and I am worried on their behalf."

"No use worrying on anybody else's behalf. They must take care of themselves."

"Are you going to explain the spread?"

"Why? It looks clear enough. Topsy-turveydom. I like that word."

"Would you consider associating the Empress, the guardian woman, with Maria?"

Mamusia went into one of her infrequent fits of laughter; not the cackling of a witch, but a deep, gutty ho-hoing. Darcourt had been mistaken if he expected her to relate her daughter to any figure of power.

"If I try to explain, I will just confuse you, because I am not at all sure myself. Your Fool-zero could be your Round Table, or that Fool-zero my son-in-law; I love him pretty well, I suppose, but he can be a Fool-zero as much as anybody else, when he gets too high and mighty. And that Great Mother, that High Priestess, could be your Platter of Plenty who can dish it out—but can she take it? I don't know. It could be somebody else, somebody new in your world."

"Couldn't Arthur be the Lover?" said Maria and was vexed to find herself blushing.

"You want him to be that, but the card is in the wrong place. Life is full of lovers, for people whose minds are set on love."

Darcourt was disappointed and worried. He had seen Mamusia discourse on a spread of cards many times, and never had she been so reluctant to speak about what she saw, what she felt, what her intuition suggested. It was not common for her to ask somebody else to lay out the cards; did that mean something special? He began to wish he had not asked Maria to bring him to the Gypsy camp in the bottom of her apartment house, but as he had done so he wanted something from the oracle that was positive, even if in small measure. He talked, he coaxed, and at last Mamusia relented a little.

"You must have something, eh? Something to lean on? It's reasonable, I suppose. Three things come to me that I would be very careful about, if I had dealt this hand for myself. The first is, be careful how you give money to this child."

"To Schnak, you mean?"

"Awful name. Yes, to Schnak. You tell me she has great talent as a musician. I know a lot about musicians; I'm one myself. I used to be greatly admired in Vienna, before I married Maria's father. I sang and played the fiddle and the cimbalom and danced my way into hundreds of hearts. Rich men gave me jewels. Poor men gave me what they couldn't afford. I could tell you—"

"Hold your gab!" said Yerko, who had been busy with the plum brandy. "Priest Simon doesn't want to hear you blow your horn."

"Yes, yes, Mamusia," said Maria, "we all know how wonderful you used to be before you became even more wonderful as you are now. You could break hearts still, if you wanted to be cruel. But you don't, dear little mother. You don't."

"No. You have embraced your fate as a *phuri dai*," said Darcourt, "and become a very wise woman and a great help to us all."

The flattery worked. Mamusia liked to be thought a wonderful old woman, although she could not have been far over sixty.

"Yes, I was wonderful. Perhaps I am even more wonderful

now. I'm not ashamed to speak the truth about myself. But this Schnak—keep her short. You people on foundations ruin a lot of artists. They need to work. They thrive on hunger and destruction. So keep this child from going on the streets, but don't drown her talent with money. Keep her short. Be careful the Platter of Plenty doesn't become the instrument of destruction."

"And the second thing?"

"Not clear at all, but it looks as if some old people, dead people, were going to say something important. Funny-looking people."

"And the third?"

"I don't know if I should say."

"Please, Madame."

"These things have nothing to do with the cards. They are just things that come to me. This third one comes very, very strong; it came when you were shivering over the Death card. I don't think I should say. Perhaps it was something just for me, not for you."

"I beg you," said Darcourt. He knew when the seeress wanted to be coaxed.

"All right. Here it is. You are wakening the little man."

Mamusia had a strong sense of the dramatic, and it was plain that this was the end of the session. So, after protestations of gratitude, and astonishment, and enlargement—there would never be too much unction for Mamusia—Darcourt and Maria returned to the penthouse and whisky, of which the abbé drank more than he intended, though less than he wanted.

Whatever Mamusia might say, he hated the Death card and it soured his feeling toward the whole of the prediction. He knew how stupid that was. If the prediction had been all positive he would have accepted it happily, at the same time retaining in another part of his mind a patronizing feeling toward the Tarot and all Gypsy vaticination. To put full trust in a sunny future would be un-Canadian, as well as unworthy of a Christian priest. But now, when he had been shown fear by the cards, that other part of his mind told him he was a fool to play King Saul, and resort to wizards who peep and mutter. Christian priest that he was, he deserved to suffer for his folly, and suffer he did.

The three random predictions he liked even less. He did not believe that artists should be kept short of money. Fat cats hunt better than lean. Don't they? Does anyone know? Poverty was not good for anybody. Was it? As for utterances by funny-looking people, he felt no response at all.

But—Wakening the little man? What little man?

The little man he knew best was his own penis, for that was what his mother had called it. Always keep the little man very clean, dear. Later he had heard it called the old man, by friends of his days as a theological student, for to those jokers it meant the Old Man, or Old Adam, whom the Redeemed Man was bidden to cast out. As a bachelor whose sexual experience, for a man of his age, had been sporadic and slight, he suffered frequent reminders from the little man that there was a side of his nature that was not being given enough attention.

His physical desire for Maria had never been overwhelming, but it was a fretting element in his life. When they met she kissed him, and he rather wished she wouldn't because it aroused inadmissible longings. But had they not agreed, when he had proposed marriage to her, that they should be friends? It had possessed deep meaning for him then, and their friendship was one of the fostering things in his life, but he was aware that there was a farcical side to it. *We are just good friends*. Wasn't that what people said when they were denying insinuations of a love affair in the press? Oh, intolerable torment! Oh, frying lust—yet not a lust that would drive him to shoot Arthur and carry Maria away to a love-nest in the East. Oh, farce of priesthood, which demanded so much that was unnatural, but failed to give the strength to banish worldly desires! Oh, misery of being the Reverend Professor Simon Darcourt, Vice-Warden of Ploughwright College, professor of Greek, a Fellow of the Royal Society, who was, in the most pressing areas of his life, a poor fish!

You are wakening the little man. Maria's mother saw through him like a pane of glass. It was ignominious. Oh, the unlit lamp and the ungirt loin! Oh hell!

[6]

ETAH IN LIMBO

YOU ARE WAKENING THE LITTLE MAN—as if the Little Man had ever been asleep! No, no, this Little Man has been wide awake in Limbo, for ever since I died I have been aware of people reading what I wrote about music, and now and then seeing **Undine**, my best completed opera, on the stage, and never forgetting my tales of wonder where, the critics say, the fantastic meets the everyday. The Little Man has certainly not been gnawing his nails because of earthly neglect.

Mine was a life of better than merely respectable achievement, but I died with one thing left undone that should have been done. That was the completion of my opera **Arthur of Britain**, in which it would have been plain to the stupidest that my apprenticeship as a composer was finished, and that I had written a masterwork. Yes, a masterwork at least as good as, and perhaps better than, the best of my dear friend Weber. But it was not to be; I had barely laid the keel of that work before I was cut down, laid out, polished off, not suddenly, but at some wretched length. It was my own doing, I admit it freely. I was unwise in my life. I emptied my purse too readily, playing the great gentleman with my health and talents. So I was cut off untimely, and that is why I find myself now in Limbo, in that part of it reserved for those artists and musicians and writers who never fully realized themselves, never quite came to the boil, so to speak. Limbo: not the worst of hereafters, for it is free of the chains of space and time, and permits its denizens a great deal of versatility and, shall I say it, some post-humous influence?

Still, not to be too delicate about it, Limbo is a bore. Should I complain? My fate is not the worst. There are artists and writers and scholars here who have had two thousand years of neglect, and would be grateful if some candidate for a Doctor of Philosophy degree would stumble on their work and seize it with joy, as material that nobody has hitherto pawed over and exhausted. The dullest thesis— and that is saying much—may be enough to release an artist from Limbo and allow him to go—we don't really know where, but we hope for the best, because to people like ourselves, used to a creative life;

boredom is punishment enough. When we were good children of the Church, some of us, we heard about sinners who roast on beds of coals, or stand naked in Siberian hurricanes. But we were not sinners. Just artists who, for one reason or another, never finished our work on earth and so must wait until we are redeemed, or at least justified, by some measure of human understanding. Heavenly understanding, it appears, is what brings us to Limbo; we never really did our best and that is a sin of a special kind, though not, as I say, the worst.

Can this be my great chance? Is this extraordinary waif Schnak to be my deliverer? I must not build my hopes too high. I did that when, however long ago it was, that curious French-German-Jew Jacques Offenbach took some of my stories as the basis for his last piece, Les Contes D'Hoffmann (thank you, Jacques, for giving my name such prominence), but it proved not to be the sort of work that gets a man out of Limbo. Tuneful, mind you, and reasonably skilled in orchestration (thank God he controlled his impulse to use the bass drum too much), but Offenbach had spent too much time writing opéra bouffe to be happy with the real thing. And he had too much French humour, which can be fatal to music. I always keep my own sense of humour, which is German and therefore deeper than his, in check when I am composing. After a man has died he understands what a betrayer of great things humour can be, when it is not in the Shakespearean or Rabelaisian mode. I am glad to see that this child Schnak has no sense of humour whatever, though she is pretty well stocked with scorn and derision, which pass for humour with stupid people.

Is this my great chance? I must do everything I can to help. I shall stand at Schnak's shoulder and push her in the right direction, so far as I can. So all those crazy guys grab her, do they? Crazy guys like Weber, and Schumann, I suppose. What about that magnificently sane guy Mozart, whose name I took as an act of homage? Is Schnak biting off more than she can chew? Schnak is going to need luck, or she will simply make a mess of my hastily scribbled intentions. I must be Schnak's Luck. Her greatest luck would be not to find that terrible libretto, in which that ass Planché was in a fair way to make a mess of Arthur when I died. Same trouble as Offenbach; too much sense of humour—English this time—too much experience of what would "go" in the theatre—meaning what "went" last time and which the public was begining to be tired of. Again, I thank God that Schnak knows nothing about the theatre and has no sense of humour. If it is possible to keep her from those two plagues I shall be at hand to do it.

Did I really die in order to save my opera from Planché's dreadful libretto? Even now I cannot tell. There are limits to what one can know about one's former life, even in Limbo.

Why did the old woman, the seeress, tell that well-meaning fellow Darcourt, and her lovely but uncomprehending daughter, that they were wakening the little man, as if that were something that should not be done? I am very happy to be awakened in this way. Luckily Darcourt thinks she meant his pizzle, egotistical jackass that he is. But does the old woman know something I cannot know, placed as I am? Is it likely?

By God, I am thoroughly awake, and I shall not rest until I have seen this thing through to the end. Then, if my luck enables me to be Schnak's Luck, I may have a chance to sleep eternally, my work accomplished.

TWO

AS A GROUP OF SCHNAK'S PROFESSORS assembled in the auditorium of the Faculty of Music to see the film *After Infinity*, Simon Darcourt heard a good deal more about Hulda Schnakenburg than he had known before, and it surprised him. Her bad manners toward the Dean had no relation to the work she did for her instructors; they admitted, with reluctance, that it was of unusual quality. Were her exercises grubby, asked Darcourt, remembering the letter she had sent to the Cornish Foundation. No indeed; they were notably clean, clear, and almost—they hated to use the word—elegant in their musical calligraphy. As a student of harmony, counterpoint, and analysis she was exemplary, and her flights into electronic music, environmental music, and any sort of noise that could be evoked from any unusual source were admitted to be innovative, when they could be distinguished from mere racket.

It was even agreed that she had a sense of humour, though not a pleasant one. She caused a sensation with a serenade she had composed for four tenors whose larynxes had been constricted to the point of strangulation with adhesive tape; there had been some cautious approval from professors who had not noticed that its performance took place on April 1. Her manners were admitted to be dreadful, but instruction in manners was not part of the Faculty's job. Nevertheless, it was agreed that Schnak went rather too far. As one professor, who had some recollection of the music-hall of an earlier day, sang in Darcourt's ear,

It ain't exactly what she sez—
It's the nasty way she sez it!

She had qualified beyond question for her Master of Music, and her reputation as a brat and a nuisance had nothing to do with the matter—apart from making her disliked and even feared by some members of the Faculty.

Predictably Schnak had not chosen to appear at Convocation, properly gowned and dressed to receive her degree at the hands of the Chancellor. She rejected all such ceremonial, or suggestion of a *rite de passage*, with her favourite term of disapproval. Shit. But she had set to work immediately on preparations for her doctorate, and when autumn came, and she presented herself at the seminars in Romantic Themes in Nineteenth-Century Opera, Traditional Compositional Techniques, and History of Performance Practice, she had already done more reading than most of the other students would do during the year to come, and she threw herself into the obligatory work on Composition and Theory Research with what would have looked like enthusiasm in someone else, but seemed more like angry zealotry in Schnak.

As well as heavy involvement in her university work, she had found time to write the music for *After Infinity,* and the auditorium was filled with students of drama, of film, and of any manifestation of the *avant-garde*. An admired student genius had written the scenario and directed the film; great things were expected. There was to be no dialogue, in order that the immediacy of the early silent film might be recaptured and any taint of merely literary values avoided. There would, however, be music, for Chaplin had given his blessing to music as an accompaniment to film, particularly when he wrote the music himself. The student genius could not write music, but he discerned a fellow genius in Schnak, and she had provided music. She had rejected the idea of using a synthesizer, and had composed her score for a piano that had been doctored with pieces of parchment fastened over the strings, assisted by a Swanee whistle ingeniously played under a metal tub, and that simplest of instruments, a comb covered with tissue paper. The effect was of a vaguely melodious but unfocussed buzzing, punctuated by shrieks, and everyone agreed that it had added much to the general effect.

The film-maker was scornful of what he called "linear" quality in a script, so his film bounded along in unconnected sections, leaving the spectators to make out as best they could what was going on. It was not too difficult. Humanity was facing the ultimate predicament; a nuclear leak had rendered all mankind, male and female, sterile. What was to become of the race? Could a woman be found, almost at the point of bearing a child, whose child would have escaped the curse of sterility? If that child could be brought to birth, how should it be nourished? Its mother's breasts would obviously—well, obviously to the film-maker—be dry, or a source of poison. Might a man, in case of dire global need, suckle a child? This question enabled several sequences to be shown in which male friends of the film-maker—the cast had all worked on a voluntary and friendly basis—strained with selfless zeal to produce milk from their flat and unlikely paps, and one of two of them actually did so, the milk being simulated very cleverly with shaving cream. But it was discovered—during one of the portions of the story that had not been thought worth filming—that one fertile female had escaped the nuclear curse. She appeared as a simple child of twelve (the daughter of the film-maker's landlady) who must take upon her the task of continuing the race, if a male could only be found still able to impregnate her. The search for a fertile male was indicated by shots of vast emptinesses; long resonant corridors up and down which there was much coming and going by unseen searchers, whose footsteps Schnak had simulated with two halves of a coconut shell. There were scenes of the anguish of a Very Wise Man (played by the film-maker's great and good friend, who chose unaccountably to do it in a Prince Albert coat and a flowing tie) who, in the culminating scene, had to explain to the twelve-year-old what Sex was, and what would be required of her. The child's face, filled with a wonderment that could also have been puzzled vacuity, was photographed from unusual angles, and she emerged as an Infans Dolorosa, a Nubile Saviour, and, of course, as a Transporting Symbol. The film was greeted in the main with solemn wonderment, though there were a few coarse souls who sniggered when the child knelt before the startlingly white bare feet of the Very Wise Man emerging from the bottom of his formal trousers, and seemed to adore them. In the great tradition of student despair the fate of mankind was left undecided at the end, which Schnak marked by three descending *glissandi* on the Swanee whistle.

Subtle campus critics professed to detect a hint of irony in the music, but the majority, while admitting that it might be so, felt that it added a dimension to a brilliant film which would, if everybody had their rights, command a variety of international awards.

When, a few days later, the Faculty met to discuss thesis topics, they were astonished that Schnak proposed to complete her work on *Arthur of Britain* within one university year. She had done her year of courses for her doctorate and nothing stood in the way except the unusually short time she had allotted to her thesis-composition. A thesis of operatic length and complexity? They demurred.

"I am through with trying to control or advise Schnak," said Dean Wintersen. "If it kills her or drives her mad, let it be so. I hope to hand over my supervision of work to a distinguished visitor."

Of course there was curiosity about the distinguished visitor, but the Dean said it was too early to talk of what was not yet assured. As always, the Faculty wished to show its academic scruple by doubt and debate.

"This thesis exercise," said a professor of musicological research; "who can say what it may involve? I am not at all impressed by this passion to complete what fate has ordained should be incomplete."

"Ah, but you must admit that it has been done, and well done," said another musicologist, who did not like the first speaker. "Look at Janet Johnson's excellent reconstruction of Rossini's *Journey to Rheims*. And what about Deryck Cooke's completion of Mahler's Tenth? What this girl wants to do is a forward, not a backward, step. She wants to display for us a Hoffmann who has never been heard before."

"I have heard one of Hoffmann's operas in Germany, which I think is something nobody else present can say, and I do not leap with joy at the prospect of another. These early nineteenth-century operas are mostly very thin stuff."

"Ah, but that's the fault of the libretti," said his enemy, who had indeed never heard a note by Hoffmann but who had a nice private specialization in libretti where nobody could challenge him. "What is the libretto for this one like?"

The question was directed to the Dean, and it gave him a chance to display those qualities which mark a dean off from ordinary professors. He did not, in fact, know anything about the Hoffmann libretto and he would not pretend that he did; if his listeners chose to think on the grounds of what he said that he had seen the libretto, the assumption was wholly their own.

"A certain amount of work will have to be undertaken before that question could be satisfactorily answered," he said. "Of course we shall have to make sure that all that side of the work is properly handled. We are not literary experts. We shall have to arrange a committee for Schnak that includes somebody from Comparative Literature."

This was greeted with groans.

"Yes, I know," said the Dean. "But you must admit that they are very thorough. I had thought of asking Professor Penelope Raven to act. Would that be agreeable?"

There were other matters to be decided, and it was nearing the time when professors feel the need of a pre-dinner drink, so they said it was agreeable.

[2]

PROFESSOR RAVEN was not pleased to be asked to join a committee supervising a thesis in the Faculty of Music; she would be the only non-musician, and she knew that the odd man out in such an academic group was expected to be modest and keep out of what didn't concern him, while lending scope and respectability to everything that was done. This looked like a job involving a great deal of work and very little satisfaction. She thought differently when she had lunched at the Faculty Club with her old friend Simon Darcourt, and had drunk her full share of a bottle of wine.

"I didn't know you were in on this, Simon," she said. "That makes a difference, of course."

"I'm not in it academically, but I'll have a good deal to say about what goes on," said Simon. Then he told Penny in extreme confidence—knowing that she was as leaky as a sieve—about the

Cornish Foundation, its support for Schnak, and its determination to present *Arthur of Britain* on the stage. He also told her that any research in which she was involved on the libretto would, of course, be generously rewarded by the Foundation. That made a great deal of difference.

"The problem seems to be that the libretto is very scrappy," he explained.

"How much have you got?" she asked.

"I've taken a quick look, and to be frank there's virtually nothing," he said. "What the chances are of digging anything up, I couldn't even guess. It isn't going to be easy, Penny."

"With my flair for research, and the money you've got your hands on, much may be achieved," said Penny, looking owlish. "I've taken a look, you know, and it was a quick look, like yours, and there's really nothing but a few notations in German, written by Hoffmann himself, because he had written quite a lot of music he wanted to use. I assumed that somebody must have some really solid stuff I hadn't seen. I gather there was some sort of dispute, amounting almost to a row, between Hoffmann and the English librettist."

"Who was—?"

"None other than the redoubtable James Robinson Planché."

"Yes, the Dean did mention that name. What was redoubtable about him?"

"Very popular nineteenth-century playwright and librettist. Just about forgotten, now. Though everybody uses a phrase of his: 'It would have made a cat laugh', he says in one of his innumerable works. I suppose the opera world knows him, if it knows him at all, as the man who wrote the libretto for the unfortunate Weber's *Oberon,* one of the resounding flopperoos of operatic history. Music splendid. Libretto—well, Schnak has a word for it."

"Shit?"

"Of the most rejectable and excrementitious order."

"Then why—?"

"I can't tell you why, and if you didn't have all that lovely money to throw around I might never find out. But I can, and I will."

"How?"

"The Cornish Foundation—I see it all now in a vision—is going to pay my expenses to go abroad and find out."

"Where will you look?"

"Now Simon, you know the research game better than that. *Where* is for me to know, and for you and Schnak and the Cornish Foundation to find out when and if I get it. But if it's to be gotten, I'm the girl to get it."

With that Simon had to be content. He liked Penny. She must have been nearer forty than thirty, but she had charm, and spirit, and in a favourite Rabelaisian phrase of his, she was "a jolly pug and well-mouthed wench". And beneath all that, she had the steely core of the woman who has scrambled up the academic ladder to a full professorship, so Simon knew that it was useless to press her further.

After lunch, in order to avoid going back to his rooms in Ploughwright, where he would have to face the heap of typescript of his life of the late Francis Cornish—the biography with that disastrous, abysmal gap in the very heart of it—he went to the Club library. He looked with distaste at the table on which were displayed a selection of the less obscure among the innumerable academic quarterlies, dismal publications in which scholars paraded pieces of research that meant all the world to them, but which their colleagues in general found supremely resistible. He ought to look over those that touched on his own subject, he knew, but outside it was spring, and he could not force himself to his scholar's task. So he strayed to another table, where unscholarly magazines lay, and picked up *Vogue*. He never read it, but he had hopes, inspired by the wine he had drunk and the cheering companionship of Penny Raven, that it might contain some pictures of women with very few clothes on, or perhaps none at all. He sat down to read.

He did not read. He looked at the advertisements instead. There were young women displayed there, in various stages of undress, but in the fashion of the time they looked so angry, so crazed, so furious, that they gave him little comfort, aroused no pleasing fantasy. Their hair stood on end or was wildly tangled. Their eyes glared or were pinched in squints that hinted at lunacy. But then he came to a picture so sharply contrasted with its neighbours that he looked at it for several minutes, and as he looked something in the back of his mind stirred, moved, was aroused, until he could hardly believe what he saw.

It was not a photograph, but a drawing of the head of a girl, in silver-point, touched here and there with white and red chalk; it was delicately executed but not weak, without any modern flash or challenge. Indeed, it was drawn in the manner, and also in the feeling, of a time at least four centuries before the present. The head was aristocratic, not haughty but modestly confident; the eyes were innocent but not simple-minded; the line of the cheek had neither the pudding-faced nor the lantern-jawed look of the models whose photographs appeared in the other advertisements. It was a face that challenged the viewer, particularly if he were a man, by its self-possession. This is what I am: what are you? it seemed to say. It was by far the most arresting picture in the magazine.

Beneath were a few lines in a clear, beautiful type, but again it was not attenuated or falsely elegant. Darcourt, who knew something about types, recognized it as a modern version of the type-face reputedly based upon the handwriting of a poet, church-man, bibliophile, scholar, humanist, and, in some respects, rascal, Cardinal Pietro Bembo. The message was brief and clear:

Your make-up is not a matter of current fashion. It is the real-ization of what you are, of that period of history to which your individual style of beauty pertains. What Old Master might have painted you, and seen you truly? We can help you to discover that, and to learn to apply the only cosmetics made to realize the Old Master quality in you. We do not seek the most customers, only the best, and our services and our products are not cheap. That is why they are obtainable only at a few selected shops from our own maquilleuses. What Master are you? We can help you to achieve the distinction that is yours alone.

The advertisement was signed, in an elegant Italic hand, "Amalie", and below were half a dozen addresses of suppliers.

Glancing around to be sure that nobody saw him doing what was academically unspeakable, Darcourt carefully tore the page out of the magazine and hurried back to his rooms, to write a most important letter.

[3]

THE MEETING between the Cornish Foundation and Schnak's parents took place late in May, in the drawing-room of the penthouse. It had better be done, everyone agreed, though nobody expected anything to come of it. Two months had gone by since the decison to support Schnak in her work to revive and re-flesh and re-clothe Hoffmann's notes for *Arthur of Britain*, and the meeting should have taken place earlier, had Arthur not been too much under the weather to do anything. Now, at the end of May, he was mending, but pale and subject to sudden loss of energy.

Arthur and Maria were supported by Darcourt only, for Hollier said he had nothing to contribute to such a meeting, and Geraint Powell was too busy with the forthcoming festival season in Stratford for anything else to claim his attention. The Schnakenburgs had been asked to come at half past eight and they were prompt.

Schnak's parents were not the nonentities Dean Wintersen's description had led Darcourt to expect. Elias Schnakenburg was not very tall, but he was very thin, which made him look tall; he wore a decent grey suit and a dark tie; his grey hair was receding. His expression was solemn and had a distinction Darcourt had not expected; this watch-repair man was a master craftsman and nobody's servant. His wife was as grey and thin as he; she wore a felt hat that was much too heavy for May weather, and grey cotton gloves.

Arthur explained what the Foundation had in mind, making it clear that they were prepared to back a young woman who was said to have great promise, and whose project appealed to the imagination. They expected that a good deal of money would be spent, and without in any way holding the Schnakenburgs responsible for the outcome, they felt that Hulda's parents should be aware of what was being done.

"If you don't hold us responsible, Mr. Cornish, just what do you expect of us?" said the father.

"Your goodwill, really. Your assent to the project. We don't want to appear to be doing anything over your head."

"Do you think our assent, or our doubts, would make any difference to Hulda?"

"We don't know. Presumably she would like to have your encouragement."

"No. It would mean nothing to her either way."

"You regard her as an entirely free agent, then?"

"How could we do that? She is our daughter and we have not given up our feeling that we are responsible for her, nor have we stopped loving her very dearly. We think we are her natural protectors, whatever the law may say about it. Her natural protectors until she marries. We have not rejected her. We are made to feel that she has rejected us." A slight German accent but carefully phrased English.

Mrs. Schnakenburg began to weep silently. Maria hastened to give her a glass of water—why add water to tears? she thought as she did so—and Darcourt decided that he might suitably intervene.

"Dean Wintersen has told us that the feeling between your daughter and yourselves is strained. And you see, of course, that we cannot interfere in that. But we must behave in a proper way, without being parties to any personal disagreement."

"Very business-like and proper of you, of course, but it isn't a matter of business. We feel that we have lost our child—our only child—and this arrangement that you intend so kindly can only make that worse."

"Your daughter is still very young. The breach may not last long. And of course I can assure you that anything Mr. and Mrs. Cornish can do, or I can do, to put things right will be done."

"Very kind. Very well meant. But you are not the people to do much about it. Hulda has found other advisers. Not of your sort. Not at all."

"Would it help to tell us about it?" said Maria. She had seated herself by Mrs. Schnakenburg and was holding her hand. The mother did not speak, but her husband, after some sighing, continued.

"We blame ourselves. We want you to understand that. I guess we were too strict, though we didn't mean it. We are very firm, you see, in our religion. We are very strict Lutherans. That was how Hulda was brought up. We never let her run wild, as so many kids do these days. I blame myself. Her mother was always kind. I wasn't as understanding as I should have been when she wanted to go to the university."

"Did you oppose that?" said Darcourt.

"Not entirely. Mind you, I didn't see what good it could do. I wanted her to do a business course, find a job, be happy, find a good man, get married—kids. You know."

"You didn't see her musical gift?"

"Oh, yes. That was clear from when she was little. But she could have done that, too. We paid for lessons until they got too expensive. We're not rich, you know. We thought she might give her music to the church. Lead a choir and play the organ. There's always a place for that. But can you build a whole life on it? We didn't think so."

"You don't think of music as a profession? The Dean says she has possibilities as a composer."

"Well—I know. He told me that, too. But is that the kind of life you want your daughter—your only daughter—to get into? Do you hear much good of it? What kind of people? Undesirables, many of them, from what you hear. Of course the Dean seems to be a good man. But he's a teacher, eh? Something solid. I tried to put my foot down, but it looks like the time for parents putting their feet down has gone."

This was a familiar story to Darcourt. "So you have a rebellious daughter, is that it? But don't all children rebel? They must—"

"Why must they?" said Schnakenburg, and for the first time there was note of combat in his voice.

"To find themselves. Love can be rather stifling, don't you agree?"

"Is the love of God stifling? Not to a truly Christian spirit."

"I meant the love of parents. Even the kindest, most well-meaning parents."

"The love of parents is the love of God manifesting itself in the life of their child. We prayed with her. We called on God to give her a contrite heart."

"Yes. And what happened?"

After a silence: "I can't tell you. I wouldn't repeat the things she said. I don't know where she picked up such language. Or—yes, I do know; you hear it everywhere nowadays. But I would have thought a girl brought up as she was would have deafened her ears to such filth."

"And she left home?"

"Walked out in what she stood up in, after a few months I wouldn't go through again for any money. Have any of you people any children?"

Shaking of heads.

"Then you can't know what Mother and I went through. We never hear from her. But of course we hear about her, because I make inquiries. She's done well in the university, I grant you. But what has the cost been? We see her, sometimes, when we take care she doesn't see us, and my heart is sore to see her. — I'm afraid she's fallen."

"What do you mean by that?"

"Well—what would I mean? I'm afraid she's living an immoral life. Where else would she get money?"

"Students do get jobs, you know. They do earn money, quite legitimately. I know scores of students who finance their own studies doing jobs that only a young, strong person could do, and keep up a program of studies at the same time. They are a very honourable group, Mr. Schnakenburg."

"You've seen her. Who would give her a job, looking the way she does?"

"She's as thin as a rake," said Mrs. Schnakenburg. It was her only contribution to the conversation.

"Do you really hate the idea of us giving her this chance?" said Maria.

"To be frank with you, Mrs. Cornish—yes, we do. But what can we say? She's not a minor, according to law. We're poor people and you're rich people. You have no children, so you can't know the pain of children. I hope for your sake it will always be so. You have ideas about all this music and art and other stuff that we don't have and don't want. We can't fight you. The world would say we were standing in Hulda's way. But the world doesn't come first with us. There's other things to be thought of. We're beaten. Don't think we don't know it."

"We certainly don't want you to think that you are beaten or that we have beaten you," said Arthur. "I wish you would try to see things a little more our way. We sincerely want to give your daughter the chance her talents entitle her to."

"I know you mean kindly. When I say we're beaten I guess I mean we're beaten for the present. But we've given Hulda something too, you know. We've given her the source of all real strength. And we pray—we pray every night, for as much as an hour, sometimes—that she will come back to that before it's too late. God's mercy is infinite, but if you kick Him in the face enough, He can be pretty stern. We'll bring our girl back to God if prayer can do it."

"You don't despair, then," said Maria.

"Certainly not. Despair is one of the worst sins. It questions God's intentions and His power. We don't despair. But we are human, and weak. We can't help being hurt."

That was that. After a few more exchanges in which Schnakenburg yielded nothing, while remaining perfectly polite, the couple left.

There was heavy silence in the room. Arthur and Maria seemed greatly put down, but Darcourt was in good spirits. He went to the bar-cupboard in the corner and set to work to make the drinks they had not thought it polite to have while the Schnakenburgs, obviously dry types, were present. As he poured, he sang under his breath:

> *"Tell me the old, old story*
> *Of unseen things above,*
> *Of Jesus and His glory*
> *Of Jesus and His love."*

"Simon, don't be facetious," said Maria.

"I'm only trying to cheer you up. Why are you so down in the mouth?"

"Those two have made me feel absolutely rotten," said Arthur. "The unfeeling, fancy-pants rich man, childless and obsessed with vanities, steals away the jewel of their lives."

"She stole herself away long before you heard of her," said Darcourt.

"You know what I mean. The overbearingness of the rich and privileged."

"Arthur, you are not well. You are open to subtle psychological attack. And that's what you've had. That man Schnakenburg knows every trick in the book to make people feel rotten who don't share his attitude toward life. It's an underdog's revenge. You are not supposed to kick the underdog, but it's perfectly okay for the underdog to bite you. One of the insoluble injustices of society. Pay no heed. Just go right on as before."

"I'm surprised at you, Simon. That man was talking from the depths of a profound religious feeling. We don't share it, but we must in decency respect it."

"Look, Arthur. I'm the expert on religion here. Don't bother your head about it."

"You are a High Church ritualist, and you despise their simplicity. I didn't think you were such a snob, Simon." Maria spoke angrily.

"In your heart you are still a superstitious Gypsy girl, and when anybody talks about God you go all of a doodah. I don't despise anybody's simplicity. But I know when a pretence of simplicity is clever play for power."

"What power has that man?" said Arthur.

"Obviously the power to make you feel rotten," said Darcourt.

"You're unjust, Simon," said Maria; "he talked with such certainty and trust about God. It made me feel like a frivolous ninny."

"Look, children—listen to old Abbé Darcourt and stop hating yourselves. I've listened to hundreds of people like that. They have certainty and depth of belief but they buy it at the price of a joyless, know-nothing attitude toward life. All they ask of God is a kind of spiritual Minimum Wage and in return they are ready to give up the sweets of life—which God also made, let me remind you. I call believers like that the Friends of the Minimum. God, who is an incorrigible joker, has landed them with a daughter who wants to join the Friends of the Maximum, and you can help her. Her parents' faith is like a little candle, burning in the night; your Cornish Foundation is, let's say for the sake of modesty, a forty-watt bulb which may light her to a better life. Don't switch off the forty-watt bulb because the candle looks so pitiably weak. Schnak is in a mess. Indeed, Schnak looks like a mess, and is an odious little creature. But the only path for Schnak is forward, not backward toward a good job, a nice husband like Daddy, and kids born in the same chains. Father Schnakenburg is very tough. You've got to be tough, too."

"I didn't know you were a stoic, Simon," said Arthur.

"I'm not a stoic. I'm that very unfashionable thing, an optimist. Give Schnak her chance."

"Of course we will. We must, now. We're committed to it. But I don't like feeling that I'm trampling on the weak."

"Oh, Arthur! You sentimental mutt! Can't you see that being trampled on is victuals and drink to Schnakenburg? In the great electoral contest of life he is running for martyr, and you are helping him. He has his depth and certainty of belief. Where's yours? You are running for the satisfaction of being a great patron. That's a reasonable cause for certainty and belief. What ails you?"

"I suppose it's money," said Maria.

"Of course it is! You people both have the guilt that our society demands of the rich. Don't give in to it! Show 'em that money can do fine things."

"By God, I believe you really are an optimist," said Arthur.

"Well, that's a start. Join me in my optimism and in time you may believe a few other things that I believe, which I never mention to you, because one thing I have learned in my work as a priest is that preaching to the poor is easy work compared with preaching to the rich. They have so much guilt, and they are so bloody pig-headed."

"We're not pig-headed! We are the ones who feel for the Schnakenburgs. You, the Abbé Darcourt, are sneering at them and urging us to sneer. You Anglican! You ritualist! You pompous professorial poop! You disgust me!"

"That is not argument. That is vulgar abuse, for which I will not even stoop to forgive you. I've played a part in the sort of scene we have just gone through more times than you can imagine. The jealousy of the humble parents for the gifted child! Old, stale goods, to me. The hitting below the belt because somebody has a bigger bank account than you, and must therefore be a moral inferior! The favourite weapon of the self-righteous poor. The use of a mean form of religion to gain a status denied to the unbeliever; they tell you the Old, Old Story, and expect you to cave in. And you do. Real religion, my friends, is evolutionary and revolutionary and that's what your Cornish Foundation had better be or it will be nothing."

"You could have been a popular preacher, Simon," said Maria.

"I've never fancied that sort of work; it inflates the ego and can lead to ruin."

"You've made me feel rather better. I don't know about Arthur."

"You're a good friend, Simon," said Arthur. "I'm sorry I was nasty to you. I withdraw pompous and even poop. But you are professorial. Let's forget the Schnakenburgs, in so far as we can. Are you making any headway with that book about Uncle Frank?"

"At last I think I am. I think I may be on to something."

"Good. We want to see the book published, you know. I joke about it, but you understand. We trust you, Simon."

"Thanks. I'm going ahead. By the way, you won't see me for a week or so. I'm going hunting."

"You can't. It's out of season."

"Not for what I'm hunting. The season has just begun."

Darcourt finished his drink, and departed, singing as he left the room,

> *"Tell me the old, old story,*
> *Tell me the old, old story,*
> *Tell me the old, old story*
> *Of Jesus and His love."*

But the tone of his voice was ironic.

"A really good friend, the old Abbé," said Arthur.

"I love him."

"Platonically, I hope."

"Of course. Can you doubt it?"

"In love I can doubt anything. I never take you for granted."

"You could, you know."

"By the way, you never told me what Mamusia told Simon while I was in hospital."

"Just that we'll all get our lumps, really."

"I think I've had my lumps for a while. My mumps-lumps. But I'm coming round, at last. I think I'll sleep in your bed tonight."

"Arthur—I'd love that. But is it wise?"

"Darcourt's doctrine of optimism. Let's give it a go."

And they did.

[4]

THE ROOM IN THE APARTMENT on Park Avenue was splendid beyond anything Darcourt had ever experienced. It was the work of a brilliant decorator—so brilliant that he had been able to make a room of modest size in a New York apartment building seem authentically to be a room in a great house, perhaps a minor palace, in Europe. The grisaille panelling had certainly come from a palace but had been adjusted, pieced out, and trimmed so that it gave no hint that it had ever been anywhere else. The furniture was elegant, but comfortable in a way palace furniture never is, and enough of it was modern to allow people to sit on it without the uneasiness demanded by a valuable antique. There were pictures on the walls the decorator had not chosen, for they spoke of a coherent and personal taste, and some were rather ugly; but the decorator had hung them to greatest advantage. There were tables loaded with bibelots and bijouteries—what the decorator called "classy junk"—but it was classy junk that belonged to the owner of the room. Photographs in sepia colouring stood on a *bonheur du jour;* they were in frames decorated with coats of arms and crests that obviously belonged to the people whose likenesses were fading inside them. A beautiful but not foolish desk marked the room as a place of business. An elegantly uniformed maid-servant had seated Darcourt, saying that the Princess would be with him in a few minutes.

She came in very quietly. A lady who might be in her fifties, but who looked much younger; a lady of great, but not professional, beauty; by far the most elegant lady Darcourt had ever encountered.

"I hope you have not been waiting long, Professor Darcourt. I was detained by a tedious telephone call." The voice gentle, and hinting at merriment. The accent of someone who spoke English perfectly, as though instructed by an English governess, but with a hint of some underlying cradle tongue. French, perhaps? German? Darcourt could not tell.

"It is good of you to come to see me. Your letter was very interesting. You wanted to ask about the drawing?"

"If I may, Princess. It is Princess, isn't it? The drawing caught my eye in a magazine. As of course it was intended to."

"I am so glad to hear you say that. Of course it was meant to attract attention. You wouldn't believe the trouble I had persuading the advertising people that it would do so. They are so very conventional, don't you think? Oh, who is going to look at such an old-fashioned picture? they said. Everybody whose eye is wearied by the gaudy, pushy girls in the other advertisements, I said. But that is the way things are being done this year, they said. But what I am advertising is not just of this year, I said. It is meant to be more lasting. It is meant to appeal to people whose lives are not just fixed in this year, I said. I couldn't persuade them. I had to insist."

"And now they admit that you were right?"

"And now they are convinced it was their idea all the time. You do not know advertising men, Professor."

"No, but I know people. I can quite believe what you tell me. Of course they have recognized the subject?"

"The head of a girl, early-seventeenth-century style? Yes, they know that."

"They have not recognized the girl?"

"How would they?"

"By using the eyes in their heads. I knew the girl as soon as you came into this room, Princess."

"Did you, indeed? You have a very keen eye. Possibly she was an ancestress of mine. The drawing is a family possession."

"May I come directly to the point, Princess? I have seen preparatory studies for that drawing."

"Have you really? Where, may I ask?"

"Among the possessions of a friend of mine, who was a gifted artist—particularly gifted in assuming the styles of earlier ages. He made countless drawings, copies from collections of such things; others from life, I should imagine, from the notations he made on the studies. There are five studies for the head which resulted in the picture you own, and which you have made public in your advertisements."

"Where are these drawings at present?"

"In the National Gallery of Canada. My friend left them all his drawings and pictures."

"Has anybody but yourself observed this astonishing resemblance?"

"Not yet. You know how galleries are. They have masses of things they have not catalogued. I saw the drawings when I was preparing my friend's things for transfer to the Gallery. I was his executor in such matters. It could be years before those particular studies are given any careful scrutiny."

"What was the name of this artist?"

"Francis Cornish."

The Princess, who had seemed amused during all their conversation, burst into laughter.

"*Le beau ténébreux!*"

"I beg your pardon?"

"That was what my governess and I called him. He taught me trigonometry. He was so handsome and solemn and proper, and I was longing for him to throw down his pencil and seize me in his strong arms and rain kisses on my burning lips and cry Fly with me! I shall take you to my ruined castle in the mountains and there we shall love, and love, and love until the stars bend down to marvel at us! I was fifteen at the time. *Le beau ténébreux!* What became of him?"

"He died about two years ago. As I say, I was one of his executors."

"Had he some profession?"

"He was a collector and connoisseur. He was very rich."

"So he had retired?"

"No indeed; he was quite active as a connoisseur."

"I meant from his work."

"His work?"

"I see you did not know of his work."

"To what work do you refer? He had studied painting, I know."

The Princess went off into another peal of laughter.

"I don't think I understand you, Princess."

"Forgive me. I was just thinking about *le beau ténébreux* and his studies in painting. But that was not his real work, you know."

Darcourt glowed with delight; here it was, at last! What had

Francis Cornish been up to during those years of which he had no record? The Princess knew. Now was the time to spill the beans.

"I am hopeful that you are going to tell me what his real work was. Because I have undertaken to write a life of my old friend, and there is a long period from about 1937 until 1945, when he became active with the commission that was sorting out all that mass of pictures and sculptures that had gone astray during the war, about which information was very scant. Anything that you can tell me about that time in his life would be most helpful. This portrait of yourself, for instance; it suggests that you knew him on terms that go a little beyond being a tutor in trigonometry."

"You think so?"

"I know a little about pictures. That drawing was made with unmistakable affection for the subject."

"Oh, Professor Darcourt! I am afraid you are a dreadful flatterer!"

So I am, thought Darcourt, and I hope it works with this vain woman. But the vain woman was going on.

"Nevertheless, I think it is ungallant of you to suggest that I can remember 1937 at all, not to speak of studying trigonometry at that time. I had hoped that my looks did not betray so much."

Damn, thought Darcourt; she must be in her middle sixties; I've put my foot in it. Never was good at figures.

"I assure you, Princess, that nothing of the sort entered my head."

"You are still too young yourself, Professor, to know what time means to women. We take refuge in many helpful things. My line of cosmetics, for instance."

"Ah, yes; I wish you every success."

"How can you say that, when you mean to expose my very special mark of excellence, my seventeenth-century drawing, as a fake? And yet I suppose you must do it, if your book about *le beau ténébreux* is to be honest and complete."

"It cannot be honest and complete unless you will tell me what you know about Francis Cornish during those years for which I have no records. And I assure you I never thought of saying anything about your drawing."

"If you don't, somebody else will.. It could be ruinous. The cosmetic business is quite sufficiently ambiguous, without any associations of art faking creeping in."

"No, no; I would never mention it."

"So long as these preliminary sketches are in your National Gallery collection, there is very great danger."

"That is unfortunate, of course."

"Professor Darcourt"—the Princess was flirting with him—"if you had known what you know now, about my drawing and the use I am making of it, would you have sent those five sketches to your National Gallery?"

"If I had thought that you held the key to the most interesting part of Francis Cornish's life, I doubt very much if I would have done so."

"And now they are utterly irretrievable?"

"You see how it is. They are government property. They belong to the Canadian nation."

"Do you suppose the Canadian nation is ever going to attach much importance to them? Can you see queues of Indians and Eskimos, and Newfoundland fishermen, and wheat-growers, standing patiently in line to look at those drawings?"

"I am afraid I do not follow you."

"If I had those drawings in my own hands, I could tell you things about Francis Cornish that would be the making of your book. They would inspire and refresh my memory."

"And if you do not get them into your own hands, Princess?"

"No deal, Professor Darcourt."

[5]

THE CORNISH FOUNDATION was assembled in full palaver. The five members sat at the Round Table, upon which was the Platter of Plenty, heaped high with the fruits of late August. Dusty purple grapes hung from the various bowls of the wondrous epergne; for once, thought Maria, the damned thing looks beautiful even to my eye.

People who live in beautiful surroundings grow accustomed to them, and even indifferent to them. Neither Maria nor the other four members of the Cornish Foundation gave much attention to the room in which they sat at the Round Table. It was a very high room, and had what the architect had called a "cathedral roof" which, in the fading light of day, seemed higher and duskier than it was; below it was a row of small clerestory windows through which the green-blue sky and the first stars could be seen; on the walls below hung Arthur's fine pictures, which were his own choosing, for the late Francis Cornish, who had enough good pictures to outfit a small museum, had left him none. There was a piano, but there was so much space that it did not dominate, as pianos sometimes do. Indeed, there was not much furniture in the room. Arthur liked space, and Maria gloried in uncluttered space, having been brought up in the more than cluttered house of her parents, even before Mamusia had reverted to Gypsydom, and established the midden in the basement beneath all this beauty. The foul rag-and-bone shop of the heart was what Darcourt had once called the Gypsy camp, and Maria had been angry with him, because it was so true.

The Foundation sat at the Round Table in candlelight, assisted by some discreet lighting under a cornice. A stranger coming suddenly into the room would have been struck and perhaps awed by its look of wealth and privilege and the elegant quietness which is one of the avails of wealth and privilege. Such a stranger was Professor Penelope Raven; she was impressed, and determined not to show it.

Expectation was high, and even Hollier had returned early from one of his expeditions to Transylvania, where he rooted for what he called cultural fossils. How handsome he is, thought Maria, and how unfairly his good looks lend weight to whatever he says; Simon isn't in the least handsome, but he does far more for the Foundation than Hollier. Arthur is handsome, but not in the distinguished mode of Hollier; yet Arthur can set wheels to turning and kettles to boiling in a way quite out of Hollier's range. I suppose I am as beautiful, for a woman, as Hollier is for a man, and I know just how little beauty adds up to, when things have to be done.

About the fifth member of the Foundation, Geraint Powell, Maria thought nothing at all. She did not like Powell, or the challenging way Powell looked at her; he was handsome in an actorly style—lots of wavy dark hair, rocking-horse nostrils, a

large mobile mouth—and like many good actors he was better
not examined at too close range. If the Cornish Foundation should
ever be presented on the stage, thought Maria, Geraint Powell
would be cast for the role of Clement Hollier; his overstated
good looks would carry to the back of the theatre, as Hollier's
fine good looks would not.

They were all present, and eager, because Professor Penelope
Raven had returned triumphant from her search abroad for the
libretto to *Arthur of Britain,* and was on hand to tell what she
had found.

"I've got it," she said; "and, as this kind of research goes, it
wasn't too hard to find. It's always like *The Hunting of the Snark,*
you know; at the very last moment your Snark may turn out to
be a Boojum. I guessed it would be in the British Museum library,
among the theatre stuff, but as I expect you know, finding things
there—if they are as obscure as this—depends a lot on research
skill, and a nose for oddities, and sheer baldheaded luck. Of
course I traipsed through the opera archives and libraries in Bamberg, Dresden, Leipzig, and Berlin—and I didn't find a thing. Not
a sausage. Lots of stuff about Hoffmann but nothing about this
opera. I had to be thorough or I would have been wasting your
money. But I had a hunch that London was where it would be."

"Because of this man Planché," said Arthur.

"No. Not Planché. I was on the track of Charles Kemble. Now
I'm going to have to lecture you a bit, I'm afraid. Kemble was a
member of the famous theatrical family; you'll all have heard of
Mrs. Siddons, who was his sister and the greatest actress of her
time; you've seen Reynolds' picture of her as the Tragic Muse.
Charles Kemble was manager and lessee of Covent Garden Theatre from 1817 till 1823, and in spite of a lot of marvellous
successes, he was always in trouble about money. Not his fault,
really. It was the theatre economics of the time. The owners of
the theatre demanded an immense yearly rental, and even a successful manager was often in hot water.

"Charles adored opera. He was always encouraging composers
to write new ones. He was really an awfully nice man, and he
encouraged anybody who had talent. He had his eye on our man,
James Robinson Planché, because Planché could deliver the

goods; he was a first-rate theatre man, and working with him meant success. Kemble had heard about Hoffmann—all the Kembles were awfully well educated, which wasn't at all the usual thing among theatre people then—and I suppose he read German, or had seen something of Hoffmann's in Germany. He persuaded Hoffmann to write him an opera, and insisted that Planché, who was still under thirty and obviously started on a successful career, should provide the libretto.

"So—the work was begun, and there was some correspondence between Planché and Hoffmann, which is lost, I fear; poor old Hoffmann was in bad health, and died before anything much came of it. And Hoffmann and Planché fought like cat and dog in the very polite epistolary fashion of the time, so I imagine Planché was relieved when the whole affair came to nothing. As it turned out he wrote a little thing to replace it, called *Maid Marian,* with music by a clever hack called Bishop.

"The story, so far as I could dig it up, was in Charles Kemble's papers in the B.M. Want to hear it?"

"Yes, we certainly do," said Arthur. "But first, can you reassure us that there actually is a libretto, of some sort, for this opera?"

"Oh there is. Yes indeed there is, and I have transcripts of it right here. But I think it would all come clearer if I read you some of the exchange between Planché and Kemble."

"Fire away," said Arthur.

"This is the first letter to Kemble that I found.

My dear Kemble:

I have exchanged letters with Herr Hoffmann, and it would appear that we are working at cross purposes, as he has only a very imperfect noting of the English theatre as it pertains to opera. But I am confident that we shall arrive at an agreement when I have explained the facts of the situation to him. We correspond, by the way, in French and I may say that his command of that language may be at the root of certain of our differences, for he is far from perfect.

As you know, I like to work quickly, and having much on my hands at the moment I wrote to Hoffmann as soon as I heard from you that he would prepare the music for a piece for the approaching Covent Garden season. I outlined a plan I have had in my mind for some time for a fairy piece which might as well be attached to King Arthur as to any other popular hero. In brief, it is this: King Arthur and his companions, wearying of the pleasures of the chase, hit upon the capital notion of establishing a Round Table with a view to raising the level of chivalry in England, which has been the source of some complaint from Queen Guenevere. (Opportunity here for a duet of a comic nature between Arthur and his Queen, who thinks herself ill-used.) Arthur knows how to deal with that, so he calls upon his enchanter, Merlin, to transfer his Court *tous sans exception* to the Kingdom of the Grand Turk, to see how ladies are treated *there,* and Merlin calls upon the Fairy Court, led by King Oberon and Queen Titania, to effect this change. But the fairy rulers are at odds, as are Arthur and Guenevere, and refuse their office. (Opportunity for a fairy ballet, which is agreed by everyone at present to be a sure card, and very pretty.) Merlin seeks assistance from Pigwiggen, the only one of Arthur's knights who is also a fairy, and they unite their enchantments to move the British Court to Turkestan. Lively end to Act One.

Turkestan is the scene of the second act, and provides opportunities which I am sure the excellent Mr. Grieve will seize upon for scenic display of a lavish and very striking order. We involve the Grand Turk, who lays siege to Queen Guenevere, arousing the jealousy of Arthur. (Great opportunity here for mischief by Pigwiggen.) To Arthur's dismay his principal Knight, Sir Lancelot, falls in love with the Queen, and he and Arthur quarrel and nothing will settle their difference but a duel. More business for Pigwiggen, who knows that Elaine, the Lily Maid, loves Lancelot and he has encouraged her. Must get Elaine onstage in Act One. The Grand Turk will have no duelling in his kingdom and, by an opportune strike of chance, Oberon and Titania appear, having resolved their dispute, and transport the whole Round Table back to Britain. I thought of a scene here in which the Fairy Court, all carrying tapers, lead the English away from Turkestan, climbing a mountain in darkness. (You are aware that Covent Garden has such a mountain among its scenes in store, which was used in *Barbarossa* three seasons ago, and could be easily refurbished to repeat the great effect it made then.) Strong conclusion to Act Two.

Act Three is again in Britain, and the duel between Arthur and Lancelot is in preparation, but first we present a Grand Parade of the Seven Champions—all played by ladies, of course—with plenty of amusing valour for St. Denis of France and St. Iago of Spain; it might be stylish if St. Anthony of Italy sang in Italian, Denis in French, and Iago in Spanish. Follow this with comical songs in characteristic dialect for St. Patrick of Ireland and St. David of Wales and St. Andrew of Scotland, with perhaps a mock combat between the three British Champions which is resolved by St. George of England, who subdues all three. Under the stewardship of St. George—a parade of Heralds at this point and a great show of heraldry, which looks splendid and costs little—Arthur and Lancelot prepare to fight—real horses, don't you think? Horses never fail with an English audience—which is halted by the appearance of Elaine, the Lily Maid of Astolat, who enters floating down a river in a skiff, apparently dead, a scroll in her hand proclaiming her to be a *petite amie* of Lancelot's whom he has jilted. Accused by Guenevere, Lancelot admits his guilt, and Elaine leaps from her bier and claims him for her own. Reconciliation of Arthur and Guenevere, assisted by Merlin and Pigwiggen, and St. George declares the triumph of chivalry and the Round Table. Grand patriotic conclusion.

I do not need to explain to you, my dear Sir, who know the resources of your theatre so well, that I have prepared this plan with singers in mind who are at once available, with the exception of Madame Catalani, who is willing to come out of retirement, and could be tempted with the role of Guenevere if opportunities for her splended *coloratura* were plentifully supplied, which presents no difficulty. If Hoffmann proved not up to it our friend Bishop could write something in his usual florid style. Otherwise, who but Braham for Arthur, Duruset for Lancelot, Miss Cause for Elaine,

Keeley as Merlin (his voice is gone but I conceive of Merlin as a minor comic figure), Madame Vestris as Pigwiggen—with a costume which would give ample play for her magnificent limbs? Wrench would do very well as Oberon as he can dance, as can Miss Paton, who would be sufficiently *petite*, despite her growing *embonpoint*, for Titania. I see Augustus Burroughs as a fine St. George. Neat, do you not agree?

Now there, I should certainly think, we have a splendid opera fitted, and chances innumerable for the fantasy and *grotesquerie* which you assure me are Herr Hoffmann's *spécialités de la maison*. But no. Oh, no!

Our German friend replies with many compliments in very stiff French—honoured to be collaborating with me, conscious of the *éclat* deriving from association with Covent Garden, etc. etc.—and then he goes on to read me a truly German lecture about opera. As he sees it, the day of the sort of opera I propose—he actually spoke of it as 'a delightful Christmas piece for children'!—is over, and something musically more ambitious is at hand. There are not to be single numbers, or songs, for the characters, with dialogue to link them together, but a continuous flow of music, the *arias* being joined by *recitativo stromentato*—so that, in effect, the orchestra never gets any rest at all, but saws and blows away all evening! And the music should be dramatic, rather than occasions for vocal display by specially gifted singers—'performers on that seriously overrated instrument, the human neck' he calls them (and what would Madame Cat make of *that*, if she heard it?)—and every character should have a musical 'motto', by which he means a phrase or instrumental flourish that signifies that character alone, and can be presented in different ways according to the spirit of the action. He declares this would make a very striking effect and signal a new mode of opera composition! As it certainly would, and empty the theatre, I am sure!

Very well. Music is his business, I suppose, though I am myself not wholly ignorant of that science, as I have shown before this. But when he laughs at my notion for the dramatic part of the piece, I think I have some cause to speak plainly.

He wants to go right back to the original Arthurian tales, and dramatize them 'seriously' he says, and not in a spirit of *'un bal travesti'*—I suppose that is a hit at my Seven Champions being represented by ladies, which I am certain would go down well, as ladies in armour are, I may say, the rage at present—partly because of legs, of course, but what of that? Spangled tights for each Champion, in the colours of the nation represented, would create a very fine effect, and give pleasure to that part of the audience which is not intensely musical. The opera house is not, and never has been, a nunnery. He speaks of the *'ambience Celtique'* of the Arthurian legend, not understanding, apparently, that the Arthurian tales have long been—by conquest, I suppose—the property of England, and therefore of her national opera house.

But do not discompose yourself, my dear friend. I am writing a reply that will explain some things to Herr Hoffmann which he clearly does not know, and we shall proceed very amicably, I am confident, once I have done so.

I have the honour to subscribe myself,

Yours very sincerely,
JAMES ROBINSON PLANCHÉ.

April 18, 1822"

"My God," said Arthur; "I foresee trouble."

"Don't worry," said Geraint. "This is all familiar stuff to me. Theatre people go on like that all the time. It's what's called the creative ferment from which all great art emerges. At least that's what it's called when you are being nice about it. There's more, I suppose?"

"Lots more," said Penny. "Wait till you hear Letter Number Two.

My dear Kemble:

When I had conquered my understandable chagrin—for I make it a principle never to speak or write in anger—I wrote again to our friend Hoffmann, in what the Bard calls a 'condoling' manner, repeating my principal points and supporting them with some passages of verse which I put forward as the sort of thing we might use in the opera. For instance, I proposed a Hunting Chorus as a beginning. Something spirited, and with plenty of brass in the orchestration, along these lines:

> *We all went out a-hunting*
> *The break of day before,*
> *In hopes to stop the grunting*
> *Of a most enormous boar!*

> *But he made it soon appear*
> *We'd got the wrong pig by the ear,*
> *Till our Fairy Knight*
> *To our delight*
> *In his spare rib poked a spear!*

—this to be followed by a thigh-slapping song for Pigwiggen (Madame Vestris, did I say?) about the hunting of the boar (with some *double entendre* on 'boar' and 'bore') and the Huntsmen to sing the chorus again.

I want the fairy element to be very strong, and Pigwiggen's power to be deft and quick, like Puck's, in contrast to the heavier comic magic of Merlin. Perhaps a song here? Pigwiggen should appeal to both the ladies and the gentlemen in the audience—to the former as a charming boy, and to the latter as a charming girl in boy's dress—a trick the Bard knew so well. I suggested to Herr H. that Pigwiggen's song might be along these lines:

> *The fairy laughs at the wisest man*
> *There's none can do as the Fairy can;*
> *Never knew a pretty girl in my life*
> *But wished she was a Fairy's wife."*

"That could get a very bad laugh in a modern opera," said Darcourt. "I don't mean to interrupt, Penny, but nowadays all fairy business has to be handled very carefully."

"Just you wait, my boy," said Penny, and went on with the letter.

"The love scenes between Lancelot and Guenevere provide the chief romantic interest in the opera, and I sketched out a duet for Hoffmann to think about. I am not a composer—though no stranger to music, as I have said—but I think this might bring out something really fine in a man who *is* a composer, as we have reason to believe Hoffmann is. Lancelot sings under Guenevere's window:

> *The moon is up, the stars shine bright*
> *O'er the silent sea;*
> *And my lady love, beneath their light*
> *Has waited long for me.*
> *O, sweet the song and the lute may sound*
> *To the lover's listening ear:*
> *But wilder and faster his pulse will bound*
> *At the voice of his lady dear.*
>
> *Then come with me where the stars shine bright*
> *O'er the silent sea:*
> *O, my lady love, beneath their light*
> *I wait alone for thee."*

"I wonder if I might trouble you for a drop more whisky?" said Hollier to Arthur in an undertone.

"Indeed you may. Much more of this and I shall want a very big one myself," said Arthur, and circulated the decanter. Darcourt and Powell seemed to need it, as well.

"I must say a word for Planché," said Penny; "no libretto reads well. But listen to what Guenevere replies, from her balcony window:

> *A latent feeling wakes*
> *Within my breast*
> *Some strange regard that breaks*
> *Its wonted rest.*
> *Let me resist, in heart,*
> *However weak*
> *What love with so much art*
> *Can speak.*

And then I suppose he means to follow with a love scene in prose, Lancelot mooning under Guenevere's window."

"Oh, not mooning, I hope," said Powell. "First fairy knights, and then mooning ladies. You'll have the show closed by the police."

"No coarse jibes, if you please," said Penny. "Not all the love songs are so sentimental. Listen to what the Grand Turk sings, when the Round Table party arrives in his court. He is immediately smitten by Guenevere and here he goes:

> *Though I've pondered on Peris and Houris,*
>   *The stars of Arabian Nights,*
> *This fair Pagan more beautiful sure is*
>   *Than any such false Harem Lights;*
> *No gazelle! no gazelle! no gazelle!*
>   *Has such eyes as of me took the measure!*
> *She's a belle! she's a belle! she's a belle!*
>   *I could ring with the greatest of pleasure!"*

"Penny, are you offering this seriously?" said Maria.

"Planché was certainly offering it seriously—and confidently. He knew his market. I assure you this is in the real early-nineteenth-century vein, and people loved just this sort of thing. It was the Regency, you know, or as near as makes no difference. They whistled and sang and barrel-organed and played *Grand Paraphrases de Concert* of stuff like this on their lovely varnished pianofortes," said Penny. "It was a time when they used to do Mozart with a lot of his music cut out, and jolly new bits by Bishop interpolated. It was before opera went all serious and sacred and had to be listened to in a holy hush. They just thought it was fun, and they treated it rough."

"What was Hoffmann's response to this muck?" said Hollier.

"Oh, muck's a bit strong, don't you think?" said Penny.

"It's so God-damned jocose," said Arthur.

"He seems to be patronizing the past, which I can't bear," said Maria. "He treats Arthur and his knights as if they had no dignity whatever."

"Oh, very true. Very true," said Penny. "But do we do any

better, with our *Camelots* and *Monty Pythons* and such? Pretending your great-great-infinitely-great-grandfather was a fool has always appealed to the theatrical mind. Sometimes I think there ought to be a Charter of Rights for the Dead. But you're quite right; it *is* jocose. Listen to this, for Elaine to sing to Lancelot when he gives her the mitt:

> *On some fine summer morning*
> *If I must hope give o'er,*
> *You'll find, I give you warning,*
> *My death laid at you door.*
> *And if at your bedside leering*
> *Some night a ghost you spy,*
> *Don't be surprised at hearing*
> *'Tis I, 'tis I, 'tis I!"*

"She sounds very like Miss Bailey—unfortunate Miss Bailey," said Arthur.

"What about the grand patriotic conclusion?" said Darcourt. "Let's see—where is it? Yes:

> *From cottage and hall*
> *To drive sorrow away,*
> *Which in both may befall*
> *On some bright happy day*
> *Reign again over me, reign again over thee,*
> *The good king we shall see!*
> *Oh! long live the king!"*

"That doesn't even make sense," said Hollier.

"It's patriotism—doesn't have to," said Penny.

"But is this what Hoffmann set to music?" said Hollier.

"No, he didn't. There is a final letter which seems to put an end to the whole business. Listen:

My dear Kemble:

I wish I had better news for you from our friend Hoffmann. As you know, I sent him some sketches for several songs for the Arthur piece, with the usual librettist's assurances that I would alter them in any way he felt necessary, to fit music he had composed. And of course that I would write additional verses for theatrical situations we agreed on, and when everything else was finished, I would pull it all together with passages of dialogue. But as you see he keeps nagging away at his *idée fixe*. I felt that any differences there were between us were a matter of language; I do not know how well he understands English. However, he has chosen to reply to me in English, and I enclose his letter—

Honoured Sir:

In order that I may make myself as plain as possible I am writing this in German, to be translated by my esteemed friend and colleague Schauspieldirektor Ludwig Devrient, into English, of which I have myself only the most imperfect knowledge. Not so imperfect, however, that I cannot seize the spirit of your beautiful verses, and declare them to be utterly unsuited to the opera I have in mind.

It has been my happiness during my life to see great changes in music, and many musicians have been so generous as to say that I have been not unhelpful in bringing such changes about. For as you doubtless do not know, I have written a great deal of musical criticism and have been happy in the commendation of the eminent Beethoven, to say nothing of the friendship of Schumann and Weber. It was Beethoven's regret that he had at last completed his *Fidelio* as an opera with spoken dialogue—a *Singspiel* as we call it. Since the completion of my last opera, *Undine,* of which Weber was so generous as to speak in the highest terms, I have thought much about the nature of opera, and now—when I assure you time is running out with me, for reasons I shall not elaborate here—I greatly wish either to write the opera of my dreams, or to write no opera at all. And, distinguished Sir, though I am sorry to speak so bluntly, your proposed libretto is no opera at all, for any purpose known to me.

When I speak of the opera of my dreams, it is no forced elegance of words, I assure you, but the expression of what I believe music to be, and to be capable of expressing. For is not music a language? And of what is it the language? Is it not the language of the dream world, the world beyond thought, beyond the languages of Mankind? Music strives to speak to Mankind in the only possible language of this unseen world. In your letters you stress again and again the necessity to reach an audience, to achieve a success. But what kind of success? I am now at a point in my life—an ending, I fear—when such success has no charms for me. I have not long to speak and I can only be content to speak truth.

I beg you to be so good as to reconsider. Let us not prepare another *Singspiel,* full of drolleries and elfin persons, but an opera in the manner of the future, with music throughout, the arias being linked by dialogue sung to an orchestral accompaniment and not simply to the few notes from the harpsichord, to keep the singer in tune. And, O my very dear Sir, let us be serious about *la Matiére de Bretagne* and not present King Arthur as a Jack Pudding.

No, I see the drama as springing from King Arthur's recognition of the noble love of Lancelot for Guenevere, and the great pain with which he accepts that love. You have all that anyone could need in your English romance *Le Morte d' Arthur.* Draw upon that, I beg you. Let us have that great love, and also the sorrow with which Lancelot knows that he is betraying his friend and king, and Lancelot's madness born of remorse. Let us make an opera about three people of the highest nobility, and let us make Arthur's forgiveness and understanding love for his Queen and his friend the culminating point of the action. The title I propose is *Arthur of Britain, or the Magnanimous Cuckold.* Whether that has the right ring in English I cannot tell, but you will know.

But let us, I entreat you, explore the miraculous that dwells in the depths of the mind. Let the lyre of Orpheus open the door of the underworld of feeling.

With every protestation of respect and regard I am, Honoured Sir,

May 1, 1822   E. T. A. HOFFMANN

Post Scriptum: I enclose a quantity of rough notes I have prepared for the sort of opera I so greatly desire, hoping that they will convey to you a measure of the feeling of which I speak—a feeling, to use a word now coming much into fashion, that is profound in its Romanticism

Now, there, my dear Kemble, what do you make of that? What do I make of that? It all sounds to me like Germans who have been smoking their long pipes and sitting up late over their thick, black beer. Of course I know what he is talking about. It is Melodrama, or verses spoken or chanted to music, and it is quite useless for the purposes of opera as we know it at Covent Garden.

But I kept my temper. Never be out of temper with a musician is a good principle, as you know from your frequent altercations with the explosive Bishop, in which you have always prevailed by your splendid Phlegm. I wrote again, trying to coax Hoffmann to see things from my point of view, which is not to push forward the frontiers of music, I assure you, or plunge into the murky world of dreams. Humour, I assured him, is what the English most value, and whatever is to be said to them must be said humorously or not at all, if music is in question. (I except, of course, Oratorio, which is a wholly different matter.) Indeed, I tried upon him a rather neat little thing I dashed off, proposing it as the song which establishes the character of the Fairy Pigwiggen (Madame Vestris):

> *King Oberon rules in Fairyland,*
> *Titania by his side;*
> *But who is their Prime Minister,*
> *Their counsellor and guide?*
> *'Tis I, the gay Pigwiggen, who*
> *Keeps hold upon the helm*
> *When their spitting and spatting*
> *Their dogging and catting*
> *Threatens the Fairy Realm*

> *Who, think you, rules in Fairyland?*
> *Not these who hold the sceptre!*
> *Nay, devil a bit*
> *Not Nob and Tit,*
> *But I, their gay preceptor!*
> *Pigwiggen, the merry minikin*
> *Is Nob and Tit's preceptor!*

Now, I think I may say, not in vanity but as a man who has won his place in the theatre with several pieces, all markedly successful, that this is rather neat. Do you agree?

Several weeks have elapsed, and I have had no word from our German friend. But time wears on, and I shall stir him up again, as genially as I know how.

Yours, etc.

June 20, 1822   J. R. PLANCHÉ

There is a notation on this letter in Kemble's hand, which says: 'News reaches me of Hoffmann's death at Berlin, on 25 June. Inform Planché at once, and suggest an immediate council to decide on a new piece and a new composer—Bishop?—as it must be ready for Christmas.' "

There was heavy silence among the Cornish Foundation, as Penny helped herself to a bunch of grapes from the Platter of Plenty.

It was Hollier who spoke first. "What do you suppose poor dying Hoffmann made of Nob and Tit?"

"A modern audience would certainly see it as jocose indecency. Language has taken some queer turns since Planché's time," said Darcourt.

"Queer's the word," said Arthur.

"Don't be too sure about a modern audience," said Powell, who seemed to be the least depressed of the group. "You recall that song in *A Chorus Line?* Rather a lot about Ass and Tit, sung by a girl with magnificent limbs? The audience couldn't get enough of it."

"I have to agree about the changes of language," said Penny. "I have spared you Planché's notes for dialogue, which he sent to Kemble. He wanted Pigwiggen to talk a lot about her Knock-ers."

"Her *what?*" said Arthur, aghast.

"Her Knockers. She meant some underground spirits who worked in the mines of Britain, and were called Knockers."

"Is there something ambiguous about Knockers?" said Hollier. "I'm sorry. I'm not very well up on the latest indecencies."

"Knockers nowadays means breasts," said Powell. "Door knockers, you know, which show up so prominently on the front. 'She has a great pair of knockers,' people say. Probably better known in England than here."

"Ah yes. I wondered if it were a misreading for Knackers," said Hollier. "Meaning the testicles. Perhaps the Magnanimous Cuck-old would be the person to talk about those."

"For God's sake try to be serious," said Arthur. "We are in very deep trouble. Doesn't anybody understand that? Are we seriously going to spend a great amount of Uncle Frank's bene-faction to stage an opera that is all about Knackers and Knockers and Nobs and Tits and gay fairies? Is my hair going white, Maria? I distinctly feel a withering of my scalp."

"As a student of Rabelais, all this sniggering, half-hearted in-decency makes me throw up," said Maria.

Penny spat out a mouthful of grape seeds, not very elegantly, on her plate. "Well—you have the music, you know. Or plans and sketches for it."

"But is it any good?" said Maria. "If it is on the Planché level, we're through. Absolutely through, as Arthur says. Was Hoff-mann any good? Does anybody know?"

"I'm not a judge," said Penny. "But I think he wasn't half bad. Mind you, music's not my thing. But when I was in London the BBC broadcast Hoffmann's *Undine* in a program called Early Romantic Operas, and of course I listened. Indeed, I took it on tape, and I have it here, if you're interested. Have you got the right sort of machine?"

It was Maria who took the tapes and put them in the hi-fi equipment that was concealed in a cupboard near the Round Table. Darcourt made sure that everybody had a drink, and the Cornish Foundation, in the lowest spirits it had known since its establishment, composed itself to listen. Nobody wore an expression of hope, but Powell was the least depressed. He was a theatre man, and was accustomed to abysses in the creative process.

It was Arthur who first was jolted into new life by the music. "Listen, listen, listen! He's using voices in the Overture! Where have you heard that before?"

"They're the voices of the lover and the Water Sprite, calling to Undine," said Penny.

"If he goes on like that, maybe we're not in too much trouble," said Arthur. He was a musical enthusiast, a bad amateur pianist, and it was his regret that his Uncle Francis had not left him his enviable collection of musical manuscripts. He would then have had the uncompleted opera safe in his own hands.

"This is accomplished stuff," said Maria.

As indeed it was. The Cornish Foundation, according to individual musical sensitivity, roused themselves. Darcourt knew what he was hearing; he had first become acquainted with Francis Cornish because of a shared enthusiasm for music. Powell declared music to be one of the elements in which he lived; it was his desire to extend his experience as a director of opera that had made him urge the Foundation to consider putting *Arthur of Britain* on the stage. Hollier was the tin-eared one, and he knew it, but he had a feeling for drama and, though now and then he dozed, *Undine* was unquestionably dramatic. By the end of the first act they were all in a happier frame of mind, and demanded drinks as cheer, rather than as pain-killers.

Undine is not a short opera, but they showed no weariness, and heard it to the end. It was then almost four o'clock in the morning and they had been at the Round Table for nine hours, but except for Hollier they were alert and happy.

"If that's Hoffmann as a composer, it looks as if we were right on the pig's back," said Arthur. "I hope I'm not carried away by relief, but I think it's splendid."

"He truly does use the lyre of Orpheus to open the underworld of feeling," said Maria. "He used that phrase often. He must have loved it."

"Did you hear how he uses the wood-winds? Not just doubling the strings, as even the best Italians were apt to do when this was written, but declaring another kind of feeling. Oh, those magical deep wood-winds! This is Romanticism, right enough," said Powell.

"New Romanticism," said Maria. "You catch Mozartian echoes—no, not echoes, but loving recollections—and some Beethovenian beef in the big moments. And God be praised he doesn't wallop the timpani whenever he wants intensity. I think it's great! Oh, Arthur—" and she kissed her husband with relief and joy.

"I'm glad we heard his letter to Planché first," said Darcourt. "You know what he's getting at, and what he hoped to achieve in *Arthur*. Not music just to support stage action, but to be action in itself. What a shame he never got his chance to go ahead!"

"Well, yes; I don't want to pour cold water," said Hollier, "but as the least musical among you, I can't forget that we haven't a libretto. Assuming, as I am sure you do, that the Planché stuff is totally unusable. No libretto, and is there enough music to make an opera. Does anybody know?"

"I've been to the library for a look," said Arthur, "and there's quite a wad of music, though I can't judge what shape it's in. There are scribbles in German on some of the manuscript which seem to suggest action, or places where action would come. I can't read that old German script well enough to say much about it."

"But no words?"

"I didn't see any words, though I could be mistaken."

"Do you think we can really turn Schnak loose on this? Does she know German? I suppose she may have picked up some from her parents. Not poetic German, certainly. Nothing Romantic about the senior Schnaks," said Darcourt.

"I don't want to nag, but without a libretto, where are we?" said Hollier.

Powell was impatient. "Surely with all the brains there are around this table we can put together a libretto?"

"Poetry?" said Darcourt.

"Libretto poetry," said Powell. "I've read dozens of 'em, and the poetic heights are not enough to make you dizzy. Come on! Faint heart never made fair libretto."

"I'm afraid I'm rather the fifth wheel of the coach so far as music is concerned," said Hollier. "But the *Matière de Bretagne* is right in my line, and I have a pretty clear recollection of Malory. Anything I know is at your service. I can fake a late-medieval line as well as most people, I suppose."

"So there we are," said Powell. "Right on the pig's back, as Arthur so Celtically puts it."

"Oh, don't be hasty," said Hollier. "This will take some time to establish, even when we've decided which of the Arthurian paths we are going to follow. There are many, you know—the Celtic, the French, the German, and of course Malory. And what attitude do we take to Arthur? Is he a sun-god embodied in legend by a people half-Christianized? Or is he simply the *dux bellorum,* the leader of his British people against the invading Saxons? Or do we choose the refinement of Marie de France and Chrétien de Troyes? Or do we assume that Geoffrey of Monmouth really knew what he was talking about, however improbable that may seem? We can dismiss any notion of a Tennysonian Arthur: he was wholly good and noble and a post-Freudian audience wouldn't swallow him. It could take months of the most careful consideration before we decide how we are going to *see* Arthur."

"We're going to see him as the hero of an early-nineteenth-century opera, and no nonsense about it," said Geraint Powell. "We haven't a moment to lose. I've made it clear, I think, that the Stratford Festival will allow us to mount ten or twelve performances of *Arthur* during its next season and I've persuaded them to slot it as late as possible. Late August—just a year from now. We've got to get cracking."

"But surely that's absurd," said Hollier. "Will the libretto be ready, not to speak of the music? And then I suppose the theatrical people will have to have a little time to get it up—"

"The theatrical people will have to be got under contract not later than next month," said Geraint. "My God, have you no idea how opera singers work? The best are all contracted three years ahead. A thing on this scale won't need the biggest stars, even if we could get them, but intelligent singers of the next rank won't be easy to find, especially for an unknown work. They'll have to shoehorn this piece into very tight schedules. And there's the designer, and all the carpentry and painting work, and the costumes—I'd better stop, I'm frightening myself!"

"But the libretto!" said Hollier.

"The libretto is going to have to hustle its stumps. Whoever is responsible for it must get to work at once, and be quick. The words have to be fitted to whatever music exists, remember, and that is tricky work. We can't fart around forever with sun-gods and Chrétien de Troyes."

"If that is your attitude, I think I had better withdraw at once. I have no desire to be associated with a botch," said Hollier, and took another very big whisky from the decanter.

"No, no, Clem, we'll need you," said Maria, who still cherished a tenderness for the man who had—it seemed so long ago now— taken her maidenhead, almost absent-mindedly. Not that, as a girl of her time, she had possessed anything so archaic as a maidenhead, but the word was suitable to the paleo-psychological spirit of Clement Hollier.

"I have a certain reputation as a scholar to protect. I am sorry to insist on that, but it is a fact."

"Of course we'll need you, Clem," said Penny Raven. "But in an advisory capacity, I think. Better leave the actual writing to old battered hacks like me and Simon."

"As you please," said Hollier, with drunken dignity. "I admit without regret that I have no theatrical experience."

"Theatrical experience is precisely what we're going to need, and lots of it," said Powell. "If I'm to see this thing through, I shall have to crack the whip, and I hope nobody will take offense. There are a lot of elements to be pulled together if we're going to have a show at all."

"As a member of the academic committee that is supposed to be midwife to this effort, I have to remind you that there is an element you've left out, that will have a big say in whatever is done," said Penny.

"Meaning?"

"Schnak's special supervisor. The very big gun who is coming to the university to be composer-in-residence for a year, for this express purpose," said Penny.

"Wintersen keeps hinting about that," said Darcourt; "but he's never mentioned a name. Do you know who it is, Penny?"

"Yes, I do. It's just been finally settled. No one less than Dr. Gunilla Dahl-Soot."

"Golly! What a name!" said Darcourt.

"Yes, and what a lady!" said Penny.

"New to me," said Arthur.

"Shame on you, Arthur. She's acknowledged to be the successor to Nadia Boulánger, as a Muse and fosterer of talent, and general wonder-worker. Schnak is a very, very lucky child. But Gunilla is also said to be a terror, so Schnak had better look out or we shall see some fur flying."

"From what point of the compass does this avatar appear?" asked Arthur.

"From Stockholm. Doesn't the name tip you off?"

"We are greatly privileged to have her, I suppose?"

"Can't say. Is she a Snark or a Boojum? Only time will tell."

[6]

ETAH IN LIMBO

I LIKE THAT MAN POWELL. He has the real professional spirit. My God, when I think what it was like for me, getting operas on the stage in Bamberg, and even in Berlin, and sometimes wondering where I would find enough musicians to make up the orchestra we needed! And what musicians some of them were! Tailors by day, and clarinetists by night! And the singers! The chorus were the worst. I remember some of them sneaking offstage when there was no work for them to do and sneaking back in three minutes, wiping their mouths with the back of a hand! And wearing their underpants beneath their tights, so that the courtiers of Count Whoever-it-was looked as if they had just stumbled in from the wastes of Lapland. Things are much better now. Sometimes I can intrude myself into a performance of something by Wagner—Wagner who wrote so very kindly of me and admitted my influence in his splendid use of the leitmotif—*and, so far as a shade can weep, I weep with pleasure to see how clean all the singers*

*are! Every man seems to have been shaved the very day of the perfor-
mance. Every woman, even though fat, is not more than five months
pregnant. Many of them can act, and they do, even if not well. No
doubt about it, opera has come a very long way since my days in
Bamberg.*

*To say nothing of money! The artists who appear in my Arthur
will be able to go to the treasury every Friday night with confidence
that a full week's salary will be forthcoming. How well I remember
the promises, and the broken promises, of opera finance in my time. Of
course, as director—and that meant conductor and sometimes scene-
painter as well—I usually had my money, but it was wretchedly little
money. These modern theatre people don't know they're alive, and when
I consider their good fortune I sometimes forget that I am dead. As
dead, that's to say, as anybody in Limbo is.*

*At last I begin to pluck up hope. I may not be in Limbo forever.
If Geraint Powell puts my Arthur on the stage, and even five people
stay till the end, I may win my freedom from this stoppage in my
spiritual voyage, this* mors interruptus *(to give it a classical
ring).*

*My own fault, of course. If I died untimely, I must admit that I
died by my own hand, though not as surely as if I had used the rope
or the knife. Mine was death by the bottle, and by—well, enough about
that. Death by Romanticism, let us call it.*

*But by the Almighty's great mercy, an existence in Limbo is not all
tears of regret. We may laugh. And how I laughed when that woman
professor—that is something new since my time, when a learned woman
might be a* bas bleu *but would never have thought of intruding herself
into a university—when that woman professor, I say, read those letters
from Planché to Kemble.*

*They were new to me. I remember his letters, and the high spirits
and assurance they gave off like a perfume. He was so certain that I,
who had not written an opera in some time—seven years, was it—
would welcome his jaunty assistance. But these letters, in which he
reported our exchanges to Kemble, were quite new, and brought back
all that trouble in a new and funny light. Poor Planché, industrious
Huguenot, with his determination to do his best for Madame Vestris
and her magnificent limbs. Poor Planché, with his certainty that an
opera audience could not be persuaded to sit still while anything im-*

portant was being played, or sung. Of course his notion of opera was bad Rossini, or Mozart defaced by that self-loving brigand Bishop. His Covent Garden was a theatre where nobody listened unless one of the Great Necks was shrieking or trumpeting; where people took baskets of cold grouse and champagne to their boxes and stuffed themselves during the music; where those of the right age—between fourteen and ninety—flirted and nodded, and sent billets doux *from box to box, wrapped around little bags of sweets; where the soprano, if the applause was sufficiently insistent, would pause in the opera to sing some popular air; after my death it was often "Home, Sweet Home", which was Bishop's monumental contribution to the art of music; where a soprano's jewels—the real thing, achieved by lying complaisantly under the bellies of rich, old fumbling noblemen—were of as much interest as her voice; as the Great Neck declined, the Grande Poitrine became the object of interest, and the bigger it was the more diamonds it would accommodate. Service medals, jealous rivals called them.*

In Germany—even in Bamberg—we knew a little better than that, and we were at work to beget Romanticism, and bring it to birth.

I wept—Oh yes, we can weep here, and often do—to hear my Undine again, done better than I ever heard it in my lifetime. How good orchestral playing is now; hardly a tailor to be heard in the music the bas bleu *conjured out of her astonishing musical machine.* **Undine** *was my last completed attempt to draw opera forward from the eighteenth century into the nineteenth. Not in the least rejecting Gluck and Mozart, but following them in our attempt to coax something more out of the unknown of man's mind into his consciousness. So we turned from their formal comedies and tragedies toward myth and legend, to release us from the chains of classicism.* **Undine**—*yes, my wonderful tale of the water nymph who marries a mortal, and at last claims him for her underwater kingdom; what does it not say of the need for modern man to explore the deep waters that lie beneath his own surface? I could do it better now, I know, but I did it pretty well then. Weber— my generous, gentle friend Weber—praised the skill with which I had matched music to subject in a beautiful melodic conception. What praise from such a source!*

Now, at long last, **Arthur** *may come to something. No libretto, they say. Only the wind-eggs that Planché blew about so confidently. Where will they turn? Again, I put my faith in Powell. I think he knows* more about the myth of Arthur than any of the others, especially the professors. Dare I hope that my music, so far as I was able to sketch it in, will set the tone for the work? Of course. It must.

I wish I understood everything they say. What does the bas bleu mean about a Snark or a Boojum? It sounds like some great conflict in the works of Wagner. Oh, this tedious waiting! I suppose this is the punishment, the torture, of Limbo.

THREE

SIMON DARCOURT sat in his study at Ploughwright College planning his crime. A crime it undoubtedly was, for he meant to rob first the University Library, and then the National Gallery of Canada. Princess Amalie had left him in no doubt; the price of the information she had about the late Francis Cornish was possession of the preliminary studies for the drawing which she was now using to sell her new line of cosmetics. She offered that drawing to the public as coming from the hand of an Old Master—though no particular Old Master was mentioned. But the delicacy of line, the complete command of the silver-point technique, and above all the evocation of untouched but not unaware virginal beauty, spoke in unmistakable terms of an Old Master hand.

Photographs of Princess Amalie had, for some years, appeared in the gossip portions of the fashionable magazines in which she advertised, and it was clear to anybody that this finely preserved aristocrat, perhaps in her fifties, was of the same family as the virgin child in the advertising picture. Of the same family, though obviously many generations separated them. Oh, the magic of aristocracy! Oh, the romance of family descent! How beauty passed, like a blessing, through four centuries! Aristocracy cannot, of course, be bought over the counter, but something of its magic might be imparted by Princess Amalie's lotions and unguents and pigments. Ladies and, it was known, quite a few gentlemen hastened to put down their names for appointments with the Princess's skilled *maquilleuses* who would (it took a whole day) discover precisely which Old Master (the range was large and came down as near to the present time as John Singer Sargent) had dwelt upon their special type of beauty and had employed colours to preserve it for the ages—colours which only Princess Amalie could duplicate in cosmetics. It was very expensive, but certainly it was worth it thus to associate oneself with the great world of art, and the great world that the greatest artists had chosen to paint. To be seen as an Old Master type; was not that worth big money? "Selling like hot cakes" was the coarse term the advertising geniuses used to describe the success of the campaign. Don't wear the look of the latest fashion. Look like the Old Master subject you are, in your deepest soul, and at your exquisite best!

Obviously, if it leaked out that the Old Master drawing of Princess Amalie's ancestor was from the hand of a Canadian who had known her as a girl, millions of dollars would go straight down the drain. Or so it seemed to the advertising world. If some Nosy Parker, rummaging in the stacks of drawings preserved in the National Gallery of Canada, were to turn up preliminary drawings for the superb imposture, from the hand of the Canadian faker and scoundrel—he could be nothing less—the Princess, again in the idiom of the advertising world, would have egg all over her beautiful face. Or so it seemed to Princess Amalie, who was as sensitive as the world expects an aristocrat to be.

The Princess wanted those preliminary sketches, and the price she offered was information which, she hinted, would be the making of Simon Darcourt's life of the late Francis Cornish, connoisseur and benefactor of his country.

Darcourt yearned for that information with the feverish lust of a biographer. Without the slightest evidence that the Princess could tell him anything important, he was convinced that she would do so, and was ready to dare greatly to find out what she knew. Surely—he felt it in his bones—it would fill in the great hole right in the middle of his book.

Much of the book was completed, in so far as a book can be completed when important information is still missing. He had written the concluding chapters, describing Francis's later years when he had returned to Canada, and played a role as a benefactor of artists, a connoisseur of international reputation, and a generous giver to the collection of contemporary and earlier paintings in the National Gallery. Indeed, he had left the Gallery all his portfolios of drawings, many of which were by undoubted early masters, and among which those preliminary sketches of Princess Amalie lay concealed. But a book about a collector and benefactor, however well written, is not necessarily a gripping story, and readers of biographies like their meat rare.

He had finished the early part of the book, about Francis's childhood and early years, and considering how little real information he had, it was a brilliant piece of work. Darcourt did not permit himself the use of the word "brilliant", for he was a modest man, but he knew it was well done, and that he had made bricks of substantial value with the wrong kind of straw. It was his good fortune that the late Francis Cornish was a man who never threw away or destroyed anything, and among his personal possessions—those which now were in the keeping of the University Library—were several albums of photographs taken by Francis's grandfather, the old Senator and founder of the family wealth. Old Hamish had been a keen amateur of photography and had made countless records of the streets, the houses, the workmen, and the more important citizens of Blairlogie, the Ottawa Valley town in which Francis had spent his early years. Every picture was carefully identified in the Senator's neat Victorian handwriting and there they were—the grandmother, the beautiful mother and the distinguished but oddly wooden father, the aunt, the family doctor, the priests, even Victoria Cameron, the Senator's cook, and Bella-Mae, Francis's nurse. There were many pictures of Francis himself, a slight, dark, watchful boy, already showing the handsome, clouded face that had caused Princess Amalie to call the adult Francis *le beau ténébreux*. On the evidence of these photographs, which the Senator liked to call his Sun Pictures, Simon Darcourt had raised a convincing structure of Francis's childhood. It was as good as much research, aided by Darcourt's lively but controlled imagination, could make it.

As biography goes, it was excellent, for biography has to rely heavily on some evidence but a great deal of speculation, unless there are diaries and family papers to provide firmer ground. But biography at its best is a form of fiction. The personality and sympathies of the biographer cannot be sifted out of what is written. Darcourt had no diaries. He had a handful of school reports from Francis's Blairlogie schools, and from Colborne Col-

lege, where he had gone at a later date; there were some lists and
records of grades from the university days. Of what was personal
there was little, but Darcourt had done wonders with what he
had.

Nevertheless, the book lacked a heart, to make it live. Did
Princess Amalie have anything of that heart, however rheumatic
or slow, that would give life to his book, and fill out the story of
those years when, so far as he knew, Francis had messed about
in Europe as an art student? Darcourt sometimes came near to
desperation. A receipted bill from a bawdy-house would have
filled him with gladness. Now, here was a chance, and a pretty
good chance, to find information that would bridge that horrible
gap between the aspiring young Canadian who had apparently
gone into hiding after Oxford, and had emerged in 1945, when
he was part of the commission that inspected pictures and works
of art that had gone astray during the war, and were to be returned
whenever possible to their original owners. The price of that
information was crime. No other name for it—crime.

Darcourt did not hesitate from moral scruple. He was a clergyman, of course, though he lived as a professor of Greek; he
still wore his Roman collar from time to time, but it had long
ceased to be a fetter on his spirit. He now regarded himself as a
biographer, and the scruples of a biographer are peculiar to the
trade. Any hesitation he felt was not about how could he bring
himself to steal, but how could he steal without being found out?
"Prof Nabbed In NatGal Heist"—he could see the headlines in
the gloating press. The exposure of a trial would be horrible. Of
course he would not go to prison. Only tax-evaders go to prison
nowadays. But he would be fined, and doubtless compelled to
report monthly to a parole officer as to how he was getting on
with his new job, teaching Latin for Berlitz.

How was it to be done? Sherlock Holmes, he recalled, sometimes solved crimes by thinking himself into the criminal mind,
and thus discovering method, if not motive. But so far as he could
adventure into the criminal mind, no solution to his problem
occurred. Whenever he tried it, all that came up on the computer
screen of his imagination was a picture of himself, wearing a black
eye-mask, dressed in a turtleneck sweater and a slouch cap, emerging from the National Gallery carrying over his shoulder a large

sack plainly marked SWAG. This was farce, and what he needed was a strong injection of elegant comedy.

Did he see himself then as a fictional figure, Darcourt the Clerical Cracksman? Beneath the sober dress of the cleric and the modest dignity of a professor of classics lurks the keen mind that plots thefts that baffle the keenest among the police—was that his character? Would that it might be so, but those smart crooks in fiction lived in a world where thought possessed absolute power, and careful plans never went wrong. Darcourt was well aware that he did not live in any such world. To begin with, he had discovered, now that he was well into middle age, that he did not know how to think. Of course he could pursue a logical path when he had to, but in his personal affairs his mental processes were a muddle, and he arrived at important conclusions by default, or by some leap that had no resemblance to thought, or logic, or any of the characteristics of the first-rate fictional criminal mind. He made his real decisions as a gifted cook makes soup: he threw into a pot anything likely that lay to hand, added seasonings and glasses of wine, and messed about until something delicious emerged. There was no recipe and the result could be foreseen only in the vaguest terms. Could one plan a crime like that?

To change the metaphor—he was always changing metaphors and trying not to mix them ludicrously—he ran off in the viewing-chamber of his mind scraps of film in which he saw himself doing various things in various ways until at last he found a plan of action. How was he to accomplish his crime?

It must be a twofold criminal job. To the best of his recollection, there were five drawings that were studies for the finished portrait of the Princess Amalie as a girl, in the large bundle of Francis Cornish's Old Master portfolios, and those were what he had to abstract and take to New York. He knew that the portfolios had not been carefully examined, and certainly not catalogued, in the storage room where they lay at the National Gallery in Ottawa. But uncatalogued as they were, those drawings had probably been seen in what he hoped was a cursory inspection, and they would be missed. But would they be remembered in any detail? They had probably been numbered. Indeed, he had submitted a loose catalogue himself when, as Francis Cornish's executor, he had sent that mass of material to Ottawa. "Pencil sketch of a girl's head"—that sort of thing. Oh, if only the hasty, determined Arthur had not been so insistent that his uncle's pictures and books and manuscripts and other valuable miscellany should be cleared out of his huge apartment and storehouse in Toronto in the shortest possible time! But Arthur had so insisted, and pinching pictures from a large public gallery was tricky work.

However—and a very big and hopeful "however" it was—a great mass of Francis Cornish's personal papers had been sent to the University Library, and among those papers were pictures that seemed to Darcourt, when he bundled them up, to be of personal rather than artistic merit. Some were pictures that belonged to the Oxford period of Francis's life, when he had been drawing from models as well as making copies of Old Master drawings in the Ashmolean Museum. Darcourt had assumed, without asking anybody for an opinion, that the National Gallery would not want such stuff, accomplished though much of it was. Could he make a switch? Could he sneak a few pictures from the Library and put them in the Gallery portfolios, and would anyone be the wiser? That seemed to be the solution to his problem, and all that remained was to decide how he might manage it.

The morning after the Round Table had met to hear Penny Raven read what existed of Planché's libretto for *Arthur of Britain*, Darcourt was sitting in his dressing-gown gazing at his interior movie-show when he heard a spluttering, snorting, farting uproar in the street outside his study window, and he knew that it could only be the noise that Geraint Powell's little red sports car made when it was brought to a halt. In a very short time there was a banging on his door that was certainly Powell, who brought a Shakespearean *brio* to quite modest daily tasks.

"Have you slept?" he said, as he pushed into the study, threw a heap of papers out of an armchair, and flung himself into it. The chair—a good one, which had cost Darcourt a lot of money in the shop of an antique pirate—creaked ominously as the actor lolled in it, one leg thrown over a delicate arm. There was about Powell a stagy largeness, and whatever he said was said with an actor's precision of speech in an unusually resonant voice, from which the Welsh intonation had not wholly disappeared.

Darcourt said that no, he had not slept very much, as he had not come home until almost five in the morning. He had found the conversation, and hearing *Undine,* exciting and his rest had been scant. He knew, of course, that Powell wanted to tell him about his own rest, as now he did.

"I didn't sleep a wink," he said. "Not a wink. I have been turning this business over and over in my head and what I see before us is a gigantic obstacle race. Consider: we have no libretto, an unknown amount of music, no singers, no designs, no time reserved with all the artificers and carpenters and machinists we shall need—nothing but high hopes and a theatre. If this opera is not to be the most God-Almighty ballocks in the history of the art, we shall have to work day and night from now until it is on the stage, and at the mercy of those rapists and child-abusers, the critics. You think I exaggerate? Ha ha"—his laugh would have filled a large theatre, and it made the windows in Darcourt's study ring—"From the depths of no trivial experience I assure you that I do not exaggerate. And upon whom are we depending, you and I? Eh? Upon whom are we depending? Upon Arthur, the best of fellows but innocent as the babe unborn in all of this world we are entering with our hands tied behind our backs. Arthur is armed only with a fine managerial spirit and barrels of money. Who next? This kid whom I have never met who is to come up with an opera score, and her supervisor—the woman with the grotesque name, who is probably some constipated pedant who will take an eternity to get anything done. There's Penny, of course, but she's an outsider and I don't know how far to trust her. Of the scholarly Professor Hollier I forbear to speak; his obvious inability to distinguish between his arse and his elbow—speaking theatrically—rules him out as anything but a pest, easily dealt with. What a gang!"

"You say nothing of Maria," said Darcourt.

"I could speak cantos of rhapsodic verse about Maria. She is the blood of my heart. But of what use is she in such a situation as this? Eh? Of what conceivable use?"

"She is the strongest possible influence with Arthur."

"You are right, of course. But that is secondary. Why did she not stop Arthur when he decided to embark on this rashest of rash enterprises?"

"Well—why didn't you? Why didn't I? We were swept away. Don't underestimate the power of Arthur's enthusiasm."

"Once again, you are right. But then you are so often right. And that is why I am talking to you now. You are the only member of the Round Table who seems to have enough wits to come in out of the rain. Excepting myself, naturally."

Darcourt's heart sank. This sort of flattery usually meant that some time-consuming task that nobody else would undertake was going to be dumped on his desk. Powell went on.

"You are the man in the Cornish Foundation who gets things done. Arthur gets ideas. He shoots them off like rockets. The rest of us are hypnotized. But if anything really happens, you are the man who makes it happen, and you can patiently persuade Arthur to listen to common sense. You know what you are, boy? They call that thing the Round Table, and if it's the Round Table who are you? Eh? No one but Myrddin Wyllt, the great king's counsellor. Merlin, that's who you are. You've seen it, of course. How could you miss it?"

Darcourt had not seen it. He wanted Powell to develop this idea, so flattering to himself, so he pretended ignorance.

"Merlin was a magician, wasn't he?"

"He looked like a magician to those other morlocks at the Round Table because he could do something besides fight and play Chase the Grail. In every great legend there are a lot of heroes and one really intelligent man. Our Arthur's a hero; people admire him and eat out of his hand. I suppose Hollier is a hero in his own way. I'm a hero, fatally flawed by intelligence. But you are no hero. You're Merlin, and I want you to work with me to get this wild scheme into some sort of workable order."

"Geraint—"

"Call me Geraint *bach*. It signifies friendship, understanding, complicity."

"Bach? You mean as in Johann Sebastian Bach?"

"Old Johann Sebastian was born a German, but in spirit he was a Welshman. The word is a diminutive. It's as if you were calling me Geraint, my darling, or Geraint, my pretty one. Welsh is a great language for intimacies and endearments. I'll call you Sim *bach*. It will signify our nearness in spirit."

Darcourt had never been aware of any special nearness of spirit between himself and Powell, but Powell was leaning forward in his chair, his lustrous eyes gleaming, and complicity coming out of him like heat out of a stove. Well, here goes, Simon thought. He could always retreat if the intimacy became outrageous.

"So what is it you want, Geraint *bach?*"

Powell spoke in a hiss. "I want a *dramatis personae,* a cast of characters, and I want it right away."

"Well, I don't suppose that presents insuperable problems. Even Planché had to agree that an opera about Arthur has to have Arthur somewhere in the cast. And if you have Arthur, you must have Queen Guenevere, and a few Knights of the Round Table. And Merlin, I presume. You can certainly count on the opera including those, whatever turn it may take."

"Aha! You grasp it at once! I knew you would. You are a golden man, Sim *bach.* And you see what that means? We must have the Operatic Four. Soprano—Guenevere, of course, though I dislike that Frenchified version of the name. I always think of her as Gwenhwyfar. Much finer, you agree? But too difficult for the thick-tongued English-speakers. Now—who's your contralto? There has to be one, you know."

"Oh, dear. Let's see? Hm. Morgan Le Fay, do you think?"

"Of course! Arthur's wicked sister. A contralto, obviously. All wicked women in opera must have those rich, enchanting low notes. Now—who's my tenor?"

"Surely Arthur himself?"

"No. Arthur must have authority. A baritone, I think. A fine, velvety bass-baritone. Make him both a tenor *and* a cuckold and you lose all sympathy, and Arthur must compel sympathy. But we need an even deeper bass for quartets as well as the plot."

"That must be Modred, who destroys Arthur."

"Precisely."

"But no tenor? Can you have an opera without a tenor?"

"Of course. The public expects a tenor. Must be Lancelot, the seducer. Tenors are great seducers."

"All right. That gives you the four you want. Five, as a matter of fact."

"So—there we are. We'll want another woman for Elaine, the Lily Maid. Better be a nice mezzo—good for pathos but not deep enough for villainy. And a few tenors and basses for the Knights of the Round Table, but they are really just Chorus, and not hard to find."

"You make it all sound simple."

"Not simple at all, Sim *bach*. I must get on the phone at once and see who I can round up for these parts. I told them so last night. Singers aren't picked up at the last minute. They're worse than hockey-players; you have to get them under contract, or at least under written agreement, as far ahead as you can do it."

"But won't the musical people—Schnak and this woman with the strange name—want some say? I know, and you know, that we have no libretto. How can you hire singers when you have no story and no music?"

"Must be done. Can't wait. And anyhow, we have the skeleton of a libretto."

"We have? Since when?"

"Since last night when I lay tossing in my bed, pulling it together. We have a story. You can't bugger about with the story of Arthur. I have a skeleton of the plot. All it needs is some words and music. And that's where you come in, old Merlin. You must hustle 'em up and get it on paper as soon as dammit."

"Powell—sorry, Geraint *bach*—have you told anybody but me?"

"Not yet. But we're to meet the great lady, the genius, the Muse, the shepherdess of Schnak, at dinner on Saturday night. Didn't anybody tell you? Well, they will. And then I'll tell her what the plot of *Arthur of Britain* is to be and you and Pretty Penny must start feeding her words as fast as you can go."

"How simple you make it sound."

"Aha—irony! I love your irony, Sim *bach*. It is what first drew me to you, boy. Well, I'm more happy than I can say that you agree, and I'll go at once and get on the phone. It's going to cost a fortune in phone bills. I send them to you, I suppose."

Geraint seized both Darcourt's hands and wrung them. Then he drew the astonished Simon to his breast and gave him a Shake-spearean hug, during which he brushed a cheek against Simon's, exhaling a lot of last night's whisky, as though in an ecstasy of relief, and dashed out the door. Surprisingly soon afterward he was heard in the street, roaring abuse at some engineering students who had gathered to snoop under the hood of his car, and with snorts and hootings he was gone.

Greatly depleted in spirit, Darcourt sat down to think about his crime. Was it a crime? The law would certainly think so. The University would undoubtedly think so, for to rob the Library would create a general coldness toward himself, though criminality might not be quite enough to justify the revocation of his professorship. A tenured professor could commit the Sin Against the Holy Ghost and get away with it, if he could find the right lawyer. Still, in decency he would have to resign. Robbing the National Gallery was something else. That was crime, real crime.

Nevertheless, the law was not everything. There was a thing called natural justice, though Darcourt was not certain where it resided. Had he not been one of the late Francis Cornish's executors, chosen by Francis Cornish himself presumably because he was expected to use his judgement in doing what the dead man would wish? And would not the dead man want the best possible story of his life written by the friend and biographer best qualified to tell it?

Well—would he? Francis Cornish had been a very odd man, and there were many corners of his character into which Darcourt had never probed or wished to probe.

That was beside the point. Francis Cornish was dead, and Darcourt was alive. A Charter of Rights for the Dead might appeal to Penny Raven, but no true biographer wants to hear about it. Darcourt had in full measure the vanity of the author, and he wanted to write the best book he could, and a good book was a better thing for his dead friend than any pallid record of scanty fact. Crime it must be, and let the consequences be as they would. The book came before everything.

As Darcourt thought in this vein, allowing all sorts of visions of crime, and Francis Cornish, and Princess Amalie, and a scene in a law court in which Darcourt defended his action to a robed judge, in whose intelligent eyes understanding could be read, he was conscious that other images were popping into view on that mental movie-show, and they were related to what Geraint Powell had said about the opera and the necessary figures to make it a reality.

There had been slight mention of Merlin. Why not? Was Merlin so trivial a figure that the plot could be managed without him? Or could the role be played by any hack, any singer recruited from a church choir at the last moment? He would have something to say about that when Geraint unfolded his opera plot at dinner on Saturday night.

Darcourt had long known that he was a man fated to do much of the world's work when other people took the credit for it, but he was not without self-esteem.

No Merlin? Was that how Geraint *bach* saw the story of Arthur? Not if he, Simon Darcourt, was to play the role of Merlin in private life. He'd show 'em!

But for the moment, crime must be given his best energies.

[2]

NO TIME LIKE THE PRESENT. Darcourt made a phone call to the librarian in charge of special collections, an old friend. A man whom he would not, for the world, deceive, except when his book was at stake.

"Archie? Simon here. Look—I've run into a little matter in connection with my book. My life of Francis Cornish, you know. I want to verify something about his Oxford life. Would there be any objection to my taking a look among the papers we sent to you?"

No objection whatever. Come when you please. This afternoon? Certainly. Would you like to use my office? No, no need to disturb you. I'll just look at them in the storage, or wherever they are.

That was the worry. Where were they? Would he have to look at them in a room with a lot of sub-librarians and other snoops hanging around? Not likely, but not impossible. With luck he might be able to use one of those little cubicles near a window, in which some favoured graduate students were occasionally allowed to spread their papers about.

Into the Library with a light step. Nod to right and left with the assurance of a well-known, greatly trusted member of faculty. Stop at Archie's room and pass the time of day. Listen to Archie's groans about the lack of funds for cataloguing. The Cornish stuff he would find just as he had bundled it up for the Library. But have no fear; it would be properly catalogued as soon as funds could be found. Might the Cornish Foundation be interested in funding that project? Darcourt assured Archie that he thought the Cornish Foundation would certainly be interested, and he would put the matter before them himself. Oh, by the way, would Archie like him to leave his briefcase in the office? Yes, yes, he knew that he was not a likely suspect—ha ha—but one should not expect other people to observe rules that one did not observe oneself. To which Archie agreed, and with each man somewhat sanctimoniously respecting the other's high principle, the brief-case was left in a chair.

Thus, cloaked in righteousness, Darcourt went into the large room, filled with steel racks, in which the Cornish papers, among many others, were stored. A young woman who was working at the slow task of cataloguing showed him where they were, and whispered—why whispered? there was nobody else in the room, but it was a place that seemed to call for whispering—that there was a nice quiet spot at the back of the room, with a big table where he could spread out the papers he wished to examine. He knew that this was not regular, that he should declare what he wanted even though it might be difficult to find; but after all, it was he who had brought the papers to the Library in the first place, and he was a generous member of the Friends of the Library, and he should be shown all possible courtesy. Nothing like a good reputation when you are about to commit a crime.

The crime took no time at all. Darcourt knew precisely which of the big bundles he was looking for, and in a moment he had opened it, and found the group of drawings he wanted.

They were drawings Francis Cornish had done in his Oxford days, and most of them were copies of minor Old Masters he had made when learning the technique which had been one of his chief sources of pride. By the most laborious and greatly talented practice, he had found the way to draw with the costly silver pencil on the carefully prepared paper. As works of art, the draw-ings were of little interest. Fine student work, no more.

There were some, however, which were in the old silver-point technique, but differently labelled—for Francis had labelled every copy of an Old Master with great care, naming the master, or that prodigiously productive artist *Ignotus,* and the date upon which the copy had been made. But several were labelled more simply: "Ismay, November 14, 1935", or some date reaching into the spring of 1936.

Several of them were heads, or half-lengths, of a girl not precisely beautiful, but of a distinguished cast of feature. Others were of the same girl, nude, lying on a sofa, or leaning on a mantelpiece. There was something about them that made it abundantly clear that they had been drawn by a loving hand. The curves of neck and shoulder, waist and breasts, hips, thighs and calves, were rendered with an exquisite care that set them apart from the work of an art student faced with a good model. Nor had the technique the Old Master remoteness: it spoke of desire, here and now. But the face of Ismay did not speak of love. In a few of the drawings it was petulant, but in most it wore a look of amusement, as though the model felt something like pity, and a measure of superiority, toward the artist. In these there was nothing of the accomplished deadness of the Old Master copies. They were alive, and they were the work of a man who had ceased to be a student.

Who was Ismay? She was Mrs. Francis Cornish, one of the many figures in his biography about whom Darcourt could discover nothing. Or very little. The daughter of Roderick and Prudence Glasson of St. Columb Hall, in Cornwall; a girl who had left Oxford (Lady Margaret Hall) without a degree after a single year; a girl who had married Francis Cornish in St. Columb's Church on September 17, 1936; a girl who thenceforward seemed to have no existence, so far as documents or other evidence was concerned. A girl whom Darcourt had come upon by accident, and identified by research, for Francis had never spoken of her.

The biographer had done his scholarly best. He had written to Sir Roderick Glasson at the Foreign Office in London, asking for details about his sister, and had received a cold reply saying that so far as Sir Roderick knew, his sister Ismay had died in the Blitz, in a northern city, probably Manchester, and that nothing was known of her, as it was impossible to identify many bodies found in that destruction, and many had never been recovered.

So this was Francis Cornish's wife as she appeared before their marriage. A girl born to fascinate, and doubtless to be loved by a man of romantic disposition. But what had happened to Ismay? She was part of the gap in the middle of Francis Cornish's life that tormented Darcourt and made his task as a biographer a nagging burden.

Darcourt could not stop long to admire. He did not want the friendly sub-librarian to approach him with offers of help, or a cup of coffee. Which to take? The heads, obviously. The nudes were too compelling to escape notice even by a hasty examiner. Darcourt, who had a weakness for female beauty that was not wholly rooted in the feelings of an amateur connoisseur, would greatly have liked to take one of them for himself, but that would be dangerous. The Clerical Cracksman must show self-denial and austerity in what he was doing. Only the heads.

So, with a rapidity that he had practised that morning as he dressed, he took off his jacket and his waistcoat—he was in clerical garb and the waistcoat was one of those broad black expanses of ribbed silk that Anglicans call an M.B. waistcoat, meaning Mark of the Beast because of its High Church and Romanist implications—and lowered his trousers. From under his shirt at the back he took a transparent plastic envelope measuring eighteen inches by twelve, slipped the drawings into it, and shoved it under his shirt again. Up with the trousers, on with the M.B., which had a convenient back strap that held the envelope firmly in place, on with the jacket, and all was completed.

"Thank you very much," he said to the sub-librarian; "I've bundled everything up ready to go back on the shelf." And he smiled in answer to her smile as he left the room.

"Many thanks, Archie," he called to his friend, as he picked up his briefcase.

"Not at all, Simon. Any time."

Out of the Library, step as light as ever, went the Clerical Cracksman, half of his crime completed. But not wholly completed. He must not go tearing back to his rooms at Ploughwright, like a guilty thing, to hide away his swag. No; he went to the Faculty Club, seated himself in the reading-room, and called for a beer. There was only one other member in the reading-room, and that member was to be his alibi, if one should be needed. The person who had seen him come there on his way back from the Library, as innocent as a new-laid egg.

The other member also had a beer, for it was a warm day. He lifted his glass to Darcourt.

"Cheers," said he.

"Here's to crime," said the Clerical Cracksman, and the other member, a simple soul, sniggered at such a jest from a clergyman.

[3]

"I LOOK UPON YOU as a daring group, a party of adventurers of extraordinary courage, set upon great risk. Perhaps the word for you is doom-eager," said Dr. Gunilla Dahl-Soot, as the Cornish Foundation sat down to dinner at the Round Table.

"That's a fine Scandinavian word, but surely rather negative, Doctor?" said Arthur, at whose right hand the guest of honour was seated.

"No, not in the least. It is realistic. You must know that never has any opera or play about King Arthur succeeded with the public, or with the world of art. Never. Not one."

"Didn't Purcell write a pretty good opera about Arthur?" said Maria.

"Purcell? No. It is not an opera. I would call it almost a *Posse mit Gesang,* a sort of vaudeville or fairy-piece. It has some interesting pages, but it has not travelled," said the Doctor, with immovable gloomy conviction.

"Perhaps we shall succeed where others have failed," said Arthur.

"Ah, I admire your courage. That is in part what has brought me here. But courage alone is not enough. Certainly not if you follow Purcell. His *Arthur* is too full of talk. All the action is in speech, not in music. The music is mere decoration. That is not opera. An opera is not talk. Indeed, there should be no talk. Music throughout."

"Well, isn't that very much under your control?" said Arthur.

"It may be so. Only time will tell," said the Doctor and drained her glass of wine at a draught. She had had her full share of the martinis before dinner; she had three at least but appeared to be thirsty still.

"Let's not begin the evening in a spirit of defeat," said Maria. "I've prepared a very special dinner. It's an Arthurian dinner.

You are going to get what Arthur's court might have eaten—making necessary allowances."

"Thank God for necessary allowances," said Hollier. "I doubt if I could get through a sixth-century meal. What are we having?"

"What a question! Don't you trust me?" said Maria. "You are beginning with poached salmon, and I'm sure Arthur had excellent salmon."

"Yes, but this Hochheimer—do you call that Arthurian?" said the Doctor. "I thought King Arthur drank beer."

"You forget that Arthur was a Cambro-Briton, with five centuries of Roman civilization behind him," said Maria. "I'll bet he drank very good wine, and took enormous care about having it transported to Camelot."

"It may be," said the Doctor, draining another large glass. "This is a good wine." She spoke as if uncertain about what might follow.

Dr. Gunilla Dahl-Soot was not an easy guest. She seemed to bring an atmosphere of deep autumn into the penthouse, though it was still no more than early September. The dinner party felt uneasily that it might decline into a hard winter if the Doctor did not cheer up.

The Round Table had not known what to expect, and nobody had foreseen anything in the least like the Doctor. It was not that she was eccentric in any of the ways that might be expected in an academic who was also a distinguished musician. She was beautifully dressed, her figure was a marvel of slim elegance, and her face was undeniably handsome. What made her strange was that she seemed to have stepped out of a past age. She wore a finely designed version of male dress; her jacket was in appearance a man's tight-waisted blue frock coat, and her tapering green velvet trousers descended toward elegant patent leather boots; she wore a very high, soft collar bound with a flowing cravat, and on her hands were a number of big, masculine rings. Her thick, straight brown hair was parted in the middle and hung to her shoulders, framing a long, distinguished, deeply melancholy face. She's got herself up as Franz Liszt before he put on his abbé's cassock, thought Darcourt. Does she get her clothes from a theatrical costumer? But odd as she is, she's dead right for *what* she is. Who is she modelled on? George Sand? No, she's much too elegant. Darcourt who was interested in women's clothes, and what went under them, was prepared to be fascinated by the Doctor, but her first ventures in conversation made it clear that the fascination might be a depressing experience.

"I'm glad you like our wine," said Arthur. "Let Simon fill your glass. Do you like Canada? That's a silly question, of course, but you must forgive me; we always ask visitors if they like Canada as soon as they step off the plane. Don't answer."

"But I will answer," said the Doctor. "I like what I have seen. It is not strange at all. It is like Sweden. Why not? We are geographical near neighbours. I look out of my window and what do I see? Fir trees. Maple trees already turning to red. Big outcroppings of bare rock. It is not like New York. I have been in New York. It is not like Princeton, where I have also been. It has the smell. It smells like a northern land. Do you have terrible winters?"

"They can be difficult," said Arthur.

"Ah," said the Doctor, smiling for the first time. "Difficult winters make very great people, and great music. I do not, generally speaking, like the music of lands that are too far south. I will have another glass of the Hochheimer, if I may."

This woman must have a hollow leg, thought Darcourt. A boozer? Surely not, with that ascetic appearance. Let's tank her up and see what happens. As an old friend of the family he had made the martinis, and his was the task of serving the wine at dinner; he went to the sideboard and opened another bottle of the Hochheimer and handed it to Arthur.

"Let us hope that you can charm some fine northern music out of the fragments of Hoffmann's score," said Arthur.

"Let us hope. Yes, hope is the thing upon which we shall build," said the Doctor, and down went the Hochheimer—not at a gulp, for the Doctor was too elegant to gulp—but without a pause.

"I hope you don't think it rude of us to speak of the opera so soon," said Maria. "It is so much on our minds, you see."

"One should always speak of what is uppermost in one's mind," said the Doctor. "I want to talk about this opera, and it is uppermost in my mind."

"You've looked at the music?" said Arthur.

"Yes. It is sketches and indications of the orchestration, and themes that Hoffmann wanted used to suggest important things in the plot. He seems somewhat to have anticipated Wagner, but his themes are prettier. But it is not an opera. Not yet. This student was too enthusiastic when she told you it was an opera. It is very pretty music, but not foolish. Some of it could be Weber. Some could be Schumann. I like all that. I love those wonderful failed operas by Schumann and Schubert."

"I hope you don't see this as another failed opera."

"Who can say?"

"But you aren't going to set to work with failure as your goal?" said Maria.

"Much may be learned from failure. Of course that is the theme of the opera, so far as I can see. *The Magnificent Cookold,* he called it. Am I right to think a cookold is a deceived husband?"

"You are. The word is pronounced cuckold, by the way."

"As I said. Cookold.—Ah, thank you. This Hochheimer is really very good.—But, now—a cookold; why is it a man? Why not a woman?"

"You are just as right to say cookold as cuckold," said Professor Hollier, who had also been getting into the Hochheimer with quiet determination. "That was a Middle English form. The French was, and still is, *cocu.* Because of the notorious goings-on of that bird." He bowed to Dr. Dahl-Soot over his raised glass.

"Ah, you are a man who knows language? Very good. Then why is it masculine? A person deceived in marriage. Are not women also deceived in marriage? Again and again and again? So why no word for that, eh?"

"I do not know how you would form a feminine from cuckold. Cuckoldess? Clumsy. Or how about she-cuckold?"

"Not good," said the Doctor.

"Does it matter? It is Arthur who is the cuckold in the Arthurian legends," said Penny Raven.

"So it is. This Arthur was a fool," said the Doctor.

"Oh, come on! I won't have that," said Maria. "He was a noble man, bent on lifting the whole moral tone of his kingdom."

"But still a cookold. He did not pay enough attention to his wife. So she gave him a big pair of horns."

"Perhaps there is no feminine of cuckold because the female of the species does not grow horns, however much she is deceived," said Hollier, solemnly.

"She knows a better trick than that," said the Doctor. "She gives him the ambiguous baby, eh? He looks in the cradle and he says, What the hell; this is a funny-looking baby. By God, I am a cookold."

"But in the Arthurian legends there is no child of the adultery of Guenevere and Lancelot. So he could not have exclaimed what you have just exclaimed, madam."

"Not madam. I prefer to be called Doctor. Unless after a long time we get on close terms; then perhaps you will call me Nilla."

"Not Gunny?" said Powell.

"I despise Gunny. But this Arthur—this stupid king—he does not need a baby to tell him. His wife and his very good friend tell him straight out. We have been in the bed while you have been lifting the moral tone. It could be a comedy. It could be by Ibsen. He was often funny like that."

Maria thought the time had come to change the direction of the conversation at the Round Table. "My next course is truly Arthurian. Roast pork, and with apple sauce. Very popular dish at Camelot, I am certain."

"Pork? No, never pork! It must be roast boar," said the Doctor.

"My butcher didn't have a good roasting boar," said Maria, perhaps a little too sharply; "you will have to put up with very good roast pork."

"I am glad it isn't roast boar," said Hollier. "I have often eaten roast boar in my travels, and I don't like it. A heavy, dense flesh and a great provoker of midnight melancholy. In me, anyhow."

"You have not had good roast boar," said the Doctor. "Good roast boar is excellent eating. I do not find it provokes to melancholy."

"How would you know?" said Penny Raven.

"I do not understand you, Professor Raven."

"You seem to be melancholy without any roast boar," said Penny, who had not been neglecting the Hochheimer. "You are depressing us about our opera, and you are disparaging Maria's wonderful roast pork."

"If I depress you, I am sorry, but the fault may not be mine. I am not a merry person. I take a serious attitude toward life. I am not a self-deceiver."

"Nor am I," said Penny. "I am enjoying Maria's fine Arthurian feast. She is Arthur's lady and I declare her to be a splendid *hlafdiga*."

"A fine what?" said the Doctor.

"A fine *hlafdiga*. It is the Old English word from which our word 'lady' is derived, and it means the person who gives the food. A very honourable title. I drink to our *hlafdiga*."

"No, no, Penny, I must protest," said Hollier. "A *hlafdiga* does not mean a lady. That is an exploded etymology. The *hlafdiga* was the dough-kneader, not the loaf-giver as you ignorantly suppose. You are muddling up the Mercian with the Northumbrian word."

"Oh, bugger you, Clem," said Penny. "The modern word 'lady' comes from *hlafdiga*; the *hlafdiga* was the loaf-giver and down through *leofdi* and thus down to *lefdi* and so to 'lady'. Don't try to teach me to suck eggs, or *aegru* if you want it in Old English. The *hlafdiga* was the wife of the *hlaford*—the lord, you pretentious ass—and thus his lady."

"Abuse is not argument, Professor Raven," said Hollier, with tipsy dignity. "The *hlafdiga* could be quite a lowly person—"

"Possibly even of Gypsy origins," said Maria, with a good deal of heat.

"For Christ's sake, are we going to get any pork?" said Powell. "Or are we going to get into an etymological wrangle while everything goes cold? I hereby declare that Maria is a lady in every sense of the word, and I want something to eat."

"There are no ladies now, thank God," said Dr. Dahl-Soot, holding out her glass. "We are all on equal footing, distinguished only by talent. Genius is the only true aristocracy. Is that a red wine you are pouring, Professor Darcourt? What is it? Let me see the bottle."

"It is an excellent Burgundy," said Darcourt.

"Good. You may pour."

"Of course he may pour," said Powell. "What do you think this is? A restaurant? That's the wine there is and that's the wine you are going to get, so shut up."

Dr. Dahl-Soot drew herself up in her chair. "Monsieur, vous êtes une personne grossière."

"You bet your sweet ass I am, Gunny, so you mind your manners and be a good girl."

There was a pause, during which Darcourt hovered over the Doctor's wineglass. Unexpectedly she burst into loud laughter.

"I think I like you, Powell," she said. "You may call me Nilla. But only you." She cast an excluding eye over the rest of the table. Then she raised her glass of Burgundy toward Powell, smiled with an elegant sweetness, and drained it to the bottom.

"More," she said, thrusting it at Darcourt, who now was attending to Penny Raven.

"You wait your turn, Nilla," said Powell.

"You are teaching me manners?" said the Doctor. "Which manners? In my country the guest of honour is allowed certain freedoms. But I see how it is. You think you are a lion-tamer and probably a lady-killer. Let me tell you that I am a lion who has eaten many tamers, and you shall not kill me because I am not a lady."

"Funny thing. That had just begun to pop into my mind," said Penny Raven. "But if you are not a lady, how do you describe yourself?"

"Not long ago we spoke of the aristocracy of genius," said the Doctor, whose glass Darcourt had hastened to fill, out of turn.

"Now Penny, no fighting," said Maria. "It isn't the custom for the lady to propose toasts, but as Arthur is busy carving this authentically Celtic piglet, I shall claim the privilege of a *hlafdiga* and propose the health of Dr. Gunilla Dahl-Soot; I declare her to be not less than a countess in the aristocracy of genius. May we enjoy the proof of her genius."

The health was drunk, with enthusiasm by all but Penny Raven, who muttered something into her glass. The Doctor rose to her feet.

"My dear new friends," she said; "you do me honour and I shall not fail you. Have I teased you just a little bit? Perhaps I have. It is my way. I am a great joker, you should know. There often lurks behind my words some *double entendre* which you may not understand, perhaps until much later. Perhaps even in the night, you wake up laughing. Ah, the Doctor, you say. She is deep, deep, deep. You have drunk to my health. I shall drink back at you. You, reverend sir, with the wine—may I have something in my glass? Ah, thank you.—Though I am not sure about wine at this Arthurian feast. I am not sure that our *hlafdiga* is

right in saying that Arthur had wine at his court. Surely it was
that stuff they made with fermented honey—"

"Mead," said Hollier. "You mean mead."

"Just so. Mead. I have drunk it. And it is nasty, sweet, awful
stuff, let me tell you. I casted up my stomach—"

"Not surprising, the way you go at it," said Penny, with a smile
which did not entirely rob her remark of offence.

"I can drink anybody here under the table," said the Doctor,
with grave belligerence. "Man, woman, or dog, I can drink him
under the table. But I want no nasty words here. I want to drink
to you all. Though as I say, I cannot believe that King Arthur
had wine—"

"I've just thought of it," said Hollier. "The Welsh did have
wine in the ancient days. You remember the old cry—*Gwin o
eur*—Wine from the gold! Not only did they have wine, but they
drank it from golden vessels. Not out of cowhorns, like a road
company doing the banquet in *Macbeth. Gwin o eur!*"

"Clem, you're drunk!" said Penny. "And that's a very dubious,
ill-founded quotation."

"And your Welsh is terrible!" said Powell.

"Is that so? If this were not a friendly gathering I'd let you
have one right on the nose for that, Powell."

"Would you, boy?" said Powell. "I dare you."

"Yes. Right on the snot-box," said Hollier. He half rose, as if
to fight, but Penny pulled him back into his chair. "The Welsh
are a despicable people," he said in a murmur.

"That's right. Real scum. Like Gypsies," said Powell, winking
at his hostess.

"Am I, or am I not, making a speech?" said the Doctor. "Am
I returning thanks for this splendid dinner, so exquisitely chosen
and so elegantly served under the lustrous eye of our *hlafdiga?*"
She bowed deeply toward Maria. "Yes, I am. So I bid all you
rowdies and learned hoggleboes keep silence, until I am finished.
I love this country; it is, like my own land, a socialist monarchy
and thus unites the best of the past and the present; I love my
hosts, they are true patrons of art. I love you all; you are comrades
in a great adventure, a Quest for something a man longed for but
did not achieve. I drain my glass to you." And she did so, and
sat down, rather heavily.

It must have been the martinis, thought Darcourt. They all drank martinis before dinner as if they never expected to see drink again. The Doctor certainly had three, because I gave them to her myself. Now, following her speech of thanks and her toast to Maria, the Doctor was silent, and ate a large helping of roast pork and apple sauce and a variety of vegetables—probably not Arthurian but nobody questioned them—in a mood that could only be called morose. The other guests murmured, more or less politely, to one another.

The Canadians—Arthur, Hollier, Penny Raven, and Darcourt—were abashed by what the Doctor had said; they closed up at any imputation of high motives, of splendid intention, of association with what might be great, and therefore dangerous. They were not wholly of the grey majority of their people; they lived in a larger world than that, but they wore the greyness as a protective outer garment. They did not murmur the national prayer: "O God, grant me mediocrity and comfort; protect me from the radiance of Thy light." Nevertheless, they knew how difficult and disquieting too bold a spirit might be. They settled to their plates, and made small talk.

In the hearts of the two who were not Canadians, Maria and Powell, the Doctor's toast struck fire. Powell was possessed by ambition, but not the ambition that puts the reward and the success before the excellence of the achievement. He meant to use his colleagues, and the Cornish Foundation, for his own purposes, but he thought the purposes good, and would provide ample reward and acclaim for anyone associated with them. He would ply the whip, and drive everyone to the last inch of their abilities, in order to get what he wanted. He knew he was dealing with a group who were primarily academics, and that the horses must amble before they could be made to gallop. But he would have his way, and in the Doctor he sensed an ally.

As for Maria, she felt, for the first time since her marriage, a stirring of real adventure. Oh, it was wonderful to be Mrs. Arthur Cornish, and to share the thoughts and ambitions of a man of fine—yes, noble, she would say noble—spirit. There was nothing she could want in a man that she did not find in Arthur. And yet—was it the northern nature, or the Canadian greyness—there was just the least hint of chill about her marriage. They loved.

They trusted. Their sexual life was a warm manifestation of love and trust. But, if only for a moment, there might be some hint of the improbable, of a relaxation of control. Maybe this opera would bring that. It was risky. It was a long time since she had sniffed the sharp, acrid smell of risk. Not since the time of Parlabane, over a year ago. Who would have thought of regretting Parlabane? And yet—he had brought something rare and pungent into her life.

What her place might be in this opera adventure she did not know. She was not a musician, though she was musical. She would not be allowed to work on the libretto; Penny and Simon had that marked off for themselves. Was she to do no more than write cheques, as an official of the Cornish Foundation? Money, as a host of grant-seekers assured her, was seminal. But it was not true seed of her seed.

Darcourt was eating and wool-gathering at the same time, a frequent trick of his. I wonder what we should look like, he thought, if a mischievous genie were to pass over this table and strike us all naked? The result would be better than at most tables. Maria would be a stunning beauty, clothed or naked. Hollier was absurdly handsome for a professor (but why? Must a professor always be a broomstick or a tub?) and without his clothes would reveal, in middle age, a Michelangelesque symmetry, agreeable to his splendid head. Arthur would be sturdy; passable but not astonishing. Powell would be less than he seemed in his clothes; like many an actor he was slight, almost thin, and his head was the best part of him. As for Penny Raven—well, there were the remains of a fine woman about Penny, but to Darcourt's probing eye the breasts were a little languid, and there was a hint of a rubber tire around the waist. The sedentary life of the scholar was running Penny down, and her jolly face was sagging a little at the chops.

As for the Doctor—well, he was reminded of a remark he had heard a student make about another student, a girl: "I'd as soon go to bed with a bicycle." The Doctor, under the fine, Chopinesque get-up, might have the wiriness, the chill, the impracticable resistance of a bicycle to a sexual approach, but she was probably interesting. Any breasts? One cannot get beneath the coat. Any hips? The skirts of the coat concealed them, whatever they might be. But an elegantly formed waist. Long, elegant feet and hands. The Doctor might be very interesting. Not that he was the man who would find out.

As for himself, Professor the Reverend Simon Darcourt, he had to admit that he did not peel well. He had been a fatty from his mother's womb and now the stretch-marks on his belly were the wound stripes of countless lost battles against overweight.

The table is almost silent, he thought; an angel must be passing. But not the stark-striking genie. The servant removed his plate and he got up to attend to the next service of wine. It was to be champagne. Who would be the first to protest that whatever wine Arthur of Britain may have served at the Round Table, it was certainly not champagne? Nobody. They accepted it with murmurs of pleasure.

Maria allowed the next course to be served without comment. It was a pretty confection of eggs and cream stiffened with something elusive.

"What is this?" asked the Doctor.

"Nobody can say that it isn't a genuinely Arthurian dish," said Maria. "Its name is washbrew."

The company was reduced to silence. Nobody liked to ask what washbrew might be, but when they heard the name their minds misgave them.

Maria said nothing for a minute or two, then she relieved their apprehension.

"It can't hurt you," she said. "It is just very fine oatmeal, with a few things to give it a nice taste. Geraint's Welsh ancestors called it flummery."

"Buttermilk and flummery say the bells of Montgomery," sang Powell, to the tune of "Oranges and Lemons".

"The flavour," said Penny. "Elusive. Delicious! Reminds me somehow of childhood."

"That is the hartshorn," said Maria. "Very Arthurian. You were probably given hartshorn candy for sore throats."

"But not just hartshorn," said Hollier. "There is another flavour, and I think it's brandy."

"I am certain Arthur had brandy," said Maria. "And if anybody contradicts me I shall send it back to the kitchen and get you some raw turnips to chew, and that will be authentically Early

Britain, and I hope it will satisfy all you purists. The champagne should help you to worry down a few turnips."

"Please don't be annoyed, dear," said Arthur. "I'm sure nobody means to be disagreeable."

"I am not so sure, and I'm sick and tired of having my dinner tested for archaeological accuracy. If my intuition tells me something is Arthurian, it's thereby Arthurian, including champagne, and that's that!"

"Of course," said the Doctor, and her tone was as smooth as the cream they were eating. "We are all being intolerable, and I demand that everyone stop it at once. We have insulted our *hlafdiga,* and we should be ashamed. I am ashamed. Are you ashamed, Professor Raven?"

"Eh?" said Penny, startled. "Yes, I suppose I am. Anything served at Arthur's Round Table is thereby Arthurian, isn't it?"

"That is what I like about you Canadians," said the Doctor; "you are so ready to admit fault. It is a fine, if dangerous, national characteristic. You are all ashamed. And I am ashamed, too."

"But I don't want anybody to feel ashamed," said Maria. "Just happy. I do wish you could be happy and not nag and quarrel all the time."

"Of course, my dear," said Hollier. "We are ungrateful beasts, and this is a delightful dinner." He leaned across Penny Raven to pat Maria's hand, but he misjudged his distance and got his sleeve in Penny's flummery. "Oh, hell," he said.

"About this opera," said Arthur. "I suppose we ought to give it some thought?"

"I've given it many hours of thought," said Powell. "The first thing we must have is a story. And I have a story."

"Have you so?" said the Doctor. "You have not seen the music, and you have not talked to me, but you have a story. I suppose we are to be permitted to hear the story, so that we little people may set to work on it?"

Powell drew himself up in his chair, and swept the table with the smile with which he could melt fifteen hundred people in a theatre.

"But of course," said he. "And you must not suppose that I wish to impose my story on anyone, and least of all on the musicians. That is not the way we librettists work. We know our place in the hierarchy of operatic artists. When I say I have a story, I mean only that I have a basis on which we may begin discussions of what this opera is to be about."

How well he manages us, thought Darcourt. He uses at least three levels of language. There is his Rough Demotic, in which he tells the Doctor to bet her pretty little ass on something, and another form of that is the speech in which he calls me "Sim *bach*", and "boy", and reverses his sentence structure in what I suppose is a translation from his cradle Welsh; and there is his Standard English, in which he addresses the world of strangers, about whom he cares little; and there is his Enriched Literary Speech, finely pronounced and begemmed with quotations from Shakespeare and the more familiar poets, and soaring at need into a form of rhapsodic, bardic chant. It's a pleasure to be bamboozled by such a man. What lustre he gives to the language that most of us treat as a common drudge. What is he going to give us now? The Enriched, I suppose.

"The story of Arthur," said Powell, "is impossible to gather into a single coherent tale. It comes to us in an elegant French form, and a sturdy, darkly coloured German form, and in Sir Thomas Malory's form, which is the richest and most enchanting of all. But behind all of these forms lies the great Celtic legend, whence all the elegance and strength and enchantment take their life, and in the brief story I offer you for this opera you may be sure I have not forgotten it. But if we are to have an opera that will hold an audience, we must above all have a strong narrative that can carry the weight of music. Music can give life and feeling to an opera, but it cannot tell a tale."

"By God, you are right," said the Doctor. Then she turned to Darcourt. "Champagne," she hissed.

"Yes! *Gwin o eur!*" said Hollier.

"Now—listen. You will agree, I hope, that there can be no tale of Arthur that leaves out Caliburn, the great magic sword; I do not like the later form Excalibur. But—economy! We cannot go back to the beginning of his life to tell about how he came by Caliburn. So I propose a device that was put in my head by Hoffmann himself. You remember how in the overture to *Undine* he strikes the right note at once by using the voices of the lover and the water-god, calling the name of the heroine? I propose that almost as soon as the overture to *Arthur of Britain* begins, we raise the curtain on a vision scene—you do it behind a scrim which makes everything misty—and we see the Magic Mere, and Arthur and Merlin on its shore. At a gesture from Merlin the great sword arises from the water, gripped in the hand of an unseen spirit, and Arthur seizes it. But as he is overcome with the grandeur of the moment, there arises from the Mere a vision of Guenevere—the name means White Ghost, as you surely know—presenting the scabbard of Caliburn; Merlin bids Arthur accept the scabbard and makes Arthur understand—don't worry, I'll show 'em how to do it—that the scabbard is even more important than the sword, because when the sword is in its scabbard there is peace, and peace must be his gift to his people. But as Arthur turns away, the visionary Guenevere shows by a gesture that the scabbard is herself, and that unless he knows her value and her might, the sword will avail him nothing. You follow me?"

"I follow you," said the Doctor. "The sword is manhood and the scabbard is womanhood, and unless they are united there can be no peace, no splendour through the arts of peace."

"You've got it!" said Powell. "And the scabbard is also Guenevere, and already Arthur is losing Guenevere because he trusts in the sword alone."

"The *symbolismus* is very good," said the Doctor. "Aha, the sword is also Arthur's thing—you know, his male thing—what do you call it—?"

"His penis," said Penny.

"Not much of a word. Latin—means his tail. How can it be a tail when it is in front? Have you no better word in English?"

"Not in decent use," said Darcourt.

"Oh—decent use! I spit on decent use! And the scabbard is the Queen's thing—what is your indecent word for that?"

Nobody quite liked to reply, but Penny whispered in the Doctor's ear. "Middle English," she added, to give it a scholarly gloss.

"Oho, *that* word!" said the Doctor. "We know it well in Sweden. That's a better word than that silly tail-word. I see that this will be a very rich opera. More champagne, if you please. Perhaps the best thing would be to put a bottle here beside me."

"Do I understand that you are telling the spectators even before the opera begins that there can be peace in the land only if there is sexual unity between the King and Queen?" said Hollier.

"Not at all," said Powell. "This Prologue tells that the greatness of the land depends on the uniting of masculine and feminine powers, and that the sword alone cannot bring the nobility of spirit Arthur seeks. Don't worry. I can get it across with some very nice lighting. There will be no raunchy shoving the sword in and out of the scabbard to please the people who think that sex is just something that happens in bed."

"More to that game than four bare legs in a blanket," said Penny, nodding sagely.

"Exactly. It is a union of two opposite but complementary sensibilities. Maybe that is what the Grail means. I leave that to the librettists, if they think it useful."

"The wine in the gold," said Maria.

"I never thought of the Grail like that," said Penny. "Interesting idea."

"Even the blind pig sometimes finds an acorn," said Powell, blowing toward her. "Now, to get into the opera proper.

"Act One begins with Arthur's evil sister, Morgan Le Fay (who is an enchantress and thus understandably a contralto), trying to worm secrets out of Merlin: who shall be Arthur's heir? Merlin squirms a bit, but he can't resist a fellow magician, and he confides that it must be someone born in the month of May, unless Arthur should have a child of his own. Morgan Le Fay is exultant, for her son Modred was born in May, and as the King's nephew he is the nearest heir. Merlin warns her not to be too sure, for Arthur loves Guenevere greatly, and a child is very likely. Not if Arthur risks his life in war, says the contralto.

"Then we have an assembly of the Knights of the Round Table: Arthur gives them their charge—they are to disperse and seek the Holy Grail, which will bring lasting peace and greatness to Britain. The Knights accept their duty, and are sent their different ways. But when Lancelot presents himself the King refuses to give him a direction; he must remain behind to govern because the King is eager to go on the Quest himself, bearing the great Caliburn; he draws it and sings of his overmastering ambition. Guenevere pleads with Arthur to let Lancelot go on the Quest, for she fears that the guilty love she and Lancelot have for each other may bring shame to the kingdom. But Arthur is resolute, and as he is being armoured for his Quest—very spectacular that will be—Morgan Le Fay steals the scabbard and Arthur, in his exalted state, refuses to wait until it is found, and goes on the Quest, declaring that bravery and strength, symbolized by the naked sword, will suffice. Everybody buggers off in search of the Grail, and Guenevere is filled with dread, and Morgan Le Fay is exultant. End of Act."

"What about Modred?" said Maria. "We haven't heard anything of him yet."

"He's one of the Knights, and he doubts the Grail," said Powell. "He can scowl and sneer in the background."

"Strong stuff, but is it nineteenth-century?" said Hollier. "A bit too psychological, perhaps?"

"No," said the Doctor. "Nineteenth-century need not mean simple-minded. Look at Weber's *Der Freischütz*. The nineteenth century had psychology too. We didn't invent it."

"Very well," said Hollier. "Go on, Powell."

"Act Two is where we get into really big operatic stuff. Begins with a scene of the Queen's Maying; she and her ladies are in the forest, gathering the May blossoms. I think she should ride a horse. A horse is always a sure card in opera. Suggests that no expense has been spared. If the horse has been given an enema an hour before curtain time, and there are enough people to lead it, even a coloratura soprano should be able to stick on its back long enough for a very pretty effect. In the forest she meets Lancelot, and they sing of their passion—after the horse and the maidens have gone, of course. But Morgan Le Fay is eavesdropping, disguised as a hag, an old witch of the forest. She cannot contain herself. She bursts upon the couple and denounces them as traitors to the King; they protest their innocence and devotion to Arthur. When the witch has gone, Merlin appears, and warns the lovers of the evil that lurks in the May blossoms, and the danger of the month of May. But they do not understand him."

"Stupid, like all characters in opera," said Hollier.

"Enchanted, like all people in love," said the Doctor. "Characters in opera are really just like ordinary people, you know, except that they show us their souls."

"If a witch and a sorcerer warned me about something, I think I would have enough wits to heed them," said Hollier.

"Probably. That is why there has never been an opera about a professor," said the Doctor.

"That is only Scene One of the Act," said Powell. "Now we have a quick change—I know how to do it—to a Tower up the river above Camelot, where Guenevere and Lancelot have gone and consummated their love. They are in ecstasy, but in the river below the Tower there appears a Black Barge guided by Morgan Le Fay, and bearing Elaine, the Lily Maid of Astolat, who accuses Lancelot of being false to her, and says that she carries his child. Guenevere is horror-struck, when Lancelot confesses that it is indeed true, but that he lay with Elaine when he was under a spell, and that he suspects the spell was cast upon him by Morgan Le Fay, who can get in a lot of very effective mockery in the ensuing quartet. But Guenevere is desolate and when the barge sweeps on, down the river to Camelot, her reproaches drive Lancelot mad. Now of course in Malory he is mad for years, and dashes about the forest banging into trees and getting into all sorts of injurious mischief, but we have no time for that, so he rages for a while. This could be quite a novelty; a Mad Scene (à la *Lucia*) for a tenor. Lancelot proposes to Guenevere that he should kill himself, as expiation for his faithlessness, even though it was not precisely his fault. No, says Guenevere; there shall be no needless killing, and she herself puts his sword back into its scabbard. As the scene concludes, a messenger arrives in hot haste, with news that there has been a great battle, and that Arthur has been killed. His body is being brought back to Camelot for burial. End of scene."

"Nobody can say that this opera lacks for incident," said Maria.

"Operas devour incident," said the Doctor. "Nobody wants to listen to people going into musical ecstasies about love for two hours and a half. Go on, Powell. What next? You have killed Arthur. That is bad. The character who gives the name to the opera should not peg out until the end. Look at *Lucia di Lammermoor;* the last act is tedious. No Lucia. You'll have to arrange something different."

"No I won't," said Powell. "The next and final Act is in the

Great Hall of Arthur's palace in Camelot, and Arthur returns triumphant, though wounded. He tells of the battle in which he has been engaged, and how a Knight in black armour appeared who challenged him to single combat. But when he seemed to be overcome, and fell from his horse, he drew his shield before him just as the Black Knight was about to give him the *coup de grâce*—"

"The what?" said Hollier.

Penny flew at him. "The *coup de grâce,* Clem. You know: the knockout. Do pay attention. You keep nodding off."

"I do nothing of the sort."

"Yes you do. Sit up straight and listen."

"As I was saying," said Powell, "the Black Knight was about to give Arthur the *coup de grâce* when he saw on the shield the painting of Our Lady, whereupon he turned and fled, and Arthur, though wounded, was spared. Arthur sings in praise of Our Lady, who saved him at need. The Eternal Feminine, you see."

"*Das Ewig-Weibliche,*" said the Doctor. "That ought to teach the masculine idiot. Go on."

"Everybody is immensely chuffed that Arthur has returned. But Arthur is uneasy. He knows he has an inveterate enemy. And this is where several Knights appear, bringing in Modred, the Black Knight, and Arthur is stricken that his nephew and the child of his dear sister should have sought his life. Modred mocks him as an idealistic fool, who holds honour greater than power, and displays the scabbard of Caliburn, without which he says honour is powerless, and the sword must settle everything. He challenges the wounded King to fight, and though Guenevere, who has seized the scabbard, begs him to sheathe Caliburn, the King will not hear of it. He and Modred fight, and once again the King is wounded. As he lies dying, Guenevere and Lancelot confess their guilty love. Now—this is the culmination of the whole affair—Arthur shows himself greatly magnanimous, and declares that the greatest love is summed up in Charity, and not in sexual fidelity alone; his love for both Guenevere and Lancelot is greater than the wound they have given him. He dies, and at once the scene changes to the Magic Mere, where we see Arthur floating out into the mists in a barge, attended only by Merlin, who sheathes Caliburn for the last time and casts it back into the water from which it first came, as Arthur nears the Isle of Sleep. Curtain."

There was applause from Darcourt and Maria. But Hollier was not content. "You drop too many people along the way," he said. "What happens to Elaine? What about her baby? We know that baby was Galahad, the Pure Knight who saw the Grail. You can't just dump all that after Act Two."

"Oh yes I can," said Powell. "This is an opera, not a Ring Cycle. We've got to get the curtain down around eleven."

"You've said nothing about Modred being the incestuous child of Arthur and Morgan Le Fay."

"No time for incest," said Powell. "The plot is complicated enough as it stands. Incest would just mess things up."

"I will have no part of any opera that includes a baby," said the Doctor. "Horses are bad enough on the stage, but children are hell."

"People will feel cheated," said Hollier. "Anybody who knows Malory will know that it was Sir Bedevere, not Merlin, who threw Caliburn back into the water. And it was three Queens who bore Arthur away. It's all so untrue to the original."

"Let 'em write to the papers," said Powell. "Let the musicologists paw it over for the next twenty years. We must have a coherent plot and we must wind it up before the stagehands go on overtime. How many people in an opera audience will know Malory, do you suppose?"

"I have always said the theatre was a coarse art," said Hollier, with tipsy dignity.

"That is why it is a live art," said the Doctor. "That is why it has vitality. Out of the ragbag about Arthur we have to find a straight story, and Powell has done so. For myself, I am very well pleased with his *schema* for the opera. I drink to you, Powell. You are what I call a real pro."

"Thank you, Nilla," said Powell. "I can't think of a compliment that would please me better."

"What's a real pro?" whispered Hollier to Penny.

"Somebody who really knows his job."

"Somebody who doesn't know Malory, it seems to me."

"I like it tremendously," said Arthur; "and I am glad you agree,

Doctor. Whatever you say, Clem, it's miles ahead of that rubbish about Nob and Tit we were listening to when Penny discovered Planché's stuff. At last I feel as if a huge weight had been lifted from my shoulders. I was terribly worried."

"Your worries have only begun, boy," said Powell. "But we'll meet 'em as they come. Won't we, Nilla *fach?*"

"Powell, you go beyond what is decent," said the Doctor. "How dare you speak to me in that way!"

"You misunderstand. The word is a Welsh endearment."

"You are gross. Do not attempt to explain."

"*Fach* is the feminine of *bach*. I say 'Sim *bach*' and it is as if I said dear old Sim."

"I want nothing to do with old dears," said the Doctor, who was again becoming belligerent. "I am a free spirit, not the scabbard of any man's sword. My world is a world of infinite choice."

"I'll bet," said Penny.

"You will oblige me by confining yourself to the libretto, which is your business, Professor Raven," said the Doctor. "Have you comprehended the *symbolismus?* This will be wonderfully modern. The true union of man and woman to save and enlarge mankind."

"But how can it be wonderfully modern if it is true to Hoffmann and the early nineteenth century?" said Hollier. "You forget that we are to restore and complete a work of art from a day long past."

"Professor Hollier, you are wonderfully obtuse, as only a very learned man can be, and I forgive you. But for the love of Almighty God, and for Our Lady whom Arthur bore on his shield, I beg you to shut up and leave the artists' work to the artists, and stop all this scholarly bleating. Real art is all one, and speaks of the great things of life, whenever it is created. Get that through your great, thick, brilliantly furnished head and shut up, shut up, *shut up*." The Doctor was roaring, in a rich contralto that might have done very well for Morgan Le Fay.

"All right," said Hollier. "I am not insulted. I am above the ravings of a drunken termagant. Go ahead, the whole pack of you, and make asses of yourselves. I withdraw."

"You mean you withdraw till next time you feel like sticking your oar in," said Penny. "I know you, Clem."

"Please. Please!" Now it was Darcourt who was shouting. "This is unbecoming an assembly of scholars and artists, and I won't listen to any more. You know what the Doctor is saying, don't you? It's been said since—well, at least since Ovid. He says somewhere—in the *Metamorphoses,* I think—that the great truths of life are the wax, and all we can do is to stamp it with different forms. But the wax is the same forever—"

"I have it," said Maria. "He says that nothing keeps its own form, but Nature who is the great renewer is always making up new forms from old forms. Nothing perishes in the whole universe—it just varies and renews its form—"

"And that's the truth that underlies all myth," shouted Darcourt, waving at her to be quiet. "If we are true to the great myth, we can give it what form we choose. The myth—the wax—does not change."

The Doctor, who had been busy lighting a large black cigar she drew from a silver case, said to Powell: "I am beginning to see my way. The scene where Arthur forgives the lovers will be in A minor, and we shall dodge back and forth in and out of A minor right until the end when the magician sees Arthur sailing off to his Island of Sleep. That's how we'll do it."

"Of course that's how we'll do it, Nilla," said Powell. "A minor comes right up out of the wax, hot and strong. And don't fuss about the opera being true to the nineteenth century. It will be artistically true, but you mustn't expect it to be literally true because—well, because a literal fidelity to the nineteenth century would be false. Do you see?"

"Yes. I see very well," said Arthur.

"Arthur, you are a darling," said Maria. "You see better than any of us."

"Well—I see many difficulties," said Hollier.

"I see the wax, and I am sure you two pros see the form, and I'm very happy about it," said Darcourt.

"God bless you, Sim *bach,*" said Powell. "You are a good old Merlin, that's what you are, boy."

"This Merlin—this magician—is more important in the story you have told, Powell, than I had expected," said the Doctor. "In opera terms, I should say he is Fifth Business, and the singer will have to be chosen with great care. What voice, do you think? We have a bass villain, and a baritone hero and a tenor lover, and a contralto villainess and a coloratura heroine and a mezzo simpleton—that deceived girl, what's her name, Elaine. What for Merlin? What would you say to a *haute contre*—you know, one of those high, unearthly voices?"

"A counter-tenor, you mean? What could be better? Makes him unlike any of the others."

"Yes, and very useful in ensembles. Those male altos are like trumpets, only strange—"

"The horns of elfland faintly blowing," said Powell.

"You seem to be pleased with the libretto just as Geraint has outlined it," said Arthur.

"Oh, it will need some small changes here and there as we work," said the Doctor. "But it is a fine *schema;* coherent and simple for people who can't follow a difficult plot, but with plenty of meaning underneath. An opera has to have a foundation; something big, like unhappy love, or vengeance, or some point of honour. Because people like that, you know. There they sit, all those stockbrokers and rich surgeons and insurance men, and they look so solemn and quiet as if nothing would rouse them. But underneath they are raging with unhappy love, or vengeance, or some point of honour or ambition—all connected with their professional lives. They go to *La Bohème* or *La Traviata* and they remember some early affair that might have been squalid if you weren't living it yourself; or they see *Rigoletto* and think how the chairman humiliated them at the last board meeting; or they see *Macbeth* and think how they would like to murder the chairman and get his job. Only they don't think it; very deep down they feel it, and boil it, and suffer it in the primitive underworld of their souls. You wouldn't get them to admit anything, not if you begged. Opera speaks to the heart as no other art does, because it is essentially simple."

"And what do you see as the deep foundation of this one?" said Arthur.

"It's a beauty," said Powell. "Victory plucked from defeat. If we can bring it off, it will wring the heart. Arthur has failed in the Quest, lost his wife, lost his crown, lost life itself. But because of his nobility and greatness of spirit when he forgives Guenevere and Lancelot, he is seen to be the greatest man of all. He is Christ-like; apparently a loser, but, in truth, the greatest victor of them all."

"You'll want a first-rate actor," said Maria.

"Yes. And I have my eye on one, but I won't tell you until I've got his name on a contract."

"It's the alchemical theme," said Maria. "Gold refined from dross."

"Do you know," said Hollier, "I believe you're right. You have always been my best student, Maria. But if you get that out of an authentic nineteenth-century stage piece, you'll be alchemists indeed."

"We are alchemists," said the Doctor. "It's our job. But now I must go home. I must be fresh tomorrow to go over all this Hoffmann stuff again with what we have been talking about fresh in my mind. I must do that before I talk with this little Schnak-enburg, whoever she is. And so I shall say good-night."

Upright as a grenadier and without a stumble, the Doctor circled the room, shaking hands with everyone.

"Let me call you a taxi," said Darcourt.

"No indeed. The walk will refresh me. It cannot be more than two miles, and the night is very fresh."

Saying which, the Doctor seized Maria in her arms and gave her a lingering kiss. "Do not worry, little one," she said. "Your dinner was very good. Not authentic, of course, but better than the real thing. Like our opera." And away she went.

"My God," said Penny, when the Doctor had gone, "did you see what that woman drank? And not once—not once in six hours—did she go to the loo. Is she human?"

"Very human," said Maria, wiping her mouth with a handker-chief. "She stuck her tongue almost down my throat."

"She didn't kiss me, you observe," said Penny. "Not that I care. Raunchy old lesbian lush. You watch yourself, Maria. She has her eye on you."

"That cigar! I'll taste it for a week!" said Maria, and picking up her glass of champagne she gargled noisily, and spat into an empty coffee cup. "I never thought of myself as attractive in that way."

"You're attractive in so many ways," said Penny, tearfully. "It isn't fair."

"When you sink into self-pity," said Hollier, "it's time for me to go home."

"I'll drive you, Clem," said Penny. "I have a large, forgiving soul, even if you are a rotten old bastard."

"Thank you, Professor Raven," said Hollier; "I would prefer not to be driven by you. Last time you drove me home we were spoken to by a policeman because of your driving."

"He was just being officious."

"And when we arrived outside my house you honked your horn derisively to waken my mother. No, Penny, no. I won't drive with you when you've got your paws in the sauce."

"Paws in the sauce! I like that! Who was falling asleep while Geraint was talking? You bloody old woman, Clem!"

"In this age of female liberation, I do not understand why 'old woman' is still considered an insult." And with careful dignity Hollier took his leave, closely followed by Penny, who was squealing incoherent abuse.

"She'll drive him, of course," said Darcourt. "Clem is as tight as the bark to a tree. He can never resist a free ride. I'll give them a minute, then I'll go too."

"Oh, Simon, when do I see you again?" said Maria. "I've got something to tell you. Crottel wants to come again and nag about Parlabane's miserable book."

"I'll be here when you need me," said Simon, and went.

"What do you make of the Doctor, Geraint?" said Arthur to the lingering guest.

" 'Oh, she doth teach the torches to burn bright!' " said Powell. "I'm mad for Old Sooty. We shall get on like a house afire— literally like a house afire."

"She won't yield to your charm," said Maria.

"Exactly. That's why we'll work well together. I despise easy women." And, kissing Maria on the cheek, he went.

Maria and Arthur looked around their large room. The candles on the Round Table were guttering. In the middle stood the Platter of Plenty, from which no guests had taken anything, whether from sixth-century scruple or not it was impossible to guess. Like all dinner tables, after prolonged dinners, it was a melancholy sight.

"Don't worry, my darling," said Arthur. "It was a wonderful

dinner, and a great success, really. But I never really understand your university friends. Why do they quarrel so?"

"It doesn't mean anything," said Maria. "It's just that they can't bear anybody else to have an advantage, even for a moment. That woman stirred them up."

"She's a disturber, no doubt about it."

"A good disturber, would you say?"

"As she said herself, we must hope," said Arthur, and led his wife off to bed. Or rather, to their separate beds, for Arthur was still not fully himself.

[4]

ETAH IN LIMBO

OLD SOOTY! *Does Powell really understand Dr. Gunilla Dahl-Soot if he can speak of her thus? Yet I believe it is meant to be affectionate, and is just his theatrical way; theatre people have little reverence— except when they look in the mirror.*

The Doctor fills me with hope. Here is someone I can understand. She knows the lyre of Orpheus when she hears it, and does not fear to follow where it may lead.

I love the Doctor. Not as a man loves a woman, but as an artist loves a friend. She reminds me gloriously of my dearest friend on earth, Ludwig Devrient. A very fine actor, and the most sympathetic and dearest of men.

What great nights we had together, in Lutter's tavern, just across the square from the house in which I lived. And why was I not in my house? Why was I not at the domestic hearth with my dear, faithful, long-suffering wife Michalina?

I think it was because Michalina loved me too much. Dear girl, when I was writing my tales of horror and grotesquerie, and my nerves were red-hot and I thought my mind might lose itself forever in the dangerous underworld from which my stories came, she would sit by my side, and keep my glass filled, and sometimes hold my hand when I began to tremble—for I did tremble when the ideas came too fast and were too frightening—and I swear it was she who kept me from madness. And how did I reward her? Certainly not with blows and harsh words and the brutality of a ruffian, as so many husbands do. When

I was a judge, I heard awful tales of domestic tyranny. A man may be the most respectable of bourgeois to his acquaintances, but a brute and a devil at home. Not I. I loved Michalina, I respected her, I gave her whatever my earnings, which were not trifling, could command. But I was always conscious that I pitied her, and I pitied her because she was so devoted to me, never questioned me, treated me as a master rather than a lover.

Not that it could have been otherwise. Too soon after my marriage I took a pupil, Julia Marc, and I loved her with all my heart and soul; all the entrancing women in my stories are portraits of Julia Marc.

It was her voice. I was teaching her to sing; but there was little enough to teach, for she had such a gift and such a voice as comes rarely in anyone's experience. Oh, I could refine her taste, and show her how to phrase her music, but as I sat at the harpsichord I was lost in a dream of love, and would have made a fool of myself, or perhaps a Byronic demon lover of myself, if she had given me any encouragement. She was sixteen, and she knew I loved her, though not how profoundly, because she was too young, and the devotion of such a man as I was seemed to her to be in the natural order of things. Very young girls think themselves made to be loved, and they may even be kind to their lovers, but they do not really understand them, and I think her secret dream was of some young officer, wondrous in a uniform, with a maddening moustache, who would turn her bowels to water with his valour and his aristocratic ways. So what was the music-master, a little man, with a strange, sharp face, who made her tune her scales until she sang with a melting purity and never strayed from the key? A nice old fellow, nearly twenty years older than herself, and at thirty-six already with some grey hairs in the parenthetic side-whiskers that framed his rat-like face. But I loved her until I thought I might die of it, and Michalina knew, and never spoke a jealous word or a reproach.

So what came of that? When she was seventeen, Julia's hardheaded, Philistine mother arranged a good marriage for her to one Groepel, who was nearly sixty, but rich. I suppose she could imagine no finer future for her daughter than to be a rich widow. What the good woman did not know was that Groepel was a drunkard of terrible assiduity. Not a roaring, heroic drinker, or a romantic melancholy drinker, but a determined fuddler. I still cannot permit myself to think what her life with Groepel may have been like. Perhaps he beat her, but it is more likely that he was coarse and sullen and abusive and never knew a single thing of any importance about what my Julia was or might be. Whatever, the marriage had to be dissolved after a few years, and it was the mercy of God that it was not in my courtroom that the process was examined and the dissolution approved by law. By that time the wonderful voice was gone, and there was nothing left of my Julia but a pitiable woman of substantial means bewailing her misfortunes to her cronies over innumerable cups of coffee and rich unwholesome little cakes. It was the lovely girl of sixteen I treasured in my heart, and now I see that she was in great part my own creation. For Julia, too, was a Philistine in her heart and nothing I could do as her teacher could touch that.

What is a Philistine? Oh, some of them are very nice people. They are the salt of the earth, but not its pepper. A Philistine is someone who is content to live in a wholly unexplored world. My dear, dear faithful Michalina was a Philistine, I believe, for she never attempted to explore any world but that of her husband, and because E.T.A. Hoffmann could not love her with the fervour of his love for Julia, that was not enough.

Was this a tragedy? Oh, no, no, no my dear cultivated friends. We know what a tragedy is, don't we? Tragedy is about heroic figures, who make their sufferings known to the world and demand that the world stand in awe of their sufferings. Not a little lawyer, who wants to be a great composer and is in reality rather an unusual writer, and his devoted Polish wife. There can be no tragedy about such ordinary people. Their lives at best are melodrama, in which the harsh realities are interspersed with scenes of comedy or even farce. They do not live under the pewter sky of tragedy. For them there are breaks in the clouds.

Such a break in the sky, such a burst of fine weather, was my friendship with Ludwig Devrient. A man most decidedly not a Philistine, but one of a great theatre family, himself a great actor, a man of such magnetism and personal beauty as might even have satisfied the girlish dreams of Julia Marc. Between us there was friendship and sympathy that perfectly suited us both, for we were both what it was then becoming fashionable to call Romantics. We did explore the world, so far as we could. And, I am sorry to say, our compass in our explorations was the bottle. The champagne bottle. In those days it was not a prohibitively expensive wine, but a wine we could apply ourselves to in seriousness and abundance. In Lutter's tavern, night after night we did so, and a group of friends would gather to hear us talk and range over that world of which the Philistines wish to know nothing.

When I died, at forty-six, of a complication of ailments of which champagne was not the least, Devrient did something that made him the mockery of those who could not understand, and won him the respect of some who could. After my funeral he went to Lutter's and made himself gloriously drunk. He was not a roaring drunk or a silly drunk or a stumbling drunk, but a man who had gone over entirely into that other world that the Philistines do not wish to explore or even to allow on the neat chart of their universe. He put two bottles of champagne into his pockets, and walked to the graveyard, and there he seated himself on my grave; and all the cool night of June 25, 1822, he talked to me in his best manner. Some of the wine he drank and some he spilled on the clay. Though I could not answer him, it was surely our best night together, and helped me kindly through the first loneliness of death.

In this woman I see Devrient, or something of him, once again. That was why, when the party was over, I walked at her side through the autumn streets of a strange but not unkindly city, until we came to her house, and there I sat by her bedside the whole night through. Did I speak to her in her dreams? Those who understand such things better than I must answer that question, but that was my hope. In Dr. Gunilla I recognized another Romantic, and though many aspire to that condition, it is a gift of birth, and we are few.

FOUR

MR MERVYN GWILT was thoroughly enjoying himself. This, he thought, was what the practice of the law should be—fine surroundings, a captive audience of distinguished people, and he, Mervyn Gwilt, advising them, for their own good, from his rich understanding of the law and human nature.

Mr. Mervyn Gwilt was every inch a lawyer. Indeed, the expression is inadequate, for there were not many inches to Mr. Gwilt, and there was an awful lot of lawyer in him. He could not have been anything else. He habitually wore a wing collar, suggesting that only a few minutes before he had whipped off his gown and bands and was attempting to reduce his courtroom demeanour and vocabulary to the needs of common life. He always wore a dark three-piece suit, lest he be summoned to court in a hurry. He particularly liked Latin; the priests of Rome might have abandoned that language as a cloak for their mystery, but not Mervyn Gwilt. It was, he explained, so pithy, so exact, so wholly legal in its underlying philosophy and its sound, that it could not be beaten as an instrument for subduing an opponent, or a client. The law had not, up to the present, shown much favour to Mr. Gwilt, but he was ready, should such favour suddenly declare itself.

"At the outset," he said, smiling around the table, "I want to make it amply clear that my client's wish in pursuing this matter carries no taint *ad crumenam* (that's to say he isn't looking for money) but is actuated solely by an inborn respect for the *ius naturale* (meaning what's right and proper)."

He smiled at Maria; at Hollier; at Darcourt. He even smiled

at the large man with the big black moustache who had been introduced simply as Mr. Carver. Finally he smiled, with special radiance, at his client Wally Crottel, who was sitting at his side.

"That's right," said Wally. "Don't think I'm just in this for what I can get."

"Let me handle it, Wally," said Mr. Gwilt. "Let's put it all on the table and look at it *ante litem motam* (by which I mean before we think of any court action). Now look: Mr. Crottel's father, the late John Parlabane, left at his death the manuscript of a novel, the title of which was *Be Not Another*. Am I right?"

Maria, Hollier, and Darcourt nodded.

"He left it to Miss Maria Magdalena Theotoky, now Mrs. Arthur Cornish, and to Professor Clement Hollier, as his literary executors. Right?"

"Not precisely," said Hollier. "He left it with an appeal that we should get it published. The term literary executors was not used."

"That remains to be seen," said Mr. Gwilt. "It might well have been implied. So far my client and I have not had a chance to examine that letter. I think this is the time for us to have it on the table. Right?"

"Out of the question," said Hollier. "It was a letter of the most intimate character, and the bit about the novel was only a small part of it. Whatever Parlabane wanted made public he sent in other letters to the newspapers."

Mr. Gwilt made stagy business of hunting in his briefcase for some newspaper clippings. "Those were the portions that spoke of his unhappy determination to take his life because of the neglect his great novel had met with."

"They were also the portions that described his elaborate and disgusting murder of Professor Urquhart McVarish," said Hollier.

"That is not relevant to the matter in hand," said Mr. Gwilt, rebuking this crude reference.

"Of course it is," said Hollier. "He knew the murder would get a lot of publicity, and draw attention to his book. He said so. 'The book a man murdered to have published' was the way he suggested it should be advertised. Or words of that sort."

"Let us not be diverted by irrelevancies," said Mr. Gwilt, primly.

"Maybe he was off his nut and didn't know what he was saying," said Wally Crottel.

"Wally! Leave this to me," said Mr. Gwilt, and kicked Wally sharply under the table. "Until we have indisputable evidence to the contrary, we assume that the late Mr. Parlabane knew precisely what he was saying, and doing."

"He was Brother John Parlabane, I believe, even though he had gone over the wall and parted from the Order of the Sacred Mission. Let's not forget he was a monk," said Maria.

"In these times many men find that they are not fully attuned to the religious life," said Mr. Gwilt. "The exact status of Mr. Parlabane at the time of his unhappy death—*felo de se,* and which of us dares point the finger—is not our business here. What concerns us is that he was my client's father. And my client's status as his heir is what we are talking about now."

"But how do we know Wally was his son?" said Maria. As a woman she wanted to get to the point, and was restless under Mr. Gwilt's ceremonious approach.

"Because that's what my late mum always told me," said Wally, " 'Parlabane was your dad, sure as guns; he was the only guy ever gave me a real organism.' That's what my mum always said."

"Please! Please! May I be allowed to conduct this investigation?" said Mr. Gwilt. "My client was brought up as the child of the late Ogden Whistlecraft, whose name is a word of magic in the annals of Canadian poetry, and his wife, the late Elsie Whistlecraft, my client's undisputed mother. That there had been a liaison of a passionate character—let's just call it an *ad hoc* thing, maybe two or three occasions—between Mrs. Whistlecraft and the late John Parlabane, we do not propose to deny. Why should we? Who dares to point the finger? What kind of woman marries a poet? A woman of deep passions and rich feminine sympathies, obviously. Her pity extended to this family friend, likewise a man of profound literary temperament. Pity! Pity, my friends! And compassion for a lonely, great, questing genius. That was what explained it."

"No. It was the organism," said Wally, stoutly.

"Orgasm, Wally! For God's sake how many times do I have to tell you? Orgasm!" Mr. Gwilt's speech was a hiss.

"She always said organism," said Wally, mulishly. "I know what my mum said. And don't think I blame her. She was my mum and I stand by her, and I'm not ashamed. You said something about that, Merv; you said it was, like, Latin, *De mortos* or something. 'Don't crap on your folks' you said it meant."

"All right! All right, Wally! Just leave it to me."

"Yeah, Merv, but I want to explain about my mum. And Whistlecraft—he didn't like me to call him Dad, but he was nice about the whole thing. He never really talked to me about it, but I know he didn't hold it against my mum. Not much. There was something he said once, in poetry—

> *Don't be ashamed*
> *When the offensive ardour blows the charge*

—as the fellow says."

"What fellow was that?" said Darcourt, speaking for the first time.

"The fellow in Shakespeare."

"Oh—that fellow! I thought it might have been something Whistlecraft wrote himself."

"No. Shakespeare. Whistlecraft was prepared to overlook the whole thing. He understood life, even if he wasn't much of a hand at the organism."

"Wally—I call your attention to the fact that there is a lady present."

"Don't mind me," said Maria; "I suppose I am what used to be called a woman of the world."

"And a fine Rabelaisian scholar," said Hollier, smiling at her.

"Aha! Rabelaisian scholar? Old-time Frenchman? Dead?" said Mr. Gwilt.

"The truly great are never dead," said Maria, and suddenly remembered that she was quoting her mother.

"Very well, then. Let us continue on a rather freer line," said Mr. Gwilt. "I don't have to remind you university people of the great changes that have taken place in public opinion, and one might almost say in public morals, in recent years. The distinction has virtually vanished, in the newspapers and also in modern fiction—though I haven't much time for fiction—between what we may define as the Okay and the Raw. Discretion of language—

where is it? Obscenity—where is it? On stage and screen we live
in the Age of the Full Frontal. Since the *Ulysses* case and the *Lady
Chatterley* case the law has had to take unwilling cognizance of
all this. If you are a student of Rabelais, Mrs. Cornish—not that
I've read his stuff, but he has a certain reputation, you know,
even among those who haven't read him—we must assume that
you are thoroughly broken to the Raw. But I digress. So let us
get back to our real interest. We admit that the late Mrs. Whistlecraft's life was in some degree flawed—"

"But not Raw," said Maria. "Nowadays we call it liberated."

"Exactly, Mrs. Cornish. I see you have an almost masculine
mind. So let us proceed. My client is John Parlabane's son—"

"Proof," said Mr. Carver. "We'll want proof."

"Excuse me, my friend," said Mr. Gwilt. "I don't understand
your position in this matter. I have assumed that you are in some
way an *amicus curiae*—a friend of the court—but if you are going
to advise and interfere I want to know why, and who you are."

"Name's George Carver. I was with the RCMP until I retired.
I do a little private investigation work now, so as not to be bored."

"I see. And have you been investigating this matter?"

"I wouldn't say that. I might, if it came to anything."

"But you don't regard this meeting as anything?"

"Not so far. You haven't proved anything."

"But you think you know something relevant."

"I know that Wally Crottel got his job as a security man in this
building by saying, among other things, that he had seen some
service with the RCMP. He hasn't. Failed entry. Education in-
sufficient."

"That may have been indiscreet but it has nothing to do with
the matter in hand. Now listen: I said at the beginning that my
client and I are relying on the *ius naturale*—on natural justice,
what's right and proper, what decent people everywhere know
to be right. I say it is his right to benefit from anything that accrues
from the publication of his father's novel, *Be Not Another,* because
he is John Parlabane's rightful heir. And I say that Professor
Clement Hollier and Mrs. Arthur Cornish have suppressed that
book for personal reasons, and all we ask is some recognition of
my client's right, or we shall be forced to resort to law, and insist
on recompense, after publication of the book."

"How would you do that?" said Darcourt. "Nobody can be forced to publish a book."

"That's as may appear," said Mr. Gwilt.

"Well, it will appear that nobody wants to publish it," said Maria. "When all the scandal blew up, a great many publishers asked to see the book, and they turned it down."

"Aha. Too Raw for them, eh?" said Mr. Gwilt.

"No. Too dull for them," said Maria.

"The book was chiefly an exposition of John Parlabane's philosophy," said Darcourt. "And as such it was derivative and tediously repetitious. He had interspersed his long philosophical passages with some autobiographical stuff that he thought was fiction, but I assure you it wasn't. Stiff as a board."

"Autobiographical?" said Mr. Gwilt. "And he may have included portraits of living persons that would have caused a fine stink. Political people? Big people in the world or business? And that was why the publishers wouldn't touch it?"

"Publishers, too, have a fine sense of the Okay and the Raw, and of that lively area where the two kiss and commingle," said Maria. "As my dear François Rabelais puts it: *Quaestio subtilissima, utrum chimaera in vacuo bombinans possit commedere secundas intentiones*. I make no apologies for the Latin, as you are such a dab hand with that language."

"Aha," said Mr. Gwilt, imparting a wealth of legal subtlety into the exclamation, though his eyes flickered with incomprehension. "And precisely how do you apply that fine legal maxim to the matter in hand?"

"Translated very roughly," said Maria, "it might be taken to suggest that you are standing on a banana skin."

"Though we would not dream of disparaging your admirable *argumentum ad excrementum taurorum*," said Hollier.

"What's he say?" said Wally to his legal adviser.

"Says it's all bullshit. Well, we don't have to take that kind of thing from people just because they have money and position. Our legal system guarantees a fair deal for everybody. And my client has not had a fair deal. If the book had been published, he would have a right to a share, if not all, of the payment proceeding from the publication. You have not proceeded to publication and we want to know why. That's what we're doing here. So I think

I'd better be more direct than I've been up to now. Where's this manuscript?"

"I don't know that you have a right to ask that," said Hollier.

"A court would have that right. You say publishers refused it?"

"To be scrupulously exact," said Maria, "one publisher said he might take it if he could put a ghost on it and make whatever could be made of the story, leaving out all Parlabane's philosophy and moralizing. He said it would have to be made sensational— a real murderer's confession. But that would have been utterly false to what Parlabane wanted, and we refused."

"I put it to you that the novel was Raw, and brought in recognizable portraits of living people, and you are protecting them."

"No, no; so far as I remember the novel—what I read of it— it wasn't Raw. Not for modern tastes," said Hollier. "There were references to homosexual encounters, but Parlabane was so allusive and indirect—as compared to his description of how he murdered poor old Urky McVarish—that it came out as rather mild stuff. Not so much Raw as half-baked. He was not an experienced writer of fiction. The publisher Mrs. Cornish has spoken of wanted to make it really Raw, and we would not degrade our old associate Parlabane in that way. What's Raw and what isn't is really a matter of taste; the taste may be pungent, but it shouldn't be nasty. We didn't at all trust the taste of that publisher."

"Do you tell me you haven't *read* the novel?" said Mr. Gwilt, with stagy incredulity.

"It was unreadable. Even a professor, who is professionally obliged to read a great deal of tedious stuff, couldn't get through it. Outraged nature overcame me at about page four hundred, and the last two hundred and fifty pages remain unread, so far as I am concerned."

"That's how it was," said Maria. "I couldn't read it either."

"Nor I," said Darcourt. "And I assure you I tried my very best."

"Aha!" said Mr. Gwilt. It was a verbal pounce. "You admit ignorance of this book, considered by its author to be one of the greatest works of fiction in the realm of the philosophical novel to be produced in history, and yet you have had the mind-boggling gall to suppress it—"

"Nobody would take it," said Darcourt.

"Please! I'm speaking! And I'm speaking now, not as a man of the law, but as a human soul peering into an abyss of snotty intellectual infamy! Now see here—if you don't produce that manuscript for our examination and the opinion of the experts we shall put to work on it, you face legal action which will make you smart, let me tell you!"

"No alternative of any kind?" said Maria. She and the two professors seemed calm under the threat of exposure and ignominy.

"My client and I don't want a stink, any more than you do. I know it may seem strange for me, as a lawyer, to advise against going to court. I suggest that a composition might be made."

"A pay-off, you mean?" said Hollier.

"Not a legal term. I say a composition in the sum of, let's say, a million dollars."

Hollier and Darcourt, both of whom had experience of publishing books, laughed aloud.

"You flatter me," said Hollier. "Do you know what professors are paid?"

"You are not alone in this," said Mr. Gwilt, smiling. "I don't suppose Mrs. Cornish would have much trouble over a million."

"Oh, not a bit," said Maria. "I fling such sums to the needy, at church doors."

"Let us keep this serious," said Mr. Gwilt. "A million's the word."

"On what grounds?"

"I have already spoken of the *ius naturale*," said Mr. Gwilt. "Common justice and decency. Let me recap: my client is the son of John Parlabane, and at the time of his death the late Mr. Parlabane did not know of the existence of that son. That's the nub of it. If Mr. Parlabane had known, at the time he made that will, would he have overlooked the claim of his own child?"

"As I remember Mr. Parlabane he might have done anything at all," said Darcourt.

"Well, the law wouldn't allow it, if he tried to cut out his natural heir. This isn't the eighteenth century, you know."

"I think it's time I put in my two cents' worth," said Mr. Carver, who had been as still as a very large cat during all that had been said. He now looked like a very wide-awake cat. "You can't prove your client is the son of John Parlabane."

"Oh, can't I, indeed?"

"No, you can't. I've made a few inquiries, and I have at least three witnesses, and I could probably find more, who had a crack at the late Mrs. Whistlecraft in her high and palmy days. If you'll pardon a bit of the Raw, one of my informants said she was known as Pay As You Enter, and poor old Whistlecraft was laughed at as a notorious cuckold, though a decent guy and quite a poet. Who's the father? Nobody knows."

"Oh yes they do," said Wally Crottel. "What about the organism? Eh? How about that? None of these guys you mention ever gave her the organism. She said so herself; she was always a very open woman. And without the organism how do you account for a child? Eh? Without the organism, no dice."

"I don't know what you've been reading, Mr. Crottel," said Mr. Carver, "but you're away off base. Take my wife, for instance; four fine kids, one of them just last week called to the bar (a lawyer like yourself, Mr. Gwilt), and she never had one of those things in her life. Told me so herself. And a very happy woman, adored by her family. You ought to see what goes on in our house on Mother's Day! This organism, as you call it, may be all very well, but it's not the real goods. So bang goes your organism. So far as it's evidence, that's to say."

"Well, anyways, that's what my mum always said," said Wally, loyal even in defeat.

Mr. Gwilt seemed to be groping in his mind, perhaps for a useful scrap of Latin. He decided to do what he could with an old one.

"The *ius naturale*," he said. "Natural justice. Are you going to fly in the face of that?"

"Yes, when it's demanded at the point of a gun, and it's an empty gun. That would be my advice," said Mr. Carver, a pussy who had not yet retracted his claws.

"Come on, Merv," said Wally. "Time to go."

"I haven't finished yet," said his lawyer. "I want to get to the bottom of why that will is withheld."

"Not a will," said Hollier; "a personal letter."

"The nearest thing to a will the late John Parlabane ever made. And why are these people refusing to produce the *corpus delicti,* by which I hasten to say I do not mean the body of the late John Parlabane, as it is commonly misunderstood, but the material object relating to the crime. I mean the manuscript of the novel about which all this dispute has arisen."

"Because there's no reason to produce it," said Mr. Carver.

"Oh, there isn't, eh? We'll see about that!"

Mr. Carver was a pussycat again, his claws well in. He used an expression perhaps unexpected in a former member of the Royal Canadian Mounted Police, and a working private eye.

"Fiddlesticks!" he said.

With a great display of indignation, and inaudible mutterings, Mr. Mervyn Gwilt rose slowly, like a man who goes, only to return with renewed strength, and, followed by his disgruntled client, left the apartment. He gave vent to his feelings by slamming the door.

"Thank God we're rid of them," said Maria.

"Rid of Gwilt, maybe. I wouldn't be sure you're rid of Wally Crottel," said Mr. Carver, rising. "I know a few things about Wally. Fellows like that can be very nasty. You'd better keep your eye peeled, Mrs. Cornish."

"Why me? Why not Professor Hollier?"

"Psychology. You're a woman, and a rich woman. People like Wally are very jealous. There's not much to be got out of the professor, if you'll excuse me for saying so, but a rich woman is an awful temptation to a fellow like Wally. I just mention it."

"Thanks, George. You've been wonderful," said Darcourt. "You'll send me your statement, won't you?"

"Itemized and in full," said Mr. Carver. "But I must say it's been a pleasure. I never liked that guy Gwilt."

Mr. Carver declined the offer of a drink, and moved out of the apartment on pussycat feet.

"Where did you find that wonderful man?" said Maria.

"I was able to do something for his oldest boy when he was a student. Taught him a little Latin—just enough," said Darcourt. "George is my key to the underworld. Everybody ought to have one."

"If that's that, then I'll be going," said Hollier. "Some work I want to finish. But if I may say so, Maria my dear, you really oughtn't to throw anything away; as a scholar you ought to know that. Throw things away and what is there for the scholars of the future? It's simple trade-unionism. Throw things away and what becomes of research?"

And he went.

"Do you have to go right away, Simon?" said Maria. "There are one or two things—Would you like a drink?"

An unnecessary question, thought Simon. In his state of authorial anxiety about his book he was always ready for a drink. He would have to watch that. A drunken priest. A drunken professor. Oh, shame!

"I will make you a drink if you want one," he said. "It seems to me you drink a great deal more than you did when you were a student."

"I need more than when I was a student. And I have inherited my Uncle Yerko's head. I'm a long way from being a serious drinker, Simon. I'll never be in the class with Dr. Gunilla Dahl-Soot."

"The Doctor is heroic in her application to the bottle. But somehow I don't think she has what Americans call a Drinking Problem. She likes it and she holds a lot. Simple."

"You won't join me?"

"I'm afraid I'm drinking too much, and I haven't got the splendid head of you and the Doctor. I'll just have some bubbly water."

"Are things getting to be too much for you, Simon?"

"This opera is worrying me, in a way that is quite absurd, because it's really none of my business. If you and Arthur want to spend hundreds of thousands on it, the money is yours. You're doing it for Powell, of course?"

"No, not of course, though it must look like that. He has certainly rushed us into the whole thing. I mean, we simply thought we would put up some money so that Schnak could do a job on the Hoffmann manuscripts, in so far as they exist. But Powell suggested that the opera might be presented, and was so full of enthusiasm and Welsh rhetoric that he infected Arthur, and you remember how Arthur went overboard about the whole idea. So here we are, up to our necks in something we don't understand."

"I suppose Powell understands it."

"Yes, but the mixture of Arthur's idealism and Powell's opportunism doesn't please me at all. The person who is going to come out on top of the heap, if the thing isn't a horrible failure, is Geraint Powell. I suppose Schnak might benefit, though how I can't pretend to see; but Powell, as the force behind the whole affair, is bound to get a lot of attention, which is what he wants."

"Why are you willing that Schnak should benefit, and so hostile to Powell?"

"He's using Arthur, and consequently he's using me. He's a climber. He's been a pretty successful actor, but he understands the limitations of that, so he wants to be a director. Because he's really very good at music, he wants to be a director of opera, and on the highest level. There's nothing wrong with any of that. He talks as if Arthur rushed everybody into this affair, but it's the other way around. He's the whirlwind. I feel he really looks on Arthur and me simply as a ladder toward his own success."

"Maria, you'd better get things straight in your head about what a patron is. I know a lot about patronage because I've seen it in the university. Either you exploit, or you are exploited. Either you demand the biggest slice of the pie for yourself, and get a gallery, or a theatre, or whatever it may be, named after you, and insist that people put up your portrait in the foyer, and toady to you, and listen to whatever you have to say with bated breath, or else you are simply the moneybags. And when you're dealing with artists of any kind you are dealing with the people who have the most gall and the most outrageous self-esteem in the world. So you've got to be tough, and insist on being first in everything, or you've got to do it for the love of the art. Don't complain about being used. Got to be magnanimous, in fact. Magnanimity, I needn't remind you, is as rare as it is splendid."

"I'm perfectly willing to be magnanimous, but I'm jealous for Arthur—Simon, I hate, and detest, and loathe and abhor the alternative title of this God-damned opera: *The Magnanimous Cuckold.* I feel that Arthur is being screwed."

"Cuckolds aren't screwed; they are deceived."

"That's what I mean."

"Arthur is most at fault, if that's what's happening to him."

"Simon, I wouldn't say this to anybody in the world but you.

You understand what I mean when I say that Arthur has a truly noble nature. But noble isn't a word that's used any more. Elitist, I suppose. But there's no other word for Arthur. He's generous and open in a way that is marvellous. But it also exposes him to terrible abuse."

"He's very fond of Powell. He asked him to be best man at your wedding, as I needn't remind you."

"Yes, and I'd never heard of Powell till he turned up then, all elegance and eloquence—full of piss and vinegar like a barber's cat, to use the old expression."

"You're getting heated, and your heat makes me thirsty. I will have that drink, after all."

"Do. I want your best advice, Simon. I'm worried, and I don't know why I'm worried."

"Yes you do. You think Arthur is too fond of Powell. Isn't that it?"

"Not in the way you mean."

"Tell me what I mean."

"I think you mean some homosexual thing. Not a bit of that in Arthur."

"Maria, for a very brilliant woman you are surprisingly naive. If you think homosexuality means no more than rough stuff in Turkish baths, and what Hamlet calls a pair of reechy kisses and paddling in necks with damned fingers in some seedy motel bedroom, you are right off your trolley. As you say, and as I believe, Arthur has a noble nature, and that isn't his style at all. Nor, to be just, do I think it's Powell's. But an obsessive admiration for a man who has qualities he envies, and for whom he is ready to give great gifts and take great risks, without grudging—that's homosexuality too, when the wind is right. Nobility isn't cautious, you know. Arthur is really Arthurian: he seeks something extraordinary—a Quest, a great adventure—and Powell seems to offer it and is, therefore, irresistible."

"Powell is a self-seeking bastard."

"And just possibly a great man—or a great artist, which is by no means the same thing. Like Richard Wagner, another self-seeking bastard. Remember how he exploited and horn-swoggled poor King Ludwig?"

"Ludwig was a crazy weakling."

"And his craziness has endowed us all with some magnificent opera. Not to speak of that totally insane fairy-tale castle of Neuschwanstein, which cost the people of Bavaria what was literally a king's ransom, and has recovered them the money a dozen times over, simply as a tourist sight."

"You're appealing to a piece of dead history, and a messy scandal, which has nothing to do with what we're talking about."

"History is never dead, because it keeps on repeating itself, though never in quite the same words or on quite the same scale. Remember what we said the other night at that Arthurian dinner, about the wax and the stamp? The wax of human experience is always the same. It is we who put our own stamp on it. These shared obsessions between patron and artist are as old as the hills, and I don't think you are going to be able to change that. Have you talked to Arthur?"

"You don't know Arthur. When I bring it up he just tells me to be patient, and that omelettes aren't made without breaking eggs, and all that sort of calm, uncomprehending thing."

"Have you told him he's in love with Powell?"

"Simon! What do you think I am?"

"I think you're a jealous woman, among other things."

"Jealous of Powell? I hate Powell!"

"Oh, Maria, haven't you learned anything in your university years?"

"Meaning what?"

"Meaning that hatred is notoriously near to love, and both are obsessions. Passions when they are pushed too far sometimes flop over into their opposites."

"What I feel about Arthur isn't going to flop over into its opposite."

"Bravely said. And what is it you feel about Arthur?"

"Doesn't it show? Devotion."

"An expensive devotion. As devotion always is, of course."

"A devotion that has enlarged my life more than I can say."

"A devotion that seems to have cost you what meant most to you in the world before you married."

"So?"

"Yes, so. How much work have you done on your edition of that unpublished Rabelais manuscript that was found in Francis

Cornish's papers? I remember your raptures when it was turned up—thanks to that monster Parlabane—and how Hollier said it would make your reputation as a scholar. Well—that's something like eighteen months ago. How's it getting on? Arthur gave it to you as a wedding present, as I recall. Now *there's* something significant: bridegroom gives bride a gift that will demand the best of her energies and understanding. Something that might mean more to her than her marriage. That would almost certainly mean reputation and scholarly fame of a special kind. A dangerous gift, certainly, but Arthur risked it. So what have you been doing?"

"I've been getting used to living with a man, and running this house, which is the exact opposite of the Gypsy *tsera* where I lived with my mother and uncle, and all the hair-raising crookedness of the *bomari* and the *wursitorea* that hung over that awful place. I only go there when you insist on it, Simon—"

"Don't forget it was Arthur who settled what was left of all that Gypsy mess in the basement of this very building where you are playing the fine lady, Maria."

"Don't be so disgusting, Simon! I'm not playing the fine lady— My God, you sound like my mother!—I'm trying to work my way finally and utterly into modern civilization, and put all that past behind me."

"It sounds as if modern civilization, which is largely rooted in Arthur, so far as you are concerned, had cut you off from what was best in you. I don't mean the Gypsy connection; forget that for the moment; but from what made you a scholar. From what drew you to Rabelais—the great humane spirit and the great humour that saves us in a rough world. I remember when you first got that manuscript; you wouldn't have called Professor M. A. Screech your uncle, and he's a mitred abbot among you Rabelaisians, I understand. And now—well, now—"

"I have by degrees dwindled into a wife?"

"You still have a nice touch with a quotation. That's something saved out of the wreck."

"I won't be called a wreck, Simon."

"All right. And I don't knock wives. But surely a woman of your qualities can be both scholar and wife? And the one all the better for the other?"

"Arthur takes a lot of looking after."

"Well—don't let him eat you. That's what I'm saying. Why do you look after him so much? He seemed to be getting on pretty well before he married you."

"He had needs that weren't being gratified."

"Aha."

"Don't say 'Aha!' like Mervyn Gwilt! You think I mean sex."

"Well—don't you?"

"Now you are the one who is being naive. Celibate priest that you are."

"And whose fault is that, may I ask? I gave you your chance to enlighten me."

"No use crying over spilt milk."

"I don't recall that we spilled any milk."

"You know perfectly well it wouldn't have done. You'd have been a worse husband than Arthur."

"Aha! Now I can say it—Aha!"

"I'm tired and you're bullying me."

"That's what women always say when they are getting the worst of things. Now come on, Maria: I'm your old friend, old tutor, old suitor. What's wrong between you and Arthur?"

"Nothing's *wrong*."

"Then perhaps too much is right."

"Perhaps. It's not that I'm panting for continual excitement and passion and all that kid stuff. But the stew could do with a little more salt."

"How about the organism?"

"In that department I suppose I rank somewhere between Mrs. Carver and the Roman candle Elsie Whistlecraft. It takes two to make an organism, you know.—We'd better stop using that word as a joke, or we'll use it seriously, and disgrace ourselves in the eyes of all right-thinking people."

"It isn't a word I find coming up much in conversation, but I suppose you're right.—So you find marriage quieter than you expected?"

"I don't know what I expected."

"Maybe you expected to see more of Arthur. Where is he now?"

"In Montreal. Comes back tomorrow. He's always dashing off on business. The Cornish Trust is very big business, you know."

"Well—I wish I had some good advice to give you, Maria, but I haven't. Every marriage is different and you have to find your own solutions. Apart from saying that I think you ought to get back to work, and have some business of your own—scholarly business—I haven't a thing to suggest."

"You don't have to give advice, Simon. I'm grateful to you for listening. We've had a real, proper *divano*. That's what Gypsies call it—a *divano*."

"A lovely word."

"Sorry if I've been a bore."

"You could never be a bore, Maria. Not yet. But unless you recover your fine Rabelaisian spirit it just might happen, and that would be dreadful."

"Fair's fair. Bore me with your own problems."

"I've said what they were. Or I've said what I feel about the opera. And of course there's the book. It never stops nagging."

"Aha!"

"Now who's being Mervyn Gwilt?"

"I am. I have something for you. Something about Uncle Frank that I bet you didn't know. Wait a minute."

Maria went to her study, and Darcourt seized the opportunity to—no, not to pour himself another drink, but to refresh the drink he had. With a generous hand.

Maria returned with a letter. "Read this, and rejoice," she said.

It was a letter in a square envelope, of the sort English people use for personal correspondence. A substantial letter, making quite a wad of paper, each sheet bearing the heading West Country Pony Club, and covered with that large, bold handwriting characteristic of people who write little, and squander their paper in a way that immediately sets the scholar on his guard. The letter itself was wholly in accord with its appearance. It said:

Dear cousin Arthur:

Yes, it's cousin, right enough, because you are the nephew of my father, the late Francis Cornish, and so we are from the same stable, if I may speak professionally. I should have written to you months ago but—pressure of business, and all that, and I'm sure you know what pressure of business means. But I only got wind of you last spring, when a Canadian colleague asked if I knew you, and it seems you are quite a nob in your own country. Of course I knew there were Canadians hanging somewhere on the family tree, because my grandfather—he was a Francis Cornish too—and the father of your uncle, who was my father—Oh dear, this is getting very mixed-up! Anyhow he married a Canadian, but we never knew him, because he was in some very hush-hush stuff which I don't pretend to understand. My father, too. The family were always very close-mouthed about him for a variety of reasons, and one of them was that he was very hush-hush too. But anyhoo (as they say) he was my father and as far as he went a very good father, because he looked after me very generously, so far as money goes, but I never saw him after I was too small to really know him, if you understand me. He married his cousin Ismay Glasson— rather a dark horse, I understand—and I was brought up on the family place—not Chegwidden Hall, but at St. Columb's because my grandmother was his cousin Prudence and that was where she lived with granddaddy, who was Roderick Glasson. Oh, crumbs, what have I said! Of course she *lived* with him because she was his wife—nothing in the least funny *there,* I assure you! St. Columb's had to be sold up, in the end, and the poor old place is a battery-hen place now, but I managed to buy the dower-house and it is from there that I ran my little stable and am rather the High Mucky Muck of the West Country Pony Club, as you see from this paper. The only paper I have, I'm afraid, because I'm up to my ample hips in the pony biz, and it's a handful—you'd never believe! But to come to the point, I'm coming to Canada in November, because I'm to be a judge at your Royal Winter Fair in the pony division—jumping and all that—and I understand you have some wonderfully keen kiddies showing and I can't wait to see them! And I'd love to see you! So may I give you a tinkle when I can get away from pony business, and perhaps we could tear a herring together and exchange family news! I don't suppose you've ever heard of me, unless somebody mentioned Little Charlie—that's me! And not so little now, let me say! So here's hoping to see you, and tons of family affection, though sight unseen!

Love—

CHARLOTTE CORNISH

"Did you know Uncle Frank had a child?" said Maria.

"I knew there was somebody called Charlotte Cornish to whom he left a quarterly allowance for life, because Arthur told me so," said Darcourt. "But I didn't know she was a daughter. Could have been any sort of old relation. The parish register recorded the marriage of Francis and his cousin Ismay Glasson, but there was no word of a child. Fool that I was, when I was snooping around in Cornwall I discovered that Francis had been married to Ismay Glasson, but when I made inquiries about her everybody shut up and knew nothing. And nobody said a word about Little Charlie or the Pony Club. Just shows that I am not much of a detective. Of course, all the Glassons had vanished, and when I got in touch with Sir Roderick in London he couldn't have been less forthcoming, and was too busy to see me. Well, well! Little Charlie is certainly no great letter-writer, is she?"

"But she's a reality. She must have heard something about Uncle Frank, even if she can't remember him. So you may have struck gold for the book, Simon."

"I'm too cautious to expect any such thing. This letter puffs and blows and giggles a bit, doesn't it? But it's a ray of light in the very dark centre of Francis Cornish's life."

"So we've both got something—not much, but something—out of the *divano*, Simon."

[*2*]

WHEN DARCOURT HAD GONE, Maria went to bed, leaving a note for Arthur, saying that he was to wake her when he came in from the airport. This was something she always did, and a request that Arthur always ignored—part of his extraordinary consideration, and his refusal to understand that she wanted to be wakened, wanted to see him, wanted to talk with him.

She did not read herself to sleep. Maria was not a reader-in-bed. Instead she set her mind to work on something that would bring sleep at last. Something substantial, some old friendly theme, but not so demanding as to keep her awake.

What should it be tonight? Darcourt had told her not to subdue her Rabelaisian nature; not to starve the full Rabelaisian humour that had been hers when she first met Arthur; not to dwindle into a wife, lest she cease to be a real wife. A good, sleepy theme might be the Seven Laughters of God. Of the angers, the vengeances, the punishments, the manifold Bellyaches of God the modern world seemed to know enough, even when it was most eager to banish God from all serious consideration. Let's have the Laughters.

The idea of the Seven Laughters was such an odd one, in the light of modern religion. Gnostic, and of course heretical. Christianity could not countenance a merry God. That God should have rejoiced, and taken delight in what He was making, and that the whole Universe sprang from delight—how foreign to a world obsessed by solemnity, which so quickly became despair. What were the Seven Laughters?

The first was the Laughter from which came light, as Genesis says. Then the Laughter of the Firmament, which our world has just begun to explore—to put a technological toe into space, and to invent bugaboos about spaceships, and Little People with antennae growing out of their heads, who might be spying on us unseen, and a sense of our inferiority in the face of immensity. Not much laughter there for us, whatever it may be for God.

What was the Third Laughter? Mind, wasn't it? Now *there* was a God one could really love, a God who laughed Mind into being just as soon as He had a place for it. Mind, the old thinkers said, was Hermes, and Hermes was a very good conception of Mind, because he was so various, so multitudinous, so many-shaped, certainly so ambiguous, but if you took him the right way, such a cheerful creation—so inventive and vigorous. Then what?

The Fourth Laughter was called Generation, which wasn't just sex, but growth and multiplicity. Nevertheless, sex was certainly a part of it if not the whole, and how God must have laughed when He confronted astonished Hermes with that pretty kettle of fish! And how Hermes, after his first astonishment, must have seized upon it as the splendid joke it was—though God and Hermes would certainly have known that many people would never see the joke. Would, indeed, spoil the joke. So, to cope with the people who could not understand jokes, God laughed again and Fate, or Destiny, came into being. The wax, in fact, upon which Darcourt insisted we all set our seal, without always knowing what the seal was.

God, rolling about on His Throne, knew Destiny would never work unless it had a frame, so—probably choking on the Joe Miller of the thing—laughed Time into being, so that Destiny would function serially, permitting people who never saw jokes to haggle about the nature of Time forever.

Last Laughter of all, when God, probably prompted by Hermes, had seen that He was perhaps being a little hard on the creatures who would inhabit the Creation, was Psyche—the Soul, the Laughter that would give creation, and mankind above all, a chance to come to terms with all God's merriment. Not to master it, and certainly not to understand it fully, but to find a way to partake of some part of it. Poor old Psyche! Poor old Soul! How our world was determined to thwart her at every turn, and speak of her—when it did speak of her—as a gloomy, gaseous maiden who did not, most of the time, know her spiritual arse from her metaphysical elbow! Never for a moment seeing her as the Consort, the true mate, of Hermes.

Well, there they were, and the effort of dredging them up from memory, where Maria had filed them some time ago, had made her sleepy. Not so sleepy, however, that she did not understand afresh what Darcourt meant when he urged her not to starve the Rabelaisian nature in herself. There were her Hermes and her Psyche, and with them she must live in truest amity, or she would cease to be Maria and her marriage would go to ruin.

She must not forget that Rabelais had known and delighted in the Arthurian stories, and had drawn upon their spirit even as he parodied them. Surely she would love her own Arthur better if she did not take him quite so seriously. Magnanimous? Of course. But a virtue in excess may slither into a weakness.

She slept. When Arthur returned, about one o'clock, he smiled affectionately at her note, and went to another bedroom, so as not to waken her.

[3]

"DO YOU WANT ME to cut your grass?"

A simple question, surely? Yet as Hulda Schnakenburg uttered it to Dr. Gunilla Dahl-Soot it was total surrender; it was Henry IV standing barefoot in the snow at Canossa; it was an act of vassalage.

Schnak had been working with the Doctor for two weeks, and this was the end of their sixth session together. The work had not begun promisingly. What the Doctor saw in Schnak was "a woman of the people", not a peasant but an urban roughneck, and she had spoken to her very much from on high. In the Doctor, Schnak thought she had met yet another tedious instructor, perhaps greatly skilled but not greatly talented, and as snotty as they come. If she had been surly and mocking with Dean Wintersen, she was rude and ugly with the Doctor, who had countered with icy courtesy. But in a short time they had begun to respect one another.

Schnak always made it her business to find out what her instructors had achieved, and what that amounted to in most cases was a respectable body of unexceptionable music, fashionably but cautiously experimental, that had been performed a few times and had won fashionable, cautious approval; rarely had it travelled far beyond the borders of Canada. It was music, surely enough, but in Schnak's expression it did not grab her. She wanted something more interesting than that. In the published work of Dr. Gunilla Dahl-Soot she found something that grabbed her, something she did not feel she could rival, an unmistakable, individual voice. Not that the Doctor was one of the world's great composers, by any means. Critics tended to describe her work as "notable". However, these were the best critics. She had been one of the better pupils of Nadia Boulanger, and had first attracted attention with a String Quartet, in which the idiom of an original voice had been discerned—a voice not that of her great teacher; Schnak had read the score with a reserve that began as derision, but that had to be abandoned, for this was unquestionably music marked by a fine clarity of thought, expressed through conventional techniques used in a wholly independent manner. It was not a long work; indeed, as music goes, it was terse, rigorous, strictly argued. But in the later Violin Sonata there was a quality even Schnak could not deride, and which she knew she would not rival; to speak of wit in music is uncritically vague, but there was no other word for it. Every succeeding work showed the same distinction of mind: a Suite for clarinet and strings, a Second String Quartet, a Symphony on a small scale (as compared with the block-busters, demanding more than a hundred players, following on the nineteenth-century masters), a body of songs that were real songs and not merely measured utterance undertaken in rivalry with an argumentative piano, and last of all a Requiem for Benjamin Britten which knocked the breath out of Schnak, and made her aware beyond a doubt that she had met her master. The Requiem was not witty, but deeply felt and poignant; these were qualities Schnak knew she lacked in herself, but which, she discovered to her amazement, she desired intensely. This was the real goods, she admitted.

Every article about the Doctor in the reference books, however, emphasized that it was as a teacher that she was most influential. She had studied with Nadia Boulanger; the musical historians said that she came nearest to imparting the spirit of her great mentor. Nobody said she was as good as Nadia Boulanger, or different; it is a firm critical principle that nobody living is quite as good as somebody dead.

A teacher, then? A teacher whom Schnak could truly respect? She had not quite known that that was what she wanted more than anything else in the world, and she came to such self-knowledge with mulish resistance. Now, at the end of her sixth session, she offered to cut the Doctor's grass. Schnak had met her master.

The grass badly wanted cutting. The Doctor had never, in her life, been a householder, but the School of Music had established her in a pleasant little house, on a street very near the university, which belonged to a professor who had gone on a year's sabbatical, taking his wife and children with him. It was a domestic little house, and the furniture, without being in ruins, spoke of a family life that included small children. It had bookshelves in every room, in which books, chiefly of a philosophical nature, were ranged tightly, with other books laid sidewise on whatever space there was above them. Small hands had marked the walls; phil-

osophical bottoms had made deep nests in every chair. There was
no complete set of any sort of china, and the cutlery was odds
and ends of stainless steel which had managed, somehow, to acquire stains. The pictures were of philosophers—not a notably
decorative class of men—and photographs of conferences where
the professor and his wife had been snapped with colleagues from
many lands. Whatever branch of philosophy the professor taught,
it was clearly not aesthetics. When the Doctor had been introduced to the house she had sighed, removed most of the pictures,
and set upon the mantelpiece her great treasure, without which
she never left her Paris flat for long; it was a small, exquisite
bronze by Barbara Hepworth. Beyond that, she felt, there was
nothing to be done.

But the grass! When she arrived, the lawn had the battlefield
look of a children's playground, and in no time at all the grass
had grown long and rank. What was to be done? The Doctor did
not know, and did not really care, but she could not ignore the
fact that the little lawns on either side were neatly trimmed. The
Doctor had never before lived in a place where grass obtruded
itself, or if it did, men came from somewhere and trimmed it. As
the grass grew, she began to feel like La Belle au Bois Dormant,
overgrown and shut in by uncontrollable herbage. As well as the
problem of the grass there was a wasps' nest over the front door,
and the windows were muddy from the rains and dusty winds of
the Canadian autumn. The Doctor had no gift for domesticity.

And here, in Hulda Schnakenburg, was somebody who seemed
to know what to do about grass!

Schnak went to the back premises where there was, of course,
a lawn-mower in a shed. It was not a good lawn-mower, for the
professor was not far above the Doctor in his understanding of
bourgeois domesticity, but it worked after a fashion, tearing up
whatever grass its ancient jaws could not chew, and with this
antique Schnak set to work to chop the lawn, if not positively to
trim it. She worked with the devotion of the willing slave, and
after the lawn had been harried into submission she raked up the
cuttings, and cut it again. She gathered the harvest and put it in
a plastic bag, which went into the garbage can, which the Doctor
regarded with disgust and used as little as she could; it was her
custom to pack the leavings from her scant meals into paper bags,

which she later, by stealth and in darkness, threw over a nearby fence into the back lawn of a professor of theology.

When at last Schnak was finished, the Doctor was standing at the front door.

"Thank you, my dear," she said. "And now, your bath is ready."

Bath? Schnak did not take baths. Now and then, under pressure from some outraged companion, she took a shower at the Women's Union, careful not to get her hair wet. She had a horror of colds.

"You are hot and tired," said the Doctor. "Look—you sweat. You will take cold. Come with me."

The bath was such as Schnak had never seen before. The professor's bathroom was not Neronian in its luxury, but it had everything that was needed, and the Doctor had banished all the smelly sponges, the balding brushes, and the celluloid ducks and rubber animals of the previous regime. The tub was contemporaneous with the house itself and was a large, old-fashioned affair with brass taps, and claw feet; it was full of hot water, bubbling fragrantly with the bath-oils the Doctor used upon herself, for she was a voluptuous bather.

What puzzled Schnak was that the Doctor seemed determined to remain in the bathroom with her, and gestured to her to take off her clothes. This was strange indeed, for in the Schnakenburg household baths were secret ceremonies, hinting of medical indecency, like enemas, and the bather always bolted the door against intruders. Schnak had stripped in front of somebody else before, because the three boys with whom she had undergone some sort of crude sexual experience were all great on what they called "skin", but since childhood she had never stripped in front of a woman, and she felt shame. The Doctor knew it, and laughing a little, but with fastidious fingers, she pulled off Schnak's filthy sweater, and nodded to her to kick off her degraded loafers and her stained jeans. So, very shortly, Schnak stood naked on the bathmat, and the Doctor looked at her consideringly.

"My God, you are a dirty child," she said. "No wonder you smell so bad. Get into the water."

Would marvels never cease? Schnak discovered that she was not to bathe, but to be bathed. The Doctor had somewhere found a large apron which she wore over her clothes, and kneeling beside the tub she gave Schnak such a bath as she had never had in twelve years, at which time she had been instructed by her mother to bathe herself. What soaping, what rubbing, what scouring of the feet in a this-little-piggy-went-to-market detail they had not known since childhood! It took a long time and the beautiful water was slick and grimy when at last the Doctor pulled out the plug and let it all drain away.

"Out with you," said the Doctor, standing with a large towel in her hands. She rubbed and scuffled Schnak's unaccustomedly clean body in a businesslike fashion that admitted of no assistance, and included intimacies that astonished Schnak, for they were not the rough maulings of her three engineering students. And while this was going on the Doctor was drawing another tubful of water.

"In you get again," said she. "Now we do the hair."

Schnak obediently stepped back into the tub, wondering greatly, but aware that out of her sight there was some very rapid undressing, and in no time the Doctor had slipped into the tub behind her, enclosing Schnak's thin body between her long elegant legs. Much dowsing of the dirty head; much shampooing with deliciously scented oil; much rinsing and at last a rough but playful drying.

"And now," said the Doctor, laughing, "you are a pretty clean girl. How does it feel?"

Lying back in the tub herself, she drew Schnak backward against her own body, and, slipping her arms around her, caressed Schnak's astonished nipples with soapy hands.

Schnak could not have said how it felt. Words were not her means of expression, or she might have said that it was paradisal. But it did float into her mind that all the books of reference concluded their pieces about the Doctor by saying that she was unmarried. Well, well, well.

Later they ceremoniously burned Schnak's discarded clothes. The Doctor wanted to do it in the fireplace, but Schnak tested the chimney by burning some paper in the grate, and the immediate belching of smoke bore out her suspicion that there was a bird's nest in the chimney. The Doctor was much impressed by this show of domestic wisdom. They burned the clothes in the back yard, after dark, and even danced a few steps around the bonfire.

Because Schnak had no clothes, she could not go home, nor did she wish to do so. She and the Doctor retired to bed, and there they drank rum mixed with rich milk, and Schnak lay in the Doctor's arms and told her the story of her life, as she understood it, in a version that would greatly have astonished and angered her parents.

"An old story," said the Doctor. "The gifted child; the Philistine parents. Loveless religion: craving for a larger life. Do you know what a Philistine is, child?"

"Somebody in the Bible?"

"Yes, but now the people who are against the things that you and I love—art, and the freedom without which art cannot exist. Have you been reading Hoffmann, as I told you?"

"Some of the stories."

"Hoffmann's life was a long fight with the Philistines. Poor devil! You have not read *Kater Murr* yet?"

"No."

"Not an easy book, but you cannot understand Hoffmann without it. It is the biography of the great musician Kreisler."

"I didn't know he was as old as that."

"Not Fritz Kreisler, stupid! A character invented by Hoffmann. One of his many *alter egos*. The great musician and composer Kapellmeister Johannes Kreisler, the romantic genius whom nobody understands and who has to put up with insults and slights from all the Philistine crew of the society in which he lives. His life has been written by a friend, and left on the desk; the tom-cat Murr finds it and writes his own life on the back of the sheets. So off goes the copy to the printer, who stupidly prints the whole thing as a unity, Kreisler and Kater Murr all mixed up in one book. But Kater Murr is a deeply Philistine cat; he embodies in himself everything that Kreisler hates and that is hostile to Kreisler. Kater Murr sums up his philosophy of life: '*Gibt es einen behaglicheren Zustand, als wenn man mit sich selbst ganz zufrieden ist?*' You understand German?"

"No."

"You should. Without German, very poor music. The tom-cat

says: 'Is there a cosier condition than being thoroughly satisfied with oneself?' That is the philosophy of the Philistine."

"A cosy condition; like having a good job as a typist."

"If that is all you want, and you cannot see beyond it. Of course not all typists are like that, or there would be no audiences at concerts."

"I want more than a cosy condition."

"And you shall have it. But you will find cosy places, too. This is one of them."

Kisses. Caresses of such skill and variety as Schnak would never have thought possible. Ninety seconds of ecstasy, and then deep peace, in which Schnak fell asleep.

The Doctor did not sleep for several hours. She was thinking of Johannes Kreisler, and herself.

[4]

THE WINE WAS VERY GOOD. Beyond that, Simon Darcourt would not have dared to speak, for he did not consider himself knowledgeable about wines. But he knew a good wine when he drank it, and this was undoubtedly very good. The bottles, as Prince Max had called to his attention, bore conservative, rather spidery engraving that declared them to be reserved for the owners of the vineyard. Nothing there of the flamboyant labels, with carousing peasants or Old Master pictures of fruit, cheese, and dead animals that marked commonplace wines. But at the top of these otherwise reticent labels was an elaborate achievement of arms and underneath it a motto: *Du sollst sterben ehe ich sterbe.*

Thou shalt perish ere I perish, thought Darcourt. Did it refer to the owners of the display of arms, or to the wine in the bottles? Must be the aristocrats; nobody would claim that a wine would outlive anyone who might be drinking it. Suppose a very young person—sixteen, let us say—were given a glass at the family table; suppose some child of a wine-drinking home were given a little, mixed with water, so that it would not feel left out at a family feast. Was it asserted that sixty years later the wine would still be in first-rate condition? Not likely. Wines like that were sold by the greatest auctioneers, not by popular wine merchants. So the boast, or assertion, or threat—it could be all or any of those—must apply to the people whose blazon of nobility this was.

There those people were, sitting at the table with him. Prince Max, who must be well into his seventies, was as straight, as slim, and as elegant as when he had been a dashing young German officer. Only his spectacles, which he somehow managed to make distinguished, and the thinness of his yellowish-white hair, so carefully brilliantined and brushed straight back from his knobby brow, gave any sign of how old he might be. His gaiety, his exuberance, and his unquenchable flow of anecdote and chatter could have belonged to a man half his age.

As for the Princess Amalie, she was as beautiful, as well-preserved, and as becomingly dressed as when Darcourt had first seen her when, during the past summer, she had made it so tactfully clear that if he wanted to know certain facts about the late Francis Cornish he must somehow provide her with the preliminary studies, from the hand of that same Francis Cornish, that had resulted in the Old Master drawing she used so lavishly, yet with such splendid understatement, in her advertisements. And that was what he had done.

The Clerical Cracksman, as he now thought of himself, had been just as adroit and just as lucky at the National Gallery as he had been at the University Library. The same approach to the curator of drawings, who was a friend and would not think of doubting Simon; the same casual, but swift, examination of the drawings in a special portfolio; a quick substitution of the drawings he had pinched from the Library, and which he carried tucked under the back strap of his M.B. waistcoat, for those that were the price of the Princess's confidence; the same cheerful greeting to his friend as he left the archives of the Gallery. The Gallery had not yet got around to putting those beastly little marks on the drawings that set off alarms when one passed certain snoopy ray machines; indeed, it looked as if nobody had looked into the portfolio since first it had come to the Gallery over a year before. It was a very neat job, thought Simon, if he said so himself, and he had been lucky in the day he chose for his robbery, because it was a day when the Pope was visiting Ottawa, and everybody who might have been snooping about was in a distant field, watching the charismatic Pontiff celebrate an outdoor mass, and utter instructions and adjurations for their future conduct to the people of Canada.

Was he dead to shame? Simon had asked himself. Was he now a contented, successful criminal, unhampered by his clerical vows? He did not attempt a philosophical answer; he was wholly in the grip of the biographer's covetous, unappeasable spirit. He was on to a good thing, and nothing should stand in his way. He would chance losing his soul, if only he could write a really good book. A deathbed repentance would probably square things with God. Meanwhile, this was Life.

"My wife is quite delighted with what you have brought," said Prince Max. "You are sure it is complete—every preliminary study?"

"To the best of my knowledge," said Simon. "I went through all Francis Cornish's drawings, his own and all the Old Masters he had copied, and I saw nothing related to the portrait of the Princess except the studies I have put in your keeping."

"Admirable," said the Prince. "I shall not say we do not know how to thank you, because we do. Amalie shall tell you all she knows about *le beau ténébreux*. And so shall I, though I did not know him so well as she. I only met him once, at Düsterstein. He made an immediate favourable impression. Handsome; modest, even witty, when wine had overcome his reticence. But you must continue, my dear. Meanwhile, another glass of wine?"

"Francis Cornish was everything Max says, and a great deal more," said the Princess. She drank little; a great professional beauty and a razor-sharp woman of business cannot afford to be a soaker. "He came into my life just as I was emerging from girlhood, and was beginning to be seriously interested in men. Seriously, I say; every girl notices men and dreams about them from the time she begins to walk. But he came to my family home just when I was beginning to think about lovers."

"It is strange to think of the Francis I knew as greatly attractive," said Simon. "He became rather an oddity as time went on."

"But I am sure it must have been a ruined beauty you saw as oddity," said the Princess. "Men do not notice such things, unless their romantic interest is in other men. Surely you have photographs?"

"He hated being photographed," said Simon.

"Then I can surprise you. I have many photographs, that I took myself. A girl's snapshots, of course, but revealing. I have one that I used to keep under my pillow until my governess discovered it and forbade it. I told her she was jealous and she laughed, but it was a laugh that told me I had hit the mark. Very handsome, and he had a nice deep voice. Not quite American; there was a Scottish burr in it that melted my soul."

"I am already jealous," said the Prince.

"Oh Max, don't be silly. You know what girls are."

"I knew what you were, my darling. But I knew what I was, too. So at the time I was not jealous."

"Odious vanity!" said the Princess. "Anyhow, we all have our early loves whom we keep in the back of our minds all our lives. I am sure you know what I mean, Professor."

"There was a girl with ringlets, when I was nine," said Darcourt, taking a sip of his wine. "I know what you mean. But please go on about Francis."

"He had everything a very young girl could love. He even had a rather untrustworthy heart. He had to keep watch on it, and report to his doctor in London."

The Prince laughed. "The heart was as useful to him as his skill with the brush," he said.

"And I am sure the dicky heart was as real as the skill."

"Of course. But we know what those reports to his doctor were, don't we?"

"You knew," said the Princess. "But I did not know, not then. You knew a lot of things I did not know."

"You are going to explain, I hope?" said Darcourt. "Bad heart. I knew something of that. Of course it was the heart that killed him at last. But was it something else?"

"I knew about the bad heart at the other end—the London end," said the Prince. "Francis sent accounts of his heart to his doctor, who passed them on at once to the right people at the Ministry of Information, because they were a code. Francis was watching the trains that passed by Düsterstein two or three times a week, carrying poor souls to a nearby internment camp—a labour camp or something of the sort. Anyhow, one of those infamous camps from which very few people escaped alive."

"Are you telling me Francis was a spy?"

"Of course he was a spy," aid the Prince. "Didn't you know? His father was a well-known spy, and I suppose he introduced the boy to the family trade."

"But *le beau ténébreux* wasn't a very good spy," said the Princess. "Lots of spies aren't, you know. I don't suppose he was a very important spy. He came to Düsterstein as an assistant to the old rogue Tancred Saraceni, who was restoring the family pictures, and if Saraceni wasn't a spy he was certainly one of the great busybodies of his time. He was on to Francis at once. And so was my grandmother."

"Nobody put anything over on the old Gräfin," said the Prince. "She was up to every dodge."

"Sorry," said Darcourt. "You've lost me completely. What was Düsterstein, and who was the old Gräfin, and what is all this spy business? I'm completely in the dark."

"Then we shall be able to pay for those drawings in full," said the Prince.

"You have the key to the missing years in Francis's life. I knew he had been in Europe for some time as a student of painting, and that he had worked with the great Saraceni, but nothing beyond that."

"Düsterstein was Amalie's family home. She lived there with her grandmother, who was the old Gräfin."

"I was an orphan," said the Princess. "Not a pitiable orphan, or a Dickensian orphan, but just an orphan, and I was brought up at Düsterstein by my grandmother, and a governess. It was as dull as could be, till old Saraceni came to work on the family collection of pictures, and not long afterward *le beau* turned up to help him. Exciting, under the circumstances."

"And he was a spy?"

"Certainly he was a spy. So was my governess, Ruth Nibsmith. Germany was full of spies during the years of the Reich. With so many spies everywhere it is astonishing that Britain made such a goat of herself as the war approached."

"He was spying on a nearby internment camp?"

"He never went near it. Nobody could do that, and certainly not a Canadian in a little sports car. No; he just counted the number of freight cars in each train that chugged along the track not far from our house. I used to watch him. It was funny, really.

There I was, in my window in a tower—sounds romantic, doesn't it—watching Francis count—you could almost hear him—as he stood at his window, invisible, as he thought, in the darkness of night. And there in the garden below, behind some bushes, was my governess, spying on Francis. I used to watch them both, almost helpless with laughter. And I suspect that my grandmother was watching too, from a room next to her business office. She was a very big farmer, you know."

"The thing about spies," said the Prince, "is that unless they are of the small number of very good ones, you can almost smell them. They have balloons coming out of their heads, like people in the comic strips, with 'I'm a snoop' written in them. One doesn't pay too much attention to them, because most of them are harmless. But if a strange, handsome young man turns up in your castle, to help a crook like Saraceni, with every credential including a bad heart, who sends regular letters to a Harley Street address—he's probably a spy."

"But Francis was a genuine assistant to Saraceni?" said Darcourt. "There was no deception about that."

"Saraceni was the soul of deception. Not, mind you, that I think he was dishonest in a trivial or purely self-seeking way. He had an artistic passion for illusion, far beyond fakery. He thought of it as playing tricks with Time. He was a very great restorer; you know that. And when he was working on a painting of value, like the pieces in the Düsterstein collection, he worked faithfully in the spirit and the mode of the artist who had made the picture. He turned back the clock. But he could take a piece of very indifferent painting, and skilfully make something fifth-rate look second-rate. That is art of a very special kind—knowing just how far to go."

"One of the best things of that kind to come from Saraceni's studio was, in fact, the work of Francis Cornish," said the Princess. "*Drollig Hansel*—you remember it, Max?"

"No, no; that was no patched-up thing. That was an original. The queerest little panel you ever saw, of a dwarf jester. Extraordinary little face; you felt it saw everything."

"It frightened me," said the Princess. "Of course I should not have seen it at all. But you know what children are. Saraceni used to lock up his studio every evening, and probably thought that all his secrets were safe. But I used to take my grandmother's key from her desk every now and then, and have a look. That dwarf seemed to me to speak of all the tragedy of human life— imprisonment in an ugly body, deformity that put him beyond the understanding of other people, the yearning for vengeance and the yearning for love. So much of the horrible pathos of life, on a panel eight inches by ten."

"Where is that picture now?" said Darcourt.

"I have no idea," said the Prince. "I believe it was in Hermann Goering's collection for a time, but I have heard nothing of it since. Unless it was destroyed—and I can't imagine anybody destroying it—it will certainly turn up some day."

"You speak as if Francis had really been a great painter," said Darcourt.

"Yes," said the Prince. "Shall we have coffee now?"

For coffee the three went into a large drawing-room. Darcourt had not been there before; his earlier talks with the Princess had been in a room she used for business, but it was so elegant that only a coarse soul would have thought of questioning any proposal of a business nature that was made there. Haggling, one presumed, was done elsewhere. But haggling there must have been, for Max and Amalie plainly conducted their businesses on a large and highly competitive level. The drawing-room seemed to occupy the whole of one side of the splendid penthouse in which they dwelt.

Darcourt was beginning to be an expert on rich people's penthouses. The Cornishes' penthouse in Toronto was wonderful because it was very modern, and some of its walls were composed entirely of glass, commanding a sweeping view over much of the city, and beyond it so that—enthusiasts insisted—on a fine day it was possible to see the mist rising from Niagara Falls in the farthest distance. But its modernity paradoxically gave it a somewhat timeless air, for it had no obtrusive architectural features, and took its character from the furnishings, many of which were in the seventeenth-century manner that appealed to Arthur and which Maria did not challenge. But Max and Amalie had chosen to give their dwelling a strong eighteenth-century character. That was why the picture that dominated the room was so surprising.

It was a triptych that hung against the damask covering of the south wall. Its subject was not immediately apparent, for it was filled—filled but not crowded—with figures dressed in the manner of the earliest sixteenth century; figures in ceremonial dress, figures in ceremonial armour, and some figures in the robes that artists have for so long used to clothe characters from biblical history. But a rather longer inspection told Darcourt that he was looking at a representation—a most unusual representation—of *The Marriage at Cana*. It was not until the Princess spoke that he became aware that he was gaping at it.

"You are admiring our treasure," she said. "Do sit here where you can see it."

Darcourt took his coffee, and sat by her. "A magnificent picture," he said. "And most unusual in terms of its subject. The figure of Christ is relegated to an inferior position, and He might almost be said to be looking in wonder at the bridegroom. May I ask if it is known who the artist was?"

"The picture is one of five or six we thought of selling a few years ago," said Prince Max. "It would have been a wrench, but we needed money badly, as I was at that time extending my wine business to North America, and you can imagine how much money that would take. The Düsterstein collection, of which we had managed to salvage some of the best pieces after the ruin and spoliation of the war, came to our rescue. We sold all but this one. Great American galleries were eager to get them. Indeed, for a time it looked as if this one might go to the National Gallery of Canada, but the deal fell through. Some trouble about finance. We had the money we needed from the other sales, so we decided to keep it."

"But you do not know who painted it?"

"Oh, yes. We know. Indeed, it was a Canadian art historian who went as far as possible into the whole question of the picture, and attached to it the name of The Alchemical Master. Because he found elements in it that suggested a knowledge of alchemy."

"The historian's name was Aylwin Ross, wasn't it?" said Darcourt.

"That was the man," said the Prince. "A very personable fellow. He helped us a great deal in placing our other pictures. You can dig up what he wrote about *The Marriage at Cana* in the files of art journals. Nobody has challenged his opinion, so far as I know.

So the picture will probably always be attributed to The Alchemical Master—unless we discover who he was. But here is our other guest."

The other guest was, like the Prince, a marvel of personal preservation. Close inspection suggested that he was well over seventy, but his step was light, his figure trim, and his teeth, though of a surprising brilliance, appeared to be his own.

"Let me introduce Professor Darcourt," said the Princess, thereby making it clear that the newcomer was, at least in her estimation, someone who outranked Darcourt. "He comes from Canada, and he has brought me the things we discussed earlier—so that is that. Professor, this is Mr. Addison Thresher. You recognize him, of course."

Darcourt did not recognize him, but the name rang a faint bell—a tinkle—somewhere in his mind. Ah, yes; one of the Grand Panjandrums of the art world, a man who advised museums, established authenticities, and struck down deceptions with a personal Sword of Truth.

"Addison has helped us so much about pictures," said the Princess. "And we asked him to drop in this evening because he is someone else who knew Francis Cornish. Professor Darcourt is writing a life of Cornish," she said to the man with the wonderful teeth. "You have often spoken about Cornish."

"Yes, indeed. I was present when Cornish leapt in a single bound from the status of a pupil of Tancred Saraceni into a place as a great detector of fraud. I saw him skewer Jean-Paul Letztpfennig. Nailed him to the cross, you might say. Exposed him as the painter of a fraudulent Van Eyck. It was a matter of an indiscreet monkey, that Letztpfennig had allowed into a picture where no such monkey could have entered by the hand of Van Eyck. The shrewdest, most elegant destruction of fraud I have ever witnessed. But he never built on it as everybody expected him to do. Not much was heard of him afterward except as a member of that commission that attempted to restore works of art to their owners after the war."

"Yes, I know about that," said Darcourt. "It is the hidden days, the Düsterstein days I suppose I may call them now, that have puzzled me. What was he like then? Can you tell me?"

"I saw him at the great scene at The Hague," said Thresher,

"and, of course, I was with him on the Commission that had the job of restoring lost or looted art after the war, but we had very little direct contact then. He was impressive, as you know better than I do. Tall, quiet in manner, but with a quality that I suppose could be called Byronic. A whiff of brimstone."

"Exactly as I remember him," said the Princess. "A whiff of brimstone. Irresistible. And Byronic."

"He ended as a shambling eccentric," said Darcourt. "Agreeable, when you knew him. But a long way from *le beau ténébreux*."

"Wouldn't you have expected that?" said Thresher. "What would Byron have been like if he had lived to be an old man? A fat, bald Tory with fearful indigestion. Probably an embittered woman-hater. These romantic heroes are lucky if they die early. They are not built for long wear."

Although the conversation continued throughout an evening that Darcourt ended by leaving sharp at eleven o'clock, he heard nothing more of significance about Francis Cornish. The talk touched on Cornish again and again, then veered away to some matter of concern to the art world, about which Thresher had an endless fund of hints and stories that might have been illuminating if Darcourt had been better informed than he was about the great sales, the great exposures, and the stupefying prices.

His evening, however, had not been quite so limited in its information as it might have seemed. Max and Amalie did their best to requite him for the drawings he had placed in their hands before dinner. They played fair in that, and when he left, the Princess gave him all her photographs of her adolescent love. But all evening his eyes turned again and again toward *The Marriage at Cana,* and when he caught his plane the next morning he was on fire to continue some research which would, he greatly hoped, tell him something about Francis Cornish that would make his book much more than a respectable, respectful biography.

[5]

WAS ARTHUR PLEASED that such an important meeting of the Cornish Foundation should be taking place somewhere other than at the Round Table? That instead of the nuts and fruits and sweets from the Platter of Plenty they were refreshing themselves from a slapdash smorgasbord Dr. Gunilla Dahl-Soot and Schnak had whipped up with a few biscuits and tins of smoked fish? That a potent aquavit was being drunk—drunk rather too freely by Hollier—with beer chasers?

No, Arthur was not pleased, but his self-control was so great that nobody would have known it, and indeed he was not fully aware of it himself, except as a generalized discomfort. He felt that control of the opera project had been taken out of his hands without any obvious snatching, and he was now an adviser only, rather than in his accustomed place as Chairman of the Board.

They had come to listen to music. There was a piano in his splendid penthouse, and if a piano was needed to learn what Hoffmann's music was like, and what Schnak had been able to make of it, why had the Doctor somewhat imperiously demanded that they come here? Schnak was playing now.

She was a competent pianist, for a composer. That is to say, she could play anything at sight but she could not play anything really well. She could play from an orchestral score, giving what she called "a notion'" of what was written there, piecing out what she could not play with her ten fingers by hoots, whistles, and shouts of "Brass!" or "Woodwind choir!" When she wished to indicate that a melody was for a singer, she sang in a distressing voice, and as there were no words she took refuge in Yah-yah-yah.

As astonishing as Schnak's noise was her altered appearance. Clean, to begin with. Dressed in some new clothes that looked as if they might have been chosen by the Doctor, for they were severe and might have had style if Schnak had worn them better. No longer haggard, but puffily plump, like someone who has been eating too much after a long abstinence. Her hair was now a respectable colour, an undistinguished brown, and flew about in uncontrolled wisps. She looked happy, and deeply engaged in what she was doing. A Schnak transformed.

Will I get a bill for those new clothes, or will the Doctor have the tact to conceal them among her own expenses, thought Darcourt. Reasonable enough. So many odd bills were reaching his desk that he began to feel like a Universal Provider. But it all made sense, in a way.

No member of the Round Table was a trained musician, but all were intelligent listeners—concert-goers and buyers of recordings—and they thought that what they heard was good. Melodious, certainly, and passionate. There seemed to be lots of it, and it was being presented in chunks of undeveloped, noncontinuous sound. When at last Schnak ceased to play, the Doctor spoke.

"That is what we have, you see. That is what Hulda must develop and stitch together, and occasionally amplify with stuff that is akin to Hoffmann without being genuine Hoffmann. He left quite a lot of notes in prose, indicating what he had in mind. But it is a long way from being an opera. What we must have now is a detailed libretto, with action and words. Words that fit these melodies. At this moment we have not even a final list of the characters in the piece. Of course we know what the orchestration will be—the sort of thirty-two-piece group that Hoffmann would have been able to use in an opera theatre of his own. Strings, woods, a few brasses, and kettle-drums—only two, for he would not have had sophisticated modern timpani. So—what have the literary people been doing?"

"We have a scheme for the libretto. That's to say, I have a scheme, pretty much like the one I outlined a few weeks ago," said Powell. "As for characters, there are the seven leading roles: Arthur, Guenevere, Lancelot, Modred, Morgan Le Fay, Elaine, and Merlin."

"And Chorus?" said the Doctor.

"For the men you have the Knights of the Round Table, and there must be twelve, to make up thirteen with Arthur. Linking it with Christ and the Disciples."

"Oh, that's very dubious," said Hollier. "That's nineteenth-century romanticism and utterly discredited now. Arthur had over a hundred Knights."

"Well, he certainly isn't going to have them in this opera," said Powell. "As well as Lancelot and Modred he can have Sir Kay, the seneschal, Gawaine and Bedevere who are the good guys, and Gareth Beaumains, who can be a pretty boy if we can find one. Then we want Lucas, the butler, and Ulphius, the chamberlain. For funnies we can have Dynadan, who was a wit and lampoonist and can be a high-comedy figure, and Dagonet the

Fool, who can be a jackass now and then to keep things lively. And the two blacks, of course."

"Blacks?" said Arthur. "Why blacks in sixth-century Britain?"

"Because if you have an opera nowadays without a black or two, you're in hot water," said Powell. "Luckily we can use Sir Pellinore and Sir Palomides, who are both Saracens, so that takes care of that."

"But Saracens were not black," said Hollier.

"They will be in this show," said Powell. "I want no trouble."

"It will be incredible," said Hollier.

"No it won't. Not when I get it on the stage," said Powell. "Nothing is incredible in opera. Now, as for women—"

"But wait," said Hollier. "Are you sending this whole thing up? Making it into a comedy?"

"Not at all," said the Doctor. "I see what Powell means. Opera presents mythic truth, even when it is about nineteenth-century whores with golden hearts. And mythic truth sets you free to do a lot of very practical things. What about women?"

"A woman for every Knight," said Powell. "They don't need names or characters. Except for the Lady Clarissant, who must be Number Two to Guenevere and carry her fan, or catch her when she faints, or whatever may be necessary. Basically, Clarissant is Chorus, though she will have to have a few more bucks because she plays a named character. So there you are. Twenty-nine in all; and a few extras for heralds and trumpeters, and of course understudies, and you'll get out with less than forty, and never more than thirty-four on stage at one time. We can't get any more on that stage in Stratford if it is to look like anything but the subway at rush-hour."

"How expensive is it likely to be?" said Darcourt.

"Expense is not our first consideration," aid Arthur. "This is an adventure, you remember."

"A Quest. A real Arthurian Quest," said Maria. "A Quest in search of something lost in the past. Let's not be cheap."

Was Maria being ironic, Darcourt asked himself. Since their talk—their *divano*—he had sensed something in Maria that was not new, but a return to the Maria he had known before she became Mrs. Arthur Cornish, and seemed to dwindle. Maria was returning to her former stature.

"I'm glad you feel like that," said Powell. "The more I think about this opera the more expensive it becomes. As Maria says, the past doesn't come cheap."

"What are the singers likely to want?" said Darcourt.

"Their figures are pretty well fixed, according to their reputations. For this job, you want second-rank singers—"

"Need we settle for that?" said Arthur.

"Don't misunderstand me. I mean second-rank, not second-rate. You don't want, and couldn't get, the biggest star names; they are booked up for three and four years ahead, and as they do a pretty restricted group of parts they wouldn't consent to learn a new role for a few performances. They aren't used to rehearsal, either. They just swoop in by plane, do their standard Violetta or Rigoletto or whatever it is without much reference to where they are or who they're with, and swoop out again, clutching their money. No, I'm talking about the intelligent singers who are also musicians, who can act and who keep their fat down. There are quite a lot of them now, and they're the opera of the future. But they're always busy, and they don't come cheap, so we shall have to hope luck is with us. I've already made a few inquiries, and I think we'll be all right. Chorus we can get in Toronto; lots of good people."

Admirable, thought Arthur. Just what he would have wanted. Lots of initiative in his friend Geraint. And yet—the business man in him would not be silent—money was being promised, and perhaps contracts offered, and who was authorizing all this? The would-be impresario and patron applauded, but the banker had nasty qualms. Powell was continuing.

"The singers aren't the only problems, let me tell you. Designer—where do you look for a designer now for an opera next summer? Far too late. But we've had a stroke of the greatest luck. There's a real comer who has been doing a lot of supervisory work for the Welsh National Opera, and she wants a chance to design something entirely her own. Dulcy Ringgold, her name is. I've talked to Dulcy on the phone, and she's keen as mustard. But there are conditions."

"Money?" said Darcourt.

"No. Dulcy isn't greedy. But she wants to do the whole thing

as if it were being done under Hoffmann's supervision at one of
his opera houses—Bamberg, for instance. And that means scene
design in the early-nineteenth-century manner, with changes managed as if we had a staff of about fifty stage-hands, when we'll
probably have ten, and they'll have to learn old techniques that
will astonish them. Because in those days stage-hands were really
scene-shifters, and not button-pushers. It'll cost a mint."

"I suppose you've closed with her?" said Hollier. The more
aquavit he drank, and the more beer he sent down to supervise
the aquavit, the more dubious he became.

"I have her on hold," said Powell. "And I hope to God you
agree with her plan."

"Does it mean monstrously heavy stuff, long intervals, mossy
banks covered with artificial flowers, and a lot of rumbling behind
the curtain?" said Arthur.

"Not a bit of it. This kind of stage dressing came before all
that nonsense. Quite simply, it's a system where each scene con-
sists of a painted back-drop, and five or six sets of wings on each
side of the stage; but they are arranged on wheels so that the
scenes change almost instantaneously—in out—in out—so that
it's almost like movie dissolves. At the end of each scene the
actors leave the stage and—whammo!—you're already in the next
scene. But it takes some very nippy work backstage."

"Sounds wonderful," said Maria.

"It's magical! I don't know how we ever changed it for all this
business of fixed settings and mood lighting that reflects nothing
much but the mood of the lighting-designer. Pure magic!"

"Sounds to me like pantomime," said Hollier.

"It is a bit like pantomime. But what's wrong with that? It's
magic, I tell you."

"You mean like the things one sees at Drottningholm?" said
Darcourt.

"Just like that."

Nobody but Darcourt among the Foundation members had
been to Drottningholm, and they were impressed.

"But why is it so expensive?" said Arthur. "It sounds to me
like a few pieces of lath and a lot of canvas and paint."

"And that's what it is. It's the paint that costs money. Good scene-painters are rare nowadays, but Dulcy says she could do it with six good art-students and herself to supervise and do the tricky bits. But it takes time and it costs like the devil."

"If it's magic, we'll have it," said Arthur.

"That's the real Arthurian touch," said Maria, and kissed him.

"I declare for it, without reserve," said the Doctor. "It will mean that I—I mean Hulda—can have many scenes, and that is wonderful freedom for a composer. Indoor-outdoor; forests and gardens. Yes, yes, Mr. Cornish, you are man of fine imagination. I also salute you."

The Doctor kissed Arthur. On the cheek. Not one of her tongue-in-the-mouth kisses.

"With such a scheme of production, I suppose you see no obstacle to using The Questing Beast," said Hollier, cheering up visibly, if a little unsteadily.

"What in God's name is The Questing Beast?" said the Doctor.

"It was the monster whose pursuit was the lifelong occupation of Sir Pellinore," said Hollier. "I'm surprised you do not know. The Questing Beast had the head of a serpent, the body of a libbard, the rump of a lion, the hooves of a hart, and a great, swingeing tail; out of its belly came a sound like the baying of thirty couple of hounds. Just the thing for a magical opera."

"Oh Clem, you genius," said Penny Raven, and, not to be left out when kissing was toward, she kissed Hollier, to his great abashment.

"Well—I don't know," said Powell.

"Oh, you must," said Penny. "Hulda could make the Beast sing out of its belly! All those voices, in wonderful harmony. What a *coup de théâtre!* No, I suppose I mean a *coup d'oreille.* It would be the hit of the show."

"Just what I'm afraid of," said Powell. "You have a very minor character, Sir Pellinore, traipsing about the stage with a bloody great pantomime dragon, and taking all the attention. No! Nix on The Questing Beast."

"I thought you wanted imagination," said Hollier, with the hauteur of a man whose brilliant idea has been scorned.

"Imagination is not uncontrolled fantasy," said the Doctor.

"The Questing Beast is a vital part of the Arthurian Legend," said Hollier, raising his voice. "The Questing Beast is pure Malory. Are you throwing Malory overboard? I want to know. If I am to have any part in preparing this libretto—as you call it—I want to know the ground rules. What are your intentions toward Malory?"

"Good sense must prevail," said the Doctor, who had not been inattentive to the aquavit. "Myth must be transmuted into art, not slavishly reproduced. If Wagner had been ruled by myth, the Ring of the Nibelungs would have been trampled to death by monsters and giants and nobody would have understood the story. I have my responsibility here, and I remind you of it. Hulda's interests must come before everything. Besides, Hoffmann has not provided any music that could in any way be turned into a four-part chorus singing inside the belly of a monster, and probably not able to see the conductor. To hell with your Questing Beast!"

Arthur felt it was time to exert his skills as Chairman of the Board, and after five minutes, during which Hollier and Penny and Powell and the Doctor shouted and insulted each other, he was able to restore some sort of order, though the heat of passion in the room was still palpable.

"Let's come to a conclusion, and stick with it," he said. "We're talking about the nature of the libretto. We have to decide the ground on which it rests. Professor Hollier is determined on Malory."

"It's simple reason," said Hollier. "The libretto is to be in English. Malory is the best English source."

"But the language, the language!" said Penny. "All that 'yea, forsooth', and 'full fain', and 'I woll welle'. Great to read but bloody to speak, let alone sing. Do you imagine you could write verse in that lingo?"

"I agree," said Darcourt. "We've got to have language that's clear, and permits rhyme, and has a romantic flavour. So what's it to be?"

"It's obvious," said Powell. "Obvious to anybody but a scholar, that's to say. Sir Walter's your man."

Nobody responded to the name of Sir Walter. There were looks of incomprehension on every face but Arthur's.

"Sir Walter Scott, he means," said he. "Haven't any of you read any Scott?"

"Nobody reads Scott nowadays," said Penny. "He's ceased to be a Figure and been demoted to an Influence. Too simple for scholarly consideration but can't be wholly overlooked."

"You mean in the universities," said Arthur. "Increasingly I thank God that I never went to one. As a reader I've just rambled at large on Parnassus, chewing the grass wherever it seemed rich. I read an awful lot of Scott when I was a boy, and loved it. I think Geraint is right. Scott's our man."

"Just about every big Scott novel was made into an opera. Not operas that are done much now, but big hits in their day. Rossini, Bellini, Donizetti, Bizet—all those guys. I've looked at them. Pretty neat, I'd say." It was Schnak who spoke. She had been almost unheard until this moment, and the others looked at her with wonder, as in one of those old tales where an animal is suddenly gifted with speech.

"We have forgotten that Hulda is fresh from her studies in musicology," said the Doctor. "We must listen to her. After all, she is to do the most important part of the work."

"Hoffmann read a lot of Scott," said Schnak. "Thought he was great. Sort of operatic."

"Schnak is right," said Arthur. "Operatic. *Lucia di Lammermoor*—still a great favourite."

"Hoffmann knew it. Probably was an influence on him, if you're hog-wild for influences," said Schnak. "Gimme some Scott, and let's see what can be done. It'd have to be a *pistache*, naturally."

"You must say *pastiche*, my dear," said the Doctor. "But you are right."

"Am I to understand that we are abandoning Malory?" said Hollier.

" 'Raus mit Malory," said Schnak. "Never heard of him."

"Hulda! You told me you did not know German!"

"That was two weeks ago, Nilla," said Schnak. "How do you suppose I got my musicology, without German? How do you suppose I read what Hoffmann wrote on his notes, without German? And I can even speak a little kitchen German. Honestly, you top people are dumb! You ask me questions like examiners, and you treat me like a kid. I'm supposed to be writing this thing, eh?"

"You're right, Schnak," said Powell. "We've been leaving you out. Sorry. You've hit the nail on the head. It must be Scott *pastiche*."

"If it's not to be Scott *pistache* I'll have to get down to reading *Marmion* and *The Lady of the Lake* right away," said Darcourt. "But how do we work?"

"Hulda will give you details about the music, and little plans that show you how the tunes go, so you can fit good words to them. And as quick as you can, please."

"I must ask to be excused," said Hollier. "If you need me for details of history, or costume, or behaviour, you know where to find me. Unless, of course, untrammelled, uninformed imagination is to determine everything. And so I bid you good-night."

[6]

"WHAT GOT INTO CLEM?" said Penny, as they drove away in Arthur's car. It was a fine car, but it was rather a squash in the back seat with Penny, Darcourt, and Powell, however politely they might try to restrain their bottoms.

"Just thwarted professorship," said Darcourt.

"Probably mid-life crisis," said Powell.

"What's that?" asked Arthur, who was driving.

"It's one of the new, fashionable ailments, like pre-menstrual bloat," said Powell. "Excuses anything."

"Really?" said Arthur. "Do you suppose I might have one of those? I've not been feeling quite the thing, lately."

"You're too young for it, my darling," said Maria. "Anyway, I wouldn't let you. It can make a man into a big baby. I thought Clem was being an awful baby."

"I've known he was a baby for years," said Darcourt. "A large, learned, very handsome baby, but still a baby. For me, the surprise of the evening was Schnak. She's coming out of her cell with a hell of a yell, isn't she? She's given us our orders."

"It's Old Sooty," said Penny. "I have my dark suspicions about Old Sooty. Do you know that kid has moved in with her? Now what does that mean?"

"You obviously want to tell us," said Maria.

"Do I have to tell you? She and Schnak are poofynooks. It's as plain as the nose on your face."

"It seems to be doing Schnak a power of good," said Arthur. "Clean, putting on a little flesh, finding her tongue, and she doesn't look at us any more as if she was just about to order up the tumbrils. If that's what lesbianism does, three cheers for lesbianism, I say."

"Yes, but haven't we some responsibility? I mean, are we delivering this kid gagged and bound into the hands of that old bulldyke? Didn't you hear 'Nilla' and 'dear Hulda' all evening until you nearly threw up?"

"What about it?" said Maria. "She's probably the first person who has ever been nice to Schnak—really nice, I mean. Very likely the first person to talk to Schnak about music seriously and not just as an instructor. If it means a few rolls in the hay, the occasional bout of kindly kissing and clipping, what about it? Schnak's nineteen, for God's sake, and an exceedingly bright nineteen. The word genius has been whispered."

"What do you think, Simon?" said Penny. "You're the professional moralist."

"I think what Maria thinks. And as a professional moralist I think you have to take love where you find it."

"Even if it means being mauled and clapper-clawed by Dr. Gunilla Dahl-Soot? Thank you, Father Darcourt, for these advanced opinions."

"I'm in the dark about this business," said Arthur. "What do they *do?*"

"Oh, Arthur, that's what every man asks about lesbians," said Maria. "I suppose they do whatever comes into their heads. I'm sure I could think of lots of things."

"Could you really?" said Arthur. "You must show me. I'll be Schnak and you be Gunny, and we'll find out what happens in the gunny-sack. A new window on the wonders of the world."

"I think you're being frivolous and irresponsible," said Penny. "I am more and more convinced that this Snark of ours is going to turn out to be a Boojum."

"What *is* all this Snark and Boojum stuff?" said Arthur. "You've talked about it ever since you came in with us on this operatic venture. Some obscure literary reference, I suppose, designed to keep the uneducated in their proper place. Instruct me, Penny;

I am just a humble, teachable money-man. Let me into your Druid Circle."

"Sorry, sorry Arthur; I suppose it *is* a private lingo but it says so much in a few words. You see, there's a very great poem by Lewis Carroll about the Hunting of the Snark; a lot of crazy creatures set off, they know not whither, in search of they know not what. The hunt is led by a Bellman—that's you, Arthur—full of zeal and umph, and his crew includes a Boots and a Banker, and a Billiard Marker and a Beaver who makes lace—probably you, Simon, because 'he often saved them from wreck, / Though none of the sailors knew how.' And there's a very peculiar creature who seems to be a Baker but turns out to be a Butcher, and he is omnicompetent—

> He would answer to 'Hi!' or to any loud cry,
>   Such as 'Fry me!' or 'Fritter-my-wig!'
> To 'What-you-may-call-um!' or 'What-was-his-name!'
>   But especially 'Thing-um-a-jig!'
>
> While, for those who preferred a more forcible word,
>   He had different names for these:
> His intimate friends called him 'Candle-ends',
>   And his enemies, 'Toasted-cheese'.

—so that's obviously you, Geraint, you Cymric mystifier, because you have us all buffaloed about this opera business. It's just about a crazy voyage that somehow, in an unfathomable way, makes a kind of eerie sense. I mean, so many of us are professors—well, Clem and Simon and me, which is quite a few—and listen to this from the Bellman's definition of a Snark—

> The third is its slowness in taking a jest
>   Should you happen to venture on one,
> It will sigh like a thing that is deeply distressed:
>   And it always looks grave at a pun.

Isn't that what we've been doing all evening? Yammering about Malory and the scholarly approach to something that is utterly unscholarly in the marrow of its bones, because it's Art. And Art is rum stuff—the very rummest. It may look like a nice, simple Snark, but it can suddenly prove to be a Boojum, and then, look out!

> 'For although common Snarks do no manner of harm
>   Yet I feel it my duty to say,
> Some are Boojums—' The Bellman broke off in alarm,
>   For the Baker had fainted away.

Do you get what I mean, Arthur? Do you see how it fits in and haunts my mind?"

"I might see it if I had your mind, but I haven't," said Arthur. "Literary reference leaves me gaping."

"I bet it would have left King Arthur gaping," said Maria loyally, "if Merlin had got off a few quaint cracks from his Black Book."

"Yes, but I see how this whole thing could go very queer," said Penny. "And I had a hint of it tonight. That poor kid Schnak thinks she's tough, but she's just a battered baby, and she's being let in for something she certainly can't handle. It worries me. I don't want to be a busybody, or a soul-saver, or any of that, but surely we ought to *do* something!"

"I think you're jealous," said Powell.

"Jealous! Me! Geraint, I hate you! I've just decided. Ever since I met you I've wondered what I really think about you, you blathering, soapy Welsh goat, and now I know. You're in this for what you can get, and you don't give a maggoty shit for anybody else, and I hate you!"

"We're all in everything for what we can get, professor," said Powell. "And if not, why are we in it? What are you in it for? You don't know, but you hope to find out. Fame? Fun? Something to fill up the gaps in your life? What's your personal Snark? You really ought to find out."

"This is where I get out," said Penny. "Thank you for driving me home, Arthur. I can't get out unless you get out first, Geraint."

Powell stepped on to the pavement and bowed as he held the door for the furious Penny.

"You shouldn't have said that, Geraint," said Maria, when they drove away.

"Why not? I think it's true."

"All the more reason not to say it," said Maria.

"You could be right about Penny," said Darcourt. "Why is such an attractive woman unattached at her age? Why is she so flirtatious with men but it never leads to anything? Perhaps our Penny is looking asquint at something she doesn't want to see."

"A fight over Schnak is just what we need to relieve the dowdy simplicity of this opera venture," said Powell. "Art is so lacking in passion, don't you think? With the Doctor and Penny contesting like the Bright and the Dark Angel for the body and soul of Hulda Schnakenburg, we shall add a little salt to the dreary porridge of our lives."

[7]

ETAH IN LIMBO

WHAT DO THEY DO? Arthur wants to know, and I, happy in my privileged position, may say that I do know.

I must be careful about my privileged position. "Is there a cosier condition than being thoroughly pleased with oneself?" I must be careful not to become like Kater Murr. Even in Limbo, I suppose, one can sink into Philistinism.

But what Dr. Gunilla and Hulda Schnakenburg do is far from Philistine, and indeed far from the anti-Philistine world as I knew it when I was a part of what is now flatteringly called The Romantic Movement. Of course there were intense and intimate friendships between women then, but whatever physical amusement they generated was not known or seriously considered. Certainly some young ladies hung about each other's necks in public; they often dressed in identical gowns; they swooned or had hysterics at the same time, for both swooning and hysterics were high among the feminine luxuries of the day, and were thought to show great delicacy of feeling. But it was always assumed that these sensitive creatures would marry at last, and after marriage the intimacy with the female friend might become even more precious. I suppose if, after the first raptures of marriage, your husband was in the habit of coming to bed drunk, or smelling of the bawdy-house, or in a mood to black an eye or give a few hard slaps to a critical wife, it was delightful to have a friend who treated you with delicate respect and who could perhaps rouse an ecstasy that your disappointing husband thought was outside the emotional range of a well-bred woman. That was how it was, you see: that special ecstasy was thought to be the prerogative of whores, and whores became expert at faking it, and thereby flattering their clients.

It was all quite different, in my day. Love was an emotion greatly valued, but it was valued for its own sake, and an unhappy love or a torturing love was perhaps even more valued than a love that was fulfilled. After all, love is an ecstasy, but sex is an appetite, and one does not always satisfy an appetite at the best restaurant in town. The bordel where Devrient and I used to go in Berlin was quite a humble affair, and the women there knew their trade and their place; they did not presume to intimacy with the visitors, who were always called Mein Herr, unless the visitors liked endearments and smutty talk, which was extra, and had to be considered in the tip. It was in Russia and Poland that people who liked that sort of thing became familiar with the whore and, in my opinion, made fools of themselves. I cannot recall the face of a single whore, though I employed many.

Why? Why did I go to the bordel, even when I was out of my mind with love for the unattainable pupil, the lovely Julia Marc? Even in my most love-stricken hours I did not cease to eat, or drink—or visit the bordel. Love was not an appetite, but an ecstasy. Whores were not women, but servants.

What about my wife? Do you suppose that when I was head over ears in love with another woman I would insult my wife, my dearest Michalina Rohrer, by seeking out her bed? Do you suppose I had no respect for her, and all she meant to me? She was a fact, and an extremely important fact, of my life, and I would not have insulted her, even if she were unconscious of the insult—and I do not for a moment suppose she was ignorant of my passion for Julia. She had a close friend, by the way, and I never made inquiry or interfered in whatever may have passed between them. Nor, I suppose, did Dante, when he was sighing for his Beatrice. Dante was a very good family man, and so was I, in the manner of my time. Romantic love and a firm domestic life were not incompatible, but they were not expected to mingle. Marriage was a contract, to be taken seriously, and the fidelity it demanded was not to be trifled with. But the obsession of love might, and often did, lie elsewhere.

Is there love between Gunilla and Hulda? On Hulda's side I am *sure it is so, and whether either of them expects it to last, as marriage is expected to last, I cannot say. It was Hulda's initiation into that sweet ecstasy; Gunilla is a woman of great experience. It was she, for instance, who introduced Hulda to what they called the Love Potion.*

It was a sort of jam, really. Jam was the heart of it; the very best raspberry jam made by Crabtree and Evelyn. With the jam was mixed honey and a few chopped walnuts. Gunilla would spread a path of it on Hulda's tender belly, beginning at the navel and extending downward. Having licked the jam out of the navel, Gunilla would lick slowly and gently in a southward direction and in time—it all had to be done lentissimo e languidamente—*to the pintle of ecstasy, and then there were sighs and sometimes cries. After a restful period of kissing, Hulda took her turn, anointing Gunilla's belly and performing the same slow ritual. With Gunilla it always ended in quite loud cries. It was she who most appreciated the walnuts, which gave, she said, a sort of traction that was very exciting.*

All innocent and delightful, concluding with a bath together (enlivened with a couple of aquavits apiece) and a refreshing sleep. Who was harmed? Nobody. And there was no resorting to the bordel, simply as a convenience.

That is what I envy them. For it was in the bordel, somewhere—I cannot tell in what city of the many where I pursued my career—it came about that I acquired the disease that was one of the contributing elements in my early death. I underwent a cure, of course, but the cures in those days cured nothing except the debts of the physicians. I thought I had been cured, but later I knew better. That was in 1818, and when I became horribly ill and died in 1822 I knew that it was not simply the liver ailment that grew from all that champagne, or the mysterious paralysis that was at last diagnosed as tabes dorsalis— *one of the many names given to the old, old disease—that carried me off. As it carried off poor Schubert, who, as I saw from the vantage of Limbo, was brought to wearing an absurd wig, to disguise the baldness that syphilis had brought upon him. And Schumann, who died of a self-inflicted starvation: but it sprang from the madness that had so long possessed him—madness that arose from the Morbus Gallicus.*

It was my legs that first became useless to me, then the paralysis settled in my hands and I could not hold a pen. I was determined to complete **Arthur of Britain** *if I could, and when writing was im-*

possible I dictated my music to my wife, my dear faithful Michalina, who was a skilled amanuensis. But I could achieve nothing but sketches for the music I wanted—the sketches from which Schnak is so cleverly divining what was in my mind. The disease that made me unable to control the pen seemed to enlarge and enrich my musical imagination; I have long believed that certain poisons—tobacco and wine, to name two of the commonest—may do that in minds of fine quality, where the poisons do not induce the usual stupor. A truly Romantic notion, some would say. But the tortures and wrenchings that came with the inspirations were terrible, and it was to them that I at last succumbed.

It is the disease of genius, many people have said, because so many men of note, and many of them my contemporaries, died of it, or were hastened to the grave because syphilis underlay whatever it was the doctors said had killed them. Would I have sacrificed my genius to avoid the pain and degradation? Fortunately there is no necessity to answer that question.

"I SIMPLY *adore* Canada! What I've seen, that's to say. Which isn't the whole thing, of course. Really only Toronto and the Royal Winter Fair. I'm going to try for a stop-over in Montreal on my way home—try out my French, you know—but I mayn't be able to spare the time. Must get back to my stud, you see. So much to be done at this time of year."

"I'm glad you approve of us," said Darcourt. "Now, about your father—"

"Oh, yes, Daddy. That's what we're here to talk about, isn't it? That's the reason for this lovely lunch in this absolutely super restaurant. Because you're writing about him, aren't you? I scribble a little myself, you know. Pony stories for children. They sell a few hundred thousand, to my surprise. But just before we get onto Daddy, there's one thing—rather hush-hush, but I know you're discreet—that I think isn't just the way it should be in Canada, and unless something is done before it goes too far it could let you down fearfully. I mean, it could bring about a drop in world prestige."

Ah, politics, thought Darcourt. Politics, which rages like the hectic in the veins of every Canadian, and quickly infects visitors—even Little Charlie, otherwise Miss Charlotte Cornish, who sat before him digging into the poached salmon.

"And what is that?" he asked, without wanting to know.

Little Charlie leaned forward conspiratorially, a loaded fork poised like a wand in her hand; there was a flake of salmon clinging to her lower lip.

"It's your farriery," she whispered. The flake was detached by the whisper and sped across the table toward Darcourt's plate. She was the sort of woman who combines acceptable table manners with obvious greed; the lapels of her excellent tweed jacket carried evidence of hasty, joyous gobbling.

"Farriery?" he said, puzzled. Had Canada's farriery gone to pot, and he had not noticed? Had the word some significance unknown to him?

"Don't imagine I'm faulting your vets," said Little Charlie. "First-class, so far as I can judge. But it's the degree below the vet; the farrier groom who is the real companion and confidant of the pony. The vet is there for the big stuff, of course: colic, and farcy, and strangles and all those dreadful things that can ruin a fine creature. But it's the farrier who gives the hot mash when the beastie is a wee bit sicky-pussy from a chill, or a tumble. It's the farrier who pets and comforts when things haven't gone just the way the beastie would like at a show. I call the farrier the pony's nurse. In fact, in my stud I have this most wonderful girl— well, she must be my age, but she's a girl to me—her name's Stella, but I always call her Nursie, and believe you me she lives up to her name. I'd trust Stella far beyond most vets, let me tell you."

"How lucky you are to have her," said Darcourt. "Now, about the late Francis Cornish, I suppose you have some memories of him?"

"Oh, yes," said Little Charlie. "But just a moment; I want to tell you something that happened yesterday. I was judging—head of the judges, really—and the most exquisite little Shetland stallion was brought in. A real winner! Eyes bright and well spaced; fine muzzle and big nostrils, deep chest and splendid withers, marvellous croup—a perfect picture! I tell you, I'd have bought him, if I could raise the cash. Won't tell you his name, because I don't want this to get around—though of course I trust you— and at his head was this groom, not a bit the kind of fellow you'd expect to see with such a little sweetie, and when the pony tossed his head—as they'll do, you know, because they know they're being judged, and they have pride—he jerked the bridle and said, 'Hold still, damn you,' under his breath! But I heard, and I tell you my heart went out to that little creature. 'Are you the farrier?' I said to him—not sharply, but firmly—and he said, 'Yeah, I look after him,' almost insolently. And I thought, well, I've seen quite a lot of that this last few days, and it sickens me. Then he jerked the bridle again and the pony nipped him! And he hit the pony on the nose! Well, of course that was that as far as judging goes. Show me a biter and I'll show you a potential bolter and probably a jibber. And all because of that brute of a groom!"

"Distressing, certainly," said Darcourt. They were moving on toward strawberry shortcake, made with tasteless imported strawberries, but that was what Little Charlie wanted, and Darcourt was trying to prime the pump of her memory. "Was your father fond of animals, do you recall?"

"Couldn't say," said Little Charlie, busy with her spoon. "It was pretty much all King and Country with him, as I was told it. But don't imagine that because I said I might have bought that stallion I'm really keen on Shetlands. Of course they sell well to people with children, because they look so sweet. But they're a deceiving kind of pony, you know. Such a short step. Keep a child too long on a Shetland and you may have spoiled her forever as a rider. What she needs as soon as she's big enough is a good Welsh, with a strain of Arab. They're the ones with style and action! They're my bread-and-butter. Not for polo, mind you. There it's Exmoor and Dartmoor, and I breed a lot of those. In fact—this is telling tales out of school but what the hell!—I sold an Exmoor stallion to His Royal Highness's stable a couple of years ago, and HRH said—I was told this very much in confidence—he'd never seen a finer little stallion."

"I won't tell a soul. Now, about your father—"

"He was a four-year-old and just coming into his best. For God's sake, I said to HRH's man, don't push him too hard. Give him time and he'll get you twenty-five to forty first-class foals every year until he's twenty. But if you push him now—! Well, you'll never believe this, but I've seen a fine stallion forced to serve as many as three hundred mares a season, and after five years he's just plain knackered! Like people. Quality, not quantity, is the root of the whole thing. Of course they can soldier on. They're wonderfully willing, you know. But it's the sperm. The sperm count in an overworked stallion goes down and down, and though he may look like Don Juan he's just Weary Willie. As Stella says—she's very broad-spoken, sometimes—his willy is willing but the trollybobs are weak. So that's it. Never, never be greedy with your stallion!"

"I promise you I never will. But now I really think we ought to talk about your father."

"Of course. Sorry, sorry, sorry. The ruling passion. I do rattle on. Stella says so. Well, as to Daddy, I never saw him."

"Never?"

"Not to remember. I suppose he saw me, when I was a tiny. But not after I'd begun to notice. But he cared for me. That's to say he sent money regularly to look after me, and all the farriery was left to my grandmother. Prudence Glasson, you know. The whole gang were related, in various distant degrees. You see, my mummy was Ismay Glasson, and her father was Roderick Glasson, who was kin to Daddy from another point of the compass. I wouldn't have bred them that way if it had been my stud, but that's all past and done with. My very first pony, when I was four—a sweet Shetland—had a ticket on his bridle, 'For Little Charlie from Daddy'."

"You remember your mother, of course?"

"No, not a bit. You see—this is the family skeleton—Mummy was a bolter. Not long after I was born she just took off, and left me to Daddy and my grandparents. Mind you, I think she was a sort of high-minded bolter; she went to Spain to fight in the war and I always assumed she was killed there, but nobody ever gave me any details. She was by way of being a beauty, but from pictures I'd say she was a bit overbred; nervous and high-strung, and likely to bite, and bolt, and jib, and do all those things."

"Really? That's very helpful. I tried to see your uncle, Sir Roderick, in London at the Foreign Office, to ask a few questions about your mother, but it was impossible to make an appointment."

"Oh, Uncle Roddy would never see you, or tell you anything if he did. He's the original Stuffed Shirt. I've given up all hope of seeing him, not that I'm keen. But don't run away with the idea that I had a neglected or unhappy childhood. It was absolutely marvellous, even though St. Columb's was running down all the time I was growing up. I believe Daddy poured a lot of money into the family place—God knows why—but my grandfather was a hopeless estate manager. Our money from Daddy was watched rather carefully by a solicitor, so it didn't go down the drain, and it still doesn't, let me assure you. My little stud is built on that, and since I met Stella—you'd adore Stella, though she is a bit frank-spoken and you are a parson, after all—I've been as happy as a lark."

"So you really know nothing about your father? In your letter to the Cornishes here you rather suggested that he had some Secret Service connection."

"That was hinted at, but not much was said. Not much was known, I suppose. But you see Daddy's father, Sir Francis, was in that, and very deep, I believe, and how far Daddy followed in his footsteps I really don't know. It was the spy connection that kept Daddy from coming to see me, or so it was said."

"Spy? Do you think he was really a spy?"

"It's not a word Gran would ever hear used. If they're British intelligence agents they certainly aren't *spies,* she said. Only foreigners are *spies.* But you know how kids are. I used to joke about him being a spy, to raise the temperature a little. You know, the way kids do. They always told me to be very secret about it but I don't suppose it matters now."

"And did you know that your father was a painter, and a remarkable connoisseur, and had a reputation as an expert on pictures?"

"Never heard a word about that. Though I was knocked endways to find out he'd left a huge fortune! I did think of asking the Cornishes if they'd like to use some of it to finance some really super breeding—you know, the very best of the best. But then I thought, shut up, Charlie; that's greedy, and Daddy has treated you very well. So shut up! And I have.—Oh, crumbs, I must be off! Heavy afternoon ahead of me. Thanks for the super lunch. I shan't be seeing you again, shall I? Or Arthur and Maria, either. I fly on Friday. They're a super pair. Especially Maria. By the way, you're a great family friend, I believe; have you heard anything about her being in foal?"

"In foal? Oh, I see what you mean. No. Have you?"

"No. But I have the breeder's eye, you know. Right away there's something about a mare that tells the tale. If the stallion's clicked, I mean.—And now I must dash!"

As well as a stout woman may, she dashed.

[2]

ARTHUR WEPT. He had not done so since his parents died in a motor accident when he was fourteen; he was stricken by the grief that overcame him as he sat in Darcourt's study, a cluttered, booky room, into which a little watery November sun made its way cautiously, as if doubtful of its welcome. He wept. His shoulders shook. It seemed to him that he howled, although Darcourt, standing by the window, looking out into the college quadrangle, heard only deep-fetched sobs. Tears poured from his eyes, and salt downpourings of mucus streamed from his nose. One handkerchief was sodden and the second—Arthur always carried two—and the second was rapidly becoming useless. Darcourt was not the sort of man who has boxes of tissues in his study. It seemed to Arthur that his paroxysm would never end; new desolation heaved up into his heart as quickly as he wept out the old. But at last he sank back in his chair blear-eyed, red-nosed, and conscious that his fine tie had a smear of snot on it.

"Got a handkerchief?" he said.

Darcourt threw him one. "Feel better now, do you?"

"I feel like a cuckold."

"Ah, yes. A cuckold. Or as Dr. Dahl-Soot pronounces it, cookold. You'll have to get used to it."

"You're a bloody unsympathetic friend. And a bloody unresponsive priest, Simon."

"Not a bit of it. I am very sorry, both for you and Maria, but what good will it do if I join you in siren tears? My job is to keep a cool head and look at the thing from the outside. What about Powell?"

"I haven't seen him. What do I do? Beat him up?"

"And signal to the whole world what's wrong? No, you certainly do not beat him up. Anyhow, you're in this opera thing up to your neck, and Powell is indispensable."

"Damn it, he's my best friend."

"The cuckoo in the nest is often the best friend. Powell loves you, as a friend may very well love you. I love you, Arthur, though I don't make a song and dance about it."

"*That* kind of love. You have to because you're a priest. Like God, it's your métier."

"You don't know anything about priests. I know we are supposed to love mankind indiscriminately, but I don't. That's why I gave up practical priesthood and became a professor. My faith charges me to love my neighbour but I can't and I won't fake it, in the greasy way professional lovers-of-mankind do—the professionally charitable, the newspaper sob-sisters, the politicians. I'm not Christ, Arthur, and I can't love like Him, so I settle for courtesy, consideration, decent manners, and whatever I can do for the people I really do love. And you are one of those. I can't help you by weeping with you, though I respect your tears. The best I can do is to bring a clear head and an open eye to your trouble. I love Maria, too, you know."

"Indeed I do know. You wanted to marry her, didn't you?"

"I did, and in the kindest possible way she gave me the mitt. I love her even more for that, because Maria and I would have made a damned bad match."

"Okay, old Clear Head and Open Eye. Why did you ask her, then?"

"Because I was in the grip of passion. There were a thousand reasons for loving Maria, and I now see there were a million for not marrying her. I love her still, but don't worry that I want to play the role that Powell has played in your marriage."

"She told me she once had *le coeur tendre* for Hollier, and that you had proposed to her. And looked a fine ninny as you did it, what's more. Every woman has these boss-shots in her past. But she married me, and now she's wrecking it."

"Balls. You're the one who's wrecking it."

"Me! She's pregnant, damn it!"

"And you're sure it's not your child?"

"Yes."

"How? You use some contraceptive, I suppose. Condoms? They're very much in vogue at present."

"I hate the damned things. There they are, the morning after, leering wetly at you from the bedside table or the carpet, like the Ghost of Nooky Past."

"Maria uses something?"

"No. We wanted a child."

"So?"

"I had mumps, you remember. Badly. The doctors told me

tactfully that henceforth I would be infertile. Not impotent. Just infertile. And it's irreversible."

"You told Maria, of course?"

"I hadn't got around to it."

"So the child must have been begotten by somebody else?"

"Yes, Sherlock Holmes."

"Must it have been Powell?"

"Who else is a possibility? You see—I hate telling you this—somebody came to me—"

"To tip you off?"

"Yes. A security man who works at night in our apartment building."

"One Wally Crottel?"

"Yes. And he said that Mr. Powell sometimes stayed late, and occasionally overnight when I was out of town, and as a convenience would it be a good idea if he gave Mr. Powell a key to the parking area?"

"And you said no."

"I said no. It was just a hint, you know. But it was enough."

"It was a mistake to underestimate Wally. So then—"

"Because of this opera business Powell comes and goes quite a lot, and if he stays late he uses our guest room. I didn't know he used it when I was away."

"Powell is a very using kind of man."

"So it seems."

"Have you told Maria now? About being infertile, I mean?"

"I told her after she told me she was pregnant. I didn't think she was as happy about a child as I would have expected, but I put it down to shyness. And I suppose I looked astonished—that's a poor word for it—and I couldn't say a word. She asked me what was wrong. I told her."

"Yes?"

"It took a few minutes, and all the time I was talking that hint from Crottel kept swelling in my mind, and at last I came out with it. Was it Powell? I said. She wouldn't say a word."

"Very unlike Maria to have nothing to say."

"She simply closed her mouth and looked as I've never seen her look before. Very big-eyed and tight-lipped. But smiling. It was enough to drive me mad."

"What did you expect? That she should fall at your feet and bathe them in her tears, and then wipe away the tears from your custom-made brogues with her hair? You don't know your own wife, my boy."

"You're damned right I don't. But it drove me crazy, and as I got hotter and hotter she just smiled that bloody smile and refused to say anything. So at last I said that her silence was answer enough. And she said, 'If that's what you think.' And that was all."

"And you haven't spoken a word to each other since?"

"We're not savages, Simon. Of course we speak. Very politely about commonplaces. But it's hell, and I don't know what to do."

"So you have come to me for advice. Sensibly, I may say."

"Oh don't be so bloody smug."

"Not smug. Don't forget I'm an old hand at this sort of thing. So shall we get down to it?"

"If you like."

"No, no; it's got to be if *you* like."

"All right."

"Well, for a starter, don't imagine I underestimate your hurt. It can't be any fun being told that you're not fully a man. But it's happened before. George Washington, for instance. Another mumps casualty, it seems. No children, though he was quite a man for the ladies. But he didn't do too badly. The Father of His Country, we are told."

"Don't be facetious."

"Wouldn't dream of it. But I refuse to take the great tragic line, either. This business of begetting children is important as one of the biological qualities of a man, but as civilization moves on, other qualities look at least equally important. You're not some wandering nomad or medieval peasant who has to have children because they are a primitive kind of insurance. This begetting business is terribly overrated. All nature does it and Man is far from the champion. If you hadn't had mumps you would probably be able to squirt out a few million live sperm at a go, and one of them might make a lucky hit. Your cousin Little Charlie's favourite stallion has you backed right off the map; he probably averages ten billion possible little stallions every time Little Charlie collects her stud fee; that's what he's for. The boar

is the real champ: eighty-five billions—and then he trots away
looking for acorns, and never gives a thought to his sow, who
turns again to her wallowing in the mire. But Man—proud Man—
is something very different. Even the least of his kind has a soul—
that's to say a lively consciousness of individuality and Self—and
you are rather a superior man, Arthur. Unfortunately Man is the
only creature to have made a hobby and a fetish of Sex, and the
bed is the great play-pen of the world. Now you listen to
me—"

"I'm listening."

"You come to me as a priest, don't you? You've made rather
a joke of that, and call me the Abbé Darcourt—the tame cleric.
The learned man on your staff. I'm an Anglican priest, and even
the Church of Rome has at last had to admit that my priesthood
is as valid as any. When I married you and Maria you had quite
a strong fit of orthodoxy, and wanted the whole thing to be on
the most orthodox lines. Well—be orthodox now. God may want
you for something more important than begetting children. God
has lots of sexual journeymen who can attend to that. So you'd
better ask God what He wants of you."

"Don't preach at me, Simon. And I wish you wouldn't drag
God into it."

"Booby! Do you suppose I have the power to drag Him out
of it? Or out of anything? Very well, simpleton, don't call it God.
That's only a shorthand term anyhow. Call it Fate or Destiny or
Kismet or the Life Force or the It or any damned name you like
but don't pretend it doesn't exist! And don't pretend that What-
ever-You-Call-It doesn't live out a portion—a tiny portion—of
its purpose through you, and that your pretensions to live your
own life by the dictates of your intelligence are just so much
nonsense, flattering to fools."

"No Free Will, then?"

"Oh yes. Freedom to do as you are told, by Whatever-You-
Call-It, and freedom to make a good job of it or a mess, according
to your inclination. Freedom to play the hand you're dealt, in
fact."

"Preach, preach, preach!"

"I damned well will preach! And don't imagine you can escape.
If you don't ask God, which is my word—my professional word—

for what we are talking about, what He wants of you, God will certainly tell you, and in no unmistakable terms, and if you don't heed, you'll be so miserable your present grief will look like a child's tantrum. You liked orthodoxy when it seemed to be picturesque. It isn't picturesque now, and I advise you to think of yourself as a man, and a very fine man, and not as a competitor with Little Charlie's stallion, or some snuffling wild boar that will eventually end up in a Bavarian restaurant as the speciality of the day."

"So what do I do?"

"You make peace with your grief and take a long, thoughtful look at your luck."

"Swallow this insult, this infidelity? Maria, the person I love more than myself?"

"Bullshit! People say that, but it's bullshit. The person you love best is Arthur Cornish, because he's the one God has given you to make the best of. Unless you love him truly and deeply you are not fit to have Maria as your wife. She's a soul, too, you know, and not just a branch-soul of your own, like one of the branches of your Cornish Trust. Maybe she has a destiny that needs this fact that you call an infidelity. Ever thought of that? I mean it, Arthur. Your business is with Arthur Cornish, first and foremost, and your value to Maria and the rest of the world depends on how you treat Arthur."

"Maria has made Arthur Cornish a cuckold."

"Then you'd better make up your mind to one of two courses. One: You beat up Powell, or perhaps kill him, and create misery that will last for several generations. Two: You take a hint from this opera that has brought about the whole thing, and decide to be the Magnanimous Cuckold. And what that may lead to, God only knows, but in the tale of Great Arthur of Britain it has led to something that has fed the best of mankind for centuries."

Arthur was silent, and Darcourt went again to the window and looked out at weather that had turned to dismal autumn rain. Such silences seem long to those who keep them, but in reality it could have not been more than four or five minutes.

"Why did she smile in that peculiar way?" said Arthur at last.

"Take heed when women smile like that," said Darcourt. "It means they have sunk very deep into themselves, far below the mind of everyday, into Nature's ruthless mind, which sees the truth and may decide not to tell what it sees."

"And what does she see?"

"I imagine she sees that she is going to bear this child, whatever you may think about it, and care for the child, even if it means parting with you, because that's the job Whatever-It-Is has given her and she knows that there is no denying those orders. She knows that for the next five or six years it will be her child, as it can never be any man's. After that men may put some superficial stamp on it, but she will have made the wax that takes the seal. Maria smiles because she knows what she is going to do, and she smiles at you because you don't."

"So what do I do about her?" said Arthur.

"Behave as if you really loved her. What was she doing when last you saw her?"

"She didn't look much like an independent soul, to be frank. She was throwing up her breakfast in the john."

"Very right and proper, for a healthy young mother. Well, my advice is, love her and leave her alone."

"You don't think I should suggest she come to you?"

"Don't you dare! But Maria will either come to me, or she'll go to her mother, and my bet is she'll come to me. Her mother and I are roughly in the same line of work, but I look more civilized, and Maria still yearns powerfully for civilization."

[3]

DARCOURT WAS NOT ACCUSTOMED to being entertained by women; not, that is to say, entertained in restaurants by women who paid the bill. It was a ridiculous attitude, he knew, as certainly Dr. Gunilla Dahl-Soot would be charging this excellent dinner to the Cornish Trust. But, even though she was a fast, efficient gobbler, whereas he was a patient muncher, the Doctor was a different person as a hostess from the obstreperous guest at Maria's Arthurian dinner. She was considerate, kindly, charming, but not particularly feminine—in a word, thought Darcourt, she is very much man-to-man.

Her notion of conversation, however, was unconventional.

"What sins would you have liked to commit?" she asked.

"Why do you ask that?"

"It is a key to character, and I want to know you. Of course, you are a parson, so I suppose you press down very hard on any sinful ideas you have, but I am sure you have them. Everybody does. What sins? What about sex? You have no wife. Is it men?"

"No indeed. I am extremely fond of women, and I have many women friends; but I am not tormented by sexual desire, if that is what you mean. Or not often. Too busy. If Don Juan had been a professor, and Vice-Warden of his college, a secretary to a large philanthropic trust, and a biographer, we should never have heard of him as a great seducer. It calls for a lot of leisure, does seduction. And a one-track mind. I imagine Don Juan must have been rather a dull dog when he wasn't on the prowl."

"The Freudians think Don Juan really hated women."

"He had a funny way of showing it. I can't imagine sex with somebody I hated."

"You don't always know you hate them till push comes to shove. I speak idiomatically, you understand. I am not talking smuttily."

"Oh, quite."

"I was married once, you know. Less than a week. Ugh!"

"Sorry to hear that."

"Why? We all have to learn. I was a quick learner. It is not my destiny to be Fru Berggrav, I decided. So—divorce, and back to my own life and my own name. Of which I am very proud, let me tell you."

"I'm sure."

"A lot of people here laugh when they hear it."

"Not all names travel well."

"Soot is an honoured name in Norway, where my Soots came from. There was a very good painter in the last century who was a Soot."

"I didn't know."

"The people who laugh at my name have limited social experience."

"Yes, yes."

"Like Professor Raven. Is she a great friend of yours?"

"I know her well."

"A stupid woman. Do you know she has been on the telephone to me?"

"About the libretto?"

"No. About Hulda Schnakenburg. She made an awful muddle of it, but it was clear she thinks I am being very naughty with that child."

"I know. And are you?"

"Certainly not! But I am coaxing her into life. She has lived a life very much—how do I say it?"

"Very much denied?"

"Yes, that's the word. No kindness. No affection. I do not say love. Horrible parents."

"I've met them."

"True followers of Kater Murr."

"Hadn't thought of him as a religious teacher."

"Oh, you wouldn't have heard of him. He was a creation of our E. T. A. Hoffmann. A tom-cat. His philosophy was, 'Can anything be cosier than having a nice, secure place in the world?' It is the religion of millions."

"Indeed it is."

"Hulda is an artist. How good or how big, who can say? But an artist, certainly. Kater Murr is the enemy of all true art, religion, science—anything of any importance whatever. Kater Murr wants nothing but certainty, and whatever is great grows in the battleground between truth and error. 'Raus mit Kater Murr! That is what Hulda says now. If I play with her a little—you understand me?—it is all for the defeat of Kater Murr."

"All?"

"You are a sly one! No, not all. It is very agreeable to me, and to her as well."

"I am not accusing you."

"But you are being very clever. You have changed the conversation from what sins you would like to commit to what sins that silly, provincial woman accuses me of. Hulda will be all right. What is it she says? Okay. She will be okay."

"A little better than just okay, I hope?"

"Oh, but you understand. She is very bad at language. She says terrible things. She says she must 'maul over' these sketches of

Hoffmann's. I look it up. She means 'mull'. And she says she will 'day-bew' with this opera. She means 'debut' and she uses it all wrong anyhow. But she is not a fool or a vulgarian. She just has no regard for language. It has no mystery, no overtones, for her."

"I know. Such people make you and me feel stuffy and pernickety."

"But she cannot be an artist in music and a hooligan in speech. You are careful about language."

"Yes."

"I know from what you have done on the libretto. It is really good."

"Thank you."

"That silly woman does not help you?"

"Certainly not so far."

"I suppose she thinks of me and it dries up the ink in her pen. And that beautiful fool Professor Hollier, who is too much a scholar to be even a very tiny poet. But what you give to Hulda is respectable poetry."

"No, no; you are too flattering."

"No I'm not. But what I want to know is—is it all yours?"

"What else could it be?"

"It could be pastiche. Which I am at last persuading Hulda not to call pistache. If so, it is first-class pastiche. But pastiche of what?"

"Now listen here, Dr. Dahl-Soot, you are being very pressing. You are accusing me of stealing something. What would you say if I accused you of stealing musical ideas?"

"I would deny it indignantly. But you are too clever to be deceived, and you know that many musicians borrow and adapt ideas, and usually they come out so that only a very subtle critic can see what has happened. Because what one borrows goes through one's own creative stomach and comes out something quite different. You know the old story about Handel? Somebody accused him of stealing an idea from another composer and he shrugged and said, 'Yes, but what did he do with it?' What is theft and what is influence, or homage? When Hoffmann suggests Mozart, as he does in some of his compositions, it is homage, not theft. So, do you have an influence?"

"If I'm going to talk to you in this way, I must insist on calling you Nilla."

"I shall be honoured. And I shall call you Simon."

"Well, Nilla, it is insulting to suggest that I am not a poet, but that I am presenting unquestionable poetry."

"Insulting, perhaps, but I think it is true."

"It suggests that I am a crook."

"All artists are children of Hermes, the Arch-Crook."

"Let me answer your earlier question: what sins would I like to commit? Very well; I have just the tiniest inclination toward imposture. I think it would be delightful to slip something not absolutely sincere and gilt-edged into a world where any sort of imposture is held in holy horror. The world of art is such a world. The critics, who themselves originate nothing, are so unforgiving if they catch an impostor! Indeed, the man whose life I am writing, and whose money is the engine behind the Cornish Foundation, once exposed an impostor—a painter—and that was the end of the poor wretch whose crime was to pretend that his masterly painting had been done by somebody long dead. Not the worst of crimes, surely?"

"So you are a crook, Simon? It makes you very interesting. And you are safe with me. Here: we drink to secrecy."

The Doctor took her wineglass in her hand and slipped her right arm through Darcourt's left. They lifted their arms, and drank—drained their glasses.

"To secrecy," said Darcourt.

"So—who are you robbing?"

"If you had to prepare this libretto, who would you rob? A poet, of course, but not a very well-known poet. And he would have to be a poet contemporaneous with Hoffmann, and a fellow-spirit, or the work would ring false. And amid the work of that poet you would have to interpose a lot of stuff in the same spirit, because nobody wrote a libretto about King Arthur that is lying around, waiting for such an occasion as this. And the result would be—"

"Pastiche!"

"Yes, and the craft of the thing would be sewing up the joins, so that nobody would notice and denounce the whole thing as—"

"Pistache! Oh, you are a clever one! Simon, I think you and I are going to be great friends!"

"Let's drink to that, Nilla," said Darcourt, and once again they linked arms and drank. Some people at a nearby table were staring, but the Doctor gave them a look of such Boreal hauteur that they hastily bent their heads over their plates.

"And now, Simon—who is it?"

"I won't tell you, Nilla. Not because I think you would blab, but because it is very important to me to be the only one who knows, and if I lose that I may lose everything. Nor do I suppose the name would mean anything to you. Not at all a fashionable poet, at present."

"But a good one. When Modred is plotting Arthur's murder, you make him say:

> Let him lean
> Against his life, that glassy interval
> 'Twixt us and nothing:
> And upon the ground
> Of his own slippery breath, draw hueless dreams
> And gaze on frost-work hopes.

I felt cold when I read that."

"Good. And you saw how it fits Schnak's musical fragment? So genuine Hoffmann is mated with my genuine poet, and with luck we may get something truly fine."

"I wish very much I knew your poet."

"Then look for him. He's not totally obscure. Just a little off the beaten path."

"Is he this Walter Scott, about whom Powell spoke?"

"Anything good you can pinch from Scott is well known, and nothing but his best is of any use."

"Surely you will be found out when the opera is produced."

"Not for a while. Perhaps not for a long time. How much of a libretto do you actually hear? It slips by, as an excuse for the music, and to indicate a plot."

"You have changed the plot Powell told us about?"

"Not much. I've tightened it up. An opera has to have a good firm story."

"And the music ought to carry the story and make it vivid."

"Well—not in Hoffmann's day. In Hoffmann's operas and those he admired you get a chunk of plot, usually in pretty simple recitative, and then the action stops while the singers have a splendid rave-up about their feelings. It's the rave-up that makes the opera; not the plot. Most of the plots, even after Wagner, have been disgustingly simple."

"Simple—and few."

"Astonishingly few, Nilla, however you dress them up."

"Some critic said there were not more than nine plots in all literature."

"He might as well have said, in all life. It's amazing, and humbling, how we tread the old paths without recognizing them. Mankind is wonderfully egotistical."

"Lucky for mankind, Simon. Don't grudge us our little scrap of individuality. You talk like that woman Maria Cornish, with her wax-and-seal. What path is she treading, do you think?"

"How can I tell till her full story is told? At which time I shall probably not be around to have an opinion."

"She interests me very much. Oh, not what you are thinking. I don't want to break up her marriage, though she is a lovely creature. But somebody will."

"You think so?"

"That husband of hers is all wrong for her."

"I'm not so sure."

"Yes. A cold fish. Not a scrap of feeling in him."

"Now Nilla, I see through you. You want me to contradict you and tell you all I know about Arthur. All I'm going to tell you is that you are wrong."

"What a man for secrets you are."

"Secrets are the priest's trade or he is no priest."

"All right. Don't tell. But that woman comes out of a very different box from Arthur Cornish, who is all money and careful plans, and Kater Murr."

"You're right about Maria. Wrong about Arthur. He is scrambling upward from Kater Murr just as fast as he can."

"Oh? So he married Maria to get away from Kater Murr? You let something slip, there. That woman is no Canadian."

"Yes she is. A Canadian can be anything. It is one of our very few gifts. Because, you see, we all bring something to Canada with us, and a few years won't wash it out. Not even a few generations. But if you are frying with curiosity, Nilla, I would be a rotten guest if I did not tell you a few things to appease you. Maria is half Pole and the other half is Hungarian Gypsy."

"What a strong soup! Gypsy, is she?"

"If you met her mother you would never doubt it. Maria doesn't hurry to admit it, but she is very like her mother. And Arthur is very fond of Maria's mother. No wise man marries a woman if he can't stand her mother."

"And this mother is still alive? Here? I want to meet her. I love Gypsies."

"I don't suppose there is any reason why you shouldn't meet her. But don't assume you are going to love her. Mamusia would smell patronage a mile away, and she would be rough with you, Nilla. She is what Schnak would call one rough old broad, and as wise as a serpent."

"Ah, now you are telling! That Maria is one rough young broad, for all her silly pretence of being a nice rich man's wife with scholarly hobbies. You have blabbed, you leaky priest!"

"It's this excellent wine, Nilla. But I have told you nothing that everybody doesn't know."

"So—come on, Simon—what about Arthur?"

"Arthur is a gifted financial man, chairman of the board of a great financial house, and a man with genuine artistic tastes. A generous man."

"And a wimp? A nerd?—You see how I learn from Hulda."

"Not a wimp, and not a nerd or anything that Hulda would know about. What he is you will have to find out for yourself."

"But what plot are he and his wife working out together? Which of the nine? Tell me, or I might hit you!"

"Don't brawl in a restaurant, it will get us thrown out. That would be deeply un-Canadian. I think I smell the plot, but if you think I am going to hint to you, you can think again. You're a clever woman; work it out for yourself."

"I will, and then probably I'll hit you. Or maybe kiss you. You don't smell bad, for a man. But you will take me to Maria's mother, at least?"

"If you like."

"I do like."

"You're a rough old broad yourself, Nilla."

"Not so old. But rough."

"I have a fancy for rough women."

"Good. And now what about cognac?"

"Armagnac, I think, if I may. More suitable to rough broads."

[4]

MARIA WAS UP TO MISCHIEF, and Darcourt knew it. Why else would she present herself in his study at half past four in the afternoon, pretending that she was passing by, and thought that he might give her a cup of tea? She knew perfectly well that he did not go in for elegant tea-drinking, and that it was a nuisance for him to find a pot, and some long-kept tea, and stew up something on his electric hot-plate. He knew perfectly well that if tea was what she wanted she would be welcome in the Common Room of her old college, where there was lots of tea. They both knew that she had come to talk about her adultery, but she was certainly not a repentant Magdalene. She was wearing a red pant-suit, and had a red scarf tied around her hair, and she smiled and tossed her head and rolled her eyes in a way that Darcourt had never seen before. Maria was not there to confess or repent, but to tease and defend.

"Arthur has been to see you," she said, after some small talk which neither of them pretended was anything but a conventional overture to real conversation.

"Did he tell you so?"

"No, but I guessed it. Poor Arthur is in a terrible state just now, and you're his refuge in terrible states."

"He was distressed."

"And you comforted him?"

"No. Comfort did not seem appropriate. Arthur is not a man to be given sugar-candy, and that's what an awful lot of comfort amounts to."

"So you know all about it?"

"I don't imagine so for a moment. I know what he told me."

"And you are going to scold me?"

"No."

"Just as well. I'm not in the mood to be scolded."

"Then why have you come to me?"

"Is it strange that I should look in on an old friend for a cup of tea?"

"Come on, Maria; don't play the fool. If you want to talk about this state of affairs, I'll certainly talk. I'm not the keeper of your conscience, you know."

"But you think I've behaved badly."

"Don't tell me what I think. Tell me what you think, if you want to."

"How was I to know that Arthur can't beget children? He never told me that."

"Would it have made a difference?"

"You simply don't understand what happened."

"In such a matter nobody understands what happened except the people directly involved, and they are not always clear about it."

"Oh, so you know that, do you?"

"I know a few things about life. Not many, but a few. I know that when a family friend plays the cuckoo in the nest it is an old, old story. And I know that when you toss your head and roll your eyes like one of Little Charlie's ponies you probably think that somebody has been using you badly. Was it Arthur?"

"Arthur wasn't frank."

"Arthur was distressed and ashamed, and you ought to know that. He would have told you, when a good time came. How frank have you been with him?"

"I haven't been frank yet. There hasn't been a good time."

"Maria, what kind of marriage have you and Arthur set up? You could have made a good time."

"A good time to crawl and weep and probably be forgiven. I absolutely refuse to be forgiven."

"You've done what you've done, and there is a price for that. Being forgiven may be a part of that price."

"Then I won't pay."

"Rather break up your marriage?"

"It wouldn't come to that."

"From what I know of Arthur, I don't suppose it would."

"It would come to being forgiven, and being one-down on the marriage score-board for the rest of my life. And I simply won't put up with that. I'm not going to spend years of saying, 'Yes, dear,' about anything important because I have a debt I can't discharge. There's going to be a child, as I suppose you know. And every time the child is troublesome or disappointing I'm not going to have Arthur sighing and rolling his eyes and being marvellously big about the whole damned thing."

"You think that's what he'd do?"

"I don't know what he'd do, but that's what I wouldn't endure."

"You have the Devil's own pride, haven't you?"

"I suppose so."

"You can never be wrong. Maria can never be at fault. Very well; live that way if you must. But I can tell you it's easier and more comfortable to be wrong now and then."

"Comfortable! You sound like Kater Murr. Do you know who Kater Murr is?"

"Why do people keep asking me that? You introduced me to Kater Murr yourself."

"So I did. Sorry. But since then I've got hold of Hoffmann's astonishing novel, and I feel as if Kater Murr had crept into my life and was making a mess of it. Kater Murr and his horrible, cosy philosophy says far too much about my marriage."

"Aha."

"Oh, for God's sake don't say Aha as if you understood everything. You don't understand anything about marriage. I thought I was happy. Then I found out what happiness could mean. For me it meant being less than myself and less than a woman. Do you know what the Feminist League says: 'A happy wife is a strikebreaker in the fight for female equality.'"

"Do they say that? But what kind of happiness are you talking about? It isn't a simple thing, Maria."

"It began to seem to me that happiness was what Kater Murr says it is—a cosy place where one is perfectly content with oneself."

"Well, for a lot of people Kater Murr is dead right. But not for you. And, as if you didn't know it, not right for Arthur. You underestimate your husband, Maria."

"Do I? Yes, and he underestimates me! It's all that bloody money! It cuts me off from everything I have been, and everything I want to be."

"Which is—?"

"I want to be Maria, whoever Maria is! But I won't find out in this marriage I'm in now, because everywhere I turn I'm not Maria; I'm Mrs. Arthur Cornish, the very rich blue-stocking whose stockings are getting to be a faded puce because all she does is be a slave to that bloody Cornish Foundation, and dish out money to people who want to do a thousand and one things that don't interest me at all. I've given up everything to that Foundation, and I've come to the end!"

"Oh, not quite the end, I hope. What about you and Arthur?"

"Arthur's getting very strange. He's so God-damned considerate about everything."

"And now you know why."

"The mumps thing? Why did it have to be mumps? Such a silly thing, and then it turns out to have a nasty side."

"Well, call it bilateral orchitis if you want a fancy label. Personally I prefer mumps, because it also means being melancholy, and out of sorts, and plagued by dissatisfaction. Which is what ails Arthur. He's thoroughly dissatisfied with himself, and being the man he is he thinks he ought to be especially nice to you because you're married to such a dud. He thinks he's a wimp and a nerd, and he's sorry for you. He knows that as he gets older his balls are going to shrivel up, and that won't be the least bit funny for him. He was afraid he'd lose you, and right now he thinks he's lost you indeed. Has he?"

"How can you ask?"

"How can I not ask? Obviously you've been sleeping with somebody who doesn't have Arthur's trouble, and you've been so indiscreet as to get pregnant."

"God, Simon, I think I hate you! You talk exactly like a man!"

"Well—I am a man. And as you obviously think there is some special feminine side to this business, you had better tell me about it."

"First of all, I haven't been *sleeping* with anybody. Not a succession of sneaky betrayals. Just once. And I swear to you it seemed to be somebody I didn't know; I have never had words with Powell that would have led to anything like that; I'm not really sure I like him. Only once, and it had to get me pregnant! Oh, what a joke! What an uproarious bit of mischief by the Rum Old Joker!"

"Tell me."

"Yes, yes—'Tell me the old, old story,' as you like to sing. But it wasn't quite the old story you think. It was a much older story— a story that goes back through the centuries and probably through the aeons, from a time when women ceased to be sub-humans cringing at the back of the cave."

"A mythical tale?"

"By God, yes! A mythical tale. Like a god descending on a mortal woman. Do you remember one night when Powell was talking about the plot for this opera, and he was describing how Morgan Le Fay appears two or three times in disguise, and makes mischief?"

"Yes. We had a talk about stage disguise."

"Arthur said that it had always troubled him in the old plays when somebody puts on a cloak and hat and is accepted by the others as somebody he isn't. Disguise is impossible, he said. You recognize people by their walk, the way they hold their heads, by a thousand things that we aren't aware of. How do you disguise your back, he said; none of us can see our backs, but everybody else does, and when you see somebody from the back you may know them much more readily than if you see them face to face. Do you remember what Powell said?"

"Something about people wishing to be deceived?"

"Yes. That you will the deception, just as you will your own deception when you watch a conjuror. He said he had once taken part in a show put on in an asylum for the insane, where a very clever conjuror worked like a dog, and didn't get any applause whatever. Why? Because the insane were not his partners in his deceits. For them a rabbit might just as well come out of an empty hat as not. But the sane, the doctors and nurses, who were living and watching in the same world of assumptions as the conjuror, were delighted. And it was the same with disguise. On the stage, people accepted somebody in a very transparent disguise because the real deception was brought about by their own will. Show

Lancelot and Guenevere a witch, and they accept her as a witch because their situation makes a witch much more acceptable than Morgan Le Fay in a ragged cloak."

"Yes, I remember. I thought it rather a thin argument at the time."

"But don't you remember what he said afterward? We are deceived because we will our own deception. It is somehow necessary to us. It is an aspect of fate."

"I think I remember. Powell talks a lot of fascinating Celtic moonshine, doesn't he?"

"You are cynical about Powell because you are jealous of his astonishing powers of persuasion. And if you are in that mood, there's no point in my going on."

"Yes, do go on. I'll promise to suspend my disbelief in Geraint Powell's ideas."

"You'd better. Now listen very carefully. About two months ago Powell came to see me about some business. You know he is making contracts with singers and stage people, and he is very scrupulous about showing them to Arthur, or me when Arthur's away, before he closes his arrangement with the artist. Arthur was away on this particular evening. In Montreal, as he often is, and I didn't know just when he might come back. That evening, late, or early the next morning. Powell and I worked late, and then we went to bed."

"Had nothing led up to that?"

"Oh, I don't mean we went to bed together. Powell often uses a room in our apartment when he is in town late, then he gets up early and drives off to Stratford before breakfast. It's an established thing, and very convenient for him."

"So Wally Crottel seemed to think."

"To hell with Wally Crottel. So—off I went to bed and to sleep, and about two o'clock Arthur came into the room and got into bed with me."

"Not unusual, I suppose."

"Not entirely usual, either. Since his illness, Arthur has a room of his own, where he usually sleeps, but of course he comes into my room when it's sex, you see. So I wasn't surprised."

"And it was Arthur?"

"Who else would it be? And it was wearing Arthur's dressing

gown. You know the one. I gave it to him soon after we were married, and I had it made in King Arthur's colours and with King Arthur's device: a green dragon, crowned in red, on a gold shield. You couldn't mistake it. I could feel the embroidered dragon on the back. He slipped into my bed, opened the dressing-gown, and there we were."

"All very much according to Hoyle."

"Yes."

"Maria, I don't believe a word of it."

"But I did. Or a very important part of me did. I took him as Arthur."

"And did he take you as Arthur?"

"That's what's so hard to explain. When a man comes into your very dark room, and you can feel your husband's dressing-gown that you know so well, and he takes you so wonderfully that all the doubt and dissatisfaction of weeks past melt away, do you ask him to identify himself?"

"He didn't speak?"

"Not a word. He didn't need to."

"Maria, it's awfully fishy. I'm no great expert but surely there are things you expect and are used to—caresses, sounds, and of course smells. Did he smell like Arthur?"

"I don't remember."

"Come on, Maria. That won't do."

"Well—yes and no."

"But you didn't protest."

"Does one protest at such a time?"

"No, I don't suppose one does. I do think I understand, you know."

"Thanks, Simon. I hoped you might. But one can't be sure. Men are so incalculable about things like that."

"You said it all yourself a few minutes ago. It's a story that roams back through the ages, and it's a story that doesn't grow old. It's the Demon Lover. Have you told Arthur?"

"How can I, when he's being so restrained and bloody saintly?"

"You'd better try. Arthur understands a lot of things you wouldn't suspect. And Arthur isn't perfectly in the clear in this affair. He didn't tell you what you had a right to know. You and

Arthur had better have a *divano*. Nothing like a good Gypsy *divano* to clear the air."

[5]

THERE IS A SPECIAL FRUSTRATION that afflicts authors when they cannot claim enough time for their own work, and Darcourt was unwontedly irritable because he was not getting on with his life of the late Francis Cornish. The sudden illumination that had struck him in the drawing-room of Princess Amalie and Prince Max demanded to be explored and enlarged, and was he doing that? No, he was involved in the unhappiness of Arthur and Maria, and because he was truly a compassionate man—though he detested what the world thought was compassion—he spent a great deal of time thinking about them and indeed worrying about them. Like most dispensers of wisdom, Darcourt was bad at taking his own medicine. Worrying and fretting will do no good, he told his friends, and then when they had left him he fell into quicksands of worry and fretfulness on their behalf. He was supposed to be enjoying a sabbatical year from his university work, but the professor who does not leave his campus knows that no complete abandonment of responsibility is possible.

There was Penny Raven, for instance. Penny, who seemed to be the complete academic woman, scholarly, well-organized, and sensible, was in a dither about whatever was going on between Schnak and Gunilla Dahl-Soot. What was it? Do you know anything, Simon? Darcourt tried to be patient during her long telephone calls. I know that the Doctor and Schnak are getting on like a house afire with this opera, and are merciless in their demands on me that I should supply new material for the libretto, or change and tinker stuff I have already done: I am in and out of their house at least once a day, fussing over scraps of recitative; I never realized that a librettist lived such a dog's life. Verdi was an old softy compared with Gunilla. They are working, Penny, working!—Yes, yes, Simon, I realize that, but they can't work all the time. What is the atmosphere? I hate to think of that poor kid being dragged into something she can't handle.—The atmosphere is fine: master guiding but not dominating pupil, and pupil blossoming like the rose—well, perhaps not like the rose, but at least putting on a few shy flowers—clean and well-fed and now and then giving a sandy little laugh.—Yes, Simon, but *how?* What price is being paid?—I don't know, Penny, and frankly I don't care because it's none of my business. I am not a nursemaid. Why don't you go and see for yourself? You were supposed to be working with me on this libretto and so far you have done sweet-bugger-all.—Oh, but you're so good at that kind of thing, Simon, and I have this big paper to get ready for the next meeting of the Learned Societies and honestly I haven't a moment. But I'll come in at the end and touch up, I promise.—The hell you will, Penny. If I do it there'll be no touching up. I get all the touching up I need from Nilla, and in English verse she has a touch like a blacksmith.—All right, if you want to disclaim all responsibility for a young person who is supposed to be in your care, at least to some extent.—Not in my care, Penny; if she's in anybody's care it is Wintersen's care, and you won't get any out-raged moral action out of him. And if you insist on sticking your nose in, you may get it punched by Schnak, so I warn you.—Oh, very well. Very well. But I'm worried and disappointed.—Good, Penny; you get right on with that. Meanwhile, do you know a two-syllable word meaning "regret" that isn't "regret"? Because "regret" isn't a word that sings well if it has to be matched up with a quarter-note followed by an eighth-note. That's the kind of thing I have to cope with. Listen—I think I've got it! How about "dolour"? Lovely word, right out of Malory, and the accent falls on the first syllable and pips off on the second. Singable! A nice big open vowel followed by a little one.—No, Simon. Won't do at all. Too olden-timesy and cutesy.—Oh, God, Penny! Get off my back, you—you *critic!*

Lots of conversations like that. Powell was right. Penny was jealous, mad as a wet hen because Gunilla had taken on Schnak as—what? As a pupil, of course, but also as a—what do you call it? When it's a man there are plenty of words. A minion, a pathic, a catamite, a bardash, a bumchum—but, when it was a woman? Darcourt knew no word for it. *Petite amie* might do. Did Penny want Schnak for herself? No, that wasn't Penny's style at all. In so far as she was anything of a sexual nature, Penny was a lesbian, but of the smothery-mothery variety, brooding possessively over the successes of her little darlings. Sexually a dog-in-the-manger, who would not eat herself, or suffer others to eat. Penny resented the buccaneering success of Dr. Gunilla, the easy command, the scorn of Kater Murr.

But every day, and all day, and sometimes in dreams, the biography of Francis Cornish nagged. Was it really fated to be such a worthy, dull, unremarkable book? The spy stuff was not bad but he wanted something bigger.

It was that picture, *The Marriage at Cana.* Where had he seen those faces? Not among the mass of drawings and rough sketches he had sent to the National Gallery. The picture was surely the lock that secured the real life of Francis Cornish, but where was the key? Nothing to do but search, and search, and search again. But where?

It was lucky that he was so very much *persona grata* at the University Library, where all the left-overs from Francis Cornish's crowded apartments were locked away, awaiting the attention of cataloguers. Certainly that material would not receive such attention quickly, because those packages were precisely what he had called them when he first transferred them to the Library. They were left-overs. Francis Cornish's splendid pictures, his enviable collection of modern art, Canadian modern art, Old Master drawings, rare books, and expensive art books, his musical manuscript accumulation (it was not sufficiently coherent to be thought of as a collection), and everything else of any value had gone to the galleries and library where they would be, in the glacier-like progress of cataloguing, put in order. But there was still the mass of left-overs, the stuff which had been glanced at, but under the pressure of time not thoroughly examined by him in his capacity as an executor with a job to do quickly.

Without any great hope in his heart, Darcourt decided that he must rummage through the left-overs. He told his friend at the Library what he wanted to do, and was promised every help. But help was exactly what he did not want. He wanted to snoop, and seek, and see if anything would crop up that would give him a hint about the astonishing picture.

The picture itself was known to the art world, though few people had seen it. But there was, of course, the definitive article that had been written about it by Aylwin Ross, and which had appeared in *Apollo* a few years ago. Before Francis Cornish died, so he must have been acquainted with it. Must surely have approved it, or at least kept quiet about it. The article was well illustrated, and when Darcourt dug it out of the Library's files of *Apollo* it troubled him with new urgency. He read and reread Ross's elaborate, elegantly written explanation of the picture, its historical implications (something about the Augsburg Interim and the attempt to reconcile the Church of Rome with the Protestants of the Reformation), and Ross had concluded that the picture was the work of an unknown painter, but a master of fine attainment, whom he chose to identify simply as The Alchemical Master, because of some alchemical elements he identified in the triptych.

But those faces? Faces that seemed in some way familiar, when he saw the picture itself, in New York. They were not so compelling in the reproductions in *Apollo,* careful and excellent as those were. But there is a quality in an original canvas that no reproduction, however skilled, fully conveys. The people in the picture were alive in a way the people in the pages of *Apollo* were not. Those faces? He had seen at least some of them somewhere, and Darcourt was good at remembering faces. But where?

Nothing to do but go painstakingly through every scrap of unconsidered material that had been cleared out of Francis Cornish's Old Curiosity Shop of a dwelling when he, and Clement Hollier, and the late unlamented Professor Urquhart McVarish had worked as executors of the dead man's possessions. Could Urky McVarish have pinched anything vital? Probable enough, for Urky was a fine example of that rare but not unknown creature, the academic crook. (With a pang Darcourt recognized that he was already far advanced in that category himself, but, of course, being himself, it was rather different.) But it would not do to assume that there was no clue to the great picture until he had sifted every possible portfolio and parcel, and the best thing would be to start at the bottom.

So, clad in slacks and a sweat-shirt in preparation for dirty work, Darcourt went to the Library, and with Archie's warm assent, began at the bottom.

The bottom was surely some stuff that neither he, nor Hollier, nor McVarish, had touched, because it did not seem to be directly

related either to Cornish's collections or to Cornish himself. A
secretary, who had been lent to the executors by Arthur Cornish,
had been asked to do the dirty work—as secretaries usually are—
and bundle up all this junk and—what? Oh, put it with the stuff
for the Library. They can throw it out when they get to it, which
may not be for years. We are in a hurry, hustled on to complete
a heavy task by the impatient Arthur Cornish.

There it was, quite a heap of it, neatly bundled and wrapped,
a proper secretarial job. Many hours of tedious search in those
bundles. Darcourt had been an active parson for almost twenty
years before he contrived to get himself appointed a professor
of Greek, and left work he had come to dislike. But the parson
years had made their mark, and as he tackled the mass, he found
himself humming.

Hums can be important. Hums can tell of a state of mind of
which the topmost layer of consciousness is unaware. Darcourt
was humming an old favourite of his own:

> Guide me, O Thou great Jehovah,
>   Pilgrim through this barren land;
> I am weak, but Thou art mighty;
>   Hold me with Thy powerful hand;
>   Bread of Heaven,
> Feed me till I want no more.

A great prayer, and because it came from the depths, and not
from the busy, fussing top of the mind, it was answered. Oh,
surely not answered? Are prayers ever answered? Can the thoroughly modern mind admit such nonsense?

The secretary had labelled every bundle in a neat, impersonal
hand. There were no letters, and anyhow Darcourt had been all
through whatever correspondence Francis Cornish had preserved.
But there were bundles of newspapers, containing reports of
artistic matters, all jumbled together but many of them about
artistic forgeries, either suspected or detected. Francis had the
horrible habit of keeping the whole newspaper, in which the
relevant item was marked with a blue pencil, instead of cutting
out what he wanted and filing it, as a man with any regard for his
heirs would have done. There were several parcels of yellowing

newspapers. Darcourt felt a biographer's guilt; he should have sifted this stuff, and he would do so, but not yet. Some of the marked articles were about the affairs, or the deaths, of people of whom Darcourt knew nothing. People suspected in Francis Cornish's Secret Service days? It could be. It was clear that as a spy Francis was sloppy and unmethodical. But here, right at the bottom, were six big packages, marked Photographs Not Personal. Surely nothing there? Darcourt had already ferreted out photographs of all the people that he needed to illustrate his book. Photographers keep very tidy files, and that had not been difficult; merely tedious. But he had determined to look at everything, and he untied the bundles, and found that they were old-fashioned family albums.

They were neat, and they were fussy, and every picture was identified underneath it in a tidy, old-fashioned hand. Ah, yes; the handwriting of Francis's grandfather, and the albums were the work, the beloved hobby, of the old Senator, Hamish McRory. He must have spent a good deal of money on them, for they had been specially made and every album was identified on its cover, in gold printing that had not tarnished (so it must have been true gold leaf), "Sun Pictures".

They were more personal than the secretary had suspected from a quick examination. The first three looked like a record of a turn-of-the-century Ontario town, streets deep in mud, or snow, or baked by summer sun, with lurching, drunken telephone poles and cobwebs of wires, and in the streets were horse-and-rig equipages, huge drays laden with immense, unmilled logs drawn by four horses apiece, and citizens in the dress of the day, some blurred because the Senator's lens had not been quick enough to stop them in action. There were scenes in a lumber-camp, where men struggled with chains and crude hoists to heave those immense logs onto the drays. There were loggers, strong men with huge beards, standing with their big woodsmen's axes beside trees they had felled, or sawn through. There were pictures of horses, giant Percherons, poorly groomed but well fed, and they too had their names carefully entered: Daisy, Old Nick, Lady Laurier, Tommy, Big Eustache, horses that dragged the logs from the forests, patient, reliable, and strong as elephants. This is where the first Cornish money came from, thought Darcourt. From lumbering, when lumbering was a very different matter from what it is today. Pictures of saw-pits, with the top-sawyer standing on the log above his monstrous saw, and the under-sawyer peeping from the bottom of the pit. Were they proud that the Senator had wanted to take their pictures? Their stiff faces betrayed nothing, but they had a look of pride in their bodies; they were men who knew their work. Fine stuff, this. A record of a Canada gone forever. Some social historian would love to get his hands on it. But there was nothing here of the faces Darcourt hoped to find.

On to the other three. This looked more promising. Priests, in soutanes and birettas, sitting in constrained postures beside a little table, on which a book lay open. A sharp-looking little man, obviously a doctor, for on his table lay an old-fashioned straight stethoscope and a skull. But this woman, in the little cap? This woman standing at her kitchen door, holding a basin and a ladle? These were the faces Darcourt wanted. Could they be—?

Yes, indeed they were. Look, here in the fifth album! A lovely girl, and certainly Francis's mother in her youth. A stiff, soldierly man, wearing an eyeglass. Beyond a doubt these were the Lady and the one-eyed Knight from *The Marriage at Cana.* Underneath, the Senator had written, "Mary-Jim and Frank, their first week in Blairlogie". Francis's parents but not as he knew them from later pictures; these were Mary-Jim and Frank as the child Francis first knew them. And then—this was a treasure, this was the clincher!—a handsome, dark-browed young man, perhaps not more than eighteen; this was "My grandson Francis, on leaving Colborne College, 1929".

So there it was! He had the key to the lock in his hand at last! But was Darcourt excited, exultant? No, he was very calm, like a man from whom doubt and anxiety had all been swept away. Patience has been rewarded, he thought, and then put the thought from him as savouring of pride. There was one album left.

"Thou hast kept the best wine till the last". The inscribed banner that floated from the mouth of that strange angel in *The Marriage at Cana* was proven by what he now turned over, with a feeling of wonder. "My coachman, Zadok Hoyle"; the fine-looking, soldierly, but—to the observant eye—unlucky man who stood by a fine carriage and a pair of bays was unquestionably the *huissier,* the jolly man with the whip in *The Marriage.* And then—

at last Darcourt lost his calm, phlegmatic acceptance of his great good luck—here, among pictures of bearded, ancient, youthful, hearty, and unstable citizens of Blairlogie at the turn of the century, was a picture of a dwarf, standing in front of a humble shop, squinting into the sun but grinning subserviently as the Senator—the local great man—took his Sun Picture. And underneath was written, "F. X. Bouchard, tailor". The dwarf who stood so confidently, so proudly, in *The Marriage* and—just possibly—the original of Drollig Hansel.

Was this—could it be—the awakening of the little man?

The kindly assistant librarian popped her head around the partition.

"Would you like a cup of coffee, Professor Darcourt?"

"By God, I would," said Simon, and the secretary, somewhat startled by the vehemence of his reply, set before him a waxed-paper cup of the liquid which the staff of the Library called, with scholarly generosity, coffee.

It was in this lukewarm, muddy draught that Darcourt drank to his good fortune. Here he sat, amid the evidence that settled a mystery of significance to the world of art. He, Simon Darcourt, had identified the figures in *The Marriage at Cana,* thereby showing it to be of our own time, telling in a finely contrived riddle the life experience of the painter. He had destroyed the fine-spun theory of Aylwin Ross and identified for all time The Alchemical Master.

It was the last Francis Cornish.

But it was not of the sensation in the art world Darcourt thought. It was of his book. His biography. It was not merely lifted out of the dullness he had feared; it had taken wings.

Like a good scholar he piled up the albums neatly on the big table in the alcove he was using. Never leave a mess. He blessed Francis Cornish and the primary precept of scholarship: never throw anything away. He would return tomorrow and make copious notes.

As he worked he was humming again. One of the metrical Psalms, this time.

> *That stone is made head corner-stone,*
> *Which builders did despise;*

This is the doing of the Lord,
And wondrous in his eyes.

[6]

OTTAWA IS NOT A PLACE to which anyone goes at the end of November simply for pleasure. Reputedly the coldest capital city in the world, in comparison with which Moscow is merely chilly, it is preparing at the end of the year for its annual ferocious assault on the endurance, good nature, and ingenuity of its inhabitants. Darcourt was glad that the National Gallery was luxuriously warm, and he scuttled between it and his hotel, his collar turned up against the sneaping winds from the river and the canal, cold in body but deliciously warm in spirit. Everything he found out from yet another and rigorous examination of what Francis Cornish had defined as his Old Master Drawings confirmed the great discovery he had made in the University Library.

Like everything else Francis had left behind him, the many portfolios and envelopes were a jumble, but a jumble of treasures, some substantial and some of less importance. The assemblages of Francis's own drawings were honestly labelled; student work, mostly; creditable in the detailed care they showed, and a little eccentric in the trouble the artist had taken in finding real old paper for his work, and preparing it for his silver-point studies. Why so much trouble for what was, after all, simply a student exercise? Each drawing was labelled, with detailed information about which original had been copied, and the date when the copy had been made. But there was about them a hint, which Darcourt took care not to allow to swell into a certainty, that the copy was almost as good as the original and in some cases was every bit as good—though it was identified as a copy. Francis, in another century and with a living to make, could have done well as one of those patient copyists who supplied wealthy tourists with copies of drawings they admired. The talent of the copyist may be very great—technically greater than that of many artists who would scorn such work and have no talent for it—but he remains a copyist.

There was one large brown envelope that Darcourt opened last, because he had a sense that it could contain what he was looking for. He wanted to tease himself, to work up an expectation that amounted almost to a fever, like a child that saves one parcel of its Christmas horde in vehement hope that it contains the gift most eagerly desired. Unlike the others, it was sealed; the gummed flap had been stuck down, instead of being merely tucked in, as was the case with all the others. It was labelled, not "Old Master Drawings", but "My Drawings in Old Master style, for the National Gallery". The Gallery authorities would probably not have allowed him to open it, or not without some Gallery representative being at his elbow as he did so, but Darcourt, who now regarded himself as a thorough-going crook, managed to sneak into the little kitchen where Gallery workers made their tea and coffee and secreted their biscuits, and quickly and efficiently steamed it open. And there it all was. If he had been a fainting man, he would have fainted.

Here were preliminary sketches for *The Marriage at Cana;* several plans for the groupings of the figures, and quick studies for heads, arms, clothes, and armour for the figures—and every head was a likeness, though not always a wholly faithful likeness, of somebody in the Sun Pictures taken by Grandfather James Ignatius McRory. No, not quite *every* head; the woman who stood in the centre panel was unknown to Grandfather, but she was very well known to Darcourt. She was Ismay Glasson, wife of Francis Cornish and mother of Little Charlie. Nor was there any source in the Sun Pictures for the figure of Judas; but he was Tancred Saraceni, caricatured in several of Francis's notebooks and plainly labelled. And the dwarf, so vaunting in *The Marriage,* so self-doubting in the photography; F. X. Bouchard, beyond a doubt. And the *huissier;* Zadok Hoyle, Grandfather's coachman. Why was he important enough to be included in the composition? Darcourt hoped that somehow he might find out, but it was not vital that he do so.

Most mysterious were the studies of that angel, who flew so confidently above the centre panel—so confidently that his influence extended over the whole three panels of the work. But here he was, and one of those drawings was identified as F. C., and although those were Cornish's own initials, this angel was certainly not Francis Cornish.—Was the drawing merely signed, in an idle moment? Or was this crazed, yet inexorably compelling and potent figure—this spook, this grotesque—some notion Francis cherished of his inner self? Had he thought so strangely of himself? Another puzzle, and Darcourt hoped he might solve it, but knew that he had no need to do so. Here were the originals of the people in *The Marriage,* and if not all of them could be equated with people Francis and Grandfather McRory had known, that did nothing to lessen the importance of his discovery. It was with a light heart that Darcourt carefully resealed the envelope, and left the Gallery, with much affability toward those who had permitted him to seek for material which they assumed, and quite rightly, was for information that would flesh out his biography of their dead benefactor.

Darcourt wanted time to come to terms with his discovery, surely the most extraordinary piece of luck that had ever come his way, so he travelled back to Toronto by train, and the journey, which would have taken just under an hour by air, filled the greater part of a day. It was just what he needed. The train was not crowded, and its alternation of simoom-like heat and bitter November draughts was vastly preferable to the "pressurized" atmosphere of a plane. What the train lacked in food—there were sandwiches of the usual railway variety—he made good with a large bar of chocolate and nuts. He had a book in his lap, for he was the kind of man who must always have a book near as a protective talisman, but did not look at it. He thought about his find. He gloated. He looked out at the sere, desolate landscape of Eastern Ontario in November, and the bleak towns, so charmless, so humble; to his gaze it might have been the Garden of Eden and all the chilled passers-by so many Adams and Eves. Sentences formed in his mind; he fastidiously chose adjectives; he rejected tempting flights into literary extravagance; he thought of several modest ways of presenting his great discovery, which wholly changed the idea the world was to receive of the late Francis Cornish. His journey passed in something as near to bliss as he had ever known.

Bliss ended with the journey. When he arrived back at his college the porter gave him a telephone message; he was to call Arthur as soon as possible.

"Simon, I've rather an important favour to ask. I know you're busy, but will you drop everything and go to Stratford at once? To see Powell."

"What about?"

"Don't you know? Don't you read the papers? He's in hospital, rather badly banged up."

"What happened?"

"Car accident last night. Apparently he was driving recklessly. In fact he was driving through the park, next to the Festival Theatre, at great speed, and ran into a tree."

"Skidded off the road?"

"He wasn't on the road. He was in the park itself, zigzagging among the trees and yelling like a wild man. Very drunk, they say. He's all smashed up. We're terribly worried about him."

"Naturally. But why don't you go yourself?"

"Bit delicate. Complications. Apparently he raved a lot under anaesthetic, and the surgeon called me to explain—and see if I had anything to say. He babbled a lot about Maria and me, and if we rush down there to see him it lends colour to a lot of speculation among the theatre people. You know what they are. But somebody must go. Indecent not to. Will you? Hire a car, of course, it's Foundation business as much as it's anything. Do go, Simon. Please."

"Of course I'll go if it's necessary. But do you mean he's spilled the beans?"

"Quite a few beans. The surgeon said that of course people fantasize under anaesthetic, and nobody takes it seriously."

"Except that he took it seriously enough to tip you off."

"There were assistants and nurses around when he was patching Geraint up—and you know how hospital people talk."

"I know how all people talk, when they think they've got hold of a juicy morsel."

"So you'll go? Simon, you *are* a good friend! And you'll call us as soon as you get back?"

"Is Maria worried?"

"We're both worried."

That was a good thing, thought Darcourt, as he sped toward Stratford in his hired limousine. If they were both worried about the same thing, and that thing was the mess they were in with

Powell, it might bring them together, and put an end to all that polite conversation about nothing. Darcourt was in a somewhat cynical frame of mind, for he had gobbled a snack while waiting for the car, and it was not sitting well with all the chocolate he had eaten in the train. Indigestion is a great begetter of cynicism. In the back seat of the car, dashing through the November darkness, he had lost the happy mood of the daytime; here he was again, good old Simon, the abbé at the court of the Cornish Foundation, the reliable old fire-engine sent off to quench a blaze of gossip that Arthur and Maria took seriously.

We live in an age of sexual liberation, he thought, when people are not supposed to take marital fidelity seriously, and when adultery, and fornication, and all uncleanness are perfectly okay—except when they come near home. When that happens, there may be uproars that awaken the gossip columnists, alert the divorce lawyers, and sometimes end in the criminal courts. Especially so among prominent people, and Arthur, and Maria, and Geraint Powell were all, in their various ways, prominent, and just as touchy as everybody else. Darcourt was of Old Ontario stock, descendant of United Empire Loyalists, and from time to time an Old Ontario saw seemed to him to sum up a situation: "It all depends whose ox is gored". The Cornish ox had been gored, and it was probably impossible to conceal the wound. Still, he must rush to stick a Band-Aid on the bleeding place.

Powell was in one of those hospital rooms which are described as "semi-private"; this meant that he lay in the part of the room nearest the door, and on the other side of the white curtain that split the room down the middle lay somebody who had hired one of the hospital television sets; he was listening to a hockey game, apparently of the first importance, with the volume turned well up. The commentators were describing the play and discussing its significance, in a high state of excitement.

"Oh, Sim *bach*, you darling man! How good of you to come! Would you ask that bugger to turn down his bloody machine?"

Geraint's head was heavily bandaged, though his face could be seen; it was bruised, but no wounds were visible. One arm was in plaster, and his left leg, swathed in some medical wrapping, was hoisted upward in a sling that hung from a metal brace attached to the bed.

"Would you please turn down the volume of your set? My friend is very ill and we want to talk."

"Hey? What did you say? You'll have to speak up; I'm a bit deaf. Great game, eh? The Hatters have got the Soviet team on the run. My pet team. The Medicine Hatters. Best in the League. If they win this one, we might get the Cup yet. Big night, eh?"

"Yes, but could you turn it down a bit? My friend is very ill."

"Is he? This'll cheer him up. Would you like to pull back the curtain so he can see?"

"Thank you, a very kind offer. But he really is suffering."

"This'll fix him. Hey—did you see that? Just missed it! Donnicker is in great shape tonight. He's showing those Russkies what defence work is. Hey—look at that! Wowie!"

It appeared that nothing could be done. The man in the other bed was gripped by the ruling passion, and it was hopeless to talk to him.

"Well, old man, how are you?" said Darcourt.

"I am at the head of the Valley of Grief in the Uplands of Hell," Geraint replied.

He's had that one ready, thought Darcourt. This may be heavy going.

"I came as soon as I knew. What on earth has happened to you?"

"Retribution, Sim *bach*. I have made an utter balls of everything! My life is in tatters and I have nobody to blame but myself. This is punishment for sin, and I have nothing to do but accept it, swallow it, suffer it, take up my cross, prostrate myself before the Throne, and die! It runs in my family; my great-grandfather and my Uncle David both died of disgrace and despair. Turned their faces to the wall. I am trying to die. It's the least I can do under the circumstances. Oh God, my head!"

Darcourt sought out a nurse; she was down the hall at the nursing-station, where she and a clutch of nurses and interns were huddled around a tiny television screen, watching the great game. But she came long enough to go to the other side of the white curtain and turn down the set of the enthusiast who shared the semi-private, who protested that his deafness required greater volume. She also, at his urgent request, brought Darcourt a glass of Alka-Seltzer to assuage his raging stomach. In the somewhat less uproarious atmosphere, he tried to soothe Powell.

"Now Geraint, don't talk like that. They tell me you are doing nicely, considering everything. You are not going to die, so put that idea right out of your head. You will be up and around in about three weeks, they say, and must be quiet and help the medical people all you can."

"A positive attitude! That's what they keep telling me. 'You must take a positive attitude, because it helps greatly with the healing, and in a few weeks you'll be right as rain.' But I don't want to be right as rain! I don't deserve it. Let the tempest rage!"

"Oh, come on, Geraint! Don't carry on like that!"

"Carry on? *Carry on?* Sim *bach,* that is a bruising expression. Oh, how my head hurts!"

"Of course your head hurts when you shout like that. Just whisper. I can hear you if I come really close. Now tell me what happened."

"Malory, Sim *bach.* Malory is what happened. The night before last I was reading Malory; it quiets the mind, and it brings me very near to Arthur—King Arthur, I mean—and his court and his great schemes and his afflictions. My book fell open at the Madness of Lancelot. You know it? You must; everybody does."

"I remember it."

"Then you know what it says: 'he lepte oute at a bay-wyndow into a gardyne, and there wyth thornys he was all to-cracched of hys vysage and hys body, and so he ranne furth he knew not whothir, and was as wylde as ever man was. And so he ran two yere, and never man had grace to know him.' "

"And that is what you did?"

"In modern terms, that is what I did. I had been having a few, naturally, and reflecting on my outcast state, and the more I thought, the more of a miserable wretch I knew I was, and suddenly I couldn't hold in any longer. I leapt out of my window— not a bay—and on the ground floor by the mercy of God. I got into my car, and drove like hell, I don't remember where, but I ended up in that park and you know how spooky woods are at night, and as I drove the feeling became more and more Arthurian and Maloryesque, and there I was, roaring around among the trees, making sharp turns and narrow circles—all at incredible speed, boy; a great racing driver has been lost in me—and I became conscious that courtly pavilions were appearing out of the woods to the right and left—"

"The public conveniences, I understand. You very nearly smashed into them."

"That be damned! It was a great pavilion, a mighty tent, with flags floating."

"That must have been the Festival Theatre."

"Armed men and peasantry were skipping about among the trees, marvelling at me."

"The police certainly. I don't know about the peasantry, but there were plenty of witnesses. That's a very easily identified car you drive."

"Don't belittle my agony, Sim *bach;* don't reduce it to mere every-day. This was an Arthurian madness—the madness of Lancelot. Then everything went black."

"You hit a tree. You were crazy-drunk and driving very much to the public danger in a public park, and you hit a tree. I've been reading the papers on my way here. Now look, Geraint: I don't underestimate your temperament, or your involvement with Malory, but facts are facts."

"Yes, but what are the facts? I am not talking about police-court facts, or newspaper lies, but psychological facts. I was in the grip of a great archetypal experience, and what it looked like to outsiders doesn't count. Listen; listen to me."

"I'm listening, but you mustn't expect me to rush off into the moonshine with you, Geraint. Understand that."

"Sim—Sim, my dear old friend. Sim, who out of all mankind I look to for sympathetic understanding, hear me. You are very harsh, boy. Your tongue is so sharp it would draw blood from the wind. Sim, you don't know what I am. I am the son of a man of God. My father, now singing a rich bass in the Choir Invisible, was a very well known Calvinistic Methodist minister in Wales. He brought me up in the knowledge and fear of God. You know what that means. You are a man of God yourself, though of the episcopal, ritualist sort, for which I forgive you, but you must have the true knowledge in you someplace."

"I hope so."

"Sim—I have never forgotten or really forsaken my early doctrine, though my life has taken me into the world of art, which is God's world too, though horribly flawed in many of its aspects. I have sinned greatly, but never against art. You know what has been my downfall?"

"Yes. Booze."

"Oh, Sim, that is unworthy! A drop now and then to ease deep inner pain, but never my downfall. No, no; my downfall was the flesh."

"Woman, you mean?"

"Not woman, Sim. I have never been dissolute. No, not woman, but Woman, that highest embodiment of God's glory and goodness, with whom I have tried to enlarge myself and raise myself. But, wretch that I am, I took the wrong path. The flesh, Sim, the flesh!"

"Your best friend's wife?"

"The last—and undoubtedly the greatest—of many. You see, Sim, God tempts us. Oh yes, He does. Don't let us pretend otherwise. Why do we pray not to be led into temptation?"

"We pray not to be put to the test."

"All right, but we are put to the test, and for some of us the test is a right bugger, let me tell you, Sim *bach*. Look here: why did God endow me with a Byronic temperament, Byronic beauty of face, a Byronic irresistibility?"

"I have no idea."

"No, you haven't. You are a great soul, Sim; a great, calm soul, but nothing to speak of in the way of physical attraction, if I may be allowed the frankness of a friend. So you don't know what it's like to see some marvellous woman and think, 'That's mine, if I choose to put out my hand and take it.' You've never felt that?"

"No, I haven't, really."

"There you are, you see. But that has been my life. Oh, the flesh! the flesh!"

The man on the other side of the white curtain was pushing it as hard as he could with his hand. "Hey, knock it off, you guys, will you? How do you expect me to hear the game if you yell like that?"

"Shhh! Keep your voice down, Sim, like a good man. This is confidential. Call it a confession, if you like. Where was I? Yes, the flesh; that was it.

> Love not as do the flesh-imprisoned men
> Whose dreams are of a bitter bought caress,
> Or even of a maiden's tenderness
> Whom they love only that she loves again,
> For it is but thyself thou lovest then—

You know that? Santayana—and there are people who say he wasn't a fine poet! That was me; my love was all self-love and I have been a flesh-imprisoned man."

Geraint's face was wet with tears. Darcourt, who felt that this interview was going all wrong, but who had not a hard heart, wiped them away with his own handkerchief. But somehow he had to reduce this outpouring to order.

"Are you telling me that you seduced Maria just to test your power? Geraint, this two-bit Byronic act of yours has brought great unhappiness into the life of Arthur, whom you insist is your friend."

"It's this opera, Sim. You can't pretend a thing like that is just a stage-piece. It's a huge influence, if it's any good at all, and this thing is going to be good. I know it. This opera has brought me back to Malory, and Maria—whom I truly love as a friend and not as a man desires a woman—is nonetheless a real Malory-woman. So free, so direct, so simple, and yet so great in spirit and so enchanting. You must feel that?"

"I know what you are talking about."

"I knew it the first time I met her. What does Malory say? 'A fair lady and a passynge wise'. But I never said a word. I was true to Arthur."

"But you couldn't stay true."

"There came that night when we were talking about disguise, and I said that the beholder in very strong situations is a partner in the deception. He wills his own belief to agree with the desire of the deceiver. And Maria was scornful of that. Which surprised me, because she is so learned in medieval things, and surely has enough sense to understand that what underlay so much medieval belief is still alive in our minds today, and only waits for the word, or the situation, to wake it up and set it to work. That is often how we fall into these archetypal involvements, that don't seem to make any sense on the surface of things, but make irresistible, compelling sense in the world below the surface. Didn't Maria know that? I couldn't think otherwise for a minute."

"Well—you may have a point there."

"And so there came that night when Arthur was away, and I had dinner with Maria and we worked till midnight at business details; contracts and agreements and orders for materials and all the complexity of stuff that is involved in a job like getting this opera on the stage. Not a word did we say that Arthur could not have heard. But from time to time I felt her looking at me, and I knew that look. But I never looked back. Not once. If I had, I think that would have been the end of it, because Maria would have understood what was happening, and she would have checked it in herself, and in me, too, of course."

"Let's hope so."

"It was when I went to bed that I found I could not forget those looks, and I could not forget the laughing, rational Maria who had made fun of my theory of disguise. There I lay in bed, remembering those looks. So—I slipped into Arthur's room, and pinched his dressing-gown, which was that very Arthurian thing Maria had made for him, when they were newly married and were still joking about the Round Table, and the Platter of Plenty and all that, and I put it on over my nakedness, and stole barefoot into Maria's room, and there she was, asleep or almost asleep. A vision, Sim: a vision. And I demonstrated that my theory was true."

"Did you? Could you swear she thought you were Arthur?"

"How do I know what she thought? But she didn't resist. Was she under a delusion? I know I was. I was deep in such a tale as Malory might have told. It was an enchantment, a spell."

"Now, just a minute, Geraint. That wasn't Arthur's Queen, that was Elaine Lancelot visited in that way."

"Don't quibble. As a situation it was pure Malory."

"She must have known your voice."

"Oh, Sim, what an innocent you are! We did not speak a word. No words were wanted."

"Well, I'm damned."

"No, Sim, you are not damned. But I think I am damned. This was more than adultery. I was a thief in the night—a thief of honour. It was breaking faith with a friend."

"With two friends, surely?"

"I don't think so. With one friend. With Arthur."

"You put Arthur before Maria, whom you seduced?"

"I know that I deceived Arthur. I can't say if I deceived Maria."

"Well, whatever the fine points are, Maria is going to have a child, and it's certainly yours. Did you know that?"

"I know. Arthur told me. He wept, Sim, and every tear was like blood from my heart. That's something I can never forget. I wish I were dead."

"Geraint, that's self-indulgent rubbish! You're not going to die, and Maria is going to have your child, and Arthur will have to find some way of swallowing the pill."

"You see it from the outside."

"Of course. I am on the outside, but I was a friend of Arthur and Maria before you were, and I shall have to do anything I can to make things work."

"Don't you think of yourself as a friend of mine, Sim? Don't I need you at least as much as the other two? Me, the flesh-imprisoned man?"

"Stop blethering about the flesh as if it were the Devil himself!"

"What else is it? The Enemy of God, the Poison of Man, the livery of hell, the image of the animal, the Sinner's Beloved, the Hypocrite's refuge, the Spider's Web, the Merchant of Souls, the home of the lost, and the demon's dung-hill."

"My God, is that what you think?"

"That is what my father thought. I remember him thundering those words from the pulpit. He was quoting one of our Welsh poet-divines, the great Morgan Llwyd. Isn't it lovely, Sim? Could you put it better?"

Powell, whose normal voice was impressive, had risen to a

Miltonic resonance and grandeur, declaiming with bardic vehemence; the man in the neighbouring, concealed bed was cheering at the top of his voice. The Hatters had won! Won by a last-minute exploit of the redoubtable Donniker!

A small nurse, big with authority and anger, burst into the room.

"What's going on in here? Have you people gone crazy? Everybody on the corridor is complaining. We've got some very sick people on this floor, if you don't know it. You'll have to go."

She took Darcourt by the arm, as he was the only able-bodied rowdy, and pushed him firmly toward the door. In his astonishment and confusion at the goings-on of Geraint, he had no resistance, and allowed himself to be, in a moderate use of the term, thrown out.

[7]

DARCOURT WAS LOOKING FORWARD to his Christmas holiday. The doings of the autumn had worn him out, or so he thought. It was true that the mess of Arthur, Maria, and Powell drew heavily on his spiritual resources; although he was not at the centre of the affair, it seemed that he was expected to be confidant and adviser to all three, and that meant that he had to listen to them, give them advice—and then listen again while they rejected it. Of the three, Maria was the least troublesome. Her course was clear; she was going to have a baby, but for a woman of brains, highly educated and with a background sufficiently unusual to put her above bourgeois conventionalities, she was making heavy weather of it, and had decided that she had wronged Arthur irreparably. Arthur was being magnanimous; he had taken upon himself the role of The Magnanimous Cuckold and was acting it to the hilt. Magnanimity can be extremely vexatious to the bystanders, for it forces them into secondary roles that are not much fun to play. Powell was enjoying himself, finding new rhetorical ways of expressing his sense of guilt, and trying them out on his friend Simon whenever he visited the hospital.

It would all have been so much simpler if all three had not been utterly sincere. They were sure they meant everything they said—even Powell, who said so much, and said it so gaudily, and enjoyed saying it. If they had been fools, Darcourt could have told them so and called them to order. But they were not fools; they were people who found themselves in a tangle from which they could not escape and for which their superficial modernity of opinion offered no solace. Modern opinion stood no chance against the clamour of voices from—from where? From the past, it seemed. Darcourt did his best and poured out comfort as well as he could.

His chief difficulty was that he did not, himself, place much value on comfort. He regarded it as the sugar-teat stupid mothers pop into the mouth of the crying baby. He wished his friends would use their heads, but was well aware that their trouble was not one for which the head offers much relief; it insists on testing the aching tooth to see if it hurts as much as it did yesterday. Because he mistrusted comfort, he could only recommend endurance, and was told, in a variety of disagreeable ways, that it was easy to tell other people to endure. Ah, well, I'm their punching-bag, he thought. They are lucky to have a good, reliable punching-bag.

His own luck was that he was able to put aside his punching-bag character and rejoice in his role as triumphant artistic detective and potentially successful biographer. He wrote to Princess Amalie and her husband, and said that he had some new light to throw on their wonderful picture. Their reply was cautious. They wanted to know what he knew, and he wrote again, offering to explain everything when he had all his material in order. They were courteous but guarded, as people are likely to be when somebody offers to throw new light on a valuable family possession. Meanwhile he was marshalling his evidence, for, although he was sure what it meant, he had to make it convincing to people who might take it badly.

No wonder, then, he was looking forward to two weeks at Christmas when he thought he could put other people's troubles out of his head, and enjoy long walks, a mass of detective stories, and a great deal of good food and drink. He had made his reservation at an expensive hotel in the north woods, where there would certainly be other holiday-makers, but perhaps not of the heartiest, most athletic kind.

He had forgotten about his promise to take Dr. Gunilla Dahl-Soot to visit Maria's mother, the seeress, the *phuri dai,* the element in Maria's background that Maria was still anxious to put behind her.

"You really ought to talk to your mother," he said to Maria, during a *divano* when they were discussing the pressing problem for, it seemed to him, the twentieth time. It was really not more than the fourth. "She's an extremely wise old bird. You ought to trust her more than you do."

"What would she know about it?" said Maria.

"For that matter, what do I know about it? I tell you what I think, and you tell me I don't understand. Mamusia would at least see the thing from another point of view. And she knows you, Maria. Knows you better than you think."

"My mother lived a reasonably civilized, modern sort of life so long as she was married to my father. When he died, she reverted as fast as she could to all the old Gypsy stuff. Of course there is something to be said for that, but not when it comes to my marriage."

"You are more like your mother than you care to think. It seems to me you get more like her every day. You were very like her the first time you came to talk to me about this wretched business, all dolled up in red like the Bad Girl in a bad nineteenth-century play. But you have been getting stupider ever since."

"Thanks very much."

"Well, I have to be rough with you when you won't listen to common sense. And I mean your common sense, not mine. And your common sense goes right back to Mamusia."

"Why not right back to my father?"

"That devout, ultra-conventional Catholic Pole? Is it because of him you've never considered doing the modern thing and having an abortion? Cut the knot, clear the slate, and begin again?"

"No, it's not. It's because of me. I am not going to do violence to what my body has undertaken without consulting my head."

"Good. But what you have just said sounds like your mother, though she would probably put it in much plainer terms. Listen, Maria: you're trying to bury your mother, and it won't work, because what you bury grows fat while you grow thin. Look at Arthur; he's buried his justifiable anger and jealousy and is giving a very respectable impersonation of a generous man who has no complaints. None whatever. But it isn't working, as I expect you know. Look at Powell; he's the lucky one of you three because he has the trick of turning everything that happens to him into art of some sort, and he is chanting away all his guilt in juicy Welsh rhetoric. He'll be off and away, one of these days, and as free as a bird. But you and Arthur will still be right here with Little What's-His-Name."

"Arthur and I call him Nemo. You know—Nobody."

"That's stupid. He is somebody, right now, and you will spend years finding out who that somebody is. Don't forget—*What's bred in the bone, etcetera*—What is bred in the bone of Nemo, as you call him? That gospel-roaring old father of Geraint's, among other things."

"Oh, don't be ridiculous!"

"Anything I say to you that makes sense to me you dismiss as ridiculous. So what's the good of threshing old straw?"

"Threshing old straw! One of your Old Ontario expressions, I suppose; one of your pithy old Loyalist sayings."

"That's what's bred in the bone with me, Maria, and if you don't like it, why do you keep coming back to me to hear it?"

[8]

DARCOURT AND DR. GUNILLA DAHL-SOOT arrived at the Gypsy camp in the basement of the Cornishes' apartment building well provided with food and drink. He had insisted on it, and the Doctor had agreed that they should, if possible, avoid the enormities of Gypsy cuisine. But they understood that if they were not to eat *soviako* and *sarmi* and kindred delights, they must take something tempting with them; they had a smoked turkey, and a large, rich Christmas cake as the foundation of their feast, and a basketful of kickshaws, as well as half a dozen bottles of champagne and some excellent cognac. Mamusia was delighted.

"This is kindness! I have been so busy these last days. My Christmas shop-lifting, you know," she confided to Gunilla, who did not blink an eye.

"It must take a lot of cleverness," said she.

"Yes. I must not be caught. Maria says that if I am caught and it gets out that she is my daughter, she will kill me."

"Because the Cornishes are so very Kater Murr?"

"I don't know what that is. But Arthur has a very respectable position."

"Yes, of course."

Mamusia went off into a fit of deep-throated laughter. "No, no, not to be disgraced by his mother-in-law." She looked inquiringly at Darcourt. "But you know all about this business, Father Darcourt."

"What business are you talking about, Madame Laoutaro?"

"Father, we are old friends, aren't we? Must we pretend? Oh, you kiss my hand, very polite, and call me 'Madame' but we have a real understanding, don't we? We are old friends and old rogues, eh? Or do we have to keep quiet because of this very fine lady you have brought with you? Will she be shocked? She doesn't look to me as if she would be very much shocked."

"I assure you I have not been shocked in many years, Madame Laoutaro."

"Of course not! Shock is for stupids. You are a woman of the world, like me. So—you understand this joke? I must not disgrace the great Arthur because shop-lifting is a sin against money, and money is the Big God. But disgrace of the bed, and the heart, doesn't count. Isn't that a good joke? That is the *gadjo* world."

The door opened and Yerko came in. Unshaven, long-haired, unkempt, he was wearing a skin cap and some sort of rough skin coat. How he is reverting to his Gypsy world, thought Darcourt; who would believe that this fellow was once a business man, a gifted, inventive engineer.

"What is the *gadjo* world?" he said, shaking snow generously in all directions from the cap.

"We are talking of the little *raklo* upstairs. I will not call him the *biwuzo*."

"You'd better not, or I'll take my belt to you, sister. And you know that it is very rude to use Gypsy words when we are talking with our friends who are not Romany. You can never keep your mouth shut about the child upstairs."

"Only because it is such a good joke."

"I do not like your joke." Yerko turned to Gunilla and bowed deeply. "Madame, it is an honour to greet you." He kissed her hand. "I know you are a very great musician. I, too, am a musician. I honour greatness in our profession."

"I hear you are a noble player on the cimbalom, Mr. Laoutaro."

"Yerko. Call me Yerko. I am all through with Mister."

"They have brought a feast, brother."

"Good! I want a feast. I have at last beaten the insurance robbers."

"They are going to give us money?"

"No; but they are not going to sue us. That is victory enough. I went to them like this, and said, 'I am a poor Gypsy. I have nothing. Are you going to put me in jail? Are you going to put my sister in jail? We are old. We are sick. We do not understand your ways. Have mercy.'—Lots of that—At last they were tired of it, and of me, and told me to go away and never come into their grand building again. 'You are merciful,' I said, weeping. 'It is Christmas. You are moved by the spirit of Bebby Jesus, and He will reward you in Heaven.' I even tried to kiss the feet of the most important man but he jerked his foot away. Nearly kicked me on the nose. I said, 'You have forgiven us, before these witnesses, whose names I have. That is all I ask.' So now they can't sue us. That is *gadjo* law. We have won."

"Wonderful! We have beaten those crooks!" In her glee, Mamusia seized Darcourt by the hands and danced a few steps, in which he followed, as well as he could.

"But what about all those magnificent instruments that went up in flames?" he said, puffing.

"All gone. It is the will of God. The people who owned them must have insured them. But simple Gypsies know nothing of such things." Mamusia laughed again. "Now we feast. Sit on the floor, great lady. That is what our real friends do."

On the floor they sat, and immediately set about the turkey and olives and the rye bread, using such implements as Yerko provided, some of them not very thoroughly washed. With plenty of champagne, Darcourt thought, it is not half bad. Gunilla, he saw, dug in with a good will, showing nothing of the refined manners he associated with her. Even so, he thought, the young

Liszt might have feasted with Gypsies. She was especially attentive to the champagne, rivalling Yerko, and taking it straight from the neck of the bottle.

"You are a real fine lady!" said Yerko. "You do not hold away from our humble meal! That is high politeness. Only common people make a fuss about how they eat."

"Not when I brought it myself," said Gunilla, gnawing a drumstick.

"Yes, yes: I only meant that you are a guest in our house. No rudeness was intended."

"You will not get the best of her," said Mamusia. "I know who she is," she said to Darcourt. "She is the lady in the cards—you know, the one on the left of the spread? She is La Force. Very great strength, but used without any roughness. You are in this opera thing my son-in-law is so worried about?"

"So you know about that?" said Gunilla.

"What don't I know? You have heard about the spread? Father Simon here made me lay out the cards right at the beginning of that adventure, and there you were, though I didn't know you then. Do you know who any of the others in the spread are now, Father? All you could think of then was that my daughter Maria must be Empress. She, an Empress! I laugh!"

Mamusia laughed, and quite a lot of turkey and champagne flew about.

"Perhaps she is not the Empress, but she may be the Female Pope. She must be one of the women in the cards."

"I think she is the third in the oracle cards; that was Judgement, you remember? She is La Justice, who tries and weighs everything. But don't ask me how. That will be seen when the time comes."

"I see you have been thinking about the forecast," said Darcourt. "Have you identified any of the other figures?"

"They are not people, you know," said Mamusia. "They are— *smoro*. Yerko, what is *smoro* in English?"

"Things," said Yerko, through a full mouth. "I don't know. Big things."

"Might we say Platonic ideas?" said Darcourt.

"If you like. You are the wise man, Priest Simon."

"Is he the Hermit? I said so then but now I wonder," said

Mamusia. "There is too much of the devil in our good Father for him to be the Hermit."

"You have left me behind," said Dr. Gunilla. "Is this a prediction about our opera? What did it say? Was it a good outlook for us?"

"Good enough," said Mamusia. "Not bad: not good. Hard to say. I was not at my best that night."

The Doctor frowned. "Are we heading toward a mediocrity?" she said. "Failure I can endure; success I like but not too much. Mediocrity turns my stomach."

"I know you are not a person who lives in the middle of the road," said Mamusia. "I do not need the cards to tell me that. Your clothes, your manners, the way you drink—all of it. Let me guess. You are funny about sex, too, eh?"

"Funny, maybe. Hilarious, not. I am myself." She turned to Darcourt. "That Raven woman has been calling me again. I had to be strong with her. 'You know Baudelaire?' I said. She said: 'You insult me. I am a professor of comparative literature. Of course I know Baudelaire.' 'Well then, chew on this,' I said: 'Baudelaire says that the unique and supreme pleasure of love lies in the certainty of doing evil; both men and women know from birth that in evil every pleasure can be found. Didn't you know that from birth? Or did you have a bad birth? A seven-months child, perhaps?' She put down her phone with a loud bang."

"Do you do evil in love?" said Mamusia.

"Good and evil are not my thing. I leave that to the professionals, like Simon here. I do what I do. I did not ask the world to judge it, or make it legal or give it a special place in the world or any of that. Listen, Madame; when I was quite a young girl I met the great Jean Cocteau and he said to me: 'Whatever the public blames you for, cultivate it, because it is yourself.' And that is what I have done. I am Gunilla Dahl-Soot, and that is all I can manage. It is enough."

"Only very great people can say that," said Yerko. "It is what I always say myself."

"Don't appeal to me as a moralist," said Darcourt. "I gave up moralizing years ago. It never worked twice in the same way." The champagne was getting to him, and also the cigar smoke.

Good cigars are not accessible to shop-lifters, even those of Mamusia's talent. The cigars Yerko circulated were more than merely odious: they caught at the throat, like a bonfire of noxious weeds. Darcourt got rid of his as soon as he decently could, but the others were puffing happily.

"Madame," he said, for his biography was much on his mind. "You had some intuitions when you laid out the cards. 'You have awakened the Little Man,' you said, 'and you must be ready for what follows.' I think I know now who the Little Man is."

"And you are going to tell us?" said Mamusia.

"Not now. If I am right, the whole world will know in plenty of time."

"Good! Good, Father Simon. You bring me a mystery and that is a wonderful thing. People come to me for mysteries, but I need a few for myself. I am glad you remember the Little Man."

"Mysteries," said the Doctor, who had grown owlish and philosophical. "They are the blood of life. It is all one huge mystery. The champagne is all gone, I see. Where is the cognac? Simon, we brought cognac, didn't we? No, no, we don't need new glasses, Yerko. These tumblers will do very well." The Doctor poured hearty slops of cognac into all the glasses. "Here's to the mystery of life, eh? You'll drink with me?"

"To mystery," said Mamusia. "Everybody wants everything explained, and that is nonsense. The people that come to me with their mysteries! Mostly about love. You remember that stupid song—

Ah, sweet mystery of life
At last I've found you!

They think the mystery must be love, and they think love is snuggling up to something warm, and that's the end of everything. Bullshit! I say it again. Bullshit! Mystery is everywhere, and if it is explained, where's your mystery then? Better not to know the answer."

"The Kingdom of the Father is spread upon the earth and men do not see it," said Darcourt. "That's what mystery is."

"Mystery is the sugar in the cup," said the Doctor. She picked up the container of white crystals the delicatessen had included in the picnic basket and poured a large dollop into her cognac.

"I don't think I'd do that, Gunilla," said Darcourt.

"Nobody wants you to do it, Simon. I am doing it, and that's enough. That is the curse of life—when people want everybody to do the same wise, stupid thing. Listen: Do you want to know what life is? I'll tell you. Life is a drama."

"Shakespeare was ahead of you, Gunilla," said Darcourt. " 'All the world's a stage,' " he declaimed.

"Shakespeare had the mind of a grocer," said Gunilla. "A poet, yes, but the soul of a grocer. He wanted to please people."

"That was his trade," said Darcourt. "And it's yours, too. Don't you want this opera to please people?"

"Yes, I do. But that is not philosophy. Hoffmann was no philosopher. Now be quiet, everybody, and listen, because this is very important. Life is a drama. I know. I am a student of the divine Goethe, not that grocer Shakespeare. Life is a drama. But it is a drama we have never understood and most of us are very poor actors. That is why our lives seem to lack meaning and we look for meaning in toys—money, love, fame. Our lives seem to lack meaning but"—the Doctor raised a finger to emphasize her great revelation—"they don't, you know." She seemed to be having some difficulty in sitting upright, and her natural pallor had become ashen.

"You're off the track, Nilla," said Darcourt. "I think we all have a personal myth. Maybe not much of a myth, but anyhow a myth that has its shape and its pattern somewhere outside our daily world."

"This is all too deep for me," said Yerko. "I am glad I am a Gypsy and do not have to have a philosophy and an explanation for everything. Madame, are you not well?"

Too plainly the Doctor was not well. Yerko, an old hand at this kind of illness, lifted her to her feet and gently, but quickly, took her to the door—the door to the outside parking lot. There were terrible sounds of whooping, retching, gagging, and pitiful cries in a language which must have been Swedish. When at last he brought a greatly diminished Gunilla back to the feast, he thought it best to prop her, in a seated position, against the wall. At once she sank sideways to the floor.

"That sugar was really salt," said Darcourt. "I knew it, but she wouldn't listen. Her part in the great drama now seems to call for a long silence."

"When she comes back to life I shall give her a shot of my personal plum brandy," said Yerko. "Will you have one now, Priest Simon?"

"Thanks, Yerko, I don't think I will. I shall have to get the great philosopher back to her home and her pupil."

"Is that the girl who is doing the opera?" said Mamusia.

"The same. Present appearances to the contrary, I think the Doctor is doing her a lot of good."

"Now she is out of the way, what about this baby?" said Mamusia.

"Well, what about it? It's a fact."

"Yes, but a queer fact. It's not her husband's."

"If I may ask, how do you know that?"

"He can't make babies. I could see it as soon as he came home from the hospital. There is a look. This actor who haunts their house made the baby."

"How do you know?"

"Wally Crottel says so."

"Mamusia, Wally Crottel is an enemy to Maria, and to Arthur, and you mustn't trust him or listen to him. He wants to destroy them."

"Oh, you don't need to warn me against Wally. I have read his palm. A little good-for-nothing, but one can find out things from such people. Don't worry about Wally. I saw an accident in his palm. Yerko is maybe taking care of the accident."

"My God, Yerko! You're not going to rub him out?"

"Priest Simon, that would be criminal! But if he is to have an accident, it had better be the right one. Leave it to me."

"This baby," said Mamusia. "Maria wants a baby more than anything. Deep down she is a real Gypsy girl and she wants a baby at the breast. Now she has a baby and she would be happy if Arthur would be happy too."

"It's rather a lot to expect, wouldn't you say?"

"In these queer days people hire women to have babies when the wife can't do it. Why not hire a father? Doesn't this fellow Powell work for them?"

"I don't suppose they thought he would work for them in quite this way."

"That Powell is not an ordinary man. I think he is the Lover in the spread. You know how that card looks. A young man between two people and the one on the right is a woman, but who is that on the left? Some people say it is another woman, but is it? They say it is a woman because it has no beard, but what is a man without a beard? Not a man in every way, but still important enough to rule the beautiful woman. That figure wears a crown. A king, of course. Every spread is personal. Maybe in this spread that figure is King Arthur, and he looks as if he is pushing the young man toward the beautiful woman. And the beautiful woman is pointing to the lover as if she is saying, 'Is it this one?' And over their heads is the god of love and he is shooting an arrow right into the heart of the beautiful woman."

"You make it sound very plausible."

"Oh, the cards can be very wise. Also very tricky. So you know who the Little Man is? And you won't tell?"

"Not yet."

"Well, be careful. Maybe the Fool is tied up with the Little Man I had that hunch about. Father Simon, have you ever looked hard at that card of the Fool?"

"I think I remember it pretty clearly."

"What is the dog doing?"

"I don't remember the dog."

"Yerko, get the cards. And maybe just a thimbleful of your plum brandy."

While Yerko was busy, Darcourt looked at the prostrate Doctor. Her colour was better, and so far as a woman of her distinguished demeanour could do so, she was snoring.

"Look now. There he is. The Fool. You see he is going on a journey and he looks very happy. He is always going someplace, is the Fool. And he has a good fool's dress, but see, the pants are torn at the back. Part of his arse is showing. And that is very true, because when the Fool comes into our life, we always show our arses a little bit. And what does the little dog do with the bare arse? He is maybe nipping at it. What is the dog, anyway? He is a thing of nature, isn't he? Not learning, or thinking, but nature in a simple form, and the little dog is nipping at the Fool's arse to make him go in a path that the mind would not think of. A better path. A natural path that Fate chooses. Maybe a path the mind would not approve of, because the mind can be a fool too—but not the great, the very fine Fool that takes the special journey. The little dog is nipping, but maybe he is also sniffing. Because you cannot nip without you also sniff. You know how dogs sniff everybody? The crotch? The arse? They have to be trained not to do it, but they forget because they have the great gift of scent, which wise, thinking Man has almost murdered. The nose speaks when the eyes are blind. Man, when he thinks he is civilized, pretends he does not smell, and if he is afraid he stinks he puts on some stuff to kill his stink. But the little dog knows that the arse and the smell are part of the real life and part of the Fool's journey, and the natural things cannot be got rid of if you want to live with the real world and not in the half-world of stupid, contented people. The Fool is going just as fast as he can to something he thinks good. What do people say when somebody goes as hard as he can for something?"

"They say he goes for it bald-headed."

"People I know say he goes for it bare-arsed," said Yerko.

"You see, Father Simon? Somebody in all this destiny that is told in that spread of cards is going bare-arsed for something very important. Is it you?"

"You have amazed me, Mamusia, and in my amazement I shall speak the truth. Yes, I think it is me."

"Good. I thought you were the Hermit, but now I am sure you are the Fool. You are going far, and instinct is nipping at your arse, and you will have to understand that instinct knows you better than you know yourself. Instinct knows the smell of your arse—your backside that you can never see.—Listen, how much does my son-in-law pay you for what you do?"

"Pay me! Mamusia, I get some expenses now and again to put back in my own pocket what I have taken out of it to serve the Cornish Foundation, damn it, but not one red cent of pay have I ever had. I am always out of pocket. And I am getting sick of it. They think because I am a friend I love working my tail off for them, just to be one of the gang. And the trouble is they are right!"

"Father Simon, don't shout! You are a very lucky man and now I know you are the Fool. The great Fool who dominates the whole spread! Don't you take a penny! Not one penny! That is the Fool's way, because his fortune is not made like other men's. They pay everybody. This Powell, the baby-maker. This Doctor here, who is very good at her job, but is just La Force, you know, and sometimes puts her foot very wrong. And that girl, that child who is being given so much money for this opera job, and it may not be for her good. But you are free! You wear no golden chain! You are the Fool—Oh, I must kiss you!"

Which she did. And then Yerko insisted on kissing him too. A prickly, smelly embrace, but Darcourt recognized now that reality and truth can sometimes be very smelly.

Thus the party broke up, and Darcourt took Gunilla home in a taxi, and delivered her, still limp and silent, into the hands of Schnak.

"Oh, Nilla, you poor darling! What have they been doing to you?" she said as she supported her wilted teacher.

"I have been a fool, Hulda," said the Doctor, as the door closed.

Yes, but not the Fool! Exhilarated as he had not been in many years, Darcourt paid off the taxi and walked home, delighting in the chill air and his new character.

Searching for words to express this exultation, this state of unusual well-being, an Old Ontario phrase swam upward from the depths of his consciousness.

He felt as if he could cut a dead dog in two.

[9]

ETAH IN LIMBO

MY HEART GOES OUT TO DARCOURT. The life of a librettist is the life of a dog. Worse than the playwright, who may have to satisfy monsters of egotism with new scenes, new jokes, chances to do what they have done successfully before; but the playwright can, to some degree, choose the form of his scenes and his speeches. The librettist must obey the tyrant composer, whose literary taste may be that of a peasant, and who thinks of nothing but his music.

Rightly so, of course. Opera is music, and all else must bow to that. But what sacrifices are demanded of the literary man!

Psychology, for instance. The watered-silk elegances of feeling and the double-dealing of even the most honest mind; the gushes of hot emotion that rush up from the depths and destroy the reason. Can music encompass all that? Yes, it can in a way, but never with the exactitude of true poetry. Music is too strongly the voice of emotion and it is not a good impersonator. Can it make a character have a voice that is wholly his own? It can try, but as a usual thing the voice is always that of the composer. If the composer is a very great man, like the divine Mozart or, God help us all, the heaven-storming Beethoven, we love the voice and would not change it for even the masterly characterizations of Shakespeare.

You see, my trouble is that I am torn between Hoffmann the poet and fabulist, and Hoffmann the composer. I could argue with equal conviction on either side. I want the poet to be supreme, and the musician to be his accompanist. But I also want the musician to pour out his inspiration, and the poet must carpenter something with the right vowel sounds that obediently partner the music without pushing itself into prominence. What great line of poetry can anybody quote from an opera libretto? Even Shakespeare is reduced to a hack, after the libretto hack has hacked his lines to suit Maestro Qualcuno's demands. And then every simpleton says that Maestro Qualcuno has shown Shakespeare how it should be done.

If the musician is really sensitive to poetry, magic is the result, as in the songs of Schubert. But, alas, Schubert wrote truly terrible operas, and Weber had the fatal knack of choosing the worst possible people to write his libretti. Like that fellow Planché, who ruined **Oberon.** *Oh, how lucky I am to have escaped the well-meaning drollery of Planché!*

Now I have Darcourt, and what a task that poor wretch has been given! To prepare a libretto that will fit existing music, or rather the music that Schnak and the brilliant Doctor can make by enlarging on my notes.

He is doing well. Of course he has to find some words that will carry the plot they have created for my **Arthur.** *It is not precisely the plot I would have wished for. It smells a little of the present day—their* *present day. But it is not bad. It is more psychological than I would have dared to make it, and I am happy with that, for I was rather a fine psychologist, in the manner of my time. My uncanny tales were not just fantasies to amuse young girls on an idle afternoon.*

But Darcourt has had a really good idea. Whenever he can, he is drawing on the writings of a true poet. A poet not very well known, he says, but I would not know about that for I never read English with real understanding, and English poetry was an unknown country to me. But I like what he has fished up from his unknown. How right he is not to tell anybody who his unknown poet is! If they knew, they would want to stick a finger in the pie, and too many fingers in pies are the utter ruin of art and the curse of drama. No; let the secret remain a secret, and if anybody wants to ferret out the secret, good luck to them and probably bad luck to him.

All artistic tinkering and monkeying is slave's work. I know. Once I undertook, as an act of friendship, to do something of the sort. I made a version of Shakespeare's **Richard III** *for my dearest friend, Ludwig Devrient. It almost cost me that friendship, for Ludwig wanted all sorts of things that my artistic conscience revolted against. But Shakespeare wanted it thus, I would say, and he would shout To hell with Shakespeare! Give me a great effect here, so that I can take the audience by the throat and choke it with splendour! And then, in the next scene, you must arrange matters so that I can choke them again, and reduce them to an admiring pulp! My dear Louis, I would say, you must trust your poet and you must trust me. And then he would say what I could not bear: Shakespeare is dead, and as for you, you do not have to go on the stage with a hump on your back and a sword in your hand, and win the battle every night. So do what I say! After which, there was nothing for me to do but get drunk. Ludwig got what he wanted, but Richard III was never one of his greatest roles, and I know why. After it was over, the audience came unchoked, and the critics told them that Ludwig was a barn-stormer and a mountebank. Whom did he blame, then? Shakespeare, of course, and me along with Shakespeare.*

I like Darcourt, and not just because I pity him. The old Gypsy woman says he will be greatly rewarded, but old Gypsy women can be wrong. Who heeds a librettist? At the party after the performance, who wants to meet him? At whose feet do the pretty ladies fall? Whose lapel do the rich impresarios seize, clamouring for more, and greater, works? Not the librettist.

The old Gypsy is wrong. Or else I do not know as much about this affair as I hope I do.

Anyhow, I must bide the event, as Shakespeare says. Or does he? There are no reference libraries in Limbo.

SIX

DARCOURT'S CHRISTMAS HOLIDAY was a success beyond his hopes. His hotel in the north woods pretended to be a simple chalet, but was, in fact, luxurious, giving him a large room with broad windows looking down over a valley of pine forest; a proper room, with a desk and a good armchair in it, as well as the bed, and—rarest of hotel blessings—a good light for reading; a chest of drawers, a closet for his clothes, and a bathroom where there was provision for everything he could need, and in the form of a bidet and a frank notice warning him not to put his sanitary towels down the plumbing, for things he did not need. With a sense of deep content he unpacked and hung up clothes that gave no hint of his clerical character; he had invested in two or three shirts sufficiently gaudy for a country holiday, and some handsome scarves to tuck into his open collar. He had a fine pair of corduroy trousers, and, for long walks, boots that were, he had been assured, proof against cold and wet. He had two tweed jackets, one with leather patches on the elbows, sure signal that he was an academic, and not an academic of the sort that likes to ski, or slide downhill on a luge, or engage in casual conversations about nothing in particular. There were young people among the guests, who wanted to do these things, and older people who wanted to sit in the bar and pretend that they would prefer to ski, or luge; but the discreet lady whose job it was to see that everybody had a good time knew Darcourt at once for a man whose idea of a good time was to be alone. So he was civil to his fellow guests, and obedient to the convention that required him to make remarks about the weather, and smile at children, but on the whole he was left to himself and settled to two weeks of his own company with a deep sense of gratitude.

He walked after breakfast. He walked before dinner. He read, sometimes detective novels and sometimes fat, difficult books that primed the pump of his reflections. He made notes. But most of the time he brooded, and mused, and looked inward, and thought about being the Fool, and what that might mean.

The Fool; the cheerful rogue on a journey, with a rip in his pants, and a little dog that nipped at his exposed rump, urging him onward and sometimes nudging him in directions he had never intended to take. The Fool, who had no number but the potent zero which, when it was added to any other number, multiplied its significance by ten. He had spoken truly in Mamusia's cellar when he said that he believed that everybody had a personal myth, and that as a rule it was a myth of no great potency. He had been inclined to see his own myth as that of a servant, a drudge, not without value, but never an initiator or an important figure in anyone's life but his own. If he had been asked to choose a card in the Tarot that would signify himself, he would probably have named the Knave of Clubs, Le Valet de Baton, the faithful, loyal servitor. Was not that the character he had played all his life? As a clergyman, loyal to his faith and his bishop until he could stand it no more and outraged nature had driven him to become a teacher? As a teacher, generous and supportive to his students, the administrative assistant to the head of his college, doing so much of the work for so little of the acclaim? As a friend, the patient helper of the Cornishes, and their crackbrained Cornish Foundation, which had embarked on such a foolish exploit as giving form to an opera that existed in no more than a few ideas, scribbled in pain by a dying man? Oh, the Knave of Clubs to the life! But now Mamusia had declared as true what he had for some time felt in his bones. He was something better. He was the Fool. Not the servitor, napkin in hand, at the behest of his betters, but the footloose traveller, urged onward by something outside the confines of intellect and caution.

Had he not felt the truth of it? Had those promptings that had led him to the Sun Pictures, and the sealed portfolio in the National Gallery hoard, not come from somewhere not accountable to reason, deduction, scholarly craft? Was not his biography of his old friend Francis Cornish, which he had undertaken as an act of friendship, and chiefly to oblige Maria and Arthur, blossoming into something that none of Francis Cornish's heirs could have foreseen? If he could piece out the jigsaw that placed the figures in Grandfather McRory's photographed chronicle of Blairlogie (unlikely cradle for a work of art) in the great composition called *The Marriage at Cana* (dated as *circa* 1550 and attributed to the unknown Alchemical Master), would he not have established Francis as, at worst, a brilliant faker, and at best an artistic genius of a rare and eccentric breed? And how would he have done it? Not by being a crook, stealing from a library and a gallery, but by being a Fool and acting on a morality not to be judged by common rules. He was the Fool, the only one of the Tarot figures who was happily in motion—not falling as in the Tower, not endlessly revolving as in the Wheel of Fortune, not drawn ceremonially by horses as in the Chariot, but off on foot, bound for adventure.

This sort of self-recognition does not come to a man in his forties in a sudden flash. It offers itself tentatively, and is rejected as immodest. It asserts itself in sudden, unaccountable bursts of well-being. It comes as a joke, and is greeted with incredulous laughter. But in the end it will not be denied, and then it takes a good deal of getting used to. Without being self-deprecatory, Darcourt had the humility of a man who had, with his whole heart, embraced the calling of a priest. He was a priest in the tradition of Erasmus, or the ungovernable Sydney Smith, who was said to have jested away his chances of a mitre. He was a priest of the type of the mighty Rabelais. But was not Rabelais a true priest and also a Fool of God? Was he, Simon Darcourt, professor, Vice-Warden of his college, unpaid dogsbody of the Cornish Foundation, and (he sometimes thought) the only sane man in a congeries of charming lunatics, really a Fool of God? He was too modest a man to greet such a revelation with a whoop and a holler.

It was thus he mused while taking his long, solitary walks through the pine forests that surrounded his hotel. He was not one of those people—do they exist anywhere except in books?— who think in a straight line, with unescapable logic. Walking helped him to think, but that meant that walking allowed him to

bob up and down in the warm bath of a mass of disjointed reflections. The warm bath had to be reheated every day, and every
day the conclusion came a little nearer until it became a happy
certainty. His fellow guests, incorrigible gossips as people in a
resort hotel always are, sometimes asked each other why the man
with the leather patches on his elbows seemed so often to smile
to himself, and not in answer to their smiles; and why, once or
twice, he laughed softly but audibly while he was eating at his
lonely table.

It was in the forest that he fared farthest in his astonishing
recognition of what he was and how he must live. Canadians are
thought of in the great world—whenever the great world thinks
about them at all—as dwellers in a northern land. But most of
them dwell in communities, large or small, where their lives are
dominated by community concerns and accepted ideas. When
they go into their forests, if they are not there to exploit the
forests by chopping them down, they are there to rush downhill
on skis, or bob-sleighs, to strain after accomplishment in winter
sports, to make decorous whoopee at the bar or on the dance
floor when the day's exertion is over. They do not go into the
forests to seek what they are, but to forget what they suspect
themselves to be. Sport numbs the concerns they have brought
with them from the towns. They do not ask the forests to speak
to them. But the forests will speak if they can find a listener, and
Darcourt listened, as he trudged the solitary trails that had been
ploughed out among the huge pines, and when—without an apparent breath of wind—powderings of snow fell from the trees
onto his shoulders, he heeded the deeper suggestions which had
nothing to do with the world of words.

He did not think only of himself, but of the people from whom
he was taking a holiday. What a muddle of concerns had been
set in action by Hulda Schnakenburg's apparently innocent desire
to piece out some manuscript notes of music, in order that she
might gain the doctorate in her studies that could lead to a place
in the world of her art! Arthur's desire to escape his world of
business and figure in the world of art as an intellectual and a
patron; Geraint Powell's opportunist scheme to launch himself
as a director of opera on an imaginative level; the seduction of
Hulda Schnakenburg by the amoral but splendidly inspiring Dr.

Gunilla Dahl-Soot; the recognition of Clement Hollier, fine scholar and renowned paleo-psychologist, as a man wholly at sea when faced with any imaginative notion that was not safely rooted in the dark and ambiguous past; the bitterness of Professor Penelope Raven, when confronted with an aspect of herself which she had disguised for half a lifetime; the uprooting of Maria, who was trying to balance her obligations as the wife of a very rich man, bound by the conventionalities of such a fate, against her inclination to become a scholar and get away from her Gypsy heritage; and of course that baby, still an unknown factor, though a living creature, who would never have come into being if Hulda, snooping through some musical manuscripts, had not come upon the skeleton of *Arthur of Britain, or The Magnanimous Cuckold.* They were driven by craving, of one sort or another, and if he were really the Knave of Clubs he was the servant of their craving. But suppose he were the Fool, driven by no craving but ready to follow his path, confident that his destiny and the mischievous little dog at his heels would guide him—was not that a vastly finer thing? The Myth of the Fool was a myth indeed, and he would live it as fully and as joyously as in him lay.

He had revulsions of feeling, as a man undergoing a great change must do. What on earth was he doing—he, a modern man, a trusted instructor of the young, a servant of the university as a temple of reason and intellectual progress—abandoning himself to an old Gypsy woman's blethers about the Tarot? If this was thinking at all, it was thinking of a superstitious, archaic nature. But then—it was so seductive, so firmly rooted in a past that it had served pretty well for millennia before the modern craze for logic. Logic, which meant not logic as a system applicable to whatever lay under the domination of inference and the scientific method, but debased logic, a means of straining out of every problem the whisperings of intuition, which was a way of seeing in the dark. Mamusia's hunches and her Tarot were only channels for her intuition, which, combined with his own, might open doors that were closed to logic. Let logic keep its honourable place, where it served man well, but it should not take absurd airs on itself as the only way of settling a problem or finding a path. Logic could be the weapon with which fear defies fate.

A word kept popping into his head which he had heard Gunilla use when she was introducing Schnak to the finer realms of musical composition. *Sprezzatura*. It meant, said Gunilla, a contempt for the obvious, for beaten paths, for what seemed to be obligatory to musical underlings; it was a noble negligence, a sudden leap in art toward a farther shore that could not be reached by the ferry-boats of custom.

Such leaps could, of course, land you in the soup. Had not Arthur's *sprezzatura,* arising probably from the first symptoms of mumps—the higher temperature, the irritable malaise—landed them all in this ridiculous opera venture? Was it a noble leap, or a plunge into the soup? Only time could show.

Was it part of the Arthurian myth, into which the Cornish Foundation seemed to have strayed, and which needed a great questing king, betrayed by his closest friend and his dearly beloved? Behind the time which was so imperiously signalled every noontide by the great observatory at Ottawa, and binding upon a million human activities, there lay the Time of Myth, the time of the mind, the habitation of all those nine plots of which he and Gunilla had spoken, and the landscape of quite another sort of life. Surely it is in the mind that we humans truly live, as animals do not; the mind, which is not the creature of the clock but of those moving planets and that vast universe whose mysteries are still, in the main, unknown to us?

Moonshine, thought Darcourt. Yes, perhaps it was moonshine, which the amateur logicians held in contempt because it threatened so much they held dear—their timorous certainty which was, when all was weighed up, certain of so very little. But they despised moonshine because they never looked at the moon. How many of the people he knew could, if asked to do so, say in which phase the moon was at the time they were questioned? Did the Fool travel by moonshine? If he did, he was in a happy state of confidence about where he was going, which very few of those who never looked at the moon seemed to be.

It was a fearful adventure to put off the servitor's livery of the Knave of Clubs, and put on the motley of the Fool. But had Darcourt, in all his eminently respectable life, ever had a real adventure? That was what the Time of Myth seemed to be urging him to do. When the time comes for truth to speak, it may choose an unfamiliar tongue; the task is to heed what is said.

When he left the forests to return to his life and its burdens, Simon Darcourt was a changed man. Not a wholly new man, not a man one jot less involved in the life of his duties and his friends, but a man with a stronger sense of who he was.

[2]

IF THE OPERA VENTURE seemed madness to Darcourt, it was more and more true and compelling to Schnak and the Doctor, who now had enough completed music to be nipped and tucked and patted and dowelled into an opera score. The final form had not been achieved but it was in sight. Not one of Hoffmann's themes and rough notes had been neglected, and the important part of the music rested upon them. But inevitably there were gaps, seams to be sewn and then concealed, bridges to be contrived to get from one piece of authentic Hoffmann to another. These were the tests that would show Schnak's quality. The Doctor suggested nothing, but she was quick to reject anything Schnak produced which seemed unworthy or unsuitable to the whole. Developing and orchestrating Hoffmann's notes was child's play to Schnak; finding Hoffmann's voice in which to devise her new material was a different matter.

The exactions of the Doctor and the exasperation of Schnak made life a hell for Darcourt. His job was to tinker scraps of language into appropriate lengths for the music which was written every day, and changed every day, until he lost all sense of a coherent narrative, or intelligible utterance. Sometimes the Doctor scolded him for the banality of what he prepared; sometimes she rejected it because it was too literary, too hard to comprehend when sung, too obtrusively poetic. Of course the Doctor, who was an artist of considerable quality, was merely expressing her dissatisfaction with herself and what she could squeeze out of her pupil; Darcourt understood that, and was prepared to put up with it. But he was not ready to take snarling impudence from Schnak, who assumed she was privileged to be rudely capricious and exacting.

"This is shit!"

"How would you know, Schnak?"

"I'm the composer, I suppose?"

"You're an illiterate brat! What you call shit is the verse of a poet of great gifts, slightly adapted by me. It's utterly beyond your comprehension. You take it and be grateful for it!"

"No, no, Simon; Hulda is right. It won't work. We must have something else."

"What else?"

"I don't know what else. That's your job. What is wanted here is something that says the same thing, but says it with a good open vowel on the third beat of the second bar."

"That means reshaping the whole thing."

"Very well; reshape it. And do it now, so we can get on. We can't wait till tomorrow while you brood over a dictionary."

"Why can't you reshape your bloody music?"

"The shape of music is something you know nothing about, Simon."

"Very well. But I won't take any more lip from this stupid kid."

"Shit!"

"Hulda! I forbid you to use that word to the professor. Or to me. We must work without passion. Art is not born of passion, but of dedication."

"Shit!"

Then the Doctor might slap Schnak across the face, or, under other circumstances, kiss her and pet her. Darcourt never slapped Schnak, but sometimes it was a near thing.

Not all the work proceeded in this high-stomached mode, but it did so at least once a day, and sometimes the Doctor had to fetch champagne for everybody. The bill for champagne, thought Darcourt, must be mounting at a fearful rate.

He persisted. He swallowed insult, and in his new notion of himself as the Fool, he frequently gave insult, but he never gave up. He was determined to be a professional. If this was the way artists worked, he would be an artist in so far as a librettist was permitted such presumption.

It was not the way all artists worked. At least once a week Powell dashed up from Stratford in his snorting little red car, and his artistic method was all oil and balm.

"Lovely, lovely, lovely! Oh, this is very fine stuff, Simon. Do you know, when I am working on my other production—I'm getting up *Twelfth Night,* you know, for a May opening—I find words coming into my head that are not Shakespeare. They are unadulterated Darcourt. You've missed your calling, Sim *bach*. You are a poet. No doubt about it."

"No, Geraint, I am not a poet. I am exploiting a poet to produce this stuff. The arias, and the long bits, are all his—with some tinkering, I admit. Only the *recitativo* passages are mine, and because of the way Nilla wants things, they are absolute buggers, because they have to have all this loose accompaniment underneath, and stresses falling in places that defy any sort of poetic common sense. Why can't the singers just speak those parts, and sound like human beings and not crazed parrots?"

"Come on, Sim *bach,* you know why. Because Hoffmann wanted it otherwise, that's why. He was an adventurer, an innovator. Long before Wagner he wanted an opera that was sung clear through, not broken up with spoken passages or recitative that is simply gabble to bustle on the plot. We must be faithful to old Hoffmann, boy. We must never betray old Hoffmann."

"Very well. But it's killing me."

"No it isn't. I've never seen you looking better. But now I'm going to talk against everything I've just said. We must have one big number for Arthur in Act Three, where he says loud and clear what Love is, and why he's forgiving Guenevere and Lancelot. And there isn't a damned scrap of Hoffmann that does it."

"And so?"

"Well, it's obvious. Dear little Schnaky-Waky is going to have to write a tune all by her dear little self, and you're going to have to find words for it."

"No, no," said the Doctor. "That would indeed be untrue to Hoffmann."

"Listen, Nilla. More operas have been spoiled by too much artistic conscience than have ever been glorified by genius. Just for the moment, forget about Hoffmann. Or no, that's not what I mean. Think of what Hoffmann would do if he were still alive. I see him now, the wonderful bright-eyed little chap, chewing his quill and thinking, 'What we need in Act Three is a great big, smashing aria for Arthur that pulls the whole thing together, and knocks the audience out of their socks. It's got to be the one that everybody remembers, and that the barrel-organs play in the streets.' We don't have barrel-organs now, but he wouldn't know

that. It's got to get the young, and the old, and if the critics despise
it the critics of the next generation will hail it as genius."

"I will not agree to anything that has a cheap appeal," said the
Doctor.

"Nilla—dear, uncompromising Nilla *fach*—there is the truly
cheap art, and we all know what it is, but there is another kind
of art, that goes far beyond what critics call good taste. Good
taste is really just a kind of aesthetic vegetarianism, you know.
You go beyond it at your peril, and you end up with schmalz like
'M'appari' in *Marta*. Or maybe you come up with 'Voi, che sapete',
or 'Porgi amor', which is genius. Or you get the Evening Star aria
out of *Tannhäuser* or the Habanera out of *Carmen*—and you can't
say Wagner dealt in cheap goods, and Bizet wrote the one sure-
fire opera. You artists really must stop kicking the public in the
face. They're not all fools, you know. You've got to get something
into this Hoffmann job that will lift it above a fancy academic
exercise to earn Schnak a degree. We've got to wow 'em, Nilla!
Can you resist that?"

"This is very dangerous talk, Powell. I'm not sure I should let
Hulda listen. These are dirtier words than any even she knows."

"Come on, Nilla. I know this is the voice of the Tempter, but
the Tempter has inspired some damned good stuff. Now listen
carefully, Nilla. Have you ever heard this?

> *Though critics may bow to art,*
> *And I am its own true lover,*
> *It is not art, but heart*
> *Which wins the wide world over."*

Darcourt, who had been listening with delight to the spell-
binder, roared with laughter. He lifted his voice in imitation of
Powell's bardic chant, and continued:

> *"And it is not the poet's song,*
> *Though sweeter than sweet bells chiming,*
> *Which thrills us through and through,*
> *But the heart which beats under the rhyming."*

"Is that English poetry?" said the Doctor, her brows raised
almost into her hair.

"Jesus, I think that's wonderful!" said Schnak. "Oh, Nilla, did you ever hear it said better?"

"I am not at home in English verse," said the Doctor, "but that sounds to me like—I will not use Hulda's word—but it sounds like crap. That is a new word I have learned and it is very useful. Crap!"

"The expression is unquestionably crap," said Darcourt. "But in the crap there is a precious jewel of truth. That is one of the problems of poetry. Even a terrible poet may hit on a truth. Even the blind pig sometimes finds an acorn."

"The professor sets us right, as he always does," said Powell. "Raw heart can't make art but woe to art when it snubs heart. By God—I ought to be a librettist! Now—will you do it?"

"I'll have a crack at it," said Schnak. "I've had about enough of writing music wrapped in Hoffmann's old bathrobe."

"I'll certainly have a crack at it," said Darcourt. "But on one condition. I find the verse before Schnak writes the music."

"Sim *bach*, I see it in your eye! You have the verse already."

"As a matter of fact, I have," said Darcourt, and he recited it to them.

"Do that again, will you," said Schnak, looking at Darcourt without suspicion and resentment for the first time since they had met.

Darcourt recited it again.

"That's it," said Powell. "Right on the pig's back, Sim *bach*."

"But is it good English verse?" said the Doctor.

"I'm not a man who awards marks to poets as if they were schoolboys," said Darcourt. "It is from the best of a very good man, and far beyond the level of an opera libretto."

"You're surely going to tell us who the very good man is?" said Powell.

"He's the man you spoke of as the base upon which we should rest this opera, the first time we discussed it," said Darcourt. "It's Sir Walter Scott."

[3]

CAN IT BE TRUE, thought Darcourt, that I am sitting in this grand penthouse on a Sunday evening eating cold roast chicken and salad with three figures from Arthurian legend? Three people working out, in such terms as modernity dictates, the great myth of the betrayed king, the enchantress queen, and the brilliant adventurer?

Does the analogy hold? What did King Arthur attempt? He tried to extend the reach of civilization by demanding that his Knights, who belonged to an undoubted Elite of Birth, should embrace the concept of chivalry, thereby becoming an Elite of Achievement. Not just power, but the intelligent, unselfish use of power to make a better world; that was the idea.

What about Arthur Cornish, who is helping himself to currant jelly across the table? He belongs to a Birth Elite of a kind; of a Canadian kind, which thinks three generations of money are enough in themselves to make a man significant, do what he will. But Arthur wants to be an intellectual, and to advance civilization by the use of his power, which is his money; or rather, the money of the late Francis Cornish, the mysterious fortune which nobody can quite explain. Surely that is an attempt, and a very respectable attempt, to advance into an Elite of Achievement? Arthur Cornish probably commands more hard cash and more power than Arthur of Britain ever dreamed of.

Queen Guenevere lives in legend as a partner in an adulterous love that brought great grief to King Arthur. Not all the legends present her as a woman troubled by love alone; sometimes she is a discontented wife, an ambitious woman of a fretful spirit, a figure more solid and varied than Tennyson draws her.

Certainly Maria fills the bill. She had told Darcourt, not so very long ago, before she married Arthur, that she had fallen in love with him because of his frankness, his largeness of spirit, and also his attractive freedom from the academic world to which her own ambitions were confined. Arthur had offered her love, but also friendship, and she had found it irresistible. Yet a woman cannot live solely in the realm of her love; she must have a life of her own; she must shed light, as well as reflecting it. It looked as if Maria's light, since her marriage, had been somewhat under a cloud. She had tried too hard to be Arthur's wife, first, last, and all the time, and her spirit was in rebellion. How long had they been married? Twenty months, was it? Twenty months of forsaking all others and cleaving only unto him? It simply won't work. No woman worth marrying is nothing but a wife, if the man is something better than a roaring egotist, which Arthur certainly is not, for all his peremptory, rich man's ways in certain matters. Darcourt, himself unmarried, had seen many marriages, and united more couples, he thought in his Old Ontario way, than he could shake a stick at. The marriages that worked best were those in which the unity still permitted of some separateness—not a ranting independence, but a firm possession by both man and woman of their own souls.

Was it any use talking to Arthur and Maria about souls? Probably not. Souls are not fashionable, at present. People will listen with wondering acquiescence to scientific talk of such invisible entities as are said to be everywhere and very important, but they shy away from talk of souls. Souls have a bad name in the world of atomic energy.

Souls were a reality to Darcourt, however. Souls, not as gassy aspiration and unreal nobility, but as the force that divides the living human creature from the raw material for the mortician's craft. Souls as a totality of consciousness, what man knows of himself and also that hidden vast part of himself which knows and impels *him,* used and abused by everybody, called upon or rejected, but inescapable.

What about Powell? Now there was a man who would assert, with passionate eloquence, that he had a soul, but who was clearly driven by that portion of his soul that was not within the range of his direct knowledge, that part of the spirit that some people— Mamusia, for instance—would call his fate. But a man's fate is his own, more than he knows. We attract what we are. And it was Powell's fate that had drawn him to seduce his friend's wife, probably—no, Darcourt was sure, undoubtedly—with the complicity of Maria's fate, just as Lancelot had seduced, or been seduced by, Guenevere.

"Do you want more dressing on your salad, Simon?" said Maria. She and Arthur and Powell had been talking while Darcourt mused.

Yes, he would like more dressing on his salad. He really must not drift off into unheeding speculation while the others were talking. And what had they been talking about?

About the impending child, of course. They talked about it a good deal, and with a frankness Darcourt found astonishing. It was five months on its way, and Maria wore becoming gowns in which she did not look pregnant, like the women Darcourt saw in the streets who wore slacks in which their distended bellies were forced upon the world, but clever gowns that enhanced, without concealing, her increasing girth.

Arthur and Geraint were rivals in solicitude. Neither had been a father before, they said, sometimes as a joke but always with an undercurrent of concern. They fussed over Maria, urging her to sit when she was perfectly comfortable standing, and rushing to fetch her things that she did not greatly want. They urged her not to drive her car, to put her feet on a stool when she sat, to get plenty of rest, to drink milk (which her doctor told her not to do), to eat heartily, to eat wisely, to drink very little wine and no spirits, to put aside the more inflammatory parts of the newspapers. They were a little disappointed that she exhibited no irrational cravings for peculiar foods; they would have been overjoyed if she had made eerie demands for pickles drenched in ice cream. These were old wives' tales, said Maria, laughing at them. But, like prospective fathers from an earlier day, they were pestilent old wives, and they grew together in old-wifery. They were better friends than ever.

Had Arthur and Lancelot, in the mythical long ago, fretted and fussed so? Of course not; they had no ambiguous baby.

"The meeting with Schnak's parents went very well," said Powell.

"Who met them? Sorry, I haven't been attending," said Darcourt.

"Nilla insisted that Schnak ask them in. Nilla is very strict with Schnak and is teaching her manners. Won't listen to Schnak's fits of bad-mouthing her old folks. You must ask them here, Hulda dearest, she said, and we must be very, very sweet to them. And that's what they did."

"Were you there?" said Maria.

"Indeed I was. Wouldn't have missed it for the world. If I may say so, I was the star turn, the cherry on the cake. I got on with the elder Schnaks brilliantly."

"Tell all," said Maria.

"Well, they turned up, in answer to a telephone call from

Schnak, which she made while Nilla stood over her with a whip, if I'm not mistaken. You've seen them. Not what I would call clubbable people, and they were all set to resent Nilla and lecture Schnak. But not a bit of it. Nilla was charming, and there was enough high-bred European atmosphere floating around for the elder Schnaks to recognize Nilla as a genuine grandee. Not just rich people, like you Cornishes, but a person of aristocratic quality. You'd be amazed how powerful that still is. She spoke to them quite a lot of the time in German, and that kept Schnak out of things, because although she understands pretty well, she can't say much in the old tongue. I don't know any more German than I need to follow a Wagner libretto, but I could tell that Nilla wsa being really gracious. Not patronizing, but speaking to them as equals, and as an older person like themselves, deeply concerned about Schnak. She talked about art, and music, and they softened up a bit under that and the rich cakes and the coffee with lots of whipped cream. They didn't soften much, although they were impressed by the huge heap of musical manuscript Schnak had piled up. Obviously the girl was working. What was sticking in their gullets was Schnak's rebellion against what they think of as religion. That was where I came in very strong."

"You, Geraint? You agreed with those bitter Puritans about religion?"

"Of course I did, Arthur, *bach*. Don't forget I grew up a Calvinistic Methodist, with a father who was a mighty shaman in the faith. I let them know that, of course. But, said I, look at me, deep into the world of art, and theatre and music, and the fatherhood and splendour of God is present to me every hour of my life, and infuses everything I do. Does God speak only with a single tongue? I asked them. Does His mighty love not reach out to those who have not yet come to the full belief, to the life of total faith? May He not speak even in the theatre, in the opera house, to those who have fled from Him into a world they think frivolous and abandoned to pleasure? Oh, my friends, you are blessed in knowing the fullness of God's revealed Word. You have not encountered, as I have, the God who knows how to speak to the fallen and the reprobate through the langauge of art; you have not met with the Cunning of God, by which He reaches out to His children who shut their ears to His true voice. Our

God is stern with those like yourselves whom He has marked from birth as His own, but He is gentle and subtle with those who have strayed into worldly paths. He speaks with many voices, and one of the most winning is the voice of music. Your daughter has been greatly gifted in music and dare you say that she is not marked by God as one of His own, to be His instrument, His harp of Zion, to draw His erring children to Him? Do you, Elias Schnakenburg, say that your child may not be speaking—I say this with humility—through her music with the voice of God Himself? Do you? Can you presume so far? Oh, Elias Schnakenburg, I urge you, I beg you, to reflect deeply upon these mysteries, and then reject your daughter's vocation if you dare!"

"By God, Geraint, did you say that?"

"Indeed I did, Maria. That and a good deal more. I even gave them a touch of the old Welsh *hwyl;* I sang my peroration. Worked like a charm."

Maria was overcome. "Geraint, you bloody crook!" she said when she could speak.

"Maria *fach,* you wound me profoundly. Sincere, every word of it. And true, what's more. Sim *bach,* you know what preaching is. Did I say a word that you would not have spoken from a pulpit?"

"I liked that about the Cunning of God, Geraint *bach.* About the rest of it I can only say that I am sure you were sincere while you were speaking, and I am not surprised the elder Schnaks fell for it. Yes—on consideration I would say that what you told them was true. But I am not sure about your intention in doing so."

"My intention was to make them like our opera, and to give them pleasure, and sew up the rent garment of the Schnakenburg family."

"And did you succeed?"

"Ma Schnakenburg was overjoyed to see her child clean and putting on some flesh; Pa Schnakenburg was, if I do not do the man injustice, glad to find Hulda in such classy company, because there is a snob in everybody, and Pa Schnak has not forgotten the elegant world of aristocratic Europe. I just put the cherry on the cake with some fancy theology."

"Not theology, Geraint. Rhetoric," said Darcourt.

"Sim *bach,* I wish you would stop knocking rhetoric. What is it? It is what the poet calls upon when the Muse is sleeping. It is what the preacher calls on when he must reach ears that need tickling to get their attention. Those of us who live in the world of art would be flat on our arses most of the time if we had no rhetoric to hold us up. Rhetoric is only base when base men use it. With me, it is the way in which I arouse the ancient and permanent elements in the spiritual structure of man by measured, rhythmic speech. Your rejection of my rhetoric springs from a mean envy, and I am disappointed in you."

"Of course you're right, Geraint; those of us who lack the gift of the gab are suspicious of those who have it. But it's just spell-binding, you know."

"*Just* spellbinding, Sim *bach!* Oh, what a pitiable barrenness of spirit lurks in that pauper's adverb *just!* I weep for you!" Powell helped himself to another piece of chicken.

"You can't weep while you're stuffing your face," said Darcourt. "Didn't the Schnaks sniff anything peculiar about the bond between Nilla and their child?"

"Such enormities are unknown to them, I imagine. My recollection of the Bible includes no instance of naughtiness between women. That's why it has a Greek name. Those tough old Israelites thought deviance was entirely a masculine privilege. They think Schnak is putting on flesh because she has come under a Good Influence."

"Speaking as a woman, I don't see the attraction of Schnak," said Maria. "If I were of Nilla's inclination I could find prettier girls."

"Ah, but Schnak has the beauty of innocence," said Powell. "Oh, she's a foul-mouthed, cornaptious slut, but underneath she is all untouched wonderment. I suppose she's been mauled by a few student morlocks, because it's the custom in the circle in which she moves, and kids fear to go against custom. But the real, deep-down Schnak is still flower-like, and Nilla's is just the delicate hand to pluck the flower. But you know what happens; or rather you don't, because none of you are gardeners; I slaved in my mam's garden all my boyhood. You pluck the first bloom, and other, stronger blooms hurry to replace it, and that is what is happening to Schnak."

"What blooms?" said Arthur. "God forbid that we should support a lesbian house of ill-fame. There are limits, even for the
Cornish Foundation. Simon, hadn't you better look into this?"

"Quite right, Arthur. The bills I've been paying for champagne
and pretty little cakes from the gourmet shops are horrendous.
Can't these women sustain their passion on hamburger?"

"You're quite wrong," said Powell. "That's not the way things
are going at all. Nilla has roused Schnak's dormant tenderness,
and let me tell you, boyos, that's chancy work. Where will it strike
next? I think she has her eye on you, Sim *bach*."

Darcourt was staggered, and not at all pleased that this suggestion was greeted with hoots of laughter from Arthur and Maria.

"I don't see the joke," said he. "The suggestion is grotesque."

"In love, nothing is grotesque," said Powell.

"Sorry, Simon. I don't suggest that you are a ridiculous love-
object," said Arthur. "But Schnak—" he could not speak, and
laughed himself into a coughing fit, and had to be slapped on the
back.

"You'll have to dye your hair and go West," said Maria.

"Simon can look after himself, and he must stay here," said
Powell. "We need him. If need be, he can take flight after the
opera is safely launched. The opera is at the root of the whole
thing. It was that poetry you quoted to her, Simon. Didn't you
see her face change?"

"You were the one who quoted poetry," said Darcourt. "You
Welsh mischief-maker, you quoted Ella Wheeler Wilcox to the
girls, and Nilla very properly gagged, but Schnak ate it up.

> *It is not art, but heart*
> *Which wins the wide world over.*

You meant it as a joke, but Schnak swallowed it whole."

"Because it is true," said Powell. "Corny, but true. And I suppose it is the first bit of verse Schnak ever heard which went right
to her heart, like the bolt of Cupid. But you were the one who
trotted out some real poetry, and gave it to her for the culminating
moment of our drama.—Simon has found the words for Arthur's
great aria," he said to Arthur and Maria, "and it's just the very

thing we want. Right period, decent verse, and a fine statement of a neglected truth."

"Let's have it, Simon," said Arthur.

Darcourt found himself embarrassed. The verses were so apt to the situation of the three people who sat at table with him; verses that spoke of chivalry, and constancy, and, he truly believed, of the essence of love itself. In a low voice—he could not bring himself to use Powell's full-throated bardic manner—he recited:

> *"True love's the gift which God has given*
> *To man alone beneath the heaven:*
> *It is not fantasy's hot fire,*
> *Whose wishes, soon as granted, fly;*
> *It liveth not in fierce desire,*
> *With dead desire it doth not die;*

> *It is the secret sympathy,*
> *The silver link, the silken tie,*
> *Which heart to heart, and mind to mind,*
> *In body and in soul can bind."*

The verses were received in silence. It was Maria who spoke first, and like a true university woman she set out on a criticism of the words which was rooted in what she had been taught; she had a critical system, unfailing in its power to reduce poetry to technicalities and to slide easily over its content. It was a system which, properly applied, could put Homer in his place and turn the Sonnets of Shakespeare into critic-fodder. Without intending to be so, it was a system which, once mastered, set the possessor free forever, should that be his wish, from anything a poet, however noble in spirit, might have felt and imparted to the world.

"Shit!" said Powell, when she had finished. And then began a very hot discussion in which Powell was strong for the verses, and Arthur quiet and considering, and Maria determined to declare all of Walter Scott second-rate, and his easy versifying the outcome of a profuse, trivial spirit.

She is fighting for her life, thought Darcourt, and she is per-versely using weapons she has learned at the university. But did anybody learn much about love in a classroom?

He kept himself apart from the wrangle. It was easy, because only by determined shouting was it possible to come between Powell and Maria. Had there ever been such a scene at Camelot, he wondered. Did Arthur, and Guenevere and Lancelot, ever haggle about what had been done, and what lay at the root of it?

If these are really modern versions of the principals in that great chivalric tale, how did they appear in terms of chivalry? The Knights, and presumably the Knights' Ladies, were supposed to possess, or try to possess, twelve knightly virtues. There were many lists of those virtues, none wholly alike, but they all included Honour, Prowess, and Courtesy, and, all things considered, these three had those virtues in plenty. Hope, Justice, Fortitude? The men emerged from that test better than Maria. Faith and Loyalty it was perhaps not well to discuss, with Maria pregnant. And it would be tactless to speak of Chastity. Franchise, now—free and frank demeanour—they had all had in their various ways. Largesse, that open-handedness which was one of the foremost attributes of a Knight, was the spirit of the Cornish Foundation. All that champagne and Viennese *gateaux* were largesse, as well as the great sums that were now beginning to appear on the horizon as necessary to get the opera on the stage. But Pity of Heart—that was an attribute which Arthur alone seemed to possess, and under all the ridiculous fussing about Maria's pregnancy it was plainly to be seen in him; Maria seemed to lack it utterly. Or did she? Was her rejection of Walter Scott just a fear of what she truly felt? *Débonnaireté*—now that was a good virtue for a Knight, and for anybody else that could achieve it; gaiety of heart, a noble indifference to trivial difficulties, a *sprezzatura*, in fact— Powell was the exemplar of that virtue, and, although he still had fits of eloquent remorse for what he had done, he was contriving to rise above it. He regarded himself as co-father with Arthur, and he played the role with style.

What is that all about, thought Darcourt. A deep Freudian would almost certainly declare that there was, between Arthur and Geraint, some dank homosexual tie, working itself out in possession of the same woman. But Darcourt was not disposed to Freudian interpretations. At best, they were glum half-truths, and they explained and healed extraordinarily little. They explored what Yeats called "the foul rag-and-bone shop of the heart", but they brought none of the Apollonian light that Yeats and many another poet cast upon the heart's dunghill. Sir Walter, so plainly writing of his darling Charlotte, knew something that had escaped the unhappily married Viennese wizard. The silver link. The silken tie.

Perhaps Arthur knew it, too. Maria was wearing out with argument, and seemed near to tears.

"Come on, darling. Time you were in bed," said Arthur. And that concluded the matter, for the moment, with Pity of Heart.

[4]

DARCOURT LONGED FOR SPRING with more than the ordinary Canadian yearning. His search for the people in *The Marriage at Cana* could not be completed until the snow was off the ground, and in Blairlogie the snow lingered and renewed itself until the middle of April.

Meanwhile he spent long hours at the Library, sifting the last scraps of what had been bundled up in Francis Cornish's apartment. It was three apartments, really, every one crammed with every sort of art object. Armed with what he already knew from his biographical burrowing and fossicking about the Cornish and O'Gorman and McRory families and their hangers-on and dependents, he was able to identify almost all of the figures in the great picture.

Some of them had been identified before. Darcourt knew almost by heart the article that had been published a quarter of a century before in *Apollo,* written by Aylwin Ross. It had put the cap on Ross's once-great reputation, and had established the beautiful young Canadian as an art historian to be taken seriously. How ingenious Ross had been, with his historical exposition about the Interim of Augsburg and the Catholic-Protestant row it had created in 1548. How convincing he was about his identification of Graf Meinhard of Düsterstein and his Lady, and Johann Agricola the scholar, and Paracelsus—this was a great coup, for portraits of Paracelsus are extremely rare—and even the jolly dwarf who was certainly, Ross knew, Drollig Hansel, who was, past question, the famous dwarf jester in the employ of the Fugger family of bankers. It was romance that might have rejoiced the heart of Sir Walter Scott. But it was all moonshine, and Darcourt knew it.

Graf Meinhard and his Lady were certainly portraits of the parents of Francis Cornish, and Johann Agricola was that school-master at Colborne College who had put Francis's foot on the path of historical study, and of whom a snapshot had been tucked into a sketchbook of Francis's Blairlogie period. What was the man's name? Ramsay, was it? Yes, Dunstan Ramsay. As for Par-acelsus, the shrewd little figure in a physician's gown who was holding a scalpel, there could be no doubt whatever that he was Dr. Joseph Ambrosius Jerome, of whom Darcourt knew little except that he had been the McRorys' family doctor, and had once been photographed by Grandfather McRory seated, with one hand on a skull, and the other holding just such a scalpel.

Sketches—there were scores of them, and many accorded with Grandfather's Sun Pictures. That dwarf was certainly François Xavier Bouchard, the little tailor of Blairlogie, seen by Grand-father fully clothed, but sketched by Francis lying on a table, stark naked and plainly dead. Was he being embalmed? Certainly there were several sketches among Francis's earliest drawings of nude figures in which there was a hint—only a few lines, but eloquent— of a figure who seemed to be the *huissier,* the man with a whip in the painting, and also the man photographed by Grandfather standing at the head of a splendid team of carriage horses; a man of ravaged good looks, always drawn with a gleam of pity in his eye; pity for the dead which was also a knightly pity of heart for the whole of mankind.

Given the sketches and the photographs that Darcourt had unearthed in the University Library and in the preliminary studies for the picture which had been, at Francis Cornish's express di-rection, sent to the National Gallery in Ottawa, the whole picture lay open. The two women disputing over the wine jars, between whom knelt the figure of Christ; beyond a doubt Francis's aunt, Miss Mary-Benedetta McRory, and her adversary was Grand-father's cook, Victoria Cameron. What could they have been quarrelling about? As they were at it, hammer and tongs, over the figure of Christ, perhaps Christ was at the root of their disagreement. But who was St. John, with pen and ink-horn? He eluded identification but might perhaps yield his secret later. There was no secret about the compelling portrait of Judas, holding firmly to his moneybag; there were enough sketches in the books Francis had filled at Düsterstein to mark him clearly as Tancred Saraceni, father in art to Francis, and an ambiguous *éminence grise* in the art world of forty years ago; a restorer of pictures of preeminent skill, who may perhaps have done a little more than restoration on some of his canvases.

There were other figures, not identifiable or not to be identified with utter certainty. That stout merchant and his wife; they could be Gerald Vincent O'Gorman, known after his Blairlogie beginnings as a very shrewd man in the Cornish Trust, and the woman must therefore be Mary-Teresa McRory, who had become Mrs. O'Gorman and, after a strong Catholic start, a shining light among Toronto Anglicans. But the woman with what appeared to be an astrological chart? No sign of her anywhere, either as a photograph or as a sketch. And those wretched children, in the background? They looked like Blairlogie children, but they had a vicious, depraved look that was dreadful to see on childish faces; they seemed to be saying something about childhood that is not often heard.

The central figures of the picture, who were plainly the wedding couple, offered no problem and admitted of no doubt. They suggested, but in no way imitated, Van Eyck's famous portrait of the Arnolfini couple; the suggestion lay in the intensity of their gaze, the gravity of their expression. Beyond a doubt the bride was Ismay Glasson, of whom Darcourt had seen almost a hundred sketches, naked and clothed, and he knew her face—not quite beautiful but more compelling in its intensity than beauty usually is—as well as he knew any face in the world. This was the woman Francis had married, the mother of Little Charlie, the bolter and fanatic; although the figure of Francis extended its hand toward her, it did not quite touch the hand of Ismay, who seemed to hold back, and her gaze was not at her husband but at the handsome young man who figured as St. John.

The husband was Francis Cornish, a confession in the form of a self-portrait. Pictures of Francis were rare; apart from this picture, he had never painted himself, and none of his contemporaries had thought him sufficiently interesting for a sketch. Grandfather's photographs showed the dark, slight boy in the hideous costume of his childhood and youth: Francis in a sailor suit, standing on a giant tree trunk, above a group of muscular, bearded timber-workers; Francis in his Sunday best, sitting beside a small table on which lay his rosary beads and a prayer-book; Francis squinting into the sun on a Blairlogie street; Francis with his beautiful mother, uneasy in a starched Eton collar; a few group photographs from Colborne days, in which Francis figured as a prize-winner; one photograph of an amateur theatrical performance—some sort of student Follies—in which a lanky, thin Francis appeared in the back row, among the stage-managers and scene-painters, hardly noticeable behind all the girls in short skirts and the boys in blazers who had obviously danced and sung greatly to their own satisfaction. Nothing at all which said anything about Francis Cornish.

In *The Marriage at Cana*, however, his was the dominant figure to which all the rest of the composition related. Not that the placing or presentation of the figure was aggressive; there was no Look At Me about it. But this intently gazing man, dressed in blacks and browns, drew the viewer's eye back to himself, however intent it may have been on any of the other figures. Most self-portraits tend to glare at the onlooker. The painter, presumably looking into a mirror beside his easel, must glare, must have one eye looking straight into the eyes of the beholder, and the more self-conscious the painter, the more intent the glare becomes. Rembrandts, who dare to paint themselves full-face and objectively, are uncommon. Francis had painted himself looking not at his wife but straight out of the canvas. Yet his eyes did not meet and challenge those of the onlooker; they seemed to be looking over his head. The face was grave, almost sad, and among the faces of the others—the Bride elusive and somewhat sulky, St. John looking like an adventurer, the Knight and his Lady looking like important figures in their world, the two disputing women painted in obvious contention, and the old artisan (Grandfather McRory as St. Simon the Zealot, with his woodsman's tools)—this face, Francis's face, was looking out of their world into some other, private world. Darcourt had sometimes seen that look on the face of the old Francis whom he had known.

Finally—no, not quite finally—there was the woman who stood beside the bridal couple, the only figure in the picture graced with a halo. The Mother of God? Yes, for the convention in which the picture was cast demanded that. But more probably the Mighty Mother of All. As the mother of everybody and everything, it was not necessary for her to look like anyone in particular. Her grave beauty was universal and her smile was of a serenity that rose beyond earthly considerations.

Was that serene smile intended to heal the hurt that was visible in the portraits of the bride and groom, in which the man extended a ring toward the fourth finger of his bride's left hand, and she seemed to be holding back, or perhaps withdrawing her hand from what he offered? To Darcourt, knowing what he knew, and immersed as he was in all the Sun Pictures and the innumerable copies, sketches, and finished drawings that were all that remained of the truth of Francis Cornish's life, it seemed as if this extraordinary picture was an allegory of a man's ruin, of the destruction of his spirit. Had the wilful bolter Ismay really hurt him so deeply? After this picture, Francis had never painted seriously again.

> *Shall I, wasting in despair,*
> *Die because a woman's fair?*

The poet who wrote that, and all the easy philosophy of love that follows it, was a hardier soul than Francis. But not all men, or all lovers, are hardy souls. It seemed to Darcourt that Francis had not died because of Ismay's determination to follow her own star, but something within him had suffered mortal hurt, and the death that had overtaken him so many years afterward, when he died alone in his cluttered flat, was a second death, and it was not in Darcourt's power to say which had been the most significant cessation of being.

Darcourt would readily have admitted that he did not know much about love. He had had no youthful affairs, except in a superficial sense. His love for Maria, which he now knew to have been a folly from which he was lucky to escape, was all that he had known of passion. But he had the gift, not often given to deeply passionate men, to understand the joys and also the heart-stopping blows of fate that afflicted other people. The more he looked at the large reproduction, and also the detailed pictures of portions of *The Marriage at Cana* that accompanied Aylwin Ross's brilliant, wholly mistaken article in *Apollo,* the more he wondered if Maria, now great with Geraint Powell's child, had struck just such a blow to Arthur Cornish. Arthur was holding up very well, if that were true, but he had lost all *débonnaireté.* Arthur was certainly The Magnanimous Cuckold. But Arthur was not the clearly defined, generous, but ruthless spirit he had been when Darcourt first knew him. If it were so, who was to blame? The more Darcourt knew, the less he was inclined to blame or praise.

The final figure in the picture, however, had to await the spring before it could be identified, so far as possible, forever.

That was the angel who floated in the air over the heads of the bridal pair and the Mighty Mother in the central panel of the triptych. Perhaps it was not quite an angel, but if not, why was it suspended in air, without angelic wings? The first time one looked at the picture it seemed to throw the whole composition into confusion. Whereas the other figures were human, painted with love, and sometimes beautiful, sometimes noble, sometimes self-satisfied, sometimes—old St. Simon was such a portrait—as wise beyond worldly wisdom, this floating creature was a comic horror. Its pointed head, its almost idiotic expression, its suggestion of disorder of mind and deformity of body, were all out of key with the rest. And yet, the more one looked, the more it seemed to belong, to be almost necessary to whatever it was the whole composition was saying.

From its mouth came a scroll, suggesting one of the balloons that hold the words in a comic strip, and in the scroll were the words *Tu autem servasti bonum vinum usque adhuc.* Not very elegant as Latin, but the words spoken to the bridegroom by the governor of the feast at the Marriage at Cana: "Thou hast kept the good wine until now." Christ's first miracle; a puzzle, for nothing in the Gospel suggests that anyone but Christ and His Mother and a few servants knew the secret.

Was this picture, then, as well as an object of great beauty, a puzzle? A joke, a deeply serious joke, on future beholders?

April brought the answer, as Darcourt had hoped it would. He made the inconvenient train journey to Blairlogie and, armed

with a shovel, a broom, and his camera, he went to the Catholic
cemetery and there, high on the bleak hill, he visited once again
the McRory family plot. It was dominated by large, tasteless
stones commemorating the Senator and his wife, and Mary-
Benedetta McRory. But there were a few humbler markers, one
of them not a gravestone but a memorial to somebody called
Zadok Hoyle, identified as a faithful servant of the family. And the
here it was—in an obscure corner behind the biggest stone was
a small marble marker, flat to the ground, and when Darcourt
had cleared away the last lingering snow and ice, and an accumulation of lichen, it read, plainly, FRANCIS.

So: here it was. Among the sketches from Francis's boyhood
years there were a number of an invalid figure, confined to a bed
which was almost a cage; the figure in the bed was a pitiable
deformity, of the sort that cruel people used to call a pinhead,
blank of eye, sparse of hair, and wearing an expression, to use
the word loosely, that would draw pity from the heart of an ogre.
These sketches, rapid but vivid, were identified only by the letter
F, except for one on which was laboriously written, in the hand
of a boy who wished to be a calligrapher but did not yet know
how, what seemed to have been copied from some royal signature,
François Premier.

Francis the First? Now, thought Darcourt, I know all I need
to know, and all I am ever likely to know. Truly the best wine
has been kept until the last.

[5]

"THE CRONES ARE COMING," said Dean Wintersen's voice down
the telephone. "They are expected today."

What crones? Was this some uncanny visitation of weird old
women? What crones? Darcourt had been roused from his work
on the biography of the late Francis Cornish, and his mind did
not readily shift to the Dean's concern. The crones? Oh, yes! Of
course! The Cranes. Had he not agreed that some people called
Crane should come from an American West Coast university to
do something or other of a vaguely defined order about the production of the opera? That had been months ago and, having so
agreed, and having it well understood that the Cranes were not

to cost the Cornish Foundation anything, he had banished the Cranes from his mind, as a problem to be dealt with when it arose. Now, it appeared, the Cranes were coming.

"You remember them, of course," said the Dean.

"Remind me," said Darcourt.

"They're the assessors from Pomelo U.," said the Dean. "It was agreed they should sit in on the production of the opera. You remember the opera, don't you?"

Oh, yes; Darcourt remembered the opera. Had he not been slaving over the libretto for the past four months?

"But what are they going to assess?" said Darcourt.

"The whole affair. Everything connected with the opera from Schnak's work on the score to the last detail of getting the thing on the stage. And then the critical and public reaction."

"But why?"

"To get Al Crane his Ph.D., of course. He's an opera major in the theatre school at Pomelo, and when he has got his assessment together he will make a *Regiebuch* and present it as his thesis."

"His what?"

"His *Regiebuch*. A German expression. All the dope on the production of the opera will be in it."

"My God! He sounds like Divine Correction out of a medieval play. Does Dr. Dahl-Soot know? Does Geraint Powell know?"

"I suppose they do. You're the liaison man, or so I understood. Didn't you tell them?"

"I don't think I knew. Or fully realized."

"You'd better tell them, then. Al and Mabel will be seeing you right away. They're eager."

"Who's Mabel?"

"I'm not sure. I think she's not quite Mrs. Crane, but she's with him. Not to worry. Al has a big grant from the Polemo Further Studies fund to look after him. This is a courtesy schools of music frequently extend to one another. It'll be all right."

How lightly the Dean took such things! Doubtless that was the secret of being a dean. When, a couple of hours after his call, Darcourt gazed at Al and Mabel Crane, as they sat in his study, he wondered if it would really be all right.

Not that the Cranes looked menacing. Not at all. They had the look of expectancy Darcourt knew so well as an attribute of a certain kind of student. They wanted something to happen to them, and they wanted him to make it happen. They were probably in their middle twenties, but they had still the unfledged, student look. Apparently they travelled light and informally. It was cool in the Canadian spring, but Al Crane was dressed as if for a hot day. He wore chinos, a much crumpled seersucker coat, and a dirty shirt. The breast pocket of the coat hung heavily with a number of ball-point pens. His bare feet were thrust into sandals that would not last much longer. He had not shaved for two or three days, and his lantern jaws were dark. As for Mabel, the one arresting thing about her was that she was monstrously pregnant. The child she carried, though still unborn, was already sitting in her lap. Like Al, she was dressed for summer, the summer of Southern California, and she too was in a bad way for footwear. They both smiled, in a dog-like manner, as if hoping to be patted.

Al, however, knew what he wanted. He wanted several days with Hulda Schnakenburg, to go over the score of the opera and examine all the scraps of Hoffmann, which he called The Documentation, and then he wanted a few days with Dr. Dahl-Soot, whose presence in the matter was, he declared, awesome. Just to talk with Gunilla Dahl-Soot would be an enrichment. He wanted access to a Xerox machine, so that he could get facsimiles of everything, every inch of Hoffmann, every draft of Schnakenburg, every page of the completed score. He wanted to go over the libretto with whoever had prepared it, and he wanted to compare it with anything by Planché, from which it derived, or did not derive. He wanted to talk with the director, the designer, the designer of lighting, and the scenic artists. He wanted copies of every design, and every rejected design. He wanted to photograph the stage that would be used, and he wanted all its measurements.

"That'll do to be going on with," he said. "Then of course I'll sit in on all the rehearsals and all the musical preparation. I'll need a full C.V. from everybody involved. But right now, we're wondering where we are to live."

"I haven't any idea," said Darcourt. "You'd better talk to Dean Wintersen about that. There are lots of hotels."

"I'm afraid a hotel would be way beyond us," said Al. "We've got to watch the pennies."

"I understood the Dean to say that you had a generous grant from Pomelo."

"Generous for one," said Al. "Tight for two. For three, I should say. You can see how it is with Mabel."

"Oh, Al, do you think there's been a slip-up?" said Mabel. She was the kind of woman, Darcourt saw with alarm, who cries easily.

"Not to worry, Sweetness," said Al. "I'm sure the professor has everything lined up."

Don't be too sure, thought Darcourt. There had been a time, before he recognized himself as the Fool, when he would have been badgered into assuming full responsibility for these Babes in the Wood. But as the Fool he had other things to attend to. So he gave the Cranes the name of Dean Wintersen's secretary, and the telephone number at which the Doctor could be reached, and, by means of well-developed professorial will-power—the spiritual equivalent of the Chinese Chi-Kung—he shifted them off his chairs and out of his sight.

They went, thanking him profusely and assuring him that they looked forward to seeing him again. It had already been a terrific experience, they said, just meeting him.

[6]

DARCOURT WAS NOT SURE how he should approach Arthur and Maria about his discovery, now his certainty, of what *The Marriage at Cana* really was. Although the Cornish Foundation was in no way underwriting his biography of Francis Cornish, friendship and a sense of decency about a family with whom he was strongly involved made it obligatory that he should tell them what he had found, before he said anything to Princess Amalie and Prince Max. The picture belonged to the New York people, and who could guess what they might say to his information about their treasure? Was it a brilliant piece of detection in the world of art history, or was it the harsh unmasking of a fake? And if a fake, what did that mean in loss of money? That was trouble enough, but the touchiness of the Cornishes about anything that might reflect, however faintly, on the integrity of the great financial house was incalculable. So he dawdled, dotting i's and crossing t's in his documentation, and hoping that a favourable moment would declare itself.

The declaration came from an unexpected source. Wally Crottel was apprehended by the police selling marijuana to schoolchildren. In the playground of the Governor Simcoe Public School, Wally was plying a brisk trade in joints at the end of each school day, and some children, with that mixture of innocence and stupidity that marks a certain sort of childish mind, were walking home puffing proudly. Before the police could put the handcuffs on him Wally made an ill-advised break for freedom and was knocked down by a passing car; he was quite badly hurt, and was now in the General Hospital, with a policeman sitting outside his room, with nothing to do but read a paperback book which Mr. Carver told Darcourt was *Middlemarch,* an unexpected choice. Mr. Carver had tipped off the police about Wally's profitable sideline, and Mr. Carver could not conceal a deep satisfaction at Wally's fall.

"But you have to admit the guy was very well organized," he said. "He was growing the stuff in a corner of a parking lot behind the boarding-house building where he lived. It was quite a small job, but you don't need an awful lot of the old Mary-Jane to make a few joints, and Wally included a good deal of dried mint with it, to make it go as far as possible, and give a flavour kids liked. Wally was doing very well, for a small operator. Where the kids got the money to pay his price I don't know, but there are quite a few rich kids in that district, and I think some of them were retailing what they bought from Wally, adulterated with dried grass and God knows what. Little bastards! Imagine kiddy pushers! But we live in a very strange world, professor."

"We do, indeed. How did you get wise to Wally?"

"There's a guy lives in the basement of that building where Mr. and Mrs. Cornish have the penthouse that I've known for years. Looks like a slob, but he's not a real slob. I think he had it in for Wally, who was always snooping around that basement apartment, trying to find out how this man and his sister came to be living there. Now, the sister's a bit of a psychic, and sometimes the cops use her, when they want one. Oh, yes; we cops are not above tips from psychics, and sometimes they're very useful. You can't discount anything you hear in the detective business."

"Will it go hard with Wally, when he comes to trial?"

"That crook Gwilt is hard at work, building up a case that Wally comes from a broken home—you know what I mean? He'll do his best to keep Wally in the hospital as long as possible, so he can do whatever he can to get Wally tried before an easy judge. Fat chance! There aren't any easy judges when it comes to pushing drugs to kids. Wally is headed for a long, reflective retirement as a guest of the Crown."

"What could that mean?"

"Well, professor, it says on the books you can get life for pushing. Nobody does, but some of the sentences are tough. Let's look on the bright side and say Wally comes out of hospital with a short leg, or a hole in his head, or something showy like that. The judge might go easy on him. He'll still go to the pen, of course, but if he's a very good boy, and squeals on a few people he knows, and sucks up to the governors and the chaplain, he might be on the street again in seven years, but not a minute less. I'd hope for nine or ten. Pushing to kids is very, very unpopular. Wally has lost face, as the Chinese say. Your friend with the book Wally was whimpering about can forget Wally. How is that nice lady?"

"At this moment, she's expecting a baby."

"Couldn't be better. If you see her, wish her luck from me."

The very night he heard of Wally's fall Darcourt hastened to the Cornishes' apartment, thinking that such news would create an atmosphere friendly to his real mission. He was not pleased to find Powell there before him, making himself very much at home. He could not possibly include Powell in any discussion about *The Marriage at Cana*. But he told Arthur and Maria about Wally, and about Carver's forecast of Wally's future.

"Poor old Wally," said Maria.

Arthur was dumbfounded. "Poor old—! Maria, don't you see? This disposes of that business of Wally wanting his father's book. He wouldn't get anywhere with a court case about that."

"Aren't the courts supposed to forget past misdeeds, when somebody has been foully wronged?"

"They're supposed to, but they don't. From henceforth, Wally is null and void."

"I'm astonished at you men. Do you want to have your own way at the expense of a fellow creature's suffering?"

"I haven't the least objection to you getting your own way at the expense of anybody's suffering. Except mine, of course," said Arthur.

"Wally is suffering becuse he is stupid," said Darcourt. "Trying to break away from the cops! Ah, these amateurs! He is obviously a criminal of no real flair."

"Wouldn't you have tried to escape?"

"If I were hanging around schoolyards, peddling dope to kids, I would hope to have more grip on my job. If I were a criminal, I would try to use the brains God gave me."

"All right. Wally is a bad boy and Wally is stupid. But it ill becomes you, as a Christian priest, to be exulting and sniggering. Where's your pity?"

"Maria, stop playing the Many-Breasted Mother, gushing compassion like a burst waterpipe. You're kidding. You're just as glad as we are that Wally's out of the way."

"I shall indeed be a mother within quite a short time, and I think a show of compassion becomes me. I know my role." Maria smiled a farcical Madonna smile.

"Good! Then I'll play my role as a Christian priest. Arthur, will you get on the phone and send Wally your own lawyer? Meanwhile I'll phone the newspaper sob-sisters and shed a few tears about Wally's sad plight. Geraint, you lodge a complaint under the Charter of Rights. Wally was an employee of this building, and thus of the Cornish Trust, of which Arthur is the Big Cheese. So Arthur must rush to the aid of a victim of our social system. Maria, prepare to appear in court, heavy with child and wearing a veil, to say what a sweet little fellow Wally always was, and how Whistlecraft's denial of his name to Wally gave him an Anonymity Complex. Wally will have to go to jail, but we can float him in and out on a flood of tears. Of course we'll keep mum about how Wally tried to shake you down for a million. Come on, let's get to work. There must be more than one phone in this palace."

"Oh, I wasn't suggesting that we *do* anything," said Maria. "I was just suggesting that we *talk* a little more compassionately."

"You don't understand modern compassion, Sim *bach*. It's a

passive virtue. I see what Maria means; let's pity Wally, and maybe send him a few grapes in the slammer. If anybody is going to be nasty to the criminal classes, it must be those horrible cops and the hard-faced men in the courts. That's what we pay them for. To make the world cosy for us. We smash Wally without having to harbour a hateful, revengeful thought; our servants do all that kind of thing for us."

"That's a new dimension of the Kater Murr philosophy," said Darcourt. "Thanks for explaining it to me, Geraint *bach*."

"After the baby is born, I think I shall write a whole volume, expanding Kater Murr," said Maria. "Hoffmann didn't begin to get all the good out of him. Kater Murr is really the foremost social philosopher of our time."

This was what Darcourt wanted. This was almost the old Maria, the woman infused with the spirit of François Rabelais, a spirit vowed to the highest reaches of scholarship and illuminated by a cleansing humour. Arthur, he thought, was looking decidedly better. Had some sort of new serenity descended on the Cornish household? Well—Powell was still there, and Powell was making himself very much at home.

"I must leave you shortly," said he, "but meanwhile I am enjoying the peaceful retirement of your dwelling. This is one place where I am sure I can't be got at by the abominable Al Crane."

"Oh, don't think you are safe here," said Arthur. "Last night Al and Sweetness turned up and he cross-examined me for two hours, taking a full five minutes to formulate each question. In the modern lingo, Al lacks verbal skills; lingually, Al is a stumblebum. He brought a tape-recorder, so that every precious Um and Ah would be preserved forever. He wanted to know what my Motivation was for putting the Fund behind the opera scheme. He doesn't believe anybody might do something for a variety of reasons; he wants one great, big, juicy Motivation which would be, he says, a significantly seminal thread in a complexity of artistic inspirations. He wants to identify all the threads that are woven into the complex tapestry of a work of art—I am quoting Al, you understand—but some threads are more seminal than others, and mine is wonderfully seminal; it could even be the warp, or maybe the woof, of the whole tapestry. I thought I would faint from boredom before I finally got him out of the house."

"Arthur did not suffer alone," said Maria. "All the time Al had him on the spot I was being bored rigid by Sweetness, who thanked me for receiving her in my Gracious Home, and then talked about what she called Our Condition. There are countless ways of making pregnancy nauseating, and I think Sweetness explored them all."

"Sweetness is delighted with you. She told me so," said Darcourt. "Because of your both being pregnant, of course. You and she, greatly in pod, are what she calls an Objective Correlative of the job of bringing this opera to birth. You, and she, and the opera all burst upon a waiting world at roughly the same time."

"Spare me Sweetness's scholarly insights," said Maria. "She is not an Objective Correlative of anything, and she disgusts me as parodies of oneself always do. She expects me to embrace her as a loving companion in gravidity, and if she gives me much more sisterly love I may miscarry. But she would be sure to interpret that as an ill omen for the opera, so I don't think I'll oblige her. Never again does she cross the threshold of my Gracious Home."

"They didn't get a great welcome in Nilla's Gracious Home," said Powell. "Nilla doesn't know what an assessor is, and I can't tell her. I always thought the word meant a judge, or somebody who estimated something. What is an assessor, exactly, Sim *bach?*"

"It is something new in the academic world," said Darcourt. "Somebody who watches something happen, and gives an enormously detailed report on it; somebody who shares an experience, without having any real involvement with it. A sort of Licensed Snoop."

"But who issues the licence?" said Arthur.

"In this case, it seems to have been Wintersen. He says watching the production process will enrich Al immeasurably, and if Al develops his thesis into a book, it will give permanency to a deeply interesting and profoundly seminal experience."

"Nilla is not pleased," said Powell. "She knows only one meaning for seminal, and she thinks Al is being indecent in a male chauvinist way. She told him flatly there was nothing seminal in what she and Schnak were doing, and when he contradicted her she was very brusque. Said she had no time for such nonsense. Sweetness burst into tears, and Al said he fully understood the mercuriality of the artistic temperament, but the act of creation was seminal and it was his job to understand it so far as in him lay, which he seemed to think was pretty far. I just hope Al does not prove to be the condom in the act of creation."

"Not much fear of that," said Arthur.

"No fear at all, really. Nilla and Schnak have worked like Trojans. In fact, I wouldn't be surprised if Wintersen weren't encouraging a deputation of Trojans to come and measure the energy involved. How does Wintersen get into this act, anyhow?"

"Dean of the Graduate School of Music," said Darcourt. "I think he sees himself as seminal in this whole project. Did you know that Al and Sweetness have been to see Penny Raven?"

"As a collaborator with you on the libretto?"

"A fat lot of collaboration Penny has done. Those Trojans had better have a word with me, when they are learning about work. But Penny is an old academic hand. She strung them along with some high-sounding nonsense, and when she phoned me about it she could hardly speak for laughing. Quoted from *The Hunting of the Snark,* as she always does."

"That Snark again," said Arthur. "I really must read it. What did she say?"

"It's an astonishing poem for descriptive quotes:

> *They sought it with thimbles, they sought it with care,*
> *They pursued it with forks and hope;*
> *They threatened its life with a railway-share;*
> *They charmed it with smiles and soap."*

"Sweetness provides the smiles and soap," said Maria. "I wonder if I shall manage not to kill Sweetness in some ingenious way. How does one get away with murder?"

"Exactly how does Sweetness come into this?" said Arthur. "Are they combining on this awful assessor game?"

"Hollier has the answer," said Darcourt. "They visited him, but they got nowhere. He examined them with great care, however, and he says that he sees Sweetness, in anthropological-psychological-historico terms as the External Image of Al's Soul."

"A terrible thought," said Maria. "Imagine looking into Sweetness's teary eyes and saying, 'My God, that's the best of me!' Al doesn't want to do anything important without her, she tells me.

I'm not sure she didn't say she was his Muse. I wouldn't put it past her."

"I wish I didn't know *The Hunting of the Snark*," said Powell. "I am up to my neck in producing this opera and I keep thinking—

> *The principal failing occurred in the sailing,*
>   *And the Bellman, perplexed and distressed,*
> *Said he* hoped, *at least, when the wind blew due East,*
>   *That the ship would* not *travel due West!*"

"You haven't got cold feet, have you, Geraint?" said Arthur.

"No colder than usual, at this stage in a big job," said Powell. "But I do see myself as the Bellman, when I wake up in the night, sweating. Everything is ready to go, you see. Got the score, got the cast, got the designs, got everything, and at last I must start on what Al would certainly call the seminal part. God grant that I am sufficiently seminal for the job. And now, with the greatest reluctance, I must leave this snug retreat, and go back to my desk. A million details await me."

He pulled himself out of his chair, with some effort. He still has a lame leg, thought Darcourt. It goes well with his generally Byronic personality. He has developed a sliding walk, to disguise his lameness, just like Byron. I wonder if it's conscious imitation—Byronic hero-worship—or if he can't help it?

With Powell out of the way, there was nothing for it but to plunge into his news about *The Marriage at Cana*. He told the tale as convincingly as he could; he wanted to open a new world to his friends, not frighten them with an explosion. For the first time, he spoke to them of his visit to Princess Amalie, to confirm that her Old Master drawing was, in fact, a portrait of herself, done in girlhood by a man on whom she had had a youthful crush. He did not think it necessary to speak of his thefts in the University Library and even in the National Gallery; these were, he now assured himself, not thefts in the ordinary sense, but adventures on the journey of the Fool, guided by intuition and governed by a morality that was not to everybody's taste. If everything worked out as he hoped, what he had done justified itself, and if he were not lucky, he might find himself in jail. With gentleness, but determination, he told of his astonishment when, in the Princess's drawing-room, displayed among a number of convincing Old Masters, and in itself convincing to any eye but his own, he saw *The Marriage,* and with shocked astonishment recognized the faces as belonging to Grandfather McRory's Sun Pictures, and to Francis Cornish's numerous, neglected sketchbooks. There could be no doubt about it, he insisted: Francis was The Alchemical Master, and the great picture was not yet fifty years old.

Arthur and Maria heard all this more or less in silence, though now and then Arthur whistled. It was necessary to come to the real point.

"You understand what this will mean to my biography of Francis," he said. "It is the justification of the book. The climax. It establishes Francis as a very great painter. Working in the mode of a bygone day, but a great painter nonetheless."

"But in the mode of a bygone day," said Arthur. "He may be a great painter, but that makes him unmistakably a faker."

"Not at all," said Darcourt. "There is not a shred of evidence that Francis meant to deceive anybody. The picture was never offered for sale, and if it hadn't been for the war, he would undoubtedly have taken it with him when he left Düsterstein, and nobody will convince me that he would have tried to palm it off as a sixteenth-century work. The Princess knows about it. The picture was stashed away in a store-room of the castle, and when the castle was taken over during the occupation of Germany it disappeared with a lot of other stuff. It was restored to the Düsterstein family after the war, by the Commission that dealt with such matters, of which Francis was a member. That's a bit fishy, but we don't know the details. And the family—that's to say Princess Amalie—has it still."

"That doesn't answer my question," said Arthur. "Why did he paint it in this sixteenth-century manner? And look at this article in *Apollo,* that explains it all. If it wasn't meant to deceive, why paint it like that?"

"That's where we come to the point that is going to be the making of my book," said Darcourt. "You don't remember Francis in any detail. But I do. He was the most inward-looking man I have ever known. He turned things over and over in his mind, and he reached conclusions. That picture is the most important of his conclusions. It represents what he thought most important in his life, the influences, the cross-currents, the tapestry, as Al Crane would say if he had a chance. In that picture Francis was making up his soul, as surely as if he had been some reflective hermit, or cloistered monk. What you see in the picture is the whole matter of Francis, as he saw it himself."

"Yes, but why in this mock sixteenth-century style?"

"Because it is the last style in which a painter could do what Francis was doing. After the Renaissance do you see any pictures that reveal all that a man knows about himself? The great self-portraits, of course. But even when Rembrandt painted himself in old age, he could only show what life had done to him, not how life had done it. With the Renaissance, painting took a new turn, and threw away all that allegorical-metaphysical stuff, all that symbolic communication. You probably don't know that Francis was an expert on iconography—the way you discover what a painter meant, instead of just what anybody can see. In *The Marriage* he means to tell his own truth, as clearly as he can. And he wasn't telling it to someone else. The picture was a confession, a summing-up, intended simply for himself. It's a magnificent thing in several different ways."

"Who's the peculiar angel?" said Maria. "You left him out when you told us who all the characters were. He's obviously somebody of the greatest importance."

"I am virtually certain he was Francis's elder brother. Only one of the sketches is labelled, but it is identified as Francis the First, and I can only guess that he was a very deep influence on Francis the Second's whole life."

"How? It looks like an idiot," said Arthur.

"Presumably it was an idiot. You didn't know your uncle. He was a deeply compassionate man. Oh, he had the reputation for being a curmudgeon, and he didn't suffer fools gladly, and often he seemed to have no tolerance for people at all. But I knew him, and he was far beyond what people mean when they say tender-hearted—which can mean cabbage-headed. He had a sense of the profoundly tragic fragility of human life that I have never known in anyone else, and I am as sure as I can be of anything that it was the knowledge of this grotesque creature, this parody of what he was himself, that made him so. He was a romantic in his youth; look at the way he has painted the girl who became his wife, and let him down so painfully. Look at the dwarf; Francis knew that poor wretch, alive and dead, and he did what he could to balance the scales of Fate when he painted him. All the portraits in *The Marriage* are judgements on people Francis knew, and they are the judgements of a man who had been rudely booted out of a youthful romanticism into a finely compassionate realism. Now Arthur, for God's sake don't ask me again why he painted this summing-up of his life in this bygone style. It was the only style that would contain what he had to say. The Old Masters were deeply religious men, and this is a deeply religious picture."

"I never heard anyone suggest that Uncle Frank was religious."

"The word is greatly misunderstood in the turmoil of our day," said Darcourt, "but in so far as it means seeking to know, and to live, beneath the surfaces of life, and to be aware of the realities beneath the superficialities, you may take it from me that Francis was truly religious."

"Uncle Frank a great painter!" said Arthur. "I don't know just how to cope with it."

"But it's bloody marvellous!" said Maria. "A genius in the family! Aren't you thrilled, Arthur?"

"There have been some rather bright people in the family, but if they were geniuses, or near it, they were financial geniuses. And don't let anybody tell you that financial genius is just low cunning. It's the real intuitive goods. But this sort of genius— For a financial family a painter is rather a skeleton in the cupboard."

"There is something about a cupboard that makes a skeleton very restless," said Darcourt. "Francis Cornish is loudly demanding to be let out."

"Your problem is going to be these people in New York. How will they like it when you reveal that their treasured Old Master— the only known work of The Alchemical Master—is a phoney?"

"It isn't a phoney, Arthur," said Maria. "Simon has been telling us what it is, and phoney is the last word to use. It is an astonishing personal confession in the form of a picture."

"Arthur is right, though," said Darcourt. "They will have to be approached with the greatest tact. I can't go to them and say, Listen, I have news for you: they must want me to come, to hear what I have to tell them. It's the difference between 'Come in, Barney,' and 'Barney, come in.' "

"I suppose that's one of your Old Ontario gobbets of folk wisdom," said Maria.

"Yes, and a very wise one, when you think about it. I can't just tell them what I know, and stop short. I must give them an idea about where this discovery might lead."

"And where would that be?" said Arthur.

"It certainly can't be the devaluation and destruction of the picture as a work of art. It must point a new way."

"Simon, I know you. I see it in your eye. I see it wriggling up your sleeve. You have a scheme. Come on—tell."

"Well, Maria, I wouldn't say I had a scheme. Just a vague idea, and I feel rather embarrassed about bringing it out, because it is sure to sound stupid."

"This modesty is just camouflage for some real Darcourt craftiness. Out with it."

So, diffidently, but not artlessly—because he had been rehearsing what he would say for several days—Darcourt told them what he had in mind.

There was a long silence. After a while Maria fetched drinks; whisky for the men and for herself a glass that looked like milk, but was of a rich, golden colour. They sipped, amid further silence. At last Arthur spoke.

"Ingenious," he said, "but I mistrust ingenuity. It's too damned clever."

"A little better than just clever," said Darcourt.

"Too many intangibles. Too many things that cannot be controlled. I'm afraid the answer must be no, Simon."

"I'm not ready to take that as your final word, Arthur," said Darcourt. "Please think about it for a while. Forget it and then think about it again. Maria, what do you think?"

"I think it's very foxy."

"Oh, please! Foxy is a nasty word."

"I didn't mean it nastily, Simon. But you must admit that it's a poopnoddy scheme, if there ever was one."

"Poopnoddy?" said Arthur. "Is that one of your Rabelaisian words?"

"Go to the head of the class, Arthur," said Maria. "Rabelaisian in spirit, though I don't know quite what he would have said in French. *Avalleur de frimarts,* or something like that. Intending to deceive the unwary, anyhow. I must have a few Rabelaisian words to counteract Simon's cataract of Old Ontario folk-sayings, about Barney and all the gang."

"If you think those people in New York are unwary, you are out of your mind," said Darcourt.

"But I think you think Arthur and I are unwary."

"If you had been wary, would you ever have got yourselves into this opera thing?"

"That's beside the point."

"I think it's the very finest end of the point. What has it brought you?"

"We don't know, yet," said Arthur. "We shall have to wait and see."

"While you're waiting, will you give some thought to my idea?"

"Now that you've brought it up, I don't see how we can help it."

"Good. That's all I ask. But I must talk to the New York people, you know. After all, I am going to explode their picture. From one point of view, that is."

"Look, Simon, can't you somehow soft-pedal the whole business of the picture?"

"No, Arthur, I can't and I won't. It isn't just the heart of my book. It's the truth, and you can't suppress truth forever. That skeleton is banging very loudly on the doors of the cupboard, and if you don't want to let it out my way, you may be sure somebody else will eventually let it out by smashing the cupboard. Don't forget all those sketches Francis bequeathed to the National Gallery."

"Will that concern us? We don't own the picture."

"No, but I shall have written the book and if I soft-pedal this material it will be shown up as a stupid, know-nothing book. I don't see why I should put up with that, just to satisfy your Kater Murr notions."

"You make a lot of fuss about your damned book."

"My damned book will be on the shelves when all of us are dust, and I want it to be the best book I can leave behind me. And I ask you, Arthur, as a friend, to think of that. Because I am going to write it, and write it my way, whatever you choose to do, and if it costs me your friendship, that will be part of the price of authorship."

"Simon, don't be pompous. Maria and I value your friendship highly, but we could live without it if we had to."

"Oh shut up, both of you!" said Maria. "Why can't men ever disagree without all this high-stomached huffing and puffing? No friendships are going to be broken, and if you and Simon part brass rags, Arthur, I'll leave you and live in sin with him. So shut up! Have another drink, Simon."

"Thank you, no. I have to be going. But do you mind telling me what that stuff is you are drinking? It looks delicious."

"It is delicious. It's milk with a good slug of rum in it. My doctor recommends it at bedtime. I haven't been sleeping well, and he says this is better than sleeping-pills, even if the milk is a bit fattening for a lady in an interesting condition."

"Marvellous! Do you think I could have a small one of those? After all, I am great with book, and I need all the little comforts of one who is about to give birth."

"Will you get it for him, Arthur? Or are you too much on your dignity to help poor Simon in his delicate state? I was drinking this last night when Al and Sweetness were here, and Sweetness was shocked."

"Shocked by rum and milk?—Oh, thanks, Arthur.—What shocked her?"

"She gave me a long, confused talk about what she called the foetal alcohol syndrome; booze in pregnancy can lead to pixie-faced, pin-headed, mentally retarded children. I knew something about that; you have to drink rather a lot to be in danger. But Sweetness is a zealot, and she's deep into the squalor of pregnancy, poor wretch. I heard all about her agonizing little balls of gas, which won't come up or go down; and how she can't do a thing with her hair—not even wash it, I thought, looking at her; and she has to be dashing off every half-hour to what she delicately calls the tinkle-pantry, because her bladder capacity is now minimal. She is paying the full price nasty old Mother Nature can exact for Al's baby. I just hope it's a nice baby."

"Did she say why they don't get married, if they are so devoted?"

"Indeed she did. Sweetness has a cliché for everything. They do not admit that their union would be hallowed more than it is, if some parson mumbled a few words over them."

"I wonder why people like that always talk about parsons mumbling a few words. I've married lots of people and I never mumble. I would scorn to mumble."

"You have no proper respect for cliché. Performing your ignominious, outdated office, you ought to mumble for very shame."

"I see. I'll remember that. Am I to mumble at the christening, by the way? I'd very much like to."

"Of course, Simon dear. Mumble, mumble, mumble."

"Have you chosen any names, yet? Always wise to be ready with names."

"Arthur and I haven't made up our minds, but Geraint keeps putting forward Welsh names that are crammed with ancient chivalry and bardic evocation, but are rather demanding for the Canadian thick tongue."

Darcourt had finished his rum and milk, and took his leave. Maria was loving and kind, and Arthur was friendly, with a hint of reserve. On the whole, Darcourt thought he had achieved about as much as he expected.

As he walked home he thought about pixie-faced, pin-headed, mentally retarded children. That was what Francis the First had been. But had Francis the First's mother been a heavy drinker? Nothing he had found in his investigations suggested it. But a biographical researcher must reconcile himself to the fact that there are many things he will never know.

[7]

"IT CERTAINLY SEEMS AS THOUGH *le beau ténébreux* had been much more shadowy than any of us suspected," said Princess Amalie.

"Frankly, I am astounded! Astounded!" said Prince Max, who liked to multiply his verbal effects. "I remember Cornish well. Charming, reserved fellow; spoke little but was a splendid listener; handsome, but didn't seem aware of it. I thought Tancred Saraceni lucky to have found such a gifted assistant; his picture of the Fugger dwarf was a little gem. I wish I had it now. And certainly the Fugger dwarf looked very much like the dwarf in *The Marriage*."

"I remember that curious man Aylwin Ross saying precisely that when the Allied Commission on Art had a chance to look at both pictures. Ross was no fool, though he came to grief in a rather foolish way."

The speaker was Addison Thresher. He is the man to watch and the man to convince, thought Darcourt. The Prince and Princess Amalie know a lot about pictures, and a very great deal about business, but this man knows the art world, and his Yes or No is decisive. Until now he has given no hint that he had known *The Marriage at Cana* in Europe. Watch your step, Darcourt.

"Did you know Francis Cornish well?" he asked.

"I did. That's to say, I met him in The Hague when he made that astonishing judgement on a fake Van Eyck. He played with his cards very close to his vest. But I had a few chats with him later in Munich, during the meetings of the Art Commission. He told me something then that clicks with your surprising explanation of this picture, that we have all loved for so many years. Do you know how he learned to draw?"

"I have seen the beautiful copies of Old Master drawings he made when he was at Oxford," said Darcourt. He saw no reason to say more.

"Yes, but before that? It was one of the most extraordinary confessions I ever heard from an artist. As a boy he learned a lot about technique from a book written by a nineteenth-century caricaturist and illustrator called Harry Furniss. Cornish told me he used to do drawings of corpses in an undertaking parlour. The embalmer was his grandfather's coachman. Furniss was an extraordinary parodist of other men's styles; he once showed a gigantic hoax exhibition in which he parodied all the great painters of the late Victorian era. Of course they hated him for it, but I wish I knew where those pictures are now. Drawing lies at the root of great painting, of course—but imagine a child learning to draw like that from a book! An eccentric genius. Not that all genius isn't eccentric."

"Do you really think our picture was the work of *le beau ténébreux?*" said the Princess.

"When I look at these photographs Professor Darcourt has been showing us, I don't see how I can think anything else."

"Then that smashes the favourite in our collection. Smashes it to smithereens," said Prince Max.

"Perhaps," said Thresher.

"Why perhaps? Isn't it shown to be a fake?"

"Please—not a fake," said Darcourt. "That is what I am anxious to prove. It was never intended to deceive. There is not a scrap of evidence that Francis Cornish ever attempted to sell it, or show it, or gain any sort of worldly advantage from it. It was a picture of wholly personal importance, in which he was setting down and balancing off the most significant elements in his own life, and doing it in the only way he knew, which was by painting. By organizing what he wanted to look at in the form and style that was most personal to him. That is not faking."

"Try telling that to the art world," said the Prince.

"That is precisely what I shall try to do in my life of Francis. And I hope I'm not immodest in saying that I shall do it. Not to unveil a fake, or smash your picture, but to show what an astonishing man Francis Cornish was."

"Yes, but my dear professor, you can't do one without the other. We shall suffer. We shall be made to look like fools, or collaborators in a deception. Think of that article in *Apollo* that Aylwin Ross wrote, explaining the sixteenth-century importance of this picture. It's well known in the world of art history. A very clever piece of detective work. People will think we kept our mouths shut to save our picture, or else that we were victims of Francis Cornish's little joke. No—his big joke. His Harry Furniss joke, as Addison has told us."

"Incidentally, that figure of the fat artist who is drawing on a little ivory tablet is Furniss to the life, now that I know what we know," said Thresher.

"Francis was not wanting in humour. I admit it. He loved a joke and particularly a dark joke that not everybody else understood," said Darcourt. "But that again is an argument on my side. Would a man who intended to deceive put such a portrait of a known artist—an artist at work—in such a picture as this? I repeat: this is not a picture for anyone but the painter himself. It is a confession, a deeply personal confession."

"Addison, what would you say was the market value of this picture, if we didn't know what Professor Darcourt has told us?" said Princess Amalie.

"Only Christie's or Sotheby's could answer that question. They know what they can get. A good many millions, certainly."

"We were ready to sell it to the National Gallery of Canada a few years ago for three millions," said Prince Max. "That was when we wanted to raise some capital to expand Amalie's business. Aylwin Ross was the Director then, but at the last minute he couldn't raise the money, and not long after he died."

"That would have been cheap," said Thresher.

"We were rather under the spell of Ross," said the Princess. "He was a most beautiful man. We offered him several pieces, at an inclusive price. This was by far the cheapest. But in the end they went to other buyers. We decided to keep this one. We like it so much."

"And you have so many others," said Thresher, not altogether kindly. "But three million was certainly a bargain. Now, if it weren't for what we have heard this evening, you could treble or quadruple that money."

This was Darcourt's moment. "Would you sell now, if you could get a price that pleased you?"

"Sell it as a distinguished fake?"

"Sell it as the greatest work of The Alchemical Master, now known to be the late Francis Cornish? Let me tell you what I have in mind."

With all the persuasive skill he could summon up, Darcourt told them what he had in mind.

"Of course, it's extremely conditional," he said when he had finished, and the Prince and the Princess and Thresher were deep in consideration.

"Very iffy indeed," said Thresher. "But it's a hell of a good idea. I don't know when I've heard of a better in forty years in the art world."

"There is no hurry," said Darcourt. "Are you willing to leave it with me?"

And that was where the matter rested when Darcourt flew back to Canada.

[8]

"I REALLY THINK one of the names must be Arthur. After all, it was my father's name, and it's my name, and it's a good name. Not unfamiliar; not peculiar; easy to pronounce; has good associations, not the least of them being this opera."

"I entirely agree," said Hollier. "As a godfather, with a right to give the boy a name of my choice, I declare for Arthur."

"No regrets about Clement?" said Arthur.

"It's not a name I've ever liked much."

"Well, thank heaven one name is settled. Now, Nilla, you're the godmother. What name have you chosen?"

"I have a weakness for Haakon, because it was my father's name, and it is a name of great honour in Norway. But it might embarrass a Canadian child. So also with Olaf, which is another favourite of mine. So—what about Nikolas? He need not even spell it with a 'k' if he doesn't want to. A fine saint's name, and I think every child should have a saint's name, even if it isn't used."

"Brilliant, Nilla. And eminently reasonable. Nikolas let it be, and I'll undertake that he uses the 'k' to keep him in mind of you."

"Oh, I'll keep him in mind of me. I intend to take my work as godmother very seriously."

"Well then—Geraint?"

This, thought Darcourt, is where the trouble lies. To be melodramatic, this is where the canker gnaws. Geraint has all the Welsh passion for genealogy, and names, and he wants to keep signalling that he is this child's true father. This is going to call heavily on Arthur's skill as a Chairman.

"Of course, I think at once of my own name," said Powell. "A beautiful, poetic, sweetly-sounding name which I bear with pleasure. But Sim *bach* advises strongly against it. Of course I wish to confer a Welsh name on the boy, but you all keep nattering about how hard they are to pronounce. Hard for whom? Not for me. To me, you see, a name has great significance; it colours a child's whole outlook on itself and gives it a role to play. Aneurin, for instance; a great bardic name. He of the Flowing Muse—"

THE CORNISH TRILOGY

"Yes, but bound to be pronounced 'An Urine' by the unregenerate Saxons," said Arthur. "Remember poor Nye Bevan and what he went through. The Sitwells always called him Aneurism."

"The Sitwells had a very vulgar streak," said Powell.

"Unfortunately, so have lots of people."

"There are other splendid names. Aidan, for instance; now there's a saint for you, Nilla! And Selwyn, which means great ardour and zeal; that would spur him on, wouldn't it? Or Owain, the Well Born; suggesting a distinguished descent, particularly on the father's side. Or Hugo, a name very popular in Wales; I propose it rather than the Welsh Huw, which might look odd to an uninstructed eye; it is the Latin form. But the one I propose with pride is Gilfaethwy, not one of the greatest heroes of the *Mabinogion* but especially appropriate to this child, for reasons that need not be chattered about now. Gilfaethwy! Nobly wild, wouldn't you say?"

"Pronounce it again, will you?" said Arthur.

"It is simplicity itself. Geel-va-ith-ooee, with the accent lightly on the 'va'. Isn't it splendid, boyos? Doesn't it smack of the great days of legend, before Arthur, when demigods trod the earth, dragons lurked in caves, and mighty magicians like Math Mathonwy dealt out reward and punishment? Powerful stuff, let me tell you."

"How do you spell that?" said Hollier, ready with pencil and paper. Geraint spelled it.

"Looks barbarous on the page," said Hollier.

Powell took this very badly. "Barbarous, you say? Barbarous, in a country where every name from every part of the earth, and ridiculous invented names, are seen in the birth announcements every day? Barbarous! By God, Hollier, let me tell you that the Welsh had enjoyed five centuries of Roman civilization when your ancestors were still eating goat with the skin on and wiping their arses with bunches of thistles! Barbarous! Am I to hear that from a pack of morlocks who can think of nothing except what is easy for them to pronounce or has some sentimental association? I pity your ignorance and despise you."

"That, by the way, is a Dickensian quotation," said Hollier. "I'm sure you could find something more bardic to express your contempt."

"Now, now, let's not come to harsh words," said Darcourt. "Let's make a decision, because I have things to say to you, parents and godparents, and we must make up our minds."

But Powell was in a black sulk, and it took a lot of cajoling to make him speak.

"Let the child have the commonest of Welsh names, if you must have it so," he said at last. "Let his name be David. Not even Dafydd, mark you, but bloody English David."

"Now that's a good name," said Gunilla.

"And another saint's name," said Darcourt. "David let it be. Now—what order? Arthur Nikolas David?"

"No. It would spell AND on his luggage," said Hollier, who seemed to be suffering an unexpected bout of practicality.

"His luggage! What a consideration," said Powell. "If you insist on this damned reductive nonsense, why don't you call the child SIN?"

Arthur and Darcourt looked at each other bleakly. Was Geraint going to let the cat out of the bag? This was what nobody wanted, except Powell, whose Welsh dander was up.

"Sin?" said Hollier. "You're joking. Why sin?"

"Because that is what he will be called by his bloody country," shouted Powell. "Social Insurance Number 123 dash 456789, and when he gets his pension in old age he will be SOAP 123 dash 456789. By the time he is SOAP nobody will have any other name except the one the God-damned civil servants have given him! So why don't we steal a march on them and call him SOAP from the start? This is a land dead to poetry, and I say the hell with it!" In his indignation he drained a large whisky at a gulp, and filled his glass again, to the brim.

It was a time to rise above passing furies and disdains, so Darcourt said, in his most honeyed tones, "Then it's to be Arthur David Nikolas, is it? An excellent name. I congratulate you. I shall pronounce the names with my warmest approval. Now, about the other matters."

"Let me remind you right away that I am a convinced unbeliever," said Hollier. "I know too much about religions to be humbugged by them. So you don't get around me with your priestcraft, Simon. I am simply doing this out of friendship for Arthur and Maria."

Yes, and because you were the first to have carnal knowledge of the child's mother, thought Darcourt. You don't fool me, Clem. But what he said was, "Oh yes, I have long experience of unbelieving godparents, and I know how to respect your reservations. All I ask is assurance of your willingness to cherish the child, and help him when you can, and advise him when he needs it, and do the decent thing if his parents should not see him into manhood. Which God forbid."

"Obviously I'll agree to that. I'll take part in the ceremony as an ancient observance. But don't ask for acceptance as a spiritual force."

"No, none of that. But if there is to be a ceremony, it must have a form, and I know the form which is appropriate. Now, Nilla, what about you?"

"No doubts and no reservations," said Gunilla. "I was brought up as what the grocer Shakespeare calls 'a spleeny Lutheran', and I am very fond of children, especially boys. I am delighted to have a godson. You can rely on me."

"I'm sure we can," said Darcourt. "And you, Geraint?"

"You know what I am, Sim *bach*. A Calvinist to the soles of my boots. I am not sure that I trust you. What are you going to ask me to promise?"

"I shall ask you, in the child's name, to renounce the Devil and all his works, the vain pomp and glory of this world, with all covetous desires of the same, and the carnal desires of the flesh."

"By God, Sim, that's very fine. Did you write that?"

"No, Geraint, Archbishop Cranmer wrote it."

"A good hand with the pen, that Archbishop. And I renounce these things for the child, not for myself?"

"That's the idea."

"You see how it is. As a man of the theatre—as an artist—I couldn't really set aside pomp and glory, because that's what I live by. As for covetousness, my whole life and work is hedged with contracts, drawn up by covetous agents and the monsters who regulate the economics of the theatre. But for the boy—for young Dafydd, whom I shall call Dai when we get to know each other—I'll renounce away like billy-o."

"Do we really promise that?" aid Hollier. "I like that about the Devil. That's getting down to realities. I hadn't realized the baptismal service delved quite so deep into the ancient world. You must lend me the book, Simon. There's good stuff in it."

"What trivial minds you men have," said Gunilla. "When you talk about artists living for pomp and glory, Powell, speak for yourself. What you say, Simon, seems to me to mean keeping the boy up to high principles. Making a man of him. You need have no doubts about me."

"Good," said Darcourt. "May I see you all at the chapel on Sunday, then, at three o'clock? Sober and decently dressed?"

When they were leaving, Powell going off to his accustomed bedroom, Darcourt took his opportunity to speak to Maria alone.

"You said nothing about names, Maria. Have you no preference as to what the child should be named?"

"I haven't forgotten my Gypsy ways, Simon dear. When the child came out of me and gave a cry, they laid it on my breast, and I named him. Gave him his real name. Whispered it into his tiny ear. And whatever you do on Sunday, that will be his name forever."

"Are you going to tell me what the name is?"

"Certainly not! He will never hear it again until he reaches puberty, when I shall whisper it to him again. He has a proper Gypsy name, and it will go with him and protect him as long as he lives. But it is a secret between him and me."

"You have been ahead of me, then?"

"Of course. I didn't think I'd do it, but just before he left my body forever, I knew I would. What's bred in the bone, you know."

[9]

EXCEPT FOR ONE MINOR MISHAP, the christening went smoothly. Only the parents, the godparents, and the baby were present; the Cranes had to be told plainly that they might not come. Al murmured incoherently about objective correlatives and the link between the birth of the child and the birth of the opera. It would, he said, make a terrific and unexpected footnote to the *Regiebuch*. Mabel begged to be allowed to come simply on the ground that she wanted to see what a christening was like. But when Darcourt suggested that she could manage that by having her own impending child christened, she and Al were quick to say that they did not believe that a few words mumbled by a parson over their child could make any difference to his future life.

Darcourt forbore to tell them that he thought they were wrong, and silly in their wrongness. He had reservations about many of the things which he, as a clergyman, was expected to believe and endorse publicly, but about the virtues of baptism he had no doubt. Its solely Christian implications apart, it was the acceptance of a new life into a society that thereby declared that it had a place for that new life; it was an assertion of an attitude toward life that was expressed in the Creed which was a part of the service in a form archaic and compressed but full of noble implication. The parents and godparents might think they did not believe that Creed, as they recited it, but it was plain to Darcourt that they were living in a society which had its roots in that Creed; if there had been no Creed, and no cause for the formulation of that Creed, vast portions of civilization would never have come into being, and those who smiled at the Creed or disregarded it altogether nevertheless stood firmly on its foundation. The Creed was one of the great signposts in the journey of mankind from a primitive society toward whatever was to come, and though the signpost might be falling behind in the march of civilization, it had marked a great advance from which there could be no permanent retreat.

Hollier had decided to accept the baptismal ceremony as a rite of passage, an acceptance of a new member into the tribe. Good enough, thought Darcourt, but such rites had a resonance not heard by the tin ear of the rationalist. Rationalism, thought Darcourt, was a handsomely intellectual way of sweeping a lot of significant, troublesome things under the rug. But the implications of the rite were not banished because some very clever people did not feel them.

Powell wanted to be a godfather with his fingers crossed. He wanted to make promises he had no intention of keeping—and indeed who can hope to keep the promises of a godfather in all their ramifications? Very well. But Powell wanted to be a godfather because it was as near as he was likely to come to being ackowledged as the real father of the child. Powell could not resist a solemn ceremony of any kind. He was one of the many, who should not therefore be despised, who wanted serious inner matters given a serious outer form, and this was what made him a true and devout child of the drama, which at its best is precisely such an objectification of what is important in life. Darcourt thought he knew what Powell meant better than Powell did himself.

He had no misgivings about Gunilla. There was a woman who could see beyond the language of a creed to the essence of a creed. Gunilla was sound as a bell.

As for Arthur and Maria, the birth of the child seemed to have drawn them nearer than they had ever been before. The blessing that children bring is a cliché. It is as corny as the rhymes of Ella Wheeler Wilcox about art. But one of the most difficult tasks for the educated and sophisticated mind is to recognize that some clichés are also important truths.

It is a cliché that the birth of a child is a symbol of hope, however disappointed and distressed that hope may at last prove to be. The baptism is a ceremony in which that hope is announced, and Hope is one of the knightly virtues in a sense that the Cranes, for instance, had not understood, and might perhaps never understand. The hope embodied in the small body of Arthur David Nikolas as Darcourt took him in his arms and sained him, was, in part, the hope of the marriage of Arthur and Maria. The silver link, the silken tie.

It was after the blessing of the child, and the saining with water, that the slight accident occurred. Following an old custom, now revived by ritualists like Darcourt, he lighted three candles from the great candle that stood beside the font, and handed them to the godparents, saying, "Receive the light of Christ, to show that you have passed from darkness to light."

Hollier and Gunilla, understanding that they did this on behalf of the child, took their candles with dignity, and Gunilla bowed her head in reverence.

Powell, startled, dropped his candle, spilling wax down his clothes, and scrambled for it on the floor, murmuring, unsuitably, "Oh, my God!" Maria giggled and the child, which had been an angel of propriety even when its head was wetted, gave a loud wail.

Darcourt took the candle from Powell, relighted it, and said,

"Receive the light of Christ, in your astonishment of heart, to show that you have passed from darkness to light."

"That was a bloody good ad lib of yours, Sim *bach*," said Powell, at the party afterward. "I've never heard a better on the stage."

"I think yours was even better, Geraint *bach*," said Darcourt.

[*10*]

THE ARTISTS AND ARTIFICERS who are assembled to put an opera on the stage make up a closed society, and no one who is not of the elect may hope to penetrate it. There is no ill-will in this; it is simply that people deep in an act of creation take their whole lives with them into that act, and the world outside becomes shadowy until the act is completed, the regular schedule of performances established, and the strength of association somewhat relaxed.

Those who are on the outside feel this keenly. As the last weeks of work on *Arthur of Britain* progressed, Arthur and Maria sensed the chill. Of course they were welcome everywhere—which is to say that nobody quite liked to ask them to go away. They were known to be the "angels". They paid the bills, the salaries, all the multifarious costs of a complicated project, and therefore they had to be treated with courtesy; but it was cold courtesy. Even their intimate friend Powell whispered to their other intimate friend Darcourt, "I wish Arthur and Maria weren't always bumming around while we're working."

Darcourt had his place in the adventure; he was the librettist, and however unlikely it was that any words would be changed at so late a point in the proceedings, he was free to come and go, and if Powell suddenly wanted him to explain a difficult passage to a singer, it was a nuisance if he were not at the rehearsal. Because of her shadowy association with the libretto, even Penny Raven appeared at rehearsals without any questioning looks. But not the angels.

"I feel as conspicuous and out of place as tan shoes on a pall-bearer," said Arthur, who was not given to simile in the ordinary way.

"But I want to see what they're doing," said Maria. "After all, we must have some rights. Have you looked at the bills lately?"

Perhaps they had expected lively doings, with Powell standing in front of a stage filled with singers, shouting and waving his arms like a policeman at a riot. Nothing of the sort. The rehearsals were quiet and orderly. The unpunctual Powell was always present half an hour before a rehearsal began, and he was stern with latecomers, though these were few, and always had reasonable excuses. The ebullient Powell was quiet and restrained; he never shouted, was never discourteous. He had absolute command and used it with easy authority. Was this artistic creation? Apparently it was, and Arthur and Maria were astonished at how quickly and surely the opera began to take shape.

Not that it seemed like an opera, as they conceived of an opera, in the first two weeks of rehearsals. These took place in Toronto in large, dirty rooms belonging to the Conservatory, and the Graduate School of Music, which had been hired for the work. In charge of these was Waldo Harris, the first assistant to Powell; he was a bland, large young man who never lost his calm in the midst of complexity, and he seemed to know everything. He had an assistant, Gwen Larking, who was called Stage Manager; she had two other girls to do her lightest bidding. Miss Larking occasionally and excusably showed some emotion, and the assistants, who were beginners, did run and fuss, and brandish their clipboards until Miss Larking frowned at them, and even hissed at them to shut up. But these young women were serenity itself compared with the three students called gofers (because they were always being told to go for coffee, or go for sandwiches, or go for somebody who was wanted in a hurry). The gofers were the lowest, most inconsiderable form of theatrical life. At rehearsals these seven clustered around Powell like iron filings around a magnet, and talked in whispers. They all dealt very largely in paper, and took notes without cease. The provision of new, sharp pencils was part of the gofers' job.

But these were all less than Mr. Watkin Bourke, who was called the *répétiteur,* or coach.

It was Watty's job to see that the singers knew their music, and this meant everything from long hours at the piano with the principals who knew their music but wanted advice about phrasing, to principals who read music with difficulty (though they never admitted this) and had to be taught their parts almost by rote. It was Watty's job to train the Chorus, and this meant the ten gentlemen, apart from Giles Shippen, the tenor lead, and Gaetano Panisi, who played Modred, who made up King Arthur's Knights, and the Ladies who were their vocal counterparts. The Chorus were all good musicians, but twenty-two good singers do not make a chorus, and they had to be gently persuaded to sing together, and not merely to sing in tune, but to sing in tune as a unity, and to vary their intonation subtly to agree with leading singers who might become the teeniest bit flat or sharp under dramatic stress. In all of this Watty, a small, hatchet-faced, intense man, and a brilliant pianist, was masterly.

Watty, like Powell, never shouted or lost his temper, though from time to time a great weariness might be seen to pass over his small, intelligent face. Such weariness, for instance, as was brought about by his encounter with Mr. Nutcombe Puckler, a bass baritone entrusted with the role of Sir Dagonet.

"I quite understand that Mr. Powell wants us to have individuality, as Knights of the Round Table," he said. "Now, the other chaps are all pretty straightforward, aren't they? Knights, you see. Just brave chaps. But Sir Dagonet is described as Arthur's Fool, and of course that's why I have been cast for it. Because I'm not a chorus singer or a small-parts man—not at all; I'm a *comprimario* with quite a big reputation as a comic. My Frosch, in *Die Fledermaus,* is known all over the operatic world. So presumably I'm cast as Sir Dagonet to get some comedy into the opera. But how? I haven't a single comic bit to sing. So something has to be introduced, you see, Watty? Some comic relief? I've been thinking a lot about it, and I've found just the place. Finale of Act One, when Arthur is haranguing the Knights about the wonders of Knighthood. It's heavy. Lovely music, of course, but heavy. So—that's surely where we bring in the comic relief. Now what's it to be—my Blurt or my Sneeze?"

"I don't follow," said Watty.

"Haven't you seen me? They're my two best laugh-getters. When Arthur's going on about Knighthood, couldn't I have a cup of wine? Then, just at the right moment, I give 'em my Blurt. I choke on the wine and spew a lot of it over the people near by. Never fails. Or, if that's a bit too strong, there's my Sneeze—just a simple, loud sneeze, you see—to relieve the atmosphere. My

Blurt is really a comic extension of my Sneeze, and of course I don't want to obtrude, so the Sneeze might be best. But you ought to hear my Blurt before you make a decision. I'd like to know now, you see, before we go into rehearsal on the floor, so I can be thinking about it and tailor my Blurt—or my Sneeze— to come in just at the right moment. Because timing is everything in comedy, as I'm sure you know."

"You must talk to Mr. Powell," said Watty. "I have nothing to do with the staging."

"But you see my point?"

"Yes, indeed."

"I don't want to be obtrusive, you understand; I just want to bring what I can to the ensemble."

"It's Mr. Powell's department."

"But may I say which you think best? The Blurt or the Sneeze?"

"I have no opinion. It's not my department."

It was an astonishment to Arthur and Maria, and to Darcourt as well, that Watty played from a full orchestral score, instructing the singers what they might expect to hear as they sang, and when they were momentarily silent; the singers worked from sketchy music, giving their vocal line and a hint or two of orchestration; the preparation of all this music, which was in Schnak's wondrous hand, had cost a small fortune.

At the musical rehearsals Dr. Dahl-Soot was present, but not a voice. She spoke to no one but Watty, and very quietly. She whispered now and then to Schnak, who was her shadow, learning her craft—learning eagerly and rapidly.

The first general rehearsal took place in a dirty, ill-lit basement room in the Conservatory. It smelled of the economical lunches that had been consumed there for years by students; there was a pervasive atmosphere of bananas in their last stages of edibility, mingled with peanut butter. There was not much space, for there were three sets of timpani stored there, and in a corner an assembly of double-bass cases with nothing in them, like a conference of senators.

"How are we going to work here?" said Nutcombe Puckler. "There isn't room to swing a cat."

"Will you all please sit down," said Gwen Larking. "There are chairs for everybody."

"As this is a new work," said Powell to the group, "and because the libretto offers some complexities, I want to begin today by reading through all three acts."

"No piano," said Nutcombe Puckler, who had a fine grasp of the obvious, as became an opera comic.

"Not a musical reading," said Powell. "You all know your music—or you should—and we won't sing for a day or two. No; I want you simply to read the words, as if this were a play. The librettist is with us, and he will be glad to clear up any difficulties about meanings."

The company was in the main an intelligent one, perhaps because it was not what conventional critics would call a company of the first order. The singers were, upon the whole, young and North American; though they had all had plenty of opera experience they were not accustomed to the usages of the greatest opera theatres of the world. Reading held no terrors for them. There were one or two, of whom Nutcombe Puckler was the leader, who could not see any reason to speak anything that could possibly be sung, but they were willing to give it a try, to humor Powell, in whom they sensed a man of ideas who knew what he was doing. Some, like Hans Holzknecht, who was to sing the role of Arthur, did not read English with ease, and Miss Clara Intrepidi, who was to be Morgan Le Fay, stumbled over words that she had sung with no difficulty in her rehearsals with Watty. The one who read like an actor—an intelligent actor—was Oliver Twentyman, and the best of the group found that by Act Two they were trying, with varying success, to read like Oliver Twentyman.

If the company was youthful in the main, Oliver Twentyman balanced matters by being old. Not astronomically old, as some people insisted; not in his nineties. But he was said to be over eighty, and he was one of the wonders of the operatic world. His exquisitely produced, silvery tenor was always described by critics as small, but it had been heard with perfect clarity in all the great opera theatres of the world, and he was a favourite at Glyndebourne and several of the more distinguished, smaller American festivals. His particular line of work was characters of fantasy— Sellem in *The Rake's Progress,* the Astrologer in *Le Coq d'Or,* and Oberon in *A Midsummer Night's Dream.* It had been a great coup to get him for Merlin. His reading of his part in the libretto was a delight.

"Marvellous!" said Powell. "Ladies and gentlemen, I beg you to take heed of Mr. Twentyman's pronunciation of English; it is in the highest tradition."

"Yes, but are not the vowels very distorted?" said Clara Intrepidi. "I mean, impure for singing. We have our vowels, right? The five? Ah, Ay, Ee, Oh, Oo. Those we can sing. You would not ask us to sing these impure sounds?"

"There are twelve vowel sounds in English," said Powell; "and as it is a language which I myself had to acquire, not being born to it, you must not think me prejudiced. What are those vowels? They are all in this advice:

> *Who knows ought of art must learn*
> *And then take his ease*

Every one of the twelve sings beautifully, and none gives such delicacy as the Indeterminate Vowel which is often a 'y' at the end of a word. 'Very' must be pronounced as a long and a short syllable, and not as two longs. I am going to nag you about pronunciation, I promise you."

Miss Intrepidi pouted slightly, as though to suggest that the barbarities of English speech would have no effect on *her* singing. But Miss Donalda Roche, an American who was to sing Guenevere, was making careful notes.

"What was that about knowing art, Mr. Powell?" she said, and Geraint sang the vowel sequence for her, joined by Oliver Twentyman, who seemed, with the greatest politeness, to wish to show Miss Intrepidi that there were really twelve differentiated sounds, and that none of them were describable as impure.

On the whole, the singers enjoyed reading the libretto, and the day's work showed clearly which were actors who could sing, and which singers who had learned to act. Marta Ullmann, the tiny creature who was to sing the small but impressive role of Elaine, came out very well with

> *"No tears, no sighing, no despair*
> *No trembling, dewy smile of care*

> *No mourning weeds*
> *Nought that discloses*
> *A heart that bleeds;*
> *But looks contented I will bear*
> *And o'er my cheeks strew roses.*
>
> *Unto the world I may not weep,*
> *But save my Sorrow all, and keep*
> *A secret heart, sweet soul, for thee,*
> *As the great earth and swelling sea."*

But it was not quite such a good moment when Donalda Roche and Giles Shippen tried to read, in unison,

> *"O Love!*
> *Time flies on restless pinions*
> *Constant never:*
> *Be constant*
> *And thou chainest time forever."*

Nor was Miss Intrepidi the celebrated audience-tamer she was reputed to be when faced with her words to the villain Modred:

> *"I know there is some maddening secret*
> *Hid in your words (and at each turn of thought*
> *Comes up a skull) like an anatomy*
> *Found in a weedy hole, 'mongst stones and roots*
> *And straggling reptiles, with his tongueless mouth*
> *That tells of Arthur's murder."*

But Miss Intrepidi was a real pro, and having made a mess of her words she cried, "I'll get it; don't worry—I'll get it!" and Powell assured her that nobody had the least doubt she would.

When the reading was completed, late in the afternoon, Gunilla spoke to the company for the first time.

"You see what our Director is doing?" she said. "He wants you to sing words, not tones. Anybody can sing the music; it takes an artist to sing the words. That's what I want, too. Simon Darcourt has found us a brilliant libretto; Hulda Schnakenburg has realized a fine score from Hoffmann's notes, and we must think of this opera as, among other things, an entirely new look at Hoffmann as a composer; this is music-drama before Wagner had put pen to paper. So—sing it like early Wagner."

"Ah—Wagner!" said Miss Intrepidi. "So now I know."

All of this, and the careful rehearsals which followed—on the floor, as Powell said, meaning that he was planning the moves and when necessary the gestures of the singers—was victuals and drink to the Cranes. (They were always referred to as the Cranes, though Mabel took pains to explain that she was still Mabel Muller, and had sacrificed nothing of her individuality—though she had obviously sacrificed her figure—in their spiritual union.) Al cornered and buttonholed everybody, and made himself conspicuous in his desire not to be obtrusive. He was on the prowl to capture and note down every motivation, and the notes for the great *Regiebuch* swelled to huge proportions. Oliver Twentyman was a Golconda to Al.

Here was tradition! Twentyman had, in his young days, sung with many famous conductors, and his training had become legendary in his lifetime. He had worked, when not much more than a boy, with the great David ffrangcon-Davies, and repeated to Al many of that master's precepts. More wonderful still, he had worked for three years with the redoubtable William Shakespeare—not, he explained to the gaping Al, the playwright, but the singing-teacher, who had been born in 1849 and had worked with many of the great ones until his death in 1931—who had always insisted that singing, even at its most elaborate, was based upon words, upon words, upon words.

"It's like a dream!" said Al.

"It's a craft, my boy," said Nutcombe Puckler, who was still waiting for a decisive word about the Blurt, or possibly just the Sneeze. "And never forget the funny stuff. Wagner hadn't much use for it; he thought *Meistersinger* was a comic opera, of course, and you should have seen my Beckmesser in St. Louis a few years ago! I stopped the show twice!"

Al was a special nuisance to Darcourt. "This libretto—some of it gets close to poetry," he said.

"That was the idea," said Simon.

"Nobody would take you for a poet," said Al.

"Probably not," said Darcourt; "when are you expecting the baby?"

"That's a worry," said Al. "Sweetness is getting pretty tired. And worried, too. We're both worried. We're lucky to be sharing this great experience, to take our minds off it."

Mabel nodded, hot, heavy, and dispirited. She longed for the move to Stratford, out of the terrible, humid heat of a Toronto summer. As she lay on the bed in their cheap lodgings at night, while Al read aloud to her from the macabre tales of Hoffmann, she sometimes wondered if Al knew how much she was sacrificing to her career. As women have wondered, no doubt, since first mankind was troubled by glimmerings of what we now call art, and scholarship.

"Will you give my feet a rub, Al? My ankles are killing me."

"Sure, Sweetness, just as soon as we finish this story."

Why, he wondered, was Sweetness crying when, twenty minutes later, he got around to rubbing her feet?

[11]

ETAH IN LIMBO

WHAT AN AMUSING DRAMA *life is when one is not obliged to be one of the characters! No, no; that sounds like Kater Murr! But I have enjoyed myself more in the past few weeks than at any time since my death. Homer was quite wrong about the gloomy half-life of the dead. The remoteness, the removal, of my afterlife is vastly agreeable. I see all the people who are preparing my opera; I comprehend their feelings without needing to share them painfully; I applaud their ambitions and I pity their follies. But as I am wholly unable to do anything about them, I am not torn by guilt or responsibility. It is thus, I suppose, that the gods view humankind. (I apologize if, by speaking of "the gods" in the plural, I am being offensive to whatever awaits me when I move into the next phase of my afterlife.) Of course, the gods could intervene, and frequently did so, but not always happily from a human standpoint.*

The trials of Powell and Watkin Bourke are very familiar to me. How often have I wrangled with singers who thought Italian was the only language of song, and who cried down our noble German as barbarous. Of course they made exquisite sounds, some of them, but they had a limited range of meanings for their sounds; Italian is a dear language and we owe much to it, but our northern tongues are richer in poetic subtlety, in shadows, and shadows were the essence of my work both as composer and as author. How I have struggled with singers whose one desire was to "vocalize"—a word that had just come into fashion and seemed to them the height of elegance and musical refinement. How deliciously they yelled when one wished that they should utter some meaning! How pressingly they would urge me to change German words to others with which they could make a prettier sound! And how incomprehensible was the word that lay ravaged at the bottom of any sound they made, as they roared, or cooed, or squalled, or sobbed with such richness of inane musicality! "Gracious lady and supreme artist," I would say to some fat bully of a soprano, "if you pronounce the word on the tone no louder than you could speak it, it will be sound enough, and replete with significance that will ravish your hearers." But they never believed me. Nothing encourages self-esteem like success as a singer.

And why not? If you can stir an audience to its depths with your A altissimo, what need you care for anything else?

Or if you can make an audience laugh, is it surprising if you cease to care how? This man who wants to sneeze, or blurt his wine in somebody's face, is different only in kind from the Jack Puddings of my time. With them all comedy was rooted in sausage; give them a sausage to eat and they would undertake to keep a sufficient part of the audience in roars of mirth for five minutes; allow them to add an onion to the sausage and it was eight minutes. How sad such merriment is! How divorced from the Comic Spirit!

I am becoming devoted to Schnak. Devoted, that is to say, only as a spirit may be; she is cleaner since the Swedish woman seduced her, but she is without charm. It is her musical genius that enslaves me. Yes, genius is the word I shall use. By that word I mean that she will have enough individual quality to impose herself upon the music of her time as a truly serious artist, and she may achieve fame, even if it follows her death. After all, Schubert is now known as a genius of the first order, yet when I became aware of his work very few people in my part of Germany had heard of him, and he did not survive me by more than five years. Of all the music I know, Schnak's, working on the foundations I laid down, most resembles that of Schubert. When she has done it best, our work together has that melancholy serenity, that acceptance of the pathos of human life, that speaks of Schubert. Dr. Dahl-Soot knows it, but the others say the music is like Weber, because they know that Weber was my friend.

That strange ass Crane is tracing all the music to Weber. He is one of those scholars who is certain that everything in art is laboriously derived from something that came before it. Much as I admired Weber, I never saw a Weber score to which I would willingly have signed my own name.

Poor Schubert, dying slowly, as I did, and of what was essentially the same disease. Nobody, so far as I know, has found out why that disease causes one man to die a driveller and a horror, and another to compose, in his last year, three of the supreme pianoforte sonatas in all the realm of music.

I should not be hard on Crane. Perhaps he is worrying about that baby, or his swollen woman, Mabel Muller. There is an erotic unction about Al that must not be ignored. Mabel, poor wretch, must be ranked low on the list of the victims of art.

There are other victims, of course, and, from my point of view, greater ones. I am sad for the Cornishes, Arthur and Maria. They long so humbly to be counted among the artists, but they are not given even the artistic status accorded to Nutcombe Puckler. Without meaning to be cruel, the artists, and even those novices in art, the gofer girls, reject them because they do not appear to be doing anything, although it is their money that is the underpinning of the whole affair. Not doing anything, when every day they write fat cheques for this, that, and the other? Writing those cheques because they truly love art and wish it to prosper! Writing those cheques because they would sing if they could, or paint their faces and join the crowd on the stage!

I sometimes saw people like them in the theatres where I worked as Powell works now. Wealthy merchants, or minor nobility, who footed the bills, and not always to gain a place in the ranks of society but because they so greatly loved those things that they could not do. A patron has one of two courses: he may domineer and spoil the broth by insisting on too much salt or pepper; or he may simply do what God has enabled him to do, and that is to pay, pay, pay! I was as bad as anyone in my time. I kissed hands, bowed low, and paid compliments, but I eagerly wished them all in hell, because they were underfoot when *my work was being done. Seeing myself as my own creation, the master-musician Johannes Kreisler, I scorned my patrons and saw in them nothing but the disciples of the odious Kater Murr! As if there were no self-seeking among artists! I wish I could comfort Arthur and Maria, who feel the subtle cold of the artists' scorn, but placed as I am, I cannot do it.*

I can see, however, that their fate is different, and who may hope to escape his fate? They are living out, in a comic mimesis, the fate of Arthur and Guenevere, but to be ruled by a comic fate is not to feel oneself as a figure of comedy. It is their fate to be rich, and to seem powerful, in a world of art where riches are not of first importance, and their power is unavailing.

Like all the others, I long for the move to Stratford.

SEVEN

WHEN THE COMPANY MOVED to Stratford and, in Powell's phrase, went into high gear on the production, it would have been easy to miss the fact that Schnak was deeply in love with Geraint. She tagged after him; but the Stage Manager, her assistants, and the gofer girls also tagged after him. She hung upon his words; but Waldo Harris, the Stage Director, and Dulcy Ringgold, the Designer, also hung upon his words. Nobody took any notice of Schnak's infatuation but Darcourt; nobody else saw the special quality in her tagging and hanging. Nobody else saw the lovelight in her eyes.

They were not eyes in which one would look for the lovelight. They were small, pebbly, squinty little eyes. Nor was Schnak a figure upon whom love sat like an accustomed garment; her motion was not graceful, because, in one of Darcourt's Old Ontario phrases, she was as bow-legged as a hog going to war; her voice was as snarly as ever, though under Gunilla's guidance her vocabulary was larger and not so dirty; she had no graces, and the least of the gofers could have wiped the floor with her in a contest of charm. But Schnak was in love, and this was not a matter of bodily awakening and bodily satisfaction as it had been with Gunilla, but beglamoured and yearning passion. This is the romanticism in which her work has drenched and soused her; I am sure she tosses on her bed and murmurs his name to her pillow, thought Darcourt.

He took his chance to ask Gunilla if she were aware of this. "Oh, yes," said the Doctor; "it was bound to happen. She must try everything, and Powell is an obvious mark for a young girl's love."

"But you don't mind?"

"Why should I mind? The child is not my property. Oh, we have had merry hours, to the great scandal of that fat busybody Professor Raven, but that was a teacher-and-pupil thing. Not love. I have known love, Simon, and with men also, let me assure you, and I know what it is. I am not such a romantic as to think of it as the great educational force—broadening her experience, enlarging her vision, and all that nonsense—but it is something everybody feels who is not a complete cabbage. I must see that it doesn't spoil her work; people seem to have forgotten that all this elaborate contrivance boils down to an examination exercise, and Hulda must get her degree, if there is not to be a great waste of money."

Elaborate contrivance indeed it was. The company was lucky in having the theatre for the last three weeks of rehearsal. Not the stage; not yet. There was still a week of performances of a play which called for only one small set, but all the workrooms and both rehearsal rooms were now devoted to *Arthur*, and during the last two weeks the stage would be available to the singers when it was not wanted by the technicians.

The technicians bulked very large. It seemed to Darcourt that they almost swamped the opera. On huge paint-frames in one of the workrooms the scenery was being painted, for Powell wanted proper scenes, and not the usual wrinkled cyclorama, suggesting a sky that had shrunk and faded in the wash.

"In Hoffmann's day there was no stage light, in our sense," he said, "and anything like a lighting effect had to be painted on the scenery. And that's how Dulcy is doing it."

Dulcy Ringgold was not what Darcourt would have thought of as a theatrical character. She was small, she was shy, she laughed a great deal, and she seemed to regard her responsibilities as the best joke in the world.

"I'm really just a glorified dressmaker," she said, through a mouthful of pins, as she draped something on Clara Intrepidi. "Just that nice little woman Miss Dulcy, who is so clever with her fingers." She did something that made Miss Intrepidi look taller and slimmer. "There dear; if you can suck up your gut the teeniest bit that will do very nicely."

"The gut is what I breathe with," said Miss Intrepidi.

"Then we'll drape this a little more freely," said Dulcy, "and maybe put a wee thingy just here."

At other times, Dulcy was to be seen with a filthy bandanna wrapped around her head, on the bridge that swayed before the paint-frame, putting special touches on huge drop-scenes that were being painted from her carefully squared-off watercolour designs. Sometimes she was in the basement, where the armour was made, not with the ring of the swordsmith's hammer, but with the chemical whiff of Plexiglas being moulded. It was here, too, that all the swords, and Arthur's sceptre, and the crowns for Arthur and his Queen were made, and studded with foil-backed glass jewels that gave a splendidly Celtic richness to post-Roman Britain. Dulcy was everywhere, and Dulcy's taste and imagination touched everything.

"I hate theatre where the audience is told to use its imagination," she said. "That's cheap. The audience lays down its good money to rent imagination from somebody who has more than they ever dreamed of. Somebody like me. Imagination's my only stock-in-trade." She said this as she whisked off a brilliant little sketch for a fool's head which was to be made in pretended metal and attached to the hilt of Sir Dagonet's sword. But it was not all of her stock-in-trade. Darcourt picked up a large book from her workbench.

"What's this?" he said.

"Oh, that's my darling and my deario, James Robinson Planché; his *Encyclopaedia of Costume,* a revolutionary book in stage design. He was the first man, believe it or not, who really cared if stage dress had any roots in the realities of the past. He designed the first *King John* that really looked like King John's time. I don't copy his pictures, of course. Strictly accurate historical costume looks absurd, as a usual thing, but dear Planché is a springboard for one's imagination."

I don't suppose even Planché knew what King Arthur wore," said Darcourt.

"No, but he would have given a jolly well-informed guess,"

said Dulcy, patting the two large books tenderly. "So I load up on dear Planché, and then I guess too. Lots of dragons; that's the stuff for Arthur. I'm putting Morgan Le Fay in a dragon head-dress. Sounds corny, but it won't be when I've finished with it."

So: the omnicompetent Planché is going to have a finger in the pie, even if we don't use his horrible libretto, thought Darcourt. He was—just a little—losing his heart to Dulcy, but so was every other man who came near her. It appeared, however, that Dulcy was somewhat of Gunilla's way of thinking about sex, and although she flirted outrageously with the men, it was with Gunilla she went to dinner.

Here is a world where sex is not of first, second, or perhaps even third importance, thought Darcourt. How refreshing.

Sex was, however, rearing its wistfully domestic head with the unhappy Mabel Muller. The weather in Stratford proved to be just as hot as it was in Toronto, and Mabel's legs swelled, and her hair drooped, and she bore her burden of posterity with visible effort. She tagged everywhere after Al, who was like a man possessed, making notes here, and taking photographs with an instant camera there, and getting in everyone's way while making obstructive efforts to avoid doing precisely that. Not that Al forgot her or excluded her; he gave her his heavy briefcase to carry, and they always ate the sandwiches Mabel brought from a fast-food shop together, while he harangued—"extrapolated" was the fine word he used—on all that he had noted, or photographed.

"This is pure gold, Sweetness," he would say from time to time. To Sweetness it was fairy gold, no sooner touched than lost.

It would be unjust to say that Al grudged the time needed to rush Mabel to the hospital when at last her pains became too much to be ignored. "They're coming every twenty minutes now," she whispered, tearfully, and Al made just one more essential note before seizing her by the arm and leading her out of the rehearsal room. It was Darcourt who found them a taxi and urged the driver to lose no time in getting them to the hospital. They had made no arrangements, had not even seen a doctor, and Mabel was admitted in Emergency.

"Something is not quite right with Mabel," said Maria, later in the day, to Darcourt. "Her pains have stopped."

"Al was back for the end of the rehearsal," said Darcourt. "I thought everything must be going smoothly."

"I'd like to brain Al," said Maria. "That's the trouble with these irregular unions. No guts when the going gets rough. I'd hang around the hospital if I could, but Arthur has to get back to his office for a couple of days and I am going with him. New developments in the Wally Crottel affair. I'll tell you later. There's really nothing for us to do here. Geraint seems to feel that we're underfoot."

"I'm sure not."

"I'm sure yes. But Simon, will you be a darling and keep an eye on Mabel? She's no concern of ours, but I'm concerned just the same. Will you get in touch if we should do anything?"

That was why Darcourt found himself in the comfortless waiting-room of the hospital's maternity ward at four o'clock in the morning. Al had left at half past ten, promising to phone early next day. Darcourt was not alone. Dr. Dahl-Soot had also turned up, after Al's departure.

"Nothing could be less in my line than this," she said. "But that poor wretch is a stranger in a strange land, and so am I, so here I am."

Darcourt knew better than to say it was very good of her.

"Arthur and Maria asked me to keep an eye on things," he said.

"I like those two," said the Doctor. "I didn't greatly like them when we first met, but they grow better on acquaintance. They are a very solid pair. Do you think it's the baby?"

"Partly the baby. A very fine baby. Maria is suckling it."

"She is? That's old style. But I believe very good."

"I don't know," said Darcourt. "As we academics say, it's not my field. But it's a very pretty sight."

"You are a softy, Simon. And that's as it should be. I wouldn't give a damn for a man who was not a softy in some ways."

"Gunilla, do you think we single people are apt to be sentimental about love and babies and all that?"

"I am not sentimental about anything. But I have sentiment about many things. That's an English-language difference that is very useful. Not to have sentiment is to be almost dead."

"But you have taken—pardon me for saying so—a decidedly anti-baby road."

"Simon, you are too intelligent a man to be as provincial as you sometimes pretend. You know there is room in the world for everything and every kind of life. What do you think marriage is? Just babies and eating off the same fork?"

"God forbid! Because it's either very early in the morning or very late at night, I'll tell you what I really think. Marriage isn't just domesticity, or the continuance of the race, or institutionalized sex, or a form of property right. And it damned well isn't happiness, as that word is generally used. I think it's a way of finding your soul."

"In a man or a woman?"

"With a man or a woman. In company, but still, essentially, alone—as all life is."

"Then why haven't you found your own soul?"

"Oh, it isn't the only way. But it's one way."

"So you think I might find my soul, some day?"

"I'd bet very heavily on it, Gunilla. People find their souls in all sorts of ways. I'm writing a book—the life of a very good friend of mine, who certainly found his soul. Found it in painting. He tried to find it in marriage, and it was the most awful mess, because he was a soppy romantic at the time, and she was one of those Sirens who inevitably leave the man with a cup of Siren tears. Rather a crook, judged by the usual standards. But in that mess Francis Cornish found his soul. I know it. I have evidence of it. I'm writing the book about it."

"Francis Cornish? One of these Cornishes?"

"Arthur's uncle. And it's Francis's money that is supporting this fantastic circus we are engaged in now."

"But you think this Arthur will find his soul in his marriage?"

"And Maria, too. And if you want to know, I think King Arthur found his soul, or a big piece of it, in his marriage to Guenevere—who was rather a crook, if you read Malory—and that is what a lot of this opera is about. *Arthur of Britain, or The Magnanimous Cuckold*. He found his soul."

"But is this Arthur a magnanimous cuckold?"

Darcourt did not need to answer, for at this moment a doctor, in his white garment and cap, came into the room.

"Are you with Mrs. Muller?"

"Yes. What's the news?"

"I'm very sorry. Are you the father?"

"No. Just a friend."

"Well—it's bad. The child is stillborn."

"What was the trouble?"

"She seems not to have had any pre-natal advice whatever. Otherwise we'd have done a Caesarian. But when we found out the foetus had a disproportionately large head for the birth canal, it was already dead. Death from foetal distress, it's called. We're very sorry, but these things do happen. And as I say, she hadn't had any previous medical attention."

"May we see her?"

"I wouldn't advise it."

"Does she know?"

"She's very groggy. It was a long labour. Somebody will have to tell her in the morning. Would you do that?"

"I'll do that," said Dr. Gunilla, and Darcourt was grateful to her.

[2]

WHEN DR DAHL-SOOT VISITED THE HOSPITAL the next morning she did not need to give the bad news. Al was with Mabel, who was hysterical.

"There was what the English call A Scene," she told Darcourt. "You see Al, that odious pedant, had not even troubled to find out whether the child was a boy or a girl, and when Mabel demanded to see the child the head nurse explained that it was impossible. Why? Mabel wanted to know. Because the body was no longer available, said the nurse. Why not? said Mabel, very fierce. Because nobody had asked for the body to be reserved for burial by the parents, said the nurse. Mabel understood that. 'You mean they've put my baby in the garbage?' she said, and the nurse said that was not the way the hospital thought of what it had done, which was what was most often done with stillborns. But she wouldn't give details, except that it was a boy and perfect except for an unusually big head. Not abnormal. Apparently it's Mabel who is slightly abnormal. You know Mabel. A fool, and weak as water, but those people can make an awful hullabaloo when they are outraged, and she was ready to kill Al. And Al— really, Al ought to have been put in the garbage at birth—kept saying, 'Calm down, Sweetness, you'll see it all differently to-morrow.' Not a tender word, not a hug, not a thing to suggest that he was involved in the affair at all. I kicked Al out, and talked to Mabel for a while, but she's in a very bad way. What are you going to do?"

"Me?"

"You seem to be the one who is expected to do something when real trouble comes up. Are you going to see Mabel?"

"I think I'd better see Al first."

Al thought Mabel was being utterly unreasonable. She knew what a load of work he had, and how important it was to his career—which meant their joint career, if they stuck together. Hadn't he gone to the hospital with her? And returned after dinner, as Darcourt well know? Hadn't the doctor said the baby might be held up for several hours because first babies were unaccountable? Was he supposed to sit there all night, and then do a day's work that he had all planned, and that would need every ounce of energy and intellect he could muster? If there hadn't been this accident—this stillbirth business—everything would have been absolutely okay. As it was, Mabel was raising hell.

The trouble, he assured Darcourt, was that Mabel had never really freed herself from her background. Very conventional, middle-brow people, with whom Al had never hit it off. They kept asking why he and Mabel didn't get married, as if having somebody mumble a few words, etc. Al thought he had pretty well lifted Mabel above all that crap, but under stress—and Al admitted that the loss of the child amounted to stress—it all came flooding back, and Mabel was once again the insurance salesman's child from Fresno. Wanted the baby given what she called "decent burial". As if having somebody mumble a few words, etc., over a thing that had never lived could change anything. Al would be frank. He wondered if the arrangement with Mabel would weather this storm. He guessed he had to face it. People on two such different levels of education—though Mabel was majoring in sociology—would never really see eye to eye.

Al wanted to do the right thing, of course. Mabel wanted to go home. Wanted her mother. Can you figure that, in a woman of twenty-two? Wanting her mother? Of course the Mullers were what is called a very close family. But Al couldn't swing it. His grant from Pomelo was enough for one, and damned tight for two, and the fare back to Fresno would screw him up. Could Darcourt persuade Mabel to take it easy for a few days, and probably see things differently?

Darcourt said he would look into the matter and do what seemed best.

That meant that he phoned Maria, in Toronto, and put the matter to her. "I'll come at once," said Maria.

It was Maria who fetched Mabel from the hospital, paid all the bills, set her up in a room near her own in a hotel, and gave Al a piece of her mind that astonished them both, so conventional was it in tone and content. It was Maria who sent Al to a druggist for a breast-pump, of which Mabel had dire need, and this was Al's lowest moment. A breast-pump! He would willingly go into a drugstore and ask for condoms. That was dashing. But a breast-pump! The squalor of domesticity engulfed him. It was Maria who drove Mabel to the airport, when she was fit to travel, and bought her ticket to Fresno and mother. Coping with Mabel, who was sentimentally grateful and woman-to-woman, and bereft-mother-to-happy-mother, tried Maria very high, but she endured all, and never uttered a word of complaint or irony, even to Darcourt. Not even Mabel's frequent, tearful hints that fate was certainly good to the rich, and tough on the poor, provoked her to any speaking of her mind. But to herself she said it was enough to turn her milk.

"You've behaved beautifully," said Darcourt. "You deserve a reward."

"Oh, but I've had a reward," said Maria. "You remember I was hinting about Wally Crottel? The most wonderful luck—the book's turned up!"

"But you said you had thrown it away."

"So I did. But that was the original—you know, that crumpled, stained, interlined, grubby mess that Parlabane left. When I sent it to the publishers, one of them thought a ghost might be able to wrench a book out of it, so he had a Xerox made—quite indefensibly, but you know what publishers are—and sent it to his favourite ghost, who reported that it was pretty hopeless. But recently the ghost sent back the Xerox, which he had unearthed on his desk—obviously a ghost of the uttermost degree of literary messiness—and the publisher, belatedly, but honourably, sent it to me. And I've sent it to Wally."

"But Wally's in jail, awaiting trial."

"I know. I sent it to Mervyn Gwilt, with a teasing, palavering letter, full of nifty bits of Latin. Told him to get it published if he could."

"Maria! You may have committed yourself to some appalling legal claim!"

"Well—no. Not really. I showed the letter to Arthur, and he laughed a lot, but then he got one of his lawyers to rewrite it, and a fine juiceless job he made of it. Not a word of Latin. Lawyers are only half the fun they used to be when they knew Latin. But apparently it's a watertight letter, admitting nothing, relinquishing nothing, but letting Wally have what he wanted, which was a peep at m'dad's book."

"And so that's that."

"As Wally seems likely to get seven years at least, that's probably that."

"Maria, you do have the Devil's own luck!"

Al said no word of thanks to Maria about her part in his crisis. It did not occur to him, so engrossed was he in his *Regiebuch,* and if it had occurred to him, he would not have dared, for a woman who could talk to him as Maria had done was somebody best avoided. The musicologist in Al came uppermost; hadn't there been an opera called *All's Well That Ends Well?* He looked it up. Yes, there it was, by Edmond Audran, whose best opera was *La Poupée,* which meant The Baby, didn't it? Remarkable how fate, and music, and life were all mixed up. It made you think.

[3]

DURING THIS INCIDENT, which did not impinge at all on the preoccupation of the company, preparations for the opera were going ahead rapidly. The play which had commanded the stage had finished its run of performances, and Powell and his forces had the full run of the theatre. Scenes were hung from the flies and all the forty-five sets of ropes that controlled them were adjusted and balanced for use. A splendid set of curtains was brought in from a rental warehouse and hung behind the proscenium, so that they could be swept aside and upward from the centre in the gloriously theatrical manner of the nineteenth century. Powell demanded, and got, a set of footlights installed. In vain did Waldo Harris demur that nobody used such things any more.

"Hoffmann's theatre used 'em, and they are very becoming to the ladies," said Powell. "We won't make all the women look like skulls, with nothing but overhead light. And get that bloody rack of lamps taken down from in front of the proscenium; it's totally out of character and we can do without 'em; the light from the front of the balcony will be quite enough."

Powell was busy, so far as was possible, transforming the small opera theatre that belonged to the Stratford Festival into a charming early-nineteenth-century house.

"We're going to use those pretty little doors that give onto the forestage," he told Darcourt, "and we'll just dim the house lights to half, because in Hoffmann's day the audience sat in full light, and everybody could see their neighbours, and chat and flirt if they didn't like the show. Flirtation's a good old sport and due for a revival."

He had worked with Dulcy Ringgold to prepare pretty cartouches which decorated the little boxes beside the stage; one bore the arms of the town, and the other the arms of the province, but so treated that they had a playful, rather than an official, air. They looked like fine plaster-work, but they were pressed in the same light material as the armour worn by Arthur's Knights.

All of this activity caused a good deal of noise, but nevertheless the singers stepped onstage from time to time and bellowed or neighed into the auditorium, and agreed that it was a nice resonant house. They were still working in rehearsal rooms under the guidance of Watkin Bourke, who appeared to put in a twelve-hour day.

The company took on new vitality when they were able to

claim the theatre as their own, and friendships were struck up, enmities sharpened, and jokes whispered behind hands.

One of these originated with Albert Greenlaw, one of the black singers, who played the role of Sir Pellinore. He had found a great toy in Nutcombe Puckler, who was a comedian by profession, but never thought of himself as a comic.

"Do you realize," said Greenlaw to Vincent LeMoyne, the other black Knight, "that Nutty gets letters from his dog? Yes, I'm not kidding, *from his dog!* The dog's in England, of course, but the dog writes twice a week. And in Cockney, what's more! 'Dear Marster, I miss you terrible, but Missus says we has to be brave and go walkies every day just as if you was 'ere. My roomatism is chronic but I takes me pills reglar, and don't have to get up in the night more than a few times, which is an improvement, Missus says. Hurry back, covered with laurels and bring lots of lovely green bones. Love from your Woofy in which Missus joins.' Can you beat it! I've known dog-nuts, but I never met a dog-nut as nutty as Nutty. Why do you suppose the dog talks Cockney?"

"It's a class thing," said Wilson Tinney, who played Gareth Beaumains. "Dog must be loving and beloved, but *not* a social equal. Certainly not a superior. Can you imagine Nutty with a titled dog? 'Dear Puckler, your wife is looking after me splendidly in your absence, and I look forward eagerly to August 12, when the grousing begins. Accept my assurance that I look upon you not as a master, but as a humble friend.' That wouldn't do at all."

"Do you know what I think?" said Vincent LeMoyne; "I think Nutty's wife writes those letters. I suspect the dog's illiterate."

"You astonish me!" said Greenlaw. "Do you suppose Nutty knows?"

There was a coolness between Miss Virginia Poole, who, as the Lady Clarissant, was the only member of the female chorus to have a named role, and Gwen Larking, the Stage Manager; Miss Poole thought she should have a dressing-room apart from the Chorus, but she had been put—"thrown" was the word she used—with them in a large basement room. She appeared in all three acts and had two costumes, and yet Marta Ullmann, who appeared in only one scene as Elaine, had a dressing-room of her own on the stage level. If this was an intentional slight, what lay behind it? If it was an oversight, should it not be put right as fast as possble?

There was a row, lasting for a day, between Powell and Waldo Harris, because a trapdoor that Powell had ordered had not been cut in the stage. But if it were cut, said Waldo, it would go down into the orchestra pit, rather than the undercroft of the stage proper. Why had he not been told earlier? demanded Powell. He wanted Merlin to appear as if by magic at that particular spot, downstage right, and Mr. Twentyman had been rehearsing for four weeks with that in mind. All right, said Waldo, he would have it cut, and it would mean reducing the size of the orchestra by five members. Here Dr. Dahl-Soot intervened, and the question was somehow resolved without bloodshed, and without the trapdoor.

"Perhaps I could come down from the flies on a wire," suggested Mr. Twentyman. "I've done it before, you know."

Oliver Twentyman had made himself popular with everybody in the theatre, without particularly exerting himself to do so. But his great age, and his charm, and above all his assumption that everyone wanted to please him, made slaves of the gofers (to whom he brought charming Belgian chocolates in pretty little packages), and convinced Gwen Larking that she was his champion and must shield him from all harm, and caused Waldo Harris to put a special reclining-chair in his dressing-room, as well as a little heater, in case there might be early autumn chill. In return Mr. Twentyman gave advice about how to pronounce English when singing, with Hans Holzknecht as an eager pupil, and even Clara Intrepidi as an overhearer, rather than a committed listener. She was still dubious about a language with so many vowels.

Thus matters moved toward the final rehearsals, and a controlled, highly professional excitement rose.

The stage was still pretty much in the grip of the technicians, but time was found to accustom the actors to singing in the theatre. Not always at full strength, Darcourt found; sometimes they "marked", which meant that they sang quietly, skipped their high notes or sang them an octave below pitch, and were altogether so intimate that they seemed determined to keep the music a secret. Watkin Bourke performed prodigies on an ancient upright piano that stood on the forestage; he was still playing from a full orchestral score, and showed great firmness in keeping Al Crane from snatching this for his own information. Gunilla, who had taken a powerful scunner to Al, was determined that he should not see the music at close range if she could avoid it, and Al whined to Powell that this was a hardship, but Powell was not to be moved. Al had as yet not succeeded in getting the copies he wanted, and was not happy when he was told that he might get something for himself once the opera was in performance.

There was great activity, too, on the part of the public relations people, who wanted tasty bits of gossip to send out to the press, which had not shown much interest in *Arthur*. The report from the box-office was discouraging; even the first night had not been sold out, and would have to be papered with passes. A few of the more learned critics, who had asked for scores to study, had not been pleased when told that none were available, as Dean Wintersen had forbade any public examination of the music until Schnak's examiners had gone over it thoroughly. As the opening drew near, the report was that less than thirty-three per cent of the tickets for all performances had been sold. If Dr. Dahl-Soot was not concerned about this, the management of the Festival was disgruntled. Darcourt, the eager amateur, wished heartily for a public success, and fretted that it appeared unlikely.

He was sitting in the balcony of the theatre, during one of the mysterious marking rehearsals, when he became aware of a presence behind him, and of a smell that he thought he recognized. It was not really a bad smell, but it was a heavy, furry smell, rather like the bears' cage in a zoo. A soft, velvety bass voice rumbled in his ear.

"Priest Simon—a word, if you please."

Turning, he found Yerko leaning forward over his shoulder.

"Priest Simon, I have been taking note. Watching with great care. Everything seems to be going well, but a vital element of opera success is still missing. You know what I mean?"

Darcourt had no idea what this large, overwhelming Gypsy could possibly mean.

"The Claque, Priest Simon. Where is your Claque? Nobody says a word about it. I have inquired. The P.Or. people do not seem to know when I speak of a Claque. But you do, surely?"

Darcourt had heard of a claque, but knew nothing about it.

"Without the Claque—nothing. How can you expect anything else? Nobody knows this opera. An opera audience must contain people who know the work intimately. Nobody will dare to applaud if they don't know where, and when, and why. They might make an embarrassing mistake—look foolish. Now listen very carefully. I know the whole business of the Claque from top to bottom. Did I not work for years at the Vienna Opera under the great Bonci—related, but not so you could talk about it, to the noble tenor of that name? I was Bonci's right-hand man."

"You mean hired applause? Oh Yerko, I don't think that would do at all."

"Certainly it would not do if you talk of hired applause. That is not a Claque; that is a noisy, untrained rabble. No, look: a Claque is a small body of experts; applause, certainly, but not unorganized row; you must have your *bisseurs* who call out loud for encores; your *rieurs* who laugh at the right places—but just appreciative chuckles to encourage the others, not from the belly; your *pleureurs* who sob when sobs are needed; and, of course, the kind of clapping that encourages the uninformed to join, which is not vulgar hand-smacking that makes the clapper look like a drunk. Good clapping must sound intelligent, and that calls for skill; you must know what part of the palm to smack. And all of this must be carefully organized—yes, orchestrated—by the *capo di claque*. That's me. We won't talk money; this is a gift from my sister and me to our dear Arthur. We give him a success! But get me twelve seats—four balcony, two on each side of the ground floor well toward the front, and four in the last two rows, centre—and we can't fail. Of course two seats for me and my sister—because we shall appear in evening dress and sit in the middle of the house—and the thing's done."

"But Yerko—it's very kind, but isn't it a sort of lie?"

"Is P.Or. a lie? Would I lie to you, my friend?"

"No, no, certainly not; but it's lying to somebody, I feel sure."

"Priest Simon, listen; remember the old Gypsy saying—Lies keep the teeth white."

"I must say it's very tempting."

"You fix it up."

"I'll talk to Powell."

"But not a word to Arthur. This is a present. A surprise."

Darcourt did talk to Powell, and Powell was delighted. "Just in the real early-nineteenth-century style!" he said. "He's right, you know. Unless the audience is led, most of it won't know when to clap or what to like. A claque's just what we need."

So Darcourt gave Yerko the approving word. This is following the path of the Fool, he thought, and, all things considered, it's good sport.

[4]

WHAT NOBODY COULD POSSIBLE HAVE CONSIDERED good sport was Schnak's examination. It affected everybody in the company, from the stage crew, who thought it a pompous nuisance, to Albert Greenlaw, who said it gave him the heebie-jeebies, and to Hans Holzknecht and Clara Intrepidi, who were told by Dr. Gunilla that they must give their best in the performance involved, and that no "marking" or saving the voice was permitted.

The form of the examination was unusual. After some haggling it was agreed that it could not take place in the School of Music, and that the examiners must journey to Stratford to do their work. They were to examine the candidate orally in the morning, in the upstairs crush-bar of the theatre, and after luncheon they were to see a performance of the opera. It made a long day for them, said Dean Wintersen. He said nothing about what sort of day it made for Schnak.

There were to be three dress rehearsals before the first night of the production, which was scheduled for a Saturday. It was on the Wednesday, therefore, that a special small bus left the Music School in Toronto at a quarter to eight in the morning, with seven academics aboard.

"I must say I find this exceedingly irregular," said Professor Andreas Pfeiffer, who was the External Examiner, a great panjandrum of musicology imported for the occasion from an important school of music in Pennsylvania.

"You mean seeing a performance of the opera?" said Dean Wintersen, who had entertained Pfeiffer at dinner the night before and had already had enough of him.

"Of that I say nothing," said Professor Pfeiffer. "I mean this business of being haled across the countryside at an early hour.

Last night I slept very poorly, thinking about what lay ahead. It is difficult to compose oneself under such circumstances."

"You must admit the circumstances are unusual," said the Dean, lighting his first cigarette of the day.

"Perhaps too unusual," said Pfeiffer. "May I politely request you not to smoke? Very disagreeable in an enclosed vehicle."

The Dean threw his cigarette out of the window.

"Ah, ah! You didn't douse it!" said Professor Adelaide O'Sullivan. "That is how forest fires are started. Can we stop? I'll get out and stamp on it."

This was done, and Professor O'Sullivan, having dodged and darted a hundred yards to the rear, amid heavy traffic, found the cigarette, which had gone out by itself on the city street, and which she trampled to bits, as a matter of principle.

This put the journey off to a start marked by underground feeling. Professor George Cooper, a stout Englishman, had already gone to sleep, but Professor John Diddear was covertly pro-Dean, as he himself liked to smoke during examinations, as a way of passing the time, and he knew that it would be impossible with Pfeiffer and O'Sullivan so strongly against it. Professor Francesco Berger, who was the examiner from the university's own department of music, and a man of peace, tried to improve the atmosphere by telling a joke, but as he was not a man with much narrative sense, he spoiled it, and made matters worse. Professor Penelope Raven, who was the seventh in the group, laughed too loudly, all alone, at the non-climax, and was stared into silence by Pfeiffer.

It took the bus a little under two hours to reach Stratford, and the driver had to put up with a good deal of cautionary exclamation from Professor Pfeiffer, who was a nervous passenger. But at last the examiners found themselves in the crush-bar of the theatre, accommodated with a large table, and lots of pencils and pads, and several jugs of coffee. Professor Pfeiffer, who never drank coffee, was given a bottle of Perrier by Gwen Larking, the Stage Manager, who had appointed herself beadle of the occasion; she left an awed gofer on the spot, to fetch, carry, and do the bidding of the academics.

The protocol of an oral examination for a doctorate in music is not extreme, but it can be severe. Schnak, who was hanging about, dressed in a skirt at Gunilla's bidding, shook hands with all of the examiners, and shaking hands was not a courtesy that came easily to her. Gunilla introduced her to Professor Pfeiffer, who made it clear that this was an honour for Schnak; he put out his hand, which she barely touched. It was like ceremonially forgiving the headsman, before he does his work.

Then Wintersen asked Schnak to go downstairs and wait until she was called; she marched off, in the charge of the jailer-gofer, who looked as solemn as eighteen can. Dr. Gunilla, the director of the thesis project, was present as an examiner, and also in the character, familiar in courts-martial, of Prisoner's Friend. She was greeted with cordiality by the Canadians, but Professor Pfeiffer, who had his own opinions about the Doctor's international reputation, managed to put a chill on her reception.

The Dean, who was an old hand at such affairs, groaned in spirit. He had been warned that Pfeiffer was a bastard but his reputation as a musicologist was great, and so he must be endured.

The Dean, by virtue of his office, was the chairman of the examination, and he began according to Hoyle, by asking the examiners if they were all acquainted. They were, and in some cases too well. He drew their attention to three copies of the full score of *Arthur* which lay on the table for ready reference.

The Dean next called upon Professor Andreas Pfeiffer, as external examiner-in-chief, to place his report before the committee.

Professor Pfeiffer did so, taking just under an hour. It was a fine late August day outside, but by the time Pfeiffer had unpacked his budget of doubt and distaste it was February in the examination room. Professor Berger, who was a genial man, and liked Schnak, managed, as internal examiner-in-chief, in twenty minutes to shove the calendar back to approximately late December, but a post-Christmas gloom was still to be felt.

The other examiners, called upon to say their say, were brief. Not more than ten minutes was taken by Penny Raven, who managed to establish that she had evolved a libretto for the opera, with some unspecified outside help from a literary man.

"I hear nothing of Planché," said Professor Pfeiffer. Both Penny and Gunilla looked at him with deadly menace, but he was impervious to any outside influence.

Now, the processions, the parades of the picadors, the recognition of the President, the preening by the matador, and all the ceremonial of the ring having been performed, it was time to bring in the bull. Dean Wintersen nodded to the gofer (by this time a thorough Shakespearean jailer), and Schnak was brought back to the table, wilted with almost two hours of solitary anxiety. She was seated next to the Dean, and asked to explain her choice of the thesis project, and her method of work in realizing it. Which she did, very badly.

Professor Pfeiffer was first let loose on her. He was a matador of immense skill, and for thirty-five minutes he nagged and harassed the wretched Schnak, who had no verbal ease, no rhetoric of any kind, and made long, unpromising pauses before most of her answers.

Professor Pfeiffer showed disappointment. The bull had no style, no pride of the ring, seemed really unworthy of a matador of his repute.

But as the torture proceeded, Schnak took refuge more and more often in a single answer: "I did it like that because it came to me like that," she said. And although Professor Pfeiffer greeted this with doubtful looks, and once or twice with disdainful snorts, one or two of the other examiners, notably Cooper and Diddear, smiled and nodded, for they were themselves, in a modest way, composers.

Now and again Dr. Dahl-Soot interposed. But Pfeiffer shut her up, saying "I must not allow myself to think that the candidate's supervisor carried undue weight in the actual work of composition; that would be wholly inadmissible." Dr. Gunilla, fuming, but tactful, remained silent after that.

When at last, by repeatedly looking at his watch, the Dean made it clear that Professor Pfeiffer must close his interrogation, Dr. Francesco Berger took over, and was so genial, so anxious to put Schnak at her ease, suggested so often that he approved of what had been done, that he almost upset the applecart. His colleagues wished Berger would not overdo it. When their time came to ask questions, they were brief and merciful.

It was George Cooper, who had dozed through much of the examination, who asked: "I notice that you have used some keys at important moments in the opera that would not perhaps have suggested themselves first to most composers. A flat major, and C flat major, and E flat major—why those? Any special reason?"

"They were ETAH's favorites," said Schnak. "He had a theory about keys and their special characters, and what they suggested."

"ETAH? Who is ETAH?" said Professor Pfeiffer.

"Sorry. E. T. A. Hoffman; I've got into the way of thinking of him as ETAH," said Schnak.

"You mean you identify yourself with him?"

"Well, working with his notes and trying to get into his mind—"

Professor Pfeiffer said nothing but made a derisive noise in his nose. But then— "These theories of key characterization were very much a thing of Hoffmann's time," he said. "Romantic nonsense, of course."

"Nonsense or not, I think we ought to hear a little more about it," said Cooper. "What did he think about those keys?"

"Well—he wrote about A flat major: 'Those chords carry me into the country of eternal longing.' And about C flat major: 'It grasps my heart with glowing claws'; he called it 'the bleak ghost with red, sparkling eyes'. And he used E flat major a lot with horns; he called it 'longing and sweet sounds'."

"Hoffmann was a drug-taker, wasn't he?" said Professor Pfeiffer.

"I don't think so. He boozed a lot and sometimes he came near to having the horrors."

"I'm not surprised, if he could talk that sort of rubbish about the character of keys," said Pfeiffer, and was ready to drop the subject. But not Schnak.

"But if that's the way he thought, oughtn't I to respect it? If I'm to finish his opera, I mean?" she said, and Professor Diddear made a noise in *his* nose, as if to suggest that Professor Pfeiffer had been caught napping.

"I suppose you explain your excessive use of extraneous modulation as coming from Hoffmann's adulation of Beethoven?"

"Hoffmann adored Beethoven and Beethoven thought a lot of Hoffmann."

"I suppose that is so," said the great musicologist. "You should remember, young lady, what Berlioz thought about Hoffmann: a writer who imagined himself to be a composer. But you have chosen to devote a great deal of work to this minor figure, and that is why we are here."

"Perhaps to suggest that Berlioz could have been wrong," said Dr. Gunilla; "he made a fool of himself often enough, as critics always do."

She knew that Dr. Pfeiffer had written an essay about Berlioz which accorded Berlioz about seventy marks out of a hundred, which was as far as the Professor was inclined to go. If she could use Berlioz as a stick with which to beat Pfeiffer, so be it.

It was one o'clock.

"Ladies and gentlemen, I remind you that our work this morning is only a part of this unusual examination," said the Dean. "We assemble again at two in the theatre, for a private performance of this opera, conducted by Miss Schnakenburg, on which a portion of your decision must necessarily rest. Proof of the pudding, you know. Meanwhile the Cornish Foundation has invited us to lunch, and we are already late."

Professor Pfeiffer did not like lunching as a guest of the Cornish Foundation. "Are they not involved?" he asked the Dean. "Is the candidate not their protégée? I do not like to use such a term, but is this an attempt to buy us?"

"I think it's just decent hospitality," said the Dean, "and, as you know, hospitality is a co-operative thing. The Romans very wisely used the same word for 'host' and 'guest'." Pfeiffer did not understand, and shook his head.

The luncheon took place at the best restaurant in Stratford—the small one down by the river—and Arthur and Maria did everything they could to make the examiners happy. Easy work with Berger, Cooper, Diddear, and Penny Raven. Easy work with the Dean, and even with Professor Adelaide O'Sullivan, who was only a bigot about tobacco. Professor Pfeiffer, however, and Dr. Dahl-Soot had thrown aside the decorum of the examination room and were going at it, hammer and tongs.

"I totally disagree with this procedure of witnessing a performance of this work," said the Professor. "It brings in elements extraneous to what we are to decide."

"You don't care if it can be seen as effective on the stage?"

"I care only if it is effective on the page. I agree with the late Ernest Newman: a great score is more finely realized when one reads it in the tranquillity of one's study than when one sits in a crowd and endures the ineptitudes of orchestra and singers."

"You mean you can do it better in your head than a hundred accomplished artists can do it for you?"

"I can read a score."

"Better than, say von Karajan? Than Haitink? Than Colin Davis?"

"I do not follow the purpose of your line of questioning."

"I am just trying to find out how great a man you are so that I can treat you with appropriate reverence. I can read a score, too. Am pretty well known for it, in fact. But it's still better when I raise the baton and a hundred and twenty artists set about their work. I am not an opera company in myself."

"So? Well—make of it what you will, but I rather think I am. No, I never drink wine. A glass of Perrier, if you please."

What Professor Pfeiffer did not drink was certainly compensated for by what the others drank. It had been a thirsty morning. Before lunch was over, all but Pfeiffer were jovial, and Professor George Cooper showed a tendency to bump into tables, and laugh at himself for doing so. They were, after all, musicians under the professorial gown, and a well-set table was one of the elements in which they lived. They all thanked Arthur and Maria with a heartiness that made Professor Pfeiffer suspect the worst. But he could not be bought. Oh no, not he.

[5]

FIRST IN THE LINE OF DRESSING-ROOMS on the stage level was a small kennel reserved for the use of the conductor, when there was one, and a quick-change room if that should be needed. Here sat Schnak, desolate and alone. She had known rejection before this: had there not been the boy who said that sex with her was like sleeping with a bicycle? She had known the loneliness of leaving home and parents. She had known the bitterness of being a loner, of not fitting into any group, while being still too young and insignificant to wear loneliness like a badge of honour. But never had she known wretchedness like this, when she was about to take a great leap forward in her life as an artist.

She knew that she would not fail. Francesco Berger had made it clear to her, a few weeks ago, that the examination was a rite of passage, a ceremonial and scholarly necessity; the School of Music would not permit the examination to take place if it were not ninety-five per cent certain to be a success. The examination was either the last and most demanding of the torments of student life, or the first and simplest of the torments of professional life. She had nothing to fear.

Nevertheless, she feared. Her experience as a conductor had been confirmed to a few bouts with a student orchestra, which was fractious enough, because inexperienced. A professional orchestra was something very different. These old pros were like livery-stable horses: they were used to all sorts of riders, and they were determined to do, so far as possible, what they chose. Oh, they wouldn't wreck the performance; they were musicians, through and through. But they would be sticky about tempi, sluggish about entrances, perfunctory in phrasing; they wouldn't be bossed by a raw kid. Gunilla would conduct at all the public performances, unless Gunilla was kind and let her do one or two mid-week shows. Gunilla knew how to get what she wanted out of an orchestra, and she had the kind of sharp tongue musicians respect—professionally severe, but not personal. What had she said to the harpist yesterday? "The *arpeggi* must be deliberate, like pearls dropping in wine, not slithering like a fat woman slipping on a banana skin." Not Oscar Wilde, but good enough for a rehearsal. Gunilla had coached her, had allowed her to conduct a full orchestra rehearsal, and had given her an hour of notes afterward. But once she lifted her baton this afternoon, she was alone. And that old hellion Pfeiffer would be watching every minute.

The dressing-room was unbearable. She wandered out to the stage, which was set for the Prologue, and as it was lighted only by one harsh lamp high up in the flies it was as charmless as an unlit stage always is. Below her, under the device of rollers, like corkscrews, that produced the effect of gently heaving waves, she heard voices: Waldo Harris, Dulcy, and Gwen Larking, arguing with Geraint.

"They work perfectly well, but they make too much noise," said Waldo. "I don't suppose you'd agree to leaving them out altogether? We could probably rig up something that would look like moving water."

"Oh, no!" said Dulcy. "These are the darlings of my heart—and absolutely authentic for the way they did things in 1820."

"They've cost a fortune to make," said Waldo. "I guess it would be a shame to scrap them."

"But what can you do?" said Geraint.

"We'd have to dismantle the three rollers and put rubber on the parts that engage. That'd do it, I think."

"How long will it take?" said Geraint.

"An hour, at least."

"Then take an hour, and do it," said Geraint. "I want to see it this afternoon."

"Can't," said Gwen Larking. "The curtain must go up sharp at two. It's Schnak's examination, remember?"

"What of it? An hour won't kill them, surely?"

"From what I hear about this morning, an hour's delay would put them in a very bad temper. Especially that old fellow who makes all the trouble. We mustn't make things difficult for Schnak."

"Oh, damn Schnak! That miserable little runt is more bother than she's worth!"

"Come on, Geraint, be a sport. Give the kid her chance."

"You mean Schnak's chance is more important than my production?"

"Yes, Geraint, from now till half past four Schnak's chance is more important than anything else. You said so yourself, to the whole cast, yesterday," said Dulcy.

"I say whatever is best at the moment, and you know it."

"What's best at the moment is that we leave this piece of machinery till later."

"This is just the trade-unionism of women. God, how I hate women."

"All right, Geraint; hate me," said Gwen. "But give Schnak her chance, even if you hate her later."

"Gwen's right," said Waldo. "I said an hour, but it could be two. Let's leave it for the moment."

"O Jesu mawr! O anwyl Crist! Have it your way then!" Geraint could be heard going off in a huff.

"Don't fuss! We'll manage the appearance of the sword! It'll do for today," said Waldo, but there was no sound of an appeased director.

Schnak threw up her lunch-time sandwich and cup of coffee into the toilet. It had turned to gall within her. When she had wiped her face and doused it with cold water, she went back to her dressing-room and looked at herself in the mirror. Damned Schnak. Miserable little runt. Yes, Geraint was right.

He'd never love me. Why would anybody love me? I love Geraint even better than I love Nilla, and he hates me. Look at me! Short. Scrawny. Awful hair. Face like a rat. Those legs! Why did Nilla say I had to wear a black jacket and this white blouse? Of course he hates me. I look just bloody awful. Why can't I look like Nilla? Or that Maria Cornish? Why is God so mean to me?

A tap at the door, and a gofer (the prettiest gofer) put her head inside.

"Fifteen minutes, Schnak," she said. "And the best of luck. All the girls have their fingers crossed for you."

Schnak snarled, and the gofer withdrew quickly.

After fifteen minutes more of repetitious self-hate the last call came—from outside the door—and Schnak made her way downstairs, through the undercroft to the stage, and into the orchestra pit. There they sat, the thirty-two villains who meant to destroy her. Some of them nodded to her pleasantly; the concert-master, and Watkin Bourke at the harpsichord, whispered, "Good luck."

If there is any applause when you step onto the podium, turn and bow to the house, Nilla had said. There was no applause, but from the tail of her eye she could see that the seven examiners had placed themselves here and there in the auditorium, and in the front row, right behind her, a full score on his knees and a flashlight in his hand, sat the ominous Professor Pfeiffer. What a seat to choose, she thought.

The little red light-signal from the Stage Manager flashed on, and at the same time the oyster eye of the closed-circuit television camera directly in front of the conductor's desk, which would carry Schnak's every movement to backstage monitors, for Stage

Management, Chorus, and offstage sound of every kind, gave a gloomy blink, like an undersea monster.

She tapped the music desk, raised her baton—one of Gunilla's own, specially made and perhaps intended as a talisman—and when she gave the down beat, the first mysterious chord of the Prologue rose at her.

The orchestra, aware of her nerves, but oblivious of her hatred, played well, and after fifteen slow bars of the Prologue the curtain swept upward to show the Enchanted Mere. In front of it stood Oliver Twentyman, splendid as Merlin, and Hans Holzknecht, armoured and cloaked as King Arthur. Merlin apostrophized the waves, and not quite on cue the great sword Caliburn rose above the unmoving waters. Arthur seized it, and invoked all the magic of the sword. Everything seemed to be going well, until Schnak felt herself being tapped—almost punched—in the back, and when she ignored this, there was a loud whistle, and Professor Pfeiffer's voice crying, "Hold it! Hold it! Repeat from Letter D, please!" Schnak dropped her baton and the music stopped.

"What's the matter?" It was Dean Wintersen's voice.

"I want to hear it again from Letter D," said Pfeiffer. "They are not playing what is written in the score."

"A minor change in rehearsal," said Gunilla's voice. "Some addition to the wood-winds."

"I am speaking to the conductor," said Pfeiffer. "If there has been a change, why is it not in the score as it was presented to us? Repeat from Letter D, if you please."

So the music was repeated from Letter D. Holzknecht, who had been pleased with his performance, was not pleased by this unexpected encore; Oliver Twentyman flashed a charming smile at Professor Pfeiffer across the footlights like someone humoring a child, and the Professor did not like it.

Nevertheless, the repeat was performed, and all went well until the end of the Prologue. It had been seen through a scrim, a transparent curtain which lent mystery to the stage, and as this was whisked up into the flies, it did not whisk obligingly, but caught on the first wing on the right side of the stage, and there was a terrible ripping. The scrim was halted in its progress, and

Gwen Larking appeared at the side of the stage accompanied by a large man with a pole who fished the scrim away from what was catching it. This did not dismay the stage crew, or the singers, who were used to such mishaps, but it struck coldly into the heart of Schnak, who was sure this would be counted against her by her merciless foe.

What happened during the long afternoon was not, as Geraint wildly cried, like the Marx Brothers in *A Night at the Opera*, but it included more than the usual number of technical troubles. What really put the rehearsal to the bad was the frequent interruption of Professor Pfeiffer, who demanded, in all, seven repeats of music which he said—quite rightly—was not entirely as it appeared in the score he had been sent three weeks earlier. When he did not stop proceedings by whistling loudly through his teeth, like a policeman, he could be heard muttering, and demanding more light to help him in making notes. The opera, which should have taken two and a half hours, without the single fifteen-minute interval, took rather more than four, and the singers became demoralized, and were far below their best. Only the orchestra, firmly professional, sawed and tooted and strummed imperturbably, and did, under the circumstances, pretty well.

Six of the seven examiners had given up the struggle before the rehearsal finished. They had heard enough, had liked what they heard, had enjoyed lunch, and were ready to wrap the affair up and get back to their homes. Professor Pfeiffer, whose eyes were fixed on his score, never seemed to look at the stage and was impatient when technical problems brought the performance to a halt. Nobody, therefore, noticed that it was not Schnak who conducted the last scene, but Watkin Bourke, who did so from the harpsichord. Schnak had disappeared, and the orchestra had assumed that she was ill and were not, all things considered, surprised.

Even they were surprised, however, when a loud siren was heard outside the fire exit on the right-hand side of the auditorium, and Gwen Larking, appearing from one of the proscenium doors, jumped from the stage to open it and admit four men with a stretcher, who hurried across the front of the theatre, trampling Professor Pfeiffer's feet as they did so, and disappeared through the pass-door on the stage left. But the music went on, somewhat rockily, until, moments later, the four men reappeared, carrying a stretcher upon which lay the body of Schnak, under a blanket. The stage had filled, meanwhile, with actors in costume, several stage-hands, the gofers, and Arthur and Maria, who stood at the footlights with Geraint Powell. The body of Schnak was carried before them, thought Darcourt, who had been in the darkness at the back of the theatre, very much as if they were looking down at it from Arthurian battlements, and their astonishment and dismay were not in the least theatrical, but real and stamped with terror. The little procession reached the door, the stretcher disappeared, and the siren grew fainter as the ambulance sped away.

There was excitement, of course, the kind of excitement over an unexpected happening that only a theatrical company can generate. What was it? Why was it? What had happened? What should be done?

It was Waldo Harris who called for order and explained. When Schnak had not appeared on the podium for the last scene, one of the gofers had gone to see what was amiss, and, not finding her in her dressing-room, had looked in the ladies' lav. And there she was, very ill and unconscious.

Had she tried to kill herself? Nobody knew, and they must not think like that until there was more news from the hospital. Miss Intrepidi let it be known that if it was an attempt at suicide, she, for one, was not surprised, after the way the poor child had been treated during the rehearsal. An Intrepidi party formed immediately, and murmured against Professor Pfeiffer, who was unaware of it and took no notice. He was anxious to continue with the examination.

"This is unfortunate," he said, "but not perhaps crucial. We can meet now, and make our decisions. I have a great many questions to ask, particularly about the libretto. Where can we be private?"

"But we can't have an examination without the candidate," said Penelope Raven.

"We've had an examination till I'm bloody sick of it," said George Cooper. "Let's give her the degree and be done with it."

"Give her the degree when there are still vital questions to be asked?" Professor Pfeiffer was scandalized. "I am far from satisfied."

"You must admit these are unusual circumstances," said Dean Wintersen. "It can hardly be said we've cut corners. We've been at it all day. Surely we can come to an agreement now?"

"Agreed! I move acceptance of the thesis and the obligatory performance as completion of the work for the doctoral degree," said Francesco Berger.

"Excuse me! As the External Examiner that is my privilege," said Professor Pfeiffer.

"Well then, for Christ's sake use your privilege," said George Cooper. "This is ridiculous! That girl may be dead, or dying."

"I fully understand the compassionate grounds for a hasty decision," said Pfeiffer; "but in my experience compassionate grounds are rarely sound grounds, and I should like to feel that this examination has been completed in proper form. Frankly, I should like to defer a decision for a week, during which we should attend at least two more performances."

"Sorry to sound like a dean," said Wintersen, "but I really must overrule you, Professor. I shall call for a vote, naming the examiners in alphabetical order. Professor Berger?"

The vote was six for acceptance of the degree, Professor Pfeiffer abstaining, and the Dean forgoing his privilege of casting a vote. The examination was over, and Schnak, dead or alive, was therewith a Doctor of Music.

The Cornishes took over. Darcourt was asked to take the examiners to dinner, as they had been detained too long. Gunilla announced her determination to go to the hospital at once, with Arthur and Maria. Professor Pfeiffer said he didn't want any dinner, but this deceived no one. The singers were shooed off to their dressing-rooms, big with the drama of the afternoon.

Geraint called Waldo and Gwen to him, and set about a long budget of notes he had taken during what was, to him, a disappointing and tediously delayed rehearsal. He would show proper emotion, he said, when everything was shipshape and Bristol fashion.

[6]

WHAT WOULD A STRANGER MAKE of this room, if he should happen in here by mistake, thought Darcourt. A beautiful young mother sits in the dim light of the only lamp, suckling her child; the long dressing-robe she wears might belong to any time during the past two thousand years. There are two very large beds in the room and in one of them, under the heavy coverlet, lie two women; one in early middle age and of distinguished, hawk-like face and the other softly pretty, her dark eyes full of mischief. The older woman's arm is around the neck of her companion, and caresses it. In the second bed I lie myself, full dressed except for my shoes, and beside me lies a man of great beauty and palpable energy; his open shirt-collar and longish curly dark hair might belong to any time during the last two hundred and fifty years. We too are partly covered, for the August night is chilly, but there is no affectionate link between us. The only other figure in the room is the man whose back is turned to us; he stands at the dressing-table, which has been turned into a pretty well-stocked bar.

The room itself? It looks as if one of those half-timbered houses, perhaps from Stratford-on-Avon or Gloucestershire, had been turned inside out. Dark beams appear to support a structure of lumpy white plaster. This style of interior finish is intended, undoubtedly, as a compliment to the Shakespeare Festival which is the chief glory of this town.

This is Maria and Arthur's room in the motel where they have been staying, intermittently, for the past three weeks observing— so far as they have been made welcome to observe—the completion of all the preparations for the presentation of *Arthur of Britain*, and they are entertaining Gunilla, and Dulcy Ringgold, and Geraint and myself. It is ten o'clock at night. We are gathered to talk about the strange behaviour of Hulda—henceforth and forever Doctor Hulda—Schnakenburg, who was borne from her doctoral examination on a stretcher a few hours earlier.

All things considered, the intruding stranger might think it an odd scene, a mixture of the domestic and the reposeful. Or was it some muddle of group sex, arranged for observers of peculiar tastes?

"She's going to be all right," said Arthur, turning to give Gunilla another strong Scotch. "But it's bound to be a little bit embarrassing when she rejoins us. The hospital people want her for a couple of days at least. Her digestive tract has suffered what they call serious insult. They've been swilling her out."

"Little fool," said Gunilla. "Nearly a hundred Aspirin and half a bottle of gin. Where would she have got the idea that it would kill her?"

"She didn't mean to kill herself," said Arthur. "It was what it is now fashionable to call a gesture of despair."

"No, no, don't patronize her," said Gunilla. "She meant to kill herself, undoubtedly. She was just badly informed, as many suicides are."

"You must admit she made a very effective scene out of it," said Dulcy. "I was moved. Blubbed quite a lot, I confess it without shame."

"She saw herself as Elaine, the Lily Maid of Astolat," said Maria. "Dying of love for the faithless Lancelot. Hulda has learned a great deal from this opera, quite apart from the music. She did it to make you feel cheap, Geraint, just as Elaine made Lancelot feel cheap. Now, Davy my pet, time to change sides." She shifted the feeding child to her other breast.

"Do all babies make that slurping noise when they are feeding?" said Geraint.

"It's a very nice noise, and no impertinent questions from you, my lad. You're in the doghouse."

"I'm damned if I'm in the doghouse," said Geraint. "You can't blame me. I won't put up with it."

"You'll have to put up with it," said Dulcy. "Of course it's unjust, but who are you to escape all of the world's injustice? This is one of those cases where the female side in the great struggle undoubtedly wins. You scorned her love, which God knows was obvious enough, and she tried to kill herself. Doghouse for you. Bitter shame upon you, Geraint Powell, you heartbreaker, for not less than two weeks."

"Bullshit!"

"Coarseness ill becomes a man in your position. You are cast as the haughty, gallant, gay Lothario, and if you have any dramatic sense at all—which is what you're paid to have—you will play the part to the hilt."

"Is nobody on my side? Sim *bach,* say a few eloquent words in my defence. How am I to blame?"

"Well, to be totally fair and even-handed, Geraint, I have seen you, now and then, casting inflammatory smiles in her direction."

"I smile at everybody, particularly when I don't mean anything by it. Perhaps I smiled—a meaningless grimace of courtesy—at Schnak now and then when she kept getting under my feet. I swear upon the soul of my dear mother, now adding a fine mezzo to the heavenly choir, that I meant nothing, nothing whatever, by it. I smile at you Nilla, and at you, Dulcy, and God knows I don't expect it to get me anywhere, you horrible old dykes."

"Dykes!" said Gunilla indignantly. "How dare you use such a word to me—to us. You are a boor, Geraint."

"Isn't he a boor, Nilla? That's precisely what he is. A boor.

> *She loved thee, boor; she loved thee, cruel boor;*

Shakespeare, freely adapted for the occasion." Dulcy was enjoying herself greatly. Indignation and Scotch were working strongly inside her.

"She didn't love me, even if she thought she did."

"It comes to the same thing."

"Yes, I fear it does," said Darcourt. "Poor old Schnak was in the grip of one of the great errors of the frenzied lover. She thought because she loved, she could provoke love in return. Everybody does it, at some time. I speak as the voice of calm reason."

"And you ignored her cruelly," said Arthur. "Doghouse for you, Geraint."

"I suppose I must make a statement," said Geraint. "What I am about to say does not spring from vanity, but from bitter experience. Listen to me, all of you. Since I was but a winsome lad, women have insisted on falling for me. It has something to do with chemistry, I suppose. Chemistry and the fact (which I state without any vanity whatever) that I am absurdly good-looking. Result, a lot of trouble for me. But am I to blame? I refuse to accept blame. Are beautiful women to blame because men fall for them? Is Maria to blame because just about everybody who sees her falls in love with her, or at least looks upon her to lust after her? I'll bet that even Sim *bach*, bloodless old turnip though he is, loves Maria. Can Maria help it? The idea is too ridiculous for discussion. So why am I to blame because Schnak, who is emotionally warped and retarded, gets silly notions about me? My beauty has been a large part of my success as an actor, and I tell you I'm bloody sick of it. That's why I want to get out of acting and into directing. I will not be sighed at and lallygagged over by audiences of hungry females. I have too keen an intelligence to value such admiration, which is simply aroused by the Livery of Hell—my physical appearance. I am close to middle age, and my beauty is giving way to a ravaged distinction. I have a gammy leg. So perhaps I can look forward to the remainder of my life in peace."

"I wouldn't count on that, Geraint," said Arthur. "You must bear your cross. Even if your looks are going, the chemistry is bubbling away as merrily as ever. But we're wandering from the point. The point is Schnak. What are you going to do about Schnak?"

"Why must I do anything about her? I'm not going to encourage her, if that's what you have in mind. I can't abide the shrimp. It isn't just that she's ugly to look at. Her voice goes through me like a rusty saw, and her impoverished vocabulary grates on me unbearably. Even if I were willing to forgo beauty, I simply must have the luxury of language. It isn't just that she looks ugly. She sounds ugly, and I want none of her."

"You make a terrible fuss about voices, Geraint," said Maria.

"Because they are terribly important, and usually neglected. Listen to you, Maria; music every time you open your lips. But most women don't even know that's possible. It is one of the three great marks of beauty. It totally changes the face. If Medusa speaks like a goddess, you can't tell her from Minerva."

"Very Welsh, Geraint," said Dulcy.

"And none the worse for that, I suppose?" said Geraint.

"There, my dumpling, that's enough," said Maria, and putting little David over her shoulder she patted his back gently. The child gave a mighty belch, extraordinary for his age.

"That boy is obviously going to grow up to be a sailor," said Arthur.

"Or a great lord of finance, like his daddy," said Maria. "Will you call Nanny, darling?"

When Nanny came she was not the stout, red-faced figure of stereotype, but a girl in her early twenties, smart in a blue uniform; David was her first charge.

"Come on, my lambie," she said, in a Scottish voice that made Geraint glance at her approvingly. "Time for bed."

She took the child over her shoulder, and this time David gave a long, reflective fart. "That's the boy," said Nanny.

"David has more sense than the lot of you," said Geraint. "He has summed up this whole argument in a masterly blast. Let's hear no more of it."

"Oh, but we must," said Maria. "You can't get out of it. Even if you didn't encourage Schnak, you must comfort her. The logic is clear, but it would take too long to spell it out."

"I'll throw up the show, first," said Geraint, and, dragging himself from under the heavy cover, he stamped out of the room. He avoided the cliché of slamming the door.

The others chewed over the rights and wrongs of the situation for quite a long time, until Darcourt fell asleep. It was midnight when they went to their own quarters. The big motel was full of people associated with *Arthur* in one way or another, and Albert Greenlaw insisted on calling it Camelot. Was there a lot of gossip at Camelot about Lancelot and Elaine? Malory doesn't say.

[7]

GERAINT WAS AT THE HOSPITAL the next day, as soon as rules permitted. Schnak was in a room for two, but by good luck the other bed was empty. She sat up in bed, wan and bedraggled, in a hospital gown that had once been blue and was now a poor grey, eating a bowl of orange Jell-O, washed down with an eggnog.

"You see how it is, old girl," said Geraint. "Just one of those unlucky things. Neither of us to blame. The working of Fate."

"I've been a selfish shit and embarrassed everybody," said Schnak. Tears did nothing to improve her looks.

"No, you haven't and you aren't. And I wish you'd take a vow to stop saying 'shit' all the time; talk shit and your life will be shit."

"My life is shit. Everything goes contrary with me."

"Mrs. Gummidge!"

"Who's Mrs. Gummidge?"

"If you're a good girl and get well soon I'll lend you the book."

"Oh, somebody in a book! All you people like Nilla and the Cornishes and that man Darcourt seem to live out of books. As if everything was in books!"

"Well, Schnak, just about everything *is* in books. No, that's wrong. We recognize in books what we've met in life. But if you'd read a few books you wouldn't have to meet everything as if it had never happened before, and take every blow right on the chin. You'd see a few things coming. About love, for instance. You thought you loved me."

Schnak gave a painful howl.

"All right then, you think you love me now. Come on, Schnak, say it. Say, 'I love you, Geraint.' "

Another howl.

"Come on. Out with it! Say it, Schnak."

"I'd die first."

"Look, Schnak, that's what comes of building your vocabulary on words like 'shit'. Great words choke you. If you can't say love, you can't feel love."

"Yes I can!"

"Then say so!"

"I'm going to be sick."

"Good. Here's a basin. I'll hold your head. Up she comes! Hmm—doesn't look too bad, for what you've been doing to yourself. Almost as good as new. I'll just put this down the john, then you have a sip of water and we'll go on."

"Leave me alone!"

"I will not leave you alone! You've got to whoop up more than that eggnog if you're to be really well. Let me wipe your mouth. Now we'll try again: say, 'I love you, Geraint.' "

The defeated Schnak buried her face in her pillow, but among the sobs she managed to whisper, "I love you."

"That's my brave girl! Now look at me, and I'll sponge your eyes. I'm your friend, you know, but I don't love you—not the way you think you love me. Oh, my dear old Schnak, don't think I don't understand! We've all had these awful hopeless passions, and they hurt like hell. But if we were romantic lovers, the kind you're thinking of, do you suppose I'd hold your head while you puked, and mop your face, and try to make you see reason? The kind of love you're dreaming about takes place on mossy banks, amid the scent of flowers and the song of birds. Or else in luxurious chambers, where you loll on a *chaise longue,* and I take off your clothes very slowly until we melt into a union of intolerable sweetness, and not a giggle or a really kind word spoken the whole time. It's the giggles and the kind words that you need for the long voyage."

"I feel like a fool!"

"Then you're quite wrong. You're not a fool, and only a fool would think you were. You're an artist, Schnak. Maybe a very good one. Romantic Art—which is what's kept you busy since last autumn—is feeling, shaped by technique. You've got bags of technique. It's feeling that kills you."

"If you grew up like I grew up, you'd hate the word feeling."

"I grew up in a boiling tank of feeling. All tied up, somehow, with religion. When I said I was going to be an actor my parents raved as if they'd seen me in Hell already. But my dad was a fine actor—a pulpit actor. And my mam was Sarah Bernhardt twenty-four hours a day. They poured it all into the chapel, of course. But I wanted a bigger stage than that, because I had an idea of God, you see, and my God showed himself in art. I couldn't trap God in the chapel. An artist doesn't want to trap God; he wants to live and breathe God, and damned hard work it is, stumbling and falling."

"I hate God."

"Good for you! You don't say, 'There is no God,' like a fool; you say you hate Him. But Schnak—you won't like this, but you have to know—God doesn't hate you. He's made you special. When Nilla is being confidential she hints that you may be really special. So think of it this way: give God His chance. Of course He'll take it anyway, but it's easier for you if you don't kick and scream."

"How can anybody live God?"

"By living as well as they can with themselves. It doesn't always look very well to the bystanders. Truth to yourself, I suppose you call it. Following your nose. But don't expect me to explain. My dad was the explainer. He could go on about living in God's light till your head swam. Duw, he was a fine preacher! A true God-intoxicated man. But he thought God had one, single, unwinking light for everybody, and that was where he and I fell out."

"Now that I've said what you made me say—don't you say anything?"

"Yes. I say it won't do. Suppose I took you up on it, and we had an affair, you loving and me using you as long as it lasted—which wouldn't be long. It would be a cheat. I haven't time or inclination for that, and when it finished you would be bitter, and you're quite bitter enough already. What about Gunilla? Did you love her?"

"It wasn't the same."

"No love ever is the same as any other. The lucky ones get the big thing. You know—'The silver link, the silken tie'—but it's not common. That's one of the big mistakes, you know—that everybody loves in the same way and that everybody may have a great love. You might as well say that everybody can compose a great symphony. A lot of love is misery; bad weather punctuated by occasional flashes of sunlight. Look at this opera we're busy with; the love in it is pretty rough. It's not the best of Arthur's life, or Lancelot's, or Guenevere's."

"It's the best of Elaine's."

"Elaine wasn't a gifted musician, so don't try that on. She had your trouble, though. 'Fantasy's hot fire,/Whose wishes, soon as granted, fly.' You set those words to some very good music. Didn't you learn anything from them? Schnak, if you and I set out on a love affair, you'd have had enough of it in two weeks."

"Because I'm ugly! Because my looks make everybody sick! It isn't fair! It's a curse! That Cornish bitch, and Nilla and Dulcy all look great and they can do anything with you, or any man! I'll kill myself!"

"No, you won't. You've got other fish to fry. But truth's truth, Schnak; you're no beauty queen and that's just something you have to put up with, and it isn't the worst affliction, let me tell you. What do you suppose Nilla looked like at your age? A big gawk, I'll bet. Now she's marvellous. When you're her age, you'll be totally different. Success will have given you a new look. You'll be a kind of distinguished goblin, I expect."

Schnak howled again, and hid her face in the pillows.

"I'm sorry if that hurt your feelings, but you see, Schnak old girl, I'm under considerable stress myself. Everybody says I have to talk to you, and be nice to you, though I protest I hadn't an inkling of the way you felt about me, and I won't take any responsibility. I can't run the risk of feeding your flame, and making things worse. So I'm talking entirely against my inclination. You know how I am; I love to talk and talk as gaudily as I can, just for the pleasure it gives me. But with you, I'm trying to speak on oath, you see. Not a word I don't truly mean. If I let myself go, I could rave on about the Livery of Hell, and the demon's dunghill, and all the rest of it. Welsh rhetoric is part of me, and my curse is that the world is full of literal-minded morlocks who don't understand, and think I'm a crook because their tongues are wrapped in burlap and mine is hinged with gold. I've been as honest as I know how. You see, don't you?"

"I guess so."

"Good. Now I must go. A million things to attend to. Get well as fast as you can; we want you on the first night, and that's the day after tomorrow. And—Schnak, here's a kiss. Not a romantic one, or a brotherly one, God forbid! but a friendly one. Fellow artists—isn't that it?"

He was gone. Schnak dozed and thought, and dozed and thought, and when Gunilla came to see her late in the afternoon, she was decidedly better.

"It must have cost him a good deal to talk like that," said Gunilla, when Schnak had given a version of what Geraint had said. "Lots of so-called lovers wouldn't have been as direct with you, Hulda. It isn't easy to be like Geraint."

[8]

IT WAS THE FINAL DRESS PARADE, on the Friday afternoon preceding the final dress rehearsal, which was to take place the same night. In Row G of the theatre sat a little group: Geraint Powell the dominant figure, with Dulcy Ringgold as his first lieutenant and Waldo Harris on his other side; in front of them sat Gwen Larking, with both her assistants, and a gofer poised to run with messages too delicate to be shouted toward the stage. One by one the actors, dressed and made up for their roles, walked to centre stage, did little excursions to right and left, bowed, curtsied, drew weapons. Now and then Geraint shouted some request to them; when they replied they shaded their eyes against the stage light, to see him if they could. Geraint whispered comments to Dulcy, who made notes, or explained, and occasionally expostulated if he wanted something that could not be managed in the time that was left before the opening.

A queer moment, thought Darcourt, who sat further back, by himself. The moment when all that is important is how the singer looks, not how he sings; the moment when everything that can be done to make the singers look like the people they represent has been done, and whatever has not been achieved must be accepted. A moment when inexplicable transformations take place.

The two black Knights, for instance, Greenlaw and LeMoyne, who looked superb in armour and the turbans Dulcy had given them to mark them as men of the East. But Wilson Tinney, as Gareth Beaumains, simply looked dumpy, although he was not an ill-looking man in his ordinary dress. His legs were too short. When he appeared without his armour he looked like a kewpie doll in his short robe. He had made himself up with very red cheeks, doubtless to suggest a life of adventure on horseback, but the effect was merely doll-like. In his robes as Merlin, Oliver Twentyman was convincingly magical, because his legs were long; he loved dressing up, and was enjoying himself. Giles Shippen, the Lancelot, looked less like a heart-breaker in costume than out of it; he was a reasonable figure, but he had Tenor written all over him, and his big chest made him look shorter than he really was.

"Did you put lifts in his shoes?" hissed Geraint to Dulcy.

"As much as I dared, without putting him in surgical boots," said she; "he just doesn't look like much whatever you do."

"Nobody will believe a woman would leave Holzknecht for him. Hans looks magnificent."

"Every inch a ruler," said Dulcy; "but everybody knows women have funny tastes. Nothing to be done, I'm afraid, Geraint."

As was to be expected, Nutcombe Puckler had a great deal to say, and was full of complaint. "Geraint, I simply can't hear in this thing," he said. He was referring to his camail, a headpiece of chain armour that hung down from his fool's bonnet to his shoulders, over his ears. "If I can't hear, I may make a false entrance and screw up. Can't something be done?"

"The effect is splendid, Nutty. You look the perfection of a merry warrior. Dulcy will put some pads under it, just over your ears, and you'll be all right."

"It fidgets me," said Nutty. "I can't bear to have my ears covered on the stage."

"Nutty, you're far too much of a pro to let a little thing bother you," said Geraint. "Give it a try tonight and if it really doesn't work, we'll find another way."

"Like hell we will," murmured Dulcy, making a note.

Among the women the assumption of costume brought about similar changes in emphasis. As Queen Guenevere, Donalda Roche looked handsome, but very much a woman of the present day, whereas Marta Ullmann, as the Lady Elaine, looked so much a creature of the Middle Ages, and so infinitely desirable, that none of the men could take their eyes off her. Clara Intrepidi, as Morgan Le Fay, looked an undoubted sorceress in her gown of changing colours and her dragon head-dress—but a sorceress who was a fugitive from some unidentified opera by Wagner. She was taller than any of the men except Holzknecht, and her appearance suggested that when she was at home she had a full suit of armour in her closet.

"Can't be helped," whispered Dulcy, "unless she consents to act on her knees, or sitting down all the time. Luckily she's Arthur's sister; great height runs in the family. Look at it that way."

"Yes, but look at Panisi," said Geraint. "He's supposed to be her son, and Arthur's son as well. Surely a child of those two would be a giant?"

"Incest makes for funny-looking children," said Dulcy. "Use your imagination, Geraint. You did the casting, you know."

The ladies of the court were, upon the whole, a splendid group, except for Virginia Poole who, as the Lady Clarissant, looked like a woman with a grievance, as indeed she was, onstage and off. Dulcy had put some of the younger women in the *cotehardie,* a tight-fitting medieval bodice that showed off a fine bust to the utmost advantage.

"You've let your natural inclinations run away with you, haven't you, dear?" said Geraint.

"You bet I have. Look at Polly Graves; it would be a black sin to muffle up such a splendid pair of jugs. And Esther Moss; an evocation of the mystic East? A whiff of Baghdad in Camelot?"

"They didn't look quite that way in the designs."

"Don't fight your luck, Geraint. These girls are for the tired business man."

"And woman, dear. I'm not complaining. Just surprised. You never know what's under rehearsal clothes, do you?"

"Primrose Maybon looks good enough to eat with a silver spoon," said Waldo.

"Too bad the women look so much better than the men," said Gwen Larking. "But our sex does have its compensations, when we can show 'em off."

"Let's see you with your trains over the arm, girls," said Dulcy. "Left arm, Etain. That's the girl."

To Darcourt they all looked wonderful, even the nuisance Puckler. Dulcy had drawn heavily on Planché's *Encyclopaedia,* and she had obviously studied the work of Burne-Jones, but the result was all her own. If not all the singers looked as well as they should in their costumes, the total effect was superb, because of the way in which colours called to one another, not obviously but subtly, in every grouping. This was an element in the opera of which Darcourt, the greenhorn in the theatre, could have had no idea.

When every costume had been seen in its final form, and all the notes made and all the complaints heard, Geraint called: "Before we break, I want to rehearse the curtain calls. Stand by, will you." And when at least these tableaux had been arranged to his satisfaction—"And of course when that's over, you, Hans, go to stage right and bring on Nilla, who takes her bow, and then, Nilla, you beckon into the wings for Schnak. And Schnak, you must come on in full fig—the fullest fig you possess—and Nilla takes your hand and you curtsy."

"I what?"

"You curtsy. You mayn't bow; not old enough. If you don't know what a curtsy is, get somebody to show you. Thank you. That's all for now. I want to see all the animal-handlers backstage right away, please."

"But why me?" said Darcourt to an unwontedly pleading Schnak, who had sidled up to him with her request when the rehearsal was over, and the singers had gone to their dressing-rooms.

"You know what a curtsy is, don't you?"

"I think so. But get one of the women to show you. It's their kind of thing."

"I don't want to. They hate me. They'd triumph over me."

"Nonsense, Schnak. They don't hate you. The younger ones are probably afraid of you, because you're so clever."

"Please, Simon. Be a good guy, eh?"

It was the first time she had ever called him Simon, and Darcourt, whose heart was not of stone, could not say no.

"All right. Here's a nice quiet place. So far as I can remember from my dancing-school days, it goes like this."

They had found a dark nook backstage, near the scene-painters' dock.

"First of all, you must stand up straight. You tend to slump, Schnak, and it won't do if you're going to curtsy. Then, slowly and with dignity, you sweep your right leg behind your left, and fit the knee lightly into the left leg joint. Then you descend, gently and slowly as if you were going down in an elevator, and when you get to the bottom, bend your head forward, from the neck. Keep your back straight all the time. It's not a cringe; it's an acknowledgement of an obligation. Now watch me."

Rather stiffly, and with perhaps too much of the dowager in his manner, Darcourt curtsied. Schnak had a try and fell over sideways.

"It isn't easy. And it's very characteristic, you know. Don't be pert, but don't be grandiose, either. You are a great artist, acknowledging the applause of your audience. You know you are their superior in art, but they are your patrons, and they expect the high courtesy of an artist. Try again."

Schnak tried again. This time she did not topple.

"What the hell do I do with my hands?"

"Keep them where your lap would be if you were sitting down. Some people wave the right hand to the side in a sweeping gesture, but that's a bit stagy and too advanced for your age. You're getting it. Try again. And again. Keep your head straight and look at the audience; only bow when you're all the way down. Again. Come on. You're getting it."

Darcourt curtsied repeatedly to Schnak, and Schnak curtsied to Darcourt. They bobbed up and down, facing one another, somewhat like a pair of heraldic animals on either side of a coat of arms; Darcourt's knees were beginning to whimper, but Schnak was learning one of the minor accomplishments of a public performer.

From above them came a sharp burst of applause, and a cry of Bravo. They looked up; suspended well above them, on the painting-bridge, were three or four stage-hands and Dulcy Ringgold, watching with undisguised delight.

Darcourt was too old and too wily to be disconcerted. He kissed his hand to the unexpected audience. But Schnak had fled to her dressing-room, hot with shame. She had much to learn.

[9]

"WE HEAR MARVELLOUS REPORTS about you, Simon," said Maria as she and Arthur sat with Darcourt in the favourite restaurant. "Dulcy says it was heart-lifting to see you teaching Schnak to curtsy. She says you were *très grande dame*."

"Somebody had to do it," said Simon, "and so few women these days are up to their job as females. I think of starting a small school to teach girls the arts of enchantment. They certainly won't learn anything from their liberated sisters."

"We live in the age of the sweat-shirt and the jeans," said Arthur. "Charm and manners are out. But they'll come back.

They always do. Look at the French Revolution: in a generation or two the French were all hopping around like fleas, bowing and scraping to Napoleon. People love manners, really. They admit you to one or another of a dozen secret societies."

"Schnak must look as well as possible when she takes her bow," said Darcourt. "Did I tell you I had a phone call from Clem Hollier? He's going to be here tomorrow night, and he wanted to know whether he should wear dinner clothes or tails. For taking his bow, you understand."

"Is Clem taking a bow?" said Maria. "Whatever for?"

"You may well ask. But his name appears on the program as one of the concocters of the libretto, and he seems to think that a clamorous audience will demand his appearance."

"But did he do anything?"

"Not a damned thing. Not even as much as Penny, who simply bitched and found fault and was cross becaue I wouldn't tell her where the best lines came from. But Penny is coming, in full fig, and I shouldn't be surprised if she expects to take a bow, too."

"Are you taking a bow, Simon?"

"I haven't been asked, and upon the whole I think not. Nobody loves a librettist. The audience wouldn't know who I was."

"You can lurk in the shadows with us."

"Oh, don't be bitter, Arthur," said Maria. And to Darcourt, "He's rather touchy because we've been cold-shouldered so much during the last few weeks."

"During the last year," said Arthur. "We've done everything we were asked, and rather more. We've certainly footed all the bills, and they aren't trivial. But if we turn up at a rehearsal and cling to the walls, Geraint looks at us as if we were intruders, and the cast glare, or smile sweetly like old Twentyman, who seems to think it's his job to spread sweetness and light even in the humblest places."

"Don't be hurt, darling. Or at least, don't show it. I expect we're on the program, somewhere."

This was a moment Darcourt had been dreading. "There was a slip-up," he said; "quite by accident the acknowledgement of the help of the Cornish Foundation was left off the program. Easily explained. The Festival generally arranges those things through its own administration, you see, and as this was a sort of special production, not quite of the Festival, though under its umbrella, there was an oversight. I didn't see a proof till this afternoon. But don't worry. Slips are being stuffed into every program at this moment, with the proper acknowledgement on it."

"Typewritten, I suppose?"

"No, no; one of those wonderful modern multilith processes."

"Same thing."

"An understandable error."

"Completely understandable, in the light of everything else that connects the Cornish Foundation with this opera. I don't know why they bother. Who gives a damn, so long as the show goes on?"

"Oh, please, Arthur, the Festival is very much aware of its benefactors."

"I suppose the benefactors take care, in the most unmistakable way, that it is so. We haven't been aggressive enough, that's the answer. Next time we must take care to push a little harder. We must learn the art of benefaction, though I must say I'm not looking forward to it."

"You thought of yourself as a patron in the old sense, the nineteenth-century sense. Not surprising, when one thinks of the nature of this opera. But better times will come. More was lost at Mohacs Field."

Arthur was somewhat appeased, but not entirely.

"I'm sorry you feel slighted, Arthur, but I assure you—no slight was intended."

"Simon, let me explain. You mustn't think Arthur is soreheaded, or pouty. That simply isn't in his nature. But he—I should say we—thought of ourselves as impresarios, encouraging and fostering and doing all that sort of thing. Like Diaghilev, you know. Well, not really like Diaghilev. He was one of a kind. But something along those lines. You've seen how it was. Nary a foster or an encourage have we been permitted. Nobody wants to talk to us. So we've played it Geraint's way, and everybody else's way. But we've been surprised and a little bit wistful."

"You've been as good as gold," said Darcourt.

"Exactly!" said Arthur. "That's precisely what we've been. As good as gold. We've been the gold at the bottom of the whole thing."

"Gold isn't really a bad part to play," said Darcourt. "You've always had it, Arthur, so you don't know how other people see it. It's no use talking about Diaghilev; he never had a red cent. Always cadging for money from people like you. You and Maria are just gold—pure gold. You are a very rich couple, and you have genius with money, but there are things about gold you don't know. Haven't you any notion of the jealousy and envy mixed with downright, barefaced, reluctant worship gold creates? You've put your soul into gold, Arthur, and you have to take the bitter with the sweet."

"Simon, that is positively the nastiest, ugliest thing you've ever said! My soul into gold! I didn't ask to be born rich, and if I have a talent for money it doesn't mean I put money above everything! Have you missed the fact that Maria and I have a real, gigantic, and mostly unselfish passion for the arts and we want to create something with our money? I'll go further—no, shut up, Maria, I'm going to speak my mind—we want to be artists so far as we can, and furthermore we want to do something with Uncle Frank's money that he would really have thought worthy. And we're treated like money-bags. Bloody, insensitive, know-nothing money-bags! Not fit to mix on equal terms with shit-bags like Nutty Puckler and that self-delighted sorehead Virginia Poole! At the first dress rehearsal I was standing in the wings, keeping my mouth shut, and I was shushed—shushed, I tell you—by one of those damned gofers when Albert Greenlaw was snickering and whispering, as he always is! I asked the kid what ailed her, and she hissed, 'There's an examination going on, you know!' As if I hadn't known about the examination for months!"

"Yes, Arthur. Yes, yes, yes. But let me explain. When art is in the air, everybody has to eat a lot of dirt, and forget about it. When I said you have put your soul into gold I was simply talking about the nature of reality."

"And my reality is gold? Is that it?"

"Yes, that's it. But not the way you think. Do please listen and don't flare up all the time. It's the soul, you see. The soul can't just exist as a sort of gas that makes us noble when we let it. The soul is something else: we have to lodge our souls somewhere and people project their souls, their energy, their best hopes—call it what you like—onto something. The two great carriers of the soul are money and sex. There are lots of others; power, or security (that's a bad one), and of course art—and that's a good one. Look at poor old Geraint. He wants to project his soul on art, and because he's a very good man it murders him when all kinds of people think he must project it on sex, because he's handsome and has indefinable attraction for both men and women. If he simply went in for sex he could be an absolute bastard, with his advantages. But art can't live without gold. Romantics pretend it can, but they're wrong. They snub gold, as they've snubbed you, but in their hearts they know what's what. Gold is one of the great realities, and like all reality it isn't all wine and roses. It's the stuff of life, and life can be a bugger. Look at your Uncle Frank; his reality was art, but art gave him more misery than joy. Why do you suppose he became such a grubby old miser in his last years? He was trying to change his soul from a thing of art to a thing of money, and it didn't work. And you and Maria are sitting on the heap he piled up in that attempt. You're doing a fine thing, trying to change the heap back into art again, but you mustn't be surprised if sometimes it brings you heartbreak."

"What have you projected your soul on, Simon?" said Maria. Arthur needed time to think.

"I used to think it was religion. That was why I became a priest. But the religion the world wanted from me didn't work, and it was killing me. Not physically, but spiritually. The world is full of priests who have been killed by religion, and can't, or won't, escape. So I tried scholarship, and that worked pretty well."

"You used to tell us in class, 'The striving for wisdom is the second paradise of the world,' " said Maria. "And I believed you. I believe it still. Paracelsus said that."

"Indeed he did, the good, misunderstood man. So I took to scholarship. Or returned to it, I suppose I should say."

"And it has served you well? Perhaps I should say you have served it well?"

"The funny thing is, the deeper I got into it, the more it began to resemble religion. The real religion, I mean. The intense yielding to what is most significant, but not always most apparent, in life. Some people find it in the Church, but I didn't. I found it in some damned queer places."

"So have I, Simon. I'm still trying. Will go on trying. It's the only way for people like us. But—

> *The flesche is brukle, the Fiend is slee*
> *Timor mortis conturbat me*

That's how it is, isn't it?"

"Not for you, Maria. You're far too young to talk about the fear of death. But you're right about the Flesh and the Fiend, even if it makes you sound like Geraint."

"I think of that sometimes, when I look at little David."

"No, no," said Arthur. "That's all over. Forget about it. The child wipes all that out."

"There speaks the real Arthur," said Darcourt, and raised his glass. "Here's to David!"

"I'm sorry I whined," said Arthur.

"You didn't whine—not really whine. You just let loose some wholly understandable indignation. Anyway, we all have a right to a good whine, now and then. Clears the mind. Cleanses the stuffed bosom of that perilous stuff that weighs upon the heart—and all that."

"Shakespeare," said Arthur. "For once I recognize one of your quotations, Simon."

"How one comes to depend on Shakespeare," said Maria. " '*What potions have I drunk of Siren tears—*' Remember that one?"

> " '*So I return rebuked to my content,*
>   *And gain by ill thrice more than I have*
>   *spent,*' "

said Darcourt. "Yes; that's a good one. Puts it very concisely."

"Thrice more than I have spent. Or rather, thrice more than Uncle Frank has spent," said Arthur. "I suppose you're right, Simon. I do think a lot about gold. Somebody must. But that doesn't mean I'm Kater Murr. Simon, we've been turning over in our minds that scheme you were talking about a while ago. That would be more in Uncle Frank's line, don't you think?"

"I wouldn't have mentioned it, otherwise," said Darcourt.

"You said you thought the New York people would listen to an offer."

"If it were put the right way. I think they would appeal to you, Arthur. Collectors, connoisseurs, but of course they don't want to be made to look foolish. Not like people who have been in any way associated with a fake. They're not Kater Murr, either. If it came out that they had been cherishing a picture which was just a simple, barefaced fake it wouldn't do them any good, either in the art world, or in the world of business."

"What is their business?"

"Prince Max is the head of an importing company that brings vast quantities of wine to this continent. Good wine. No cheap schlock, adulterated with Algerian piss. No fakes, in fact. I've seen some of his things on your table. Probably you didn't notice the motto on the coat of arms on the bottles: 'Thou shalt perish ere I perish'."

"Good motto for wine."

"Yes, but the motto is a family motto, and it means Don't try to get the better of me, or you'll wish you hadn't."

"I've met some of those in business."

"But you must bear in mind that the Princess is a business woman, too. Cosmetics, in the most distinguished possible way."

"What's that to do with it?"

"Dear Arthur, it means simply putting the best face on things. That's what they'll want to do."

"So you think they'll want a whopping price?"

"This is an age of whopping prices for pictures."

"Even fakes?"

"Arthur, I may be brought to crowning you with this bottle—which isn't one of Prince Max's, by the way. How often do I have to tell you that the picture isn't a fake, was never meant to be a fake, and is in fact a picture of the most extraordinary and unique significance?"

"I know. I've heard all you've said about it. But who will convince the world of it?"

"I will, of course. You're forgetting my book."

"Simon, I don't want to be a brute, but how many people will read your book?"

"If you follow my suggestion, hundreds of thousands of people will read it, because it will explain Francis Cornish's life as a great artistic adventure. And a very Canadian sort of adventure, what's more."

"I don't see this country as a land hotching with artistic adventure, or deep concern about the soul, and if you do, I think you're off your head."

"I do, and I'm not off my head. I sometimes think I'm ahead of my time. You haven't read my book. It isn't finished, of course, and how it ends hangs entirely on the decision you make. The ending can be fantastic, in both the literal and the colloquial meanings of the word. You don't know what a good long look at your uncle's life brings to the surface, in a mind like mine. You've got to trust me, and in this sort of thing you don't trust me, Arthur, because you're afraid to trust yourself."

"I trusted myself in this opera venture. I hustled the Foundation into doing something that hasn't worked out."

"You don't know if it has worked out, and you won't, until long after tomorrow night. You have the amateur's notion that a first performance tells the whole story about a stage piece. Did you know the St. Louis people are already interested in *Arthur of Britain*? If the opera doesn't cause a stir here, it may very well do so there. And in other places. Of course, you hustled us into this job. And now you think it was just the beginning of your mumps. But great achievements have sprung from stranger things than a dose of mumps."

"All right. Let us proceed. With caution. I suppose I'd better take over, and see these New York people."

"And I suppose you'd better do nothing of the sort," said Maria. "You leave it to Simon. He's a downy old bird."

"Maria, you are beginning to sound like a wife."

"The best wife you'll ever have," said Maria.

"True. Very true, my darling. By the way, I'm thinking of calling you Sweetness, in future."

Maria put out her tongue at him.

"Before you degenerate into embarrassing public connubiality," said Darcourt, "let me call your attention to the fact that the dress rehearsal must now have almost completed the first act of this opera Arthur has decided to hate. We'd better get over to the theatre, and be slighted and neglected, if that's the way it goes. As for this other thing, shall I go ahead?"

"Yes, Simon, you go ahead," said Maria.

Arthur, characteristically, was calling for the bill.

[*10*]

IT IS THE FIRST NIGHT of *Arthur of Britain*.

Gwen Larking speaks through the intercom to all dressing-rooms and the Green Room: "Ladies and gentlemen, this is your half-hour call. Half an hour till curtain, please."

The early birds have been ready long since. In his dressing-room Oliver Twentyman lies in his reclining-chair. He is made up and dressed, except for his magician's gown, which hangs ready to put on. His dresser has tactfully left him alone, to compose himself. Will this be his last appearance? Who can say? Certainly not Oliver Twentyman, who will go on appearing in operas as long as directors and conductors want him—and they still want him. But this will probably be his last creation of a new role; nobody has ever sung Merlin in *Arthur of Britain* before, and he intends to give the audience something to remember. The critics, too, those chroniclers of operatic history, upon the whole so much more reliable than their brethren who deal with the theatre. When Oliver Twentyman is no more, they will say that Merlin, under-taken when he was already over eighty, was the best thing he had done since he sang Oberon in Britten's *Dream*. He liked being old—and still a great artist. Age, linked with achievement, was a splendid crown of life, and took the sting from death.

> . . . *an old age, serene and bright,*
> *And lovely as a Lapland night,*
> *Shall lead thee to thy grave.*

Wordsworth knew what he was talking about. Oliver Twentyman murmured the words two or three times, like a prayer. He was a praying sort of man, and often his prayers took the form of quotations.

ONSTAGE WALDO HARRIS was having the last, he hoped, of many sessions with Hans Holzknecht about Hair on the Floor. Many years ago—Holzknecht would not say how many, nor would he identify the opera house (though it was a great one)—he had found, during the last act of *Boris Godunov,* that he was choking. Choking so that he could scarcely utter. Something had invaded his throat and was strangling him. Instead of singing he was on the verge of throwing up. It was a situation in which the best of the artist must unite with the best of the man to overcome a difficulty all the greater because it could not be identified. Some-how—there were times when he thought it must have been Di-vine intervention—he had sung his way—sung well and truly, though in agony—to the end of the act and then, when the curtain was down, he had rushed to his dressing-room, and called for the theatre doctor, who, with a forceps, had removed from his throat a twenty-inch human hair! From a wig? From some shedding soprano in the chorus in an earlier scene? Whatever the source, there it was, a hair of great length which had, in its situation, behaved with the malignance of an animate thing! In one of his great intakes of breath while lying, as the distraught Tsar, on the floor, he had sucked up that hair, and he had it yet, preserved in a plastic bag, which he showed to every stage management in every theatre where he appeared, as a warning of what could happen if the stage were not properly swept, not once, but at every possible time, during a performance. He did not want to be a nuisance, nor did he wish to appear neurotic, but a singer meets perils of which the public knows nothing, and he begged— begged with all the authority of his place in the company—that he might have the assurance of Waldo Harris that the stage would be properly swept whenever the curtain was down. Which as-surance Waldo gave, sympathetic, but also wishing that Holz-knecht would accept one positive answer, and shut up about hairs on the stage.

In the Prompt Corner, Gwen Larking was fussing. She would not have thought of it as fussing, but as she was redoing and perfecting things that had already been done, and done to perfection, there is no other word for it. Gwen was, in herself, the perfection of a Stage Manager, which meant that she was impeccable in her attention to detail, alert for any mishap and capable of meeting it, and a monument of assurance to nervous artists. And the greatest fusser of them all, beneath an impassive exterior.

She was dressed for her work in an expensive pant-suit, and a blouse of deceptive simplicity. She had made her two assistants and the three gofers dress themselves similarly, as near as it was in their destiny to come to her own stripped-down elegance. Art deserves respect, and respect is mirrored in proper dress. Let those members of the audience who so wished appear in the theatre looking as if they had just come from mucking out the cowshed; it was up to the stage crew to dress as if they were about important work. The gofers had to be warned about bangles and chains that jingled; of course such things could not be heard on the stage but they might be distracting in the wings.

The Prompt Corner was called so because of tradition; nobody could possibly have prompted anyone onstage from it. Indeed, the stage could not be seen from it, except fleetingly. But over Gwen Larking's desk, which looked like the conductor's own, lay a full score of the opera, in which every detail of the production was recorded, for instant reference. This was what Al Crane would have given an ear to get his hands on, but Gwen guarded it jealously, just as she guarded the conductor's full score, which lived in the safe in Waldo Harris's office.

Gwen Larking twisted the lucky ring on the fourth finger of her left hand. Nothing would have persuaded her to admit that it was a lucky ring. She was a Stage Manager, devoted to certainty, not luck. But it was in truth a lucky ring, a Renaissance cameo, a gift from a former lover, and all the gofers knew it, and had somewhere found lucky rings of their own, for Gwen was their ideal.

DARCOURT DID NOT HEAR the half-hour call, because he was in the favourite restaurant, entertaining two eminent critics. Arthur and Maria had refused to do anything of the sort, but the line between eminent critic from New York and distinguished guest is so fine that Darcourt had decided he had better give them dinner. Very, very eminent critics can eat and drink any amount, without in the least compromising their impartiality of opinion, and have indeed been known to bite the hand that has fed them, without noticing. Darcourt was aware of this, but thought a modest dinner would give him a chance to provide the critics with some information.

In the case of Claude Applegarth, who was undoubtedly the most popular and widely read of New York critics, information was cast on stony ground, for Mr. Applegarth had been a critic of the theatre arts too long to be concerned with the background of anything. The wisecrack was his speciality; that was what his readers expected of him and was he not, after all, himself a popular entertainer? He would not have attended *Arthur* if it had not been that his annual visit to the Shakespearean portion of the Festival coincided with this opening so closely that it could not decently be neglected. Not that opera was his thing, at all; it was in the criticism of musicals that he was felt as a great and usually blighting influence.

It was a different matter with Robin Adair, whose word on opera was—well, not law, but rather the judgement of the Recording Angel. A notable musicologist, a translator of libretti, a man of formidable culture, and—rarest attribute of all—a real lover of opera, he was avid for any information Darcourt could give him, and questioned like a cross-examiner.

"The details I have received are just vague enough to provoke a thousand questions," he said. "The libretto, for instance. If Hoffmann had gone no further than sketching the work, how much of a libretto existed? Had Planché any hand in it? I hope not. He ruined *Oberon* with his jokey nonsense. Is there a coherent libretto?"

"I gather from Dr. Dahl-Soot that the word 'sketch' is somewhat too dismissive for what Hoffmann left in the way of music. There was a good deal of it, all of which is in the score. The basis of it, in fact."

"Yes, but the libretto. It can't have been finished. Who has done it?"

"As you will see from the program, I have."

"Ah? And on what basis? Original work of your own? You see, of course, that if this is to be considered as the completion of a work by Hoffmann—dead in, when was it, 1822?—the libretto is of greatest importance. There must be a congruity of style not at all easy to achieve. Do you think you have managed that?"

"Not really for me to say," said Darcourt. "But I may tell you this: by far the greatest part of the libretto is either drawn exactly from, or slightly adapted from, the work of a poet of undoubted genius who was Hoffmann's contemporary and devout co-religionist in romanticism."

"And his name is—?"

"I am sure that a man of your reputation for out-of-the-way scholarship will recognize his hand at once."

"A puzzle? How delightful! I love a puzzle. I shall see you afterward and give you my guess, and you must say if I am right."

"Do you think we might have just a little more champagne?" said Mr. Applegarth. "Now listen: whoever wrote the bloody words, there has never been a good play or musical about King Arthur. Look at *Camelot*. A turkey."

"A fairly tough old bird by now," said Mr. Adair.

"Nevertheless, a turkey. I said it then and I say it now. A turkey."

"Tell me something about this Cornish Foundation," said Mr. Adair. "I understand it's a man and a woman with a dummy board. They have ambitious ideas about patronage."

"They can't have enough money for anything really big," said Mr. Applegarth, who now had a second bottle of champagne and was somewhat less morose. "The modern Medici! That's what they all want. Won't work in the modern world."

"Oh, surely fine things have been done by patrons even during this year," said Mr. Adair.

"Listen," said Mr. Applegarth. "Patronage only worked when artists were humble. Some of 'em wore livery. An art patron today is a victim. The artists will crucify him and mock him and caricature him and strip him naked, if he hasn't got the drop on them from the start. Only when the Medici or the Esterhazys had their heel on the artist's neck did it work. Admit artists to equality and the jig's up, because they don't believe in equality. Only in their own superiority. Sons of bitches!" he said, gloomily filling his glass.

"The Cornishes have tried very much to leave the artists to their own devices in this affair," said Darcourt. "I must admit they feel that they have been somewhat shouldered aside by the artists."

"You don't surprise me at all," said Mr. Applegarth.

"Ah, well—the artistic temperament. Not all sweetness and light," said Mr. Adair, rather as though he felt he had a foot in the artist's world.

"I see that it's half past six," said Darcourt. "Perhaps we should be getting to the theatre. Seven-o'clock curtain, you know."

"I hate these early curtains," said Mr. Applegarth. "They ruin dinner."

"Oh come along, Claude," said Mr. Adair. "It's for our benefit you know. Early curtain so the critics can make their deadline."

"Not on a Saturday night," said Mr. Applegarth, who had passed from the morose, through the sardonic, to the combative stage of critical preparation. "Bloody *Arthur*. Why can't they leave him in his grave?"

"Nobody knows where his grave is," said Mr. Adair, Scottish fount of information as he was.

"It'll be on this stage, tonight," said Mr. Applegarth, obviously ready to assure that it should be so.

GWEN HAD CALLED the quarter-hour. From the dressing-rooms could be heard the humming, the buzzing, now and then the full-throated vocalization, of singers getting their voices under command. In front of the curtain early birds among the audience—the kind of people who like lots of time to study their programs—could be heard arriving. Up and down the corridors among the dressing-rooms walked Hans Holzknecht, wishing the company good luck. "Hals und beinbruch!" he shouted, and if it was a man, he gave him a sharp knee in the rump.

IN THE WINGS, out of earshot of Gwen Larking, Albert Greenlaw was about his favourite sport of instructing the gofers in the lore and tradition of the theatre. They stood about him, devouring the fine Belgian chocolates they had been given earlier by Oliver Twentyman, who believed in first-night presents, especially to the humbler members of the company.

"I don't know if I ought to tell you," he said, "because it is not the thing little girls ought to know. But if you're *really* set on a stage career—"

"Oh yes, Albert. Be a sport. Tell us."

"Well then, honey-child, you ought to know about critics. There are some in the audience tonight who are of the cream of that very creamy cream. And you can tell those real ones from the fellows who are just from local papers by one infallible sign, and it is this." His voice sank to a whisper. "They never go to the john."

"Not during the show?" said the prettiest gofer.

"Not *ever*. From womb to tomb—not *ever*. Nobody has ever met a critic in the Men's, anywhere on this earth."

"Albert, that can't be," said a dubious gofer, but in a tone that betrayed that she very much wished it to be so, and thirsted for marvels.

"Would I kid you? Have you ever known me to kid you? I'll tell you something that will be invaluable to you when you are all happy wives and mothers—or maybe just mothers, in these carefree days. When your child is born, take a look right away at where its teeny-weeny exit ought to be. If it isn't there, honey, you've borne a critic."

"Albert, I don't believe it!"

"Fact. Medical fact. Imperforate anus, it's called, in medical circles. And it's the mark of the critic. The real, top-flight critic. They have two or three of them, pickled, in the medical museum at Johns Hopkins and there you can observe the phenomenon as plain as if it were labelled No Exit. The little fellows, they're like you and me; they have the normal disposal facilities. But not the biggies. No, no, no. Remember your Uncle Albert told you."

"THEY SAY CLAUDE APPLEGARTH is here tonight," said Schnak. She and Dr. Gunilla were in the small dressing-room reserved for the conductors. It was very close, for the Doctor was smoking one of her black cigars.

"Who is Claude Applegarth?" she asked.

"He's supposed to be the most influential critic in New York. And I suppose that means the world," said Schnak, who had all the Canadian awe of New York.

"I do not know his name," said the Doctor. "And I blow my nose in his hair," she added. This was to encourage Schnak, who was trying to dissemble her terror. Gunilla would conduct in the pit tonight, of course, but Schnak was to be offstage conductor; when the Chorus sang in the wings, it was she who must direct them, taking her time from a monitor on which appeared a ghostly, grey Gunilla. She must do this with an unwieldy baton that was, in fact, a small red lamp on the end of a metal stick, and her beat, never elegant, became ridiculous when she waved what the Chorus called her fairy wand.

Conducting! Oh, conducting! Would she ever master it? Conduct the libretto, not just the score, Gunilla was always saying. Easy for Gunilla, tall, elegant, romantic figure. In the evening dress that Dulcy had rigged up for her, Schnak felt like a scarecrow. With a razor she had painfully hoicked the hair from her armpits, and now, in Dulcy's creation, they did not show. But they hurt. At this moment, Schnak would gladly have forgone any future as a public performer.

"Five minutes, please, ladies and gentlemen. Overture and beginners in five minutes." Gwen's voice, low and clear, came from the speaker on the wall.

"Perhaps you should go to your post," said the Doctor.

"I haven't anything until after the Overture."

"But I have," said the Doctor. "And I should like to be by myself."

DARCOURT, STANDING IN THE FOYER, saw that at the five-minute call, which he could not hear but which he knew was being given, a special group of people arrived, and quickly dispersed themselves into twos and threes. There was nothing positively disturbing about them, but they seemed somewhat overdressed for the occasion. Of course, many of the people who had already entered the theatre were in evening clothes—dinner suits and dinner frocks—but several of these men wore full dress and white ties that spoke of antiquity. The ladies tended to be dressed in plushy materials, well worn and somewhat sprung in the seat. One had a plume in her hair, and another sported a metal headpiece studded with impressive, but not totally convincing, gems. It was the Yerko Claque, and in the midst of them Yerko rose like a mountain in shirt and tie that had grown yellow with time, and a coat, the tails of which hung to his calves; beside him was Mamusia, and it was she who wore the paste jewels and kid gloves that had once been white; they reached well above her elbows. The group comported itself with a stateliness rarely seen on the North American continent, and certainly never in Stratford.

Yerko's eye met Darcourt's, without a spark of recognition.

Well, God help us, here we go, thought Darcourt, and went inside to claim his seat.

ARTHUR OF BRITAIN

AN OPERA IN THREE ACTS planned and sketched by E. T. A. HOFFMANN and completed from his notes by Hulda Schnakenburg under the direction of Dr. Gunilla Dahl-Soot.

CHARACTERS

King Arthur of Britain	Hans Holzknecht
Modred, the King's nephew	Gaetano Panisi
Sir Lancelot	Giles Shippen
Merlin	Oliver Twentyman
Sir Kay the Seneschal	George Sudlow
Sir Gawaine	Jean Morant
Sir Bedevere	Yuri Vollmer
Sir Gareth Beaumains	Wilson Tinney
Sir Lucas, Butler	Mark Horrebow
Sir Ulphius, Chamberlain	Charles Bland
Sir Dynadan	Mark Luppino
Sir Dagonet, the Fool	Nutcombe Puckler
Sir Pellinore	Albert Greenlaw
Sir Palomides	Vincent LeMoyne
Queen Guenevere	Donalda Roche
Morgan Le Fay, sister to the King	Clara Intrepidi
The Lady Elaine	Marta Ullmann
The Lady Clarissant	Virginia Poole

Ladies of the Court: Ada Boscawen, Lucia Pozzi, Margaret Calnan, Lucy-Ellen Osler, Appoline Graves, Etain O'Hara, Esther Moss, Miriam Downey, Hosanna Marks, Karen Edey, Minnie Sainsbury

Heralds: James Mitchell, Ulick Carman

Attendants: Bessie Louth, Jane Holland, Primrose Maybon, Noble Grandy, Ellis Cronyn, Eden Wigglesworth

· · ·

Costumes and settings designed by Dulcy Ringgold, and executed in the
    Festival workshops.
Scenic Artist: Willy Grieve
Head Carpenter: Dicky Plaunt

· · ·

Lighting Director: Waldo Harris
Stage Manager: Gwenllian Larking
Concert-Master: Otto Klafsky
Répétiteur and Harpsichordist: Watkin Bourke
Director: Geraint Powell
Conductor: Gunilla Dahl-Soot

· · ·

The Libretto realized by Simon Darcourt, assisted by
Penelope Raven and Clement Hollier.

The public relations people had done their job efficiently. The
house was decently full and not with an audience of despair,
recruited from nurses' residences and old folks' homes. Darcourt
found himself sitting next to Clement Hollier; he reflected that
he had never seen Hollier in evening dress before, and the learned
man stank pungently of some spicy toilet water or after-shave.
This may be hard to endure, thought Darcourt. But he could not
ponder long on this, for the house lights dimmed, and Dr. Gunilla
Dahl-Soot strode into the orchestra pit, shook hands with the
concert-master, and bowed elegantly to the audience.

The audience responded eagerly. They had never seen anything
like Gunilla, with her masculine good looks, her magnificent
green tailcoat, and her ample white stock, and their expectations
for the evening rose. The show, they felt, had begun.

Gunilla raised her baton, and the first heavy chords, stating the
theme of Caliburn, were heard, and gave way to a firm but melancholy theme, the theme of Chivalry, which was developed for
perhaps three minutes, until the point in the score marked by
Letter D was reached; then the splendid red curtains swept upward and back, to disclose King Arthur and Merlin standing on
the brink of the Enchanted Mere.

This was something for which the audience was wholly unprepared. Geraint, Waldo Harris, and Dulcy Ringgold had laboured
faithfully to reproduce the stage dressing of the early years of the
nineteenth century—the stage as Hoffmann would have known

it. From the footlights—for there were footlights—the stage rose in a gentle rake which reached backward to the full forty feet of stage space, and on each side were six sets of wings, painted to represent a British forest in springtime as perhaps Fuseli might have imagined it; at the back, in front of a splendidly painted backcloth, the rollers which had been so much trouble a few days before were revolving silently, giving an impression of gently heaving water. It was a perspective scene in the nineteenth-century manner, designed to be beautiful and to complement the stage action, rather than to persuade anyone that it mimicked some natural reality.

An "objective correlative" to the music, thought Al Crane, and scribbled a note in the darkness. He was not entirely sure what the phrase meant, but he thought it meant something that helped you to understand something else and that was good enough.

The audience, which had never seen anything like it, burst into loud applause. Canadians are great applauders of stage settings. But Gunilla, who was not aware of this national custom, turned upon them with the face of a Gorgon. She gave a hiss of menace and waved a hand as if to quell the sound. Assistance came from an unforeseen quarter; there were gentle shushings, not angry but politely rebuking, from all over the house. Yerko's Claque had moved into action and from then onward it directed the applause with fine certainty of taste. The clappers were quieted, and the voice of Oliver Twentyman, high and pure as a silver trumpet, was heard invoking the power of Caliburn to elevate and refine the life of Arthur's Court, and to give a new meaning to Chivalry.

Darcourt breathed with relief. A very tricky corner had been turned. He gave himself up to the music, and in time the curtains closed, and the Overture—for it was a true Hoffmann overture, employing the voices of singers—moved to its completion.

When the curtains rose immediately on Act One, the scene was a hall in the Court of Arthur, and a fine sight, but not one that suggested chivalry, particularly; the Knights and their Ladies had not that look of stricken consecration which is associated with chivalry on the stage. Nutcombe Puckler was, as Geraint had directed him, "horsing around and playing the goat" with a cup-and-ball, but not too distractingly. The Knights paid him little heed. The Ladies—Polly Graves' splendid jugs well downstage and Primrose Maybon equally prominent—declared themselves, and their situation, in the best operatic manner. Darcourt was well pleased with the old ballad he had adapted to a theme of Hoffmann's and which put the opera off to a somewhat folkloric start.

> Arthur our King lives in merry Caerleon
> And seemly is to see:
> And there he hath with him Queen Guenevere
> That bride so bright of blee.

Thus sang the Knights. "So bright of *what?*" hissed Hollier in his ear.

"Blee! You know—*blee!* Complexion. Shut up!"

The Ladies took up the ballad strain:

> And there he hath with him Queen Guenevere
> That is so bright in bower:
> And all his brave knights around him stand
> Of chivalry the flower.

The Knights, pleased with this handsome compliment, make what might be called a statement of policy, joined by the Ladies:

> O Jesu, Lord of mickle might,
> That died for us on rood,
> So maintain us in all our right,
> For we come of a noble blood.

But they are not permitted to take their ease in this Kater Murr conception of their society. Preceded by four pages holding in check four very large Irish wolfhounds, King Arthur and his

Queen appear, and Arthur tells them of the revelation at the Enchanted Mere:

> *Leaf after leaf, like a magician's book*
> *Turned in a dragon-guarded hermitage*
> *By trees—dishevelling spirits of the air—*
> *My plan unfolds.*

And he charges them with his chivalric code, in which noble blood must be partnered by noble deeds. Let them henceforth be *bons, sages et cortois, preux et vaillans*. And as an act of good faith, he pledges himself to the service of the Christ of Chivalry, and in only slightly less degree to the service of his Queen, as the Vessel of his Honour, the scabbard of Caliburn. The scene ends when the Knights bind themselves in the same terms to their Ladies.

This was received with warm approval by the audience, and Darcourt began to feel somewhat more at ease. But—what is this? Darcourt knew, but the audience did not, and Darcourt could not have foreseen their astonishment when, with no interfering curtain, and the barest minimum of mechanical sound, the scene changed visibly from Arthur's Court to a nearby chapel, where Morgan Le Fay and her son Modred were plotting the theft of the scabbard of Caliburn. What happened, if you knew, was that the twelve wings that flanked the court scene were drawn silently back out of sight, and wings suited to the ruin were left in view; at the same moment a drop scene was lowered at the back of the stage, and the great hall seemed to have melted imperceptibly into its successor.

"Those nineteenth-century people knew a trick or two," whispered Hollier.

Indeed they did, thought Darcourt, but he said nothing, for the scenery-applauders were hard at it, and Yerko's Claque were quietly reducing them to silence.

Morgan Le Fay and her son plotted. Good stuff, thought Darcourt, as Modred—Gaetano Panisi, a splendid bass, though a stumpy figure—gave velvety utterance to his scorn for Arthur and the chivalric ideal:

> *. . . Let him lean*
> *Against his life, that glassy interval*
> *'Twixt us and nothing: and upon the ground*
> *Of his own slippery breath, draw hueless dreams,*
> *And gaze on frost-work hopes.*

Back to the hall in the Court—another swift transformation. Back to Arthur, charging his Knights to undertake the Holy Quest for the Grail, which shall be the heart and splendour of his new chivalry. He lifts the great sword to ask a blessing on it, and while he does so Morgan Le Fay steals the scabbard. Splendid scene of mounting vigour culminating in a great Chorale of the Grail, almost Wagnerian in conception.

"Going well," said Hollier, as he and Darcourt made their way up the aisle. But when Darcourt went into the little room behind the manager's office he found Geraint, drinking whisky in huge swigs, and furious.

"What in the name of God do those morlocks think they're up to?" he said. "Applauding the scenery!"

"It's very fine scenery," said Darcourt. "Most of them have never seen such scenery. It was outlawed sixty years ago when there was all that blethers about letting the audience use its imagination. A fat lot of good that was!"

"I think it's the acting they like," said Hollier. "Do you remember what Byron said? 'I am acquainted with no immaterial sensuality so delightful as good acting.' You must remember, Powell; you're a great Byron enthusiast. That little chap Panisi is marvellous. And Holzknecht, too, of course, but one always admires villains more than heroes."

It was plain that Hollier had something on his mind, and after he had accepted a drink he overcame his diffidence. "Geraint, about curtain calls—I suppose it will be expected that those of us who have provided the libretto for the opera should make some appearance? Not that I am anxious to do so. I really hate all this sort of public nonsense. But if it's expected—?"

"Just go around through the pass-door when the final curtain comes down," said Geraint. "Gwen will show you what to do, and you'll have lots of time, because there will be plenty of applause—that's guaranteed. When Gwen shoves you on, you'll be blinded by the lights, so don't fall into the orchestra. Try not to look any more of a mutt than literary people usually do on a stage full of actors. Just bow. Don't do anything fancy. And don't leave the stage till all the hullabaloo is over."

"You'll be there, yourself, of course?"

"I may, or I may not."

"But you're the director!"

"Indeed I am, and since this afternoon at four o'clock I have been the most unnecessary creature involved in this opera. Nobody needs me. My work is done. I am wholly superfluous."

"Surely not!"

"Surely yes! If I cut my throat at this minute the opera would progress through its appointed number of performances not a whit the worse."

"But you've made it."

"I have not made it. Hoffmann, and Gunilla and Schnak, and all those singers and musicians have made it. And even you fellows have made it. I have supplied the trickery and whoredom of the show. The stuff that appeals to people who don't care much for music."

"Rubbish, Geraint," said Darcourt, who saw a fine Powell tantrum coming. "You've been the energy and encouragement of the whole affair. We've all warmed ourselves at your fire. Don't think we don't know it. You're indispensable. So cheer up."

"I know you, Sim *bach*. In a minute you'll be rebuking me for self-pity."

"Perhaps so."

"You don't know what an artist is, you nice, controlled, reasonable man. You don't know the shadow of the artist—the sieve of vanity, the bile of bitterness, the bond of untruth that is bound with icy chains to all the sunlight and encouraging and he's-a-jolly-good-fellow of being an opera director. I am exhausted and I am not needed. I am sinking into such a slough of despond as only an artist whose job is finished must endure. Go on, both of you! Go back to your seats. Float in the warm waters of assured success. Leave me! Leave me!" By this time he was drinking straight from the bottle.

"I really think we'd better go," said Darcourt. "I couldn't bear to miss what's coming next. But do try to pull yourself together, Geraint *bach*. We all love you, you know."

What was coming next, to begin Act Two, was the scene of The Queen's Maying, over which Powell, and Waldo, and Dulcy had toiled and contrived for months. As the curtains drew back, after a brief and lovely prelude, it seemed to the audience that they could see immeasurably deep into a grove of hawthorn trees in snowy bloom. Far in the blossom-misted distance appeared Queen Guenevere, mounted on a black horse, riding at ease in her side-saddle, as a page led the horse forward. One by one, wearing white mantles, the Ladies of the Court made their way into the front of the scene, but never so far as to obscure the figure of the distant Queen. They did not sing; they seemed enchanted, as the whole scene was one of enchantment, and while the music rose and fell, they grouped themselves in a tableau of expectation. They carried garlands of May blossom. Something truly wonderful was happening.

Darcourt knew how the effect was achieved. He had attended most of the rehearsals and heard many of the arguments during which the notable scene had been planned. Nevertheless, he was caught in its magic and he understood, what he had not known before, that much of the magic of a great theatrical moment is created by the audience itself, a magic impalpable but vividly present, and that what begins as trickery of lights and paint is enlarged and made fine by the response of the beholders. There are no great performances without great audiences, and this is the barrier that film and television, by their utmost efforts, cannot cross, for there can be no interaction between what is done, and those to whom it is done. Great theatre, great music-drama, is created again and again on both sides of the footlights.

He enjoyed the extra pleasure of the man who knows how it has been done. It had been the suggestion of Waldo Harris, not to the casual eye an imaginative man, that for this scene the forty-foot depth of the stage should be increased by opening the huge sliding doors to the storage rooms, and beyond them into the workshops, so that in the end a vista of a hundred feet could be attained. Not a great depth, surely, but with the aid of perspective painting it could be made to seem limitless. And—this had tickled Waldo and Dulcy so that they giggled for days—when first Queen Guenevere was seen, at the farthest distance, on her black steed, it was not Donalda Roche, a woman of operatic sturdiness of figure, but a child of six, mounted on a pony no bigger than a St. Bernard. At a point perhaps sixty feet from the footlights the midget Guenevere rounded a grove of trees to be replaced by a larger child, mounted on a larger pony, led by a larger page. This Guenevere, forty feet from the footlights, disappeared for a moment in May blossom and it was Donalda Roche from then onward, on a black horse of normal stature. Behind her, pages led two magnificent white goats with gilded horns. Waldo and Dulcy had played with this illusion, and refined it, until it changed from a simple trick of perspective into a thing of beauty.

Of course, it would not have been possible without the finest pages in Schnak's score. There had been three related themes, obviously meant as the foundation for an extended piece of music in Hoffmann's notes, and Schnak and Gunilla had decided that these should be developed into a prelude to Act Two, a preparation for the scenes of love and betrayal in which Guenevere and Lancelot, under the malign influence of Morgan Le Fay, would consummate their passion and suffer a double remorse, for Lancelot had also been tricked into a union with the maiden Elaine. But when Geraint heard the first developments of the prelude, he demanded that it should be the music for The Queen's Maying, and overbore the musicians, who of course wanted it as pure music. This was the passage which, at her examination, had persuaded Schnak's examiners (all but the difficult Dr. Pfeiffer) that Schnak was certainly a doctor of music, and probably a good deal more than that.

So here it was, not as a symphonic piece, but as an accompaniment to an act of lovely trickery, or, if you prefer, a masterwork of stage magic.

When it was being rehearsed, some of the singers were not pleased that what was probably the finest part of the score made no use of their voices. Nutcombe Puckler, indeed, referred to it as "this *silent* music", and Hans Holzknecht had some hard words about pantomine. But it proved itself masterly in performance.

The audience, partly quelled by Yerko's Claque, which had been stealthily teaching them to wait for their cues, and partly because they were enthralled by what they saw and heard, were still as mice until the end, when the Queen, joined by her special Knights, bearing white shields, moved gently off the stage to the place where Gwen had cleared space for what was—Queen, horse, Knights and Ladies—rather a crowd which must on no account be halted in its progress. Then they broke into three minutes of sustained applause. Three minutes is a long time for furious clapping, and when the first minute had passed Yerko let loose his forces in every part of the house, and their cries of Bravo were so heart-lifting that several non-claquers joined in. But as they were not trained mid-European bawlers, they had little chance against the professionals in approbation.

Was a voice heard to cry, "Bravo, Hoffmann"? There was, and it was the voice of Simon Darcourt.

Gunilla, though not by inclination apt to recognize an audience except with frosty courtesy, bowed again and again. Gunilla was, after all, a great artist, and such approbation is very sweet to the performer's ear.

"That's fetched 'em," shouted Hollier in Darcourt's ear. "I think we've got 'em now!"

We? thought Darcourt, applauding till his hands smarted. Who's we? What had you to do with this? What had I to do with it? The music, of course, is Hoffmann-cum-Schnak, and very fine, too. But this magic belongs to Geraint Powell, and to Dulcy and Waldo, whom he fired and inspired with his own sense of theatre.

And to Hoffmann. He had raised his voice for Hoffmann. Not solely Hoffmann the composer, who might not have been as good a musician as Schnak, but Hoffmann who lived and died when Romance was blossoming in all the arts. To the spirit of Hoffmann, indeed. This was certainly the Little Man who had been aroused by the Cornish Foundation and all the people it had touched.

The Second Act moved rapidly. The scene outside Merlin's cave, where the enchantress Morgan tricks the good old man into the revelation: Arthur can only be destroyed by one born in the month of May. The exultation of Morgan, for it is her son—also,

by incest, the son of Arthur, though Arthur does not know it—
who is the May-born. The fateful words of Morgan:

> *The trembling ray*
> *Of some approaching thought, I know not what*
> *Gleans on my darkened mind. . . .*

And Modred's response:

> *I feel it growing, growing*
> *Like a man's shadow when the moon floats slowly*
> *Through the white border of a baffled cloud:*
> *And now the pale conception furls and thickens—*

The temptation of Guenevere by Lancelot. His declaration of
love and her sad cry:

> *Oh no! I'll not believe you; when I do*
> *My heart will crack to powder.*

The revelation to the lovers Guenevere and Lancelot that the
Maid Elaine, whom Lancelot deflowered when under Morgan's
evil spell, must die of her love, but die gladly:

> *Oh, that sweet influence of thoughts and looks!*
> *That change of being, which to one who lives*
> *Is nothing less divine than divine life*
> *To the unmade! Love? Do I love? I walk*
> *Within the brilliance of another's thought*
> *As in a glory.*

And Lancelot's recognition of the treachery of his love, and his
bitter acceptance of implacable destiny:

> *I never felt my nature so divine*
> *As at this saddest hour.*

The audience—not, one would have supposed, greatly susceptible to Arthurian romance—were now wholly in the grip of

the opera, and the buzz of enthusiasm at the interval was heartening.

Darcourt had something very much on his mind.

"Penny," he said, cornering her in the foyer, "will you let Clem have your seat for the Third Act? I'd like you to be with me for at least a part of this."

"Nicely said, Simon, but I know what you mean. I've been talking with Clem, and whatever he has been dousing himself with, he's overdone it. I was almost asphyxiated, and I know what you must have been going through. 'A bundle of myrrh is my well beloved to me: he lieth all night between my breasts'. But not if I can help it. I'll be delighted to relieve you. We've pulled it off nicely, don't you think?"

We, again. What have you done? thought Darcourt. A few sessions of bitchy criticism of my work.

"My guess, for what it's worth, is that our Snark is really a Snark, and not a speck of a Boojum. Did you ever hear such enthusiasm? In Canada, I mean, the Home of Modified Rapture."

"It is certainly going well," said Darcourt, who had sighted Yerko leaning, with pachydermatous elegance, over a very small but excitable lady with orange hair. "Let's go in. Third Act any minute now."

The Third Act was very much as Geraint had outlined it, so long ago as it now seemed, when they had dined unhappily on Maria's Arthurian feast. Perhaps inevitably the emphasis was different. The music for Merlin, when he denounced the villain Modred, was arresting:

> *Thy gloomy features, like a midnight dial,*
> *Scowl the dark index of a fearful hour. . . .*

And later:

> *Transparent art thou as a poisoned glass*
> *Through which the drinker sees his murderer smiling.*

Then Modred's unrepentant, properly villainous death:

Why, what's the world and time? A fleeting thought
In the great meditating universe;
A brief parenthesis in chaos.

But it was Hans Holzknecht, as the King, who had the best of it. Fine actor, fine singer, he drew the most from the shattered Arthur's recognition of his unrecognized incest, the bitterness of his son Modred's hate, and—heaviest of all—the betrayal by his beloved wife and his beloved friend. But his invocation to Love, as a charity beyond even the poetry of fleshly possession, was his best moment, and his conclusion—

It is the secret sympathy,
The silver link, the silken tie,
Which heart to heart, and mind to mind,
In body and in soul can bind.

—moved many of the audience, somewhat to their embarrassment, to tears.

Walter Scott is very good, but Schnak has raised him to another level, thought Darcourt. I wonder if she really understood what she was setting to music? If so, there's hope for her, tormented child as she is. But with musicians you can never be quite sure.

At the death of Arthur, the scene melted magically again to the shores of the Enchanted Mere, which had not been seen since the Overture. But it was not quite the same scene, for this was deeply autumnal; leaves, and a few snowflakes, scudded across the stage where the Knights stood, leaning on their swords. They sang:

The wind, dead leaves and snow,
Doth hurry to and fro,
And once, a day shall break
O'er the wave,
When a storm of ghosts shall·shake
The dead, till our King wake
From the grave

The body of Arthur—but not the living Holzknecht—was placed in a shallow craft in which it sailed across the water, and as it disappeared Merlin flung after it Caliburn, now safely in its scabbard, and an armoured hand rose from the waves and seized it. The great chords that had introduced the opera were heard again, and the curtain fell.

Marshalled by Gwen Larking, Penny Raven, Clement Hollier, and Simon Darcourt appeared during the final curtain-call. Nobody knew who they were or why they were there, but at the end of every operatic first night a few people make inexplicable appearances, and the charity of the audience includes them.

Geraint, surprisingly steady on his feet, was thunderously applauded. He appeared to be in excellent spirits and looked wondrously romantic in full evening dress. He and Gunilla were, indeed, the commanding figures in the rather untidy tableau at the final curtain.

Schnak, Darcourt observed with satisfaction, managed a number of curtsies without a stagger.

[11]

ETAH IN LIMBO

CHAMPAGNE! So much of it, and not a drop for me. It is one of the inconveniences of Limbo that one retains all one's carnal appetites but is utterly debarred from satisfying them. So, as I move unseen through the party that follows the first public performance of my Arthur, I am aware of brimming glasses and full bottles everywhere, and because of my spiritual condition—we are very chaste in Limbo, oh yes, very chaste—I am denied even the elfin satisfaction of tipping a few glasses down shirt-fronts and into the crannies of bosoms. I, who once drank champagne from pint pots! But I gather that the wine has gone up in the world and this crowd sips it reverently.

I suppose this is my night of triumph. My opera, projected but never finished, has now been finished indeed, and on the whole to my satisfaction. Am I a little jealous of the Schnakenburg child? Certainly she has a deft hand with orchestration, and what I sense to be a developing gift for melody, but I do not feel the true Romantic fervour in her, not yet. Perhaps it will never come again, as we knew it who first felt its pain and beauty; we, of whom it was my luck to be among the foremost.

Did I like the performance? Ah, there we move into a realm where I cannot be sure of my answer. The music was played and sung vastly better than it would have been in my Dresden days. The orchestra far outshone the assemblage of villains I had to put up with, and the Dahl-Soot woman had much of the daemonic spirit of my own Kapellmeister Kreisler. The stage pictures were thrilling. The singers, marvellous in the telling, could act, and did so, even when they were not singing. What would the Eunike family—three of whom I had to use in my production of Undine—have said to that? This was indeed a music drama, performed with a unity of style and intent quite impossible in my time.

But—one is a creature of one's time. I missed elements in this production that were familiar, rather than good.

The prompter, for one. Oh, those prompters of my time, who all seemed to have been born old, all born with a cold in the head, all addicted to snuff and brandy, all foul-tempered and all soured from the nape to the chine with their personal failure as composers, or singers, or conductors! They crouched in the little hutch among the footlights, which was shielded from the audience, as a usual thing, by an ornamental shell, bent forward into a hood. Only their heads showed above the stage level, and their heads were heated to roasting-point by the oil lamps in the footlights. Below stage level they were frozen by the draughts of the under-croft of the stage, and every time the stage-hands set a trap in action there was a rush of air as some god or demon was whisked upward onto the stage, and the prompter was choked with the dust of years. In this living hell the prompter hissed his directions to the singers and flung them their cues just before they were to sing, often giving them the note in the cracked voice of a man dying of phthisic, complicated by snuff and the scenery dust—which some of the more spiteful singers took care to kick in his face.

Why would I miss the prompter? Believe me, one often misses the afflictions and inadequacies of the past as truly as its splendours. I knew many prompters, and attended the funerals of several, and these singers who are such good musicians that they can manage without him seem to me to be, somehow, unnatural.

I miss the backstage life. The Green Room, where the singers congregated when they were not wanted onstage, and where one's consequence in the troupe determined with mathematical exactitude how near one might sit, or stand, to the stove. But even more I miss the dressing-rooms, so tiny, so characteristically redolent of the scent preferred by the singer, beneath which might often be discerned the reek from the chamber-pot, which lived in a little cupboard by itself, on top of which was the basin and ewer so the singer might wash his hands, when he could persuade his servant to bring him some hot water from its only source—the carpenter's room under the stage. The stove in the Green Room was very precious to the poorer folk of the theatre, for the dressing-rooms, if they were heated at all, had only a little iron box in which some charcoal could be burnt, and charcoal cost money and had to be fetched by servants who had to be tipped.

What complexity of romance and delicious intrigue took place in those dressing-rooms, the best of which contained a couch or even, sometimes, a bed for one, which could, with some contrivance, become a bed for two!

This handsome theatre is so much better than any I ever knew. This audience is so much more polite—yes, polite and well-bred, as audiences in my day never were—and I swear this audience was more musically receptive than any I could count upon. They hardly needed a claque, though the one they had was efficient. The spirit of Kater Murr was present—indeed, when is that ultra-respectable Philistine ever absent from public performance—but Kater Murr has learned much with the passing of time. His fur has a new gloss. Yes, yes; times change, and in some things times even grow better.

But—one is a creature of one's time. Does the divine Mozart, I wonder, ever look in on the countless presentations of his operas, so psychologized and philosophized? Could it be that he feels as strange, as wistful, as I have done at the realization and presentation of my Arthur?

Shall I hear it again?

I suppose I could hang about, but I do not think I shall do anything of the kind. I have watched Arthur brought into being, I have watched the complexities it has introduced into so many lives, and, as an artist, it becomes me to know when enough, even of one's own art, is enough.

Besides, I have had intimations from—I do not know who whispered, and am too tactful to inquire—that my time in Limbo is completed. After all, it was a piece of unfinished work that brought me here, and that work is now done. Arthur is done, and sufficiently well done, and I'm off and away.

Farewell, whoever you are. Remember Hoffmann.

EIGHT

THE COMPLETION of Darcourt's poopnoddy scheme took almost three years from the fall of the final curtain on *Arthur of Britain*. Government bodies, great galleries, connoisseurs of art, publishers of books, and great sums of money all move with the uttermost deliberation, and to persuade them all to fit into a coherent plan calls for the extreme of diplomacy and tact. But Darcourt did it, and did it furthermore without ulcers or heart palpitations or too many private bouts of hysteria. He did it, he told himself, by pursuing the path of the Fool, marching merrily on his way, trusting to his intelligent nose and the little dog of intuition nipping at his rump to show him the path, overgrown and tortuous as it was.

So, on a December afternoon, in the presence of a distinguished assembly, the Francis Cornish Memorial Gallery was officially opened by the Governor General, and was agreed by everyone— or almost everyone—to be a notable addition to the National Gallery of Canada, to reflect the greatest credit on everyone concerned, and especially upon Arthur and Maria Cornish, whose names, as the prime movers in the plan, were never allowed to escape the notice of the public. If the contribution of the Cornishes to the opera production had been under-prized, and if their understandably hurt feelings had not been adequately salved, they were thanked to the point of embarrassment in the establishment of the Francis Cornish Memorial Gallery.

Of course they protested; of course their modesty was outraged, and they were entirely sincere in their protests and their sense of outrage. Nevertheless, it is very sweet to be recognized as public benefactors, and to be compelled to protest and feel outrage. Sweeter by far than to feel overlooked, under-prized, and intrusive when one is sincerely trying to do something for the furtherance of culture—for the hateful word, so much licked and pawed by Kater Murr, cannot conveniently be avoided. Arthur and Maria were modest, and were not displeased that the world should see that they were modest.

Darcourt, too, was modest, and for the first time in his life he had something of substantial public interest to be modest about. His book, the long-projected life of the late Francis Cornish, had been published a year earlier, and had received attention not only in Canada but throughout the English-speaking world, and indeed everywhere that books about extraordinary painters are read. Not all of the attention was flattering, but his publishers assured him that the attacks and the disparagement also had their value. Critics do not lash themselves into a high aesthetic tizzy about things that are insignificant. Nor were these critics all concerned with painting; many of them were critics of culture in a more general sense, and several of these were tarred with the recently fashionable Jungian brush, and had even read some of the writings of Jung. What delighted these, and enraged many of the art critics, was the Introduction to the book that had been contributed by Clement Hollier, whose reputation in such matters where art, time, and the enduring and many-layered human psyche kissed and commingled, was very great indeed. Clem, so hopelessly out of his depth in the creation of an opera libretto, was a very big gun in the world where Darcourt's biography took its place. Paleopsychology and the history of human culture was what the knowing ones called it, and it was not everybody who could follow Clem in its overgrown paths. Thus Darcourt found himself a significant explainer in a number of important worlds, and invitations to lecture—which were in some cases demands that he appear to defend himself—were piling up on his desk.

Such invitations had to wait until the Francis Cornish Memorial Gallery had been shaped, and assembled, and formally opened to the world. After that, his Old Ontario folk wisdom told him, it would be time enough to cut a dead dog in two.

The work was not easy. First of all, Prince Max and the Princess Amalie had to be persuaded to sell *The Marriage at Cana* to the National Gallery. There had to be assurance that they would not, under any circumstances, be accused of having harboured a fake, and shown it to the world as a genuine painting dating from the sixteenth century. They had never offered the picture for sale under false pretences; but on the other hand they had never denied the interesting explanation of the picture that had been contained in that persuasive article by Aylwin Ross, and which was there to be consulted in the authoritative pages of *Apollo*. It was in the light of this splendid piece of art detection that they had allowed it to be exhibited in a great American Gallery, which had for a time considered buying it. They must not seem guileful, only reserved, and it must be apparent to everybody that their hands were clean. This could be managed, and it was managed, by the brilliant critic Addison Thresher, who washed their hands and laundered the picture—though the hateful word "laundered" was never, never used—and set the price the Cornish Foundation paid for it. If a percentage of that awesome sum later passed into the hands of Addison Thresher, surely it was to be expected that he would be recompensed for his work, and his great reputation which set at rest all, or nearly all, doubts.

This involved delicate negotiation, but it was as nothing to the work of persuading the National Gallery of Canada that it should accept a picture of such curious provenance, and show it with pride in a room specially devoted to it, even if it did not cost the Gallery a cent.

People who control important galleries are very far from being stupid, but they are not accustomed to thinking of pictures psychologically. If the picture, whose beauty they readily acknowledged, were the work of a Canadian who had painted it less than fifty years ago, why had he painted it in a sixteenth-century style, on an authentic old triptych, with paints that defied any of the tests that had been used? Yes, yes; the picture was a masterpiece, in the old sense of being a work undertaken by a painter who wished to prove himself a master. But what kind of a master? Francis had been a pupil, certainly the best pupil, of Tancred Saraceni, who was himself a supreme master of picture restoration, and so much a master that it was suspected that he had revised, or even recreated, some old pictures into forms that were vastly superior to what they had originally been. People whose lives and reputations are devoted to pictures have fits at any suggestion of faking. Faking is the syphilis of art, and the horrid truth is that syphilis has sometimes lain at the root of very fine art. But connoisseurs and great galleries shrink from saying to the world: Here's a fine, poxy piece of painting, beautiful, uplifting, sincerely describable as great—though of course, because of its ambiguity, not precisely the sort of thing you can safely recommend to Kater Murr. For him and his kind, everything must be Simon Pure—or, if you prefer the term, kosher. Kater Murr is very active among the connoisseurs and the galleries.

It was here that the testimony of Clement Hollier was invaluable. If a man wants to paint a picture that is intended primarily as an exercise in a special area of expertise, he will do so in a style with which he is most familiar. If he wants to paint a picture which has a particular relevance to his own life-experience, which explores the myth of his life as he understands it, and which, in the old phrase, "makes up his soul", he is compelled to do it in a mode that permits such allegorical revelation. Painters after the Renaissance, and certainly after the Protestant Reformation, have not painted such pictures with the frankness that was natural to pre-Renaissance artists. The vocabulary of faith, and of myth, has been taken from them by the passing of time. But Francis Cornish, when he wanted to make up his soul, turned to the style of painting and the concept of visual art which came most naturally to him. He did not feel himself bound to be "contemporary". Indeed, he had many times laughed at the notion of contemporaneity in conversation with both Hollier and Darcourt, mocking it as a foolish chain on a painter's inspiration and intention.

It must be remembered, added Darcourt, that Francis had been brought up a Catholic—or almost a Catholic—and he had taken his catholicity seriously enough to make it a foundation of his art. If God is one and eternal, and if Christ is not dead, but living, are not fashions in art mere follies for those who are the slaves of Time?

All of this had been thoroughly explored by Darcourt in his

life of Francis Cornish, but he had to go over it many times in person, before many committees of solemn doubters.

The bigwigs of the National Gallery, who regarded themselves quite reasonably as the guardians of Canada's official artistic taste, hummed and hawed. They heard; they understood; they admitted the adroitness of the argument; but they were not convinced. A man who painted in a bygone style, and who had the effrontery to do it with an accomplishment and imagination notably absent among the best modern Canadian artists, was not someone they could readily embrace. He had played the fool with one of the most sacred ideas still left to a world where the notion of sacrosanctity had become abhorrent—the idea of Time. He had dared to be of a time not his own. Surely such a person was either touched in his wits or else—this was grave fear—a joker? Government bodies, the worlds of connoisseurship and art, dread jokes as the Devil dreads holy water. And when a joke also involves great sums of money—money, the very seed and foundation of modern art and modern culture—the dread quickly mounts to panic, and Kater Murr has catfits.

Nevertheless, Darcourt, staunchly aided by Hollier, and supported at every turn by Arthur and Maria, prevailed at last, and on that December day the Francis Cornish Memorial Gallery was opened.

It was a gallery in the sense that it was a large room devoted solely to the triptych of *The Marriage at Cana* and, on the other walls, a display of supportive material that showed what the Canadian origins of the picture were. Grandfather McRory's Sun Pictures, enlarged so that they could be studied in detail, and the people of Blairlogie, the people of Grandfather's household, and the medieval isolation of that backwoods town could be made apparent to anyone who chose to look. On another wall were Francis's careful studies in Old Master style, as evidence of how the extraordinary technical skill of the great picture had been acquired. And on the third wall the most intimate of all Francis's drawings—hasty sketches done in the undertaker's workroom, quick impressions of Tancred Saraceni and Grandfather's coachman which linked them with Judas and the *huissier* in the great picture, and the arresting studies—drawn with so much adoration—of Ismay Glasson, clothed and naked and, plain for all to see, the Bride in *The Marriage*. Not all the figures in the great picture were represented in the sketches and drawings, but most of them were, and perhaps the most arresting were the photograph of F. X. Bouchard, the dwarf tailor, by Grandfather, and the pitiful figure of the dwarf naked on the embalmer's table, drawn by Francis; the most casual looker could not fail to see that this was the proud dwarf in parade armour who looked out at the spectator from the triptych.

It had been agreed by Arthur and Maria and Darcourt that the sketches which identified the grotesque angel as Francis the First should not be shown. Some mystery must be left unexplained.

With these exhibitions were explanatory notes, written by Darcourt, for what Hollier wrote was not plain enough for the widest possible public. But what could be plain only to visitors who had understood what the whole room said were the words painted in handsome calligraphy on the wall above the great picture:

> *A Man's life of any worth is a continual allegory—*
> *and very few eyes can see the Mystery of his life—a*
> *life like the scriptures, figurative.*   JOHN KEATS.

[2]

"ARE YOU HAPPY WITH IT, Simon?" said Maria. "I do hope you are. You've worked so hard to make it happen."

She and Arthur and Darcourt sat at dinner after the grand opening. The Governor General and his entourage had been thanked and bowed into their cars; Prince Max and Princess Amalie and the ever-attentive Addison Thresher had been escorted to the airport and seen off with many expressions of goodwill, as well as some whispered words to Darcourt from the Princess in which she thanked him yet again for the tact with which any connection between her own Old Master drawing from Francis's hand (now so widely seen in her cosmetic advertisements) had been avoided; Clement Hollier and Penny Raven had been watched as they disappeared down the chute toward another plane to Toronto. The captains and the kings and the scholars had all departed, and the three friends were happily alone at their table.

"As happy as it's in my nature to be," said Darcourt. "A kind of golden glow. And I hope you're happy, too."

"Why wouldn't we be?" said Arthur. "We've been lauded and complimented and petted beyond our deserts. I feel rather a fake."

"It was all the money," said Maria. "I suppose it's silly to underestimate money."

"Uncle Frank's money, almost every penny," said Arthur. "The cupboard is nearly bare. It'll take a few years before the cistern has refilled to the point where the Foundation can do anything else."

"Oh, it won't be forever," said Maria. "The bankers think about three years. Then we shall be able to do something else."

"What's going to be your attitude?" said Darcourt. "Are you going to be the Sword of Discretion or the Gushing Breast of Compassion?"

"The Sword every time," said Arthur. "Offer the breast and somebody will bite it. Until you've tried it, you can have no idea of how hard it is to give away money. Intelligently, that's to say. Look at this Gallery. What a fight we had to get it."

"Oh, but a very genteel, high-minded fight," said Darcourt. "What a tricky balancing of egotisms of various weights, and varying interests, some of which you're not supposed to know about. What a lot of jockeying so that nobody has to say thank-you in such a way that they lose face. I'll bet old Frank is laughing his head off, if he knows anything about it. He was an ironic old devil. And his big secret—that loony angel who was his parents' first attempt at a Francis—is still a secret, though it's almost certain that some toilsome snoop will root it out sooner or later. Not everything is on those apparently explanatory walls."

"It's been an adventure, and I've always hankered for adventures," said Arthur. "And the opera was an adventure, too. That was Frank's doing, and we shouldn't forget it."

"How can we?" said Maria. "Isn't it still going on? Schnak is doing well, in a quiet way."

"Not so quiet," said Darcourt. "The opera hasn't been done again; not yet, but there are nibbles. But that big central passage—

The Queen's Maying—has been played several times by very good orchestras, and always with a note that it comes from the opera. Schnak is on her way, and there is even some renewed interest in Hoffmann as a composer, Nilla tells me."

"You know I hated Nilla when I first met her," said Maria. "She was so awful at that Arthurian dinner. But she's the perfection of a fairy—or I suppose I should say lesbian—godmother. She sends Davy the most wonderful wooden toys, trains and farm carts and things, and she's determined we must take him to Paris for her to see. Not like that stinker Powell. He writes now and again but he never mentions the boy. Just his own dear little self. Mind you, he's doing marvellously well. A terrific *Orfeo* in Milan, when last heard of. Even Clem is a better godfather. He's given Davy a wonderfully illustrated book of the Arthurian legend, which he will be able to read when he's about ten. And Penny has given him a first edition of *The Hunting of the Snark*. Have these professors no understanding of what a child of three is?"

"Perhaps it was really meant for you," said Darcourt. "The Snark was a pretty fair comment on that opera job, and in the end the Snark was only half a Boojum."

"I've never got around to reading that poem," said Arthur. "Simon—lighten my darkness, I beseech you. What the hell *is* a Snark? And a Boojum? I suppose I ought to know."

"You won't ever know if you don't read it," said Darcourt. "But just for the moment, a Snark is a highly desirable object of search which, when found, can be unexpected and dangerous—a Boojum, in fact. All Snarks are likely to be boojums to the unresting, questing Romantic spirit. It's a splendid allegory of all artistic adventures."

"Allegory. Allegory—I know what an allegory is. Simon, you've put that quotation from Keats right over Uncle Frank's picture. 'A Man's life of any worth is a continual allegory'. Do you really believe that?"

"Haven't I convinced you?" said Darcourt. "It's one of those magnificent flashes that Keats popped into letters. That comes from a gossipy letter to his brother and sister. Just a piece of a letter, but what an insight!"

"You've convinced me several times, but I keep coming unconvinced. It's such a terrifying thought."

"Such an enlarging thought," said Maria. " 'A Man's life of any worth'—it forces you to wonder whether your life is of no particular worth, or if it has a mystery you can't see."

"I think I'd rather say my life was of no particular worth than face the idea of a pattern in it that I don't know, and probably never will know," said Arthur.

"You mustn't dream of saying that your life is of no particular worth, my darling," said Maria. "Because I know better."

"But an allegory seems such an extraordinary thing to claim for oneself," said Arthur. "It's like commissioning a statue of yourself, stark naked, holding a scroll."

"Keats wrote at the gallop," said Darcourt. "He might equally well have said that a man's life has a buried myth."

"I don't see that making it any easier."

"Arthur, you are sometimes remarkably obtuse—not to say dumb," said Darcourt. "Now—I think I've had enough of this excellent Burgundy to ask you a very personal question. Haven't you seen your own myth in all that opera business? Your myth, and Maria's myth, and Powell's myth? A fine myth, and as an observer I must say you all carried it through with style."

"Well, if you want to cast me as Arthur—though how do you know it isn't just a trick of the name?—Maria has to be Guenevere, and I suppose Powell is Lancelot. But we weren't very Arthurian, were we? Where's your myth?"

Darcourt was about to speak, but Maria hushed him. "Of course you don't see it. It's not the nature of heroes of myth to think of themselves as heroes of myth. They don't swan around, declaiming, 'I'm a hero of myth.' It's observers like Simon and me who spot the myths and the heroes. The heroes see themselves simply as chaps doing the best they can in a special situation."

"I flatly decline to be a hero," said Arthur. "Who could live with that?"

"You haven't any choice," said Darcourt. "Fish up a myth from the depths and it takes you over. Maybe it's had its eye on you for a long time. Think—an opera. What was it Hoffmann said?— you dug it up, Maria."

" 'The lyre of Orpheus opens the door of the underworld'."

"He must have been a wonderful little chap," said Arthur. "I've always thought that, though of course I couldn't have put it like that. But I still don't see the myth."

"It is the myth of the Magnanimous Cuckold," said Darcourt. "And the only way to meet it is with charity and love."

After a long silence, and reflective sipping of wine, Arthur spoke.

"I choose not to think of myself as magnanimous."

"But I do," said Maria.

READ MORE IN PENGUIN

In every corner of the world, on every subject under the sun, Penguin represents quality and variety – the very best in publishing today.

For complete information about books available from Penguin – including Puffins, Penguin Classics and Arkana – and how to order them, write to us at the appropriate address below. Please note that for copyright reasons the selection of books varies from country to country.

In the United Kingdom: Please write to *Dept. EP, Penguin Books Ltd, Bath Road, Harmondsworth, West Drayton, Middlesex UB7 ODA*

In the United States: Please write to *Consumer Sales, Penguin USA, P.O. Box 999, Dept. 17109, Bergenfield, New Jersey 07621-0120.* VISA and MasterCard holders call 1-800-253-6476 to order Penguin titles

In Canada: Please write to *Penguin Books Canada Ltd, 10 Alcorn Avenue, Suite 300, Toronto, Ontario M4V 3B2*

In Australia: Please write to *Penguin Books Australia Ltd, P.O. Box 257, Ringwood, Victoria 3134*

In New Zealand: Please write to *Penguin Books (NZ) Ltd, Private Bag 102902, North Shore Mail Centre, Auckland 10*

In India: Please write to *Penguin Books India Pvt Ltd, 706 Eros Apartments, 56 Nehru Place, New Delhi 110 019*

In the Netherlands: Please write to *Penguin Books Netherlands bv, Postbus 3507, NL-1001 AH Amsterdam*

In Germany: Please write to *Penguin Books Deutschland GmbH, Metzlerstrasse 26, 60594 Frankfurt am Main*

In Spain: Please write to *Penguin Books S. A., Bravo Murillo 19, 1° B, 28015 Madrid*

In Italy: Please write to *Penguin Italia s.r.l., Via Felice Casati 20, I–20124 Milano*

In France: Please write to *Penguin France S. A., 17 rue Lejeune, F–31000 Toulouse*

In Japan: Please write to *Penguin Books Japan, Ishikiribashi Building, 2–5–4, Suido, Bunkyo-ku, Tokyo 112*

In South Africa: Please write to *Longman Penguin Southern Africa (Pty) Ltd, Private Bag X08, Bertsham 2013*

READ MORE IN PENGUIN

A CHOICE OF FICTION

The Ghost Road   Pat Barker
Winner of the 1995 Booker Prize

'One of the richest and most rewarding works of fiction of recent times. Intricately plotted, beautifully written, skilfully assembled, tender, horrifying and funny, it lives on in the imagination, like the war it so imaginatively and so intelligently explores' – *The Times Literary Supplement*

None to Accompany Me   Nadine Gordimer

In an extraordinary period before the first non-racial elections in South Africa, Vera Stark, a lawyer representing blacks' struggle to reclaim the land, weaves an interpretation of her own past into her participation in the present. 'With great dexterity and force Gordimer combines all these stories – career, colleagues, political struggles, sexual love, identity, family – into a compelling narrative' – *Daily Telegraph*

Of Love and Other Demons   Gabriel García Márquez

'García Márquez tells a story of forbidden love, but he demonstrates once again the vigor of his own passion: the daring and irresistible coupling of history and imagination' – *Time*. 'A further marvellous manifestation of the enchantment and the disenchantment that his native Colombia always stirs in García Márquez' – *Sunday Times*

Millroy the Magician   Paul Theroux

A magician of baffling talents, a vegetarian and a health fanatic with a mission to change the food habits of America, Millroy has the power to heal, and to hypnotize. 'Fresh and unexpected . . . this very accomplished, confident book is among his best' – *Guardian*

English Music   Peter Ackroyd

'Each dream-sequence is a virtuoso performance on Ackroyd's part. In his fiction he has made a speciality of leap-frogging time, so that the past occupies the same plane as the present. Never before, however, has he been so chronologically acrobatic, nor so confident' – *The Times*

READ MORE IN PENGUIN

A CHOICE OF FICTION

Felicia's Journey   William Trevor
Winner of the 1994 Whitbread Book of the Year Award

Vividly and with heart-aching insight William Trevor traces the desperate plight of a young Irish girl scouring the post-industrial Midlands for her lover. Unable to find Johnny, she is, instead, found by Mr Hilditch, pudgy canteen manager, collecter and befriender of homeless young girls.

The Eye in the Door   Pat Barker

'Barker weaves fact and fiction to spellbinding effect, conjuring up the vastness of the First World War through its chilling impact on the minds of the men who endured it ... a startlingly original work of fiction ... it extends the boundaries not only of the anti-war novel, but of fiction generally' – *Sunday Telegraph*

The Heart of It   Barry Hines

Cal Rickards, a successful scriptwriter, is forced to return to the Yorkshire mining town of his youth when his father, a leading voice in the 1980s miners' strike, suddenly becomes ill. Gradually, as Cal delves into his family's past and faces unsettling memories, he comes to reassess his own future.

Dr Haggard's Disease   Patrick McGrath

'The reader is compellingly drawn into Dr Haggard's life as it begins to unfold through episodic flashbacks ... It is a beautiful story, impressively told, with a restraint and a grasp of technicality that command belief, and a lyricism that gives the description of the love affair the sort of epic quality rarely found these days' – *The Times*

A Place I've Never Been   David Leavitt

'Wise, witty and cunningly fuelled by narrative ... another high calibre collection by an unnervingly mature young writer' – *Sunday Times*. 'Leavitt can make a world at a stroke and people it with convincing characters ... humane, touching and beautifully written' – *Observer*

READ MORE IN PENGUIN

A CHOICE OF FICTION

Grey Area Will Self

'A demon lover, a model village and office paraphernalia are springboards for Self's bizarre flights of fancy . . . his collection of short stories explores strange worlds which have mutated out of our own – *Financial Times*

A Frolic of His Own William Gaddis

'Everybody is suing somebody in *A Frolic of His Own* . . . Among the suits and counter-suits, judgements and appeals, the central character, Oscar Crease, scion of a distinguished legal family, is even suing himself for personal injury after his aptly named Sosumi car runs over him as he hot-wires the ignition . . . Like all satire this is a very funny but also a very serious book' – *Independent on Sunday*

The Children of Men P. D. James

'As taut, terrifying and ultimately convincing as anything in the dystopian genre. It is at once a piercing satire on our cosseted, faithless and trivially self-indulgent society and a most tender love story' – *Daily Mail*

The Only Problem Muriel Spark

Harvey Gotham had abandoned his beautiful wife Effie on the *autostrada* in Italy. Now, nearly a year later, ensconced in France where he is writing a monograph on the Book of Job, his solitude is interrupted by Effie's sister. Suddenly Harvey finds himself longing for the unpredictable pleasure's of Effie's company. But she has other ideas. 'One of this century's finest creators of the comic-metaphysical entertainment' – *The New York Times*

Small g: a Summer Idyll Patricia Highsmith

At the 'small g', a Zurich bar known for its not exclusively gay clientele, the lives of a small community are played out one summer. 'From the first page it is recognisably authentic Highsmith. Perhaps approaching her lesbian novel *Carol* in tenderness and theme, it has a serenity rarely found in Highsmith's world' – *Guardian*

BY THE SAME AUTHOR

The Papers of Samuel Marchbanks

No one has better captured the spirit of the age than that cantankerous old devil – the celebrated columnist Samuel Marchbanks.

From this compendium volume Robertson Davies has selected from his friend's writings to give us a feast of anecdote and opinion, liberally spiced with scorn, spleen, irony and wit. Here is Marchbanks on railway dining, on spy scares, on hay fever, on honesty, Beethoven and Christmas cards – Marchbanks, in short, on everything under the sun. All annotated by the incomparable Robertson Davies.

A Voice from the Attic

Essays on the Art of Reading
Revised Edition

An urbane, robust, and wonderfully opinionated voice from Canada, sometimes called 'America's attic', speaks here of the delights of reading, and of what mass education has done to readers today, to taste, to books, to culture. With his usual wit and breadth of vision, Robertson Davies ranges through the world of letters – books renowned and obscure, old and recent; English, Irish, Canadian and American writers both forgotten and fondly remembered.

'This book of essays and observations bestows . . . multiple benefactions, and anyone picking it up is bound north to pleasure and profit' – *The New York Times Book Review*

BY THE SAME AUTHOR

The Salterton Trilogy

Tempest Tost · Leaven of Malice · A Mixture of Frailties

People who do not know Salterton call it dreamy and old-world. They say it is the place where Anglican clergymen go when they die. The real Saltertonians, however, know that there is nothing quaint about the place at all. With its two cathedrals, its one university, and its native sons and daughters busily scheming for their dreams, Salterton is very much in the real world.

'Ingenious, erudite, entertaining ... Davies displays all the qualities of a latterday Trollope and shows us what modern Canada is like' – Anthony Burgess in the *Observer* Books of the Year

The Deptford Trilogy

Fifth Business · The Manticore · World of Wonders

Who killed Boy Staunton, elegant, rich philanthropist and public servant? Why did he drown at the wheel of his car with a stone in his mouth?

Around this central mystery is woven a glittering, fantastical, cunningly contrived trilogy of novels. Luring the reader down labyrinthine tunnels of myth, history and magic, *The Deptford Trilogy* provides an exhilarating antidote to a world from where 'the fear and dread and splendour of wonder have been banished'.

'His books will be recognized with the very best works of this century' – J. K. Galbraith in *The New York Times Book Review*

BY THE SAME AUTHOR

The Cunning Man

Dr Jonathan Hullah is the 'cunning man': unorthodox healer, amateur dramatist and narrator of his life's story. Interviewed for a series of articles entitled 'The Toronto That Used To Be', he compiles a Case Book to aid his memory, recalling his childhood, his boyhood friends, and the fateful events surrounding the death of Saintly Father Ninian Hobbes.

'Cerebral gusto and humane enjoyment make this novel irresistible. ... Robertson Davies presides over another wholehearted and sharp-minded celebration of . . . the Great Theatre of Life' – Peter Kemp in the *Sunday Times*

Murther and Walking Spirits

Connor Gilmartin is a ghost in search of vengeance . . .

Unceremoniously murdered by his wife's lover, respected journalist Connor Gilmartin finds himself seated beside his murderer in a darkened room at the Toronto Film Festival. Suddenly a mysterious film appears on screen, visible only to himself. Connor Gilmartin is about to embark on a fantastic journey into his past . . .

'An extraordinary tapestry of a book – richly layered, embroidered with detail and stitched together with skill and style' – *Time Out*

'Davies's devotees will recognize at once the master's sharp ear for proverbial wisdoms, his relish for fantastical and dark linguistic corners, his magpie accummulations of odd bits of lore and historical tidbits' – *Observer*